Leslie
Thomas

Leslie Thomas

Tropic of Ruislip

Dangerous Davies

Bare Nell

That Old Gang of Mine

Tropic of Ruislip first published in Great Britain in 1974 by
Eyre Methuen Limited
Dangerous Davies first published in Great Britain in 1976 by
Eyre Methuen Limited
Bare Nell first published in Great Britain in 1977 by Eyre Methuen Limited
That Old Gang of Mine first published in Great Britain in 1979 by
Eyre Methuen Limited

This edition first published in Great Britain in 1988 by

The Octopus Group Limited
Michelin House
81 Fulham Road
London SW3 6RB

Reprinted in 1991

ISBN 0 413 60960 X

Distributed by Methuen London Limited

Printed in Great Britain by The Bath Press, Avon

Contents

Tropic of Ruislip

Woe unto them that join house to house,
that lay field to field, till there be no place.

ISAIAH 5:8

CHAPTER ONE

For a man facing both Monday morning and utter defeat he did not feel too bad. The morning sun, beaming like a cheap salesman, burst from the direction of Breakspear Crematorium (a reminder that Nicholas Breakspear, the only English pope, was of these parts), there was a wide optimism about the sky and the grinning fields, and the girl from Cowacre, the one with the bum like a deftly closed tulip, was walking by on her way to the station.

Andrew's double-glazed kitchen window was higher than all the others at Plummers Park, for his four-bedroomed house (garage and carport, Blo-hole heating, bland picture windows, sun patio, old tree incorporated into the garden wall) was on the prow of Upmeadow. From his sitting-room a variety of sunsets could be witnessed through the seasons, a ritual dipping which, the estate agent had assured him, would be an asset if he ever decided to sell. From the place where he stood this first working morning of a June week he could look, in fact he had no choice but to look, out on to the flat roofs of all the other houses on the estate, scattered in the valley like bamboo rafts on some wide eastern river.

The girl from Cowacre wore a pale shirt, tight across her brassy little breasts, their noses prodding through the material. His coffee-cup immobilized at the tilt, he watched her stride by, her legs long, her face clean and confident as the sun, and waited in anticipation for the promised view of her backside.

Scarcely more than a remnant of blue denim had gone into that skirt, a mere pantile at the front, so tight behind that her buttocks pushed at it like imprisoned faces jostling for a view. They collided beneath the light blue fabric with each neat, blatant step. The road before her extended vacantly to the horizon, to the junction of Upmeadow with Risingfield, and she walked as though she were happy but alone in the world. Behind her in ragged file followed Mr Brewster, Mr Reynolds, Mr Burville, Mr George Jones and his brother Mr Henry Jones, Mr Shillingford, and poor old Mr Henty trying to keep up.

'I swear they crouch behind their front doors until that kid passes by,' said Audrey. She was standing a yard behind him, on her toes to see what he was seeing.

'Which kid?' he asked, innocence always being his first reflex.

'The one that made you spill your coffee down your shirt,' she said, wiping at the stain. 'If you're going to ruin your clothes with mental sex then it's time I had a new washing-machine. The man says this one is going to blow up at any moment.'

'I'll try and finish my coffee before she goes by in the morning,' said Andrew. There was no heat in their discussion. They knew how they were.

Audrey bit into a piece of toast and considered the men following the girl. 'You're as bad as that sorry lot,' she observed. 'You stand on that same spot every morning waiting for her. Her and her arse. It's wonder the lino isn't worn into a hole.'

She laughed with off-hand bitterness. 'Dirty lot of sods,' she said. 'Just look at old Shillingford dodging about so that horny Bertie Reynolds doesn't block his view. If she were older, if she had a bit of know-how, she would turn round suddenly. I bet they'd all fall over in fright.'

'If she were older maybe they wouldn't be following her,' argued Andrew.

'They wouldn't know what to do with a girl like that,' she said, sharpness hardening her voice. 'And nor would you. She'd scare the life out of you.'

He nodded solemnly. 'I wouldn't know what to say to her,' he agreed. He did not believe in fighting in the morning – or at any time if he could avoid it. The best thing about defeat was that there was no more war.

Suddenly Audrey laughed. To make a joke was frequently her way out of their disputes. 'Imagine if one fell out,' she said. 'One of her cheeks. Can't you see it bouncing down the road?'

'There'd be a scramble,' he agreed, glad of the let-out. 'Like a rugby scrum.'

'Please can I have my ball back?' mimicked Audrey, but not sounding like a young girl.

They both laughed, and he put on his jacket. He said, 'It's going to be hot again. And I'll be in the lousy magistrates court.' His basset hound, Gladstone, a hung and drawn dog, saw that he was going out. Its face sagged even lower. Andrew stooped and examined the perpetually red eyes, shaking his head in mock sadness at the diagnosis.

'That creature stank like a hayrick all day yesterday,' said Audrey. 'I don't mind when it's Sunday and you have to smell him too. But on Mondays he's got me to himself. You'll have to bath him or have him destroyed.'

Andrew looked into the hound's ravaged eyes. 'Action-Dog,' he said to the sagging face. 'You are not wanted. You and I will run away together. The world calls us. We will voyage to the Land Where The Bong Tree Grows.'

'The Pong Tree,' corrected Audrey. 'And the furthest you'll get today is Bushey Magistrates Court, so stop building up my hopes.'

'Nine years,' grumbled Andrew. 'Nine years before the bench. Nine years of Monday and Thursday mornings. Soon I'm going to carve my initials on the press table.'

'It's a wonder you haven't before this.'

'Ah, well, I wasn't sure I was going to stay.'

'Is that why you haven't carved your initials anywhere in this house?' she asked, apparently absently. She had turned away and was brushing her fingers against some flowers on the kitchen table, touching them into a token arrangement. And Andrew put out his hand to her shoulder and another on a chair. 'I'd hate to damage the place,' he said. 'Anyway, I think you've got me for ever. Like the *Journal*.'

'Hooray,' she said quietly, still keeping her face from him. 'At least you've made it clear. At last I can plan my life too.' She walked to the tear-off calendar on the kitchen wall and tore off another day which she rolled up deliberately, kissed, and dropped into the waste-bin. 'Goodbye, June the second,' she sighed.

'Stop it,' he said. Sometimes he felt sorrier for her than he did for himself. 'It's a nice day.'

Audrey glanced at him almost coyly, then smiled and went towards him, her step apologetic. She said, 'So it is,' and put her arms limply about him. 'Poor old us,' she said. She was tall; his eyes only had to descend a fraction to meet hers. She had kept a good figure but her face had a sort of tired patience. They embraced and he pressed her crowded chest into his for a spasm of familiar comfort but, as though by tacit agreement, they did not kiss.

They relaxed their arms, and as though that were a signal for the resumption of normality she bit into her toast again. She said: 'Listen, Lizzie wants to go up to the canal again tonight with this youth group they've started. She says they want to do some more work on the barge. Do you think it's safe?'

He was on his way out and he stopped. 'She can swim,' he said simply.

'Christ,' she groaned. 'For a newspaperman you're really dim at times. I didn't think she was going to fall into the canal, you idiot. She's fifteen, if you've had a look lately, and she's up there with two or three boys inside a boat where, by all accounts, they just about have to lie down because there's no room to stand up. Now do you understand?'

Andrew nodded thoughtfully. 'She's all right,' he said. 'Lizzie's not stupid. Ask her if she can work up the mast. Let them have a look at her knicks.'

'You casual sod.'

'Well, what do you want me to say? Perhaps we ought to tell her to keep away from boys and barges.'

'All right, all right,' sighed Audrey. 'I couldn't help thinking they've been spending a hell of a lot of time up there, that's all.'

'Maybe it's a big barge.'

'Perhaps we ought to go and have a look at it. Just to see.'

'All right,' he agreed. 'Let's go up tonight.'

'Do we let her know we're coming? She's out to tea, so I won't be seeing her.'

'We'll play fair,' he said. 'We'll sing as we walk along the tow-path. Give her time to pull her pants up.'

'Shut up. Don't be so bloody nasty.'

He was going out of the door now. 'Nasty, nothing,' he retaliated. 'Just want to give the kid a sporting chance.'

He walked down the front path, his feet among the marigolds which had gone on the rampage. She called after him, on impulse, desperately, as though she had to shout something before he went. 'You!' she called without venom. 'You're mad, you are, Andrew Maiby!' It sounded like a child's taunt.

'So are you!' he returned blithely. 'Mad!' He had the sudden pleasing awareness of the sun on his face. 'We're all mad! All of us!' He spread his arms to take in the multiple boxed houses of the estate. 'Look,' he exclaimed. 'Look where we live!'

Each of the thousand flat roofs had a quaint tin chimney projecting from it, the antithesis of the bare and functional boxiness of the rest of the house. It was like a stove-pipe sticking up and was topped by a pert pointed hat, like the chimneys of prospectors' cabins in gold-rush days or the pixie houses in children's books. In cold weather wraiths of smoke wriggled out as the Blo-hole central heating puffed. This fine morning they were smokeless and Andrew could clearly see the farming fields on the other side of the main road running from Harrow to Watford. He enjoyed seeing the busy smoke rising from the little chimneys and lolling in the valley on frosty mornings. It made the place look inhabited.

Plummers Park was thirty miles from Central London, in the latitude of Ruislip, in the country but not of it. The fields seemed almost touchable and yet remote. Wild roses bloomed and blew in seclusion just out of reach; rooks and flashing magpies in elm and rowan were merely distant birds in distant trees; the fox and the rabbit went unseen from the human windows. On Sundays the people had to drive out in their cars to witness a pig. The estate was the strangest crop ever to grow on that old Hertfordshire farming land. When it was built some trees were permitted to remain like unhappy captives spared because they are old. They remained in clusters, sometimes embedded in garden walls as selling points for house-buyers desiring fresh air, twigs, greenness, and autumn acorns for their children. It was rumoured that the builders had a mechanical squirrel which ran up trees to delight, deceive and decide prospective purchasers.

The streets had, with commercial coyness, retained the sometimes embarrassing names of the various pastures and fields that now lay beneath concrete, crazy paving and statutory roses. Cowacre, Up-meadow, Risingfield, Sheep-Dip, The Sluice, and Bucket Way. Some of the new people said they found it embarrassing to give their address as Sows Hole Lane – provided for a policeman it always provoked suspicion – but others liked the rustic sounds.

This was the home of Flat-Roof Man, and Flat-Roof Man had topped the agrarian names with his own fancies. As Andrew walked that morning he passed gates labelled 'Ponderosa', 'Khartoum' and 'High Sierra'. One, called 'Dobermann Lodge', was both a name and a dog warning, while his own uncompromising cube bore the name 'Bennunikin', old Navajo Indian for 'The Wigwam on the Hill'. In these houses lived men who played patience and others who played fast and loose; women who wanted love and others who desired only an automatic dishwasher. Dreams were regularly dreamed, ambitions thwarted, folded away or modestly attained. Love visited and sex sniffed around. Pottery and French classes were popular in winter; people booked their summer holidays as an antidote to the cold terrors of each New Year. Husbands polished cars; wives polished windows or finger-nails. On summer and autumn evenings sunset gardeners burned leaves and rubbish, the smoke climbing like a silent plea for deliverance that forever went unanswered.

The estate was divided from a monster council-housing development, built to rehouse families from slum London, by the fortuitous incision of a railway line raised on an embankment like a dyke or a dam.

At the top of his own street, where it met Risingfield, at its junction with Upper Herd, Andrew was able to look down the residential slopes to the frontier-line of the railway and beyond that to the council estate where the terrace houses lay like long grey ships. There were no garages over there but the trees in the streets freely canopied, in season, the lines of cars outside the houses; the churches, the shops and the schools, except the primary schools, were beyond the embankment on the wrong side of the tracks. But the morning sun visited there only after it had spread across the squared, castellated fortress hill of Plummers Park. Those people, whoever they were, in that hinterland, had to wait for it.

The main rush of morning movers, head-down for the station, had eased, the streets had almost emptied. Soon they would be left to tradesmen, occasional housewives and lonely-eyed infants scraping the pavements on tricycles. Andrew had to travel only one stop to the *Journal* office in Watford, so he could take his time. There were some stragglers, though, and some with easier hours, still making the downward journey from the summit of Plummers Park to the station established like some border post in the valley.

Beneath the station burrowed a pedestrian tunnel nervously joining Plummers Park to the council estate. To venture through it was to leave one country for another: on one side fuchsias, and on the other sheets of newspaper drifting in the street winds. The path though the tunnel was their only direct link. Vehicles had to drive south or north and take the roads joining through neutral territory. Trouble was rare between the tenants of one side of the railway and the residents of the other (except for one violent morning in the launderette where some council clothes and some private garments became somehow mixed in a washing-machine). Otherwise the people were not well enough acquainted to fight. They were merely strangers.

From the gate of 'Eagle's Cranny', as Andrew sloped towards the station, emerged Simon Grant whose brand new wife Ena had the breasts at any party within fourteen miles. (At Uxbridge, it was whispered among the men, a better pair had been spied, but this was hearsay.) The indigestible elation with which the young man was filled even at the mundane outset of a working week was emphatic in the way he closed the gate and waved with jaunty triumph at the farewell hand, slender and disembodied, from the bedroom window.

'Great morning, Andrew!' he exclaimed. Then he sighed as though viewing a private memory: 'Fantastic. Just fantastic.'

'It's going to be a hot summer,' nodded Andrew, staring up at the window in the hopeless hope he might see something forbidden.

'No! I don't mean the weather,' chortled the young man. He fell in beside Andrew with a nudging excitement. 'Christ, Andrew, you ought to wake up every morning and see what I see.'

Andrew glanced half behind with assumed innocence. 'Wouldn't have thought the view was all that much this far down the hill,' he observed. 'We've got the whole valley, the farm, the golf course, the crematorium . . .'

'Stop playing games, mate,' beamed Simon wickedly. 'You don't *want* to know what I see in the mornings. I'm talking about what's right in front of my peepers. Soon as I open them. Right under my own private bedclothes. There *they* are . . .'

'Oh, yes, I see. I get you,' said Andrew, hurriedly. 'Yes, that must be a nice sight.'

'Better than the crematorium,' smugged Simon. 'People around here don't know what sex means. They've no idea, Andrew.'

Andrew did not feel at all hurt. Instead he said: 'Oh, I don't know, Simon. Who knows what passions are broiling in the breast of a man washing his Ford Cortina on a Sunday morning?' Then he asked: 'How long have you and Ena been married now?'

'Ten months last Saturday.' Simon almost hugged himself. 'And listen, just listen to this! On our anniversary she's promised to buy a black body-stocking with a hole between the legs. As advertised in the Sunday paper. How about that, then!'

'How *about* that,' agreed Andrew. He was relieved to see another late-leaver opening his rose-cluttered gate twenty yards further down the hill. Normally he might have groaned at meeting Ernest Rollett so early in the day and the week, but he knew that the additional companionship to the station would douse the hot young man who now walked with him.

'Oh God,' breathed Simon. 'Earnest Ernest. I wonder what the week's good cause is? Petitions to the council, the Ratepayers' Ragtime Ball, or the fouling of footways by other dogs than his?'

''Morning, 'morning, 'morning,' Ernest challenged in the way of one briskly disposing of a paltry argument.

'Nice week-end?' Andrew recited the acknowledged Monday greeting.

'Worried,' said Ernest, dropping his tone eighty per cent. 'Damned worried. You've *heard*, of course?'

'I could have done. What was it?'

'I jolly well hope your paper is going to do something about it.'

'Yes, we might. What is it?'

'The waste land.'

'Eliot's poem?' said Andrew deliberately.

Ernest stared at him malignantly. 'I'm talking about the waste land behind my house,' he grated. He nodded fiercely at Simon. 'And yours.'

Simon became abruptly serious. 'What's it about?'

'School for maladjusted kids,' announced Ernest with dread triumph. 'Plans all ready, all drawn up behind our blasted backs. They'll start building in the spring unless we stop them!'

He glowered at the other two. 'You know what that means, don't you? Drugs. Violence. Delinquents. Madness even.'

'You think we've got enough of that now,' suggested Andrew.

'No, I blasted well don't!' hooted Ernest. A ring of sparrows meeting on a square of lawn hummed off in hurt formation. 'You always seem to have some fool answer, Andrew,' he growled. 'This is bloody serious. Unmarried mothers, shoplifters. That sort of type.'

'Sounds like it's going to be a big place,' observed Andrew. 'How come you know about this?'

'I was told. Someone at county level,' said Ernest bumptiously. They were levelling out at the bottom of the hill now. Ernest's voice took on a piteous tone. 'We need play space for our children . . .' he began.

'Didn't know you had any,' said Andrew.

Ernest flushed. 'I'm talking generally,' he said huffily. 'Or I thought they might use it to build a church. Why not? We haven't got a church over this side of the railway. We could do with a nice church.'

'A church?' repeated Simon as though the idea shocked him more than the maladjusted children. 'A church – over here?'

Andrew laughed: 'In this pagan place?'

Ernest argued: 'Perhaps it wouldn't be pagan if we had a church. That vicar from the thing on the council estate seems frightened to come under the tunnel.'

'Don't blame him, mate,' said Andrew. 'This is cannibal country.'

'And here's one of the cannibals,' said Ernest dolefully, looking ahead. 'For God's sake, he's still swinging that invisible golf club.'

'Gorgeous George,' smiled Simon, glad to see him. 'The hole-in-one man.'

'Wish I were, old chap,' laughed George waiting for them to catch up. 'Had the flaming Hole-in-One tie stuck in my wardrobe for two years now, you know. Still not entitled to wear it.'

'Why don't you just wear it and say you've done a hole-in-one?' asked Simon reasonably.

George looked quietly aghast. 'But that's lying,' he said. 'You can't lie – not about a thing like that anyway.' He shook his head as though saddened by a whiff of great evil.

'Didn't see you up there at the week-end,' he said to Andrew.

'Oh, I get cheesed off with the game,' shrugged Andrew. 'It's too difficult.'

George nodded agreeably. He was a man like a pile of sand. He had gingery hair and a moustache exploded like cordite at each end, pale brown eyes and a baggy fawn suit. 'Cheesed off, that's right,' he said.

'Nobody gets more so than yours truly. Unfortunately I just can't leave it alone.'

'Some things get you like that,' agreed Simon, glancing at Andrew as if they had some private secret.

'Have you heard about the waste land?' asked Ernest irritably. 'Or have you spent the entire weekend in a bunker?'

George was pacing beside them now, and the remark set him off on a series of sand iron shots as he walked. 'Waste land? What's that about, Ernie?' he said.

Ernest bridled at being called Ernie. 'Behind the houses,' he said, haughtily pointing over the flat roofs like someone who alone knows an odd and remote region. 'Not on your side of the road, of course. But you'll be affected like the rest of us.'

'What's going to happen?'

'Just a school for maladjusted kids,' sighed Ernest portentously.

'Damn,' exclaimed George. 'I thought that might be just the size for a pitch-and-putt course. Very handy that would be.'

'Then *you'll* have to fight,' pronounced Ernest, swallowing his inclination to wrath. 'We'll *all* have to fight. I intend to call a meeting as soon as possible. And I'm telephoning your editor this morning, Andrew. We must get the paper involved. It's got to stop before it starts.'

They paused while a small and apologetic sports car, the top pulled raggedly back, emerged rear-first from a scarred double gate. The house was one of the oldest on the Plummers Park Estate, all of ten years (when they were cheap), and they did not know the owner's name. His privet hedges were sturdy and cluttered with summer dust. A wan-faced middle-aged man tugged nervously at the wheel of the car as it backed in jerks. His hound eyes rolled towards them, as though in urgent mute warning. At that moment a rainbow of wet salad, potato peelings and carrot tops curved through the air from somewhere behind the privet hedge. Obviously projected by an expert it lobbed over the windscreen of the little car and covered the man in the driving seat. 'Fuck off!' screamed a raw female voice from the hidden house door. 'And don't fucking well come back!'

Andrew, Ernest, George and Simon stood in almost military rank, transfixed alongside the car. The driver, hung with lettuce and festooned with long potato peelings sat as though about to weep. Weakly and apologetically he turned to them, seemingly confident they would understand, and shrugged: 'Monday morning.'

Politely they said nothing as the trembling man backed the trembling car into the road and there stopped it while he miserably picked the vegetable debris from his head and clothes. They walked on, in silence, Andrew, Simon and George not daring to look at each other, and the proper Ernest, feeling it only decent to ignore the drama, returned to his former subject. 'No,' he affirmed loudly and conclusively, 'We've got no place for the maladjusted in Plummers Park.'

Audrey Maiby was a quietly sensual woman married to a lazy man. In her teens she had been more promiscuous than either fashion or safety had recognized. She had met Andrew one night on a riverboat shuffle on the Thames, and they watched the growing dawn while sprawled amid the damp dock leaves and dewy dandelions of Temple Island. She and he, hung against each other, drunk with exultation and the unused smell of five o'clock sun, had walked the bank along the length of the Henley Regatta course, she carrying her damp knickers in her hand. Now they lived at Plummers Park like all the others who had merely held hands in the cinema. The wild times had gone. The winds had been thrown to caution. She, who had so perilously enjoyed her love, was securely on the pill.

She watched him leave that airy morning, sixteen years after Temple Island, still worth looking at, his longer hair not looking incongruous as it did on some of the other men, but his stride now eased to something like a shuffle, and no riverboat shuffle either. He spent a lot of his time reading. That far night among the dandelions, as they lay wet against each other, he had told her rhymes and things he had heard and what he had dreamed. He seemed to have read every book in the world, and he knew words, quite short words, of which she had never suspected the existence. 'You,' she had said in her teenage way, massaging her fingers around his uncovered loins. 'You're a poet you are, you know. And I've heard poets are dangerous.'

Now, she thought with a comfort, wry and contrary, he was about as dangerous as one of the pied milking cows she could see mooning in the slanting fields beyond Plummers Park, and at times she had caught him wearing the same expression. And yet he would worry if they had not made love for a week; she had sensed him, in bed, mentally calculating the days and wondering whether he ought to ask. He had once run off with an extraordinary and attractive woman, but he had come back because, she suspected, he missed their furniture, the colour television, his books and his smelly dog.

Gladstone, the brown bolster, the emitter of noises and odours, lay now, already defeated by the growing sun, having watched his master walk towards the station with the smashed expression of one convinced that a beloved one has gone forever.

'You ought to go with him,' she suggested to the basset. Then spitefully: 'You ought to have gone with him last time.' The tubular dog looked up with a red hung eye and ingratiating smile. She closed the front door on him, stood indecisively in the hall, then went into the kitchen to finish her coffee. She stood, as he had stood earlier watching the girl from Cowacre, looking out over the emptied estate. Andrew was always one of the final husbands to leave, and it seemed that the entire valley had been quit by its people because of some plague or disaster and not merely by the daily necessity of employment. It was left flooded with the silence of sunshine, populated by toddlers, routine housewives and, with the exception of the French onion man, unexciting tradesmen.

On this morning, however, there were two early and abnormal interruptions. First Herbie Futter, the taxidermist, left his house later than usual, with a smothering embrace for and from his ash-grey wife on the step. She reflected on the way Jewish people said goodbye as though they never expected to see each other again. She had once asked Herbie to change a five pound note in the Watford supermarket, and he had produced his wallet and proceeded to kiss, both feverishly and fervently, fading pictures of his wife and grown-up children before finally giving her the change. He was a perpetually nodding man, followed, sometimes pursued, by dogs attracted by the smell of the chemicals he used in his trade. Especially in hot weather. He had come to Plummers Park because, he said, he despised the regimentation of the German mentality in his own country. It was not so much the gas chambers, he once complained, but the indignity of lining up for them.

Now he walked quite briskly along the paraded ranks of English houses, free he believed, towards the station and then to his workshop where he was engaged in stuffing a bison, a tiring and exacting task for someone no longer young.

He had only just completed his exit from the wide screen of her kitchen window when from the other edge appeared Hercules, the singing tramp, bent like a tactful enquiry over the laden perambulator which he pushed all day, all week, all year, all life, on some mysterious and never accomplished journey. He was the Flying Dutchman of Plummers Park, restless, unresting, regarded by the new people as something quaint and traditional, to be fed and preserved. He lent atmosphere to the place.

'Hang on a minute, Hercules,' Audrey said to herself, and tugging her dressing-gown round her she went out of the door. She thought she would call him first, but since he travelled at something below a mile an hour she refrained and hurried instead under the carport and to the garage at the rear. Wedged at the side of her white mini was what had been, in its heyday, an elegant baby-carriage. Now it was scratched and dusty and the wheels complained as she moved it. She withdrew it from the garage and then pushed it down the front path.

Hercules was singing in his plodding voice, his head down as if he were tired or ashamed:

When I survey the wondrous Cross
On which the Prince of Glory died
My richest gain I count but loss
And pour contempt on all my pride.

'I say,' she called, 'I wonder if you'd like a new pram.' She did not call him Hercules, because that was just a nickname which people around there had given him. She did not know whether he knew it or would like it.

He stopped walking and singing, bent so low he was scarcely half her height. His face turned upwards. It was like a piece of bruised fruit, but his eyes were black and bright. 'It squeaks,' he pointed out at once. 'I heard it squeaking when you wheeled it.'

'That old thing squeaks too,' Audrey said, nodding at his rusted pram piled with sacks and blankets and with socks hanging over its side like the fenders of a tugboat. They were rumoured to be full of gold sovereigns.

'Right,' agreed Hercules. He swivelled on both heels, a miniature military movement, to view his present pram. She noticed that, apart from a minimal parting from the knees downwards as he walked, his short legs were kept close together all the time. 'It squeaks as well,' he conceded. 'But I'm used to this squeak, ain't I? I don't reckon I could change it for another squeak, not now, missus. Mine's regular. Sends me to kip sometimes when I'm on the road.'

'I wondered why you never got any speed up,' she said, hurt that he viewed her gift with such off-handedness. 'Well, do you want it, or don't you? It's not been used for a few years but it's all right.'

'It squeaks,' he said doggedly. 'Better the squeak you know than the squeak you don't. Let's have a look at it, anyway.'

'I don't want anything for it,' she said hurriedly, in case he thought she was trying to sell it.

'You won't get nuffink neither,' he confirmed, without change of expression. 'I can't see me taking it off your hands. I'm very busy just now.'

He mistook her incredulous expression for disappointment. 'Okay, all right, missus,' he said reassuringly. 'Let's see what it goes like.' He waddled towards her and she pushed the pram a little nervously his way. 'The tyres ain't much good,' he said.

'God, you'd think you were a second-hand car dealer!'

'I was once,' he said, glancing over the bodywork. 'That's why I'm on the road. Too easy-going I was, missus.'

'Look,' she said in exasperation. 'Do you want the damned pram or don't you? If you don't, just say, and I'll get rid of it elsewhere.'

'Where?' he inquired challengingly. 'The dustmen won't take it, and the council will charge you to take it away.' He had shuffled round the rear end by now and she saw with alarm and embarrassment that he was so bent by his years of pushing his low pram that he could not reach the white polished handle of hers. He turned accusingly as though she had perpetrated some cruel joke. 'I can't get my 'ands up that 'igh,' he protested.

'Shit,' she said angrily to herself.

'I can shit, missus. Shitting's nuffink. But I can't reach that 'andle. My old one's a foot lower.'

'All right,' Audrey sighed. 'Let's forget it. I'll take it back.'

'Naw,' he said, with a sudden surging smile of generosity, black teeth projecting over his lips like cigarette stubs. 'Naw, I'll take it off your 'ands. I like the look of you.'

She stared at the innocent wickedness of his face. 'Listen,' he said. 'Don't you worry. I'll tow it behind. I might be able to get rid of it for you.'

'Oh good, all right then,' she said.

She thought he was going to ask her for money, but he merely said: 'I can't stay chatting all day, missus. I'm way behind schedule already. I'll 'ave to go or I'll be in trouble.' Still far from understanding, she nodded seriously and watched him attach the newly acquired pram to his boyscout belt by a piece of cord. Then, one conveyance ahead and another behind he recommenced his eternal journey. For the first time she noticed he had a bunch of wild flowers in a jam jar in the hull of his pram.

She returned gratefully to the house, but for some reason turned at the door and looked out. The bland sunshine seemed wasted on such an empty place. The houses looked like crates waiting on a wharf. On the most distant road, Hedgerows, she could see a post-office van like a ladybird. By her own front path the dew remained like glass on the roses. Birds were sending their summer songs from the oak tree incorporated in their garden wall, which itself was constructed of *old* bricks. That tree and the rough wall put five hundred pounds on the house. The primrose telephone rang in the hall and she went in.

'In the street accosting men,' whispered the accusation. '*I* saw you.'

'Hello, Cynth.' She smiled to herself. 'You and all the neighbours, I bet.'

'Old Hercules might be fun.'

'You haven't seen his teeth.'

'Come to think of it, I don't think I've seen his face,' said Cynthia Turvey. 'He's always got it facing the road as he pushes that pram. Do you think he'll take our old pushchair? You do hang on to these things, but I can't see us needing it now.'

'He won't look at it,' said Audrey, as though Hercules were a fine art dealer. 'He was doing me a big favour, believe me.'

'Fancy the poor bugger being all bent up like that,' sighed Cynthia. 'Have you seen Bill Shillingford? He's getting like that. They say he's digging an extra room out of the earth. He can do it because he's got a split level on his side of the hill.'

'Really. I must tell Andrew, though I can't see him ever doing anything like that.'

'You have to actually be on the *side* of the hill,' pointed out Cynthia pedantically. 'Apparently if you go round there he's liable to walk through the lounge stripped to the waist and wheeling a wheelbarrow full of clay.'

Audrey said, 'Come to think about it, I wouldn't mind seeing Andrew hauling a few barrows about. He spends all his time reading, thinking great thoughts or playing football with the kids over the waste ground. He comes back soaked with sweat and boasting he's scored three goals.'

'He'll have more kids to play with soon,' said Cynthia, in the manner of someone who knows something.

'How do you mean?'

'They're going to build a place for retarded children over on the waste land, didn't you hear?'

'No! They wouldn't do that!' She felt the leaden sensation in her stomach that arrived whenever there was a threat of any kind to the security that so bored her. 'Who told you?'

'It's all over Plummers Park,' said Cynthia glibly. 'They're starting work any minute.'

'Oh, Christ, Cynth, that's terrible. It'll knock thousands off these properties. Just our damned luck.' Her fear flamed easily into anger. 'Didn't Andrew know anything about it? I thought *he* would.'

Audrey sighed. 'He's usually the last to hear even though he's on the paper. Maybe he knew and forgot to mention it. He would. He didn't tell me that Greta Humphries had committed suicide until everybody else for miles around knew. He said it wasn't the sort of thing he thought ought to be bandied about because of her kids.'

'Well, he's very thoughtful, very kind, old Andrew. You know where you are with him. Safe.'

'Old Andrew, indeed,' agreed Audrey. 'He was being nice and thoughtful this morning when that girl, what's her name, Hewkins, from Cowacre came by, with half the men in Plummers Park sniffing after her like randy dogs. You're lucky Geoff goes off early and you don't have to put up with that.'

'He gets his thrills in the office,' said Cynthia confidently, then added a cautious 'I expect'. 'They think nothing of it. It's part of being male. They'd kick up murder, though, wouldn't they, if *we* went around fancying *men* left, right and centre?'

'*Don't* you?'

'Don't I what?'

'Fancy men, Cynth?'

'Yes, I suppose I do, really. I fancied Geoff when he was married. Do you?'

'Naturally I do. Isn't it funny how they think only *they* get the urges. They think we're not the same, we're not allowed to be.'

'I suppose you're right, Audrey.' Cynthia sounded as though she was becoming wary of the conversation. 'Listen,' she continued quickly, 'tonight, if it stays decent, we thought we'd go out and have a drink somewhere in the country. Do you two want to come?'

Audrey waited. 'Well, we'd thought of going out ourselves,' she said cautiously. 'Lizzie is up on the canal renovating that old barge with the other children and she keeps asking us to go up and see what they've done. You've got to show willing, haven't you, when they ask? So we thought we'd wander up there and have a look.'

'Oh, yes. Perhaps we could come with you.'

'No.' It came out more sharply than she had intended. 'Well, you know what kids are. They'll think we've brought the whole neighbourhood up.'

'Oh, all right then.'

'No, but you do understand, don't you? Kids are funny these days. They don't like the idea of grown-ups breathing down their necks. Listen, why don't we meet you and Geoff in that pub up there, the one with the seats in the garden and the old mill-wheel . . . The one with the funny name. Remember we laughed about it?'

'The Jolly Grinder,' said Cynthia, but still coolly. 'All right, I'll ask my

Geoff if he wants to go there. He might have somewhere else in mind. You understand that, don't you?'

'Of course I do, Cynthia. Andrew's the same. I always like to ask him. Anyway, maybe we'll see you in the garden.'

'All right. 'Bye, Audrey. Sorry about the home for maladjusted kids.'

'So am I. It's a liberty. 'Bye, 'bye.'

Audrey went up to the bathroom. They had knocked the lavatory and the bathroom into one so that it was now a tufty-white carpeted room of a good size. They had found some dignified Delft tiles in an antique shop and put them into the wall to give the area around the lavatory pan more character.

One of the results of making the two rooms into one was that the only place for a full-length mirror was now directly in front of the lavatory and anyone squatting there was faced with their own reflection. She had put a coy flowered curtain on the wall so that visitors could pull it across the mirror if they felt embarrassed by their own presence. She sat naked on the pan and regarded herself seriously in the glass. You could hardly expect to look better every day, not when you were a day older, but the summer tan helped. She smiled at herself and was glad to see that her good teeth showed very white against the deepening brown of her face. Two fatty rolls lay across her stomach, so she folded her arms, formally, as though in a photograph, to hide them.

When she had finished she turned on the bath taps and then felt her breasts for lumps as she did every day, as instructed in the Sunday supplements. None had appeared. The breasts were full but dull, strong but with a touch of sloth about them, like her husband. Andrew enjoyed her breasts. He still told her so, and when he felt like feeling her affectionately that was always where his hands went. Now, when they had overcome the natural laziness of familiarity, they sometimes lay on their sides, face to face, in bed, while he sucked at them, holding her buttocks in his considerate but firm grip.

She now rolled them firmly with her hands, enjoying the minor sensation, and then laughing at her reflection in the mirror. She struck a series of odd poses, like a Balinese temple dancer, legs akimbo, arms and hands projecting like angled wings, head clicking from side to side. She turned and adjusted the cold crystal bath tap. She put the lid of the toilet down and sat on it, the candlewick cover comfortably soft against her buttocks. She took a bottle of almond oil and began to rub it into the broad tops of her legs, where the week-end sunburn was blushing and sore.

Afterwards she stood in the bath and soaped herself and then lay down in the warm water and let her eyes close. The house seemed very vacant and quiet. She stopped moving and the sudsy water around her settled to stillness. Now through the left-open door she could hear the chronic movements of the clock from their bedroom, the birds outside the window, and miles away the half-sound of a lofty aeroplane. No one was there but her, no one to see or care or listen. It hardly seemed to matter what she did. If she simply drowned herself she wondered if Andrew would keep the truth from Lizzie. Would he be so considerate with a suicide of his own as he had been over Greta Humphries? The solitariness and the frustration gathered within her like indigestion. She felt like having a good swear, but instead she began to sing, like Hercules:

When I survey the Wondrous Cross
On which the Prince of Glory died
My richest gain I count but loss,
And pour contempt on all my pride.

Then she began to cry. It was brief, and she wiped the tears quickly into the bathwater. 'I'm mad,' she thought lucidly. 'I must be potty. I thought I had another ten years or more before I started this sort of thing.'

She climbed from the bath and began to dry herself. 'You ought to snap out of it, my girl,' she told herself loudly. 'You ought to get out and do some charity work.' She would not mind helping with the maladusted children, she thought, if only they would build their rotten place somewhere else, over the railway line perhaps. Or maybe she ought to go to London more often. It was three months since she had been to London.

She dressed, did her hair and her makeup, and then went down to the kitchen and made another cup of coffee. She turned the radio on and allowed Jimmy Young to twitter three sentences before turning it off again. Then, through the window, she caught sight of the French onion seller.

He was the most beautiful man anyone had ever seen in Plummers Park. Tall, slim, black-haired and dark-faced, with violinist's eyes, everything about him was exciting, sexual, even the onions hanging from his bike. He toured the English streets once a month, he and his wares, leaving tears in many eyes. He wore the *bleu de travail*. He was said to come from Normandy and he had little English. He had never been seen to enter any woman's home. She watched with womanly cunning from the spot a yard inside her window and saw the housewives come to their doors and simper as they purchased his onions. Two were in bikinis and another was in her nightdress. He did not appear to notice. Poor drunken Mrs Burville was already in her garden walking in circles among the flowers, trying to pick a few stems. She was wearing a fat nylon overall and white knee-length socks belonging to her brilliant daughter Sarah. She made little darts at odd roses as if trying to capture a butterfly, but after several indecisive circles picked only one bloom which she gave with the caring smile of the truly inebriated to the French onion man. He accepted it courteously and gave her a single onion in return. Then he turned, crossed the road, and made straight for Audrey's door.

She pretended not to take a glance at herself in the mirror as she went to the door, but she caught herself doing it. She opened the door and he stood there smiling, his dark hair curling down his brown neck and his forehead, and his arms festooned with naked onions. He had left his bike on the road.

'Not today, thank you,' she said firmly.

He looked theatrically concerned. 'A long time,' he said, 'You have not onions.'

'We're not great onion eaters,' said Audrey politely. 'My husband doesn't care for them.'

'And you, madame?'

'No, nor me either.'

He shrugged and his onions shrugged with him. 'It is a pity,' he said. He paused and looked at her with blatant steadiness. Christ, she thought, those eyes are ridiculous. 'Perhaps, my dear, there is something else?'

Audrey felt her blush cover her face and her chest. 'No. I don't think so, thank you. Not today.'

He went and she retreated into the house bubbling like a spring inside. She sat in an armchair and laughed unbelievingly into her hands. Dear Jesus, there was nothing like an onion man to make you feel like a desirable woman.

CHAPTER TWO

Andrew went directly from the station to the magistrates court, a cool and carbolic place, the high windows letting in the murmurs of a June morning to those who would be brought from the cells to the dock. Clean sunlight slanted tantalizingly from the upper windows, but the lower panes were frosted as though not to aggravate the envy of the prisoners and the others who had to be in that serious position on that fine day.

He collected the charge list from Sergeant Fearnley, the officer's bald, official head bronzed from his garden. He carried it to where Big Brenda, the girl reporter from the opposition paper, squatted at the press table. She was a red, chatty soul, who had once been reprimanded by the chairman of the magistrates for clicking her knitting needles throughout the preliminary hearing of a murder trial.

It was a meagre press table and it was their Monday habit to squeeze together on the bench, their thighs wedged in the confined space between the bulbous table legs. No words were ever said about this comforting tradition. Big Brenda was hung with woollen garments, whatever the season. She knitted most of them herself, often beneath the reporters' table during long and doleful cases. The work finished, she would appear dressed in these sheepish scraps, a bobbled hat, a shaggy scarf, a cardigan growing wooden buttons, toggles, acorns, and, in the meanest part of winter, bright red mittens on her bright red hands.

Andrew placed the charge list on the table between them, and Big Brenda's large fuchsia lips flopped into a smile of genuine greeting. They leaned forward to study it together, nudging hard against the table's legs and each other's, her swollen, woollen bosom resting on the oak top like two bags of damp laundry.

'All the usual,' sighed Andrew, running his eye down the list. 'Drunk, drunk and indecent, drunk and not indecent, drunk and incapable, drunk in charge of a bicycle . . . that could be all right . . . theft from a gas meter, non-payment of arrears . . . parking without lights . . . thrill upon thrill . . . everything but knocking on doors and running away . . . theft from Waitrose Supermarket . . . theft from W. H. Smith's . . . theft from MacFisheries . . . looks like this chap did a round tour . . .'

'Strange for it to be a man,' murmured Brenda. 'They're usually women, shoplifters. And he's seventy-four. Charles White, seventy-four. Morrison Way. That's your direction, isn't it?'

'Other side of the railway,' replied Andrew immediately, and surprised at his own defensiveness. 'On the council estate.'

'Where else?' said Brenda. 'You'd hardly expect anyone from your bit to nick half a pound of hake from the fish-shop.'

'We have other faults,' said Andrew. 'False idols, fornication . . . getting up the Joneses.' She giggled primly and his voice trailed off. The court had been filling, and now the elevated oak-panelled door opened in a mildly dramatic way and, to the bellow of 'Rise, please!' from Sergeant Fearnley, the three magistrates made an entrance of modest majesty.

Andrew's eyes turned idly around the court. It looked like the stage of a bad amateur theatrical company, as though people had been hastily gathered from the street, briefly told their parts, and put into the scene. Some characters were constant, Sergeant Fearnley; his coughing constable; an old boy who always sat in the oaken public gallery, side-on like someone sitting up in their coffin, pouring himself relays of tea from a grim flask; Miss Bishop, the probation officer, an anguished soul screwing up pieces of paper and leaving them on the floor like a castaway's pleas for help. Then there were the witnesses and the relatives of the various accused, sitting resigned, tired, frightened, puzzled or amused, and Mr Henry, the court clerk, his nostrils so close to his large ledger that in the winter dewdrops from his nose seemed to join him like tacky glue to the legal pages. Above him, in the manner of a trio of coachmen above a lone, head-hung horse, were the magistrates: on one flank Mr Walter Brownlow, a baggy seed merchant, and former mayor, who left trails of barley and oats dripping from his pockets and trouser turn-ups wherever he went; on the other Mrs Matilda Prentice, a sexily severe young woman who peered with a sharp but beautiful face from beneath a variable but gay hat at accused men who had never so much as touched one of her kind; at their centre the chairman, Mr John Osmund, a scraggy man who uttered thin comments to himself throughout the hearing of a case and doled out sentences either sadistically severe or idiotically liberal as the mood or the morning took him. Andrew watched them without sensation until he fell to thinking that because of the enclosed gallery on which they sat he had never seen Mrs Prentice's legs. She was the type of woman who still wore stockings and a small suspender belt.

'Number one, sir. John Smart,' Sergeant Fearnley called.

John Smart, sparse and dun, tired, a shred of coloured tie tight around the neck of a grisly army shirt, the very denial of his name, blinked through sore eyes from the dock. He seemed anxious to get the matter done. ''aving a piss, sir,' he announced loudly towards the magistrates.

Mr Osmund leaned pedantically over towards the back of his clerk's head. 'What did he say?' he inquired. Andrew saw how much the magistrate and the accused were physically alike, the meagre heads jutting forward, but one a small, demanding pump, the other a hopeful, hopeless nod.

The clerk rattled his throat, half rose, half turned, and replied: 'He says he was . . . er relieving himself, sir.'

'Oh, for goodness' sake, why can't we start at the beginning, in the proper way?' sighed Mr Osmund.

'Of course, sir,' replied the clerk. He turned from the one sparse man to the other. 'John Smart,' he began . . .

'Just 'aving a piss,' reaffirmed the accused almost smugly.

'*John Smart*,' said Mr Henry doggedly. 'You are charged with being drunk and indecent at Church Lane last night. Do you plead guilty or not guilty?'

'Guilty, sir,' sighed the red-eyed man as though at last they understood. 'Just 'aving a piss.'

He was fined a pound, which he did not have, and so was sentenced to one day in prison, which meant he sat down in court and watched the other drunks and miscreants with the scorning amusement of one whose debt is paid.

The pathetic Monday morning carnival trailed through the official room. To some, thought Andrew, it was probably the best room in which they had ever been. A man with a black eye wept in the dock; two earthy young women, wild as gipsies, sniggered and then fell upon each other with unashamed laughter as a police constable produced two groundsheets, said to be an essential part of their open-air trade; a youth with a broken arm nodded dumbly when it was suggested that he fell down the steps of the cells and was never pushed; a man found at midnight with a glass-cutter adjacent to a neat hole in a shop window protested that it was a tool of his trade, that he was entitled to carry it and had merely been testing its sharpness on the window. It was a poor parade even for that petty area, and the advent of Charles White, aged seventy-four, charged with shoplifting, did little to raise the general tone. Except that with him, sitting in the public seats, watching with studied anxiety, was a girl, small and serious: a round, conventionally pretty, salesgirl face framed with fair hair. She was shadowed below the eyes as though she did not sleep well. When the old man in the dock spoke her lips formed the words with him, as if together they had rehearsed every line.

Mr Henry read the monotonous accumulation of charges. Two tins of cling peaches and a plastic tube of cocktail sticks from Waitrose Supermarket, two paperbacks and three coloured pencils from Smith's, a cod cutlet and a live eel from MacFisheries . . .

'Peaches, cocktail sticks, paperbacks, cod and eel,' muttered Brenda as she wrote in her slow shorthand.

'Ivory, and apes and peacocks, sandalwood and cedarwood and sweet white wine,' sighed Andrew quietly.

'Do you plead guilty or not guilty?' inquired Mr Henry lifting his head from his big ledger, as if annoyed at intrusion into some personal and private study.

'Guilty,' the old man almost shouted. Andrew watched the girl's lips say it with him. 'I . . . I . . . I'm guilty all right.'

'Yes, yes,' said Mr Henry impatiently. 'Evidence, please.'

A young constable was in the pouch of the witness-box, crouching at the neck, holding the Bible above his head as though sheltering from a local shower. He took the oath with religious care and then proceeded to describe the crimes and apprehension of Charles White, aged seventy-four, now standing like a failed suicide, dying of consumption, in front of a firing squad. The old man sported three worn and pathetic medals on his chest, one bravely pulling the lapel of his weary coat forward like a derisive tongue.

'A *live* eel?' said the magistrate. Andrew nodded to himself, grateful that the chairman had brought it up. It was the best part of the story.

'Yes, sir,' replied the constable, carefully referring to his notebook. 'Live. Extant, your honour. This is why the accused was apprehended, sir. A woman complained to me that the accused had dropped the eel on to her baby in the pram. He was trying to make his escape from the fishmongers at the time. The accused, that is, sir.'

'Guilty, guilty,' insisted the dry old voice from the dock, wanting to get it done.

'The supermarket, Smith's, MacFisheries,' recited the chairman. 'Went on the rampage, didn't you?'

He glanced towards the press bench, making sure they were writing 'on the rampage' down. He liked to see his notable phrases in the paper. 'Why did you do this?' he demanded towards the dock.

'Forgot to pay,' said Charles White. He pushed forward one side of his chest so that his medals gave a brief jangle. Mr Osmund ignored the action. Old men were always jangling medals in court.

'You forgot to pay in three shops,' sniffed the chairman. He glanced at the court generally. 'Is there any other evidence?'

'His grand-daughter's here, sir,' said Sergeant Fearnley, touching the girl on the shoulder. 'I think she would like to say something.'

The girl and the grandfather in the dock exchanged quick, trapped looks. 'Take the oath, then,' sighed Mr Osmund. The girl, slight in a red dress, walked nervously to the witness-box and whispered the words on the card before her.

'I swear that the evidence I shall give will be the truth, the whole truth

... and nothing but the truth ...' She stumbled along the trite lines and it seemed that she was going to cry. Brenda had gone scarlet with pity. Andrew leaned forward.

'Come on, come on, young woman,' said Mr Henry, with soft severity. He liked young girl witnesses. 'Don't let's have any tears. Lots of people have read that oath.'

'*I* haven't,' said the girl, jerking her head up and staring defiantly at him. 'Not before.'

The clerk seemed unable to find an argument. 'What's your name?' he asked impatiently.

'Bessie White,' she whispered.

'Speak up, girl. Everybody wants to hear you. The magistrates, the press, everybody.'

'The press?' breathed the girl, her face hardening. 'What's the press got to do with it?'

Andrew had often wondered that himself. Now Mr Henry and all three magistrates turned, grinning knowingly at him and Brenda, and they dutifully returned the stupid grins.

'The press are always in court,' said Mr Henry with bland pride. 'Now let's have your name again.'

'Bessie White,' she repeated, staring across at Andrew as though she could scarcely credit her eyes.

'That's Elizabeth, is it? Bessie?'

'Bessie,' she replied firmly.

'I see. How old are you?'

'Eighteen. Nearly nineteen.'

'And you live at 22 Morrison Way, Attlee Park, with the accused?'

'He's my grandad,' she said hurriedly, and looking around for understanding as though anxious to correct any wrong impression.

'Quite, quite so,' murmured Mr Henry. 'Now, you have heard him plead guilty to this charge . . .'

'Guilty! Guilty!' croaked the old man gladly from the dock.

The girl and Mr Henry both looked at him sternly but in different ways. He dropped his forlorn eyes and began to rub one of his medals with his sleeve. '. . . you have heard him plead guilty,' repeated the clerk.

'Guilty, guilty,' muttered the man.

'Shut up, Grandad!' cried the girl suddenly and fiercely. Her voice, which had been soft, touched with an edge of Cockney, flew like a knife. The old man dropped his ashamed chin on his chest.

'Thank you,' said Mr Henry. 'Now, what have you got to tell us?'

'Just that he didn't mean it,' she said. 'He's just an old fool. He just saw the things and he took them. What does he want with cocktail sticks?'

'We appreciate you coming to espouse him.' It was the sharp young Mrs Prentice leaning over her wooden parapet to look down at the girl. 'What sort of person is he?'

'He's an old man,' shrugged the girl as though it answered everything. 'He's even older than he is, if you see what I mean. He just walks around and does silly things. I don't want his name in the papers.'

Andrew looked up sharply from his notes and saw her hard expression directly at him. He began to scribble aimlessly. Brenda's thigh nudged him. Mr Brownlow, the corn merchant magistrate, a kind man, took out a great handkerchief to blow his nose and ejected with it a scattering of barley seeds which fell, bounced noisily on the bench and trickled on to the half-bent head of the clerk below him. Mr Henry privately closed his eyes.

'I'm afraid, young lady,' said Mr Brownlow heavily, ignoring what he had done, 'that we have no power to tell the press what to publish or what not to publish.'

'I don't want it in,' she repeated as if it were an order or a threat.

'Do you wish to say anything else about the accused?' asked Mr Osmund impatiently.

'No, nothing,' she said, turning her expression slowly to him. 'It's just that he's an old man. You can see that.'

Sergeant Fearnley moved towards the girl and touched her arm as she descended from the witness-box. She glanced at her grandfather and then looked again at Andrew. Then she sat down.

'Anything known?' asked the chairman, eyebrows going towards the constable.

The policeman stepped back into the witness-box and consulted some spread papers. 'Previous conviction, sir, for stealing thirty-five newspapers from a vendor's stand, fifteen *Stars*, five *Standards*, and the rest *Evening News*es, sir. Put on probation for three years. Acton magistrates court, sir.'

'That must have been years ago,' pointed out the kindly Mr Brownlow. 'The *Star*'s not been published for ten or twelve years now.'

'Yes, sir,' agreed the constable. 'The conviction was in 1950, sir.'

'Why didn't you say so then?' said Mr Brownlow.

'I was going to, sir, when you spoke.' The policeman looked at the corn merchant steadily and the corn merchant, abashed, picked up one of his previously scattered grains lying on the bench before him, and ate it remorselessly, rolling it in exaggerated manner about his rural cheeks and gums.

After the pause the policeman said with studied firmness, 'There is another conviction – for cruelty, sir.'

He glanced up to see the court stir at that. Andrew was watching the girl again and saw the disbelief and alarm on her pale face.

'Cruelty?' queried Mr Osmund, looking sternly at the old man in the dock and then returning to the constable. 'What cruelty?'

'Apparently, sir, he was fined five shillings at Acton for painting a sparrow yellow, sir, and attempting to sell it as a canary.'

The grim man who always sat sideways like someone in his coffin in the public gallery began to honk with laughter, the first time he had made a sound in court in years. Others were grinning or laughing. Andrew could feel Branda rolling inside like warm water in a plastic bag and he briefly turned his own face down to the table. When he looked up there was still the pale, laughterless face of the girl.

'Sparrow? Canary?' muttered the chairman.

'Very unkind,' said Mrs Prentice severely.

'Guilty, guilty,' cried the man in the dock.

'It was a long time ago, sir,' said the constable as if sorry it were not more recent. 'Nineteen twenty-one, sir.'

'That's all there is?' inquired the chairman wearily. 'This seems to be getting out of hand.'

'Yes, your honour, that's all,' said the constable. He stepped down.

'Charles White,' sighed Mr Osmund, as though considering every syllable of the name. 'You have admitted this charge and we have heard your previous record. Is there anything else you want to say?'

'Guilty, guilty,' said the old man with dry doggedness.

'I am going to fine you twenty-five pounds.'

There was a moment when the grandfather half-turned and looked at the girl. She nodded and reached for her handbag.

Outside the magistrates court, at the top of the warm summer road, was a café called The Bombardier owned by a former regular soldier and painted in camouflage streaks of khaki and green. Big Brenda said she had to return to her office and rolled away down the hill, while Andrew walked idly up the incline towards the café. The work he had done that morning would take an hour to write, and after that he would probably be free to go home to Plummers Park. Sometimes Burton, the editor, gave him evening jobs to do, but not many. He was working at twenty-five per cent of his capacity and he knew it. He was living at the same rate. Two years before he had gone to live for six sexual weeks with a beautiful and crazy girl in three damp rooms overlooking the Thames. Every minute of every day and every night was taken. They had lived, feasted off each other then finished. They walked away leaving the washing-up of their last meal in the sink. He had gone back to slow compromise with his wife. When he had nothing else to think about, which was quite often, he thought about the girl. If he went to London he pretended he might even see her among the hundreds in the streets. But he never did. She had probably gone to America. Audrey thought about her too but she was hardly ever mentioned.

Bessie White left the magistrates court, pulling her grandfather after her like an old handcart. She nagged him up the road and followed Andrew into The Bombardier Café where he was sitting at one of the tables covered with decorated oilcloth depicting badges of Britain's fighting forces. The bombardier himself, short-haired, thick-armed, festooned with memorable tattoos, stood behind the counter watching the steaming spout of a tea-urn as in other days he had watched what he liked to call the smoking arse of a twenty-five-pounder gun.

Andrew looked up from his table and tea and felt a short startled sensation as the girl came through the door. It was as if she were some kind of threat or vengeance. She was ushering the old man before her now. His face was set with elderly indifference and Andrew saw that his medals had gone. Andrew thought the girl was going to sit opposite him at his place, but she knew where she was going. She and her grandfather sat at the next oilclothed table staring directly at him. He tried to look deep into the revolving tea in his cup but he knew that the young face and the old face were both irrevocably in his direction, so he looked up and grinned foolishly.

'Where's his medals, then?' he asked with uneasy friendliness.

'He had to give them back, didn't he,' said the girl with the London rhetorical question.

'How do you mean?'

'They didn't belong to him,' she replied easily. 'Never done a day's fighting in his life, except with my gran or the neighbours.'

'You . . . you just . . . borrowed them?' asked Andrew carefully. She had steady hazel eyes, and they were watching him with an implicit challenge. 'Just for the duration of the case, as it were?' he added.

'As it were,' she repeated with a little curl of mockery. 'The other one was wearing them, the one who was drunk and having a pee. I gave him a pound to lend them to me. He's got them back now.'

'God,' said Andrew. 'You've got a nerve.'

The tea arrived for her and her grandfather, and she peeped around the thickness of the bombardier's embossed forearms to reply. 'Yes, that's one thing I have got, a nerve.'

'I've never heard anything like it,' said Andrew.

'I suppose you're going to shove *that* in the paper now,' she said. Her hostility rose like a spike. A pink spot appeared on each of her pale cheeks.

'No,' he assured her. 'No, I won't be doing that.' He regarded the strange pair. The girl neat and sharp, the old man staring at him and beyond him, punched with age and indifference. 'Can I come and sit there?' said Andrew, getting up and taking his cup and saucer in his hand. He had taken a pace, but the girl put up the flat of her hand to him, a slim white hand like a trout's belly.

'Why don't you stay where you are,' she suggested, to his discomfort. 'There's plenty of room to talk like this. Anyway, you could scare the old boy and he'll spill his tea. He spills things all the time.'

'All right, if that's what you want,' grumbled Andrew uncomfortably, edging back to his seat. When he looked up, having slopped his tea from thick cup to thick saucer, feeling as he had felt when as a teenager a girl had declined to dance with him, she was smiling.

'Don't take offence,' she said. 'It's not your fault you've got a job like you have. Telling about people.'

'Oh, come on,' he said, roused as he invariably was by any attack on the profession he loathed. 'You'd be the first one to read this sort of case if it wasn't your grandfather involved. You'd have a good laugh and a gossip about it in your street.'

'Do you know where we live?' she asked.

'Morrison Way,' he muttered, as though ashamed he knew. 'I live over that area myself. I live on the hill. Upmeadow.'

She grimaced with puzzlement, then laughed as though he had told a shoddy joke. 'Oh, Christ!' she exclaimed. 'Over the other side. Well, you'll really *know* all about us, then, won't you? Like you know about the Chinese.'

'Listen,' said Andrew, Flat-Roof Man rising to battle within him, 'I've seen a girl in riding gear leading a bloody *horse* out of the front door of one of those council houses. So don't give me all the poor people stuff.'

'Remember *you're* the one who pays my dad's rates,' she mimicked accurately.

'I've got more to do than argue with the likes of you,' he said angrily, getting up. He saw that his zip fly was hanging undone and that she was looking at it. He zipped himself up fiercely and defiantly, but caught a piece of his shirt in the metal teeth and it stuck. He tugged up and down violently but he could not move it. The girl was laughing into her hands, still watching him through slight, open fingers. The old man just continued to stare as though he did not understand.

He sat at his desk staring so emphatically at a picture of steelworks on a wall calendar that the ring of the telephone almost lifted him out of his seat.

'Hello,' he said, still blinking with the shock. 'Maiby here.'

'You've got a funny name,' she said. 'Maiby. It sounds like you're not sure what it is.'

'I'm *not* sure what it is sometimes,' he said. 'And that's not all I'm not sure about either. What do you want?'

'This is Bessie White here.'

'I know. What do you want?'

'Well, to start with, you got up in such a huff from that caff that you forgot to pay for your tea. I paid for it.'

'Thanks,' he said ungraciously. 'If I'd known I'd have had a cheese roll as well. What do you want?'

'Christ,' she suddenly laughed. 'You didn't half look funny trying to get your flies done up. You got yourself in a right tangle.'

'Flies are things that sit on the wall and rub their feet together,' Andrew told her. 'The thing I was trying to adjust was my *fly*. It's not plural. What do you want?'

'I don't care if it's a fly or a centipede,' she said easily. 'It was still funny. I want to talk to you about keeping my grandad's case out of the paper. You went off too fast . . .'

'No chance,' he said.

'I'm willing to pay,' she said seriously. 'I'll give you a fiver if you'll do it.'

Andrew laughed. 'A fiver! My God, you are flashing your wealth about. First you pay for my tea, then you start dishing out bribes . . .'

'It's all I've got,' she replied simply. 'All I've got now, anyway. I had to pay the old sod's fine, didn't I? And that was my holiday money. If it's going to cost more, then you'll have to wait and trust me to pay you.'

'Listen,' he said more gently. 'There's no way either you or I can keep it out of the paper. I've made it as short as I can but I just can't . . .'

'You've not put it in already!' she cried.

'Well, it's written,' he said uneasily.

'Oh no,' she breathed, her voice hardly carrying over the wire. 'You've got to stop it. Can't you understand, Andrew? I can't let my mum and dad know about it, or the bloody neighbours. If they read it they'll boot him out in the street. Honestly. Can't you see?'

'They don't know, your parents?'

'No. I've kept it from them. I was having a day off sick at home when the police came, and they were both out. So I didn't let on. They'll chuck him out.'

'Listen, Bessie,' he said earnestly. 'Even if I could stop it – and take it from me, I can't – what will happen when it appears in the other paper, the *Chronicle*? My editor will want to know why *we* haven't got it.'

'Jesus wept,' she said bitterly. 'You would think it was a war being declared or a big burglary or something, not an old-age pensioner stealing a live eel.'

'I'll tell you something,' he said defensively. 'In normal circumstances I would have telephoned the story over to the evening papers too. An old man stealing a live eel is a good laugh.' Then he added: 'Unless it happens to be your grandfather.'

He could hear her sense of outrage coming over the phone. 'They would put *that* in the evening papers?' she said incredulously. 'A thing like that? And they'd pay you for doing it?'

'It's a rough world,' he shrugged. 'But anyway I didn't. I don't know why, but I didn't. I'm lazy, put it down to the fact that I'm lazy.'

'*You* could stop it going in the *Chronicle*,' she said, her voice changing craftily. 'That should be easy for you, Andrew. That big fat bird sitting next to you in the court, she was from the *Chronicle*, right?'

'If you mean Miss Perry, yes,' he said firmly.

'Miss Perry, that big fat bird,' she confirmed. 'Well, listen, mate, you won't have any bother with her. She'll keep it out of her paper if you tell her. Give her an extra rub of your leg under the table.'

Andrew's head retreated and stared at the mouthpiece as though he were staring at her. 'Really,' he said eventually. 'Honestly, I don't know what to say to you. I've never come across anyone like you before.'

'And I'm only eighteen,' she mimicked bitterly.

'What's the use?' he sighed. 'Listen, girlie, carefully. There is no chance of keeping this case out of the *Journal*. I will go to the editor, but I hold out no hope at all. Okay?'

'What if I said I would sleep with you?' she said.

That stopped him. He said nothing for a moment. Then he pulled all his strings in. 'You,' he said, 'are just a little older than my daughter.'

'That should make it all the nicer,' she said.

'Look, Bessie, you are a remarkable girl. I'll give you that. But I think you'd better get off the line and forget it. I'll do as I promised – I'll ask the editor, but there's not a hope in hell. I know what he'll say.'

'No,' said the editor.

'Okay,' nodded Andrew. 'I promised it would be put to you, that's all.

But I told the old man's grand-daughter there was no chance of keeping it out of the paper.'

'You were quite right, as usual,' said Burton. 'There *is* no chance.' He was an abrasive man, and Andrew never argued with him. He was a street-born North Londoner, but now on the suburban hem he liked to give an agricultural effect by wearing ginger tweeds and jodhpurs. He made his face a country red by panting across ragged fields behind his house every morning and by frequently pinching his cheeks in private, which also made his eyes watery. Now he was seated astride a chair as on a horse, his heels digging impatiently into the legs.

'That's all we want to say about that, then, isn't it?' he said.

'Yes,' nodded Andrew. 'That's fine by me. I told her I'd ask, that's all.'

'Well, you asked,' said Burton. 'Now, let's move on to something else. I had a call from a man called Ernest Rollett – said he was a neighbour of yours. He was on about a home for maladjusted kids planned for a spare site on your estate. Said he's already mentioned it to you.'

'He filled my ear with it this morning,' replied Andrew. 'He's one of these petrified pricks who sees a motorway coming through his precious rhubarb patch every time somebody wearing a black raincoat turns up with a tape measure.'

'He sounded very concerned to me,' said Burton.

'The man wears his hypocrisy like his Sunday suit,' shrugged Andrew.

'He said he was a friend of yours.'

'He's a neighbour,' said Andrew logically. 'He's *got* to be a friend. At Plummers Park you do not quarrel with your neighbours. Hate their guts but don't quarrel. Be nice to them, admire their roses, pat their dog, smile, but don't leer, at their wife. In good old-fashioned suburbia people who didn't like each other never bothered to speak, and in the slums they settled it with their fists, but not in a place like Plummers Park. It's an estate, and you don't do things like that on an estate.'

Burton was regarding him cagily. 'Sounds like something you've got strong feelings about,' he observed. 'Why don't you write a feature about it, or a series. "The Hate Behind the Sandersons' Curtains".' He stopped and smiled with thin satisfaction at Andrew's growing expression.

'God, I couldn't do that,' pleaded Andrew. 'I've got to live there . . .' He glanced up to see that Burton had been baiting him, and felt the shame and the relief mix inside him.

'You could always ask the editor to keep it out of the paper,' said Burton. He got up from astride the chair and turned away from Andrew, taking short stiff strides like a horseman in a stable. 'Listen, anyway,' he said reaching his desk and giving it a pat. 'Look into this other thing, the plan for the maladjusted kids place. See how firm it is at county level and then have a wander around Plummers Park asking people for their reactions. This man Rollett says he's going to call a protest meeting.'

'He will,' said Andrew confidently. 'I'll get on with that this afternoon, shall I?'

'Yes, I should. That's if you've finished all the court cases you want to allow in the paper.'

CHAPTER THREE

When the telephone sounded, Ena Grant was reading the *Daily Express* fashion page, sitting naked in the growing sun on a G-plan dining-room chair placed strategically just inside the open door of her french windows. The new non-peep fence, which her husband Simon had erected because he liked the idea of her brown all over, protected her on both sides of the narrow garden. The waste land stretched from the infant rose-trees at the bottom of the plot, curving away from her view so that the flat tops of the houses over there were only just in sight, like regular tombstones lying in a hilly cemetery. She could quickly see anyone approaching from that direction.

She let the phone ring fifteen times, counting the tones carefully on her fingers. Then she stood, first placing the newspaper over her front, like a breastplate, and then quickly sliding it around to cover her rear, as she turned and walked into the room. It had sounded three times more before she reached it.

'Hello,' she said calmly. 'Plummers Park 9834.'

It was a deliberate rearrangement of the correct number. If it were Simon he would think that she had merely got the digits in the wrong order. He always credited her with that virtue of the beautiful blonde – dippiness.

'North Thames Gas Board,' answered the voice.

'How are you, North Thames Gas Board?' she asked.

'One day it will be,' said Geoff Turvey. 'And that's the day you're going to make some fitter's life very happy.'

'For all you know,' she said deliberately, 'I may already be making some fitter's life very happy.'

'You'd better not,' he threatened. 'Or I won't pay my gas bill, and I'll tell your husband not to pay his.'

'He doesn't pay it now,' said Ena. 'He thinks if the gas man comes to cut off the supply and I get to the door all smiles and wobbling bosom, the man will stagger away sobbing.'

'Good thinking,' acknowledged Geoff. 'For Simon.'

'I've told you before,' she said without heat. 'Don't be snotty about him. He's got time to improve. At your age you haven't.'

'In my case there's very little room for improvement,' he replied blithely. 'Anyway, stop defending him.'

'Somebody's got to,' she said. 'Did you want anything apart from an argument?'

'How about a nice Monday intercourse?'

'You are too romantic.'

'Listen, it was all I could do to tone it down to "intercourse". This afternoon?'

'All right.'

'I love you.'

'For two hours at a time,' she said.

'Same place. One o'clock.'

'All right,' she said. 'I love you too.'

She was waiting in her car in the parking space behind The Jolly Grinder when he arrived, curving his white MGB a trifle flamboyantly on the gravel and coasting it to a standstill six inches from hers, pointing in the opposite direction, so that from their open windows their faces were within whispering distance.

'That was a bit flash,' said Edna. 'It's only an MG not an Alfa.'

'Where I work,' said Geoff smiling easily, 'and where I live also, mark you, missus, the MG is still a symbol of freedom and status, a sweet bird of youth and affluence. Where we lived before, at Northolt, it was the Triumph Spitfire. Tomorrow – maybe the Alfa, in Kensington.'

'If we get nabbed you'll be lucky to afford a bike,' she said practically. 'Cynthia would soak you for every penny.'

'Stop it. You may persuade me to turn right round and head for Hemel Hempstead, where I am supposed to be spying out some building land.' He leaned across and so immediately did she and they kissed briefly. As they came apart their faces stopped six inches from each other and his settled eyes and her young full face met seriously. 'Stay there a minute,' he muttered. 'I'm coming across.'

He jumped from the car and strode around to her far door. He opened it and almost fell in with her, clasping her and pushing his face into her neck and the spectacular breasts beneath the summer blouse, his palms going to their heavy bottom lobes. She responded at once, pulling his head closer as though they both needed the comfort desperately, her open lips against the shaggy sides of his hair, biting him without using her teeth. He suddenly relaxed and looped his hands around her waist. 'All right?' he said.

'Yes, I'm all right,' she replied softly. 'If you are.'

'Christ, I look forward to this,' he said. 'Do you?'

'Every time,' she said. 'I thought it might wear off, but I think I get worse.'

'Good. So do I.'

'Do you think it's really safe here?' she said, glancing around. 'It's only ten miles away and people do come up here from Plummers Park, you know.'

'Now and again,' he agreed. 'But only in the evenings. Nobody is likely to be around here now.' He kissed her quietly again. 'Sit out in the garden. Go around the corner there, by the mill-wheel. I'll get a drink. What would you like to eat, love?'

'Anything they've got. I'll sit over there.'

She walked across the open space to the garden and sat in the bower created by some flowering shrubs and the solemn wheel which came from the days when the inn was a mill. It felt safe and sunny there. She sat gratefully, happy with the anticipation of the next few hours, but already with the seeds of guilt and sadness that she knew would grow once the evening came.

'What did you do today?' Simon would demand, muffled in the folds of her chest. 'Chasing off all the men?' And she would make up some mundane lie. She was an expert liar and she preferred not to face him while she was telling them, so she kept his face pressed to her breasts and uttered them over the nape of his happy neck. And he thought it was the clutch of love.

Geoffrey returned with a bottle of white wine, two glasses and two plates of cold meat and salad. They sat, content for a while in their lives, having a picnic on a day full of the trifling sounds of summer.

They were hidden by the mill-wheel as though it were the side of a great armchair, but there was no one else about anyway. A tortoise-shell cat was trying to catch a butterfly on the pub lawn, but that was all.

'Don't let's go to the motel today, Geoff,' she suggested.

He glanced at her. 'Where do you want to do . . . Where do you want to go then?'

'Oh, I don't know. It seems like such a lovely day to be playing Mr and Mrs Smith in a motel, and it's always so nasty having to pack up and go at five in the afternoon.'

'They're used to it,' he shrugged. 'That's the best thing about motels. At least you pay first, so you don't have the embarrassment of creeping down to the desk and saying you've suddenly got to leave because your Auntie Emma is dying in Darlington.'

'There are times when you sound horribly like the voice of an experienced adulterer,' she said.

'No, not at all,' he began to protest. 'Adultery is an older man's pastime. This is love.'

She waved his voice away. 'I don't want to know, anyway,' she said. 'I'm not exactly innocent, am I? As long as you stay faithful to me.' She wagged a finger at him. The wine and the sun worked quickly on her. 'Nobody else – understand? Except your wife.'

He smiled at her. 'You're a little bugger, really,' he said. 'All right. Where are we going to have it today?'

She waved her glass airily at the fields inert beneath the heavy June sun. She elevated it so that she could look at the rays through the wine. 'Out of doors,' she said finally. 'In the fresh air.'

He stared at her grin. 'In a cornfield, that sort of thing, you mean?'

'Yes, why not?'

'It would be cheaper,' he agreed, smiling.

'Naturally,' she said tartly. 'You can put the money you save towards some plants for your garden or a new tin-opener for the kitchen.'

He glanced at her with sharpness, but then he shrugged and laughed and she returned the laugh. He caught her hand and the wedge of bitterness was blunted. 'All right,' he said firmly. 'To the woods.'

They left her car in a lane near the inn and they took his due north until they reached the downs at Dunstable, great green lumps of mid-England, lying with vacant expressions under a sky hanging with summer heat. It was a place for gliding, and they watched the wide silent wings of the gliders like white hands against the blue.

'Do you think they can see us from those things?' asked Ena as they lay in the ferns and crowded grass. They were stretched easily together, side against side, faces up into the large sky.

'I expect they can,' said Geoff. The smell of her and the humid afternoon was going like smoke through his head. 'But they won't come down to get a closer look because the whole object is to get those contraptions up as high as possible. That's where the whole thrill is.'

'I know something else like that,' she giggled. He glanced at her.

'That was a cheap, nasty little suburban joke,' he reproved gently.

'I'm a cheap, nasty little suburban joker,' she said. Her face became abruptly pinched and sad. 'Oh, Geoff,' she whispered, leaning into his shirt. 'Why is it arranged so it's so difficult? It's all so much trouble.'

He put his face against her thick hair, his nose going right through to her ear. 'All life is trouble,' he said. 'It's death's no trouble.'

She looked up slowly. 'That's very profound coming from you,' she said.

'Thanks very much. It's *Zorba the Greek*,' he told her. 'Went to see the film the other night with Cynth.'

'With Cynth,' she repeated miserably. 'Poor Cynthia, poor Simon. They haven't done any harm, Geoff.'

'Errors. They've made errors. Marrying us,' he said. He took her face in his hands and kissed her deeply. 'And it's a fabulous day, and we're out here alone for a couple of hours. Can't we leave it at that and not ask why?'

'All right,' she nodded. 'I want that too. Do you think anyone will see us here?'

He glanced around. They were in a depression, embraced by ferns on the flank of one of the matronly downland hills. Between their upturned feet, hers shoeless, the flat counties ran to the Midlands, distant trees like puffs of smoke, houses and farms and fields disintegrating in the haze.

He looked then at her resting form, her profile stretched beside him on the dry summer hill, her sweet landscape against distant Bedfordshire. Her cascading fair hair tumbled over the grass, her forehead touched by the sun, the green material of her dress pushed up by her gorgeous breasts, then dipping to her flattened lower body; her bare legs and brown feet were pointed slightly out towards Woburn Abbey and Whipsnade Zoo respectively. He turned on his hip, and she looked at him with hardly a blink, as though she had been warned to watch him carefully, while he undid the buttons down the length of her summer dress. He stroked her flat naked stomach with his right hand and turned the fingers around the honed curve of her waist. They turned inwards and moved close, their faces sweating on each other. Her hands went to his zip and she parted his trousers at the front like a banana before putting her topmost hand in to stroke. Somewhere in the air about them an observant skylark began a song and a snail paused in his green journey along a stem.

'You're a dirty little pig,' Geoffrey whispered, kissing her messily. He wiped his chin and then, using the other side of his hand, wiped hers also. She was wearing a pink brassière with a button between the cups so that when he released it the nylon flapped away like the ears of a flying helmet, leaving her breasts blinking in the sunshine.

He examined, surveyed them for a moment before putting his hands and his lips there. Using both hands he could scarcely circumnavigate one – thumb to thumb and little finger trying to touch little finger. With his tongue against the wrinkles of the right nipple, he glanced with low eyes towards the horizon of the other mound across the valley. It seemed miles away. She had caught him below, but was using her hands easily as though she were washing them and thinking of something else.

The lark was noisy and occupied in the nearby air, but the snail had witnessed enough and was continuing on his slimy journey up the stem. Two hundred yards away four little girls were walking down the hill.

'Don't overdo it, love,' groaned Geoff. He had gritted his teeth, only just remembering to remove them from her nipple in time. She eased her manipulations obediently, took his fingers and coaxed them down to her pelvis. Like someone lowering a flag he lowered her pants. Her eyes were tense on his face. Fifty yards away the four little girls were making daisy-chains.

Geoffrey pulled his trousers back from his backside and hot-faced rolled on top of Ena. They were together in a trice, faces clenched with the anxious work, pushing together, pulling away, and pushing again, the shunting of love, until eventually with only a brief pause to regain breath, they collided hard and joyously, and the lark was gone.

The couple lay together, in the lap of adultery and peace. They were there for minutes, with no more worry or hurry than if Bedfordshire were otherwise uninhabited. Geoffrey could feel the sturdy sun baking his backside and he was about to mention it when the snail, which had been mounting the stem during the normal course of its day, was thrown sharply and accurately and bounced on the springy flesh of his right buttock. It had been thrown by one of the quartet of little girls, who were now seated intently on the ridge above the secluded depression, hung with interest and daisy-chains.

'What you doing then?' asked the child who had projected the snail.

Geoff felt Ena go to stone. He remained with his face buried beside her like a soldier under fire.

'They're dead,' said the second girl confidently. 'I bet they're dead.'

'Why's the man got his bum showing?' asked the third.

A snort of scorn and realization came from the first. 'They're making a baby. That's what they're doing.' Then with an air of throwaway wisdom. '*I* know.'

The fourth child began to cry.

'What's the matter, Daff?' inquired the second.

'I don't feel very well,' sniffled Daff. 'I saw my mum and Uncle Ginger making a baby once and my mum said if I ever told, or if I ever saw it again, I'd turn to salt. I don't feel well, Lesley. I think I'm turning to salt.'

'Don't be so soppy,' said the first scornfully. She called down to Geoffrey. 'Mister, we can see you. We know you're not dead.'

The snail, shaking its head in a dazed fashion, was hurrying away in the manner of one who does not want to be further involved. Geoff, hot-faced, looked up and saw the quartet squatting above.

'Go away,' he ordered. 'Go on. Go away.'

'What you doing then?' insisted the first girl. 'Tell us.'

'This lady,' croaked Geoff, 'is very ill and I'm a doctor. Now go away and get an ambulance, will you. Please – it's an emergency.'

'Why you got your bum showing?' inquired the third, unimpressed. 'I never seen a doctor with his bum showing.'

They burst into merry laughter, apart from Daff who was still crying and feeling herself all over for signs of salt. Then they began to chant as children do:

I like sherry, I like rum,
Give me some and I'll show my bum!

'I'll kill these little fuckers,' grated Geoff close to Ena's ear. He looked at her and saw she was white.

'Listen to 'im!' howled the leading girl, outraged. 'Little fuckers! We'll tell the police! We'll tell the parkie!'

'Go on then,' snarled Geoff, still unable to move without completely exposing himself. 'Go on, tell the police.'

'Daff,' ordered the first girl. 'Go and tell the copper or the parkie.'

Daff departed, snivelling, still examining her legs and arms, and pinching her nose. The other three, their crumpled daisy-chains still hanging from their small sweaty hands, sat motionless intently watching the equally motionless couple below.

'Offer them money,' whispered Ena.

Geoff turned a gluey smile round to the children. 'Why don't you go to Whipsnade Zoo?' he persuaded. 'It's very nice there. Bears and lions. I'll give you the money.'

'We bin to the zoo,' said the spokesgirl. 'We don't reckon it.'

'It whiffs,' said the second.

Geoffrey had lost the remnants of his erection and now he lost his temper too. Turning swiftly so that his back swivelled towards the girls he tugged up his trousers and, in his shelter, Ena began buttoning her dress. With a roar he got to his knees and made a rush up the bank. But not before the three witches had taken off, screaming down the hill, their excited terror echoing over the sloping summery ground. The adulterers adjusted their clothing quickly and climbed hurriedly the other way.

CHAPTER FOUR

In the same manner that Hercules, the tramp who wheeled his croaking pram around the boxed roads of the estate, was regarded with distant but proprietorial affection at Plummers Park, so the back wall of the saloon bar in The Case Is Altered public house was revered because it dated, it was alleged, from medieval times. In a place of such shining newness, populated with shiny new people, age and quaintness were things to be treasured and exhibited.

Even before he entered the bar Andrew heard the guided-tour voice of Barney Rogers, 'That's very old stone, that is,' and knew there were strangers present. The pub was built two years before in a mock nineteen-thirties style, and the mouldering lump of wall, wearing its proud plaque like a dog collar, was, with both business sense and sentiment, incorporated into the building.

'Old stone . . .' The hushed American voice was loaded with respect as Andrew walked in, past the juke-box, the fruit-machine and the pile of plastic sawdust that was regularly spread across the floor to give the place a rural feel underfoot. It was almost three in the afternoon and apart from Barney behind the bar the only people there were a young American couple, Jean and Harry Solkiss, and Dormouse Dan, a pensioner who slept on a remote stool with a half-pint of cider standing like a patient night-light at his elbow. He was always there from opening to closing time, curled in sleep, his beverage hardly disturbed through the hours, although he occasionally slumped to the floor and had to be replaced on his stool.

The Americans were from Kingman, Arizona, and everywhere they went in this foreign place of England and Plummers Park they held hands.

'Old stone,' breathed Jean Solkiss, putting out lean fingers to touch the mystery.

'Stone *is* old,' shrugged Andrew. 'There's nothing it can do about it. All stone is old.' They turned and saw him and smiled recognition and puzzlement together. He had met them a week earlier when they were moving into their rented house on the estate, having come straight from Arizona to Plummers Park.

'This is sure *old*,' went on Harry like an archaeologist who had recently excavated the remnant himself. 'We just don't *have* old stone like this back home.'

'I would have thought the Grand Canyon had one or two old stones,' observed Andrew. 'Pint please, Barney.'

'The Grand Canyon is *not* a wall, though, is it?' said Barney with a truculent smile. Mounted above his head was the dead face of a fox with the same expression. 'That's a *wall*. There *is* a difference, you know.'

'It's great,' sighed Jean Solkiss. 'Just great.' She was already holding her husband's hand tightly, a habit of several years which had curiously resulted in his becoming left-handed. She smiled at Andrew with her arranged American teeth and frank full eyes. She was a bony girl, with a light brown tan, and a thick cable of black hair down her back. Harry was tall and thin and shy, looking through rimless glasses with what appeared to be a plea for truth and simplicity. He wore a Marks & Spencer sweater and jeans. He was a junior officer at the United States Air Force base at Ruislip.

'How's the defence of our realm going?' asked Andrew lightly. A brief frown of warning went from wife to husband as though afraid he might have secrets to tell.

'Great,' replied Harry. 'Real great. Never saw a realm defended better.'

'It's the Zeppelins,' sighed Andrew with drama. 'If we can stop the Zeppelins, we can win.'

The young woman did not appear to understand immediately, but when she saw her husband laugh easily she laughed too. Andrew bought them a drink.

'But this wall is sure interesting,' reverted Jean touching the damp plaster with her fingers once more. 'Just imagine, Harry, this was built when our country was inhabited by savages.'

'There were savages around here when the rest of the pub was built,' observed Andrew. 'A couple of years ago. Some are still in the vicinity.'

'Andrew's always kidding, kids,' said Barney from across the bar. 'He's just trying to scare you. Plummers Park is very, very nice.'

'Very, very nice,' nodded Andrew with exaggeration. 'Very, very, very nice. Heaven in Hertfordshire.' He recited:

Bring your kids, bring your dogs,
We've nice fresh air, and we've got no wogs.

Nobody laughed, and the Americans looked at him unhappily. Eventually Jean said: 'Is the fox head a hunting trophy?'

'In a way,' said Andrew before Barney could reply. 'Found stone dead by some dustbins in Hedgerows one morning. Poisoned by a local woman's cookery.'

Harry characteristically sought peace. 'The inn sure has a strange name,' he said.

Jean glanced at him gratefully. Barney, putting a warning glance Andrew's way, said: 'Well yes, I can tell you about that. It was like this . . .'

Andrew wished Barney could afford some teeth that fitted. They clattered away as he spoke, never seeming synchronized with the movements of his jawbone. It was like a man walking with the sole of his shoe flapping. '. . . an inn in Spain was called Casa Alta, or the House on the Hill,' instructed Barney. 'During the Peninsular War, in Spain, see, the men of a local regiment rested at this place and when they came back several of them took pubs and called them by the same name – Casa Alta. Over the years it's changed to The Case Is Altered. Now isn't *that* interesting?'

'Gee, I'll say,' breathed Jean Solkiss. She wrung her husband's fingers and he grinned a wincing agreement at Barney.

'My house is called Bennunikin,' announced Andrew. 'That's Navajo Indian for "The Wigwam on the Hill", same thing.'

'Gee, you are so *funny!*' said Jean Solkiss, thinking he had made a joke. Then she sighed seriously: 'Everywhere's so full of history.'

Andrew added for her: 'And the policemen don't have guns and the little kids have such rosy cheeks.'

The couple laughed again uncertainly. 'Sorry,' he said. Then: 'Talking about kids with rosy cheeks, how do you feel about maladjusted children?'

'Terrible,' said Barney before they could answer. 'Terrible.'

Andrew took out his notebook and wrote 'Terrible. Barney Rogers, Publican', at which Barney became frightened, for nothing frightens people so much as writing their names in a notebook.

'It's nothing to worry about,' consoled Andrew. 'I'm merely doing a story for the paper. There's some plan to build a home for maladjusted children on the waste ground up the top of the estate, and I'm getting people's opinions.'

'Could we visit with them?' suggested Jean anxiously. 'Oh boy, we both would love to do something like that, wouldn't we just, Harry?'

'Sure, sure, when's it going to be?' asked Harry with genuine eagerness, his cowboy eyes bright with decency behind his glasses. Barney was straining across the bar like a man about to say the wrong thing.

Andrew restrained him with a stiffened glance and touched the young couple on the shoulders. 'That's very good of you,' he said. 'They haven't finally decided about the place yet, but I'll let you know.'

'Oh thanks,' said Jean. 'We'd sure like to help.'

'Right,' emphasized Harry. 'Any way we can.'

They said they had to go. Holding hands tightly, as though one or the other had just been reprieved from a death sentence, they went from the bar. Immediately they had turned away, her head, it seemed automatically, fell slightly sideways against his elongated arm and they walked out like that.

'Isn't that nice?' observed Andrew, looking challengingly at the publican.

'Why does she call him Hairy?' grunted Barney, his professional good fellowship gone with the custom. 'He's not got a hair on him. He's like a skinned rabbit.'

'It's just the way she says his name,' said Andrew. 'He's called Harry. But it sounds like Hairy.'

'Sending out boys to do a man's job,' muttered Barney, gathering the glasses. 'Fancy *him* having to let off the bomb.'

'Oh, I don't expect it's actually *him*,' said Andrew in his irritatingly soothing fashion. 'They probably have a much heftier chap to do that. He probably just helps.'

'You're a cynical bugger, you know, Andrew,' muttered Barney. He glanced at the clock, like a hint. But it was five minutes from time.

'Cynical? Not at all,' argued Andrew amiably. 'I've just seen something most uncynical go out of your door. True love, that is, Barney. Before your very eyes. You don't often see that these days.'

'Ah, yes,' said Barney immediately. 'And talking about love and that – did you know we've got a flasher in the district?'

Andrew regarded the unromantic man behind the bar, his beer almost to his lips. 'A flasher?' he inquired into his tankard.

Barney leaned forward with horrified eagerness. 'Yes, Andrew, a bloke flashing his plonker. He's been seen this week-end charging around Fairy Copse with his dickie in his hand. No woman is safe.'

'Most of them around here are dead safe,' observed Andrew. 'Who told you this, Barney?'

'Mrs Sissing. She was in yesterday,' Barney fairly hissed across the bar. 'She saw him on Saturday.'

'Take her a month to get used to her Bert again I should think,' said Andrew. 'And where did this revelation take place?'

'Up at Fairy Copse, like I told you,' continued Barney. 'Long mackintosh, opens it out – and there it is! One morning in the week he was seen by some children. I've warned our June. You ought to warn your girl, too, Andrew. Maybe we ought to get together, some of us, and hunt the bugger down.'

'The police know all about it, I suppose,' said Andrew. 'I'd better go and have a word with them.'

'They know, all right,' confirmed Barney. 'Mrs Sissing was able to give them a full description.'

Andrew said: 'I bet.'

He had almost forgotten how bright and hot the day had grown. He walked from the coolness of the pub and the sun seemed to pick him out. Taking off his jacket he sat for five minutes on one of the rusting rustic benches outside, trundling a Skol umbrella across to provide himself with shade. The street was an afternoon desert, the void that inhabits such dormitory places in the day, filling it to the house-tops with emptiness. At the far end some brightly-clothed infants, like little coloured bugs, scraped around on tricycles and in plastic cars. He had often thought about children playing like that, remembering his own lonely games in the grit of summer or the mud of a thousand winters ago.

As he watched them at their remote pretending, microbes in a huge world bounded by unapproachable fields, untouchable roads, and with planned trees and flat roofs holding up a sky of nursery blue, he thought briefly of his solitariness as a child; that inward tightness, a refusal of something to let go or give way; a strong and secret box he knew was still there and still locked. When he was dead perhaps they might open it and find him – crouching.

Bessie White had said, 'What if I said I would sleep with you?' She had come straight out with it, with blunt courage and no bungling, because she was someone who could make up her mind about things. All he had needed to say was 'Yes'. One baby word. If he had said it then *something* would have happened, even if it was only a farce and not a fuck. But no, not him. He had whinnied his way out of it, scrambling to put it aside as though he were above such thoughts and things.

'You are just a little older than my daughter,' he mimicked aloud in the exact prissy way he had said it on the telephone. Christ, why do it? Why sling up frantic defences and feel like hell when a girl of eighteen makes an offer like that? Why? 'That's you all bloody over,' he accused himself aloud. 'You did it once before and then what happened? You ran.' The three miniature motorists and tricyclists, on a long trip, had squeaked and trundled along the hot pavement from the far end of the road and were now level with him and observing his selfish conversation. He looked up and saw them seated in or astride their vehicles, regarding him with that dead-eyed, snotty-nosed, droopy-lipped curiosity that grows on the faces of small children.

'Who are you saying to?' inquired a girl in a plastic Jaguar.

'Saying to?' questioned Andrew, regarding them suddenly and guiltily. 'Oh, I see. Yes. Well, I was talking to myself.'

'Why?' She was determined. One day she would have a real car like that.

'I've got a lot of worries,' he replied. Children always accepted that.

'My daddy's got a lot of worries,' nodded a boy like a half-grown apple, giving his tricycle a scuff around the pavement. 'So's my mum.'

'All daddies and mummies have,' intoned Andrew as though he knew the very answers to life. 'Aren't you a long way down the street from your houses?'

'We're having an adventure,' said the girl triumphantly. 'We're going now. Goodbye.'

She led them off, a confident convoy, the boys revving up with junior splatterings of spit, the girl hanging out a casual female hand as a traffic signal before they crossed the vacant, dusty road. Andrew watched her. Another woman. Christ, and they wanted liberating.

He suddenly remembered, thirty years before, strutting with the sudden confidence of the trickster, picking out special children who, he told them, were to be guests at his birthday party. ('You can come, so can you. But you can't . . .') They had to bring their own cups and saucers and knives and spoons, he had said. At that Gloria Penny, her drawers, as ever, sagging like a sporran, her face scarlet with scorn, scoffed: 'You ain't having a party, Andrew Maiby. You *never* have a party!' Nor was he, of course, nor did he. Ever. The guests, secreting on his instructions the crockery and cutlery from their own homes, sat on his patch of council-house back garden and drank water and ground their teeth on iron-hard ship's biscuits which his father, a merchant seaman, had brought home as emergency rations in case the war was further prolonged. He had wanted to play some games but they left him and all went home early and grumbling.

That was the last adventure for him. He never again risked it. Exactly nine years later, on his sixteenth birthday, Mrs Bigbury, his mother's great white friend, had asked him to call around to her house on his way to the weekly parade of the Air Training Corps. Her husband had died fighting the Germans (even after the war she called them 'the common enemy' as though it were some social slur), and as Andrew had been chopping her firewood and running her errands she said that she was going to give him a birthday present.

He arrived in his itchy air-force blue uniform, with the motto 'Venture Adventure' glistering on his badges, to find that Mrs Bigbury had apparently recently left her bath and was awaiting him in an aura of steam and a long and frilly robe. This garment, although in retrospect a trifle on the grubby side, seemed to him at the time to be the most glamorous wrapping he had ever seen, trailing visions of Maureen O'Hara and other unreachable stars even as it trailed along Mrs Bigbury's kitchen floor. It descended around and about her in shades and folds of pink, containing at the top the considerable bulk of her fine untrammelled breasts. From its folds her fat damp knees kept emerging and withdrawing like red-faced men in hiding, as she walked steaming and beaming towards him. Her heavy blonde hair, with its tidemark of black, was suspended like some Valkyrie's mane. She did not look right in a council house.

'Little Andrew!' she exclaimed, her arms opening as barn doors open. 'Happy birthday! Happy birthday!'

'Thank you, Mrs Big . . .' he had trembled. He remembered even now how the remainder of whatever he had intended became merely 'glubby . . . glubby . . . glub . . . glub . . .', like the globular sounds of a drowning mouth, because she had grasped him and slammed his innocent's face into her mature breasts, and he was suddenly engulfed with her boiled flesh and Woolworth's perfume. She rocked him to and fro with her hefty forearms, banging his frightened cheeks against the fat ramparts of her bosom, his saliva from his smothered sentences running down her red valley.

During this passion she somehow noticed his cap badge and bellowed: 'Venture Adventure! What a lovely motto, Andrew!' The powerful clamps of her arms crashed around him again and he was back in there among the titty and the spit, his hands desperately grasping the soft material of her fluffy robe. But then, curses (even now after all these years, curses and more bloody curses) he began to fight to get away.

Somehow he pushed her off, ducking under the booms of her arms, and forced a gulf between them. Her face broke up in a strange way he could not understand. He smoothed his tunic and straightened his cap. Then, in a moment of chivalry, he produced his clean air-force blue handkerchief and, while she stood stiff, he wiped his spittle from her chest. Stepping back like an Air Marshal who had just conferred a medal on the breast of a brave but foolish pilot, he said: 'I must go now, Mrs Bigbury. I shall be late on parade.' And then, like the little cunt he was, *he saluted her*, turned, and fled.

His sad and embarrassing memories caused him to sink reflectively into his seat outside the pub. The sun was burning his face and the heat was getting inside his collar and down his shirt. He dozed uncomfortably and inelegantly for a few minutes and was roused by revolving and regular squeaks. He thought as he woke that the infant adventurers were returning. Instead, across his opening vision, progressed an invalid chair bearing an old lady of such regal demeanour that she might have been a queen in a carriage. Her face was set as though in a cast and her silver hair was built up like a Tibetan temple. She was being pushed by Freddie Tyler, the Plummers Park station master, an amiable, olding man, and was immediately followed by a young slender woman piled high and hung low with boxes and bags.

'Wagons Ho!' called out Andrew sleepily from his seat. He stood up and felt a quick riddle of sweat run down inside his shirt. Old Tyler looked round, his lined face wet with effort. The elderly lady looked round too, more of a glare. The other woman tried to see him over the top of her load like someone trying to surmount a stone wall.

'Want a push,' said Andrew. 'I expect you do.'

'Not much,' said Mr Tyler. 'She's a bit beefy to push on a day like this.'

'I am *not* beefy!' protested the old lady at this ungracious remark. 'It's all the other stuff I'm carrying.'

She was right. The vehicle was festooned with household things in the manner of a tinker's cart. In the lady's lap were three large, old-fashioned flat-irons. Everyone had stopped now, and Andrew took the top two boxes from the pile borne by the younger woman. 'We're just moving house,' she explained, now fully in view. She was dark and tight-looking, but her smile of thanks softened her face.

'It's easier with a moving van,' observed Andrew.

'You're dead right,' agreed Mr Tyler. He was hanging over the handle of the invalid chair, heaving with exhaustion. 'I never thought one old dear would be such a load, Andrew, straight I didn't.'

'Now you know what Hercules feels like with that pram,' said Andrew, winking at the old lady reassuringly.

'He's not pushing anybody in it, that's for sure,' groaned Mr Tyler. 'I just happened to be going home when this lot arrived.'

Andrew saw the younger woman open her mouth sharply, but he restrained her with a pleading glance, unloaded some of her burden and, giving Mr Tyler a hold-all and a carrier bag to manage, he took the rest in one hand and pushed the old lady's conveyance with the other.

'Needless to say, we *did* have a removals van,' the young woman pointed out as they made better progress. 'But it's always the bits and pieces that get left behind. They take up the time and make the trouble. We had a lot of bother with mother's flat-irons on the train.'

'Where I go, they go,' announced the old woman to the bare pavement ahead of them. 'How else could I iron my Herbert's shirts?'

Her daughter leaned near to Andrew's ear. The boxes she was still carrying nudged against him and he could sense her. 'She's a little bit dippy,' she whispered. 'She still irons my father's shirts every night.'

He nodded. She was so close he thought his forehead had almost touched her hair. 'That stops him catching cold anyway,' he observed.

'It's too late,' she whispered. 'He's been dead twenty-two years.'

'Stop swapping secrets with that man,' snapped her mother from the wheel-chair. 'I can hear you, my girl. Whenever there's something in trousers around, you start your whispering.'

Andrew looked wryly at her daughter, and the neat face grimaced back over the boxes. 'Here it is,' she said then. 'This house.' It was one of the older, phase one Plummers Park houses, now in need of attention after ten Hertfordshire winters.

Old Tyler opened the door, and they helped the elderly woman from the invalid chair into the hall. She stumped away as though eager to explore. Tyler decently went with her. Andrew went into the house and saw furniture and carpets left anywhere, books piled on the floor, and a huge and beautiful mirror, heavy with carved ormolu, standing on the floor against a wall. As soon as they walked in, his dusty shoes and the younger woman's sandals were reflected in its oblong.

'You'll need some help to get that on the wall,' observed Andrew.

'I don't have a man around the house, if that's what you mean,' she answered.

'Well, I wasn't prying,' he replied awkwardly. 'It's just that it looks as though it weighs a ton and the old girl doesn't look all that strong.'

She laughed and said: 'You're odd.' Then decisively: 'Well, look, you might as well spread the good news around, because this is the sort of place, I imagine, where people like to know a bit about you. My name is Joy Rowley. I am a Mrs, but there's no Mr Rowley. That should stop the lace curtains being pulled aside too much in the hope of catching a glimpse of *him* anyway. But now everybody will watch to see if I have other men staying the night.'

'They might well do that,' said Andrew sagely. 'They like to keep an eye on their neighbours around here.'

She nodded that she had expected that, and then she said: 'Now you want to know if we're divorced. Well, we're not. He's deceased, as the lawyers say.'

'Oh, I see. I'm sorry.'

'Save your tears. We were divorced and then on top of that he went and died. He was always one for exaggerating a point.'

'I see,' grinned Andrew. 'Now if anyone asks me I can let them know. The dear old place wouldn't be the same without gossip. I have an idea I've seen you somewhere before. Is that possible?'

'It's even probable,' she nodded. 'I'm a faded actress. Faded before I bloomed really. I do the odd commercial on television. By some joke of nature I, who am childless and husbandless, have the loving-mother image that they need. You'll see me baking cakes, washing the boys' football shirts, putting Harpic down the pan, and all sorts of riveting things like that. The station-master called you Andrew . . .'

'Sorry. It's Andrew Maiby, M-A-I-B-Y. I live at Upmeadow, on the top of the hill. I'm on the local newspaper, God help me.'

'God help *me*,' she corrected. 'Now I've told *all* to the press.'

'Your secret is safe with me,' he smiled. Old Tyler came back to the room. 'She's ironing,' he said in wonderment. 'Soon as she got in she had the stove on and the ironing board up and she starts ironing. I've never seen that before.'

'She does it all the time,' said Joy. 'Dashing away with the smoothing iron.' She looked reassuringly at Tyler. 'It's a sort of hobby with her. She's ironing away her sorrow.' She said it naturally and with a smile at him.

'I see, I see,' replied old Tyler. His tone implied that he didn't know what the district was coming to. 'Yes, well I'm on my way then, Andrew.'

It was almost as if he prudishly insisted that Andrew must go with him and not be left with this woman.

'I'll be with you,' replied Andrew obligingly. 'I'm going up the hill.'

'Well, thanks for your help,' said Joy. 'It's nice to know you've got helpful neighbours.'

'At Plummers Park,' said Andrew at the door, 'we rely on respect, esteem and the helping hand, with the odd bit of treachery thrown in to make it interesting. See you again.'

'Of course,' she smiled. He could see that she had a face that was used to trouble. He glanced up at the house. 'They're pretty good houses,' he said as if to give her confidence. 'As houses go these days. And you can see the sunset from here. If you sit on the roof.'

'I'll watch for it,' she promised.

He ran his eyes over the flat front again. He could not know then that one night he would face death at that very place.

The nearest that Plummers Park would ever come to a traditional English corner shop was Gomer John's sub-post office, near the station, on the opposite side of the railway from all the other shops. It stood beside a narrow lane which led to the higher houses, and, at the bottom of this, three iron bollards which, although not old, were of antique form, like the upturned barrels of cannons. They, at the foot of the oddly unplanned lane, and the shop were the meeting place for the children and teenagers of the district. There was nowhere else.

Gomer's father had been Welsh; the sub-postmaster himself was a long-drawn-out young man with hair so fine and fair that in a certain light he looked bald. Andrew bought the early editions of the London evening newspapers which arrived, bringing tips for races already run, by the 3.30 ghost train, the empty afternoon service before the evening rush hour.

'I wanted to ask you what you thought about the idea for a school for maladjusted children on the estate,' said Andrew.

'I heard,' said Gomer lifting his pale young eyes guiltily, as though a serious accusation had been indicated. He had been twenty years out of Wales, but he still had the accent. 'You understand that it's difficult for me to say anything, being in an *official* capacity, you see, but if you'll be so kind as to come to the back I'll talk to you away from the counter, in my private room and as a private person. You've never been in my room, have you?'

Andrew had not. He walked in now, the curtain opened like the door of some secret place, and found himself in the cabin of a ship's captain: a heavy desk, a sextant, a porthole looking out on a tight sunless yard, books, and walls covered with charts.

'Ahoy,' he said quietly. 'My goodness, Gomer, what a place!'

'You like it, don't you?' inquired Gomer, indicating it was important that he did.

'Yes, of course,' replied Andrew. 'It's extraordinary.' He blinked around again. 'I was just surprised, that's all.'

There was a sharp gleam in the fair man's face. 'I wear this sometimes,' he blurted out. He picked up a cap with a badge anchored on its forepeak and placed it excitedly on his head. He sat at the desk and spread his arms in a strong pose, then looked at Andrew with renewed anxiety. 'You don't think it's silly, do you.' It was a plea not a question.

'Silly? God, no, Gomer,' said Andrew, patting the thin shoulder that would never carry anything but the command of a sub-post office. 'You must let me write a piece for the paper about you.'

Gomer looked at him with sincere alarm. 'Oh, no, Mr Maiby. Nothing like that, please, whatever you do. It's only for my own amusement, see, and I don't want any publicity.' He dropped his tone. 'I always think the Post Office might turn a bit funny about something like this. They're a bit strict because of their special responsibility, see.'

'Right you are,' Andrew assured. 'Not a word then.' It occurred to him that all day he had been dealing with people who did not want to appear in his paper.

With a carefully-stitched smile Gomer removed the captain's hat and, brushing the badge with his slim fingers first, laid it on the desk. 'There's no secret about it,' he said. 'People know it's my hobby, but I'd like to keep it local if I can.'

'Naturally,' said Andrew. 'Tell me, what's it all about?'

'These charts,' said Gomer, moving with a distinct nautical roll to the wall. 'They're anchorages in the South Seas. Polynesia, Micronesia, Melanesia. Small islands and atolls, harbours that only see a trading schooner once a month. And such names, Mr Maiby, such names!' His chalk finger wriggled its way around an inked coastline. 'Look here, on the island of Morfuti. Bourgainville inlet, Green Parrot Creek. There's ten fathoms there.'

'You know how deep the water is?'

'Every current, every tide,' said Gomer. 'I've sailed this room, this sub-post office if you please, into many a distant and tropic anchorage.'

'Who would believe it?' said Andrew, meaning it.

Gomer darted forward. 'I've got all the books,' he said. 'Look, rows of them. And I've read them all.' His weak hands ran along the bindings built along the wall. '*Burleigh's Navigation Guide to the Pacific, Trade Winds in the South Seas, Jason's Seasonal Weather Charts, Two Years Before the Mast*, all of them.' He stared at Andrew as though daring him to laugh, then, almost in a whisper, said: 'I could smuggle you, on the darkest night of the year, 23 October to be precise, on to a lonely beach in Morluka, in the Windrift Islands, without even the natives knowing. Do you believe that?'

'I believe you could,' replied Andrew. 'If I'm ever thinking of doing that I'll let you know.'

'Now you're making fun,' said Gomer, his face collapsing.

'No, no, Gomer, I'm sorry. I think it's a fantastic hobby. I like your porthole.'

Gomer shrugged. 'It only looks out on to the yard – bloody place is full of pop bottles, but as far as I am concerned it looks right out to the horizon of the ocean.' He avoided Andrew's eyes shamefully. 'It's just a pastime,' he apologized again. 'It stops me being lonely. Can you understand that?'

'We're all lonely in some way,' replied Andrew. 'It's the great ailment of the world.'

'Listen, listen to this,' said Gomer, encouraged. 'You're a man of words and letters, even if the sea is not in your blood. I think you'll like this.'

To Andrew's further astonishment the young sub-postmaster turned the switch of an old-fashioned winder gramophone in one corner and the room was at once filled with the sounds of a storm at sea. Gomer stood there, eyes half closed, visibly swaying to it, side to side, his knees bending and flexing to the movements of his imagined vessel. Andrew blinked at him in some alarm, as one might regard a person who has suddenly thrown a fit. But Gomer's eyes opened and he smiled. 'It's a wonderful thing and I don't think it's any sillier than dancing or football or golf. Do you?'

'Not sillier, just rarer,' Andrew admitted.

'I'm one of the few subscribers to *Lloyd's Register of Shipping* in Hertfordshire,' confided Gomer proudly.

'Yes, I can imagine that too.' The storm on the record now stilled and its sounds quietened to the slapping of an easy swell against the hull, the shouting of gulls and the crooning of wind in rigging. Compassion and embarrassment brought a lump to Andrew's throat. He felt himself blushing.

'I thought you would understand,' said the sub-postmaster. 'You're a sensitive man.'

'Will you ever go?' asked Andrew.

Gomer's glance went along his charted wall. 'To these places?' he sighed. 'No, I wouldn't think so. I might even be disappointed if I did. They'd probably be full of tin cans and television sets, and all that. I've never been abroad at all, you know. Not even on holiday. There's my mam upstairs and her leg and her dog, that sodding dog. I *can't* go. It's job enough to get anyone to help in the shop and the sub-post office. I'd planned to go to Ostend one day last year, on one of those day trips, but it was all messed up at the last minute. I don't know which will go first, the dog, my mam's leg or my mam, but whichever it is, it will be too late then. It's too late now, I suppose.'

As a final, defeated gesture, he threw a passport on the desk. 'I've had a passport for ten years, see. Two renewals and filled with visas. Look at these.' He flicked the pages like a picturescope, and Andrew saw that the coloured visas with their stamps and signatures covered each page. 'Impressive, very pretty,' nodded Gomer. 'New Caledonia, Indonesia, Philippines, Thailand. There's nothing to stop you getting the visas even if you never go. It costs a bit, but then all hobbies do, don't they?'

Someone was calling from the shop: 'Gomer, I want *Woman's World* and a packet of Smarties.' He went out. Andrew waited sadly, turning to the porthole and seeing, strangely to his own disappointment, only crates of empty pop bottles. Gomer returned and apologized for taking all his time.

'I hope it's not embarrassed you,' he said.

'Not for a moment,' said Andrew. 'It's nice to know somebody in this place has got a spark of poetry in them.'

Gomer nodded shyly. 'Now, you came about the plan for the school. For the maladjusted is it?'

'That's it. Nothing's fixed yet, but I'm just getting a few quotes for the paper. How do you feel?'

'Well, listen,' said Gomer apologetically. 'I've been thinking, Mr Maiby, perhaps it would be better if I *didn't* say anything. I'm in a public position, as I say, and I'm afraid I'm not a very adventurous person.'

Mrs Polly Blossom-Smith – as her name indicated – lived in a better, older, nobler house than the others at Plummers Park. She was a full, handsome woman, a sculptress of some talent and note, rumoured to have an Arabic proverb tattooed at the very top of her right leg.

The house had been one of the estate homes in the days when townspeople stayed in their natural towns and farmland grew unmolested from London to the folds of the Chiltern Hills. Fairy Copse sprouted about it like an Edwardian beard, and its own acre and a half of garden was amok with tangles and weeds, lawns gone gratefully to meadow, and stone urns and statues draped with natural tendrils. The growth this summer had become so thick that even birds familiar with the locality had difficulty in locating the two bird-baths.

There was one clearing, hacked to stubble by some frenzied amateur with a scythe, an area of about ten yards in diameter, and in this hollow on this increasingly hot afternoon sprawled Mrs Polly Blossom-Smith on a sagging canvas bed. Andrew thought how grandly she lay: grand as a piano is grand, handsome, with a fine patina and exaggerated curves. She was in her mid-thirties, but her very stature and presence made her seem more senior than anyone who visited her at 'The Sanctuary'. She had layers of black hair, and thick muscular fingers strengthened through the kneading of tough modelling clay and the chipping of marble. She was wearing a cheap turquoise bikini and her trembling torso was slicked with suntan oil. At the top of her right leg was clearly tattooed an old Arab proverb.

This much Andrew observed after timidly creeping round the dull red walls of the house to the rear garden. He approached the elongated Mrs Polly Blossom-Smith side-on, and was able to see and appreciate the large expanse of her. Her hair, built up in the front, lolled like a funeral drape over the back of her bed, her ample, beautiful face was lifted slightly towards the sun, the nose a little superior, the lips fruity, the neck like one of her own well-sculptured pedestals. Some men, Gomer for one, he reflected, would have been proud of shoulders like that, and the breasts sat atop the body like two separate tureens. The stomach was not without fat but ran away smoothly to the swathe of turquoise around her pubis; the motto was clearly embellished just where the leg of the bikini rounded her thigh; then the legs strode away, slightly arched with a distinct underhang below the thigh and calf but looking fine and shapely and glistening under the sheen of Ambre Solaire. Pound for pound she was as fine a woman as you would see anywhere in Hertfordshire on that summer's afternoon.

Andrew allowed himself a little time to take in the vision (and to remember Mrs Bigbury for a second time that day) before announcing himself with a cough across the indolent buzzing of the garden. She turned her face without hurry, her breasts wobbling fractionally his way a moment later. 'Ah, Mr Maiby – Andrew,' she called. 'How lovely. Come on over.'

She sat up to greet him, and two fleeting riddles of sweat and sun-oil ran down her stomach like bandits heading for the forest. 'It's weeks since I've seen you,' she said. 'Not since that beastly party at the Thingies. That awful woman was sick on the parrot, remember. Excuse my bikini, won't you.'

'Don't worry,' smiled Andrew. 'You look um . . . very neat.'

'Neat! Moses, you newspaper people! Always the *mot juste*.' She laughed extravagantly, like someone pouring water from a bucket.

'Anyway I hope I'm not disturbing you too much,' he said. 'I did ring at the front door, but there was no answer.'

'Staff non-existent at the moment, love. I had old scrawny Annie for a few weeks but she kicked up about having to pose in the nude.' She smiled at him. 'But I'm glad to see you, anyway. For a moment I rather hoped it might be the Phantom Flasher.'

'Oh, you know about the Flasher?'

'Know about him! My sweet, I can't wait to get an eyeful of him. All clothed in a heavy raincoat with just his knob hanging out of a trapdoor in the front of his trousers. Very Magritte. When I heard you cough I thought I might look up and see him holding his testicles.'

'Sorry to disappoint you, Polly.'

'Life's full of 'em, dear. Let me get you a drink. Will you have a gin or something?'

'With lots of tonic, please. It's early.'

'All right.' She moved towards the open french windows of the house, where some flowered curtains were sagging into the garden as though trying to get a breath of air. For a big woman her backside was compact, unsagging, like a professionally wrapped parcel. She went in and he remained in the garden, looking around at nature taken leave of its senses in what had been once a place of geometrical order.

'I take lots of gin and a little tonic,' she bellowed from the shade of the room. 'I think tonic weakens the resolve. Want some ice?'

'Please.'

'You'll have to have a bit off the floor, I've just dropped the sodding lot,' she cried happily. 'It's not too bad though, just a few carpet hairs and a bit of cat fluff on it, that's all.'

'I prefer hairy ice,' he called back.

She appeared almost immediately with the slopping drinks, flinging the jaded curtains royally aside. 'You really are a *very* nice man, you know,' she exclaimed. Then: 'Would you say you're a happy man?'

The frank inquiry took him by surprise. He sipped his drink first. 'Well,' he said slowly. 'It's a lovely day and I'm not ill, nor am I entirely broke, and I've got a family and . . .'

'You sound like somebody counting up how many points they're stuck with at the end of a hand of hundred-and-one rummy,' she laughed. She sat on the canvas bed and placed her square bare feet on the ground like a mother paddling at the seaside. 'I've heard that all men over forty are afraid of death,' she said. 'And especially on lovely summer days like this. Would you say that is true?'

'Auden said it's like the rumble of distant thunder at a picnic,' he replied.

'Of course, *he* would do. That's enough to turn you off picnics for life. Perhaps that's where I've been mistaken about you, Andrew. I always think you look so unhappy, but perhaps it's just the poet in you. You've always looked so thoughtful. When I've seen you at parties and what-have-you.'

'Well at that last thing I *was* feeling a bit unhappy about that poor parrot,' he said. 'You would have thought that the silly bitch could have thrown up somewhere else, wouldn't you? Cleaning it was a hell of a job.'

'Yes, very tiresome,' she agreed. 'Nasty mixture, spew and feathers. But you were the one who did it. Everyone else was too convulsed with their idiotic laughter. It was very kind of you. I'm sure the parrot will always remember it. Have you got much of a tricep, Andrew? Upper arm?'

'Pardon?'

'Sorry, I will dodge about so. Will you let me have a decko at your upper arm muscle, there's a good chap? I'm doing a composite man, you know, modelled from bits and pieces of all the males around here. Flat-Roof Man, the twentieth-century phenomenon. In centuries to come he will be gazed upon and studied by people in museums in the same way as we today ogle at the cave-dwellers.

'Yes, I'm sure he will, Polly,' he replied.

'Let's have a look then, will you.'

Doubtfully he put down his glass, took off his jacket and rolled his shirt sleeve. He folded the arm, watching the muscle grow as he had watched it with doubt when they had contests at school. Mrs Blossom-Smith looked quickly disappointed. 'No,' she sighed. 'It's not that interesting. As muscles go it's neither one thing nor another.'

'I tend to be like that – generally,' he shrugged. He replaced his coat.

A thrush bounced on the lawn. Polly clasped her hands before her like the folding of a pair of bellows. '*Turdus philomelos!*' she exclaimed. 'An embarrassing name for a nice little bird.' She looked up as though she had been talking to herself. 'Would you like to see the work?' she asked. 'It's nowhere near finished. As you will see, there's all sorts of bits and pieces, his dickie for one, to be stuck on. But he's coming along slowly. Come and take a peep.'

Blithely, like some magnified summer nymph, she led the way across the untidily matted grass towards the house. He felt a strange and unjustified thrill following this expansive, rolling woman into the dimness of the cluttered house. He had been inside before, once to a party where he had laid a jam sandwich (Mrs Blossom-Smith served jam sandwiches at her parties) down on a plate and had picked it up coated with vintage dust. Furniture was piled rather than arranged, paintings sagged on the walls like victims of a firing squad, in one corner was a rolled carpet standing upright as a warning finger. A flight of disturbed bats would not have surprised him.

'It's in my bedroom,' she hooted over her shoulder. 'You won't mind coming into my bedroom, will you, Andrew? Will Audrey mind?'

'I won't tell her,' he forecast confidently.

'Well, you're quite safe,' she replied, heavily charging the stairs. 'I've set my heart on the Phantom Flasher. Here we are, this way.'

The stairs had become a gallery and she led him from the gallery into a bedroom, rudely bare except for a single-size iron bed, its covers screwed and churned, and a life-size clay model of a naked man, minus several essential parts.

The bed and the model were only a foot apart and Mrs Blossom-Smith immediately apologized for this. 'It's just that I get taken with the urge to muck about with him in the middle of the blessed night,' she explained. 'And I can't be bothered to get out of bed. Do you like him?'

Andrew described a tentative sideways movement around the bed until he was facing the clay man. 'Hey Presto! Flat-Roof Man!' announced the sculptress and switched on a spotlight which hit and lit the model squarely.

'Christ,' said Andrew softly. 'It's Geoffrey Turvey!'

'Right first time!' enthused Polly. 'Well, the face and head are Mr Turvey. He has that sort of weekend face which typifies the species. Only on Saturdays and Sundays does it really become apparent with life.'

'It's very good of him,' breathed Andrew admiringly. 'Did he take a lot of persuasion to pose?'

'Trapped him, like the rest,' said Polly with quiet triumph. 'The legs you might find difficult to recognize because, of course, they are normally just a pair of trousers, but they belong to Bertram Reynolds, a trifle knobbly and lacking in flesh as you can perceive. Then the ears belong to Mr Henry Jones and Mr George Jones, respectively, the chest and the abdomen are Mr Shillingford's, and the bum is someone whose secret I have sworn to respect.'

'Geoff Turvey,' ruminated Andrew, gazing at the mute face of his friend. 'The old so-and-so. He didn't tell me.'

'Now you will be able to trouble him with hints,' she smiled. She was looking at him quizzically. 'I'd like to give you a part, Andrew,' she said like a casting director. 'But there's not a lot left. There's the arms and hands, the feet, and the genitals. We've discussed your arms. Your hands are too good and your feet look too big even from here, and I really do want to see if The Flasher can fit with the other bits.'

'Please yourself,' laughed Andrew bemused by her. 'Posterity will have to do without Andrew Maiby.'

'You like him, though, don't you?' Polly asked with genuine anxiety. 'Naturally I don't display him to every Tom, Dick or Harry.'

'Just to Geoff, Bertram and Henry,' said Andrew.

'I do believe you're jealous,' she said, giving him a heavy friendly push. 'Come down and we'll have another drink. You haven't told me why you came to see me anyway.'

'After all this, I'd almost forgotten,' admitted Andrew. He followed her down through the grimy house again and out into the garden sunshine. She poured them each another drink. 'Old Geoffrey looks great, really life-like,' he said reflectively. 'He must have sat for you a long time.'

'Most of the time he was stretched out on the bed,' she said airily. 'He gets very tired. Can't think what he does to get like that. But I thought his head was quite right. It's a mildly *worried* head and it's even a little flat on top. He really looks like Flat-Roof Man.'

'He does too,' nodded Andrew. 'I'd never really thought about his flat head before.'

'I saw it immediately,' she said. 'It was as though nature had designed him for his house. Now, tell me why you came.' She lolled back on the scruffy canvas garden-bed again like Goya's Duchess. Andrew felt very strange. He pulled up a small collapsible seat and squatted on it. He could not somehow imagine himself wanting her sexually. She was too jolly. But when she stopped fluffing and laughing, when her jokes and chatter had been taken into account, there she was, waiting to be taken, like a large lump of marginally over-ripe fruit.

'I'm afraid that the reason I came to see you seems a bit ordinary somehow, after all this,' he said.

'All what?'

'Well, arriving here and seeing that model and drinking gin and bits of carpet fluff. It's all a bit exotic.' He paused, then said bravely: 'Listen, Polly, can I ask you something really personal? Is that really an Arab motto on the top of your leg?'

'My tattoo? You came to see me about my tattoo?'

'No, no. Nothing like that. I'll ask you about the other thing in a minute. It's just a thing for the paper. It's not important.'

She pulled the flesh of her leg tightly round so that she could peruse the blue words. 'Yes,' she said as though satisfied she had deciphered it correctly. 'It's an Arab proverb. Well, the sort of introduction to it. I was at school in Damascus at the time – my father was in the embassy there – and I went off and had this done. I was a bit of a little cow in those days. I got found out before it was finished, so I never got the job done properly. It's supposed to run right round the top of the leg. Like a garter.'

'And what's it say?'

'Well, truthfully, I was a bit disappointed with it. I was very young and full of dreams and ideals and I asked this Syrian tattooist to write something profound about the world and our existence. Well, his idea of something profound and mine were a bit different, so, in a way I suppose, it's just as well he never got around to finishing the sentence.'

'What is it?'

'Oh, it's quite a well-known Arab proverb,' she shrugged. 'It says, something like: Life is like a cucumber – the moment you think you have grasped it in your hands it's up your arse.'

His poker face wrinkled and then exploded with laughter. 'My God, Polly,' he eventually choked. 'There's not too many people like you around.'

She hesitated as though afraid of his laughter, but then she laughed too. 'No,' she agreed enthusiastically. 'I don't suppose there are. I really *am* a cheery great thing, aren't I, Andrew!'

He laughed with her in agreement, but her mirth stopped abruptly and she asked: 'Andrew, will you tell your wife you've been to see me?'

Andrew, surprised, said: 'Yes, I suppose I will.'

'I thought you might. You mean someone might have seen you arrive here?'

'Yes, that's about it,' he agreed honestly.

'But you wouldn't say about my model or going to my bedroom?'

'No.' He realized she was asking the questions like a social surveyor. He added carefully: 'Not everybody's as . . . as free as you, Polly. Inside most women, especially married women, is a rotten apple. It's called suspicion.'

'Fear, more like it,' she said with understanding. 'With women, especially as you say, married women, it goes with love.'

CHAPTER FIVE

They walked along the towpath, some guilty giggling between them, the barge lying like a tethered hippo three hundred yards up the straight run of bank and water. The sheen of evening had settled on the canal, stilling it so completely that they seemed to be walking into a painted landscape. Even the suspended gnats and water-flies appeared almost stationary in the cooling air.

'It's lovely,' said Audrey, stumbling along the path, catching hold of his arm. He pushed away some dangling blackberry thorns so they could get by. She said, 'Thanks,' and he was surprised to see a blush on her cheeks.

'Birds everywhere,' said Andrew joining in the game. 'Listen. Hundreds of them. And to think that we don't know the note of one from the croak of another.'

'It's very nice,' she said looking around. 'And to think it's here all the time.'

'Amazing how it stirs you,' he acknowledged. 'My God! A couple o' pints o' cider, my girl, and I'd be throwing 'ee into nearest hayrick.'

'You farm lads all be the same,' she said, attempting to mimic too. 'You be only wantin' us maids for one thing.'

'Ye be a stocky wench,' he said roughly, standing away and quizzically regarding her suburban face and her best coat. 'Ye look like ye could carry a coupla churns.'

'I be promised, zur,' she said with a rustic curtsey.

'Who you be promised to, the French onion man?'

He knew he had spoiled it. Her expression changed. 'Oh, shut up, Andrew,' she said. 'We were having a good time then. One of us always has to ruin it.'

'Right,' he acknowledged. 'I'm sorry. Still, we can't play yokels for ever. Even those birds are really screaming to other birds to keep off their property.'

They had walked almost to the barge now. 'Do you think it would work for two people to go away somewhere isolated together and try to get to know the *good* things about each other?' she asked thoughtfully.

'Only if they've never met before. Only strangers might. People who are familiar can't. Once you've tasted blood . . .'

'Stop it,' she said again, pleading now. 'We were happy only a minute ago. Don't let these kids hear us fighting.'

'No, they mustn't,' he agreed. Awkwardly he clambered aboard the barge. He noticed, with slight unease, that the plank of wood that did service as a gangway had been pulled on to the deck. He swivelled it out so that Audrey could walk on it, and then called quickly, before, he thought, she could tell him to hush. Their glances met anxiously as he shouted.

'Anyone aboard?' called out Andrew again.

There was a delayed scraping movement from the stern of the barge and a foggy voice replied. They walked along the deck planks and reached a companionway with worn and uncertain steps going down to a door painted in the curly, vanished hand of the canal people.

'Hang on, please, Mr Maiby,' came the boy's voice from within. 'The door's a bit stuck.'

Andrew was going to hold back, but Audrey's foot went out and gave the door a push to which it responded squeakily. 'Open sesame!' she exclaimed with accentuated brightness. 'That wasn't stuck very much.'

'It's easier from that side,' said the embarrassed boy.

'That's all right, Tim,' said Audrey. She examined him quickly, and Andrew looked at him over her shoulder. He was a hollow-faced kid, the twelve-year-old product of Bertram and Gloria Reynolds, both people with oddly curved features. He had long fair hair, lying lank across his shirt which was open to the waist. Around his neck he wore an old half-crown on a silver chain.

'Why shut it?' asked Audrey. 'It's a lovely evening.'

'I was just starting to paint the inside,' said the boy.

'Sorry,' said Andrew. 'Is it safe for us to come in?'

'Yes, Mr Maiby.'

'I meant . . . I thought there might be paint and lord knows what around.'

'Come on in,' called Lizzie. They could see her now, or half of her, in the dimness at the fore end of the long covered hold of the barge. She was standing in the well of an open trapdoor, her hands above her head fixing something to the dark low roof.

'It's half a woman,' laughed her father, bent almost double in the low space. He squatted down on his haunches. With her hands above her head like that, her new breasts swelling her light sweater, she looked more than half a woman. Her hair was fair and brief and curly. It had been a week since he had been prompted to notice she had been to have it cut.

'Hello, daddy,' she called easily to him. 'Why didn't you say you were coming? We would have piped you aboard.'

'It's a bit dim in here,' said Audrey. She was squatting down now as well. 'It's a wonder you can see to work.'

'Oh, you get used to it,' said Lizzie, remaining in her hole, still intent on the work above her head. 'There's enough light coming through the little window up here, and Tim has only just started on the door, so it's been open until now. We were going to pack in soon anyway.'

'Where's everybody else?' asked Andrew. 'I thought there was a whole gang of you.'

'Billy is down below,' said Lizzie. 'Tim's brother.' She curved slightly and called down. 'Billy! My parents are here on an inspection trip. Give them a bang.'

There were three loud bangs on the floorboards almost beneath their feet. 'He can't come up,' interposed Tim. 'He's plugging the hull and if he leaves it too long the barge starts to sink.'

Audrey looked immediately anxious, but Andrew laughed.

'All right,' he said. 'We'll abandon ship.' He touched his wife's elbow. She glanced at him as though she wanted to stay, but then she followed him on to the outside ladder. 'Why don't you knock off and come and have a drink?' Andrew suggested, poking his head back into the dimness.

'All right, dad,' Lizzie called back. 'You go over to The Jolly Grinder and we'll follow. We won't be a couple of minutes.'

He hesitated, then said: 'As you like, Liz, we'll see you in the garden.'

'Right, daddy.'

Andrew and Audrey balanced along the narrow walk of the deck. They stopped when they came to the dirty little window in the deck housing and Andrew knocked gently with his toe. Their daughter's young face, indistinctly smiling through the grime and cobwebs peered out at them. Audrey waved to her and Andrew blew her a kiss and she laughingly poked out her tongue at them.

'They haven't done very much,' said Audrey when they were on the canal bank again. 'Not considering the time they've spent up here.'

'They've done a bit on the outside,' said Andrew, pointing to the newly painted prow. 'And they're following the old sign, which must take a bit of time. All those curly bits. She's all right.'

'You think so? You don't think there's anything going on there?'

'Oh, come on, Audrey. We're showing our age, love.'

She shrugged unhappily: 'If you say so.'

'Anyway, I don't think we need worry about the two Reynolds kids. Lizzie's miles ahead of them. God, that Tim's got a face just like his mother. It curves inwards like a bowl. And his old man's got a face that's convex, it swells out. You remember when we saw them dancing at that dinner-dance. Their faces looked as if they could fit into each other. Like one porridge bowl into another.'

Audrey turned and looked back at the barge. 'I still don't reckon they've done a lot. Not to the barge, anyway,' she said.

'They're gone,' said Tim Reynolds. 'I can see them walking along the bank.'

'God,' breathed Lizzie, still standing in the wooden hole. 'That was really scary. Fancy them creeping up on us like that.'

She clambered from the well in the deck. She was wearing nothing from the waist down. The boy stared at her. Her sweater finished in wrinkles about her middle and her slim legs and rounded buttocks looked luminous in the dim light of the barge.

'Did our Billy have his look?' inquired Tim earnestly. 'I haven't had my look yet.'

'We can't now,' said Lizzie. 'I'd better go over to the pub.' She bent over the hold, the seam of her backside pointing straight towards the boy. His eyes wide, he moved forward as though to put his hand on her but he hesitated and in that moment she had retrieved her jeans and pants from below the deck and was getting her feet into them. 'Sorry, boys,' she said, 'we'll have to do it another day. They would, just when we'd started.'

Billy's plate face appeared from the hatch. He looked flushed even in the dimness. 'Christ almighty,' he said profoundly. 'Was I bloody scared. I was shivering under there, trying to get my things on. I reckon I've got a spider in my pants. I can feel it.'

'Go on!' the girl exploded with delight. 'You haven't.'

'I reckon I have.'

'Not a spider!'

'There's *something* in there,' said Billy. He pulled his trousers out at the waistband and stared down. 'And it's not my dinga either.'

'Let me put my hand down,' suggested Lizzie excitedly. 'I'll find out what it is.'

Tim, the twelve-year-old, stared with excitement and apprehension as his elder brother nodded dumbly and the girl put her fingers down inside. She and Billy were standing close and Tim was at a spectator's distance. Her jeans and pants had dropped down to her ankles again and her backside was chubby and curved only two feet away. He thought how thin her legs were at the top. His mother's legs were like sides of beef.

'*That's* not a spider,' muttered Billy as the girl, a wicked smile filling her face, explored.

'I can tell that,' she burst out. 'It's more like a lamp-post!'

They all fell into childish laughter at this joke and Lizzie stepped back and said: 'Take it out then, go on, like we said. And I'll show you mine. But, we'll have to get a move on.'

'All right then,' answered Billy carefully. 'But Tim had better keep a look-out at the door.'

'That's just like you, mate,' protested his brother. 'Tim can keep a look-out. Good old Tim. He won't mind. Maybe I want to have a butchers as well.'

'You've seen my thing plenty of times,' replied Billy artfully.

'Get off! I mean hers. I haven't seen hers, have I?'

'Go and keep watch, kid,' ordered Billy.

Lizzie smiled beguilingly at the younger boy. 'Go just for a minute,' she persuaded. 'And then you can come and see as well.'

Head bent venerably because of the lowness of the roof towards the after part of the barge, Tim went off to his post. He pushed the door cautiously open and, half hanging out on to the deck, looked round the corner at the empty towpath. He glanced back. His brother and the girl were kneeling down on the rough boards. He decided to abandon his post right away.

'There's nobody there,' he reported, scampering back through the splinters and dust. 'Honest. They're gone to the pub.'

Billy had taken his member from his trousers, white and solid, and the girl was bending down in the dimness to examine it.

'Harry Phillpot's got a bigger one than that,' announced Tim maliciously. 'Twice that.' He was staring, though, wondering how his brother could have made it so impressive.

'No he ain't,' said Billy, glaring up. 'Nothing like. I'll give him a bloody contest any day.'

'I want to touch it,' said the girl. 'May I?'

Doubt spread across the boy's face for a moment but then he nodded as though he had weighed up the question. 'Be careful though,' he said.

Lizzie pressed down on the end of the penis with her middle finger, pushing it down like the key of a cash register, then releasing it so that it jumped up.

'It's ever so springy,' she observed. Her voice was thoughtful.

'It goes better than that,' boasted Billy. 'Give it a good press. I put a conker on it once, ask our Tim, and it jumped about three feet.'

Lizzie pressed the contraption again, right down as far as she could, using two fingers now, and let it go so that it flipped up strongly. 'It's like the school diving board,' she said. 'Do you like me doing that?'

'It's not too bad,' said Billy strangely. 'Now let's have a decko at yours.'

'You can see mine if you like,' interpolated Tim, touching the girl's shoulder hopefully.

'She don't want to see yours,' argued Billy disdainfully. 'Once you've seen one in our family you've seen them all. Except his is smaller.'

'I'll have a look if you like,' offered Lizzie. 'I don't mind, really.'

The younger boy unzipped his trousers and out flopped a flaccid little willie. All three stared at it in the dim light.

'What's the matter with it?' asked Lizzie. Billy began to laugh cruelly.

'It would! It sodding would!' bellowed Tim. 'Just my sodding luck.'

'Put it away before it gets cold,' advised Billy. 'Come on, Liz. Let's see like you promised.'

'I'll just look at the door,' said the younger boy. He scuffled away, his eyes near tears, angry and humiliated. He stared out but he could scarcely see down the towpath because of the moisture in his eyes. Billy glanced at Lizzie in the dark. 'He's all upset,' he said knowingly. 'But he's only a little kid.'

'I know. I understand,' said the girl. She stepped out of her jeans and pulled them towards her to make a seat on the ragged floorboards. Demurely she sat, arranging the jeans for comfort, and then opened her slight legs. 'There you are,' she said.

There was a mouselike scamper as Tim came back through the dark. His brother warned him off with a hand. 'Don't rush, sonny,' he said. 'You can have a peep in a minute.' He rolled forward on his knees and peered up the shafts of her legs like a plumber looking for a leak. He shuffled forward, almost on his stomach and she obligingly opened her thighs further. 'I can't see nothin',' he announced eventually. 'It's too dark.'

'I'll get the torch,' said the ever eager Tim. He went to the back of the barge and returned with the hand torch. 'Do you want me to shine it?' he asked. 'I'll shine it if you like.'

'No need,' said his brother with an impatient sigh. 'Give it 'ere. I can manage.'

He switched on the beam so that it shot up the tanned flesh of the girl's legs to the narrow, white bottleneck of her thighs. 'Can you see it now?' inquired Lizzie.

'Er, yes,' Billy muttered doubtfully. 'Yes, I think I've got it. You've got quite a few hairs, haven't you?'

'Of course I have, silly.'

'I didn't think you'd have as many as that. They're getting in the way a bit. That's why I can't see it clear.'

Lizzie shifted on her bottom, drawing her knees up higher. 'Is that better?'

'A bit better.' Billy's voice was like someone in a tunnel now. 'Can I move some of them to one side?'

'No you can't,' said the girl very firmly. 'I'll do it. But you're not to touch me, Billy Reynolds.'

Billy's face emerged from his endeavours between her legs. 'You touched *me*,' he protested. 'I let you.'

'You're a boy. It's different with a girl. You're not to.'

'*I'll* look without touching,' interrupted the hopeful Tim. 'I'll be able to see. I've got good eyes.'

'Shut up,' ordered his brother. 'Wait your turn.'

'That's right,' grumbled the smaller boy. 'You're always bleeding first. *You* have what you want on the telly. *You* get a new bike and *I* have to wait until it's too small for you. Every time it's like that.' He nodded at Lizzie for sympathy and she touched his hand with hers. 'It'll be your turn soon,' she said soothingly. 'It'll still be there.'

'I'm not sure it's there now,' grumbled Billy, still shuffling for a better position.

'Oh, Christ,' muttered the girl. 'If you can't see it now you never will.'

There was no sound from Billy. A prolonged, profound silence. Then he backed out carefully and handed the torch to his brother. 'Go on then,' he said. Then, cautioning, 'It's different to what you think.'

Tim went down between her legs like a mole in a hurry. The girl shifted impatiently. 'Don't be long, Tim,' she called down to him. 'We've got to get going.'

Tim eventually emerged. 'Cor,' he said. 'That's fantastic! That's the first one I've seen.' He saw the expressions of his brother and the girl. 'Close up,' he added.

They dressed hurriedly and, laughing, went out on to the deck of the barge and along the plank to the shore. The sky was in its final shade of day, but the birds still sounded and the water had become thick with diminished light. 'It's half-past nine,' said the girl, looking at her watch. 'Come on, you two. I'll race you to the end of the path! Last one's a silly nit!'

They ran.

Even when the day had almost seeped away it was still warm. In the garden of the inn the landlord had hung four lanterns, and moths and other evening creatures came to flutter blissfully against the light.

Geoffrey and Cynthia were already there when Andrew and Audrey arrived. They were sitting in the little arbour formed by the mill wheel. Geoff was sitting in the place where he had sat earlier that day, and his wife was sitting where Ena Grant had sat. He was drinking beer and she a Martini. She had wanted to go there and he had reluctantly agreed, although he was apprehensive. There were other people distributed around the garden that had been empty in the early afternoon sun; sitting on the bench outside the door of the saloon bar, anonymous kids holding hands and having a shadowy fumble and kiss, young executives, in their evening skins of suede, or carefully stitched jeans, laughing in young executive manner, old people crouched vacantly over a solidified pint of a night-black Guinness, inwardly comparing that dusk perhaps to other dusks long ago.

Under what had once been an apple tree, but was now only a soured trunk, sat a man and his daughter, close together but not conversing, both drinking lemonade.

'We were just saying,' said Cynthia to Audrey, while Andrew went for the drinks, 'they're a funny pair, those two. Always together like man and wife.'

'Who is it?' said Audrey peering through the dusk. 'I can't see properly.'

'The Burville girl and her father,' said Cynthia. 'Sarah.'

'Oh yes. I see. I saw her mother this morning, poor soul. She was sloshed then by the look of it. Trying to pick flowers and she couldn't cope with that. No wonder those two stick together. I suppose they have to rely on each other a lot, having her in that state all the time.'

'The girl's very bright.'

'Yes, clever,' agreed Audrey. 'Mrs Burville does mad things, so they say, and she can be very nasty. Apparently she went round to her husband's office in Ruislip and fisted the commissionaire. Apparently she gets violent as hell. They had to carry her out.'

'Did you hear the dogs kicking up all that row in the street tonight?' said Cynthia. 'They all went for old Herbie Futter as he was going home.'

'They've done that before,' said Audrey. 'It's the smell of the stuff he uses stuffing those animals. It sends the dogs mad in the hot weather.'

'Well,' went on Cynthia, 'they would have had him for tea tonight if Gerry Scattergold hadn't turned his garden hose on them. They were as vicious as anything. There was a horrible big black thing. But he must pong. I wouldn't like to sit next to him in the train.'

Andrew had come back and set the drinks down. 'It's the big black dog from Hedgerows that's out to get Herbie,' he said. 'There's a personal feud there.'

'If they actually set on him, instead of just barking, then he'd have no chance,' said Geoffrey. He had not contributed much to the talk for he was disturbed at being in the garden again. He glanced sideways at Cynthia, her slightly sagging chin over her glass. She was his second wife. Not many people knew that, although Andrew and Audrey did. They had a little girl, Tania, who was five. Now he was spending his afternoons screwing again. He looked at Cynthia's chin again and remembered that's how he got her – afternoon screwing.

'How are they getting on at the barge?' asked Cynthia.

'Oh yes. Just fine,' replied Audrey easily. 'Lizzie will be here in a minute. They were just finishing some painting.'

Cynthia paused over the rim of her Martini. 'Everything proper and above-board?' she inquired.

Audrey felt herself flush and Andrew glanced fractionally at the other woman. 'God, yes,' Andrew said for his wife. 'We only wanted to see what they were doing to the barge.'

'Of course,' smiled Cynthia through the gloom. 'That's what I meant.'

'She's there with the two Reynolds boys,' said Audrey.

'Oh, I see. Well, you've nothing to worry about with those two. God, those kids look so dim they make their parents seem positively bright.'

'We weren't worrying,' insisted Audrey. 'We just wanted to have a look, that's all.'

'Just to show an interest,' confirmed Andrew.

'Andrew went to see Polly Blossom-Smith today, didn't you, Andrew?' said Audrey. She had curious ways of steering a conversation.

'Yes,' said Andrew to the others. 'I've already confessed to my wife. She was in her bikini too, a stirring sight.' He caught a new anxiety in Geoffrey's eye and he gave the briefest shake of his head in reassurance.

'Does she have a tattoo, like they say?' asked Cynthia.

'An Arabic proverb,' confirmed Andrew. 'At the top of her leg.'

'You didn't tell me you'd seen that,' said Audrey.

'The suspicions of women,' sighed Andrew. 'She was in her bikini, I couldn't help seeing it. It's something about life being like . . .' He hesitated. '. . . like a bowl of cherries.'

'Very Arabic,' sniffed Audrey.

'Well something like that,' said Andrew. Her innate suspicion was such, he knew, that she could not have accepted that the true translation was told to him by a woman in a friendly manner. A cucumber up the arse could only be the words of an intimate.

'I also went to see Gomer John,' said Andrew. 'He's busy navigating the sub-post office around the world.'

'It's all done out like a ship's cabin,' said Cynthia. 'His mother told me. She thinks he's mad.'

'Just one of the maladjusted we'll be having at Plummers Park soon,' said Audrey. 'That'll do the property values no end of good.'

'It's only a vague proposal,' sighed Andrew. 'It's just old Ernest getting two legs in one knicker leg again.'

A man emerged through the incandescence of the garden lanterns. It was the landlord of the inn. He looked uncertainly for a moment and then leaned towards Geoffrey and held out his hand.

'Open your hand, sir,' he said as though he were about to perform magic.

All four looked bemusedly at him from their seats. Geoffrey, with an accommodating grin, put out his hand and the man put a fifty-pence piece in his palm.

'What's that for?' asked Geoffrey.

'Lunchtime, sir. You didn't take your change at lunchtime. I recognized you getting out of the white MG.'

'Not me,' said Geoffrey stiffly through the silence of the others. He pushed the coin back towards the man. 'I'll take it if you like – money is money. But it wasn't me.'

The man leaned forward again as though he were peering through smoke. 'Not you?' he said. 'I could have sworn it was . . .' He caught the look, the iron look, and drew back. 'Oh no, sir. Well, now I come to see you I realize it wasn't.' He looked around accusingly. 'These lamps are a bit dim, for a start. Sorry about that.'

Geoffrey laughed easily and held out his hand. 'I'll still have it,' he said. 'I'll keep it if you like.'

'No, sir,' said the landlord taking the coin. 'But I think I'd better wait till the right gentleman comes in. If he don't then it can go in the polio box.'

The man backed away and the three looked at Geoffrey. He laughed again. 'What about that? I could have been fifty pence to the good.'

'You shouldn't be so honest,' said Cynthia choosing her words.

'The best policy, they say,' said Geoffrey. 'Who wants another drink?'

'Here come the children,' said Audrey. 'Could you get some lemonade for them?'

'Andrew.'

'Yes.'

'Wasn't that strange at the pub. That man bringing out the fifty pence. Do you think it was really Geoff?'

'No. He said it wasn't. Geoff wasn't there at lunchtime.'

'You don't think so?'

'Audrey love, if he says he wasn't, he wasn't.'

'It just seemed funny, that's all. He seemed so certain.'

'Oh, I don't know. The light was very dim. I didn't realize it was Burville and his daughter sitting across the way from us until someone pointed them out.'

'I suppose you're right. I mean, Cynth's his second wife, isn't she?'

'Look, if Geoff's playing around he's hardly likely to go to the same place twice in one day, is he? He's not that daft.'

'I told Cynthia that we were going there. Perhaps he couldn't get out of it.'

'Why don't you forget it, love. It was nothing. Nothing to do with us anyway.'

They lay with just a sheet over them. The night was close. They had left the curtains open and they could watch the stars above Plummers Park, with the roving lights of stacking airliners over Watford waiting their turn to go into London Airport.

'Andrew.'

'Yes.'

'You wouldn't leave me again, would you?'

'No. That's all finished. You know that.'

'But you wouldn't. For anybody. I get afraid, you know. Married women do get afraid.'

'I get afraid too. I'm afraid all the time.'

'It's not too bad together, is it?'

'No. It's fine.'

'Andrew, put your hand around my bum.'

'All right. Is that okay.'

'That's fine. I love you, you know.'

'I do you too. I love you, I mean.'

'Good. Goodnight, love.'

'Goodnight, baby.'

'Geoff. Come on to bed.'

'Just coming.'

'Geoff.'

'Yes, love?'

'Wasn't it funny that man thinking you'd been there at lunchtime.'

'A bit embarrassing. Good job he realized.'

'Yes, he *did* realize.'

'It was nice up there, wasn't it?'

'Yes, we ought to go again, Geoff. It's not far.'

'What about the two Reynolds boys, Cynth? Have you ever seen a couple of thicker-looking kids? They have that prehistoric look about them. Polly Blossom-Smith should use them as models.'

'What about Lizzie though? She's a beautiful kid, isn't she?'

'I'll say. She's going to be a stunner.'

'She's well on the way now. Andrew and Audrey are going to have trouble with her.'

'All life's trouble. It's death's no trouble.'

'That's very true.'

'It was in *Zorba the Greek*. Don't you remember?'

'No. I can never remember anything like that. Once I'm out of the cinema it goes.'

'It's not often I do. But that stuck.'

'Perhaps it means something to you.'

'Me? Not me. It's Andrew remembers things like that.'

'Good old Andrew. Do you think they're happy?'

'Andrew and Audrey? Oh, they're all right. The same as all of us.'

'We're all right, aren't we?'

'Us? Of course. You ought to know.'

'I do. Of course we are.'

As she said it he turned round at the side of the bed, away from her, standing naked. And she wondered sleepily why his buttocks were so pink. Almost sunburned.

CHAPTER SIX

Susie Minnings was an anguished young woman with a booming cloud of red hair like coloured smoke rising from the combustion of her extraordinary face. The flying arches of her eyebrows, the banging black eyelashes, the zooming eyes, the thick fiery lipstick and the pink cheeks gave her a perpetual expression of surprised explosion. Tonight she was having a party.

Her clothes were purples and puces, and heavy beads, rarely smaller than walnuts, flew on strings about her neck like a dangerous whirligig. She wore beads all the time, even in bed, and her swinging of them, by accident or design, sometimes injured her small children. Her size-eight feet, clad, on this the night of her reunion party, in emerald Aladdin slippers with tingling bells on the toes, were set like the hands of a large clock at ten to two. 'Do you know,' Andrew confided to Geoffrey as they watched her, 'I could never bring myself to have an affair with a woman whose feet stuck out like that.'

'Up! Up! Everybody!' Susie cried scattering her guests from the settee. 'Time to feed the hammies!' Three snot-encrusted children in foul nightwear jogged around her excitedly, each one ducking with almost synchronized reflexes the scything of her beads. In her off-white hands with their mauve finger-nails she clutched a fire shovel loaded with grain which she shovelled down the seam at the back of the settee. 'Listen to the little sods now!' she shouted with delight. 'Can you hear them scampering after it?' She smiled around in her smashed fashion. 'All right, you can sit down again,' she invited. 'The hamsters don't mind. If one gets caught in the springs you'll soon know. They let out the most Christlike squeak.'

'How many hamsters are there, Susie?' asked Andrew.

'He-llo, Andrew,' she said kissing him. He wiped his cheek because a kiss from Susie looked like a nasty wound. 'How many? Hamsters? Don't know, dear. Half a dozen at least. They've lived down there for generations. They never come up and I can't say I blame them.'

Her three infants were congregating just out of swinging range of the beads. Two were sharing a glass of wine. 'Come on!' Susie bawled at them. 'Up in the bath, you lot! Let the nice neighbours see you do have a bath now and again.' She shooed them off. 'Then go to kip. Dry yourselves first.' The children went, and she turned to Andrew and Geoff. 'Last time they went straight from the bath into bed. Didn't bother to dry themselves. They're mad. They're like their bloody father.'

'Where is their bloody father?' asked Geoff. 'Wasn't this a reunion party for you two?' Before she answered, Audrey and Cynthia had appeared from the cloak room and were hovering near their husbands, nodding oddly at Susie, as timid spectators might nod at an exotic zoo animal known to be dangerous.

'Hello, girls,' she replied blithely. She looked at Geoffrey and then quickly at Cynthia again. 'You two haven't gone and got in the club again, have you?' she inquired loudly. She poked Cynthia's stomach. 'Or is that just a good lunch?'

She stopped. Her eyes revolved like a fruit-machine at the aghast couple. Andrew had a quick drink and Audrey covered her mouth. 'Oh shit,' said Susie. 'I've done it again. Sorry, love. Don't take any notice of me.'

'I don't,' said Cynthia bitterly.

'Good for you. Christ, I say the maddest things. I judge everybody by me. A hamburger and a couple of pints and I swell out like I'm having triplets.'

'What about Doug?' asked Andrew quickly. 'Is he around?'

'Oh, that craven bastard. Well, he's buggered off back to his black bint in Wembley and good luck to her. He's been shacking up with her for a month – one of his usual capers – but he came back and that's why I put it around that this was a reunion party. Now he's gone again. It was too late to cancel the reunion so I thought I'd make it a separation party instead. Thank Christ it's only a party. When he came back once we had a celebration kid – that brat Regina.'

'She's the one who breaks the eggs in the supermarket, isn't she?' said Cynthia tartly.

'They all do that,' answered Susie. 'Little swines. Anyway, Bollock-chops won't be here tonight, so you're spared him.' She waved extravagantly to them and went off like an armed raider through the crowded room.

'She's damned well impossible,' said Audrey. She glanced sympathetically, but with something funny in her eye too, at Cynthia. 'Poor Cynth. Fancy her saying that.'

'Silly cow,' muttered Cynthia. 'It's just this dress. I'd have spat in her eye and cleared off right there and then, but I didn't want to bring myself down to her level.'

'I'm glad you didn't,' said Geoffrey. 'We might have missed something.'

Cynthia leaned over the side-table by which they were standing and wrote 'Do Not Disturb' in the dust.

In a shed in the garden next to the Minnings house, across the fence from the coloured lights hanging from the line-posts and the children's swing, a paunchy acne-splattered youth called Brian Harvey, known as Brain Harvey, was crouched at the controls of his specially-designed baby-listening network. His receiver was connected to twenty houses in the area where children were sleeping, each one with a small microphone in the bedroom. Parents who paid fifty pence per night for the service made periodic visits from the party, and at the pull of a switch Brain could tell them whether or not their offspring slept undisturbed.

Geoffrey was making his second check call of the night and found himself going in the same direction as a young woman who was a stranger. 'I think I'm the only person who's doing this in reverse,' she said as they waited for Brain to make contact with her house. 'I'm a child checking on my mother.'

'That's a new twist,' admitted Geoffrey. 'Does she cry much at night?'

'No. She irons shirts. All the time. It's a sort of fad with her and I thought I would take advantage of this idea to listen in and make sure she was all right.' Brain pulled the switch and the woman leaned forward. 'Ah, yes. She's okay. I can hear her singing.'

'How do you know it's not the radio?' asked Geoff.

'They don't sing "Goodbye, Dolly Grey" much on the radio these days,' she said. 'She sings that all the time.'

'Are you ready for contact Mr Turvey?' inquired Brain. 'Shall I attempt to get through?' He crouched and fiddled with anxious sweat like the eternally pessimistic wireless-operator in jungle war films. He was very serious about his function.

'Roger,' said Geoffrey, and Brain smiled at him appreciatively. The young woman gave an amused twitch of her nose. He thought he recognized her from somewhere. Brain operated the switch and Geoffrey leaned forward to hear the blameless breathing of his child. He smiled fondly, as even adulterous fathers do, and patted Brain on his rubbery shoulder. 'Roger and out,' he said.

He walked with the young woman across the garden, back to the party. 'My name's Geoffrey Turvey,' he said. 'We haven't met.'

'Just moved in,' she said. 'I'm Joy Rowley. You're a friend of Andrew's, aren't you? I saw you talking.'

'Andrew?' echoed Geoffrey, not querying the name but the fact that she knew it. 'Old Andrew. He didn't tell me . . .'

She laughed engagingly. 'Why should he? He helped me to carry some of my belongings to my house the other day. With the station-master. Is that your wife next to Andrew? And that's his wife, I imagine.'

'Yes, sure, come on over,' said Geoffrey.

He led her across and watched for the little arch of suspicion to shoot up on Cynthia's face. It appeared immediately but dropped quickly again when Andrew stepped forward and in a friendly way held the younger woman's hand before introducing her.

'This is Joy Rowley,' he said. 'She's a famous dramatic actress and she's come to live in Plummers Park.'

'He's kidding,' laughed Joy. She was so easy that the other women relaxed. 'I'm the Sarah Siddons of the washing-machine. I do the occasional television commercial, that's all.'

'A celebrity!' exclaimed Audrey, only half-mocking.

'We could do with a few more around here,' said Cynthia seriously. 'A couple of pop singers and somebody who's on telly regularly and gets in the scandal columns. The property values would go up like mad. You're a start anyway.'

'Thank you,' said Joy politely. 'I try to be as scandalous as possible.'

'Is Mr Rowley here?' asked Audrey.

'If he were he'd be a sensation,' Joy replied. 'He's dead.'

'Oh dear, what have I said? I'm sorry.'

'Don't worry. Don't be silly.'

'I often wonder which is best, or worse, a divorce or a bereavement,' ruminated Cynthia seriously. 'Even a divorce doesn't seem quite so final as the other thing. People have been known to get back together after a divorce.'

'It's difficult after death,' admitted Andrew sagely.

'Well, we were both,' said Joy. 'Divorced – then he died.'

'I bet that made the estate difficult,' said Cynthia, sticking her nose forward. 'Did he have another woman to keep?'

'Cynthia!' laughed Geoffrey not very convincingly.

His wife looked stupidly surprised, first at him and then at the others. 'Oh, I'm sorry. I didn't mean to pry,' she huffed. 'I like to know where people stand, that's all. The problem pages are meat and drink to me, I'm afraid.'

'Have you had a chance to meet many people around here yet?' asked Audrey.

'She means besides me,' said Andrew.

'I didn't at all,' denied Audrey tartly. 'For all you know I might have meant the onion seller.'

'The onion seller?' laughed Joy. 'Who's that?'

'Most fantastic man in Plummers Park, next to Hercules the tramp,' put in Andrew. 'Has the wives round here in tears. I don't know whether it's frustration or the onions.'

'Well, I've got that pleasure to come,' Joy assured them. 'This is the first time I've really been anywhere. I met Susie in the post office. She hit my mother across the head with her beads. She certainly knows how to entertain.'

'She's made an effort this time,' sniffed Cynthia. 'She's even taken the dead moths out of the light bowl in the hall.'

Gerry Scattergood, who lived across the road from Andrew and Audrey, was a contraceptive salesman, a young bulky man, fair-haired, waist and paunch overhanging his belt, a large laugh and a quiet sniffy wife called Min who was childless. He sat cross-legged in the centre of a circle of Susie's guests in the manner of a man selling snake medicine. 'The spoggie,' he announced seriously, 'the french letter, the condom, the sheath, the noddy, the bladder, the nosebag, the Friday night blessing and the vicar's friend, whatever you like to call it, is a remarkable contraption that has afforded great benefit to mankind, and womankind incidentally.'

'Prophylactics,' said the tall American voice of Harry Solkiss. He and Jean were holding hands on the fringe of the audience and he spoke without stretching over the heads before him. The English people turned with a collective slow pout, as they do with foreigners.

'The same to you,' said Gerry looking up. His neighbours laughed.

'Yes, sir, that's smart,' agreed the amiable Harry, laughing more than anyone and shaking his head at the unbounded wit of the Englishman. 'Real smart. I meant that *we* call them prophylactics.'

'Yes,' said Gerry carefully. 'Yes, I suppose you would. But it's not something that would catch on over here. I mean, by the time you'd said that mouthful you'd have forgotten what you were supposed to be doing with it.'

'Right!' exclaimed Harry with polite over-enthusiasm amid the laughter. 'I guess you would!'

His wife squeezed his tall, thin hand and laughed her confirmation. 'You sure would, Hairy.'

'Today,' pronounced Gerry Scattergood, with a glance at the Americans which did not invite further interruptions, 'this evening, ladies and gentlemen, spoggy-users all, I trust . . .'

'Not likely!'

'You'd be lucky!'

'What about the pill?'

Gerry stared about him, hurt astonishment cracking up his face. 'Please, please,' he implored softly. 'Ladies and gentlemen. Do not mention such things. Do not upset the performer. The pill? The pill? A gob-stopper, madam, a sugared bon-bon. *I* speak, sir, of no chemist's concoction, but of a game for two, of titillation and technique, something as engrossing as a toy and as much fun, an art form . . . poetry . . . joy.'

He revolved his wide eyes round the amused faces with challenge. His trousers, from habit, had parted from his shirt at the back and the great melon of flesh was bulging out. 'An art form,' he repeated softly. 'And I demonstrate.'

From his waistcoat pocket he produced with a professional flourish a wriggle of purple rubber which he put to his lips and blew into expertly. It expanded with a squeak like something rudely awakened, and became before everyone's eyes a little plum-coloured dragon with bright eyes and pointed horns.

'The Purple People-eater, our new model,' he announced modestly. Women had their hands across their mouths and regarded him and the rubber dragon with hilarious but fearsome fascination. Gerry let go the end and, with a quick raspberry like a rude comment to the watchers, the dragon disappeared, to be replaced, with the facility of a conjuror, by another rubber creature, its head covered with small horns and ticklers.

'An importation from Honolulu called Invitation to Love. Note the colour – Pacific Twilight.'

'The Japanese Gorilla,' he said immediately, producing another condom from his waistcoat. He glanced about him sternly. 'Not to be used, gentlemen, unless there is a full moon – and only if you love your wife very, very much.' The laughter burst out again, all around.

'And here,' he said, hanging out what appeared to be a small three-fingered rubber glove, 'Is the triple-teat treat.' He glanced about him mischievously. 'For doing it left, right and centre.'

'Note our array of colours,' he continued with a new burst of energy. 'Black Midnight, Passion Puce, Sligo Green – our line for the Republic of Ireland – and this lovely new creation, a tender pink, which we call After The Ball.'

Most of the party guests were crowding about now; the Indian music from the record-player was not altogether inappropriate to Gerry's market-place posture. 'And strength!' he attacked again. 'Such strength, ladies and gentlemen. Not only do you have the enjoyment of trying these products in private, of adding a new dimension to your marriage, a new width to the bed, if you like, but . . . but . . . you have the famous assurance of my company – Joy Through Strength!'

'Talking about Joy,' Geoffrey said as they stood watching Gerry Scattergood gather his wares at the conclusion of his act. 'You didn't tell me you knew her.'

Andrew grinned. 'Joy? Well, I have some secrets. Don't we all?'

'What's that mean?'

'Who's been modelling his lovely self for Polly Blossom-Smith then? Whose magnificent brow is to be immortalized as Flat-Roof Man?'

'Christ, she told you?' Geoffrey's eyes darted around with abrupt alarm not quelled until he saw Cynthia safely at the distant end of the room.

'She didn't just tell me, old friend. She showed me.'

'Ah, she's done you then, as well. You slimy bugger. If you tell on me, I'll tell on you.'

'No chance, son. She's not "done" me, whatever you may mean by that. But she did show me her masterpiece – and there *you* are. Well, bits of you.'

'Has she got the cock on it yet?'

'You thought that might be my contribution?'

'Boasting again.'

'The function of this statue, as far as I understand it,' said Andrew calmly, 'is to depict *typical* Flat-Roof Man. He is far from Superman. In fact from what I saw of it he looks very much like Homo Sapiens Gone Wrong.'

'Cheeky bastard. Just because she didn't use you.'

'Not at all. No bit of him is there because it's the biggest or the best, but because it's typical of our breed. So it's open to argument whether the sexual organ would be big or indifferent from neglect. Some have it, some don't. It's obviously a matter for Polly to ponder.'

'It's a point,' conceded Geoffrey. 'Perhaps she ought to use Gerry

Scattergood, as it's in his line, so to speak.'

'I think she's intrigued by the Phantom Flasher,' said Andrew. 'If she can capture him she'll be well pleased. She'd broadcast it everywhere around Plummers Park.'

'God, yes, what about that? Who do you think it is?'

'It's not me,' shrugged Andrew. 'I won't go to a public urinal unless there's nobody else there.'

'It's certainly not me.'

'No, I'm sure of that. Half the women around here would recognize you immediately.'

'I should be so lucky. With Cynthia around I couldn't so much as raise my hat let alone unzip my fly.'

'What about the other night at The Jolly Grinder?' asked Andrew. 'The landlord coming over like that.'

'A mistake,' said Geoffrey, looking at him firmly. 'A case of mistaken identity.'

'Here's Ena,' said Andrew, suddenly looking across Geoffrey's shoulder. 'And Simon close in attendance.'

'As ever,' said Geoffrey turning to see her. 'He never lets her out of clutching distance.'

'Would you?' asked Andrew. 'They don't grow many like that around Plummers Park.' They stood, glasses in hand, admiring her together, as others were.

She wore a pink dress that flowed spectacularly about her. She bent minutely forward to catch something a man was saying and her breasts beamed at them. Her fair hair was piled high. She was genuinely beautiful. She looked too good for the party.

A few yards away their wives were watching. 'Diamond Lil,' sniffed Cynthia.

'That dress,' said Audrey. 'It's not very suitable for here, is it? They say *he* chooses all her clothes.'

'I reckon he pumps her up when she's in them too,' said Cynthia.

'Oh, Cynth!'

'Well, I ask you. You'd think she was going to Buck House instead of 43 Hedgerows.'

'Where's Buck House?' asked Audrey genuinely.

'Oh Audrey, for goodness sake. Buckingham Palace.'

'Oh I see. Well I didn't know. I never go there.' The look she returned to her neighbour said: 'And neither do you.' But the comment remained a look.

Cynthia turned her back to the french windows through which Simon and Ena had entered and where they were now talking with the bead-whirling hostess. 'I can't look,' she said. 'She's like a prize from Hampstead Heath fairground.'

Geoffrey had looked away too and was staring bitterly into his drink. He was tempted to tell Andrew. To say simply: 'I've had her, Andrew. I have her regularly. I've had those breasts in my mouth. I've had those lips and my hands full of that hair, and I've been right inside that lovely flat belly.' Instead he said: 'Have you played much golf lately?'

'Golf?'

'Yes, you know, golf.'

Andrew laughed. 'Sorry. I was looking at her. She certainly is pretty spectacular. I think she's truly beautiful.'

'Our wives don't,' said Geoffrey, nodding across. 'There's blood dripping from my loved-one's fingernails. Look at her. Don't you think women are ugly when they get screwed up with jealousy?'

'Do you want to talk about golf or women?' asked Andrew.

'Women,' agreed Geoffrey reluctantly. 'I don't really know much about golf.'

'But you know about women?'

'Sometimes I think I do. At others I think I know more about golf.'

'You're miserable about something,' said Andrew.

'I was okay,' said Geoffrey, swirling his drink around in his glass. 'Until I looked up and caught that sneer of envy on Cynthia's face. That hatred. Only women have that sort of hate. And only *some* women. I'm married to one of them. That's what has pissed me off so suddenly.'

Andrew shrugged: 'The best you can hope from marriage is a good clean fight,' he said.

'Christ,' Geoffrey said, 'I sometimes think I'll run away, abroad, somewhere tropical, where all the women have nice light-brown titties and pleasing smiles.' He let a thought drop into his glass, then looked up. 'You and Audrey fight, don't you?' he asked as though seeking reassurance.

'All the time. Well, we don't really fight, we skirmish.'

'I retreat,' said Geoffrey. 'I'm always on the retreat or behind my defences. I don't want to fight. This is my second bash at it.'

'I know. I've never asked you about it. What was the first one like?'

'The wife or the marriage? Well, they were the same really. Both excruciating boredom. Every day I used to get on the train to go into London and I'd be sitting there wondering what the hell I was going to do to escape, and every day, on the dot, that bloody great overcrowded cemetery at Kensal Green used to straggle past the window. I tried not to look but I still used to. Miles of it. Sometimes I thought I could hear the sods laughing at me. So one day I met Cynthia and I ran off with her. Just to get away. I thought it was my last chance. I might as well have gone to work by bus and missed seeing the cemetery.'

'That's a hard thing to say.'

'It changes, Andrew. Don't you agree? Before your very eyes, it changes. That bitter woman over there is the one I used to wait for with a banging heart.' He looked at Andrew accusingly, as though anxious that he too should confess. 'You went off with that girl, didn't you? But you came back. Why did you come back?'

'I missed my home,' shrugged Andrew. 'Straight up, I did. I missed the furniture and the new prints we'd bought in Watford. That sort of daft thing.'

'What about the bird?'

'She flew,' said Andrew. 'Off she went and vanished into the world. She'll be all right. She was terrific, sexy and really unusual.'

'And you let her go. You preferred your chairs and your prints.'

'I was afraid. I couldn't handle the situation. I scuttled back in a blind panic – and there was Audrey standing on one of our chairs trying to bang a nail in the wall for one of the prints.'

'Did you ever see her again. The girl?'

'No. I used to walk around looking for her in the streets, in London, imagining I would see her face in a shop window. But I never saw her and after a year or so I stopped looking.'

'Was she a good talker?'

'Yes, she was. She had a marvellous voice too. We used to lie in bed and talk for hours.'

'And you used to tell her how decent and beautiful your wife was. And your lovely daughter. And all about your neighbours and friends. And about the furniture and the prints.'

'That's it. She was very patient too. And I was the one who cleared out. It's funny, isn't it?'

'What are you going to do now? Settle for it?'

'Of course, settle for it,' said Andrew. 'Audrey has.'

'You could always start digging out a new room beneath your house, like old Shillingford.'

'Ah, I suppose so. But with him it's a hobby. If I did it Audrey would think I was trying to tunnel out. To escape.'

'You would be, wouldn't you?'

Someone took Susie's wandering Indian music off the record-player and replaced it with Sinatra's worn 'Songs for Swinging Lovers' which haunted Plummers Park parties like the ghost of youth. People began to dance, at first an obligatory shuffle with their household partners, but then, as at a silent signal, in the arms of the husband or wife they wanted and who had a fancy for them. It was a game they played at every party: the fresh chest pressed to the fresh breast, the lights dimmed to the jokey laughter of the dancers and to their relief. But, immediately, in the shadows came the clutch in earnest, the suddenly nipping lips and the soughing breath on necks, the touching of bosoms. Hands that daily polished brass door-knockers rubbed recklessly at hardening trouser fronts. Few of the semi-detached people would venture the risks, tribulations and expenses of a real love affair, and this was the next best thing. But like all games it was for a set duration. The following morning it would be remembered but remain untouched, undisturbed, until the next time Sinatra sang songs in some suburban sitting-room.

Andrew and Audrey always backed away from this dancing. Once when they had given a party Lizzie and a young boy from Risingfield had stood watching these married dancers, clutching and kissing, while the record played 'The Second Time Around'. The girl and the boy had gone from the room and Audrey had found them in the kitchen. 'It makes me sick,' Lizzie had said, 'seeing all that. We don't do that at *our* parties. All that pawing from people that age.' Now they stood at the ringside, watching with half-amused embarrassment the increased fumbling of half-recognized shadows which shuffled and turned and groaned with slow enjoyment and feigned despair. It was as if she and he feared to become involved, like two people who have saved hard for years standing and watching a game of high-stakes roulette.

They danced briefly, and properly, together and they smiled at each other as though in recognition, but that was all, and they were relieved to be interrupted. 'Been up there lately, Andrew? Haven't seen you,' said the voice.

Amidst the sexual fraudulence Gorgeous George was indulging in his own pretence, swinging his eternal, invisible, golf club, slowly back and taking care to follow through. He took up a deliberate stance in front of Andrew and the bemused Audrey, addressing an unseen ball, adjusting his wrists and his feet, then looking up and seeing their expressions.

'Sorry,' he said cheerily. 'Been trying to get it right. Think I'm turning the wrists over at the last moment or something. What do you think, old boy?' He performed an imaginary swing.

'Wrong club,' suggested Andrew, nodding at George's empty hands. 'That's a four iron and you played it more like a nine.'

George grinned beneath his exploded cordite moustache with genuine pleasure at the mild joke. 'You're a funny devil, Andrew,' he nodded. 'Should get you to speak at the annual dinner.' He turned to Audrey. 'Don't you think he's jolly funny?' he asked.

'A constant hoot,' she agreed dolefully. 'I can't get my housework done for laughing at him. An absolute tonic.'

'Been trying to line up the putts better, recently,' continued George, actually going through the motions of replacing one imaginary club in a non-existent golf-bag, taking out an unseen putter and putting a phantom ball at his feet. 'All the boys at the club say I'm not lining the thing up right. Playing tomorrow, Andrew?'

'Tomorrow? Tomorrow? No, I don't think so. Is it anything special?'

'Mixed foursomes. Have to play with the girls. Mixed gruesomes, you know. The boys don't really like it, but it's only now and again. It's a different game with the girls, a totally different game.'

'It usually is,' said Andrew. He felt Audrey glance at him quickly.

'Hear about old Fowler?' asked George. 'The head greenkeeper. They're giving him the push.'

'Fowler? The push?' Andrew leaned forward, genuinely astonished. 'Why, for God's sake? He's been there donkey's years. He must be on retirement anyway.'

'That's just it,' said George with a strange triumph as though at last he had made a remark of some true interest. 'The Committee thought they'd move him along before they had to keep him for the rest of his life. They can get a jolly good rent these days for that cottage of his.'

'That's bloody scandalous!' exploded Andrew. 'I've never heard anything like it.'

George looked taken aback at the outburst. He said: 'Well, it's life, Andrew old chap. Like golf, life is a difficult business.'

He went off suddenly through the crowd, after first replacing the invisible putter in the ghostly golf-bag which he put across his shoulder.

'Rotten swines,' said Andrew. 'If they do that they can stick their miserable golf club up their arse as far as I'm concerned. I'll see that gets in the Sunday papers too.'

Audrey was grinning wryly at him. 'Oh, we're aroused are we? Growling, for God's sake! What *have* those naughty *boys* and *girls* at the golf club done!'

Geoffrey Turvey and Ena Grant never danced together or anywhere near each other at parties. Not since the party at which they first met. Tonight he was dancing with Susie Minnings's beads wound about his neck like a hawser around a bollard. Susie's children in disgraceful night clothes were charging about the room blowing up Gerry Scattergood's products like coloured balloons. Simon was dancing with his wife, his nose hovering over the scent of her breasts, before leading her in a proprietorial fashion off the floor and towards Andrew and Audrey. It was only in male company that he talked about the extravagance of his wife's personal parts. With other wives around he gained the air of an earnest young man, anxious to discuss serious issues, local, national and terrestrial, and celestial, with considered opinions and firm nods of his head.

Ena was towed to the fringe of these discussions and left there, never asked, expected or even allowed to join in. It was as though she were some luxuriously upholstered vehicle tethered for use once the serious discussions had concluded. If she attempted to make a remark in general company, as distinct from any side-talk among the women, she was given a fond little tug of the wrist or ear-lobe and silenced by Simon's affectionate sentence: 'But I don't think you understand, darling.' It was after one such rebuff in one such deadly conversation months before that Geoffrey had touched her hand and taken her to the floor to dance. Cynthia was in bed with tonsillitis at the time of that party. The first words Ena ever spoke to the man who was to become her lover were: 'There are times when I think I am married to the world's biggest prick.'

Now Simon trawled her through the drinking guests. People were bending this way and that, rolling and staggering too, with the dubious red and white wine that the Minnings provided, plus a bottle of scotch passed secretly around after being burgled from a locked cupboard. Simon only permitted her to drink tomato juice in company, although at home he encouraged her to drink quite extravagantly on some nights. He pulled her in like a tugman pulling in a rope, and immediately engaged Andrew in conversation about the home for maladjusted children. Andrew contributed little but watched the young man, swaying around on a firm base like some sort of talking toy. 'As far as I can see, and I've thought damned carefully about this, Andrew,' he affirmed, 'it's not only a matter of people's comfort up here, and the price of their assets, but their safety too. Maladjusted kids are maladjusted kids no matter what fancy names you would like to call them. Now take this, as an example, and I'd like you to listen damned carefully to this . . .'

Audrey turned slightly to Ena. 'Only a tomato juice?' she inquired, nodding at the young wife's glass.

Ena lifted it past her half-exposed breasts and drank it deeply. She smiled at Audrey. 'I've been looking forward to that all day,' she sighed.

Cynthia came from the bathroom and automatically surveyed the room for her husband. The cold nose of a nasty feeling poked into her as she saw him dancing with Joy Rowley. She did not trust actresses. Cynthia crouched and waited for them to move in front of the table-lamp by the far window. She spied carefully and was relieved to see that there was light between their bodies. But they were talking deeply. She was distrustful too of women who could talk deeply. Creeping around the edge of the dancers she sprang out on them like an ambusher. 'Oh, there you are!' she cried, making both jump. Then: 'Oh, Geoff, go and listen for Tania, will you, darling?'

'Sure,' he said, his face only tightening a fraction. 'After this dance, I'll go.'

'No, please go now,' suggested Joy easing herself away from him.

'Perhaps you'll listen for my mother too, will you . . . er . . .'

'Geoffrey,' filled in Cynthia. 'And I'm Cynthia.'

'Of course. I'm sorry, Geoff.' She turned sweetly to Cynthia. 'I've had the listening service hooked up to my house for my mother,' she said. 'She's alone and she's a bit strange, you know.' She smiled fully at the wife. 'A bit potty, I'm afraid. Irons my dead father's shirts all the time. You ought to come round one afternoon for some tea, Cynthia. You'd like my mother.'

The other woman's panicky polite and only half-comprehending smile was interrupted at that moment by the appearance at the french windows of the impressive and fiery form of Mrs Polly Blossom-Smith, a gin bottle in each outstretched hand. She always took her personal gin to parties. Her face was in the light and splattered with excitement. 'Invasion!' she cried dramatically. 'Invasion! Plummers Park is invaded! There's a whole lot of blackies coming up the road!'

That stopped the party in mid-dance, mid-laugh, mid-kiss. Mrs Polly Blossom-Smith was more exotic than Susie Minnings, and larger, and she now filled the doorway, a scarlet robe hanging from her like the evidence of some recent massacre. Then the garden outside was bobbing with black faces. Polly turned and, screaming 'They're here! They're here!', tumbled into the crowded room.

'A demon! It's a demon!' the leading negro retaliated, pointing a long finger at Polly hanging on to the guests like a battered heavyweight on the ropes. 'It's the Bad Red Zombie!' He walked easily into the room, a strong humourous-looking man wearing a good suit and pork-pie hat which he courteously doffed about him. He was followed by further coloured men and women, and eventually, solving the mystery, by Douglas Minnings, Susie's husband, arm around the waist of a bouncing West Indian girl.

'You lousy bastard!' Susie's voice hooted from the back of the crowd. She wriggled her way through for a confrontation with her cheerful husband. 'What do you mean bringing this tribe here like this?' She glared at the West Indian girl, doubling the expression on her already explosive countenance. 'And her! Fancy bringing her!'

'Ah, Dorcas,' said Douglas, as though he had suddenly remembered something. 'This is my wife Susan. Susie, this is Dorcas.'

To everyone's astonishment the two women shook hands almost formally, but immediately Susie spun about and, catching her husband by the lapels of his light jacket, howled: 'Come on, get this lot out of here. We're having our reunion party – or don't you remember?'

'Sure, sure,' soothed Douglas. 'That's why I *had* to get here. I thought I'd bring a few of the gang from Wembley and we could gee it up a bit. Parties here tend to get a bit stodgy. We've brought some rum and soda water and some bits of chicken, and Alfonse over there has got his mouth-organ, and Boney's got his drum. We're going to have a great time.'

'No you are not!' argued Susie. 'You are taking this minstrel show back to Wembley. And now.'

'And who's going to throw us out?' asked Doug.

'My friends here,' said Susie, recklessly swinging her arm about. The faces of the Plummers Park men took on uneasy shades. Their womenfolk looked at them for bravery and reassurance and were, without exception, disappointed.

'Doug! Doug! Doug!' The three Minnings children rushed from the direction of the kitchen like raiding bedouins and embraced their father's legs. He lifted them all at once, like bundles of disreputable rags. 'Look at this, Dorcas! What about these then?'

'Sure, what about them?' replied Dorcas ambiguously.

'Hello, Dorcas!' Hello!' the children enthused. 'Are you sleeping with our daddy?' inquired the eldest.

'Not right now,' answered Dorcas, eyeing Susie.

'We put Mrs Brown's tom cat down the toilet,' exclaimed the middle child.

'And pulled the chain!' added the youngest as though anxious to complete the news. 'We pulled the chain! We pulled the chain!'

'Listen,' demanded Susie, 'are you getting this lot out of this house?'

Douglas touched her soothingly. 'This house, baby,' he pointed out, 'is my house. Ask the solicitor. And I'd just like some of my friends to join the party, that's all. If you and your friends don't like it I suggest they go out into the garden or piss off home.'

'All right,' breathed Susie. 'Let them stay. But *this* is *my* party. If you want your own party, have it at the other end of the room. We'll push up this end. You have the other half and a gap in the middle.'

'What a great idea,' enthused Doug, kissing his wife on her truculent nose. He walked the width of the room making a corridor with his hands. At the end of this he was confronted by his own children again. 'Give these three machine-guns and they can patrol it like real life,' he suggested.

'No need for that,' replied Susie. 'We'll keep to our bit if you keep to yours. And no banging that bloody bongo thing louder than our record-player.'

Everyone, the Plummer Park whites and the Wembley coloureds, allowed themselves to be recruited into the farce by the husband and wife whose entire existence was built on battle and compromise. They shifted and shuffled, pushing against each other, making space, clutching glasses and loved ones closer, so that in the end there were two distinct ethnic groups at each end of the room, with the vacant corridor between them. Sinatra, the high and unseen priest of Flat-Roof Man's culture, remained incanting the older songs at one extreme, while at the other the West Indians swayed so quietly it was almost a slow tremble to the sound of the drum touched and tapped unprovocatively. But it was an uneasy armistice. The whites had been drinking all the evening and the blacks now began to distribute the rum among themselves. The corridor became narrower as each side tried to gain a few inches of extra room. The atmosphere was becoming hostile when Mrs Harrington, a woman like a frigate bird, who was in the front-line position, stood to spontaneous and courageous attention and began to sing flatly: 'There'll Always Be An England.'

She bleated through the first bars before anyone on either side recognized the song, and then other voices joined in, the West Indians as well, all chorusing the words about country lanes and turning wheels and a million marching feet. The black voices were not only of better quality than the whites but they were louder and expressed the patriotic words with infinitely more feeling. As they bawled at each other, 'Red, White and Blue, what does it mean to you?' the little Minnings children appeared, charmingly bearing trays of small glasses filled with green liquid. 'My God, they've found the crème de menthe,' shouted someone, and hands, black and white, came from all sides to grab the glasses, some to be sipped, but some, in that charged and alcoholic atmosphere, to be brazenly swallowed at a gulp.

Screams and cries and bubbles followed immediately. People staggered for the kitchen, the bathroom and the toilet, or made for the open air, while clouds of bubbles great and small bounced and danced and squirted about the room. 'Don't drink it!' screamed Susie. 'The little bastards! It's Fairy Liquid!'

The washing-up solution had people everywhere clutching their throats and holding their stomachs. The rainbow bubbles, from both sides of the room, burst and flew. In the middle of it all Doug and Susie Minnings clutched each other with helpless laughter, and their children danced with the excitement of life.

In her bedroom, with the light of the street-lamp eyeing her over the drawn curtains, Tania Turvey stared through the dimness towards the loudspeaker they had fixed on her wall as part of the listening network. She was hearing strange voices, screams and ribald laughter coming from that direction. It was difficult for her to understand but she was not afraid, for she was a composed and intelligent five year old.

Brain had left his post at the switchboard to go for his supper and drunken hands were trying the switches at random. Eventually Tania sat up in her small bed and said loudly: 'Hello Wall, what in God's name do you want now?'

CHAPTER SEVEN

Dormouse Dan hung over the bow of the bar in The Case Is Altered. It was Sunday morning and he had been the first customer. His half pint of cider now lay dead and flat in its glass and he was snoring mildly.

'They're going to put a preservation order on that bit of wall, you know,' Barney Rogers said, leaning towards Gomer John from his side of the counter. 'It's very fragile, very fragile indeed. After five hundred years it's got a right to be, of course. What it wants is a sort of iron grille around it. Stop people leaning against it.'

'It's a lovely bit of wall, Barney,' agreed Gomer, after letting his lips barely brush the surface of the beer in his half-pint mug. For a young man he was a notoriously slow drinker. Barney eyed the token sip with disdain and looked towards the door for the vanguard of the Sunday morning people from the newer houses. If he needed to live on the likes of Gomer he would starve. Still he had not long opened the doors and let the Sunday sunshine fly in on the plastic sawdust, and there was no one else to talk to unless he woke Dormouse Dan, and he had only just dozed off.

'S'pose you've heard about the Flasher?' said Barney.

'Oh yes, at the sub-post office we hear about most things, you know. That's the sort of brain centre around here. Seems a funny occupation to me, running around displaying your private parts to the opposite sex. In the Pacific, of course, in the Fogufu Islands in Melanesia, they have a sort of Flasher's Festival – I suppose you could call it – where the young men, at a certain day in the year, or night time I expect, rush around the various villages showing themselves off in the most indecent way to the women.'

''ave you been there then?' asked Barney suspiciously.

'No, no, I haven't,' admitted the pale sub-postmaster guardedly. 'But I make a study of it.'

'What? Flashing?'

'No, for goodness sake, Barney. The Pacific. The islands and the customs of the people, navigation and all that.'

'Of course he does,' said Andrew, walking in from the sunshine. Geoffrey followed him and made a drinking sign to Barney for their usual pints. Barney looked grateful for their arrival. Andrew put his hand on Gomer's thin Welsh shoulder. 'Round the world in eighty threepenny stamps, isn't it, Gomer?'

'It's only a hobby,' mumbled Gomer. 'It's a private hobby, that's all.'

'Sorry, Gomer,' said Andrew genuinely, seeing he was hurt. 'I wasn't making fun. Here, let Geoffrey buy you a drink.'

'Thank you,' said Gomer, quickly taking the first definite bite out of his beer. 'I'll have a pint, please.' He looked with slight embarrassment at the half-pint mug he had put down. 'I always have a half when I first come in,' he said uncomfortably. 'I like to start off a bit gradual, see.'

Others, nearly all male, came in from the heat of the Plummers Park forenoon until the bar was filled, and there were people sitting all around the terrace. It was the expression of Sunday ordinariness so beloved of the middle-class Englishman, when in his carefully casual clothes he drinks beer with others of his tribe and they can talk as men.

'How it is that all the au pair girls in this area look like the bum of a buffalo? I'll tell you why. Because the women around here pick them to look like that. Anything decent and she's pushed off very smartish. The one we've got has hair on her arms . . .'

'. . . I don't see why we should pay our rates to subsidize those layabouts over the railway. Everybody's got a car over there, council houses or not. The money that's going in some of those houses. Someone saw a damned horse being brought through somebody's front door the other day . . .'

'. . . That new six-cylinder job is just beautiful . . .'

'. . . So this Irishman takes the nun's panties down with a spanner . . .'

'. . . We found if you just went up the coast a bit you hardly found any English people, Majorca or not . . .'

'. . . The one with the big knockers in our Costing Department . . .'

'. . . The Government should stamp on them right away . . .'

'. . . All right, why don't we organize a race for naked au pair girls? A tenner for the winner. Run it at midnight along Hedgerows . . .'

'. . . Nuns don't have panties. Whatever they have it's not panties.'

The men moved very little as they talked, but they performed a very slow revolving dance, a suburban saraband, so that the one whose turn it was to next buy the drinks in that group found himself at the right moment adjacent to the bar. Women came in occasionally from the terrace to have their own glasses replenished or buy crisps for the children. They were greeted and kissed by their husband's friends and then ushered out again so that the conversation could continue. Andrew was listening to the joke about the Irishman and the nun when he saw Bessie White sitting like an apparition on the oak settle near the door. She was regarding him with the same pale, engrossed expression as when she had looked at him in the magistrate's court.

He looked away at once, telling himself that he had not seen her, then admitting that he had, but reasoning that whatever she was doing there it was nothing to him. He returned to listening to the joke. '. . . so the nun said, "I'll recommend you to the Mother Superior" . . .' and looked back at the girl again, as though he were reasonably confident that she would not have vanished. A fat man was blocking his view. He leaned marginally backwards to look round the man's rump. She was still there. Regarding him.

Well, there was nothing to prevent her coming into the place, was there? Maybe she had just taken a walk under the station tunnel because it was a nice day. She could drink there if she liked. They usually kept to their own pub over there, but she could come over and have a drink. There was no law against that. It was just that she wasn't drinking. Just looking at him. He felt he was sweating more than the others.

The girl had not moved. He began to suspect that she was there only as a prelude to something else, and he was right. A big, ham-faced man sauntered into the bar, his frame almost filling the doorway. He wore a dark blue suit with white open collar, with his muscled neck projecting from it like the trunk of a banyan tree. It was easy to see he was from the other side of the railway.

'Ah, you're 'ere,' he said loudly to the girl. 'You might 'ave bleedin' waited for me.' Conversation crumpled all around. Everyone looked towards him but he remained cockily unaware of it. 'Is the geezer 'ere?'

'Yes,' said Bessie. Andrew saw her rise beyond the fat man. 'He's over there.'

'Mind your backs, gents,' advised the man as he worked his way through the drinkers. The weekend executives turned and stared at his wide-suited shoulders as he went past. The men in Andrew's group were at the most distant extremity of the bar and they sensed the intruder was making for them. Geoffrey's pint was fixed halfway to his mouth, Gerry Scattergood, who had been telling the joke, was frozen at the last line, Gorgeous George had just joined them from the golf course, and sitting at the little table across the sacred old wall were Harry and Jean Solkiss holding ritual hands across their two half-pints of cider. Barney was leaning over his bar with that incredulous reactionary glare of his kind witnessing the arrival of a four-ale bar type in the lounge of his pub.

The man got to Andrew's group. 'Who's Mr Maiby?' he said to Geoffrey.

'It's him,' swallowed Geoffrey, nudging his beer gratefully towards the paled Andrew. All eyes now turned to Andrew.

'Ah,' said the man, on the half-turn. 'It's you.'

'It's me,' admitted Andrew.

The visitor glanced about him with working-class haughtiness. 'I've got a bit of business with you,' he said. His voice had dropped but was so hard and grating that it was heard easily throughout the now almost silent bar. 'But not in 'ere. Would you care to step outside?'

It said much of Andrew's friends and neighbours that they fell back to a man, making an avenue through which he walked with the man behind him. The man had said, 'After you,' and waved a great horny paw. Andrew walked like someone riddled with guilt at the moment of arrest.

The tracking eyes went to Bessie, who from her prim seat had risen and now followed the two men out to the terrace. Once they had gone the voices and the eyebrows went up.

On the warm terrace the trio emerging from the door provoked less attention. The wives and children were out there, a concoction of gossip and gin, cries and crisps, sitting at the iron tables beneath the Skol umbrellas and on the imitation rustic benches. Andrew looked behind him, uncertain which way to turn, as though the other man were pushing him forward on the end of a shotgun.

'This'll do,' said the man. They stopped under the board which said 'Gentlemen'. Bessie walked to them, and the three faced inwards towards each other.

'I'm Bessie's dad,' said the man.

'Bert,' added Bessie glancing at her father as though he had forgotten his lines. 'Bert White.'

'Hello, Bert,' said Andrew uncomfortably. 'What's the trouble?'

'There's no trouble, mate,' said Bert. He appeared appalled at the suggestion. 'I just wanted to give you this.' He pushed out a hand clenched downwards in the manner of a schoolboy giving a toad to a nervous girl. Andrew automatically, but tentatively, put out his hand and found two ten-pound notes pressed into it.

'Twenty quid,' said Bert. Bessie nodded her fair hair as though encouraging Andrew to take it.

Andrew stared at the notes. 'What's this for?' he said.

Bert's matey, iron hand touched his shoulder. 'For keeping the old boy's name out of the papers,' he answered. 'It's to sort of pay you off. I found out about the court an' all. There's not much they can keep from me in our 'ouse. Anyway, there it is.' He glanced up truculently. 'Is that enough?'

'Yes, yes,' Andrew assured him. 'But I don't want this. I didn't even . . .'

'Yes you do,' insisted Bert as though he recognized a direct lie when he heard it. 'Everybody wants money. If it ain't enough, say so, mate, and I'll put another fiver to it.'

'No,' argued Andrew feebly. 'It's not that. You see I didn't . . .'

'Tell it to Bessie,' said Bert shortly. 'She's got to buy you a drink out of her own money. I've told her that, Mr Maiby, and she's got to do it.' He glanced at the pub and the garland of faces at the door. 'I can't come in,' he said with no regret. 'I got a darts match at our boozer and I got to get to that.' He turned, slapped his hand powerfully on Andrew's shoulder, smiled a jagged smile and then, with a curiously sweet ''Bye, 'bye', crunched about and strode away.

Andrew glared at the composed and smiling Bessie. 'What the hell was all that about?' he insisted.

'Christ, Andrew,' she giggled. 'You ought to have seen your face. He's a big bloke, isn't he?'

Andrew looked down at the twenty pounds held in his hands like some ill omen passed to him. He thrust them towards Bessie. 'You take this back,' he said. 'I don't want it.'

She half glanced to the right of his shoulder. 'All your friends are looking,' she said. 'I wouldn't make any more bother if I was you.'

Andrew looked too. The faces, Geoffrey, Gerry and the others, were grinning now. Ill-temperedly he thrust the notes into his pocket. 'How do you think that damned-well looked?' he said to Bessie. 'You being there and that big, hulking so-and-so dragging me out of the pub? I've got to live around here you know. They'll be thinking all sorts of things.'

'And your wife will find out,' she said smugly.

'Find out? It wouldn't surprise me to see her belting around that corner any minute. And none of this is my doing. I didn't keep your grandad's name out of the bloody paper. I didn't even notice the story wasn't in.'

'Well, it wasn't,' said Bessie simply. 'And it wasn't in the other one either.'

'It was nothing to do with me,' said Andrew angrily. 'So get that straight for a start.'

'You're getting all upset,' soothed Bessie. 'Let's go in and I'll buy you that drink.'

'You keep out of there,' growled Andrew. 'That's my pub, that is. I have to drink in there.'

'In that case I reckon you *ought* to take me in. At least you can tell them the truth, or something anyway. Just so's it don't look like you've got me pregnant or something and my old man came up to sort it out. I mean, it did look a bit funny.'

Andrew groaned and wiped his damp forehead. She was still smiling. 'Listen,' – he leaned towards her nastily – 'they *saw*. They *saw* your old man give me money. I'll show them. Nobody, not even your lot, goes around giving money to men who have seduced their daughters.'

'Our lot? What's that mean, our lot?'

He was immediately embarrassed. 'Well, your family.'

'You didn't mean that,' she said. 'You meant "our lot" from the other side of the railway, didn't you?'

'I didn't mean that at all. But, I ask you, what a way . . .'

'I'll come in and buy you that drink,' she said briskly. 'Or you can go and buy it and I'll stand out here if you think I'll spread some sort of disease in your rotten pub. But I'm going to buy it for you because my old man told me to. Otherwise he'll belt me.'

'He'll belt you?'

'That's right. They still hit the kids over there, see.'

Andrew sighed. 'All right. Come on in and we'll have a drink.' He looked at the notes again. 'I can't take this, though. I mean, I didn't . . .'

'Put it in the poor-box then,' suggested the girl. 'If you've got one on this side.'

'Come on,' he said glaring at her.

'All right,' she replied blithely now. 'I'll behave. I won't let you down, Andrew. Honest.'

They took two paces towards the door. All the heads were immediately pulled in. Bessie was slightly behind him. He stopped and turned. 'I thought you guaranteed that your father would never know about the old man being in court. That didn't last long, did it?'

'Sometimes things go wrong,' she shrugged. 'Even with me. You know I told you that I'd given the medals back to the other bloke. Well, I didn't actually do it myself. I told grandad to do it. I thought he had, but the thieving old bugger kept them. Nicked them. The other bloke came around the house to get them back and all the story came out. My dad went mad.'

'A regular old magpie your grandfather, isn't he?' said Andrew bitterly. 'Cocktail sticks, wasn't it? And live eels . . .'

'*A* live eel,' she corrected. 'There was only one. Don't make it worse than it is.'

'All right, *one* live eel. Now some poor old soldier's medals. He certainly collects things.'

'He's not going to be collecting his pension for a few weeks,' said Bessie. 'Not all of it, anyway.'

'This twenty pounds is coming out of his pension, is it?'

'Too bloody right it is. Two quid a week. He's lucky my dad let him off so lightly. Even then he cried, the old sod. He's always crying. But he won't get out of it. The only way he's going to get out of paying is to croak.'

'Give it back to him,' said Andrew, feeling for the notes which he had put in his pocket.

'You're joking,' she said, genuinely shocked. 'It'd be more than my life's worth. Do what you like with it, but don't expect me to take it.'

Andrew thrust it away. 'You people,' he sighed in his annoyed way.

'Us people,' she said, looking at him.

'I'm sorry,' he said. 'Let's go and have that drink. My reputation is already smashed beyond hope; standing here talking to you won't make any difference, I suppose. Bruiser enters pub, accosts respectable man. Young girl weeps in the background. It's a melodrama.'

She laughed in her bright way. 'You ought to write that in your paper,' she said.

'And that's another thing. *I* didn't keep that out. And I certainly didn't stop it getting in the opposition either. I don't know how it happened.'

'Go on,' she teased. 'I thought you'd been around giving a bit of comfort to that fat bird on the other paper.'

'Well I haven't,' he said. 'And I wouldn't. Even I have my standards, you know.'

'Oh, you admit that you do 'ave a look around then. I thought you were all married and that.'

'I *am* all married and that,' replied Andrew. 'And I need a drink. This is all getting too much for me.'

They walked into the lounge bar, and through the dimness and the contrast from the sun outside they could see the smiles standing out on indistinct faces. 'Cheshire cats,' muttered Andrew, as they went through the smirking men. His own group had retreated to the distant end of the bar and were waiting for them. Andrew purposely stopped short and turned the girl towards Barney's bar. 'What would you like, miss?' he asked with his back to his friends.

'No,' insisted Bessie. 'I got to buy you one.' She did it purposely, he knew, in her squeakiest Cockney. Andrew grimaced. 'Just a pint of bitter, please,' he said carefully.

'You don't want no egg-flip nor nuffink?' she inquired.

'A pint, please.'

'Pinta bi'er, please, mate,' smiled Bessie at Barney. 'An' drop o' port an' lemon for me.'

Andrew leaned close to her. 'Will you please, *please*, pack up this Eliza-sodding-Doolittle stuff,' he grated. 'What are you trying to do to me? And *I'll* pay for the drinks. You can pay me back outside if you feel you must.' Even as he admonished her he was aware of her sweet, fresh, open smell that belied the slum accent. Barney, with a knowing smile, handed the drinks over the bar. Andrew was about to pay for them with one of the ten-pound notes when he realized what it was. Unthinking, he pushed them towards the girl and said: 'You'd better have these.' He felt the landlord's eyes glow, turned, swallowed in anger and confusion, and thrust the notes back into his own pocket.

The drinks in his hands, he turned her towards the watching smirks of his own friends. 'This is er . . . a young friend of mine, Miss White,' he began.

'Bessie White,' she completed with a wide, bright smile.

'Bessie,' Andrew continued, 'this is Geoff and Gerry and George. And those two over there are the nice people around here, Harry and Jean Solkiss. They're Americans.'

Everyone nodded at the fair girl, and Harry and Jean, looping their held hands over the table, stood and joined the group. No one seemed to know what to say to her but she did not appear at all uncomfortable. She stirred her foot among the sawdust on the floor.

'What's this stuff for?' she asked.

'Well, it's to sort of give the place a traditional air,' said Andrew. 'I suppose.'

'What? Sticking sawdust on the floor!' she said. 'That's a joke.'

She gave the sawdust a stout kick sending a little spray of it over Gorgeous George's suede boots. He backed off, but continued to stare at her as though she were from some outer world. 'In our pub,' she continued, 'they've got those nice modern lino-tiles. It's easy to mop the beer up afterwards, I s'pose. It's a very good pub, really. Juke-box and a couple of fruit-machines and there's usually a singsong or a bit of a knees-up. Do you have singsongs here?'

'Not generally,' said Geoffrey. He was regarding her with quiet disbelief. 'Nor knees-ups. I've tried it once or twice but nobody will join in.'

'Oh, in our pub the trouble is stopping them when it's chucking out time,' smiled Bessie. 'They're a boozy lot.'

'Where is this pub of yours, love?' asked Gerry. He was firm and more confident than the others as if, through his varied trading journeys, he had come to know her type and learned her native tongue.

'Bull and Bush,' she answered. 'Cross the line.'

'The line?' It was George leaning forward now. They were like missionaries questioning a little captured savage.

'The railway,' explained Andrew. 'Over the railway.'

'I live over there, Attlee Park,' said Bessie, pointing over Barney's head.

'Ah,' they said, looking at her even more closely. 'Ah, do you now,' Geoffrey continued for them all. 'Whereabouts?'

'Morrison Way,' she replied. 'Know it?'

'No,' Geoffrey disclaimed hurriedly. 'No, I don't actually.' The others all shook their heads. Harry and Jean had failed to detect any difference in the girl's accent or demeanour from that of any other English person they had met. To them the exchange seemed to be some sort of stark and absorbing ritualistic play.

'It's the street that goes up from the cake-shop,' said Bessie as though that would fix it, and it apparently did for they all nodded.

'How do you know our Andrew?' asked Geoffrey lightly. The two men each sent a fraction of a glance towards the other.

Bessie put her hand on Andrew's sleeve and recited in the manner of a line from a film: 'It's a long story. You tell them, Andrew.' Andrew sensed his mouth and throat contract. He felt sure that Audrey was going to stalk into the bar at any second. He changed hands with his glass so that her fingers slipped away from his arm.

'Well,' he said. 'It was a bit complicated, really . . .'

'Take your time,' advised Geoffrey enjoying it, watching him profoundly.

'I will, I will,' muttered Andrew. 'It was Miss White's . . . Bessie's grandfather, you see. He was in a little trouble . . .'

'With the narks,' added Bessie.

'Er . . . yes. Well, he was unfortunate. You see he was in court and I was there for the paper. Yes, he was in court . . .' He tailed off lamely.

'Heroin pushing,' nodded Bessie.

The others fell visibly away before Andrew laughed in a strange abandoned way and said: 'No, No. Nothing like that.' He grimaced at Bessie. 'You and your inimitable humour,' he said. He returned to the others. 'No, the old chap was in court. No fault of his own really, just bad luck in fact. One of these technical offences . . .'

'Well, what?' asked Gerry after some moments of vacuum.

'No lights on his bike,' said Andrew desperately.

'And aiding and abetting prostitution,' added Bessie.

'No!' Andrew howled it so loud that all the pub's customers turned to look. He stifled his voice. 'No. She's only fooling. No lights on his bike and . . . er . . . yes, um stealing by finding. Yes, that was it. He found the bike at the side of the road and thought somebody had abandoned it so he rode it home.'

'So it wasn't *his* bike?' pursued Gerry.

'No.'

'But they charged him with having no lights on it?'

'Oh, for God's sake! Listen, I was there. I can't remember it all. Anyway he was fined twenty pounds, but he didn't have the money so my paper, the editor, decided to pay the fine for him. It was a touching sort of story, as you can see.'

The group nodded sagely. 'Very touching,' said George.

'And that's about it. Bessie's father got to hear what had happened and he's brought the money back to be repaid to the paper. He's a proud man, her father.' He took a triumphant drink of his pint and regarded them challengingly.

'He's a big bloke too,' said Geoffrey.

'Very touching I must say,' added Gerry Scattergood.

'I said it was,' replied Andrew.

'You English,' sighed Jean Solkiss. 'You're so . . . so . . . noble in such little ways. Aren't they just, Hairy.'

'They surely are,' agreed Harry. 'I guess *noble* is the right word.'

'It's the big things we're not noble about,' said Andrew. He was relieved now the explanation was over. It sounded so convincing that he would hardly have minded if Audrey had put in an appearance.

'Pity your old man couldn't 'ang around for a drink,' said Gerry, slipping easily into the patois. 'He looks an interesting bloke.'

'He does demolitions,' said Bessie. 'Knocks down buildings and that.'

'He looks as though he could do it with his fist,' nodded Geoffrey giving Andrew another glance. 'I wouldn't like to get in a rough-house with him.'

'He can be ever so nasty,' agreed the girl. 'Once he knocked my Uncle Tom right through our reeded-glass kitchen door. Not a scratch on him, he went through so fast. He had to go off today because he had a darts match. Anyway he wouldn't drink in here. He said this wasn't no pub, it was a pansies' parlour.'

This information had such a stunning effect on the group that nobody said anything for more than a minute. Bessie seemed serenely ignorant of the chasm she had cut. She smiled privately into her drink. Eventually George rumbled: 'We don't think it's too bad. Bit of atmosphere here, anyway. Do you like the fox's head over the bar? That was actually caught on this estate.'

Bessie lifted her small nose and smiled at the fixed grin of the fox. 'Hello, Bruin,' she said. Andrew closed his eyes quietly.

'That wall,' continued George portentously, pointing at the relic, 'is said to date from the Middle Ages. It's part of the old inn that stood here then. Mind how you touch, it's very fragile.'

The girl had leaned forward to put her fingers on the wall and as she did so Andrew saw how slim and finely arched her body was, the backside tight in red trousers, twin small bumps, and the hooped front of her summer blouse sagging as she leaned so that for a moment he could see the first gentle white risings of her breasts. Bessie dug her fingers into the powdery stonework. George's eyebrows rose apprehensively. But she withdrew before he could say anything.

'When we lived in Kilburn,' she sniffed, 'before we moved out here, all the bloody walls of our house had damp like that. You could stick your finger through into next-door, just about. They used to say it was only the wallpaper keeping them up. Nobody wanted to show *them* off, I can tell you.'

She smiled around at the group, a pure, lovely smile, as though she were some princess talking to a group of commoners. 'I've got to be on my way,' she said. 'Blimey, my mum goes beserk if we're not there on the dot for Sunday dinner. Thanks kindly for the drink.'

'I must go too,' said Andrew. That quick movement from Geoffrey's eyes again. 'I'll walk you down to the . . . tunnel.'

'Right you are,' she laughed. 'I know my way from there. I'm in my own country, like.' She blew a quick series of kisses all around and made for the door with the reddened Andrew following. As they went he sensed the eyes and the curving mouths all around. The conversation dropped like a breeze at sea. He was relieved that at least the terrace was less occupied now.

He and the girl walked silently in the widespread sun. She was on the outside but he let it stay like that. 'Funny how different it is over here,' she said. 'Especially when it's really only a few yards. One day I'd like to live somewhere a bit posh. I'd like to live somewhere where . . .' she paused thoughtfully, '. . . where people don't plant their old Christmas trees in their gardens and expect them to sprout.'

'A graphic ambition,' he said. For some reason he now felt calm and unworried. He did not want to say anything about the things she had said in the pub. It did not matter.

They reached the entrance to the tunnel. 'Do you want me to walk through with you?' he said.

'No, dafty,' she laughed. 'There's no need to fall over yourself for me. I've been coming through this tunnel ever since I was eight and nothing's ever happened to me yet, worse luck.'

'I'll walk through anyway,' he said. They started forward together, a few inches dividing them, and went into the cool gloom of the tiled arches. 'I honestly had nothing to do with stopping that story getting into the paper,' said Andrew, his voice booming strangely around them. Some council house boys were playing on small bicycles at the distant end, black against the vivid sunlight of the exit arch. Together they shouted 'Bollocks' and the word bounded and bounced the length of the tube. The boys cawed like crows and turned their cycles away. The girl did not seem to have noticed them or heard their shout.

'Pay the money into some kids' charity or something then,' she said. She was walking very straight, very upright, almost marching through the tunnel. At the far end they paused and she said openly: 'When it's a fine day I take my sandwiches into the churchyard in Watford and eat them there. Why don't you come there as well?'

He looked at her. She was turned towards him now, the fresh face upturned, the fair hair drifting a trifle in the small breeze that always lived in the tunnel. Christ, he thought, this is *it*. This is where you run as you ran from Mrs Bigbury when you were young. Now it's the ages reversed. Go on, *run*.

'All right,' he heard himself saying, his voice making a minute echo against the tiles. 'Perhaps I'll come on Tuesday.'

She nodded seriously. 'Right you are. See you then, Andrew. 'Bye.'

He watched her walk up the slipway and stood there until she gradually went from his view as though she had descended a ramp on the far side. On impulse he went to the top of the slipway and saw her talking to the two boys who had shouted 'Bollocks' from their bicycles. He could see all three were laughing. The council estate seemed barren to him even in the sunlight. Great sheets of Saturday night's newspapers were lying like corpses in the road. He retreated and made his way back to his own familiar territory.

'Christ, what have I done?' he whispered to himself as he went towards his flat-roofed house on the hill. A grin forced itself on to his face and stayed there.

CHAPTER EIGHT

The girl from Cowacre walked tightly along Upmeadow to Risingfield on her Monday morning way to the station. Mr Brewster, Mr Reynolds, Mr Burville, Mr George and Mr Henry Jones, Mr Shillingford and poor old Mr Henty followed at their appointed paces. Andrew stood on his spot and drank his coffee like a casual general reviewing a familiar parade. Gladstone circled his legs like a hairy pipe. 'Action-Dog,' said Andrew, 'I am watching my world go by.'

Herbie Futter smothered his wife with kisses before taking the daily risk of parting. Cynthia Turvey folded Tania's vest and shorts for the school sports. Simon Grant, eagerly opening a parcel from the postman, found the anniversary body-stocking for Ena had arrived a week early. His eyes shone. Gorgeous George was practising pitching and putting on his lawn but his thoughts were elsewhere. Ernest Rollett was beginning a week's holiday during which he intended to properly organize the protest against the school for maladjusted children. The youngest and grubbiest of the Minnings family had caught her head in the springs of the settee while trying to view the hamsters. An ambulance and the Watford fire brigade had arrived.

Joy Rowley was setting out to do a television commercial, taking her mother with her. They let her mother do ironing in the wardrobe department. Gomer John, trembling, opened an envelope in his sub-post office and saw the words: 'So You Have Applied To Join The Royal Navy'. Mrs Burville was pouring her first drink of the day and measuring herself against her wartime ATS uniform hidden in a cupboard. Big Brenda, her knitting-bag slung like a papoose over her shoulder, trundled to the magistrates court where she would press her weekly thigh against Andrew. Mr Brownlow, the oat-growing magistrate, was preparing for the same court with a bad conscience. Mrs Polly Blossom-Smith was telephoning the police station:

'Hello, hello. Ah, there you are. I thought I'd never get you. Mrs Polly Blossom-Smith here.'

'Oh, yes. Hello, Mrs Blossom-Smith. I'm sorry we didn't answer. We're very busy.'

'Lots of crime?'

'Crime? Oh no. It's just it's Monday. It's the start of the week.'

'A fantastic deduction, officer. Is the station sergeant or somebody of rank there?'

'He's ever so busy, Mrs Blossom-Smith. But I'll tell him. He'll come for you, I expect.'

'Tell him I've been raped and mutilated.'

'Yes. All right. I'll pass the message.'

She waited. 'Station Sergeant here,' said an eventual voice.

'Did your constable give you my message?' asked Mrs Blossom-Smith.

'Yes.'

'He told you I'd been raped and mutilated?'

'Yes. Do you wish to make a complaint?'

'Oh, sergeant, you are terribly funny.'

'Thank you. What was your call about, Mrs Blossom-Smith? We're up to our ears here. There's three lollipop men haven't turned up for work and the panda car has broken down.'

'It sounds like toytown,' said Mrs Blossom-Smith brightly. 'No, sergeant, I was merely ringing about the . . . this man who is dashing about exposing himself.'

'Ah! Have you seen him?'

'No. Not yet.'

'Oh, I see. You're just worried.'

'Anxious more than worried.'

'Yes, well living with all those woods around you I expect it's a nasty feeling. He's been seen twice this weekend. Once at the back of the golf course and on Sunday evening, late, down at the Sheep-Dip where he stopped a young girl, exposed himself, and then asked the way to the Catholic church. The girl, with great presence of mind I must say, gave him the required directions without even looking at the exposed part of his body. Fortunately she was a Catholic and knew the location of the church. It's in Watford so the directions were quite complicated.'

'It's a marvellous thing, religion,' sighed Mrs Blossom-Smith. 'So you think he might be around today?'

'We don't know. He appears mostly at night or at weekends, so he must have a job to go to.'

'He's just a part-time flasher, you mean?'

'Er, yes. It would seem so. If there's an outbreak of occurrences during the day we'll know he's on his annual holiday – and then we've got him! We check on every man in the district who's on holiday.'

'Ingenious, sergeant.'

'We're paid to be, Mrs Blossom-Smith. But don't worry. I don't suppose he'll bother you.'

'How kind you are.'

'Well, I like to be reassuring. But don't count on it. You'll know him if you see him. Medium height, raincoat, furtive look.'

'Any other distinguishing features?'

'Oh, well. Only the obvious one. He exposes himself.'

'Easily recognizable, what?'

'Oh, you'll know him if you see him. And don't worry. We're nearly always here, and when we've got the panda mended we'll come and have a snoop around Fairy Copse.'

'I'm sure the fairy cops will be pleased to see you. Goodbye, sergeant.'

'Goodbye, Mrs Blossom-Smith. *Who* will?'

But she had gone.

Monday was the day of destiny, decided the Reverend Malcolm Boon; the day when he would cross the tracks and attempt something which until then had eluded him and his predecessors in the parish of St James the Less, Plummers Park. He would go, from his vicarage safe among the council houses, and journey into the land of Flat-Roof Man, and there try, at least, to establish some contact for Christ.

The mission seemed to him to be fully accommodated within those terms. The people about him he knew and understood. The girls were always white brides in his church, he baptized their children (sometimes spectacularly soon after the wedding) giving them the names of Cheyenne, Darren, Scott, Desiree, Crystal, Melody, Ossie, or whatever was the fashion or the footballer of the moment. Generally they did not bring their dead to the church but took them straight to the cemetery chapel, for which he was grateful. Funerals were even untidier than weddings. The local teenagers had cheerfully excommunicated him. They inhabited the coffee and hamburger places of Watford, caring nothing for eternity. For them, he had reflected glumly, the world was less likely to end with a bang than with a Wimpy.

Some of the older people actually attended church on other occasions too, and the Sunday School was what he, a gentle man, liked to describe as robust. One volunteer teacher had a lawsuit outstanding against the parents of one of the pupils, and two others had left not only his church but Christianity in general because of what they suffered at the hands of little children who had come unto them.

But those people beyond the railway line were of another country. There was no church over there and not even a list of souls who would be glad to see one established. He prayed long and hard late on the Sunday night while his wife kept shushing him because she was watching an Edward G. Robinson film on television, and on Monday he set out on his mission.

He set out dressed, not inappropriately, in a khaki bush-jacket and camouflage green shorts, his clerical collar and bib poking coyly from the open shirt neck, with blue woollen socks and open-toed sandals. He abandoned the idea of taking a scout stave with him as being a trifle too theatrical. It was not very far.

Timidly he left his departure until the bulk of the morning march to the station, through the tunnel, would be finished. He was not one to meet the heathen head-on. By ten o'clock, however, they were all departed and, after a quick prayer in his own church for blessing on his project, he set out in the Monday sunshine.

He went through the tiled coolness of the tunnel and emerged into the emptiness of the Plummers Park estate. He knew only one person there by name, Mrs Polly Blossom-Smith with whom he had judged a children's art contest in Watford the previous year. She had not, it was true, struck him as a likely disciple but she was a kind if somewhat awry woman who might be able to give him names and addresses. In such a manner, he told himself comfortingly, did Christ begin his church. Contacts.

Sheep-Dip, the road that led from the station, was vacant except for an anguished man trying to re-inflate the flattened tyres of an elderly open sports car. He looked up at the vicar's approach, his face running with a confluence of tears and perspiration. He appeared to come to an immediate decision, as though the Reverend Boon had been sent especially.

'I wish *you'd* have a word with her,' he implored. 'Anything.'

'Who? What?'

'In there,' shuddered the man, pointing at the house.

'What about?'

'This. This sort of thing,' he sobbed, nodding at the car as though it were some injured human. 'Letting down the tyres, now. Or she throws things, muck, anything, at me, or she scratches the paintwork – look at that there – or pulls wires and things out. She'll ruin it one day.'

'I'm terribly sorry,' said the Reverend Boon inadequately. 'Terribly, terribly sorry.'

'You are a minister, aren't you?' inquired the man. 'I mean, you're not dressed up for something?'

'No. No. I'm a clergyman.'

'Go and see her then, will you? It might appeal to her better nature if she saw your collar. She's superstitious like that.'

'Well, er, no,' declined Mr Boon. 'I have to be getting along.' Disappointment crumpled the man's face. 'I'm visiting the sick,' lied the vicar desperately.

'Well, you could start right in there,' said the man, nodding again vigorously at the house.

'No, I must be off.' He nodded helplessly at the defunct tyres. 'I hope you get them up.'

He walked briskly off, the weight of guilt and defeat banging around in his stomach like the clapper of a cold ball. He decided to avoid the

climbing pavements of Risingfield and Upmeadow and to continue to
the boundary of the estate with the main road, where a screen of trees had
been left, a slim plantation that bulged eventually into the wider expanse
known as the Fairy Copse.

He liked it in there: the enclosed grass and the cosseted wild flowers,
the trees, slender as organ pipes, the sun flicking through the leaves, the
birds hidden and singing. He saw a squirrel and raised a hand to it. It
would have been nice, he thought, to have been St Francis or Robin
Hood, or someone else who inhabited a forest.

Mrs Polly Blossom-Smith, he knew, lived in the Victorian house called
'The Sanctuary' edging the copse. He felt a little shy at approaching her
property through the trees, but he intended to call from the fringe to see if
he could attract her attention. This was not necessary, however, for Mrs
Blossom-Smith leapt out upon him as he approached the edge of the
woodland with such enthusiastic ferocity that he was severely shaken.

'Mr Boon!' she exclaimed. 'Not you!'

'Yes, yes,' the vicar assured her. 'It's me.'

Her enthusiasm deflated quickly, he was sad to see, and she shook her
head. 'No, not you. I'm dreadfully sorry. I thought it was someone else.'

'Oh, you were expecting someone.'

'Well, more anticipating them, shall we say. Never mind. What a
lovely day again! Will you come and have some coffee?'

'Thank you. I would love that. I came over because I need your help.'

Polly led the way across the wild lawn. She was disappointed it was
only the vicar, but she hid it. She was wearing a large yellow outfit of
trousers and blouse, with a hat shaped like a grand buttercup shading
her face down to the end of her nose. She looked at the clergyman
sideways from its deeper shadow. 'How can I help, vicar?'

'Well, truthfully, you are the only person on this side of the railway line
that I know at all. Since all Plummers Park estate is officially my parish I
feel I ought to do something about . . . well . . .'

'Colonizing it,' suggested Polly sympathetically.

'Claiming it, I suppose,' nodded Mr Boon. 'I am neglecting my duty if
I do not. I need to know some people over here who would form the basis
of a church, who would serve on committees and say the occasional
prayer. Do you think that would be too much to ask?'

'I don't know,' sighed Polly sincerely. 'I'm afraid if you gave these
people the choice of the Kingdom of Heaven and a fortnight in Benidorm
they'd be down the bank getting their pesetas like a shot.'

'I was afraid it would be like that,' said the vicar gloomily. 'It's going
to be very difficult.'

He sat in the garden while she went for the coffee. He liked it there in
the hushed sunshine with the enclosing green and the flowers and the
squirrel he could still see floating in the trees. St Francis had certainly
been very fortunate. How would he have fared with Plummers Park?

It was very warm. He undid the back button of his clerical collar and
let it sag around his thin neck like a ring about a prize on a hoopla stall.
He would do it up later when he went into the streets again, for nothing

looked sloppier than a vicar with a drooping collar.

'Yes, vicar, it's a great task that faces you,' boomed Polly cheerfully as she returned with the coffee. 'I'm afraid there aren't many paid-up Christians around here. Still, when Jesus started I suppose he felt very much the same.'

The Reverend Boon pondered this for a moment. He sipped his coffee tentatively. 'How do you feel about it, Mrs Blossom-Smith?' he asked. 'You would be the sort of pilllar of strength the church would need over here.'

She smiled extravagantly from beneath the huge buttercup hat. 'I'm very touched that you should ask,' she assured him. 'But I have to confess to being an agnostic, I suppose.'

'How do you mean – "I suppose"?' he inquired with hope.

'Well,' she hesitated. 'I'm not really a *practising* agnostic. I think, quite honestly, that the best thing I can do is to give you the names of a few people who might be of some help to you.'

'It's as though we were trying to start up some entirely new religion, isn't it?' said Mr Boon sadly. 'Not something that's been going on for two thousand years. It's my fault, I suppose. But I've never been able to think of a way to make contact with the people over here. It's not as though they die or get married. They're married when they get here and they're not ready for death yet. The generations haven't had time to move up. Are there many babies, Mrs Blossom-Smith?'

'Oh yes, quite a few latish ones I think,' she said. 'But most of the wives are reaching their thirties, so they're past the first rush on babies. And when they get here they're all for having a dishwasher and going out to nice places to dinner, so the late addition frequently never arrives in Plummers Park. It's a bit like the London evening papers.'

'What is?'

'You know, how they come in by train and sometimes they never arrive at all. Late editions or late additions, it's all the same.'

He looked at her a little glassily over the small curve of his coffee cup. 'Yes, yes, I see,' he wobbled.

'The first wave of Plummers Park kids is not quite old enough to start begetting yet, although by the look and demeanour of some of them it won't be too long. Whether the trade will come your way, I don't know. They seem to like to get away from here for such things as christenings and weddings. They go back to the places they came from originally. I don't know why. I suppose they think things are more *established* there.'

'Like the Church of England,' sighed Mr Boon.

'Everything,' said Polly consolingly. 'This is such an unreal sort of place. It's manufactured and it's slow to grow. It's just been dumped here in the middle of all these fields and chewing cows. People come here for big sitting-rooms and bright kitchens and something called Blo-hole heating. But it'll take years to puff the breath of life into this baby, vicar. And the people don't expect it. They know it's prefabricated. That's why they go elsewhere for their traditions.'

'What about the people on my ... the other side?' he asked. 'They have the breath of life. They've been dumped here, as you put it, too.'

'Ah, those are evacuated cockneys,' she said. 'They're different. They'll always *live* as long as there's enough of them to keep each other warm. They live on each other just as they always did when they were in London. They know, by instinct, how to keep the fire burning. Their doors are always open, neighbours in and out, fights and all-pals-together. All that sort of thing. The people over here don't barge into each other's houses to borrow a squeeze of the bluebag or half a pound of margarine. Even if they live next door they talk on the telephone. They're a new breed, you see, and even *they're* not sure what they're like.'

'My goodness, you seem to know them very well,' said the vicar, professional admiration lighting his sombre face.

'Oh, I've had a good look at them,' she laughed. 'They all think I'm potty, of course. I've got a funny name and I live in this draughty old house and I do clay modelling and sculpting and that sort of suspicious activity.' She looked at him uncertainly. 'Actually, vicar, I've made a special study of Flat-Roof Man, as I call him, and I'm modelling him at this moment. Would you like to see him?'

'Yes, I really would,' said the Reverend Boon sincerely. 'It might help me to recognize him, as it were. I'd also be very grateful for those names and addresses, Mrs Blossom-Smith.'

'Of course. Let me tell you now. I don't know these people's religious convictions, you understand. It's not something that's very widely discussed here. If you asked me their feelings about the rates or the preference in motor-cars I might be able to help. But they're the *sort* of people who could be useful, if you know what I mean.'

'I understand very well,' said the Reverend Boon. He produced a pencil, which he wet with a businesslike flick across his tongue.

She watched the small action with amused curiosity; he looked up and saw her expression and realized immediately why she smiled. 'Wetting the pencil,' he acknowledged with a sigh. 'Yes, that must come from working on the other side. Over here, I suppose, only meter readers and plumbers do that sort of thing. It sort of gives me away, do you think?'

'Over here,' said Polly kindly, 'the felt pen is the thing right now. Licking the end of the pencil might *just* put them off a shade.'

'It would betray me,' he agreed sadly. He smiled at her: 'This is something like training as an agent to drop into Occupied France during the war. It's exciting in that way too, I suppose.'

'If you knew all about the latest Alfa Romeo or you could claim to have met one of the Beatles it might help to gain sympathy, to identify with them,' she said helpfully.

'The Beatles? But surely, aren't they old hat now? The teenagers over the other side laugh when you mention the Beatles. I've tried it.'

She nodded. 'Exactly. That's the difference. Over here they're busy beatifying them. They are spoken of in the very same breath as Mozart.'

'Ah,' he said. 'Now we may be on to something. In a modest way I'm considered to be something of an expert on chamber music. I even wrote a small tract on Vivaldi. Would that be a let-in, or wouldn't it?'

'Vivaldi might be taken for the ice-cream man. Stick to Mozart,' she advised. 'And then only in relation to the Beatles.'

'I see. I shall have to tread warily, won't I?'

'You may be all right,' she said, regarding him carefully. Then she added: 'As a sort of curiosity.'

He looked down the front of himself from the witless grin of his sagging clerical collar through his crumpled khaki bushshirt and olive-green shorts to the woollen socks and sandals projecting from the ends of his white straight legs. 'A curiosity?' he said.

'Yes, and a good thing it would be for you. The people here, well, they like to grasp on to *something*. They're all seeking something because they're so new to it all. It sounds very patronizing I know, vicar, and I don't mean to be, but that would be your major chance. They might *take* to you because you are part of something *old*, something *established*. There's a piece of wall in the pub which is said to be medieval, although I have my doubts. Believe me, St Albans Cathedral is not more sacred. *That* could be your way in.'

'Could I have the names, please?' asked the clergyman.

'Oh, now I've upset you,' said Polly, truly concerned. She reached out and patted him on his bib. 'I didn't mean to. I'm so sorry.'

'No, not at all, Mrs Blossom-Smith,' he replied. 'It's just that the whole operation looks more complicated than even I had believed.' He paused and spread his pale hands. 'As you say, they're a new breed of people. They're not like my people over the line, they're not like settled suburbanites, they're not like people who live in old places like St Albans. They're something completely new and different. I suppose I should pray about it.' He glanced at her. 'Later, of course.'

'Let me tell you the names,' she said hurriedly as though he might fall on his knees immediately. 'First there's a man called Ernest Rollett. His name suits him. He undoubtedly is a rather earnest man. Always canvassing for this or protesting about that. I can't vouch for his Christianity, but I feel sure if you offered him some sort of official position, as church secretary on this side or something of that nature, he might well be your chap.'

Wetting his pencil again, looking up guiltily, and then pressing the lead with unseemly hardness into his notebook, the Reverend Boon took note of the name.

'Simon Grant,' added Polly. 'He's another. Always talking very seriously at parties and what-have-you about local issues. Very opinionated, but he's young and he has an attractive wife. She would get the children to Sunday School, especially the lads. He lives just down the road from Mr Rollett at Risingfield, although you'll have to ask because I don't know the exact numbers. Then there's Gomer John at the sub-post office. He's a bit wet, I always think, but he's Welsh and they're often religious, aren't they?'

The vicar wrote industriously. 'Yes, I've seen the chap in the sub-post office. He asked me once about how one became a missionary in Polynesia, but I didn't know. He's certainly a possible. Anyone else?'

Polly hesitated. 'Well, there is,' she said. 'It's a long shot though. His name is Andrew Maiby. He's a reporter on the newspaper in Watford and he lives at Upmeadow. I don't know why I'm suggesting him. It's just he seems to be a thoughtful person, and I think he's kind. I believe he would like to be a good man. He's certainly looking for somewhere to go.'

'You mean he's moving from here?'

Polly nearly said: 'No, stupid fool!' Instead she said: 'No, I mean spiritually. He's a bit lost, I think.'

'I will make you fishers of men,' quoted Mr Boon writing down Andrew's name.

When he had finished his jotting, Polly said: 'Would you really like to see my sculpture? It might give you some notion of recognizing your quarry, so to speak.'

'Yes, yes, I would love that. That's very kind.'

'It's upstairs,' she said, leading the way. 'In my bedroom, I'm afraid. Still, I suppose you are used to going into strange bedrooms.' Decently she added: 'Visiting the sick and suchlike.'

'Oh yes, indeed,' agreed the Reverend Boon, trying to remember the last time anyone asked him into a bedroom. He hurried after her, sniffing familiarly at the churchy dust hanging in the gloomed air of the house. She banged up the stairs ahead of him shouting, 'I sometimes work from bed, you see. Whenever I get inspiration.'

'Oh yes,' he called after her. 'I do the same.'

She stopped and turned around: 'You work from bed?'

'Oh no! When I get the inspiration.'

'Ooooops! Sorry. Right, here we are.'

The curtains were open wide and the first thing the vicar saw was the spread and sunlit view of almost the whole of the Plummers Park landscape. He went to the window and looked on it. 'And the devil took him up into a high mountain and showed to him all the Kingdoms of the Earth,' he mused aloud.

'Thank you, vicar.'

'Oh dear, my dear Mrs Blossom-Smith. We seem to get at cross purposes all the time! I was merely quoting. I didn't mean that you were the . . . er . . . devil.'

But he saw she was laughing. 'I'm afraid the view isn't all the Kingdoms of the Earth either,' she said. 'Just Plummers Park estate.' She sighed and fitting her big hands into her substantial hips she viewed it with him. 'It's like a tented city, isn't it?' she observed. 'Wake up tomorrow and they might have all crept away in the night.'

'That would solve the problem for me,' said Mr Boon wistfully. 'Now please let me see your sculpture.'

She was standing beside her untidy bed and with a little flourish, one of the few *small* movements of which she was capable, she flicked away a drape from her model. 'Presenting Flat-Roof Man,' she announced.

The vicar was both impressed and nonplussed by what he saw. The work was strong and individual. 'Very fine,' he nodded. 'Really very fine. You are most talented, Mrs Blossom-Smith.'

She swallowed the compliment easily. 'I'm not bad, I suppose,' she beamed. 'The different parts of the anatomy were taken from different models. All residents here on this estate.'

'Real men?' he exclaimed. 'And they came up here and . . . and . . . sat for you?'

'Loved it,' she confided. 'It's curiosity value, you see. This is what I meant. The face and the head are from a chap who lives at Upmeadow, and the trunk and the arms and legs are spread out all over the place. It's like a dismemberment in reverse.'

'Indeed, indeed,' said the vicar sagely.

'You notice that he is incomplete, vicar.'

The Reverend Boon found himself backing away from her.

'Yes,' he said, 'I had observed that.'

She gave a fat giggle. 'Don't worry, I'm not asking for volunteers. I have someone in mind. The difficulty is – capturing him.'

'Of course,' agreed the vicar as though he understood fully. 'Flat-Roof Man would look very odd left like that.'

'I suppose I could exhibit him as he is and suggest that Flat-Roof Man is sexless,' she said. 'But it would not be true. There's even an individual form of sexuality about here. It's not the Saturday-night grunt and groan of your other parishioners, vicar. Nor is it the prim jiggery-pokery of ordinary suburbia. Here, vicar, it looks so . . . so bland, look out of the window and see.'

He turned and they both walked to the window. 'Bland,' she repeated. 'But it seethes with unsatisfied demands and emotions. If this place ran amok, vicar, the Borgias would look like tea-party people.'

He looked at her, worried, and saw she was serious. 'It looks innocent enough,' he said. The raft roofs floated down and up and down again over the crammed landscape, trees and telegraph poles and street lights projecting between them like the arms of drowning people. All was sun and silence. 'All those people,' he whispered wistfully. 'Hundreds of souls. Waiting, just waiting for something.'

'I'd get out there before someone like the Hare Krishna rabble do,' she advised. 'If people don't believe in something they'll have anything.'

Hercules the tramp, hunched like the perpetual handle over his dogged perambulator, progressed along Cowacre below them. The air was so quiet they could hear the rhythmic squeak of the pram's wheels.

'Hercules,' nodded Polly in introduction. 'The conscience of Plummers Park you could call him. He pushes that pram around here day in and day out and the people give him things. He's their charity, their let-out. But only him. He's the *local* tramp. Another one would be ignored or hounded out.'

'I wonder if he's a Christian?' mused the Reverend Boon. 'He would be most valuable.'

'If cleanliness is next to Godliness, I doubt it. Anyway, he used to be a car dealer. But he's been *adopted* around here. If you could be adopted like that . . .'

'I see, I see,' sighed the vicar. 'To be accepted. That's what it needs.'

'We have another itinerant,' said Polly. 'A French onion seller, the most gorgeous man. Eyes, hair, biceps, the most magnificent thorax you ever did see. He's Mephistopheles, I think. Yes, Mephistopheles, with his dangling onions and his bicycle. You can almost imagine the man wearing wicked horns. The women are mesmerized and terrified by him.'

'In other words he's a moral danger?'

'No. In a strange way I think not. It's the Plummers Park thing again. I can't see any housewife around here bringing herself to have an affair with a man who habitually uses a bike.'

CHAPTER NINE

Miss Dora Jankin, a short, rude woman, was headmistress of Plummers Park Primary School, which many of the young of the estate attended. Later, if they did not attain a grammar school scholarship, they were often farmed out to surrounding private schools, thus circumnavigating the necessity for them to attend the local secondary modern school with the children from the council houses.

It was school sports day and all about her children ran knock-kneed with eggs balanced on the ends of spoons, fell heavily over ropes they were intended to leap, and scampered races urged on by the screams of competitive and near-hysterical mothers. She viewed it all with distaste. Mothers and children, in that order, were the reasons why Miss Jankin had never married and had a family. Children in baggy shorts snivelled and hung around her as she made a tour of the picnic panic of the sports field. Her school, behind her shoulder, was one of those which might easily have been assembled from a kit. She was not in the best of tempers and she would be greatly glad when the holidays arrived so she could give full attention to the miniature dachshunds she bred so devotedly. They were much more rewarding than children.

She snorted like a compact dragon when she saw the Reverend Boon approaching across the sports field, smiling like a lost imbecile, patting infant heads indiscriminately. He walked unheedingly into the three-legged race just at the moment it had started and wondered why his blessings and benedictions aroused such fury in both children and parents.

He looked up from his reckless route at the second steamy snort from the advancing headmistress. 'Ho, ho!' shouted Miss Jankin. 'All things bright and beautiful! Look what the sun's brought out!'

He dithered across to her, knowing that of all the oddments on the field his shorts were the baggiest and his legs the whitest. 'Good afternoon, Miss Jankin,' he said. 'What a lovely day.'

She snorted aside the greeting. 'If you did at Kempton Park what you've just done to our three-legged race you'd be warned off the damned course,' she told him.

'Oh dear, what was that? What did I do?'

'Messed up the start doing your blessings bit,' said the headmistress. 'That's a very dangerous race to interrupt too. Pride can be hurt, bets lost, and little legs broken.'

'That's terrible,' agreed the Reverend Boon, his hand going to his mouth. 'I must go back and apologize.'

'Don't do that,' she warned. 'They've just got their limbs sorted out. They're starting. The mothers might ravage you.'

The clergyman considered her miserably. He had not had a good day. He was sweating and he wished now that he had acknowledged the cowardice of his convictions and worn an open-necked shirt instead of his collar and bib. He had undone the back button and it was damp and sagging now. Nor had his visits been greatly successful. Mr Ernest Rollett, whom he had found at home, had agreed to become an officer of his church as soon as they built the church right behind his house instead of the school for maladjusteds. Neither Simon Grant nor Andrew Maiby had been at home and Gomer John had said that he intended to join the navy if his mam would let him.

But he gazed around the field with attempted ecclesiastical benignity. 'What a lovely day for it, headmistress,' he observed.

'For what? This rubbish?' She glared at him as though he were mad. 'As far as I am concerned it's one day nearer the holidays when I can get out of this howling biscuit-tin they call a school and look after my dogs. What are you doing over on this side anyway? I'm surprised you haven't got a native guide with you.'

'Yes, yes, Miss Jankin, I fear you are right,' admitted Mr Boon dolefully. 'That is the reason I'm here. I have failed so thoroughly with these new people. I thought if I came over and made some contacts, it might encourage people to come to church.'

'You'll be lucky,' she leered brutally. 'The blinding kids only come to school because it's the law. The parents are so damned indulgent they'd let them squat in front of a television set all day if they could. It would save the mothers having to get up early. Some of them want a fleet of buses to tour the district to bring the brats here and take them back in the afternoons, thus relieving the parents of further responsibility.'

'That's not true of all the people, surely?'

'It's true of enough of them,' she replied. 'And then because little Johnny can't read like the kid next-door who's three years older, and brilliant, they come up and threaten me with their fists.'

'Oh dear, oh dear, headmistress, you sound so bitter. Surely middle-class children like this . . .'

'Middle-class my backside! I've worked in the East End and it was easy-street to this. At least you knew where you were with the slum kids.

They were rough but you accepted it and there were ways of handling them. These kids are so sneaky. I caught a nine-year-old boy urinating in the bloody staff teapot the other day.'

'How revolting!'

'It didn't make the Typhoo taste any better, believe me.'

'You tasted . . . you still used the pot?'

'I made the little sod wash it out but I wouldn't be surprised if he wee-weed in it again afterwards. Elevenses tasted dreadful and Miss Thornby had stomach pains in the afternoon.'

'Oh dear.'

'Vicar, for Christ's sake, stop saying "Oh dear".'

'Really, Miss Jankin.'

'Yes, really. I'm sorry, vicar, but I can't deal in your ephemerals. It's all happening right here, around my blasted feet. Go about your missionary work, with pleasure, but I have to go and organize the sack race. The way I feel I might put the bags over the little swines' heads.'

She strode away and the vicar, further defeated, went dejectedly out into the field, smiling this way and that, trying to engage wary mothers in conversations which he hoped would, by some touch from God, turn in the direction of local religious life. But no help arrived and when he blatantly opened the subject himself he found the women evasive. They could not promise anything regarding anything, particularly church, before consulting their husbands on their return from work. Others made excuses. The church was too far, Sunday school would entail their children walking through dangerous streets on the other side of the railway. There were other difficulties. 'If church was any other day but Sunday it wouldn't be so bad,' a young mother sighed.

The vicar wandered disconsolately to where a man was selling ice-cream at the school gate. The vendor was cheerful but blunt. 'What you want then, mate?' he inquired.

Mr Boon thought a Strawberry Trinity sounded appropriate and ordered one. Because of the heat it ran very quickly and he had splashed some on his bib before he caught up with the drippings. Two older girls in the summer uniform dresses of the local grammar school watched him working his tongue around the confection while they waited for their own ice-creams. He smiled with embarrassment and, having contained the pink flow, nodded acknowledgement. 'You're from St John's,' he said.

'Yes, sir,' replied the shorter of the two, who smiled at him brazenly. 'We're helping with the junior sports.'

'Ah, good,' smiled the vicar. He knew that a pimple of pink ice-cream was suddenly sitting like a joke on the point of his nose. He could feel its coldness. He squinted and confirmed it. The girls had seen it too, of course, and were restraining a giggle. He wiped the ice-cream away. 'It's very nice to see older children assisting the young,' he continued.

'We got the day off to do it,' replied the taller girl. She had a dark and serious face and she regarded the vicar's forlorn appearance with real interest. 'You're the Reverend Boon, aren't you. From the church.'

'Yes,' acknowledged the vicar, pleased that he had been recognized. 'I shall be at your prize-giving, with the bishop, at the end of this term. Now, who are you?'

'I'm Lizzie Maiby,' said the shorter girl.

'And I'm Sarah Burville.'

'Ah, yes, now I've heard of you,' said the Reverend Boon. 'Do you have some prizes to come this term?'

'Yes, I believe so.'

'She's won everything,' said Lizzie without envy. 'Haven't you Sarah? She's won so many things she'll have a job to carry them home.'

'Ah, yes, yes,' said the vicar trying to remember. 'I'm sure your headmistress told me something about you last year. She hopes you will go to university. But your mother's ill, isn't she? Your head did say something about her. Is she better?'

A scarlet blush rushed across Sarah's face. Lizzie stared at her. She trembled in the sunshine. 'Yes, thank you,' she said eventually. 'She's much better.'

Simon Grant was home early from work. The afternoon children were only just returning from school and the sports field when he walked from the station. His jacket and his tie were off almost as he entered the house.

'Have you tried it on yet?' he asked Ena eagerly.

'No,' she hesitated. 'No I didn't.'

'Well, why not, darling?' She had been sunbathing. Now she was wearing a short light dress. He caught her brown forearms and pulled her to his shirt. He unzipped his trousers and let them fall ridiculously about his ankles as he embraced her.

'You don't hang around do you?' she said. 'You've only been in the house twenty seconds. Don't you want a drink or a cup of tea or something?'

'Let's have the something,' he smirked boyishly. 'All the way home I've been sweating in the train and thinking about you in that body-stocking. I thought you would have tried it on. Why didn't you?'

'I thought it was for our anniversary,' she said.

'It's here! Don't let's wait, baby. Come on, let's go up now.'

'All right,' she agreed with a sad patience he failed to notice. 'Let me give the kitten a drink. He needs a drop.'

'So do I,' said Simon coarsely. He picked up his trousers from the floor and went upstairs. 'Don't forget to bring the right pussy up,' he called down to her. 'And the parcel.'

Ena closed her eyes momentarily, miserably. Still, it was a change for him to pick up his own trousers. She poured the kitten's milk into the saucer and looked out to the garden and the sun-blue sky over the houses. She wondered where Geoff was. She felt very lonely in this house with her husband. Reluctantly she picked up the unwrapped parcel and touched the nylon garment inside with distaste. Then she walked up the stairs.

Simon was lying in the middle of their king-size bed, still wearing his shirt with his penis standing up from beneath it like an admonition. The curtains were closed and the room was humid. The sun seemed to be pushing against the blue curtain fabric, trying to force its way in. From outside came the 4.30 sounds of the Plummers Park children going squeakily home to tea.

'See how I feel,' said Simon nodding down from the pillow to his projection. He was so insensitive he did not even notice how his insensitivity injured her.

Ena nodded: 'I noticed.'

'You don't seem very enthusiastic, darl. Is anything wrong?'

'No, nothing. I've just been a bit tired today, that's all. I thought we were going to leave it until our anniversary. It will be a bit hot wearing that thing.'

'Oh come on, sweetie,' pleaded Simon. 'Don't let me down now. Give me your hand.'

She stretched her fingers towards him smiling wanly through the muted light of the room. He caught them and twirled them about his erection. 'They're cool,' he said. 'Your fingers.'

'Anything would be cool against that,' she said. 'It's burning.'

'Like a poker,' he agreed. 'How can you expect me to wait?'

He pulled her forward while she still grasped him and guided her lips to his. He felt the large breasts, under the short light girlish dress, roll freely forward. He took his mouth from hers and while she still arched above him undid the top pair of buttons of the dress and with both hands pulled out the big right breast from the thin brassière that held it, like a man lifting a puppy from the litter. He laid his tongue against the supple nipple. She released him and his member nuzzled its way under the short skirt of her dress and between her glossy legs. Simon put the breast away and lay back on the pillow, his wife's lovely face and falling fair hair a few inches from his eyes. 'I'd love to have you now, darl,' he said. 'But I'm going to control myself. Will you put the thing on? I want to see how you look in it. I wouldn't mind having a drink.'

'A drink? I thought you said you didn't want one.'

'Well, I sort of fancy just lying back here like a sultan sipping something cool and watching you walk about in the body-stocking.'

'All right,' she sighed. 'I'll get you something. Do you want me to put that garment on in here?'

'No! For goodness sake don't do that,' he said anxiously. 'You'll spoil the effect. Put it on in the other room and put your negligee thing over it. The pink fluffy one that I like. Then you can sort of take it off.'

'In other words, a striptease.'

'Aw, you don't mind, do you?'

'No. No, I don't mind. I'll get you a beer.'

'*Not* a beer! I can't watch my wife cavort while I'm drinking a measly beer. Have we got a lime juice? That's a bit more exotic.'

'We've got some tinned shandy,' she said. 'Will that do?'

'If I didn't know, I'd swear you were trying to mess this up.'

'I'm not. I'll go and get it and put the body-stocking on for you.'

She went and he lay luxuriating in the private, dimmed warmth of the room and the anticipation of what was to come. He looked down at his penis with proprietorial satisfaction and rolled his body one way and another so that the member dipped and rose like the mast of a small boat in a choppy sea. He thought of his wife's fine untiring body, and smiled. He was a happy man. There were not many wives around Plummers Park who would look anything in a body-stocking.

He tried to imagine what it would be like. The advertisement in the Sunday paper had indicated it was the last word in glamorous garments, with an erotic aperture for each breast and what the wording described as enticing divided legs.

She came back into the bedroom then, lovely in the pink robe he liked so much, her hair arranged, a glass in her hands, her legs black-nyloned. He took the glass from her. 'No shoes?' he said. 'Why don't you put those very high heels on.'

'Will you want me to do high kicks so you can see the grating they've left between the legs.'

'Oh, don't be so mean, Ena darling.'

'Well,' she said more softly, 'it *is* a bit of a creation, Simon. I was embarrassed to put it on. Do we *need* this sort of thing . . .'

'You promised,' he pointed out. She was standing at the bottom of the bed now and he had to keep peering around his own upstand to see her properly.

'All right,' she sighed. 'Do you want me to reveal it all now – in a flash?'

'No wait,' said Simon, half sitting up, his drink balanced in one hand. 'Do it properly, lover. With a bit of show.'

She smiled at him for the first time. 'You really are a boy, you know, Simon. You enjoy it so much, don't you? All this.'

'Of course I do. Better than having some sort of formal sex every Sunday afternoon like half the people around here. My God, you know we've seen them wearily drawing the curtains. Right after the Big Match on television. It's fun like we do it. Don't you think it is?'

'Yes,' she said, still smiling a trifle pityingly at him. 'Right, are you ready for this?'

'I'm ready,' he sighed, lying back again. 'On with the show.'

She went along with his wishes now, swaying theatrically and turning her head and then pushing the negligee away from her shoulders, inch by inch until it slipped and droped away from her. Simon stared at her. Her splendid body – always a surprise and a thrill for him – was entirely cased in the tight black nylon except for the two gaping holes at the front from each of which her breasts thrust spectacularly, the flesh rounded, the tips rosy. She smiled at him. 'How do I look?' she inquired.

'Good God? How do you look?' gasped Simon. '*How do you look?*'

'Coo-ee. Cooooooooooooeeeeee. Cooo . . . Cooooooeeeee.'

The sound came from outside the house and then immediately from within. Someone was yodelling up at the window and then poking their head into the hall.

'Oh, Christ, what's that?' demanded Simon.

'Wait, wait, I'll see,' she whispered.

'Not like that! He'll see.'

'I know, I know.' She caught hold of her dress from the adjoining room and stepped quickly into it.

'Coooeeee. Who's at home?' came the voice from below.

'Fuck,' swore Simon. 'Bloody fuck.'

'Quiet! It's a clergyman,' said Ena, peering down through the curtains. 'You must have left the front door open. He's looking in.'

'Nosy bastard,' complained Simon. 'What are we going to do?'

'You stay here,' said Ena. 'I'll go down.'

'Keep him outside the door, then,' said Simon. 'Once those buggers get in you can never get shot of them.'

She went from the room as the third 'Cooooooooeeeeee' hooted through the house. Simon lay fuming, his manhood collapsed, his fists clenched with frustration.

Swear words hissed from him like short escapes of gas. He could hear the voices from below, the professional hushed bray of the clergyman and the agreeing sounds of Ena. Eventually he heard her coming upstairs. There was a suggestion of amusement on her face as she entered the room. 'You'll have to come down for a minute, Simon,' she said. 'He knows you're in.'

'What in Christ's name does he want?' demanded Simon in a whisper, unconscious of the aptness.

'I think he wants you to become a leader of the church,' replied Ena. 'You'd better get your trousers on.'

Simon was such that, sexually interrupted though he had been, the thought of some recognition from the church, or any other well-known body, quelled his bad temper. He sat on the side of the bed and a sudden vision of himself in the raiment of an archbishop came to him. Standing like a golden bird before thousands. Quickly he put his lolling organ into his trousers, slipped on his shoes and socks and followed his wife downstairs.

The Reverend Bonn, dangling apology, was sitting in one of their Stag armchairs. His shorts hung from his legs like abject flags, his sun-flushed face was choking from his clerical collar which he had buttoned again in the interests of propriety. He greeted Simon with a damp church hand.

'I sincerely hope I am not intruding at an inconvenient time,' said the vicar.

'Not at all,' Simon assured him with a beam.

'When you get in from the city it must be very nice just to put your feet up for a few minutes.'

Ena, who had retreated to the kitchen to get the vicar a lemonade, heard the remark and muttered privately: 'Don't give him ideas about his feet.'

She returned to find her husband and the Reverend Boon in profound and friendly conversation. 'Certainly if I can be of any assistance, as a lay preacher perhaps . . .' Simon was saying.

Ena smiled grimly to herself again. 'What does a lay preacher do, Simon?' she inquired innocently.

'Now, now, darling,' he said putting up his barrier hand. 'If you start getting involved we'll be here for hours. The vicar wants some help in establishing a church over here, that's all.'

'That's all,' repeated the vicar doubtfully. He got in before Simon could speak again. 'What we need is a group of people as a foundation, a rock, a beginning. I think that a young couple such as you could be a great help and influence in Plummers Park.'

'I'm sure we would be delighted,' said Simon blandly. 'Ena is good at organizing teas and suchlike, aren't you, baby?'

She nodded, not so much puzzled as amazed by him. The rampant sultan had been turned with a few ecclesiastical words into a missionary. The vicar, finishing his lemonade, rose politely.

'I won't intrude on you any further,' he said. 'I must get back for my confirmation class anyway. If I'm not there they all escape and go home. I'm afraid enthusiasm is not a strong point at St James the Less.'

'Good name for a church,' said Simon in a businesslike way. 'It's got a sound about it. Did you pick it yourself?'

'No, no,' answered the vicar cautiously. 'That's a matter for the higher authorities. I must be off. Goodbye, Mrs Grant, Mr Grant. God be with you. I shall contact you quite soon.'

They saw him to the front gate and then returned to the house. 'You can't be serious,' said Ena.

'About the church? Of course I'm serious.'

'But you . . . me . . .?'

'Listen, think of the contacts you make that way. Once you're in you get invited to this, that and the other thing. Dinners, garden parties and the like. You'll have to cover up your boobs, but we could get a lot of kudos like that. Meeting Lord this and Lady that and the odd bishop here and there. It's like in business, you have to *know* people.'

Five minutes later they were on the bed again. 'Now for St Simon the Most,' he boasted. She lay and closed her eyes and felt him enter her. She wanted to tell him she was pregnant but even when they had finished she could not bring herself to do it. She knew how it would upset him. And he was having such a good time.

Andrew left the office with studied casualness and walked along the main street. He decided he would stroll by the churchyard, not through it, just to see if she had meant what she said. It was a cooler day with a short furly wind mixing with the sunshine.

The old graves in the churchyard had been grassed over, and girls and men from the offices and shops now lay there sunbathing above the former inhabitants lying in similar positions in the darkness beneath.

Three times he sauntered deliberately by the wise, worn steps of the entrance but he could not see her. Then, glum with doubt, he turned in through the gate and went slowly along the old path, crazed with the tombstone slabs of two centuries before. Bessie was sitting on a wooden bench talking with a young man in jeans with his shirt open to his navel. Andrew almost walked by but she rose easily and said to the youth, 'I've got to be off now.' She walked alongside Andrew over the old stones.

'Do you think these people who were buried underneath the stones would mind us treading on them like this?' she asked without a greeting, as though they had been conversing for hours.

'They're not really in a position to mind, are they?' Andrew pointed out.

'No. It's a shame really, I think. Having people walking all over your name.' She smiled at him. 'I wondered if you'd come,' she said.

'Oh, I was going through anyway,' he said absently. 'I thought I'd keep a look-out for you.'

'You walked past the gate three times,' she grinned. 'I spotted you. Have you got any sandwiches or anything? I've eaten mine.'

'Er . . . no . . . I don't generally bring sandwiches. I have something in the pub as a rule. That's where I was going. Why don't you come and watch me eat my pork pie? I'll buy you a drink.'

She had stopped and was looking at a memorial tablet on the church wall. 'Have you ever read that, Andrew?' she asked. 'I often look at it.'

'Never read gravestones,' he advised. 'It's fatal. Whatever advice they give, it's too late. A forlorn afterthought. What last-gasp goodies has this one got?'

He leaned forward and read aloud: 'The wonder of the world, the beauty and the power, the shape of things, their colours, lights and shades; these I saw. Look Ye also while life lasts.'

'It's really nice,' said Bessie sadly. 'I think it's ever so nice.'

'It has an icy ring about it when you get a bit older,' answered Andrew.

'You talk as though you're eighty,' she said. 'From the minute I first met you, mate, I could see you were getting the miseries about your age.'

He glanced at her sharply. She was watching him in her half-laughing manner, her face clean with youth, the town sun on her gentle hair. She looked lithe and carefree. Her hand came out to him encouragingly. He felt a groan of joy growing within him.

'Who was that chap?' he asked.

'What chap?'

'The one you were talking to on the bench.'

'I don't know. I was just chatting to him.'

'You kids talk to anybody today, don't you? When I was your age you wouldn't start a conversation with someone like that unless you had *intentions*.'

'What's that mean? Intentions?'

'Well, unless you thought there was something *in it*. It took a lot of guts when I was young to just sit down and talk to someone of the opposite sex and in your own age group. You swallowed several times and then . . .'

'I know – she dropped her lace handkerchief and you picked it up!'

'Go on, have a good laugh. If you want to know the truth, when I was eighteen I *carried* a lace handkerchief around with me – so that if I saw a girl I fancied I used to drop it and pretend I thought it was hers. I'd belt after her and ask her if she'd dropped it.'

'Blimey,' she said admiringly. 'That's not bad. I bet you pulled a few like that.'

'Pulled a few? My god, the richness of the language these days. You make it sound as though it's something to do with teeth.'

'All right, you *had* them then. Is that better?'

'Not much,' grunted Andrew. 'And I didn't *have* them anyway. It wasn't like it is now, or what I'm told it's like now. In those days if you got a kiss on the third date you went home walking three feet above the ground.'

'That's nice,' she approved. 'It's a pity you couldn't talk to people though. Me, I'll talk to anybody.'

'I've noticed. Are you sure you didn't *talk* to anybody at my newspaper? I've tried to find out who stopped that court report going in, but nobody seems to know.'

'Grandad was just lucky,' she shrugged. 'Not that it made much difference: my dad found out dead easy anyway. But at least the neighbours didn't know.'

'Well, *something* happened. You don't get the same thing omitted from both papers by coincidence. I could believe you'd seduced my editor, but the other editor is an old woman.'

She laughed. 'I'm not particular,' she said.

'But you're rude,' he replied. He almost said 'crude' and he changed it at the last syllable.

They had reached the far end of the churchyard now, where the traditional yew tree shaded out over a paved area with tables outside the public-house. She drank half a pint of beer with him and watched him eat his pork pie, refusing to have anything more to eat.

'How do you reckon you get to be a saint?' she said.

He looked up from his pie, not so surprised at her now, to see she was studying the gold lettering on the church notice-board.

'You're too late,' he observed. 'I wouldn't bother if I were you.'

'No, but I mean Saint Adrian, like it says up there. Who was he when he was home?'

'Mostly away,' said Andrew. 'His real name was Nicholas Breakspear and he came from around this area. Probably the council estate.'

'Don't be funny. I'm trying to learn. Did they call the crematorium after him?' she said.

'Yes, they did,' he said encouraged. 'But the name is all around here. He was Adrian, the Fourth or Fifth, I can't remember, the only Englishman ever to become Pope. He had a white palfrey and the Emperor Frederick of Germany kissed his foot in the stirrup.'

'Is that a horse?'

'A palfrey? Yes. Frederick led the horse while Adrian rode it.'

'He must have been a good bloke. I wouldn't mind being a pope if I could have a white 'orse and be led around by an emperor who kissed my feet. I'd reckon that.'

'You've got no chance,' he said.

'Listen,' she added thoughtfully. 'I was thinking about you at work yesterday and I thought it seems a bit funny really – like you being so clever and yet you're only working on a tinpot local rag. Why don't you work for the *Daily Mirror* or one of them?'

'Thanks,' sighed Andrew. 'You sound just like my wife.'

'Your wife's bound to ask you. Can't say I blame her.'

'To start with I don't think I'm clever. I know a few things which I've read in books – all about Nicholas Breakspear for instance because he was a local chap – but whatever I know or I can do is counterbalanced by the fact that I'm bone lazy. I do the easiest thing, the minimum effort for the most amount of pay I can get. Does that answer the question?'

She nodded. 'I'd worked that out already,' she said. 'And I bet you're like that with everything, not just your job.'

'Well, I don't keep a lace handkerchief to drop if I see somebody I fancy. Not now.'

'You ought to read that thing on the tomb again, Andrew,' she advised. 'About looking while you're alive.'

'Oh, I look. Don't get the wrong idea. I'm *looking* all the time.'

'It's just you don't move your arse to *do* anything?'

'A fair assessment.'

'I've got to get back to the shop,' she said rising suddenly. 'It's my half-day tomorrow. Do you want to meet up and go somewhere?'

'Go somewhere?'

'Yes. Just go somewhere. I don't know. Do you want to, or not?'

'Yes,' he said. He hesitated then added. 'Here about the same time?'

'All right,' she nodded. 'I'll be here. I'll try not to talk to anybody.' She bent and picked a daisy at the gate to the churchyard. 'You know why they call this a daisy?' she asked.

'No, I don't.'

'Thank Christ for that. Well, it's because it used to be called the day's-eye. People said it looked at the day from the very minute it opened in the morning. They learned me that at school, anyway.'

The next day was suddenly drooping with cloud after two weeks of hot weather. The wind increased about the town and there was a trace of rain at noon. Andrew went to the churchyard and saw her sitting alone in the deserted place, a large carrier-bag on the seat beside her.

'New clothes?' he said.

'No. Some old ones,' she said cheerfully. 'They're for you.'

'Me? Why?'

'Well, I thought, Andrew, you might like to come around to my house for a cup of tea, and since we've got so many nosey bleeding neighbours I thought you wouldn't mind putting these things on.'

'A cup of tea?' he said.

She looked at him steadily. 'Yes, that's what I thought. Nobody else will be in except grandad and he's stuck to the television all the time.'

'What are these things?' He stared at the bag.

She said doubtfully. 'It's a sort of gas-meter reader's outfit. You know, a cap and a long mackintosh and that. It's a good job the weather's gone off. You'd have looked a scream wearing that heavy mac if it was still hot.'

Andrew touched her arm. It felt very slender under her light coat. 'Here, now, just a minute, Bessie. Isn't all this a bit elaborate?'

'Do you want to come or don't you? To my house?'

'Yes.'

'Have you got a car?'

'No, well yes, but my wife uses it. I don't drive.'

'You don't drive? How do you manage for your work then? Do you run to the scoops?'

'No. We have an office car with a driver. I use that sometimes. We don't have to hurry so much when it's a weekly paper.'

'Christ,' she said studying him. 'I reckon you get worse.'

'I'm sorry, but I don't have a car.'

'I thought everybody had a car.'

'Well, I haven't.'

'Right you are. We'll have to go on the train,' she decided. 'I'll go first. You catch the next train after me and come down the road in this gas-meter man's outfit and come to the front door.'

'Look, couldn't I just be the insurance man, or something?'

'No. If you're in ordinary gear they'll still want to know who you are. It will get around to my dad in no time.'

'I'm getting to like this less all the time.'

'Do you, or don't you?'

'Yes, all right. I've said so. But why don't we go to a hotel . . . and . . . have some tea.'

She looked aghast. 'Hotel?' she whispered as though it were unmentionable. 'If you think I'm going to start creeping into hotels with you, mate, you're mistaken,' she said hotly. 'I'm going now. I'll go home and if you're not at the door in half an hour then I'll wash my hair and forget about it.'

Bessie went. He watched her, the decisive legs, the straight hair dropping over the slim back. She turned towards the station at the churchyard gate and did not look back. Andrew sat down dejectedly with the carrier-bag. He looked with misgivings inside. Folded, the raincoat weighed like a stored tent. The cap was greasy. There was a record book with a wooden back and a pencil. He was amazed and disgusted with himself, but there was an unfamiliar excitement too and he knew he was going to wear it.

He knocked at the door and she must have been standing directly behind it because she opened it right away and almost tugged him in. He could hear the old man's ratcheted voice calling: 'Who is it, Bessie? Who is it?'

'Nothing, grandad,' she called after leaving a pause. 'Wrong house.'

She put her finger to her mouth and, eyes laughing at the sight of him in his disguise, she beckoned him quietly from the hall through the small living-room, within a couple of feet of the old man's back. Her grandfather was watching a programme in Spanish on a huge colour television set. It was a crammed room, with narrow channels between the furniture and across one a bamboo and walnut bar, with bottles in clips like ammunition, and bull-fight posters on the wall. He went from the door, through the room and out of another door without the old man knowing a thing. The stairs were linoleumed and he climbed them tentatively until at last he was in her bedroom and the door closed behind them.

'Oh, Andrew,' she whispered, enthralled. 'You look fabulous. I'm crazy about men in uniform.'

'God,' he breathed. 'I never thought I'd ever get involved in anything *quite* like this.'

'You're *not* involved yet,' she said, smiling quietly at him. He returned the smile and she helped him from the great tarpaulin raincoat.

'Where, in God's name, did you get this stuff?' he asked.

'My Uncle Brett,' she said. 'But he don't use it now because he's in the nick. He kept the money from gas meters. It's been hanging in the hall ever since he went.'

'It's a wonder the Gas Board didn't want it back,' said Andrew.

'Well,' she said cautiously. 'He never actually worked for them. That's why he got done. He just made out he did and emptied the meters. The cops brought the mackintosh and the cap and the book back after he'd gone. Don't ask me why. Maybe they're hoping to nab him again as soon as he gets out.'

'There's never a dull moment with you, is there?' He was regarding her carefully. She had a white sweater curving modestly over her bust and a pair of flared red velvet trousers tight around her thighs.

'You say nice things,' she said. She sat on the bed. It was a small room with space enough only for the single bed, a dressing table and a wardrobe. On the wall was a childish painting of a Dutch windmill. The curtains were pulled across the window.

'All right,' he said. 'Where's the tea then?'

'There ain't no tea. It was a trick to get you here.'

He leaned quickly down to her then and they kissed, tenderly, her quiet lips against his grown mouth, their hands friendly on each other's forearms. He bent at the knees and crouched beside her. 'I honestly don't know how all this has happened,' he said. 'But it's doing something for me.'

'I know,' she acknowledged softly. 'It's doin' the same for me. Ever since the time I saw you in the courtroom I wanted this. I don't get much fun living here.'

'There's such a difference between us, ages and everything.'

'That's why I wanted to have you,' she said firmly. 'It's the *difference*. One thing I don't want and that's to talk. I'm going to take my things off. Close your eyes. I'm shy.'

'Now you're *certain*?' he said, touching her face.

'Christ,' she sighed. 'I told you, didn't I? I'm *sure*. If you're not then you'd better get out before I start undressing.'

He kissed her again. She cut it short. 'Close your eyes now,' she said. 'Go on.'

He sat on the edge of the childish bed. 'Can I talk?' he asked.

'You usually do,' she said. 'Don't start on anything too long though. I won't be a tick.'

'You're amazing,' he said sincerely. 'I've never known anyone like you. Honestly, Bessie, I don't know what to do about you.'

'Would you like to adopt me?' she giggled. She paused. 'Now, take a decko.'

He opened his eyes and saw her standing at the foot of the bed, slender, white, naked, smiling at him, her breasts small, their nipples like pink flowers, her stomach long and curved inward and then out to the pubic hill with its brief copse of fair hair. 'There's not much of me,' she apologized.

Andrew found he was trembling. He stood and put his hands out to touch her. She smiled uncertainly, then said brazenly, 'Get your trousers off,' but then, in a moment, fell against him and he engulfed her in his embrace. He felt her, skin and lively flesh, against his chest, her legs slotted between his, her face and hair crushed into his neck. 'Come on Andrew,' she nagged breathlessly in her cockney voice, 'let's see you. Be fair.'

Quickly he undressed. He looked at her and saw a strange blush coming to her face. Eventually they were naked and facing each other. He pulled her to him again and felt his penis spring and lodge easily between her thighs. He was gentle with her, the points of her breasts barely touching his lower chest, her stomach resting against his loins.

'You're sure?' he whispered.

'I'll give you my knee in your crutch if you ask me that again,' she answered. 'I'm *sure*. I'm *sure* I want it. I'm *sure* we're going to have it. I'm *sure* the old boy won't come up the stairs. Anything else you'd like to check.'

'It looks a small bed,' he said mischievously.

She seemed oddly hurt. 'It is, but we don't all live in posh houses. It had to fit the room, didn't it?'

'I didn't mean it like that. I wondered if it would hold us, that's all.'

'It's all there is. I'm scared to use my mum and dad's bed.'

'So am I,' agreed Andrew. He eased her back and she lay, at that moment half afraid it seemed, thin and pale, a half-stopped smile on her lips, anxiety in her eyes. He eased her legs apart and leaned forward and kissed her on her clump of hair.

'No,' she said immediately. 'I don't want any of that. I want it properly.'

They had it properly. There were few preliminaries. He merely leaned towards her and sank deep into her, seeing the expression of relief and gladness flow across her face as he did so. Still arched away from her with most of his weight on his forearms he dropped his head forward so that his face fell into her hair and her neck. They lay savouring the suspended luxury of it for a while and then he began to move. She was very undemonstrative through it all. As though she were intent on committing it to memory. When they lay together after their climax, she said: 'It took forty-three before you fired. Well, forty-three and the last one which you could reckon to be a half, I suppose.'

'Fired? Oh, you counted?'

'Yes, I nearly always do.'

'I see. Was I up to standard?'

'Lovely,' she said, kissing his face. 'I had a fabulous come.'

'Good.' He eased himself away from her. Then without looking directly at her he said: 'Have you done this a lot then.'

'A fair amount,' she answered readily. 'Have you?'

'I'm married,' he said.

'Excuses, excuses,' she giggled. 'Answer the question. Have you?'

'Well, yes. On and off, I suppose.'

'I bet you've never had anyone as young as me. Eighteen.'

'No. I haven't.'

'I've never had anybody as old as you either,' she said, cocking her head as though trying to remember. She glanced at him and smirked at his expression. 'Worse luck,' she assured. She leaned towards him on her elbow, her small breasts dropping to the left only slightly like the eyes of his dog when it looked to one side. 'When you're old, well older, does it make you very tired having sex?'

'Tiredish,' he said.

'It makes me feel I could run up to the sky,' she said. 'Honest.'

'I don't think I've got much time to drop off, and neither have you for running up to the sky,' he observed. 'I don't think I ought to hang around too long.'

'You're *not* going yet,' she said stubbornly. 'What do you think this is, a bit behind the bike shed?'

'But what if anyone comes back, your parents?'

'They won't. They're both on overtime tonight. They're going to Spain next week and they're grabbing all the money they can. They won't be back yet.'

He was about to mention the old man sitting downstairs when a disembodied voice groaned up through the landing: 'Bessie, Bessie.'

'What d'you want?' she called back unruffled. She put her face only a little closer to Andrew's and said: 'He'll never get up here, don't worry. He did once and the silly old sod fell arse over tip all the way down. So he won't now.' She turned her mouth away from him again and shouted: 'Grandad, what's the matter?'

'I want some fags, Bessie,' came the painful voice. It sounded as though it were coming from a deeply-welled spiral staircase instead of a few feet from the bedroom door. 'I want some fags. I ain't got no scratch.'

'He's got scratch all right,' she muttered, crawling on all fours from the bed. 'He's always bleeding scratching.' Andrew watched her from the bed. She went like a wraith across the linoleumed floor to where her handbag was sitting on the dressing table. She took some money from her purse and went lightly to the door. ''Ere y'are,' she called, and tossed the coins down the stairs. Shutting the door quietly and firmly she returned to the bed.

'Bessie!' complained the voice again. 'Bessie! It's another three. I ain't got nuffink.'

'Christ,' she swore. She slipped across the bed again and looked in her purse. 'I haven't got three,' she said to Andrew. 'He'll never bring back the change from ten. Have you got any?'

'Have a look in my gas-man's coat,' he advised. 'I put my small change in the pocket when I changed into it.' She laughed, mischievously and silently at him and felt in the wide, rough pocket, producing some brown coins. She examined them. 'Blimey,' she said. 'There's one of the old pennies in here. That's not yours, is it?'

'No,' he answered. 'I cashed all my old ones in.' His head was on her pillow which was embroidered with a bluebird, and he watched her with a subdued amazement. She went to the door, stepping like a fawn. ''Ere?' she bellowed down the stairs. ''Ere's the other three. Now bugger off. I'm washing my hair.'

She flung the coins and Andrew heard them bounce on the linoleum and then the old man's grunts as he sought to retrieve them. She waited by the door and after a minute or so opened it a fraction and looked down through the aperture. Satisfied that her grandfather had gone she turned with her wan smile and regarded him. 'You asleep?' she inquired softly.

'No,' he said. 'I was watching you.'

'Do I look all right without no clothes?'

'Beautiful,' he replied.

'That's gone to sleep even if you're not,' she said, coming on to the small bed on all fours, her little breasts hanging below her like an animal's. She put her finger under his penis and lifted it. 'Poor Tired Tim,' she said. 'Let me give him a kiss.'

She put her lips softly to the implement's head and laughed at the reaction under her nose. 'That woke him up, didn't it just?' she said.

He thought she might do something further, but she did not and he was willing to lie and watch her do what she wished. She lay flat on him, her thin form hardly brushing his flesh, then began to crawl upwards, an inch at a time until their faces were together. 'Let's have a bit of a lie like this,' she suggested. He nodded against her cheek and put his hands protectively over the small humps of the backside. 'Put him in,' she said. 'But don't do nothing yet. Let's have a chat.'

She felt under her as she was speaking and catching his member in her right fingers guided it like a short hose to her place. Then she backed up, moved on to it, and they lay there hooked in the dim afternoon light of the small room.

'Now don't do anything silly,' she warned. 'Just have a natter.'

'What do you want to talk about?'

'Anything.' She came to a decision. 'Where did you get changed into the gas-man's stuff?'

'That wasn't easy,' he grunted. 'God, if anybody had told me yesterday I'd be walking up Morrison Way in a thick mac and a peaked cap I'd have said they were mad.'

'Wasn't it worth it?'

'Every frightened step,' he smiled. 'I've still got to get out of here yet.'

'Blimey I hadn't thought about that. What you going to do, Andrew?'

'I'll go out like I came in,' he said like an old campaigner. 'And I'll take the stuff off in a phone-box just up from the station. I put it on in there and it doesn't take a moment. You'll have to follow me and pick it up from the phone-box.'

'Right. That's good. I reckon you're really enjoying this.'

'Well, you're winning me round,' he smiled.

'What else shall we talk about?'

He thought, then suggested. 'Where are your parents going on holiday?'

She gave a brief laugh. 'Parents?' she said. 'It's funny but over here we never call them parents. They're mums and dads. It's when you get over your side they're called parents.'

'I see. Your mum and dad, then.'

'They're going to Spain. They always go to Lloret. They like it there because there's pubs and things. They always go to the same hotel and they come back ever so brown and they win the frog races and the tango championship.'

'I see. It's well worth their while going then,' he said eventually. 'To win the frog races and the tango championship.'

She examined his expression anxiously. 'You're not taking the piss, are you?' she inquired.

'No, of course I'm not.'

'Well, you'd better not. They practise all the winter for their holidays. They have strings stretched out along the passage and they jerk these cardboard frogs on them. Every time you jerk the string it sort of jolts them along, and when they're at Lloret they have races in the hotel and they always win it, easy. They win quids like that. And they really like the tango. Love it, they do. They practise it downstairs, in and out of the furniture.' She moved her head violently one way, then the other, as tango dancers do, but she was very serious about it – poised over his body, her head just lifted, her nipples nibbling his chest.

'They must be pretty good then, eh?' he said. 'And yet, somehow, your dad doesn't look the tangoing sort, does he?'

'Oh, they're fabulous,' she sighed. 'I wish I could do it. My mum's ever so small too. She's only a squinchy five foot and you've seen how big he is. He whisks her around all over the place.'

'He'll whisk me around all over the place if he catches me here,' said Andrew.

'He would too,' she replied as though she would approve, 'my dad. They won't be back yet, though, so stop bothering.' She looked at him sagely. 'Do you want to start doing it again now?' she inquired.

'We could try it.'

'I reckon we could. You lie still and let me do the moving. I want to start and stop and keep on starting and stopping until we can't stand it any more.'

She began to move, very slightly, on him and then rolled easily from one side to the other, before jerking hard at his loins with sharp predatory jabs. He felt her bottom going like a small powerful piston. Then she stopped and looked down at him, smiling brightly. 'Is it nice?' she asked.

He sighed. 'if I'd known it was going to be like this, Bess, I'd have joined the Gas Board years ago.'

CHAPTER TEN

By evening the heavy clouds had queued away to the east and the remainder of the day's sun lingered across the uncaring cattle in the back fields, mellowed the Plummers Park houses, and touched the trees with selective grace. Some people were in their small-portioned gardens, and children were playing on the waste land and by the sub-post office, but the place was still largely empty. The cars had been nosed into garages and under carports, the homing trains had emptied and now the Englishmen were in their boxed castles again, most of them not to emerge until morning.

'Where did you go this afternoon?' asked Audrey. 'I rang the office and they said you'd gone out but they didn't know where.'

He was quickly grateful she had added the second sentence. It gave him time to think. 'Oh, *they* wouldn't,' he said with more ease than he felt. 'They never know a damned thing. I went up to have a chat with old Fowler, the greenkeeper at the golf club.' It was a risk, but he did not think she would check. He had been to see the man the day before.

'The one you were so upset about? Are they going to give him the boot?'

Andrew shook his head. He picked up the evening paper so that he did not have to look at her. 'They think they are, but they're not.'

'Why not?'

'Because he's been there longer than anyone else – and he's clever. He's got a trump card. He knows something – I don't know what it is but he does. He's not worried. He's not as simple as they think.'

'He sounds like the man with the key to the lavatory,' she observed.

'I think he is. Or the key of Life. Maybe both. Maybe they're the same thing.'

'Where else did you go?'

Now he was tempted to face her but he resisted it. God, the intuition of the married woman. He knew if he did not panic, then it would be all right. She didn't know anything but she felt something.

'I had a sniff around after the infamous Plummers Park Flasher,' he said. He walked to the windows so he would not have to look directly at her for a few moments more. He told his heart to be quiet and made sure his voice was normal and regulated. 'I had a natter with them at the police station but they're not exactly Scotland Yard calibre across there. They're more worried because they're a couple of lollipop men short at the moment.'

'Do you think it's someone who lives around here?' she asked. He knew then that he was safe, like a man who has trodden the last stepping-stone. She had rejected her intuition, her suspicion, and was ready to push along with the conversation.

'It's got to be,' he said. 'The way he keeps popping up and vanishing so quickly, he's got to live in this area.'

'It's nasty, though,' she grimaced. 'It's not nice for the kids.'

'I expect most of the girls around here would have a laugh at it,' Andrew said. 'I can't see them being very frightened. He must look ridiculous.'

'Lizzie would,' she interrupted brusquely. 'She'd be scared.'

He caught her expression. Her face was a little flushed, half angry. Lizzie always had her tea immediately she came in from school, before doing her homework and then usually going out again. Her parents always ate their evening meal together at the kitchen table, half watching the portable television in between any conversation. Tonight it was on but the sound was switched to below a mumble. 'Lizzie's not been going up to the barge lately, has she?' asked Andrew.

'Not as much,' said Audrey. 'She went up there tonight, though, with Sarah Burville and that fair-haired boy from Sheep-Dip.'

'Sarah Burville, well that's an improvement.'

'I'll say. They were helping at the little school sports yesterday. They seem to be pretty pally. She's a nice kid. It's a crying shame about her mother. I feel sorry for her father too. Fancy coming home to that every night. Anyway, Lizzie and Sarah have gone up there with the boy, what's his name, Whiting, Keith or Ken I think it is. The Reynolds kids seem to be out of it now.'

'Just as well. The rate they were working it wouldn't have been ready before the Flood.'

She smiled. 'I'm not sorry either about the Reynolds boys. She would never have got into any trouble with them, but God help us . . .'

The sentence was truncated by an abrupt howling of dogs outside the window. 'Herbie,' said Andrew, getting up from the table. 'It sounds like the whole pack tonight.'

They went to the window to look out. 'God, Andrew, they've got him!' cried Audrey. 'Rollett's Alsatian's there!'

As she called, Herbie Futter was pulled down by the savage attack of a dozen dogs. The Alsatian, which was normally fenced in Ernest Rollett's garden, and the big black dog from Hedgerows were on top of him. They had caught his coat and he stumbled, and in a moment all the animals were at him and on him barking and biting and rolling him over. Andrew ran for the door calling, 'Get Gerry, over the road.' He took a broom from the cupboard in the hall and ran down the garden path and along the road to where Herbie Futter was almost buried by the savage pile.

Andrew ran at them with the broom held like a lance. He caught the Alsatian in the ribs as he arrived and lifted another animal with his foot, sending it howling. But the pack instinct in them was fully roused and they snarled and bit at him as he tried to get to the old man crouched beneath the pile bleeding hands over head, like a rugby player in the middle of a dangerous scrimmage. Andrew was panting and fearful. He was making no impression on them. Shouting, he swung the broom and then jabbed them, kicking out and trying to grab at the bristling hair with his hands, but they would not back off. The black dog tore his shirt sleeve down and he felt blood running on his forearm. He waded into them then, dropping the broom and flinging them angrily aside, trying to get to Herbie. A small dog went for his face. He kicked the Alsatian again. He was very frightened now. Sweat and blood were in his eyes. He felt the teeth of one against his ear and he punched another on the end of the nose as though he were fighting another man. Then Gerry Scattergood arrived with a hosepipe, picked up at the run from his front garden, charging and squirting the heavy stream of water as he advanced. The dogs, howling still, backed away as Gerry soaked them. With his free hand he was hurling clods of earth and Andrew, relieved now, joined him in the bombardment. Eventually they had all gone, standing barking at the junction with Risingfield, as though regrouping for another attack.

'Bastards,' breathed Gerry. 'Mad bastards.'

Gently he and Andrew picked up Herbie. The old man's face was paper-white and smeared with blood; he was half breathing, half sobbing, his clothes wet from Gerry's hose; he was trembling so much his bones seemed to rattle. Andrew said: 'Take him over to my place, Gerry.'

'I'll carry him,' said Gerry. He lifted the old man up and bore him easily up the path to Andrew's house. 'I'd take him in my place,' he added, 'but my missus is out. So's his wife, I think. I saw her go by about six.'

'Take him in then,' said Andrew. 'We ought to get him looked at in hospital. He's no youngster.'

'No, no, no,' Herbie Futter protested feebly, rocking his head. 'My wife will do it. She will do it.'

They took him inside Andrew's house and gave him some brandy. When he had taken a drink, Andrew, who realized he was shaking too, took a swig of the bottle. Cynthia and Geoffrey had come across, and Cynthia bathed Herbie's head while Audrey did the same with the bites and scratches on his face and hands and neck. His trousers and coat were torn. Andrew sat down, pale-faced, with a towel around the gash in his forearm. Audrey saw him and pulled the torn shirt back and saw the wound. She kissed him quietly on the cheek and bathed the blood away.

'I think you'll both need a bit of stitching up,' said Geoffrey. 'Gerry's getting the ambulance I think.'

Herbie stared at them, black eyes set in ashen face. 'Fucken dogs,' he groaned. 'I sorry, ladies. Beg pardon. But I kill those fucken bludda dogs.' He lay back heaving. Audrey gave him another sip of brandy and then handed the bottle to Andrew.

They all watched Herbie anxiously. His eyes were closed as he lay back frailly in the chair. The cuts on his forehead and cheek still ran blood. Eventually he looked at his neighbours and gave them a crooked smile. 'You know,' he said slowly. 'In the First World War, in Germany, my fadder he had a suit made of the stuff they call shoddy. Yes, shoddy. My two brothers, his sons you understand, killed at the front, and he was walking in Hamburg in his shoddy suit and it rained, you see, and the suit fell to bits on him.' He gave a little shaky laugh. 'Like a funny man. First a sleeve, then a leg from the trousers. It all fell to bits in the rain. And his sons were dead. He sat in the gutter and he cried, my fadder. So what's a little thing like this, hey?'

Audrey suddenly began to cry and so did Cynthia. To Andrew's intense relief he heard the ambulance siren and in a moment the vehicle stopped outside. Gerry came in with the two ambulance men.

'Savaged by dogs,' wondered one as they persuaded Herbie to lie on their stretcher. One of them looked at Andrew's arm and nodded for him to go also to the ambulance. Andrew felt rather foolish walking through the small assembly of neighbours and excited children who had gathered on the pavement. He could hear children shrieking excitedly down the street. 'Savaged by dogs,' repeated the ambulance man as he and his companion carried Herbie into the vehicle. 'I don't know what the country's coming to.'

Jean and Harry Solkiss, thin as pipes in jeans and Western shirts, their cusomary fingers intertwined, sauntered along Sheep-Dip going towards Risingfield and the meeting which Ernest Rollett had called to discuss the establishment of the school for maladjusted children. Their normal peace was not with them, both were aware of this. Only Harry knew why.

Joy Rowley came from her house and they heard her call back: 'Don't iron too late, mother. He won't need all those shirts this week. 'Bye, 'bye.'

She saw them and smiled. 'Going to the meeting?' she guessed. 'It seems such a nice evening, it's a pity to occupy it gassing.'

'Gassing?'

'Talking,' she said. 'Chin-wagging. But it's got to be done sometime I suppose.'

'Gassing,' said Jean studiously, taking out a dwarf notebook. She wrote the word. 'I guess it's spelt like it sounds?' she asked. 'G-a-s-s-i-n-g?'

'That's right. You're compiling an English oddity dictionary, are you?'

'Right. It's real interesting. Yesterday I found out that twig was not just something on a tree. It means to realize something.'

'You twigged it,' said Joy.

'And chin-wag, I've just got to have that beauty.' She wrote it down.

Harry laughed. 'I've been thinking maybe I'd tell her some of the crazy words from the base, but she said she didn't go in for that sort of classification.'

'I think air force words ought to be kept in the air force, like at twenty thousand feet,' Jean answered. 'It's the typical English I'm rooting out.'

Joy Rowley said thoughtfully: 'I hope you don't think *this*, this around here, is typically English. It's a strange thing to all of us, all these big windows and flat roofs and carports and lost-looking people, all just dumped here in the middle of the fields. We're strangers here ourselves. Nowhere else in this country would a self-respecting street allow itself to be called Sheep-Dip, for instance.'

'Yeah, I guess we've worked that out,' agreed Harry. 'It's a little like being on a US base in a foreign country. You're kinda lost. And so are all the other guys.'

'*You* don't seem to belong here,' Jean said to the other woman as though she had just realized. 'It's not the sort of locality . . .'

'To find a wicked actress living without a man,' Joy finished.

'Oh, please, don't get me wrong.'

'Not at all,' said Joy. 'I know you didn't mean that. But I'm an oddity here, even more than most. I hear about it. In a place like this, rooted wives and restless men, I'm as good as a scarlet woman.'

'Oh, please. I really didn't mean that at all!' exclaimed Jean.

'No, Jean didn't mean that,' confirmed Harry. 'She just meant that we imagined an actress would live in some area like Chelsea. Like she said, you don't seem to belong here.'

'Sure,' agreed Jean anxiously. 'That's what I meant.'

'I'm sorry,' smiled Joy. 'Jumping to conclusions, that's me. I'm probably a bit touchy about it at the moment. I came out to this district purposely because I thought there might be some sort of magic about open green fields. English people actually believe that, you know. Like a fool I believed the builders' advertisements.'

'And now you regret it?'

'No, not altogether. I don't suppose I will ever find what I want unless it's on top of a mountain where no one's ever been.' She grinned. 'And then I'd never get my mother up there. Not with her ironing-board and everything.'

'We feel real settled here,' sighed Jean. She glanced at her husband to note the enthusiasm of his nod. It was screwing her up because she knew he was keeping something from her that day. 'We try to keep open minds about everything and to listen and find out what makes a place like this operate go.'

Joy nodded seriously. 'In that case,' she said. 'When you've drawn some conclusions perhaps you'd let the people around here know. They don't know now. This evening, I fancy, we are to enjoy the spectacle of some fine old English middle-class hypocrisy. Smuggery at its best.'

'Smuggery?' asked Jean, reaching for her notebook.

'An invention of mine, I'm afraid. You're welcome to it if you think it's apt. It means mugging with a smile. They'll say all the right things and then turn the whole thing upside down so that they'll die rather than have a load of maladjusted children on their doorsteps.'

The young Americans stopped walking and looked shocked. 'Oh, no,'

Jean said slowly. 'We were going along to see if we could help to get it *established*.'

'You Americans are such nice people,' said Joy. 'Watch for the British tiger.'

'That's sure come as a shock,' ruminated Harry. 'It's a good thing you warned us.'

'Just do some of your watching and listening this evening,' advised Joy. 'It will be an interesting lesson.'

'I wondered why people kinda clammed up when we seemed so enthusiastic about helping,' sighed Jean. 'I guess we should have watched and listened more carefully.' She shook her pony-tail thoughtfully. 'On the other hand that nice guy, Andrew, the newspaperman – he didn't seem to be against it, or against us for accepting it like we did.'

'Ah, Andrew,' said Joy. 'I don't know him very well. He seems to want to do the right things but he can't get the steam-up to do them. He flaps his hands at the universe. He's like Don Quixote without a lance or a horse.'

'But he tries,' said Jean.

'He *thinks* about trying,' amended Joy. 'And then sometimes he does try. On Monday he tried to fight off some dogs who were attacking some old boy and he got bitten, so I heard today. Generally speaking I don't think he has a lot of luck.'

'That's terrible,' said Harry. 'Poor guy. Is he okay?'

'I believe so. He'll be there tonight I expect. Maybe he could rally the forces of humanity and carry the day for the maladjusteds.'

'*You* support the idea?' asked Jean cautiously.

'Yes,' nodded Joy. 'But they'll say it doesn't affect me because I don't have any kids, because I live some distance away from the site, and because I've got a maladjusted mother anyway. In the same way they would say that you were only supporting it because you thought it was the progressive, smart thing to do. And anyway, by the time it's built you will be safe back in America.'

'Jeeze, I never thought I'd hear anyone use the phrase "safe back in America",' grinned Harry.

They had reached the point where Sheep-Dip made an angle and its last section turned towards the tarmac hill of Risingfield. The man with the old open sports car was sprawled on his back in the road, half under the carcass of his vehicle, trying to untangle a fist of barbed wire wound around the front wheel.

His mauve face shuddered from beneath it as they passed. He glowered at them as they nodded, but said nothing and again inched under the running board.

'That was barbed wire,' whispered Harry as they went on. 'Did you see that? Nobody gets barbed wire around a wheel by accident. Not wound around and around like that. That guy's been sabotaged.'

'His wife,' said Joy confidently. 'So I gather. She hates him and she hates his car, although I'm not certain in which order. It's one of those incompatible situations. She's violent and he's peaceful. He'd be better off going to live in sin with the car.'

'Wow, that's really terrible.'

'Revenge,' said Joy thoughtfully, 'echoes through these parts like the sound of somebody chopping trees in a wood. A man, so I heard, burned all his household furniture in the garden, and a woman drilled holes in her husband's bath.'

'That's real sneaky,' agreed Jean.

They turned and walked up the gradual slope of Risingfield, the American wife in her jeans and pony-tail and with the sharp face looking like a small girl alongside the measured maturity of the Englishwoman. Harry, stooping with the everyday embarrassment of every exceptionally tall man, strode oddly beside them, trying to shorten and adjust his wide strides to their short steps. Risingfield was empty apart from a man hosing down his Austin, and two small children sitting on a low wall, surrounded by the excessive roses of someone's front garden.

'It's so peaceful,' enthused Jean. 'Don't you feel it, Hairy?'

'Empty,' corrected Joy. 'People vanish in these parts. Just disappear. There's a legend that their riches turn to rags after eight in the evening, British Summer Time. But there should be a few at Ernest Rollett's place.

'Does he have a big house?' asked Harry.

'Same as everybody else,' replied Joy. 'But it won't be in the house. Not the meeting. You can bet it will be in the garden. People will go because they like to have a nose around in their neighbour's places, just to see what they've got, but from what I hear Mrs Rollett will turf them out, if you'll excuse the pun, on the lawn. She'll make the excuse that they thought there would be too many people for the house and as it was a nice evening they thought it would be pleasant in the garden. Then she doesn't have to do too much clearing up afterwards.'

'You seem to have gotten to know this location real quick,' observed Harry.

'Instinct,' said Joy. 'Pure instinct.'

They reached the high fence of the Rollett house and heard the talk of people on the other side, the muffled talk of people at a failed picnic. The American couple glanced acknowledgement at their companion. The high gate was ajar and they walked through to find a vapid group of about thirty sitting self-consciously on small school-like benches sipping the most wan orange squash poured into their glasses from a long enamel sanitary jug.

'Wow, drinks!' enthused Joy secretly to Jean.

Jean smiled, unsure how the remark was meant. 'I'm sure thirsty,' she said politely, and her husband nodded from the top of his stoop. 'Me too, honey.'

The Englishwoman gazed, rapt, into the pale potion plopped into her glass, as though trying to detect a trace of orange in it. 'Is it a fly?' inquired Mrs Rollett, who was dispensing the liquid from the jug like a relief worker at a disaster.

'No, no,' replied Joy. 'No, it's perfectly clear, thank you, Mrs Rollett.' Mrs Rollett went along the ranks of her neighbours seated on their forms, jerking her jug in the manner of someone ministering to the poor and wounded. 'Cheers,' said Joy to Jean and Harry Solkiss.

'Cheers,' they replied, their response stranded between politeness and embarrassment.

'They're bound to have a collection after this,' said Joy. 'To defray expenses, as they say, and to start the fighting fund to stop the maladjusteds in their tracks. Nothing brings out the Dunkirk spirit in the British so much as a threat to their property values.'

Andrew and Audrey came through the gate followed by Geoffrey and Cynthia. Andrew, his arm bandaged to the elbow, smiled at Joy and the Solkiss couple, surveyed the people, the straight forms and the orange squash, and said: 'Blimey, it's Sunday school!'

'How's your arm?' asked Joy. She was already aware of Audrey and Cynthia watching her like the twin muzzles of a shotgun.

'It's like a bit of embroidery,' answered Andrew with a grin. 'Mr Rollett's dog has an artistic bite.'

'It was *his* dog, was it?'

'The starved monster that normally inhabits this garden,' said Andrew evenly. 'But which has been removed to some refuge tonight in case I get my boot up its jacksie.'

'Good evening, Andrew, Audrey, Geoffrey, Cynthia,' intoned Ernest Rollett as he moved to the front of the crouched assembly. 'Arm all right, Andrew?' And then: 'Good evening, everyone.'

The talking stumbled at his opening voice, to an eventual silence spoiled only by Andrew taking a long sucking drink from his glass of insipid orangeade. Ernest looked at him with annoyance as the faces turned towards the sound. 'My God,' said Andrew with loud cheerfulness. 'I *needed* that drink.'

'Perhaps,' pouted Ernest, 'we can get the meeting started.' He looked about him truculently, challenging any disagreements, and was almost immediately interrupted by the arrival of the Reverend Boon, who charged through the high gate like some guilty cleric in a French farce. Faced with thirty strange and instantaneously half-hostile expressions, he smiled through his sweat and mouthed the silent 'Good evenings' while making short stabbing bows from the waist in all directions. He accepted a glass for his orangeade. Mrs Rollett had measured well. The great narrow jug was lifted until it was all but upside down and the final drip of the pale refreshment had riddled into his glass. 'In the nick of time, Mr Boon!' chuffed Mrs Rollett. 'In the nick of time!'

Her husband was beginning the proceedings. 'Ladies and gentlemen, friends,' he began, 'this meeting has been called tonight to discuss the proposed establishment, in the very midst of our homes, of an institution for the maladjusted. The plan is that the open land at the rear of this house, and abutting many of your houses, should be used for the erection of this place. Need I say that such a happening would have a disastrous effect upon this community, upon our daily lives, on the value of our property . . .'

'They've called it off.'

It was Andrew's casual remark. It stopped Ernest a few sentences short of his appeal to launch a fighting fund. Everyone turned and looked at him.

'What's that?' asked Ernest brusquely.

'They've abandoned the idea,' repeated Andrew. With some difficulty he took a piece of paper from his inside pocket with his uninjured hand. 'I only heard tonight. I rang my contact at County Hall and told him about this meeting and he said that the plan has been dropped.'

Ernest's mouth had sagged. 'Why . . . why didn't you say?' he demanded.

'I've just said,' pointed out Andrew. 'I wanted to hear a bit of your speech, that's all, Ernest. But you're wasting your breath, old lad. The county council committee decided this afternoon that the environment at Plummers Park would not be suitable for the establishment of the home for maladjusted children.'

Somebody began to clap, and Ernest, determined to lead something anyway, applauded with loud exaggeration and urged the others to join in. The sound of the hands was strange over the evening void.

As the applause diminished, Andrew held up a hand. 'I had not quite finished,' he said, glancing at the paper. 'The committee felt that the environment here would not be conducive to the well-being of these children under their care.'

He turned to go out through the gate not bothering whether Audrey or anyone else was following. At the fence he turned and called back. 'Thanks for the drink, Ernest.' Some fool, even then, began to clap.

The Reverend Boon walked towards the railway, and the tunnel that led to the council estate, still deeply puzzled by this curious land and these outlandish people. It was dark now. He had spent the last two hours playing chess with Andrew Maiby and tasting the first scotch whisky of his life.

The drink had left him a little light in the head and he hummed a snatch of 'All People That On Earth Do Dwell' to a strong rock beat as he went down Sheep-Dip.

There were few lights in the windows now and apparently nobody about. Then, ahead of him, through the night, four large, white, trotting, naked girls appeared, giggling and wobbling as they ran. He pressed himself back against a hedge in horror and astonishment. They bounded by, pounding, pounds of undressed flesh, great feet smacking on the road. He was witnessing the Plummers Park Nude Au Pair Girls Derby, heavily backed and with twenty pounds to the winner.

The clergyman pulled his jacket about him and fled for the tunnel which led to the country he knew and understood.

CHAPTER ELEVEN

Bessie climbed the stile with the awkwardness of a non-rider trying to mount a difficult horse. 'Listen,' she said sulkily. 'I didn't want a bleeding walk in the country. I've seen all this stuff before.'

'The canal?' said Andrew helping her down. She descended gracelessly, as though she had four legs. 'You've been along here before then?'

'No, but I've seen it all on the box, haven't I? It's the same. Water and grass and insects buzzing around. At least with the telly you don't get bitten by the things. Andy, I'm not this sort of girl . . .'

'Call me Andy again and I'll give you a nudge into the canal.'

'Sorry, I meant Andrew. But for Christ's sake, Andrew, tell me where we're going. We're wasting a lovely afternoon messing about out here in the country.'

'See that barge just up there. We're going on that.'

'That? You must be joking, mate. You're not getting me on that?'

'Why not, for God's sake?'

'Crummy old thing, that looks. It might take us straight to the bottom.'

'I'll go straight to your bottom in a moment.'

She flushed and then laughed as though released from her anxieties. 'Oh, all right. Anything for a giggle. Is there a bed on it?'

'No. But we'll manage. We might get the odd splinter but we'll pull them out for each other.'

'Shut up! You give me cold shivers.'

'What can I do?' pursued Andrew. 'You won't go to any hotel and I can't do all that carry-on with the gas-man's outfit. Not again. I couldn't think of anywhere else apart from this, except the mortuary, and I thought you might grumble about that.'

'Too bloody right I would,' she grimaced. 'How did you know about this barge thing? How do you know it's not all locked up?'

'A relative of mine has an interest in it,' he replied carefully. He put his arm around her waist, thin and curved sharply inwards beneath her summer dress, her hip-bone projecting like a horn. She pushed herself closer to him and he dropped his fingers so that they slipped into the hip-bone's groove, and then he pushed them further down so he could feel the bun of hair beneath her summer dress and knickers. The towpath was cross-banded with sunshine and the obese shadows of the edging trees. As they walked the shade and the sun moved across them like a slow, moving belt.

'Have you had a lot of affairs, Andrew?' she asked casually.

'You are witnessing the final threshings of a randy old fish,' he muttered.

'Never mind the fairy tales. Have you?'

'I lived with another woman for a while a couple of years ago,' he said. 'Just for a few weeks.'

'Who left? You or her?'

'I left. Not that there was anything wrong with her. We were really absolutely right for each other.'

'Why go back then?'

'Because of my wife, I suppose, and my child. All the reasons people do go back.'

'They're mad. I always think they're mad, going back just because they think it's the right thing to do,' she said. 'I wouldn't go back unless I *wanted* to go. It's no use doing it and then being sorry is it? You screw up everybody then. You've got to do what you want to do. In the end it's best for everybody, all round.'

Andrew nodded and watched the path ahead. 'To yourself be true,' he muttered.

'Well, if you put it like that, yes.'

'Shakespeare put it like that.'

'Well, he was talking sense. He probably had some bother himself. Everybody has bother at some time. But if you meet somebody and they feel just right, then I reckon you ought to stay with them, you see what I mean.' She paused and then said with almost comic misery: 'We don't feel right together, do we?'

He stopped and turned her shining face to him and kissed her gently. They were alone except for a water-rat beginning to swim across the canal. 'We don't even *look* right,' smiled Andrew.

'There's a rat!' she screamed stamping her feet like a baby. 'Oh God, look at it, Andrew! Yuk! It's all sloppy and wet!'

'So would you be if you lived in there,' pointed out Andrew calmly.

She said 'yuk' again, but subdued now. They watched the animal stroking determinedly and, reaching the other bank, scramble out and disappear into the summer undergrowth.

'He knows where he's going anyway,' said Bessie, the stiffness leaving her frame once the animal had vanished. They walked a few more paces. They were almost at the barge now. 'It's funny,' she mused, 'but my mum and dad are ever so happy. All around we've got neighbours who fight. The people next-door, they throw bloody great heavy metal things at each other – at three o'clock in the morning. You can hear them screaming, effing and blinding and you can hear the things bashing against the wall. I've never worked out how they get their hands on things like that in the middle of the night. Buckets, all sorts of stuff. I mean, you don't have buckets in the bedroom do you? My dad reckons they take their ammunition upstairs with them every night and then when they have a set-to they bring it out from under the bed and start chucking it.' She laughed. 'He's really funny, my dad. And my mum's nice. And they're happy.' Her voice dropped. 'I'm the only one who's not right in our house.'

Andrew pressed her to him again. They had reached the crude gangplank to the barge. He said. 'You're sure you want to go on.'

'You're always asking me whether I'm *sure* of this or I'm *sure* of that,' she complained. 'I ain't sure of anything. But I'll do it anyway. Did you mean "go on" with you or "go on" this ship?'

'Both,' he laughed. He helped her up the wobbling plank and held her nervous hand as they inched their way along the narrow wooden walk, the wall of the low deck housing pushing against the backs of their legs. Andrew stooped and peered through the odd window at the end, where he and Audrey had seen Lizzie. It had been cleaned and cleared of cobwebs and he could see rolls of sunlight hanging on the walls.

'The door should be open, I hope,' he said as they reached the painted companionway.

'Cor, this is pretty, init?' said Bessie, touching the serpentine decoration on and about the door. 'I go for colours like that. Greens and reds and yellows all flyin' about.'

He almost said: 'So did the barge people.' But he stopped himself and said: 'They're the sort of traditional colours and patterns of the people who used to work and live on the barges in the old days. They even painted their kettles and watering-cans like that.'

'Ever so nice,' she repeated. 'Nice and cheerful.'

'They were cheerful people,' said Andrew. The door was unlocked. He turned the handle stiffly. It opened and they peered into the half-light of the long, dry, low cabin.

'Blimey,' she said, poking her head forward to look further inside. 'Cheerful? I reckon they didn't 'ave much choice. There's no room to scrap in here.'

She shuffled in timidly with Andrew just behind her. He saw that the children had cleaned the inside thoroughly, Sarah Burville's hand he thought, and there were some beer crates, probably purloined from The Jolly Grinder, arranged like chairs in a conversational circle and topped by cushions. An oil lamp hung from the middle beam and there was a second on the floor; in one corner was an indistinct bundle.

'Where're we going to 'ave it?' asked Bessie bluntly.

Andrew, bent like a pilgrim because of the lowness of the roof, shrugged. 'I thought we might manage something,' he confessed. 'But it looks a bit bare, doesn't it? Let's see what this is.' He went to the pile in the corner and found it was a small inflatable rubber dinghy, clean, flat and folded and with a single nylon sail rolled under it.

'It's a dinghy,' he said. 'We could put that down.'

She grinned like an urchin. 'By the time you've blown that up, mate,' she observed, 'you won't have any puff left for nothing else.'

'There's a foot-pump,' he said triumphantly, turning the folded rubber over. 'We'll use that.'

'I hope I don't get seasick, that's all,' she said. 'I generally 'ate boats.' Then, as though the matter was now settled to her satisfaction, she undid the buttons of her dress and pulled it away from her shoulders. It was held about her waist by a belt and it hung down while, without fuss, she unhooked her bra, ran her hands over her nipples and gave herself a furious scratch under the armpit.

Andrew's eyes remained on her. He dropped the foot-pump and, still arched beneath the ceiling, moved towards the girl. She laughed at his stance. 'You look like a hunch-back,' she said.

'I feel like Quasimodo,' he admitted.

'Well I still reckon you look like a hunchback,' she said. 'Or a big ape. You could really be quite scary.'

He stopped because there was a trace of alarm in her face, as though she had suddenly realized, because of the ape posture, that she hardly knew anything about him. He bent forward, not touching her with his hands, and kissed her cleanly, giving her confidence. 'Let me pump this thing up,' he suggested. 'When we're lying down it will be more comfortable.'

'Your trousers are getting all dusty,' she pointed out. 'Why don't you take them off.' She was still naked only to the waist, her dress hanging over from its middle band. As though to get it done quickly before he made any reply, she walked forward, unzipped his fly and tugged his trousers down his legs. Then she knelt and put her narrow arms about his legs, pushed her face and rolled her hair into his groin. 'You've got thick legs,' she muttered with her mouth brushing the end of his agitated penis imprisoned in his underpants. She now reached up and pulled these down so that they joined his trousers in a ruffled pool about his ankles.

'Let me get these off, love,' he said softly. 'Then I'll get this contraption pumped up. It doesn't take a minute.'

The acknowledgement in the final sentence that he had undertaken the operation before, the feel of the pump pedal under his bare feet, once he had got rid of his shoes and socks, brought back to him abruptly the last time he had pumped a rubber dinghy – on the beach at Weymouth when Lizzie was four years old and he and Audrey were content together.

He brushed the image away, annoyed with himself for having conjured it up at all, and pumped steadily with his foot. Bessie, her hands on her narrow naked middle, grinned at him. 'You don't half look funny,' she said. 'Doing that in your shirt tails.'

'It feels a bit strange, Bess,' he said.

'Do I look funny?' she asked, suddenly anxious.

'No. You look . . . sweet. Yes, sweet.'

He had half inflated the dinghy, so that it breathed flabbily. He picked up the nylon sail and threw it across the upturned rubber floor of the boat. 'Your couch, my lady,' he announced.

'That's ever so clever,' she acknowledged. 'Are you sure you haven't done this here before with some other bird?'

'It's not experience,' he said. 'It's ingenuity. If we were on a desert island, Bess, I would surprise you with the things I can do.'

'*You'd* be more surprised at me,' she promised.

'Come on, love,' he said softly.

An unusual intensity came into her face, as though she had been hiding something, ashamed of it, and was now about to relieve herself of that burden. She moved forward half stumbling on to the sagging rubber with its covering sail, knees first, then hands and knees, the dress still like some voluminous skirt about her lower half. Then she eased herself over and lay there smiling up at him in the dry dimness of that enclosed place.

Andrew undid his shirt, threw it off and went down on his knees at the side of her makeshift bed. She put a fond hand on his penis, stroking it as though it were some pet. He reached forward and kissed her nipples, briefly first and then taking each breast and enclosing as much of it as he could accommodate in his mouth. While he was occupied at that end of her she put her hands to her waist and pushed and wriggled her way out of the rest of her clothes. His head still lay across her chest; he moved his extended palm down the straight course of her body, feeling her ribs corrugated beneath the cool layer of skin, feeling the abrupt little hill of flesh that was her stomach and then, with his hand travelling like a train over a smooth country, he pushed his fingers down in the culvert between her barely opened thighs. He rubbed her furrow gently for a while, never taking his head from her breasts, and felt her body's response to his finger tips.

'You don't arf get me worked up, mate,' she breathed.

'Let me lie beside you,' Andrew muttered, easing himself on to the rubber boat. There was room for them both since it was a dinghy normally meant to carry five persons in a calm sea. He felt his large man's body touched by the slightness of her form, the light sweet smell of her filling his head. His arms encircled her to him as though they sought mutual protection. He felt her flesh at points all along his body. They settled into each other.

'Why do you call me Bess, Andrew?' she asked drowsily.

'You ask questions at the most inconvenient times,' he replied. 'Do I call you Bess?'

'All the time. Always Bess. Is it because it sounds better, well posher, than Bessie?'

'No,' he said, considering the point guiltily. 'Nothing like that. I just like Bess, that's all.'

'I'm silly,' she said. 'There was I thinking it was for the other reason. Like you don't like me calling you Andy instead of Andrew.'

He eased himself a fraction from her. There was already a little sheen of sweat between their bodies and it parted like a cobweb as they came away from each other. 'Have we come here to argue over names?' he said. 'Or would anything do?'

Bessie regarded him sorrowfully. 'I'm sorry,' she said. 'I'm doing my best to bugger it up. I always try to spoil things, even the things I want most. Come back, right up close, Andrew.'

As he moved back to her he felt his compassion stir. 'You're as lost as I am, aren't you, Bessie?' he said.

'Call me Bess,' she whispered.

'I thought you didn't like it.'

'I didn't say that. I was only asking you *why* you did it, that's all. I like to hear it come from you. Do it again.'

'All right, Bess.' He smiled so close to her cheek that she felt his mouth parting. 'Do you want to call me Andy then?'

'No,' she whispered. 'Let's keep it a bit posh. I'd like it to be like that.' Her voice assumed an attempted refinement. 'Do you wish to have intercourse now, sir?'

'If that's what we're calling it today, yes,' he smiled. He eased himself above her, making sure his weight did not press on to her, and then lowered himself into the recess of her legs. They loved immediately and easily, and they paused and she whispered: 'Can I come on the top deck now, skipper?'

'Aye, aye,' he said. Without taking himself from within her he turned his body carefully below and eased her weightless form up with his arms and a shove or two of his thighs until they had revolved and she was suspended above him. They smiled, congratulating each other on their accomplishment and then she dropped her cheek on his jawbone and said: 'Andrew, can I ask you something?'

'You usually do at this juncture,' he observed, looking up patiently. 'What is it now?'

'Do you like Christmas?'

'Christmas! What a time to ask.'

'Well, I thought I would.'

'Er . . . well, no I don't actually. Now you ask. In fact I would exchange Christmas, New Year, and Pancake Tuesday for just one afternoon of a summer's day. Particularly this afternoon.'

'You're lovely, you are, Andrew.'

'You're not bad yourself.'

'I wasn't really going to ask you about Christmas.'

'I thought you weren't.'

'No, I was going to ask you something else. But I got scared.'

'What is it?'

'We know each other very well, don't we, *really*?'

'Yes, I'd say that,' he agreed patiently. 'Better than some people know each other all their lives.'

'Will you do something then? One thing?'

'All right. What do you want me to do?'

'Smack my arse.'

'What!' He half jerked up from the horizontal in his amazement, but she pushed him flat again with surprising force.

'Sorry, I mean my bottom.'

'Christ. You are the limit.'

'Well, will you? Quite hard,' she continued hurriedly. 'I've wanted to ask someone before, but if you ask some boy your own age he's bound to think you're kinky or something.'

'Yes,' agreed Andrew, still startled. 'He might too.'

'Go on,' she encouraged. 'Do it then. You've got a big hand.'

'Oh, Bess, what am I going to do with you?' he moaned.

'Smack my arse, I hope.'

'I can't.'

'Go on. Please, I want you to.'

He sighed. 'All right. But I'm not doing it hard.'

'Quite hard,' she insisted quietly.

His hand went around her buttocks from each side, each warm globe just over a handful for him. He held them and rolled them gently, feeling them wobble and brush against each other. Then he withdrew his hands and felt, to his anxiety, her body stiffen with anticipation. He drew his right palm back but it was as though another hidden hand was holding him and he kept it there, a foot from her expectant buttock.

'Come on, then,' she said cheerfully. 'What you hanging around for?'

'I *can't*,' he croaked. 'Honestly, Bess, I simply can't.'

He felt her inner muscles giggle. 'You can do it,' she encouraged wickedly. 'Just force yourself.'

He brought his hand down with a weak flap like the tired movement of a bird's wing and said: '*There*, was that what you wanted?'

'Is *that* all there is?' she inquired.

She eased her face up from his body pushing her hands out for leverage and stared at his confused expression. She was pink-cheeked but confident as ever. 'Are you a man or a wet flannel?' she asked. 'If you're a man do it proper.'

She relaxed against him again and lay there waiting. He gritted his teeth as though it was he who was to get the blow. Then he pulled his right hand back and brought it down smartly on her backside. She gave a truncated squeak and began moving against him. 'Do it again love. A few more.'

He did, bringing his hand up and down against the small portion three times and then again on the other side. It opened a great door in him and he felt his whole sexual gases vibrating and heaving as she plunged more savagely against him with each smack. They climaxed together very quickly and they lay there drained and sweating. He screwed his eyes together and felt his hands caressing the area he had just chastised. Bess began to laugh happily against his neck. She stopped and kissed his jugular vein and said: 'You know, I really enjoyed that.'

'You make it sound like a steak and kidney pie,' he observed wearily from beneath her. His arms went around her strongly then, around her back, and he crushed her to his wet chest with a great feeling of love and regard, kissing her face, and her hair and her eyes.

'Get off,' she protested bashfully. 'You'll muck up me eyes.' He stopped and studied her with an expression short of belief. She returned his look seriously: 'You're ashamed of me, I bet,' she said.

He kissed up at her with tenderness. 'No, Bess,' he said. 'I feel a bit ashamed of myself for doing it, that's all.'

'But I *wanted* it,' she replied, looking down. 'Don't you go and blame yourself. It had to be someone like you. Somebody older.'

'Kraft-Ebbing would understand, I suppose.'

'Don't you go tell *anybody*,' she said alarmed. 'You did it, don't forget.

It takes two.'

He laughed. 'I wouldn't tell.'

She looked at him with pleading. 'You liked it as well, didn't you, Andrew? A bit?'

He nodded fondly. 'Of course I did, Bess,' he assured her. 'I don't like the idea of hurting you, that's all.'

'It's not hurting,' she insisted. 'It's like having an icy cold shower. It's a sort of thrill. That's what my parents, my mum and dad, get from the tango. A thrill.'

She eased herself away from him entirely and he looked down the stretched length of her body, the colour of planed soft wood, arched above him as though she were doing press-ups, and admired it again in its slimness, in the unblemished flesh, the cheekiness of the breasts, and the indomitable smile that crowned it. She rolled from him and knelt on the floor. 'Is my bum red?' she asked. She had turned it in his direction and now she shuffled backwards so that he could view it more conveniently. The insides of the backs of her legs were wet, glistening. He touched her with both hands.

'You're a bit pink,' he said. 'But if you don't go around showing people it ought to be all right soon.'

She turned about, still on her hands and knees and bent towards him, kissing his stomach and his groin and then moving her lips lower. 'Sleepy head,' she said.

'I want a cup of tea,' announced Andrew, sitting up.

'Oh, blimey,' she said. '*You*, Andrew! With muffins and strawberry jam, I s'pose!'

'That wouldn't be a bad idea,' he confirmed. 'I'm all for doing things to excess. Get your clothes on.'

She began collecting her garments while he let the air escape from the dinghy, helping it out by pressing his foot on the walls, and began to fold it. Then she found the piece of paper by the beer crate where she had left her shoes.

'Looks like somebody's been here before us,' she said studying the paper with amusement. 'Kids too. Little buggers.' She handed it to Andrew. It was a crude crayon drawing of a naked girl facing a naked boy whose penis bridged the gap between them ambitiously. In the middle was another girl, face on, big breasted, watching them. Above the first girl was the name 'Lizzie', above the boy 'Ken', and the girl in the middle was labelled 'Sarah'.

Andrew felt a sickness surge in his stomach and his hand trembled as he crushed the paper. Bessie was not watching him. It was nothing to her and she had turned to retrieve her skirt. He crushed the drawing so hard he felt his nails digging into his palm.

'Fancy kids getting in here and doing that,' said Bessie blithely. She was pulling her dress up her body, wriggling into the waist. 'Still, I s'pose everybody's got to start somewhere.'

He almost shouted at her, but he restrained the impulse and turned away from her so that she would not see his face. She was quickly dressed and, telling him cheerfully to hurry, she hopped out of the companion-way and climbed like a child herself on to the roof of the barge. He could hear her running about above his head. Miserably, slowly, he put his clothes on, and then taking a match from the box at the side of the oil lamp on the floor he lit the piece of paper, and then the lamp. He carried it to the trapdoor at the far end of the long cabin, the same well in which his daughter had been standing up to her waist on the evening he had gone there with Audrey. Below was a pile of sacking and a scattering of paint tins. He suspended the lamp over the hole for a moment and then deliberately opened his fingers and let it drop. It broke and the flame burst out. He watched it a moment then shut the trapdoor on it and walked out.

The girl was already ashore on the towpath. 'Tea and muffins,' she called to him as he walked along the deck.

She had not noticed his face and now he attempted to compose it. 'Tea and muffins,' he agreed.

'Cor, Andrew, we're doing all the exciting things today!' she laughed.

They walked along the flower-decked towpath without looking back. Had they done so they would have seen a sliver of smoke seeping out of the timbers of the barge.

CHAPTER TWELVE

Plummers Park Golf Club always had a splendid view of the evening. Its clubhouse was far from sumptuous, more like a large bungalow with pieces added without thought to each end, but it spread itself with the grinning comfort of a satisfied man in an armchair on the highest plateau in southern Hertfordshire with views as far as the Chiltern Hills in the north-west and London to the south. Had this been Red Indian country it would have been the natural place to observe smoke signals from Hampstead Heath.

It crouched benignly overlooking fairways dropping away all around, like the pleats of a voluminous skirt. In the dulcet light of the final two hours of the summer's day the greens looked rich, emerald shading to olive; the distributed trees, ash and elm and birch on the course itself, and doyen oaks all around, were draped with late sunshine, and even the difficult bunkers smiled a sandy smile.

Groups of members were out on the course, as slow, distant and indistinct as the crunching sheep in the farm fields beyond. They were observed from the terrace by other members drinking and playing a serious but juvenile game of trying to recognize the identities of players on the remote greens. As pairs and quartets of players completed their contests at the eighteenth hole beneath the clubhouse, they were addressed with the gentle and meaningless buffoonery that is part of an imaginary world.

'Humbled again, Percy!'

'She's killer, that Clementine!'

'You took so long to play that putt I thought you were dead, old boy.'

The players, the majority into middle age but some elderly and some young, walked ritualistically, all smiling, up the path to the terrace and with pleasant weariness joined the drinkers, talkers and watchers there. They were joined by Group Captain Fernie Withers, the secretary, a man with the fierce expression only attained with a florid face and a wall-eye, both of which he had. He ruled the club and the course like a little king, and with a rough charm that is the acquisition of his breed.

'Damned beautiful out there tonight, isn't it, Cartley?' he inquired of one of the returning players, an older man in unsuitable multicolours. The member grinned respectfully and agreed it was, damned beautiful. Since the club was far from exclusive and its members mostly drawn from the minor professional people living in the Ruislip latitude, the secretary treated almost everyone with a sort of jocular aloofness, which they accepted as a part of his former rank of Group Captain.

Bertram Mason, the captain of the club, nicknamed Mauler, was under-sized, bald and mean-eyed. He strode with all the self-importance of a small man in authority on to the terrace, wearing the hues of a varied hors-d'oeuvre, clasping to his little chest a full pint of beer in a tankard that almost obliterated his Shetland pullover.

'We'd better have a word with Fowler this evening, don't you think? Better get it over with,' he said to Withers.

The Group Captain regarded him doubtfully. 'Yes, I suppose we should. You definitely want me to be there, do you?'

'Of course,' replied Mason in his hot small voice. 'Dammit, you're secretary of the club. We'll do it together. We can't let sensitivities stand in the way, you know. He's past it now, he's as good as useless on the course, and we could use that cottage of his. We'll have a good whip-round for him, don't worry.'

'All right,' said the secretary. 'He's working on the third tee. I'll get somebody to fetch him over.'

At that moment the Plummers Park police panda car made as dramatic an entry to the club car-park as it is possible for a panda car to make. It rolled in quickly like a large blue and white ball, sent up a modest hail of asphalt as it came to a skidding halt, and sat panting as two members of the constabulary jumped out.

'Hello, hello,' said Group Captain Withers. 'What's the excitement?'

'Sorry to interrupt you, sir, but it's the Flasher,' said the sergeant in the lead. He glanced with quick alarm at the ladies turned towards him in their terrace seats, and amended it. 'The exposer, sir. We think he's on the golf course.'

'Good God, that indecent chap?' exploded Group Captain Withers.

'On the course. And some of our girls are out there.'

'We'll get him, don't you worry,' vowed the sergeant. 'Before he can do much harm.' He turned to his companion constable. 'Right,' he ordered. 'Fan out.'

The lone PC blinked at this difficult instruction but set off, nevertheless, at a good professional jog, down the first fairway. Before the sergeant could embark in the other direction, Mason slammed his pint of beer down on the rustic table and said: 'We'll assist you. We've got to catch this beast.'

'Indeed!' howled Group Captain Withers, a sudden bloodlust lighting his retired face. 'Come on, chaps. Ladies – inside the clubhouse and stay there until it's safe.'

The men, most of whom had just walked five miles round the course in the sun, began getting hesitantly to their feet. Within a minute Withers and the minute Mauler Mason were leading the posse, each brandishing a golf club and a courageous expression, on a wide encircling movement to drive the Flasher into the waiting net of justice.

The Flasher stood trembling behind a holly bush at the back of the thirteenth green. By the very nature of his vice he disliked holly, blackberry or any form of bramble, but this provided his only chance of concealment.

He was dressed in a long fawn mackintosh beneath which he wore only the legs of a pair of trousers. These covered his shins but terminated above the knee, where they were held by elastic. He wore plimsolls and no underwear. Over his face he had pulled the recognized disguise of a nylon stocking which gave his features the look of plasticine, and on his head was a light-coloured canvas hat which he thought he would replace when winter came with a warm cap. He was trembling because he was afraid, as he always was, not only of those who hunted him but of his own compulsion. He had tried most things, gardening, learning German, taking cold baths, reading good books, and in the end, miserable and excited, he always crept back to the old mac and the topless trousers.

The four ladies now approaching the thirteenth green were at once his prey and his predators. He knew that the moment he had accomplished what he had to do he would be on the run like a hare. He had only rarely worked the golf course before for many reasons, one of which was that it was too open. After uncovering he needed quick cover.

Four was also a good number at one exposure. It provided a proportionately greater thrill than the single victim, but was not so many as to turn the quick deft act into a performance for the mass. He judged their ages to be about right too, three of them young women and the fourth mildly round with middle-age. To display it in front of old women was, he felt, unnecessary generosity.

The quartet dithered a little short of the green and one lady had to pitch her ball out of a bunker, but eventually there were four balls on the green. In a moment, the Flasher thought with a quiver, there would be a couple more.

One of the younger women was hunched over the ball, preparing to putt it three feet to the hole, and the other two were intent on her actions, so that it was only the older of the quartet who observed him walk casually from behind the holly tree and open the front of his mackintosh to reveal all his private hangings. With true golf grit and tradition she did not scream, or indeed utter a sound, until her opponent's putt was safely made. Only after the ball had plopped into the hole did her frenzied cry break through the murmurs of approval for the accurate play.

They turned with her pointed finger and saw him standing. He pulled the curtains of his mackintosh wide again and let his appendage look at them and they look at it. Four screams, frightened or baffled at first, then strengthening to sheer fury, issued from the peaceful green. He was an experienced flasher and he knew that this was the time to leave. He bowed politely to the ladies, gave them another quick glimpse, and then in an almost leisurely fashion, trotted away.

Behind him he heard the urgent, ambiguous cry: 'Was it a member?' Then the summons: 'After him!' which made him increase his pace through the beard of woods. Then he realized he was in trouble. There was a police car on the road behind the course, which was his escape route, and he saw a line of bright men fanned out to cut his retreat the other way. Suddenly frightened he turned and ran through the gorse and undergrowth in the opposite direction, causing untold discomfort to his naked regions. Letting out little squeaks of pain he had covered two hundred yards across this punishing terrain when he saw the unmistakable blue blob of the law ahead. The policeman did not see him, so spinning about he doubled back and then made off at yet another angle. Plunging and sprawling through ever more agonizing undergrowth he suddenly found himself confronted by a police sergeant and the golf club secretary. In panic he turned again as they saw him and ran back towards the other policeman. Sweat was sticking the nylon stocking to his face and his tears of fear were soaking it also. He quivered as he ran, abject terror now making him unheeding when the brambles caught him. The one thing he must not be: exposed.

There was no doubt they were closing in on him. He could hear the men golfers and the unnaturally excited women calling to each other in the thicket. One policeman was blowing his whistle. He decided to make a brave break through the open golf course itself. Fearfully he worked his way along the fringe of the undergrowth and then at the edge of the twelfth fairway essayed his run. His audacity paid off and he was able to make about a hundred yards or more across the open grass before anyone spotted him. Then they were after him in a howling pack. The older ones were tiring, but two younger but fortunately overweight golfers were running with masculine fierceness after him, and one of the young women from the quartet, who must have been something of an athlete, was speeding like a gazelle on an almost parallel course to his. He must not let *her* catch him. That would be ignominy indeed.

His big advantage was his almost total lack of clothing beneath the mackintosh, and the plimsolls on his feet. The golfers without exception were in heavy studded golfing shoes. He went like a ragged hare over the course, his pursuers baying through the quiet evening. He knew that they were enjoying it now. He distinctly heard someone shout 'Tantivy!'

At the incline on the long arm of the course leading up to Fairy Copse his breath began to sag. He turned and saw they were nearer. On the road to his left he observed the pale blue top of the panda car bouncing like an Easter egg beyond the hedge. Sobbing with fear and gulping for breath he stumbled into the thick copse, paused with panicky uncertainty, then turned right, hoping to reach the open sheep fields beyond. But he heard running voices as he reached the fringe of the wood and he knew his escape that way was impossible. The panda car, he reasoned quickly, would be on the road to his left. There was no way to go but straight ahead. The half-idea had been in his mind for some time, now there was nothing else for it. The rumours had reached him. He ran, fell, picked himself up, and then ran again until he reached the rear of the house of Mrs Polly Blossom-Smith. Above the arch leading from the copse to the dusky garden were the vivid words 'The Sanctuary'. The Flasher went in.

'For God's sake, sergeant, why didn't you bring tracker dogs?'

The policeman regarded the Group Captain with morose patience: 'We've only got one, sir, Rexie, and he's on leave.'

'On leave! Don't tell me the bloody dogs have leave.'

'They've got to, sir. Regulations. We'd be done by the RSPCA otherwise. The only dog we've got at the station is a stray Pomeranian, and he's not trained for this type of work, sir.'

'There's no need to be facetious, sergeant,' interjected Mauler Mason. 'We are aware that a Pomeranian would not have been suitable. The fact is the swine got away. Four of our women violated . . .'

'Violated, sir?'

'Yes violated, sergeant! Visually violated. It will be rape next.'

'I doubt it, Mr Mason,' intoned the policeman. 'The man who flashes is very rarely the man who actually *does*. They're a different kettle of fish altogether.'

Group Captain Withers glowered at him: 'We don't have time for amateur psychology now, sergeant. We've got to *do* something about this chap. The girls will be too frightened to go out on the course until he is caught.'

'Human frailty is a difficult thing, sir,' said the sergeant shaking his head. 'I often think that if it was only the other way around – females indecently exposing themselves to males – skirt-lifters instead of shirt-lifters if you see my point, sir – there would be a lot less complaints.'

The secretary and the club captain looked at each other with exploding astonishment. 'Christ almighty, sergeant,' protested Mason. 'Don't sit there philosophising. What are you going to do? Maybe you had better call in the Yard.'

The sergeant scratched his head industriously. 'We can't do that, I'm afraid, Mr Mason. Anything less than a murder and they get upset and fidgety. He must have given us the slip before he got to the house. Mrs Blossom-Smith had not seen him. I've asked my constable to check on your groundsman, sir.'

'Fowler? For heaven's sake, it wasn't Fowler. He's too old to run like that.'

'I didn't assume it *was* him, sir. It's just he might have some ideas.'

'Well, you'd better ask him soon because he's not going to be here long,' said Mason maliciously.

'Oh, sir?'

'He's retiring,' said Group Captain Withers waving the matter away.

'I see. Well, I suppose he would be. He's getting on. Been up here years, hasn't he? Before all the houses were put up or all these people lived around here. I've always thought he was here first and they built everything around him. Grand old chap.'

He did not seem to be looking at either of the other men, so the embarrassment and annoyance that flew about their faces missed him. He got up slowly in the unique manner of disappointed policemen everywhere and shook hands with quiet finality first with Mauler Mason and then the Group Captain, as though he could not reasonably expect anything further from the investigation. 'If Chummy returns, sir, then you know . . .'

'Chummy? Who's Chummy?' asked Mason blindly.

The sergeant appeared surprised. 'Chummy? The criminal, the suspect. It's a police word, sir. We call them all Chummy.'

Withers humphed. 'Well, sergeant, if this particular Chummy does return, what chances have we of catching him next time?'

A shrug enveloped the sergeant's body like a wrinkled glove. 'I can't give guarantees. Not for anything. We're watching all the time, but we have our problems too. We've had three lollipop men away and we've had to put constables at the school crossings. And the car keeps playing up.'

'Somehow it all seems a long way from the police series we see on television,' commented Mason.

'It is, sir,' agreed the sergeant sadly. 'It is. If you cared to drop into the station one day you would perceive that a policeman's lot is the pursuit of the trivial. Lost property, lost children, men flashing themselves. Even the houses around here don't attract burglars. They're not established enough. We would welcome a nice murder, sir, just to break the monotony. Our Black Museum, at the moment, has only got the relics of suicides. That's the nearest we get to violent death. No killer to hunt. The victim and the killer are one. It's a story without an end, so you can't tie it up nice and neat.' He turned with a professional weariness to each man and shook his hand again; then, straightening his cap at the door as though he expected someone important to be outside, he went. A moment later they heard him trying to start the panda car.

'What a miserable so-and-so for a policeman,' said Mason.

'The rot's set in right through the country,' agreed Withers. 'They don't seem as enthusiastic as they did before the War.'

Mason glanced at the window. 'Here's Fowler,' he said. 'Will you tell him, or shall I?'

'We'll do it together,' answered Withers unsatisfactorily. 'Don't worry.'

'I'm not worried,' returned Mason sourly. 'I've got more to do than worry about an old man.'

Fowler knocked and came into the office at the secretary's call. He had obviously been home and washed his thin red face and combed the outcrops of hair about his ears. He was a little man, brown and red, but with a wise jauntiness about him like a small old tree.

'Ah, Fowler,' boomed Mason, who was even shorter than the green-keeper. 'Ah, Fowler, Fowler, Fowler . . .' He paused as though he had forgotten the next line. Then he said: 'Sit down, old chap.'

There was a smile arranged on Fowler's face, as though he were puzzled by the invitation but rather hoped it would turn out for the best.

'Fowler,' began Group Captain Withers when it seemed that nobody else was going to speak. 'Just how long have you been with Plummers Park Golf Club?'

'Many years, Captain,' said Fowler enigmatically. 'Years, years.'

'Yes, well we thought it would be about that. You don't seem to have even signed any sort of formal agreement, any contract, with the club when you came here, terms of employment and suchlike. We can't find anything in the records.'

Fowler lifted his contented eyes. 'No, there wasn't one, Captain. It was a gentleman's agreement.' He turned and smiled at both with confidence and pride as he said the final two words.

'We've been talking about your retirement,' said Mason bluntly. 'You're well over sixty now, aren't you?'

'Well over, sir. Seventy-four.'

'Good gracious! You look jolly well on it,' said Withers.

'It's the nice atmosphere around here, sir. That's what's done it.'

'Yes,' put in Mason, sharply again. 'Now – retirement.'

'I'd like to retire, Mr Mason,' said Fowler quickly, but moving his head slowly to follow the words like a ventriloquist's dummy. 'I've thought about it, I can tell you. I know how these old bones feel early on a frosty morning. But I feel it would be letting you down, sirs. Letting the club down . . .'

The two listeners adopted looks of pretence, surprise and pleasure as he spoke and were both ready to interrupt, but there was something dogged about Fowler's delivery, something that advised them he was not going to be interrupted. '. . . You see, Mr Mason, Captain Withers, I worried a lot about this. I knew I ought to retire because I've worked since I was twelve and a body needs a rest. But I'm worried about the drains.'

An unsurprising silence greeted this remark. Then Withers ventured: 'Drains, Fowler? What drains?'

'The drains of the course, Group Captain. The lot. All the system, all over the course. I'm the only one what knows where they all are. Every inch of them. And I know them by instinct, as you might say. Nobody else knows them. A little bit here and a little bit there, maybe. But I knows every pipe, every cock, every bend. I'm afraid if I went you'd have the course flooded in no time. One storm and that would be that. I couldn't have that on my conscience, now could I?'

Withers turned to see the suburban anger was bursting to get out of Mason's tight mouth. 'Oh come on, Fowler,' said the little man, controlling it. 'Surely there are plans of the drainage system.'

'Disappeared before the War, sir. Vanished. Never found. That's what's been worrying me. I'd draw a plan for you, sir, and then I could retire happy and contented, but I'm no hand at drawing and I wouldn't get it right. It's all done by instinct, now. Like playing the violin, I suppose. By touch, if you understand me.'

The two men understood him. He shook his head, for his sorrow seemed to have deepened. 'The only thing I can offer, sir, is to try and teach somebody younger the lay-out.' Their faces brightened but fell again when he added: 'A little bit at a time.'

'How long would that take?' asked Withers.

'Years, sir. I only hope I'm spared to pass on all the knowledge.'

'We hope so too, Fowler,' said the Group Captain, glancing sideways at the thoroughly depressed Mason. 'Don't we, Mr Mason?'

'Yes, oh yes,' nodded the club captain bitterly. 'Of course.'

If they thought Fowler had finished, he had not. 'But, as I say, Mister Secretary, I do feel the cold in the mornings once the year goes on. I thought the club might be kind enough to let me sort of half retire. I could be in what they call an advisory capacity, don't they? I could start a bit later and finish a bit earlier, if you see what I mean.'

They gave no reply, but he did not need one. He rose. 'And one more thing,' he smiled. The two officials backed involuntarily away from what might come next. Fowler said: 'That bloke what was being chased across the course tonight.'

'Yes, Fowler. What about him?' said Withers.

'I think he was a club member, sir. I didn't say as much to the policeman, but I think he was.'

'Good heavens! Whatever makes you say that?' exclaimed Mason.

'He jumped right over the new bunker on the twelfth, sir. And you just can't see that bunker when you're going towards it, from the back, like. It just looks like a hump of grass and there's a whole lot of little humps just there. But he *knew*, sir. He knew it was there, all right. He went over it like the favourite at Beechers Brook. And another thing. Even though everybody was on his trail he ran *round* the tenth and the thirteenth greens. It would have been a sight quicker to run across them. But his golfer's feelings, like his instincts was too strong. He ran round the putting surface and so did everybody else chasing him, except the police sergeant, who has got big boots I must say. That green will need watering and rolling tomorrow. But that gentleman, whoever he was and whatever he had been up to, was a sportsman, sir.

I'll say that for him.'

'Geoff.'

'Yes, darling?'

'Can you take your leg off mine for a minute? I've got cramp.'

'You're getting old. Do you want me to rub it for you?'

'Yes, would you?' said Ena.

He reached below the motel sheets and smiled into her eyes as he played his hands into the tightened muscle of the leg until it was soft again.

'All right now?' he asked.

'Yes, thanks. That's better. It felt very nice.'

'It felt all right for me too.'

They were naked and face to face in the impersonal bed. The curtains cut out the afternoon light and she had the sheet pulled almost over her head like a veil. Her face and her shoulders and the mounds of her breasts looked luminous.

'Here we are again,' she smiled sadly. 'These motel bills must cost you a fortune.'

'We have had to postpone the new fitted carpet for the lounge,' Geoff grinned. 'Perhaps we could have wall-to-wall motel bills instead.'

'Poor Cynthia,' she said.

'Oh, don't start "poor Cynthia-ing" again,' he pleaded. 'Nor "poor Simonizing". We're here to enjoy ourselves.'

'But *why* do we do it?' she insisted softly. 'Why do we creep away and have sex and then go back with a big innocent smile?'

'Why? Christ, trust a woman. Because we like it. I like it, and you like it, and our lives would be empty without it. That's why.'

'Your emptiness and my emptiness,' she said thoughtfully. 'I suppose if you pour two lots of emptiness into a pool you still get an empty pool.'

'There are times when going to bed with you is like going to bed with *Old Moore's Almanac*,' he grumbled.

'I'm sorry, Geoff. It's just that I feel I would like to do other things with you – for you – for a change. You may laugh at this, but I'd like to go to the cinema together or bake a cake for you. Do you understand?'

'We are *not* spending our illicit afternoon making cakes,' he said firmly. 'Or at the pictures.'

Ena smiled and pushed her face and the top of her body to him. His went down to the full barrel of her breasts. She scratched his head. 'It's silly, I know. But this always seems so temporary. There's no conclusion with it.'

'There's a salesman I know,' sighed Geoff, 'an old boy, been in interior design for years, and he's fond of saying: "Geoff, my boy, never forget the four Ws – wine, wool, wood and women. There's nothing that tastes or feels like any of them." What he doesn't say is that the first three don't argue.'

'I'm not arguing,' she argued. 'I'm worried, that's all. I'm worried about you and me, you and Cynthia, me and Simon. What's to become of us?'

He kissed her anxiously. 'Do you remember that party the night we met? The leaf-sweeping party at the Reynolds.'

She giggled reluctantly. 'A leaf-sweeping party,' she mused. 'Have you ever heard anything like it? And you made me laugh when you said most of the women had ridden in on their own brooms.'

'A leaf-sweeping party,' repeated Geoff. 'Good old Plummers Park. We didn't worry too much about conclusions then, did we?'

'That wasn't the time to worry about them. We needed each other so badly.'

'Don't we still?'

'Yes, of course. I was really at a low when I saw you for the first time. I knew before we had spoken two sentences that we would be doing this. It's funny how all the things you say to each other then, clever or idiotic, all point down between your legs.' She sighed. 'I never told you then but it was my birthday three days before, and do you know what Simon had given me?'

'At a quick guess – an album of photographs of himself.'

She smiled tiredly. 'Not quite. He had set up a treasure trail. All over Watford and Stanmore and down to Northwood and Ruislip. You know, clues in little notes. It started from home and I had to follow up each clue on to the next one. They were in shops and pubs and even a book in the library. I thought it was very romantic and it took me two days and goodness knows how much in bus fares. And the prize was at the end of it in an electrical shop in Watford. It was an electro-vibro massager.'

Geoff whistled noisily under the bedclothes. 'What every woman wants for her birthday,' he said.

'He said it was to keep me in trim, as he put it, but the first night he wanted me to use it on him.' Suddenly to Geoffrey's astonishment she erupted into tears, sobbing and thrusting her head hard against his chest, her breasts banging against him as she sobbed. 'Oh, Geoff,' she cried hopelessly, 'I'm pregnant and he wants to move to Wimbledon.'

Geoffrey felt his breath tighten. He said nothing for a few moments, then eased her away and looked down into her rainy face. 'That could be a funny line in some plays,' he said. 'You're pregnant and you're moving to Wimbledon?'

Snivelling she nodded her head. 'It does sound a bit comic, doesn't it? she wept. 'But it doesn't seem like that to me.'

'It could be *my* baby,' he said.

'It could be. I got all careless with my pills, silly fool that I am. Those little bastards, they wriggle inside you so sneakily.'

'The human sperm does not know the meaning of sportsmanship,' said Geoffrey glumly. 'What are you going to do?'

'Move to Wimbledon and have a baby, I suppose,' she sniffed. 'Simon's been offered a promotion but it would mean moving down there. Unless you do something I'll have to go.'

'Unless *I* do something?'

She hesitated, then looked at him directly. They moved away

fractionally from each other because when they stared so closely it made
them go cross-eyed. 'Unless you and I put this on an honest basis and go
off together. You leave Cynthia and I'll leave Simon and we'll go
somewhere else and live together. Anywhere, New Zealand if you like.'

'New Zealand?' he whispered. 'This is getting serious.'

'It *is* serious,' she replied. 'I've told you how serious. Unless I get out
now there's going to be *no* getting out.'

'Wimbledon and motherhood,' murmured Geoffrey. 'A nasty
combination.'

'You're so sodding flippant about it.'

'I'm trying to be,' he said. 'It gives me time to think. God knows I
adore you. I look forward to these times we have together like mad. I
even thought we might be able to sneak a holiday together later on. But
. . . Christ, Ena, you *know* I've made one mistake. I've quit one marriage,
how can I do it again?'

'You've made *two* mistakes,' she pointed out. 'Otherwise we wouldn't
be lying naked in this room. What you're afraid of now is correcting the
second mistake. A third marriage is not a disgrace. The disgrace is being
unhappy in the second but still hanging on.'

'I'm afraid,' he said.

'I know,' she agreed softly. 'So am I. Bloody afraid. Can you imagine
what it would do to Simon?'

'I could make a rough guess,' he agreed miserably. He pulled her
warm body to him. 'I'm stunned,' he said. 'I can't think.'

'Do you want to make love now? she asked. 'I'd like to. It may be the
last time.'

He nodded and without another word they closed to each other in the
dark beneath the sheet. Afterwards they lay in silence until eventually
she said: 'I'd have an abortion if you were worried about the baby.' She
began to cry again and turning to him said: 'Oh, Geoff, I love you so. It's
not fair, is it? Nothing's arranged properly in this life.'

No, he thought, it isn't.

CHAPTER THIRTEEN

Thursday 18 July was an important and dramatic day for two members
of the Plummers Park community: it was the day Sarah Burville had her
prizes and the day Herbie Futter had his heart attack.

The prize-giving happened first. The summer-ginghamed girls of the
Grammar School scraped chairs and giggled in rows, watching carefully
the sunshine boxed in the big windows of the school hall, as though they

feared it was about to vanish forever. In two days they would be released for the holidays. Parents and other visitors were accommodated in the rearmost ranks. The governors, staff and select visitors were ranged in a wide morose arc across the stage like a large and losing football team. The Bishop was there, wrapped in thought and gaiters, and so too was the Reverend Boon, banished to the extreme wing and, to his discomfiture, placed next to Miss Jankin, the headmistress of the Plummers Park Primary School.

'Ah,' whispered the vicar as though it were some rude secret. 'I see from the programme, Miss Jankin, that we are to have some songs from the Elfin Choir of the Plummers Park Primary School.'

'They're hideous,' sniffed Miss Jankin at once. 'Unreservedly hideous.'

'Oh dear. I would have thought you'd have been rather proud of them.'

'Mister Boon, I have told you on a previous occasion how I feel about my school. Almost every activity, apart from hometime and the blessed breaking-up for the holidays, fills me with dismay and not infrequently disgust.'

'But you're so uncharitable,' he complained.

'Before you speak of charity, vicar, wait until you've heard the Plummers Park Elfin Choir. There ought to be a registered charity for schoolteachers who have to suffer like this. Miss Simister – known, not undeservedly, as Miss Sinister in the school – who conducts them is not only excessively furtive, she's deaf as well.'

'But I understand they have gained a certain amount of popularity in this district,' argued the vicar unhappily.

'Notoriety,' Miss Jankin grimly amended. 'They had them up at the old folks home to complete the misery of the inmates last Christmas. The matron at the general hospital wisely curtailed their concert there to prevent the further spread of gloom and despondency.'

'Surely you exaggerate.'

'Just wait. You've never heard such a lot of tuneless little swines. Not that they're completely without entertainment value. Jason Farley, a child who far from hunting for a golden fleece will be fleeced himself regularly throughout life, sometimes provides a diverting moment.'

'Oh good. What does he do?'

'Wets himself,' said the headmistress uncompromisingly.

'Miss Jankin!'

'Straight up. He doesn't always do it, but he mostly does. He's what you could call an unknown quantity. He's left his indelible stain on half the platforms and stages in Hertfordshire.'

The Reverend Boon rolled his eyes miserably. Miss Jankin said with her nasty eagerness: 'Here they come now. I think Miss Simister has encouraged Jason to pee during the songs rather than between them so that it's a bit less obvious. You can't actually *hear* him doing it anyway.'

'I'm glad, I'm glad,' nodded the vicar haplessly. Then: 'I must say they look very sweet.'

Miss Jankin snorted, but her neighbour joined enthusiastically in the applause for the fifteen small children who now clopped on to the stage. The motherhood barely latent in the girls in the audience burst out and there were sighs and fond eyes as the Elfin Choir, dressed in green crêpe-paper costumes with pointed hats framing their infant expressions, formed a half-circle.

Mrs Mappin, the headmistress of the Grammar School, a steady-looking woman in a pinstriped suit, strode out to the front of the platform on resounding shoes and announced: 'My Lord Bishop, Councillors, Governors, Ladies and Gentlemen, girls. To start off our annual prize-giving this year we have the Elfin Choir from Plummers Park Primary School, and I think you will agree, very pretty little boys and girls they look.' There was applause for this compliment, and the choir stood moon-faced, simpering, holding hands apprehensively and badly wanting to remember the first song.

Mrs Mappin continued: 'With their choir-mistress Miss Simister at the piano they will sing three or four songs for us. Miss Simister has asked me to explain that unfortunately she has suffered an unfortunate accident to two of her fingers which are I see encased in sticking plaster.'

The dairymaid Miss Simister held up the two fingers, bound so excessively in plaster that they resembled toffee-apples, to the assembly in a sort of indomitable victory-sign. Miss Jankin sighed. 'Silly bitch left them on the keyboard and little Bertie Ringling slammed the lid down on them.' Mr Boon, defeated now, nodded.

Mrs Mappin continued: 'So I am sure you will understand that the piano accompaniment might not be all that it usually is. We have offered to provide an accompanist, but Miss Simister and her Elfin Choir are such a team that they feel they would rather persevere even under these difficulties.'

There was further applause at this news. As it died and the children stiffened themselves for the attack on the first song, Miss Jankin whispered: 'I hope you're ready for this, vicar.'

The performance started badly even by the low standards of the Elfin Choir. Miss Simister's two toffee-apple fingers hit the notes like the hammers of a xylophone player, each blow causing her to jump with pain, and each jump lifted her a few inches from her stool in the manner of a rider mounted on a difficult pony. The children, never over-confident, stumbled over the first few bars of 'Sumer is icumen in', started again, muffed it again, re-started, and eventually trampled through it in great confusion and haste.

The applause was more sympathetic than polite.

'That was written by a monk, you know, in the thirteenth century,' whispered Mr Boon informatively.

'May he return and haunt them,' grunted Miss Jankin.

There followed the choir's decimated version of 'Linden Lea', during which Miss Simister chose to continually remind the audience of her disability by holding up her two plastered fingers at them whenever she could, a sort of 'look, one-handed' sign, causing the girls in the audience to blush and snigger. Then appropriately in the next song, 'The Rain It Raineth Every Day', the risky Jason Farley wet himself spectacularly, a spreading emerald patch appearing on the front of his paper elfin trousers, ever widening, until the paper itself sagged and parted and eventually rolled and fell about the small boy's knees, leaving him staring down in disbelief. The occurrence fortunately came at the end of the song and the near hysterical applause covered both the mishap and the reaction to it.

The small choir was led off the stage, and their mistress did a further innocent V-sign as she was about to disappear into the wings. Miss Jankin dried her eyes on the vicar's shoulder. 'My God, that was their best ever, vicar. I've never seen it all happen at once before. The way that silly cow kept lifting her fingers!' The heaving headmistress attempted to illustrate her point by thrusting her own two middle fingers up until the Reverend Boon almost forcibly restrained her.

He had never been so angry. He feared the Bishop might have caught a glimpse of those uplifted fingers and would think that their owner was something to do with him. 'I really don't know, Miss Jankin,' he gritted, his head low, 'why you ever became a schoolteacher at all. It does *not* appear to be your vocation.'

She was un-angry, unruffled. She laid a comradely hand on his shoulder. 'You don't seem to be much cop as a vicar, not to me,' she said. 'I bet you only went into the Church in a fit of devilment.'

The Reverend Boon's indignant retort was snuffed by the rising once again of Mrs Mappin. She straightened the skirt of her pinstripe and banged her boot on the stage for silence among the girls.

'I am sure that we would all like to thank Miss Simister and the Elfin Choir for er . . . performing here this afternoon,' she said doggedly. 'And to let them know that we appreciate the various difficulties under which they were working.' She came to an almost military attention on the stage and then opened one leg like the prop of an old-fashioned blackboard, thumping her foot down noisily.

She then introduced the Bishop, who gave a condensed lecture on Life, his voice flapping big and slow around the hall like the circular flight of a large tired bird. The Bishop ended with a joke he imagined he had heard when he had tuned in by mistake to a disc-jockey programme one morning. It was meaningless to him but he thought it sounded as though it might be funny because the disc jockey laughed a lot. So he repeated it as well as he could remember, but at the end he knew he had been under some misapprehension, for the entire young audience remained gazing at him with bored respect with not an inch of a smile at the corner of any mouth. He blinked with disappointment, thought about repeating the final line in case nobody had heard, gave it up, treated them to a quick blessing and sat down.

Mrs Mappin stood again and said how marvellous it was to have a bishop who understood young people and their world. She went on to summarize the school year and, finally, announced: 'We have had this year a pupil who has been more than merely outstanding. Never in my experience as a teacher and as a head have I come across a girl with such a unique academic ability – and, I might say, a very modest and pleasant nature to go with it. Everyone will know that I am talking of Sarah Burville.'

There was huge applause at the name, and shouts from the girls in all the rows. Sarah sat crimson-faced among her classmates while they clapped.

'I would hesitate to say that Sarah has "hogged" all the prizes, for hogging is very far from her nature. I think she is as popular with her classmates as she is with the staff. A rare combination, if I may say so. She has not had any undue educational advantages, just an outstanding ability and a modesty which makes her work as hard as anyone in this school. I think it is indicative of her attitude to school and life in general that although she has never claimed to be more than proficient on the sports field, she represented the school at both tennis and swimming this year and was a member of the team which won the county relay at the swimming gala last month.'

She paused and looked across the heads of the six hundred girls. 'I know I am embarrassing Sarah. I can see it from here.' The girls laughed and looked round. 'To save her the further embarrassment of having to troop up to this platform half a dozen times to collect her prizes I propose to read out the list and, if Sarah can carry them all at once, she can come and get them all at once – or in a couple of journeys anyway.'

Laughter came readily from the hall. The guests on the platform nodded and beamed. Andrew arrived at the school at that moment. He had been delayed in the office and had telephoned Audrey to say he would join her at the prize-giving.

He had walked into the front lobby of the school when a car pulled up raggedly outside, and behind him, through the main door, staggered Mrs Burville, sodden drunk and wearing her wartime ATS uniform from which she burst and bloated at every button. He saw her as she clattered against the door and hung on to it with one faltering hand while covering her face with the other. Andrew stared uncomprehendingly. The khaki tunic was bulging and the buttons, bright with Brasso, strained. Her skirt was so tight it forced her middle-aged knees together so that she could hardly hobble, and her peaked cap was smashed on her head like some comic headgear. Andrew moved towards her, his hands going out ineffectually in case she should fall.

'Don't you touch me, you smug bugger!' she shouted. Her hand came away from her face and he saw that it was almost purple, the bitter red eyes sunk so deep it was as though they were looking from behind a lurid carnival mask.

'Mrs Burville, Mrs Burville,' he pleaded helplessly.

'They didn't tell me!' she cried. 'They're fucking well ashamed of me. I had to read it in the paper. My own girl, my Sarah, and even she didn't tell me. God help me, I'll show them who's her mother! It's me! I'm her mother . . .'

Andrew attempted to catch hold of her. But with surprising swiftness she had taken a large silver sports cup from its display-shelf in the lobby and held it above her head like a weapon. 'Let me go by or I'll smash this on your bloody head,' she swore. 'You can't understand. Get out of my way!'

He still made the attempt. Instead of striking him with the cup she flung it furiously. He ducked but it bounced on his shoulder and smashed through the glass door of a display cabinet. That was the first those inside heard.

She went through the gap he had left like a rugby three-quarter, head down. She burst through the double swing-doors of the school assembly hall just as her daughter stood on the stage, books in her arms and about to receive another from the headmistress. Mrs Mappin was saying: 'And yet another First Prize – this for English Literature . . .'

'Sarah! Sarah!' Mrs Burville screeched from the back of the hall. Everybody looked. Mrs Burville was hanging there by one of the brass handles, legs askew all over the polished floor, the ridiculous ATS shoes toes up, skirt torn halfway down her hip, tunic like a lumpy bag, hat fallen backwards, held by a pin, hair wet over red drunken face.

'My Sarah!' she squealed again. 'You di'n tell me. I *wanted* to come! I *wanted* to come!'

'Oh, God,' said the girl, ashen-faced on the platform. 'Oh no, God.'

'Your mother,' said the headmistress quietly.

'Yes, my mother,' said the girl, speaking as though to emptiness. 'She's ill.' The prizes began toppling from her hands on to the platform. She looked through icy tears to see the nightmare woman advancing knock-kneed, arms flailing, down the polished centre aisle, crying like a ghost. Nobody in the hall moved.

Sarah, calmly now putting the rest of the books at her feet, walked down the steps from the stage and advanced towards the sliding woman. They faced each other for a moment, like the two women they were, tears and anger and pity on the girl's face; blank guilt, panic, on the countenance of her mother. 'Come on, mum,' said Sarah. 'It's over. I'll take you home.'

She put her young arm round the heaving shoulders and turned her mother around to face the door. Turning back momentarily to the platform where the headmistress and the others remained like a frieze, she called: 'She's not at all well.'

They stumbled together to the door. The abject Andrew was there, head down, to open it for them and they went out towards the playground sunshine.

No one in the hall moved. Some of the girls and some of the mothers were crying. Mrs Mappin hesitated, then moved to the front of the stage. 'As an emergency measure,' she announced trying to keep her voice straight, 'I am going to ask for another song from the Elfin Choir.'

'Christ, Jesus,' muttered Miss Jankin into her hands. 'Haven't we had enough suffering for one afternoon?'

Harry Solkiss and Gerry Scattergood, the tall, thin, loping man and the broad, striding man, adapting their different paces, walked from The Case Is Altered. It was seven o'clock. Most of the men were home by now and Plummers Park had its familiar air of evening hollowness.

'Don't often see you having a drink without your wife,' said Gerry. 'Can't ever remember seeing one of you without the other, come to think of it.'

'You're correct,' agreed the American dolefully. 'Jeanie and I are real close. In fact I was having that drink to kick up my courage. I have to break something to her.'

Gerry nodded incuriously. 'Telling women things can be very difficult,' he said philosphically. 'There's a lot they don't want to know.'

'Sure. This is going to be tough. Hell, it is. Every day I bus to the base and every night I come home and it's cosy, and up till now that's been fine with me. But they've offered me a job flying around, going to Paris and Rome and places like that, maybe four or five times a month.'

'That sounds great,' nodded Gerry. 'But you don't think she's going to be very sweet on it?'

'I know she won't. We've seen each other every day since we married and I've never slept away from my own bed and my own wife. It's going to come hard.'

'And she'll be thinking that you're having a great time with the birds in Paris while she's worrying at home.'

The boyish American grimaced. 'Not me,' he said seriously. 'I wouldn't do *anything* like that. But she'll sure worry in case I do.'

'Women do worry,' nodded Gerry understandingly. 'And a lot of them in Plummers Park have good reason. Don't believe in it, myself, all this playing around. I suppose selling contraceptives as I do, you get to the basics, if you know what I mean, behind all the romantic mush. In the end it boils down to the same bits meeting the same bits. It don't matter if they're film stars or poor people or a couple of railway trucks, they all couple up in more or less the same way.'

'Is there a deal of it in this neighbourhood? Playing around, I mean.'

'A fair amount. They're all at the stage when they're looking around to see what they might have missed first time.'

'You mean wife-swopping?'

Gerry considered it but shook his head. 'I doubt it. Not your direct *blatant* swop. They have a nibble here and a nibble there but nothing is *organized*, if you see what I mean. Come to think of it that's the one thing they haven't been able to organize around here. Some of the husbands wouldn't mind another man's wife in their bed, but it would upset them to see her cooking the breakfast. See what I mean?'

'I get it. We have these problems at home too, in Arizona,' said Harry anxious, as ever, to politely spread the guilt. 'Some of the girls there get wed at fifteen and by the time they're twenty they're rooting around like little pigs.'

'Maybe that's better,' said Gerry, considering it. 'If you get married at fifteen then at least you're still young enough for another start at twenty. Here, when they start itching, it's generally getting too late to scratch.

I'm very settled, myself, like I say; my job keeps my feet on the ground and off the bed. Mind, I *have* buggered about. In the past. When I first got married I was a real tearaway. But I was selling baked beans then. I had a different philosophy, a different outlook on life. One night I went out on the razzle and I woke up next morning stark bollock naked with this terrible ugly bird, also stripped, in the back seat of my car. I couldn't remember anything about the night before, not even her. We were parked right outside a bloody railway station too and there were hundreds of people going to work and gaping in at us through the window. That just about cured me, I can tell you.'

'I imagine,' said Harry, who had begun to stare with disbelief at the tale. He shook his head. 'And to think, back home people really believe that all the British do is to sit weaving in the fog.'

Halfway up Risingfield they heard the violent howling of the dogs. 'Jesus,' said Gerry, hurrying his pace. 'That sounds bad. It's old Futter being ambushed again.'

He began to run, and the long lean Harry ran easily beside him. 'That's the old guy who always gets the dogs at him?' he asked.

'He's a taxidermist and they go for the smell.' Gerry did not take long to pant and he was puffing heavily by the time they reached the privet hedge corner of Risingfield and Upmeadow. The dogs – a dozen of them were in the road – were still baying and barking, but were backing away from the swinging brooms of Mrs Futter and Audrey Maiby. Gerry's wife Min was running up the road, unravelling the garden hose like an auxiliary fireman as she ran. Andrew Maiby was kneeling over the rumpled figure of Herbie Futter.

'Blimey, they've got him this time,' said Gerry running forward. He and Harry went in among the dogs with boots and shouts and the pack eventually retreated to the far side of the road. People were coming from their houses and looking from their windows. The old taxidermist looked as though he had been assassinated, lying mouth open to the clear blue evening sky. Mrs Futter knelt on the opposite side to Andrew and began to sway and weep. Andrew looked up and saw Gerry. 'He's out cold,' he said urgently. 'I can't get any response.'

Harry Solkiss kneeled down. 'I know a few things,' he said. 'But I guess what he needs is a doctor.'

'He's been called,' said Andrew. 'But he's got to come from Watford. Why the hell we haven't got a doctor here, I don't know.'

Harry began massaging the old man's heart. Someone brought out a bright aluminium sun-bed and they eased him on to the ironically vivid canvas and carried him to his house, with Harry massaging on one side and Mrs Futter howling on the other.

They took the sagging old man to his house. Nobody in the neighbourhood had ever been inside that house, and now as they carried the improvised stretcher over the threshold their sense of amazement all but overtook their concern for Herbie. For within the uncompromising square Plummers Park walls was a small, ornate palace, a place of rich carpets, chairs with curly backs and cabriole legs.

'On the table,' said Harry ogling around. Then he caught Andrew's glance and turned and saw the exquisite ovalled wood and fine shining surface of the Regency table, with a gigantic candelabra hanging above it, the two pieces taking up almost the entire space of the modest modern room.

'Maybe not,' amended Gerry.

'On the table,' cried Mrs Futter. 'He likes that table.'

They put him on the rare wood, his quaint button-boots sticking out like the hands of a clock, his old-fashioned trousers spread pathetically, his shirt open to the scraggy neck, and Harry sweating as he continued to try and bring some life to the heart.

'Where's that sodding doctor?' cursed Andrew impotently. 'You'd think it was miles.'

'It *is* miles,' said Gerry. 'You ought to get your paper on to that one. We're like a flaming outpost of Empire here.'

As though he had been waiting for the right moment Herbie opened his eyes. He stared around at the anxious faces of his neighbours and reached out his uncertain hand for his trembling wife. 'Bludda fucken dogs,' he said to Andrew. He closed his eyes again. Audrey said, 'He'll be all right,' and took Mrs Futter hunched across the road.

Andrew, Gerry and Harry stood awkwardly around the prostrate old Jew. 'I'll get a mirror,' said Gerry, 'to see if he's breathing.'

He went to the bathroom and returned with a small round mirror. He held it in front of the old man's mouth but no breath showed. At that moment the doctor came in. 'Watch he doesn't wake up and see himself,' he observed casually. 'He looks terrible.' He bent and examined the old man. 'He's gone,' he said. 'Dead.'

'What do we do now?' Andrew asked the doctor. It suddenly came to him that very few of them had known any dealings with death. Plummers Park had not reached the age when people died within their houses.

'Well, you can't leave him on that table for a start,' said the doctor. 'Not a Regency table. It's like Blenheim Palace in here, isn't it?'

Andrew was about to make some angry rejoinder when he caught the doctor's eyes and saw that he *did* know something about death. Instead he said: 'He'd better go to his bedroom, I suppose.'

'That's more usual than leaving him on the dining-room table,' said the doctor. 'Somebody will look after his wife, won't they?'

'My wife will,' said Andrew. 'She's taken her across to my place.'

'In the bedroom then,' said the doctor. 'You take the other end. He's only a little one.'

Herbie was like a fragile shell. They carried him easily up the stairs and pushed open the first door. 'That's not it,' said the doctor. 'That's a spare room.' He hesitated at the door and said: 'Good God, there's a stuffed dog in there.'

They put Herbie in the next room, and with some brief embarrassment arranged him on the bed as though they were making him comfortable.

'There,' said the doctor as if he were satisfied with some good task.

'He'll be all right there.' He stood back and regarded the dead Herbie. 'Just to think,' he muttered almost to himself, 'whatever we do in this life, we all end up on our backs, staring into space.'

Andrew immediately thought of Bessie. He nodded with brief bitterness and they left the room. He stopped at the first door they had opened and, glancing at the doctor's back retreating down the stairs, pushed it quietly. It opened. There in the middle of the floor was the big black dog from Hedgerows, dead, stuffed and stitched, standing quite elegantly, feet apart, head raised, vacancy shining from its brown glass eyes. Herbie Futter's revenge! Andrew's shock was more than he had felt about Herbie's death. His face paled. He closed the door and went down after the doctor. At the front door, red from his bike, was the Reverend Boon.

'I heard,' he said breathlessly. 'I heard from Mrs Blossom-Smith on the phone. Someone's had a heart attack. Can I be of some help?'

'He's dead,' said Andrew simply. He took hold of the clergyman's arm. 'He's not only dead, but he's Jewish. Or was. Is someone still Jewish when they're dead? I suppose they are.'

'Oh dear,' said the vicar. 'What a shame. What a great shame.'

He shrugged, mounted his bicycle, and free-wheeled disconsolately down the hill. Andrew watched him go. 'You're another one who doesn't have any luck,' he said aloud.

CHAPTER FOURTEEN

There were rooks in the churchyard and cars in the street. Bessie sat eating her egg sandwiches, and Andrew, after carefully surveying the lunch-time people on the grass, sat beside her. They talked, and he ate one of her sandwiches. He was worried about her. He said, suddenly: 'Do you have any plans?'

'You know I'm working this afternoon,' she answered in her shopgirl way: 'I can't just buzz off when I like. Not like you. I wonder how you manage it, really. Don't they ever ask you where you're going or what you're up to?'

'I tell them I'm making inquiries,' he said blandly. 'General calls and inquiries. That's how I put it on my expenses.'

'Christ, you get expenses for it as well!'

'I *have* to charge expenses, otherwise they'd think I wasn't doing anything, wouldn't they? Anyway, I didn't mean this afternoon, I meant generally. You know, in the future.'

'I never look to it much,' she said. She bit crudely into an egg sandwich and left a tail of crust hanging out of her mouth which was gradually munched inside. The next sentence came through a mouthful of bread. 'I get up in the morning and I go to bed at night. Sometimes I see you and sometimes I don't.'

'That's not much of a life for a young woman,' he said.

She examined him suspiciously. 'What're you trying to get at, Andrew?' she said. 'You want me to "make something of my life" do you? Sounds just like my teacher at school. Make something of your life, plan your life, construct your life, she used to say. You'd think it was a bleeding skyscraper. I just let it happen.'

Andrew sighed. She had given him a bit of her sandwich, tearing it off and handing it to him without saying anything. He shared his portion with some path sparrows. 'I get worried about you, that's all,' he said. 'I feel, well, in a way I feel responsible for you.'

'I'm not up the spout if that's what you're getting at,' she said bluntly. 'That's why I couldn't go to bed with you last week. I'm on the pill, in good nick, and everything's working.'

'Not that,' he said. 'Just generally. I ought to be ashamed of myself really, having an affair with someone your age. Taking advantage.'

'Cradle snatching,' she grinned.

'That's right. We used to call it that too.'

'When you lived in *your* council house?' she said mockingly.

'That's correct,' he said hardening. 'When I lived in *my* council house. I told you before you're not the only one who's had the privilege, you know.'

'But I've got the privilege *now*,' she smiled, annoying him. 'I like to see you wriggle.'

'Thanks, I thought you might.'

'Don't let's fight,' she said. 'I've got to be back in ten minutes.' She became quiet, sitting there with one egg sandwich left in its wrapping on her lap. She looked at it, curled up her nose and said: 'Do you want the last one, Andrew?'

'No thanks, Bess,' he said.

She looked straight ahead across the churchyard over the heads of the people on the summer town grass. 'You don't have to worry about me, Andrew,' she said. 'I'm having a good time. And you don't have to worry about us, neither. When the bus stops, I'll know where to get off.'

'I didn't mean anything like that,' he protested.

She bent, touched his shoulder, and said gently: 'I've got to push off. I'll be late back. Is Wednesday all right?'

He looked at her, studied her face. 'I'm very lucky, you know,' he said.

'I know you are,' she replied simply. 'Is it all right?'

'Yes, I'm fixing something.'

Andrew waited until everybody but Burton, the editor, and the office cleaner had gone home. He could see Burton roving behind the frosted panes of his room and the cleaner rummaging among the untidy papers at the far end of the editorial room. He picked up the telephone: 'Will you get me County Hall at Hertford please,' he asked the operator. 'Mr Culler.'

She called him back. 'Mr Culler on the line.'

'Thanks. Hello, Dick, Andrew Maiby.'

'Andrew! Nice to hear you. What secrets can I tell you?'

'No secrets, this time, Dick. Thanks for the thing about the school for maladjusted kids, by the way. I was able to give them the news – and the reason about the environment – just as they were starting a collection for protest expenses.'

'Ha! A most opportune moment, I'd say.'

'It was. You ought to have seen the looks on their faces. The trouble was that when I told them that the environment was not considered to be right for the children, some of them thought it was a compliment to *them*!'

'God, you must live among a fine bunch.'

'No, I wouldn't blame them, not altogether,' said Andrew. 'I'm one of them, I suppose. There's no villains. But they've got something, a house and a few possessions, and they get afraid they'll lose them, that's all. I know how they feel.'

He could almost hear the other man nodding. 'Maybe you're right,' he replied. 'We all get like it. I can't sleep at nights because somebody leaves a bicycle in the hall downstairs. It annoys me. I gnash my teeth and tell myself it lowers the standard of the place.'

'That's what I wanted to ask you about. Not the bike, your flat.'

'What about it?'

'When I come up to the county council meeting on Wednesday, do you think I could borrow it for an hour or so.'

He heard the breathing silence at the other end. Then, eventually: 'You old devil. What are you up to? Have you met up with that marvellous girl again?'

'No. It's not her.'

'You old devil,' Culler said again. He did not sound enthusiastic. 'But I take it I'm right in a general sort of way?'

'Yes,' said Andrew uneasily. 'I could say I wanted to borrow the flat to read the council minutes, but you wouldn't believe me. Yes, you're right in a general sort of way.'

'I wish I could operate like you operate,' said Culler without admiration in his voice.

'You *are* single,' Andrew pointed out. 'Adultery is the *prerogative* of the married man.'

'And married woman.'

'Yes, and her. Them.'

There was another pause. Andrew could tell he did not like doing it. Then he said: 'Yes, you can have the flat, Andrew. I'll be in the council chamber with my boss, so I'll pass the key to you beforehand. Without knowing any more about it than I do now, I'd say it was a better way of passing the afternoon than listening to some of the fatuous duffers who'll be doing their usual spouting at the council.'

'Thanks. I'll leave it tidy. There's no point in my being in the council chamber all the time, anyway, as you know. I'm only interested in the stuff that affects my local area, and that's right at the end of the meeting by the look of the agenda. I'll get one of the other press boys to give me a ring when it looks like coming up.'

'Such cunning. You've got it all planned.'

'Yes, it sounds like that, doesn't it? Dick, you don't mind, do you?'

'No. It's all right.'

'You don't sound very enthusiastic.'

'Well, it's not me that's having it, is it? I shall think of you when I'm pressed up against some fat borough planning officer on Wednesday.'

'I'm sorry. It's all right then?'

'Yes, Andrew. I said so.'

'Good. Thanks very much.'

'You're welcome. Have a good time.'

'Blimey,' said Bessie. 'We do get some changes of scenery, don't we. I'm never looking up at the same ceiling twice.'

'Don't grumble,' said Andrew. 'You refuse to go to a hotel.'

'No, I told you. There's something nasty about going to hotels. It's immoral.'

Andrew groaned. 'Sometimes I lose track of your arguments, Bess. We've got to have somewhere. It was just our bad luck that barge catching fire and sinking like that.'

'We must have been hot stuff,' she laughed. She was undressing casually, her eyes drifting around the room. 'Who is this bloke anyway, the one what has this place?'

Andrew was sitting on the edge of the bed watching for the moment when she took away her brassière and those pretty nipples blinked in the light. He had not undressed. He said: 'He's an old friend. He works for the county council.'

'Does he know what we are going to do here?'

'Well, he knew I didn't want to lie down because of a headache, but he didn't ask too many questions.'

'But what about your work? You supposed to be at this meeting.'

'You're always going on about my work,' said Andrew. 'You worry about it more than I do.'

'Well, I worry about *you*,' she said simply. 'I worry about your job in case you should get into trouble, not doing it. Screwing me instead.'

Andrew sighed. 'Bess, it's all arranged, so don't worry. I will not miss a county council scoop. They'll be gassing for a couple of hours before they reach anything that concerns me. I've fixed for one of the other reporters to give me a ring from the press room when the time comes.'

'You've got it all nice and planned,' she said. 'All for me.'

'All for me too,' he said. She was nude now and she lay back with ease and familiarity on the double bed. But there was a remoteness about her too, as if she were only posing. She spread her feet apart but her knees moved towards each other to form a steeple and she closed her eyes as though she were sunbathing. Andrew, remote too, like a voyeur, in his clothes, sat on the side of the bed and eventually put his hand on the upturned bowl of her stomach, then moved it down and rubbed his fingers gently into her hump of hair and against the angles and flats of her bent legs. She opened her eyes. 'What's the bloke like,' she said, 'what lives here?'

'He's a nice chap. About twenty-eight and he's not married. He works in the development department.'

'Building houses and things,' she said.

'Yes, sort of.'

'He had some nice records in the other room, on the player,' she mused. 'What's those cups for on top of the wardrobe? For sex?'

'For squash, I imagine,' said Andrew. 'He plays squash.'

'So do we,' she said, looking at him quickly to see if he approved of her joke. 'Are you doing it with your shirt on today?'

He stood and began to undress. She watched him, her hands going behind her head and her small breasts flattening out with the movement. 'Do you reckon he's had lots of women on this bed?' she asked suddenly.

'Possibly. I don't know. He's a bit of a quiet, thoughtful type.'

'That didn't stop you,' she pointed out easily. She looked around again. 'It's funny somebody from the council living here and having pop records and things, cups and all that, because when you get letters from them they don't seem human, do they?'

'Well, he is,' said Andrew naked now, easing himself on to the bed, crouching beside her. 'And so am I.'

'I can see that,' she said. As though with a sudden idea she opened her mouth and put it low to him, hanging on madly, cradling him beneath, moving him in and out like a piston. She was a girl full of impulses. Andrew's head dropped forward with the acute sensations she gave him so that his forehead rested against the fine skin of her back. They bent, curved into each other, fitting together like the figures in a Japanese ivory carving. He felt as though she was drawing his whole being away through a straw. His teeth gritted and he said tensely: 'Stop it, Bess, no more now.'

Not for the first time he thought what a remarkable girl she was. She pulled away from him, laughed up at him wet-lipped and wicked, and then eased herself back on the bed. 'If we packed up early,' she said in her joking, matter-of-fact way, 'we could go out and do some sightseeing. I wouldn't mind having a look around Hertford. I don't see many old towns. Do you think people in hundreds of years, like, will walk around where we live and think how interesting it is?'

'I can't see the houses on my side staying up that long,' said Andrew.

'Ours will,' she said with confident pride. 'They'll be up. They're not fancy like yours, and they have to be strong because council house people fight and have lots of kids.'

'That sounds like a contradiction in terms, but I'm not sure.'

'What's that?'

'Well, people fighting but having lots of kids.'

'Oh, I get you. Well they do. They fight and they still have kids. Kids is not always to do with love, you know.'

'No, I think you're right.'

'I am, generally.'

'I think you're right there too.'

'Come on top,' she suggested.

'Will you want to be tanned today?'

'Ah, I thought you liked that. We'll have a bit of that later on. I hope these walls aren't too thin.'

'I don't expect they are.'

He embraced and kissed her and they rolled with ease to each other, her knees nudging his thighs, hips and groins locked, the points of her breasts rubbing his ribs, her face against his neck, his lips on her hair. They moved smoothly into and against each other and then, when they paused and lay for a while, she said: 'Did you notice something just now?'

'What should I have noticed?'

'When I said about the walls. I said "I hope they aren't thin" instead of *ain't*, or turning the words arse about face, like I usually do with you, so I don't need to say it at all.'

'You make me feel like Professor Higgins,' he said. He was still buried in her and had leaned forward against her again after their brief conversation, ready to recommence, when the telephone rang. Andrew cursed. 'It can't be,' he said. 'Not yet.'

'Pick it up,' she said. 'I can't stand it ringing.'

Andrew did. It was Audrey.

'Audrey!' he cried. Then croaked: 'Audrey.'

'Yes. *Andrew*, whatever's the matter?'

His eyes were bulging, his flesh was trembling, his erection had withered at breathtaking speed like a released balloon. Several croaks creaked from his throat. Bessie watched him with horror. He thought she was going to say something so he put his shaking hand across her mouth, very hard, until she wriggled from beneath it and retreated across the bed, silent and staring.

'N . . . noth . . . nothing's the matter, love. Nothing.'

'Where are you?'

'A flat,' he said aghast still. 'A friend's flat. I didn't feel too good so he let me come up here. Dick Culler. You don't know him.'

'You're ill? What's wrong?'

'Oh, I don't know.' He was steeling himself now, trying to force his voice into its proper groove, trying to think. 'I almost fainted at the council meeting. Something I had to eat, I expect.'

'Good God! You! You've never fainted in your life. And nobody said anything when I rang County Hall.'

'Oh. Oh, you rang there?'

'Yes, of course. Andrew what *is* the matter? You sound very strange. Very odd.'

'No, I'm all right, thanks, Audrey,' he said weakly. 'But I felt pretty bad and I went off to sleep and the phone woke me. You know how the phone scares you sometimes.'

He heard Bessie whisper behind him: 'And you can say that again.' He made frantic signals to her to keep quiet.

'What did you say?' asked Audrey. 'What was that?'

'Oh, wait a minute,' said Andrew feigning anger. 'I can't get my thoughts together. It was a surprise hearing you, that's all.' He feared suddenly that Bessie would remark on that too, but she didn't. She lay on her back, revolving her thumbs, a look of disgust and sadness on her face.

'Listen, Andrew Maiby,' said Audrey brusquely. 'Don't you get ratty with me. I rang the press room and somebody said you'd be at that number, so I rang. I don't understand why you sound so funny.'

'I told you, Audrey. I feel ill. I feel terrible.'

'Have you called a doctor?'

'No. No I haven't. If I rest for a bit I'll be all right and I'll make my way home. Why did you ring anyway, love? Anything urgent?'

'Fairly urgent,' she said. He could still hear the suspicion hissing around at the other end. 'I wouldn't have tried to get hold of you otherwise, would I? You'd think I was checking up on you.'

'Yes, of course. What was it?'

'About your birthday.'

'My birthday?' His incredulous voice sounded miles away from him. The phone was slippery in his hand. He glanced back at Bessie and saw she was lying like a corpse on the bed.

'Yes,' said Audrey, annoyance spiking the words. 'You have a birthday, don't you? And it's next week. You are thirty-seven, or don't you remember?'

'Of course I remember. Don't turn nasty on me. I'm not feeling up to it.'

'All right.' Her voice calmed, but he knew she was making an effort. 'It's just that I wanted to make sure we were definitely having the dinner party on Thursday – that's the actual day. Geoff and Cynthia have to know this afternoon because they've got to make some other arrangements right away. Do you want me to ask anyone in particular besides?'

'Anybody,' he replied still weakly. 'Gerry and Min. How about them?'

'You don't sound as if you care very much,' she retorted.

'Christ, I told you. I don't feel well, love.'

'All right. I won't ring again. You can get back to bed, or wherever you were.'

She rang off abruptly and he replaced the phone and lay sickly back on the bed. 'I don't feel well, love,' mimicked Bessie with disgust from alongside him. 'Oh dear, I do feel ill, oh dear, oh dear. Yuk, yuk, yuk.'

'What did you expect me to say?' he demanded. 'That I was here having it away with you?'

'Bloody 'ell,' she laughed sarcastically. 'I've never seen anybody so bleedin' scared. You looked like you'd seen your grandad's ghost.'

'I *was* scared,' he confessed miserably. 'I was so scared I still feel sick. Fancy picking up the phone and hearing her. She's never done that before.'

'She *knows* something,' said Bessie in a disinterested voice. 'She doesn't ring up with your birthday plans when you're supposed to be working and you're screwing instead. She's got the sniff on you, mate.'

'You're always so poetic,' he muttered.

'Well, whatever I am,' she turned and shouted at him, '*I'm not pathetic like you*! If you could have seen yourself writhing and crawling. If you'd turned around and told her to fuck off she'd have gone like a shot – *and* she'd have believed you. I know how a woman thinks.'

'I am not in the habit of telling my wife to fuck off!' he snarled.

'Ho, ho, listen to us. We don't use nasty common language like that on *our* side of the railway. Not to our lovely wives.'

He hit her suddenly and hard across the face. She jumped up from the bed, white-cheeked, with the red mark of his hand bright on the skin. He recoiled. 'Oh, Bess, I'm sorry! I'm sorry darling.'

'Bessie to you,' she said evenly. 'If anyone else had done that, Andrew Maiby, I'd have torn their bleeding eyes out. But I wouldn't like you to go home to your mummy all scratched now, would I?' She moved towards her clothes and began to dress quietly.

'Don't go, Bess, please don't,' he pleaded.

'You don't like wasting the room,' she jeered. 'Well, mister, I don't like being knocked about. Not even by somebody better-class than me.' She paused, standing in her pants with her bra in her hand. 'I might as well tell you something right now,' she continued bitterly. '*I* stopped that bit about my grandad in court getting into the papers. *I* went across and cheered up that silly old bugger who's a magistrate – the one who's got all the bloody cornflakes in his pocket.'

'You? Mr Brownlow. You went to see him?'

'That's right. He seemed a decent sort so I went to see him and let him put his arm around me and pat my arse a few times and he promised to see if he could get it kept out of both papers. He said he used to be mayor and he could pull some strings. And he did.'

'Jesus Christ, you're amazing.'

'I thought you were a bit different too,' she said sadly. 'I fancied you from the first minute because you looked different and dependable and nice. I'm trying not to cry. I didn't want to take you away from your wife. I just wanted to have you to myself a bit now and again. I thought that would be something decent anyway. Now you've hit me. Any fool can hit me.' She put her face in her hands and sat on the bedside chair, still naked to the waist, bent forward into her palms. When she looked up she was red about the eyes but there were no tears.

'Come back, Bess. Come back to bed. I'm sorry. I wouldn't do that again.'

'You're not going to get the bloody chance,' she said bluntly. 'This is the last time we're doing this.'

'But, for God's sake . . .'

'I'm getting married,' she said airily.

'Married! You're not! You're lying!'

'No I'm not lying,' she said. 'I'm telling the truth.'

'But . . . no! Who to!'

'Bloke in our road. Kenny Broad. We've been sort of half engaged for a long time and he keeps on at me to get married, so I thought the other day that I would. I told him last night.'

'Oh, darling, for God's sake you can't! If you don't love him . . .'

'Who told you that?' she said smartly. 'I didn't say I didn't love him.'

'But, what about . . .? How *can* you love somebody when . . .?'

'You love your wife, don't you? Go on, deny it. You kept calling her love, darling. You won't ever leave her. Well, this bloke might not wait around forever. And he's all right. Not all the good people come from your side of the lines, you know.'

Slowly she had been getting dressed. He watched the breasts disappear into the bra as though they were toys being packed away for the last time. He dropped his head in his hands. 'I can't believe it,' he groaned. 'I just can't believe it.'

'It's got to happen sometime,' she said almost blithely. She had put her dress back on and was looking through her handbag for a comb. 'I wanted you for something and you wanted me. We've had each other and that's that. We knew it couldn't go on forever.'

'But that telephone call convinced you, did it?'

'Yes, that was the knock. There's no time like the present. I'm going now. I'll get a train about four o'clock, I expect. 'Bye, Andrew.'

She walked briskly from the room leaving him sitting on the side of the bed like a stunned boxer on a stool. He heard the outer door of the flat shut. He did not go after her. He knew that the longer he sat there the better it would be. The phone rang again and he jumped almost to the ceiling. But it was only the reporter from the Hertford paper. 'Your stuff's coming shortly,' he said. 'Did you get the call that came for you?'

'Yes, I got it all right.'

'Good,' said the man innocently. 'It was lucky I could tell her the number.'

'Yes, it was. Thanks. I'm just coming across.'

He dressed slowly. He looked at his haunted face in the mirror. His thoughts were not of Bessie. Only how he could compose himself in front of Audrey when he walked in that night.

CHAPTER FIFTEEN

Two magpies patrolled the garden in a constabulary way, numerous other Plummers Park birds sat around in hawthorn, privet and miniature peach tree, singing the songs that kept others from trespassing on their territory or their mates.

'You've been having sex with somebody else in this area.'

'What in the name of God are you talking about?'

'I've had my suspicions for a long time, you crafty bastard.'

'Oh have you? Well, your nasty little suspicions are wrong. *You* ought to know how to detect bloody adultery – after all, that's how I got you!'

The voices of Cynthia and Geoffrey Turvey clattered untidily out of the french windows on to the summer-morning lawn. Adding their complaints, the magpies flew off at the first-flung accusation, the other birds backed away. Neighbours on both sides stopped in their tasks and listened eagerly.

'Adultery's too good a word for you!' Cynthia sneered. 'You're like a greedy little boy: you can't leave something extra alone, can you? What are you trying to prove – at your age?'

'Listen,' said Geoffrey. 'I'm going. I'm going to work. I don't want to discuss this any more.' His voice had dropped to a low threat, a disappointment to the neighbours. They had no such problem with Cynthia.

'You don't want to discuss it any more!' she screamed. 'I should think you bloody wouldn't either!' She bent closer to him with a strangely confiding attitude, as he was arranging some papers for his brief-case. 'Listen, *chum*, you forget that's how *I* got *you* as well. And I know your tricks, because I was on the other side of the fence last time. Never admit anything – that's what you used to say. Lie until your teeth drop out. If you're cornered get out of the house as quick as you can. Christ, I can hear you saying it. So, you're getting out. Go on, clear off to work – so that you can think of something clever to say when you get back, so that you can warn her to cover her tracks. Well, you've got the wrong girl here. I *know*!'

The front door slammed to coincide with the final word. She heard him start the car and she watched from the window as he backed it from the carport. He turned it sharply and drove down the hill. Suddenly she felt very solitary. She turned dejectedly back into the lounge and looked around her at the possessions they had accumulated since they had come together and married. Tania had gone to infants' school, the house was hollow and quiet except for the calls of the birds drifting in from the garden and a muted and crackly disc jockey on the portable radio in the kitchen. Anger and hurt were now joined by a bitter sadness inside her. She decided to go and see the other woman right away. Two minutes later she was on her way to the house of Polly Blossom-Smith.

She was undecided as to her approach. A direct attack? Some reconnoitring conversation? A skirmish? Her anger drove her towards 'The Sanctuary' like a small but powerful motor. She seethed and closed her eyes for yards at a time as she strode, once almost trampling over a small child, one of the aimless morning tricyclists under school age, who emerged from a front gate into her blind and fuming path.

'Sorry, little boy!' exclaimed the stumbling Cynthia, trying to blow some cheerfulness into a glassy smile.

'I'm Roddy,' said the child, apparently hoping to prolong the conversation because he was lonely. 'I'm going to hospickle to have my winkie seen to.'

'I know somebody who could go with you,' thought Cynthia. She patted the child on his sparse hair and continued. He pursued her, hopefully, apparently bursting with further private information, until she outdistanced him and he returned to his solitary wheelings along the dusty pavement, beneath the laburnum and the baby beech trees. He had been warned by his mother that the seed pods of the laburnum would poison him and he wondered whether it would be worth trying. He might get some attention that way.

At the main gate of 'The Sanctuary' Cynthia hesitated, but a small booster explosion of wrath within her propelled her forward quickly and she strode up the path and banged on the hideously grinning gargoyle knocker. She poked her tongue fiercely at its metallic amusement and then steeled herself as she heard the catch being rattled within.

She had determined to keep a civilized front before launching into her accusations, but her tactics were immediately baulked by the appearance at the door not of Mrs Polly Blossom-Smith but of a thin scraggy old woman wearing a girl's bikini. She had a void expression and a feather duster which she continued to flick unambitiously around her as though seeking to do some token work.

'I'm the daily,' she said. 'Mrs Blossom-Smith's not in. She'll be back soon. Do you want to wait?'

Cynthia had hardly recovered from the first sight of the woman. She must have been seventy and her hips stuck up each side of her like the pommels of a saddle. The bikini which sagged like a hammock between her loins and drooped emptily across her chest was bright pink satin. She looked like a bone tied up with ribbon.

'I'll wait,' decided Cynthia.

'Come on in then,' muttered the grey woman. 'You'll 'ave to excuse my swimming suit but that was 'er ladyship's idea. She's doing some sort of statue and she studies me as I walks about doing the 'oovering and suchlike. She reckons it 'elps her get the bone structure right. Well, she can see every one of mine.'

Cynthia nodded understandingly, then craftily said: 'She uses live people for models all the time, doesn't she?'

'I'll say she does. You want to see the bloke up in the bedroom. Balls and all, 'e is.'

A cold hand touched Cynthia's stomach. 'In the bedroom?' she inquired.

'That's where she's got 'im,' nodded the old lady. 'I ain't never seen nuffing like it and I ain't led a sheltered life I can tell you.'

'I'd like to see that,' said Cynthia. She reached for a handkerchief from her purse and dropped it, a pound note floating down at the same time. The old woman, who seemed to know exactly what to do, picked up the handkerchief and the money and returned only the former. She tucked the note into her bikini pants with all the adroitness of a stripper at a stag party.

'The missus told me to feed the birds,' she sniffed. 'So I'll go and get on with it. Make yourself comfy.' She glanced around the moribund house. 'If you can,' she added. She stuttered down the passage like the victim of some famine, turned at the end and nodded helpfully towards the upper landing. 'Door right in front of your nose,' she said.

She vanished to the garden and the birds, and Cynthia stood, momentarily afraid, at the foot of the stairs. Then her bitterness began knocking again, so with a determined breath she mounted the Victorian stairs two at a time and without hesitation threw open the door.

The model of Flat-Roof Man was standing like a braggart beside Mrs Blossom-Smith's bed: Geoffrey Turvey smiling out at the window on to Plummer Park. Her breath shuddered and she crept towards it as though she needed to catch it unawares. She stopped three feet in front of it, feeling as though something had suddenly hollowed out her inside. Geoffrey, her husband, standing naked in clay, grinning confidently into her face. Her gasp went audibly around the room. She stood back, as though she feared it, and put her hands protectively across her blouse. It was Geoffrey right enough, just as she had heard, the face she had loved enough to throw away a marriage. It seemed to nod its grin at her: 'I told you so.' Her eyes went inevitably down to the loins and the detailed appendage hanging there.

Abruptly the model was flooded with white light and Mrs Blossom-Smith's voice said: 'Do you think it's a good likeness?'

The whole gigantic effrontery of the thing suddenly exploded before Cynthia's baffled eyes. The eyes narrowed and then went wild. 'You great cow!' she screamed across the room. Polly's expression collapsed. Cynthia turned back towards her clay husband and with a vicious grab she tore away the modelled penis and flung it like a flying sausage at Polly whose face filled with a scream for her creation. 'It's not his!' she protested. 'It's not his!' She caught the clay roll with both hands close to her stomach. Frantically, her artistic reflexes overcoming her wrath she began to try and remould the member from memory.

'Stop! Stop!' she pleaded. Cynthia was amazed that the big woman had not rushed her, but merely hung by the door begging for the life of her creation. A frontal assault might have been more effective from Polly's point of view, for Cynthia, encouraged by the disinclination to attack, turned upon Flat-Roof Man again and with an echoing cry of vengeance drew back her housewife's fist and smashed it into the grinning face of the immortalized Geoffrey. The nose bent comically and the eyes almost closed with the blow. She laughed without restraint, as though this were some sort of recommended and enjoyable therapy. She hit him with a left then, flattened the cheek and withdrew with the right ear dangling pitifully. Then Polly came across the floor at her like an unbraked railway train. Cynthia tore the head from the clay shoulders and threw it at the sculptress as she rushed. It caught her square on and caused her to stagger sideways. With an abandoned whoop Cynthia leapt the bed, ran around its foot and out of the bedroom door. She half fell down the stairs. She reached the sunshine and continued to run. The bedroom window was flung open behind her and Polly's howl followed her through the unoccupied morning air: 'Vandal woman! Vandal! Philistine!'

Cynthia did not mind. A great exultation gripped her heart; freedom seemed to fly around her. As she ran she laughed, her feet skipping above the pavements of Plummers Park. The small tricyclist with whom she had conversed on her downward journey watched her coming with lonely interest. He began to pedal towards her hopeful of some more brief companionship. 'The doctor won't hurt my winkie!' he called in advance. 'Mummy says it won't hurt.'

Geoffrey sat with triumphant if surprised composure on his satin settee. Cynthia had poured him a concerned vodka and tonic and he manoeuvred the ice about in the foot of the glass with enjoyment of the moment. Mrs Polly Blossom-Smith had just left. Cynthia was huddled, very chastened, on the chair opposite.

'You should have told me, Geoff,' she complained. 'If you'd told me I am sure I would have understood. I'm not that jealous.'

'It was going to be a surprise,' he said easily, making his hurt sound convincing. 'When it was unveiled, there I would be – for posterity.'

'And it truthfully wasn't your thingy?' she pleaded, looking coyly from the rim of her glass.

'Couldn't *you* tell that, of all people?' he smirked.

'Well, I didn't look that close. When I could see it was your face, just like I'd been told it would be. Mrs Reynolds told me. That old gossip. You might have wanted to keep it a surprise, but it was all round the estate. And I had the feeling, which I know was wrong now, that you were having an affair.' She began to sniff plaintively. He thought the time had come to put his arm about her. He called her over to the settee and she went obediently and sat beside him wiping her eyes. 'When I thought about it, you know, about the man at The Jolly Grinder saying you'd been up there that day, and one night – this might seem really silly – when you were undressing I notice all your bum was red, almost as if the sun had been on it. I thought nothing of it at the time, but when all this suspicion started growing in my mind it suddenly came back to me. I thought you'd been out in a field with somebody.'

If she had watched her husband's face she would have seen the pleased look quickly replaced by a sick expression. He skilfully managed to dismantle this by the time she faced him. By then he had replaced it with a measure of incredulity. 'You thought I was in a *field?*' he repeated, as though he could not believe his ears. 'A *field?* Me? With Polly Blossom-Smith? Christ, Cynthia, you want to go and get somebody to examine your head!'

'I know, I know,' she acknowledged miserably. 'But I'd got myself into such a state I'd believe anything. It sort of festered inside me.'

He composed a hurt sigh and released it. 'How could you do it beats me. I thought she was very decent about it.'

'Yes, yes, she was,' admitted Cynthia. 'I felt such a fool.'

'There were bits of men from all over Plummers Park in that model,' said Geoffrey. 'You must have seen it wasn't all me.'

'Whose was the thingy, I wonder?' ruminated Cynthia.

'The Flasher,' answered Geoffrey dramatically.

Cynthia's astonished face came up to meet his eyes. 'The Flasher? That man . . . who . . . You mean the indecent exposurer?'

'That was the story,' said Geoffrey smugly. 'She wanted that bit reserved for him. Somehow she must have got him. All I can tell you is it wasn't me.'

'How amazing,' acknowledged Cynthia. 'But, then, she's an extra-ordinary woman. And she was very nice about it really, wasn't she? Sitting down here and not getting mad. I really took to her. I wonder what happened to *Mister* Polly Blossom-Smith? Nobody's ever asked that, I bet. She seems so, well, *complete* without a man, doesn't she? She's a very clever woman and not only in her work either. I was glad when she said she wasn't very happy about the model anyway and she had thought about starting again with just the inspiration floating about in her mind. It must be marvellous to be able to do that, Geoff. Marvellous. Perhaps I'll go to pottery classes again in September. I used to be quite good.'

Apart from Dormouse Dan and Barney Rogers the publican, the bar of The Case Is Altered was empty when Andrew walked in. Barney pulled the pint he ordered then walked through to the back of the bar, to his private quarters where Andrew knew, by the steaming smells, his early evening meal was cooking.

Andrew sat and opened the evening paper. After a moment he sensed someone looking at him and glanced up to see Bessie White's father in the doorway. Apprehension fluttered inside him.

'Well, well, it's Mr Maiby,' said the man.

'Hello . . . Mr White, isn't it? Nice to see you. Have a good holiday?'

'Who said I'd been on my 'olidays?'

'Oh, well, nobody. But you look nice and brown. Will you have a drink?'

'No, I drink in my own pub, thanks.'

'Did you want to see me?' Andrew's smile was hung with trepidation. 'I put that money in the paper's polio fund, incidentally. I couldn't keep it.'

'Very good of you that was. Yes, very decent. I came to see you about our Bessie. She's been cryin' at nights and I never 'eard her cry before, not since she was a nipper. You've been seeing a bit of her, 'aven't you?'

'Seeing her?' Andrew felt his inside solidifying. The man's attitude was menacing but matter-of-fact. Andrew shrugged: 'Well, I do see her some lunchtimes when she has her sandwiches in the churchyard.'

'You're a married man,' said Mr White. 'She's a young girl. You upset her, mister, and you'll be in the fucking churchyard for more than your sandwiches.'

Andrew rose guiltily and looked over his shoulder in fear that Barney might be back at the bar. The other man saw his glance and knew what it meant. 'Don't worry, mate,' he said. 'Nobody's heard. It won't get back to your missus.'

'Now, look here,' said Andrew with as much whispered outrage as he could summon. 'What do you want?'

'Our Bessie's getting married on Saturday to a kid in our road. So I've come to tell you to keep to your own side of the railway line, mate. If you get busy with her again I'll knock all the piss out of you. And there's a lot to knock out.'

He reached out and gave Andrew a short push. Then, as though deciding all at once to do it, he reached forward, caught Andrew by the lapels and threw him violently the length of the bar.

Andrew careered backwards through the empty chairs and tables, crashing them to each side. Dormouse Dan awoke and looked at the scene with gradually focusing eyes. Andrew had fallen near the medieval wall, and picked himself up wondering whether he would be wiser to stay down. White strode through the chairs after him and caught hold of him easily in immensely powerful grips and flung him back again. All the breath went from him in a great wheeze. A darkness banged through his brain and he could hear Barney's voice shouting: 'The wall! The wall! Be careful – that's an old wall!'

Mr White stared at Barney for a moment, then turned on the wall and with four mighty blows with the sole of his boot he smashed a great hole through the old powdery stone and plaster. Barney howled his horror and tentatively reached for the telephone.

'Put that thing down, guv'nor,' said Mr White with menace, 'or I'll make a *bigger* hole in you.'

Barney prudently replaced the receiver. 'But it's five hundred years old,' he whispered piteously. 'Five hundred.'

Mr White turned to the debris again. Some of it had fallen across the prostrate Andrew. The man from the council houses gave it three or four more kicks sending the rotten materials tumbling again. Then he picked up a piece of plaster and examined it, smelled it, crumbled it in his fingers, and eventually tossed it away.

'Listen, mate,' he said to the speechless Barney. 'I'm an ignorant bloke, but I know about walls. I'm knocking them down all fucking day. I'm in demolition, see. That wall is no more than a hundred years old. You can smell the plaster and tell that, dead easy.'

'What . . . what about the damage?' stammered Barney.

'Sorry,' said Mr White. 'I got carried away. There's a lot of things I don't like over this side and that wall was one of them. It's about as bleeding straight as most of the people. But don't worry about the damage, old friend. I'll come over with my mate on Saturday morning and we'll have it all built up nice for you in no time. All right?'

'No. No, don't bother,' hurried Barney. 'I'll get it done.'

'Please yourself, squire. But no talking to the coppers about it, either,' warned the other man. 'One word and you might find this boozer a bit more crowded on Saturday than you likes it to be. And then you might find *all* the fucking walls knocked down. Got that too?'

'I have,' nodded Barney, thoroughly frightened by the threat. 'Nothing will be said. Are you going now?'

'Yes, I'll be on my way.' He turned easily to Andrew who was retching among the debris. "Night then, Mr Maiby. I'll think about you on Saturday. 'Bye, 'bye.'

CHAPTER SIXTEEN

He was considering his reflection in the blade of a table knife, the rubbery, spread face, the blobbed nose, the eyes drawn out orientally. A good likeness, he thought. He gave it a cursory polish and set it on the dining table beside the cork place-mat with the picture of Old London Bridge.

'Andrew,' Audrey called through the hatch from the kitchen. 'You *do* want this dinner party, don't you?'

'Want it? Yes, of course. That's a funny question at this stage.'

'You don't seem over pleased. Is there anyone else you would have liked to come? Your girlfriend, perhaps?'

He dug a kings pattern fork into the palm of his hand with exasperation. 'If you keep on about this mythical girlfriend,' he called back controlling his tone, 'I shall go out and obtain one. I'll get some little scrubber from the council estate and bring her.'

The moment he said it, he felt ashamed, not because of Audrey but because of Bessie. He blinked away a momentary picture of her.

'Good idea,' she echoed from the kitchen. 'She might bring a little fresh light into our lives.' He nodded miserably. 'You don't seem to be looking forward to this very much,' Audrey went on. 'After all it is for you. It's your birthday.'

'Age is nothing to applaud,' he answered carefully. 'Even the most stupid people get it. As for me, I can see forty squatting on the dark horizon like a large malicious moon.'

The telephone rang. He answered it. 'Audrey,' he called. 'It's from Cynthia. She wants to speak to you.' As Audrey came wiping her hands from the kitchen, he added: 'She sounds bothered.'

He returned to laying the places at the table. Audrey put the receiver of the phone down on the hall table and walked through to him. 'Geoff's parents have turned up. Nobody expected them. Cynthia says they're horrific and she and Geoff don't mind staying away tonight. But I said bring them over. Is that all right?'

'Yes, of course,' said Andrew. 'Maybe they'll bring a little fresh light into our lives.'

She poked her tongue out at him. 'Not these two, if Cynth's anything to go by,' she said. She returned to the phone. 'Andrew says you've got to bring them. He wants somebody fresh to impress. Yes, he means it. See you at eight.'

She returned to Andrew. 'That's going to be great,' she sighed. 'He's sixty-nine and she's sixty-two. She keeps showing people photographs of Geoff's ex-wife who she thought was lovely. They're from Lancashire, you know. He used to be a miner.'

She paused and looked down at Gladstone slothfully patrolling the table legs. 'Is it possible that Action-Dog could be shut up somewhere this evening?' she requested. 'You know he gets under the dining table and makes those sickening smells.'

'How can we shut him up anywhere?' answered Andrew. 'He'll howl the damn place down. They'll think we've got the Hound of the Baskervilles locked up.'

She sighed. 'If you ever do decide to leave again,' she said, 'will you take that bloody dog with you?'

'I wouldn't be without him,' he replied.

'Listen, pal,' confided Geoffrey almost as soon as his parents had been ushered into the lounge. 'Let me warn you. These two are dynamite. She's been sitting in the garden all the afternoon waving her hankie to the airliners stacking over Watford. She's convinced that the passengers hang out of the windows and wave back. And given encouragement he'll give you the history of the northern coalfields.'

'I haven't got any beer,' said Andrew.

'Beer? Don't worry about that. They order like they drink in the Savoy every lunchtime. I don't know where they get it. He'll tell you about Tufton Main pit disaster while sipping an extra-dry Martini.'

Andrew cautiously served the drinks. Mrs Turvey, bright red from her afternoon's plane-waving, her corrugated hair banging as though it were on springs, said she would like a Cinzano Bianco with a twist of lemon, soda and three ice cubes, an order which Andrew received with gradually ascending eyebrows. Mr Turvey, already settled back in the armchair, his short legs jutting from his brown suit in the forlorn ambition of touching the ground, had a vodka and bitter lemon with two ice cubes.

'Ah,' the old man sighed, a strange crackling coming from his chest as he moved in the chair, 'it's like paradise down 'ere, lad. Seems a shame that folks 'ave to die when there's places like this.'

'Alf's right,' agreed his wife. 'All these houses with these contemporary flat roofs, fields right next-door, and two cars in every alleyway, and people with lovely contemporary homes like this, and divorces. It's like America. Like you see on the television.'

The chimes rang, and Gerry, bursting from a pair of scarlet trousers, and Min Scattergood arrived. Gerry coaxed Andrew aside just within the door and whispered. 'I just want to pop into the dining-room a minute. A birthday surprise for you.'

Andrew smiled, and put his hand on the suet shoulder. 'Not a lifetime's supply, I hope?'

'No chance,' said Gerry. 'You'll see soon. You can't come in. It's got to be secret.'

Andrew grinned gratefully and waved an invitation at the dining-room door. He returned to the lounge. Geoff's father was saying to his son: 'Mind, we don't like the idea of flat roofs in the north, do we, Annie? It don't seem right some'ow. God meant roofs to be pointed.'

'Like on Noah's Ark,' confirmed his wife. 'They tried to 'ave these contemporary flat roofs up our way but the folks didn't take to them. They had to build pointed roofs on top, didn't they, Alf?'

They were obviously accustomed to confirming each other's statements and Alf nodded and said: 'Aye, they did that.'

The old man put his lips to the edge of his glass and sucked loudly. The ice crowded to the rim. Andrew wondered how low a chair would have to be cut before his feet touched the ground. He could imagine him in a coalmine. More crackling came from the man's chest.

'Were you in the pits all your life?' asked Andrew.

'Aye, same seam for twenty-eight years.'

'I bet you were glad to be out of that.'

'No, fair do's. There's nowt wrong with workin' in the pit. It were a bit damp . . .'

'Water up to your knees,' muttered his wife.

'Damp,' said her husband firmly. 'But it were nowt to grumble about. There's no germs down pits, you know, lad. And no women either.'

'Well there was *something* down there,' said Cynthia. 'Listen to your chest.'

'Aye, I've got a bit of a crackle,' he agreed.

'He used to wear a hearing-aid,' said Geoff. 'He wasn't a bit deaf but he used to pretend the crackle came from the battery.'

'Ah, I was vain then, lad,' said his father. 'Now I don't care what folk think.'

'That's one of the compensations of age,' smiled Andrew. 'I'm beginning to feel like that.'

'He's thirty-seven today,' retorted Audrey. 'He talks as if everything's over.'

'Many 'appy returns,' offered the elder Mrs Turvey.

'An' many of 'um, lad,' said the husband, raising his glass. He adroitly continued the upward movement to give Andrew the glass to be refilled. Andrew took it with a grin.

'Geoff left his Mary on her birthday, didn't you, Geoff?' Mrs Turvey said as though she had just remembered. 'When you went off with Cynthia.'

'Andrew came home with a black eye the other night,' said Audrey conversationally.

They were around the table. Beneath it lay the elongated Gladstone, a tube seething with captive gases. Andrew watched Audrey making regular sniffs but the hound had contained itself so far.

'You had a fight in the pub or something, didn't you?' asked Gerry Scattergood. 'Some bloke was smashing down the old wall and you tried to stop him.'

Andrew raised his eyebrows, not displeased at the rumoured explanation. 'Some character from the council estate,' he shrugged. 'A big one too, unfortunately. Suffers from what I call agro-phobia – love of agro. Just looking for trouble. A nasty bit of work. Came in and started kicking the old bit of wall about and I told him to be careful. The next thing I knew he's knocked me down *and* the wall.'

'What I simply could not understand,' said Audrey, 'is why it had to be you.'

'Like the mountain,' said Andrew simply. 'Because I was there. It was me either me or Dormouse Dan, and he was kipping. All I can say is I'm glad he didn't use his boot on me like he used it on that wall.'

Geoff laughed: 'They're now saying it's not old at all. After all the fuss old Barney used to make about it being medieval.'

'Early Fred Astaire's more accurate, I think,' said Andrew, and Audrey said: 'It's amazing how things never seem what they are at Plummers Park. Nothing.'

Geoffrey's father had been silent at the table. He had made a pleased examination of everything in the room, nodding and smiling at prints, ornaments and the furniture as though in considered approval. Now he turned to his wife and said: 'They 'ave some right funny candles down 'ere, don't they, lass?'

'Aye,' she replied without emphasis. 'I was wondering about them meself.'

The attention of everyone went to the two single candles in their stainless steel sticks.

'Dear God,' said Cynthia eventually when she was certain. 'Do you see what I see?'

'But . . . but I only bought the usual candles,' gasped Audrey.

Andrew began to laugh. He dropped his face into his hands and looked out between his fingers at the two objects. They had been burning for several minutes now, but the wax had melted to a peculiar design so that now exposed on the table were two phallic symbols, upright, domed, leaving no doubt as to what they were supposed to represent. 'Gerry,' laughed Andrew accusingly. 'Your birthday surprise?'

'Gerry!' exclaimed Min. 'You didn't . . .? You *did*, you rotten pig! Fancy doing that!'

Gerry began to laugh, but only he and Andrew seemed to be doing so. Geoffrey was grinning sheepishly, Cynthia and Audrey were staring with awe and fascination at the objects running with hot wax, while the old couple nodded in unison as though this was just another facet of the decadent southern life they had been shown.

Gerry now looked confused and said: 'Sorry, but I saw them when I was getting an order at this sex shop in Paddington and I thought they were a great laugh. You should have seen all your faces!'

He looked around again as though to confirm his first impression but,

Andrew apart, the expressions remained cool, glum or puzzled. 'Oh, come on,' he said uncertainly. 'It was only a bit of a joke. Wasn't it, Andrew?'

'Of course,' shrugged Andrew. 'I thought it was funny anyway.'

'A *bit* of a joke, is what it was,' said Min tartly. 'I wish you wouldn't bring your work home, Gerald Scattergood.'

'Now wait a minute . . .' began Gerry, becoming angry.

'Wait nothing,' soothed Andrew, making a calming motion with his hands. 'Don't let's fall out about the candles.'

'I'll move them,' said Min determinedly. 'Where are the proper candles, Audrey dear?'

'I hid them,' muttered Gerry unhappily. 'They're in that cupboard over there. I'm sorry, Audrey.'

It was Audrey who went to the cupboard and retrieved the normal candles. She stood at the side of the table, one in each hand, waiting for someone to blow out the phallic candles and take them from their holders. There was a funny awkwardness, and then Gerry, grunting with annoyance, blew them out and took the offending objects from their sconces.

'If it's not a rude question, what shall I do with them?' he inquired.

Andrew laughed at his discomfiture, standing sorrowfaced at the table, a big white penis in each hand. 'Listen,' he said reasonably. 'I think it's funny and it's *my* bloody birthday party – so there. Here, Gerry. I'll take them. I'll put them in the kitchen.'

Audrey glanced at him quickly. 'Don't leave them where Lizzie will see them,' she said. 'She'll be in soon.'

'Give them to Polly Blossom-Smith,' suggested Cynthia airily. 'She's always looking for models.' She smiled with craft and sweetness at her husband.

Geoffrey's father, who after carefully tasting Andrew's red wine was drinking it thirstily, suddenly said: 'If no bugger wants them I'll 'ave 'em. It'll be a laugh at Christmas, won't it, lass?'

'I'll wrap them for you,' promised Andrew. 'Now will everybody have some more wine and let's get on with my birthday party.'

The old man took another long swig of the wine and said philosophically, 'It's damned 'ard to make a woman laugh, yer know. The only time we ever did see eye to eye with women is when we're layin' inside 'em.'

'Go on,' said his wife good-humouredly. 'We've 'ad some good times.'

'Aye,' he agreed. 'We didn't have much but we 'ad some good times.'

'We never seemed to want much,' she said.

'No, tha' right, lass. And you could always leave your door unlocked. We never locked our door.'

'No,' confirmed his wife. 'Nobody stole from you in those days.' She looked at her son and then at Cynthia. 'Whatever you 'ad was yourn.'

An atmosphere of frosty inebriation settled around the table. Andrew leaned back and regarded his guests and their wives. 'She was a lovely kid, that Mary,' said old Mrs Turvey. 'I could never fathom it. I've got some snaps 'ere.' She fumbled in her handbag and passed around a photograph of a young woman in a garden. She even showed them to Cynthia, who had seen them before.

Then, as though on cue, from below the long table seeped an insidious smell, drifting up around the edges until the guests were looking around suspiciously at their neighbours. 'There's a bit of a niff,' said Geoffrey's father.

'Andrew,' said Audrey grittily, 'get Gladstone out from under the table. He's letting off again.'

Andrew got his head under the table with difficulty. There between the trousers and the shoes and stockings of his guests was the basset facing him, its face riven with sorrow and apology.

'You've done it again, Action-Dog,' he said, patting the dog on its patent-leather nose. 'You've got to go. Come on out.'

The animal moaned an apology, but Andrew dragged him out like a half-filled sack. 'I'm sorry, friends,' he said. 'I'll just eject him.'

'By Christ,' said Geoffrey's father with some admiration. 'I swear I've never niffed anything like that since they opened the old coal seam at Preston Main Number Five.'

Andrew dragged the dog to the door and pushed him out into the garden. It was a warm night with the stars mounted above Plummers Park and a bored moon just rising over the railway line. He was glad to be away from the table. He allowed himself one flying look across the flat roofs of the estate to where he knew, a mile away, Bessie would be trying on her wedding dress before her bedroom mirror.

Andrew, packed with wine, sat back and dimly and grimly perceived Audrey sitting opposite him. The others had gone now, early because it had not been the most successful of evenings. The lights of Plummers Park were going out in little spasms, leaving the night to the local stars.

They had gone out on to the terrace for it was still warm. Drunk as he was he knew he had to keep his voice down out there. They were sitting in deckchairs facing each other like old people in armchairs each side of a fire, their years of marriage tying them, their sprouting hostility screaming for them to get away.

Audrey said sadly: 'Do you remember, when this house was just foundations, coming up here and sitting on piles of bricks, trying to think how it would be?'

'I remember, I remember. The day this house was born,' he recited drunkenly.

'And yet we're so unhappy half the time,' she said.

'Who isn't?' asked Andrew. 'The only people who weren't fighting tonight were the old couple, and they're not match-fit. You have to be fit for marital combat like you have to be fit for football. Anybody around here knows that.'

'*Some* people are happy,' she persisted pleadingly.

'All right,' he challenged. 'Let's count them. The only pair I know are the Yanks, Jean and old Hairy.'

'She's had the onion man in,' sniffed Audrey.

'Get off!'

'So I was told. Her husband's flying off all over the place and she had the onion man in. His bike was outside twenty minutes, they say.'

'The whole world's crumbling,' groaned Andrew. 'I'm pissed off with it anyway. Personally I don't understand why it was arranged that men have to have anything to do with women.'

'I'll second that,' she said. She looked hard at him: 'You're frightened because it's your birthday.'

'I begrudge every damned one, Aud,' he admitted. 'I begrudge every Christmas and every New Year and especially every birthday. Soon the hair starts to come out and then the teeth rattle loose and clatter on to the floor. It's a wonder that, as the final insult, God didn't arrange for a man's chopper to fall off as well.'

She stood up. 'I'm going to bed,' she sighed firmly. 'I can't listen to any more of your great thoughts. I'm tired.'

'I'm going for a walk,' he said.

'A walk? Now?'

'Yes, now. I'll trot old Gladstone for an inspection around Plummers Park by night. I'll be like a watchman making his tour. Perhaps I'll peep through a few windows.'

'Why don't you come to bed. You've had a hell of a lot to drink.'

'I'm going for a walk,' he insisted.

She leapt up from her chair in a burst of anger. 'Oh, get stuffed!' she snarled at him. 'Go for your walk. Go and see what you can pick up.'

'You never know your luck,' he retorted viciously. She strode through the french windows slamming the metal door behind her and drawing the curtains emphatically. At the moment before the drapes finally came together he caught a swift view of his lined and coloured books and the prints on the wall. Then he was left standing on the terrace like an actor on a stage. He called the dog, and, hunched and doleful both, they set off down the slope of Upmeadow.

It was only just past midnight. The late train rattled its lights along the Metropolitan line, the trees fidgeted in their sleep, a dog howled like a coyote in the Hertfordshire night. At the bottom of Risingfield he saw the small, old, open sports car standing by the pavement, and just short of it the defeated figure of its persecuted owner. He was sitting with his feet in the gutter, his left hand patting the wheel of the car as though he were comforting a sick animal.

Andrew felt very drunk, his walk was haphazard, and he needed to shuffle every thought and each word. He stopped short of the man. 'Camping out?' he said.

'Locked out,' said the neighbour pathetically. 'I can break in easy enough, but I'd just as soon stay out here. There's nobody in there anyway. She's gone off, the lady wife. Gone off with her amour, her lover, you understand.'

'I've heard of such things,' nodded Andrew sympathetically. 'Well, you've still got the car.'

The man nodded. He was not looking at Andrew. 'Yes,' he said hoarsely. 'The car I've still got. Just she's gone.'

He stood up and walked with no further word into the darkened enclosure of his front garden. A moment later a pane of glass broke, the door opened and quietly shut again.

Andrew walked about the vehicle twice and Gladstone urinated against both front wheels. Andrew shambled on, not knowing where he was going, only knowing that now, as he shambled and ambled, he was only howling distance from Bessie's window. He felt tempted to climb the railway embankment and to shout 'Bessie! Bessie!' from his side to hers, but he knew it was too late.

Gomer John was standing by the pillar-box just outside his sub-post office, an instrument held in his hands and up to the sky.

'Hello, Gomer,' said Andrew. 'Waiting for the eclipse?'

The thin young Welshman jumped nervously. 'Oh Mr Maiby! That was a scare. Didn't expect anybody to be about as late as this.'

'What are you doing?'

'Taking a fix on the stars,' answered Gomer, returning professionally to the instrument. 'With my sextant, see.'

'Making sure the old sub-post office is not off course, eh?'

The young man brought the instrument down. 'I don't blame you laughing, Mr Maiby. My mam thinks I'm mad. But it's a passion, see, and even in Plummers Park people have passions.'

'Here more than anywhere,' agreed Andrew soberly. 'I wasn't making fun, Gomer. Do you think I could have a go? Could you show me how to do it? Let me look at the stars. I've had my feet in the gutter too long.'

'You really want to?'

'Yes, of course. I've never tried to fix the stars before. Nor anything else come to think of it.'

'Well, well, who'd have thought you'd be interested?' said Gomer warmly. 'I'd like to show you. It's all a matter of angles, see. The word sextant means to measure in one-sixths.'

'It's nice to hear it used that way,' nodded Andrew.

Gomer showed him how to look through the telescope eyepiece of the instrument, but only a moment after he had begun to squint through the aperture the young man caught his arm. 'Mr Maiby,' he said, 'I don't think I'm mistaken, but does that look like a house on fire over there?'

There was a terrible idiocy about that night which was never to leave him. Even when he had hours and days to relive it in the hospital he was never able to think of it as more than a drunk's dream, long and stretched out in places, yawning yards of it, and then quickened to the pace of Mickey Mouse voices in the smoke and the bruised glow of the fire. And, on top of that, there was Gomer.

It was Joy Rowley's house. As they ran he counted the staggered walls and realized it was hers. There was a deep glow in the upstairs windows like the light thrown by a red table-lamp. From one of the big swivel windows, swung open, black smoke uncoiled like a long pipe reaching into the street.

'Gomer, I'll go!' shouted Andrew to the younger man who was running ahead of him. 'You get on the phone.'

Gomer pulled up. 'All right, Mr Maiby,' he panted. 'Are you sure?'

'For God's sake hurry!'

There was a phone-box outside Gomer's own sub-post office. He ran and opened the door but called after Andrew again: 'I haven't got any change.'

Andrew stopped, fooled. Then he bellowed back: 'It's free; you bloody idiot!'

He ran on. For some reason it had never occurred to him that there would not be a crowd at a fire. He had always associated crowds with fires. But there was only him. The houses on either side slept undisturbed. There was hardly a light in the street. For once nobody was watching.

The upstairs floor of the building was burning like a torch, but the downstairs rooms were strangely quiet and untouched. He looked into the sitting-room. It was still and dark with the shapes of the furniture hardly distinguishable. He began to ring on the doorbell, almost politely. Something inside stopped him shouting fire. On the garden path Gladstone, hunched like an oriental bridge, was straining over a turd.

Then at the closed upstairs window he saw Joy Rowley. He waved both hands to her. She was wearing blue pyjamas and he felt surprised that she should wear pyjamas. He had always concluded she was a nightdress girl. It seemed as though his voice had left him for he wanted to start shouting, but somehow no words were coming out. She stood like a ghost in the window, then bent to the catch and opened it. It swung out. They stood like some old Romeo and Juliet, facing each other. 'I can't reach the stairs, Andrew,' she said almost conversationally. 'My mother's at the back of the house somewhere. I can't get to her.'

'The fire brigade is coming,' said Andrew hopefully. 'You'd better get out of there, Joy. Do you think you could jump? I'll try and catch you.'

'I've got the door closed,' she answered calmly. 'But the wall started burning when I opened this window.' He could see the glow behind her increasing.

'Jump,' he urged her. 'Listen, climb over the window ledge and drop feet first. It's not that far. I'll catch you.'

'What about my mother? She must have left the iron on. I've only just let her use the electric iron.'

'I'll see if I can get her. But you come on out now.'

She turned her back on him and cocked one leg over the window ledge, then the other, supporting herself by her elbows. She looked very slim and small in her pyjamas. He had the odd thought that it was like a child escaping from a school dormitory. 'As you drop,' he called, 'shove yourself away from the wall with your arms and feet. You won't hit anything on the way down then.'

'Andrew,' she suddenly called in a stifled voice, 'I must get my mother.'

'Come down!' he shouted, almost screamed. 'I'll see to her. I told you.

Come on – now!'

She jumped backwards and he caught her. He gave at the knees but her dropping weight astonished him, knocking him over on to the front lawn. They sprawled there like some knockabout acrobats, and Gladstone, sensing some fun, loped around them, his clownish face rough with excitement.

Andrew had a passing sensation of her body, a waist as slim as Bessie's, the slim kicking legs in the blue pyjamas. He was sprawled beneath her, for the fall had left them breathless, but she remained calm.

'I'll see if I can get to your mother,' he said, helping her to her feet. 'You go and bang on some doors. Do they all take bloody sleeping pills around here?'

'You'd better have this,' she said. 'It's the front-door key. I remembered to pick it up.'

'Good, that's fine,' he said. 'Go on now. Go next-door. Gomer John is calling the fire people.'

He felt somewhat foolish opening the door of a burning house in such a conventional way. He turned the key and pushed the door open before him. Smoke was loitering in the hall and a heat came out from the enclosed space but there was no fire. First he took his jacket off and then realizing it was a fire not somebody drowning he put it back on again. He wished he was not drunk. He poked his head in the sitting-room, then went through the hall into the kitchen at the rear.

A wide path of moonlight was coming innocently through the big window, illuminating the tiled floor, the dish-washer, the packet of Persil on the draining board, the two pairs of tights hanging to dry. In the moonbeams smoke wandered unhurriedly as though having a good look around before consuming the place.

He had a notion to switch the lights on, but he desisted since he had no idea what effect that might have. Instead he took a tea-towel and put it under the cold tap for a moment. Hardly a cupful of water soaked into it, but the inadequacy did not occur to him at the time. He put it around his mouth like a bandit's mask and, after a moment at the bottom of the stairs, ran up into the fire.

It was the most terrible and terrifying thing. In a second he was engulfed by hot red air. No flames, but a monstrous glow that burned his clothes and his hair. The shock was so great when he realized what he had done that he cried out and the tea-towel fell from his face and he felt the red-hot air rush into his mouth and against his face. Black smoke was thick as fur about him with the crimson glow at its centre. He knew his coat and his hair were on fire. His face was stinging, his lungs full of oily smoke.

'Mrs Rowley!' he shouted once, as though he was crying for her to rescue him. 'Leave the ironing, Mrs Rowley.' Then he had to get out. He knew it was that or death. His bare skin was blistering all across his chest. He wondered where the front of his shirt had gone. He couldn't see. His mouth was full of smoke like oil. Heat was searing up his legs. His shoes were on fire. He stumbled forward in the blackness and his hand miraculously touched the top pedestal of the stairs.

He launched himself into the blackness and tipped and rolled screaming down the stairs. There were a collection of people at the bottom and he plunged through them, tumbling among the faces so they parted and let him roll through. He could hear Gomer's voice shouting, 'I'll go, I'll go.' In terror and pain and panic he picked himself up and ran like a burning ghost out into the indifference of Plummers Park night.

Some of the people began running after him now, pursuing him, and he ran madly at the head of the grotesque chase. His body was in rags, he could feel his skin sagging like chewing gum. He wept as he ran. From behind he could hear the shouts of his neighbours and the baying of Gladstone who was running joyfully with them. There was no sense or object to his flight. He went madly along Risingfield, through gates and gardens and finally rolled and rolled in the dew of Gorgeous George's front lawn. Even in his state he knew where he was lying because of the golf holes cut into the grass. He threshed about in the dew and then sat up, cross-legged, his skin hanging, his hair gone, his clothes charred shreds, like a leper begging in some eastern street. There was a strong smell of hamburger.

'Oh Bessie!' he howled loudly. 'Oh Audrey, Bessie, Audrey! Oh, what the fuck have I done now!'

Audrey sat down patiently but awkwardly, as people do in hospitals, that deep trench between the visitor and the sick, the uncomfortable chair, the watching the clock for the time to go, the sensation of an interview.

'When do they say you can read?' she asked.

'Next week, they promised. They're going to have another look at my eyes to make sure they're really all right and then the sister says I can read the papers and have a squint at a book.' He held up the panda-like hands, covered in bandages. 'They put a strap around one paw with a thing like a knitting needle attached to it. You turn over the pages with that. It's marvellous what you can do without fingers.'

'Thank God you're not without them for good,' said Audrey. 'They told me today they've only got one more lot of skin grafts to do.'

'Yes, a couple more bits of jig-saw and I'm a complete picture. And all new skin like a baby.'

'You were very lucky.'

'I know.'

They waited uncomfortably.

'What's happening?' he said eventually.

'At Plummers Park? Nothing much. Let's think. Oh yes, you know Mr Shillingford was digging out another room.'

'Yes. Has he finished?'

'Struck an underground stream,' said Audrey with satisfaction. 'It poured through the lounge. They had to have the fire brigade.'

'We're keeping them busy at Plummers Park,' said Andrew.

They both waited again.

'Are you all right?' said Andrew eventually.

'Fine, thanks. Yes, fine. So is Lizzie. She's got a new boyfriend. That nice Cowley boy. And . . . oh my goodness, yes! . . . that golfing chap, the one you call Gorgeous George. He was in court yesterday. It was in the paper. Indecent exposure. Long raincoat . . . everything.'

Andrew's start made his skin hurt. 'Oh no,' he muttered. 'George. The Phantom Flasher. Poor George.'

'Arrested by a woman police constable too,' added Audrey with female satisfaction. 'Cost him a hundred pound fine.'

'And drummed out of the golf club,' sighed Andrew. 'Poor George.'

'You keep saying "poor George",' she said, and at once they were aware that, even in the hospital, they were sliding towards one of their arguments. Audrey sniffed: 'After all it's not a very nice thing to do.'

'Flashing was just his hobby,' said Andrew patiently. 'Golf was his life.'

They fell to silence, both unwilling to fight. Then she asked lamely: 'What do you do all day?'

'Checking up on me again,' he grinned ruefully. 'I'm safe in here. My only female indulgence I have is listening to Woman's Hour.'

The yawning gap opened between them again, she on the small wooden chair, he swathed in the bed. It was as though they had never known each other, never been close, had nothing, no common experience about which to converse. She dropped a glance to her watch.

'Only five minutes gone,' he said.

'Don't. I didn't look for that.'

'If you're ever in hospital I promise I won't visit you,' he said. 'We sit here like two bad actors trying to remember our lines.'

'I know,' she said miserably. 'It's funny how we run out of conversation so quickly. Don't you want me to come?'

He reached out with a quick sympathetic paw. 'Yes, of course. I'm only saying it to hurt you. As usual. God knows why I do it. The hours go slowly enough in here. Five weeks and another three, four or five, to go.'

'You seem to be much more cheerful when other people come. They say you're always making jokes,' she said. 'Would you like Joy Rowley to come and see you again? I think she wants to.'

He caught the old warp of suspicion in her eye, the hurt inquiry. 'Why do you say it like that?' he asked. 'If she'd like to come I'd like to see her.'

'She says she wants to explain about her mother. When she came last time you were too ill for her to tell you. But I told her you knew what had happened.'

'What, about the old girl being in the house down the road all the time?'

'Yes, I saw those people yesterday. They felt terrible about the whole thing. They said they weren't sure who she was when she knocked on their door at midnight. God knows why she went there. She seemed quite batty. She had gone to tell them that the house was on fire because she'd left her iron on, but when she got talking to them she forgot all about it. She said she was having such a good time chatting with them it went right out of her head.'

'Why didn't she tell Joy?'

'You can't get any sense out of her. She says she went up the road to tell the people there because she was afraid her daughter wouldn't understand.'

'Silly old cow,' he said bitterly. 'Gomer died for nothing.'

'There was no need for you to have been in there at all,' she said. 'It was a terrible mess-up all round.'

'Poor Gomer,' said Andrew. 'Getting lost in there. And he wanted to be a navigator. Whatever will I say to his mother?'

'She's potty as well,' said Audrey. 'She's apparently furious because she found out after the fire that he'd been planning to go in the navy for ten years. She's more upset about that then the fact that he's dead.' She sniffed sadly. 'The vicar, what's his name, Boon, was a bit put out because Gomer turned out to be a Methodist. Apparently he was very annoyed.'

'Robbed him of a hero's funeral, eh?' grinned Andrew. 'First old Futter, then Gomer. I'm Church of England and I didn't die.'

'Shows even a vicar can't have everything he wants,' she replied, not looking at him. 'But Gomer's mother was the worst. She was really angry about the navy.'

'Strange logic,' he agreed.

'None of it's very logical,' she replied bitterly. 'I nearly lost my husband an hour after his thirty-seventh birthday. Or had one crippled and disfigured for the rest of his life.'

He felt ashamed. 'I should have thought about you first,' he nodded. 'And Lizzie. God only knows what made me go in there. Stupidity, bravado? I don't know.'

'Suicide,' she said flatly. 'You were in the mood for it that night.'

He said nothing to that. Instead he said: 'The ward sister was saying that she thinks you have behaved remarkably.'

'Me? What did I do?'

'You stayed with me,' he replied simply. He felt a lump in his throat stretching his sore skin painfully. 'She says it's far from unknown for a wife to come and see her beloved burned to a frazzle and to piss off forever the same day.'

'That's more reasonable than it sounds,' she nodded. 'I wouldn't do it because I love you.'

She said it just as simply but he felt the tears suddenly begin to rise in his face. She spared him by getting up and going to the window. It had been raining all day. He had spent hours watching drips of rain working to bend a rose thorn just outside the pane.

The silence between them sagged like a rope bridge across a chasm. He could think of nothing but to splutter with his sore mouth, 'I love you too. You know that.'

'You always say "You know that" when you say you love me. As though we were having an argument,' she said, still not turning about.

'Sorry. I'll remember not to say it.'

She remained at the window studying the rain intently. 'There's some wicked buggers at Plummers Park, you know,' she said suddenly. 'The story has gone around that you were inside the house with Joy Rowley when the fire happened. I don't believe that's true, but that's what's going around.'

He felt himself go dry. 'That's a bloody terrible thing to say,' he whispered. 'A terrible thing. Especially with Gomer dying like that. Audrey . . . you don't believe that do you? Have you asked Joy?'

'She came and told me it wasn't true,' said Audrey. 'When she explained about her mother.'

'You don't believe it, do you?'

'No, I don't. It's just the sort of story that gets around.'

She turned casually. 'Geoffrey and Cynthia are talking about moving,' she said. 'Just talking about it. They had a look at a house down at Southfields last Sunday. He says he would like to go down there.'

'Southfields? That's Wimbledon way, isn't it?'

'Yes. He says he'd like to go south of the river.'

'Half the neighbourhood are moving south of the river,' he said. 'Simon and Ena went down there. It must be the attraction of Victoriana after Plummers Park.'

'Somebody's moved into Simon and Ena's house,' she said, just remembering. 'From across on the council estate. She's a blonde girl. I think they've just got married. It shows that as soon as they can afford it they hop across the railway line as quick as they can. As long as they don't have washing hung everywhere it will be all right, I suppose.'

He stared at her through his sore eyes, but they were so red she did not notice the difference. She said she had to go. She kissed him on the new skin on his cheek. For weeks she had been unable to bring herself to do more than peck her lips near him.

She walked to the window, a neat dark woman nearing middle age. She sighed at the rain. 'I suppose the summer's gone now,' she said. 'I don't suppose we'll see another one like that.'

Dangerous Davies

The Last Detective

To Eric Hiscock
who encouraged me at the start

CELIA: Well, the beginning,
    that is dead and buried.

As you like it

CHAPTER ONE

This is the story of a young man who became deeply concerned with the unsolved murder of a young girl, committed twenty-five years before.

He was a drunk, lost, laughed at and frequently baffled; poor attributes for a detective. But he was patient too, and dogged. He was called Dangerous Davies (because he was said to be harmless) and was known in the London police as 'The Last Detective' since he was never dispatched on any assignment unless it was very risky or there was no one else to send.

CHAPTER TWO

Daybreak (they did not have dawns in those parts) arrived over the cemetery to a show of widespread indifference. A laburnum dripped unerringly, cats went home, and the man lying on the tombstone of Basil Henry Weggs ('He Loved All Other Men'), late of that parish, stretched with aching limbs and desolate heart. A wasted night. No one had attempted to blow up the graveyard.

It was not something he had reasonably expected to occur for it would not only have been pointless but so difficult as to verge on the impossible. Nevertheless the scratchy note delivered at the police station had to be treated with some demonstration of seriousness and, naturally, they had sent him. It had proved an uncomfortable but not particularly haunting night. Wrapped in his enormous brown overcoat and spreadeagled on the unyielding stone, Davies had wondered, in a loose sort of way, what the odds were on the morning heralding The Day of The Resurrection. He imagined the stones creaking open and everybody climbing out, rubbing their eyes. But nothing had happened and he was not surprised. It was not his fate to be present on great occasions.

With the day, and its banishment of even the remote chances of both saboteurs and spectres, he dozed briefly and awoke when the cemetery caretaker gave him a vicious push just after eight o'clock.

Davies opened gritty eyes. 'Shouldn't sleep on the slabs,' said the man. 'How can you expect anybody else to respect the fucking place if the law don't?'

Creakily Davies stood up. His overcoat was spongy with dew. The caretaker brushed the tombstone clean as though it were a settee. 'Is that your load of junk outside the gate?' he inquired.

'My car? Yes.'

'What's that in the back seat?'

'It's a dog. He lives there.'

The man appeared to accept this with reluctance. But he did not pursue it. Instead he said: 'You shouldn't park it here. Not in front of the gates.'

'I didn't think anyone would be going out,' remarked Davies. 'I'm surprised you bother to lock the gates.'

'That's to stop people getting *in*,' argued the caretaker, 'Vagabonds and the like.' He regarded Davies with suspicion. 'Are you sure you're the law?' he said suspiciously. 'In that coat?'

Davies looked down the long, wet, sagging length of his coat. His shoes poked beneath its hem as if peeping out from below a blanket. 'Very good for tomb-watching, this coat,' he said gravely. 'Very warm, down to the ankles. I got this at a police sale of unclaimed property.'

'I'm not surprised it was unclaimed,' said the caretaker. He sniffed around in the cold air. 'Anyway, are you going? I've a lot to do.'

'I expect you have,' said Davies. 'Tidying up and that.'

'That's right. You're off then?'

'Yes, I'm off. No bombs, nothing went bump in the night.'

The man could scarcely withhold his disgust. 'I should think not,' he said. 'You must be mad. Who'd want to blow up this place?'

'Search me,' shrugged Davies. He began to shuffle down the path. 'Good morning.'

He made towards the gate. The caretaker wiped his nose with his fingers and watched the long, retreating, brown overcoat. 'And good riddance,' he said just loud enough for Davies to hear.

Davies was almost out of the gate when he paused by a massive, flat tombstone which had sunk spectacularly at one corner. 'Hoi,' he shouted out at the caretaker. 'Here's one that needs straightening!'

'Up yours too,' said the man unkindly.

At 10 o'clock, notwithstanding his uncomfortable night-duty, Davies was due to give evidence in court. (The Queen versus Joseph Beech. Attempted felony, viz a pigeon loft.) Because he disliked testifying in court, he often wished the pubs opened at breakfast time. Too frequently he found his sympathies on the side of the accused.

First he took the Lagonda and its torpid dog to the garage where he kept them. Kitty growled ungratefully when roused from beneath its tarpaulin for breakfast. The dog was a heavy animal with a rattling chest, a cross between a St Bernard and a Yak. Its chest vibrated nastily and it cleared its throat. While it ate he tried to pull a few bits of debris from its matted and tangled coat, but the animal rolled a threat from its throat. Davies desisted. 'Sod you,' he said in disappointment. 'You'll just have to miss Crufts.'

A few hundred yards short of the court was a café painted the appropriate hue of H.P. Sauce. It was called 'The Copper Kettle', although the original kettle had been stolen long ago. It was that sort of neighbourhood. The establishment was owned by a villainous couple. Mr and Mrs Villiers, who nevertheless made a sensible cup of tea and attracted a clientèle of constant interest to the police. Davies had once good-naturedly bought a tea and a round of bread and dripping for a man in there who appeared to be in some need. He was, in truth, impoverished, mainly because he had failed in an attempted armed robbery on a post office only the day before. Davies's kindly and typical indiscretion might have gone unnoticed but for the fact that the man, when arrested and charged in court, made public thanks to his benefactor from the criminal dock.

Davies drank his tea from a large stony cup and winced as the proprietor, behind the sodden counter, took an investigative bite of the five-pence piece he proffered in payment. He did that every time and, for Davies anyway, the joke had grown cold.

Nevertheless he was greeted with friendship at the court. As he went through the outer hall minor malefactors of all persuasions, drunks, shoplifters, threatening-words-and-behaviourists, wilful damagers and obscene exposurers, bade him a familiar good day.

'Morning, Dangerous.'

'God bless you, Dangerous.'

'They nabbed me at last, Dangerous.'

He walked, smiling and nodding to each side like the popular manager of a happy factory. Jealously other officers frowned.

The magistrates courtroom seemed to him, at times, like a small amateur theatre, with the public spectators, the police, the press reporters and the witnesses playing their clumsy parts, eager for every trivial, shocking exposure, always nodding knowingly as evidence accumulated, always laughing at some dry joke of a magistrate. At times even the accused would join in the laughter and then Davies was tempted to warn him it would not ingratiate him with the trio of looming justices on the bench above.

After the drunks had been processed the courtroom was redolent with the odour of morning-after. A lady magistrate held her handkerchief to her imperious nose. The warrant officer made a disgusted face but, pulling himself together, called: 'Case of Joseph Beech, sir, Number 23.' Davies sighed, pulled off his overcoat as though he were reluctantly stripping to fight and shambled, in his large old blue suit, across the courtroom to the witness box. He stood, Bible poised, ready to make the oath, the suit hanging forward like a threatening avalanche. The magistrate eyed him with a disapproval not far elevated from his examination of the prisoner Joseph Beech who, having ascended the stairs from the cells, now rose as if by some magic in the dock. He shouted

'Guilty!' before anyone had asked him.

Davies took the oath. Then recited: 'Acting on information received, your honour, I went to 23, Whitley Crescent, and there found the accused apprehended by the householder, a Mr Wallace who said to me: "I have just caught this bastard trying to nick my pigeon loft."'

'Tell them *who* you received the information from then, Dangerous,' prompted the man from the dock eagerly.

'In good time, Mr Beech,' replied Davies, embarrassed.

'Tell them. Go on,' said the insistent accused.

Davies glanced at the magistrate for help. 'Tell us, for goodness sake, Mr Davies,' said the Chairman impatiently. Each time Davies gave evidence in court it seemed to develop into some kind of farce.

'I'm sorry, sir,' said Davies politely. 'In fact I received the information from the accused himself. I would have included that in my evidence, of course, if he had given me time.'

'From the accused? He *told* you he was going to steal this pigeon loft?'

'Yes sir. I told him some years ago, sir, that if he ever felt the urge to commit a felony then he could telephone me first so that I could dissuade him, sir. I saw it as a method of keeping him out of prison.'

'It did too,' confirmed Beech smugly. 'I used to ring him up and he'd come and stop me. But this time he was too slow and the other bloke copped me first.'

'I was in the bath,' Davies said apologetically.

'All right, all right,' said the magistrate impatiently. 'Let's not turn it into a performance.' He glanced at Davies and then turned to Joseph Beech. 'You stand a good chance of going to prison for three months,' he said.

Joseph Beech sighed happily. 'I'd like a bit of stir,' he nodded. 'Last time in the Scrubs I made a model of Buckingham Palace out of bits of wood. A working model. It was ever so good, wasn't it Dangerous?'

At the police station he went into the airless C.I.D. Room to write his report on the night in the cemetery and to do his football pools. Hardly had he sat down when the telephone rang. He picked it up.

'Dangerous,' said the duty sergeant. 'There's a West Indian run amuck, or whatever it is they do, in Kilburn. He's in his lodgings and threatening to burn the dump down. The squad car's leaving – they want you along too.'

'Who else?' sighed Davies. He rebuttoned his overcoat and went out to join the two policemen in the squad car. They took only three minutes to the address in a street of downcast lodging houses. Four policemen from another station were already grouped at the door. There was a scattering of expectant watchers in the street. Davies trudged up the broken outside stairs. 'What's this?' he said approaching the policemen. 'A procession of coppers? What are you waiting for – the band?'

'Assessing the situation, Dangerous,' sniffed the sergeant.

'Waiting for me to get my head caved in again, more like it,' said Davies. 'Where is he?'

'Top room. Right at the head of the stairs. He's a tough bugger by all accounts.'

'How about arms?'

'He's got arms and fists at the end of them.' The laden voice was of the wild man's landlady, a sniffling Irishwoman with a malevolent wall-eye. 'He's twice as big as you,' she continued reassuringly. 'And black. They're stronger when they're black.'

Davies eyed her unenthusiastically. 'Why won't he come out? What's he doing up there in the first place?'

'Drunk,' she said solidly. 'Drains a bottle of whisky and a bottle of rum every day. I've told him he'll end up like an alcoholic.'

'Very likely,' agreed Davies. 'Have you got a bucket, missus?'

'I have,' she said. 'Would you be wanting a mop as well? Is it for the blood?'

'Just the bucket,' sighed Davies.

She dragged herself into the dark house and returned to the front with a bucket.

'What's his name?' Davies asked the sergeant.

'Bright,' answered the sergeant looking at his notebook. 'Pomeroy Bright.'

'Pomeroy?' said Davies wearily. 'There's never a Bill or a Ben among them, is there. Okay. Give me the pail, missus.'

The Irish woman handed it to him. First he leaned up the stairs and shouted. 'Pomeroy, it's the police. Will you come down, please.'

This reasonable request was greeted by the most colourful cascade of Caribbean abuse. Davies felt his eyebrows go up. 'I don't think he's coming down,' he confided to the sergeant.

'Pomeroy,' he called again. 'You can't win, son. Come on down and let's sort it out down here. Why don't you be reasonable?'

'Because I ain't fuckin' reasonable, man,' came the response. 'I'se waiting for you to come and get me. Come right up, man. Come right up.'

'Shit,' said Davies quietly. He turned to the sergeant. 'I'm going up,' he said. 'Will you make sure your storm-troopers are just behind me and not a tenpenny bus-ride away.'

'We'll be there to catch you,' said the sergeant unpromisingly. 'What's the bucket for?'

'What d'you think it's for? I'm not going milking. It's to take the brunt of whatever this nut's going to sling. It's what they call bitter experience. You're sure he's not got a gun?'

'I'm not sure, but I don't think so,' said the sergeant comfortlessly.

Davies groaned, held the bucket in front of his face like a visor and said, 'Right, come on then.'

He charged up the stairs like a buffalo, yelling into the echoing bucket, his overcoat flapping about his ankles. The Irish woman fell back and crossed herself hurriedly, the police squad, taken aback by the abrupt frenzy, hesitated and then went gingerly up the stairs after Davies.

He threw himself against the door which to his astonishment gave easily. It had not been locked. Pomeroy Bright was waiting for him two paces into the room. He was a huge man and he held a full-length framed wall-mirror like a bit. He was entirely amazed at Davies's entry behind the bucket and stood immobile for a moment.

Davies stopped inside the door and, not being attacked, lowered the bucket. It was then that Pomeroy swung the long mirror. He batted it horizontally at Davies's head. Davies, his protecting armour lowered, had the unique vision of his own consternation reflected in the glass the moment before the mirror hit him. He fell to the dusty floor and was trampled under the boots of his fellow officers rushing in to overpower the West Indian.

When it was over and they had stopped his forehead bleeding he was helped out by two immensely cheerful ambulancemen to desultory applause from the grown and appreciative audience in the street.

Davies let them take him to the hospital in the ambulance. He was conscious of his right eye swelling.

'Never mind,' sympathized the ambulance man as they travelled. 'The mirror didn't break so there's no need to worry about the bad luck.'

It had been a difficult summer for Davies. Not only had the London months been untypically hot and arid but, by the autumn (or The Fall as he, a natural pessimist, preferred to call it) his personal and professional life had deteriorated even further than he, one of the world's born stumblers, could have reasonably expected.

His comfortable and long-standing affair with a Tory widow in Cricklewood had been terminated upon his mistakenly climbing into her teenage daughter's bed, while drunk, and finding himself surprisingly welcome, but later discovered by the Tory widow herself.

Life in 'Bali Hi', Furtman Gardens, London N.W., a shadow-ridden boarding house overseen by a Mrs Fulljames, was far from serene. His wife Doris also lived there, but separate from him, occupying her own quarters and glaring at him over the communal table. Other lodgers included a Mr Harold Smeeton (The Complete Home Entertainer), who sometimes sat at dinner dressed as a clown or a maharajah; Mod Lewis, an unemployed Welsh philosopher; Minnie Banks, an outstandingly thin infants' school teacher, and a passing parade of occasional lodgers of all manner of creeds and greeds.

Professionally, it was no use denying it, his activities had been less than glamorous. The arson of the confessional box at St Fridewide's Catholic Church, the theft of a pigeon loft, and even less glorious cases descending almost to instances of knocking-on-doors-and-running-away, was scarcely big crime. It might be asked, indeed he frequently wondered himself, for he was an honest man, why he was retained in the Criminal Investigation Department of the Metropolitan Police, except for the necessity for having someone available in his division to lead the police charge on hazardous occasions. Davies had been thrown down more flights of stairs than any man in London.

He was also utilized for routine checking tasks involving endless plodding of the streets and the asking of repetitious and usually fruitless questions. Through these urban journeys he had become known to a great many people and he himself knew some of them. His nature was such that suspicion only dawned on him by degrees, his view of the stony world he walked was brightened by a decent innocence. He was kind even when drunk.

He was, however, drinking too much, even by his standards, and he had twice been the victim of ferocious attacks by his own dog, Kitty.

Davies, a long man, thirty-three years old, inhabited his tall brown overcoat for the entire London winter and well into the spring. By the first frosts he was resident again.

He was to be seen at the wheel of his 1937 Lagonda Tourer, forever open and exposed to the weather, the hood having been jammed like a fixed backward grin since 1940. It was a car which prompted envy in many enthusiasts, almost as much as it evoked their disgust that such a rare prize should be kept in so disgraceful a condition. It was rusty and ragged. Its fine great brass lamps wobbled like the heads of twin ventriloquists' dummies. Its metal was tarnished to brown, its elegant seats torn and defiled with rubbish. In the back lived the huge and unkempt dog, as foul and matted as the rest of the interior.

His area of operation, if it could be termed that – his 'manor' in police parlance – spread out in a ragged hand from London to the north-west. Fortunately his efforts there were reinforced by many other policemen.

It was a choked place, a great suburb of grit and industrial debasement. Streets spilled into factories and factories leaned over railway yards. A power station, its cooling towers suggesting a touch of Ali Baba, squatted heavily amid the mess like a fat man unable to walk a step further. In winter the air was wet and in summer the sun's brightest and best was rarely more than bronze. Spring might bring an inexperienced cuckoo in from the country but he soon fled for there was nowhere for him. Trees and flowers were born to fight and lose.

There were factories for the making or assembling of soup, dynamos, home electric organs, rat poison, bicycles and boot polish, conglomerated in all their various grimes. Smoke hung about and the dust had no time to settle on Sunday before it stirred again on early Monday. In the old days the district had been quite famous for its watercress.

Lying amid it all, like an old man's outstretched arm, was the Grand Union Canal, grand in no way now. Its greened unmoving water divided the whole region, its modest but still ornate bridges pinned the banks together. Almost parallel with the canal there were several main, mean, shopping streets, jointing in the way a drainpipe joints at a change of direction. The people of the place were Irish, Indians, Pakistanis, West Indians, Africans and some of the original British. Few of them liked it. It was somewhere to be, to work.

It was evening by the time Davies left the Casualty Department of the hospital with his stitches, his black eye and his aching head. He reported to the police station, where his injuries hardly raised a glance, and then walked to a public house called 'The Babe In Arms' where it was his homegoing habit to drink as much as possible with his fellow lodger and friend Mod Lewis, a Welshman named Modest after Tchaikovsky's brother. Mod was happy to be known as a philosopher. His great talent was loyalty (he had been faithful to the same Labour Exchange for twelve years) and he knew many unusual and useless things, for he had read half the books in the public library.

Mod viewed his smoked eye with resigned sympathy. 'Been leading the charge again, have we,' he sighed.

'Once more into the breach,' agreed Davies heavily. He examined his eye and the plastered forehead in the mirror across the bar. 'The eye is nothing,' he said. 'You ought to see my body. Covered in coppers' bootmarks. I'm a sort of human draw-bridge. They have me knocked down and then they all run over me.'

Although it was not dole-day Mod bought him a beer and he drank it gratefully but not without some pain.

The public bar was as tight as a ravine, only narrowly escaping being a corridor. Along the windows onto the street was frosted glass, curled with Victorian designs. At that time of the evening, with the lights still on in the fronts of the shops across the road, the homeward figures of the workers passed like a shadowgraph. A rough woman came in and put a coin in the juke box. She played the same tune all the time, 'Viva España', and when she had taken a few drinks she would sing and dance to it as well. She winked at Davies as though they shared some private love, joy or secret. The sound of the record overcame the cries of Job who dolefully sold his evening papers at the corner crying: 'Tragedy tonight! Tragedy tonight!' It was a statement never challenged and indeed frequently true.

'You know,' said Mod the philosopher, pulling his pint glass from his face with a slow strength that suggested it might have been glued there. 'Injured as you are, you're a lovely drinker, Dangerous. Lovely.'

Davies thanked him seriously.

'No, but you are,' pursued Mod. 'I've been watching you lifting that pint. It's like a bird in flight.'

Davies was accustomed to the poet's fancies. He acknowledged it with an encore of the drinking movement which Mod duly stood back to admire further. The demonstration drained the glass and Davies ordered refills.

'It's a pity to see you in such poor way, especially since your jug-lip has finally healed,' remarked Mod accepting the beer gratefully as though it were an unexpected pleasure. 'It looked very nasty. Just like a spout. It was painful to sit at the table and observe you attempting to drink soup.'

It's the first time you've mentioned it,' said Davies pulling down his lip and examining it in the mirror across the bar.

'Well, I didn't like to before, boy,' said Mod. 'And neither did our fellow lodgers. Indeed it's nothing very new to see you come injured to the dinner table. Tonight they will have a new array to intrigue them.'

'Part of the job I suppose,' shrugged Davies. 'I seem to have spent half my police life looking up from that floor into the face of somebody intent on murder.'

Mod sniffed over the rim of his beer. 'If you ask me that's why they keep you. You're no detective, I can tell that.'

'You've mentioned it before.'

'No offence, Dangerous. But even you must realize that. When did they last give you a decent, wholesome crime of your own to solve? They either have you trekking around knocking on doors or leading the charge up the stairs to some madman's door. For example where may I ask, did you come by the jug lip?'

'A disturbance of the peace,' said Davies. 'A fracas. The sort of thing you're bound to get in this sort of place. Have you ever thought how many people around here are actually at war with each other? We've got two religious lots of Irish, hostile African tribes, Indians and Pakistanis, Jews and Arabs. That's how I got the lip, the Jews and the Arabs. Some fool at St Saviour's Hall got the bookings mixed up and let the place to the local branch of El Fatah and the Jewish Lads Brigade on the same night. And I got in the middle of it.'

He pulled down the lip again and peered over to the mirror. 'It's gone back all right, though,' he said. He began to think of dinner. 'What time is it?'

'The clock just above your head says six-thirty,' observed Mod.

'Oh yes, the clock. I forgot it was there.'

The rough woman had drunk enough to inspire a trembling of her heels and heavy calves. She began to emit small Iberian cries. The record of 'Viva España', which she had already played twice, swooped again onto the turntable at her touch of the selector button.

'Let's go before Flamenco Fanny starts splintering the floor,' suggested Davies.

'Indeed,' agreed Mod. 'My stomach, if no other part of me, draws me to Mrs Fulljames.'

People were gratefully going home from work, tramping in tired quiet lines along the dusty fronts of the small shops. It had been a warm autumn day and the industrial sky was gritty, glowing red over the cooling towers of the power stations as the sun quit. The roofs of the terraced houses hung like parched tongues, smutty privet hedges enclosed tight little gardens, dull windows sat on low window-sills. Many of the people who passed were West Indians, Indians or Irish. The lights of the Bingo Hall began to glimmer promptly at seven.

'Bali Hi', Furtman Gardens, was a larger house, ponderous Victorian with a monkey tree in the front garden. Mod used his key to open the door and they walked in on the rest of the residents already sitting with gloomy expectancy at the evening table. Doris, Davies's wife, was staring at her bread-and-butter plate in the manner of one expecting invisible writing to materialize; Minnie Banks, the thin schoolmistress, sat head down like a safety pin, while Mr Smeeton, The Complete Home Entertainer, was dressed in the leather trousers and braces of a Bavarian smack-dancer, in readiness for a later engagement. It was rarely a festive board but tonight seemed even more subdued than ususal. To Davies it appeared that they had been awaiting him. He and Mod muttered general greetings and sat down into the silence. Then Mrs Fulljames came powerfully from the adjoining kitchen. She regarded Davies with controlled contempt.

'I thought you're supposed to be a detective,' she began truculently, thrusting her jaw at him. 'That's what I thought.'

'It's a general misapprehension,' said Davies removing his face.

'Don't be rude,' Doris said to him from the opposite side of the table.

'I take it from whence it comes, Mrs Davies,' sniffed Mrs Fulljames. She revolved heavily towards Davies again. 'A *detective*,' she repeated.

'What seems to be the complaint?' asked Davies.

'*Complaint? Complaint? Crime*, more like it! And right under your nose. Detective indeed.' Her bosom soared as though steam was being pumped into her.

'I've rung the police station and they said to tell you when you got in,' the landlady continued tartly. 'I could hear the idiots laughing like girls. They said no point in sending a copper around if there's one in the house already.'

With deliberation Davies took out his notebook and licked the end of his police pencil. 'You can put that rubbish away,' rasped Mrs Fulljames. 'There's no time for writing things down. There's a suet pudding done in the kitchen.' She glanced suspiciously over her shoulder. A skein of steam was coming from the open door like a ghostly hand trying to attract her attention. She wavered between polemic and pans and decided the pans could not wait. She revolved rather than turned and pounded into the cooking regions. Davies put his notebook away. He glanced earnestly around the table. 'What seems to be the trouble?' he inquired.

Doris, as though doing a reluctant wife's duty, said: 'There's been a theft in the house, that's what. A theft.'

'Good God, I didn't there was anything worth nicking here,' replied Davies honestly.

'The brass bedstead,' said Doris trumping the remark. 'The antique brass bedstead in Mr Sahidar's room. It's gone. Antique.' She was someone who always needs to add an extra word.

Davies checked around the table. 'And I perceive that Mr Sahidar is also no longer with us. Am I right in deducing that he and the bedstead went together?'

'Both gone,' sniffed Doris. 'And right in the room next to yours. I wouldn't mind, but it's *right next door*. It makes me feel small, I can tell you.'

'Mrs Davies,' said Davies. 'You can hardly expect me to keep vigil through the night in case a fellow guest makes off with his bed. It's not something that you can cater for. In any event I spent last night in the comfort of the cemetery.'

'All we know is it's gone,' sniffed Doris. 'Mrs Fulljames went in there this morning and all she found was a pile of bedclothes and the smell of incense. That bedstead was worth a hundred pounds. It used to be Mr Fulljames's bed.' She performed her customary pause, then added:

'When he was alive.'

'A relic, indeed,' muttered Davies.

'Antique,' put in Mrs Fulljames arriving from the kitchen with a frightening cannonball of suet on a steaming plate. It looked so heavy that she gave the impression of pushing it rather than carrying it. 'Antique, Mr Policeman.'

Mrs Fulljames attacked the suet pudding with a murderous knife. Davies edged away, half expecting it to scream. She served everyone else first and smashed the final lump on his plate. She went to the kitchen and returned with boiled potatoes, carrots and a jug of Oxo. 'Priceless,' she muttered. 'That bed.'

No one answered. Minnie Banks looked frightened. Mod knocked the suet pudding around his plate and the leather-costumed Mr Smeeton stared upwards as if in dreams he saw the Bavarian mountains. Suddenly Mrs Fulljames dropped her face into the steam of her dinner and sobbed among the vapour. 'It belonged to Mr Fulljames!' she cried. 'The late Mr Fulljames.' Doris leaned across to pat her hand but the sentimental moment soon flew. 'How?' she barked at Davies. 'How?'

Davies fought to dispose of a hot mouthful of suet and meat. He felt it drop burning into his inside. 'I don't know,' he said bitterly. 'How do I know? Mr Sahidar was a Persian. Maybe he *flew* it out of the window!'

Mrs Fulljames regarded him fiercely, an expression helped by half a carrot protruding from her lips like the tongue of a dragon. 'I take it,' she said taking the carrot out with her spoon and laying it among its friends on her plate. 'I take it you will carry out a serious investigation. Tonight.'

'In one hour,' he promised. 'I'll have this place swarming with police.'

CHAPTER THREE

Inspector Vernon Yardbird looked sourly across the threadbare rooftops from his office on the fourth floor of the police station. In thirty years in the force, and in that same division, he had viewed the same area, although he had during that time ascended from the Police Constables' room in the basement, next to the cells, to his own elevated office.

He considered he should have gone much further. Not upwards but sideways, in the direction of Scotland Yard. He had always considered that he had a Scotland Yard name. After all, top policemen always had Scotland Yard names. Hatstick of the Yard, Harborough of the Yard, Todhunter of the Yard. What better than Yardbird of the Yard? It had a *sound* to it.

Unfortunately others had seen his prospects differently. He had always been a painstaking policeman, even pedantic, but generally thought to be lacking in imagination. Today he was awaiting a visit from a man from the Special Branch. He did not approve of the Special Branch.

During the summer it had not been unentertaining to look from his window for there was a students' hostel across the first bank of roofs and the girls used to lie out sunbathing on the hot, gritty days. He did not approve of students, but he did not mind having them under surveillance and to this end he had brought a pair of racing binoculars to the office. But now their disporting was done. They had retreated with the sun and even a brief burst of Indian summer had not brought them out again. Now, after a few fine days, dank autumn was sprad over the roofs. He did not approve of autumn.

Downstairs the desk sergeant was attempting to placate an old but vibrant widow who had come with a complaint that her neighbours were terrorizing her with almost incessant use of their lavatory chain. He saw the Special Branch man walk in and politely interrupted the catalogue of flushings to speak to Inspector Yardbird upstairs. He told the Special Branch man to go up.

Yardbird did not know him. Detective Sergeant Herbert Green. What a *name* for the Special Branch. It was packed with upstarts, anyway, and this upstart had the name *Green*. He had no time for them these days. Some of them even came from Universities. He did not approve of Universities.

Green turned out to be a pale and diffident young man, almost apologetically placing a file on Yardbird's desk as soon as he came in. 'Ramscar,' he said. 'Cecil Victor Ramscar. Aged 45.'

'I know him, I know him,' sniffed Yardbird impatiently. 'He was born around here, baptized, went to school, joined the scouts, and did his first bank robbery all within a couple of square miles.'

'Good,' said the Sergeant easily. 'Then you'll know who to look for.'

'He's back, is he? The bastard. I thought we'd got shot of him forever.' He slung his hook a few years ago.'

'Right. He's been in Australia and in America. Getting his fingers dirty with various things, but he's come back. He didn't come in through any normal channels or we would have spotted him quicker. But we think he's back on your manor Inspector. He's gone to ground around here.'

'What do you want him for?'

'We don't know.'

Yardbird looked up petulantly. 'That's a bloody good start, I must say.'

Green shrugged. 'It's no start at all,' he agreed. 'But we've got nothing on him. Nothing. We might get him for illegal entry, if we could find him, but we might have trouble in sticking that on him.'

'In that case, what d'you want?'

'We just want him located. And tagged.'

'For nothing.'

'It's nothing at the moment. We think it will be something.'

A thick banging came at the door, no sharp knock with a hand, but a dull contact with the wood. Yardbird called and in came a canteen woman with two cups, thick as chamber pots, sitting on equally substantial saucers. Green saw the mildly red mark on her forehead and knew that she had banged the door with her forehead. They took the tea and the woman shuffled out.

'What's Ramscar up to then?'

'We think he may be going fashionable and doing a little bit of abduction, hi-jacking, hostaging or something like that. He's been involved in some fairly major league things in Australia and in California and he hasn't come back to London for nothing. We think he's lined up in partnership with a dissident group. For money, of course, not ideology. We think he could be the heavy man in a political kidnapping.'

Yardbird sniffed. 'You don't know very much, do you? There's a hell of a lot of ifs and buts and maybes.'

'That's all we have,' shrugged Green. It was not all they had but he was not telling Yardbird any more. 'What we're asking,' he said. 'Is that Ramscar is located.'

'Why don't you do it yourself?' asked Yardbird. 'You've got enough people in your office, surely.'

'We could have a couple of men going around this district,' agreed Green. 'But it was thought better that somebody local should do it. Somebody who knows his way around.'

'It was thought better?' inquired Yardbird. 'Who thought it better?'

'The Commissioner,' smiled Green laying down a good card.

'Oh, I see. Well in that case he's probably right.'

Green drank his tea at one attempt and replaced the heavy cup and saucer on Yardbird's desk. 'Christ,' said Green. 'They need to have thick cups to keep that stuff in.' He smiled in a confiding way at Yardbird. 'It won't matter if absolute secrecy is not possible in this,' he said. 'In fact I think that in a way the clumsier the inquiries, the better. If they can be conducted in such a way as to stir up Mr Ramscar, worry him, make him break cover or play his hand hurriedly, then that might be what we want.'

'One man will be enough?' said Yardbird.

'Have you got somebody like that, somebody who will set up the ripples? Somebody really clumsy?'

Yardbird nodded. He picked up the phone. 'Get hold of Detective Constable Davies,' he said.

The everyday working smoke had sauntered away across the industrial horizon, leaving the sky with a mildly puzzled expression. Davies walked towards the police station. It was not often he was called in to see the Inspector. He did not hurry although they had apparently been attempting to contact him since late afternoon. He had been feeding the ducks by the canal. There were not many people in the streets at that evening time, they had mostly returned from their employments and had not yet gone out to their enjoyments. Even the main road was subdued, giving Davies the feeling that he might be walking in the country. The cemetery which he skirted seemed almost busy by comparison.

They had secured the formidable gates for the night causing him to wonder once again on the reason for his moribund security. Few would want to go in after dark and certainly nobody was getting out. He paused at the big gates and peered in at the dusty greenery strangling the incisive sentiments of stone-masons. He touched his forehead in salute, said a private 'Goodnight all' and continued his course to the police station.

He toyed with the fantasy that Inspector Yardbird was calling him in to investigate something spectacular, a murder perhaps. Davies had frequently thought how he would handle such a matter. Not that they *would* ask him – not unless the remainder of the Metropolitan Police Force had been wiped out by typhoid fever. Even then they would bring someone in from, say, Devon County rather than entrust it to him. Anyway there had been no homicide in the area that day or for some preceding weeks; not, in fact, since a belligerent Pakistani had stuck a quiet Irishman dead in front of the Labour Exchange using a tell-tale Eastern dagger to accomplish the felony. Davies had not been required to take any great or glamorous part in that investigation. In fact the brief inquiry he was instructed to make at the Labour Exchange he conducted with such diffidence that he was mistaken in his intention and, after an hour's wait, was offered a job in a laundry. Not for the first time he had determined to put more authority in his approach. He had even been loudly reprimanded by the Labour Exchange manager in front of its doleful customers, for failing to call it the Social Security Department. He had tried to convince himself that he was meticulous in his inquiries but even he had to admit that, for all the time he took, he left a good many buttons undone.

At the next corner to the police station he saw the early prostitute standing against the laurel bush that she always hoped and imagined would frame and enhance her dubiuous appeal. She was faithfully there at that hour. Her name was Beryl Suggs but he always called her Venus because, he said, she was like the evening star.

'Hello love. Done it yet?' he inquired solicitously.

'Nothing moving yet, Dangerous.' She returned the smile, drawing back vermilion lips, the bed for a row of ragged teeth. She sniffed the dubious evening air as though it might give her a clue. 'Somebody'll be along in a minute,' she forecast. She looked at him curiously. 'You're out a bit late. I always see you in the afternoons. You're down there feeding the ducks.'

'I'm allowed out until it gets dark,' confided Davies.

Venus laughed and he walked towards the despondent laurels at the police station steps. Somebody, he saw, had written 'Clean up the Police!' with an aerosol spray right across the front of the notice board outside the main door. He ran his finger along the dust of the laurel leaves and thought that the cleaning might well start there. At the base of the steps he paused and felt for his notebook and pencil. He was not going to be caught wanting for them. On one occasion, in the grim presence of a superior officer, he had found it necessary to ask several passers-by for the loan of a pencil and any spare scrap of paper they happened to have on their person. When this proved fruitless he had turned desperately first to the frosty Inspector and, when no help was forthcoming there, to the accused man who had obligingly held out both pencil and paper.

Davies steadied himself at the police station door, in the manner of a wanted man going to give himself up, then entered with what he hoped was a show of confidence. The duty sergeant was at the counter reading out a list of road accidents for the local newspaper reporter who was writing them without excitement in his notebook. 'Anthea Mary Draycott, double tee,' recited the sergeant. 'Minor injuries . . . 'evening Dangerous . . . St Mary's Hospital. Not detained.'

There were two elderly people sitting on the hard bench of the front office, crouched and anxious as people are in police stations even if they have nothing to fear, and a further set of trapped eyes looked over the top of the frosted glass in the charge room. There was some fresh blood on the wood-block floor of the corridor but Davies deduced, correctly for once, that P.C. Westerman's nose had been bleeding again.

Davies followed the trail of red into the C.I.D. Room where the haemorrhaging constable was hung over the washbasin. His eyes swivelled. 'Get the keys, will you Dangerous,' he pleaded.

The cell keys were hanging on their accustomed hook and Davies, knowing what was required, took them and dropped them obligingly down Westerman's heavy back. The constable gave a small start at the touch of the cold metal, but it stopped the nosebleed.

'Thanks, Dangerous,' he said. He looked up. He appeared to have been eating strawberry jam. 'Funny how the keys always stop it.'

'Just don't ask me to get them out,' said Davies. 'Better wash your face off. It'll look as though we're torturing the staff as well.'

Westerman bent and washed his face in the basin. 'I'm glad it was you and not old Yardbird. I couldn't have asked him. Not again. He's such a bloody misery.'

'Is he upstairs?' asked Davies. 'I've been sent for.'

'That's right, I was forgetting. No, he's gone home. He wouldn't wait past six, you know that. But I think the sarge has got some message for you.' He looked up and regarded his pink lower face in the mirror. 'Thanks for the keys anyway, Dangerous. I'd better go in the bog and fish them out.'

Davies went to the police station counter. The local reporter had gone. The sergeant had put a solid folio on the desk before him. 'This is for you, Dangerous,' he said. 'Came up this afternoon from Criminal Records. Ramscar. Cecil Victor. Heard of him?'

'Vaguely. What's he done?'

'Two years, three years and five years,' answered the sergeant. 'Anyway this lot is for you. Yardbird says you're to read through it, peruse it, he says, and go up to see him in the morning. He was a bit grumpy that he couldn't get hold of you this afternoon, but there, that bugger's always grumpy.'

'What's it for? Any idea?' asked Davies.

'Ramscar used to be a bad boy around here years ago. Nasty lad. Then he went off somewhere to the big times. It looks like he's back and they want you to find him.'

Davies brightened. 'Well, well,' he said. 'That's a change anyway. Looking for a real villain. Better than larceny of a pigeon loft.'

The sergeant laughed, picking up a mug of tea and allowed the laugh to serve as a blowing action to cool it. 'What did he get, the bloke that nicked the pigeon loft? What's his name?'

'Beech, Joe Beech,' said Davies, '55, plumber. Got the three months he wanted. He's going to make another working model of Buckingham Palace.' He picked up the file from the desk and frowned at its bulk. Then he walked towards the C.I.D. Room.

The sergeant called after him: 'How in Christ's name can you have a *working* model of Buckingham Palace?'

'Don't ask me,' returned Davies. 'I'm just a simple copper.'

The staff of the Criminal Investigation Department who operated from the station often complained that their communal room was the worst in the entire building, not excluding the cells. It was cold, green-painted and windowless, a high and dusty fanlight excepted. Shut in there a man could lose track of the tread of time. The seasons were only marked by the death-drop of flies from the ceiling in winter and the buzz of their descendants in the spring.

Spread around were some necessary but basic tables and chairs, a couple of disgruntled desks, and some scratched personal lockers. There was a consumptive gas heater and next to it a gas ring with a kettle and a collection of tea mugs. There were three wall adornments: a dartboard, a United Dairies calendar showing a milkmaid and a stupefied cow and a framed representation of 'The Martyrdom of St Peter'. The saint hung uncomfortably upside down on his cross. His face was not always the most morose nor the most puzzled in that office. There was nobody there now except Davies.

The canteen was still open and he had provisioned himself with a mug of coffee and three flecked pastries. Sitting down he struck his head against the hanging ceiling light. He let it swing balefully and silently like some untold bell. When it had stopped he opened the file on Cecil Victor Ramscar.

He began at the back. Everything that was known about Ramscar was there, every conviction, every suspicion, every inquiry. There were the criminal blotches of his finger prints and the photographs taken in prison, getting progressively younger until the final one showed him as a hard-looking lad in the Borstal hockey team. The first entry (theft of clothing coupons) was in 1945 and the last (suspected armed robbery, not proven) in 1968. After that there was nothing but a note: 'Believed to be resident in Oakland, California. F.B.I, information (Ref: F.B.I.

384A) January 1972.'

Twenty-five years back in the folder there appeared a single typewritten sheet of paper. Davies leaned forward in the poor light. Across the top was a penned note: 'Statement by Cecil Victor Ramscar. Reference Missing (believed dead) Celia Norris.' It was dated August 15th, 1951.

Davies read it studiously. It was, as were most of Ramscar's statements in the file, a complete denial. It gave his movements for the evening of July 23rd, 1951 and for several subsequent days. Ramscar, so he said, had been at the races and spent the night of July 23rd at a hotel in Newmarket with two strippers. Davies raised his eyebrows. Ramscar admitted to knowing Celia Norris because her father was a business associate, but denied he had spoken to her or seen her for the week preceding July 23rd or ever after that date.

The statement had been accepted by the police after checking. It was stamped and acknowledged at the bottom by a Detective Inspector whose signature Davies failed to decipher. He remained blinking at it. He had never heard of the case of Celia Norris. He rose slowly in the drab room and walked out to the desk sergeant at the front counter.

The sergeant was a shiny sort of man with no hair. Davies knew he would be retiring within a few months. 'Ben,' he asked. 'You've been around here since the Flood. Ever hear of the case of Celia Norris? Vanished in July 1951?'

Ben had a habit of smoothing down a non-existent fringe. He did so now and said: 'Oh yes, I know that one, Dangerous. Young girl, sixteen or seventeen, going home from a youth club, on a bike, I think. Just disappeared. Thin air case.'

'Never found?'

'No, not a trace. Not a sausage. I can't remember it all now but I think her clothes turned up somewhere.'

'Did we treat it as murder?'

'No. Not at first, only after; everybody thought she'd just gone off like young girls do go off. With some bloke or other. She'd done it before and her home was nothing to shout about. In fact, now I come to think of it, Dangerous, her old man was a bit of a villain around here, into all sorts of petty larceny and fiddling. That sort of stuff. I haven't heard of him for a few years. He's probably inside.'

'And it never got off the deck?'

'No, God, they couldn't even find a proper suspect, if I remember rightly. Pulled all the usuals in, but nothing. There was a lot of fuss, in the papers and all that rubbish. The C.I.D. here couldn't have solved a bloody crossword puzzle in those days and after they'd hooked in one or two obvious prize choices and let them go, the thing just fizzled out. It's still on the file. I'm surprised you've never heard anyone talk about it. Why did you want to know, anyway?'

Davies had no time to reply. The swing door whirled and in fell a weeping woman holding her head with one hand and a large saucepan with the other.

'That fucker's done it again!' she howled at Ben. 'Bashed me on the head with this! Right on the bleeding head!' Davies backed away. The woman took her hand away to reveal a spectacular bump. The sergeant opened the ledger on his desk with a long sigh which seemed to be repeated by the pages of the book itself. 'Mrs Goodly,' he recited aloud. He wrote it down. 'Vera. Which number Hawthorn Street?'

'Twenty-seven,' she said obviously thoroughly familiar with the ritual. 'The fucker. I'll swing for him yet.'

Davies padded heavily away. He helped himself to a key from the board behind the counter and went down the corridor to a door marked 'Local Records'.

Even then, at that initial moment, he was aware of something germinating inside him. Something moving with caution, but nevertheless moving. He switched on the light and went along the tin-boxed files. It had an entire file to itself: 'Norris. Celia. 1951–'

With his unknown thrill growing, he took the box down and put it on the central table. It creaked open. He pulled out the contents, hundreds of sheets, statements, browning newspaper cuttings and photographs. In a separate envelope was an enlarged picture of a pixie-faced girl licking an ice cream. A dab of vanilla had got onto her chin and she knew it was there and was laughing about it. On the back was a caption. It said: 'Celia Mary Norris. 5ft. 1 inch. 7 stone 10 lbs. Aged 17'.

For the next two hours he sat hunched in the enclosed room and read through the file. Down the corridor he could occasionally hear the evening life of the police station going on, the drunks, the threats, the weeping, and twice the echoing clang of the doors to the cells. By the time he had reached the last inconclusive page – the whole thing, left, abandoned, run out, exhausted but unfinished – it was ten o'clock by the station clock which he could see at the distant end of the corridor. He folded the documents and replaced them in their tin-box. He went out, returning the key to the desk sergeant who had just taken over from Ben.

Outside it was raining. He pulled the huge overcoat closer about him and trotted clumsily to 'The Babe In Arms'. The rough woman was lying on the bar floor having just cracked an ankle during her flamenco. Mod was trying to lift her but when he saw Davies he let her drop to the floor again. 'For Jesus sake, where have you been?' he demanded. 'I've been stuck here buying my own beer.'

Davies asked for two pints but Mod still regarded him accusingly. 'Fine bloody evening, I've had,' he complained. He nodded towards the rough woman who was now being lifted, howling, towards the door by three strong men. 'Spent all night trying to explain about Spain to that lunatic female. She's never heard of Franco or Don Juan Carlos. All she knows is that "Viva España" thing. She thinks Granada is a fucking television station.' He pulled up and began to look steadily at Davies who was smiling. 'Something's been and happened,' Mod said carefully. 'You've been up to something, Dangerous. What is it?'

Davies let his smile travel over the surface of his beer. 'A murder,' he said quietly. 'I've got myself a murder.'

Mod looked with amazement. 'Your own murder!' he breathed. 'They've given *you* a murder?'

'No,' corrected Davies firmly. 'They didn't *give* it to me. I . . . I sort of appropriated it.'

'You . . . what?'

Davies grinned: 'I'm not going to tell them about it.'

CHAPTER FOUR

Breakfast at 'Bali Hi', Furtman Gardens, was a fragmented affair. Thin Minnie Banks, the school-teacher, attempted to correct some abysmal exercise books for the day's lessons, while drinking her weak tea. Mod, undoing *The Guardian*, sat down to his toast, glanced over her shoulder and remarked: 'Training the future unemployed, I see.'

'You can talk!' Her voice was as piping as her frame. 'Since when, Mr Lewis, have you done a day's work?'

Mod sniffed like a managing director and spread his paper. 'It takes a great deal of skill and technique to remain unemployed,' he observed. 'I doubt if your pupils would ever reach the required standard.'

Davies came downstairs and Mrs Fulljames heard him from her kitchen where she ate her breakfast not so much in privacy as secrecy. 'Any sign of my bed yet, Sherlock Holmes?' she called.

'Inquiries are proceeding,' Davies shouted back woodenly. 'You will be informed of any progress.'

'I'll be bloody lucky,' she retorted. 'Who tried to blow up the cemetery then?'

'Nobody,' sighed Davies. He poured himself some tea and splashed jam on a round of stony toast. Mrs Fulljames, cup in one hand, the *Daily Mirror* in the other, appeared at the door of her citadel. '*Anybody* could have told you that,' she jeered. 'How could anyone blow up a cemetery? How?'

Davies lowered his toast. 'It was the misreading of a handwritten message,' he said wearily. 'We had received a warning but it was incorrectly written down, scribbled, in fact. I thought it said something was going to happen in the graveyard with a bomb. But 'bomb' was badly written and I didn't correctly read it. It should have been 'tomb'. But nothing happened to any tombs either. I just got double pneumonia.'

'Police!' jeered Mrs Fulljames returning to the kitchen. 'You'd make better girl guides. God knows what would happen if there was ever a murder around here.'

Davies caught Mod's eye and set his teeth to fight the toast. He hoped the grinding and the grunts would reach Mrs Fulljames. If they did she took no heed.

Later he fed Kitty, who was prostrate, as usual, in the back seat of the Lagonda, but he left the car and the wheezing dog in the tin garage at the foot of the street and walked, his thoughts full, to the police station.

It was a wan morning with most people by now behind the gates at their work, stragglers at the bus stops, steam curtaining the window of the 'Copper Kettle' Café, and shopkeepers yawning behind their counters. He heard compressed coughing from the waiting room of the doctor's surgery, a milkman on a float clanked with his hazardous load, and two boys, playing truant, squirmed their way through the fence by the railway embankment. For a large place it was often as empty as a village.

At the police station some midnight miscreants were being taken from the overnight cells to the court. There were some familiar faces among the drunks, the drunks and indecents, the drunk and disorderlies and the drunks and incapables, and they saw Davies as a friend.

'Morning all,' he said as he went through to the C.I.D. Room. They rumbled their own greetings and stumbled frowstily forward. After they had gone out, shivering in the early air to walk to the courthouse around the corner, the desk sergeant took out an aerosol spray and played it around extravagantly. 'Yardbird wants to see you at ten, Dangerous,' he called down the corridor. 'He was shitty because he couldn't get hold of you yesterday. Wanted to know what you were up to.'

'Inquiries,' Davies called back down the corridor. He had half an hour so he went to the canteen and bought a cup of solid coffee and two cakes. Then he returned to the C.I.D. Room and took the file of Cecil Victor Ramscar from his locker. He had intended to go through it again but he turned instead to the one statement concerning the disappearance of Celia Norris. He read it, with an odd guilt, as though he were looking through something forbidden. Then, just as guiltily, he purloined the key of the 'Local Records' Room and took down the Celia Norris file. He felt a sharp unreasonable thrill as he opened it again. There she was, laughing up from her photograph, the ice cream dab on her chin. He ran his fingers thickly down the edges of the documents and statements. All this, and nobody ever found.

Clipped to the front of the wad was a summary of the case and an index of statements. Davies took an absent-minded bite of one cake, and began to read again. He did not like the cake. It stuck to the roof of his mouth. He put the rest in a random file he took from the shelf. One day someone would find a cake in a file. He read through the summary.

Celia Norris had spent what was almost without doubt, the final afternoon of her life planning her future. At 4 o'clock on 23 July, 1951, she had gone to the youth employment office in the town to inquire about the possibilities of becoming a nurse. She had gone afterwards to her home at Hunter Street, almost under the rims of the Ali Baba jars of the power station, had a meal and then left for the youth club at St

Fridewide's Catholic Church. At ten o'clock, or shortly after, she had left there on her bicycle. Her boyfriend, William Lind, had remained behind for a sports meeting and anyway his bicycle had a puncture and he had to walk home. So he did not accompany her. To reach her home she would have cycled along the main road to its junction with Hunter Street and turned there, or perhaps taken the short cut, which she had been known to do, being a girl of no nervous disposition, along the towpath of the canal, later joining the main road and completing her journey as before.

After that night nobody reported seeing her. The bicycle was never discovered. Her clothes were found, except her pants. A lipstick she was known to have carried in the pocket of her dress was missing. A youth called Andrew Parsons, a known underwear thief, was arrested on a call from the attendant of a twenty-four-hour public convenience in the High Street who had seen him handling some girl's clothing in the establishment. The clothes, a green gingham dress, white bra, white socks and brown Louis-heeled shoes, were identified as those worn by Celia Norris on the night she disappeared and presumably died. Parsons, a nocturnal moocher, told the police he had originally taken the garments from the public lavatory where he found them stuffed behind a cistern at one o'clock one morning in July. The shoes were inside the cistern. He believed it was July 24th. When three weeks later he saw in the newspapers that the clothes were the same as were described as belonging to the missing girl, he panicked and decided to return them to the place where he had found them. The police had questioned him for two days and then let him go. He was kept under surveillance but nothing more came from this.

The finding of the girl's garments, and the fact of the missing knickers which Parsons (who was found to have a collection of 234 pairs of assorted women's pants in a cupboard at his lodgings) swore he had never taken or even seen, had turned a desultory search for a wayward teenager who had previously strayed, into a hunt for a body and a murderer. Neither were ever found. Nor was Celia's bicycle.

And it had happened, by all the evidence, at ten o'clock on a summer evening – a warm summer evening too – and yet no one had come forward to say they had seen a girl in a gingham dress on a bicycle. In that, anonymously crowded but somehow vacant place, when it was just growing dark, as it would have been, it was not so strange as it might at first seem. People did not stroll in those streets for there was nowhere to go and it was too early for the exodus from the pubs or the cinemas. Television was still a compelling novelty. There was a regular police van patrol taking in the High Street and the canal towpath (policemen on foot beat had recently been replaced) but neither Police Constable Frederick Fennell nor his colleague P.C. James Dudley, who were driving their small vehicle in the area until midnight, saw the girl or reported anything unusual. Celia Norris had mounted her bicycle at the Catholic youth club and ridden away into nothing.

Davies remembered yardbird and opened the door to look at the clock down the corridor. He still had seven minutes. His coffee was looking even more muddy and was now cold. He attempted a drink and screwed up his face. He took a football pools envelope from his pocket (he had resolved to seek his fortune that season) and noted on its back the names of those who had made statements in the case of Celia Norris:

Elizabeth Norris, mother; Albert Norris, father; William Lind, boyfriend; Ena Brown, a friend; Roxanne Potts, another friend; all members of the youth club; David Boot, youth club leader; Andrew Parsons, underwear thief, and the name that had begun it all for Davies; Cecil Victor Ramscar, described as a friend of the girl's family. There were other names, statements made by people who thought they might be able to assist, but mostly nebulous, and, lastly, the negative report of P.C. Fennell and P.C. Dudley, who had been on duty in the police van that night.

The clock along the corridor said three minutes to ten. He still had time. From the file he took the envelope containing the various photographs collected during the investigation. They were pathetic little snapshots, sepia now, moments in a life that had not long to run. Celia with her mother, Celia with her dog, Celia at the seaside with a chisel-faced youth wearing a paper hat, possibly William Lind, and, finally, one that must have lodged in the envelope when he had first opened it the previous night. It showed Celia and another girl at what appeared to be a fairground or fete. Both wore summer dresses and were laughing. Standing between them, ten inches taller than either in an open-necked shirt and badged blazer was a bronzed man, grinning. At first glance it seemed he had his arms about their young waists. But Davies hurried into the desk sergeant and borrowed the magnifying glass the station clerk used for reading small print.

'Don't forget Yardbird, Dangerous,' the sergeant reminded him.

'No. No. Just going up,' answered Davies hurrying back down the corridor. He put the magnifying glass on the photograph. He saw that although the man's hold on the girls seemed conventionally friendly, his fingers, in fact were curved higher and touched the undersides of their breasts. He pursed his lips. That, he decided, might be David Boot, youth club leader.

Inspector Yardbird was grouped at his window, hands clasped Napoleonically behind his back, legs astride, shoulders square, a growl on his face. He was gazing over the creased and crowded roofs as though he were considering conquering them. He had called aloofly to answer Davies's knock but he remained with his back to the room for two minutes until a subdued cough caused him to turn to see the Detective Constable.

'Glad you could make it,' remarked Yardbird caustically. 'Searched everywhere for you yesterday. Where were you? At the pictures?'

'Inquiries, sir,' said Davies.

Yardbird sniffed. 'Well, I've got some further inquiries for you. And this is bigger stuff than you've been asked to handle before. Much bigger. It seems to me you've been rather falling behind in the general run of things, Davies.'

There was nothing but for him to agree. 'Yes, sir,' he answered. 'I've had that feeling myself. I thought I was being, sort of, overlooked.'

Yardbird sat on the edge of his desk. His left foot just reached the floor. He thought he caught a movement from the window of the girl students' hostel and he tried to get a firmer look without Davies noticing.

'Hah,' smiled Davies amiably. 'Do those girls still live across there, sir?'

Yardbird spun so quickly he all but spilled from the desk. 'Girls? For Christ's sake, which girls?' He turned and sat down behind the desk, and, without being asked, Davies sat pensively in the visitor's chair. The Inspector rubbed his face in his hands. 'I don't know, Davies,' he grumbled. 'I really don't know. I consider you for a big job, but I honestly can't tell whether I'm doing either of us a favour. I still can't get the police garden party out of my mind. Those fucking raffle tickets blowing all over the show. And when you'd got back from collecting them somebody had nicked the raffle money.'

'I was a poor choice for the raffle, the wrong man,' admitted Davies. 'It seemed to go from bad to worse, didn't it.'

'The Commissioner thought you were some kind of clown we had hired. I might as well tell you that here and now, Davies. It made me feel pretty stupid I can tell you.' He sighed and thrust his broad chin into his broader tunic. 'On the other hand I was always one for giving somebody another chance. And that's what I'm offering you. Another chance. Did you look through the Ramscar file last night when you came in?'

'Yes, I did, sir.'

'Nasty bugger that,' muttered Yardbird. 'He's been around ever since I was a young constable in this division. A finger in every criminal pie, a real villain. Larceny, grevious bodily harm, vice, protection rackets, all sorts of things. And very active in the old London gang wars. Mr Ramscar's put bullets through a few kneecaps I can tell you.'

'He's got a big file, sir,' agreed Davies. 'What's he done this time?'

'Nothing,' replied Yardbird. 'Nothing that our splendid Special Branch can prove. And it's them that wants him. They just know he's back in London from abroad, where he's been involved in some big villainy and they think he's come back for a good reason. They think he might be up to political crime now. He likes to keep in the trend. Anyway they want him found but they don't want to set an army looking for him. They just want somebody to track him down. And you're the some-body. Because they think he's come home. He's in this area. You find him.'

'I see. Find him.'

'That's it. Get around his old haunts and his old friends. Ask a lot of questions. We don't mind too much if he starts flapping his wings. I'm going to detach you from other duties. Just see I get regular reports. It shouldn't take you long, a couple of weeks at the most.'

'Yes,' said Davies. 'I see.'

Yardbird looked up. It was time for Davies to go. 'Anything else?' asked the Inspector. 'You've got the whole picture, now.'

'No . . . No, nothing else, sir. Just one thing. Can I use my own transport? My car?'

Yardbird, who had never seen Davies's Lagonda or the dog, nodded brusquely. 'If it's decent. If it doesn't let down the force. And . . . Davies.'

'Yes sir.'

'Keep the expenses down. If you have to go to the West End go by bus. And not too much boozing in those clubs. Remember, you're not in the Flying Squad.'

Davies thanked him and went out, down the stairs and into the C.I.D. Room A detective sergeant called Myer was going through three hundred pornographic pictures. Two other C.I.D. men looking over his shoulder, examined them for clues. Davies got the Ramscar file and sat down to go through it again. He came to the Celia Norris statement and read it minutely. He took a deep breath and plunged into the rest of the history. But in his mind he could see only a girl with a blob of ice cream on her chin.

Davies had few notions about locating Ramscar. It appeared obvious that if he were in hiding he would hardly visit his once habitual haunts, although he would undoubtedly contact old associates. Davies thought if he walked about loudly enough and asked a great many random questions then Ramscar might come to him.

In the afternoon he went to Park Royal greyhound races and backed for spectacularly losing dogs, one at evens. He made conversations with a number of shifty men, mentioning Ramscar and showing his picture but it appeared to mean nothing. In the toilet he approached a fellow urinator and waved the photograph but the man, white-faced, retreated, still making water, and with a quaint leap-frogging motion along the troughs. As soon as he reached the door he ran and reported Davies to a policeman.

It was not at all a promising first day. At five o'clock he returned to the police station and, unable to help himself, almost mesmerized, he again took down the file on Celia Norris. He kept looking over his shoulder experiencing the same sensations as when he had, as a boy, secretly examined the illustrations in 'First Aid To The Injured', fearful that his mother would catch him enslaved by a drawing of a woman receiving artificial respiration. He felt contracted inside reading through the unfinished story again, looking at the photographs. He found himself making a stupid little movement with his hand trying to brush that nib of ice cream from the laughing girl's chin. He reacted with horror when he realized what he was doing. Eventually, unable to help himself, he returned the file and very secretly went out and began to walk the twenty-five year old trail of Celia Norris.

Although there had been demolitions and developments on the London fringe of the district, the area of the High Street and the canal were all but unchanged. The cemetery occupied a good many acres at the base of this region and that was as immovable as cemeteries generally are. The canal formed a wedge through the centre and provided another hard argument against change. On the far side the small workshops and bigger factories had been so busy making goods and money during the nineteen-fifties and sixties that few thought of making any improvements. Now they had slowed with the recession, those who operated them were unwilling to finance re-planning or expansion. The High Street, grey and crowded, ran, roughly on the same line as the canal, although it curved quickly to cross the waterway at its uppermost end before the power station. It was locked between the immovable and the immutable. To the south the cemetery, to the north the power station, to the west the canal and to the east the solid, three- and four-storey houses of the original Victorian town, including 'Bali Hi', Furtman Gardens (formerly called 'Cranbrook Villa' but renamed after Mrs Fulljames had fallen in love with Rosano Brazzi in the film version of 'South Pacific'). It would be half-a-century before anyone thought of pulling those down.

And so the stage remained largely as it was that close night in July, 1951, when Celia Norris began her cycle journey home from the youth club. It was now a gritty October evening. Davies left the police station and after courteously declining the offer of a free intercourse from Venus, the evening star, he set off on foot for St Fridewide's Catholic Church.

The youth club had been in the grounds of the church, indeed it still was, and the girl would have cycled from the main gate. He walked thoughtfully from there to the junction with the southern end of the High Street. The cemetery occupied about ten acres, fronting on the main road, at that point, all dead land. He went at a steady pace (he would cycle it, he decided, at some later time) but increased his step past the graveyard gates because he did not want to be forced into making an explanation to the miserable keeper about the misreading of the word 'tomb' for 'bomb'. The man was bound to be uncharitable. He should introduce him to Mrs Fulljames one fine day.

At the conclusion of the cemetery there was the customary stonemason's yard with a nice display of crosses and weepy angels, to catch the passing trade, and from this the haphazard High Street began its course. The smart, big, bright stores that grew up in the years of plenty, in the sixties, had found their home in other easier thoroughfares in Kilburn, Paddington and Cricklewood, leaving this street to the small grocers, the tobacconists, the fish-and-chip merchants, the humid cafés, the bright, cheap clothes shops, the betting shops, of course, and several long stretches occupied by the showrooms of second-hand car dealers, the vehicles and the salesmen smiling identical smiles from the open fronts of the premises.

The local newspaper, the *Citizen*, was uncomfortably accommodated in a house, once the residence of the neighbourhood's only famous son, Miles Shaltoe, a writer of somewhat dubious novels who enjoyed a vogue in the early nineteen hundreds. There was a plaque commemorating his occupation under the fascia which proclaimed 'North West London Citizen' and in smaller letters 'Every Friday'. There were also several ladies' hairdressers, one boasting the title 'Antoinette of Paris, Switzerland and Hemel Hempstead'. There were numerous public houses interpolated along the street, with the 'The Babe In Arms' occupying a favoured position adjacent to the public conveniences, two cinemas, the more palatial of which now only featured Indian films, a West Indian Bongo Club and an English Bingo Club, a pawn shop, its avuncular balls first hung in 1896, and 'The Healing Hands' massage parlour, an establishment of more recent roots.

Despite attempts with paint and plastic to brighten it, the street was decayed and tired, sighing for the euthanasia of the demolition man's flying ball. Davies walked along it, as he had many times in his past five years in that town, but now examining the upper windows and wondering if any eyes had looked down from their vantage on the final journey of Celia Norris.

The upper floors, while mostly curtained and closed, with lights behind them at this time of evening, had the occasionally noteworthy difference. There were the premises of Madame Tarantella Phelps-Smith, High Class Fortunes Told, the Winged Victory Ex-Servicemen's Club, the ubiquitous snooker hall, and the Quaker Meeting Room, undoubtedly reeking with the rising odours of the Take-away-Curry shop underneath.

The husky evening itself was layered with odours – Guinness, chips, work and dirt. There was a municipal tree at the junction with Jubilee Road, one of the Victorian offshoots. It was donated by the Rotary Club – and had a plaque to prove it – to commemorate the Coronation of Queen Elizabeth II and, despite being protectively caged in an iron waistcoat, it was stricken as though by some long-term lightning.

Davies walked the length of the High Street twice in forty minutes. It was busy with buses and homeward cars now, and with people scurrying from their work, thinking of freedom, food, television or possibly love. He ended his thoughtful patrol at 'The Babe In Arms' and went into the elongated bar. Mod was predictably peering into a half pint, which he had purchased with his own money. He was glad to see Davies for he was anxious to know further about his private murder case and his glass was running low.

'I've started,' said Davies when they were drinking. 'I've started on the case.'

'How far have you got.'

'Nowhere.'

Mod nodded at his beer and at the logic of the reply. 'Will you keep me informed, Dangerous?' he asked. 'I have a lot of time to think, you know. I may just come up with something.'

'I'll tell you,' promised Davies. He glanced up and down the bar. 'She's not in then? Flamenco Fanny.'

'No,' confirmed Mod. 'I think she must have broken her ankle last night when she fell down. With any luck.'

The door opened on cue and the rough woman, her untidy leg in a hammerhead of plaster-of-paris, stumped in supported by a massive walking stick. 'Olé!' she cried.

'Oshit,' said Davies.

Even with the annoyance of the rough woman stumping around all night in the bar on her enormous plaster cast it was only with some difficulty that Davies managed to entice Mod to leave and to walk with him to the canal bank.

'If I am to be your Dr Watson, I wish you could arrange for our investigations to be outside drinking hours,' complained Mod. 'If you don't mind me saying so, I can't see how any clues to this conundrum – there, I said it too, beered as I am – are going to be lying around by the canal twenty-five years after the event.'

A man loitering in a shop doorway opposite saw them leave the bar and, after allowing them fifty yards clearance walked in the shadows behind. He watched them make for the entrance to the alley between the pawnbroker's and the massage parlour, then hurried down a service road alongside some neighbouring shops and climbed a fence to reach the canal bank. He ran through the towpath mud, passed a man fishing in the dead of night, and turned up the alley from the canal end. Davies and Mod were wandering towards him.

'It's not clues, it's geography I want to be sure about.' Davies was saying patiently. 'On her way home she might have cycled down this cut and gone along the towpath to the road bridge. I just want to cover the ground, that's all.'

The man who had followed them now approached from the foot of the alley. They looked up from their talk and saw him come, coat-collared, towards them. Davies felt an instinctive touch of nervousness as the silhouette came nearer, as though his new role had given him a sharper edge. They had almost to touch to pass each other and, as people do in such awkward circumstances they muttered almost into each other's faces as they passed.

'Goodnight,' said Davies.

'Nighty-night,' added Mod.

'Night,' responded the man, a short blast of beer emitting with the word. Davies saw nothing more of him than a pale triangle of face jutting from the collar and pinpoint eyes squinting through rudimentary spectacles. The man had gone to the upper end of the alley before Davies realized that there were no lenses in those glasses.

The alley performed a mild curve and beyond the angle the limp lamplit water of the canal came into their view. The damp, rotten smell was at once heavier. They stood and took in the confined scene. If the girl had gone that way she would have had that same view in the same light as she rode carefully on her bicycle. The helmeted lamp had hovered above the bridge for many years. It was as if it had lost something in the water and was taking a long time to find it.

Davies and Mod were contemplating the chill view, hearing the bored glugging of the water against its old banks when, dramatically, a figure ascended from behind the elevated hedge on their right. They jumped

like a pair of ponies. The figure squeaked nervously. 'Oh . . . oh . . . ever so
sorry, mates . . .' he said eventually. He stood upright against the hedge
five feet above them because of the variant in the ground levels. Davies
and Mod regarded him as they would have regarded the appearance of
Satan. Davies contained his voice. 'Don't worry,' he laughed hollowly.
'Didn't see you there, that's all. Made us jump.'

'No you wouldn't, not from down there,' acknowledged the man.
'Completely hidden from down there I am, I bet.' He performed a brief
demonstration crouching behind the hedge and calling to them. 'There,
can you see me now?'

'No, not a thing. Can't see you at all,' obliged Davies.

'What are you doing anyway?' inquired Mod, more to the point.

'The allotment,' said the man rising and nodding over his shoulder
into the vacant darkness. 'Only chance I've got of getting down here. By
the time I get home from work and that. I'm just getting a few veg.'

'Good job you know where everything is,' observed Davies.

'All in nice straight lines,' said the man. 'I've got a torch but the
batteries went. I've done now, anyway. Finished.'

They continued looking up at him. He was like a politician with a
small audience. 'Any good, these allotments?' asked Davies.

'Not bad. Not as good as the power station plots, but not bad either.
Here it's always dampish, see. Because of the canal. But the power station
stuff gets the spray from the cooling towers. But you get good stuff in
both.' He began to heave a sack over the hedge. Davies and then Mod
moved forward and helped him to bring it to the ground. He thanked
them, wished them a cheerful good-night, then shouldered the sack and
went towards the top of the alley. 'He must have a lot of mouths to feed,'
observed Mod.

They continued to the end of the cut, the air closing damper with each
step. The canal water, near black by day, was in its night-time guise,
appearing in the streaky light of the lamp as limpid as a tropical pool.
Sitting on the bank, quite close to the bridge, was Father Harvey, the
priest of St Fridewide's. He was fishing.

'Now I've seen the lot,' Davies said to him. 'Up there was a chap
digging his allotment in the dark, and now you fishing. Caught
anything?'

'If I do I'll have you as witness to a holy miracle,' murmured the priest.
'I am only seeking peace. Unfortunately canal banks have become areas
of suspicion and a bachelor priest might find it embarrassing to merely
walk or stand along here at night. So I fish.'

Davies grinned in the dark. 'I was thinking of nicking you for
poaching, father,' he said.

'Chessus, now, I never thought of that,' replied the priest. 'I suppose I
could always plead that I was fishing for souls.'

'You'd need communion bread for bait,' suggested Mod. Davies told
Father Harvey who Mod was and the Father nodded up and Mod
nodded down.

'We passed a man up there in the alley who was wearing glasses with no lenses in them,' said Davies.

He heard the priest sniff. 'There's a lot of poverty about,' he observed.

'Or maybe it was a disguise.'

'It could have been that,' agreed Father Harvey. 'There's that place of degradation the council have allowed them to open at the top of the alley – the so-called "massage parlour". Hell masquerading as hygiene. He might have been going there and not wanting anyone to recognize him. The pawnshop and the massage parlour are both full of the unredeemed.'

'Good point. You should be in the force.'

'Thank you, my son,' said the priest laconically. They were silent for a while watching the deadpan water as though expecting a pike to bite at any moment. Then the priest said: 'I take it you haven't found out who burned down my confessional box?'

'No,' admitted Davies. 'We haven't got very far on that one. But I don't see it as an act of desecration.' He could see the priest's nose profiled like a triangle.

'I might have told my flock it was a sign from Heaven, or Hell,' said the priest. 'But experience tells me it was boys smoking in there.'

'It won't be easy to find out,' interpolated Mod. 'You won't get it out of them at Confession because you haven't got a confessional box. It's like the chicken and the egg.'

The priest showed no outward reaction. He appeared to be trying to analyse something in the water. 'You know, Dangerous,' he said coming to a conclusion, not turning his head. 'I can't help thinking that you're not really cut out for being a detective. If you could cut your drinking by half, I'd suggest the priesthood.'

'That's a pretty general opinion,' agreed Davies, with doleful sportsmanship. 'But, it happens, I am on an important inquiry at present.'

'Oh, and what would that be? Or can you tell?'

'I think I can. After all you're a man of secrets.'

'It goes with the job,' agreed the priest.

Davies crouched on the dank bank. Mod remained standing as though keeping watch. Davies asked: 'Father, do you remember Celia Norris?'

'Celia Norris,' nodded the priest. 'The girl was apparently murdered. A long time ago.'

'Twenty-five years,' said Davies. 'I've reopened the case.'

'Chessus,' said Father Harvey. 'It was when I first came here. In fact I only knew the girl a few weeks. I can't even remember her face.'

Davies could. 'It was never cleared up,' he said. 'It was just left.'

'You didn't come down here looking for footprints, by any chance, did you?' asked the priest.

'Not quite. But I thought I would just wander along and see if I could get any ideas.'

'She was at the youth club. And they never found anything,' said the priest.

'Her clothes,' said Davies. 'They found those. Except her . . . underpants.'

'Ah, her knickers,' agreed Father Harvey. 'Yes, I recall that fact.' He gave the fishing line a few ruminative jerks. 'Perhaps, now, she wasn't wearing any.'

'Father!' Davies said it. Mod began to whistle in the night.

'Well, like I said just now, there's a lot of poverty about. Twenty-five years ago it was no better.'

Davies considered again the priest's nose. In silhouette it appeared a lot longer than in daylight. 'Do you know where Mrs Norris, her mother, lives these days?' he asked.

'Yes, yes. Let me see. Hunter Street, by the power station. She still comes to church, sometimes.'

'Dave Boot,' said Davies. 'Remember Dave Boot, the youth club man, father? What was he like?'

'Muscles,' said Father Harvey decisively. 'All muscles. He did all this training nonsense. Chessus, he used to make me feel envious. I had a few muscles myself in those days, but I was required to hide them under my cassock. One of the sacrifices of spiritual life, you see. But there were times, I must confess when I would have swopped all the vestments of a bishop for a string vest.'

Davies laughed sombrely in the dark. Mod, who did not have a top coat, shuffled in the cold. Davies took the hint.

'We'll be going then, father,' said Davies.

'Right you are,' sniffed the priest. 'I wish you well with your mouldy old murder. This one's not only dead, it's been dead a long time. Cold ashes, Dangerous, cold ashes. You might find it's better left like that.'

'It's not an official investigation,' said Davies. 'I am doing it myself. In my own time.'

'Like a hobby?' said the priest still watching the water.

'Yes, you could say that. Like a hobby.'

CHAPTER FIVE

He began to rake the cold ashes by going to Hunter Street. It was one of the streets grouped around the cooling towers of the power station, midgets crowding giants. The stream and vapour from the towers kept it a perpetual rainy day. But it had compensations, for when the sun came out it filled the damp, melancholy streets with rainbows.

Davies stood at the front of the terraced house, the same as all the others but more in need of a paint. The door hung like a jaw. Months before someone had planted a Christmas tree in the patch of front garden hoping to defy God and make it grow. God had won. It stood brittle,

brown, shivering at the first fingering of another autumn. Davies
knocked at the door and several pieces of paint fell off. It appeared that a
whole system of locks was undone before the thin woman's face
appeared.

'What d'you want?'

'Mrs Norris?'

'That's right. What d'you want?'

'I've . . . I've come to have a talk with you, if I can. About your
daughter.'

'Josie. What's Josie done?'

'No. Not Josie. Celia.'

The eyes seemed to sprout quickly from the face. 'Celia?' she
whispered. 'Who are you then?'

'I'm a policeman.'

'You've . . . have you . . . found our Celia?'

'No. No we haven't.'

'Well go and have another look,' she said suddenly and bitterly.
'Bugger off.'

The door slammed resoundingly in his face and several more pieces of
paint fell off. He backed away because he was unsure what to do next. If a
door were shut during an official investigation then there were methods
of opening it again, even if it meant asking politely. But when it was just a
hobby it was more difficult.

He went out of the gate and began to walk thoughtfully along the
street. Approaching him from the power station end appeared a
wobbling motor scooter. It skidded noisily, slid by him and then was
backed up. It was ridden by a girl, small and dark. She pulled her head
out of her yellow crash helmet which had 'Stop Development in Buenos
Aires' written on it, and shook her hair. She only needed the ice cream
blob on her chin.

'Josie,' said Davies. 'You're Josie Norris.'

'You scored,' she said. 'Who are you? I saw you coming from our gate.'

'I'm a policeman,' he said apologetically. 'Detective Constable
Davies. Your mum just threw me out.'

'She would do,' nodded the girl confidently. 'Are you going to nick the
old man. He said he was considering going straight.'

'No. It's nothing to do with your father. It's Celia.'

'Christ,' she breathed. 'You haven't found something?'

'No. But I'm hoping to.'

'Hoping? Hoping?' she sounded incredulous. 'And I'm hoping to do a
straight swop with this scooter for a new Rolls Royce. When I'm
eighteen.'

'How long is that?'

'Eight months and three days. I'm free then. You're free when you're
eighteen now.'

'So I'm told. I seemed to have missed it.'

'You want to chat to my mum, do you?'

'Yes. Will you fix it?'

'You're serious about it,' she said thoughtfully. 'I mean you're not
going to bugger her about and then just drop it again. She's had enough
already.'

'I'm serious,' nodded Davies. He hesitated and then said. 'I don't
think it was ever properly investigated.'

'Why is it being investigated now?'

He decided to lie. 'New information. A man in prison has talked.'

'What did he say?'

'I can't tell you that.'

She looked at him on the angle. 'All right,' she said. 'I'll get her to meet
you. There's a Lyons Caff in the High Street, just by the florists.'

'I know it.'

'Make it three o'clock in there. She shut the door on you because my
dad's at home, I expect. But she'll be there.' She regarded him squarely,
a small, confident face protruding from a yellow oilskin jacket. 'But,
mister . . . promise you won't screw her up.'

'Promise,' said Davies.

The afternoon closed early as though it were anxious to be quit for the
day. Drizzle, the real thing from the sky, not from the cooling towers,
licked the shop windows in the High Street and buses shushed by on their
way to Cricklewood. Davies loitered across the road from the café,
imagining that he merged with the background shadow, his face almost
buried by the bowsprit of his overcoat. He felt quaintly confident in his
obscurity and was shaken when three apparent strangers wished him
good-afternoon, by name. Mrs Norris approached, unseen, and unerringly picking him out, announced: 'I'm here.'

Davies, disgruntled, followed her across the rainy road, and into the
café. She indicated that she was running the situation by nodding him
towards a corner table. Obediently he shuffled off to the marble slab
while she joined the self-service line. He watched her from his distance.
She had been tall but, although she was only in her fifties, her back was
beginning to bend. The face was fatigued and fixed, looking straight at
the neck of the woman before her in the queue, her eyes flicking around
occasionally but only briefly before returning to the stare. Davies sat and
opened the buttons of his coat. An Indian at the next table ate Heinz
spaghetti and double chips and was anointing it with whorls of brown
sauce. He sang quietly to himself, some song doubtless born in cool
faraway hills, interrupting the plaint to slurp loudly from his cup.

Mrs Norris arrived with the tea, her eyes sharp. 'All right, then,' she
sighed tiredly when she had seated herself opposite him. 'What's going
on about our Celia?'

'New information has come to light, Mrs Norris,' he said in the
policeman's manner he sometimes practised before his bedroom mirror.
'A man has talked. I can't tell you what he has said but he has talked.'

'Why can't you?'

'These things have to be proved,' he replied uncomfortably. 'Without
pre-conceived ideas.'

'Pre-conceived ideas,' she snorted into her tea. 'They was talking about them twenty-five years ago. Is it the same lot of ideas or a new lot?'

He nodded sympathetically. 'Yes, yes,' he said. 'I can guess what it's been like for you.'

'No, you can't,' she whispered, her eyes and nose almost in her cup. 'Nobody can. She was a good girl, Mr Davies. Very good. She used to bring me flowers and not many kids do that. And they tried to make out she was some kind of prostitute just because they never found her drawers.' She sniffed and when she raised her eyes, Davies saw they were smudgy.

'Don't cry, Mrs Norris,' he said with hurried helplessness. 'Not in Lyons.'

'I won't,' she promised. 'It's not so easy as you think to cry. Not after all this time.' She paused then looked at him with sad hope. 'How far have you got?'

'I've only just started. But I believe that after all this time, people will say things they only *thought* twenty-five years ago, or things they didn't even *realize* they knew.'

She nodded. 'People do change their tune,' she agreed. 'I know that. Too well.'

'How?' he said. 'In what way?'

'Well, you know. They're all sympathy and that at the time, then they avoid you and the whispers start going around. About my girl . . . And they're still at it. I mean, you know she went off once before. She was headstrong like that. One of the bloody Sunday papers brought the whole thing up again a couple of years ago, "What Happened to Happy Celia?" That was the headline. They sent some bloke to see me. I chucked a bucket of soapsuds over him.'

'You do want the answer, don't you?' he said.

'Yes I do, but not that way. Not all over the bleeding newspapers. Muckraking that's all that was. It's got to be done a bit on the quiet. That's the only way you or anybody else is going to find out anything.'

'When she went off before,' said Davies, 'Was that with a man?'

'I don't know,' she replied almost sulkily. 'When she came back she didn't say. She said she had been away for a change. I never asked her after that.'

The café was almost empty for it was mid-afternoon. Steam rose from the dishes at the counter which had not been in favour at lunchtime. Odours wandered from the back regions. A tramp came in and, after politely taking off his hat and giving his ragged hair a pat with his hand, sat down at a table near to the counter. At that distance he examined the brightly illuminated food like a patron at an art gallery. He knew his timing.

'Shepherd's pie for ten pence? That's less than half price,' suggested the woman across the counter. The tramp shook his head. 'I only got six,' he answered. 'All right, six,' sighed the woman. 'No wonder they reckon you're a millionaire.'

Davies said: 'They ought to do a tramp's pie and sell it to shepherds.'

Mrs Norris did not smile. 'There's some good-hearted people around,' was her only comment. She returned her face to Davies.

Eventually he said: 'Mrs Norris, do you think you could bear to go through it again? To tell me about that one day. I've seen the statements, but I want to hear it from you.'

'All right,' she said wearily. 'Can I have another cup?'

He rose. 'I could do with one myself.'

'I expect it'll go on expenses, won't it?' she asked genuinely.

'I'll fiddle it and make a profit,' he said. He went to the counter and got the teas. The tramp said: 'Hello Dangerous.'

Unprompted she began when he had returned to the table. 'It was the 23rd of July. She was at home in the morning, helping me. She was very good like that. It was a very hot day. There'd been about a week of hot weather. In the afternoon she went to the Employment place. It was only a little office in those days, not that great big place they've got now.'

'Times change,' he nodded. 'She was interested in nursing, wasn't she?'

Mrs Norris nodded. 'She'd have been a credit. She was a very kind-natured girl.' Her voice was without inflection, as though she were merely reciting something she had said many times before. 'They had a talk to her about nursing but she came to have her tea and went straight out to that bleeding youth club. She said she'd tell me all about it when she got back that night. And, she never did get back.'

'You didn't like the youth club?' he said.

'I don't know,' she shook her head. 'Nothing was ever said, but there was something *rotten* about it. Father Harvey never watched it like he ought to have done. But he was new here then. But I think he feels guilty about it. I think he knows how I feel about that.'

'You didn't care for Mr Boot?' suggested Davies.

Her eyes came to life, as though, in a moment some faith in him had been kindled. Then she subsided again. 'No, I didn't like that one,' she admitted. 'I expect you've seen the pictures.'

'Yes, the one of Mr Boot, Celia and another girl at some sort of garden fête.'

'Ena Brown,' said Mrs Norris. 'As was then. She's Ena Lind now.'

'Lind? Lind? Who else was called Lind?' he said trying to remember the names on the statements.

'Bill Lind,' she filled in flatly. 'He was our Celia's boyfriend. Just a friend. Like they are at that age. Not really a boyfriend.'

'And he married Ena, Celia's friend?'

'Yes. About three years after. They told the newspaper in that article . . . they said they had been "drawn together by the tragedy" or some bleeding muck like that. Drawn together! She was pregnant more like it. They've got one of those council maisonettes now. She looks like a tart and when I see him in the street he turns the other way. Makes out he don't know me.'

'And you didn't like Mr Boot?'

'No, I didn't care for him, neither.'

'Any idea where he is these days?'

'He's at Finchley or Mill Hill or somewhere like that. I saw in the paper he used to run a sort of disco place. And now, I saw an advert the other week, he's got one of these sex shops. Suit him, it should.'

'Still in youth work, eh?' sniffed Davies. He paused. The tea in his cup was beginning to congeal. He drank it quickly and made a face. 'Did they er . . . give you her clothes back . . . eventually?'

'The police? Yes, I got them back. I've still got them. It wasn't much because it was hot weather, like I said. It was a green gingham dress, a bra and her white socks and shoes. Like everybody knows, her lipstick, just a little Woolworth's lipstick, and her drawers were missing. Everybody.' Her voice was dead.

'You've still got the clothes, Mrs Norris?'

'Yes, but they're hidden away. I'm not showing them to you or nobody else.

'I see. I understand. Er . . . the youth that found the clothes in the toilet and took them home. Did you know him?'

'Poor little devil,' she said unexpectedly. 'That boy Parsons. The police gave him a hard time. They had to get their hooks into somebody, I s'pose. But he didn't do it, Mr Davies. I didn't know him before that time but I've seen him around since. He plays in the Salvation Army band now. I've seen him in the market. He always nods to me.'

'What did Mr Norris think about it all?' he asked.

'What d'you mean – what did he *think* about it?'

'How did he react?'

She considered the question again. 'He was like he always is when there's aggravation, shouting his mouth off, charging around, screaming for the police to do something.' She laughed bitterly. 'Come to think of it that's the only time I can ever remember him *wanting* the police to do something. He was upset, 'course he was, but he shows it different. I woke up in the night and heard him crying downstairs. He felt it all right, same as I did.'

'What's he *like*, your husband?'

'Bert Norris is all right, at times,' she said. He could see her selecting the words with care. 'He's a layabout, that's all. Work-bloody-shy. He's done time, like I expect you know. Silly things. He likes to think he's big. He was like it when I married him but I thought he'd grow out of it. He used to nick ration books then. Now it's car log books.'

'A man who moves with the times,' observed Davies. 'Do you love him?'

She seemed incredulous at the question. 'Love . . . him? Love him? Christ, that's a funny thing for a copper to ask. I don't know . . . I live in the same house with him if that's what it means. He's not somebody you can love. You don't sort of connect the word with Bert . . . not with my husband.'

'He's a friend of Cecil Ramscar, isn't he?'

The remnants of her stare from her surprise at the last question were still on her face. They solidified.

'Ramscar? He went off years ago. Never heard of him since.'

'He's back,' said Davies, deciding to take the chance.

'Back is he,' she muttered. 'I thought there was something going on.'

'With your husband?'

She backed away from the question by returning to the original. 'Ramscar – he used to come around and muck about when Celia was there. He always had his hands around her bottom and that sort of thing, but there, he would have a try with any female between eight and eighty. He reckoned he was big. He tried it on me once or twice....' She glanced at Davies uncomfortably. 'I . . . I was younger then, of course, I didn't look quite such an old ratbag. . . .'

Davies protested with his hands, but she stilled him with hers. He felt they were as hard as dried figs. She went on. 'He used to tell Bert that he'd like to 'ave me and our Celia in the same bed at the same time. That's how he was. All mouth and bloody trousers.'

'Do you think he could have caused Celia's death?' asked Davies quietly.

'God knows.'

'He was checked out by the police,' Davies pointed out.

'So was Jack the Ripper, I expect,' she muttered without humour.

She looked up from the depths of her tea cup. 'I'll have to go,' she said. 'The shops will be closing. If you want to ask me any more, tell Josie. She works in Antoinette's, that hairdresser by the clock in the High Street.

'Right,' he said. 'I will. I'm sorry it's been so painful for you. I hope I can do something.' He thought for a moment. She was gathering up her handbag and her coat. 'One thing,' he finished. 'People don't seem to move from this district very much. Most of those who were here then are still here or roundabout.'

She smiled more softly. 'No, people don't seem to move away very much from here,' she said. 'It's very homely and friendly, really.'

CHAPTER SIX

That night Dangerous went out with Mod and got seriously drunk at 'The Babe In Arms'. Mod was at his most loquacious and informative, extemporizing on the poisoned arrows used, he said by certain tribes in Upper India, the sexual taboos of the first period Incas and the history of tramcars in Liverpool. On their stumbling way home to Mrs Fulljames's house they found a horse walking morosely along the street. They recognized it as belonging to a local scrap merchant. Mod said they ought to inform the police so he reported it to Dangerous, who took brief notes. They eventually tied the horse to the doorknocker of a neighbouring house and went home to bed.

The following day Davies went to seek out Dave Boot. The sex emporium was not difficult to locate. It was called 'The Garden of Ooo-la-la'. There was a large sticker across the window announcing: 'Sale'. Davies, who had never visited such an establishment, inspected it with ever-ascending eyebrows. A willowy youth was swaying behind the counter, moving to muted music. Davies approached him: 'What's in the sale?' he inquired.

'Everything, love,' replied the youth. 'Absolutely everything. Depends what your requirements are really, don't it.'

'I'm not sure what they are,' said Davies.

'Ooooo, you lads do get yourself in a state, don't you,' marvelled the assistant. 'How about a Japanese tickler, slightly shop soiled.'

'Are the rubber women in the sale?' inquired Davies.

'Some of the older models are,' shrugged the boy. 'They perish.'

'Where's Dave Boot?' asked Davies.

The youth's aloof expression sharpened with the hardness in Davies's voice. 'Dave Boot . . . oh, Mr Boot. He's doing something at the disco.'

'Detective Constable Davies,' said Dangerous showing his card. 'Get him eh?'

The young man brushed his hair away from his fair eyes and dithered with the telephone. Davies wandered to the back of the shop and, on impulse, slid through a curtain into the back room. He was intrigued to find a partly inflated rubber woman with an attached foot-pump, lolling against a desk. Unable to resist it he depressed the pump and then let it go, then depressed it, and continued with the sequence, watching to his fascination as the woman inflated to life before his eyes. She grew to full size, then to outsize and then to enormous proportions. Mesmerized, Davies could not stop. He went on pumping. The woman grew fatter and fatter. Her eyes, her cheeks and her breasts all bulged hugely. He could hear the rubber creaking. He went on pumping. Her expanding backside knocked a chair over.

'Stop!' The cry came through the door. A tall, thick man in a tight denim suit rushed forward and pulled out a valve in the buttocks. The woman shrivelled horrifyingly.

'If she'd have exploded you'd have killed yourself,' said the man. 'Stupid bloody thing to do.'

Davies was gazing sadly at the collapsing rubber figure. 'Now I know what God feels like,' he said. He turned and smiled without warmth. 'Nice place you've got here.'

'We fill a need,' sniffed the man. 'What did you want?'

'I'm Detective Constable Davies.'

'Yes, Tarquin said. I'm Dave Boot. What was it?'

'Can I sit down? I'm puffed out after that pumping.'

Boot picked up the chair which the woman had knocked down. Davies sat on it gratefully and Boot sat behind the desk. The youth Tarquin came through the curtain and asked if they would require coffee. Boot was going to send him away but Davies said he would like some and smiled his advanced thanks.

'Right, two,' said Boot at the head issuing through the curtain.

'But don't stir it with your finger.' Davies called after him.

Boot grimaced. 'I'm pretty busy,' he said. 'What did you want?'

'Me too,' said Davies amiably. 'Ever so busy. I wanted you to tell me about Celia Norris.'

White astonishment flew into Boot's face. 'Celia . . . Celia Norris?' He got it out eventually. 'Christ, that was years ago.'

'You still remember, don't you?'

'Yes, yes. But why . . . why now?'

'There's never any particular season.'

'Yes, but . . . aw come on. What is all this? The police went through it all at the time. Christ, hours of it. They cleared me. They had nothing. . . .'

'I didn't say you *did* anything.' Davies pointed out quietly. 'I only asked you if you remembered. Nobody's come to arrest you.'

'I shouldn't bloody well think so, either,' said Boot, his skin hardening. 'I think I want my solicitor along here. I can't afford trouble. I'm a businessman.'

'So I see,' said Davies looking down at the deflated rubber woman.

'And there's nothing you can touch me for here, either,' said Boot following his glance. 'Nothing. It's all legal. Anyway, I'll call my solicitor.'

'Call him if you like,' offered Davies with more confidence than he felt. 'But you'll be wasting your money. Nobody's putting any pressure on you, Mr Boot. We've reopened the case of Celia Norris and I've got the job of checking on people who made statements at the time. That's all there is to it.'

Boot subsided. 'All right then, if that's all it is. But what difference it makes, Christ knows. I told them everything at the time.'

Tarquin came through the curtain, curiously knocking on it as though it were a door. He was carrying a cardboard tray with two plastic beakers of coffee. He smiled wanly at Davies. 'There, Inspector, that's yours.' Davies and Boot took the beakers. The youth backed out. 'I didn't stir it,' he smiled. 'Not with my finger, anyway.'

Davies stared into the swirling coffee and wondered what he had stirred it with. He put it untouched on the table.

'You remember the night when it happened, I take it,' he said leaning towards Boot. 'When she went off and vanished.'

'Well, of course I remember it. It was bloody years ago though . . . how long?'

'Twenty-five,' Davies told him.

'Yes, well, I mean. Twenty-five. It's not like it was yesterday. But I remember it all right. I'm not likely to forget it am I?'

'I'm hoping you might remember bits now that didn't seem important at the time, now you've had a while to turn it over in your mind.'

Boot glanced at him under his puffy lids. 'All I knew I told then,' he grunted. 'Every single thing. God, I went over it enough with them.'

Davies nodded. 'I've seen your statement,' he said. 'You saw her at the youth club, she went off on her bike and that was that. You didn't even know she was missing until one of her friends told you some days later.'

'That's how it was. Exactly. I said it then and I say it again now.'

Davies mused. He picked up the coffee absent-mindedly and took a sip. Horror rolled across his face as he realized what he had done. Boot laughed sarcastically. 'Don't worry about the coffee. He probably just stirred it with a Japanese tickler.'

Davies grimaced. He pushed the beaker out of reach across the table so that he would not be moved to pick it up again. Then he leaned again towards Boot, confidingly. 'Statements are just sort of catalogues of fact, see. I did this at such and such a time, and then I did that. They're not very filling, if you know what I mean, Mr Boot. A lot of bones and not much meat. They never tell you how people *feel*. I want to find out that. How they *felt* about Celia Norris. How did you feel about her?'

'Feel?' Boot shrugged and spread his hands. 'Nothing. Nothing at all. She was just a kid at the youth club.'

'You didn't fancy her then?'

Boot glared. 'Sod off, I'm going to get my solicitor. Like I said. I should have before.'

'Don't bother,' reassured Davies. 'I'm going now. I only wanted to have a look at you. Just let me ask you one more thing before I'm off.'

Boot sulked and said nothing but Davies pretended not to notice.

'How would you have described her behaviour, Celia's, sexually. She was seventeen. Do you think she was a virgin?'

Surprisingly, Boot thought about it. 'I don't know about her virginity, I'm sure. They used to keep it longer in those days, didn't they?'

'So I understand.'

'Yes, so do I. But they were all full of it. You know . . . flirty.'

'Flirty,' smiled Davies. 'Ah, Mr Boot that's a lovely old-fashioned word, I think I'll write that down.' He took out his notebook carefully, while Boot watched impatiently, and wrote down 'FLIRTY' in capital letters and with great care. He stood back and considered it as though it were some prize etching. 'Flirty', he repeated. 'Lovely.'

'Well, she was,' said Boot, unhappy that he had said anything, but somehow drawn to continue. 'We used to say they were P.T.s didn't we, Mr Davies? Prick teasers.'

'Did we!' exploded Davies. 'Did *we* now? And why should we say that? Prick teasers. Just a minute I want to write that down too.' Boot swallowed heavily as Davies wrote the words painstakingly beneath the word 'FLIRTY'. He regarded the prase as he had regarded the single word. 'My goodness,' he said mildly. 'That takes you back, doesn't it, Mr Boot? It really takes you back.'

'Not me, personally,' muttered Boot. 'It was just a saying at the time. Yu must know that.'

'Flirty prick teasers,' mused Davies rubbing his chin. 'Celia Norris.'

'Yes,' said Boot stubbornly. 'Celia Norris.'

'And why would you say that about her?'

'Because I've got eyes,' said Boot desperately. I could *see* what she was like couldn't I? She had a boyfriend there. . . .'

'Bill Lind,' prompted Davies. 'Good old Bill Lind.'

Boot stared at him hard. 'That's him. That poor bugger used to go crazy. But they were all the same, those girls. Today at least, they're honest. They *give* something.'

'Do they?' asked Davies his eyebrows ascending.

'Surely even you know that. The kids now are more straightforward about sex and that. They don't have the frustrations we used to have.'

'Didn't we just, Mr Boot,' said Davies. He looked again at the three words he had written, studying them as though he thought they might be an anagram. 'Flirty old Celia Norris,' he grinned.

'Flirty Celia Norris,' nodded Boot savagely.

'And Ena Brown, said Davies. 'Flirty Ena Brown?'

There was no vestige of colour in Boot's face now. 'Ena Brown,' he muttered. 'Her as well.'

At 'The Babe In Arms' a representative of the Spanish Tourist Office was making a presentation to the rough woman who had broken her ankle while dancing to 'Viva España'. It was followed by a similar presentation from the juke box company. The ceremony was attended by press representatives and embryo celebrities who had come to try and get their pictures in the newspapers. The landlord beamed on the scene.

Davies and Mod left the bar early and in disgust, for the evening meal at 'Bali Hi', Furtman Gardens. 'I think I would prefer the silence of that lonely room to the false glamour we witnessed back there,' said Mod sorrowfully as they walked down Furtman Gardens. 'Vanity, vanity, all is vanity and publicity.'

'Commerce,' corrected Davies. He had been telling Mod about his visit to Dave Boot. 'Can you imagine a shop like *that*? Floor to ceiling with sexual fantasy.'

'And he probably does very nicely from it too,' nodded Mod. 'They say that in Arabia there are men who sell *shade* to pilgrims walking the hot road to Mecca. They put up an awning or rent a bit of wall and they charge people to stand in the shade for a few minutes. It's supply and demand.'

At 'Bali Hi' they found a new lodger established at the table, an Indian, Mr Patel, who was soon engaged by Mod who asked about tribal customs of the North-West Frontier about which Mr Patel knew nothing since he came from Tottenham. Thin Minnie Banks squeaked girlishly at the error but Mr Smeeton, on this evening disguised as a harlequin, showed renewed interest.

'One of my acts is a sort of conjuring extravaganza,' he said. 'I wouldn't mind a bloke in a turban to be Gilly-Gilly, the funny assistant. Would that interest you?'

Mr Patel politely refused the offer on the grounds that he was busy with his job as a lecturer in Metallurgy and he did not possess a turban anyway. He apologized that he knew nothing of the tribal customs on the North-West Frontier.

This was digested in uncomfortable silence. Doris knocked her fork onto the floor and they all jumped. Davies said diplomatically: 'I think the tribal customs of North-West London are probably a good deal more primitive.'

'He's a detective,' said Mr Smeeton caustically nodding his harlequin head towards Davies. 'But he's no bloody good. Not from what we hear, anyway.'

Mr Patel smiled agreeably. 'It is very nice to be in a household where everybody speaks so frankly.'

'Detective!' snorted Mrs Fulljames appearing from her kitchen cavern with a cauldron of stew. 'Detective!' The pot seemed to be pulling her along like a steam engine.

'Don't tell me you've lost another bed,' observed Davies wearily.

'No. But the other one hasn't been found either,' she sniffed. 'Antique. And I suppose you slept all through the racket last night. All the screams and everything. It woke the whole street up but not you.'

'What did I miss *last* night?'

'Somebody tied a horse to Mrs Connelly's door knocker. Somebody's idea of a joke.'

A glance each from Mod and Davies crept across the table.

'A horse?' protested Davies. 'I'm a policeman not a groom.'

'It was a crime,' said Mrs Fulljames firmly slopping out the lamb stew. Davies saw Mr Patel looking at it doubtfully. So did Mod. 'It's quite all right, Mr Patel,' said Mod, his voice booming ghostlike through the vapour. 'It's sheep not sacred cow.'

'Thank you, thank you,' muttered Mr Patel.

'The upset!' said Mrs Fulljames, still pursuing the horse. 'It kept banging on Mrs Connelly's door knocker and neighing or whinnying or whatever they do. And that poor woman came down in her nightdress and the animal walked straight into her front hall. Petrified she was, and who can blame her?'

'Who indeed,' said Davies staring into the volcanic stew.

'Well *you* didn't hear it,' complained Doris. 'People miles away must have heard it, all that screaming and the horse making a terrible noise. But not you.'

'It went right in, right in the hall,' said Mrs Fulljames sitting down with her plate sending its veil to her face. The meal was beginning to resemble a séance. 'And it trod on Mr Connelly's foot when he came down to see what was going on. He's off work for a month.'

'A month at least, knowing Mr Connelly,' commented Davies. 'What did they do with the horse, shoot it?'

'It belongs to that terrible man down the town, Scribbens isn't it? The rag-and-bone merchant. They got him to come and take it back. Disgusting business altogether. Poor woman.'

They paused to eat and the steam subsided as they emptied their plates. Eventually Mr Patel said: 'A detective, Mr Davies, most interesting, most. And what, if it is possible to divulge, are you investigating at this moment?'

'Apart from my stolen bed,' sniffed Mrs Fulljames.

'Well,' Davies hesitated. 'A sort of missing person.'

It was early closing day but Antoinette (Paris, Switzerland and Hemel Hempstead) Ladies' Hairdressers remained stubbornly open. Davies loitered in the lee of a telephone box across the street until Josie came out for her lunch at two o'clock. He was, as usual, disconcerted when she immediately walked across the road to him.

'How did you spot me?' he inquired unhappily.

'Spot you? Blimey half the shop saw you,' she laughed. 'You'd be surprised how well-known you are in these parts, Dangerous. Marie – that's my friend in the salon – you nicked her brother for stealing scrap metal a couple of years ago, but he got off because of some technicality. You'd lost your notes or something.'

Davies sighed. 'I seem to remember that,' he admitted.

'They do, too. Marie said they still have a good laugh about it.'

'Thanks.' They had begun to walk apparently aimlessly along the shut street.

'Then the lady whose perm we were doing said you'd found her front door swinging open one night and you walked in and her old man smashed you over the head with a chair, because he thought you was a burglar.'

'Yes, I recall that too. He broke the chair.'

'Bertha – that's Antoinette – and most of the customers and staff knew you in some way or another. Didn't you see them crowding to the windows to look at you trying to hide behind that phone box?'

'Well, I did think you had rather a big crowd in there for a small place,' admitted Davies. 'I thought it was your busy morning that's all.'

'You talked to my mum, didn't you,' she said.

'Yes.'

'She trusts you, she does. Are you still working on the thing about our Celia?'

Davies arched his eyebrows. 'Of course I am. I've only been on it a few days.'

'What's that after twenty-five years?' shrugged Josie. 'I've got some sandwiches. I was going to get a bus and sit up by the Welsh Harp. My scooter's got a puncture. I'm going by the reservoir. As it's a decent day.'

It was too. There had been a smattering of October sun through the morning and, miraculously it now grinned over the entire sky.

'You can come as well if you like, Dangerous,' said Josie. 'I won't eat all my sandwiches myself.'

'All right,' he said. They walked along the closed faces of the shops. The white bodices of the cooling towers looked strangely clean in the sunshine. They were comfortable in each other's company. The bus arrived opportunely and they boarded it, sitting without speaking on the cross-seats on the lower deck. They reached the Welsh Harp, a shapely lake shining benignly beyond the reach of the factory fumes. Three small sailing dinghies, one with red sails, swam across its easy surface. Davies and Josie walked to a seat overlooking the water and sat down. She opened a packet of sandwiches and gave him one. It was cheese and pickle.

'Your mother,' said Davies through his bread. 'She's never got over it, has she?'

'You don't have to be Maigret to see that,' she commented, but not directly at him. 'She'll never get it off her mind. When the anniversary comes round she's almost mental.' She paused as though weighing up whether to add something. She decided she would. 'It sounds a silly thing to say, I know,' she ventured. 'But it's . . . it's almost, sort of, given her something to live for.'

Davies glanced sideways at her and whistled softly to himself. 'That's a strange remark,' he said.

'I said it was, didn't I,' she pointed out. 'But it has, Dangerous . . . You don't mind me calling you that do you? What's your proper first name?'

'Percival,' he lied.

She regarded him seriously. 'Dangerous . . .' she said. She bit fiercely into her sandwich. She had a sharply pretty face and gentle hair. She had opened her coat and her small breasts just touched the surface of her sweater. The sun blew across her colourless urban face.

'Yes Josie?' he said.

'Dangerous, you really *want* to do this don't you?'

'Yes, I do.'

'Why? I mean, why all of a sudden? I don't believe all that cobblers about some bloke talking in prison, even if my mum does.'

'I don't like to see something left,' he replied defensively. 'Just abandoned. Don't you think I ought to find out?' He hesitated. 'If I can.'

'Who is it in aid of, Dangerous?' she asked quietly. She opened the top slice of her sandwich and said to herself. 'No pickle in this one.' She returned her small face to him. 'Who is it for?' she repeated. 'Is it for Celia or my mum? Or is it for you?'

He felt a shaft of guilt. 'It's not *for* anybody,' he protested. 'All I know is that somebody is walking about free today – with blood on their hands.'

'Dried blood,' she sniffed. 'He'll hardly remember it now. Have you ever done a murder case before?'

'No.' He did not look at her. 'This is the first.'

'Did your inspector, or whoever it is, tell you to do it? Or are you just doing it off your own bat?'

'On my own,' he mumbled. He examined the sandwich in his hand and, carefully selecting a site, bit into it.

'I thought so,' she said. 'It's like a hobby, then.'

Father Harvey had said that. The repetition of the word stung him. 'It's *not* a hobby!' he said angrily. 'I'm going to find out who killed Celia!'

'Don't get out of your bloody pram,' said Josie. She was looking at him calmly. 'I don't know whether it's going to make anyone better off, that's all. I might as well tell you, I'd have nothing to do with it. But my mum seems to think you can do something.' She looked up and then held his sleeve. 'Christ,' she said. 'That little boat's turned over, Dangerous. The bloke's in the water.'

'They do it all the time,' answered Davies looking up. 'People ring us and the fire brigade and God knows who else. But we tell them not to worry because it's part of the sport. They enjoy it.'

'You leave *them* be, then,' she said pointedly.

'We do,' he said. 'One day one of them will drown and everybody will moan and say why didn't we do anything.'

She sighed sadly and threw a whole sandwich at a loitering bird. It flew away in fright, but then returned cautiously, hardly able to believe its luck. 'How far have you got?' she said. 'Anywhere?'

'Bits and pieces,' he shrugged. 'It will take a while. Do you want to help me?'

She eased her eyes. 'All right. But don't let it bugger up my mother, will you. She's had twenty-five years of it.' She seemed undecided whether to tell him something. 'Even now, and this sounds mad I know, even now she seems to think that somehow you're going to bring Celia back – alive!'

'Oh Christ, no.'

'Oh Christ, yes,' she said. 'You can see what I'm getting at. I was a sort of replacement for her, you see. I'm a sort of second-hand Celia. They had another baby after she went but it was stillborn. That didn't help.'

'I bet,' nodded Davies. The man had righted his dinghy and was climbing back aboard. He was wearing yellow oilskins and a life-jacket. Davies said. 'You said a funny thing about your mother. . . .'

'About Celia giving her something to live for? Yes, it sounds funny, I know, but that's just how it seems sometimes. If it had not happened, her disappearing, Celia would have grown up like anybody else, got married and cleared off. In a way she's been much more of a daughter for my mum, since she's been dead. If she is dead. No matter what I do, Dangerous, I'll never make up for her.'

He patted her hand with his half-eaten sandwich. 'I see,' he nodded. She smiled in her young way. The sun was still on them. 'It's a pity you never knew Celia,' he added.

'Knew her!' Her laugh came out bitterly. 'I've spent my whole life with her, mate.'

'You don't like her very much do you?'

'There's nothing to like or dislike. You can't dislike a ghost. I never saw her, did I, or 'eard her speak. She's just a name to me. But it's a name that keeps coming up if you know what I mean. If my mum could do a swop, me for our Celia, she'd have 'er every time. I'm stuck with that, see.'

Davies nodded. 'I see.' He waited. 'Do you think your mum knows who did it?'

'I think she thinks she does,' said Josie wiping a stray bean from her chin.

'How about Cecil Ramscar, for a start?'

'She's never said as much.'

'What do you think?'

'Christ knows. I wasn't around twenty-five years ago. But he could have. He sent a wreath.'

CHAPTER SEVEN

He went back to the police station thinking about Ramscar. When he reached there he discovered that the Ramscar file had been locked in a cupboard with the divisional sporting trophies, the supply of tea bags and the tear-gas cannisters. The keys were with an officer who was attending the magistrates' court so Davies walked around there.

It was a busy day in the court and as was usual a lot of ordinary innocent people had come in to sit and watch for a while. There were loaded shopping baskets and loaded expressions in the public seats. He entered as stealthily as he could, falling over a wheelbarrow which was being used as an exhibit in the case being heard. Everyone turned to see him. The public laughed, the police and the magistrates sighed, the man in the dock pointed a stare at him, a look threaded with uncertainty. Davies nervously recognized him as the man he had helped with the sack of vegetables over the allotment hedge a few nights previously. He sidled out of the accused's sight.

The prisoner was being called from the dock to give evidence on his own behalf in the witness box. He dismounted one stand to mount the other, reading the oath in a suitably earthy voice. Davies looked around for the sergeant who had the key to the police station cupboard.

He saw him squatting at the end of a row of policemen waiting to give evidence in the court's crowd of cases. Davies advanced with dainty clumsiness, hunched low in the way of a soldier moving under fire, until squatting in his piled overcoat by the officer he persuaded him to surrender the key. He was aware of the court proceedings freezing all around him. He looked up to see the Godlike faces of the magistrates high on their dais regarding him sourly. The rest of the people were either standing or leaning, trying to get a view of the dwarf in the voluminous raincoat who had wafted so clumsily across the floor.

'Mr Davies, is it?' asked the chairman of the bench, knowing perfectly well that it was.

'Yes, your honour,' replied Davies still crouching criminally.

'Will you be long?'

'No sir. Sorry sir. Just getting the key to the police station cupboard.' He looked up beggingly to the uniformed sergeant, who red to the cheekbones, searched and eventually found the key and delivered it to him. Davies began to retrace his progress through the court still at his midget's crouch.

'Mr Davies,' called the chairman. 'There's no need for you to continue with this impersonation of the Hunchback of Notre-Dame. You may walk normally.'

There was laughter in court. Davies, hung with embarrassment, rose to his proper height and bowed at the bench. He backed away and was about to collide with the wheelbarrow when he was pulled firmly into a vacant seat by the court warrant officer. 'Sit down for a bit,' said the exasperated official below his breath. 'Just sit down.'

Davies gratefully sat down. The case proceeded. From the witness box the prisoner was making a histrionic plea. 'That allotment, your lordship, has been in our family for years. My father and my grandfather 'ad it. Then me. It was like our heritage. I took it on, carrying on the tradition, but then I was on the sick for months and I couldn't keep it up and the council comes along and takes it off me. After all those years. . . .'

Davies found himself nodding sympathetically. 'They gave it to some other bloke,' said the accused brokely. 'My land.'

The chairman leaned over logically. 'So you think that entitles you to go in the darkness and steal his produce?' he suggested.

'I manured that allotment,' said the man bleakly.

The courtroom door opened to Davies's right as someone came into the chamber. The duty officer nudged Davies and he took his cue and shuffled out. As he did so the garden gangster was returning to his accused place in the dock. Davies did not know why, but he let himself take a final glance.

When Davies returned to the police station his way was barred by a rowdy phalanx of boys, all noisily disputing the ownership of a ravaged-looking tortoise which squatted neutrally before the desk sergeant on the counter. The sergeant silenced the din with a single shout. Davies ducked and felt it go over his head.

'Now – who found this ugly bugger in the first place?' demanded the sergeant. Through the conflict that followed he called to Davies. 'There's another file of Ramscar stuff come from the Yard, Dangerous. The Inspector said to look through it and then go up and see him. It's in your locker.'

Davies fought his way through the squabbling lads. Several of the smaller ones had begun to cry. He shut the door of the C.I.D. Room behind him. A policeman who had been concerned with traffic duty for as long as Davies could remember, was sitting masticating over the collection of pornographic pictures which Detective Sergeant Myers had been investigating.

'Hello, hello, hello,' said Davies in his deepest police tone. 'Looking for suspected traffic offenders, eh?' The policeman grinned sheepishly but rose and put the pictures back in a cardboard box. 'It's all right for you lot, Dangerous,' he sighed. 'All I see all day is idiot bloody motorists and lollypop women.'

He went out sadly and Davies took the new Ramscar file from his locker and set it out on the table. It contained reports and photographs from Australia and from America. He went through the material conscientiously, sniffing along the lines of the written summaries and examining the photographs, taken over a period of years, with Ramscar getting thicker and more prosperous as time elapsed.

There was a photograph in a separate envelope marked 'Return to Criminal Records Dept. New Scotland Yard, London.' Davies opened it. To his surprise he found himself looking at a wedding-day picture of Ramscar. He attempted a whistle, another accomplishment beyond him. Nothing but hushed air came out. On the back the picture was stamped 'May 14th. 1965'. Davies turned it over slowly. It was an immobile wedding group, everything fixed from feet to smiles, with Ramscar, then in his thirties, hugging a big clouded blonde, whose hair, hat and bouquet were being dragged away by what appeared to be a near-gale. The trousers of the men in the group blew out stiffly like flags. Ramscar had a flower in his lapel and another waggishly between his teeth. Grouped around him were a team of London criminals and their loved ones. Mrs Norris was there, clay-faced, and next to her was a furtive man who, he correctly guessed, was Albert Norris. In front of the group was a dainty girl in a bonnet holding a posy and simpering as small girls do at weddings. At first Davies hardly noticed her but then he looked, and put the photograph under the magnifying glass he once more quickly borrowed. The expression was unmistakable. It was Josie.

He eventually folded the file and carried it up four flights of stairs to Yardbird's office. He knocked and waited for the customary two minutes before Yardbird answered. He had been by the window for there was new cigarette ash on the floor and there was a girl standing on the flat roof of the students' hostel looking out over the streets. But now he was back behind his desk and trying to give the impression he had been working heavily there all the time.

'I've been through these, sir,' said Davies putting the file on the edge of the desk. 'Ramscar's new file.'

'Did they tell you anything?' asked Yardbird without looking up from the report he was ostensibly writing.

'This and that,' shrugged Davies. 'I've got a pretty good picture of him now. All I have to do is find him.'

'Yardbird said with off-hand tartness. 'That's all you had to do from the beginning, Davies. We don't want you to write his life story, we want to know where he is.'

'I've been making inquiries, sir, as well. All over the place. It won't be too long before I run into him, I expect.' He paused, then decided to go on even though Yardbird was still writing, his eyes fixed down. 'He's been in bother everywhere, hasn't he,' said Davies.

'We all know that,' sighed Yardbird. 'All sorts of villainy. I told you that at the very start.'

Davies rose and took the file from the desk. 'I'll keep this then,' he said. 'I'll keep it with our own file. There was enough in that to hang him.'

Yardbird eventually looked up. 'What are you going on about, Davies? he asked wearily. 'Christ, you gabble on like an old woman, sometimes. Can't you see I'm up to my ears in work?'

'Sorry,' said Davies moving towards the door.

'What was it anyway? You were just saying?'

Davies kicked himself afterwards, but it seemed to come out of its own volition. 'He looked fair game for a murder charge, once,' he said. 'Remember the Norris murder?'

'He's been close to murder . . . *which* murder?'

'Norris. Celia Norris. Seventeen. July nineteen fifty-one. Never solved.'

Yardbird put his pen down. 'Now listen, Davies,' he said angrily. 'Don't let's have any of your usual frigging things up. I sent you to find a man, not scratch about with bloody history. I had my doubts about your ability to handle this Ramscar thing, and I should have had a few more. I can see that now.'

'No, sir,' protested Davies. 'I'll find Ramscar.'

'Well *find* him then. Get out and find him, man. And stop mucking about with things that don't matter any more.'

Davies went outside. 'Fuck you for a start,' he said below his breath. 'It matters to me.'

It was a chill afternoon for anyone to be stripping. Davies felt a pang of pity for the girl on the apron stage as she went through the traditional ritual of her work. Her face was distant, her movements never quite synchronized with the music that wheezed from somewhere amid the coloured light bulbs that fringed, but hardly illuminated, the perform-ance. There was little style about the audience either.

There were three overcoated businessmen, curled like moles. A fourth snored voluminously. There was a butcher's delivery man, whose pulpitted bicycle Davies had observed parked outside. He sat in his blotched and striped apron, watching the girl almost professionally. There were two lank-haired youths both of whom Davies recognized from their appearances in court. Sitting on one of the unkempt chairs also, occasioning in Davies a certain surprise, was a Red Cross nurse.

'What's she for? In case anyone faints with excitement?' Davies asked the bouncer.

'Nah, she ain't a real proper nurse,' replied the guardian. 'She couldn't stick a plaster on your arse. She's part of the show.'

'What does she do then? The kiss of life?'

'Nah. She takes 'er duds off, don't she. You know, black stockings and that gear. Nurses strippin' is a favourite.' He nodded disparagingly at the tableau of watchers.

A small, featureless man with dangling arms had been despatched to find Albert Norris. The messenger now returned ambling across the stage, passing within an inch of the performing girl's ramshackle bottom, and approached them like an obedient chimpanzee. "'E's gorn,' he said. 'Just gorn out the back way.'

Davies stepped between the turgid customers, whose trance he failed to disturb, and strode briskly onto the stage, excusing himself with a bow to the occupant, and then went out into the street through an exit situated within inches of the plywood wings. He failed to close the door fully and was followed by a howl from the girl: 'The door! Shut the bleeding door!' He mumbled an apology and turned but she, naked as she was, emerged half way through the opening into the street, made a violent remark, and slammed the door.

He was in a long road, a service access, behind some shops, and he immediately saw Norris, who had reached the end and was turning into the main road. Davies went at a hurried amble after him. Norris, a small man, was, however, wearing a check overcoat and was an easy target. Davies reached the junction with the main road just as Norris turned to see if he was folllowing. Norris paused, then went into a cinema, following a series of pensioners waiting to pay their reduced afternoon prices at the box office. By the time Davies had reached the foyer Norris was inside.

Davies paid for a ticket. He stood and as his eyes came to terms with the surroundings he could see that the place was ranked with empty seats with an island of twenty or so patrons gathered together, as though for mutual protection, in the centre. Davies trod cautiously towards them. When he reached the small colony he saw that it consisted of old age pensioners, softly chewing, faces rapt, spectacles reflecting the spectacle which was now dawning on the screen. The exception was the chequered figure of Albert Norris sitting incongruously among them. There was an empty seat in the row before him.

Davies pushed along the row of sharp knees and hands and sat in the seat. He turned immediately and looked at Albert Norris. 'Can you see all right?' he inquired politely.

'What you following me for?' asked Norris bluntly.

'Shush.' 'Shut up,' chorused the aged people.

'Sorry,' apologized Davies generally. He watched two minutes of the film then returned to Norris, the weasel face set among all the small rabbit faces.

'I wanted to have a chat with you,' he said at just above a whisper.

'Shush.' 'Hush.' 'Shut your mouths,' complained the old folks. The crone next to Davies dug him in the ribs with her spiked elbow. He kept looking at Norris.

'Chat?' asked Norris. 'What we got to chat about?'

'All sorts of things,' answered Davies. 'Ramscar for one.'

He saw the man's face change even in the dimness. But then his shoulder was seized and he turned to see the angry expression of an aged man standing over him. He wore a bowler hat at a threatening angle.

'Why can't you poofters go and sit somewhere else?' demanded the man. 'Comin in 'ere spoiling the fillum for decent people.' A chorus of threatening support came from all around.

'If you want to hold 'ands or whisper sweet bleedin' nothings go and do it in the park,' the spokesman went on. 'If you don't pack it up we'll set on you.'

'Set on them!' quivered a voice.

'I think we'd better move, angel,' said Davies.

'Funny bugger,' glowered Norris. He got up and pushed his way past the elderly. Davies did likewise. The old people pummelled them and struck them with sticks and umbrellas as they went by.

'Nancies!'

'Bum-boys!'

The old fashioned taunts pursued them up the central aisle. Davies put his arm affectionately around Norris's waist. Norris shook him off and they made their exit to a wild chorus of raspberries.

They walked, a yard apart like friends who have recently quarrelled, along the towpath of the canal. The afternoon had become dimmer and on either side the houses and the backs of shops and small factories stood in a cold frieze.

'Where's Ramscar?' asked Davies.

'How in the 'ell do I know?' returned Norris. Davies decided that all Josie had inherited from her father was her smallness. His eyes were hard-bright.

Davies watched the aimless water of the canal. Norris said 'If you don't pack up bothering me and my missus and my daughter I'm going to complain. Even a copper can't keep 'arassing you, or didn't they ever tell you?'

'Harassing?' said Davies heavily. 'Harassing? This is the first time I've had the pleasure of your company, Mr Norris.'

'But you been at the wife and Josie,' argued Norris. 'I hear what's going on. And I don't bloody like it. I'm clean. I 'aven't done anything in two years. No, my mistake, four years. So you got no reason.'

'You know why I'm checking, then, I take it?'

'Our Celia, so you reckon,' said Norris. His hard small face turned to Davies. 'She's dead and nobody knows who done it. So don't give *me* all this crap about digging the whole bloody thing up again. It's bleedin' cruel, disgusting, the way you coppers go about things sometimes.'

'Did Ramscar do it?' inquired Davies quietly.

'Oh Christ! No, no, no, he didn't do it.' Norris stopped on the towpath. He caught Davies's sleeve fiercely. 'Listen, mate,' he said firmly. 'Ramscar *didn't* do it. Let me tell you that for gospel. He was at Newmarket. Do you think I would have kept it quiet? She was my girl, you know.'

Davies stared at the bitter face. 'Where's Ramscar now?' he said.

'Norris began to walk on angrily. 'I told you, I don't know. He cleared off abroad years ago. I thought even the police knew that.'

'I've heard he is back,' replied Davies. A duck moved unemotionally along the canal and was followed by its mate, cruising under the bridge.

Davies wondered if their feet ever got cold.

'Well you know more than I do,' said Norris. 'I ain't seen anything of 'im. You'd better ask somebody else.'

'What happened to his wife?' asked Davies. He could see that Norris was genuinely astounded.

'Wife! Christ almighty, that only lasted a month. Fuck me – his wife! I'd forgot all about her. God only knows where she's gone. I don't.'

'What was her name?'

Norris stopped and spread his sharp hands. 'I don't know, Mr Davies, I don't know. Straight up. Elsie or Mary or something, I don't know. I hardly knew her. It was bloody years ago.'

'May fourteenth, nineteen sixty-five,' recited Davies. He was disappointed that this incisive knowledge had no effect on Norris. All Norris said was, 'Very likely was.'

'What did she do, this Elsie or Mary. For a living.'

'Oh, Christ. I don't know. If I knew I've forgot.'

'Was she on the game, perhaps.'

Norris considered it. 'No, not that. Cecil was very particular.'

He pulled up short as if he realized he was talking too much. They had reached the part of the towpath where the humped bridge with its lamp intervened across the canal and the tight lane ran up to the pawnshop and the massage parlour in the High Street.

It was a natural place to pause and they stood on the rise of the bridge, looking down at the inclement water.

'Why did Cecil Ramscar send a wreath?' asked Davies.

Norris nodded in a dull movement. 'My missus, I suppose, or Josie. One of them told you.'

'Why did he?'

'You're so fucking clever,' said Norris nastily. 'With your questions and bloody answers. Cecil didn't mean to send a wreath. He's not thick. He asked another bloke, a dopey bugger called Rickett, to send some flowers. Sort of sympathy, just like you'd send flowers to somebody if they wanted cheering up. Cecil reckoned it would be nice and he got stupid bloody Rickett to send them. And Rickett got pissed at the pub and sent a wreath instead. Cecil got narked and had Rickett seen to.'

'Seen to?'

'Sorted out. He don't walk proper now.'

'Mr Norris,' said Davies. 'Could you just run through the events of the day that Celia vanished.'

Norris looked deflated. 'Oh bloody Christ,' he moaned. 'Do I have to? You've heard it all from my missus. I wouldn't mind if it was really Celia you was trying to sort out. But you're just having a sniff around for other things. I know, mate, I know.'

Davies dismissed it. 'I'm investigating the disappearance and presumed death of Celia Norris,' he said formally. 'Will you tell me what the events of that day were.'

Norris leaned on the bridge and gaped at the unremarkable canal. 'What happened that day?'

'It was when I was working for a car firm. In the West End,' said Norris patiently. 'I saw her in the morning just before I went to work and I didn't see her again. That's all. I told the coppers everything at the time. But they've never done nothing have they?'

His voice had subsided and the final words came out wistfully. Davies said: 'We're still trying. That's why I want to see Ramscar.'

'Back to him,' said Norris his suspicion returning at once. 'You'd rather see Cecil than anything, wouldn't you? This whole thing wouldn't be some copper's plan to get at Cecil, would it? You wouldn't be using our Celia to try and get him, by any chance?'

To his amazement Davies saw that Norris's small frame was flooding with emotion. His face shook. Suddenly he turned away and leaned on the parapet of the bridge put his head in his elbows and wept. Embarrassed, Davies stood back. He pushed out a tentative hand and then withdrew it. Norris continued to sob.

A small girl and an older boy appeared on the towpath and began to walk across the bridge. When they saw Norris they stopped and regarded him with huge interest. Davies made ineffectual movements with his hands.

'What's the matter wiv 'im then mister?' asked the boy. The little girl had curved over and was now arched under Norris's bent body attempting to look up into his face. It was athough she were peering up a chimney.

'He's upset,' mumbled Davies. 'You two run along.'

'What's he upset for?' inquired the girl. She was smaller than the boy, but she had jam on her face and she looked determined.

Davies shrugged. 'He's lost something precious in the canal,' he said unthinkingly.

Norris looked up slowly. His eyes were blood red, his skin puffed and wet. 'I suppose you think that's bloody funny don't you?' he said. 'Copper.'

CHAPTER EIGHT

Gladstone Heights was a vantage point above a stiff hill at the back of the town. The council flats at its brow had a view and, as though to celebrate their prestige, the housewives had washing hanging like banners and bunting high up there, exalted, where the air was almost clear.

Arrayed below were all the streets, curving like fan vaulting, the dull blade of the canal cut through the hunched houses, the factories making plastics, steels and alloys, paint and fertilizer, cosmetics and baked beans.

Each added its own puff of smoke to the congested sky, each ground relentlessly, grafting and grubby. Particles of grit performed a saraband above it all.

The flats – for some environmental reason – could only be reached by a steep footpath, the road terminating far below. Davies left the Lagonda and Kitty on the lower slope and began to walk. He bent like a large sherpa as he tackled the tarmac hill. The view expanded with every pace. It was said that Mr Gladstone, when Prime Minister, used to come to this spot for solace and rural refreshment. Now the fields and country trees did not begin for another ten miles.

Ena and William Lind lived on the crown of Gladstone Heights. It was Davies's second ascent. The first time there had been no one in their flat and he descended disconsolately on the steep road, thinking that a watchman's hut in telephone communication with the summit might be a reasonable expense upon the ratepayers.

This time he had, at least, the assurance that there was someone at home because he had carefully calculated the location of their flat among the piled widows and he saw now that, like a welcome lighthouse, there was illumination in the window. Davies thought how useful the situation would be for anyone wishing to send signals down into the town.

As a compensation for the gradient walk, each block of flats had its lift and Davies waited gratefully on the bottom landing for it to descend. Also waiting was a man who complained of the wind that rifled through the concrete doors and corridors.

'Sometimes up here,' moaned the man. 'You can actually 'ear it whining through your trousers. Whistles everywhere. What a place to put human beings, I ask you.'

'It's a long way up,' agreed Davies.

'Stand up on this hill,' the man pursued. 'Face east and the wind blows straight from Russia and up your legs. There's not another higher hill between here and the Ural Mountains. And this is where they put us.'

The lift, like a biscuit tin, came down and opened. A woman got out with a shopping bag and pulled her collar up around her face before launching herself outside. She emitted a muffled reply to the old man's greeting.

'That's not, by any chance, Mrs Lind, is it?' asked Davies half way in the lift.

'Mrs Lind? No that's Mrs Cotter. Mrs Lind's better than that.' The resident eyed him with fractionally more interest. 'Going to call on Mrs Lind are you?'

'Yes.'

'Fourth floor. Number thirty-six,' he said.

Davies thanked him and got out at the fourth landing. As he left the lift the man muttered enigmatically: 'Very nice too.'

Nevertheless Davies was surprised when his doorbell ring was answered by a woman in a leopard-skin play-suit. Her face was carefully put together and her blonde hair assembled like a creamy confection. She idly held a large glass of crème de menthe in one hand and a copy of

Vogue was tucked under her opposite arm. From the flat's interior came a full, but not indelicate perfume, and the sound of Elgar. It was eleven o'clock on a Monday morning.

'Oh, hello,' she said. 'Can I help you?' The tone was modulated cockney.

'It is possible you may,' replied Davies straightening his own voice. 'I am Detective Constable Davies. I wondered if I might take a little of your time.'

'A detective!' She coincided a purr and an exclamation. 'How terrifically thrilling.'

She performed a quick, practised, sequence. She let him in, poked her face out of the door, looked once each way and withdrew. She saw that he had seen her.

'Am I being followed?' he inquired to relieve her embarrassment. She laughed throatfully. 'You never know who's poking their nose in your business around here,' she answered. 'Council places.'

She led him into the room. It astonished him. Everywhere was lime green. The walls, the tons of curtains, the undulating three-piece suites, the carpet. On the settee was a green cat. 'We call this the green room,' she explained seriously. 'Would you like a crème de menthe?'

'Er,' Davies hesitated. 'Yes, yes. Thank you. It's a bit early in the week but I will.'

'It's never too early,' she smiled going to a cocktail cabinet with a maw that lit musically when it was opened. 'I love the Green Goddess.'

'Yes, it's nice,' agreed Davies lamely.

There was a colour television in a green casing in one corner and a stereo deck next to the cocktail cabinet. He looked around for the speakers but they were well concealed. 'I think Elgar's such an enigma,' she said returning with the drinks and jerking her head in the direction of the music.

'Yes, I suppose he is. Was.'

'Is,' she said. 'I sit here, listening, just listening, wondering what he is trying to say.'

'My whole life's like that,' agreed Davies.

'Ah yes, your police life.' She moved closer and handed him the green glass. He could feel a warmth from her.

'Let me take your coat,' she said. 'I'm afraid I like a bit of a fug in here. And you have to turn council heating right up before you can even feel it.' He rolled off his great ungainly overcoat and she almost fell forward with the weight of it. She carried it to a bedroom that glowed pink as she entered it. 'Did anyone see you come up?' she called.

'An old chap and a lady going shopping,' he replied.

She tutted as she re-entered the room. 'They're so nosey, you see,' she said. 'Did they know that you were coming here? Actually here?'

'Well, yes. The old chap. He directed me. Funny old boy. Said the wind comes straight from the Urals.'

'Mr Bentley,' she said confidently. 'Silly old sod. Excuse me, but he is. Goes around talking like a professor but he hasn't a clue really. Straight from the Urals. What's the Urals, anyway?'

'Mountains in Russia, I understand,' said Davies.

'In that case he could be right,' she acknowledged. 'I heard his wife going on about it but she's as ignorant as shit, if you'll excuse me again. She was saying the wind came from the urinals. Anyway he saw you.'

'I'm afraid he did.'

'It'll be all over the flats by tonight,' she said confidently. 'No privacy. Why don't we sit down. Move over Limey.' She gave the cat a firm push.

'Good name, Limey,' offered Davies. He hesitated. 'I've never seen a green cat before.'

'It's pricey to get him dyed,' she sighed. 'But he's something to talk about when people come to dinner.'

'I imagine,' said Davies. He finished his drink. He was aware of her nearness on the settee. He sat with his hands on his knees, as though he were in a railway carriage. 'Perhaps I'd better tell you why I am here,' he said.

'Ah yes,' she replied as though it were only of minor importance. She smiled fully as he half turned to her. Her teeth were smooth and menacing, white versions of her finger nails. 'I'm not afraid,' she added. 'I know I haven't been wicked. Well, not in a way the police would be interested.' She leaned forward abruptly and the heavy breasts, scarcely contained in the catsuit bulged as though they wanted to view him also. 'It's nothing my husband has done is it?'

'No. He's not in trouble.'

'I thought not,' she said with disappointment. 'I don't think he's capable of getting into trouble. What's it about then?'

'Remember Celia Norris?'

There was no quick reaction from her. He watched for it and all that occurred was a slight roll of the breasts. Her face was half away from him, however, staring at the cat which had begun to wash itself hysterically on the green carpet, perhaps in some forlorn foray to rid itself of its hue.

'The police are not still raking around with that?' she commented eventually in the same assumed modulated tone. 'That's all a bit old hat now, isn't it, Celia Norris?'

Davies clasped his hands firmly before him like an insurance salesman trying to make a selling point. 'Oh no, not really,' he said. 'Look at it this way – there's somebody walking around free today who did away with that girl. I'm trying to find out who that person is.'

'But it's years!' It sounded like exasperation. It was in her face, the lines suddenly cracking through the accurately applied make-up. Her arms folded tightly in front of her in the manner of a washer-woman, pushing her breasts up towards her chin. 'Years,' she repeated getting up and walking away from him across the room. 'What good can it do now?'

Davies elevated his eyes to see her standing above, confronting him. His steady expression stopped her. She sat down, not lightly, not with studied elegance, as she had done before, but with a heavy middle-aged clump.

'It keeps coming up,' she sighed. 'And I suppose it always will keep bleeding well coming up.'

'Until it's solved,' observed Davies.

'All right, have it your way. Until it's solved.'

'It came up a couple of years ago, didn't it?' he pointed out quietly. 'In the newspaper.'

'That. Yes, that's right.' She hesitated. 'Well they offered me two hundred quid and I jumped at it. *He* went mad of course, my husband. But then he would. He's such a wooden bastard, you know.'

'No I didn't.'

'Oh Christ, *him*. You've never met anybody like him. If he picked his nose it would be on his conscience for life.'

Davies was watching the cat. It had finished its desperate licking and was now running its green tongue around its chops.

'Your husband, Bill, that is . . .'

'William,' she corrected purposefully. 'He likes to be called William. See what I mean?'

'Yes, I see. Well, William Lind, your husband. When you were all in your teens, those few years ago, he was Celia Norris's boyfriend, wasn't he?'

She nodded. 'For what it was worth.' She laughed sharply. 'She didn't know what a lucky escape she had.' Immediately she glanced guiltily at him. 'I didn't mean it like that,' she said.

'Was he always so . . . wooden?'

'Yes, always. Even as a kid he was a prissy bugger.'

'But you married him. Didn't you have a baby?'

She smiled a pale smile. 'You've been checking up haven't you? I lost the baby. I was always a loser.'

'Sorry, I'm stupid,' he said, embarrassed.

'That's all right,' she sighed. 'Anyway, I married him like you say. I knew what he was like but I thought he had a bit up top, you know, as well. Brains. I thought he might get somewhere. Make life a bit comfortable.'

'And he hasn't?'

'Ha!' The snort was almost masculine. 'If you call a capstan operator "getting somewhere."'

Glancing at his glass Davies was moderately surprised to see that he had finished his crème de menthe. She saw the action but made no offer to refill it. 'I've got a friend coming in a minute,' she said hinting that it was in explanation. 'A girl friend, of course, Clare. We get up the West End three or four times a week. Walk around the shops, go to the pictures and that. It's harmless enough.'

'I would think it is,' agreed Davies blandly, wondering why she had said it. 'I won't keep you long. Really I just wanted to ask you to recall, in just a few words, what happened on that evening. When Celia disappeared. Just as you remember it.'

She sighed. 'Well I've done it all before. Another time won't matter. She was at the youth club playing table tennis with Bill. . . .'

'William?'

'I call him Bill behind his back,' she shrugged. '. . . . and off she went home on her bike. It was about ten o'clock. Just getting dark. Nobody ever saw her again.'

'Bill, William, stayed behind for a football meeting didn't he?'

Scorn quickly accumulated on her painted face. 'Football! He didn't play football or go to football meetings. Afraid of getting kicked. No, he stayed for something. Probably a netball meeting, that's more like it. He liked to see the girls playing netball.'

'Why was that?'

'Probably liked to see their drawers.'

'Oh, I understand.'

She glanced at him suspiciously. 'Here, don't think *he* did it. I've got no bloody time for him, but he wouldn't do that. Not that sexual sort.'

'The sexual sort?'

'Well you don't have to be a detective to work out that she wasn't done for her money, Celia. But *not* Bill Lind. He was there, in the club, for a good half hour afterwards. Anyway, not him.' She turned to him determinedly. 'You're talking about a man who even now won't have a bath unless he's wearing his swimming trunks!'

'Swimming trunks?'

'His bloody swimming trunks. And I've told that to nobody else. Not even Clare, who's my mate. I'd be too ashamed. He wanted to lock the door at first, but I wouldn't have that. Not in my own home, with just the two of us here, so he put on his swimming trunks. Every time he has a bath he's in there like bleeding Captain Webb.'

Davies wanted to laugh but her face was crammed with unhappiness. 'He comes from that sort of family,' she sighed.

'I've heard his mother talk about a *chest* of chicken.' She rested her face in her hands and Davies sat embarrassed, wanting to touch her sympathetically.

Instead he said. 'What about this man Boot? Dave Boot?'

Her head came up slowly as if it were on a lever. She was about to answer when a melody played at the door. 'Clare,' she forecast. She stood up and composed her face into the smile it had carried when he had first walked in. 'I'll give you a call,' she said. 'At the police station?'

'I'll give you the number,' he said, writing it out for her. 'We'd better fix a time. I don't like being in there longer than I can help. It's miserable.'

She smiled like some genteel hostess. 'All right. Eight tonight. I'll use the phone box on my way home.'

'Eight?' he said. 'You won't be home to get your husband's dinner then?'

'No I won't,' she said. She moved towards the door as the melody warbled blandly. Davies thought how much the bell suited her.

She paused inside the door before opening it. 'I don't do a lot for him,' she said across her shoulder. 'But then he doesn't do much for me.'

Because the call was promised for eight o'clock he had to miss dinner at

Mrs Fulljames's, he sat moodily in the C.I.D. Room eating a hapless sandwich. He was wondering whether to eat the crust when the phone rang.

Ena was mildly brazen in a giggling sort of way. He thought he could smell the ruby port and lemon drifting over the wires.

'Listen,' she said confidingly. 'I reckoned it would be better on the telephone, but I've thought about it again. What the hell, I don't care. I'll tell you face to face. Can you meet me somewhere?'

'Now?'

'Yes, before I change my mind.'

'All right. Where are you?'

'I'm in a phone box at Willesden Green Station, Clare's gone off home.'

'I could be there in ten minutes,' he said.

'Come to the pub across the road from the station, The Lame Elephant. I don't mind waiting in there. I'm not proud. I'll be in the saloon bar but I won't get a drink. I'll wait for you, then you can buy it.'

'Right. I'll be right along.'

He needed two hands to pick his overcoat up from the adjoining chair. It had been raining and the coat was porous, doubling its already considerable weight and bulk. It was like pulling a wet walrus onto his back. He went out, raising a heavy hand to the sergeant on the desk. His Lagonda stood, as ever, open to the rain but Kitty had crawled below the green tarpaulin. The dog lay in the back seat like an ominously covered cadaver. Davies got in and started the engine and Kitty growled with it. The great headlamps of the car careered grandly through the drizzle and the dreary streets as Davies drove towards The Lame Elephant. He wondered why, if Ena Lind despised her husband so much, she talked about them having people around to dinner.

She was waiting in the saloon bar, enfolded in a coat of dyed rabbit, the space on the knee-high table before her cleared suggestively.

'Double port and single lemon,' she said. 'You're all wet. You look like a sponge.'

'My car leaks,' he explained going to the bar. He got her double port and single lemon and a scotch for himself and carried it back to the table. 'No crème de menthe?' he said.

'They wouldn't know what that was in here,' she sniffed. 'If the masses don't drink it, they get confused. They're all bloody Irish anyway.'

Davies rolled off his coat again, considered the reliability of a coathook on the wall and decided not to burden it. He hung it on the chair next to him. Ena Lind regarded him doubtfully.

'You're a bit of a mess, one way and another,' she sniffed.

'Haven't you got anybody to look after you?'

'Well,' he said drinking his scotch. 'I do have a *sort* of wife. We live in the same house – it's a kind of boarding house – but we don't live *together*, if you understand what I mean.'

'I understand all right,' she said, 'Very well indeed.' She studied the inside of the saloon bar. It was the period of the evening when it had begun to swell with people and with smoke.

'If people had homes,' she murmured. 'The pubs would be out of business for a start.'

'True, true,' he agreed. 'But if there was a vote on it, homes or pubs, I bet the pubs would win. Will you have another?'

'You've soon swallowed that.'

'Yes, I tend to get through the first one quickly.'

'I can see.' She disposed of her drink. 'Right-o then. But this one's on me. No arguments.' She pressed a pound into his hand and closed his fingers around it. Her hand felt dry on his damp skin.

'All right,' he nodded. 'Thanks very much.'

'Have a double,' she suggested. 'I expect you'd have got a double for yourself, wouldn't you? Might just stop you getting pneumonia.'

He grinned gratefully and ordered the drinks. He returned to the table and raised his glass.

'Cheers, Ena,' he said.

'Here's to Celia Norris,' she replied soberly.

He looked at her on the sharp angle. 'Well,' she said catching his askew eyes. 'Why not? It's been a long time. She's *still* dead. Maybe, wherever she's got to, she'll like us to drink her health.'

'All right,' he agreed. 'I thought it was a bit late for that, that's all.' He pushed his glass upwards. 'To Celia Norris, then.'

'Yes,' she affirmed. Her glass ascended a few inches. '*Our lovely Celia.*'

'What's that mean?' he inquired quickly. 'Saying it like that?'

'Well she was,' replied Ena Lind with assumed conviction. 'Lovely. Nice little figure, pretty little face, suffered spots, but still pretty. Tiny bottom. The boys used to enjoy to watch her playing table tennis, or better still netball, so they could get a glimpse at her arse.'

'Only the boys?'

'And some men, of course. That's what you meant isn't it?'

'Yes. Men. Like who?'

'Let's have another drink. If I'm going to tell you I don't want to hold myself responsible for it.'

'That's a good excuse. All right. Same?'

'Same,' she smiled. She looked quite attractive in a full, forty-year-old way. Her teeth were large and splendid and her face rounded and smoothed with the wrinkles well subdued. The stitched and tinted rabbit skins looked plush on her. She sensed his thoughts and opened the fur down to her middle so that her breasts lounged indolently against it. She smiled and he turned and went to get the drinks. He bought himself another double scotch.

'Do you always drink that?' he asked putting the double port and single lemon on the table before her.

'That and crème de menthe,' she said. 'Mostly when I'm out I drink this. It warms me up. Green's very cold, don't you think?'

He sat down. 'Now tell me,' he said turning towards her. 'About the men?'

'There was only one really, one who *did* anything,' she said. 'Could you guess who that was? Come on, let's see if you're really a good detective.'

'Ramscar,' he guessed.

Her etched eyebrows jumped with genuine surprise. 'Fancy you saying that,' she said softly. 'Ramscar. Blimey I'd forgotten all about him.' She thought about it. 'Yes . . . I suppose you *could* be right, too. I must say I hadn't thought about it like that. He used to hang around Celia a bit. Flash bugger. Wandering Hands Society, you know what I mean. He was a friend of her father's, and he was a crook you know. Still is, I expect. No, I wasn't thinking of Ramscar.' Her voice trailed as though she had conjured new possibilities from old memories.

'Boot then,' prompted Davies. 'He's runner-up.'

'Right, second time. Dave Boot. He'd had Celia.'

'*Had* her? Sexually?'

'Is there another way? He'd had her and he'd had me and some of the other girls as well. We were all fifteen when we joined there, at the youth club and I reckon he got around us all in a couple of years. We used to think he was terrific. Terrific. I don't mind telling you now. It's all gone a long time ago for me.'

With blunt wistfulness she added: 'I could do with him now, these days. Instead of that dud sod I'm married to. Oh, he was manly, Dave Boot. You know, sports singlet, muscles, fair hair, tanned. He used to go up and lie in the grass by the Welsh Harp every day in the summer because he only worked in the evenings, see. I came across him up there one day when I was mooching along by the water. He had pieces of tin, sort of squares, like the sides of a biscuit tin all around him. He told me it was to catch every bit of sun, reflecting it.

'We used to think he was great. And there wasn't many of us he hadn't fucked by the time he'd finished. He only left the really pimply girls or the fat ones alone. And we all knew who he was having. We used to fight about him.'

'Dave the Rave,' murmured Davies to himself.

'That's what they call him now,' she nodded. 'I've seen his picture in the local papers. He's got this disco at Finchley. I've fancied calling in and surprising him. But he wouldn't know me now. I bet he's still having them as young as ever. Could I have another drink? Here I'll pay for this one. I don't want to cadge. Please.'

He nodded, reluctant to break her story, and took the money to get the drinks. The barman winked at him, looked across at Ena, her prow heaving like an ice-breaker, grinned and gave the thumbs up sign. Davies ignored him.

He had another double for himself and found the short journey back to his seat took slightly longer than before. He would have to watch it. He didn't want to lose her now. For a moment, after regaining his seat, he thought he *had* lost her. She sipped at her drink then leaned back and closed her eyes. Her face was set and passive. He gave her a nudge.

'What's the matter?' she inquired, curiously opening only one eye.

'Oh, sorry, Ena. I thought you'd dozed off.'

'No, no. I was just thinking about it. About Dave.'

'He . . . . he definitely had sex with Celia then? You're pretty sure of that.'

'Not pretty sure. Very sure. I was there, mate, I was there. He had us both at the same time. The first time, anyway.'

'Oh.'

'Well, we were only kids and we thought he was Mister Wonderful.' She had closed her eyes again as though trying to recapture the intensity of Boot's muscles. 'The two of us, Celia and me, being friends, used to giggle about it and make out what we'd like him to do to us. And then, one day, he did it. Just like that. It was a bit of a shock, but a nice shock, if you see what I mean.' She glanced at him to ascertain if he had seen what she meant. His whiskeyed eyes were attentive. He nodded her on.

'Funny thing was, it was afternoon. It must have been in the holidays because we was at school then. We'd gone around to the church which was where the youth club was, as you know, to do something or other, like help getting things together for a church fête. We helped to put a sort of sideshow together and Father Harvey, who'd just got there in those days, was helping us, farting about like he still does, but eventually he went off to pray or something and suddenly, in the vestry Dave put his arms around our waists. Celia had been bending over getting something and he gave her a pat on the bottom, just playing, and I bent over, laughing like, so he could do the same to me. I remember saying something like: 'Not one without the other, Dave.' So he smacked me too. That seemed to start it. We went out of the vestry and all three of us ran across the grass to the youth club, where he had a key to a storeroom. I remember being so hot and excited. I felt like I was flying. I was scared too, of course, petrified. But I could see Celia was just the same, excited but frightened, and I thought then "*She's* not having anything *I'm* not having." And that's how it was.'

She had given the appearance of reciting to herself. Now she waited and looked at Davies. He leaned towards her like a peckish dog. Her returned expression indicated that she required him to say something.

So he said: 'I'm glad he didn't do it in the vestry.'

She shrugged seriously. 'He thought Father Harvey might come back, I suppose. It was nothing religious. He wasn't all that religious, Dave wasn't.'

Davies felt weary because of the drink but he still managed to raise his eyebrows. 'Do you want me to go on?' She inquired mischievously. 'I bet you do.'

'I'd like you to,' he admitted.

'I'll need another drink, I think,' she said apologetically. 'I'm under a bit of a strain.'

Davies got up carefully as though not to disturb her train of thought. He had run out of money but the publican knew him and told the barman to go ahead with the drinks. 'Another copper in his pocket,' said the man caustically as he poured them.

'Piss off,' muttered Davies and returned equally clumsily to Ena.

'Really,' she said. 'It does me good to talk about it. It's years since I was able to talk about it to anyone. In detail.' She smiled expansively. The port on her breath met the whisky on his half way between them in an invisible but potent alchemy. He intended only to nod to her, signalling her to recommence, but his head seemed overweight and it dropped forward and collided with her shoulder and her cheek. She patted him affectionately. 'Now don't you doze off before I've finished. This isn't a bedtime story.'

He forced himself away from the rabbity comfort of her shoulder and cursed the curse of drink. 'I'm listening,' he mumbled. 'Very carefully, I'm listening.'

'You'd better. We're getting to the really wicked bit now. Where he fucked us.' She giggled. 'Not that we would have used a word like that *then*. Not in those days.' She almost bit into the double port and single lemon. Davies had the nous to reflect that it appeared to have a less wearing effect than scotch. 'You want me to go on?' she said.

'I can't wait.'

'So, as I said, we went across to this storeroom and there he undressed both of us. We just stood there like a couple of nits, hands hanging down by our sides, not daring to look at each other or move, and he took our clothes off for us. First he took one thing off Celia, then he turned to me and took something from me. Celia was wearing her first bra, but I was already two cup sizes ahead, I remember feeling quite proud of mine. He took his time over it, that Dave, the devil. I remember the sun coming in the window, watching it, because I was too nervous to even look at his face. Then we stood there, stark naked, Celia and me, sort of shivering like you do. Nervousness. I could feel goose pimples all over me. We both felt a bit stupid just *standing* there with him looking us over. Celia – she couldn't help it – started to giggle and so did I. But he told us to stop laughing and he was serious, very stern, so we did. We would have done anything he wanted. I remember wondering what was going to happen next and whether I could get pregnant. But I didn't think about that for long. He hadn't touched us, not our skin, not sexually, only to get our clothes off, but then he suddenly took down his track suit trousers – he always wore a track suit, sometimes a blue one, sometimes red, and then his support whatsit, his jock strap, and out came this great *thing*. It seemed enormous to us then, and even now, allowing for always remembering the good things, you know, even now I reckon it was something frightening.

'We still didn't know what to do. I could see Celia was scarlet and I could feel my face burning. Then, bold as you like, she reached out and touched it. I was bloody amazed, I can tell you. But she did. She put out her hand and sort of patted it on the end and then she caught hold of it in her fingers, wrapping them right around it. I thought. "Right, you're not being left behind, Ena." So I grabbed hold of his whatsits.'

'Whatsits?' asked the bemused Davies.

'Oh God, you know. Underneath. Testicles. Is that clear enough?'

'Yes, yes. Very clear.'

'Right, well I did. And I grabbed *hard*, all eager not to be outdone, and

Christ, he nearly went through the ceiling! I mean, I didn't know, not at that age, that men are tender under there. Poor Dave. He tried to screech, but he had to keep his voice down at the same time in case anybody heard. You should have seen his face. It was like a horror film with no sound. You can imagine. I was really ashamed and embarrassed, especially as Celia was doing so well. But after a bit, he felt better, and water went out of his eyes, and he started playing about with us, and us with him and eventually he got us over to the club trampoline and had us both on that.'

'Trampoline?' uttered Davies from his fog. 'Trampoline?'

'Right. He had a few minutes with Celia first and then a few minutes with me. It didn't half kick up a dust too, on that thing. I remember all the bits of dust floating in the sunshine coming through the window.' She paused as though remembering particularly the sunshine. 'And that was that,' she said. 'The first time. After that it happened on and off. Not regular. Just on and off. And never me and Celia together again.'

'When did it stop?' Davies remembered to ask.

'After Celia. After she'd gone. He never did it with me again after that. I suppose he thought it was unfair, that sort of thing. One without the other.'

Their glasses were empty. Davies confident of the publican's co-operation rolled to the bar for a last refill. It was a minute to closing time. He returned to her. She had her painted lids closed again and once more he thought she might be asleep. He had some difficulty in focussing her. But the sound of the glasses clunking on the table caused her to open her eyes again.

'Did you think that was interesting?' she inquired in the manner of a popular lecturer.

'Most informative,' he said cautiously. 'And there were others?'

'Lots,' she agreed. 'Celia and me saw him having it with a girl called Potts, Roxanne Potts, one night. He had her across the vaulting horse in the club.'

'He used all the equipment then?'

'Dave was a trained gymnast,' she said seriously. They drank their glasses quickly and went towards the door. Shakily she helped him to get his ponderous overcoat over his arms and shoulders. Then, to his astonishment, she said: 'But you don't suspect him, Dave, of course, do you? Not of murdering her. He wouldn't do a thing like that.'

It had ceased raining, but the night air was smeary and damp. He drove her to the foot of Gladstone Heights and she rolled herself close to him in the front of the Lagonda. 'Doesn't the top go on this thing?' she inquired hazily.

'Not since the war,' he said. 'It's stuck and I haven't had time to fix it.'

'What's that lump under the canvas thing in the back seat. It's not a dead body is it?'

'Sort of. It's my dog, Kitty. He might as well be dead. He hardly ever stirs. Only his bad chest and jawbone when he's eating.'

'How old are you?' she decided to ask.

'About thirty-three or five,' he said. 'I'm not sure.'

'I'm older than you,' she grumbled as though it were his fault. 'At least three years.'

'It happens to everybody,' he said to comfort her. He stopped the Lagonda at the foot of the mountainous path to the council flats. He did not feel inclined to walk up but he could not let her stagger the gradient alone. They rolled drunkenly out of the car, and like old pals, their arms about each other they trudged up the climb.

'Is that a light in your window?' inquired Davies looking up to the rearing buildings against the watery stars.

'He leaves it on,' she sniffed. 'To guide me home. He ought to have been a bloody coastguard.'

Talking was an effort. Their spirited breaths puffed into the night air like the snorts of dragons. They reached the entrance to the flats gratefully. Davies kissed her on the plump cheek. ''Night Ena,' he said. 'I'll be trundling down.'

'Wait,' she insisted quietly. 'See me up in the lift. Just to the door. He'll be asleep. He leaves the light on but he goes to sleep.'

He eyed her with what suspicion he could muster, but her face was as roundly innocent as before. He took her elbow and then went to the tin lift. It arrived at a quick rattle and they stepped in. She pressed a button and the door closed but the awaited sensation of ascent did not follow. He looked at her, puzzled, and saw she was opening her coat and quickly her blouse. A protest engulfed his throat but she worked like lightning. Her big pink brassière was hooked in the centre of its cups and she had flicked it open in a moment, her voluminous breasts tumbled out, and without waiting, she caught hold of the back of his head and violently smashed his face into them. His cries were smothered by warm, scented flesh, but he could hear her making short gasping requests. 'I want you. I've got to have a *real* one! A real one!'

'I'm not free! I'm promised!' Davies howled desperately from the clutch. She pulled his head violently away by the hair. His senses were revolving. He knew he had the horn.

'Don't you like them?' she demanded. 'Not good enough for you?'

'Yes, yes,' he pleaded. 'They're nice, Ena. Really super. Big. But Ena. . . . Put them away!'

Her reply was to smash his face down into her bosom again, grabbing the back of his hair and wiping him up and down as though he were some kind of hand mop. She released one hand and it dived to his trousers. With a cry of triumph she caught his enclosed penis in a fierce grip and, amid it all, he suddenly knew why Dave Boot had screeched out all those years ago. It was an iron grip.

His hands were thrashing about like a penguin off balance. One set of fingers found the control panel of the lift. He pressed everything he could find. Three times the lift went up and three times down while he struggled with her hunger and wrath. They were thrown off balance against the metal sides and then on the floor. From that position like boxers who have delivered simultaneously damaging punches they gazed at each other. Her white balloon breasts were still swinging from her front, their reddened nipples glaring resentfully. It was nothing to the fierce look in her eyes. She came at him with her nails and her handbag. He tried to rise and she flung him against the wall. His panicked fingers found the buttons and the lift dropped spectacularly, throwing them over again as it bounced on the ground floor. This time Davies scrambled up first. He found the 'Door Open' button and pressed it furiously.

The door opened and outside was his dog, Kitty, a great wet-matted mound of hound, howling terribly. With unerring instinct it had sensed the battle and, rousing from its stupor, had lumbered from the car and pounded up the hill. Now, with the same unerring instinct, it fiercely attacked Davies, knocking him to the ground, snarling in his face and finally biting him on the arm. Davies collapsed. The dog saw what it had done and leapt on his prostrate body howling apparently with remorse at its error.

Ena Lind, weeping from every pore, shovelled her breasts back into her garments as she pounded violently up the concrete stairs. Doors were beginning to open and lit squares jerked into windows but it did not stop her sniping from the first landing.

'Serve you bloody right, you sexless berk!' she cried. 'I hope the bloody dog screws you!'

'Please lady,' muttered Davies lying against a cold wall. 'Don't put ideas into his head.'

CHAPTER NINE

Among his unnumbered shortcomings as a detective was the fact that he neither harboured suspicion nor cultivated caution in the appropriate proportions at the important moment. He reflected deeply on these absent traits during his vacant days in hospital following the violent attack on him by two men using a dustbin.

The invitation to the attack was lying on the front door mat that night when Davies reached 'Bali Hi' after so narrowly fighting off Ena Lind and his own dog. The dog's teeth, soft and mouldering fortunately, like the remainder of the creature, had impressed his arm but it was the fiery memory of Ena's wanton breasts which clutched his thoughts more deeply on his journey to Mrs Fulljames's front door. He had permitted himself a long medicinal draught of scotch from a bottle which he kept secretly in the Lagonda before garaging the car and Kitty for the night.

Then, before his hazy eyes they appeared – those breasts floating like cream, pointed balloons, wobbling just beyond reach, disturbing and hot in the chilly night.

His hands felt pulpy as he reached for his key outside the door had he considered once more what a narrow escape from rape he had experienced. Calamities he knew like old familiars but being raped was something new and hardly the thing for a Metropolitan Police detective constable to have to admit even to himself.

The note on the doormat had to be taken out and read by the street light, for lights-out in Mrs Fulljames's house meant what it said. Under the lamp Davies perceived the pencilled invitation. 'For important information be by the canal bridge at 23.45 hours.'

He wondered if the message could have come in some roundabout fashion from Father Harvey. Although that conclusion did not fit the twenty-four hour timing. He did not think the Roman Catholic Church had yet got around to writing '23.45 hours'. 'After Vespers', perhaps.

Nevertheless the note seemed frank enough. Somebody trying to help him. Somebody with information to give or to sell. The thought of a trap or an ambush never occurred to him which, to some considerable extent, was why his professional career was so generally scattered with physical injury. Davies always thought the best of people.

He had perceived that the perspex of his watch which that night he had remembered to wear had been dented and starred in his struggle in Ena Lind's lift. He held it under the street lamp and, having distinguished the hands from the cracks, he saw that he had only five minutes to fulfil the rendezvous by the canal. He would need to walk, for, having put the Lagonda away, he knew that neither the car nor the dog liked to be disturbed once they had been stabled for the night. He turned up his deep damp collar once more and strode towards the High Street and the sloping alley that led to the canal.

They saw him coming as soon as he began passing the illuminated shop windows in the main street. They had been arguing in criminal undertones about the wording of the message they had dropped through his door. One thought that it was a mistake to say '23.45 hours', but the other held that because it looked more official it did not engender so much suspicion. No felon, he argued, would be suspected of using twenty-four hour divisions. It was a clever detail.

The thought had come firmly to Davies that it might be some sort of official communication, the time quotation being the basis of this consideration. Perhaps after all, it *was* Father Harvey, using man-made time in his off-duty life. He remained with the notion while he turned between the pawnshop and the massage parlour, both closed and cold, and entered the alley. The ambushers began to move in then, closing behind him, tip-toeing, the dustbin suspended between them as if they were some fairy refuse collectors. Davies heard nothing until the swift swishing sound and a stunning clang as the dustbin was turned over his head and he was engulfed in a dark, closed, curry-smelling world with his head and shoulders jammed firmly and his hands flipping helplessly.

They could not have found a better fit if they'd measured him.

He revolved in confusion and alarm, the darkness and the stench revolting and revolving with him. Then they went into the next stage of the attack, producing pick-axe handles from the verge of the allotment fence and belabouring the dustbin with them. Davies had never been so hurt or so frightened. The blows battered and rained on the metal, smashing him from side to side so that his head clanged against the sides like the clapper of a voluminous bell. His attackers, after the first close flurry of blows, and knowing how helpless he was, stood back and took good long swings at him denting the tin walls with each violent blow. They belaboured his hands too, crushing them to his sides, but not his legs. That was for later.

Davies pirouetted like a large ballet dancer. Separate from all he could feel his ankles turning like cogged wheels. Each man dealt him a final blow. They then caught him by the sides, took the dead weight, and dragged him grunting towards the canal. One of the pair retained his pick-axe handle. They stood Davies on the bank of the canal and while one held his dropping body steady the other took a final cruel swing and brought the wooden weapon violently across the backs of his legs. He toppled forward and went gratefully into the canal. The two men left, collecting the other pick-axe handle on the way. They might need them again.

It was Father Harvey who heard the discordant campanology of the blows upon the dustbin (others did too, but it was not a neighbourhood where people, in general, investigated disturbances the same night). The priest had been sitting late in his study, in thought spiced with modicum of prayer, studying a plan for a do-it-yourself confessional box. The arson of the former box had caught both the insurance company and the ecclesiastical authorities in a niggardly mood and the weeks without a place to unload sins had resulted in an accumulating backlog of guilt throughout his parish. He was thus considering erecting a temporary structure himself and was biting his clerical lip over the plans when he heard the clanging of the smitten dustbin. He went to the door of his house, ascertained the direction of the resounding metal and returned to get his fishing rod. It was, truly, an excuse for being abroad late at night, and it could be a handy weapon.

He heard the heavy splash as he reached the canal bank and looked and saw the two hurrying shapes by the humped bridge. He walked quickly and bravely in that direction and reached the bridge in time to see a curved flank of the dustbin, illuminated by the bridge lamp, gradually submerging like some secret submarine. His first thought was merely that some rowdy youths had dropped it into the black water as a joke, but before he turned away he took a final look, and saw a pair of trousers and attached boots break the surface surrounded by glugging bubbles.

Father Harvey had, in his youth in Ireland, been one of the best swimmers in Dingle, County Kerry (not as distinguished as it might appear since his contemporaries were fishing lads who preferred to keep a hull between themselves and the water and never went into the sea, except by accident). Now he did not hesitate to take off his encumbering black priest's gown and his black patent leather dancing pumps which he wore as slippers. He stood there in his vest and long underpants. Then came the hesitation. He looked over the parapet of the bridge to make absolutely sure he was not too late, and would be jumping for nothing. He saw the same trousers and bobbing boots, sighed a prayer, crossed himself and then eyes closed, plunged clumsily into the cold canal.

Dropping blindly, he struck the dustbin with a spectacular splash and clang, legs wide like a knight leaping onto the back of a steed. It sank at once with Davies trapped within it and the priest astride. They gurgled down into the cold, dank tunnel of water. The icy blow took Father Harvey's breath away. Then the stench of it surged up his large dilated nostrils. But his flailing arms immediately caught the projecting legs and he hung onto them. He knew that once he let go he would never find them again in that awful place.

The priest burst to the surface. His snatched prayer of gratitude was truncated by a full mouthful of canal, which he spat away before launching himself for the bank mercifully only a yard away, towing the dustbin and its contents behind him. He was a strong priest and – more than that – determined, unwilling, despite his supplications, to wait for Providence to perform miracles on his behalf. He reached the edge and hung on and shouted at the height of his soaked voice. His cry was heard by a man sitting through the night, guarding his allotment (there had been much rustling on the vegetable patches in the area since the rise in shop prices and the publicity given to the court case involving the vegetable robber). The man hurried to the bank. He was, fortuitously, a strong man, used to digging the London clay, and he eventually pulled Father Harvey from the canal. Together they then got hold of Davies's dustbin and brought that to dry land. They pulled it away and Father Harvey emitted a wet gasp when he saw who was inside. 'Dangerous,' he said addressing the unconscious face, running with fresh blood since there was now no water to wash it away. 'Dangerous, what in the name of God are you up to?'

Father Harvey went to visit Davies in Park Royal Hospital, three days later when they had completed pumping him through, stitched his wounds and opened his eyes as far as possible.

'It's no wonder the water went straight through you,' remarked the priest eyeing him. 'You're full of bloody holes.' He glanced guiltily sideways down the ward because of his swear-words.

'I leak all over,' agreed Davies dreamily.

'Ah, you're a strong, tough man, I'll give you that,' said Father Harvey. 'I thought we would be preparing for your wake. Even on the canal bank I got to wondering what religion you pursued. I didn't know, but I gave you the last rites just in case. One thing about us men of God, we know our rites.'

Davies attempted a smile. 'It would have been more to the point if you'd tried the kiss of life,' he remarked.

'Every man to his calling,' replied the priest unruffled. 'It's fine to see you're still with us on this side, anyway. I wouldn't guarantee you much of a future over there, beyond, you know. Not being a policeman.'

'If it wasn't for you happening to be out swimming at that time of night I would be most certainly beyond,' said Davies. He moved his hand gratefully towards the priest who, glancing privily around the ward first, patted it with his own.

'A very nasty business,' said Father Harvey. 'I suppose the police force must be combing the area, whatever that may mean.'

'They'll hardly think to give it a scratch,' said Davies with certainty. 'An attack on a copper – particularly *this* copper – is nothing special. The Inspector, Yardbird, probably had a good laugh and asked the lads to watch for anything suspicious on their way home from work.'

'Charity rarely begins at home,' agreed the priest. 'Do you know who might have done it?'

'I've got a fair idea,' said Davies, a light coming from his reduced eyes. 'All I have to do is find them . . . him.'

'It's a wonder they didn't crack your skull even before drowning you. It must be even thicker than I thought.'

Davies tried a bigger smile but it hurt him all over his face. 'One of my copper colleagues tells me the bin came from the Indian Restaurant,' he said. 'It had a lining of dried curry. Tough stuff that curry, especially from that dump. It saved my life.' He regarded Father Harvey through his bruises and stitches. 'You're a good bloke,' he said genuinely. 'Thanks. When I've got this lot over with I'll find out who burned down your confessional box.'

'I'm thinking of building a temporary structure,' the priest told him. 'There's a nasty backlog of unforgiven sins piling up, and my superiors are not being very sympathetic, nor is the insurance company. If you happen to know of any reasonable wood lying around that I might make some use of perhaps you'll tell me. I saw some very decent planks in the yard of Swindell's the undertakers, but I'm not sure that would morally be quite correct. Sitting there tight surrounded by the best cedar would make me feel uncomfortable. I'll be long enough in my coffin when I truly get there.'

'Better than being scuttled in a refuse bin,' said Davies. 'Did you run up any expenses, by the way? You know, with your clothes being waterlogged and everything?'

The priest shook his head. 'My underwear was dry by the morning. I put it over the church boiler. The only charge will be for the dry cleaning of my clerical gown which I threw off before throwing myself into the canal. Unfortunately I tossed it into a particularly filthy puddle. I'll send you the bill. At the cleaners they always charge it as a maxi-coat.'

Mrs Fulljames and Doris came through the door of the ward and stood there in plastic truculence; one pink and one sky blue crinkly and crackly raincoat with transparent overshoes of the same synthetic material tied about their ankles, imprisoning their feet like specimens. They remained stiffly at the door, the raindrops dripping from their gulleys and gutters like melting ice. They examined Davies at that distance, squinting their eyes and screwing up their faces, backing their heads away, as though trying to get a true perspective of his injuries. He sat taut and propped in bed, wondering why they had come.

'Fine bloody mess you look,' snorted Mrs Fulljames from the door.

'Yes, a fine mess,' confirmed Doris loyally.

Davies believed he heard Mrs Fulljames snap her fingers and the two plastic dragons advanced on him, their scales creaking as they strode. But he was spared. A voice croaked at the distant end of the room and caught his landlady's attention. 'Oh, just look, Doris,' she said in a pleased way. 'There's that polite Mr Wellington, who used to be our milkman.'

'So it is. Mr Wellington,' agreed Doris. When she smiled Davies sometimes thought he caught a distant glimpse of her youth. But it was soon gone. 'Wonder why he's in?'

'Let's go and see the poor soul,' said Mrs Fulljames. She wheeled stiffly, luffing like a sea-soaked sailing barge and made for the extreme end of the ward. Doris, with not so much as a splintered glance at her husband, followed obediently. They waved wet waves to Mr Wellington as they went. Davies astonished himself by experiencing a touch of jealousy. He eased himself up in his bed and saw the milkman sitting up in real excitement and anticipation.

It was almost ten minutes before they returned. 'Such an interesting man, that,' chuffed Mrs Fulljames, as though that was an entire and acceptable excuse for their divergence. 'He's so polite, isn't he Doris? And he's been everywhere.'

'Milkmen usually have,' observed Davies painfully.

Doris stared at her husband's dented and stitched countenance. 'He's eaten your Smarties,' she said bluntly, as though wanting to get it over with. 'I brought you some Smarties, but Mr Wellington's had them.'

Once more Davies felt illogically hurt. He scowled and the pain told him not to do it again. 'Thanks for bringing them anyway,' he muttered. 'It's the thought, really I suppose.'

'Of course it is!' interpolated Mrs Fulljames extravagantly. She hovered across his sheets now as though enjoyably anticipating performing an operation on him.

'And he's *so* interesting,' echoed Doris, still with a hint of guilt. 'He's done *so* many things.'

'He's eaten my fucking Smarties for a start,' grumbled Davies bitterly.

Mrs Fulljames held up a restraining arm like a point-duty policeman. Some rain, as if retained by capillary action in the creases of her pink plastic sleeve, now drizzled onto his sheet. 'We will send some more,' she said in her final way. 'So stop being a misery. You don't look as though you could manage a Smartie anyway.'

'I expect they feed you by tubes, don't they?' agreed Doris. 'You'd never get a Smartie down a tube.'

'Anyway, you know what *you* did, don't you?' asked Mrs Fulljames.

'I gather,' said Davies wearily. 'That I got a dustbin put over my head, was then bashed about something fearful, and finally knocked in the canal.'

'You also left the front door open,' said Doris frostily. 'Your key was in it.'

'Oh?'

'And somebody walked in and stole the hallstand,' Mrs Fulljames finished it for her, perhaps afraid Doris might not achieve the right emphasis. 'My antique hallstand.'

'Antique?' queried Davies. 'That object was antique?'

'It belonged to Mr Fulljames,' muttered Doris indicating that was a mark of authenticity. 'The late Mr Fulljames.'

'Perhaps that Persian bloke – the one who nicked the bed – has been on the prowl again,' suggested Davies dismally.

'You're being frivolous,' said Mrs Fulljames haughtily. 'I'll bet you're laughing all over your face behind that mess. Anyway we didn't come here to argue. How long will you be in?'

'Christ knows. The embroidery class is coming back tomorrow. I reckon they're going to try and keep me as a demonstration model or something.'

'How long?' insisted Doris. 'Tell Mrs Fulljames.'

'I don't know!' He managed that most difficult of all vocal achievements, a quiet shout.

'Do you want your room kept? That's the point.'

Davies was horrified. 'My room? You *wouldn't* let my room?'

'It's economics, Mr Davies. That's how we have to live. Surely even you know that.'

'Jesus wept. Don't let it. I'll keep paying.'

'In that case, all right,' sniffed Mrs Fulljames indicating a load had been taken off her mind. 'We'll discuss the hallstand at some other time. I don't feel up to it now.'

'Nor me,' muttered Davies trying to slide under the sheet.

She produced a newspaper from her plastic folds. 'I brought you this,' she said as though they had reached a truce. '*Evening News*. Last night's. But in here it makes no difference, I suppose.'

'None at all,' he agreed defeatedly. 'The world hardly exists.'

They backed towards the door. Then Doris, unexpectedly gave a little birdlike dart forward and kissed him on his sore cheek. A final minor cascade of trapped rain escaped from her hat onto his face. 'Bye, then,' she said, then anxiously: 'You've, you've got your insurances all paid up, haven't you?'

Mod Lewis came through the door like a felon. 'I'm not all that keen on this place,' he explained on tip-toe when he reached to the foot of Davies's bed. 'I was a porter here once, you know, during a crime wave. Someone kept stealing the patients' false teeth. By night, see.'

He rolled his eyes melodramatically. 'Everybody was suspect, boy. Even the consultant surgeons. Everybody got left with a nasty taste in their mouths. Especially the patients.' He advanced around the side of the bed to Davies, as though his experience as a porter had given him some professional knowledge. 'Aye, that's better,' he said surveying the swollen face approvingly. 'Nice job they've done there, those sutures. It'll all go back in place eventually. It's subsided even now.'

'You've been in to see me before?'

'Oh yes, man. Course I have. The first morning, as soon as I heard. It was a good excuse for not going to the library. But you looked very poorly, Dangerous. Never saw a face like it. Your head was all swelled up. Reminded me of the old globe of the world we had at school. That was knocked about too. I sat with you for an hour or more. You were right out and since I had nobody to talk to I amused myself by tracing the major rivers, sea and air routes on your face – and the railways, of course, most interesting.'

'That's one thing about me, I'm never boring,' said Davies. 'Do you think you could get a message to a young woman for me.'

'Josie,' said Mod confidently. 'She's coming in tonight. She read it in the local paper and she came into "The Babe In Arms". Nice little girl. Bit skinny. Bit young for you. She wanted to come this morning but I said I'd come first. Just to see you were passable.'

'Am I?'

'Passable,' nodded Mod, but with some doubt. 'You're sort of going down from when I last viewed you. Who did it?'

'Ramscar, his lot. It must have been,' said Davies quietly. 'Out to kill me, I suppose.'

'Davus sum non Oedipus' quoted Mod looking at him glumly. 'Publius Terence, Roman poet.

'What's it mean?' asked Davies.

'I am a simple man, no solver of riddles,' obliged Mod. 'I read it yesterday and I thought how fitting it was.'

He had been standing but now he pulled the small visitor's chair confidently to the bedside. 'But you must be standing on *somebody's* toes, that's for certain,' he said.

'In my blundering sort of way,' agreed Davies.

'Ever thought that's maybe why you were put onto the Ramscar business in the very beginning,' suggested Mod. 'Maybe they didn't want anybody who'd be too . . . well . . . subtle.'

'Everybody who comes in here is so kind,' sighed Davies. 'Is anybody feeding my dog?'

'Mr Smeeton, the Complete Home Entertainer,' Mod told him. 'I tried to feed the foul thing but it bit me. So I sent Mr Smeeton. He went along in his dog outfit, on the way to one of his performances. He says he is coming to see you.'

'Not in one of his costumes, I hope.'

'Probably,' said Mod. 'He said he'd come by on the way to work. So you know what that means. One of his extravaganzas.'

'I can't wait.'

A silence dropped between them for a moment, as it does at hospital bedsides. Mod wanted to say something. 'You've heard about the hallstand being nicked, I suppose.' he said eventually. Davies sensed that he had intended to say something else.

'They came in, you know,' he replied. 'Mrs Fulljames and Doris. It was terrifying. She even gave my Smarties away.' He looked at Mod through his bruises. 'What else was it you were going to say?'

'Well, nothing really. I was just wondering . . . not prying into your business as a police detective or anything. I was just wondering how it was going. The Celia thing.'

Davies had spent his prostrate hours going through it all portion by portion. 'I keep turning up stones, and finding wiggly things underneath. Very odd things some of them too. Very nasty, some. But they don't seem to have any connection. A couple of hours before I was duffed up I thought I'd found a good lead, something that's been reeking for years and, sure enough, out it came.'

Mod continued thoughtfully, 'Perhaps, begging your pardon, Dangerous, perhaps blundering about like you're apt to do, you've stirred up more than one dirty pond.'

'Listen Mod,' Davies said. 'When I feel more up to it, I'll tell you what I've found so far. It's a lot, but it's nothing, if you see what I mean. You might be able to see something that I can't.'

The Welshman nodded. 'That's more than probable,' he accepted. 'In the meantime, I've done something on your behalf. I thought while you was stuck in here I'd take over on the case of Celia Norris for a few days.'

'And what?'

'Oh, I've done nothing really. Nothing at all. And I don't want to interfere, if you understand me, casting aspersions or anything. But I did *notice* something. I'm not going to tell you what it is because it might be putting ideas into your head – and at this stage they might not be the right ideas. They certainly wouldn't be very welcome ideas, take it for gospel. I'll point you in the right direction and then you'll have to make the same conclusions yourself.'

Davies stared at him. 'All right. What is it for God's sake?'

'I've just looked up the account of the Norris murder in the files of the local paper, in the *Citizen*. I take it you've done that?'

'One of the first things,' confirmed Davies. 'The press cuttings are all in the dossier. I read that right through.'

Mod got to his feet. 'Well, when you get out of here go and take another look – in the files. See if you can see what I think I saw. All right?'

'Can't you tell me now? Come on Mod. You're supposed to be my pal.'

'Thank you, but no. Have a look yourself. I'm not being the cause of any unpleasantness. Good-bye Dangerous. Hope you're better when I come in next time.'

'Rotten bastard,' muttered Davies. But Mod just laughed and went out.

Mr Smeeton, the Complete Home Entertainer, materialized at the ward door that evening, as Mod had forecast, his feet hoofed, his chest chestnut and a life-sized horse's head tucked beneath his arm.

'I've taken on a partner,' he confidingly said as he came across the floor. Visitors' conversation in the ward stopped. 'I've left him outside. He's the back-end.'

'Where else?' agreed Davies. 'Nice to see you're branching out. Taking on staff. You'll have to be a bit careful, though, won't you about who you employ for the arse. It seems to me that could be a bit risky.'

'It's a clean show,' said Mr Smeeton primly. 'And I employ only clean people.' He put the horse's head down on its ear on the bed. It grinned at Davies glassily. Mr Smeeton carefully examined him. 'Nasty,' he breathed eventually. 'Very nasty. I knew a bloke in a knife throwing act who went off with his partner's wife. I remember going to the hospital. He looked just like you.'

'I do an act with a dustbin,' said Davies. 'Followed by a spectacular dive into icy water.'

'So I understand,' said the entertainer morosely. 'And you left the front door open and the hallstand was stolen. We've had nothing but moans about that around the table ever since you've been in here. She's a hard woman that Mrs Fulljames. She would never make the grade as a theatrical landlady. No kindness in her. Somehow I can't see her lifting a midget up to the lavatory chain.'

The face ached as Davies grinned. He adjusted it again. 'No, somehow Mrs Fulljames doesn't fit that picture,' he agreed. 'Thank you for feeding Kitty, by the way.'

'Glad to help,' said Mr Smeeton kindly. He stamped his hooves on the floor. They sounded real. People looked up again. 'I'll have to be going. Our show begins at eight. I hope you're out soon.' He picked up his horse's head from the blanket and swivelled one of its eyes. 'See you then. Toodle pip.'

As he reached the door, the head wedged awkwardly under his arm, Josie walked in. Her small face looked very pinched. Her stride was jerky. 'I suppose he'd been to see you,' she guessed. 'Him with the horse's head.'

'Right,' nodded Davies. 'They keep trying to make me laugh.'

She looked at his face. Then she sat down heavily on the little chair, took both his hands in hers and began to cry on them.

CHAPTER TEN

As it was Sunday evening it had begun to rain. The Salvation Army band formed their circle, their small Stonehenge of faith, outside their Citadel, and turning their blue backs on the rest of the town and the world, began to play inwardly.

It was the wrong season for it to be anything much more than a private gathering. In the summer they often had people in the dry street, loitering, offering advice or ribaldry, while they sang their songs of love. There was, at that season, a man who contrived to do a Cockney soft-shoe shuffle to their tunes. But now, in the dumb autumn dusk, there were only two outside the circle who took any notice of their burly playing or heard the hope in the words they proclaimed.

The first man was always there, at any time or term, an active simpleton who enjoyed conducting the band behind the true conductor's back. He had followed every sweep of the hands and arms for years and, in truth, performed them faithfully and well. This shadow had also acquired a Salvation Army cap from an Army Surplus Store and it gave his corded face a certain peak of religious authority. Sunday night was the gladdest night of the week for him, not because he heard and accepted their salvation, but because it was the only night of the week when he was not alone. The other witness was Dangerous Davies.

They had discharged him from the hospital with the well-meant advice to be more careful in the future. He had walked painfully that evening to the police station to write the required official report on the attack and his comrade officers had gathered around him, inspecting his injuries, poking him as though he were some manner of specimen, and discussing among themselves various wounds suffered by policemen in the past. He was grateful to return to the rain. He had walked under it in the direction of the shuttered High Street and heard, through the veil of the evening, the sounds of the Sabbath band.

Davies had always admired and enjoyed the Salvation Army. Even on this evening, drear and dun, they seemed to puff out warmth, as though the fervent breath emitted through the oom-pah instruments was pumped from some special Christian boiler. Standing there by the telephone box, on the second day of his two-day convalescence, the street lights through the squared post office panes making a guard across his damaged face, he remembered years ago how his mother had dearly wanted to join the Salvation Army. But his father had disliked the bonnet and had forbidden her to wear it. They were both dead and gone now and he wondered idly whether part of his father's purgatory was to sit and watch his mother wearing an eternal hat of Booth's blue and red.

Davies was observing Andrew Parsons, pumping warm low notes through a tuba. He was a cubed man with a serious and solid face (which anyone who plays a tuba must have since it is an instrument which precludes a smile) level shoulders, legs planted surely astride; a long way travelled from the bag-eyed lad who had stolen ladies garments from half the washing lines in the neighbourhood. Davies approved.

The commandant of the little band stopped the music for a prayer. Presumably as a privilege of rank he was handed an umbrella, ringed with the army's blue and red, and clutching it between his hands in the manner of some different faith with a crucifix, he said a compendum of prayers. He then commenced a sermon, taking predictably as his text (and not for the first time, Davies imagined) the assurance about where two or three are gathered together in His name, there will He be also. Now that they were not playing their instruments, the band seemed to sink lower in the street almost as though the drizzle was quietly melting them. The sermon was too long for the liking of the pseudo-conductor outside the circle and he began shouting: 'Get on with the hymns!' and 'Stop the bleeding rabbitting!' which finally provoked a bassoonist to turn and threaten, in a thoroughly unchristian fashion, to close him up for good.

Likewise Davies found that wisdom and water were poor mixers, so he slyly slotted himself into the telephone box, pretended to be making a call, and observed Parsons from there. The commandant, he perceived, seemed to shout all the louder for his benefit, or perhaps to cast his words to the windows of the street, alight and uncaring all around. His mouth opened so wide that the rain dropped in. But nobody heeded. He was a wilderness crying in a voice.

Eventually the band played again and, as if God were also relieved that the sermon was ended, the rain eased and the faces of the bandsmen dried out. At the end came a prayer and Davies emerged from the telephone box to meet the demanding eyes of Parsons who was making the collection in his hat.

'Hope you've enjoyed it, sir. Would you like to contribute something?' He asked in a way that indicated that Davies owed an admission fee. Davies looked down at the floor of the hat. The simpleton had placed two milk bottle tops in there and Davies added the twopence which he had held in the cause of realism during his bogus phone call. Parsons, who, from experience, had accepted the milk bottle tops without argument, stared at the two pence and then at Davies, shaming him into putting a further ten pence piece. The coin lay like a silver moon in a black sky.

'Thank you sir,' said Parsons looking down into the black-bottomed hat. 'We're saving up for a new concert hall.'

The money was nevertheless, religiously counted and after another humphing hymn and a prayer, so quiet it was almost an aside, the cordon bleu broke and its members went off through the damp dark, nursing their instruments like infants. The banner was examined and Davies heard the portly woman who had borne it, sigh 'Sopping wet again. Take all week to dry.' He turned and followed Parsons through the streets.

'Pity there weren't a few more of us there,' he observed chattily, catching up with the square, striding man. Parsons looked round quickly and grinned grimly. 'Can't expect it this weather,' he said philosophically. 'It takes all our faith to keep us out there. Be much easier in a nice warm citadel.'

'Still it was enjoyable even in the rain,' said Davies. 'I couldn't see the Catholics having High Mass in those sort of conditions.'

'No, that's true enough,' agreed Parsons thoughtfully. 'You couldn't burn incense or candles on a night like this could you.' He walked a few more yards and then asked: 'Are you a Christian?'

'No. I'm a copper.'

Parsons showed no surprise. He continued walking and nodded quietly. 'Yes, I thought so. I've seen you around. Your face seems to have changed, though.'

'It's old age,' answered Davies. They had reached some untidy steps leading up to one of the narrow Victorian houses. There were odd curtains in every window. 'You live here?' he asked.

'Yes. Up the top.'

'Can I come in for a minute. I wanted to ask you something.'

Again Parsons did not seem to think it was unexpected. Davies thought that perhaps he never thought anything was. 'Yes, if you want,' he said starting up the steps and manoeuvring his tuba to get his key. 'About Christianity is it?' he asked unconfidently.

'No. I'm afraid it's about crime.'

Parsons opened the front door carefully. 'All right,' he responded keeping his head to the front where it was almost touching the red and yellow diamond glass. Briefly he appeared to rest his forehead against the pattern. 'But keep the noise down, will you,' he asked over his uniformed shoulder, 'I don't want the landlady to know I've got anybody in. Especially the police. She's not an admirer of the police.'

'Mine's the same,' answered Davies truthfully. He crept through the front door after Parsons. They went up the dim stairs quickly but with stealth, along a corridor hung with cooking smells and shadows, and eventually, when Parsons had unlocked a further door, into a bed-sitting room, tidy but tired.

'Never married then?' inquired Davies sitting in a cold armchair while Parsons bent to light a gas fire.

'Wouldn't be stuck up here if I did,' replied Parsons again not put out by the question. 'I've lived here thirty years.'

'Man and boy,' added Davies. He leaned back. Sitting on the chair was like sitting on the lap of a large, clammy woman. He drew his wet coat closer to him. 'You must have been here when you had the trouble.'

'The trouble?'

'You know, Andrew. The bother about Celia Norris.'

Parsons stood up slowly, still facing away from him towards the gas fire which was now spluttering around his shins. There was a mirror suspended above the fire and he looked at Davies in that. 'Oh God,' he said resignedly. 'Won't you ever leave me be?'

'I know mate, I know,' nodded Davies with genuine sympathy. 'These things follow you.'

'Hardly anybody knows about my stupidness in those days. I keep hoping it's all past and done and over. What's your name anyway?' He turned away from the wall and the mirror.

'Davies. Detective Constable.'

'Ah, you're the one they call Dangerous Davies.'

'Everybody knows,' sighed Davies.

'It can't be very important if they send you,' said Parsons bluntly. 'Not a constable.'

'Routine,' said Davies not allowing his annoyance to appear. 'Purely routine. Something's come up, about the Celia Norris case, that's all. Maybe a new lead.'

'After – what is it – after twenty odd years? I would have reckoned all the leads were as dead as she is,' muttered Parsons. He sat down in an identically worn armchair opposite Davies so that they flanked the gas burner. Only one element was burning.

'People change their minds, think about things differently, say things they wouldn't have said at the time.' Davies repeated, as much to reassure himself as inform Parsons.

'That is all very well,' said Parsons his tone weary. 'But you look at it from my point of view. I've tried to live it down, forget it. People have just about forgotten it now, around here, and I don't want them remembering.' He looked up with a small fierce desperation at Davies. 'It's taken me two years to learn to play that tuba,' he said.

'I'm really sorry,' answered Davies. 'But there's no need to worry. If we can get through this now it will be all over, done, and nobody will ever know any different.'

'Until the next time.'

'There won't be any next time,' urged Davies leaning towards him. 'Not if we can clear it up this time, with your help and the help of others, then it will be over for ever. It's going to be painful, for you, I understand that very well, but it needn't take long.'

Parsons sighed and clasped his hands before him. Then he rose and put his tuba away in a cupboard as though to keep it from knowing what was going to be said by and about the man who blew into it. Parsons returned to the chair. 'I don't drink,' he said. 'So I can't offer you anything.'

'Forget it,' said Davies. 'I'm thinking of packing it in myself.'

'Does you no good,' said the Salvation Army man firmly. 'No good at all. Rots your inside, strong drink.'

'Agreed. Now, will you just tell me, as you remember it, what happened. I've read the statement that you made at the time, like I've read all the others, but I'm asking people to repeat them because now, after all this time, they may just possibly say something different that will provide a lead.'

'All right, but there's just one thing, Mr Davies. I don't *do* that any more. Understand? You know, the knickers thing. It's all gone and I'm cured. I was only a kid then and I was lonely. You never think of youngsters being lonely, do you? It was the loneliest time of my life. Now, what with the Salvation Army and the tuba and everything, I've got plenty to keep my mind occupied. No more knickers.'

'Just go on,' Davies encouraged. 'I understand all you've said. We all do things we're embarrassed about at some time in our lives. Me, not excepted . . .'

'Oh,' said Parsons interested. 'What have you done?'

Davies knew he was beginning one of his familiar spirals. The suspect was interrogating him. 'Never mind,' he said firmly. 'Just start off *now* and tell me how you remember it.'

It took twenty minutes. How he had found the girl's clothes in the all-night toilet, but minus the knickers. How he had kept them until he realized, from the newspapers, that they were the garments of Celia Norris. How he had taken them to the toilet again and been seen by the attendant. It had not become any the less pathetic over the years, nor diminished because a grown man was talking about the foibles of a boy. The story was retold in a flat voice. Parsons sat, his head almost between his knees, never once looking up. When he did, at the conclusion, raise his head, Davies saw that his eyes were streaming.

'All right,' said Davies getting up and patted him on the level shoulder. 'I'm sorry, Mr Parsons. Thanks for going over it. I just wanted to get the public bog thing straight, that's all.'

'Is that all now? Is that the lot?'

'Well, I hope so. I can't promise I won't be back. There may just be one or two points. You never know. Anyway thanks.' He felt it would be wrong to offer the man his hand so he turned and went out of the door and along the corridor. He had gone down the first three stairs when Parsons called after him from the door, in a sudden burst of tears. His voice trembled as he tried to cry out and keep it quiet at the same time. 'And good riddance too! To bad rubbish!'

Davies waved his hand sadly in the shadows and continued down. Parsons closed the door and quietly sobbed against its panels. 'Next time put something decent in the collection too,' he sniffled. 'Mean copper.'

He went, almost dragging himself to the bed, and began to take his stiff uniform off. He took off his tunic and trousers and folded them over a chair. He shivered and he saw that the single bar of the gas fire had gone out. It was cold standing there in his brassière and panties.

The police station charwoman was languidly washing down the notice board when Davies arrived in the morning. The front steps had also been washed down and the brass handle on the door shone with odd brilliance. It was almost as if they had cleaned up the place to welcome him back.

'Waste of time this is,' said the cleaning woman, eyes drifting aloft as she washed the grime from the glass of the notice board. 'No sooner it's done than it's filthy again. This was always a dirty station, Mr Davies.'

'At least you can see through the glass now,' observed Davies chattily. She made a swift examination of his damaged face but made no comment, apparently concluding, not unreasonably, that it went with the job. He leaned closer examining the several newly-revealed photographs of Wanted Criminals. 'It's time it had a clean,' he joked. 'According to this we're still looking for Charlie Peace.'

'Good luck to him, I say,' she replied, his observation foundering. 'It's a wonder you lot catch anybody. Not the way this place is run.'

Inside the station, the duty sergeant patiently tried to assemble the physique of a lost dog. He had taken the chart of known breeds from the wall and was holding it up for a wiry old lady to point out the type most approximating to her missing friend. 'He's got a head like that . . . and, let me see . . . a body like that and . . . oh, yes a nice stubby tail like that . . . and long legs – like that one there.'

'That makes him a camel,' murmured the sergeant writing patiently in his book.

A haunted pair of eyes leaned over the top of the charge room door and two mislaid children awaiting their mother, sat on the corridor bench playing 'Find the Lady'.

Police Constable Westerman had been stricken with another nose-bleed and was sprawled in the C.I.D. Room looking like a riot casualty while someone went to get the cell keys to drop down his back.

'The gov'nor wants to see you, Dangerous,' he said bravely through the blood. 'Are you feeling better?'

Davies was touched that the first inquiry after his health had come from one who was so riven with suffering. 'Much better thank you,' he smiled painfully. 'You're not too good, I take it.'

Westerman decided not to risk taking away the scarlet handkerchief again, so he merely rolled his eyes tragically. Davies went upstairs, knocked on Superintendent Yardbird's office, and, at the call two minutes later, went in.

Yardbird looked at his scarred face but his expression did not change. There might have been more reaction if Davies had been wearing a different suit.

'We're all very pleased,' said Yardbird.

'Oh good, I'm glad,' said Davies painfully. Every stitch seemed to hurt.

'Well these things happen when you're a policeman,' said Yardbird. He got up from his desk and went, as though by habit towards the window. The rooftops were like a frozen sea. There was no sign of movement from the Students' Hostel. 'All good experience for you, Davies.'

'Yes sir. Splendid.'

'And it shows that you've stirred him up. Ramscar. It shows he's worried. That's what the Special Branch are pleased about. I bet he's had you followed ever since you started asking questions about him.'

Davies nodded. He remembered the man with no glass in his spectacles. 'I expect they have, sir,' he muttered.

'If you'd kept your eyes open you wouldn't have walked into it. And, for Christ's sake man, fancy just falling in their laps by taking any notice of a note put through your letter box. And going alone. That was the stupid thing. Sometimes I don't think you'll ever make it, Davies.'

'Sometimes I think that myself, sir,' Davies had to admit.

'Well, anyway, all's well that ends well. We know at least that they've risen to the bait.'

'Yes,' nodded Davies. 'Even when I'm the bait.'

'Listen Davies,' said Yardbird turning from the window. 'You can jack this in, if you wish. I'll get somebody else on it. I was thinking about doing that anyway.'

'No, no, I'll be all right, sir,' protested Davies. 'I've got a little score to pay back to Mr Ramscar now. Nobody puts a dustbin over me and gets away with it.'

'All right,' said Yardbird. 'And I take it you're concentrating on this now and not digging up old murders.'

'Yes, I am.'

'Good. Christ, if every copper in the Metropolitan Police spent his time raking up unsolved crimes the Ramscars of this world would have a bloody marvellous time. It would be mayhem. Get your priorities straight, for God's sake. I hope you won't be wanting sick leave because of this?'

'I'm working now,' said Davies evenly. 'When it's over perhaps I'll take some leave then. Let the stitches heal properly. I think I'd like to go and see my uncle in Stoke-on-Trent.'

'Good,' said Yardbird returning to his desk. 'Might do you the world of good. Now, go and find Ramscar.'

CHAPTER ELEVEN

That night Dave Boot was wearing his best hair, a reddish confection clouding to orange around his clay face. His suit of lights danced and his body lit up with violent, violet flashes, as the console before him hammered out its songs of popular wisdom and illumination. He was pleased to see a big crowd, but not entirely surprised since Mondays was free entry when he hoped to salvage at the bar what was lost at the turnstiles.

From his rostrum Boot was thinking how tall teenagers grew in these times. He could see them standing silhouetted like trees against the vermilion walls at the back of the room. Then the tallest and widest tree of all swayed forward clumsily through the wobbling dancers and Boot saw that it was Dangerous Davies.

Boot found himself shaking within as well as without. He watched Davies come nearer, trying to dance but all out of beat, treading and kicking the young people around him so that they pushed and elbowed him in retaliation. He was shepherding a small pinched, dark-haired girl. They neared the flashing hues of the rostrum. The illuminated Boot leaned over angrily. 'What business have you got here?' he demanded.

Davies looked up cheerfully, his grin now, at last, the deepest gash in his face. 'I'm a golden oldie, love,' he answered. 'A rave from the grave.'

Performing an adapted valeta, he jogged Josie away. 'So that's Mr Boot,' said Josie quietly. 'Celia's mate.' Davies did not know how she meant that. He had told her nothing. 'What a bleeding sight,' she added. 'Like a fairground gone mad. I hate all this stuff, Dangerous.'

'I thought all young people liked this. It's pop,' Davies said. 'I wish I could do it. It would be somewhere to go on a Monday night.'

Josie curled up her nose disdainfully in the half-dark. 'I can't stand it,' she repeated. 'I'm folk.'

'Oh, are you,' he said. 'What's that? Folk?'

'Folk,' she repeated carefully. 'Folk music. I've got eighty-three long players. There's a club called "The Truck Drivers" I go to.'

Davies nodded. 'I've seen that. In Kilburn. I always thought it was a transport caff.'

She gave a half-inch grin. '*This* is the transport caff,' she said. 'Bloody orange hair. Look at him up there.'

'I think we'll just quietly hop out now,' murmured Davies. 'The dog has seen the rabbit and the rabbit the dog. That's all I wanted. He'll be worried now. We'll go and have a pint or something and see Mr Boot later. Thank you for the dance, Josie.'

He despatched Josie home in a taxi before going back to find Boot. He paid the driver in advance and then saw that she was gesticulating behind the window in an impersonal way. She had edged the window down by the time he had fumbled with the door. Her small face had appeared framed in the aperture. 'Now Dangerous,' she warned seriously. 'Don't – please – get into any more bother. And don't get drunk. And don't stay out late.'

'No,' he replied to all three demands. She pushed her face through the gap and kissed him inaccurately on his top lip. He patted her face clumsily and then waved to her as the taxi went away.

He returned to the club and strolled in, conspicuously incongruous, among the slight teenagers in the shadows. Boot had gone.

'He's off early,' shrugged the lady in charge of the cloakroom. 'He sometimes takes sort of half a night off on Mondays because they don't pay do they? He's gone. But he's only just. You might catch him in the car park.'

Davies went out hurriedly. The lines of cars at the back lay inert. There was only a motor cyclist, bowed under the egg of his helmet, kicking his machine to a start. Davies walked quickly around the cars to make sure that Boot was not merely lying low. He disturbed three back-seat couples (in one car a recumbent girl had her feet pressed against the ceiling in confined ecstasy), before the motor cyclist droned by and he saw in the car park lights the orange wig curling out of a bag strapped behind the seat.

Boot was beyond the gate before Davies's belated shout escaped. Davies turned and scampered clumsily towards his Lagonda, upsetting his sleeping dog with the urgency of his arrival and the bursting noise of the starting engine. Kitty began to cough irritably. A young voice called out 'Peeping Tom!' as he made for the gate. He saw that Boot was held up at the traffic lights at the foot of the hill.

Boot had now seen him and he drove the motor cycle smartly along the main road hearing the animal roar of the Lagonda emitted behind him. It occurred to Davies that there was a lot of traffic coming in the opposite direction for a night so early in the week. He kept Boot's ruby rear light just in sight and was surprised to see it sag and suddenly wobble as the machine was turned off the road and into the car park at Neasden Underground Station. He became wedged in some traffic at a junction. He noticed it was swelling from the direction of Wembley. The delay was enough time for Boot to leave the motor cycle and walk into the entrance of the tube station.

Hurriedly, if humanely, Davies threw the canvas sheet over Kitty, who snarled, and then went in pursuit of Boot. He ignored the ticket office and clumped in disarray down to the platform where at once he saw Boot, clutching his crash helmet like a trophy beneath his arm, at the far end. A red train was snaking into the station and Boot kept calm. As Davies stumped towards him he stepped aboard. As Davies hurried the length of the train he saw that it was crammed with men. He reached the final door, the one which Boot had entered, and stepped resolutely inside, forcing himself among the tight, overcoated, enscarved, en-capped and encapsuled bodies. There were protests over his entry and his bulk, but the doors closed, crushing him into the mass and that was the conclusion of any arguments.

'What you fink of the twin-strikers, then, mate?' asked the man next to him.

'Rubbish,' said Davies, making a guess. 'Powder puffs.' He could not see Boot in his immediate vicinity. He stood on tip-toe until several of his abutting neighbours told him to stand proper. The man who had asked him about the twin-strikers stared at him, having, in fact, addressed the query to a companion beyond Davies's shoulder, a companion who now emerged and, after joining his questioner in a haughty look at Davies's face, settled into a further discussion of the game.

England, Davies perceived, had been playing, not very competently, at Wembley Stadium. 'I reckon that referee's a wanker,' said the fan closest to Davies's left ear. 'And the linesmen. Both wankers.'

'S'no use calling them wankers, mate,' replied the man next to his right ear, having overheard the confidence. 'Not when all the bloody forwards are wankers. And the fucking defence.'

The first man told him to shut his face and there came a verbal altercation followed swiftly by a fist fight, with Davies jammed between the two antagonists. One had, with swift initiative, grabbed the other's England rosette and was trying to ram it into his mouth. A kick landed on Davies's ankle and another apparently found a target somewhere else because cries were folowed by a renewed outbreak of fighting. All at once Davies felt like an elephant trapped in a river by crocodiles. He lumbered about trying to keep out of the way while the tight battle jabbed and butted all around him. A scarf was being tightened around a reddening neck. He was trying to avoid revealing he was a policeman but when he was forced to shout this revelation the only reaction was that somebody kneed him in the valley. The entire jammed carriage seemed to be swaying with the battle, arms and fists, heads and oaths, flew about the tubular space. Davies tried to reach for his warrant card but he could not free his hand, trapped beneath an anonymous but hard armpit.

The mêlée was resolved abruptly and simply by the train's arrival at the next station, the doors opening and the bursting battle, or a fair proportion of it, being spilled on to the platform, where it rolled about with increased gusto. When the doors slid to a close again one-third of the original passengers were gone. Such fighting as was left in the train reduced itself to incomplete skirmishes and bitter looks.

A morsel-sized man, almost smothered by his England muffler and rosette, had been pummelled into one corner by the fierceness of the engagement, and now squatted on the floor trying to reassemble his spectacles. 'I wouldn't mind,' he complained. 'But they're all supposed to be supporting bleeding England.' Standing immediately behind him, watching Davies, was Dave Boot.

Davies moved close to him. Even the mutterings all around had now descended to sullenness or attempts at a sane analysis of the game. Davies said to Boot: 'Do you come here often?'

'Only when there's a football match at Wembley,' replied Boot. 'Then the roads get jammed. Now where would you be going?'

'With you,' said Davies simply.

'Listen, you're not following me to my place. I live with my mum,' said Boot unexpectedly. 'And I don't want my old lady upset by the police.'

'Where do you live?' asked Davies.

'You'll have to wait and see where I get off.'

The train arrived at another stop and more men disembarked. Some waved their rattles in melancholy defiance in the damp lamplit air.

'I don't mind asking you a few questions here,' said Davies, who did mind. Boot knew it was a bluff. A sharp expression seeped into his eyes. Both were aware that the men around them had all produced newspapers from behind the creases of which they were listening avidly.

'Go on then,' challenged Boot. 'Ask.'

Indecision swamped Davies. He looked around at the ears projecting from the papers. 'I can wait,' he said. 'I can wait until we get off.'

'How's your murder?' asked Boot loudly. The eyes joined the ears ascending from the edges of the pages. 'Fancy you being involved in a nasty business like that.'

Davies glared up at him. 'Shut up,' he demanded throatily. 'You're showing us up.'

'Grisly thing, murder,' continued Boot unconcerned. 'Especially being involved so deep, like you are.'

'I'll arrest you and drag you out at the next station,' whispered Davies. 'I'm not kidding.'

'What for?' asked Boot more quietly. 'You've got nothing to arrest me for. What's the charge – being cheeky to a copper on the London Underground?'

They were interrupted by the formidable entry of a ticket inspector at the next station. As though he had been purposely briefed he homed straight on Davies. 'Ticket please,' he boomed. Others around began fumbling.

'I haven't got one,' muttered Davies. 'I was . . . I would have paid.'

'They *all* say that. They *all* want to pay once they're nabbed,' boomed the Inspector. 'That's why London Transport is losing money. People like you.'

'I didn't know how far I was going,' explained Davies hurriedly. He put his head close, almost affectionately next to the inspector's bristly neck. 'I'm a police officer,' he whispered.

'Oh, are you now? I've heard that one as well,' claimed the inspector with a booming grin. 'Well, sir, can I see your warrant card?'

The entire compartment now stood expectantly grouped to watch Davies produce his warrant card. Those without a good vantage, stood on the seats or levered themselves up on the hangers. Boot stood watching Davies and his discomfiture with an adjacent smile.

'Warrant card?' said Davies. 'Oh, all right. This is very inconvenient I can tell you,' Even as his hand went to his pocket he knew it would not be there. He remembered last seeing it on his bedside table back at Mrs Fulljames's. The hand returned empty-handed. The other hand went into the other inside pocket and then to the outside enclosures of his coat. 'I had it,' he protested desperately. 'Somebody must have picked my pocket.'

The inspector laughed knowingly. 'You haven't got a warrant card, you haven't got a ticket, and you don't know where you're going until you get there. Does that sum it up, sir?'

Davies nodded miserably. 'I'm afraid it does. But I am a policeman, honest.'

'He's a friend of mine,' nodded Boot. 'I can vouch for him. And I've got a ticket.'

'Are you a policeman, sir?' inquired the inspector looking at Boot with a respect that he had not wasted on Davies. 'No. But I can identify myself.' He went quickly to his pocket. 'These are my business cards. And here's a letter from the Mayor of Neasden in connection with some charity work I am performing. It has my address on it.'

Davies, on instinct, tried to get a sight of the address but the inspector, giving him a quick, foul look, took it out of his view. 'Mr Boot!' said the inspector. 'Ah yes, I know you! From my boxing days in Willesden. Remember you well, Mr Boot.' He glanced, still disparagingly at Davies. 'Well, if you can vouch for him, that's good enough for me. He'll have to pay his fare though. He won't get away with that.'

'I'll see he pays it to the ticket collector when we get out. We don't know how far we're going yet.'

'Oh, all right. I'll trust him then,' said the inspector. He turned to the white-faced Davies. 'Now I'm putting you in Mr Boot's charge,' he said. He wagged a big, red finger. 'And just remember – you're on your honour.'

Passengers left the train at every station and few boarded to take their places. When the adjoining seats became vacant Boot enjoying himself, rolled his eyes suggestively and Davies grumpily followed him to them. Eventually there remained only a mothy-looking woman near them and two men, both wearing England rosettes as big as their faces, who sat at the extreme end of the carriage, on opposite seats, contemplating each other in antagonstic silence.

Davies frowned at the passing stations and then at the map. The train was under the Thames and heading for home at the Elephant and Castle. Boot was clamped in silence, taking a newspaper out of his pocket and reading it minutely. Davies sat uncomfortably. The mothy woman stood up and gathered her spreadeagled belongings to her, eventually, and got from the train. Now there only remained the two men and they were at the far end. 'All right,' sighed Boot, folding away his paper. 'What's it all about?'

'I hope you enjoyed your fun,' replied Davies sourly.

'I saved you from being thrown off the train for not paying your fare. You might have even been arrested,' Boot pointed out.

'Yes, very good of you, mate. Now where exactly are we getting off?'

'I'm not getting off,' said Boot firmly. 'You can if you like. But I told you, I don't want any copper following me home and upsetting my mum. It's not as if you've got a warrant or anything. Like I told you before, my solicitor ought to be present.'

'She means a lot to you, your mum,' commented Davies.

'Funnily enough she does,' replied Boot sharply.

'Did you use to go home to your mum in the old days – in the good old days, remember? Did you go home to her after screwing Roxanne Potts on the vaulting horse?'

'Who the hell . . .!'

'Roxanne Potts, now there's a name to conjure with.'

Boot looked miserably thoughtful. 'Jesus, you've been busy digging them up, haven't you. Roxanne Potts. She must be forty-odd now.'

'She was fifteen then,' said Davies quietly. 'So was Ena and so was poor dead Celia Norris. Remember the trampoline? Nobody could accuse you of not using the equipment.' He made a bouncing movement with his hands. 'Davy go up, Davy go down. Davy go up . . .'

'Pack it in, will you, you bastard,' snorted Boot. He looked along to see if the men at the far end of the carriage were listening. They had stood up to get out. The train was at the end of the line. They looked around curiously at Davies and Boot, then stepped down and hurried away with collars pulled around their ears. As each of them walked past the window their eyes came around the sharp end of their collars to look at the two who remained in the train.

'Elephant and Castle,' said Boot, half getting to his feet. 'It stops here.'

Davies eased him back into the seat. 'But I don't,' he said. 'Now we've travelled so far together I want you to listen for a while and then I want to hear your story too. I suggest you do it now, Booty, because later it could make things much nastier for you.'

Boot sat down. 'We can't sit here,' he argued lamely. 'The train's finished for the night.'

'We'll wait until they throw us off,' said Davies cheerfully. 'It's warm and comfortable and it's quiet. We can talk.'

'Who's been talking to you?' asked Boot. 'Roxanne Potts?'

'No. I haven't had the pleasure of meeting Roxanne. Try again.'

'That Ena.'

'That Ena it was,' approved Davies. 'Ena Brown that was. Ena Lind that is. She married dashing Bill Lind, you know, and now lives in a council penthouse overlooking the entire world. You know, she's even got a green cat.'

'Sometimes,' observed Boot. 'You sound like you're drunk when you're not.'

'You don't believe she's got a green cat? I'll take you along to see it if you like. It's really something to see.'

'No. No thanks. I'll pass on that one.'

'Ena would love to see big muscled Dave again. You could wear a singlet and a jock strap. She'd know you meant business, then. Take a trampoline along and – provided you could take it up in the lift – you could have a rare old time together. Just like the old days.'

'You can't touch me for that, Davies. It was years ago.'

'So was the murder. I could touch you for that.'

Boot's face stiffened as though he had suddenly realized the magnitude of the business. 'And murder is a wound that time won't heal,' encouraged Davies close to his ear. 'You'd better tell me all you know, Booty.'

'I told you, I didn't have anything to do with it. Not killing her,' said Boot dragging the words out. 'Straight.'

'All the more important that you should tell me what you did have to do with then,' urged Davies quietly. 'Otherwise I might think you *did* do that bad thing.'

A London Underground man strolled along the platform, a languid West Indian, buried by life below a cold city. He was supposed to check the train but as he passed the carriage where they sat his attention was caught by a new cinema poster. He examined it casually, quietly embroidered the heroine with a curly moustache, and continued his echoing patrol without seeing Boot or Davies. They did not see him either. Boot was whispering to Davies about teenage girls who had seduced him in the days that used to be. Davies was listening. He was waiting. The doors of the train slid together in a sleepy embrace and it moved. Boot looked up, but now he had begun he seemed reluctant to let anything get in the way. For his part Davies would have detained him on the train even if he had known it had just begun a journey to Addis Ababa.

Eventually Boot had told everything he knew or remembered or cared to relate. He had not been looking even occasionally at Davies's face. Few people do when they are telling something difficult from their past. When he thought he had come to the conclusion of the story, he did glance up as if he thought Davies might have dropped off to sleep. But the big, scarred face was still watching him. The brown overcoat had settled around the policeman's shoulders like a mound of damp earth.

'We're moving,' Boot said nodding at the darkness that was stumbling by the window. 'God knows where we're going now.'

'It's no bother,' yawned Davies. 'These things find it difficult to get out of London. You hadn't finished had you?'

'Yes,' hesitated Boot. 'I think I've told you everything, officer.'

Anger gathered in Davies's face like an extra bruise. 'Don't you fucking "officer" me, Booty,' he threatened. He stood up and grabbed the other man's lapels, lifting him from the seat. 'Tell us about your boxing days then,' he said. Boot's face stretched tight and he began to say something. Davies, however, picked him up and threw him the length of the carriage. He landed, half-sitting in the open area by the doors. 'It's all right, inspector, I can vouch for him. I'll see he pays his fare,' Davies called up after him. Boot, his features drained, looked along the seats from his place on the floor. 'You're out to get your own back for that,' he whispered. 'You're like all of those police buggers. All for yourself in the end. You're going to do me over because I made you look small.'

Davies at once beamed into a real smile. 'No, I wouldn't do that, Booty. Not to *you*. Not while we're having such a useful talk.' He walked over and hauled Boot up from the floor with excess gallantry, brushing him down and replacing him in his seat. 'But,' he said when they were seated again. 'But, I want to tell you something. For your own comfort and convenience. If you don't think of a bit more of that story, the bit you've left out, I'm going to chuck you down to that other gangway next time. That furthest one up there. And then I shall come and stamp on you for taking the piss out of me in front of all the football fans. All right. You've got that clear?'

Boot's head went up and down as though it were on a hinge. 'What *else* then?' he asked.

'The night, Booty,' said Davies, his nose almost in the man's ear. 'The night of July 23rd, 1951.' His face dissolved and he broke into a fragment of song. 'That perfect night, the night you met, there was magic abroad in the air. . . .'

'Celia?' said Boot.

'Too bloody right, Celia,' confirmed Davies quietly. A little smoke of excitement began to rise within his heart. Boot watched his fists close. 'That night.'

'We had it,' said Boot. 'Sexual intercourse, that is. She pestered me. They all did. Christ, I was on the point of exhaustion sometimes.'

'Rotten lot,' murmured Davies.

'And she kept on at me. It was her turn, she said. So . . . so . . . that night I told her to come to the store after she had told everybody she was going home. And I saw her there.'

'Why did you kill her Booty?'

'I DIDN'T KILL HER!'

His shout echoed strangely through the carriage. The train was clattering and curving on its nameless journey. Davies reached for the lapels again, picked up Boot and flung him the distance to the far doorway. He lay on the ribbed wooden floor looking around him, trying to find his breath.

'There, I told you I could do it,' Davies remarked. He walked, swaying with the train towards Boot. Boot sat up and hid his head in his hands like a frightened boy in a school playground. Davies hung above him on the straps. 'Now,' he said. 'Do you want me to throw you back again?'

Boot spoke from his sitting position, his face still enclosed in his hands. 'I had her knickers,' he said. 'I got rid of them after. But I didn't kill her, Davies. Straight I didn't. She was all right when she went from me. She went off on her bike.'

'Leaving you with the prize pants,' said Davies. The smoke within him had become a small fire of triumph. He had *solved* something!

'She ran off without them,' muttered Boot. 'We'd had a row, a dispute. . . .'

'About what, Booty?'

'Oh, for Christ sake. It's twenty-five years ago. . . .'

'What about?'

'I wanted her to do something, you know what I mean, and she wouldn't. She suddenly turned all Catholic and said it was a sin. And I started to kid her about it, just kidding, and she got wild as hell . . . and . . .'

'I don't know what you mean,' said Davies. 'You said I'd *know*. But I can't even guess. What did you have the fight about?'

'You are a bastard,' muttered Boot. 'You just want to hear me say it, don't you.' He looked up as he felt the damp sole of Davies's shoe pushing him in the shirtfront, an inch below his Adam's apple.

'That's right, I want you to say it,' said Davies. 'My imagination is a bit limited about things like this.'

'I wanted her to . . . give me a gobble,' said Boot his head going back to its hiding place between his hands. He looked up and his expression collided with Davies's look of outraged disbelief. 'You know . . .' Boot mumbled. 'A gobble. You know what a gobble is.'

'It's a noise a turkey makes,' said Davies.

'Oh, Christ. Stop it. I wanted her to take it in her mouth. But she wouldn't.'

'I don't blame her,' said Davies. He had become outwardly even more calm. 'I wouldn't like to give you a gobble either.'

Boot's head was trembling in his palms. 'And that was it. She got all ratty and slapped my face and I caught hold of her wrists to stop her. I was only playing, really, but she took it all seriously. Then she kicked me, hard – very nastily too – and rushed out. I saw her get on her bike and she went. That was the last I saw of her.'

'Leaving you with her bloomers. Something to remember her by.'

'That's the lot,' said Boot miserably. 'That's all. Make what you like out of it.'

Davies stepped back and sat on one of the seats. 'All those years ago,' he said shaking his head at the wonder of it. 'And you can still remember how hard she kicked you. And all over a little thing like a gobble. . . .'

Boot squealed as the big man jumped at him. Davies picked him up and thrust him back against the swaying curved walls. Three times he banged him against the wall. Then he turned and threw him half the length of the carriage again. Boot lay on the floor, moaning. He got up as far as his elbow. 'You . . . you fucking hypocrite,' he howled. 'You only do this because you've never had a gobble in your bloody life!'

He was saved from almost certain death by the lurch of the train. Davies stumbled and stopped. He sat down heavily on the cross seats not doing anything. Suddenly he felt very cold. He could see fingers of rain hitting the windows and extending down. 'Look at that,' he called to Boot at the far end. 'It's pouring. We've been nice and dry in here, anyway.'

One of the doors communicating with the next carriage opened noisily and an overalled and undersized man poked his head through. He took in the scene as though it were not entirely unfamiliar. 'Ere,' he inquired. 'What you doin' still on the bleeding train? This train is in the washing shed.'

He made a short bow, like a man having delivered a brief but important oration, and vanished behind the closing door. He returned in five minutes with two other longer men. 'There,' he said, 'That's them. Look, that one's got blood all down him. They been having a fight.'

Davies had, by then, fixed Boot in the seat beside him and had put his arm affectionately about his shoulder. 'L'il disagreement,' he informed the trio. 'Few drinks then the argy-bargy. But we're all right now. Mates again, ain't we Booty?' The head in the arm nodded as it was powerfully squeezed. 'And we'll go orf 'ome quiet. Thank you, gentlemen.'

'This way then,' said one of the men ungraciously. 'You got to go right though the train to the end. You can get out there. And don't be sick, somebody's got to clean this train. You're trespassing anyway, you know that?'

'I know it, but I can't say it,' grinned Davies stupidly. 'Come on old mate. Let's get going. We'll wish these kind gentlemen a fond goodnight.' He lifted Boot out of the seat with his one enclosing arm and then staggered with him along the central aisle and into the next carriage. The London Transport men followed them at a carriage-length. Davies and then Boot, in response to another squeeze of the arm, began to sing drunkenly. 'Dear old pals, jolly old pals . . . Give me the friendship of dear old pals.'

CHAPTER TWELVE

He and Mod had a profound drinking session in 'The Babe In Arms' the next evening. Mod held forth vigorously and variously on the flaws in Darwin's Theory of Origins, produced a logical explanation of the miracle of Moses striking the rock to bring forth water, and related how, in Edwardian times, it was a common embellishment to have goldfish swimming in the plate glass lavatory cisterns of great houses. It was not until they had been deposited, like clumsy sacks, on the wet midnight pavement by the Irish publican and two eager barmen that the matter of the murder was mentioned.

'Is this an opportune moment to inquire as to whether you pursued my investigation into the local newspaper coverage of the late melancholy event?' Mod asked in the posed manner he often affected when drunk. He struggled up from the pavement, confident he could stand and at once toppled again. Davies was leaning against the wall the public house spread across the bricks as if he feared it was about to fall. He looked at the horizontal Mod. He seemed a long way down.

'You get yourself in a bloody deplorable state, Mod Lewis,' Davies reprimanded. 'Why are you wallowing on the pavement?'

'Because I can't get up, Dangerous,' replied Mod practically. 'I do believe my legs have finally gone. After all these years. Oh, I shall miss them a terrible lot. They've been good pals, these legs have.' He looked at Davies and measured the distance between them. 'Friend,' he inquired calmly. 'Do you think you could get over here and lift me?'

Davies calculated the yards also. 'No,' he decided, 'I don't think I could make it. Not that far. But . . . now listen Mod, don't despair. . . . If you crawl over here and I hang on to this drainpipe, then you can hoist yourself up, using me and the drainpipe to hang on to. Once you're on your feet you're generally all right.'

'Lovely idea. Brains, brains,' murmured Mod. He eyed the gap between himself and Davies's feet like a careful coward about to opt for unavoidable heroism. He used his head to count the pavement stones, nodding a greeting at each one. He dared not take as much as a supporting finger away. 'Do you really think I *could* make it, Dangerous?' he whispered fiercely.

'Mod,' said Dangerous, clutching the drainpipe. 'I *know* you can, boy, I know.'

'Faith,' muttered Mod. 'Can move mountains. I'm but a mound of flesh. All right, I'll give it a whirl.'

He did not whirl, but moved over the cold stone squares on hands and knees, stumbling twice, even from that lowly posture, before reaching the neighbourhood of Davies's ankles. From there he began to climb, periously like a man attempting the Eiger's North Face, hanging on to the pockets, belt and loopholes of Davies's commodious brown overcoat.

'Watch the coat,' warned Davies seriously. 'You'll ruin the bloody thing.' Mod's face drew level with his neck and he knew he was as upright as he would ever be. 'Now grab the drainpipe,' instructed Davies. They hung together like men on a ledge with a thousand foot drop beyond their toes. Mod's hands touched the rough metal of the downward pipe and grasped it hungrily. It moved under the additional weight (it was already supporting 20 feet of rotten guttering plus Davies) but Mod thought the unsteadiness was within himself.

'Another hand and I'm there, old friend,' he muttered courageously. 'One more swing.' Davies encouraged him to make the attempt. He did so, staggering across the front of Davies and hanging violently onto the pipe with his other hand.

It was a sober drainpipe but old and infirm. Under the force and weight of the four grasping hands it sagged and sighed as it came away from the wall of the public house. Davies and Mod felt it at the same moment and identical cries issued from each of them. They looked up and saw the entire upright pipe and its attached guttering from the roof toppling from above like an avenging cross. It hung wobbling, apparently trying to regain its ancient balance, while their appalled faces looked up. Then, uncompromisingly, it crashed, snaking like a metallic rope right across the road. The old cast-iron made a fine noise as it shattered. Davies and Mod cowered to the pipeless wall. Lights went on in the windows above the shops, sashes were pushed up and, more disturbing, from behind them, in the saloon bar they could hear someone fighting to open the chains and locks. Some fool across the street shouted: 'Shrapnel! There's shrapnel on the road. The guns have opened up. The guns!'

With that mysterious power, the drunken man's adrenalin, that disaster or danger brings to those who were previously incapable, Davies and Mod ran away. They even had the restored wit enough to dodge around the side of the public house and make up a brief alley that joined it to a parallel street. Over the housetops they could hear voices and very soon the yodelling of a police car. 'They've got the boys out of bed,' observed Davies. 'Somebody must have thought it was a smash and grab.'

They began to walk towards Mrs Fulljames' lodging house, bow-legged but now beginning to laugh. They sniggered at first, in the schoolish manner of the inebriate, and then let it go, bellowing, howling into the ear of the urban night.

As they approached 'Bali Hi' their natural caution became restored and they stopped laughing and slowed their pace cautiously. Ahead, in the dark, they heard something and almost at once up the street came the nocturnal wandering horse of the rag-and-bone-man. It approached in the welcoming manner of one who is warmed by meeting a fellow creature on a dank night.

'Should be tethered,' said Davies heavily, looking along the black hill of the horse's elongated face. 'Constitutes a danger to traffic.'

'Now, whose door knocker will it be tonight?' inquired Mod secretly. 'The same as before?'

'No. Somebody else,' whispered Davies.

'Dangerous,' grinned Mod, the idea flooding him. 'Why not Mrs Fulljames's?'

Davies smiled a serene smile in the dark. 'We'll have to clear off quickly,' he said. 'But it's a lovely idea, Mod. That woman is cruel. She'd take the last Smartie out of your mouth.'

Mod gave a schoolboyish jerk of his head, as much to the horse as to Davies, the trio mooched along the privet hedges until they reached the door of 'Bali Hi', Furtman Gardens. Then Davies noticed the horse had no halter.

'Bugger it,' he swore. 'We've got to have something to tie it to the knocker.' He looked about him.

'Wait,' cautioned Mod. 'Hold fast a minute. Why just tie him to the door? Why don't we push him inside?'

The great pleased look that dawned on Davies's face almost shone through the dark. 'What a bloody fine thought,' he whispered. 'We'll shove him in and clear off quick.'

Drunkenly they fumbled until Mod found his key. They tip-toed to the door and the horse, as though eager to enter into the conspiracy, seemed to tip-toe also. The key was revolved and the big Victorian door swung into the entrance hall. Davies gave the horse an accomplice's nudge, and seeming to know what was expected, it tip-toed into the passage. They closed the door after it and escaped, first at a drunken walk, then a trot, and then a wild hooting run. They staggered and ran, overwhelmed with the enormity of what they had perpetrated, until they came to 'The Moonlight Serenade' an all-night coffee stall hard by the railway station. This was owned by a man called Burney who divided his time between serving coffee there and serving time in Wormwood Scrubs. He and Davies were old friends.

'If necessary,' said Mod cautiously to Davies. 'I expect Mr Burney would provide us with an alibi.'

Davies shook his head, doubt hanging from his face. 'Nobody would believe him,' he decided. 'He's past the credibility stage. He's priced himself out of the alibi business.'

Mod drank his second mug of coffee. 'Mind you,' he said thoughtfully. 'I know where we could get a genuine alibi. Someone anybody would believe. Mr Chrust at the local paper. I think you ought to go there anyway. Remember what I told you. About the report of the murder?'

'He lives above the office,' agreed Davies, still rocking on his feet with the laughing and the drink. 'He won't like being got up. But if we say it's an important inquiry. And there's nobody would doubt his word about us being there. And who is going to check the time by the minute? Yes, let's go and see him.'

'Mod,' said Davies as they thumped along the echoing street. 'I had a good look at the cuttings again, old friend. Read them right through, minutely. Nothing. I couldn't see a single thing. Are you sure you weren't pissed again and read the wrong murder?'

'Listen,' said Mod stopping in mid-stride. He let his foot drop gently to the pavement. He was still drunk and so was Davies, but the helplessness was wearing off. The coffee was still comfortable within them. 'Listen . . . and I mean listen. I told you the *files* of the *Citizen*, *not* the cuttings. You'll never make a detective, you know. Not as long as you've got a hole in your arse.'

'That's anatomy,' protested Davies mildly. 'And don't keep insulting my professional ability. Or do you want a fight? Fists?' He doubled his big fists and swayed uncertainly.

'No. Not now. We're nearly there anyway.'

He nodded ahead to the *North-West London Citizen* office, in its converted house in the High Street. It had a bayed shop window full of photographs, pinned grinning civic dignitaries, unnoteworthy amateur opera singers and triumphant school prizewinners. The newspaper's photographer was under a standing instruction to include as many people as possible in every photograph he took, since more people would want to see themselves in the paper, thus sending up or, at least, keeping up, the circulation. The photographer, a man who understood orders – if focuses were occasionally a mystery – once missed a vivid picture of a smash-and-grab raider escaping with his loot. He had failed to press the button because he felt there were not enough people about to make it worth while.

'He lives upstairs then,' said Mod, meaning Mr Chrust, the editor and proprietor. 'Let's hope he's not deaf.'

Mr Chrust was not. They had scarcely finished their fourth ring on the front door bell when the windows above them became squares of light. The curtains of both squares were pulled away and both sashes went up. Two middle-aged women, both wearing mop caps looked out. Even from the ground level Davies could see that each potato face bore a resemblance to the other. 'Excuse me, ladies,' he called up. 'Is Mr Chrust at home?'

'Who wants him?' they inquired together.

'Police,' Mod replied for Davies. Then, not wishing to be accused of impersonating an officer, he pointed at Davies and added: 'That's him.'

Both heads went in as if pulled by the same string and the voices could be heard encouraging Mr Chrust to get from his bed because he was wanted by the police. Mr Chrust apparently took some time to be convinced or to be dressed because the two doughy faces again appeared at the windows and looked down on Davies and Mod for a full two minutes before Mr Chrust appeared. Then, like obedient handmaidens they vanished, leaving him to conduct the dialogue from the sill.

'Mr Davies, isn't it?' he said peering down on Dangerous. 'It's really a police inquiry then?'

'It is, Mr Chrust,' confirmed Davies, not very firmly for he was beginning to regret the venture. 'Sorry to have disturbed you and . . . er Mrs Chrust.'

'We aren't disturbed, we aren't disturbed,' Mr Chrust replied ambiguously. He was a peanut of a man, with short bristles protruding from his face and otherwise bald head like the airy white fluff of a dandelion clock. 'I'll just be down.'

Through the fanlight of the front door they saw a procession of shadows follow a fitful light down the stair. Then the bulb in the hallway went on and the door was opened. Mr Chrust stood there in a dressing gown across the front of which a Chinese dragon snarled. With him were the two ladies in woolly dressing gowns and mop caps.

'Mrs Chrust passed away last February,' said Mr Chrust hurriedly once they were inside. He seemed to want no misunderstanding. 'These are her sisters. It's a very big flat, upstairs you know. They look after my wants.'

Davies nodded to the tin moons of Mr Chrust's firmament. It occurred to him that the editor might think that the visit was in connection with immorality charges so he hastened to ask if they could look at the newspaper files for 1951. Mr Chrust beamed with patent relief and the bristles danced blithely on his face.

'If you just show us where they are,' said Davies. 'We'll just take a quick peep and be off. It was most urgent, you understand. Please go back to your bed . . . beds.'

'Of course, of course,' said Mr Chrust agreeably. He began to push the nightdressed ladies up the stairs like a lean sheepdog nudging fat ewes towards an upland meadow. He turned after they had waddled away from the landing. 'I don't want to pry, Mr Davies,' he whispered. 'Not into police inquiries. But naturally, we of the press like to know what's going on, under our very noses as it were. Perhaps, when you are free to do so, you will drop a hint of it in my ear.'

'With pleasure, Mr Chrust,' answered Davies. The drink was still loitering around him. 'Now you go off to bed before you get lonely . . . well, cold. Goodnight Mr Chrust. We'll close the door when we leave.'

'Please do,' nodded Mr Chrust backing up the stairs. 'The sisters get nervous.'

He went up the staircase and the excited noises of the ladies, which had been filling the upper part of the building like the chattering of fat pigeons in a loft, were stilled. Davies and Mod counted three separate twangings of springs. Mod raised his eyebrows and said: 'I bet he's got a story he wouldn't print in his paper.' Davies hushed him and ran his unsteady finger along the bound years of the newspaper fixed into shelves along the wall of the back office.

It stopped accurately on 1951 and he and Mod pulled the great cardboard slab out between them and eased it on to a table. A new excitement was added to the qualms of the drink. His fingers fumbled and Mod helped him to fold sheaves of pages until they arrived at the date of the week they were seeking.

Carefully Davies turned the front page. Celia Norris's young, faded face, the likeness aged with the paper, looked out of the page. The narrative took up a modest six inches of print under the heading 'Local girl missing.' Davies read it carefully again. There was nothing new he could see.

'It's the same cutting as we have in our files,' he protested to Mod, who remained standing back. 'What's it you can see?'

'It's not the cutting,' insisted Mod still withdrawn behind him. 'It's the *page*. Look at the little morsel in the last column. At the bottom.'

Davies did. It said unarrestingly: 'Policeman's Farewell'. Beneath it sat three dull paragraphs describing the retirement of an apparently popular policeman, Sergeant David Morris and a farewell function held for him at the local Sturgeon Rooms.

'All right, so they had a farewell drink for a retiring copper. So what? It often happens.'

'But murders don't – not on the same night,' pointed out Mod hoarsely. 'It was the same night Dangerous.'

'Yes. Yes, all right them. But . . .'

'There's a picture on page three,' said Mod relentlessly, enjoying himself in the chilly light of the little room.

Davies turned the page and looked at the picture. A group of policemen, pictured at the farewell to Sergeant D. Morris, said the caption. Above the photograph was the heading: 'Cheers, say Policemen' and below it a panel of names of the officers who raised their glasses for the cameraman and for posterity.

'All right,' said Davies. 'But I still don't see . . .'

'Read the names,' said Mod. 'Go on, read them!'

Davies read them. Two names made him swallow so hard he had a fit of coughing. 'P.C. James Dudley and P.C. Frederick Fennell,' he said eventually. After a silence, he added: 'And they were supposed to be in the patrol car in the High Street when she vanished.'

'But they weren't, were they,' said Mod.

'I've seen the duty slips and reports they signed,' said Davies. 'And they were drinking with the boys. They lied for a start.'

'And nobody noticed the lie,' said Mod. 'Or nobody cared to notice.'

An apologetic shadow appeared on the stairs. It was Mr Chrust. 'How are you getting on, gentlemen?' he inquired. 'Making some headway? I'm afraid the ladies are so excited they can't get back to sleep.'

'We're just off, thank you Mr Chrust,' said Davies, his thoughts miles, years, away from his voice. 'Just going.'

He and Mod folded the file and heaved it up into its slot on the shelf like a piece of masonry. Mr Chrust walked over and shining his lantern-torch along the bindings pedantically made sure that the years still ran as ordained. 'We sleep above history here, Mr Davies,' he smiled fluffily.

'You certainly do,' agreed Davies his mind still on what he had seen. They had reached the outside door. 'Thank you very much,' he called back. 'Sorry to have disturbed you. Goodnight.'

To his astonishment further 'goodnights' came from above and he looked up to see the two plump ladies girlishly framed in the upstairs window, the sashes thrust up.

Their progress home towards 'Bali Hi', Furtman Gardens, was hung with guilt, slowing their steps and causing them to dawdle at street corners more than was justified by the damp blanket of drink that still loosely enwrapped them. Neither mentioned the horse until they reached the final right-angle, the turn that would take them into Furtman Gardens and a view of whatever there was to be seen. Then Mod leaned back against a privet hedge, causing its dust to fall like pollen, and shook a cowardly head. 'Dangerous,' he said hoarsely. 'I can't go any further. I'm afraid to look.'

Davies tried to hold on to the hedge as one would lead against a wall but his hand kept sticking into the prickly twigs. He found he could stand upright without aid, however, and pleased by this improvement, he confronted Mod.

'We're going home,' he ordered sternly. 'We're *both* going home. We've got to face this together, Mod. After all we've got an alibi and if I turn up and you don't they'll be sure to think you did it by yourself.'

Mod nodded miserably, acknowledging the logic. 'I wish you wouldn't keep buying me drink, Dangerous,' he mumbled. 'If you didn't buy them I wouldn't be able to drink them. Aw, Christ, come on then. Let's face the foe.'

There was a fire engine, a police car, a horse ambulance and the rag-and-bone man's cart outside the house of Mrs Fulljames. Each was toting a red or blue revolving light, even the rag-and-bone man's cart which had no navigation or warning appliances of its own and had borrowed a spare revolving blue light from the sympathetic attendant of the horse ambulance. From the distant end of the street they could see the crowd gathered and individual shadows moving with the various emergency lights bleeding and bleeping above them. It looked, at that distance, like a modest but busy fairground.

Davies and Mod approached to within a few yards with seemly caution. The horse, looking elated, was being led by its owner to the shafts of the cart. It blinked at the revolving light but otherwise went quietly. The horse ambulance attendant was unemotionally inspecting a kicked door on his vehicle, the front door of 'Bali Hi' was also bereft of its lower panels. Firemen were washing down the path, possibly feeling that since they had been summoned they ought to contribute something. All around were the faces of police and people, trying not to laugh.

The front room bay window on the first floor was open and backed with orange light. Mrs Fulljames, Doris at her side, stood in impressive silhouette as though she were about to jump or make a speech. With unerring aim she spotted the loitering Mod and Davies as soon as they came to the penumbral verge of the incident.

'Did you put that horse in my house?' she bawled hysterically. 'Did you two do it?'

Their faces, innocence and amazement fighting for possession, elevated themselves to the voice. She gave them no time to deny or even reply. 'There's shit everywhere!' she howled. 'Every bloody where.'

Some people in the crowd, neighbours who had to keep the peace with Mrs Fulljames, turned away and hid because they were laughing too much. 'Up the passage, on the stairs, in the front room!' she continued. 'Shit!' The very force of her bellow seemed to draw her forward and people below cried a warning, possibly fearing for themselves as much as her. 'Better get the jumping sheet,' Davies said to an enthralled fireman. 'I think she'll topple over any minute.'

Doris even from the window saw the brief conversation. 'Are you listening to Mrs Fulljames?' she shouted. 'Do you care? That thing has smashed the sideboard in the front room. Antique that was. Antique!'

'Belonged to Mr Fulljames, I bet,' whispered Davies to the speechless fireman.

'That belonged to Mr Fulljames,' screamed Doris obediently. 'The late Mr Fulljames.'

Mrs Fulljames, somewhat ungraciously, pushed Doris violently back into the room and then leaned out menacingly. She looked like Mussolini pressing a point. 'Mr Davies, Mr Lewis,' she demanded. 'Did you get that horse in here? Did you? I want to know.'

'Mrs Fulljames,' shouted Davies mildly. 'You are making a scene. I have been out on police inquiries of a serious nature and Mr Lewis has been accompanying me.'

His landlady clamped her mouth angrily and then pulled down the window with a sound almost as loud. Davies's fellow policeman, having seen the horse between the shafts and taken its name and that of its owner, now returned. 'This is where you live is it, Dangerous?' inquired a young officer. Davies nodded, still looking up at the finality of the slammed window.

'Seems a nice cosy little place,' murmured the policeman. 'Bit on the quiet side, but cosy.'

'Nothing ever happens,' shrugged Davies. He turned to Mod. 'We'd better go in and see if we've still got beds. Goodnight officer,' he added formally.

'Goodnight, Dangerous. I'll be glad when we've finished tonight. We've already had two bloody hooligans pulling down the drainpipe at the pub.'

CHAPTER THIRTEEN

Mrs Edwina Fennell lived in a dying caravan anchored at the centre of a muddy field, ten miles from the streets and the industry her husband had patrolled as a policeman on occasions when he was not in bed with the lady palmist who lived and foresaw the future in the High Street.

'She's over there,' pointed out the farm man from whom Davies had asked directions. He indicated, with a dungy finger, the caravan across the soggy field. 'It'll be a bit damp underfoot, but it's a good job you didn't come in the real winter. Sometimes she gets cut off altogether.'

Davies commenced to sludge across the field. Sometimes the cowpats seemed firmer than the surrounding earth. He had a quick recollection of walking into the front hall of 'Bali Hi', Furtman Gardens, early on that same morning, after the horse had been taken away. He winced partly from the thought and partly at the spasm of a mean wind which was searching the open land. It was a flat and unpoetic place, no hills, few trees, just muddy fields holding up a muddy sky. He was glad of his faithful overcoat, bravely opposing the cut and buffet of the wind. He looked up and saw he was still only half way to Mrs Fennell's caravan, wheelless and listing listlessly, like some sorry shipwrecked raft.

In such circumstances he was surprised to see an illuminated door chime affixed to the peeling door of the caravan. He pushed it and released a globular melody not inferior to that which had heralded his entrance to the council penthouse of Ena Lind. It was necessary to stand in the morass of the field while he awaited a response, for there was no step. The caravan had subsided so far into the field, however, that Edwina Fennell, when she opened the door was on almost the same level. 'Sorry I was a long time,' she sniffled. 'I get so fed up with people coming and ringing the bell.'

Bemused, Davies quickly looked around to see if he had missed a city on his journey. But the field remained disconsolate all about. 'Yes,' he replied carefully. 'It's a bit of a drag to have to keep answering the door. I hope I won't keep you long. I'm Detective Constable Davies. I'm at your husband's old station.'

'Oh that,' she said, as though it were of only remote interest. 'Well he's not here. Not any more.'

'I see,' said Davies. She remained resolutely in the small entrance, thin arms folded over a pallid pinafore. 'I wanted to have a word with you as well, Mrs Fennell. Do you . . . could I possibly come in? I think I'm sort of sinking here. The water is getting through into my shoes.'

'Wipe your feet then,' she said dully backing away from the entrance. He stepped out of the chilly mud, each foot emitting a reluctant sucking sound as he pulled it clear. Within the doorway the floor was covered by a piece of coconut matting. He thought he would destroy it if he wiped his shoes so, mumbling as one performing a rite, he took them off and left them in the field, walking into the interior in stockinged feet.

There was little difference in the temperature in the caravan to that of the outside. It was cold and cloying, the fittings damaged and the plastic furniture unkempt. There was an unlit oil lamp and a hand-wound gramophone with a pile of old-fashioned records. They had a damp sheen on them. Mrs Fennell had been occupied in cutting a great careful pile of sandwiches assembled from a sizable joint of cold beef and three long sliced loaves of bread.

She was a rejected-looking woman in her sixties. Her sunken eyes seemed incapable of rising to look at him. She went behind the barricade of sandwiches and began to butter some bread. 'It gets very muddy out there sometimes,' she said absently. To his surprise she emitted a cackling laugh. 'Sometimes I think I hear the bell and I think it must be one of my million lovers at the door. But when I go they've vanished and I think they must have sunk down in the mud.'

'Yes, it's a trifle damp,' said Davies awkwardly. He wondered if his shoes would still be there when he went out. He nodded towards her sandwiches. 'Looks like a picnic,' he said.

'Foxes', she replied. 'I cut them up every day for the foxes. They come around after dark and sit and wait. They're so handsome. And it didn't seem right, dignified if you see what I mean, to just chuck bits of food out to them, so I do it properly, in sandwiches and they each have their own plates. You should see them eating. It's a lovely sight when it's a full moon.'

Davies sincerely said he could imagine it was. He half hoped she might offer him a sandwich for himself, but the thought obviously never came to her. 'What did you want then?' she prompted. 'What did you want with Fred Fennell?'

He knew that when a woman called her husband by both Christian and surname he was not in any kind of favour. 'Well, just a few memories of his police days, really,' he said. 'I'm checking on something that happened a long time ago and I thought I might pick his brains.'

'There's not a lot to pick,' she sniffed bluntly. 'He's lost all his brains. He's in the looney house, Mr Davies. The mental hospital. St Austin's at Bedford.'

Davies felt his heart plummet. 'Oh, I'm sorry about that.'

'He's not. Loves it. Every minute. He thinks he's Peter the Great. Well he did last time I went to see him.'

'When was that?' asked Davies.

'Last year,' she cut into the bread fiercely. 'Twelve months ago.'

'Why did you stop?'

'Reasons.' She seemed to be gritting her teeth, trying not to cry. 'I couldn't stand it. All the horrors in there. I couldn't stand hearing him giving orders to the bleeding Russian court and the like. I couldn't face it. I stopped going.'

She stopped cutting the sandwiches. It occurred to Davies that the foxes were in for a feast that night. 'It's horrible in that place,' she said. 'So horrible I can't tell you. You'll see if you go.'

He got up. The smell of the fresh bread and the cold beef was overpowering. 'I'll be off then,' he said. 'What shall I say if he asks when you're going to see him?'

She hesitated, then cleaned the crumbs from the knife with her fingers. 'Tell him . . . tell him I'll come after the Revolution,' she said. 'That'll do.'

Immediately he went beyond the gates of St Austin's Hospital, Davies experienced the guilt of the sane going to visit the insane. He drove the Lagonda with consideration through the arched gatehouse and nodded in an agreeably humble way to everyone he saw. At first he was in a wide expanse of playing fields and woodland, but it felt different; it was as if he had entered a strange country. In the distance he could see the bent backs of the buildings among greenery like giants kneeling at a game of dice. He realized that this was a no man's land. There was another, higher wall ahead.

Autumn was thinning the trees and through a belt of white and shaky birches he could see moving coloured figures. Some men with ropes were sawing loudly in an oak tree around which the road curved. They waved to him from their perilous branches and he gladly waved back. As he turned the curve he saw that a football match was being played ahead; a proper match with goalposts and nets, corner flags, and with the players decked in correct shirts, shorts, socks and boots. A referee, in regulation black, danced around controlling the game. The scene pleased Davies immensely. It was Wednesday morning and he was glad to see them playing at that time of the day and the week.

He slowed the car, stopped it almost opposite one of the goals, a few yards from the touchline which, he was again glad to see was being overseen by a proper linesman in black shirt and shorts holding a bright orange flag. The linesman smiled at Davies and proceeded to pretend he was walking a tightrope along the whitewashed line. Davies laughed heartily at his joke and called; 'Good match?'

'First rate,' responded the linesman soberly, balancing on his imaginary tightrope. His arms went out like stabilizing wings and he prepared to spin slowly and go back the other way. 'Two good teams,' he added before revolving. 'Best teams in the world.'

'Oh,' said Davies uncomfortably.

'Brazil and England,' said the linesman secretly. 'Playing for the World Cup.'

There came a burst of action in front of the adjacent goal. A heavy forward of the yellow team trundled the ball through and, having unceremoniously pushed the advancing goalkeeper away with both hands, scored easily and went dancing joyfully down the pitch to the arms and kisses of his teammates.

Davies shouted from his driving seat. 'Foul! Foul!' The linesman turned with worried, white face, 'You think so?' he inquired.

'He just pushed the goalie out of the way,' Davies pointed out.

A player in the red team standing near the touchline heard him. 'No goal!' he bellowed across the pitch. 'A foul! This man says it was a foul!'

An icy fear caught Davies's heart. The linesman was staring at him drop-mouthed, and across the football pitch twenty-two shouting, arguing, pushing players charged at him with the referee and the other linesmen funeral figures far to the rear.

Kitty, sensing something important was taking place, looked out from below its tarpaulin and, seeing, the advancing shirted horde, howled dismally. The sound jerked Davies into fortunate action. 'Must be off!' he shouted handsomely, jabbing the accelerator. 'Play up!'

The Lagonda ran forward quickly. At a safe distance he looked in the mirror and saw them standing in a coloured bunch all shouting at each other. The referee was sitting alone under a tree, one linesman was kicking the ball and the other was still tip-toeing the line.

He found he was trembling. Kitty burrowed below the tarpaulin once more. The road was leading towards a great wooden gate, set in a formidable wall, it curved to an apex like the entrance to a castle or a prison. Set into it was an infant door. Davies stopped the car and walked to it. The sadness of the place was settling upon him. There was a silence too, holding everything, the walls, the peeping roofs, and the grimy sky. Against the inset door was fixed an iron ring-handle, inhospitable to the hand. He turned it and, somewhat to his surprise, it opened without resistance and the little door swung easily in.

Davies was confronted with a framed scene, much as Alice was through her looking glass. Stretching as far as he could see were desolately well-tended lawns and flower beds, set out in squares and oblongs. They appeared perfectly cultured and kept but looked as though no sun ever shone upon them. Set into this there was a solitary human figure, a woman, a bent back and downturned face overlooking some minute job at the corner of the border just beyond the gate. Unhappy, Davies stepped through.

There was no sign or notice of the way he ought to follow. He was within a few feet of the woman, enthralled by a few daisies she had dug from the flower bed with the prongs of a table fork. 'Oh, excuse me, madam,' Davies said.

Her face came around first, old but ageless, bright-eyed. It was followed by the muzzle of a gun, a pistol of nasty aspect, which she held secretly against her blue overall. 'Stick 'em up,' she demanded quietly.

Davies raised his hands above his head. The blood seemed to run down his arms and into his stomach. He stared at the gun. It looked real. 'I saw you,' she said rising slowly from her knees. 'I detected you coming in.'

'Oh . . . oh, yes,' nodded Davies stiffly. He felt, arms up as he was, that his trousers might fall. 'I've come to see the superintendent, Doctor Longton. Do you know. . . .?'

'Keep 'em up,' she warned grimly. 'And walk.'

He looked wildly about him. There was no other person in the entire walled garden. It was as though it had all been prepared as a trap for him. She nudged him with the gun and he began to march with his hands held above his ears.

She nudged him through another archway and into a stone corridor, wide, with windows and doors on either side. A man came out of an office with a clipboard in his hand. Davies tried to say something but the man walked by studying the clipboard and taking no heed of the gunwoman or the man she pushed before her. Other people appeared, some in white coats, but his extraordinary progress along the corridor aroused no interest whatever. Some actually wished his captor 'Good Morning'. Eventually they turned into a large hall where a physical training class was taking place. An instructor was demonstrating a bend to thirty or so people who watched and then bent with dedication. The woman marched Davies right across the floor at gunpoint and still nobody made a mention of it. Eventually they arrived in front of a short tubby woman with a steady, red face.

'Matron,' said the gunwoman. 'An intruder. He wants Dr Longton.'

The matron hardly glanced at Davies with his hands still hovering in the air. 'He's in his office,' she said. 'Hurry and you'll catch him.'

The muzzle of the gun banged into the small of Davies's back and he was forced to jog across the floor to a further corridor and the entrance to an office. The gunwoman reached around and knocked at the door with the butt of the weapon. A pleasant voice, the voice of someone happy with his work, called out: 'Come in, come in.'

Relief had replaced consternation in Davies by now and he stood sheepishly with his arms still up as his captor ushered him into the room. Doctor Longton smiled understandingly. 'Ah, you came in the back way, I see,' he said. Then to the woman. 'It's all right, Marie. I'll take over. Thank you very much.'

The woman went out without a word. Davies said: 'Can I put my arms down now?' He lowered them. 'That looked like a real gun to me.'

'Oh it was,' the Superintendent said. 'She needs it. We tried giving her a toy but she wouldn't accept it. So we got that one, and she's happy with that. We've taken a few parts out of it, of course, and she has no access to any ammunition. It's her status symbol, if you understand.'

'Yes, I see,' blinked Davies. He introduced himself and they shook hands. 'It was just a bit of a shock, that's all. Unexpected.'

'We expect the unexpected here,' said the doctor as though that was the limit of the discussion. 'You've come to see Mr Fennell?'

'Yes, I went to see his wife. . . .'

'It's a pity *she* doesn't come to see him,' said the other man. 'He misses her terribly.'

Davies nodded unhappily, knowing that he was treading where he would prefer not to walk. 'She said she won't come,' he said.

Dr Longton scratched his nose. He was slim and gently bent like a feather. 'A thousand pities,' he said.

'I think she found it too much for her,' said Davies. 'The whole thing.'
'Most people do,' said Dr Longton. 'But not as much as the patients.'
'Yes, I can understand that,' nodded Davies.

'Mr Fennell is not too bad now, though. He has very good days. It seems to be arrested. His delusions of grandeur, being royalty and suchlike, are less pronounced. I think he would like to see you, Mr Davies. And if you get chance perhaps you could get his wife to come and visit him. It would make his life much brighter.'

Davies nodded uncertainly. 'I'll go and see her again,' he promised. 'I'll see what she says.'

'Good. I've arranged for you to see Mr Fennell away from the ward. If the others saw you talking they would all want to tell you their troubles. They become stored-up, as it were, here. There's a small consulting room where you can talk.' He hesitated. 'Without prying too much into police business,' he ventured. 'Would it be possible for you to tell me something of what this is about. I'm thinking of the patient, you understand.'

Davies nodded. 'Of course. I see that. Actually it's a murder inquiry. It's not quite so dramatic as it sounds because it happened twenty-five years ago. Mr Fennell was a police constable in the area at the time and had some part in the inquiries.'

'You want to see if he remembers,' said the doctor. He seemed to be considering it. 'I'd be grateful if you could tread carefully,' he said. 'Be very careful with him. If he doesn't remember I'd be glad if you'd call it a day and not press him.'

'I will,' promised Davies gently. 'I don't want to mess anything up.'

'Thank you. And don't make it too protracted, if you don't mind. It's a big day for him, you know, having a visitor and it could be emotionally tiring.' He stopped and thought out the points he had made. 'Right,' he concluded. 'I'll take you along there.'

They went on a short journey as near to a nightmare as Davies had been in waking hours. Each door they reached was double-locked and unlocked, each corridor seemed to go deeper and deeper into the throes of the building. He heard screams and shouts, and faces, faces pallid with amazement appeared at side windows as they walked by. Eventually they reached a door set apart from the others.

'He's in here, waiting,' said Longton quietly. 'Something I forgot to ask, Mr Davies. Does he actually *know* you?'

'No,' replied Davies. 'We've never met. He had left the police before I arrived in the division.'

'I see,' said the doctor. He knocked courteously and a voice inside bade them anxiously 'Come in'. Even from behind Davies knew that Longton was smiling as he entered. He could tell by the wrinkles at the nape of his neck. An ashen-faced, ancient, shaking man sat on a wooden chair by a plain table. 'Mr Davies to see you, Mr Fennell,' announced Dr Longton.

Fennell stood irresolutely. His face trembled and, as though it could not hold him, finally crackling into gigantic tears. 'Oh, thank you for coming,' he said to Davies holding out his hands. 'My old friend, thank you for coming.'

CHAPTER FOURTEEN

Madame Tarantella Phelps-Smith, High Class Gipsy Fortune Teller, was a flitting figure in the town. Over the years less had been seen of her, not merely because she made her outdoor appearances infrequently, but because she seemed to be getting smaller as her life went on. Beryl Adams, as she was before she was touched magically by a Gipsy Soothsayer at a fair on Hackney Marshes, had once lent an exotic touch to the labouring surroundings of the district. She flowed about in robes that moved like a coloured sea. She had rings on her fingers and bells on the long curly toes of her embroidered shoes. Davies had always thought of her as a tall person; even her face seemed to be tall, a high forehead and a deep chin; her eyes were vertically elongated, her eyebrows aloft and arched and her mouth a perpetual upright oval as though she received an amazement every moment of her life.

She used to be seen in various parts of the town dispensing ready magic and telling the futures of the inhabitants who, in that hard and gritty place, always hoped that things might improve. But the years had dimmed her eye and her ambitions and by the time she came to Davies's professional notice she contained her outside forays to dashes to the off-licence and the fish-and-chip shop. By this time her back had bent, her tall arms hung and swung almost to the pavement, and her shoulders were forever hunched.

'It's the years I've spent leaning over this bloody crystal ball,' she complained to Davies. 'It's a risk of the job I suppose. Like miners get that disease, whatever it's called, soothsayers get bent backs and hunched shoulders.'

'You get a lot of business?'

'No, but I have to practise, otherwise you get rusty.'

'Policemen get flat feet,' he sympathized. 'And a pain in the neck. I went to see Fred Fennell yesterday.'

Madame Tarantella seemed unsurprised. 'Fred Fennell,' she mused as though only days had passed since she last read his palm while they lay unclothed in her patchworked bed. 'Dear Fred. How is he? Getting old now, I suppose.'

'He's keeping pace with the rest of us,' agreed Davies. Her room was above a men's plain outfitters, Mr Blake's, who had clothed half the working force of the district, mostly by weekly instalments. As they sat there, Davies could hear the sturdy clothes being moved from their racks which were fixed just below Madame Tarantella's floor. Madame

Tarantella herself sat in what she called her driving seat, the little bentwood chair seeming to cling like a child around her skirts. The room was professionally dim with drapes and tassels on the curtains and the signs of the Zodiac on illuminated panels around the wall. On the table with the crystal ball was a used coffee cup, an ashtray full of massacred stubs and a copy of the daily paper open and marked at the racing page.

'You ought to be on a winner every time,' observed Davies nodding at the newspaper. He was sitting in the client's chair, his overcoat opened because of the closeness of the small room.

'Horses? No damn fear,' she sighed. 'If I could see the winners, I wouldn't be sitting here now, Dangerous. When I try to focus it on Epsom or Sandown Park it turns rogue and gives me one of the back-markers. A gift's a gift but it won't get you rich at fifty-pence a gaze. The only fortune that comes up here is somebody else's.' She looked at him speculatively. 'You wouldn't like to have a consultation while you're here, would you?'

Davies smiled solemnly. 'I've already met two dark mysterious men,' he said. 'I've still got the scars.'

'You'll meet them again, beware,' she warned abruptly. 'But you will be saved by a beast. Do you have a police dog?'

'Not a *police* dog. I've got Kitty, a damn ratbag of a thing that spends its life sleeping in my car.'

She nodded. 'Ah yes, I've seen the beast. You should give it a wash sometime. Look after it, Dangerous. You will need it.' She seemed tempted to take a quick plunge into the crystal but she resisted. 'And what did Fred Fennell have to say?'

'You . . . you knew him pretty well a few years ago? So he told me.'

'Oh come on, Dangerous,' she replied good-humouredly. 'You and me are in the same basic business. Knowing about people. You know he was my lover or you wouldn't be in this room now. But it was donkey's years ago.'

'He's not so bad . . . physically. In the circumstances.'

'It's a mental hospital then,' she said quickly. 'I *felt* he was ill, but I didn't get a fix on a mental hospital.'

'Well he is. At Bedford.'

'Oh my. Poor Fred. He was always the big virile policeman, you know. I've seen him standing in this room many a time wearing nothing but his hobnailed boots. A fine sight.'

'I bet,' said Davies. He wanted her to go on.

'What about that wife of his then?' she said. 'Cruel bitch, she was. She had a thing about animals. She'd go out and poison cats and dogs at night. The family had to use force to keep her away from the zoo. Apparently she was in somebody's house once and she tried to strangle their goldfish.'

'That's not easy,' conceded Davies. 'Well she must have reformed because she feeds foxes now – on beef sandwiches. Unless she spreads poison with the butter. I hadn't thought of that.'

'Dreadful woman. Fred used to weep about her. I liked him,

Dangerous. But I couldn't see a future for us together.'

'If you couldn't, who could?' acknowledged Davies. 'Do you remember, years ago, the case of Celia Norris. She vanished.'

'Oh her. *That* girl. Yes, I remember, I've still got her bicycle.'

Davies almost fell off the chair. Sweat burst out all over his face. He stared at her. She was idly running her tall fingers over the crystal ball. 'Her bicycle?' he managed to say.

'That's it,' she said practically. 'It's down in my shed somewhere. There's a lot of junk in there but I know it's there.'

Davies tried to keep himself calm. 'How . . . how did it come to be here?' he asked forcing his voice to be slow. 'How?'

'Fred brought it in,' she said simply. 'There's no harm in telling you now. If he's in the bin they can't touch him and I bet you'd find it hard to arrest me.'

'I won't arrest you,' Davies promised desperately. 'Nobody will, ever. Just tell me.'

'It was the time of that Norris girl thing. The same night as she disappeared. Fred was up here. I remember it very well. He used to pop up for half an hour or sometimes more when he was on duty. He used to be in the little van that went all around the streets, with another policeman, and they used to arrange so that one of them could hop off for a while. They would take turns. The other chap used to go somewhere, I don't know where, and Fred used to come up here. It started off when he came in to have his future foretold – well, that's what he said. It was his excuse for getting to know me. I was young and rather handsome then. And once he'd given me his hand to hold professionally, I found I couldn't let go of it. It happens, Dangerous, even to us who have extra powers.'

Davies nodded solemnly. He wanted to dance around the room with her but he kept his seat in the chair.

'He'd had a few drinks that particular night. Been to some police booze-up, again on the quiet because he was supposed to be on duty. They were devils in those days. I wouldn't have trusted a policeman, believe me, except Fred of course.'

'Terrible lot,' agreed Davies. He did not want to stop her. She was staring at the racing page as if trying to conjure some vision of Mr Fred Fennell from Tipster's Selections from Market Rasen.

'Yes,' she went on eventually. 'That night he'd had a few and he only came up for a while. Then he went down and not long afterwards he came back with the bike. It's been here ever since. All these years.'

Davies said: 'Why did he bring it here?'

'Well he had just found it. He didn't know whose it was, of course. It was lying by the wall of the cemetery. He'd come across it lying in the grass and he'd brought it here. He was quite clever, Fred, for an ordinary police constable who never got promoted. Or crafty. His idea was to keep it here and then if ever he was found out, you know, if they discovered him here or his wife got suspicious and followed him or had him watched, then he could say he had come after a report of a missing bicycle being found. I would say that I'd found it and hand it over and no one would be any the wiser. It was just a sort of safeguard for him being in here, see.'

'But didn't he realize whose bike it was?'

'No. Of course not. He thought it was just a bike – any bike. Lost or thrown away by somebody who had stolen it. It wasn't until later, when the hue and cry was on, that he realized that it belonged to the girl Norris. And by that time it was too late. He was too scared to take it in.'

Davies hardly trusted his mouth to open. 'Tarantella,' he said pushing his hand across the table and resting it on hers. Her hand felt cold, dead. 'Can I see it? The bike?'

'It's in the shed,' she told him, rising. 'I'll show you. There's years of rubbish down there. It's behind all that.' She led the way from the stuffy room, down a back staircase and into a corrugated iron shed in the miniature yard behind. 'The rest of the building belongs to Mr Blake of the outfitters,' she explained pulling back a rusted bolt. 'But the shed was in with the flat. It was in the lease.'

It was damp and cold in the yard. Davies tugged his overcoat around him and his hand felt his fiercely beating heart. Growing triumph and fear banged like two clappers in his chest. A stale smell came from the shed. 'I've put a lot of my old things – props and that sort of thing – in here,' she said. 'You know how fashions change even in this game.' She was pushing aside some painted screens. 'And here's my clairvoyant stuff, my trumpet and my smoke machine. I packed that in. Gave me the creeps.' She was clearing a way ahead. Davies took the pieces from her as she handed them back.

'Here it is. I can see it. At the back. Could you get across there, Dangerous?'

'Try and stop me,' he thought. He moved her gently aside and clambered through the lumber. Then he stopped, surrounded by dust and relics, and looked. It was there. Celia's bicycle. He almost choked with excitement. His arms, as they went across to grasp the handlebars, were vibrating. His face was streaming sweat. Then he got it. He touched the cold, dusty metal. He had got it!

Firmly he lifted and pulled the bicycle away from its surroundings. It was pathetically light. He knew it was the right one. He knew that machine as well as its sad owner had known it. He touched the saddle upon which she had ridden those last minutes of her seventeen years. Carefully, despite its urgency, he lifted it clear of the surrounding junk, and eventually rested it on the clear floor. Madame Tarantella looked at it unemotionally. 'Both tires have gone down,' she said flatly.

Davies did not know what to do next. He began to wipe the dust away from the frame with his fingertips. Then he leaned the tubed metal against his thigh and opened the buckles of the saddle bags.

Like a shock it hit him. Inside, brown and broken and brittle, were the remains of a bunch of flowers.

'They were in there when he brought it,' said Madame Tarantella beyond his shoulder. 'Chrysanthemums and a few irises. They had a card with them, but I threw that away. I think she must have got them from the cemetery.'

'Her mother said she brought her flowers,' murmured Davies. 'I wondered where she's picked them.'

'Flowers,' said Mod softly. 'Well, well, fancy them still being there.' He was looking into his glass, both he and Davies keeping their heads down from the suspicion and bale in the face of the landlord. He knew who it was who had demolished his drainpipe.

'She must have gone into the cemetery regularly on her way home from the youth club,' said Davies. 'To take flowers to her mother. I was wondering where she could have picked the flowers in this neighbourhood.'

'That means she went over the wall or the gates. Being at night,' said Mod.

'She must have.'

'That night without her knickers.'

'Apparently so.'

'Where are we then?'

Davies sighed. 'Yes, where are we! Well, we've got three neo-suspects. None of them fit but they're all vaguely in the running. Just vaguely. Start from the back. Our friend Boot. Now Boot did some naughty things, and to Celia Norris among others. But he says he didn't kill her.'

'That's a fine recommendation,' mumbled Mod his face semi-submerged in his beer. When he peered over the surface of the drink he looked like an otter swimming half below the top of a pool. 'You'll take his word for it?'

'No. But he told me everything, well, nearly everything, the other night. By the time I'd done with him I had him banging on his mum's door crying to be let in. Not a pretty sight. I don't think it was him, despite all the other bits and pieces, unless he's been craftier than I think he is. But one thing he won't tell. He won't say what he did with her pants. He says he can't remember.'

'And you believe that?' Mod grumbled. 'If you'll swallow that you'll swallow anything.'

'I could swallow another pint,' said Davies absently. Mod braved the landlord's eye and asked for more beer. The landlord filled the glasses with ill-grace and slammed them down in front of them on the bar. 'Drinking I can understand,' he said bitterly. 'Vandalism, I can't.'

Mod and Davies exchanged expressions brimmed with innocent incomprehension. 'Some people never know when they've had enough,' Davies called agreeably at the publican's retreating back. He returned to Mod. 'No, he remembers what he did with them, all right. That will come. He may have gone with her from the youth club – at this distance nobody can remember seeing him or not seeing him that night. It's twenty-five years after all. He could have walked with her as far as the cemetery wall and there the dirty deed was done. I don't know, Mod. But I somehow don't think so. I don't think he did it. But I've still got him on the string. I don't think he's having a very carefree life at the moment.'

The rough woman who sang 'Viva España' her foot still a club of plaster charged her way like a squat bull through the bar door and made for the juke box. She could have pressed the tab with her eyes closed. Her heavy hips began to jerk even as the first bars of the song shot from the machine. She banged her way down the bar clapping her hands above her head like blocks of wood.

'Then Ramscar,' said Davies determinedly. 'It might *really* have been Ramscar. He could have fixed that alibi, no trouble. And he bobs up all the time, except nobody knows where he is. He knows I'm looking for him. Who but our Cecil would have arranged the dustbin blitz on me? Only Ramscar has that sort of mind or organization.'

Mod was watching the rough woman's performance with calm scorn. 'One day,' he forecast. 'She's going to drop dead right in this bar. And I for one will go and stamp up and down on her prostrate body. He returned to Davies. 'How about Parsons? Reformed undie-thief? Perhaps it was his Salvation Army mates who shanghaied you.'

'I haven't finished with Parsons, either,' nodded Davies. 'We'll have another chat before long. And we've still got Bill Lind.'

'Ah, the boyfriend. I was wondering when he would come up.'

'Madam,' called Davies to the rough woman. 'If you don't stop carrying on in that manner I will arrest you for being disorderly in a public place.'

'Bollocks,' replied the lady of Spain. 'At least I don't go pulling people's bloody drainpipes off the walls.'

'Bill Lind,' said Davies, returning at once to Mod. 'Well I'm going to wait until Bill Lind comes to me. I'm sure he will.'

'And . . .' said the woman now truculent, leaning towards them, all the pride of Andalucia gone. 'Nor do I put a fucking horse in somebody's fucking front passage either. *And* I don't dive in the fucking canal with a fucking dustbin on my fucking head!'

She did not wait for them to react or reply. She stumped towards the door and with a final smashing of her hands above her head and a sluggish whirl of her dirty hung skirt, she went out. They observed her shout 'Bollocks' from the street.

'That,' observed Mod. 'Is known as the Iberian clap.' He brought his hands together above his sparse dome.

'And that brings me to Fred Fennell,' went on Davies. 'What about Fred Fennell? A strange tale. And Celia's bike being there. *Did* Fred do her in after creeping, heavy with police party drink, unsatisfied from the arms of Madame Tarantella? He was only a few minutes, remember. He and James Dudley always shared that nice, cosy little duty, cruising around in that van. One would go off and do his thing, then the other. A convenient and simple arrangement, and it passed the lonely hours. That night, as we've seen, they both called into the Police farewell party and had a few, despite the fact that they were supposed to be on duty. That's nothing new. Policemen can be very unofficial at times.'

Mod said: 'He could have gone out of the flat and walked up the street, past the cemetery and seen Celia, with no pants, coming over the wall with a bunch of nicked funeral flowers. It all happens then. Afterwards he quietly wheels the bike to Madame Tarantella's place.'

'It doesn't sound bad,' Davies agreed. 'Not bad at all. But it could just as easily have been the other copper, who did it – Dudley. Remember, nobody remembers seeing Celia from the time she left the youth club. People were asked to say if they'd seen a *girl on a bike*. Well, she wasn't on her bike. That was left outside the boneyard. She could have been in the police van with P.C. Dudley.'

'And what's happened to him?' inquired Mod. He had drained his glass and was moving it around, revolving it, in a fidgety way. Davies steeled himself to look at the landlord and two more pints were grudgingly delivered.

'Dudley, James Dudley, took himself and his family off to Australia. Emigrated twenty years ago. He liked the seaside. They wanted to go to Torquay but they couldn't afford it. He joined the police force in Sydney and worked with the vice squad until eight years ago, when he died when a brothel caught fire.'

'Died on duty, eh?' Mod nodded.

'Off duty,' corrected Davies. 'He'd been suspended on suspicion of accepting bribes.'

'Oh dear,' said Mod as if he knew the man personally.

Davies spread his hands. 'And that's about the lot. I've told you everything now, friend.'

'Celia,' ruminated Mod. 'She appears in *As you Like It* and she's in Spenser's *Faerie Queene* also. Derived from "Caelia", Latin, which means "Heavenly girl". I looked it up.'

'It's grand living in a library,' acknowledged Davies. 'Heavenly girl, eh?'

Mod looked up at the clock. 'Nearly closing time,' he observed. 'We must get back at the proper hour tonight.' He raised his voice so it carried to the landlord. 'Otherwise you get the blame for all manner of incidents and accidents.' Then quietly he said to Davies. 'You know where I think she's buried.'

'Where they're all buried,' sighed Davies.

'In the cemetery.' said Mod.

'That's what I thought,' said Davies.

CHAPTER FIFTEEN

Josie was lying in wait for him outside the saloon bar, insinuated in the doorway like a loitering child. She was wearing an oilskin and a sou'wester against the commonplace evening drizzle.

'Did you guess it was me?' she asked when she and Davies were walking hunched towards the town. Mod had bidden them goodnight and trudged the other way.

'I mistook you for a small lifeboatman,' replied Davies. 'Where are we going?'

'I'm going to show you something,' she said pushing along in the dark. She seemed very slight at her side. 'I've been looking for you from the window at work but you don't seem to have been around.'

He did not know why he felt so guilty about her. 'I've been kept busy,' he said. 'Inquiries. I'm still on the trail of Mr Ramscar – except there's no trail. I've done the grand tour, strip joints, clip joints, dip joints, places I wouldn't like to tell my mother about. I've been to. . . .'

'Ramscar's been threatening my mum,' she interrupted bluntly. 'She won't be able to speak to you any more.'

'Ramscar!' He halted like a guardsman in the road. They were just crossing and a bus, like a bright, businesslike dragon, came hissing at them. Josie pulled him across. 'Ramscar?' he said when they got to the pavemen not noticing the bus driver shaking his fist. 'Where is he hiding? Do you know?'

'Nobody knows,' she shrugged and continued walking. 'He just sends messages. My old man is petrified. He's scared to go out of the house. They know he talked to you.'

'Tell your mum and dad not to move,' said Davies. He was worried now. 'We ought to get a copper to watch the house.'

'No! That would be worse. They won't move, don't worry. I have to take food into them.'

'Ramscar,' he muttered again. 'I'd really like to know where he is.' Suddenly aware of her smallness and vulnerability he said. 'What about you?'

'Oh me,' she laughed. 'Ramscar don't worry me, Dangerous. I'd just tell him to piss off. Him or any of his mates.' She turned around in the rain, the bright sixpenny face framed in the outsized rim of the oilskin hat, brash, cheeky, confident and without defence. Celia again.

'You lie low,' he said. 'And if you get a whiff of trouble ring me, or anyone at the nick, at once. All right?'

She grinned at him. 'All right, Dangerous,' she said. 'He's not after me, don't worry. But I'll let you be a big brother if that's what you want.' She took some keys from her raincoat pocket. 'We're going in the salon,' she said seriously, walking on ahead of him. 'There's something I think you ought to see.'

'What is it?'

'Wait for it. It's a hoot,' she said. 'You'll see.' She opened the downstairs door and walked concisely up the narrow stairs to the first floor. She was just ahead of him, the still wet rim of her raincoat almost touching his nose. 'You've been avoiding me,' she grumbled confidently as she went up. 'You've been keeping out of my way. And it's not *just* Ramscar, either.'

He felt hollow and heavy and old. 'I told you I've been busy,' he muttered. 'Anyway you're seventeen, Josie.'

She halted on the stairs one leg just ahead of him and looked back scornfully. 'Seventeen,' she said. 'Is not *seven*. At seventeen you can do all sorts of things, you know. Look at Celia.'

'All right, all right,' he said wearily. She had begun to step up the stairs again and, on reaching the landing, switched on the lights and walked into the hairdressing salon. He followed her and looked around. The chairs were lined up like a battery of anti-aircraft guns, each one with its attendant hairdrier like a doused searchlight. 'Take that awful overcoat off,' she said. 'If ever I marry you, Dangerous, that overcoat's going to be the first to go.'

He ignored the remark and sat tiredly in one of the chairs. He read the reversed lettering on the windows facing him. Josie had gone somewhere into the back of the salon. He called out to her. 'Why does she call herself Antoinette of Paris, Switzerland and Hemel Hempstead? How come Paris and Switzerland?'

He could not see her. She was doing something in the shadows behind him. 'It's just a bit of swank,' she called out. 'She went to winter sports in Switzerland once and she didn't like the snow. She kept falling down. So she stayed in the hotel and did people's hair. I don't know what she did in Paris. Did a shampoo and set there once, I expect. Probably for herself.'

'What are you doing back there? he asked from the chair. He was regarding himself in the ladies' mirror and thinking how pale and bulky he looked. She called back. 'Won't be a minute. Just on the wall in front of you is a switch, Dangerous. When I tell you, you switch it on. Not till I tell you, though.'

'Playing games,' he grumbled.

'How's Kitty?' she called from the shadow.

'Bad chest and bad disposition.'

'How's Mod? I like Mod.'

'You've only just seen Mod. . . .'

'Right, Dangerous. Now. The switch!'

He did as she had instructed, leaning out of the chair and putting down the switch. The salon fell into darkness and a moment later a spotlight from the ceiling hit the floor by the entrance, fifteen feet away.

He waited.

Josie jumped like a child dancer into the light. He cried out, horrified, when he saw her. She was wearing her murdered sister's clothes. The green gingham dress, the white socks and the brown shoes buckled across the instep. She stood, grinning in the saucer of light. Celia Norris!

'Oh . . . oh, Christ,' he said and tried to back away further into the chair. 'Oh . . . why . . . what did you do that for?'

'I found them,' Josie said triumphantly. 'I found where my mum had hidden them. And I tried them on and they fitted. To the inch, Dangerous!'

She turned daintily in the circle. He still sat dumbstruck at what she had done. 'It's like one of them identi-kit things,' she laughed then paused, leaning forward to peer from the light to the dark at him. 'Are you still watching?'

'Yes I'm still watching,' he said, his mouth like stone. There was a trembling within himself, as if he were a mountain.

'Watch this then,' she laughed. He knew too well what she would do. She twirled like a little dancer and let the short skirt of the dress fly out. 'No pants,' she giggled eerily. 'No pants, either.' He stared desolately at her. She revolved more slowly a second time. The slim legs down to the ankles and the white socks and shoes, and up to the miniature thighs. Daintily she held the skirt and pirouetted once more. The globes of her bottom were small, contoured in the light and shadow. Again she turned. The slightly protruding belly and the darker shadow of hair at the top of her legs.

'Stop it!' he bellowed rising from the chair. He caught his head an idiotic clanging blow on the over-hanging hairdryer. He heard her laugh like an echo and cried again: 'Stop it, Josie. Do you hear me. Stop. . . .'

She did as he asked. She stopped and walked from the light to the dim towards him, on tip-toe. She stood in front of him in the thin dress. He squeezed his eyes together. 'You shouldn't . . .' he muttered. 'For God's sake. . . .'

'I thought I told you to take your coat off,' she answered practically. She bent over towards him and he could smell the mothballs from the dress. He wanted to touch it, to feel the material, but his hands would not move. She undid the clumsy buttons on his overcoat and divided it open. Then, she climbed on to his lap, in a kneeling position, her thin knees on his trousers, her body like a twig, her arms slim around his thick neck, her face looking intently into his. He could not stop himself then. He allowed his hands to touch her bringing them around, still encased in the ridiculous tunnels of the overcoat sleeves, and resting his fingers on her hips. The feel of the gingham went through him like a shock. So thin he could feel her hipbones protruding like a cowboy's guns. 'Oh hell . . .' he said hollowly. 'Oh bloody hell.'

At that she moved her face to his, smooth against tough, and pressed her thin body into his chest. His hands fell down the murderous dress and enveloped the softness of her naked bottom. He held her there while they both trembled. He could feel her young tears running down his face. He pulled her away and looked at her. Her smudged face and the clothes. Had Celia wept that night long ago?

In the C.I.D. room at the police station the detectives were all trying on suits, the proceeds of a thwarted robbery. There was an atmosphere akin to the fitting room of a busy tailor's shop, with comparisons of cloth, style and cut, being bandied about. Davies sat down quietly and wrote a short and almost entirely fanciful report of his efforts to locate Ramscar.

'Pity there wasn't an overcoat among this stuff, Dangerous,' observed one of the young, successful, detectives, smart in a pinstripe. 'Yours is going green with mould.'

'It's comfortable,' shrugged Davies putting his report in the file for Inspector Yardbird's office. 'I've sort of settled into it now. I don't think I could get used to a new one.' He left them to their fashions and went out and walked towards the cemetery.

It was a good day for visiting the dead. A damaged sky scattered over his immediate area of the world, a sky black but riven with chasms of jagged sunshine, a sky shrieking with dark winds. Wagner might have put it to music.

Davies, however, whistled a simple but jaunty sea-shanty ('Come cheer up my lads, 'tis to glory we steer') as he parked the Lagonda in the half-circle of road at the cemetery gates.

The grave keeper came immediately from his small mausoleum-like house at the gate and pointed at the car. Kitty, the unfumigated Kitty, raised itself blandly and blindly in the back seat, looked around and with a surge of disinterest fell down again to customary sloth.

The keeper pointed at once an accusing finger at the car. 'Can't you dump that thing somewhere else?' he demanded. 'It gives this place a bad name. And I can smell that dog, or whatever it is, from here.'

'I suppose I've got used to him,' grimaced Davies mildly. 'I won't take a couple of minutes of your time.' He was tempted to add 'I just want to inquire about digging up a few graves.' But tact prevented him.

'What is it?' demanded the man. He stood posed between a large laurel and a weeping elm. Davies realized how well trees and shrubs did in this particular plot and felt a distant shudder. The keeper sniffed. 'I hope you don't want to hang around the cemetery all night again, like last time.' he laughed, almost a snarl. 'Whoever heard of anybody threatening to blow up a place like this!'

'Ah,' said Davies, 'I am glad you mentioned that, friend. I'm afraid that was an administrative error.'

The man got half-way to putting a protective hand on the nearest bent headstone, but stopped himself. 'What is it you want, this time?' he asked.

'I wondered if I could just have a look at the registers, the Record of Burials, or whatever they're called in the profession,' asked Davies. He smiled grandly as though requesting a list of prizewinners. 'You've got them, I take it?'

'Of course, we've got them,' replied the man. 'Otherwise we wouldn't know *who* was bloody *who* would we?'

'That's logical,' agreed Davies.

'It's official police business then?'

'Naturally,' lied Davies. 'Would I do this for a pastime?'

The keeper turned and went back to his house, leaving Davies looking around him at the memorial stones, the final imprint of men upon earth. Some of them were quite old and he had to get close to read the inscriptions. Keys sounded behind him making him start. 'It's around the other side,' said the keeper. 'The registry.'

On the short journey to the place where the records were kept he seemed to unbend a little. Perhaps he was one of those persons who cannot bear to walk in silence with anyone, even in a cemetery. 'It's fucking cold ths morning,' he said.

Davies remembered him swearing the time before and wondered whether foul language came readily to people who worked among those who cannot listen. It was the man's only comment, however, and he unlocked the registry door with a surly twist of the keys. They walked into a long, icy room lined with racks and heavy ledgers. There was a writing desk with a green baize top, an inkstand and an ominously empty chair. Davies imagined the skeleton figure of Death crouched there at night over his ledgers. He declined the keeper's invitation to sit down.

'Who was it, or when was it?' asked the man.

'Who – I don't know,' said Davies awkwardly. 'But it would be July 1951. About that.'

'About that!' retorted the keeper. 'You don't know *who* it is – and you don't know *where* and you don't know *when*!'

'We're struggling a bit on this one,' admitted Davies. He pulled at his nose thoughtfully. 'Can I ask you – how long before a burial is the grave actually dug?' He wondered why the man showed no arousal of interest in the inquiries.

'Depends,' was the dull answer. 'If we're going to have a rush we might get them done a few days in advance, but normally it's just the day before. It's a business that just ticks over.'

'Well, in that case,' decided Davies. 'Could we check the burials for the 24th, 25th, 26th of July, 1951.'

The man assumed his customary crumpled expression, sighed, but went along the racks until he came to the appropriate book. Davies watched him and looking along the moribund shelves fancifully thought that tasteful notices saying 'Thrillers' 'Romances' 'True Life Adventure' might cheer the place. The man came back with a thick ledger. 'Quarter for July to September,' he said thumping the book down. 'I'm glad it wasn't a winter quarter, this is bleeding heavy enough.'

Davies took the occupational grumble with an understanding nod. He sat at the empty chair, now without thinking, and with compressed eagerness began to turn the pages. He reached July 24th, three entries, two on the 25th, three again on the 26th. He borrowed a pencil from the keeper and finding, for once, his notebook wrote down the names.

'Would these graves be all in more or less the same area?' he asked.

The keeper nodded. At last a touch of interest was germinating in his face. 'What's it all for anyway?'

'Just routine inquiries,' replied Davies convincingly. 'Which part of the place?'

The keeper checked the book over his shoulders, looking at the serial numbers. 'North-west corner,' he said. 'It's not used now.'

'By the wall?'

'Yes. Well more or less. There's a bit of green this side of the wall, then the path, then this section.'

'Where are all the tools kept?' asked Davies suddenly. 'The spades and such like.'

The man was beginning to look surprised. 'Tools? This is a funny business, isn't it? Tools? Well, they're supposed to be kept in the central store shed, but more often than not they're left out. The blokes you get on this job, they just leave them against the wall or even in the grave. They haven't got a lot of interest or pride in the work and bugger off as soon as they can, leaving the tools until the next day. Half the gardens around here have been dug with spades nicked from this cemetery.'

'It gets better,' said Davies to himself. He looked at the man. 'So if that area of the cemetery was being worked, as it were, eight burials in three days, then the tools might well be left there.'

'They could have been.'

'Right,' said Davies rising. 'Thanks very much. I'll be off.'

The man was now eager to ask about it, but Davies, wrapping his overcoat like silence about him made only non-commital answers. As they approached the gatehouse again he noticed the yellow splash of an excavator a few hundred yards away across the petrified causeway of headstones.

'What are they doing over there?' he inquired.

'Doing some business with the road,' replied the keeper. 'They've had to move the wall over. And dig up some old graves. I don't hold with that, digging them up.'

'Nasty job,' commented Davies.

'In the olden days,' replied the keeper, apparently glad to dispense some graveyard history. 'They had to get the labourers drunk on whisky before they'd take it on. It was very smelly and so on. But now they've got chemicals and suchlike. But I still don't reckon it.'

They had reached the gate now. 'Ever had an exhumation order carried out here?' Davies asked casually.

Shock smothered the keeper's face. 'Oh no,' he said. 'This is a respectable cemetery. Not for donkey's years. Long before my time.'

'Be quite difficult to get *eight* exhumation orders, I imagine,' said Davies beginning to walk towards the car.

'Eight!' The keeper appeared likely to faint. 'Eight exhumations! Over my dead body!'

'That's what I thought,' said Davies. 'Thanks anyway.'

Without answering the man turned towards his house, glancing back suspiciously towards the exiting Davies. 'Mad', he said. 'Absolutely fucking mad.'

Davies got into the Lagonda and thoughtfully started the engine. But he did not put the car into gear. There was something wrong. Slowly he turned and, leaning over, lifted the edge of the tarpaulin and exposed the crouching Kitty underneath. Kitty was gnawing a large bone.

'Listen,' said Davies to Mod. 'If our idea is right, if our murderer caught Celia Norris in the cemetery when she was stealing the flowers, or saw her going over the wall, or coming back, or whatever, did his nasty business, and then buried her in an already dug grave, then we've got to dig up eight coffins.'

'A formidable task,' agreed Mod. They were slouching along to 'Bali Hi', Furtman Gardens, having had to miss their evening drink because Mod had been kept late at the Labour Exchange. An emergency matter had arisen and there was a strong threat that he might be offered a job. He had managed to overcome it, however, before he left for home.

Mod, who never wore an overcoat, never having owned one, was walking comfortably in a sagging purple sports jacket and an open-necked shirt. Davies was curled like a large, walking chrysalis in his brown coat. 'The trouble is,' said Davies. 'No matter how far fetched it seems, the opportunity and the props were all there. That was the part of the cemetery beng used at that time, there were several open graves, and the tools were most likely left lying about. He could have raped her, or whatever, killed her and then dug a foot or so deeper into an already dug grave and buried her in there. So that the next day the coffin it was intended for was put in on top of it, and the whole lot buried for good. And the whole thing could have been done in the best possible conditions – at night and in peace and quiet. There's nowhere more private than behind a cemetery wall.'

'Who, for God's sake, is going to let you dig up eight graves?' said Mod.

'Nobody,' admitted Davies. 'I wouldn't even like to inquire.'

Mod glanced at him unhappily. 'And don't think I'm going to help you dig them up on the quiet,' he said. 'Because I'm not. I'm not allowed heavy manual work. I'd have got a job long ago if I was.'

They reached 'Bali Hi' Furtman Gardens. On the coat-rack in the hall was pinned a note for Davies. It said: 'Mr William Lind wishes to see you at the Police Station.'

The evenings had become enclosed and dark now and on his walk to the police station Davies passed only five other people, and three of those were walking dogs. He reflected once more how, even in that tightly populated place, the streets were emptied at evenings. In some countries, it would be the time for people to be out promenading, parading themselves, but here it seemed that once the factories had stopped for the day people shot like moles into holes and vanished. Even on a hot summer evening, like the one on which Celia Norris was seen for the last time, there were few people actuall out walking. There was the matter of television, of course, but also there were few outdoor places to go. A few small parks and the dead banks of the canal. People did as they did in the winter, they went into the pubs or stayed in their rooms. The only difference was that in the summer they left the windows open.

Venus, the evening whore, waved a customary hand to him from the end of the police station street. She looked lonely, exiled, as only a whore can look. For once the police station interior looked welcoming, its official light optimistic in comparison to the overwhelming weariness of the street. The duty sergeant was leaning over the inquiry counter and, at the safe distance, attempting to comfort an elderly lady who regularly reported being followed by salacious men with long fingers. 'My trouble, officer,' she whinnied, is that I look so young *from the back*. They always follow me.'

'She should try walking backwards,' muttered the sergeant when she had gone out complaining and full of anticipation into the awaiting night. 'That would scare them off. Your bloke is in the charge room, Dangerous.'

Davies thanked him and went into the bleak charge room. William Lind was sitting there, biting his lip. He rose as Davies walked in and knocked his wooden chair over backwards, then jumped violently as it sounded on the floor.

Lind's face looked shocked, as though he had committed a recent malpractice. He fumbled and righted the chair. Davies sat down at the opposite side of the wooden table his overcoat draped around him like a wigwam. 'Mr Lind,' he said steadily, 'Now what can I do for you?'

'Well Mr Davies, I heard . . . I understand from my wife, that is. You're looking into the Celia Norris business.'

Davies glanced over his shoulder to make sure he had shut the door. The Metropolitan Police did not like you doing your own work or your hobby on their premises. The door was closed. A policeman passed by and, out of habit, glanced over the frosted glass horizon into the charge room. But the semi-head floated away and Davies returned to the drawn face of Bill Lind.

'What was it, Mr Lind?' inquired Davies. 'Bill?'

'Just this,' said Lind. He felt into his pocket and produced a plastic bag from which he took Celia Norris's light green knickers. Davies almost fell backwards over the chair.

'They're hers, Celia's,' said Lind. 'They've been kept in mothballs.'

'That's almost the full house,' said Davies aloud but to himself as he reached across to take the small garment. 'It seems like everything has been kept in mothballs.'

'What . . . what's that mean?' asked Lind.

'Forget it. How did you come by these?'

'I found them,' said Lind simply. 'Straight up, Mr Davies. In the saddle of my bike. The day after she vanished. I opened it up and there they were.'

'How did you know they were hers?' inquired Davies.

'Ah, you can't catch me like that,' said Lind. The denial was made with something near waggish triumph. A finger came up but he stopped short of shaking it. 'I'd seen her in the club, like playing table tennis and netball and that, and all the boys used to have a look. See a flash of the girl's pants. You know, like lads do. . . .'

'Yes, yes, they do,' agreed Davies solemnly. 'But you were her boyfriend, weren't you, Mr Lind? Her regular?'

'Well sort of,' said Lind doubtfully. Davies could visualize him wearing swimming-trunks in the bath. 'But that's not the reason I know they were Celia's. It wasn't like that, see. I was a bit of a gentleman, you understand, and I liked to be decent about things. I still do. I thought of her in a . . . well pure sort of way.'

'Except when she was playing table tennis or netball. Then you had a look with the other lads?'

Two small red spots, almost like those of a clown, appeared on Lind's white cheeks.

'Now, now, Mr Davies. I didn't come here to have you accusing *me*,' he said primly. 'I came because I wanted to help.'

'It must be a long walk,' commented Davies drily. 'It's taken you twenty-five years. Why didn't you take this article to the police at the time, Mr Lind? You knew they were looking for her clothes.'

'Not right away, I didn't know. Because it was some time before they started to get really worried about her,' said Lind hurriedly. 'I kept them first of all because I knew they were hers and I just . . . wanted them. I wanted to keep them. Can you understand that?'

'Why didn't you go to the police station at the time?' insisted Davies heavily. 'You must have known it was the proper thing to do.'

Lind put his face against his fingers. He had strangely effeminate hands for a capstan operator. 'I was scared to. The coppers . . . the police came and took statements and I was frightened out of my life. I thought if I'd shown them these they would have jumped to the conclusion that *I* did it. And they could hang you in those days, Mr Davies. I didn't want to hang by mistake. So I didn't tell them. . . . I'm beginning to wish I hadn't told you now.'

Davies ignored it. 'Where have you kept them?' he said. 'Hidden.'

'In the loft,' said Lind. 'In an old suitcase, with a lot of other stuff.'

'You live in a flat,' said Davies. 'How long have you had a loft?'

'At my mother's place,' said Lind smartly with that little touch of triumph recurring. 'You didn't give me time to tell you, did you. In my mum's loft. That's where they've been. I spend quite a lot of time at my mum's. In fact I may go there for good soon. My wife's getting on my nerves, you see. A couple of weeks ago she was actually *fighting – fighting* with some man on the stairs outside the flat. None of the neighbours think she's any good, Mr Davies.'

Davies tried not to swallow hard but he did. He retreated into the overcoat to hide the lump as it went down. 'How did this garment get into your saddle bag then?' he asked.

'Somebody put them there,' said Lind simply. 'As a joke or something. Before they realized that something had happened to her, I thought she'd done it herself. It was the sort of teasing thing she'd do.'

Davies said, 'She was a bit of a . . *teaser*, wasn't she?'

'*I* would never say that,' sniffed Lind. 'I didn't think like that. And I still don't. I used to think of her very purely. That was the trouble.'

Davies nodded. 'Very gallant I'm sure. Right, it looks as though I'm going to have to get all this down in a statement at some time. Is there anything else, Mr Lind?'

He had asked the question with no hope, but immediately he was overjoyed he had put it. Lind half decided to say something, then thought not, then, looking up to see Davies's eyes jutting out at him, he ventured: 'Yes, there was, sort of.'

'Well, what, sort of?'

'It might be nothing, Mr Davies. But my mum reckons that about ten or twelve years ago she was sitting in one of those shelters in Glazebrook Park, you know the little round shelters, kind of divided into compartments. She was sitting there, having a rest walking back from the shops, when she heard two women talking in the next bit, the other side of the wooden dividing piece.' He glanced up to see if Davies was interested. The policeman's eyes were on him. 'And my mum says she heard one woman saying to the other that her husband had seen Celia walking along the canal towpath with a man. And this bloke had his arm around her. And this woman reckons her husband told the police, when they was asking for information, but she heard nothing more about it. Don't you think that's funny, Mr Davies?'

Davies closed his eyes as if it might stop his heart beating so loudly. 'This woman,' he asked. 'Did your mother know who she was?'

'She saw the two women as they got up and walked away,' said Lind. 'And she knew one of them slightly. But she didn't know which was the one who had said it. The woman she knew was called Mrs Whethers, and she lived somewhere down by the Kensal Green Empire, that was. It was years ago mind. She might not be there now.'

CHAPTER SIXTEEN

Guiltily Davies filled in his required official report at the police station, borrowing a Yellow Pages Directory, for suitable addresses, bookmakers establishments, drinking clubs and the like, where he might have been expected to go in quest of Ramscar. Indeed he had been moved by conscience to pursue some genuine inquiries but these had proved predictably pointless. He believed Ramscar might come to him in the end. In the meantime he found it impossible to think beyond Celia

Norris. He filed the report for Yardbird, wondered glumly how long it would be before the inspector began to complain, and then left the station to find Mrs Whethers.

Mrs Whethers was a comfortably heated-looking lady, a flush occupying her face as she hobbled out into the afternoon air on her journey to the Over Sixties Club in the Kensal Rise Pavilion. A transfixed fox stared glassily from around her neck as if it had jumped there and died. She carried it like a hunter bearing his prey. She had a substantial coat which she had worn for many years but which seemed to have thickened instead of thinned and now had the texture of compressed wood shavings. It banged solidly against her elderly legs as she made her familiar journey down her street.

Davies observed her leave her gate and followed. She reached a bus stop in the main road and stood there substantially. Davies then approached her. 'Mrs Whethers,' he ventured. 'I wonder if I could have a word with you?'

As some people get old their curiosity seeps away and nothing matters. She seemed not very surprised or interested. 'If it's insurance, the Conservatives or Jehovah's Witnesses, I don't want to know,' she said firmly. 'Or soap powders.'

Davies smiled. 'None of them,' he replied. 'Are you going to get a bus from here?'

She sniffed hugely. 'No, I'm waiting to see if Lloyd-George comes along. I haven't got time to talk to you, young man. I'm on my way to my club.'

'Perhaps I could come with you.'

She regarded him with doubt. 'It's over sixties,,' she decided. 'But you look a bit threadbare so I expect they'll let you in. Where, for God's sake, did you get that terrible coat?'

'In a sort of auction,' he replied lamely.

'You were done, son,' she told him firmly. 'Diddled. What did you want anyway?'

'I'm a policeman. Plain clothes.'

'Plain is the word,' she agreed surveying the garment again. 'Never saw plainer.'

'Here's the bus,' he said glad to change the course of the talk.

'I don't need the bus,' she said briskly. 'I'm just having a breather. I'm off now. It starts at half past two.'

She hobbled away at a large pace and Davies hurried after her. 'I wanted to ask you something, that's all.'

'I've got nothing to fear from the police,' she said. She was puffing a little. 'And I want to be in time for the dancing lesson.' She stopped and faced him, as though knowing that walking and talking together were too much for her. 'So if you are making police inquiries you'd better come with me and when I get a spare minute I'll see if I can answer them.'

That was definitely that. She slung her bad leg forward and he had to be content to lope along beside her until they arrived. He did not mind very much. He was glad to have found her. He was relieved she was alive.

The Over Sixties Club was in a corrugated iron church hall, its roof pointed timidly to heaven, its well-used door touched by a simple stone table which said 'Mary Ann Smith. Laid by the Grace of God. December 15th, 1919.'

With some doubt Davies followed Mrs Whethers into the hall. It was jolly with old people, limbering up for a dancing lesson about to be expounded by an extensively-built woman in her fifties, wearing a rose in her hair and a long feather boa which curled affectionately about her neck and big, blunt bosom.

'Gather round, gather round,' instructed the lady flapping her hands at them. 'Today it's the Argentinian Tango.' The old people all breathed 'Aaah!' The lady's skirt, for the occasion Davies imagined, was cut like that of a girl gaucho. It reached to the middle of her short shins. She had legs like logs.

The old folks, about twenty women and seven smug-looking men, shuffled forward so they could see the demonstration. Their skins were folded and used, their hands shaky, their understanding uncertain, but their eyes were bright. Dancing was a popular afternoon.

'Gaiety, that's what we must have, gaiety,' announced the instructress. 'And élan! That is what the Argentinian Tango is all about. So I want you to abandon yourself to the music and the romance. Mr Bragg, the gramophone if you please.'

Obediently an ancient man broke away from the eager crowd and edged painfully towards the wind-up gramophone. He looked so feathery that Davies felt inclined to help him with the weight of the record. He managed that, but puffed out his cheeks violently as he wound the handle. Into the wintry room, with its exhortation to 'Love Thy God' emblazoned on the far wall, seeped the wheezing sound of South America, played below distant stars many, many years before.

The instructress demonstrated first the basic tango step, the forward glide and the dip of the foot and the body. Davies, standing largely among the small old people, was not difficult to see but she was apparently not surprised at his presence. Now she paused in her Latin progress and asked him to step forward. He felt himself go pale under his coat but the old folks began to shout raucous encouragement and he was pushed forward firmly to the centre of the floor.

'Perhaps it would be better,' suggested the lady surveying him. 'If you danced without the er . . . garment.'

'Yes, yes . . . all right,' agreed Davies. He peeled himself out of the coat. The frail Mr Bragg stepped forward to collect it and at once fell to the floor under its weight. Two other men came forward and bore the coat and Mr Bragg, who kept shouting that he was all right, from the arena.

Davies was instructed to enfold the stumpy lady in his arms. She rolled her eyes provocatively. He had to bend into a question mark to embrace her and this impeded his first-ever attempt to dance the Argentinian Tango even more than would have been the case. For a short woman she was very powerful and she dragged him along like a shunting engine with a heavy load. He somehow concluded the sequence with one knee on the ground in an attitude of gallantry.

'You are most clumsy,' she said loudly rejecting his clutching hands. 'For a young man, most clumsy. What are you doing here anyway?'

'I'm a policeman,' he muttered helplessly. They all heard him and hummed and tutted between themselves about the well-known clumsiness of the police. He vacated the floor with the single applause of Mrs Whethers, who apparently felt some responsibility towards him.

'Most of this lot couldn't do any better,' she confided. 'Silly old sods.'

There was further instruction and then the elderly watchers were told to take their partners for a trial tango. The seven old men were grabbed like prize gigolos and Mrs Whethers claimed Davies and pulled him to the floor. The dusty rhythm began again and he rambled and stumbled with her staggering like someone trying to dance in a storm at sea. There was a familiar smell about Mrs Whethers. Mothballs.

There was a good deal of jolly laughing and clapping after the dance and cheerful cups of tea were passed around. The dance lady put on her coat and went out, her stint done, and Davies found himself sitting on a Sunday School chair almost knee to knee with Mrs Whethers.

'All right, then, what is it?' she said.

She had quite a powerful face for an old lady, not pink and fluffy like some of them, but girded with deep straight lines as though her head were held on with string. The tea they drank was in enormously thick cups. He wondered whether elderly people, gnashing their teeth perhaps or trying to reassure themselves of their strength, bit through more delicate china.

'Celia Norris,' he said. 'Do you remember?'

'I remember,' she said without showing surprise. 'Never been found. Not a sausage.'

'Right,' he confirmed. 'Now I've got the job of digging the whole thing up again, Mrs Whethers.'

'How's that?' she inquired enjoying her tea with a serene sucking sound. 'It's been a long time.'

'Sometimes these things take a long time,' he said attempting to sound wise. 'Anyway, I've heard whisper that your husband made a statement to the police.'

'My late husband, Bernard,' she agreed. 'Yes he did. He was willing to swear it on oath too. But he never heard another thing from them, not a word.'

'Raffle.' The disembodied voice came from behind his shoulder. Mrs Whethers began wrestling with a handbag the size of a cat and produced two ten-pence pieces. 'You'd better get some tickets as well,' she advised Davies. 'They don't like it if everybody doesn't put in.' She said it as if they were a foreign tribe indulging in strange insular customs.

Davies burrowed into the pockets of his overcoat. The wasted lady who stood behind him held the book of tickets threateningly like a witchdoctor with an omen. Davies handed her two ten-pence pieces.

'You have to *give* something as well,' Mrs Whethers advised. 'A packet of tea or a tin of beans or some cake mixture.'

'I forgot to bring them,' said Davies. I knew there was something. . . .'

The ticket lady said: 'Well, you've got to give something. Them's the rules. Right, Mrs Whethers?'

Mrs Whethers nodded grimly. 'If you don't put something in you can't have anything out, even if your ticket wins. Have you got a pound note?'

Davies began reaching into what appeared to be the very fastnesses of his body. 'Yes,' he affirmed. 'Yes, I've got a pound.'

'Good, put that in. It's a good prize. They'll like that.'

Davies gave the hovering lady the note and turned again to Mrs Whethers. To his annoyance she had risen from her seat and was hobbling up and down like a lame sea captain pacing his bridge. 'I've got to do it,' she explained over her shoulder on the outward run. 'It goes dead. My funny leg. I have to get the blood moving again.'

Davies sighed got up and began walking alongside Mrs Whethers. She pushed him away. 'Sit down,' she said brusquely. 'It will be circulating in a minute. You can wait until then with your questions. And after the raffle.'

Davies sat down impotently. He could sometimes understand how police officers were accused of intimidating witnesses. Mrs Whethers returned to her seat, her perambulations accomplished, and thrust out a sturdy but damaged leg at him. 'Feel that,' she invited. 'Feel the blood moving through it now.'

He obliged patiently. 'Oooooooo Mrs Whethers! There's a nice young man!' bawled a gummy old hag in the next tribal circle. 'Ask him to give me a rub of mine!'

The old ones swayed with merriment but the raffle mercifully intervened. 'Eyes down, look in,' called a limpid pensioner in a gravy-stained jacket. He called the numbers and the old people pressed forward eagerly to claim the prizes they themselves had provided. 'Ninety-seven, red,' he called and Davies looked down to see he had the number in his hand. 'Go on,' urged Mrs Whethers. 'See what we've won.'

The raffler was holding the pound note which Davies himself had contributed. When he saw Davies coming towards him he quickly switched the prize to a large tin of garden slug pellets. 'You can't have the pound,' said the stained man firmly. 'If you put it in, you can't take it out.' He turned to the ancient tribe. 'It's the rules innit?' he said. 'It's the rules,' they chorused in return. Davies went back with his slug pellets and sporting applause. 'You should have slipped the ticket to me,' whispered Mrs Whethers. 'You're a bit slow for a copper.'

'That's what they all say,' agreed Davies. He leaned forward. 'Now tell me about what your husband saw.' Around him the groups had dissolved into conversation, the pound having been miraculously won by the raffler himself. Mrs Whethers at last looked businesslike.

'My husband, Mr Whethers,' she said formally. 'Was walking home at about ten o'clock on that night, whenever it was. It still wasn't quite dark

because it was in the summer. And he said he saw that girl going down
the alley towards the canal with a man.'

Davies nodded gladly.

'A man,' she nodded firmly. 'In a dark suit. And not wearing a hat.
And he had his arm around the girl's waist. That's what he saw.'

'You say he made a statement to the police to that effect, Mrs
Whethers?'

'As soon as all the fuss started and it was in the papers, my Bernard said
what he had seen, but he didn't go to the police. He was a great one for
minding his own business. He liked to live and let live. But the rumour
got around the neighbourhood, like the one about what Mr Harkness
saw, and this policeman turned up out of the blue and took a statement.
But he said the law would take its course or one of these things policemen
say. And that's the last that came of it.'

Davies felt his heart move again. 'Mr Harkness,' he said. 'Who was Mr
Harkness?'

'A very old man. We told the police about him too but he was very ill
then, and he used to drink, so I don't suppose they took much notice of
him. I mean – how long ago was it now?'

'Twenty-five years,' said Davies.

'Well, he would have been seventy-six *then*, old Harkness. So I don't
suppose they put much store by him. But he was reckoned to have seen
something. But he was ill and old. . . .'

'Did he have family? asked Davies. 'Around here now?'

'They moved. To Bristol or somewhere. I didn't know any of them
very well. I just heard.'

All around them the encampment was breaking up, the elderly tribe
gathering its chattels and making for the door. A man approached and
asked Davies if he needed the slug pellets and on hearing that he did not,
relieved him of them. Davies went towards the door with the hobbling
Mrs Whethers.

'Mr Whethers and me,' said Mrs Whethers. 'We always wondered
why we never heard any more. Not a dicky bird.'

At three o'clock on almost any afternoon he knew where to find Mod. He
went to the public library, warm as a loaf in the middle of the chill
November afternoon. Davies had been into the library on other
occasions but he had never appreciated how comfortable as well as
improving it was. Mod had studied there for years.

The entrance hall served also as a small museum where were displayed
various objects of local history. A fragment of mosaic, Roman, an axe-
head, which had an air of late Woolworths about it but was sworn to be of
the Middle Ages; a spade used by minor royalty to plant a commemora-
tive tree which had died a good many years before its planter; a set of
tradesman's ledgers from the seventeenth century, and a policeman's
helmet which Davies noticed was significantly dented.

On the walls was an assortment of iodine-coloured photographs, none
of them hanging straight. They were of groups of councillors with mayors

in Nelsonian hats and attitudes; the official opening of several buildings including the library itself, celebrations for coronations and jubilees, a scene of wartime bomb damage in the High Street and the local company of the Home Guard crouched at the side of the canal apparently in the strong belief that Hitler would launch his invasion of Britain via that waterway.

There was a potted palm at the library door, the only hint of exotica for miles about. On such a winters' day it was pleasant to brush against it as Davies went into the library. His overcoat immediately caught the assistant's notice and he knew he was under observation as a possible book thief. He saw Mod sitting snug beneath a benevolent reading light over a table at the far end of the Reference Room.

'Lovely,' he sighed approaching Mod. 'What a fine bloody life.'

'Hush,' said Mod with the traditional library caution. 'Would you care to sit down?' Davies sat at the opposite side of the table. It was like visiting some senior businessman in a large office. Mod leaned forward attentively, his elbows on the table, his fingers touching thoughtfully. 'And what can I do for you?' he inquired in a library whisper.

'Christ, you sound like the Chairman of Shell International,' muttered Davies. 'It's a great life, I must say. Sitting here in comfort, drawing the dole, while the likes of me traipse the streets in the rain.'

'I'm studying,' explained Mod simply. 'This world is enriched by study, not by tramping the streets.'

'You could be right. What is it?' he nodded towards the books, their pages open like the palms of many hands on the table.

Mod leaned over conspiratorially. 'There are still courts in this country,' he whispered. 'Which can impose the punishment of the stocks or a journey in a cart of dung. Have you ever come across anything so amazing?'

'Frequently,' muttered Davies taking Celia Norris's knickers from his pocket. He took them out of the plastic bag. 'How about these?'

Mod was stunned. 'Good God,' he said. 'You've *found* them!'

Davies sniffed. 'Quite a collection we're getting,' he said. 'We've got her bike and her pants. All we want now is the body and the murderer.'

'Where did you get them?' asked Mod his voice hushed with wonder and the requirements of the library. 'They sniff of mothballs.'

'The whole case docs,' commented Davies. 'Our friend Bill Lind. He decided to come clean after all these long years. He says they were put in the saddle-bag of his bicycle and I think he's telling the truth. You can bet your life that they were put there by Dave Boot. Our Bill's had them hidden away all this time in his mummy's loft.

'Why did he keep them? asked Mod. 'A sort of relic?'

'He says not.'

'Why do they smell of mothballs, then, Dangerous? He must have meant to preserve them.'

'He says they were in a trunk of old clothes in the loft and the mothballs were among the clothes. You know what people are like around here, not ever throwing anything away.'

'What are you going to do now? Apply for those eight exhumation orders?'

Davies grinned wryly. 'I might as well apply for promotion to detective chief inspector,' he said. 'Anyway I, I've changed my mind about that, Mod. I don't think she's in the cemetery.'

'Why not?'

'She was seen walking down the alley by the pawnbrokers – towards the canal – with a man in a dark suit. That night. I've got a witness.'

'Jesus! A witness?'

Davies held out his hands for restraint. 'Well, he *was* a witness. A Mr Bernard Whethers. He's gone where he can't give evidence, unfortunately. He's dead. There was somebody else too. An old man called Harkness, but he's dead too. He was seventy-six then, twenty-five years ago.'

'They're not going to say much now,' agreed Mod morosely.

'Mr Whethers made a statement, his widow says. He didn't volunteer it, but rumours get around and apparently a copper turned up on the strength of these rumours. It doesn't take long for things like that to get to our ears, not when we're searching around. But that statement was never recorded at the police station I know. I made another check and it's not in the file, or ever mentioned.'

Mod looked at him across the books. 'Miasma from the police station again,' he said.

'The man Mr Whethers saw with a girl he thinks was Celia was wearing a dark suit. So he said. And no hat. It need not rule out a policeman, our friend P.C. Dudley for example, because it was almost dark and Mr Whethers was some distance away. The uniform would look like a dark suit and he could have been carrying his hat, or even left it in the police van. They teach you at police school, you know, to take your hat off if you want to gain somebody's confidence.'

'Do they now?' said Mod interested. 'The only time I've had dealings with a copper without a hat is when I knocked it off. What good's a statement of a dead witness anyway? Especially when it's not been recorded at the police station.'

He looked up and whispered 'Watch the knickers.'

Confused, Davies failed to act in time. A stony lady library assistant, journeying past the table, saw the green gingham lying there. Quickly Mod picked up the little garment and pretended to fiercely blow his nose with it. He then folded the books in a muffled way on the table and, stretching himself indulgently, announced that he believed he had worked enough for the day. With casual familiarity he turned out the table lamp and unerringly returned the volumes to their various places on the shelves. Studying him, Davies could not avoid the impression that he would shortly open a cabinet and pour them both a drink from a comprehensive selection of spirits.

Members of the library staff nodded affable goodnights as he and Mod walked towards the door. 'Hadn't you better remind them to lock up?' Davies suggested.

Mod sniffed potently. 'You may well take the piss,' he said quietly. 'But it's my presence here that, to a great extent, justifies the continued operation of the reference section of the municipal library. I am the doyen of the place, you understand. Every now and then a deputation of councillors comes snooping and I have to hurry out and get a few friends in from the streets to sit and peruse the books for a while. That's why I'm appreciated here, Dangerous. There's no waste of the ratepayers' money while Mod Lewis is studying.'

Davies let the perverse logic roll over his shoulder. He pointed to the policeman's helmet in the foyer. 'Did you, by any chance, dent that?' he inquired.

'General Strike,' recited Mod without a second look. 'Attack on police at the Clock Tower. No, I was not present, owing only to the fact that I was yet unborn. Otherwise I would have been there. I like a good attack on the police.'

Davies said: 'Listen, let me talk this whole thing out to you, Mod. Right from the beginning. And let's walk from the Catholic Church to the cemetery, along the High Street, then down to the canal and along the bank. Just to see if it does anything.'

Mod acquiesced thoughtfully. 'Right,' he nodded having apparently made some mental calculation. 'Even walking slowly – and thinking – that ought to see us at "The Babe In Arms" as they open the gates.'

'We'll keep to that,' promised Davies. They walked. A pinched wintry dark had overcome the town. Window lights and shops lights shone bravely but only a few feet above the ground the pall of late November had laid itself inclemently across the roofs. The first of the home-going cars were on the roads, there were thickening queues at the bus stops. Davies, not for the first time, wondered what economics inspired West Indians and Indians to come and live, and queue for buses, in such a clime. They stood, with the natives, their faces merged in the gloom, not a snake charmer or a calypso singer among them.

Davies turned his huge coat collar up. It was like a giant's arm about his neck. Mod pulled up the stumpy collar of his sports jacket and thrust his hands into his shallow pockets but did not grumble.

Turning from the main road they continued as far as the Catholic Church. It was uncompromising shut and dark, as though the faith had gone bankrupt. But there was a modest parcel of light coming from the window of Father Harvey's house and, at first, Davies made towards it, going down the gravel path with Mod hanging behind. Mod did not like the vicinity of religions. It had been Davies's half-intention to talk briefly with the priest before they began their thoughtful journey, but on looking through the window they saw that he was engaged in hammering together some large sections of wood. His hammering was violent but not more so than his expression. His holy robe was hitched around his waist like the skirt of a washerwoman. Davies thought that a tap on the window would probably cause him to hammer his own thumb, so he began to turn again.

Mod, peering around his overcoat, saw the interior industry also.

'What's he making?' he whispered as they went away. 'An Ark? Do you think he knows something we don't know?'

'It's a do-it-yourself confessional box,' Davies said confidently.

'I would have considered that the confessional was one of the things you could *not* do satisfactorily by yourself,' said Mod pensively. 'Like making love or playing shuttlecock.' He thought again. 'Not that I have a great experience of either.'

Davies pointed to a square roofed shadow beyond the church. 'That's the youth club,' he said. 'It's a new building but it's on the site of the old one. So we can say that Celia Norris began her last bicycle ride from there. Her cycle would have been in the yard and she would have come out through this gate and made off towards the cemetery to get her mum the flowers.'

They began there and followed the trail humped as a couple of slow bloodhounds. At the cemetery entrance they were inevitably confronted by the graveyard keeper who peered through the gloom and the gates. 'Oh, Christ, it's you again.' he said regarding them as he might have regarded Burke and Hare. 'I hope you haven't got that stinking dog with you.'

Davies immediately worried that they had discovered the missing bone. It was still, violently gnawed, in the back seat of the Lagonda. Every time he had attempted to recapture it Kitty had growled spitefully. 'No, No,' he assured. 'No dog today. Just taking the air. This is Mr Modest Lewis.'

'Funny place to take it,' said the man ignoring Mod. 'The air around here.'

'Mr Lewis is a famous pathologist,' added Davies trenchantly. The graveyard man was at once impressed. 'Oh, very pleased to meet you,' he said in the manner of one greeting a worker in the same trade. He pushed his hand, white as a bat in the winter darkness, through the bars of the gate. Mod never unready to assume a part, took it, examined it carefully and let him have it back.

'That's a cold hand,' he said frowning professionally.

'Is it?' said the man with a hint of worry. 'Is there . . . is there anything I can do for you Mr Lewis? We don't have that many pathologists visiting us. Anything you'd like to see, perhaps?' He sounded as if he were quite prepared to start digging.

'Nothing, nothing at all,' replied Mod carefully. 'But you just look after your hands. They're very cold.'

'I will, I will,' promised the man apprehensively. 'I'll warm them in front of the fire.' He hurried away with his palms thrust beneath his armpits.

Mod grinned in the dark. 'I enjoyed that,' he said as they continued their trail. 'I've always thought I might like to be a pathologist, you know. No one gets nearer to the human being than the pathologist. Imagine, one day, performing a post mortem – *and finding a man's trapped soul!* Fluttering away there like a snared butterfly. Now that would be a thing, wouldn't it, Dangerous?'

'If you'd like to start on the ground floor,' observed Davies wryly. 'I can give you a human femur. If I can get it out of Kitty's jaws. She nicked it from the boneyard last time we were here.'

'Dear, dear,' said Mod shaking his head. 'That dog will get into trouble yet. Just imagine some poor soul limping through eternity without a thighbone.'

They had paused beneath the cemetery wall. Somewhere there P.C. Frederick Fennell had found the abandoned bicycle. It was a ragged patch of ground, a gathering place for tufted grass and weeds, although sweetened by daisies and dandelions and visited by occasional desperate bees in the summer. The light of the street lamps touched hanging ears of ivy on the brick wall. 'That ivy must have been here then,' said Mod knowledgeably. 'If it could only talk.'

'I'd be glad if some humans would talk, never mind the ivy.' grumbled Davies. He began to walk again in the direction of the main shopping street. The lights were going out all over the World Stores, David Greig's and the Home and Colonial. Men dodged into a small furtive shop for cigarettes and at the corner Job, the newspaper seller, called mournfully 'Tragedy tonight! Big tragedy!' as he peddled his gloomy wares in the gloom.

As they walked Davies related the events, as he knew them, appertaining as he officially put it, to the disappearance and undoubted murder of Celia Norris. Mod walked beside him grunting and listening. They turned eventually down the alley path between the pawnbrokers and the 'Healing Hands Massage Parlour', and plunged into the damp darkness of the canal cut. Davies climbed the bank of the allotments and surveyed the dankened rows of cabbages and sprouts. A platoon of bean poles stood guard in the dark. He got down again and they paced the towpath carefully, Davies still talking, Mod leaning over to look into the oily water as if hoping some clue or inspiration might still be given from there. They walked the half mile length until they reached the road bridge that transversed the canal. Their journey had been frowned upon by the rears of warehouses and shops and a few terrace houses with their backs to the waterway. Somebody had even parked a little boat by the dead water. There were romantics everywhere.

Back on the road Mod's nose began to twitch towards the distant junction light of 'The Babe In Arms' and they hurried towards the early evening brew. After their customary three pints they repaired to 'Bali Hi' Furtman Gardens where Mrs Fulljames had created tripe and onions for dinner and Mr Smeeton was appropriately disguised in Breton costume. 'French Club tonight,' he mumbled enigmatically. Mr Patel was explaining a metallic bending of a fork to Minnie Banks and Doris who were looking on entranced.

After dinner Davies went to his bedroom. Covering the bedside lamp with a vest (Mrs Fulljames did not approve of lights burning in all parts of the house) he wrote down with great care everything he knew about the case of Celia Norris. Then, on another sheet of paper, borrowed from Minnie and headed 'Kensal Green Primary School', he wrote everything he *thought* he knew, and on a third, the things he *wished* he knew. He folded his work and put it inside a shoe (an odd shoe, the survivor of a battle at an Irish goodwill party) in his wardrobe.

At ten o'clock he thought he would stroll to 'The Babe In Arms' before it closed. It had become misty merging on foggy. He spent only a few minutes in there chiefly because of the woman who sang 'Viva España' and then returned back to Furtman Gardens. Halfway down the foggy street, beneath its only tree, he was violently attacked by three, possibly four men. He was struck on the head and was aware of blows coming from all directions. Even in his pain and confusion he thought he detected the familiar blow of a pick-axe handle. He fell to the pavement and was then gratefully aware of a distant panic among his assailants. At once the blows ceased. He thought they were running away and there was another sound of heavier running, then hot, smelly breathing into his battered face. It needed all his strength to open his eyes once. He found himself looking up into the worried face of the rag-and-bone man's horse.

CHAPTER SEVENTEEN

As he hung across a stretcher in the casualty department at the hospital Davies opened his eyes and smiled a grating smile at the young doctor nosing over his injuries. 'Could I have my usual room, please?' he asked. He was aware of another figure prostrate on a trolley-stretcher a few feet away. He half-turned and even to his blurred vision the face looked familiar. The man seemed to sense he was looking and scraped his head to the side so that he could face him. It was Josie's father.

'Hello Mr Norris,' muttered Davies. 'What are you in for?'

'Same as you, you fucking berk,' said Mr Norris unkindly. 'I told you to lay off.'

'Ramscar as well, eh?'

'It wasn't Father Christmas. I told you what would happen. I hope they've duffed you up good.'

The young doctor looked annoyed. 'Will casualties please stop quarreling among themselves,' he said petulantly. 'It's not a mothers' meeting, you know.' He turned as two orderlies came into the area. 'This one,' he said pointing to Davies. 'Dressings and observation.' Then he nodded at Norris. 'That one, theatre number two. In half an hour.'

Davies's heart fell. He thought at once of Josie. 'Sorry Mr Norris,' he whispered.

'So am I. Ramscar will nail you, you just bleeding wait. I'm staying inside here for as long as I can. By the time I'm out maybe you and the rest of the berks will have got him. I bloody doubt it, though. I doubt it.'

Davies was beginning to personally doubt it himself. He ached from the waist up, but he knew they had not hurt him as much as before. He decided to buy the rag-and-bone man's horse a complete cabbage once he was released from hospital.

It was his last conscious thought until next day. He awoke in the early afternoon when a pale, round nurse asked him if he would like a bedpan and some custard. He declined the custard.

Mercifully neither Doris nor Mrs Fulljames came to visit him. That would have been beyond his patience. But Mod did, sitting moodily watching his bandaged face with doubt and consternation.

'I suppose,' remarked Mod with Welsh solemnity, 'That a powerful police dragnet is at this very instant closing around the perpetrators of this new outrage against your person.'

Davies grinned and winced. 'I have no doubt that the Metropolitan Police have been moved to vast inactivity,' he said. 'They sent a sergeant over here to get all the thrilling particulars and the cops' doctor came and looked me over. It's been terrific, believe me. My God, by now they'll have enough men in the hunt to throw a cordon around a phone box.'

'A disgraceful situation,' grumbled Mod. 'They seem to have no regard for you at all. Still, I suppose they're so accustomed to seeing you bashed about that the novelty's worn off.'

Josie came to see him too. She sat by the edge of the bed regarding him sorrowfully but saying nothing. He felt like an archer looking through a small slit window. 'You've got a job lot to visit now,' he joked with difficulty. 'How's your old man?'

'In a mess,' she shrugged. 'Worse than you, and that's saying something, that is. Christ, you must have three miles of bandages round your head.'

'Sorry, Josie,' he mumbled. She looked lost. She put her hand on the bedclothes. 'Don't go blaming yourself, Dangerous,' she replied softly. 'He's been skimming around in that mucky pond for years. First with Ramscar then with others like him. Some time or other he was bound to get done. And you were doing your job as a copper. What else can anyone say?'

'What about your mother?'

'She's got the wind up. It was she who found the old man on the doorstep. He'd gone to the door. I've shoved her off to her sister's in Luton.'

'Is Luton far enough away?' asked Davies. 'From Ramscar.'

'It's got to be. The next nearest relative's in Australia.' She laughed making the joke, but her face was crowded with fear. 'It's got to stop some time,' she said. 'Or else somebody's going to get killed. And it looks like you're favourite, Dangerous.' She suddenly laid her head against the white bedcover, her face small and pinched. He touched her thin shoulder with his fingers and she put her hand up to hold them.

'Do you think it's just Ramscar?' she asked, still with her head on his legs. 'Or is it something to do with that Celia thing? Somebody trying to stop you.'

'It could be both,' he sighed. 'Maybe there're the same thing. Maybe Ramscar did it after all. The more I find out the less I know, Josie. Do you think your father knows where Ramscar is hiding out?'

She laughed wryly. 'If he does there's no bloody way he's going to tell anybody *now*. Not the state he's in. It's a miracle they managed to sew him together again. He's like a patchwork quilt. It's sodded up his looks for good, and he never looked much anyway.' She looked up from her crouching position, slowly, then quickly, as though awakening after a nap. 'Dangerous, have you found out *anything* about Celia? What happened to her.'

He had never told her. He paused a moment now, then he said. 'I've got her bike, Josie, and I've got her pants.'

He thought she was going to fall off the chair. 'You've got what!'

'Her bike and her pants,' repeated Davies carefully.

'Christ! However did you . . .?'

'Listen,' he said. He tried to lean forward but it hurt too much. 'Listen Josie, I've turned up all sorts of things. I'll tell you soon, promise. Not now, because it's too public here, and I feel too rough right now. But I'll tell you before long exactly *what* happened to your sister. Perhaps I'll know *who* did it too.'

Josie continued to stare at him in deep disbelief. 'I . . . I can't believe it,' she said. 'Honest, I just can't believe it.'

'You didn't think I could do it?'

'No . . . No, it's not that. I just didn't think *anybody* could do it. And you've still got the bike?'

'Still in working order,' Davies said quietly. 'A bit creaky but nothing more. I've even got the remains of the flowers she was taking home to your mother. She got them from the cemetery, you know.'

She appeared to be unable to digest the information. She slowly got to her feet. 'I've got to go,' she said. 'I've got to think about this.' She looked at him doubtfully. 'You're sure,' she said. 'I mean you're not having me on. . . .'

'I'm sure,' nodded Davies. 'Very sure. See you Josie.'

'See you,' she almost stuttered. She moved forward quickly and kissed him on the piece of cheek that was showing. As she moved away she produced a small smile. 'You're brighter than I reckoned,' she said.

'Thanks,' he replied. 'Sometimes I surprise myself.'

She went without looking back. He realized that his head was throbbing from the encounter. He slept briefly and then lay, in the night dimness of the ward, thinking about Celia Norris and her bicycle journey to eternity twenty-five years before. He followed every turn of the pedals by those brown shoes. From the youth club to the cemetery. He saw her brazenly climb the wall, knickerless, and steal the flowers from a grave. He knew she would be capable of that. He could see Josie doing it. And then what? Waiting outside the wall, or just approaching it as she climbed over again in the gloom, was the mooching police van. At its wheel, a policeman who had been drinking at the social function shortly before; alone in the van while his colleague spent time with his fortune-telling lover.

What did he do that policeman? Did he get out of the car and stand waiting under the wall while she climbed over? Did he see then that this seventeen-year-old girl was wearing nothing below her gingham dress? Was he stern with her and did he take her into the police van, not seeing her bicycle left in the dandelions and weeds? Did they drive slowly up the High Street that humid summer night? And while they drove did that inebriated policeman suggest to that young girl that they went down by the canal bank together? Did he cajole or threaten her?

Davies saw them walking in the dusk, the policeman without a hat, as Mr Wethers had seen. Down to the foot of the alley and by the bank. And then it happened. That policeman raped Celia Norris and murdered her. And disposed of her body. But not her clothes. Disposed of her body . . . but not her clothes. . . .

Suddenly Dangerous Davies shot up in bed so fast that his head sang with pain. He clasped it with a cry that was almost exultation. A man across the ward called out eerily: 'Are you all right? Shall I get the nurse?'

'No, no,' warned Davies hoarsely. 'Nothing, thank you.'

The last thing he wanted was the nurse. He looked at his watch. It was only ten o'clock. They closed down early in hospitals. He slid clumsily out of bed, stood up and put his pillow beneath the sheet. His head banged in protest as though somebody were trying to get out through the bandages. There was an ante-room just outside the ward and last time that was where they had kept his clothes. He went painfully but hopefully across the polished floor of the ward, his head feeling like a turnip. But his hope was realized. His suit and his overcoat were keeping each other forlorn company on a single iron hanger. His shoes were in a locker beneath, but he could not find his socks, his underwear or his shirt. He took the clothes and the shoes and went into the toilet. He put them on over his pyjamas, and pulling the faithful overcoat up around his plastered ears he crept heavily towards the corridor. There was no one there. The night nurse was in a side room and the doorway to the outside was only a few yards down the passage. He gained it in three strides and let himself out into the chill air.

He was a mile and a half from the single room of Andrew Parsons of the Salvation Army, which is where he wanted to be. Not even the most optimistic of taxis ever patrolled that threadbare area and he was thinking he might have to walk or to steal a bicycle when he saw a bus illuminating in the distance. The bus stop was just outside the hospital. No one at the gatehouse took any heed of him and he timed his walk so that he gained the pavement just before the bus. Gratefully he boarded it, miraculously found some coins in his overcoat pocket, and sat on the cross-seat feeling relieved and elated. He thought he knew where Celia Norris was.

At the next stop a couple, arms entwined, boarded the bus and sat opposite him. Their interest in each other was gradually transferred to him. At first they studied his heavily embalmed head, intently as though following every whorl and curve. Then the girl's gaze dropped to his ankles. Awkwardly he followed her eyes down and saw that his pyjama legs were protruding below the turn-ups of his trousers and that immediately below that incongruity he was showing segments of bare feet.

He smiled feebly across at them. 'Night shift,' he said as though confident that would explain everything.

They nodded dumbly but continued to stare until he left the bus in the High Street. When he last saw them, as the vehicle made off into the latening evening, they were with their faces pushed to the window, together with that of the conductor, to whom they had obviously reported the phenomenon. Davies waved to them as he crossed the road.

He kept into the best shadows of the terrace houses until he came to the front door of Andrew Parson's lodgings. He knocked with misgiving which was justified by the beginnings of a scream which came from the flowered-overalled woman who answered. He tried to smile through the bandages which made matters worse, but fortunately he arrived at an explanation before she arrived at a screech. 'Mr Parsons, please,' he pleaded. 'Salvation Army. It's an emergency.'

To his relief and her credit, she subsided. 'It looks like an emergency too,' she commented. 'I'll call him. He's up there with his cronies. Blaring away.' She advanced to the bottom of the stairs and bellowed 'Mr Parsons!' up into the gloom. She called twice more and eventually a phase of light showed that a door had been opened. 'Mr Parsons, there's somebody for you. Says it's an emergency.'

'Emergency?' Davies heard Parsons return. 'Who is it?'

'Don't ask me,' she bawled back. 'Looks like the Invisible Man.' She turned to Davies. 'Go on up,' she said. 'I can't stand here shouting my head off.'

Davies thanked her and advanced up the stairs. When he had gained the first landing, Parsons, on the third, called doubtfully again. 'Who is it?'

Davies chanted:

'I am the ghost of General Booth,

'I've come to make you tell the truth.'

He was pleased with his extemporaneous effort. He heard Parsons give a quick sob in the gloom and he knew he had been recognized. Parsons almost tumbled down the stairs to meet him. 'Mr Davies . . .' he said. Then seeing Davies's state. 'Oh my goodness . . . what happened?'

'I tripped over a collection,' said Davies in the dark. 'I want to have a chat, Andy. I've come specially to see you. Can I come up?'

'Oh, for God's sake,' pleaded Parson 'Not now. Not in the room. We've got bandsmen practising.'

As though to corroborate the statement a subdued trump issued through the open door above. Then a piping whistle noise. 'All right,' whispered Davies. 'Tell me something, exactly and no bloody lies mate, and you can go back and get on with Crimmond, otherwise we go up and talk about it there.'

Parson's head had dropped. He was muttering, perhaps praying. 'What? What is it then?' he asked.

'Right,' Davies moved closer to him on the landing. 'Where did you *really* find those clothes. *Not* in the public bog. Come on tell me – they were *not* in there, were they?'

'No,' nodded Parsons. 'Dear God, I knew it would all come out one day. I'm trying to live it down. . . . The Army. . . .'

'Where?' asked Davies stonily.

'No, not the convenience. I took them to the convenience when I tried to put them back, after I'd realized that they were that girl's things. But I lied about finding them there. I was just all confused and upset, Mr Davies.'

'Where?' repeated Davies grimly. His heart jerked when Parsons said. 'By the canal. They were just lying there. I nicked them. But when I heard about the girl I panicked and took them to the convenience. That's when they copped me. I couldn't tell them the truth about where I got them. I was already on probation, and they knew I collected things from lines and that. They tried to get me for that girl, Mr Davies, and I didn't do it. I stuck to my story, every detail. And they couldn't break me.' A small triumph had entered his voice. Davies leaned out in the half-dark and caught him by the collar. Parsons stifled a squeak. 'They could . . . you know . . . hang you in those days,' he stammered.

'That's what they all say,' said Davies remembering Lind. 'Now *exactly* where, Mr Parsons? To the inch.'

Parsons face was shining with sweat in the dark. 'Yes, yes,' he nodded. 'Exactly. Just at the bottom of the alley. Where the old wartime blockhouse used to be. Just there. I was walking down the alley, towards the canal and I saw them. I was tempted by Satan and I picked them up. God, how many times I've regretted that weakness.'

Davies could feel himself smiling painfully within the helmet of his dressings. 'Lovely,' he breathed. 'Lovely. At the bottom of the alley, right. At the foot of those gardens, allotments.'

'It was there,' nodded Parsons. 'By the allotments.'

'Right,' said Davies. 'You can go back to your oompah-pah, now. Have a good blow. But don't piss off to any band festivals or anything. I want to know where I can find you.'

'That's all then?'

'Yes, that's all. Why was there anything else?'

'No. Oh no. I'll be going back.'

Davies said: 'All right. Play a tune for me.'

Parsons ran gratefully up the grimy stairs. To satisfy his friends in his room he called over the banisters. 'Goodnight Mr Davies. And God Bless. I'll pray for you in your trouble.'

It was eleven-thirty when Davies roused Mr Chrust and his two sisters-in-law from their beds above the newspaper office. The same lights and the same entranced faces materialized. They shuffled about and opened the door for him, a strong family politeness apparently preventing them asking how he came to be swathed in ghostly bandages. He did not keep them long from their rest. It was merely a matter of checking the recent issues of the *Citizen* for the report of the prosecution of the vegetable garden thief. Davies noted his name, George Tilth, 47, Harrow Gardens. He thanked Mr Chrust and said a muffled goodnight to the ladies of the place. Then he went to see Mr Tilth.

He was relieved to perceive that it was not yet bedtime in the Tilth household. There were lights downstairs in the modest terraced house and Mr Tilth answered his knock fully clothed and appropriately cradling a squat potted plant.

'I don't suppose you remember me?' began Davies.

'I can't see you for a start,' replied Mr Tilth reasonably. 'Not through all that first-aid stuff. Who are you anyway?'

'Police,' said Davies. 'Detective Constable Davies.'

The man went white as lime. 'I've done nothing, officer,' he protested. He glanced down at the pot-plant as a woman might look at her nursing baby. 'This is mine. I grew it all by myself.'

'All right, all right,' calmed Davies. 'I haven't come about anything like that. You're the man who knows all about gardens and I want some information.'

'Information? Horticultural information?'

'Yes, you could say that. Can I come in for a moment?'

Mr Tilth nodded. 'Yes, all right,' he agreed. 'I've got nothing to conceal, Mr Davies. But perhaps you wouldn't mind just waiting here for a moment.'

Davies loitered while from the front room of the house came the sounds of furtive but urgent movements. He was tempted to step in but he knew he coud not spoil it now for anything. Eventually Mr Tilth returned, a guilty flush replacing the former pallid countenance. 'Yes, it's all right now. To come in. Just wanted to get the place tidy for you. You don't expect visitors at this time of night, do you? Not generally.'

'Not generally,' acknowledged Davies. He walked in. Even through his mask of dressings he could smell a greenhouse damp. He went into the front room where a table was covered with newspaper, flower pots, plants and scattered compost.

'Taking cuttings,' explained Mr Tilth.

'Messy job.' Davies glanced around as he was guided towards a chair at the table. A large clothes-horse hung with towels had been awkwardly placed in the corner of the room, strategically, but not so strategically that it completely concealed the fronds of a palm tree coyly curling over its edge. Davies sat down. 'Mr Tilth,' he said firmly. 'This visit is unconnected with any dealings you may have had with the police previously. I want to assure you of that.' He hesitated then rephrased it. 'No, that's not strictly true. It *is* to do with that.' He watched the consternation cram into the man's face. 'But not in the way you think. I want your help.'

'Well, what is it, Mr Davies?' asked Mr Tilth, still not convinced.

'Your allotment. The one by the canal.'

'As was,' said Mr Tilth. 'It's not mine any more. Like I said in court, the Council took it away from me. After all those years of work.'

'Yes, it's the years I'm interested in. Your ownership went back to 1951 didn't it? Before that even.'

'Back to the nineteen forties,' asserted the man a glimmer of pride rising in his eyes. 'In the dark days of nineteen-forty, when Britain stood alone. And it was my old father's before that. Like I told them in court, it's been our 'eritage, that allotment.'

'You remember when the wartime blockhouse that was built along the bottom, by the canal.'

'Blimey, I'll say. We had our nursery bed there and they came and built that bloody thing. I had a real row with the Home Guard captain or whatever he was. Told him, I did, that I was doing more for the war-effort than him and his tin bleeding soldiers. And he tried to tell me that it was there to *defend* my sprouts and my spuds from the Germans. Load of horse-shit.'

Davies let him finish. 'When was it knocked down?' he asked.

'Oh, a couple of years after the war,' considered the man. 'About forty-seven, forty-eight, I'd say.'

Davies felt his hopes sigh as they deflated. 'Not later. Not nineteen-fifty-one?'

'No. Definitely not. My dad died in forty-nine and it was gone then. I remember I was annoyed when they knocked it down in the end because it was useful for keeping tools and that. But it was gone in forty-nine because I remember putting the garden shed what we built and the cold frames we had. I remember putting them on the base of the thing, the concrete foundation.'

'Oh, what a pity,' muttered Davies.

The man regarded him, for the first time, with some measure of curiosity. He sniffed thoughtfully. 'And that was in forty-nine,' he repeated. 'Definitely.'

Davies rose wearily. His face was beginning to ache. The soreness below the bandages was making him shudder. 'Right then,' he said. 'It was just an idea I had that's all.'

'It must have been an important idea, Mr Davies, for you to come around here in that state,' He glanced apprehensively towards the corner where the palm, like a disobedient child, was poking its head around the clothes horse meant to be concealing it. 'It wasn't for nothing else, then, was it?'

'No, no,' Davies assured him. 'Nothing else.' He went to the front door. He wondered why the man had not asked him to go into the kitchen since the front room had proved such an embarrassment. Perhaps the kitchen would have been even more so.

At the front door they lingered for a moment. The night air felt cold coming in through the triangular eye, nose and mouth gap of the dressing. 'That bit of the allotment was never any good for growing things,' said the man reflectively. 'It wasn't just the concrete floor. We might have got that up, I suppose. But underneath there, that was another room, see. . . .'

The poor man thought Davies had attacked him. He jumped clear from the ground as he was caught by the detective's hands. 'A room? Underneath?' demanded Davies hoarsely. 'A room?'

'Let me go!' pleaded Mr Tilth. Davies dropped him. From his enclosed face his eyes shone. The garden man trembled. 'Yes, that's right, a room underneath. It was a sort of command post, I suppose, for the Home Guard. Like an air-raid shelter would be. There was a trap door, a sort of metal cover, like a manhole.'

'And when they knocked the blockhouse down, they left the other bit under the ground? So it's still there? And there's a trap-door?'

'Still there,' confirmed the man more steadily. His anxiety was now becoming overtaken by curiosity. 'Why?'

'Come on,' said Davies taking his hand like a child. 'We're going down there.'

'What now?' The man backed away. 'At this hour of night.'

'There's no better time,' insisted Davies. 'Come on. Now.'

'I'll . . . I'll get my coat and tell the missus,' said Mr Tilth. He backed away still staring at the glowing Davies. A female voice called down the stairs. 'I'm getting my coat,' the man called up. 'I'm going out.'

'Are they taking you in?' inquired the woman, as though it was thoroughly expected.

'Shut up, for God's sake,' Mr Tilth called back. 'I'm going to help the detective.'

'That's what they always say,' returned the woman stoicly. She came down two stairs from the top and Davies could see her thin shins trapped in large furry slippers. 'Helping the police with their inquiries,' she taunted. 'That's what they say.'

'Mr Tilth is not being arrested for anything,' Davies called up to her. 'He has some valuable information for the police, that's all. We won't be long.'

As they went out into the street she creaked open an upstairs window and leaned out. 'It's a bleeding trick mate,' she called to her husband. 'Don't you admit nothing.'

'Go to bed for Christ's sake,' ordered the gardener.

'All right,' she returned angrily. 'But don't expect me to wait for you to come out of prison this time. Don't say I didn't warn you.'

'Silly mare,' commented Mr Tilth. They said nothing more. It was about ten minutes' walk and they went silently through the hollow streets. Davies was conscious of a shiver in his stomach. He increased their pace. They crossed the main road and then went down along the bank of the canal. It was a dark night and they could not see the water, only sense it and hear its fidgeting. The lamp at the bridge stood in the distance like a mariners' lighthouse; under it there was a reflected yellow sheen on the dull water and its illumination touched the boundary hedge of the allotments.

'I'm glad I'm with you,' said Mr Tilth. 'The magistrate told me that the next time I came here I'd get three months minimum.' He looked at Davies and even in the dark Davies could discern the question all over his face. 'It *is* all right, isn't it?'

'Don't worry,' Davies said ambiguously. 'We won't be here long.'

'I wish I knew what we're going to do.'

'Well, we've not come after turnips or sprouts,' said Davies. 'Not this time.'

The man obligingly showed him the easiest place to climb over the hedge and then followed him into the garden. It was an inhospitable patch, draped with cold darkness, damp rising to the knee. In a strange manner the crammed town seemed to have vanished. They might have been standing in a bog. Davies's attention went straight to the end of the plot.

'He's got his greenhouse on it,' sniffed Mr Tilth. 'Rickety old thing.'

Davies walked slowly along the garden path. The greenhouse stood like a beached ship, a faint light coming through its ribs. The ground around was muddy, but Mr Tilth scratched the surface expertly with his shoe and Davies touched the concrete underneath.

'Where was the entrance, the trap door?' he whispered.

'About here,' said Mr Tilth. 'He's got the greenhouse over the top of it.' He took a pace forward and opened the wheezy door of the wooden-framed building. Davies saw the whole structure wobble at the touch.

'Bloody awful old thing, this,' the other man complained. 'Rotten. The wooden ones always fall to bits in the end.'

'Is it inside, the trapdoor?' asked Davies anxiously. He shone the torch to get his answer. It illuminated a small glade of pots and plants.

'A mess, just like I thought,' grumbled Mr Tilth. 'Look at that Fatsia, Mr Davies. Ever see such a disgrace?' He pulled at a large leaf like a hand and it obediently came adrift from its stalk. He looked to the floor. 'It's all wooden boards,' he said. 'I thought he might have concreted it over again, but he wouldn't bother. Not him.'

'Good for him,' remarked Davies. 'Where's the trap door then? Where is it?'

'Let's see. It would just about be at the far end, as I remember.' He bent with the torch. 'He's got a whole lot of Pelegorams overwintering just there.' He sniffed. 'This lot won't see the spring, anyway.' He began to shift the pots without care, tossing them to both sides. There followed some seed boxes and then a brief struggle with some rotten planks which formed the floor. The debris began to pile up on the side. Eventually Mr Tilth straightened up. 'There it is,' he said simply.

Davies almost fell forward, stumbling in his bulky coat over the short planks, seed boxes and plastic flower plots. Mr Tilth was shining the torch downward. It illuminated a rusty metal cover, a yard square, fitted deep into the ground. Davies felt a frightening expectation. 'We'll need a shovel and a pick,' he whispered. 'Can you find them?'

'I might have to break the toolshed lock,' said Mr Tilth with patent hope.

'Do it then.'

'Right. Won't be a minute. The shed's rotten as well. This bloke's got no idea. No idea at all.'

He went out leaving Davies crouched in almost prayer-like attitude in front of the rusty metal square. He leaned forward, tapped it with his fist and backed minutely away as though expecting an answer.

A busy splintering of wood came from the darkness outside and then a grunt of accomplishment. Mr Tith loomed behind them with a spade and a pickaxe. 'You'd better let me do it,' the gardener suggested. 'I know the best way. And with your face all like that. . . .'

Davies did not ponder the logic of the statement. He stood back and let the man go to work with a nocturnal professionalism. In that confined place it was like digging in a coal mine. Small cargoes of stony earth came back as Mr Tilth cleaned the fringe of the metal plate. Eventually he stopped and remarked quietly over his shoulder. 'There's a sort of metal ring at one end. If we can hook the toe of the pickaxe into it we might be able to see if it's going to shift.'

Eagerly Davies passed the pickaxe to him. He was feeling sweaty now, with the inherent warmth of the greenhouse, his heavy clothes, his bandages and his mounting excitement. Mr Tilth took the tool and manoeuvred while Davies shone the torch between his legs, the only convenient aperture. The point of the implement eventually engaged the ring and Davies heard it creak as the ring moved on its hinge. 'Right, let's give it a try,' suggested Mr Tilth. 'Let me have a go first.' His small muscular body bent in the dimness but there was no answering scrape from the horizontal trap. He tried again, fiercely, but then gave it up. 'Good and fixed,' he panted. 'Been fixed for too long.'

'Let's both have a go,' suggested Davies. With difficulty he found space beside Mr Tilth, pushing plants and pots roughly aside to make room. There were two benches now confining them, one on each side. Mr Tilth straightened up and with dark enjoyment tipped one of them on its side sending a further avalanche of nurtured greenery to the floor. Davies took the cue and capsized the other. 'Serve the bugger right,' muttered the deposed gardener happily.

They now had room to both hold the pick. The area of the trap had been cleared but it seemed to have rusted into the very earth. The point of the pick was still engaged in the corroded ring. 'Right,' said Davies. 'Let's try it.'

They both bore down on the handle, seeking to lever the plate from its setting. Nothing happened. They eased off and rested, panting, then tried again. This time they felt it move. 'Steady a minute,' said Davies. They relaxed. 'Next time it'll come.'

It did. They felt it shudder and then begin to move upwards towards them. Davies knew he was shaking with anticipation. 'Keep it up,' he snorted. 'Another good one.'

Then the handle came out of the pickaxe. They were heaving their utmost when it happened and the release sent them violently staggering back. The considerable weight of Davies, followed by Mr Tilth, collided with the flimsy end wall of the greenhouse behind them. The rotting wood bulged, buckled and collapsed, splintered and split all about them, the panes of glass sliding like a glacier over a precipice. With a sigh the rest of the greenhouse followed the collapse, sagging forward and easing itself gratefully to the ground. It fell with no great sound as though it had been awaiting the moment for years. It stretched itself out, some of the glass breaking, but most of the panes simply slithering away. Davies and Mr Tilth found themselves lying under a blanket of wreckage.

'Oh dear.' said Mr Tilth inadequately. 'That's fucking done it.'

Davies dragged himself clear and he and the gardener got to their feet beside what now appeared to be the debris of some disastrous Zeppelin.

'Come on,' said Davies limping around to the rear of the wreckage. Mr Tilth, who was patently enjoying himself on what he saw as some sort of licensed destruction, wiped the wood-dust from his eyes and followed. 'Ah, that's good,' said Davies. Mr Tilth followed his downward look. The wall's falling the opposite way had almost cleared the metal plate. It required only a few random pushes with their shoes to clear away some stray wood and glass and there it was as exposed as before. 'Can you get the pick,' said Davies almost absently.

'The pick's no bloody good,' answered Mr Tilth. 'The man can't even look after his tools. Anyway we've loosened it up, what we want now is some wire. There's some hanging outside his shed. Hang on, Mr Davies. Just hang on.'

He returned quickly with the wire, it was stout and tough. They hooked and bent it around the upturned ring and then moving to the side, clear of the debris, they heaved on it like a tug-of-war team. They felt the metal shift, scrape, then shift again. Another effort, another taking of the strain, and they heard the whole plate come away. Just ahead of them, in the dark, was a hole.

'Now what?' asked Mr Tilth.

He looked through the night in surprise. Davies was merely standing there, stiff, as though unable to make the final move. 'Now what, indeed,' he said and his voice trembled over the few words. They had put the torch on the ground and now he reached for it and went deliberately towards the square aperture they had opened in the earth. Mr Tilth stood back, wondering, in the manner of someone watching a secret ritual they do not comprehend. Davies reached the hole and stood looking down, still not shining the torch into the opening. Then he did.

It shone immediately on the bones. A pathetic, lonely pile of cold, damp bones. Davies kneeled and looked closer. The torch wavered in his hands. He felt a huge engulfing sadness rising in his throat. Tears flooded his eyes. 'Oh, Celia,' he muttered. 'What a rotten trick.'

CHAPTER EIGHTEEN

In the morning the ward sister stopped by his bed and said: 'Ah, there, now you look a whole lot better for a good night's sleep.'

Since he had not returned to his bed before three o'clock he raised his eyebrows as far as he was able. She could only see the triangle of his face between eyes and point of chin, a small area from which to judge that someone was looking better, so he concluded that it was just hospital small talk. Nevertheless after two hours a doctor examined him and said he could go home but had to return every day to the out-patients' department. He went gladly.

Mod was at his desk in the library, like an archbishop wallowing in his books. As Davies walked into the foyer, and paused to smile gratefully at the Home Guard photograph on the wall, he could see a girl from the staff taking Mod a cup of coffee at the distant end of the reference room.

He walked in, evoking disapproving looks from staff and customers, people in bandages apparently being unwelcome. Mod saw him coming and smiled felicitations.

'All better, then, son?' he whispered drinking the coffee above the pages of the open volume before him. 'Glad to see you out.'

Davies sat down and stared from the aperture in his bandages. 'I've found her,' he said simply. 'I've found the body.'

Mod jerked a wave of coffee over the side of the cup and on to the printed page. His sharp and guilty look was followed by a swift sweep of his sleeve to wipe it away. 'Where?' he asked.

Davies told him where and how it had taken place. 'I remembered that Home Guard photo out in the lobby there,' he said. 'It's got a picture of the blockhouse that used to be along by the canal. It's been knocked down, but it had a basement room, a kind of concrete operations room. That's where he put her. Down there.'

Mod's library whisper whistled across the table. 'What did you do?'

'I left her there,' Davies said simply. 'I pulled the cover back and left her there. I've told the gardening bloke, Mr Tilth, that if he says a word to anyone I'll investigate the theft of a palm tree, which he's got standing in his living room at the moment. That scared him. He won't tell.'

'You won't do anything? Not report it?'

Davies shook his head, still a painful achievement. 'I'm going to risk it, Mod,' he said. 'I've got *her* but I haven't got *him* yet.'

'It looks more and more like our policeman friend,' muttered Mod. 'Police Constable Dudley. And he's dead. So you'll never get him,' He touched the coffee-damp pages of his book then closed it. 'Nobody will open that again for a few years anyway,' he shrugged. 'By that time it won't matter, will it.'

'Sounds like a summing up of our case,' said Davies. 'I don't know what to do next, Mod.'

'You would have thought that places like that underground room would have been searched when they were looking for the girl,' said Mod thoughtfully. 'You know police with tracker dogs, like you see on the television.'

Davies said: 'Well, to start with nobody took her disappearance all that seriously for about a month. I mean she was seventeen, it wasn't a little kid vanishing, and she'd gone off before, remember. There was a search but we'll never know how thorough it was. Perhaps P.C. Dudley got that area allocated to himself during the search. That wouldn't be all that difficult. Remember a *policeman* actually went to see Mr Whethers, but nothing was ever done, as far as we know, about that statement, or about following up whatever the other old chap, Mr Harkness saw, or thought he saw. Was that policeman P.C. Dudley as well? Remember Mr Whethers never actually reported what he saw. The policeman *came of his own accord* after hearing the stories going around the district.'

'Perhaps *nobody* at the police station wanted that evidence to come out,' sniffed Mod.

Davies looked at him steadily. 'Yes,' he said slowly. 'I hadn't thought of that. I suppose that's possible.'

'On the evidence,' added Mod. 'Half the force were pissed out of their minds that night. One, who should have been on duty, was screwing a fortune teller, and another, who was also on duty, was committing rape and murder. Join London's police for a worthwhile career.'

Davies scowled at him. 'All right, all right. It's all "mights and maybes" though, isn't it.' He paused, then inquired. 'I don't suppose you've got your dole money yet, have you?'

'Social Security,' corrected Mod. 'No. I get paid tomorrow.'

'I thought so. I was toying with the idea of you buying me a drink.'

'I'll accompany you,' said Mod closing the books with finality. 'And, if you'll honour me with a loan, I'll buy the drinks, repaying the debt tomorrow.' He looked doubtfully at Davies's head. 'I can't see you getting a pint glass in that little window in the bandages,' he said.

'I'll have to drink shorts,' replied Davies. He waited while Mod replaced his books on the various shelves. 'Amazing, you know,' said Mod as they made for the door. 'The period from 3000 B.C. to 500 B.C., two thousand five hundred years in Britain was a time of almost uninterrupted peace and progress.'

'I'm pleased to hear it,' replied Davies soberly.

'Due to the fact that nobody really *wanted* anything,' said Mod. 'There were only a few tribes, and lots of land for their needs and plenty of room for invaders. It has also been said that the people turned from worshipping the Gods of War, which had always attracted the menfolk, to worshipping the Gods of Fertility and the like, which were kind of

Women's Lib. Gods.'

'I bet the police force was crooked,' suggested Davies. He tapped the Home Guard picture affectionately as they reached the foyer. Mod nodded at it sagely. 'What are you going to do next?'

'Well, one thing I want to do and that is tell Josie nearly everything.'

'Nearly? You won't tell her you've found the body?'

'No. I won't tell her that.'

They walked along the shut and shadowed street. It was eleven-thirty and urban cats were beginning to sound and wander. Once more everybody for miles about seemed to have gone home and locked their doors against the night. The crowds were in their beds. They had abandoned the town to the dark.

Josie's footfalls progressed deftly along the pavements while Davies's large feet made only a muffled scraping in the gutter. He chose to walk there so as to bring their heights somewhere into proximity although, even with the adjustment he still looked down at her.

His overcoat hung largely about him while she was small and neatly wrapped as a package. They walked without touching or speaking. He had not told her that he had found her sister's body.

Close to her house was one of the district's innumerable alleys, afterthoughts, shortcuts, planning compromises, sprouting through the lines of streets. As they went past she caught his large hand and encouraged him into its darkness. He stood there, awkward as ever, she with her back to somebody's fence, he facing her but only touching her by placing his hands lightly about her waist. She regarded him morosely in the gloom.

'Oh, Dangerous,' she said. 'You'll never make a teenager.'

'I can't remember being much of a teenager even when I was one,' he confessed wryly. 'And now I'm a bit far gone for necking against fences.'

'God,' she sighed. 'You stand there like a dummy from Burton's window. Have a go at kissing me. Go on.'

He eased forward from the waist and her face rose to kiss him. They had taken some more of his bandages off that day so that his face was now exposed although he still looked oddly like a man peering through a window. With the kiss she pushed her slight body closer to him, unbuttoning the overcoat, briskly as she did so. He folded it protectively about her. They had spent half an hour that evening going over his notes written on the paper appropriated from Minnie Banks, the school teacher.

'I'm glad you've told me everything,' she said. 'About Celia.' Then she repeated: 'That's if it is everything.'

'There are further inquiries,' he said looking down at the crown of her dark hair.

'Further inquiries,' she mocked gently. 'You can't help sounding like a copper, can you?' Then she said: 'You remember that day by the Welsh Harp you told me that Percival was your proper name. Well it's not, is it.'

'I lied,' he said. 'It's Peregrine.'

'Bugger off,' she sighed.

There was a long enclosed silence from within the coat. Then she said: 'Dangerous, I've got something to tell you.'

'He laughed gently and patted her on top of her head. 'What is it?' he asked.

'I've found something out.'

'What?'

'My father *does* know where Ramscar is.'

He eased her away and looked down at the defined, pale face. 'Where is he?' he asked.

'I said *he* knows, *I* don't,' she replied. 'I wasn't going to tell you. You've had enough beatings-up as it is. But I've begun thinking you ought to know.'

'What's he told you?'

'I didn't tell you before, but he had a heart attack yesterday. In the hospital. Brought on by being duffed up. It wasn't much as heart attacks go, but it's scared the living daylights out of him. He thinks he'll die if he has another one. I went to see him and tonight he was in a terrible state. He's got all confessional. He started doing the "my dearest daughter" act,' she laughed caustically. 'After all these bloody years.' She glanced up at his chin. He was still waiting. 'Ramscar's up to something very big, according to the old man. And very soon.'

'What sort of thing?'

'I don't know. Even the old man doesn't. But I reckon he's got a good idea where Ramscar is hanging out. That's why he feels safer in hospital.'

'He's probably right,' nodded Davies. He looked at her steadily. 'Will you find out for me?'

She did not reply at once, but remained hidden inside his coat. 'I'll think about it,' she told eventually. 'But I'm not making any promises.'

'If we know where he is we can wind up the whole business,' said Davies. 'Get him.'

'Will you put your hands inside my dress for a minute, Dangerous?' she asked. 'If I undo the buttons.'

Bemused at her habitual change of direction he did not say anything. But she undid the buttons on the front of her dress, carefully, and took his hands and pushed them inside against some material covering her small breasts. He could feel the brief point of each nipple. He bent forward and kissed her on the face. 'What's this thing you've got underneath?' he asked.

'A vest,' she responded simply. 'My mum makes me wear a vest this weather. Even now she's up at Luton I still wear it. A promise is a promise. She knitted it herself. Yards of it. It goes down for miles, Dangerous. Here, go on, give it a pull.'

Smiling, he did as she instructed. Using both hands he began to tug at the vest and it came up, and continued coming up, from somewhere in her nether regions. Josie giggled. 'I told you. There's yards of it. It's like a bale of bloody cloth.'

Eventually the garment was assembled above her waist, making her dress bulge spectacularly. She laughed quietly and gave a mischievous wriggle. It fell down, dropping beyond her skirt and hanging to her knees. Davies clasped her to him. 'Do you want to come in the house?' she asked. 'It's empty.'

'I thought you were staying with some other family,' he said anxiously. 'I hope you're not in the house by yourself.'

'I'm not,' she assured him. 'I'm living with the Fieldings two doors up. But I've still got our key.'

'It's time you got some sleep,' he said gently. He put his arms protectively about her. 'When it's all done,' he said. 'All finished. Then I'm going to take some leave.'

'And you'll take me too?'

'If you'll come. When I was a boy I was sent to Stoke-on-Trent once. I've always thought of going back.'

'It sounds dreamy,' she said. 'I've still got a week of my holiday to come. Stoke-on-Trent.!'

'You'd better go,' he said. They kissed seriously and he helped her to tuck the extraordinary vest away. Then they walked along the street to the house where she was staying. He said goodnight and she went into the house. He had walked a few yards down the street when the door opened behind him and Josie came out again to the pavement. 'Dangerous,' she called. There was something different in her voice. 'The hospital phoned. He's had another heart attack. I've got to go.'

He waited until two o'clock in the painfully familiar surroundings of the hospital. It was cold and desolate in the waiting room. When she came out he saw that she had dried tears smudged about her eyes.

'He snuffed it,' she said. 'Six minutes past one.'

He had often wondered at the curiosity of people recording the exact weight of a baby at birth and the precise time of death. Why not the time of birth and the weight at death? 'I'm sorry, Josie,' he said drawing her kindly to him.

'He thought I was Celia,' she shrugged.

He telephoned a taxi and they sat in the waiting room until it arrived. They said very little either there or on the journey to the house of her friends. As she got out of the taxi and the front door of the house opened, she kissed him dumbly on the cheek. 'Ramscar's at a place called Bracken Farm,' she said. 'Uxbridge way.'

It was ten miles away, part of the dead land between the town and eventual country, a place of pig farms, scrap yards, small untidy fields and struggling hedgerows. Davies collected the Lagonda and drove out there through the cold, early hours. Kitty moaned grotesquely for the first part of the journey, taking unhappily to being disturbed, but then settled to a bronchial sleep under the tarpaulin once more. Davies did not tell anyone he was going. It hardly occurred to him. He had his own score to settle.

He had telephoned the Uxbridge fire brigade to find out the farm's location. He did not want to ask the police. It was at the end of a rutted

lane off the main Oxford road. He drove down it carefully, headlights
out, threading the Lagonda between piles of rubbish, wrecked vehicles
and other peripheral trash. There was a gipsy encampment one field
away and his approach set some dogs baying. He cursed them. He could
see lights ahead, a high illuminated window, which he thought might be
a watching point. He pulled the car close into a farm gate and went
studiously forward on foot.

Everything about him smelled damp. Mud eased from beneath his feet
with stifled sighs. There were two big cars standing in the yard of the
farm. The house looked substantial but unkempt even at night. Apart
from the light in the high upper window there were two lit but red
curtained windows on the ground floor. He moved, large but silent, into
the yard. He touched the bonnet of the nearest car. It was warm. So was
the next one. He intended to try and get to the window, but he guessed
there would be someone left outside to keep guard. He saw the man come
around the corner of the house while he was shadowed by the cars. The
man was lighting a cigarette and grumbling to himself. Davies got on his
hands and knees and shuffled to the door of what looked to be an outside
lavatory. It was a coalhouse. His eyes were accustomed now to the dark.
There was a scattering of coal on the floor and a coal shovel by the wall.

Davies could hear the man moving about outside. Then he walked
right past the open door of the outhouse. Davies picked up the shovel. It
was the normal household implement, fashioned from one piece of metal,
the handle formed by turning the metal into a short tube. Pointing the
tube forward, Davies left his concealment. The man was standing only
four yards away smoking and looking out to the anonymity of the ragged
night. Davies approached and pushed the circular end of the shovel into
the pit of the watcher's back.

The man went stiff, but he could feel the round impression well
enough. 'Drop your shooter on the ground,' said Davies. 'Behind you.'
With a shrug the man reached in his pocket and dropped his gun on
Davies's toe. Davies picked it up.

'Right, we're going to walk towards the house.'

The man spoke. 'The whole lot's in there,' he said quietly as if trying to
convey a favour. 'If there's any shooting, mate, I don't want to be in it. I
don't reckon this fucking thing at all.'

'How many?' asked Davies.

'Seven,' said the man.

'I've got the place surrounded by hundreds,' Davies told him. 'Just
walk. Now.'

The progressed gingerly along the narrow path of the farm's front
garden, like partners on a high wire. Fifteen feet from the door was an
empty dustbin. Davies noted it grimly. Then he whispered for his captive
to stop. 'I'm going to make things difficult for you, son,' he said quietly.
'But, get this, if you try anything, or make a row, I'll shoot you. Got that?'

'Got it,' nodded the man. Davies bent and sweetly put the dustbin over
the man's head and shoulders. The man shivered and staggered for a
moment, but recovered and stood there like some strange midnight

robot. Davies jogged him forward with the coal shovel. He had the gun but he used the shovel in case the man should know the gun was not loaded. They went to the door.

It was a big Georgian door and Davies saw with satisfaction that his dustbinned prisoner would be able to get in. There was a low brass doorknob. He turned it and the door swung in. He pushed the man forward into the room. 'My old man's a dustman,' he announced walking into the room. 'Anyone move and they're a goner.'

A group of men were sitting around a table eating fish and chips. All the faces came up and around to him. He recognized Ramscar at once. 'I've come for you, Ramscar,' he said.

'Fuck it,' said Ramscar taking a chip from his mouth.

A small, tanned man, sitting at the nearside of the table suddenly jumped up and, with a wild cry, ran towards Davies. Davies banged him on his approaching head with the coal shovel, but the diversion had been enough. In a moment they had rushed him. They came like a rugby scum flying across the room. They hit him from all directions at once and he felt himself reeling. There were shots and he felt his legs burning. Then lights. But somehow more logical than the usual exploding lights in his head. Someone shouted: 'Piss off, there's coppers outside.'

Before he tumbled to what he now recognized as unconsciousness Davies looked up to see the face of a strange police inspector. 'Just right,' Davies managed to smile. 'Everything okay?'

'Great,' grunted the inspector. 'Except the bloke you crowned with the shovel is a bloody American ambassador.'

The desk sergeant was looking through the crime book for the local reporter when Davies propelled his wheeled chair through the police station door. The lady cleaner and Venus, who was just on her way to her evening patrol had helped him up the outside steps.

'Interesting one here,' said the sergeant. 'Theft of rare minute palms from Kew Gardens. General to all stations, this . . .'. He saw Davies and came round the counter to shake his hand. 'So glad you're all right, Dangerous. The old man's upstairs. I'll help you with the lift.'

The sergeant and the reporter got him into the lift. He knocked on Inspector Yardbird's door with his toe and after the customary pause Yardbird called him to go in.

His wheeled chair rolled through the office door. They had re-bandaged his head and set his right leg and left ankle in plaster. There as not much they could do about the bruising on his ribs except let it heal. The nurses had given him a joke season-ticket to the hospital.

Yardbird looked up from behind his desk. 'Ah, jolly good. I think we did jolly well, Davies,' he said.

Davies moved his head gingerly. 'Yes, sir, I think we did.'

'We . . . ee . . . ll, we got Ramscar, which was the whole object of my plan from the very beginning, as you will appreciate, Davies. And that's a feather in the cap of the division. On the other hand to hit a United States diplomat on the head with a coal shovel was pretty unfortunate.'

'I'm sorry,' shrugged Davies. Every movement seemed to hurt. 'I didn't know who he was. I thought he was one of the gang. Nobody told me.'

'We *couldn't* tell every Tom, Dick and Harry, Davies,' yawned Yardbird. 'It would have been gossiped all around the place. We knew that Ramscar was lying low because he was involved in something big, much bigger than anything he had done before. We knew he had become involved with what we call "Overseas Interests" you understand.'

'Yes. I understand,' said Davies.

'And these Interests had decided to kidnap this American wallah on his way to the Airport. Which they did, of course, but fortunately we nailed them.'

'Oh yes, we nailed them,' replied Davies.

'Quite a feather in the cap of the division, as I mentioned.'

'Yes sir, you said.'

'Once I'd got you to actually concentrate on the proper job in hand, it worked like a charm, didn't it? We got Ramscar.' For the first time Yardbird got from behind his desk. He kicked the wheel of the invalid chair as though to make sure it was safe. 'Well,' he said. 'As I've said before this is all good experience for you.'

'Great experience,' agreed Davies.

'How long will it be?' He pushed his expression in the general direction of Davies's injuries. 'Couple of weeks?'

'Two months, they say,' said Davies. 'And a bit of convalescence just to get the feel of my legs again. I may go to Stoke-on-Trent.'

'You'll like that,' muttered Yardbird absently. 'In the meantime perhaps you'd like to give your thoughts to the business of who stole that brass bedstead from your lodgings. And the antique hall stand. That landlady of yours, what's her name, Mrs Brownjohn?'

'Mrs Fulljames,' said Davies.

'Yes, her. Stupid old cow. Button-holed me at the Chamber of Commerce Dinner the other evening and demanded that something be done about it. It does look a bit bad, I suppose, actually having a C.I.D. man in the house and having unsolved crime hanging about. Have you given it any consideration at all?'

'I've thought of very little else,' replied Davies. It did not appear to penetrate. Yardbird appeared submerged in worries.

'And there was another thing, while you're here. That idiotic dog of yours. It bit three policemen during the raid on the farm.'

Davies nodded. 'I know. It doesn't like coppers. It's had a go at me before now.'

'Well you must control it, you know. If not, have it put down. Might be the best way in the end. Get you into no end of bother.'

Davies said: 'Right, I'll see he behaves. And I'll think about the brass bedstead. Can I go now, sir? My arms get tired.'

'Yes, yes. Off you go. I'm busy as hell. And . . . Davies. . . .'

'Sir?'

'Keep out of aggravation, eh?'

As he went through the corridor Davies could clearly hear Yardbird laughing at his own joke.

Father Harvey trundled Davies in his wheeled chair alongside the canal. Davies was glad of the privacy because their progress through the High Street had been approaching the triumphal. People he did not recognize, but who clearly knew him intimately, approached to inquire about his injuries and to shake his hand. Mr Chrust appeared at the door of the newspaper office and had shown hiim a copy of the *Citizen* embellished by Davies's chair-borne photograph, while from the upper windows the sisters-in-law waved in bright sympathy. Madame Tarantella Phelphs-Smith hooted greetings from her door and shouted clairvoyant encour-agement: 'You'll be better soon. Your lucky colour is blue! Blue!' Even his wife Doris, shopping with Mrs Fulljames, had come out of the bakers and given him a jam doughnut. 'It's getting like the Entry of the Queen of Sheba,' commented Father Harvey.

Josie joined them at the canal bridge and helped to get the wheel chair down the inclined path to the canal bank. She walked with them hungrily nuzzling a lunchbag.

'I hear through my excellent intelligence services that a police award is to be made to you,' mentioned the priest. 'So your wounds will not have been entirely in vain.'

'Listen, Yardbird wouldn't recommend anyone for a sick pass let alone an award,' observed Davies. It was a nice day for that town at that time of year. Ducks followed the fitful sunshine on the straight water. Josie emptied the crumbs from her lunchbag into the canal. The ducks clamoured as though it were already spring.

'Somebody over the top of Yardbird has put you up,' said Father Harvey. 'I get to know these things. The confessional is not merely for the telling of sins, you know, Dangerous. It is useful for handy tit-bits of information.'

'How's the confessional box anyway?' inquired Davies over his shoulder.

'The new one is fine. Never heard better confessions. But the one I built myself was more frail than the parishioners, I'm afraid. Mrs Bryant, who becomes a trifle histrionic during the unburdening of her soul, put her elbow through one of the panels. So I rang the bishop and kicked up bloody hell and they've sent a new portable effort, in plastic you'll know, pending the arrival of a proper replacement. It was there, in that plastic shell, that I heard the whisper of your impending award.'

'Award?' grinned. '*I'm* the mug who did it all wrong. If Josie hadn't telephoned the police to say I was on my way to Bracken Farm I'd still be there now. Buried under the cow-shed.'

His voice slowed as they approached the footbridge, the three of them, the priest, the policeman and the poppet, and fifteen yards away, beyond the allotment hedge, Celia Norris was buried. He glanced at Josie. She was devouring a yoghurt from a small tub. 'I thought you'd have the sense to go with other coppers,' she said. A strawberry blob squatted on her chin, like Celia again. She wiped it away. 'I thought even *you* would have the bleeding gumption to do that, Dangerous. But then, when I got in the house, I thought probably you *wouldn't* have the bleeding gumption. So I rang nine-nine-nine.'

Although they talked, Davies's awareness of their location and his sadness because of it, seeped to the others. They turned at the bridge and, now silent, went back the way they came. The ducks, spotting their return, queued up hopefully. A water rat dropped without fuss into the brown depths. 'Dangerous,' said Josie suddenly. 'How old is Doris?'

'Doris? God knows. thirty or thereabouts.'

'And Mod?'

'Mod's in his forties. I think.'

'You think. Do you know the age of *anyone* in that house of yours?'

'No . . . no, I don't think I actually do.'

'Father Harvey,' she pursued. 'How old do you think I am?'

'Ah, it's a game,' decided the priest. 'Well, let me see. Oh, you're a young girl. What nineteen, twenty or so.'

'It's funny,' she said thoughtfully. 'When my father died the other week, I didn't know how old he was. And I'm not sure about my mother. I'm seventeen.'

'Davies was eyeing her. 'What are you getting at, Josie?'

She laughed. 'Blimey, you look like Chief Ironside in that chair, Dangerous. On the television.'

He did not pursue it then. The priest got the invalid chair up to the road and then left them. Josie was to push it along the street to the library for the afternoon and Mod was to propel it to 'The Babe In Arms' at the opening time and then to 'Bali Hi', Furtman Gardens. The sunshine persisted uncannily. Around the power station cooling towers played small cherubs of steam. 'What was all that about people's ages' he asked.

Josie waved to a friend in the street. Then she began speaking as she pushed. 'It was just you said a funny thing, Dangerous. Before all the farm business, when you told me all about Celia. Or you *reckoned* you'd told me all. You remember when we went all through your notes? All on that school notepaper?'

'Yes, of course. What did I say?'

'About that old Mrs Whethers. You'd written down everything you remember her saying, right?'

'Right.'

'The old man. Mr Harkness. How old did she say he was when it all happened with Celia?'

'Seventy-six,' he said. 'And that was twenty-five years ago.'

'But according to her, she hardly *knew* him. She'd just heard that he'd seen something that night and she knew he'd been ill. *But to know that he was seventy-six, twenty-five years ago is very odd.* Not seventy-five, nor anything else. Exactly *seventy-six*.' She had halted the chair in the middle of the shopping street now and Davies was painfully half-turned around to her. She went around to the front of the chair and knelt, pretending to rearrange the rug around his legs.

'What did she say, exactly, this Mrs Whethers?' asked Josie. 'Have you got those notes?'

Davies hurriedly thrust his hand into the deep inside pocket of the overcoat. 'My favourite reading,' he said. He began to turn over the crammed scrawled pages of school paper. 'Here, it's here,' he said. 'Mrs Whethers. Ah, yes. She asked me how long ago the Celia business was and I said twenty-five years and she said. . . .'

'Mr Harkness was seventy-six,' Josie concluded. 'She knew his *exact* age, but she didn't know how long ago the murder was. What a funny thing.'

'She calculated it by deducting the twenty-five years. She was in no doubt, either. Seventy-six.'

'All I'm saying,' said Josie. She had gone behind and begun to push the chair again. 'Is that it's strange she knew his right age, but she didn't know him well. We've just tested you and Father Harvey out. People hardly ever know other people's ages. Sometimes not even their own family and friends.'

'So,' he said. 'There's got to be something special about Mr Harkness, so that she is quite sure of his age.'

She nodded. 'You've tumbled. I reckon he's still alive, Dangerous. And he's a hundred and one.'

CHAPTER NINETEEN

Mod pushed him all the way from the library to the Kensal Green Old Folks Club. It was the hardest afternoon's work he had done for twenty years.

The ancients were doing a *paso doble*, stamping worn feet and cracking rheumy hands over their heads, led by the fat and fiery dancing teacher. Mod was astounded at the activity. 'I wondered why none of them ever gets to the library,' he said.

They all stopped sympathetically when they saw him in the chair. 'Oh dear, oh dear,' said the dance teacher. 'Whatever have you been up to?'

'Practising,' said Davies.

'I knew you'd do yourself an injury,' she replied confidently. 'Altogether too unsupple. No rhythm.' She returned to the elderly class. 'Right old people,' she called. 'Finish for today. Let's all have one good clap and leave it there.'

They banged their hands together and those that had not already stiffened up during the pause stamped their feet a few token times, then spread out about the hall for teatime. Mrs Whethers, clucking sympathy, brought a free cup of tea for Davies but Mod had to pay for his own. They sat down in a triangle.

'Mrs Whethers,' said Davies. 'I'm sorry to bother you again but I wanted to ask you one more thing.'

'Fire away,' she said jovially. 'I didn't do it.'

'Indeed not. But, Mrs Whethers, is there any chance that Mr Harkness is still alive?'

She looked at him in astonishment. '*Of course* he's still alive!' she exclaimed. 'I took it for granted you knew that. He's a hundred and one. It was in the local paper back in the summer. He lives in Bristol with his daughter or somebody but she sent the bit of news to the *Citizen*.'

'He was seventy-six twenty-five years ago,' nodded Davies. 'That's how you knew his exact age. Because of his being a hundred and one.'

She smiled in an old way. 'I always was good at sums,' she said.

'And I thought we were talking about somebody who was dead,' he sighed. 'I must go and see him.'

'You'd better get those wheels turning, then,' she laughed. 'At a hundred and one you don't know where you'll be from one day to another. How about buying a ticket for the raffle?'

St Fridewide's Church had a van, fitted with seats for use on parish-outings and it was in this, with Father Harvey driving, that Davies journeyed to see Mr Harkness at Bristol. Fortunately the centenarian lived in a ground-floor flat and with Mod, who had never been to Bristol but had eruditely lectured on the place throughout the journey, pushing, the invalid chair was manoeuvred through the small entrance hall and into the old man's sitting room.

'He's still getting dressed,' his elderly daughter said. 'He takes his time at his age, you understand, but he won't let me help him. He says I'm too old to dress myself.' She was a grey tub of a lady. Davies wondered what her father would look like.

It was a pleasing apartment, its expansive front window framing the choppy water of the Bristol docks, with the enclosing land easing itself up from the shore on all sides. They could see the hull of Brunel's fine old ship *The Great Britain* lying in her special berth.

'That ship and my father are both over a century old,' she said. 'They sort of keep each other company.'

She asked them if they would like coffee. Father Harvey had parked the van and gone to visit a retired priest, a drinking companion of former days.

'Mr Harkness will be very glad to see you,' smiled his daughter. 'He was very excited when I told him you had telephoned. He loves to talk over old times. I told him you were a policeman and he seemed more taken with the idea than ever. This is quite a big day for him. He'll probably wear his red velvet jacket.' She went and listened at the door and then returned. 'Normally that's for birthdays only, his velvet jacket, although I don't suppose, at a hundred and one, he can hope to get a great deal more wear out of it now.' They were aware of a movement in the passage outside the room. 'Ah, I think he's arrived,' said the lady. She turned warningly. 'One thing I must tell you. Mr Harkness is deaf.'

Through the door shuffled the centenarian, almost pixielike in his smallness, a jovial pointed face, bright china eyes, and pink-cheeked. A little dewdrop dangled like a decoration from the tip of his nose. He wiped it away with the sleeve of his red velvet jacket. 'Hello, hello,' he greeted them. 'I'm Charlie Harkness. I'm a hundred and one years old.'

His very presence made them glad. Davies smiled, so did Mod. The daughter looked pleased.

'Sit down, sit down,' called the old man blithely. 'I'm a bit on the short side. They won't have to dig out much earth for me.' He cackled at his joke. They sat down grinning. He said he would like his morning milk with a few drops in it.

'I'm supposed to be deaf,' he confided when the lady had gone from the room. 'But I'm not as deaf as I make out. I only pretend to her because otherwise she rambles on all day, and I don't want to listen. You know how women get when they're knocking on in years. But if you get close enough to my left ear I'll be able to hear you fair enough. And I've got all my nuts and bolts too. So I'll know what you're talking about.' Davies had a mental picture of him in the witness box.

Mod was looking at one of a series of sere military pictures on the wall. 'You fought in Zululand, then Mr Harkness?' he remarked.

'Zululand? Oh, yes I was there. Fighting. Not that it did much good. They're all in Bristol now, you know. Last summer I went out for a bit of a stroll and there's blackies all over the place! I thought to myself at the time, last time I saw a Fuzzy-wuzzy as close as that he was stuck on the end of my lance.'

His daughter brought in a tray with the cups of coffee and the beaker of milk. Mr Harkness sniffed the milk to make sure she'd splashed the scotch in it. 'I heard what you said,' she reproved. 'About blackies. You can be sent to prison for saying things like that, these days. And Mr Davies is a policeman.'

'Blow it,' returned the old man. 'There's not a prison could hold me.' He stopped and considered Davies. 'Oh yes, you're from the force. I'd forgot that. What are you after, young man?'

Davies felt relieved that he had been saved the approach. 'It's something that happened a few years ago,' he said moving close to the ancient's ear. 'And I wondered if you would remember something about it. Back in London. Do you remember a girl called Celia Norris. . . .?'

The name did not register. Davies could see that. 'Oh I've known a few girls in my time. . . .' began the old man with customary joviality.

'She disappeared,' continued Davies. 'In fact it seems she was murdered.' He saw the alarm jump into the woman's face and she began to move forward protectively. But Mr Harkness pushed her away excitedly. 'Ah that. Oh, I remember that, all right. The night I fell in the canal.'

'What can you remember about it?' called Davies, relief warming him. 'Tell us everything you can remember.'

'Oh, I remember, I remember,' said Mr Harkness making a little song of it. 'I used to drink a little drop in those days. Well, I was a youngster then, in my seventies, I suppose. But that night just about put the end to my drinking, my big drinking anyway. Because I fell in the bleeding canal and I went home in wet things and I got bronchitis and pneumonia and all the rest of it. They thought I was going to collect my cards, I can tell you.'

'That was when I took him firmly in hand,' interrupted his daughter. 'I nursed him better and I kept him away from the bottle. My husband had just passed away and Mr Harkness was all I had. I've kept him well. Well enough to see a hundred and one.'

'For Christ's sake, don't go on so, Dulcie,' said Mr Harkness irritated. 'They've come to hear *me* not you. Why don't you take the cups out?'

'No,' she replied firmly. 'I'd like to hear what this is about. It all sounds a bit unpleasant to me.'

Davies nodded to her. She sat down and folded her hands in her rounded lap. Mr Harkness ignored her. 'Yes, I remember it.'

'Mr Harkness,' said Davies creeping close to the fragile ear. 'What exactly did you *see* that night? Did you see a girl?'

'I'd been to the Labour Club,' recalled the old man, determined to tell it his way. He closed his eyes reflectively. 'We used to have some very good times there at the Labour Club. You could get pissed there for a couple of bob in those days. Easy.' Dulcie drew in a deep breath but Davies's hand asked that she should not interrupt. The breath softened to a sigh.

'And that night I was drunk as a monkey. Hot summer that was and I'd taken on a load of ale, I can tell you. That's why I tumbled in the canal. Blind drunk. Blotto. I used to go home along the canal bank, like it was a short cut for me, and I was leaning over, I remember, trying to see myself in the water. Just where that lamp is on the bridge. Or was, I don't know whether it's there now.' He stopped. He seemed breathless. Davies turned to his daughter. 'Is he all right?' he whispered. 'I don't want to distress him.'

'Are you still listening?' demanded the old man. 'I'm just getting to the interesting part.'

'Still listening,' nodded Davies.

'Well listen then,' said Mr Harkness. 'Next time you come I might be dead and gone so I won't be able to tell you a sausage, will I?'

'Please go on.'

'Where was I? In the water? No, looking down at it. Anyway in a trice I was *in* the bloody water. I just fell in. That sobered me up a bit. I can still feel the cold now. It stinks too, that canal. Everybody's shit goes in there. Dead cats and everything.'

Davies nodded agreement.

'And it was while I was in the water, hanging on to the bank actually, that I saw them.'

'Them? Who?'

'The policeman and the girl,' said Mr Harkness patiently. 'On the bank. I was in the dark, hanging on to the bank and they was on the path at the side. At first I thought I was in luck there being a copper handy. I mean, generally you can never find one when you want one. But there he was and there was me in the canal. But I was just about to hollar and I saw he was kissing the girl. I thought, oi oi! There's little of what you fancy going on here. So I stayed with my head out of the water and they were on the bank. At first I thought they was cuddling, but I couldn't be sure about that. Because he sort of pulled her away towards the alley that goes up to the pawnshop.'

'Towards where the old Home Guard blockhouse used to be?'

'That's it. That's just it. I forgot that was there. I think they'd knocked it down by then, but it used to be just there.'

'And you're sure you saw all that?'

'Sure? Of course I'm sure. I wouldn't be telling you would I? I thought somebody would come around to see me from the police station because I told Dulcie here what I'd seen. After all the fuss about the girl, I mean.'

'I thought he was rambling,' said his daughter. 'He was ever so ill. Bronchial pneumonia. He wasn't far from dead. It was a year before he was really right. That's when we moved out here to Bristol. I'm glad we did. Bristol air's kept him alive.'

'How dark was it?' asked Davies. Mod was sitting staring at the photographs of the Zulu wars. He got up to inspect one closely as though he did not want to listen to what was not his business.

'Not very dark,' said Mr Harkness thoughtfully. 'Except under the bleeding water. That was smelly and dark. But it was summer, like I said, and it was quite light really. And there was the light from that lamp on the bridge.'

'So you're sure in your own mind,' ventured Davies. 'That it was a policeman and a girl. Not just a courting couple?'

Mr Harkness smiled felicitously. 'Oh, it was a copper all right. I'd been in court for drunk and incapable so many times that I knew a copper when I saw one. I even saw *who* it was.'

He paused. Davies, tight as a drum inside, stared unbelievably. Mod was standing and staring too. With my luck, thought Davies in dead-pan panic, Mr Harkness will now drop dead.

'Well,' said Mr Harkness, more alive than any of them. 'Do you want me to say who it was?'

'Er . . . yes, please,' nodded Davies with stiff calmness. 'that would be most helpful.'

'Well I knew him because he'd run me in so many times,' said the old man. 'Some of the young coppers were all right, but he was a miserable bugger. Yardbird, his name was. Police Constable Yardbird.'

All the way home in the back of the church conveyance Mod had to keep hold of the wheeled chair to prevent it careering carelessly about when Father Harvey took a bend, accelerated or applied the brakes, all three of which he was inclined to do with some violence and a degree of after-thought. On the outward journey to Bristol an abrupt halt at some traffic lights had resulted in Davies being propelled fiercely from one end of the vehicle to the other. After that Mod held tight to the chair.

'Yardbird,' Davies kept saying. 'Yardbird. Christ, whatever are we going to do now? He might just as well have said it was the Prime Minister or the Archbishop of Canterbury.'

'Your duty is clear,' Mod said ponderously. 'You must walk into his office and formally charge him with murder.'

Davies grimaced at him. 'Apart from not being able to stand up, let alone walk, at the moment, I doubt if I'd ever be able to say the words. Not to *him*.' He tried in a quivering voice: 'Inspector Yardbird, I charge you that on the night of July 23rd, 1951, at Canal Towpath, London N.W.10 you did murder Celia Norris. . . .' He shook his head miserably. 'He'd have *me* in the bloody cells before I could finish it off.' Mod rocked the invalid chair minutely to and fro like a nurse with a worrying child. 'Mr Harkness would make a grand witness,' he said without conviction.

'If he lives that long,' grumbled Davies. '*If* he can hear, *if* they've got an oxygen machine handy. Christ, Mod he's a hundred and one and the betting is about the same odds. A couple of nifty adjournments by the defence, a sharp draught coming through the court-room door, and our witness is no witness because he's dead.'

Mod nodded his sympathy. He stood and opened the small aperture to the driver's cabin. Father Harvey was singing a Gregorian chant, a difficult task while driving at speed along the motorway. Mod closed the panel without saying anything.

'I've got a body, exhibits including the girl's bicycle, a witness and an accused, and I still don't know why the hell I became a detective in the first place,' said Davies miserably.

'It's something I've often asked myself,' agreed Mod uncharitably. 'Can I make a suggestion?'

'You want me to forget the whole thing?'

'No indeed not. Not now. You're nearly there, boy. But think, is there anybody, anybody you've already talked to or anybody you think you should have talked to, who might just give it that extra couple of yards it needs? Anybody?'

Davies remained gloomy. The rest of the journey was made in general silence with Father Harvey's muted praises, punctuated by curses directed at other drivers, filtering through to them. Mod took out an antique copy of *Clarendon's Rebellion*, Volume Three and read it assiduously. Davies thought but nothing happened.

When they reached 'Bali Hi', Furtman Gardens, Mod wheeled Davies into the downstairs front room which Mrs Fulljames, with some grudging generosity, had put at his disposal for the time of his incapability, and at only a small extra cost. On the mantleshelf was a letter. It was from Frederick Fennell in the St Austin's Mental Hospital, Bedford. It said simply: 'Come and see me again for interesting news.' Beneath his signature was the drawing of a girl's bicycle.'

Fortunately it was the off-season for outings from St Fridewide's and

Father Harvey was able to bring the church vehicle around the following day so that Davies could be transported to see Fred Fennell. 'I'll see you get repaid one day,' Davies promised the priest. 'If all this becomes official police business.'

Father Harvey, who had shown remarkable incuriosity for a priest, nodded generously as he and Mod guided the invalid chair into the open rear of the vehicle. 'I'd quite like to have one of those blue flashing lights on the roof,' grunted the priest as he heaved the heavy load up an improvised ramp. 'And maybe a police siren. Oh yes, I'd certainly like that.'

As they drove towards Bedford, Mod again rocked the chair moodily. 'What d'you hope to get from this?' he sighed. 'Another witness? Your case gets better and better, Dangerous. One witness over a hundred and likely to pop off during his evidence, and another who's convinced he's Peter the Great.'

'It's not much of a line-up,' acknowledged Davies. 'But there's got to be something. Something somewhere.'

Father Harvey helped them to disembark then obligingly went off to see the hospital chaplain whom he knew from an occasion when they had taken part in a religious brains trust in Wandsworth Prison. There was no question of the wheeled chair going through the main door, so Mod, on Davies's guidance, took it through the rear garden gates. The solitary lady was still prodding at her private weeds with a table fork. Davies had warned Mod of what might occur so they were not surprised to be marched to the Superintendent's office at gunpoint. Davies raised both hands, but Mod only one since the captor acknowledged that he needed the other to push the chair. Davies gave her a disarming smile as she delivered them to the main office and the Superintendent took them to see Frederick Fennell sitting calmly in the room where Davies had first met him.

'Oh god help us, you're in a state,' said Fennell when he saw Davies. 'I was told you'd been in a dispute.'

'Described to a nicety,' acknowledged Davies. 'This is Modest Lewis, my assistant on this case. How did you hear about me?'

'Tarantella, Madame Phelps-Smith, came to see me,' said Fennell. He talked quietly and rationally. His face was no longer haunted. He smiled at the memory of her visit. 'She said that she had shown you the bicycle. So I thought I ought to tell you the rest.'

Davies fidgeted forward in his chair. 'Yes, Fred,' he said steadily. 'That would be very useful.'

'My wife's been to see me too,' continued Fennell. 'She came because you went back to her and asked her. I'm very grateful to you. That's why I want to tell you.' He paused and smiled, almost secretly. 'Funny thing, I've been stuck in this nuthouse all this time and nobody's bothered and all at once they both came to see me.' He sighed. 'I've had to tell Tarantella that it's all over between us, of course. I think I'll be on my way out of here before too long and then my good wife and I will start somewhere again. She brought me some nice cold beef sandwiches last time.'

'In that case you're definitely back in favour,' said Davies firmly. 'What else did you want to tell us?'

'Oh yes. You don't want to listen to all my personal gossip. When you came here last I wasn't sure what you were after. You didn't tell me in so many words. But Tarantella filled it all in. Anyway, if it's any use to you, I've got something. By the way, did you like Edwina's little place in the country?'

Davies remembered the swamped caravan. 'Oh yes,' he murmured. 'Very rural.'

'I want to sell it. Get right away from here. Down to Cornwall, somewhere fresh.' He caught Davies' glance. 'Yes, well that's me, again, isn't it. Sorry, but so many things have happened. I feel like I'm alive again.'

'You're looking a great deal better,' said Davies truthfully.

'And thanks to you. It was like the sun coming up . . . Anyway listen. I've got something for you. Edwina brought it in to me. I told her where to find it in my old police relics. Here – it's for you, Mr Davies.'

He held out a registered envelope. Puzzled, Davies took it. Mod was watching over his shoulder. 'Registered,' said Fennell. 'See it's registered London, N.W.10, 20th August, 1951. And it's never been opened.'

'What's in it?' asked Davies.

'A statement by P.C. Dudley,' said Fennell undramatically and simply. 'He was a careful bloke, Dudley, and he wanted to be sure to cover himself. He wrote this when they started treating the Norris girl business as murder. He wrote it all down and then sent it to himself by registered post. If it remained unopened that would be proof that it was written at the time the registered post label was dated. Got me?'

'Yes. But we can't know what's in it without opening it ourselves. And that would destroy its value as evidence.'

'Right. But he made a copy. I've got that too. It was sealed up with sealing wax and I've opened it. They came from Australia, after Dudley died in that fire. A solicitor in Melbourne sent them to me. He said Dudley had lodged them with him with instructions that they were to be forwarded to me in the event of his death. He was in all sorts of trouble, you know. Maybe he planned to commit suicide. But anyway that fire settled it for him. And these arrived in the post.'

Fennell smiled wryly. 'It was about the time when I went off my head.' He glanced in a suddenly embarrassing manner as if he thought that Mod might not realize why he was in the building. 'The envelope got stuck away with my other things and, to tell the truth I forgot all about them. I had enough trouble remembering who I was!' He laughed. 'You won't believe this but I actually thought I was Peter the Great. And he's been dead years!'

Davies glanced at him with alarm. But it was a joke. Fennell grinned knowingly at that. 'Here's the second envelope.' He handed a foolscap envelope blotched with sealing wax to them. Davies took it. He was surprised to find himself so calm.

'It's about that night,' said Fennell thoughtfully. 'The night the girl disappeared. We'd been to the party for Davie Morris who was leaving the force and had had quite a few drinks, even though we were on duty. You could get away with, well sort of unofficial things. Anyway we, that's Dudley and myself, we were supposed to be on duty in the little van. I sneaked in to see Tarantella and when I went out again I walked up the street towards the cemetery because that's where I thought Dudley would be waiting. We used to meet up there. One of us would park the van by the cemetery gates and let the other go off for an hour. On this night the van wasn't there, but there was this bike lying by the wall. I'd had it in the back of my mind for a long time to kind of have a bit of evidence standing by, you know to produce if anybody wanted to know what I was doing in Tarantella's place. And my wife was getting suspicious. I would say that Tarantella had found it and I'd gone there in response to her call. The bike was some *solid* evidence, if you know what I mean. It all seems so bloody paltry now . . . and so far away.'

'What happened to Dudley that night, do you think?' Davies did not want him to slip away now.

'Don't worry,' nodded Fennell. 'I'm coming to that. I suppose we were just young coppers and up to all sorts of roguery. And we were allowed to get away with it. Anyway, this bike. I took it into Tarantella's place and then I went back to find Dudley in the van. It was parked in the main road by the alley leading to the canal. By the pawnbrokers. Dudley was in the front but was still feeling terrible. He never could take his drink. In fact, you'll see in the statement, he'd only just got there. He felt so bad that he'd been lying down in his girlfriend's flat. There's more about that in the statement. Anyway I told him to clear off early and I did the rest of the stint myself. I signed in for him when I got back to the station. There was never any difficulty about that either. It was easy.'

'So Dudley was in the car when you got there?' said Davies. In imagination he could see Mr Harkness cheerfully spilling false evidence in every sentence. He sighed wearily.

'Yes, he was sat there. I remember how bad he looked. Silly bugger had been drinking rum. But . . . but something else had happened. Something . . . he's put in the statement. You've got to read that for yourself. Even though we used to share that duty nearly all the time, and we'd fixed it to fiddle time off, we were never very pally. We never really trusted each other.'

'But it was to *you* that he arranged to have these envelopes sent.'

'Because I was *there* that night. That's the reason. In a way I was *in it* with him. Whatever it was. Read it. Go on read it.'

Fennell leaned forward, eagerness overcoming his carefully arranged calm. He watched Davies open the thin envelope. Davies read aloud.

'At the top it says: "This is a true copy of my statement of 20th August, 1951, sealed in a registered envelope also in possession of Maxley Davidson of Flinders Street, Melbourne. The statement is as follows:

'"On the night of July 23rd, 1951, I was on duty with P.C. Frederick Fennell, patrolling the area of the High Street, London N.W.10. There was a police social function at the nearby 'Sturgeon Rooms', a farewell party for a colleague, David Morris, who was leaving the force. During the course of our patrol in the police van P.C. Fennell and I called into this function and had some drinks. I drank rum which always has a bad effect on me and I felt ill. P.C. Fennell left before me and, as he often did went to visit a woman friend. We arranged to meet at the gates of the cemetery an hour later. Sometimes one of us would take unofficial time off and sometimes the other would do the same. The one who remained with the van would be at the cemetery entrance at a prearranged time. We had done this for more than a year and nothing had gone wrong with the arrangement.

'"But on this night, I felt so bad after drinking the rum that I did not think I could drive the van to the rendez-vous. It was then that P.C. Vernon Yardbird offered to take over the duty for me. He had been drinking with the rest but he seemed to be all right. I let him take over and I went to the flat of a friend in the district and had a cup of coffee and a lie down. After about an hour I felt better and I walked to the cemetery gates intending to meet P.C. Yardbird with the van. It was not there and I walked along the High Street until I finally spotted it near the pawnbroker's shop. There was no one in it. I could see someone moving down the alleyway leading to the canal. Someone was in the verge by the allotments.

'"I called and eventually P.C. Yardbird came up the alley. He looked very strange, white-faced, sweating and there was blood on his cheek as though he had been scratched, and he told me he was going home because he thought he had drunk too much. I thanked him for doing me the favour and I got into the driving seat of the van. On the floor by the passenger seat I found a lipstick. I put this in my pocket but later I threw it away in case my wife found it. It is not until now – a month later – when the case of Celia Norris's disappearance has come into prominence, that I have begun to think that the lipstick and the state P.C. Yardbird was in that night might have had any bearing on the case. The lipstick was a type sold in Woolworth's and was of the same type that Celia Norris was said to have had. This statement is true."'

Davies looked up at the others. 'He's signed it. James Henry Dudley, P.C. Aug. 20th. 1951.' He held the registered envelope in his hands, as though weighing it. 'And that is a duplicate of the statement contained in this package.' His natural pessimism asserted itself. 'I hope.'

CHAPTER TWENTY

It was difficult to hold a cosy gathering at the police station. Nevertheless the cleaning lady had dusted the charge room for once and had put a bunch of dried flowers on the table which, remembering Celia's flowers, Davies thought was accidentally appropriate.

Detective Sergeant Green of the Special Branch helped Mod to get Davies's wheeled chair up the front steps to the station. He had come out purposely and leaned close to Davies's ear when they had reached the top step. 'What have you been doing to Yardbird?' he inquired quietly. 'He's bloody livid. He's supposed to make this presentation to you this morning but something's happened. I think he'd rather strangle you.'

'Oh dear,' said Davies mildly. 'I think I must have embarrassed him.'

'Christ, you've done more than embarrassed him. Apparently went berserk in his office half an hour ago and he said he wasn't going to make the presentation. But my boss Bob Carter, has insisted that he does it. And Yardbird won't say why he's blowing his top.'

'I see,' said Davies. 'I think I know why he's so upset, Mr Green.'

'What is it?'

'I'll tell you soon. Would you do me a favour?'

'What?'

'After our little ceremony is over – as soon as I give you the eye – would you take your boss, Detective Superintendent Carter into the C.I.D. Room. I'll come in very shortly after with Inspector Yardbird. I have something I would like to say to him in your presence.'

Green nodded silently. He was a man well accustomed to the odd twists of life. He let Mod push the wheeled chair towards the charge room when the duty sergeant, the shiny Ben, appeared like a substantial shadow and pulled him aside.

'Very quickly,' whispered Ben. 'I don't know what you've been up to, Dangerous, but the old man is fucking furious. It happened first thing this morning, as soon as Yardbird came in. I gather there's been a complaint against you from somebody called Boot. Says you've been terrorizing him, beating him up, he says. Anyway he's been telling tales on you. Then old Yardbird comes down to the C.I.D. Room and gets the key to your locker, which he empties all over the floor. And he went out frothing at the bloody mouth with a photograph of some young girl. I didn't see this, but P.C. Westerman was in there with a nosebleed. He said it was a photo of a girl.' Ben looked at Davies curiously. 'You haven't been dabbling in indecent pictures, have you, Dangerous?'

Davies smiled. 'Sort of,' he said.

Ben stared at him but said nothing more. He helped Mod to wheel the chair into the charge room which was full of people drinking Cyprus Sherry. As he came in they all clapped and he gave a short, embarrassed wave. Then through the door came Detective Superintendent Carter and Detective Sergeant Green of the Special Branch, and stiff-faced, Inspector Yardbird.

Davies sat in his chair, feeling its wheels vibrating from his own trembling. Mod stood one side of him and Josie on the other. To his amazement Doris and Mrs Fulljames then arrived, both extravagantly kissing him before retiring to a short distance, looking smug and apparently not noticing Josie or her proximity to Davies.

He knew that Mrs Fulljames was pleased because the rag-and-bone man had that day restored the brass bedstead to 'Bali Hi' Furtman Gardens. Davies had seen the piece in the yard when he had gone to give the horse a cabbage for saving his life. He purchased it, at a special police discount, the man alleging that he bought it from an honest-looking Persian who was in a hurry.

It was Detective Superintendent Carter who made the speech. Inspector Yardbird stood behind like a wax figure.

'This is in the nature of a very private function,' Carter said. 'The implications in the matter which was concluded at Bracken Farm, Uxbridge, are still going on. Mr Ramscar and others are still to go for trial, as you know. But I felt, and I know others did, that in some personal and private way we should make some presentation to Detective Constable Davies, known to you all as Dangerous Davies. Official recognition of his performance may well follow. That's not for me to say. But this is our own private show. As we can all see he has been severely injured in this affair, although I am glad to hear that he will soon be walking again. I hope that this small presentation from his colleagues will make up for some of it. I will ask his own station inspector, Inspector Yardbird, who himself has known the unique difficulties of a policeman's life in this particular district, for a good many years, to make the presentation.'

Yardbird staring at Davies stepped forward. Davies wheeled the chair across the floor. His hands trembled on the rim of the wheels. The Inspector shaking more than Davies, presented a silver marmalade pot, plate and spoon. He said no word. Davies thanked them all from his wheeled chair, shook hands with Carter and then held his hand out to Yardbird. Yardbird pushed out a freezing hand. Davies held it strongly.

All around there was more applause and the Cyprus Sherry began to flow. Davies was in his chair next to the stiff legs of Yardbird. As Yardbird was about to move away, Davies reached up and tentatively tugged the edge of his tunic. Yardbird looked down into a big stony smile.

'Sir,' Davies said diffidently. 'Do you think I might have a few words with you? In private?'

Bare Nell

'Tis Pity She's a Whore
JOHN FORD

CHAPTER ONE

Even as a young girl in the West Country of England I realized that I was intended for an unusual life. In the school I was clever with words and I was pretty in what they call in those parts a 'fruity' way. I knew that one day I could become perhaps a famous writer or a famous whore. It was my spelling let me down.

From the beginning I was called Bare Nell; little Nelly Luscombe, naked and brown, her body just podding, paddling in the village stream, or squatting there, trout wriggling about her thighs. In 1943, American soldiers waiting to go to war would toss money and chewing gum to me and ask where my mother was. They would sit on the stream bank and watch me for hours, looking wistful.

Oh, my dears, I have lived a full, sexy, merry and sad life. More even than *full*. Overflowing! I remember how the minister used to bawl at the harvest festival, up in the pulpit, throwing his arms out over the loaves and the turnips and suchlike (he was a thoughtful man who would escort nervous young choirboys to their homes on dark Devon nights). 'What bounty!' he used to cry (at the harvest festival, that is, not on the dark Devon nights). 'What bounty!' I have always remembered that. For what bounty I have known! And not just bread and turnips either.

In this life I have known, loved, lived for, lived on, lived off, laughed and cried over, many men. Most are nameless (as well they deserved to be), others, such as Lennie the Lizard of the Lounge, I would prefer to forget.

My mother used to say: 'Have no shame in your life Nell,' and I have done nothing that causes me shame. I have worn white at all my weddings and I did *not* (Scotland Yard, please note) poison Pierre Arthur Bickerstaff.

In fact I would like to clear up the misunderstanding about Pierre Arthur Bickerstaff and the way he went, before I tell of anything else in my life. Pierre Arthur Bickerstaff died by swallowing sulphur which he ate in mistake for custard powder when he was drunk one New Year's Eve. He died so close to midnight that there was some doubt about which year should be mentioned on his gravestone. He was trying to make Crème Caramel. When he was sober he was quite a good cook. His grave can be seen in Kensal Green Cemetery in London and I place a posy of seasonal flowers upon it whenever I am in that area. The headstone is very nice, with a pair of strutting birds carved on it which, considering the custard powder tragedy, is just right. Indeed, so attached was I to

Pierre Arthur Bickerstaff (as I have said repeatedly at the Yard) that I have put a deposit on the next burial plot to his, so that when I go, which I hope will be getting towards the end of the next fifty years, I can lie comfortably beside him. It will be quite like old times, but quieter. I have also deposited a sum of money with Pleesum, Squeezem, Filth and Foulenough, solicitors of Bognor Regis (a disguised name to protect the innocent), for the carvings of a headstone for me. It will be a lump of red Devon rock topped with a female equestrian figure and the inscription: 'She rode the horse of Life'. I made that up myself.

For a long time I have wanted to put my life on paper because so many books have been written to give the whore a bad name. The bed has been my workbench. There all life is horizontal. Nothing that has happened has made me want to change my feeling that man's goodness outweighs his badness by an important half-an-ounce. I was born and I have lived as a romantic. As a little girl I could not understand why the sun did not go down with a roar.

I was born in the front room of Number Three Chapel Cottages, Upcoombe, a village over a red hill from Hopewell, in the county of Devon. My father, who was only five foot two and painfully thin, would shout every Friday: 'I'll knock this house down with my fists.' In my first years I really believed he could do it and I used to eye him cautiously and edge nearer the front door. It also occurred to me that if he actually carried out his threat, then the cottages on either side – and those on either side of them – would fall down too, since they formed a slanting terrace down the lane to the stream. I wouldn't have minded Mr Wormy Wood on the lower side finishing up under his house, because he used to swear at my mother, but on the upper side was Granny Lidstone who was sweet and old and only had one tooth and I would not have liked anything to have happened to her. I used to go into her house and she would make me toffee apples. One day I could stand it no longer and I warned her to be ready to get out of the house at a moment's notice because my father had the power to demolish the terrace, but she did not seem very worried. 'Your dad couldn't knock down a skittle, m'dearie,' she said, ''specially on a Friday.'

My mother spent her days boiling other people's washing in a gigantic copper vat. To me, looking into it was like looking into the centre of the earth. She seemed like a bundle of washing herself, round, done up with string around her waist, her hair plastered around her forehead and neck, her face sweating and like tallow. When she was not washing the clothes, she was ironing them, with more steam rising about her from the iron. She spent her life in vapour. Even as a little girl, I thought there must be some better way of living. My sister Mary and I would sit and watch her enveloped by the steam as if she were a ghost appearing at a seance. Mary, who was four years older than me, whispered one day: 'I'm not going to do that, Nell, not when I get grown.'

'Me neither, Mary,' I agreed. 'I'd rather go on the streets.' I was about eight at the time. I must have heard the expression from somewhere. Mary must have been impressed by the sound of it because I remember she said: 'And me.' She never did. She went to work in a bakery.

Ah, but it was a lovely place to be a child. The little Devon hills were all around, red earth and green meadows, the lanes were deep and banked with primroses as soon as the year's first sun came out. If I climbed onto my bedroom windowsill and stood outside the house, holding onto the old guttering, I could glimpse a patch of the sea. Hopewell was only a mile away but to me it seemed like a distant place. It meant climbing the hill out of Upcoombe village and then going down the other side to the creek and the place where swans used to reflect themselves in the still water. The main street rose from there to the spire of the church on the next hill. I remember now climbing from our village on a morning at the beginning or the end of the year and seeing the point of the church and a few of the taller roofs nosing up through the mist that had gathered over the small town. It was a lovely place.

The stream that ran at the foot of Chapel Cottages was never more than a few inches deep. It ran over soft pebbles, polishing them more and in summer it had giant sunflowers on its banks, growing against the walls of the chapel and the end cottages. In those days I never gave a thought to where the stream came from or where it went. All I knew was that I could see clearly down through the water to my toes. It came in fact from a spring above the village and it ran eventually into the creek at Hopewell and then down to empty into the sea.

I was six when the war began. It seemed to make no difference, except that men went off, even my father eventually, which I thought was a masterstroke on the part of our Government because, provided with enough cider, he could undoubtedly do untold damage to enemy houses and property. Nothing seemed to change except that my mother was happier with my father absent. In fact I think she believed that Hitler could not be all bad to have brought about such a relief to a hard-pressed woman.

But the village and the town, season by season, went their ways, just as quiet and slowly as before. At the small school we had gas-mask drill and we were told to save paper, tins and water. I remember going to the stream and getting water in several containers, jugs, basins and a small bucket, and saving it in the front room of the house. I expected that someone would come and collect it for the war effort but they never did. Men from the town and the village died in battle, or course, and my mother would see their names in the local newspaper and shake her head and sometimes cry for they were often the friends of her younger days. She always read about the casualties. Sometimes I thought she was looking to see if my father was mentioned.

Growing up had never occurred to me, which I suppose is very odd for a child. I was content with the sameness of each day and the everyday things it brought. Nothing seemed to change. My own changes I was the last to notice.

Towards the middle of the war soldiers began to gather in the South Hams. A few at first but then more and more, thousands and thousands, mostly Americans riding in jeeps and tanks and floating on boats and barges in the Hopewell Creek.

Even then, as a child, I thought that under the helmets and in spite of their guns and blackened faces the soldiers seemed, for the most part, young and lost and lonely. Apart from the black faces, it's the sort of look you see in brothels the world over.

Some of the women from Hopewell, and some from our village and the others around us in the South Hams, used to keep the Americans company, but the women who did not used to gossip and watch them spitefully. The women who went with the Americans had stockings and butter and gum and this caused jealousy. Sometimes there were fights in the town pub and the vicar of Hopewell began praying in the services, asking God for peace in the world and also in the town.

There were soldiers, as I said, who would come and sit on the bank of our stream when I was paddling there as I often did in summer. I had never thought I should wear anything to cover me in the stream and apparently neither had my mother because at one time there were only the villagers to see me and they had known me since I was born. Now these foreign American young men came regularly and sat there. They were very funny and kind and gave me chewing gum and sometimes a few pennies. I showed them how I could catch my trout with my fingers and they would ask me about my mother (Was she young? Was she pretty?) and if my father was away at the war.

Then one evening I had stayed in the water a bit later than usual because my mother had gone to collect somebody's washing and had remained for a gossip about the Americans, and my sister Mary had gone to work as a housemaid in Hopewell Manor. She would go straight there from school and help until seven o'clock. They gave her half a crown a week for that.

So I was in the stream, naked as ever, with the day drawing away over the fields towards the sea. Some flies and midges came around for the air was warm and they liked the water and my skin. I was wondering if that night I could stop in the stream later than I had ever done before (already my feet were growing dim) when down Chapel Lane came the American soldier. It was the one who had told me that he was a cowboy before they took him for a soldier. He was alone.

'Hiya, Nell,' he called as soon as he saw me. 'Kinda late for that.'

'I'm waiting for my mum,' I said as though I always waited in midstream.

He squatted on the bank. 'Gee, that stream sure looks good,' he said. 'Is it cold?'

'No,' I said. 'What's your name?'

'I'm the one they call Bronco, Sergeant Bronco,' he said. 'I was a cowboy.'

'You told me that before,' I remembered. 'But I didn't know your name. Where's all the others gone?'

'Gone to chow,' he said. Then quickly, 'I feel like I could just get in that stream myself, Nelly. My feet are howling like dogs. We been marching.'

He took his shoes and socks off and then, mildly to my surprise, his trousers. I wondered why he could not just roll them up, but I thought he had to keep them smart for parades.

The evening was very dim and silent around us. I did not feel afraid, only curious. Thoughtfully I sat down in the stream, letting the water rise and run over my legs and gurgle around my waist. It was such a natural things for me to do, almost like absently sitting in a chair, that I hardly noticed the feel of the water. Sergeant Bronco looked down at me and then jogged his chin up and down as though he had come to a decision about something.

'I just feel I might come and sit down there with you Nell,' he said slowly. His face was becoming dim but I could see his eyes shining.

'Ah,' I replied with childish aplomb. 'Then you'll get your drawers wet, won't you?'

'Right,' he smiled. 'Right. Okay. I'll take them off I guess.' And he did. Right there in the stream in the evening light. He moved a little closer and I smelled drink on him, a familiar enough sensation for a girl who had lived years of Friday nights with my father. But he was smiling his friendly American smile and he took his drawers off as naturally as he might have taken off his hat. I was intrigued but not anxious.

It was the first male organ I had ever viewed. It dangled like some sort of third leg. I stared at it in the dusk.

'What you be calling that?' I inquired, pointing my finger carefully towards it.

'That?' He seemed quite surprised I should have seen and looked down at it as though he had never noticed its existence before.

'Well now . . . what would you guess, Nell?'

I thought it was a reasonable inquiry. I'd been asked sillier questions at school. 'Well now,' I said slowly in my Devon way. 'I think it looks like a jumbo.'

'Great,' he laughed, but not loudly. He lowered himself into the stream and his face changed in the half light as the water closed around him. 'Gee . . . ze. This is a little cool.' But we were there now, sitting in the water, the soldier and the naked little girl. He would soon be going to the war and I would stay in the village to grow up. Around us it was nearly dark and the only noise was the sound of the late insects and the slipping of the stream.

'Jumbo,' he repeated pensively. 'That's a great name for it.' He shuffled towards me, his bottom scraping the river bed. The tail and front flaps of his army shirt were trailing in the stream but he did not seem to notice. He came to a stop only a yard away. His big legs spread open with me sitting daintily between them. Now he was close I could see his face was worried.

'Nelly,' he said hoarsely. He kneeled up, bringing his torso out of the water. 'Nelly, will you hold Jumbo for me?'

I cannot recall being shocked or even thinking it an unreasonable request. Maybe I was meant for the life I eventually led. 'Hold it?' I inquired, however. I looked down. Despite the cold water, now running in streams down his skin, the implement was still long and thick, hanging down. 'Hold it?' I repeated. 'Now what would a maid like me be wanting to hold that great thing for?'

'It's to help . . .' His voice was now a pleading croak. 'It's to help in the war against Hitler.'

Even after all these years and all my experience, I still think it was the best excuse I have ever heard.

It must have impressed me because I looked down again. His legs were arched. It was hanging like a bell in a belfry, its end just brushing the stream.

'Well, I don't know,' I hesitated. 'I bain't done that before. I'll go and ask my mum.'

'No,' he replied hurriedly. 'I'm getting real cold here.' He reached forward and took my hands in his, but gently. His eyes were anchored on my brown, bare face. He was still smiling but it was a trifle fixed. I let him take my hands and I felt them touch, then close around the jumbo. It was hot! I was amazed. Then further amazed as it began to grow and stiffen in the most magic way. It was like the inflating of a bicycle tyre. I thought he was performing some sort of conjuring trick (which of course I suppose he was in a way of speaking) and my big eyes grew bigger in the dark as I felt the life pushing through it. 'Sergeant Bronco,' I whispered uncertainly, 'it's moving.' I had a notion it might even wriggle off downstream.

'Sure, sure.' His voice was like grit now. 'Hold onto it honey and it won't be going nowhere.'

I should confess now that I liked the feel of it and it is a pleasure that has never left me. Its silken strength, its homely warmth, its mind of its own. I began to run my fingers over it and the small palms of my hands. I had stiffened like the stalk of a bullrush. I was amazed by its capacity for growth. The man looked all out of proportion. 'Will it get any bigger?' I inquired, pushing my face down towards it to get a better view.

'It could try,' he said. But his voice now was like the last gasp of somebody being strangled. I looked up to see the most tremendous torment in his face. Instinctively I rubbed my fingers up and down. The expression tightened, as though someone was pulling together a strong bag. 'Jesus . . . I'm coming,' he whispered.

'Don't die!' I cried in misunderstanding. I had genuinely thought he was about to expire and that his remark was his warning to Jesus that he was on his way. My Auntie Dolly had said a similar thing before she went.

He was not dying but in the next moment he threw himself towards me and clutching my small body in his arms he crushed me to him. Ridiculously he hung onto me for a minute or more and then collapsed into the stream, his torment washed away with the innocent water. His face was running with tears. He pulled himself from the water and pressed his young man's cheek tenderly to mine.

'Nelly,' he said. 'Great Nelly.'

I never saw him again. He must have gone off to the war and perhaps he lived and perhaps he died. I promised I would keep our secret (and I have until this day) and I went home as usual, had my supper and went to bed. My mother came up to hear my prayers and I prayed especially hard for the sergeant, which amused and puzzled her. But I, Nelly Luscombe, knew that I had already done something in the fight against Hitler.

'Mum,' I said before I went to sleep. 'We're going to win the war.'

By the finish of June all the soldiers had gone and the countryside had fallen silent. No more tanks in the lanes or guns in the streets. It was as though they had taken their war completely with them. Aeroplanes passed distant in the sky, like needles shining on a blue cloth, but they seemed to have nothing to do with us or our lives.

The Americans were missed by some, of course. By the publicans and the shopkeepers and the women they used to keep company with. No more gum or stockings, no more grappling in the alleys of the town. The women seemed lost, missing the Americans more, it seemed, than they missed their true husbands who were away fighting in some other part of the war. I left the village school that summer and had to go into Hopewell to the town school and on afternoons while I was waiting with the other children for the bus that went into the villages, I would sometimes see these women, half a dozen or so, sitting on their seats by the creek where they had once sat to meet their lovers. Now they were subdued and just crouched there throwing stones at the swans. Some of the other women who were in the town would not speak to them.

Once I saw one of the lonely women hit one of the swans with a quarter brick and it took off from the creek in a terrible fright with all the other swans following it. They set out down the water towards the sea, in a long vee-formation, the air creaking out from under their wings. They looked lovely; just like bombers. But the women just sat and stared at them until they were out of sight.

Then one of them began to cry and wail. All us little children waiting for the bus heard her plainly cry: 'Oh Wilbur! Oh Wilbur! Where be you now?' And she got up and tried to throw herself bodily into the creek. The others all grabbed her and stopped her before she got to the edge, but the upset spread to all of them and another cried out: 'Oh Hank, my Hank.' And a third. 'Benjie! Benjie boy!' And before long they were all crying out and wailing on the seat on the very edge of the creek. It was a very curious sight to see. I could not understand it, all howling and hanging onto each others necks like that, while we children and the townspeople stood and watched. I suppose it was the first time any of the poor women had really been in love.

But it was summer and I was a young girl. The noises of wasps about in the faces of the sunflowers, the warmth of the air, the smell of the fields, all went unappreciated by me. All I knew was that they were there, all about me. Every day I woke early, always it seemed to the fresh sun. I dressed in one of my three dresses for school. I continued to bathe in the stream each afternoon now uninterrupted, and always naked. Now I come to consider it, my wardrobe was so sparse I could hardly have bathed in any other way but nude. Not that anyone ever said 'nude' in those parts at that time. I never heard the word until I was working under more sophisticated, but still naked circumstances. In the stream I was bare.

My adventure with Sergeant Bronco had interested me, and I thought about it from time to time, but it had given me no feeling of disturbance. It was not necessary for me to go to any great effort to keep it secret because it did not lie in my mind. I was more moved, I think, the first time I ever saw a farmer's fingers on a cow's udder and more alarmed the first time I saw a carthorse crap in the road. Many years later a psychiatrist became deeply interested when I told him these true facts.

In those summers we had three weeks off from school in August and another three weeks in later September and earlier October, so that we children could help with the harvest. That was a good time for us, in the fields with the men, really helping with the threshing and the corn. The days always seemed to be hot and red and I can smell the dust of the corn now. Rabbits and rats would run in terror from the island of grain that got ever-smaller in the middle of the field. The dogs would chase them in furious excitement and the men would often shoot the rabbits and take them home to be skinned and cooked.

The men used to bring hunks of bread and cheese and slices of onion in muslin cloth and as the day wore on they sweated more and would drink pint upon pint of rough cider. This was provided by whoever owned the field and was known in the locality as Farmer's Revenge because of the tremendous diarrhoea it caused. The men were used to it, of course, but if any of us children drank it we would soon be seen streaking across the cut field as fast as our small legs would carry us. I can still remember the awful sensation of believing that I would not reach the hedge in time and the agony of hearing the great guffing laughs of the men as I ran. The psychiatrist was very interested in that too.

What used to be worrying was that as the evening got near the men used to get very fruity on the cider and start making to catch some of the older girls and young women who were up there working with them. My mother would always come and fetch me from the field at six o'clock because she knew that the raw cider made the men feel mazed and randy. Then, to my surprise, she started coming up to the fields to work herself, bending with the rest of them and having an occasional swig of the cider flagon. It did her real good. Her face lost its steamy look and her cheeks got brown and her eyes bright. She had always been on the rounded side, but I could see this pleased some of the men who would pause to look down her brown neck to her large breasts when she was bending and working. One day I noticed three farm men all timing their own bending so that they were upright as she bent down. It was like a sort of slow barn dance. When she realized what they were about she pretended to be annoyed but after a minute she laughed as merrily as any of them. I had never seen her like this. It was as if she felt young again.

There was a young man called Luke, big and red as a plum, with curly hair, who had bad eyes which kept him from the war. He could see my mother well enough, though, and I could see that she liked him, for they always laughed together and it was his cider flagon she always drank from. They used to make silly jokes and hoot like owls about them. I stood aside and wondered why she had never laughed with my father like that and, as well, why my father, who was undersized, should have been sent to fight Hitler, while Luke, just because he had got sheep dust or corn dust in his eyes, should be there in an English field gathering the harvest with my mother.

I was further mystified when, one noon when everyone was taking their dinnertime and the dogs were lying under the bellies of the horses in the shade, I wandered off to the far edge of the field away from the place where we were working. The corn was still standing there and I went around the edge, feeling the ears of grain tickling under my armpits. My hair and my forehead must have been just above the level of the crop. I was going to a bank of honeysuckle or something (to think I have forgotten honeysuckle) and I was sniffing the air to get a scent of it when I smelled an unmistakable stench of raw cider. Then I heard a growling laugh from somewhere ahead and then a guilty chuckle that I knew was my mother's voice.

'Now, Luke Lethbridge,' I heard her whisper. 'We shouldn't be a-doing of this. These corn stalks are sore on my arse.'

I moved a yard further into the grain and I could see them wallowing. I could hear him groaning and sweating. Then, to my astonishment, a great pink, male rump rose above the corn like a whale coming to the surface of the sea. It rose and fell several times and I heard Luke Lethbridge grunting happily and my mother making sweet groans. I did not run, I wandered away, worried and wondering.

Bravery has always come naturally to me. That evening when it was getting dim and everyone was just about going home, I went to Luke and stopped him with my small hand on his thick belt.

'Luke Lethbridge,' I said, 'what were you about with my mum in the crop?'

He had fair hair and fair bushy eyebrows (very bushy, come to think of it; perhaps that's why he couldn't see enough to go and fight in the war). His face was round and red with the work. He stopped and thought about it, as though he wondered if it was worth an answer.

'Rastling,' he said at last. 'We was rastling, maid.'

'Rastling? Rastling?' I remember saying bitterly. 'How be it you take your bags off your arse for rastling?'

'It was 'ot, maid,' he said. Devon farm labourers rarely take offence. 'It was 'ot when we was about it.'

And then he clumped away, his big boots banging the earth, his coat over his shoulder, his shoulders swaying like a farm cat heading for his wife and his tea.

The matter came to an end in a very odd way. There was another man working in the fields, a man called Daniel Pentecost, as dark as Luke Lethbridge was fair. He was short and wide, like an anvil, and just as strong. He must have taken more than one glance at my mother too because he and Luke became enemies in the harvest fields that year. When I think of it now, it is amazing the attraction she had, rough and full as she was, for these country men.

I don't know if my mother paid any heed to the lust, love or jealousy of Daniel Pentecost, but he was driven to do the thing he did only because of her. Daniel had charge of one of the teams of big horses which pulled the reaper through the standing corn or the waiting hay. They still used them then, their retirement to make way for tractors put back by the war, and they were handsome things, with bowed heads and big shoulders, pulling the farm machinery. Years later some crazy man showed me an obscene photograph involving some of these noble horses and I was so upset that I burst into tears and struck him on the ear with a three-quarters-full bottle of gin. It was no more than he deserved.

There were two horses in Daniel's team and he would drive them from his perch on the reaper (or the plough at the onset of the year) with shouts of 'Hup, Samson! Hup, Goliath! Come on ye big bastards!' He never said very much else, even at the village pub. It seemed he could only talk to horses.

One dinnertime towards the end of the harvest days Daniel sat eating and swigging from his flagon, beneath his horses' belly, like the dogs, shading himself from the noon sun. (In winter, when he was ploughing, he had been known to shelter below the horses when there was heavy rain. He was quite at home there.) I had been scampering with the other children through the hedges and the honeysuckle and returned to that place where the workers were all gathered to see at once that my mother and her lover Luke were missing. I remember how loaded my heart felt. I sat down beside one of the wagons and considered setting the corn afire. Daniel's thoughts must have been on the same subject. He rose from beneath the horses' stomachs and quietly began to hitch them to the reaper.

'Ho, there, Dan'l,' one of the other men shouted. 'You no need to be startin' yet! 'Tis only one!'

'Knackers to you, Brian Brewer,' Daniel replied slowly. 'I be startin' now.'

They must have realized what he was about, because everyone stopped eating their bread and cheese and the cider was stopped on the way to men's lips. The women and children grouped closer together as they do in a crisis. But I stood apart from the others and watched him tut and turn his horses off to the fringe of the grain where he had been cutting before dinnertime. The reaper turned over quietly behind him.

'Ho, Samson! Ho, Goliath! Come on ye big bastards!' he called and leaned forward like the captain of a ship searching for something ahead.

He had gone right to the distant side of the field before I, in my childish way, realized what mischief he was about. If the others knew truly what it was, then they still did not move, but stood like stones watching him. Then it came to me. He was heading those horses and that great whirling reaper for the hiding place among the grain of my mother and Luke Lethbridge. 'No you don't, Dan'l Pentecost!' I suddenly cried. 'Don't you go a-cutting of my mother!'

I started to run screaming across the stubble. The stalks cut my ankles and my legs as I ran. There was a long gap behind me and then something released the others from their trance and they all started to fly after me. It must have been a rare and curious sight to see us all charging across the stubble, me half-naked at the front, women with skirts up, men stripped to the waist ploughing on with heavy boots, following, and a long tail of excited children, eager for the sight of blood, coming along behind.

Luke must have been giving my mother a good seein'-to, because they did not hear the approach of the horses and the reaper and they did not hear us shouting. Our agricultural training was such that we ran in a broad angle around the edge of the uncut grain, not daring to go through it, or knowing that it would be too thick to penetrate.

Daniel and his horses moved on. I was running like I had never run and yelling in my piping little voice. Daniel heard me and turned in his seat. Then he looked forward again and urged Samson and Goliath, the big bastards, on with further relish.

They say it was Goliath that stepped right in the middle of Luke Lethbridge's back. It was certainly Goliath that reared up first, bringing the other horse up with him in the shafts. Like some daytime demon, Daniel urged them so the blades of the machine he was trailing would pass over the couple in the grain. As it was, the horses nearly accomplished his wicked plan for they flew up and then plunged down. But they had slewed to one side and Luke and my dear mother just escaped the full weight of the iron hooves, which can give you a nasty knock at the best of times.

Daniel got himself down from the seat of the reaper and took off across the fields; nobody chased him. They say he was crazed. They say he reached Exeter the next day and joined the Navy.

The villagers got hold of the horses and then lifted poor Luke from on top of my mother. It was a strange sight there in the sunny field. He was without his trousers, and right in the middle of his back, like a blacksmith's sign, was the imprint of the great horseshoe. My dear mother had been pressed several inches into the field and actually left a hole when they pulled her out. I had feared she might be bare. She was not but she might as well have been. Her skirts were up and her drawers were down and her breasts were bulging out of her bodice like loaded goatskins. Nobody seemed to be able to do anything about it so I pushed my way between them all, the staring fools, and heaved her breasts back where they belonged and pulled her skirt decently down.

'God bless you Nelly darling,' she gasped, opening her troubled eyes. 'Your mother was just having a rest.'

One odd result of my mother's injuries, which were not very serious (neither were Luke's. A lot of local men said coarsely that he had got the horse to help him 'get in'), was that my father was given compassionate leave from the war to go and see her. It was the only bit of compassion he had ever had anything to do with.

He turned up in his army clothes and it turned out that he had not actually been at the war at all but somewhere like Aldershot. In a cookhouse. He had soup on his trousers. They had not bothered to give him much of a uniform and he arrived looking like a furtive whippet, his tunic collar miles too big. Nobody told him what actually happened in the cornfield, or if they did he had too much caution to get tangled with big Luke, and all he did was mutter some words of sympathy to my mother and pat myself and my sister Mary on the head. He had funny, heavy hands for such a weedy man and his patting always hurt like someone hitting you with a piece of wood. At times this sign of affection set us both crying, which made him surprised and often very angry.

It did not take him long to find his way from the house and smartly up Chapel Lane to the pub. We watched from the cottage windows and saw his comical figure going jerkily up the cobbles, the uniform seeming to hang in heavy layers about him. He came back brimming with cider bombast and threats. One of his threats was nasty and very dramatic, since he made it clear that he now had the power to blow us all up. In the past his promise had been to tear down the house with his hands, but the army had now taught him how to explode it. Before our alarmed and helpless faces – Mary and I were crouched against the kitchen table and our mother was sitting white as her own washing in the rocking chair – he proceeded to make preparations for the disaster.

It seemed enormously simple. From his army pack he produced a metal oblong box, formed by two army mess-tins (although we didn't know they were mess tins), one fitting inside the other. He placed them carefully on the table and we stared at them.

'TNT,' he said. 'Explosives.'

'Percy,' my bruised mother said from her corner. 'You mustn't frighten our little girls like that. Or me.'

'I'm going to blow us all up,' he replied, hardly turning to her. He smiled his ghastly cider-stained smile in our faces. 'It's something I've always wanted to do.'

There didn't seem much answer to that, but I tried. 'Daddy,' I said trembling. 'You'll be disturbing Granny Lidstone next door. And her'll be in bed.'

'Her'll soon be out of it, the old cow,' he replied wickedly. His teeth were so rotten and he had that fearful smile. He looked around at us, to see, it seemed, if we were paying attention.

'TNT,' he said again. 'Packed solid with it my dears. Now the fuse.'

He took from his pocket what looked uncommonly like a bootlace – and it was in fact a bootlace – and this he deliberately dipped into the paraffin of one of the two lamps we had in the house. 'The fuse,' he said, holding it up like a conjuror.

'Percy.' My mother was shaking. She was trying to get out of the rocking chair. 'Percy you must not blow this house up. You've had too much scrumpy.'

He turned and gave her an easy push which sent her back into the chair and the chair to rocking. 'This is my house, you are my wife, and these are my little maids,' he said smugly. 'I'll blow them up if I like. And I ain't had too much scrumpy. It's like mule's piss at Aldershot.'

None of us had tried to escape. It was as if he had mesmerized us. But now, to give added effect, the swine went up to the kitchen door and locked it with great show. He grinned like a pantomime demon around the table. Mary put her hand out and held mine. 'Now . . . the matches,' he said.

'Percy, mercy, God help us,' moaned mother.

'You'll be with God in a few minutes,' he said, smug as ever. A thought struck him. 'On the other hand we ought to tell him we're on the way. Let's have a prayer.'

The lousy bastard made us kneel and we prayed in faltering voices for our everlasting life. Mother tried to put in a word about saving us from the bomb, but dad turned quickly and slapped his hand over her mouth before the message was half out. When we had finished the prayers he grinned around at our faces and then said again: 'Matches.'

He struck three before he got one alight and I swear he was doing it purposely to prolong the agony. His bomb was sitting on the table with the bootlace fuse hanging from it like a wet tail. While he was fumbling about with the matches I pushed it across the table towards him but he saw me and pushed it back again. Mary began to cry and I joined in and then my mother began to howl louder than any of us.

He carefully lit the third match and put it to his fuse. It flared with a blue flame and travelled slowly, but fast enough for us, up the length of the lace towards the mess-tins. We all stared, our eyes bright with fear, I should think, in that lamplight. Then the flame reached the bomb. We clenched our eyes together and Mary almost broke my fingers of my hand.

'Bang!' shouted my father. We all screamed and fell down. But we were not dead and lying there it crossed my mind that he had been up to his sodding tricks again. Trembling we got up and looked over the edge of the table. He was sitting grinning. He opened his bomb, taking out some cheese sandwiches and began to munch them. What a bastard.

CHAPTER TWO

The school at Hopewell was down an old cobbly street and then up again to where the playground was slanted on the side of a hill, a good place for roller skates, cart-wheels and sliding on frosty mornings. At the bottom of the playground incline was the school wall and often, in all seasons, children were sent to the Cottage Hospital after colliding with the wall.

From outside villages the pupils came in by buses to school. My memories of the place are of droning voices chanting out multiplication tables into close summer afternoons, of the smell of floor polish and cabbage, blackboard chalk and the various country smells brought by in the children and the farms. In class I sat next to a boy called Bertie Hannaford who reeked of pigs. It was not his fault – as he told me tearfully when I complained about it – because he had to work in his father's sties before setting off for school each morning. I think this crisis between us sparked off our love affair. It made me sorry to think of him wallowing in all that swill on early mornings, and, fighting every inch of the way, I forced myself to sit even closer to him in class, in assembly and even at the tables at dinnertime when all the other children would keep themselves as far away as possible. He was eleven and I was ten.

After we had realized we were in love, we would walk hand-in-hand from the school, his palm as soft as mine (the result, I suppose, of dipping it daily into pig buckets), and the most terrible foul stench coming from his simple clothes. I kept promising to kiss him and, when I could put it off no longer, I took a deep breath and almost staggered into that first, and as it happened, last kiss. It was not the piggy nature of that kiss, or the boy, that stopped the romance. In fact he kissed very well, powerfully and with a certain amount of gnawing, surprising in a young lad like that. I suppose that might have come from watching the pigs too.

No, the thing that stopped our affair was the result of his male desire to show off. Only a few minutes, in fact, after that first kiss, while I was still gulping for air, he picked up an acorn from beneath a tree under which we had romantically embraced.

'Oi can put this right up my snout,' he said, beaming with simple vanity. 'True as true, oi can.'

Even at ten I remember feeling unimpressed at this bragging. Putting an acorn up a nose seemed to me to be both stupid and the sure sign of a big nostril. Years later a man tried to tell me he could put a pigeon's egg in his ear and I could not find any interest for that either.

'Don't you bother Bertie Hannaford,' I said. 'It don't make any odds to me whether that acorn goes up your snout or not.'

'You don't think oi can do it,' he grunted. 'But oi can. Sure as shit oi can.'

'Oh go on then,' I sighed, 'Bertie Hannaford.' I sat down under the tree, putting my elbows on my knees. Just to make a further impression he started to do some kind of what you might call limbering-up exercises, running around in tight circles, his thin legs like sticks out of his ragged, baggy shorts.

'Why be you a-doin' that, Bertie?' I asked him. By then I must have begun to wonder what romance I had seen in him in the first place.

'Oi be getting a sweat-on,' he replied, still whirling about in little rings. 'If oi get a sweat on then 'ee slips up easier, don't un?'

I cupped my chin in my hands and watched him, feeling very dull. It's a mood that has come over me many times since, for I never have been able to like men who show off. Eventually his whirling slowed and then he stopped, standing, panting. The smell of the sty came from him in strong waves.

'Now,' he panted. ''Ere goes.'

He held up the big brown acorn for me to see. I nodded and sat watching. 'Da-ta-taaaa . . .' he imitated a sort of fanfare, then, first squinting down at the acorn, pushed it up his nose. I was surprised how easily it slid up there. It bulged underneath his skin making him look as though he had a boil or growth.

'There then,' he said proudly, spreading out his hands like some act in a circus. His voice sounded strange. ''Ow about that, Nelly Luscombe?'

'Ever so good,' I answered, then quite impressed by the performance. I paused and looked at him standing there. 'Now let's see you get it down.'

He laughed what was supposed to be a reckless laugh. 'Oi'll get 'ee down, all right,' he reckoned. 'That bain't any bother for oi.'

He put his thumb to the outside of his nose and pressed downwards. Nothing happened. Then two fingers also pushing down. The acorn stayed up there. Then two fingers pushing down and one from the other hand up inside the nostril. Nothing came down. Slowly he turned towards me with terror in his face.

'Oi'll be fucked,' he trembled. 'It be stuck!'

Stuck it was. We tried everything, pushing, pulling, trying to lever it out with his penknife. I even thought of banging him on the side of the nose with a stone to try and splinter the acorn, but he backed away just as I was about to hit him. He burst into tears and I had to take him back to school. We were late for the afternoon lessons and the teacher, a sharp, short-sighted woman, yelled at us and made us sit down at our desks. All the other children began to snigger. Bertie was still sobbing but the teacher purposely took no notice of him. She went on with the lesson. My hand kept half going up and down again but she ignored me too. Then Bertie howled dramatically. 'Oi be dyin'! Oi got an acorn stuck up my nose.'

She became very angry because she thought at first that he was playing-up, but then she saw the swollen and bruised nose and the blood around the nostril and she bent down and had a look. She went to get the headmaster who had a further look and eventually sent for the town ambulance. Bertie was taken to the Cottage Hospital where they got the acorn down and sent him home.

Somehow the business had irritated me and I decided I had been wrong about him. I realized I could never love anybody so foolish as to put an acorn up their nostril and not be able to get it down again.

In country places like that they look on children, or used to look on them, with the same sort of quaint mind that they would look on livestock. A boy might have a good eye for a furrow or show promise in the making of a fence; a girl would be considered in the same way, as something useful, or something that would be useful one day. I remember going to a harvest supper and dance, making myself look all shining and pretty in a red dress with a white frill at the hem. I had lovely full hair and a pretty face and brown arms and legs and the beginnings of the bust that was to make me famous. At the dance I knew that some of the boys and more of the men were watching me. My mother dropped her purse and I purposely bent over from the waist to display all my rounded parts and healthy legs. Behind me, I heard two farm men discussing the view.

'Ah,' one of them said, with Devon slowness. 'That little Nell Luscombe be growing fast. Won't be long afore 'er'll carry a couple o' good churns.'

They were great nights, those. The harvest supper and dance, the Christmas supper and the Easter Barn Dance. I remember them better than all the grand events of later years. The war was far away outside the walls of the village hall and inside all was rosy and comfortable, with enough to eat and drink and with all sorts of dancing and the village people doing turns on the stage. Even the local gentry would come along. Sir Waldo Beechcroft, his wife, Lady Martha, and sometimes their idiot son Parsifal. Parsifal was a poor young lad, mazed as they said locally, who turned the same hollow ghastly smile on everyone.

Rumours were put around that he sat for hours in Sir Waldo's barn flipping beans in the air from the end of his erect penis, a story I later found the be correct. Lady Martha talked to herself a great deal and was said to be in direct communication with ghosts. Her other son, who was sane, had been killed in the battles in France.

Sir Waldo was then in his late fifties. He was thin and hairless and had a long damp nose. It was rumoured that he liked wild dancing and young girls. It was his nose the drew my eyes. It seemed to start high up on the baldness of his head and descend like a long toboggan run. Fascinated I stared up it while we were partners, for we had come together in a progressive barn dance, the Lord and the little girl.

'Now who are you, gel?' His voice seemed to fall down to me.

'Nelly Luscombe,' I said. 'From Chapel Lane.' I thought I had said it in my normal voice, but perhaps I had whispered it because I was shy (although I doubt that) or perhaps the village band's music was too loud. Anyway he called down that he had not heard me. He asked me again. But he still did not hear. So he put his hard arms around my waist and lifted me up to him. I ended up with my legs around his thin ribs and his hands making a seat for my bottom. Everybody laughed at his kindness and liking for children.

'Now *who* are you?' he repeated. 'Pretty.'

'NELLY LUSCOMBE!' I bawled in his face. I heard the consternation of the villagers all around me and I heard my mother squeak over everybody else. But Sir Waldo pretended to laugh sportingly (the laugh shot down his nose too) and put me down to the floor again. I was glad of that.

'When you're a bigger girl, Nelly,' he snorted, 'you must come and work at the house. You'll like that.'

I was not at all sure that I would like it but I said a proper, grateful 'thank you' to him before he moved on to the next partner. My mother took me home that night and we walked, with my sister Mary, along the moonlit road. My stream was lying all silvery at the foot of the lane and owls were about in the roofs. My mother was upset.

'Nell,' she said as we went up the lane. 'You're a wicked girl.'

'Why am I, mum?' I asked surprised.

'You should never, *never*, shout in the face of the gentry,' she said. "Tis not proper.'

When I think now of all the faces of the gentry, I have shouted at, and worse, I have to laugh. But she meant it, poor creature. She did not know any better.

When I was very young I attracted the red eye of many middle-aged husband who wandered my way, and now I am casually coming to middle age myself it is the young men who find me to their liking. It is strange how the fancies go.

The headmaster at the town school was a gentle, eccentric and grey man, Mr Bunn, who in attempting to bring home to us in that peaceful place the fact that there was a war on would sometimes walk about the school wearing the gas mask. One day, in assembly, he insisted that all the other teachers wear their gas masks on the platform and he read the lesson from the Bible and said muffled prayers through the black piggy snout of what he called the respirator. The children began to snigger and then, for we could not help ourselves, laugh outright. The school was in uproar. The next day he made us all wear our gas masks through assembly. We sang 'God has blotted them out' and it must have sounded very strange. It was also very difficult and some children fainted. Mr Bunn said it was all to make us aware of the war.

Mr Bunn should have retired long before but because of the shortage of teachers in those times he stayed on. But he became increasingly unusual. Even further obsessed with the war effort he had his pupils ranging from the countryside gathering in the waste paper and old tins and other rubbish he imagined would defeat what he called the Hordes of Hunland. None of this salvage was ever collected and it stood like a giant rubbish dump in the school playground for months until the sanitary authorities removed it. He encouraged us to Dig for Victory and could be seen himself, far into the night, digging up old waste pieces of ground, apparently thinking that they would be useful for growing food. The vicar had a battle with him when he wanted to start digging up the churchyard and one summer evening he stood beside the bowling green, grinning and holding a garden fork. The police were called to warn him.

One Christmas Mr Bunn wrote a nativity play for the school which caused controversy because it included the figure of Hitler who arrived in the Bethlehem stable with the object of putting Jesus down and was attacked with a sickle by the Virgin Mary.

For me the idea seemed to be exciting and I was the first to volunteer to play Hitler and when this was rejected, put my hand up for the second-best part of the Virgin Mary and was accepted. My mother was very pleased when she heard the news (she had some belief that anything like that gave you credit with God). She was puzzled and doubtful about the inclusion of Hitler but, since she accepted unquestioningly every decision made by authority or by anyone socially higher than herself – which was almost everyone – she reasoned that it had to be all right. She offered to make me a Virgin Mary outfit from a pattern but Mr Bunn said they had suitable costumes in the school store and it was the object of seeing if they would fit that one afternoon he called me from class.

He was a nice, feathery old man, I thought, although that day he was upset because some boys had written 'Mr Bunn is a Hun' on the school lavatory wall. I was content to follow him to the storeroom and even to hold his friendly, shaky hand for the final part of the ascent up the school stairs.

'There,' he breathed when we had finally reached the store-room. He closed the door behind us. It would give us more space that way, more leeway. I couldn't understand why space was needed to be fitted out with a few flowing bits of cloth, but I did not ask. He turned his face around the shelves. It was not a very large room but it was stacked with school junk. Eventually he said: 'Ah, yes, Nelly. There it is. The Virgin Mary.'

There was a box on a high shelf and he said he could not reach it. He would have to go and fetch a step-ladder.

'Don't, Sir,' I said helpfully. 'I could reach it. If you lift me up.' I must have been a dirty old man's dream. I was always being lifted up.

Mr Bunn seemed amazed and delighted at the suggestion. 'Now I would never have thought of that,' he said, looking cheered. 'Let's put a chair up against the door so nobody comes in unexpectedly and knocks us all over like skittles.' He got a chair (it was then I began wondering why he didn't simply stand on the chair as he had to go and fetch one anyway) and fixed it under the door handle. Wheezing a bit he crouched down and I climbed onto his old shoulders. The first thing I felt were the bristly grey hairs at the back of his neck sticking into the skin of my legs.

'Upsidaisy,' he growled jovially as I rose in the air. He held me just above my podgy knees. I did not know the exact box which contained the Virgin Mary outfit and he seemed to have forgotten, or lost it, so for a while we waltzed back and forwards, with me jogging against the nape of his neck. I could feel him beginning to sweat. It was very odd being like that in that small, tall store-room.

But he was quite elderly and I think the weight and the strain of one thing and another weakened him because after about five minutes he saw the box we needed and I managed to take it from the shelf. He lowered himself like a giraffe and I climbed off his neck. I rubbed the sore parts of my legs.

'Now, let us see,' he said, opening the box. 'One Virgin Mary costume. That's it.' Out came a white silk dress and a blue robe with a cardboard halo which had been worn by generations of girls on the school stage. The same costume, without the halo, was used for the May Queen when we had the maypole dancing in the summer.

'Let's see if it fits,' he said cheerily. I put the costume up against me, but he said I ought to take my dress off to make sure it was right all around, and I thought there was nothing improper about this. After all, he was the headmaster. He made a fuss about undoing the buttons at the back of the dress and I had it off in two wriggles. I stood there only a little embarrassed, in my drawers and vest. Mr Bunn hinted that it might not be wise to mention this to my mother, although, I am sure, her only thought would have been to thank heaven that I was clean underneath, as she used to say.

'Oh dear, oh dear,' he said. 'Your legs are very red.'

''Tis the hairs on the back of your neck, Mr Bunn,' I said boldly. 'They're stiff as a hedgehog.'

'Oh dear, oh dear,' he said again and sportingly rubbed the red parts, briskly like a football trainer. He did this for some time and then looked up thoughtfully. 'It's time I had my gas mask drill,' he said. 'I don't suppose you've got yours, Nelly?' I admitted that I had not brought it. 'Never mind,' he said forgivingly. 'I'll have my practice and, so that we won't be wasting time, keeping you from your lessons too long, we'll say a prayer for God's blessing on our King, our Country, and our Nativity play and your part as the Virgin Mary.'

All this, coming from Mr Bunn, sounded not unreasonable to a girl only just ten. I watched him put his respirator on and take a few practice deep breaths. Then he knelt by the side of a large tin trunk and motioned me to join him. We bent there, next to each other, the old man in his gas mask, the girl in her vest, and prayed for all the things he had suggested. When we eventually rose he took off his gas mask and his face was covered with sweat. But that seemed to be it. I put the dress and the cloak and the halo on and took them off and replaced them with my own dress and in no time I was on my way back to the classroom.

Then, when almost at the door, I realized I had left in the storeroom an exercise book which I had carried from class. I went back and opened the door. He was sitting, crumpled, head in hands, shaking his face back and forwards. And he was crying, really crying and repeating to himself: 'Bunn the Hun. Bunn the Hun.'

He did not know I was there for he had not heard me open the door. I stood, suddenly overwhelmed with sadness for him, for I could see he was in trouble although I could not understand why. I backed out and closed the door and went thoughtfully back to the classroom.

Our lives went on peaceably in our narrow lane, in the insignificant village outside the small town, with not much to bother our days. Things were still done in the steady old ways. Change had always been slow and the war made it slower. Horses pulled in the fields and in the steep streets of Hopewell too; people worked long days and went home tired to listen to the news of battles far away. About us the farms and fields altered only with the year, shrugging off the seasons, and some strange olden customs were still followed. One day I saw a farmer, wearing no trousers, squatting thoughtfully in a ploughed field, testing the warmth of the earth to see if it was sowing time. What seemed to us to be exciting things happened, of course, as they do in all places. Wall-eyed Willie, the Upcoombe simpleton, went seriously mad in the middle of August and tried to chop his mother to pieces. It took eight neighbours to hold him down while the rest of the village gathered around shouting advice and encouragement, some of it intended for Willie himself. I stood with Granny Lidstone and watched the spectacle, feeling very unhappy for Willie whose eye was the only frightening thing about him. His mother was proudly showing the people the axe with which the attack had been made, while poor Willie was gurgling under the weight of all those people sitting on top of him. The axe was quite small and one that did not look as though it could have done much damage to the outside of Willie's mother, who was the largest and hardest woman in the South Hams, well-known for her tunnel-like mouth. Granny Lidstone held my hand and nodded wisely at the scene. 'They've been and sent for the Sanity Inspector,' she said.

There were other rural sensations. Farmer Swanley, who lived at Rotten Hill all solitary and in a house that fell more to bits every winter, was found dead in bed with a pig lying beside him. People said that he had the habit of taking the pig to bed to keep him warm. It was put around that it was a suicide pact.

Weddings and babies occurred regularly and not always in the correct sequence, the forces of nature always being stronger in those who live next to the ground. The people seemed to sense the rising of the sap. There was a field next to Totnes Road which was always full of couples of a spring evening when the urge was very strong on them. We children used to stand in the gate and count the boots and bottoms. I remember it was called Fallingfield.

But it was always death that was of the greatest interest. We would stand petrified, entranced, in the street or watch from windows as a bright coffin was taken by to the 'gravy-yard', as Granny Lidstone used to call it. It was frightening but very thrilling to know that someone you had seen walking about that very place was being carried boxed on the shoulders of those grave men. Village people loved to add tit-bits of fairy tale to the deaths of their neighbours. 'Oi looked out in the night and there I seed an angel standing knocking at Flossie's door. And oi thought "Ah, that Flossie will be agone come the morning", an' she was.'

The departure that caused the most interest was that of Mr Rush, a fat, rolly man who had been a sailor in his time. He died, so they said, of a disease that made you swell something terrible even after you were gone. They put him in his coffin and he swelled so much he exploded in the night in the front room of 12, Holmedale Villas. Granny Lidstone swore that she actually heard him blow up. The coffin was shattered and his wife said the wallpaper looked as though it was covered with roses.

My sister Mary would come home breathless from working at Hopewell Manor and have to sit, absolutely bursting to tell me something, but forbidden by my mother (who always said she knew what was right and what was wrong) to tell a word. Once we had gone to bed, though, and all the lights were doused, Mary would creep out from the blankets and open the curtains to let the moon in and we would lie, curled up, stifling laughter in our bed while she related what oddness she had seen.

The Manor was often visited by people in important-looking uniforms who arrived with cars with stars painted on them. There was a lot of eating and drinking done and on one occasion an Admiral was reckoned to have dropped down the well in the grounds and to have very nearly drowned before being pulled out. Sir Waldo apparently always went around talking gibberish, peering down the chute of his nose, and indecently assaulting any of the staff whom he managed to seize unawares. Lady Martha knitted long scarves for Russians. When they had their dinner parties with generals and other high-ups they used to plan the battles of the war on the table and often left it covered with drawings and maps and scraps of paper scrawled with figures and secrets.

While these things were taking place at the Hall, not very far away in the bar, Parsifal, the idiot son, was enslaved by his pastime 'Oi seed 'ee,' Mary whispered to me in our moonlit bed. 'With moi own eyes oi seed 'ee do it.'

One placid afternoon just before tea-time, a lost German bomber flew over the town and then the village and dropped one bomb which blew down all the houses in Chapel Lane and killed the three people who were in them at the time. Wormy Wood, Granny Lidstone and our mother.

I was on my way home from school when this thing happened and I got off the bus in the village to see the smoke and people all crowding round Chapel Lane. I nudged my way through the crowd and saw what it was like. The air raid wardens and the fire-brigade and all the rest of them were pulling and tugging at the pieces of what had been our house. Our sofa was strangely sitting there in the rubble and the fireplace and the chimney breast were still standing. People rushed and shouted. The terrace was so flat you could see my stream at the bottom of the lane.

Standing a bit apart from all the other people was my sister Mary. She was by herself, ever so still, and I went over and stood next to her and watched with her. For a long time we didn't say anything but just stared at what was going on, but not in any sort of panic or anything. It was as if we were watching men doing some road-repairing. I did not realize it was a bomb that had dropped and I said to her: 'Mary, did our dad do that?'

'No,' she said, still staring ahead. 'A German bomb done it.'

The men were shouting and pulling stuff away from one corner of our house, where the kitchen used to be. At the back our dresser was sticking up out of all the mess.

'Is our mum in there?' I asked Mary quietly.

'I reckon 'er is.' she replied.

'Will she be all right?'

''Tis doubtful,' said Mary shaking her head. She was fifteen at the time.

'Who'll look after us?' I said.

'I'll be looking after 'ee, Nell,' she said seriously. 'So don't you go causin' me any trouble.'

When at last I went back, after all these unruly years, I went to the library in the main street by the church gates (they used to lock these during the war, it was said as a defence against enemy parachustists, something which puzzled me even as a child). Walking there again I felt sure that somebody would recognize Nell Luscombe, but nobody did. Nor did I get a glimpse of a face I might have known. I kept trying to imagine what my childhood friends would look like after all these years, trying to fix their faces onto the faces that passed me by. But the population were all strangers and nobody looked at me. In the library I asked to see the files of the *Hopewell Chronicle* and I turned the dry pages until I came to the report of the bombing of Chapel Lane on that wartime afternoon.

Because of all the secrecy of those times they could not even mention the name of our village, but called it merely a hamlet in the South Hams. The victims were named: Mrs Amelia Lidstone, aged 78; Mr Algernon Barker Wood (what an important name for old Wormy) and Mrs Joan Annie Luscombe, aged 32, the mother of two little girls. The report was almost brief, just the spare details and somebody praising the work of the air raid wardens which was strange because nobody was rescued and all they had to do was clear the mess. I did not expect much to be in the newspaper but I expected more than that. But in those days, I suppose, they did not want to encourage the enemy just when we were on the point of winning the war.

It seemed extraordinary, but the paper was full of things that were nothing to do with the war, whist drives, reports of the crops, a new vicar at some church, a dance organized by the Red Cross, plans for new drainage, cooking recipes and sewing hints, somebody wanting help with looking after some stables, a letter complaining of the poor biting quality of wartime false teeth, and another recalling the history of the Hopewell darts league. The Germans had dropped their bomb in the middle of all that.

Feeling empty I turned the pages to the following week's issue. There was a whole column about the three funerals, our mother's the last of them, written about just as though it was the burial of someone who had fallen down stairs. The list of mourners brought back names in my memory, some of whom I could picture from my childhood. One of the coffin bearers was Luke Lethbridge, her lover from the harvest field. A single sentence said that the widower – serving in His Majesty's forces – followed the cortège in uniform.

What it did not say was that my father trailed behind the coffin oozing cider, marching in his ridiculously baggy uniform and on his shoulder a shotgun borrowed from one of his public bar friends. I can see him now, like some army dwarf, striding out below that greatcoat, his eyes floating emotionally way in front of him, with the shotgun held as if it were the funeral of the King. Over the open grave he let off both barrels into the surrounding trees, disturbing the rooks not to mention the vicar and the mourners, and then burst into gusts of tears. The bloody bastard.

Another item in the newspaper said that a collection among friends and neighbours in Upcoombe had amounted to the fine sum of thirty-one pounds, seven shillings and elevenpence and that this was to alleviate the suffering of the motherless children. It was handed to my father and, needless to add, went only to alleviate his suffering.

After the funeral, we went, surrounded by mourners, to the house of Miss Timms, a drunkard from the village whom dad knew although until that afternoon we had not realized how well he knew her. There he held court with a glass of whisky in one hand and the other hand around Miss Timms waist. She was a good-sized woman, swollen by cider, and his short arm hardly came out the other side of her. Mary and I looked at each other doubtfully.

The drinks and cold meats went down the surrounding throats in steady quantities. They sat all around the walls, like a sort of shadow show, enjoying themselves and gossiping about other funerals they had enjoyed. There were some uncles and aunts and some other bits and pieces of family. One uncle, whom I can never remember seeing before or since, made me sit on his lap and squeezed me between his legs in play, which I did not like although he seemed to.

'Mind 'ee,' said one of the aunts in mid-guzzle, ''er didn't suffer. I allus thinks it be not so bad if 'ee don't suffer.'

'Naw,' said another, her face sunk in a sandwich. ''Ee sure don' suffer if 'ee gets struck by one of them bombs.'

'Naw,' my father agreed with a wise sniff, his mouth awash with pie and whisky. ''Er didn't suffer one minute.' He had made her suffer for years. 'In war,' he said, looking around like somebody essential. 'In war, people die. All the time they be dying. I know.'

''Ow is you know then?' asked my Aunt Ella, whom I liked a bit. 'Oi thought you was tucked up safe in Aldershot or somewhere. 'Ow could you know about dying?'

That upset my father. 'I be on *secret* work,' he rasped. His voice dropped like a stone and he stared around at everybody as if he thought we might all be spies. 'On His Majesty's Secret Service, I be.'

They knew him too well to be impressed. 'What is it, this secret work?' Aunt Ella demanded. 'What be you about?'

My father glowed angrily. You could see it even though the room was reverently dim. His sharp cheeks were like spiteful coals. 'I can't tell 'ee, can I?' he snorted, whirling around, sending pie crumbs spraying around the room. ''Ow can I tell 'ee? Not if it be secret.'

'We *all* be family 'ere, Percy Luscombe,' grunted Aunt Ella. 'There be no need to keep it from us. 'Tis my opinion that there bain't be any secrets. You be in the army cookhouse, and don't deny it either. All the secrets you have is what goes in the bloody soup.'

My father went mad. He rushed up to Ella, throwing his khaki arms about and shooting her with pie crust. She wiped it away carefully and looked him in the eye. 'Go on,' she said. 'Deny it.'

'I be a fightin' man!' he howled. It was the whisky howling. 'I be in dread mortal danger!'

'Aye,' sniffed Ella. 'Dread mortal danger of dying of drink.'

'I got a gun! You seed my gun today! I fired 'un over the grave of my poor wife.' He stopped, fell to his knees and began to sob, pounding his fists against the sofa. He had done it so many times that it had no effect. The relatives just sniffed and carried on with the food and drink.

'Gun?' put in Uncle Herbert, who was Ella's husband. 'That bain't be no army gun. That were a bloody rabbit gun you had there George Luscombe. And I knows where you got it. From Jed Brown at the pub.'

My father got to his feet. 'Drinks!' he shouted. 'Everybody 'ave a drink. It's all on me.' He jumped out of the whole argument just like that. He always did. And because they all knew him they didn't go on with it either. They forgot the gun and the Secret Service and all of it and set to drink and eat as much as they could in memory of my mother. Mary and I sat and watched them wolfing. Somebody gave us a pie between us, asking us not to let the jelly run on our dresses, and we had one sip of sherry each. Then they all got up and trooped out to go to the pub, my father and Miss Timms following behind, him with his head bent almost double with grief to the benefit of the neighbours. No one said anything to Mary and me. We just stood in the room with what they had left scattered all around us. She looked at me and I looked at her. Nobody wanted us.

CHAPTER THREE

The next day a woman with a black moustache took us to St Bernard's Institution at Bristol, a city we had only heard tell about. We did not know we were going to a place like that until we actually arrived at the iron gates. My father had said that he was sending us on a holiday and innocently Mary and I had begun to collect the buckets and spades which we had kept since the pre-war days when we had been able to go down to the Devon beaches. Helped by Miss Timms he piled up the lie, saying that despite the lateness of the year it would still be warm in Bristol and there were several good beaches nearby. We packed everything we had, which was not a long job, and set out for the station with the moustached lady who came especially to fetch us. She was a miserable-faced creature (although women with moustaches always have a hard struggle to smile) and she hardly said a word to us. But she kept staring at the buckets and spades and eventually, after we had changed trains and were on the last part of the journey, she leaned over and said meanly: 'What you be wanting with those things?'

We were amazed that she had never seen a bucket and spade and apparently did not know their use. Mary explained that they were for digging sand castles and the woman listened for a minute, her whiskers twitching, before sniffing up the length of her nose and grunting, 'You won't be digging sandcastles where you're going.'

We came separately to the same conclusion that she was jealous because she was too old and crabby to enjoy beaches and things like that. It was only when we walked up the hill towards the place where we were going that it began to dawn on us that something was wrong. The building was outside the city in untidy fields and yet for some reason its walls and windows looked hung with soot.

For two village children grime was unknown and we stood on the hill and gazed up at the dark gates against the dark sky. The iron letters, like a black rainbow, curved against the sulky clouds. ST BERNARD'S INSTITUTION it said. Mary dropped her bucket and spade causing Whiskers to jump. The bucket rolled, lop-sided down the hill. We had been tricked.

The first thing the matron, who was called Mrs Fagence, did was to have all our clothes burned. We were hurt about this because our mother had always kept us decent, but Mrs Fagence said they were falling to bits. 'They're only fit for the incinerator' she said. They gave us some stiff pyjamas, odd bottoms and tops, and sent us to be bathed and have our hair combed for nits.

A boy from Plymouth had arrived just before us and he was having his clothes burned too. All three of us stood stark bare on the landing; then the boy rushed naked after the woman taking his trousers to the incinerator and fought small hand to large hand with her until he got the trousers back. He hung onto them and turning away from her he started to get something from one of the pockets. The old cow smacked him across the backside leaving the print of her hand there. But he had got what he wanted, his penknife. He was crying and the woman seeing the penknife, began to howl 'A knife! A knife! He's got a knife!'

'It's my penknife,' said the boy. 'I want it.'

'Don't you dare stick it in me.'

'I don't think it would,' he said simply, walking back towards us. 'It's not sharp enough, missus.'

This boy, David Lenny, was ten, a year younger than me. In later life he was to become my lover.

It was strange that when I first saw him he was wearing no clothes and that's the way I remember him best. They put us in the bath together and we sat opposite each other, neither of us shy, but our lives full of catastrophe, both present and future.

'I come from Plymouth,' he said. 'Where you from?'

'Upcoombe.'

He did not ask me where that was.

'My mum died in hospital,' he said next.

'A bomb hit my mum,' I said triumphantly.

'My dad got torpedoed. He got drowned.'

That was difficult to trump. But I tried.

'My dad goes on secret missions. I expect he'll be dead soon.'

'Did they burn your clothes as well?'

'Yes.'

'It's bloody terrible here,' he said.

'Yes. I'm going to hate it.'

'Me, I'm going to escape,' he said. 'That's why I wanted my penknife. I'll be needing that.'

'Can I come with you?'

'If you like.'

We stared at each other up the length of the bath. It was in the middle of a great tank of a room with half a dozen other baths in it. We had to keep our voices low to stop them echoing around. I could see he was looking at me more intently. He pointed his finger at my girlish breasts.

'Can I have a touch of those?' he asked politely.

'Why?'

'I never touched any before.'

'All right. If you're quick.'

He moved forward in a sort of studious way, his eyes on my pale blunt nipples. His fingers came out of the water and he examined each breast in turn, running his touch over the swellings, and tapping each nipple with his middle finger like he was sounding it to see if it was hollow. He had the talent for it even then and I felt the little electric thrill run from my teats down my stomach. I could feel myself blushing in the steam. Then he looked at me and grinned in the way I came to know so well in later years. He pressed the right titty harder with his finger and said: 'Ding-ding.'

We both giggled, then laughed. Then another miserable woman (the place was stocked with them) came in and stared at us because she could not understand why we were laughing. 'What's all the joke about?' she said. She had been eating and she had some macaroni cheese hanging on the front of her blue overall and another bit on her eyebrow.

'Nothing,' said David. 'We was just laughing for nothing.'

Not long after we had been sent to that disgraceful place for children, I had a nasty and frightening adventure with the mayor of a nearby town and his white mouse. All sorts of dignified people used to go in processions through the home and stare at us and nod when something was explained to them about us by somebody on the staff. We used to be sitting there, munching our meal or washing up or in the dormitory, dusting or putting polish on the floor. And they would troop around like groups of pigeons, most of them senile and snobbish, screwing up their lips as they inspected us, trying to smile as if they could well remember the times when they were in an institution.

After a few weeks you got used to it and you just carried on with what you were about, giving them a quick grin to order, or holding some old pigeon's hand when it made her feel better. They used to contribute to the place, so they liked to come and see what good their money was doing us.

But, even at that age, I must have had some sort of eye and taste for the glistening things of life, because when the mayor and his wiry wife, and another clutch of mumblers, were shown around one day, I looked at his

chain and wondered to myself how much it might fetch in the right
hands. He saw me looking and he whispered to Mrs Fagence and she
called me away from the washing-up sink, telling me to wipe my hands
dry. 'We can't have you wetting the mayor,' she said. I was wearing a
miserable sort of striped pinafore and I rubbed my hands down that. He
looked dignified, as if he was sucking his cheeks in, and his smile was like a
crack in an eggshell. He tried to tempt me forward as if I was a puppy or
something, holding out this golden chain with its lumpy badge on the
end.

'You know I think she would like to see this,' he said patronizingly to
the people around him. 'Would you girl?'

Since there was no chance of getting my hands on it permanently I was
not over eager, but it was the richest thing I had ever seen at close
quarters and I was interested, and always have been, in rich things.
Standing before him just under his waistcoat I looked up at it dangling
just above my eyes, without saying anything and without moving.

'You can't see it properly like that,' he huffed. 'Let's see . . .'

He glanced around in a way that hinted he was used to people running
about and getting chairs for him and somebody quickly brought a chair.
He sat down, spread his black-trousered leg like a plump spider, and
when he was all smoothed out and set, he reached over and lifted me onto
his knee. All the children were watching and I sat stiffly and began
swinging my head mechanically from side to side like a ventriloquist's
dummy. I was very good at that sort of mimicry and it has proved very
useful during my career. It is shocking what some perverted men do to
helpless ventriloquists' dummies. I knew a man in Antibes once, who had
a whole cupboard full of them, all ragged and shagged, poor things.

As I sat, like wood, on the mayor's lap, twisting my head one way and
then the other, the other children burst out laughing. David laughed
bigger than anybody – because he was very brave and defiant for a small
boy – but after joining in for a minute because they felt they had to, the
grown-ups stopped and Mrs Fagence gripped my upper arm viciously
and told me to stop clowning.

The mayor chortled in a pompous town-hall sort of way, but he soon
stopped. It was like water running away down a plug-hole.

The grip Mrs Fagence had on my arm shot tears to my eyes. I stopped
my acting and just sat there. He had put a buttery hand around my waist
and now he tightened it a bit.

'Ah,' he said in his resounding official voice, like somebody talking into
a chamber pot. 'So it's the mayor's old dangler you're wanting to see, is
it?'

He held out the end of the chain and even at that age I could see it
wasn't even true gold, just some metal done over with gold. I pretended
to be fascinated by the tatty buckles and badges around his sweaty neck.
I ran the chain through my hands and he explained what the coat of arms
meant on the end. My eyes kept going to the tide mark running around
above his collar, making it look as though his head were detachable.

He put me down eventually and after all the usual pattings and pettings they cleared off to their cars and left us to get on with the washing-up. David whispered to me that he was making plans to escape from the place and asked me if I wanted to go too. I nodded excitedly over the soapsuds. Where would we go, I wondered. Perhaps over the ocean. Perhaps to kind people who would take us and protect us.

Mrs Fagence called me the next day into her office which smelled of floor polish and wet sheets. 'Oh you're a lucky girl, Nell Luscombe,' she bawled. 'You're going to tea – with the mayor! He's sending his car. His car!' I nodded calmly.

'I hope you're grateful,' she said pursing her mouth. 'You ought to be grateful.'

After school in a fresh, flowered dress produced from some secret store kept for such emergencies, and nearly new buttoned shoes (taken from a girl who had arrived wearing presentable clothes) I waited for the mayoral car. While I stood stiffly, Mrs Fagence gave my hair a final examination for nits and chanted instructions on eating correctly and not picking my nose. She seemed to think I ought to be all agog and nervous, but I was not. Occasions like that never did worry me. I have been led to the bed of a perverted Crown Prince without a tremor.

The mayor lived in a small town about half an hour's drive away and I sat grandly alone in the back seat of the car with the chaffeur stiff as a new boot in the front. At first I sat on one end of what seemed an enormous seat and then on the other, bright in my dress, my legs sticking to the leather. Then I sat in the middle, like royalty, balancing myself with my hands pushed out like props on either side. But that seat was made for larger bottoms than mine and I could not get comfortable. Eventually I simply stood on the seat and looked out through the little back window, poking my tongue out at two young army officers following behind in a car.

The mayor's home was heavy and quiet in the main street of the town. Outside it was covered in creepers which even fell over the windows. It had been raining and drops fell from the top of the doorway onto my dress.

I was eleven years old and I had no idea what sort of power a mayor actually had. Vaguely I thought he must rule everybody around in the town and the countryside and have many running servants, so I was surprised to find him alone in the house.

Even the chauffeur backed out and went away and I was left there with the mayor. He said I could call him Uncle Dick. He took my hand and showed me around the house which was big and boring and not nearly as warm as Granny Lidstone's was before the bomb hit it.

But after a while we went into a room where a good fire was burning and two padded sofas faced each other in front of the grate. There was a short table and a tea tray on the table with cakes and sandwiches the like of which I have never seen even in shop windows. I thought perhaps in his position he might get special rations. The sofas faced each other and Uncle Dick suggested that we placed ourselves one on one side and one on the other. When I sat down the table came just below the bulges of my knees. Straight away the dress they had given me rode up my legs. I did not think it was immodest or even important, and after one try at pulling it down, only to see it climb again, I did not think about it again but began filling my mouth with peanut butter sandwiches.

The mayor asked me if I preferred tea or milk and I said I would like milk. I saw his hand was trembling with the jug and it slopped over. He filled a cup for me and handed it across. I could see he was still shaking and I remembered being told at Sunday School about the man in the Bible who was sick of the palsy.

'Do you suffer from the palsy?' I asked politely.

His eyes bulged and he blew crumbs from his mouth and choked. Then he laughed, without any meaning, and bent over and patted my knees. We continued to sit there, facing each other across the fireside. Now he did not seem to know what to say and I did not care very much. I was craftily trying to race him to the last cream bun. He had poured himself some tea and the cup rattled again in the saucer.

'Your mummy is dead,' he said eventually.

'A bomb got her,' I said casually through the cream of the bun which I had succeeded in capturing. 'A German one.'

'What a shame. What a pity,' he sighed. 'And what about your father? He's in the army, isn't he Nelly?'

For some reason I was quite chilled he knew my name.

'Fighting in the war,' I said blatantly. 'Secret operations.'

'Do you get letters from him?' He was leaning towards me again.

'No,' I shrugged. That was another thing that had not occurred to me. 'I don't reckon 'ee knows where to write. Anyway I 'spect 'ee be busy fighting.'

'I'll make inquiries,' he said importantly. 'I'll find out where he is and make sure he sends you letters.'

'All right, if you like,' I repeated off-handedly because it truly did not matter to me. And he never *did* do anything anyway because we didn't get any letters from our father.

There was another scrap of silence. Then I dropped a dollop of cream on my exposed knee and I must have opened my legs as it landed. As I flung them apart I heard a funny quick sound from the mayor. Granny Lidstone could draw in her gums and make that noise. I looked up at him to see him staring right up my legs. I could not believe it. *He was staring right up my legs!* His eyes were all stuck out and I was frightened to close my legs so I left them open. It had never occurred to me that a man would want to look up there.

'Would you like the cream horn?' I asked politely.

He jumped out of his stare. He was pink in the cheeks and his lips had gone all rubbery. 'Er . . . no. No thank you . . . Nelly,' he managed to say. 'You have it. I'll be back in a minute.'

As soon as he had gone I grabbed the cream horn and locked my knees tightly together. I had another good try at pulling the dress down over them but it was no good. He was gone a few minutes and when he came back he had got his mayor's outfit on, a long red coat with fur down the front of the sleeves, the forged gold chain I had seen before and a three cornered hat which I thought made him look odd.

'Don't you think I look grand?' he asked me, gleaming pomposity.

I must have thought about it. 'Oh yes,' I said after studying him. 'Just like Mr Punch.'

He was not overpleased with this and his face went hard about the edges. But then he put his smile back like somebody replacing a clock on a mantlepiece and walked forward, until he was standing above me, the robes seeming to block out the light like a heavy curtain. 'Feel the fur, Nelly,' he said. 'Do you like fur?'

I reached out to touch the edge of his sleeve and jumped as a small, white face nudged out of the drooping sleeve. It was a mouse.

'That's Perkins,' said the mayor. He touched me again on the legs and I moved up to make room for him on the couch. In those heavy garments and in front of a roaring fire I could see he was beginning to sweat. 'Do you like mice?' he panted. He brought the thing out of his sleeve, held it and invited me to shake its paw.

'Shake hands, Perkins,' said the mayor. 'Shake hands with the pretty young lady.'

The mouse was as reluctant as I was, but we put a little show of shaking hands. Then the mayor took my hand, selected a finger and helped me to stroke it down the mouse's back. He seemed to get more enjoyment out of this than either Perkins or me. His face had grown very fat and florid and the sweat was oozing. I thought perhaps the chain was hanging too heavy on him.

'You're a bad lad, Perkins,' he breathed on the mouse. It did not seem to care. 'You're always escaping and running in the most inconvenient places.'

I had the last peanut butter sandwich half way to my mouth but the uneasy feeling came on me and I stopped with it poised in mid-air. The mouse could smell the peanut butter and its whiskers were vibrating.

At that moment that bastard mayor let his rotten mouse run right up my leg. It was the most amazing and terrifying thing. Even now I can feel it making a dash for my drawers. I hardly had time to break out of my freeze and scream before the mayor in his furry robes was on top of me and grabbing at my dress and my bottom and my legs. 'Perkins! Perkins!' he was shouting. 'Come back at once! Naughty mouse!'

His weight knocked me back onto the couch. I screamed really loudly then. I could feel the creature charging about up there.

I was screeching and jumping about and the mayor was just about smothering me with the weight of his fucking ermine, and grabbing now at my drawers making out he was trying to grab the mouse. 'Perkins! Perkins! Naughty mouse! Naughty naughty mouse!'

Even now I can see me kicking back on the couch, my legs flying about in the air, the mayor howling, sweating and grabbing all over the place. I can hear that cry of 'Perkins! Perkins! Naughty little mouse!' echoing down the years into my trembling ear.

He finally trapped it. 'Got him!' blubbered the horrible mayor. 'It's all

right, Nelly. I've got naughty Perkins now.' He fumbled around under
my skirt until he had the mouse firmly in his hand. Slowly he drew it out.
'Perkins,' he said, holding it up. 'Perkins, the mayor is ashamed of you.'

I had collapsed back on the couch, everything drained from me, and I
began to sob.

'Don't cry, Nelly,' he said. He took advantage of the sympathy to put
his hands on my legs again as he leaned over. 'Have another sandwich.'

He handed one to me and I automatically accepted it and began to
bite it through my tears.

The mouse had gone back up the sleeve of the robe, having no doubt
found the experience just as trying as I had. 'Perkins is a very bad mouse,'
muttered the mayor. He looked flabby and deflated and I'll wager he
was. 'Wherever will he get next?'

'Anywhere,' I managed to say through the crumbs and the crying. ''Ee
can go anywhere as long as it bain't up my dress.'

It was the later days of spring when we made our escape. David had
planned it for a long time but he said, in his wise youthful way, that we
ought to see what the war situation was before we went, since the
authorities might think we were saboteurs or spies. But on a night in
April he crept to me in the dormitory and kneeling by my bed he
whispered: 'The war's nearly over, Nell. We'll make a run for it soon.
You're sure you want to?'

I remember pushing my hand from beneath my blankets and it
touched his worried face. 'I want to come with you Davie,' I said. I felt
him bite my arm gently and then he went off between the dark beds,
crouched like a dwarf.

We decided to give my sister Mary a chance to go with us but we were
going to tell nobody else. Mary said she did not want to come because she
had obtained the job of clearing the staff room which meant that she
could eat what they had left at the table and there was a good chance that
she would soon be a prefect at the school. She always was one for
advancement.

It was not easy for us though. It needed a lot of bravery. Children who
had run away were caned when they were caught and they never did it
again. In fact I thought that David was wavering, although he kept
winking and nudging me because of our secret. Two or three weeks went
by without any signal for us to go. I was impatient.

'All right then, when are we going to bunk?' I challenged him in the
school playground. 'I'm waiting.'

'Any day,' he said out of the corner of his mouth. 'When the time is
ripe. I'll tell you. We'll need clothes and food and money.'

The clothes were easy and the food not that much more of a problem
because I could pick the lock on the storeroom door in one minute ten
seconds, which was faster than anyone else in the place. But the money
was a different matter.

'How we going to get the money?' I asked.

'Grab it. Steal it,' he said casually.

Even so it needed something drastic finally to make us run away from St Bernard's. It happened one afternoon at the end of April when I was walking with some girls toward the boot room where the children had to clean shoes or boots ready for the next day's school. We went around the corner and there I saw Davie hanging out of the windows of the Superintendent's study which was two storeys up. He was screaming in a strange whistling way, suspended from the sill, with Mr Fagence framed in the window holding Davie's wrists and shouting at his face: 'Thief! Thief! Little swine thief!'

I screamed out and ran to the base of the wall because I had some idea of catching him when he fell. The other girls just stuck open-mouthed and stared up at the sight of Davie's legs kicking above them.

'Confess!' shouted Mr Fagence. 'Confess!'

'Yes! Yes I did, Mr Fagence!' Davie yelled back.

Then it came to me that, unbelievably, the bastard man was hanging the boy out of the window on purpose. He was not trying to rescue him: he was risking his neck.

'Stop it, Sir!' I bawled up at the window. I scurried back from the wall so that I could see him and he could see me. 'Stop it. Pull him in!' I howled madly. Tears were spreading all down my face and over my mouth. 'I'll tell the bloody police! You'll be in prison for this! I'll tell on you!'

It was a rash threat, but it seemed to bring the man to some sort of sense. He glared down at my upturned weeping face but then shouted back as though he had to explain: 'A thief! I won't have thieves at St Bernard's!'

But at least, he started to haul Davie back inside the window, scraping his face and knees up against the ragged brickwork. I was still sobbing and shaking. I turned savagely on the other girls. 'You saw that. You're witnesses, remember!' Then I ran through the nearest door and up the stairs. The Superintendent's door was shut and locked. Wrathfully I banged on it with my fists. To my surprise it opened at once, and Davie came out, his cheek grazed and bleeding, his face ghost white, his eyes bulging like a calf's.

We stood helpless, facing each other. Nobody else was in the corridor. I put my arms about his thin body and held him to me like my mother used to hold me. He wasn't crying now but his body was stiff as if he had frozen and he would not talk, only shake his head. I began to walk with him down the corridor. We were almost at the far end when the door opened behind us and Mr Fagence, sheet-faced as well, came out into the corridor and yelled after us: 'Thief! Thief!'

My fury swamped my fear. I turned back, keeping my arm about Davie's shoulder. 'Shit! Shit and more shit to you, Mr Fagence!' I shouted. I thought he was bound to come after me, but to my surprise and relief he turned angrily, went back into the room and slammed the door. Then I could hear his fists pounding it from the other side. He was not fit to look after rats.

Gently I took Davie down to the ablutions and washed his face in cold water. He was sick in the wash basin. I took him to the toilet because he wanted to sit down. He sat on the pan with his head held in hands. He still said nothing but eventually he drew his face up and stared at me standing by the door.

'I reckoned I'd had it then, Nelly,' he whispered. 'Thought I was done for.'

'We'll tell the police,' I said decisively. ''E's not allowed to hang boys out of windows. He be a cruel bastard.'

'The door was open,' sniffed Davie. 'And I thought I'd take the chance and get some money for our bunking off. I'd just got my hand in his cash tin when the sod walked in. He went right off his head. He knocked me all over the place. Then he punched me right in the stomach and while I was doubled over he picked me up and hung me out of the window. Fuck, I was so scared Nelly.'

I took a step towards him as he sat in the cubicle and put my hands on his head again. I just pulled it to my stomach, feeling its hard roundness against my belly. 'We've got to tell the cops, Davie,' I said again, looking at the pipe up the wall. 'We can't be lettin' the sod get away with that, now can we?'

'Wearily he rubbed his head against my pinafore. 'That's no good,' he whispered. ''E told me. When 'e got me back in the room, 'e told me. If I told the coppers then 'e would reckon that 'e caught me hanging onto the windowsill, like I was trying to climb out because I heard him coming. It'd be only his word against mine. And you know who'd win.'

I sighed: 'What we goin' to do Davie?'

'We goin',' he decided. 'We're certain goin' now. I got an idea.'

'What idea?'

He shook his head. 'Bain't tellin' you right now, Nell, because I need to have a shit. And a bit of a think. Shut the door Nell.'

For a moment, his head still against me, he put his arms around my legs. I could feel him trembling still. Then he sat up and began to unbuckle his snake belt. I left him there and shut the door.

At school we had been learning lessons about some peasant revolt years ago in history. The teacher always told us we could learn from history because history always came around a second time. I found it all boring and dry, but Davie, who sat in the desk across the aisle from me, seemed to pay a lot of attention. He told me he was trying to learn how to be great.

'It's us,' he said, as though finally deciding, as we walked back to St Bernard's from school. 'We're just like them peasants. We've got to revolt, Nelly, we've got to rise up against them. We'll do it tonight. And while everyone's revolting I'm going to creep in and nick the money from the office.

It was a marvellous rebellion. We talked everybody into taking part although Mary said she would not do any actual attacking but would stay at the far end of the corridor to keep watch. 'I don't want to be gettin' myself into any trouble,' she said. She ought to have been born in

Switzerland that one.

Davie planned it painstakingly. He had one boy, a little kid from Cornwall called Blackie, who was small but very clever at jumping, running and tipping head over heels. I often wondered if he ever became a clown or a tumbler in a circus. He would jump from or over anything. There was a swing bridge down by the docks in Bristol and, when we were allowed out for Sunday walks with one of the staff, he would slide off and climb over a fence and leap from one bit of the swing bridge to the other just as it was opening. He left the jump too late one day and had to be rescued from the dock by the bridge keeper. Even while they were still in the water he accused the bridge keeper of speeding up the opening so that he would miss the other side.

This acrobatic boy was put on top of a wardrobe just behind the dormitory door. He was an ugly little soul and he crouched there like one of those gargoyles, grinning and waiting.

Also on top of the wardrobe was a little girl who was a bit slow and mental. She was called Mad Martha. She was about seven and she did not remember her parents or even know where she came from. She just went around with a kind of damp smile on her face, gentle and silly, although one day she strangled three rabbits. She had just got into somebody's garden and seen the rabbits in their cage and taken them out one by one and strangled them. She was like that.

We had put her behind the boy Blackie and told her what to do. It was not difficult to persuade her to get up there because she did everything anybody asked, nodding that everlasting, mad smile.

When everything was ready Davie gave a signal and all the other children started a riot. It was in the boys' dormitory and the girls were never allowed in there so we knew that the mixture of voices would soon bring Mr Fagence to see what was happening. The children loved it, shouting and cursing and throwing things. It must have taken less than two minutes for the Superintendent to take the bait. He charged up the corridor, obviously having come straight from his evening meal because he had a handkerchief tucked into his trousers and his mouth crammed with macaroni cheese.

'Whaht, whaht, whahtsh going on?' he shouted through the food. 'Shtop . . . shtop it! Shtop it at oncsh!'

At that moment little Blackie launched himself through the air and caught Mr Fagence square across his shoulders. He went down like he had been hit with a telegraph pole. Then all the eager boys piled on top of him. While he was kicking and choking underneath the mound I grabbed the fork from his hand which was sticking out of the side and gave it a good shove straight up his arse. I enjoyed that.

The second part of Davie's plan was still to happen. Davie stood apart from the pile of boys now entirely hiding Mr Fagence on the floor. He had calculated beautifully. Mrs Fagence had not yet arrived but we knew she would not be long. Davie eyed me and I nodded. All the girls were ready and waiting.

Along the corridor she came, the bloody old ginger harridan, bellowing and throwing her wicked arms about. She had two pieces of macaroni cheese hanging over her lower lip like devil's fangs. They suited her. At first she thought it was just a general fight and did not realize that her husband was underneath the pile of boys.

'Beasts!' she screamed. 'Animals! Stop, stop!' She began kicking the nearest boys with her pointed shoes and then bending over and belabouring them. On Davie's signal, and it had been well rehearsed, the boys rolled away revealing the smashed Mr Fagence underneath. It was as though twenty pigs had rolled on him.

'Mr Fagence!' screamed Mrs Fagence. 'Oh, Mr Fagence!'

Davie nodded to Mad Martha smiling on top of the wardrobe. She may have been dim but there was nothing wrong with her timing. She flew through the air like a fat bat, striking Mrs Fagence between the shoulder blades with the same accuracy that Blackie had shown with Mr Fagence. It was wonderful to see. The old cow pitched forward with a terrible croak and then all the girls pitched in, whooping like red indians. The boys then fell on Mr Fagence again, jumping up and down on him as if he were a trampoline. I thought they might even squash him to death but I did not care. I went over to the female pile, with Mrs Fagence prostrate underneath, pulled her handbag away from the rubble, took her purse out and the key to the office. I gave the key to Davie so that he could get at the cash box. We went quickly from the dormitory, bursting with success and joy. At the end of the corridor Mary was concealed in her watching place. It would not be long before other members of the staff would come running. Mary wanted to be clear of the trouble by then. She saw us and then looked away as though she did not want to be a witness.

'Bye-bye, Mary,' I laughed, holding on to Davie's hand.

'You'll come to no good, Nell Luscombe,' said Mary, her face still turned away from me. 'Mark my words.'

'I know,' I laughed. I think I did too.

CHAPTER FOUR

It was wonderful to be free. I have always found stories of elopements enjoyable because of the excitement and the making for freedom and I suppose, young as we were, this was a kind of elopement. I really trusted Davie. I believed that nothing could go wrong with us and our plans as long as he was with me. In those days he had what you could only call a deep confidence, amazing in a boy of his age, very silent but sure.

We went on the bus to Bristol, paying our fares out of the four pounds eight shillings and eight pence, all in silver and copper, which we had taken jointly from Mrs Fagence and the office cash box. The coins weighed down the pockets of our overcoats and clanked as we moved.

On the ride down the town and through the streets, the money weighing us down like donkeys, we said scarcely a word to each other. Inside I was pent up like a balloon and I could see by his fixed face that Davie felt the same way. When he gave the conductress the money for the fare his fingers were shaking but the rest of him was in control.

We got to the bus station in Bristol and sat eating cold meat pies in the waiting room. I let him do all the deciding. It was good to have someone to depend on again. 'We got to get away from 'ere Nell, as quick as lightning,' he said. 'They'll start the police looking for us soon and we're sure and certain to be picked up in Bristol.'

'Where'll we go then?' I whispered. We were sitting on benches in a dark part of the waiting room and a bus woman from the office, wearing a cap too big for her, kept poking her head around the door and looking at us. After a bit she examined us harder and said: 'I hope you two aren't up to mischief.'

'We're waiting for the bus, madam,' answered Davie in a marvellous sort of upper-class voice. He sounded as though he'd come from Harrow instead of St Bernard's. I was astonished because I'd never heard him do that before. It was not just the high-born tone of it but it was so aloof, like someone who is used to ordering servants about. It stopped the nosey woman. I swear that she did a little half-curtsy and mumbled that she was sorry before disappearing. Full of admiration, I grinned at Davie. He just shrugged and said: 'We need a map, Nell. I tore one out of the atlas at school but it's not big enough.'

'There's a map on the wall,' I pointed out.

It was a bus route map stretching all over Somerset, Devon and Gloucestershire. All maps had been taken away when they thought the country was going to be invaded by Germans, but now the war was nearly done they had put them back in such places as bus stations. This one was fixed behind a glass plate and was framed with wood. Davie did not say anything further. He scarcely bothered to look around. He just stood up and went to it like a cat. There was no one else in that part of the waiting room. Down the far end a man was dozing on a bench, his snores mumbling towards us.

It took less that two minutes. Davie took out his penknife, levered away the side frame and easily drew the map out. It was like a picture thief in an art gallery. I'm certain that even then he used to *enjoy* stealing things. The map was folded and stuffed in my knickers. He quite often put stolen things there.

'We'll get on any bus,' said Davie. 'Go up on the top deck and we'll look at the map there.'

Poking our heads from the waiting room we saw that a bus was just about to leave, its windows alight and its engine starting. We did not bother about its destination but just jumped aboard and went upstairs. Then, when we had stared, we realized with a sickening feeling that we were going back the way we had come – towards St Bernard's.

There were only two other people on top of the bus and they were right in front so they did not see us duck low as we went by the iron gates. Davie could not resist a brief look. He prised he head up a couple of inches and looked out. I followed him.

'Christ,' I breathed. 'What we gone and done?'

Every light in the place was on and the main door was open. Two policemen stood outside by their car and an ambulance was just drawing away. The fear of the fugitive fell over me. 'Do 'ee reckon we killed them, Davie?' I said.

'Might have done,' he shrugged. We were past now and we sat upright once more. He sniffed confidently. 'But they can't hang us Nell. We're too young.'

I had some idea about making our way back to my village. It seemed the natural thing to do and one place was very much as good as another. I thought I might find help for us there, perhaps someone who would take us in and be kind and let us live there with them. I also had some strange notion that our house might, by now, be rebuilt.

The weather was warm for our journey. The first night we slept in a pile of sacks in a field just outside Bristol. They had been used for fertilizer or something and just left lying there. They smelled to heaven and back but we were tired and it was late so we made the sacks into a bed, the mattress several layers thick and the rest over us like a smelly blanket. But they were warm and we lay wearily down together.

Apart from my sister and my mother I had never slept with anyone before. It was funny because we were suddenly nervous of each other, not letting our bodies touch, lying a foot apart, a sort of no-man's land between us. Then an owl started and there were other noises. I began to feel afraid – I sensed Davie was on edge too.

'Davie,' I whispered in the darkness of the field. 'Don't these sacks pong?'

'They'll do that, Nell,' he said seriously. ''Tis fertilizer. It makes things grow but it pongs like 'ell.'

'Davie, do you think they'll catch us?'

'Over my dead body,' he said strongly. 'Nobody's going to catch us Nell. We'll get somewhere safe.'

I felt reassured and glad I was with him. We were still lying a foot apart.

'Is there *anything* you're afraid of, Davie? Anything at all?'

I felt him half turn under the sacks. He seemed to be thinking about it. Then he said quietly: 'Lockjaw. That's the only thing I'm afraid of. Lockjaw.'

'What's it do to you?' I asked. 'Lockjaw.'

'If you cut yourself or something,' he whispered in the dark, 'it goes to your jaw and you can't move it. It locks tight. You can't speak and you can't eat. So you die. It's a killer. 'Tis the only thing I reckon I'm afraid of, Nell.'

We were silent for a while, then I moved first. I pushed myself to him and he put his bottom into my lap. My arms went about his waist and we slept.

All the silver and copper we had taken weighted our pockets down and slowed us on our journey. We dare not ask anyone to change it into notes in case two children having cash like that aroused people's suspicions. It hung down in our coat pockets like lead as we trudged on our journey.

Davie carried most of it in the pockets of his worn overcoat and it bulged out at each side and made his walking difficult. The second day after our escape we came to a neat place with a river and some rowing boats drawn up against a wooden pier. We stood looking at the boats. There was not a soul around, no sound except the ducks on the water and a breeze, pushing against a clump of overhanging trees. The sun had fallen behind some clouds and it was very warm.

'I used to go out in boats like that once,' said Davie looking at them expertly. 'All the time. I was always rowing somewhere, you know, Nell. I can do anything in a boat.'

Because I believed everything he said I nodded. It was not until that day I knew he had an unsteady side to his nature, a leaning towards what you would call romancing. 'Could you row one of those?' I asked.

'Easy,' he said. 'Dead easy.'

We stood on the bank in our hanging coats, dirty faced, I expect, although we had decided to try and keep ourselves washed since seeing a poster which said: 'V.D. is dangerous. Clean living is the real safeguard.' We didn't know what V.D. was or why it was dangerous, but we decided that if we were going to look after ourselves, we ought to have some sort of a wash each day.

'I bet you wouldn't row me across the river,' I murmured.

'There and back in five minutes,' he boasted. 'Come on Nelly, there's nobody around.'

He gave the nearest little boat a push with his foot and it slipped without trouble into the water. He had another quick look around and picked up a pair of oars from the next boat along the line.

'Jump in Nell,' he said. 'And I'll show you how I do it.'

The boat wobbled wildly when I stepped in but I only laughed because I did not want him to see I was nervous. He held my hand like a gentleman and I staggered to the square end and sat down, my eyes fixed on Davie. He did not seem to be completely at home, not as much as I had expected, and he had a lot of trouble getting the oars fixed. But eventually there we were, very romantic, a young girl and boy in a boat on a placid river in the spring. He pushed the boat out from the bank and gave a couple of clumsy tugs on the oars. The water came up and hit him in the face. I started to laugh because he looked so funny with his soaked face and wet hair and his head sticking out of his overcoat like a tortoise.

'Don't you make fun of me, Nell Luscombe!' he shouted angrily.

It was such a shock to hear him so quickly bad tempered like that. I just stared at him, suddenly frightened. He saw my amazement and calmed down. 'It's just these oars, that's all,' he said in a quieter way but still huffy. 'They're the wrong size, see.' Then his face went funny and tight again and he almost shouted once more. 'So don't you go laughing.'

'Sorry, Davie,' I said, knowing my tears were rising. Then a different expression fell on his face. 'Christ Almighty!' he exclaimed. 'We be sinking!'

We were too. The bottom boards of the boat were letting water through like a grating. I cried out with fright and he started to pull wildly back to the bank. 'Pray for us Nell,' he said in a choking way. 'I can't swim.'

All children in those days were taught to pray. I flung myself into the bottom of the boat and began to ask God wildly to save us and forgive us our trespasses, particularly attacking Mr and Mrs Fagence and stealing the money. The only answer was the cold unstoppable water climbing up past my bent knees. It came up in a rush then, so that we were sitting awash with it, bursting with tears, both howling like mad, and the boat going down. The river seemed to take one last bit at the boat and then gobbled it up. Then we were in the freezing stream of it and our shouts stopped as it took our breath away. Then I saw the oar floating in front of me and I grabbed it. Davie did the same thing at the same moment.

'Coats,' gurgled Davie. 'Get them off.'

I don't know how we managed it but we both got out of our coats and their weighty loads of coins. The river current sucked them down. It was terrible. But now we found the oar would keep us afloat. We began to kick towards the bank which was only a few yards away. There was still nobody around. We could have drowned and nobody would have seen.

Fortunately the bank was easy because it had been made so that the boats could be launched and brought from the river. We crawled out and stood shivering and weeping in the mud. 'The money,' I howled, realizing now. 'Now we bain't got any money.'

Davie looked thin and cold. He was like a skeleton. But he was not one to delay. 'There's a house over there,' he shivered. 'Let's go there. Say we fell in.'

'We did fall in,' I said, trying to make a little joke of it. He did not laugh.

'Come on Nell,' he said, getting up. 'We'll be freezing to our deaths.'

Stiffly we got up and stumbled along the bank of the river. The house was only a cottage, with a garden crammed with flowers and a cat asleep on the window sill. But, cold as I was, I remember how it made me stop, a chillier feeling coming over me. It was a house, somebody's home, just the same as I had had not many months before. Davie apparently felt nothing of the sort. He opened a small pointed gate and went to the front door. 'Don't say anything about the boat,' he whispered before knocking. 'It might have belonged to them.'

I shook my head, trying to get myself out of my trembling. He knocked at the door. It sounded old. Nothing happened. He tried again and then a third time. There was still no answer.

'Let's have a look around the back,' he said coolly. I sensed that he was, even then, quite capable of anything and it frightened me. But I simply nodded and followed him. At the back of the cottage was a vegetable garden and a small arched door lolling with flowers. On the whitened wall a tin bath was hanging. Davie knocked with his knuckles on the door, then banged on the bath with his hand and called: 'Anybody home?'

Nobody replied. By now my teeth would not keep still because of the wet cold all over me, and my legs vibrated so much I could hardly stand. To my astonishment Davie tried the door. It opened. He poked his head through the opening and called again. 'Excuse me. Anybody home?' Even from there I could hear a clock ticking like a sharp hammer in the room beyond the little corridor where we found ourselves. Davie strolled in. I was amazed and my hand went out to warn him not to do anything wrong. But he did not seem to feel it. He just walked in, a couple of careful steps first and then straight into the room as if he owned the place.

'Davie,' I whispered. 'Davie, we'll get caught.'

'No we won't,' he said surely. 'There's a note left here on the table. The woman won't be back until six o'clock. She left the note for her husband.'

'What about him then?' I asked 'What if he turns up?'

'He won't,' he said, a touch impatiently. 'The note says he's to put the potatoes on the stove if he gets home before her. And she's not due until six.'

'You're very clever, Davie,' I said.

'I'm very cold, Nell,' he replied, accepting the compliment. We glanced around. 'But we can have a good time here, can't we? Let's have a look around.'

I was still doubtful. 'Be careful, Davie, whatever you do.'

'Nelly,' he said turning around quickly on me. 'Shut up.' I looked at him. I did not know whether I admired him or was frightened of him. It was the same all through the time I knew him. But he had thought of everything.

'If anybody comes,' he said, spreading his hands, 'we'll just say that you fell in the river and I rescued you and we came in here because of being wet and you being half drowned.'

'Rescued me?' I said, a bit annoyed. 'You can't even swim.'

'THEY won't know that WILL they?' he replied, almost shouting the two words in his impatience. 'Now stop worrying. Let's have a look around.'

I could still hardly believe that he was doing it. But there he was, with me trembling behind him, going through the house like a professional burglar.

We went up the narrow cottage stairs. There were only two bedrooms with a small landing and a row of coat hooks with a flannel dressing gown and a man's jacket hanging from them. Davie took them down. 'These'll do for the minute,' he said, handing me the dressing gown. Without a second glance at me he began to take off his clothes. Then he saw me looking and stopped. Although we had been put in the same bath together on the night we arrived at St Bernard's, we had not seen each other naked since. And this, being by ourselves, in somebody's house, seemed somehow different.

'Oh, all right then,' he said, sensing my look. 'Turn around, back to back. Unless you want to be going in the bedroom, Nell – in case I spy what you got.'

'No, Davie,' I said, trying to sound unconcerned. 'Back to back be all right.'

We stood on the small landing, facing opposite ways, and took our cold wet clothes off. Mine were sticking to me and I heard Davie's trousers slosh on the floor. When I had taken off everything, including my shoes and socks, I just about tunnelled myself into the big woman's dressing gown. I felt better then. 'Are you ready, Davie?' I said over my shoulder before turning around.

'Ready,' he answered. 'But don't you laugh, Nell Luscombe.'

It was a job not to. He was slim and quite small and the man's jacket swamped him, coming down below his knees and his arms hanging like apes. 'It don't fit very well, do it?' he said in a sulky way. 'But there, it don't matter. There be nobody to see me – excepting you.'

'It's all right,' I said, hurt by the casual remark. 'I don't reckon it matters.'

Davie was going through the pockets. Some cigarette papers and a few ends of tobacco came out and some butt ends. 'No money,' he grumbled. 'I wonder if there's any around about.'

'Davie!' I exclaimed because I felt shocked. This was different to stealing from Mr and Mrs Fagence.

'What'll be the matter with that?' he said. 'We ain't going to get any further without money, that's for sure. Unless we can fish it up from the bottom of that river there. And I ain't trying that. So we got to see what we can get in here. Stands to reason.'

He went back downstairs and went straight to the dresser in a space next to the fireplace. There was a two shilling piece there on top of an insurance book. He flipped it expertly into his pocket. 'Come on, Nell,' he said half turning. 'Don't be standing starin' like that, you get looking.'

'Yes, Davie,' I nodded. I started slowly but he was so fast he had gone through the room before I had looked in a couple of drawers and found nothing. 'I got a wristlet watch,' he said holding it up triumphantly. 'We could sell that and here's a sort of ring. Could be gold.'

'That'll be a wedding ring, Davie,' I said sternly. 'God'll send us bad luck if you take that wedding ring.' It was very big for a wedding ring. It was probably a small curtain ring.

'God ain't sent us that much *good* luck yet,' he pointed out, dropping it into the jacket pocket. His thin shins and feet sticking out from beneath the outsized coat made him look oddly like a black and waddling duck. 'See what be in the larder, Nell. We might as well fill ourselves up.'

I went to the larder in the small kitchen. There was not much there but we took half a loaf of bread and some margarine and some cheese and a jug of milk. We sat down at the kitchen table and without speaking a word wolfed the lot. There were some onions and a pot of jam which we also took for our journey. It was now about two o'clock. 'Nobody'll be back for a long while,' said Davie when he'd finished the last drop of milk. 'Then they'll have to go out and get some more milk.' He laughed wickedly and I laughed too but I had to make myself.

'Why don't we go and 'ave a bit of a lie down on the bed upstairs,' he suggested. 'I wouldn't mind being in a bed for a change.'

I could not believe his nerve. 'But Davie they might come back.'

'Who's bin a-sleepin' in my bed,' he giggled.

I sniggered into my hands, 'You wouldn't dare,' I said.

'You know I would,' he replied straight away. I knew he would too. 'Listen, I tell yer, they *won't* be back. Not till five anyway. I saw an alarm clock by the bed. We'll set it to make sure anyway. 'Tis easy.'

I nodded through my last mouthful of bread and margarine. 'All right then,' I said. 'I'm worn out.'

We went up the short stairs together. 'After,' he said. 'we'll look for some proper clothes.' We looked into the smaller bedroom. 'It's a girl's room,' I said. 'That's not going to help you much, Davie.'

'You get a bit of sleep,' he said. 'I'll still have a look around. Never know what I might find. I don't feel that tired anyway.'

'You said you did,' I reminded him. 'Only a few ticks ago.'

'I said I wouldn't mind being in a bed,' he said. 'But I bain't all that tired. You close your eyes and I'll come and lie down in a minute.'

'Shall I get into the bed?' I wondered. I had gone to the second door and stood looking at the big downy bed.

'Get in,' he said after a second's thought. 'Might as well be killed for a sheep as a lamb, Nelly.'

'I don't want to be killed for anything,' I said. I still hesitated. It seemed criminal to get into somebody's bed. Worse than stealing.

'Go on,' he said, giving me a small push on my way. 'Get in.'

'All right. But I'd better keep this thing on.' I sniffed down at the flannel dressing gown. 'Just in case.'

'Do what you want,' he said. 'I'll keep my eyes open anyway.'

I walked into the bedroom. Its low ceiling and its bent walls made it seem, I remember thinking, like the inside of a loaf. The bed looked clean and soft. It made me feel even more tired. I sat on the edge and it curled down under my weight, soft below my bottom. There was an old-fashioned long mirror by the wall, on a stand and swivel. I moved along the edge of the bed so I could see myself in it. To my surprise, my face had gone quite brown in a few days in the open air. I pushed my hair into some sort of shape and smiled hopefully at my reflection. The dressing gown almost drowned me. I moved my leg and my knee came through the gap. I nudged it further and my leg came out. From the end of my toes to the top of my thigh. I had never thought much about legs, but now I looked at it and I thought it did not look bad at all. The terrible food at St Bernard's and the work had slimmed all my podginess away. With more curiosity, like someone unwrapping a parcel, I opened the front of the dressing gown, a fraction at a time, looking over my shoulder first to see if Davie was around. I could hear him moving in the house but he was not near the door. I let the dressing gown drop open.

My body surprised me. I had not seen it in a full length mirror before. My breasts were really ripening, pink and full with their small blind nipples showing against the young skin. I glanced up at my face and I saw that I was blushing. Tugging the dressing gown around me I moved away from the mirror and pulled back the corner of the bed. But I could not resist going back to the glass for another look. Davie was still roving around downstairs. Guiltily I inched the dressing gown open and had another look at myself, one breast at at time. The nose of the right one came round the edge of the flannel material like a puppy sniffing around a corner. The breast was full enough to make the material slip away down its outside slope. I looked at it with a certain amount of pride. The nipple was closed like a sleeping eye, but the skin was pure and creamy with not a blemish or mark upon it. I made the other one appear in the same way, the flannel going up one slope, over the soft point and falling away down the other. The valley between the two was curved at the bottom, but there was no girlish sagging with my breasts. They stood of their own accord bright and full. I was very pleased with them. I felt sure they would help me in my life. I was going to need them.

At my middle there was still a bit of roly-poly flesh, but I breathed in, expanding my bosom and making my stomach flatten. As it backed away the newly-grown bush of hairs around the crease at the tops of my legs rose. I had begun to notice it some months before, and, because I knew nothing of how a girl grew, and since at St Bernard's there was no one I dared ask, not even our Mary, I worried in case I was turning into some sort of monkey. I had watched my face anxiously for any sign of hairiness there. Then I had found a couple of little bushes under my armpits and I went mad with anxiety, imagining I would be swinging through the trees in no time.

I was saved from thoughts of suicide by discovering a picture postcard of a naked lady concealed between the pages of a pious book, in the room at St Bernard's which we used as a chapel and a library. There were a few dozen broken books in there for the children to read and this picture had fallen out of one when I picked it up. This person was standing with a few flowers dangled around her but her pubic hairs and her bosom clearly on display. After noting with relief that she was far hairier in that place than I was, and making up my mind to ask my sister about it, I stood wondering where I could put the picture to get the most fun. At the end of the room was a thick reading stand with a Bible on it. Mr Fagence used to read from it every evening after tea. I put the nude lady in the middle of the Bible. I remember watching his expression when he turned right away to it that evening at prayers. He gave a start, made a quick guilty glance around and then put it slyly into the inside pocket of his jacket. Then he read the lesson.

My little collection of hairs was quite pretty, I thought, gazing at them in the mirror. Fair and springy, like the hair on a doll. I was enjoying looking at myself now. I let the dressing gown fall right off and had a view of my arms and shoulders: then, turning around, at my bottom, and finally at the front of me again. Just as I had been glad at the way my bosom was forming, I felt glad that my whole body was not fat any longer, that my legs were becoming slender and my skin was clear and fair.

The feel of the soft bed under my bottom again reminded me that I had intended to sleep for a while. I heard Davie coming up the stairs again and, because for some reason I did not want to disobey him, I put the dressing gown on and climbed between the covers.

My weariness caused by being without proper bed for three nights sent me to sleep almost right away. I tumbled straight into it, but I had only been dozing for a few minutes when the sound of something falling and breaking woke me. At first I was frightened, not realizing where I was. Then I knew it must be Davie up to something. It was.

Climbing swiftly from the bed I went out onto the short landing. The noise had come from the other bedroom. I went in and was shocked to see a girl, about my age, standing there. She was facing away, wearing a grey pleated skirt and a short coat with what we used to call a pixie hood over her head. She had white ankle socks and white buttoned shoes. On the floor was a broken china money-box, which had been a pig. I could tell because the head was still in one piece. The coins from the box, mostly pennies with a few silver coins, were spread around the floor. The girl stooped to pick them up.

This I took in while I stood mesmerized at the door. I could not move but my sudden breathing made her turn around. I cried out aloud. It was Davie!

I don't believe I have ever been so stunned since. 'Davie,' I managed to get out. 'Davie what you up to?'

'Disguise,' he said calmly. 'Good innit? Nobody will be lookin' for two *girls*, Nell.'

'But . . .' I stared at him. I didn't know why but it seemed so creepy. There was something bad about it that I did not understand. Somehow it was not funny, like dressing up.

'I'll keep the pixie hood up,' he said. 'So it covers my hair. Then I look as good a maid as you.'

I nodded, still dumb with surprise. But he did truthfully make a good girl. He had blue eyes and small features and even dimples.

Then, I don't know why, something in me I suppose, made me ask him: 'You got everything on? Of 'er's? Like underneath?'

Boldly he lifted the hem of the pleated skirt.

'Fancy putting them on! I almost shouted. I was aghast. 'Her drawers.'

'Why not?' he replied. 'My pants are soaking anyway. And if you're going to do something, I reckon it should be done all proper.'

They were white flannel. He lifted his skirt higher and I could see him bulging through the material.

'They're all right,' he shrugged. 'Just the same as mine, 'cept I'll have to pull 'em down to be havin' a pee.'

I couldn't find anything else to say about it. 'Fancy breaking the money pig,' I said. 'That's somebody's. It belongs to her.'

David stared at me with those biting blue eyes. They seemed even sharper coming from beneath that hood. 'What you expect then?' he asked. 'You expect me to get it out with a knife? There bain't be time for that. I reckon we ought to be going. On our way see?'

'All right.' Now I know that somehow I felt insanely jealous of his wearing that unknown girl's clothes, especially underneath.

'Well don't be so durn flighty about it,' he said. 'You'd think they was your things.'

That, I realized, I would not have minded. 'We'd better go,' I said. 'They might come back early.' He looked at me in the overloaded dressing gown. 'You'd better get some of her clothes for yourself,' he said. 'There be plenty in that wardrobe thing. Her drawers is in the drawers.'

He sniggered because he had made a joke. I just sniffed. 'It's a pity she's got no brother,' I said haughtily. 'I could be wearin' his trucks and things. I reckon I'd look alright in boys' trucks.'

I thrust my leg out of the dressing gown, right up to the top as I had done before the mirror. His eyes went right up it and I saw that he coloured under the pixie hood. 'Naw,' he said. 'That wouldn't be any use, now, would it? We'd still be a boy and a maid, and that be what they be lookin' for.'

Still hardly able to believe what he had done I said, 'What we goin' to call you now then? Be no use callin' you Davie. Not with you dolled up like that. Somebody might be listenin' in.'

He took the idea seriously. 'You're right Nell,' he said. He gave it a bit of thought. 'Daphne, I reckon,' he said.

I started to laugh. I could not help it. But he cut me short bad-temperedly. 'Well, what's wrong with that?' He demanded. ''Tis a proper maid's name innit? And it sounds a bit like Davie, anyway.'

His face was odd, really nasty under the pixie hood. 'All right then,' I said, ' . . . Daphne.'

CHAPTER FIVE

During my strange and busy life, I've had a good many odd days and a great number of odd nights, but never so odd as when Davie (or Daphne) and I made our way through the countryside in the early May of 1945. At first I found it difficult to say anything at all. It was like travelling with a new person, someone I did not know. When I called him Davie he would look around to see if anyone might be listening and give me a warning look. When I called him Daphne he was just as difficult, saying that I did not need to call him that all the time. In the end I found myself just clearing my throat and saying 'Hmm' before I spoke.

We made our way by bus and often on foot, keeping to the map we had managed to dry out. I would never have found my way but Davie – and under the pleated skirt and the blouse he was still Davie to me – was very clever with things like maps and directions, even using the sun to calculate our way. He should have been an explorer. Dressed in a different way.

On the second day after we had changed our clothes we came to places that I knew were near my home because, although I had never been to them, I had heard people talk about them in everyday conversation. Newton Abbot, Buckfast, Totnes market. In the afternoon Davie decided he wanted to go to the picture house. It meant using up a lot of our money but he wanted to see the film which was a war film about Japanese bombers. He suggested that to conserve our funds he should pay to go in and then help me through the lavatory window. It's difficult to know why now, but this struck me as a reasonable enough plan, and I made no suggestion that *I* should go in and *he* should get through the window. He could persuade you to do things.

'Be careful of your voice then,' I told him before he went into the cinema foyer. 'Don't forget you're a girl.'

'One sixpenny, please,' he mimicked from under his hood. He had worn that hood so long now that it was like travelling with a small monk. If it had not been, that is, for the ankle socks and the pleated skirt.

I was not surprised that his girl's voice was so good. He seemed to be able to do anything. 'Put a hankie to your nose, just in case,' I advised. But I knew it would not be necessary. Looking from under the rim of that hood he looked just as much a girl as I did. 'How will I know the window?' I asked him.

'It's bound to let out into the alley down the side there,' he said pointing. 'Wait down there and I'll go into the lav and throw something out of the little window. If there's a big window and I can get it open, I'll do it. If not you'll have to get through the small top one. Now you understand, Nell, don't you?'

I said I understood and he went into the foyer of the cinema. I hung about outside and I heard him make his Daphne voice. It sounded convincing enough to me and the girl at the cash desk did not even look up. I counted to a hundred and then I went around to the side alley. Nothing happened for five minutes and I worried that I had made a mistake or something had gone wrong. Then, mercifully, a piece of newspaper floated out of a small window three parts of the way down the alley. I hurried to it.

'Davie,' I whispered. Then ' . . . Daphne.'

'Nell. Come on.' His hand was waving at the small fanlight window at the top. 'You've got to get through 'ere, Nell,' he said hoarsely. 'I can't get the other bugger to open. It's all rusty.'

In all my life I had only been to the films two or three times and then never through a toilet window. But climbing was nothing to me. I got a foothold on a water pipe and then a knee on the sill before pulling myself up to the window. It was a squeeze, and I hoped that no one would come along the alley and see my bottom bent over as it was, but I was soon dropping head first down inside and there was Davie, standing on a toilet pan to help me down.

'It's a good job you remembered to come to the ladies' place,' I said when I was on my feet. 'I meant to tell you.'

'You should have,' he grunted. 'That's why I was such a long time Nell. I didn't think about being dressed up. I went straight into the men's lav and stood there while some old man finished pissing. I forgot I was supposed to be a maid. It was ever so strange. When 'e'd done 'ee turned hisself around, with his old thing still hanging out and 'ee just stared and stared at me. 'Ee must have thought that t'was 'ee in the wrong lav. Then he looked at the troughs what they only 'ave for men and 'ee knew 'ee hadn't made a mistake.'

I had begun to giggle, but Davie said sharply, 'Don't mock, Nell Luscombe, t'was dead serious, I tell 'ee. There 'un was with the old pig danglin' out from 'is trucks and there was I dressed like this. And the dirty old gaffer just stood and a big smile came all over him. All bad teeth 'ee 'ad too. 'Ee took 'old of that thing and began swingin' it around like a rope. And just smilin' straight. T'were nasty, I tell 'ee, Nell.'

'T'was terrible, Davie,' I said trying to keep my face straight. 'What went on then?'

'I give un a shove,' said Davie. 'Pushed him right back into the pee troughs. I pushed 'un a bit hard because 'ee sat down in all the wet. Then I buggered off fast and came in 'ere, in the maid's lav.'

'Is he gone, I wonder Davie?'

'I hope so. Let's go in quiet. It be dark anyway.'

We went from the toilet into the main part of the cinema. Even in the dark you could see it was almost empty. We crept sideways down a row in the middle and sank down into the seats. The main film was just starting and I could see Davie's eyes, bright points of anticipation. I watched for a few minutes, but the weariness of being without a bed came over me and in the dusty warmth of the picture palace I sank lower and easily into sleep.

I don't know how long I slept but I was roused by a dig from Davie's elbow. When my eyes had focused I saw that sitting by him was an old man with a bald head and a nasty overgrown moustache.

Davie saw I was looking. "Ee be back,' he said flatly. 'The old sod from the lav.'

'What 'ee be up to?' I asked, still drowsy.

"Ee be feeling of my leg,' said Davie in a matter-of-fact way. 'Rubbin' like.'

'What you goin' to do then?'

'Got a pin or anythin' like that?' His voice went down to a whisper.

'I got a safety pin,' I said. I found it in my pocket and handed it to him in the dark. He nodded his thanks.

Nothing happened for a while and I began to think that the old man had gone back to sitting quietly watching the film. Then Davie leaned towards me. "Ee be gettin' 'un out now,' he confided. "Ee's fumblin' for it.'

The elderly molester, I could see, was having some sort of struggle. Then he leaned over closer to Davie and I could see his randy old eyes twinkling.

Well, then they stopped twinkling because Davie stuck the pin in his dick and he let out the biggest screech you ever did hear from any man on earth. He jumped up like he was on springs and as he did Davie stuck the pin up his backside and he howled like fury again.

'Oh! Oh! Oh!' he blubbered and went hopping down the empty row of seats like a castrated kangaroo. We held on to each other for laughing but we knew that it was time to get out. Soon the manager and maybe the police would arrive and we did not want to be there then. We marched steadily to the far exit and let ourselves out into the street. Still laughing we went through the market place and beyond the town to where the open road leads to the south and Upcoombe.

It was in the evening when I first saw something I recognized, the spire of the church at Hopewell poking, as it always did, through the easy mist that came from the creek. We were coming from a strange direction for me but I felt the thrill of thankfulness that it was still there, as I remembered it, and that I was nearly home.

From the high ground where we looked out we could see the South Hams, fields green and red and curved beyond the town, coloured by the evening light and after the fields, in one triangle, the sun setting on the sea, sailing away like a ship. I held Davie's hand.

'We be nearly there now,' I said. 'This is where I went to school.'

'Will they have built that house of yourn that quick?' he asked. "Tis not a year yet.'

'They will,' I answered confidently. 'They work hard down here and it was only a little house.' I glanced unsurely at him, not wanting to give the impression that we had lived in poverty. 'But it were a very *good* house,' I said. ''Tis always possible my dad is back there now. Back from the army.'

'I thought your dad was on secret missions,' he said. ''Ow could he be on secret missions and sittin' in your house at the same time? 'Ee couldn't. Stands to reason, don't it?'

This made me a bit sulky. 'The war's nearly over so they say. Maybe he got out first because of us to look after. Mary and me.'

He sniffed unbelievingly. ''Ow far is it?' he asked. 'Much further? My feet are barkin'.'

'Oh it's only a couple of miles,' I told him. 'No way at all. Come on. Let's get there afore it's dark.'

We left by the familiar road at Hopewell and went though the snaking lanes hanging with scents, and we came to the head of the little hill at Upcoombe. I felt full and strangely frightened now. Frightened by what we might find. Or what we might not find. We walked down towards Chapel Cottages past the houses where lived the people I knew. I did not want to show myself right away, so we kept low and ducked out of the way if we heard voices. Then I heard something else, the sound of my stream. My stream where I had spent so many hours paddling and playing. It made me smile to hear it and I stopped Davie and told him to listen too. But he was impatient. I suppose there's nothing more boring than other people's nostalgia.

It seemed to me, though, that the stream sounded very clear. I thought at first, that this might be because I had not heard it for so long, it was coming new to me. Then I wondered if there had been a lot of rain and it was in flood. But then, the real answer came like a chill. The reason I could hear it so plain was that the houses, our little row of houses, which had shielded the sound in the days before, were no longer there. They had not built them again. We had come all this way for nothing.

We reached the brow of the village and looked down to where Chapel Cottages had been. It was just black debris. They had not even bothered to clear away our burned-out kitchen dresser and the coconut mat from our passageway was lying rotten among the bricks and broken wood. I walked towards it all, in the light that was just going for the evening. I don't know what I felt, disappointment, despair or the deepest loneliness, but the tears were dripping down my face and onto my chin. Davie hung behind and shuffled down after me. We stood in the old, damp-smelling rubble. I went and stood in the place where the kitchen had been, just where my mother used to do the ironing and we used to sit by her. I looked around me and then across the unbroken space to where dear Granny Lidstone's house had been. Now she and mum were both in the gravy-yard. Davie kicked his shoes into the thick mess. 'Not much here,' he said hollowly. 'Better be goin' Nell. Somewhere else.'

'Yes,' I tried to sniff back the tears so he would not see them. 'Let's go somewhere else.' We trod over the rest of the mess and back onto the lane. It was almost dark and the stream was gurgling loud at the bottom of the lane. Where would we go? I did not know. I left it to Davie.

On the day that the war was ended, the German war that is, we arrived in Plymouth. We had some idea that we might be able to get a ship from there to some place where we could be happy and no one could ever find us.

For a girl of nearly twelve whose only experience of the war was one bomb, even though that bomb killed her mother, it was astounding to walk into a city where hardly one stone seemed to be left standing upon another. From the flattened buildings the odd wall stood up like a ghostly tree. But people went about as if nothing had happened. Even a child could see for miles through the open spaces. The smell of the sea came right off Plymouth Hoe and went inland without nothing to stop it. 'This is where *I* used to live,' said Davie with a funny bit of oneupmanship. 'There weren't just one bomb here. Look at it.'

I did not argue with him because you did not when he said things as strongly as that. Some things I had already learned. People were gathering in the centre of the ruined town to celebrate the last day of the war. They started singing and as they got towards later evening there was music booming from a van with a loudspeaker and everybody seemed to be drinking from bottles and dancing, and then they all began an orgy of kissing and hugging.

Davie and I had bought some chips and eaten them. We must have been looking scruffy and rough by now because more people were looking at us with curiosity. I had tried to get Davie to put his own clothes back on, but he insisted that we had to keep up the disguise. 'When we're free,' he said in that important way he managed to put on. 'And only when we're free, Nell. Then I'll be Davie . . . again.'

The jolly crowd in the centre of the city drew us towards them. By the time it was dark there must have been thousands singing, dancing and cheering. A message from Mr Churchill was broadcast over the loudspeaker and they all went mad. People were crying and laughing at the same time but Davie said that was because they were drunk, which was probably true. There were lots of men and women in the mob in uniform, especially sailors of course, with some soldiers and airmen. I had a quick look at one or two of the soldiers in the hope – or rather in the *idea*, not the *hope* – that it might be my father. But wherever he was going beserk that night it did not seem to be in Plymouth.

We found ourselves gradually dragged into the celebrations and we began to enjoy it. After all, we had been a week on the run, keeping away from people and living rough, and now here we were in the middle of a great big party and feeling as though we were welcome. A lady gave me her bottle of stout which I tried to drink but could not swallow, although she kept telling me it was black champagne. Davie was smoking a cigarette – a Camel – which an American had given him from a packet. I was worried in case we got separated by the mob and I called out 'Davie' towards him. His scowl shot at me from yards away. Then I realized what I had said. 'Sorry,' I cried. 'Sorry, Daphne!'

I moved towards him through the jostle and then, at the moment I reached him, we were grabbed by two big and jolly land army girls. They were wearing fat farm breeches and their green knitted sweaters bulged like the udders on a couple of prize milking cows. They had great mouths and red faces that glistened, all ruddy in the many lights. The caught hold of us and shouted roughly, 'Come on girls – let's all dance!'

Well, I didn't know about a lot of things and it seemed all right, even if it was a bit embarrassing to be dancing like that with another female. She caught hold of me and smashed me into her voluminous chest with arms like gateposts around me. My eyes wobbled and my body bounced and I could see Davie caught by the same agricultural grip. He was trying to keep his pixie hood on so that she would not see his hair.

We did some wild prancing dance with the two landgirls chortling like fiends and us two little ones crushed and suffocating in their sweaters. 'Hoik! Hoik! Hoik!' mine was shouting, just as though she was trying to turn some old pig on its back. She rubbed me violently right across her bulging front from one tit to the other and back again. I could feel them rolling against my face like bags of hot water. It was terrifying.

Then, just when I though I would pass out through lack of air, they let us go, having seen some of their friends swigging cider in the distance. I staggered to the edge of the crowd and Davie followed me dizzily.

Our faces were thick with sweat, my hair was sticking to my forehead and Davie's pixie hood had almost been torn from his head. We were still panting when two equally rumbustious sailors came towards us. They waved bottles of brown ale, and, gasping as we were, we accepted a swig each. Used to drinking rough cider, I drank my mouthful, but I noticed, with some sort of smugness, that Davie spat his out.

We handed the bottles back to the sailors, but they did not move off. It was obvious by their faces that they wanted some repayment. They stood beaming expectantly at us while the creeping feeling that further trouble was on the way grew in my breast – the appropriate place for it, because the sailor in front of me was staring down at my girlish swellings just like he was looking into the deepest waves of the sea.

'Righto, girls!' he boomed suddenly. 'I'm Jack and he's John. Let's 'ave some dancing.'

There was only chance for one wild glance between Davie and me before we were again carted off into the crowd, our trembling legs only just scraping the ground. Jack crushed me close to his barrel chest almost as fiercely as the landgirl had. Then he started sloshing great big kisses all over my head and face. Horrified, I screwed my eyes around to see if the same thing was happening to Davie. It was. I began to bleat with worry.

'Come on my darlin',' encouraged my sailor. 'Give us a kiss.' I thought if I did he might be satisfied so I held my lips up, only to find the lower half of my face and then my neck engulfed with great wet smacks. It was like being hit with a jelly.

He loved every sloshing minute of it. He had me tight, bouncing to the music, alternating with gurgles from his bottle of beer.

'You can call me Handsome Jack,' he shouted above the din of the

celebrations. It was impossible for me to call him *anything* because I had
no breath for two words. I wagged my head at him while he banged me
up and down like a rag doll. 'I bet you'm enjoying this,' he bellowed into
my face.

Handsome Jack hauled me through the great jumping crowd. It was
like being dragged through the waves of an ocean. His big chest heaved
against me, his bristling chin scratched my forehead and his great booted
feet pounded the ground all around my thin shoes. From head to toe he
was a constant threat. Desperately I tried to see what had happened to
Davie, but he had been washed away by some other human current. I
wondered if I would ever see him again. Jack's enormous round knees
were now pummelling my middle like pistons.

'Jack! Jack!' I managed to cry. 'Stop. It's killing me.'

Immediately he stopped and became all concerned. 'M'dearie,' he
said, his trunkish arms about me. 'What be the complaint?'

I began to cry and he led me with overdone gentleness to the edge of
the crowd. There he found a shipmate waving a bottle of whisky. He
grabbed at his like it was a passing gull, held it and poured some down my
gasping throat. I felt like I was on fire. It hit the bottom of my belly and
seemed to rise up through me in hot streams. While I was still gasping he
poured another mouthful into me.

What happened after that I was not very clear about. Somehow
Handsome Jack got me into the back yard of what must have been a
brewery and there he tried to rape me across a beer barrel. Rape, I
suppose, is too strong a word. I had no resistance. Exhaustion and the
whisky had seen to that. In any witness box I would have had to confess
that my protests were feeble. Jack, presumably to cover himself in case of
prosecution, kept bellowing at me: 'Say you be sixteen, Nelly! Say you be
sixteen!'

'I be sixteen!' I cried out in panic. I thought it was the only way to stop
him shouting and battering me with his giant caresses. We were against
the barrel which was on its side, with some sort of wedge beneath it to stop
it rolling. His horny hand went up my skirt and he began hauling at my
knickers.

'No, Jack, no!' I pleaded. 'What you be about?'

'You know what I be about darling,' he leered. The booze on his
breath was so overpowering that, even in those straits, I wondered
whether it was worth arguing if he was going to rant as well as rape.

'Handsome Jack. Now you stop it!' I tried again. I used his full name to
try and please him.

'Not now, I bain't stoppin',' he bellowed. ''Tis for the war, Nelly, for
the war!'

Christ, I thought bitterly, not that one again. ''Tis finished, Jack,' I
protested. ''Tis done. The war's over.'

'Against Japan,' he bawled with leering triumph. ''Tis for that war.'

By now I hardly cared which fucking war it was for. He had me naked
to the waist. I was wriggling like a fish but I could feel my strength
sapping. 'Now there's a pretty thing,' I heard him say as if to himself.

Then he produced what was anything but a pretty thing.

God it was like a white gun! From my position pushed back on the beer cask I could see it coming towards me in the gloom. His hands felt me out. They were like blocks of wood and about as gentle. He opened my legs and I felt the night air rush up them. His beer burped horribly and I could see his big broken teeth gnashing with enjoyment and naval lust.

Then that great, girt thing was pressed up between my thighs. It seemed to fill the whole space from one leg to the other. The rounded wood of the barrel was splintering against my buttocks and the backs of my legs. But I had no fight left. Handsome Jack would have his way.

He was having some drunken trouble in finding the proper place. 'Where be it maid?' he kept demanding. 'Where you gorn and hid it?' He pushed my legs further astride. I thought he must split me in two. Then, with a grin you could have seen a mile away on a dark night, he connected and began to push his jumbo into me. I closed my eyes.

Then, like the heroines in all the girls' stories I should have read but haven't, I was saved from this fate by fate itself. He was rocking the barrel now with his shuttling movements, trying to get himself home. I felt it move beneath me and on the downward stroke my feet touched the cobbles of the yard. I waited for the next time and once I felt them touch I pushed with every atom of strength I had left, pushed and then threw my head and my weight backwards over the barrel.

It worked brilliantly. The barrel rolled back a complete turn, taking us with it. With a horrible cry Handsome Jack was pitched over the top of me. I had a memory of seeing his shape flying through the air above me, his jumbo standing up as though in shock. A short but amazing sight.

I landed on the back of my neck on the cobbles, my legs still over the barrel and pointing up at the Plymouth stars. Jack had flown yards further and had pitched on his head somewhere behind. I pulled myself together, kicked the barrel away and turning around kneeled up, pulling my drawers up with one hand as I supported my trembling self with the other. Looking back I saw what had happened to Jack.

Now he looked far from handsome. His head must have struck the ground first for he was cradling it in his hands, crouched down with his white rump stuck in the air like a big boiled egg.

Staggering to my feet I still had enough conscience to whisper 'Jack . . . Jack . . . are you all right Jack?' His reply was to slide slowly sideways and lie curled on the cobbles. I completed pulling my clothes into shape and ran quickly out. I heard his groans echoing from the yard. Poor Handsome Jack. He was the first man I had left groaning. But far from last.

It took me a tearful hour to find Davie again. I went through and then around the fringe of the crowd which was pounding about in the street, even bigger in numbers than before. It was amazing how many servicemen came to offer their services or to ask if I'd like to celebrate the end of the war with them.

Eventually I found Davie sitting in a large cardboard box in a shop

doorway. Only his head was showing and he eyed me with dull suspicion.
I had to speak first.

'What you be doin' in that box, Davie?' I said. 'You cold or what?'

'Hiding,' he said sulkily. 'Hiding these girl's clothes. Men keep trying
to get me.'

'Get you?'

'Well, you know, *get* me. You're a girl, you ought to know.'

'I know,' I sighed. I sat on the step beside him. The sounds of the
celebrations floated over the roofs around us. 'I know all right. Oh Davie
. . . that sailor tried to be filthy . . .'

He looked at me without his expression changing. 'What d'you think
mine did, then?' he sulked. 'Black and blue I am Nelly.'

'At least he couldn't *do* anything to you,' I said innocently. 'I mean
you're a boy. You're different to a girl.'

'That's what I told 'im,' said Davie.

'And what did he say?'

''Ee reckoned it was better.'

I did not understand this but I was so hurt and confused now, and I
was getting cold, that I did not ask him any further, except to find out
how he had escaped. 'Well 'ee went and give me his bottle to have a drink
like. So I banged him over the head with it. They took him off in an
ambulance.'

'We'd better get away from here,' I said. 'We'd better find somewhere
safe.'

He stared at me, his head sticking very strangely out of the box.
'Where's safe?' he said hopelessly. He began to stand up. His girl's clothes
were muddy and torn now and he had lost his pixie hood. I felt over come
with pity for him – he always had that effect on me when he was downcast
– and I put out my hands and helped him from the box. 'Where we goin'
to go Nell?' he asked, all assurance gone now. 'Where'll be safe?'

We found the answer amazingly quick. Only a few yards along the
street a small door was swinging open. Someone must have left it to hurry
to the dancing in the streets. We looked in carefully. It was a sort of
storehouse with boxes and crates standing in piles like dark walls. No
sound came from the shadows. We walked carefully through the
corridors of goods. Then I put my hand to one side and touched
something soft. 'Davie,' I whispered. 'There's some mattresses piled up
here. Let's climb up.'

He seemed uncertain. 'We got to get right *away* from 'ere, Nell,' he
said. 'Abroad. We've got to stow away or something. We can't go on like
this.'

I patted him in the dark. His shoulder felt hard and thin. 'Let's lie up
'ere for a while, Davie,' I said. 'Then we'll work out what to do.'

I sensed his nod. We climbed up the pile of mattresses and fell into
them. Then we rolled protectively towards each other. His body felt
damp and warm but small next to mine. I put my arms about his neck
and put my face next to his cheek.

We felt each other trembling but, lying like that, we seemed to calm and before long we went to sleep. It was some drunks shouting and singing in the alley behind the building that woke us up. We did not speak but lay there listening to them and, when they had gone, to the wind rustling in the darkness of the store.

'Davie,' I whispered. 'Do you think they'll be back to shut the door?'

'Don't known, Nell.' He stirred. We were warm and luxurious in there, away from the noise and the dangers of the world outside. It seemed nothing but natural that we should turn to each other and embrace. I could see his eyes looking at me in the dark.

'Do you know how they do it?' he asked quietly.

'What, Davie?'

'You know what Nell. Like the sailors tried to do.'

'No Davie,' I said. 'But I expect 'tis easy. I don't reckon it's anything you have to be clever for. Anybody can, even simple-minded people.'

'You want to have a try, Nell?'

'Aye, Davie, if you like,' I whispered.

He stirred against me and pushed his face against my chest. It was very strange because we were still both in the clothes of girls. We made no attempt to kiss each other but we began to touch, explore and rub each other with our hands. He rubbed my breasts, gently and around and around, as though he had a polishing rag. I felt the blood hurry through me and I put both my hands down to his bare legs under his skirt. First I rubbed his knees and then worked my way up until I felt his sturdy little jumbo inside the girl's drawers. I stroked it with my fingers and felt it give a throb. A great feeling of suffocation came over me. I rolled onto my back, my legs open for a second time that night. But this was different. We were that rare thing, instinctive lovers. His right hand went around to my bottom and his left slid along the cleft of my legs. He stroked it back and forward. It was though we had planned it and rehearsed it many times.

Davie withdrew his face from me and said as though in ordinary conversation: 'Nell, I reckon we ought to stop playing about now and do it proper. Do you still want to?'

He saw me nod in the dark. He brought himself to his knees and lifted both our skirts up. Then he pulled my knickers down and did the same with his. I could almost see his penis glowing in the dark. I reached out and touched it. It was a like a warm velvet pencil. I was trembling again, with anticipation, not fear now, and I released him so that he could guide it to me. He was careful, so accurate you would think he had done it all his life.

I moved my bottom and opened my thighs wider. He found the place with no trouble, first time. Thousands would have missed. I was still sore from Handsome Jack's efforts, but I ignored that. I felt it enter, its head poking into my darkness, then the body followed. I don't remember any pain. All I remember was that delicious young rod travelling up inside me. It was all I could do not to cry out with the unusual pleasure. I wriggled beneath him and he began to withdraw.

'No, Davie, no. Don't do that.'

He was collected as ever. 'I be taken 'un out to see if us both is all right,' he said mysteriously. 'T'will go back in you soon, Nell, you see.'

He withdrew it and shifted up to his knees and looked down at it in the dark. 'Is 'un all right, Davie?' I asked him anxiously.

'Dunno. 'Un seems all right. But I can't see 'un proper.' He looked at me beneath him in the gloom. 'I reckon us'll have to be wed, Nell, if we go on like this now.'

I laughed and I heard him chuckle. Then he began feeling around in the pocket of his skirt. 'I got that there weddin' ring we found in the house by the river,' he whispered, still fumbling. "Ere 'un is. I'll put it on you finger.'

He did too. It was miles too big of course (I am certain it was a curtain ring). I moved it around my finger. Then I did a truly amazing thing.

I took the ring in one hand and his small jumbo in the other, and I slipped the ring over the head of it just as easily as if it had been a finger. We both went into gusts of laughter, rolling about on the mattresses like a couple of pups.

'Nell Luscombe,' he threatened, 'now I'll show you.' And he threw me back, mounted me again, and thrust himself home, still wearing the ring. We started laughing again at the thought of the ring inside me. He bent over and for the first time we kissed lip to lip.

Then from behind us, and slightly below, a torch shone at our backsides. A policeman and two other men were standing staring at the amazing sight of two half-naked schoolgirls in bodily embrace.

'God 'elp me, Fred,' said the policeman. 'Now I seed everything.'

CHAPTER SIX

Davie and I were never taken back to St Bernard's. But we were separated the day we were caught and we did not see each other again for many years. They took Davie off to some place in another part of the country and I went to a big downtrodden house in Cornwall, a sort of hostel for difficult girls. I liked it there. It was an exciting place to be, high on some cliffs where it was always misty, or windy, a shaggy old house that looked haunted. Inside it was exciting too, because some of the inmates were very delinquent and kept setting fire to the place or having intercourse with soldiers, or chasing each other with carving knives or kettles or boiling water. There was a riot once and some of the bigger girls made the matron take off all her clothes, pick up a shovel, and stoke the boiler with coke.

I was younger than most and much quieter. I was constantly

interested in what was going on but I was always in the background. Some of the girls were very strange, I thought at the time. One came into the bathroom once, when I was in the bath, and asked if she could wash me. I refused, and then she begged me to allow her to kiss me on the breasts. Very shocked, I would not allow this either and she went out weeping and tugging her hair. Not much trouble came my way though, and I was regarded as an inoffensive child, which indeed I was. I only got into trouble once and that was due to a mistake. The girls had to go and have their hair cut short at a scruffy old woman's place in the nearest village. Each was given a ticket with a special rubber stamp on it and when the old woman had cut her hair, she would hand in the ticket and the woman would be paid at the end of the month.

After I'd been in the hostel a week or so one of staff gave me a ticket and said brusquely: 'Get your hair done.' And, unknowing, I took her at her word and went to a proper salon in the neighbouring town; I sat there, feeling like a duchess, had a shampoo and set and a special styling and then (never being one who knew when to stop) I had a manicure as well. When I handed them the ticket from the hostel and explained that it was instead of payment they went crazy, telephoned the matron and caused me all sorts of bother. My pocket money was stopped for two months, but I was able to walk about, among the basin-headed girls, with my hair looking beautiful.

It was at the hostel, however, that they discovered I could sing. It was a discovery for me too. When I was with my mother at home, I used to sing around the house and to myself when I was paddling in the stream. Absent-mindedly I suppose, for I used to hate singing in school because it meant tedious warbling up and down scales. Since then I hardly sung at all because I had not had much to sing about.

But I was glad to join the choir because this meant that you went to people's houses and to church halls and the like, to give performances, and people gave you gifts or cakes or sometimes money. We went into some quite grand places and the audiences used to sit with damp expressions on their faces while we harmonized songs and things like 'Abide with me'. It was while they were held in this sort of charitable trance that some of the choir used to lift bits and pieces from the tables and sideboards and pocket them. There was a pawnbroker in the town who had no scruples about buying anything they brought.

It was through this singing that I first met the Commander, one of the few men I have honestly loved. It was approaching Christmas and we were told that we were going to sing carols at a special hospital for wounded officers. The delinquent girls liked the sound of this because they thought they might do themselves some good from the social point of view.

But when we went to the place and we were taken into the ward, we all came to a stop inside the door just as if we were afraid of moving another step. It was terrible to see them, the poor men, lying broken and wounded by the war. In one moment I saw how horrible it had been and would now always be for these officers. They would not be able to live again. Some were blinded and others could not speak; others had ghastly burns and scars, no arms or legs. One man was in a bath of oil because he had been burned so much.

I almost choked with tears while we were doing the carols. The poor souls were trying to sit up and listen to us and some tried to sing with us. One officer, all covered with bandages so that you could hardly see he was a human being, sang like someone calling out for help when they have been gagged. His bed was quite near to where I was standing. The hem of my dress was caught on the bedside chair, showing the backs of my legs, and I was going to pull it away, but for some reason I did not. It was my instinct, I suppose, and I think he knew I had left it hitched up there on purpose.

It was terrible when they tried to applaud, bandaged hands going together all muffled and strange, and distorted noises coming from their mouths. Some of the girls were frightened and when we had finished, they hung around in a group like ewes, waiting for someone to take us out. But I looked at the man in the nearby bed and I could see by his half-buried eyes and the way the dressings were shaped around his mouth that he was smiling. I smiled back. He patted the side of his bed and without a tremor I went and sat by him.

'What's it like inside there?' I said.

'Dark,' he replied. His voice was faint, not because of the bandages but because apart from everything else he had a throat wound. It came out in a faint croak. 'Dark and hot.'

'How did you do it?' At the time it did not seem like a silly question, even allowing for the fact that *he* didn't do it, the Germans did. It seemed a natural way to carry on a conversation. After all you can't start by asking somebody trussed up like that if they've had an interesting day.

'Fell downstairs,' he joked from his hollow. 'Drunk.'

I must have laughed because his hand, which was outside the bandages, in fact was one of the few parts of him that seemed to be uncovered, patted mine. It seemed to be quite a young hand.

'How long?' I asked him. 'How long until you're better?'

'Don't know,' he answered simply. 'Have me fixed up in time for the next war, I expect.'

He suddenly leaned back on his pillows as if the conversation was too much effort. I asked him if he was all right. He nodded but did not speak. It was time for us to go. One of our staff came in and started making a fuss because I was sitting on the officer's bed, but a nurse from the place told her not to worry and then smiled nicely at me. Encouraged, I said to the officer: 'Would you like me to come and see you again?'

He nodded but did not seem able to speak. The nurse was on the other side of the bed. She looked at me quickly. 'Would you like to?' she said. 'Really?'

'Yes,' I answered. 'That's why I said.'

'We could get someone to fetch you from the hostel,' she said. 'And get you back.'

'There's a bus,' I answered. 'I'll get on that. It's not far.' The other girls were all standing like ravaged virgins, open-mouthed at this conversation. All this time the officer in the bandages kept nodding encouragement to the nurse and to me.

'You could come on Saturdays, if the hostel people will let you,' said the nurse. 'We play housey-housey then. The Commander needs somebody to shout for him when he wins. He keeps missing out. You could do that.'

I nodded. 'Right, I will,' I told her. 'I'm allowed out on Saturdays.'

None of the other girls said anything to me until we were outside the hospital. Then one young slut said: 'Jesus Christ, fancy doing that.'

'Doing what?' I replied. The others were crowding around very ominously.

'Well, what you just done. Gettin' yourself in with the officers.'

'Bleedin' cheek she's got,' said another.

Then the first one again. She was a low, conniving sort of girl. Her face came right up to mine. ''Ow d'you know what he looks like?' she rasped. ''Ow can you tell under all those bandages?'

My heart went cold. I was tempted to hit her in the face. Instead I said simply: 'Go and get fucked.' I bet she was too, thousands of times. It was the first occasion I had ever used that word to anybody.

From that day I would get the Saturday afternoon bus to the hospital and sit by him while we played housey-housey. Because of his wounds he could not hear the numbers very well and for the same reason he could not shout if he won. But I sat on his chair or on the edge of the bed and we played it like that. Quite often – for there were only twenty or so players – we would win sixpence or sometimes a full house of half-a-crown. I would take a penny from the sixpence or sixpence from the half-crown as my commission and to help with my bus fares. They were very unusual and peaceful, those afternoons, and I used to look forward to them. He was still inside all those bandages, like a man inside a hollow tree looking out, and I could see by his eyes that he was always pleased to see me.

When I think of it now, how odd it was that I had no idea what he looked like, how old he was, or even his name. I never asked. I simply called him the Commander. That was good enough for both of us.

When he had enough strength in his voice he would ask me about my life and I would tell him about my mother and the bomb and some of the other things that had happened to me. I was now twelve.

I went to the hospital throughout the winter and into the spring. One day, I remember, I saw some daffodils blooming in somebody's garden and quietly stole half a dozen to take to cheer him. Then they told me at the hostel that I was to go back to Hopewell. My sister Mary, having been retrieved from St Bernard's at Bristol, had been taken into full-time service at Hopewell Manor, and it was decided that I should go to, returning to the village school until I could leave at fourteen, and living with the other staff in the manor house.

Even bearing in mind that it meant I would have Sir Waldo Beechcroft breathing down his long nose at me like some pale dragon, I would have been glad to go. I missed my sister sometimes and it would be fine going back to my old school after all my travels and adventures. But my first thought, when they told me, was that I would have to leave the Commander.

'It's a pity you have to go away now, Nelly,' said the nurse who used to look after him. 'In a couple of weeks he will have his bandages off and you'll be able to meet him properly.' Then she said thoughtfully, to herself rather than to me: 'But maybe it's just as well.'

'I'll come back and see him,' I promised. 'It's not all that far, and I'll be earning some money when I start at the manor. I could still come.' The tears were forming in my eyes. I managed to stem them.

'You don't even know his name do you?' she asked.

'No,' I shrugged. 'I've never thought to ask. But I'll have to know now. I reckoned on writing to him to tell him how I'm getting on.'

She smiled. 'Good. I hope you will, Nelly. After you've finished housey-housey today come and see me and I'll write down his name for you to take with you.' Then she did a surprising thing. She said: 'You're a lovely girl.' And she kissed me on the cheek.

It was terrible that last day. I could hardly speak for sadness and inside that great cocoon of bandages, I knew the Commander was upset too. We won sixpence and I took my usual commission. And then it was time to go. I stood up. Once more I was going to be alone.

'I'll write you a letter as soon as I get there,' I said, trying to choke back the crying. 'Nurse is giving me your name and address.'

He seemed surprised at this because the bandages gave a little jerk. It's interesting how you can see people's reactions even when their covered up like that. I remember that very day I was leaving, when I got to the door of the ward and looked back, he was sort of sagging in his sitting-up position in the bed, just like a bandaged thumb bent over.

'Write then, Nelly,' he said in his firmest and best croak. 'I hope we'll meet again.' I walked back to him. He patted his hand against mine. I leaned over and kissed the dressings in the general area of his forehead and he kissed me with the charred lips that lived in the hole in the bandages. I hurried out with only that brief look back at him. I had to go into the toilet and have a cry before I was able to come out and get the name and address from the nurse. She had written it on a card. It said: 'Lieutenant Commander Sir Frederick Harrie-Young, R.N., G.C.' and the address of the hospital, which I knew anyway.

Nothing in the world would have made me ask about the 'Sir'. Instead I said: 'What are the letters? I know the R.N., but what are the others?'

'The G.C. is the George Cross,' she said.

'And he's got that?' I said. 'A medal like that?'

'That's right,' she said bitterly. 'He's got that Nelly. Instead of a face.'

It was more than a year later when I saw him properly for the first time. I had kept my promise and written careful letters to him, writing on the flap of the envelope S.W.A.L.K., sealed with a loving kiss, and when he wrote to me he put the same letters on the flap of the envelope too. Mrs

Chandley, the housekeeper at the Manor, used to ask me who would write such rubbish on the back of an envelope. She thought it was 'some silly boy' because his handwriting was ugly and difficult since he could not hold a pen properly, something I had not realized before.

But the letters were wonderful. It must have been so painful and difficult for him to write at all because of the damaged tendons in his wrist, and each letter took him a week or more to complete, so that he had just finished one and my next one would arrive and he would have to start all over again.

He would write about the most amazing and beautiful things. Even though he was trapped in those bandages and imprisoned in that ward behind the gates of the hospital, he sounded so free. Everything that happened in the ward he found worth some comment, including the results of the housey-housey sessions. He had not replaced me as an assistant but had made an arrangement where he was allowed to bang an enamel cup on the metal part of the bed to show that he had a full house or a complete line. Although there was only the one window near him, and he had difficulty in working his way around to look out of it, the *things he saw*! The birds and the aeroplanes and the shapes in the piles of clouds were truly astonishing. And he noted them all and wrote to me about them. These letters always arrived on a Monday and, while I was still in school, I would sit in lessons, the unopened letter warm in my pocket, waiting for playtime so I could go to the lavatory and read it in peace. I was always astonished at the amount of things he could write about. Although I was much freer, I did not seem to have half as much to say.

All these letters he simply signed 'The Commander' and, after thinking about it, I never used his title or his full name or his decorations on my letters to the hospital. But they reached him anyway.

In between all the other things he would write about, he would sometimes mention that he had begun what he called his 'jig-saw-puzzle' operations, skin grafts and the like, and that they were 'getting the pieces to fit quite nicely'. They had taken his bandages away, or most of them, and I was especially glad about this. I had been lying in bed thinking about how dark and lonely it was inside all that wrapping.

But I was never able to visit him. My sureness that it was only a bus-ride away was demolished when it turned out to be fifty miles and many buses and more money than I had. I thought I might see if I could get permission to take two days to go and see him, but nobody would listen and I began to think I would have to run away again to do it. But he wrote, promising to come and visit me as soon as he was 'all ship-shape', as he joked, and when the time came he kept his promise.

I guessed the time was drawing near because his letters had more news about his operations and how he had gone outside for the first time and sat in the autumn sun in the hospital garden. Because his skin was all new – like a baby's, he said – he had gone back into the ward with quite a brown face. In my kiddish way I began to imagine him as a bronze handsome man in naval uniform dripping with medals. A thousand times I must have romantically imagined our reunion, me an almost

grown girl now, not all that far off being a woman, and he a hero of . . .
how old? I did not know how old he was. Nobody had ever told me. I had
never asked and parcelled up like he was in the hospital there was no way
I could judge. I thought he could be twenty-five or he could be forty. In
fact he was forty.

He came to see me one day towards the end of the year. It was raining
and I was doing my afternoon job of cleaning the cutlery with silver
polish. Mrs Chandley came in all of a flap and said: 'Nelly, there's a
gentleman to see *you*. None of the family is home except Master Parsifal so
he couldn't have told *them* he was coming. But he's left his card for the
master and he's Sir something-or-other.'

I thought my heart would jump from my body. My face had gone
scarlet. I could feel it burning. But I tried to treat it in a matter-of-fact
way. 'It's Sir Frederick Harrie-Young, Lieutenant Commander, R.N.,
G.C.' I recited. I had never forgotten that. 'He's my friend.'

'Your friend?' she said unbelievingly. 'Your friend?'

'That's right, Mrs Chandley,' I said, getting up and putting the knives
back in their box. 'I know lots of Sirs, you know; hundreds of them.'

As I went from the room I heard her loud cowish sniff behind me. She
said: 'He's got a very odd face. Very odd.'

I trembled but I walked on through the passage until I came to the
room near the front door. Callers were always shown into there. I
hesitated and then knocked on the door. His familiar croak answered
and I went in.

I had never seen him standing before. That was something I had
forgotten. He was quite tall, close to six feet, and he must have been well
built at one time. Now he looked as though there were wires holding his
body together. He was in naval uniform and it hung about his frame. He
was standing, but leaning against a table, and he had positioned himself,
purposely now I realize, in the darkest part of the room because of his
face. It was badly damaged but it was not ugly. His jaw and the lower
parts of his cheeks were stretched with new tight skin, discoloured at the
edge of each patch and square where they had done the grafting. His
neck was a general mess and on the right side he had no ear.

But his eyes were clear and blue, his forehead very strong and
handsome and his hair dark and thick. I smiled at him, standing as I was
near the door.

'Hello Nell,' he said. 'How do I look?'

'Taller,' I said, trying to prevent myself shaking. 'Much taller than I
thought.' I couldn't help myself then. I rushed towards him, the tears
spouting down my face. I threw my arms around his waist and held him
tighter than I have ever held anybody in my life. His arms went around
my head and he held it against his chest. I could feel him trembling too.
After a full minute he was trying to say something.

'Let's go out and have some tea shall we, Nell? Then we can have a
talk. Can you come out now?'

Drawing myself away from him, and turning my head swiftly so he could not see my stained cheeks, I went towards the door. 'I'll get my coat,' I said. 'Mrs Chandley will let me come. Just wait here for me, Commander.'

I got my coat and announced to Mrs Chandley that I was going out. She knew better than to argue when someone important was involved. She gave one of her sniffs and said: 'Don't forget your manners then.'

Now I felt excited and glad. I hurried back to the front room and I remember how he walked forward quite naturally and helped me to put my coat on.

He had a taxi waiting outside and it took us into the main street of Hopewell where we went to the Queen Anne Cake Shoppe, which was somewhere I had gazed at with ambition ever since I was old enough to want the better things of life. It was quaint and chintzy and even during the war had served teas and home-made cakes and sandwiches. We went in there and I sat down dumbly and looked around at the comfortable people. We had a proper tea with sandwiches and pastries. I told him what I had been doing, which did not take long, and he told me what had happened at the hospital, which did not take much longer. But we were not uncomfortable or embarrassed in each other's presence and he told me some good jokes and made me laugh with my mouth full of bread and butter. Afterwards we went to the picture house where we sat together in the dark and watched *Strike Up the Band* with Mickey Rooney and Judy Garland. It was shown on television not long ago and I kept a cabinet minister waiting while I watched it and had a cry.

When he took me home in another taxi we were both feeling sad. He said he was waiting to hear if he would be going back to the Navy, which he wanted, or whether they were going to throw him off the deck, as he put it. He told me he would keep writing to me and he asked me to write to him also. Sir Waldo was still not home, so he left his card and his compliments with Mrs Chandley, and drove away. We kissed each other on the cheek before he went and I waved until the taxi was gone into the gloom at the end of the drive. With him that was how it would always be.

It was true what they said about Parsifal, the mad son of Sir Waldo. He was a poor simple wretch, a boy of about fourteen, who spent most of his time crouched in the barn launching beans into the air from the end of his stiff penis. He never seemed to get bored with this and, naturally, it was a great matter of interest with the young housemaids around the place. It was my sister Mary, who was now eighteen, who promised to take me to see the unusual performance and with two of the other girls we hid in the bales and watched him at his lonely pastime.

He had a great strong member and very springy too, probably because of the way it was constantly put to use. He would crouch and bend it like a catapult placing a flat bean on the end of it and then letting it go so that the bean flew up in the air. The poor lad would make little whoops of happiness if the bean flew a long way. The other three girls were all laughing in their hands, but although I giggled with the rest of them at the first sight of the oddity, I felt very downhearted about poor Parsifal and the thing that he was doing. His parents never seemed to speak to him or care what he was about. His father simply ignored him and his mother grieved over the loss in the war of her other, normal son. You could see she wished it could have been Parsifal, but of course he had been too young to go to the war, and in any case, they did not take mad people. I used to see her watching him while they sat at breakfast (all his other meals he took in the kitchen with us), sloshing his food about, but otherwise eating in a sort of crazy silence, with everything going on around him completely unnoticed. His mother's eyes would go across the table, full of agony, towards him while he spooned his porridge everywhere but his mouth. His father hardly ever looked beyond his newspaper.

After the first time watching him in the barn, I would not go and spy on him again, although Mary, who always appeared so right and proper, was always prepared to go and have a giggle provided some of the other maids would go with her. Then one morning, when I was taking some waste to the chickens, I had to walk past the barn door and I heard him doing his bean flipping, making little grunts of satisfaction or disappointment depending on how far the bean was flipped.

Foolishly, and only because I felt so sorry for him, I went in through a low side door. There he crouched, his member stretched out like a springboard at a swimming pool. He had a pot of beans at his side and he fumbled inside it and took a bean – after throwing away a couple he must have thought unsuitable – and placed it carefully on the flat head of the thing. He pressed it back an amazing distance (I've since known men who could do quite extraordinary tricks with erections, but I've never known one who could do what Parsifal could do) and then leaning back so as to be out of the way in case the bean sprang back and hit him, he released it and it flew in a high curve, several yards across the barn floor. My heart swelled with pity for him. I could not help it. Coming from my hiding place I walked across the floor towards him and stood a few yards off so he could see me. He looked up but he showed no shame, no embarrassment, not even caring that I was there. He just selected another bean and did it again and then glanced up at me to see if I thought it was clever.

'Parsifal,' I whispered. 'Why be you doin' that all the time?'

'Ah,' he said as if he had a secret he was willing to share. 'It's my bean flipper.'

''Tis not a bean flipper,' I said soft, approaching him. ''Tis not for that, Parsifal.'

'It's my bean flipper,' he said sternly.

Now I was just in front of him. He was sitting on a wooden box. I bent at the knees in front of him and looked into his barmy eyes. He was just like a little cow to look at in the eyes. He looked at me puzzled and nervous because I was so close. But I smiled at him and a softer look came over his boy's face. 'You want to touch my bean flipper?' he said. 'Look, this is it.'

I just nodded and I put out my hand and touched it on its soft nose. His expression altered to one of excitement and surprise. He took my hand, uncertainly at first, but then firmly, and ran it along the skin. I remembered doing that, when I was a little girl in a stream, for the poor lonely American soldier, and now I was doing it for a mad boy. First I let him guide my fingers up and down, but then I put my other hand to it and began to work them all over. He had gone puffy in the face and his eyes were nearly jumping out of his head. He was making purring noises way back in his throat. His hands went out and touched my face. I did for him what I had done for the American soldier. I caressed and rubbed him until the last seconds and then I cradled him.

I went outside and dipped my hands in the rainbutt. Inside the barn there was a great silence. And then, to my shock and horror, there came the most horrible cry. I looked through the door and saw him running about in crazy circles, his hands on his little thing, and crying: 'Oh, my bean flipper! Oh God! Oh God! That girl's broke my bean flipper!'

The incident that sent me away from Hopewell Manor for ever happened at breakfast time; after being there two years I was considered old enough to wait at table. It was well-known among the maids that Sir Waldo was apt to behave very wicked in the early part of the day and more than one had returned to the kitchen in fear and tears because of some gross but casual indecency performed on her person while she was serving or waiting at the breakfast table. A complaint to Mrs Chandley only brought scornful disbelief or the opinion that 'Sir Waldo is a bit absent-minded in the mornings.'

It was true he performed these evil things in what seemed to be an absent-minded way, usually when he was reading *The Times*, but the general opinion among the kitchen staff was that he knew what he was doing all right. The maids, and there were five of us including my sister Mary (who, typically, was inclined to put down the assaults as 'accidents'), used to draw lots and the unlucky one had to serve breakfast. This lottery used to take the form of closing our eyes and putting our hands in the silver draw and selecting a knife, fork or spoon. We would then look at the silver marks and whichever had the lowest letter of the alphabet as its date-letter had to do the chore. I managed to avoid this by concealing a piece of cutlery with a high letter up the sleeve of my dress and dropping it into my hand when I was making my selection.

Unfortunately I overplayed my hand and it was quickly noticed by the other girls. One morning they made a combined rush at me and pinning me to the table found a teaspoon in my sleeve. After that I had to run the gauntlet for a week.

On the first morning, Sir Waldo's mile-long nose came out of his newspaper like a trunk as I busied myself around the table. I imagined that I saw a nasty bright light come into his eye but I looked away quickly and went around the other side of the large table where Madam was cracking dry toast in her teeth while staring blankly at the wall. Parsifal was moonily slopping porridge over the table cloth.

But nothing happened until my third day, when Sir Waldo took me firmly by the wrist and instructed me to stand at the side of his chair. I did so trembling, frightened at what might occur, but unable to prevent it. My whole body vibrated and my feet were hot in my shoes. Hopefully I looked at Madam but if her husband had thrown me to the carpet and raped me repeatedly, it is doubtful if she would have noticed it over her machinations with the toast. And as for Parsifal, all you could have counted on from him was a mad faraway smile.

And so I stood, like some little sentry, at the side of Sir Waldo's chair, waiting. He was in no hurry. In fact perhaps that was part of the pervert's pleasure, his delaying and my suspense. Eventually he made a move. He leaned around the outside of his paper and whispered: 'How old are you, gel?'

'Fifteen, Sir,' I mumbled. I kept staring at the paper. I remember it said: 'Attlee Anxious About Next Move.' So was I. I concentrated on reading the words underneath the headline, anything to keep my mind off what I knew was about to take place. There was nothing I really understood because, until then, I had no great interest in politics. Then he began putting his hand up my dress.

God I can feel it now. Just like a spider climbing up the spout. Oh you *low* man, I thought. You dirty, *low man*. Strangely enough my shaking ceased. It was probably the uncertainty that caused it. Now I stood rigid, letting him do it, suffering it.

The maids all wore black lisle stockings, held up with garters. His hand went up the rough material and touched the naked flesh at the top of my leg. Not for a moment did he look up from his newspaper, which he managed to balance expertly in the other hand. The thin fingers went inside the garter and hung there for a moment or so. Then they continued the journey to my private places wrapped inside my drawers. A scream was trapped in my mouth. Silently and closing my eyes tightly I began to pray. 'Oh Almighty God, our heavenly father, who sees all things, please in Thy mercy stop this dirty man doing what 'ee be doing right now. For our Lord Jesus Christ's sake. Amen.'

Nothing happened, which was much as I expected. I've learned not to put too much faith in praying, especially in emergencies, since prayers seem to take longer than they ought to reach their destination. And by that time it's usually happened.

While I was still muttering privately to God, the hand went further with its explorations. First it massaged the outside of my drawers right below the arch of my legs, then it wheedled its way up the leg, breaking the elastic as it went. Wartime elastic was never very strong. It was amazing that this was going on and yet nothing in the room was moving. He continued with his newspaper. I stood stiff and terrified, Parsifal was scooping some of the blobs of porridge off the cloth, and the only sounds were the explosions of Madam gnashing her toast.

Thinking of it now I am amazed that I did nothing. My memory is that I braved it out, hopelessly, in the way that you fight your way through a nightmare, knowing that there is nothing that you can do to change it. Eventually he removed his hand and folded his newspaper.

Madam looked up as though she had seen me for the first time. She had finished all her toast and I suppose that is what made her look across to me. Perhaps he had timed the end of the assault on me to coincide with the last crust. He knew exactly what he was doing. 'Go and get some more toast girl,' she said sharply. 'Don't just stand there as if you'd been struck by lightning.'

I stumbled out of the room thinking I would have preferred lightning. At least it never struck in the same place twice. Returning with the toast I set it on the table and then looked up just in time to see his randy eye lifted above the edge of the paper. Then, at the moment, I thought: 'Right, you filthy bastard, I'll get you tomorrow.'

From the moment I had the thought I knew I would see it through. In fact, once I had formed my plan, I could hardly wait until the next day to carry it out. It would be necessary for me to make a quick escape and to have everything ready for that. Fortunately it was the day after we received our monthly pittance from the hands of Mrs Chandley, so with a pound or so I had saved, I knew I would be able to travel and exist for at least a week until, with luck, I found some refuge. I was very cool about it. I packed everything I had in a cardboard box and tied it with string before putting it under my bed in readiness for my flight. I put my street coat with it. It was a good plan.

The other maids, including Mary, stood grinning stupidly, as I carried in the trays to the breakfast room.

The scene was as before, indeed it never seem to alter. It was like a working model in a wax exhibition. He was reading *The Times*, the idiot boy was distributing porridge and his mother was munching on the toast. I did what I was supposed to do and, sure enough (and to my relief, because I had a feeling that perhaps that day, of all days, he would not be feeling filthy enough to make his indecent assault) he caught me by the hand and held me at the side of his chair. He continued with the newspaper and I found myself reading a speech by a man called Ernest Bevin which had upset Conservative members of the House of Commons. A few more days like that, trying to take my mind off what was about to happen, and I might have become a political expert. But, right on time, the wandering hand left Sir Waldo's side, as though going off of its own accord, and found its way to the hem of my skirt. Up it crawled, up the servants' black stockings, a slight twang of the garter and then a busy fingering of the flesh of my thighs. That was the moment.

I closed my legs, quietly but firmly, trapping the hand between them. A little start came over him, but he was conceited enough to think I was enjoying it and joining in. A wicked smile sniggered beneath the long nose and he looked at me questioningly, taking care to stay under cover of the newspaper. Now I had him. From beneath an extra tureen on the serving table on my other side, I produced a primed mousetrap. He did not see it, so taken was he with my co-operation. I did it beautifully. I thrust it up my skirt and held it against my thigh. As his fingers crept up my leg the trap was sprung and caught his hand.

Christ, you ought to have heard him! He screeched out and shot a foot up in his chair. The howl actually froze on his face as he pulled his hand away and the mousetrap was still clamped on his fingers. He bounced up and down in agony, tugging at the contraption to get it off. He collapsed on his chair. I leaned over, calmly picked up Parsifal's bowl of porridge and emptied it over his father's head. What pandemonium!

Madam went beserk, firing toast crumbs all over the place in her frenzy, letting loose a terrible high howl. Parsifal banged his gruel spoon on the table and screamed: 'She broke my bean flipper! She broke my bean flipper!'

It was time to go. I did not rush or even run. I turned briskly and walked out, passing an avalanche of servants heading in the opposite direction to see what had happened. Upstairs I took my cardboard box from beneath my bed, kissed Mary's pillow (as a substitute for taking farewell of Mary herself) and went out of the back door. It was a fresh early winter's day. I could smell freedom. Through the garden and out into the lane I went and ran down the airy hill towards the town. All the way I was laughing and crying at the same time. People turned and must have thought I was very odd. I suppose I was really.

This time I was on my own. There was no Davie to help and guide me. From the moment he had been hauled away, I had heard not another thing from him. Three times I had written and I sent him a Christmas card and a two shilling postal order as a present, but he had not replied. It would be a long wait before I saw him again. The Commander had gone back to sea, he had written to tell me so. ('Dearest Nell, I am now sailing to Gibraltar, en route for the Suez Canal and the Orient. It is very lonely being the captain of a ship.') So I could not turn to him, and in any case I would not have gone to him in any trouble. There only remained my father and, even if I could discover where he was, I knew that after the first emotional play acting, the kisses and the rubber tears, he would have sent me straight back to Sir Waldo or handed me over to the police and asked for a reward.

So I went alone and blindly at first, just wanting as many fields between myself and Hopewell as possible, and quickly. My happy childhood had turned sour. Instinctively my first flight was in the direction of the bus station, thinking that this was where Davie would have headed. Just as I reached there a bus was pulling out and on the destination board it said 'Exeter'. That seemed far enough away for a start. I ran and jumped aboard. I sat on the top deck and watched the Devon lanes and pastures go by, just as though they were running away from me, not me from them, and the red winter furrows, and cattle, and smoke fingering up from chimneys and blowing slowly through the cold air. People in the villages and small towns that we passed all seemed to belong to the places and to each other; they had a set sure life, somewhere to live and somewhere to work; family and the friendship of the other human beings. It did not seem a lot to want. My cardboard box of belongings lay very light on my lap. But I got to thinking about what I had done in the breakfast room in Hopewell Manor. I began to giggle, and I was still giggling when the conductor, a spherical, red-faced man with a little tuft of white hair, came up the stairs.

'Ah,' he said. ''Tis nice to see people laughing. Even if 'tis by theirselves. Where be you going m'dear?'

'Exeter,' I said firmly. 'Just Exeter.'

'Now, which part?' he asked. 'I bain't want to be charging you to much for the ticket, do I?'

That caught me. 'The middle part,' I filled in hurriedly. 'As far as the bus goes.'

He looked at me strangely. Then he said. 'Going to see somebody be 'ee?'

'N . . . no, I bain't. I be . . . going for a job.'

He gave me the ticket slowly, then said. 'Well, m'dear, I 'ope you get it.'

Then he went downstairs. I cursed a country that was trained to look out for spies. The normal Devon man's curiosity was enough without adding anything. I felt sure he was suspicious of me. Perhaps a cordon had been thrown around the district to capture me for the police. I took a pair of sewing scissors from my box. I had reckoned that I ought to be entitled to a going away present from the Manor, so I had helped myself to these, intending to use them as a defensive weapon. The rough memory of Handsome Jack the sailor still lingered.

But nothing worrying happened. The bus went through what was already foreign land to me, even though it was only a few miles from the place where I was born. Rivers broadened and the hills became flatter and eventually we drove through the streets of Exeter, again all crumbled from the bombing of the war. It astonished me. To think that all around there had been such destruction and that we in our village had seen nothing of it except the bomb that put paid to my mother and my childhood.

At the terminus at the centre of the old town the conductor said goodbye to me and, in an odd, knowing way, wished me good luck. It encouraged me for a while but that feeling and the enjoyment of my freedom soon went as the day drew on and the afternoon closed in, dim and damp. Everyone around me seemed to have plenty to do and places to be going, while I wandered aimlessly through their busy day. I went to a steamed-up café and had sausage and chips and a cup of tea. It cost me more than I thought and I knew that if I were to survive I would need to conserve my money better than that. On the other hand it was not, this time, all in pennies and half pennies, so there was no question of it weighing me down as it had when I escaped with Davie.

Probably because it was the only place I felt any connection with, I wandered back to the bus station. I had some vague idea of looking at the route map in there, and the waiting room, bleak though it was, seemed more comfortable than the chill of the bare street.

I bought a tacky bun from the refreshment counter and sat in a corner of the waiting room, wondering what to do next. Then I saw the conductor of the bus I had been on, coming across the floor towards me. I tried to hide behind the paper bag and the bun.

'You still here then?' he said, standing a couple of yards away and looking at me kindly.

'Yes.'

''Tis because you be lost.'

'I bain't be lost. I just don't know where I be going.'

''Tis cold.'

'Aye, 'tis gettin' that way.'

He leaned forward and took me by the hand. He was not someone you could fear or be suspicious about, so I went with him. I did not think he would take me to the police or hand me over to anybody else. And he did not. We walked instead through the chilly old streets, me silent, holding my cardboard box against me as though it kept me warm, and him whistling cheerfully through his teeth. After reaching a small street we turned into an alley and went to the front door of a house, almost a cottage even though it was in a city. Dark though it was I could see that the outside was carefully kept and there were things growing neatly in the patch of garden at the front.

His wife, who looked so much like him she could have been his twin sister, made a cup of tea. Somehow I did not feel nervous telling them my story, even to the embarrassing parts. They sat one each side of me, with the fire on all our faces, while I related what had happened that day. When I got to the part about Sir Waldo's indecency towards me they kept shaking their heads to and fro just like clockwork. I looked from one to the other but I could never get a full face at one time. Then when I told them about the mousetrap they pealed with laughter and hung onto each other's shoulders, reaching across me and holding each other. 'Oh that's a good one!' the bus conductor chuckled. ''Tis indeed a good one.' When I had finished the lady began to cry a bit and her husband patted her. Then she got up and cooked us all sausage and chips.

I could see they did not know what to do with me. After the meal they allowed me to sit in an old deep chair with another cup of tea and listen to Tommy Handley on the radio. I sat and laughed. They went into the kitchen and did the washing up, refusing my offers of help, and I could hear them discussing my plight – and theirs now – in their fruity voices. They had no idea what they should do with me and, at that moment, I thought I would have to save them the trouble by leaving the house in the early morning and going on my way.

It was not difficult. I awoke automatically at six-thirty because that was the time all the servants got up at the Manor. The cottage was cosy and quiet. I could hear the clock clucking downstairs. They had put me in a little room, almost filled by the bed, and there in the dark, I got dressed and, taking my cardboard box, inched my way down the creaky stairs. There were still embers in the fire from the night before and their big white cat was rolled up like a cushion on the mat. It was a really homely place and I was sorry I would have to go. But there was nothing for it.

First I wrote them a note which just said *Thank you. God bless.* and with two kisses after it. Then I quietly let myself out into the small garden and crept to the gate. It was still dark and everywhere was cold as iron. I reached the gate and, turning around, I saw an oil lamp lit in the upper window. He was looking right down at me. For a moment neither of us did anything. He must have been thinking, weighing things up. Then he just waved goodbye to me, a small wave as if he thought a bigger one might wake his wife. And I thought I saw the shadow of a smile. I waved back, gratefully, and went on my journey.

CHAPTER SEVEN

Why I went to Weymouth I do not know. It was just that the roads seemed to lead that way and in some unconscious manner I felt happier and safer if I kept to the seacoast. By the time I reached there I had only two shillings of my money left. I would have to do something definite before long or surrender.

My hand was on that two shilling piece, just as though I was keeping it warm and it was doing the same for me, as I walked aimlessly along the chill seafront of Weymouth. The beach was empty and so was the sea, except for gulls and other December birds. A couple of minutes of sun occurred, pale as lemon, and a few old people, stiff and freezing, came out walking, trying as they do to keep healthy and have a longer life.

All that was in my mind was to find somewhere to *be*, somewhere where there would be no trouble, no cruelty, no fear. Somewhere certain.

There was a nudging hunger inside me and I stopped outside the café by the side of the small port, all comfortably steamed up and full of men who worked on the ships in the docks. It was my last two shillings, but as I stood there the door opened and the smell of frying wafted out. Two grinning, satisfied-looking men came out and before they had time to close the door I was inside.

It was too early for the main midday meal and in that sort of place anyway breakfast just ran on to supper time with hardly a break. In one corner, away from the rest, there was a table, yellow marble cracked like a spider's web, and I sat there alone. An easy-looking man in an apron all splodged with tomato sauce, fat and tea-stains came and asked me what I wanted and I ordered fried egg, chips, bread and butter and tea, which I calculated from the chalk menu on the wall came to exactly two shillings. Some of the men around me looked at me curiously and I expect some made a few guesses at what I was doing there, but they left me to myself and I ate hungrily what I knew could be my last decent meal for a long time. The appearance of a solitary sausage on the plate worried because I had not ordered it, nor did I have the money to pay for it, but it looked glistening hot and, although I had half an idea to take it back when I had finished the rest, I could not resist the aroma and I sliced it up and ate it. Having now gone over the top of what I could afford to pay for, I might have then decided to be hung for a sheep as a lamb and ordered a second helping of everything with treacle pudding to follow. But my nerve failed. Even then, as I stood up to go to the counter, I felt my legs tremble.

'Two and tuppence, lady,' said the woman behind the till. Her hair was sticking to her forehead in the way my mother's used to do when she was steam-ironing. She had fat forearms and heavy elbows as ladies in that sort of café seem always to have. Her apron was stained in the same kind of pattern as the man's, like an artist's palette.

'I've only got two shillings,' I said. 'I thought it would come to two shillings.'

'Two and tuppence,' she repeated. Then she called: 'Harold!'

Harold was the man who had served me. 'It's two and tuppence, dear,' he nodded.

There was nothing for it but to stand my ground. 'I didn't *ask* for that sausage,' I pointed out. 'You put it there without me asking.'

'You scoffed it,' Harold pointed out amiably. 'How much have you got?'

'Two shillings,' I replied. 'And that's the lot.' I knew that all the men had stopped eating now and were looking around behind me.

'Aw, Christ,' said Harold with a sigh. 'I'm not going to be arguing about tuppence. Two bob it is. The sausage is freeman's.'

'Thanks. Very kind of you I'm sure,' I said. I put the coin on the counter and turned to walk out in as dignified a way as I could. When I had reached the door the lady called after me. 'Want to do the washing up dear? There's plenty of washing up.'

I heard some of the men laugh and I thought she was making fun of me because I had no money. That was very nearly the last straw because on top of the embarrassment of the whole thing, the memory of the meal was already fading and there was a space in my pocket where the two shillings had once been. Turning quickly I was just about to give them some choice thoughts when I saw that they were looking at me in a friendly way through the steam. I stopped myself.

'Yes,' I said instead, relief filling me. 'I'll do it. Anything you've got.'

All the men clapped and laughed at this. One of them shouted: 'You pay 'er union rates, Flossie!' and another smacked my bottom in a friendly way as I went back to the counter. Not thinking, I put my cardboard box down on the counter and they stared at it, realizing then that it was my luggage. 'There's a lot of it,' said the woman in a low sort of voice. 'Mountains.'

'But we'll feed you and pay a bob an hour,' said Harold. 'Is that all right?'

I grinned at them. Their grins came back at me through the vapour.

Gladness filled me like their tea. 'That's all right,' I whispered. 'I'll start it now.'

The months that followed were, in many ways, amongst the most settled in my young life. Everything was so simple. I worked in the café, washing up at first, then they got an old woman to help with that and I became the waitress. I slept in a room above the café and they paid me a shilling an hour and all my food. For me it was contentment, almost luxury.

The winter of that year was arctic. The harbour froze and even the edge of the beaches had what looked like thick fingernails of ice. Everything became very still, nothing seemed to move from one day to another, as though the air and the whole of the Weymouth and the world was frozen solid. The café was steamy and warm, a good place to be, and the heat drifted up through the ceiling into my little room above making it as warm as a nest. I began to be very happy.

Every afternoon I was allowed an hour off and I always went down to the frozen beach. My feet, warm inside a pair of sailor's socks and wellington boots which had been given to me, would crunch on the sharp sand. The sea broke the ice at its edges as it came in with the tide but the coating soon formed again as soon as it came to the ebb. There were no winds and no storms. The cold air and the cold sea seemed to be joined together. Gulls still flew, their wings creaking.

Harold and Flossie Crouch, the couple with the sauce-splashed aprons who ran Hal's Café ('always something hot') were as kind as parents to me. At first they made no inquiries about where I had come from, or why, at just fifteen, I should be wandering about with no roots and apparently no family. Then, one afternoon when it was snowing freshly and it was too cold for me to go out, I sat in the little kitchen behind the café and told Flossie my story. I can see her now, wet-browed, cigarette bent and broken in her nicotined hands, leaning forward to hear every word of what I had to say. She was quite overcome by the things that had happened to me and twice she had to call me to stop because she had begun to cry uncontrollably and had to blot the tears with her stained apron. When I told her about Sir Waldo and his deadly wandering hand her eyes burned with amazement and anger and she kept muttering: 'The bastard, the foul bastard,' and jabbing the point of a huge breadknife into the top of the table. It was as well for Sir Waldo that he never dropped into Hal's Café for a cup of tea and two slices of bread and dripping.

Because I was afraid my new life might be discovered and I would be dragged away to somewhere, I did not write to Mary. By this time I knew that I could not rely on her as a sister, or her on me, and that we would not grow into life by our separate ways, me, as it turned out, to be an international whore and her as a pastrycook in a baker's shop.

I did, however, write to the Commander, at the hospital, hoping they would forward it to him as he had returned to sea, but no reply came back which made me sad, although somehow I knew that we had not seen the last of each other. I would wait for him.

The winter had really bitten deep into everything that year. There was snow and ice until the end of March and then the frozen weather was broken up by the spring tides and storms. The café was almost on the harbour front and it was thrilling for me to lie in the enclosed warmth of the loft and hear the wind and the waves throwing themselves across the shore. And then, one morning, most unexpectedly the spring arrived. The storms and the cold went almost at once and I was awoke to the huge sun, a long sky and the blue channel. It was to grow into one of the most beautiful of all summers.

Naturally a great many of the men who came into the café from their work on the docks or the boats became familiar and friendly. I was the sort who could laugh off their bantering remarks and their well-intended pinching. I could give as good as I got from any of them. Waltzing around the tables with my arms loaded with hot plates, brushing of the rude jokes and reaching hands, I was completely happy. I knew that some of the young fishermen who came in smelling of haddock and mackerel looked at me with a more serious interest. I often caught them glancing at the line of my bosom as I went about my work or heard the banter stop abruptly when I bent my bottom over. I was pleased and flattered and indeed several of them I felt were very appetizing themselves, young and strong with bright eyes and always with a laugh. If it had not been for the overpowering smell of fish they would have attracted any woman.

One of these easy lads was called Rainbow by all the others. He worked a small fishing boat with his father who was small and creased and quiet. His father was also deaf and, as far as I can remember, was known as Hooter. They would come in after a night in the Channel, niffing to heaven, and sit and eat huge hot breakfast. They lived together in a house at the back of the town with no woman there because old Hooter's wife had died.

Rainbow was very lively and popular, always raising a shout or a laugh from the other men when he arrived in the morning from his boat. The old man used to slouch in after his son, looking very miserable and blank-eyed, not seeming to take any notice of anyone there. Sometimes the customers would shout: 'Where did you catch him then, Rainbow?' and everybody would roll about laughing, although the joke was well worn. Rainbow would reply, and always the same reply: "Un got caught in the net. I thought 'un was one o' they mermaids.' And that would get a rousing laugh too. They were simple men and they never asked a lot of life.

I guessed that Rainbow liked the look of me, particularly as he always spoke softly to me without any of the loudness I got from the other lads. He seemed almost shy. Of course it did not take the other's long to catch on to this and they would always banter us. Flossie said to me one day: 'You want to beware of young Rainbow, Nelly. He's got a look in his eye. And he ain't spotted a shoal of mackerel neither.'

Nor had he. He began to come into the café in the evenings sometimes, before he and old Hooter took their boat out for the night and, in truth, I used to look forward to seeing him, because he was a handsome boy and I liked him too.

Then one night in the spring, just as the evenings were lighter and you could see far across the sea even at nine o'clock, Rainbow asked me if I would go out fishing with Hooter and him. I guessed he meant nothing innocent because he did not look at me when he said it but kept his head half turned away and asked me from the corner of his mouth.

'All right, Rainbow,' I agreed. 'I never been on one o' they boats. I'll come with you.'

It was true. Although I had always lived within a whiff of the sea and I was familiar with tides and storms and gulls, I had never actually been on a boat. My only experience of a vessel of any kind was the little skiff that sank beneath Davie and me in the river, and since we were only aboard it for about two minutes it was scarcely worth counting.

I told Harold and Flossie I was going and Flossie frowned with doubt and repeated that I ought to watch young Rainbow carefully. But Harold said he was all for it, provided I arrived back in time to do my work in the morning and I did not fall asleep over the breakfasts. So at ten o'clock, when the last bar of silver had gone from the channel, I waited for Rainbow's boat in the harbour. He came whistling through the darkness with a little lantern swinging in front of him and old Hooter grumbling along behind. It was Hooter who was carrying the nets. Rainbow was delighted and seemed surprised to see me, as if he thought that I might change my mind. The old man, although he had come into the café dozens of times, stood and looked at me in the light of the lantern asking: 'Be this the one? Be she? Be she?' He took the lantern from his son and ran the lantern up and down to get a good look at me from head to foot. Apparently he liked what he saw because he muttered: ''Tis all right,' and turned and climbed down to the deck.

Rainbow's boat was called *Dainty Girl* and she reeked of fish. She was short and stubby, and the winter's new paint had already been knocked off in great patches by the clumsy sea. But the narrow wheelhouse at the back, like a watchman's hut, looked very jaunty and Rainbow said that although we might run into a 'bit o' a sea' that night the trip should be a good one. He helped me very courteously onto the deck and I could feel how powerful his hands and forearms were as he held me. His almost Spanish face looked very romantic in the lantern light, gentle but with some sort of threat in it. I felt wonderful.

Rainbow sat me in the wheelhouse right beside him and the old man went below and started the engine. Rainbow kept calling short instructions to him down a small brass tube, giving a whistle before every order. Since Hooter was supposed to be stone deaf I did not know how this worked. Later I got the suspicion that it was all done to impress me and that Hooter never even answered the other end of the tube but got on with starting the engine on his own. But impressed I was. The sky was ragged with clouds and the sea came at us with a steady slap as we left the harbour. Sitting there, next to handsome Rainbow at the wheel, watching the land and the sky move on, made me feel like some glamorous star of a film about the Spanish Main.

As we left the stone harbour and the channel spread all around us, Hooter came up to the deck with three mugs of tea. He took his and began busying himself with the nets on the deck. It felt grand being out there in the night, drinking tea, warm in a large woollen jersey. There was a pane of glass missing in the window of the wheelhouse and the wind ran through it and blew at my hair. How wonderful it all was. Then the sea began the get heavier. I laughed when it pitched over us the first time, but the laugh was thinner when it threw us the opposite way the next moment. I had finished my tea and I could feel it swilling around like bilge in my stomach. Then the wooden nose of the boat went straight up in the air, just like it had suddenly scented something far off in the oceans. I tipped backwards. The tight wheelhouse was suddenly rattling and shuddering and the stench of fish assailed me in gusts.

'Oh Rainbow, oh God,' I remember saying, although my voice seemed miles away from my body. 'I bain't feelin' all that healthy.'

Rainbow was all surprise and consideration. He tied the wheel with a piece of string and shouted something to his father who was stumping about on the deck as easily as he would walk about a Weymouth street. Then, supporting me firmly about the waist, he took me down the few steps to the deck and told me to breathe the wind. But the more wind I breathed the more fish I breathed as well. Then the boat pitched again and despite his support I tipped over and slithered away across the scaly deck. A cowardly wave gushed over the side and hit me when I was down. I began to cry.

It took both Rainbow and old Hooter to get me up this time. They held me to the side so that I could be sick. One of them, and I suspected it was the old chap, had his hand on my arse, the horny fingers flattened out like a seat. Not that I cared. The whole world was spinning and dipping and the air full of noisy gusts.

'Down,' I managed to get out. 'Down, down.'

'Down? Down?' They started to repeat it to themselves like a pair of comedians. 'Down? Down?'

'Under,' I belched. 'Below. Down below.'

That was their language. They got me across the deck, shaking with sickness, wetness and cold, and helped me through the tight hatch to the place under the deck. God, there it was worse!

The reek of the engine oil and the increased smell of fish had me reeling again. And it was so low and confined. Like a coffin. But there was no going back. With Hooter's hand still three parts of the way up my bottom and with Rainbow holding me conscientiously under the breasts, I was almost frog marched to the middle of the boat and there heaved up onto a bunk.

'You 'ang on there, m'beauty,' said old Hooter in the dark. It was the first time he had ever spoken a sentence that long in my hearing. Rainbow heaved my bosom onto the bunk as if it were a kit bag. Then he hung a foul old fish bucket from a hook on the side of the bunk and said if I felt sick that was the place to put it. Then they slumped off back onto the deck.

I hung there spread out like some stricken flatfish, unable to see anything but only knowing the terrible black movement all around. It was like being in your grave in an earthquake. But a sort of coma came over me. I became drowsy and dozy and eventually the movement itself seemed to rock me to sleep. When I awoke there was a lantern burning in the cabin, the sea had calmed and the boat was moving sedately. And there was Rainbow sitting stark naked on the stool beside the bunk.

My eyes took him in. His body was powerful and the lamplight made it smooth and olive. He looked at me as though ashamed and said: 'Durn it! I went and got wet.'

'It gets wet at sea,' I said logically. 'Did you come down to change, Rainbow?'

'Aye, that's it,' he agreed. 'The wind 'as dropped off now. The old man's got the nets over the side. I got a bit o' spare time.'

On his body he had several strange tattoos and these he showed me, holding up the lantern to illuminate the various places. He had some daggers and hearts on his forearms and the words 'love and death' and these I had seen before. But over his heart he had a heart in red ink and below his belly-button a sort of scroll with the words: 'For good girls only' and some little arrows pointing down to his fine, dark jumbo. Then he turned about and I sat up in the bunk and held the lantern to see what he had to show me there. It made me laugh. Sailing across his bottom was a fleet of tattoed fishing boats, the leading vessel just disappearing into his backside crack.

'You're just like a picture show,' I said. I knew my voice sounded croaky, but I was not sure whether this was because of my recent sickness or because I knew what was going to happen. He was very gentlemanly, his jumbo was hanging quietly during all the conversations just as if he wanted me to see that he did not expect too much.

But he was a handsome lad and I was primed for someone like him. 'I'll show you what *I* got, Rainbow,' I was throatily. 'But 'tis not tattoos.'

While he squatted there dumbly I wriggled out of the tight trousers I was wearing, pulling away my drawers at the same time. I could just about sit up in the bunk, with my head bent forward a little. In this way I pulled the jersey away from my body and took off all my other things.

Rainbow sat staring as if he could not believe what he saw. Then when I was naked he stood up and held the lantern so that he could see me properly. I could almost feel it making shadows across my body. 'Be I all right then, Rainbow dear?' I asked.

'Aw, Nell,' he said in a respectful whisper. 'Aw Nell, you certainly be a real pleasant sight.'

This was my first really grown-up sex and, in some ways I now see, it began a new life for me. All the things that have followed have stemmed from that one night in a little boat on an abruptly windless sea.

It was amazing how calm it had become. The vessel now moved about as easily as a cow strolling across its meadow. All my sickness had gone with the waves, although it made me feel weak. But not all that weak. I looked at the comely Rainbow with his now upstanding jumbo and his fine smile and waited for him to climb upon me.

'Be it all right then, Nelly?' he asked with his fisherman's politeness.

''Tis all right,' I whispered. 'I'm true fond of you, Rainbow.'

He climbed up with hardly an effort, just easing himself from the floor and lying half on top and half alongside me, keeping most of his weight off my body, a politeness I have always appreciated in a gentleman. I could feel his member burning eagerly against the top of my leg. My fingers went to it and encouraged it. Considerately, with my other hand I put my nipple between his lips. He sucked for a while like a child and became very excited in a powerful but contained way.

There was not much room for romance. Every movement needed some guidance and encouragement. I was pleasantly surprised to find how good I was at it. Although my experience had until then only covered an American soldier and poor Parsifal (neither of which could be counted as the real thing), the drunken efforts of Handsome Jack the Plymouth sailor and the juvenile love of Davie – although that was all, I seemed to be moved by instinct.

I moved below him, gently pushing his stomach up until his body was arched above me, his chest wide and with a pretty tuft of hair flowering at its centre, and his tattoes animated. A quick dance with my bottom and I was directly below his anxious eyes, his arched stomach and his eager pointed lance. It seemed to glow with anticipation. I could feel myself glowing too, a flush on my skin, my breasts warm, and between my legs like an oven. I opened them wider and guided him to me. It was amazing. He seemed to fill my belly with himself. He slid home with never a moment's hesitation and all in one deep breath. There was no doubt he was a splendid and healthy lad, even if he did smell fishy.

Having run in for his entire length he did nothing else but just lay there like some landed fish himself. I turned and looked at his comely face just at my shoulder. His eyes clouded and then closed and I had a short silly fright that the experience might have killed him. I did not want that to happen on my first real time. But his face was moving and he seemed to be trying to say something.

'What is it Rainbow dear?' I whispered. 'What be you on about?'

'I be prayin' Nell,' he said simply. 'I be prayin' to thank the Lord God for this thing we be up to.'

I let him pray, although I would have preferred to have got on with it. But, perhaps, I thought, it was like grace said before a meal. It was the only prayer he knew but worded approximately for us he prayed: 'Oh God, bless us who go down to the sea in ships and occupy our business in great waters . . .' Now, after all this time, I can appreciate how charming it was, but then I must confess, I thought it a bit strange and only caused an avoidable delay. When he had done he opened his seaman's eyes and began moving like a piston engine. What a thing he possessed. I truly thought he would burst me at the seams. He began to sweat busily and his grunts of young pleasure were in rhythm with the beat of the boat's little engine. His fish-cutting hands had my buttocks held so fiercely that it was all I could do not to cry out, and I feared he might damage me for he had a strange liking for banging my buttocks together like cymbals in a band. His thighs rolled on mine and his gasping open mouth on my neck.

He blew out as quickly as the storm and lay there wallowing lazily like the boat in the easing sea. To my surprise he wasted no time before slipping fast asleep and began to snore unmusically. At that time of course, I knew nothing of the strange disinterest of men once they have had what a few minutes previously they wanted before anything else in the world. I did not like to wake him although I was getting cold and stiff in the bunk. I pulled a blanket around us and dozed myself, letting the moving of the sea and the rasping snores of my young lover become a lullaby. When I awoke again he had gone from my side and was bumping about the deck with his father.

I searched about for my clothes, washed my face in a bucket of reasonably clean water and, straightening my hair and my expression, I climbed the ladder up through the companionway.

As I reached the open deck the knifey air caught me and the new morning's sun fell on my face. It was a great salty sunlit sight, the sea reclining bright blue towards the green land only a short distance away. Seabirds were whirling and squawking around the mast and the funny little wheelhouse and there were baskets of silver fish on the deck.

'Did you catch much last night then, Rainbow?' I called as he was sorting the nets at the stern.

He returned the look gravely and steadily. 'Aye,' he said.

Old Hooter did not glance from the land ahead. He was at the wheel and he stared straight over the bow as though he had never entered Weymouth harbour before. Being a useful sort of girl I turned and went below and found the kettle and the teapot and made three mugs of tea. I took them above and father and son accepted them without a word. We stood together on deck and watched the land closing on us, like Columbus coming to a strange world.

Before long we slipped around the stone breakwater and into the early-morning harbour. Other fishing boats were heading in and we waved to several crews. One man shouted, 'Did you do all right then, young Rainbow?' and I heard him and the others laughing across the summery water. I glanced at Rainbow and saw that he was flushed and angry for that moment and he turned away and went and did something with the ropes at the stern. The old man took the boat alongside the jetty and they tied up.

'I've got to go now,' I said to both of them at once. They were standing awkwardly on the deck, wearing high boots and dim expressions. A seagull came down and grabbed a fish from one of the baskets. Rainbow shouted something at him in fisherman's gibberish. 'I got to,' I said. 'I promised I'd be back to help with the breakfasts.'

It seemed there was something else. Something they wanted to do. I smiled at them and went to climb up the ladder to the jetty.

Rainbow said something sharp, quickly to old Hooter and then turned and went in a hurry down below. The old man simply stood on deck, caught in some indecision.

'Bye, bye,' I said as cheerfully as I could. I climbed the scaly ladder to the jetty and turned to wave again. Then, as I turned to walk towards the town, old Hooter shouted: 'Girl!' I turned to see something bounce on the stones. It rolled and then stopped and shone in the sun. I took two paces towards it, hesitated, stooped and picked it up. It was half-a-crown.

Quickly I put it in my pocket, turned and walked away. Not for the first time in my life, I did not know whether to laugh or cry. Still I took it. I clutched it in my hand as I began to run along the cobbles.

That was the start of it all. I had done it for money. I was a whore.

After that I began going out on the boats of Weymouth with various fisherboys and sailors. Often I could be seen making my way, in a quietly brazen manner, down to the harbour as the night came on and the same watcher would have seen me return on the peaceful tide with a deck full of mackerel and satisfaction on the face of some wholesome seafaring lad.

Never again did I go with Rainbow and Hooter on their boat. It turned out that I had been an eighteenth birthday present for the boy from the old man because despite his brave tattoos, until that night he had experienced even less than I had. But after that he stuck to fishing and even when he came into Hal's gave no sign of those rocky hours we had spent in each others arms. But the word had gone round, of course, and various lads asked me to go out to the Channel with them and I often went. Naturally my charges went up with the increasing demand. One sunset I sailed with three jolly brothers and during a force nine gale blowing nor' nor' west I obliged each in turn. I stepped ashore with over a pound.

Needless to say this new career was not helping my work at the café. Sometimes I was so dog tired I would drop off to sleep over the till while waiting for someone to take the money from their pocket to pay for a meal. Once I fell into a big pan of potatoes and another time let the washing up sink overflow and flood the kitchen floor.

Harold and Flossie were most patient with me. They realized from the beginning what was going on. One night, when I was in bed, I heard them arguing about me. I was very surprised because they seldom had a cross word and it upset me that I should be the cause of any disagreement.

Their room was next to mine and the walls were only plywood. It was rarely they said much after they had gone to bed because they worked such long and heavy hours and they were exhausted by that time.

Occasionally they would murmur some reminder to order more potatoes or grumble about the late delivery of the eggs (it was strange, but they never served fish on the principle, I suppose, that fishermen don't enjoy eating what they've caught). On this night, however, I heard my name mentioned and I lay, suddenly awake in the moonlight spreading from my window, listening to them.

''Tis a thorough bad life for a girl, Flossie,' he said. 'A carnal life like that for somebody so young. It might be money, but it's trouble and in the end it's shame as well.'

Flossie used to wear a heavy cloth nightdress, so heavy that I swear I could hear her putting it on even though there was a wall between us. 'Shame? Rubbish!' she replied. 'After what's been done to 'er, who can blame the girl.'

I felt glad that she should come to my defence in that way. 'She's never 'ad a morsel,' she continued. 'And she never will 'ave, 'tis certain, washing up in a place like this. But she's got *one* thing. She's 'andsome, Harold, she's real 'andsome. It's the girl's gift. I don't see why she can't be using it to make a bit o' money.'

''Tis immoral,' he argued. 'There's nothing good about it. She'll find no good in her life if she goes about at prostitution.'

The word came through the wall like a bullet. Somehow I had never used it when I thought about what I was doing. It's a foul word anyway. *Prostitute.* Even in those early days, and little as I knew, I tried to think of myself as a courtesan (a term I had found in a romantic novel), which sound so much more elegant. It has a palatial air about it; it sounds like fine dresses, string music, and ladies curtsying.

But that is what Harold said: 'Prostitution.' I buried my face in the pillow, a lifetime of furtive street corners and stained beds suddenly confronting me. Then I heard Flossie again. 'She'll be the best, that one, you mark my words, Hal. She's got carriage and beauty and she'll learn because she's clever. Take it from me it's her only chance to make good.' The bedspring harped as they got beneath the blankets. 'Look at us,' she said. 'Work till midnight and what are we? Poor as a couple of shithouse spiders.'

They must have been facing away from each other because I heard the bed twang again as one of them turned. 'You sound as though you'd have liked to do that yourself Floss . . .' Harold said accusingly, but softly enough.

I heard her laugh croakily. 'Me? Oh, Hal! I don't reckon I'd have done much good as a prossie. I would have had to have been a bargain.'

'Oh I don't know,' he said good-humouredly now. 'I reckon I'd have spent a bob or two on you.'

'Go on,' she giggled. I smiled now in my moonlit bed. 'I'd never have charged you for it, love.'

The next day in the shadows at the back of the café Flossie came to me diffidently and said: 'I'd like to be giving you some advice Nelly dear. Now you're growing.'

I felt myself blush but she was as practical as she was kind. She placed in my surprised hand a small square packet.

'Give one of these to the lad,' she said secretly. 'And make sure he uses it. You don't want no babies.'

It was the most touching and the most useful present of my life. All through the years that followed I had no child. More's the pity I think now. My good sister Mary had five. I like to think that she had mine too.

CHAPTER EIGHT

My time at Hal's came to an end, as it happened, in an unexpected way, although abrupt conclusions and quick beginnings have been part of my life since then. From time to time a larger vessel than the everyday fishing boat would come into the harbour, perhaps a coaster of several hundred tons, and it was aboard one of these, the *Charlie Harry II*, that I sailed unintentionally from England.

I was by everyone's account a fine-looking girl with a ready smile and a generous heart. My early apprenticeship aboard the boats was over and I had a greater control of what I was about. My charges went up to ten shillings (I now had nearly fifty pounds in the Post Office Savings Bank, the rewards of loose living in the trawling grounds and a sum which delighted the old dearie in the Weymouth Post Office who thought I was earning such good money at the café) and, in addition, I had become accepted in that small, salty world. I went out at the start of the season (the fishing season I mean. My work was continuous.) with the little fleet to hear the Bishop pray from the bow of a boat, for God's blessing on the catches and the men who caught them. I prayed with my eyes as tightly shut as the next person.

A hot summer had settled on the southern coast, days of huge skies and easy seas, when the people started going back to the beaches now the war was over. They came to Weymouth in their thousands although the barbed wire and the buried mines were still in some places, and watching the busy children on the sands with their mothers and fathers made me, for a moment only, sad because of what I had missed.

But I was making up for it now. I am afraid I was to be found in some of the lower public houses of the town, laughing and drinking and not thinking of either yesterday or tomorrow. I had, at last, written to my sister Mary and she replied and told me how well she was getting on at the bakery in Hopewell, where she had gone after the disaster at Hopewell Manor (well reported in the newspapers, of course, and hardly needing detailed repetition here) when poor Parsifal poisoned both his parents at the breakfast table and had to be taken away to a refuge for the simple-minded. Neither Mary nor I ever heard a word from our father, although Mary was told that he had been seen in Plymouth with a one-legged woman. It was of no great interest to me. Then, however, before the affair of the *Charlie Harry II,* I received a letter from the Commander. He had gone to Hopewell and inquiring after Mary had traced her to the bakery and had obtained my address. He wrote and asked me to go and see him in London, enclosing three pounds for my first class railway fare.

I was full of excitement and a sort of compressed terror. What if he should find out about the life I was now leading? I trembled in my bed to think of it and I refused to go out in the boat for a whole week before I went to London in case there should be signs of debauchery in my face; also I did not want to smell of fish because there was no doubt that a whore takes on the aroma of her customers very quickly when she works in a certain area or among men of a certain profession. Charlotte the Harlot, who I knew in later years in London, had worked in the region of a tannery for years and always had that niff of hide about her, something which put off quite a number of potential customers. In fact it ruined her for general practice in the end and she had to go to the chemical works area in the Midlands where it did not notice so much.

Anyway, I was bubbling over by the time the day arrived for me to go to London. I had never been there in my life, of course, and it was like setting out for a different and distant country. There must have been a dozen of my friends at Weymouth Station to see me off, with much anxious advice about keeping hold of my money and watching for pickpockets and pimps who preyed on innocent girls from the country and sea.

All the journey I sat rigid as a virgin in the corner seat, not speaking to anyone and even refusing haughtily the offer of a young man opposite who wanted to give me a cucumber sandwich. I hoped he thought I was some fine lady, even though I was travelling third class. (I couldn't bring myself, when it came to it, to buy a first class ticket.) England looked lovely though, from the carriage window. I had not travelled by train very much (not, in fact, since Mary and I were taken from Hopewell to Bristol in our early forlorn days). It was May and everywhere seemed breathing happily and freely now there was no war. There was blossom on the trees and cows in the fields, houses and rivers and people and bicycles. Some people, not just children but grown-ups also, stood at the side of the line and waved at our train. It was just as though they had never seen a train before and they had come out specially to see us. I waved back, a bit haughtily, just the merest turn of the glove at my wrist. In a way I felt like a queen.

Mind you, I did this partly to show the young man with the cucumber sandwiches that I was aloof and aristocratic and when I opened my corned beef sandwiches from their greaseproof paper I took only dainty bites at them, munching the mouthful like a lady, the lips tightly together, and wiping the crumbs off my mouth with a flick of my imitation lace gloves.

I thought that the young man was duly impressed by all this high-class behaviour, but I was mistaken because we reached Winchester and he got out, raising his cap (which pleased me, of course), as he opened the door. But then he stood on the platform, just outside the open window and, leaning in, kissed me fully on my surprised lips and said: 'I reckon you'd make a fine shag, my love.'

He strode away jauntily, leaving me trying to be aghast for the benefit of the other passenger, an elderly, nodding man. 'I don't know what manners are coming to!' I sniffed with all the high disdain I could find.

'Aye,' said the elderly, nodding man looking me in the eye. 'But he's right though.' In those days I never knew how men could tell.

He was there to meet me at the station, not the tall, gallant naval officer I had imagined in my girlish fantasies, but an ever-wounded man, his face aged with pain and scars, a man supported on two sticks with legs as stiff as the sticks themselves.

But his voice was strong and gentle as ever. I walked, then unable to help it, ran along the platform towards him, my happiness at seeing him again almost flooding away the sadness of his condition. I scrambled all my first words together in my confusion and was stood, a pace apart, him smiling, me choked with emotion. Then, very carefully, for I was afraid I might topple him over, I put out my arms and folded them around him. It was the first time we had touched as adults. His body was as meagre as a pole. He could not return the embrace because he could not let go of his walking sticks. He stood rigid, as though helpless with shock, while I pressed myself to him and put my face against his damaged face. There was nothing I would not have done for him. He was someone I loved.

'I have a taxi,' he said hoarsely in my ear. 'It's waiting.'

It was the first time I had seen a London cab, a black box on wheels, but I understood how useful it was for him because he was unable to bend his legs at the knee and in the back of the taxi there was room for him to stretch out in front of him. We sat while the cab set off through the wonderful strange streets to an address he had given. But now it seemed that we did not know what to say. It was as though everything that we had in common had been said in that embrace at the station.

'I've got some change for you,' I said eventually, awkwardly.

'Change from what, Nell?' he asked.

'From the train,' I explained. 'I couldn't bring myself to come first class. It seems such a waste. So there's twenty-five shillings change.'

He laughed in his throat-crackling way. I often wondered what his laugh was like before he was hurt.

'With that, Nell,' he decided. 'you must buy yourself a hat. I think you would look beautiful in a hat.'

'Where are we going?'

'To the home of a friend,' he said. 'Diana Seagram. We will stay there.'

A sudden coldness came upon me at the mention of another woman, an immediate jealousy such as I had never experienced in my life. And she sounded rather grand too, this Diana Seagram, with a house in London. I looked at him, half afraid, half accusing, as if I had any claim on him. He still thought of me as a child. He smiled into my face.

'You'll like her,' he said, not understanding my look. 'She has a very pleasant house too.'

'Commander,' I said, deciding to blurt it out. 'Is she . . . is she . . . your . . . lady?'

He laughed joyously, and I felt myself flush to my neck.

'My lady?' he repeated, enjoying it. 'No, she's not Nell. She's just a friend. She's the widow of a man I knew in the war. He was killed on my ship. She's wonderful but she's not my . . . er . . . lady.' He laughed again and put his arm about my embarrassed shoulder. 'You're my only lady, Nelly Luscombe,' he said.

The house was near Westminster. It had been damaged in the bombing but despite the patching up it was pleasing and comfortable. The lady was the same; sweet-faced, middle-aged, slim and assured in a gentle way. I stood in the hall when we first arrived, staring up as she came down the fine staircase, feeling once more like a little country housemaid. But her eyes were kind and soft, and she took me to my room talking all the time to make me feel at ease. It was amazing the things she knew about me.

'He told you all these things?' I said.

'Yes all of them,' she answered. We had gone into the room, the best room I had ever slept in, until then. Diana drew back the curtains and the sun fell in. Outside was a walled, small garden. There were bees walking on the window sill.

'You were very important to him,' she said simply. 'When he needed some help. Did you know that Nell?'

'No,' I answered truthfully. 'I didn't do anything. I just played housey-housey with him, that's all.'

'It was very important,' she said. 'Almost everything.' She touched me on the shoulder. I felt I liked her very much. 'You helped him survive all that.'

That afternoon they both took me to Bond Street and I bought the hat he had promised. I can remember it exactly now and it makes me smile. It had a little lacy veil, like a small fishing net, that dangled over my forehead and my eyes and made me feel very beautiful and cool. We went into other marvellous shops, the Commander sitting down, his legs stuck out in front of him ('like a damned wheelbarrow,' he said), and Diana and I looking at and trying on the clothes. She bought herself an expensive, tasteful blouse and she wanted to buy me a skirt, but I would not allow her to do so. I had some of my immoral earnings from Weymouth, which I had drawn from the Post Office Savings Bank the day before, and in one shop I bought myself a pair of gloves which I paid for with my own money. I had never paid so much for anything in my whole life. But I did not show it. My face, I know, was composed, I gave the assistant the money and thanked her with what I hoped sounded like a rich voice. Diana and the Commander were watching me closely and they both smiled and nodded.

In the street once more I caught up with the fresh thrill of that exciting and expensive place. The shop windows were draped and displayed with things the like of which I had never seen, the road was full of cars and buses and those taxis like squat hearses. The pavements flowing with people.

There were also strangely loitering ladies in the street, wearing smart suits and shoes, but who seemed to be on some kind of patrol, walking and waiting and then walking again, and conversing with random men. I watched them and their expensive clothes and faces and I saw that here there must be better pickings than among the fishing boats of Weymouth. Trying to hide my interest from the Commander and Diana, I nevertheless was able to see what these ladies were about and how busy they became even in the middle of the afternoon. Nobody seemed to notice or mind.

They filled me with an irrepressible and illegal thrill. I wanted to see them again and find out more about them. I was shy and unsure but not afraid. The following day Diana had to go out and the Commander said he would take a rest because his legs were painful after the previous afternoon's excursion. Did I mind amusing myself? I said truthfully that I would be glad to do so and I went out saying I was going to visit the zoo. But, as soon as I was clear of the house, I brazenly got into a taxi (it is amazing how quickly even a country girl slips into such easy city habits) and told the driver to take me to Bond Street.

On edge with anticipation, I walked along the crowded pavements and saw again the elegant prowling ladies. Then I took to some of the side streets, being careful not to lose my soundings (as they say among seafarers), and I was amazed to find even more expensively dressed loiterers down where there were fewer shops and more privacy. Eventually I found myself in Curzon Street and then in the narrow courtways of Shepherd Market. Wandering women were on the loose everywhere, waiting outside smart shops, taking afternoon tea in the small cafés, and making secret signs and signals to each other as they cruised around.

Amazed and fascinated, I tried to overhear what conversation went on between them. It was basic, trade talk, like signals to one another.

'Done it yet Emmy?'

'Three times love, one double time.'

'You're so lucky, darling. Had to go to bloody Marlborough Street to pay my licence. Haven't had a thing since.'

Breathlessly I listened. Licence? Was a licence needed in London for this sort of occupation? Did it permit the business? I hung about, watching and walking up and down the pavement. Eventually a buxom and handsome lady, in a red costume and with a fascinating blackened eye, took to watching me and after a while approached me.

'Why don't you fuck off?' she suggested.

I was dumbfounded. I felt a flush fall over my face like a curtain.

'Why?' I managed to say. 'I'm not doing anything.'

'Listen dearie,' she said, leaning close so that I could smell her powerful perfume and see the lines protruding around the black eye. 'We've got enough girls on this stretch as it is. There's no more room. Where you from?'

'Paris,' I decided brilliantly and followed it by a string of gibberish which I hoped might be taken for French.

'Well just fuck off back there,' she advised. 'There's too many working this pitch. And, anyway, this is the pricey pavement. Two quid a time here. If you want to work in London go and try Soho, all right?'

I replied with a further stream of gibberish and minced off with a pounding heart within me and what I hoped was a show of utter disdain without. Soho? Ah, I had heard of Soho. The Weymouth fishermen talked of it as something in their dreams, in the same way as they might talk of a huge catch of mackerel, or a chance of a salvage prize money. It was something beyond them.

I stopped another taxi. 'Take me to Soho,' I said with polite highness, and sat back in the seat feeling stifled with the thrill. Driving through London streets I knew that my future was there.

Soho did not frighten me at all. Considering that I had been born and brought up among the good clean fields of Devon (where, certainly, there was sin, but in a secret and silent country way), I found the streets, the brassy lights and the strange foreign people only fascinating.

Leaving the taxi, I wandered entranced by the aromatic alleys and delighted by the doors from which strange sounds and dark movements came. It was a warm afternoon, and the Soho ladies were lolling from open windows or walking the narrow pavements. They were not so well tailored as the Curzon Street women, they wore common red shoes and chewed gum. But furtive men stalked them along those streets. I wondered how much money they made on an afternoon in a heatwave.

The way I was meandering about, taking my time and looking at everything with such intense curiosity, made me a target for several men mooching through the courts and alleyways. I had the fresh, fruity look of the country girl, bright eyes and my hair at its finest, with my bosom bursting beneath my blouse. I soon had a little contingent of prospective and eager customers following obediently. Three times men coming in the opposite direction fell conveniently over their own feet as they neared and lurched into me full of apologies and pleasure.

A squat, swarthy fellow I took to be an Italian kept popping up out of doorways and turnings all over the place. He would slide from one opening and walk towards me, eyes almost revolving, go past and then a minute later emerge from yet another exit twenty yards ahead. He had a magician's moustache and was wearing on overcoat despite the warmth of the day. I began to laugh because of his antics and this encouraged him to approach me.

'How much you want – only to talk?' he whispered.

I may have been from the country but I was not slow. 'How much you pay?' I asked sweetly.

His face beamed at my willingness. 'Only to talk for ten minutes,' he repeated reassuringly. 'I give you two pounds.'

This seemed like a very reasonable proposition. 'Where do we talk?' I asked, suspecting there had to be more to it. 'Where do we have to go?'

'Here-a in da street,' he nodded encouragingly. 'Just-a walk and just-a talk. I give you two pounds.'

'What do you want to talk about?' I said. 'Anything special?'

'Oh-yes, verra special,' he nodded. He was taking two pound notes out of his crocodile wallet and pushing them towards me insistently. I took them and put them in my bag. 'Now we talk,' he said. 'Me - I talk.'

So we walked along the street, my arm casually through his like old acquaintances. There were people everywhere. We walked through the vegetable market and then along Old Compton Street. He began to speak in a steady confiding tone. 'I would like-a to peess all down your beautiful back,' he began.

Now this surprised me. There was no chance of me allowing such a thing – in those early days I only knew the plain and simple ways – but the very idea amazed me. I turned quickly to him. He hardly glanced at me but said: 'I pay two pounds. I talk 'ow I like. Okay?'

There was nothing I could do but nod and we walked for ten minutes through the by-ways of Soho with his amazing one-way conversation going on in my left ear. He spoke in the same low voice and with the same low thoughts. What he said he wanted to do with me was enough to make my young rural eyebrows go up and down as if they were on strings.

My face, I knew, was scarlet with embarrassment, but I walked solidly on with him until he had apparently attained the satisfaction he acquired in this most curious way. At that point he bowed politely and shook my hand, inquiring whether I would care to meet him for further conversation the following day. I hesitated but he forestalled any refusal by putting the fee up fifty percent. Three pounds was three pounds in anybody's life, so I agreed to meet him in the same place at the same time.

The following day I made an excuse to be by myself in the afternoon and the Commander and Diana smiled knowingly. 'I think you have met some nice young man,' the Commander said, sitting stiffly in his chair. 'You must bring him here, mustn't she Diana?'

Diana smiled in agreement and I had a brief picture of the Italian whispering that he would like to peess all down her beautiful back. So I denied meeting anyone but said I wanted to buy some presents for the people in Weymouth. Half an hour later, my ears now plugged with cotton wool, I walked round and round the little garden in Soho Square while the small Italian talked earnestly of his strange ambitions and interests. I heard hardly any of it, and at the end of the stroll I was three pounds better off, more than some people earned for a weeks's work in those days. It seemed an easy enough way of making a living.

He wanted me to return on the following afternoon but it was to be my last day and I was looking forward to spending it with the Commander. The Italian took great umbrage at my refusal and there in the street began to get awkward and angry. In the end the only way to get rid of him was to give him a mouthful of West Country curses. He looked shocked and answered primly: 'Don' you talk-a to me like-a that.' I thought it was a trifle odd coming from him. He went away still muttering.

On the afternoon following I took the Commander boating on the Serpentine. It was my treat. He had taken me to several restaurants and to see *Annie Get Your Gun* and now I insisted that I would take him to tea by the lake and for a row along its summery green water.

I can see him now, as though in a happy dream, stretched almost full out in the boat, his unbending legs sticking out, while I rowed between the ducks. I had become quite good at handling small boats, for the Weymouth fishermen sometimes asked me to assist them in more than my usual way. The London sun shone on us and he joked and pretended that his stiffened legs were the barrels of twin naval guns. He fired them in all directions giving orders and instructions to a make-believe gun crew. It is strange how men are such great pretenders.

That hour is so pictured in my memory in soft colours like an old miniature painting. To be in his company was always a pleasure. To laugh and float about like that under the sky and the overhung leaves was pure joy. I felt I loved him so much.

'Commander,' I called from my rower's seat. 'Have you ever had a wife?'

His legs stopped firing. He seemed to wait an eternity before answering and I was fearful that I had said the wrong thing to him. But his voice returned eventually, as careful and calm as ever.

'Yes Nell,' he said. 'I had a wife. But we separated. She's married to someone else now.'

There was another silence, only the simple splashing of the oars and the talking of the ducks making any sound. I was afraid to say more. Eventually he said: 'She did not want a husband like this.'

CHAPTER NINE

From London I returned to Weymouth feeling empty, sad and suddenly lost, but my adventure aboard the *Charlie Harry II* soon put all other things out of my mind and my life was once again changed.

Until that time I had only occupied my business in small waters, among the crews of the little fishing boats that had their homes in Weymouth bay. Larger vessels, of course, came into the port and I had occasionally stood on the quay and watched them and wondered about their possibilities as far as business was concerned. About this time also the ferry service from Weymouth to the Channel Islands was resumed after being stopped by the war, and it crossed my mind that, if it could be arranged with the more or less permanent booking of a cabin and that sort of thing, I could make a steady living from likely men going on that passage. The crossing, in those days, took about ten hours.

I did, in fact, make one experimental trip (my journey to London having made me keen to travel and to find new opportunities) and booked a cabin on the overnight boat. On board was a Welsh rugby team and their supporters going to play in Jersey. I caught the eye of a square, randy-looking fellow first and eyed him to my cabin where, at the door, I asked him if he wanted to spend some money. Either he had taken too many drinks or they did not practice prostitution in Wales, or he was plain stupid, but whatever it was he did not seem able to understand the proposition. Eventually, fearing our doorway discussion might be spotted by someone in authority, I pulled him into the room and demonstrated what charms I was making available. A bright light dawned on his dumb face and he said: 'Oh, it's a shag you're wanting, lovely! Oh fine, all right. Always ready for a shag. You look as though you're panting for it.' Then he piled on top of me as though he was going into one of those scrum things they have in rugby, gave me a terrible seeing-to, pulled up his trousers and marched out with a triumphant grin all over his Welsh face. I couldn't seem to make him understand that I wanted paying for my services. He seemed to think that it was *he* who was doing the favour.

The news, needless to say, was passed around quicker than the ball they play with. While I was still lying back panting and cursing my luck and lack of business sense, there came a knock on the door and outside I found the rest of the team and a number of supporters. I found one man who was not so drunk as the others and who seemed to understand English and explained that I was doing this as a living and not as a charity. Appropriately enough (although I did not appreciate this at the time because the word was unknown to me), this man was the hooker of the team. He shut the others out, passed over a pound – which he was careful to explain was payment also for the original fellow who turned out to be his brother – and pushed me back on the narrow bunk. I felt a lot better about this and he seemed to enjoy it, the only drawback being I was almost smothered by the thick rugby scarf which he insisted on leaving wound around his neck. To take it off he indicated between lurches and grunts would be bad luck for the team.

Afterwards he went outside and explained to those that remained (some had gone back to singing at the bar, for Welshmen have strange priorities) that it was on a commercial basis and that he would collect the money. I stepped very quickly outside and said I would prefer to collect it myself and the collection would take place immediately before giving my services.

'Oh, all right then, lovely' he said amiably. 'I was only seeing you wasn't going to be cheated, that's all.'

During the course of that evening I think I must have seen to the whole team, the reserves, the secretary and the treasurer, who cried all through his fuck because he was something to do with the chapel and he didn't think he ought to enjoy it. I was exhausted but richer by some nineteen pounds seven and sixpence. The shillings and pence came from one of the reserves, a cherub of a lad, only sixteen, who pleaded with me to accept the reduced fare saying it was all he had, his father was on the dole and his mother had left home with the coalman. It was a heart-rending story, accompanied by a smattering of Welsh tears, and he looked so comely that I accepted the seven and six. He had wiped his eyes with the hand that held the coins and they were wet with his sobbing when he handed them over. I was very touched. But then he came at me like a young pig and gave me the most frightful going over before strolling out whistling some song they sang in their bloody valleys.

I was tired by the time the ferry reached Jersey. I stayed ashore for two days, recuperating, and then returned to England with the same team. If I thought I was going to get richer I was mistaken. The team had lost heavily (and some of them had the effrontery to put the blame on me) and the entire return trip was accompanied by maudlin songs and dismal drinking. Indeed, I ended up crying and singing with them, as plastered as any, and finished the night with the club captain and the secretary sharing my little bunk, at the conclusion of which I was given a life-long honorary membership of Abercowan Rugby Club, which entitled me to go and see any of their home matches free.

It was now obvious and inevitable that there was for me no escape from a wicked life. If, in the solitary nights I had, I experienced any pangs of worry and remorse I soon dismissed them and went soundly to sleep. I liked the physical demands and the interesting varied men and I hoped right from the start it would lead to more rarified things. If I was not born to it then I adopted it and it adopted me with equal willingness. As Flossie had said that night, it was using the one talent and advantage I had – an enticing and willing body and a giving nature. And through this horizontal life I have risen from being a homeless waif to become a famous lady. My bed has been shared by a Prime Minister, three international footballers, a circus strong man, several millionaires and powerful industrialists, the editor of a Sunday newspaper, sundry actors *and* actresses, and a sly rural dean. All on different nights of course.

Within a week of my return to Weymouth – where my work at Hal's Café had, of necessity, become part-time – I was standing on the quay when the *Charlie Harry II* chugged into port. There were few things very handsome about her – and that went for the captain and crew as well – but she looked quite jaunty as she pushed through the harbour mouth on an August evening's tide. As she passed she gave me a little toot-toot on her siren and I waved and laughed because I was sure it was intended for me.

As it happened I was right. The crew of this vessel, which had been plying in and out of Weymouth for a year of more, had seen me serving in Hal's and had heard from the local fisherboys of my other activities. This had interested them a good deal, especially the mate who missed his wife a lot, and they had decided to entice me aboard their ship.

That evening they came into Hal's and sat eating their chips and eyeing me. I was not worried for I had been surveyed many times before and when the mate (Jock they all called him – it was that sort of informal ship) invited me to accompany him and two others for a drink in the town I went along easily as I always did. I was still particular, but not as particular as when I started. Most men look alike if you close your eyes and count your money.

They seemed a very friendly bunch, laughing and joking a lot, and buying rum and whisky and port for me. Port, appropriately now I think of it, was my favourite drink. It never failed to lull me into a receptive mood.

They were sailing around the coasts of Europe, going wherever there was a cargo to be hawked, taking their old leaky ship in and out of harbours along the English Channel, down through Biscay and into the Mediterranean ports. She was an old vessel, damaged several times during the war, and apparently quite unsuited for the cargoes she carried. Bits fell off and sank or floated away regularly but the crew sailed on.

'One day,' forecast Jock the mate confidently, 'the wee old tub will sigh and slide below the waves and we'll all be left to swim. I'll give her twelve months and no more.'

He was eleven months short in his estimation.

There is little I can remember of the next few hours. Lifting the glass of port became difficult and I began to laugh a lot. The next sensation was an aching head and the familiar roll of a vessel under my bottom. I wondered which of the fishing lads I was voyaging with that night.

But there was an unfamiliar atmosphere and a strange hot smell about the darkness to which I woke. The place felt to have more room. I could sense it all about me, and there was no smell of fish. I stirred and realized I was lying naked in the warm darkness.

I felt around with my foot, touching the wall by the wide bunk in which I lay. My toe touched a switch and I pushed it down. A dim, electric light bulb, as naked as I was, glowed in the bulkhead. I looked over the hills of my breasts, between them and around them, still lying flat on my back surveying the place with caution. There was a man lying in another bunk across the cabin. I could see he was watching me. It was Jock the mate.

'Och, so you're awake, lassie,' he said.

'Where's my clothes?' I said quietly.

'Dryin' out,' he replied simply. 'Ye fell out of the wee dinghy when you were coming aboard.'

'I don't want to be here,' I said. Like Venus I put my hand modestly over my pubis. 'I want to go back.'

'Lassie,' he said. 'Ye wanted to be here last night. You wouldna' be any place else, and that's a fact.'

'Somebody gave me something,' I said adamantly. 'Put something in my drink. Where are we going anyway?'

'South by south west,' he said. 'Unless the captain's drunk again. Heading for Finisterre. Then down the Bay to Bilbao, then who knows where lass? Who knows where?'

The news staggered me. 'I can't,' I said, sitting bolt upright. He stared at my breasts. I lay down and covered them with my spare forearm. 'I can't go to Bilbao, wherever that is. I haven't even got a passport.'

'Stowaways don't as a rule,' he replied simply. 'Would you have a liking for some coffee?'

'Stowaway!' I howled. 'You Scotch bastard! You shanghaied me! I've been kidnapped!'

'Keep your voice low lass,' he said urgently. 'The skipper doesn't know. Yet.'

'Then he's got to know,' I said sitting up again. This time I drew a blanket up between my legs and held it around the back of my neck. I sat in the dim light like a prehistoric woman in a cave.

''Tis better he doesna' know,' warned Jock. 'He's a hard man. Especially with girl stowaways.'

'I'm not a bloody stowaway,' I said, prudently keeping the protest below a shout. I didn't like the sound of the captain. 'You drugged me and brought me aboard this fucking hulk.'

'Hulk is correct,' he nodded wisely. 'Fucking? Well, we shall see. Meself I'm wondering if she'll last the trip. There's more water inside her than outside. The pumps are going all the time. And as for whether you're a stowaway or not, the matter is of no matter. All stowaways say they've have been shanghaied. That's the story they all tell. But maritime courts, if it ever got that far, are inclined to believe the officers. I'm thinking that the furthest this will go will be the captain. And that would be bad for you Nelly, lass. I told the truth. He's a bad one with girl stowaways.'

I felt myself collapse hopelessly within, and I sagged in the blanket. He handed me a mug of coffee which I took without thinking and drank. It made me feel better. 'You make it seem as if you had a lot of girl stowaways,' I said dully. 'That's how it sounds.'

'Aye,' he agreed, having thought about it. 'We seem to have a wee few. They seem to be attracted by us.'

'What do I have to do?' I asked, knowing full well.

He advanced heavily on me. 'For a beginning,' he said with throaty romance, 'you can comfort a man who's far distant from his lovin' wife. That's me.' He was bare chested and wearing an old pair of dungaree trousers.

'I charge you know,' I said, thinking I might just as well make the most of the situation. 'I do it for money,' I wondered how far Bilbao was.

'And you'll be paid lass,' he said. 'Paid right well, I promise.' He waited, his face quickly sad. ''Tis my pretty Jeanie McAllister from Glen Donal that I miss. That I'm yearning for. Be pretty Jeanie McAllister for me, will ye?'

'Aye,' I replied, getting right into the game (this is a talent you need to have in the business).

'Hoots,' I murmured as he slipped his trousers down. 'There's a grand sight. Hoots again.'

To be honest he was a fine looking chap with that sort of hungry look about his body. He closed his eyes and he closed with me and came into me muttering. 'In the glen, sweet Jeanie. In the heather in the glen.' I had not the heart to ask him about money then, but I thought it would be all right.

I lay back and closed my Devon arms about his Highland back and brought him to my breasts. There were only a few occasions when I truly relished it, I had already got over that, but I must say his fatless body and his Scottish mutterings were not without enjoyment.

'Dear Jeanie,' he kept saying and I dutifully muttered back. 'Aye, aye, I'm right here in the glen with ye,' and all sorts of pantomime like that. At one point he paused to correct my pronunciation of a word, which made me understand how important it all was to him. Then the pipes started, at least that's what he said, because he could hear them through the mountains and the mists.

'The pipes, aye, the pipes. The Campbells are coming,' he cried.

The Campbells weren't the only ones. He was a fraction before them and we lay exhausted as the hills and glens vanished and were replaced by the dark bunk in the pitching sea.

'Ah, that was grand, Nell,' he said kissing my face. He levered himself up and watching him, I wondered why Jeanie McAllister allowed him to roam so far from home.

'Now,' he said stepping towards the other side of the cabin. 'Ye have to be paid.' He returned and pressed into my hand what looked like a small brown coin with a hole in its centre.

'What's this?' I asked staring at it. 'I want some money!'

'Hush woman,' he said. 'The captain will hear ye – and then there's trouble. He does terrible things to girl stowaways.'

'What *is* it?' I demanded, but whispering.

'A token,' he smiled. 'Everything on board is paid for by tokens ye see, you'll be able to buy things with it. Tobacco, sweeties, all sorts of merchandise. It's worth all of five shillings.'

'Five shillings! I charge more than that.'

'That's just from *me*,' he pointed out. 'I'm the mate on this ship and if I tell the others it's ten shillings a time, at the end you'll have a wee fortune in those tokens.'

'Others?' I said. 'You expect me to do it for the others? For tokens?'

'Aye,' he said. 'There's six others. Fine gentle lads, all o' them. All missing their dear wives and sweethearts. They'll be glad to have you aboard, Nelly.'

It would not have been so bad and at least it would have helped my pride a bit if perhaps just *one* of the crew had called me Nell and not pretended that he was with someone he loved, or said he loved. Sailors are terrible romancers and hypocrites. The loneliness of the sea gets into them and they cry easily as they drink and pray and then are often remorseful.

During the next few days in that leaky and lumpy little ship, I was called so many names in the welter of passion that I began to wonder who I really was. True, Jock the mate came back three times and I was Jeanie McAllister each time, so at least he was faithful in his fashion. But the charade I played with the others sometimes verged on the edge of treachery.

First the bosun's mate, a horny type of bandy man with a bright eye, came into the cabin and, having deposited his token, stood looking at me like a ferret staring from a rabbit hole. 'I'll call you Dorothea,' he said, a surprisingly high voice coming from such a low slung body. 'Or Rose.'

'Make up your mind,' I sighed, leaning back. 'It's all the same to me.'

'Torn between them, I am,' he sniffed, 'Dorothea in Tilbury and Rose in Gibraltar.' He thought about it. 'No, I think I'll call you Maggie,' he decided.

I surrendered then and became Maggie for the next ten minutes. When he had finished he was in penitent tears and trembled, 'Oh Audrey, how could I do these things to you?'

In those few days I took on the names of twenty far-flung women and had a few real surprises. One deckhand kept murmuring, 'Granny, oh granny,' in my ear and the cabin boy, a sweet lad, howled for his mother and his Uncle George.

After almost a week I was weary, bored, robbed of identity and worrying about where I could change the pile of brass tokens I had accumulated. Then there came a private knock on the cabin door and in came the mate and the rest of them, like a deputation, and stood bashfully around the door. Seen together they made a pathetically downtrodden bunch. Jock had been voted as the spokesman and he stood grappling for words and moving his hands like paddles.

'Jeanie,' began the mate pleadingly. The others followed all together.

'Dorothea.'

'Rose.'

'Beryl.'

'Zara.'

'Audrey.'

'Kate.'

'Pussy.'

'Granny.'

'Mum and Uncle George.'

'Nelly!' I bawled at them. 'Won't you learn. I'm Nelly Luscombe from Weymouth!'

'Ah yes,' nodded Jock. 'And who else could you be, lass?' He waited while they all muttered 'Nelly, Nelly, Nelly,' like some prayer of the seven dwarfs. They were still all cluttered together looking embarrassed by the cabin door. 'Nelly,' went on the mate. 'We've come to ask a favour of you, just one wee favour.'

'I should think I've done enough favours,' I said glancing at the pile of brass tokens by the bed. 'I've got enough of those things to keep me in sweeties to the rest of my days.'

'It's just one thing,' he insisted. 'One favour.'

'What is it?' I asked impatiently. I was getting fed up with all of them.

'Do you think you could do a bit of darning for us? Darning and mending. We're none of us any good at it.'

Nothing surprised me any longer. I leaned back and sighed. At least it would mean working with my hands, which would be a welcome change. I nodded.

'And the cook on the ship is a madman,' went on Jock plaintively. 'He'll kill us all yet. He leaves the giblets in the chicken, doesn't he boys?'

'He leaves the giblets in the chicken,' they echoed like slaves.

'So you want me to cook as well?'

'Just now and then. So we can have a decent meal. We'll get him drunk, which will be no trouble, and give you the run of the galley.'

'All right. All right,' I sighed. 'But if I cook and sew I want a rest from working on this bed. Is that agreed?'

They agreed with unflattering eagerness. My body was being willingly swopped for mended socks and edible food. Inwardly I shrugged.

'And we'll keep the donkeyman away – promise,' piped up the dim cabin boy. The others nudged him furiously. He looked shamefaced.

'Who?' I demanded. 'Who did you say?'

'Er . . . the donkeyman,' he blushed.

I looked at Jock. 'Who's the donkeyman?' I demanded.

'Och, 'tis only the laddie that works the donkey engine,' he said. 'He's a wee bit crazy. He keeps wanting to come in here, ye see, like to . . . well, to join in the fun. But we won't let him in. We took all his tokens away. And we won't let him get at the drink. Just so he wouldna' bother you.'

'Thanks,' I whispered. The thought of a crazy donkeyman coming in was unnerving. 'Just keep him out of my way then.'

'We will, we will,' they all recited and then they shuffled out. The first consignment of socks was in my cabin in ten minutes.

I locked the door carefully, for now I was fearful that the hideous donkeyman would come wandering down. In my cabin I darned socks and mended shirts for two days. It was getting stuffy but I dare not show myself in case I should be seen by the donkeyman or the captain.

In the event the weather on deck, according to the crew, was spiteful for the season. The vessel pitched about a good deal but this no longer worried me. Whatever else I had lost I had found my sealegs. What did concern me was the awful creaking and straining of the vessel. At night she groaned like someone dying.

Half the crew's time seemed to be spent in trying to keep the pumps working and there were bets struck that we would reach the bed of the sea before Bilbao.

They did, however, manage to pour enough drink down the unresisting gullet of the cook and I was smuggled into the galley to prepare a meal for them. I had never been much of a cook, but what I gave them seemed to them like a feast and for a while made everyone forget their loved ones far away and the fact that the ship was falling to pieces by the hour.

The cabin boy was told to help me with the washing of the dishes but we had only just started clearing the galley table when there came a terrible roar from the companionway and Jock the mate came tumbling down backwards followed by an enormous and wild man, oil all over his face and dungarees. His eyes were blazing and oaths tumbled from his monstrous mouth. When he saw me he howled like a gorilla.

'The donkeyman!' cried poor Jock, trying to get up from the floor.

'The donkeyman!' howled the cabin boy.

I stood transfixed. The crew came tumbling pathetically downstairs after the wild man, trying to catch him and hold him, but he was brushing them aside like King Kong.

I backed away stiffly. He was clear of the crew, who were left sprawling in all directions, and now there was only the cabin boy between his desires and the object of them – Nell Luscombe. Soon there was no cabin boy either for he went gallantly under the galley table. I turned searching frantically for an escape, for a weapon. It was my fortune that I picked on the best weapon I could have wanted – a bowl of washing up powder standing by the sink. I threw the lot in the donkeyman's face and followed it with a bowl of water, a combination which resulted in the amazing sight of the frenzied creature blowing coloured bubbles all over the galley.

It was enough. I went over the top of the table like a deer and ran along the lower gangway. I dashed up a flight of stairs and found myself on the open deck. It was dark and the ship was pitching about, apparently without hope, in a strong sea. There was a light on the bridge. There was nothing for it but to go there.

Up the ladder I went, the furious sounds of battle coming from an open hatch as I passed. Flinging open the bridge door I discovered the captain standing there, peaked cap, black beard and woollen combinations tucked into sea boots.

'I'm a girl stowaway,' I said.

We met the donkeyman on the companionway as we set off for the captain's cabin, leaving the bridge in charge of a myopic crew member who, logically, had been given the charge of the wheel. This old fellow had actually been introduced into my cabin by Jock – it was his idea of an act of charity, although not towards me – and was so short-sighted that he failed to see me in the dimness. I kept very still and he struggled out again complaining about people making jokes with old men who were nearly blind.

The donkeyman came charging up the stairs and there was a confrontation between him, the captain in his 'combs', and me trembling behind that powerful, flannelled posterior.

'I want 'er,' growled the donkeyman. 'She was promised.'

'Out of the way,' the captain bellowed in his face. 'Get back to your duty or I'll have you in chains!'

The donkeyman hesitated. The captain's big hairy leg took a step towards him. 'While I wear the uniform of the captain of this ship,' he said strangely. 'I am in command. Back to your duty or its mutiny.'

The huge oily man retreated, growling and cursing, and we went once more towards the captain's cabin. By now I was glad to be with him.

We went into his pitching cabin. A photograph of an old lady on the wall was going to and fro like a pendulum. He sat on a stool and held me at arm's length before him.

'Now, let us have a look at you,' he growled amiably. I felt reassured. He held out his hands and took mine, keeping me at a distance like a large uncle. The opening at the front of his flannel combinations gaped like a mouse-crack in a wall. His beard was like a huge bunch of seaweed.

He reached back and took a half full bottle of whisky from the table behind him. The level had been swaying from side to side with the ship. Still holding me by one hand he took a gigantic swig of the scotch.

'Can you sing, girl?' he roared to my astonishment. 'Can you dance?' Then: 'What's your name anyway?'

'Nell,' I said carefully, 'Nell Luscombe.'

'Well what about singing and dancing?'

'I can a bit.'

'Do you know "The Good Ship Lollipop"?'

'No, I don't.'

'Shirley Temple sang that. What a pretty little girl.' He seemed to make a decision.

'Come on, sit here on my lap and *I'll* sing it to *you*.'

'Now?' I said incredulously.

'Yes, come on girl, now.'

Hardly able to believe it I sat on his lap, my face close to his reeking beard, his arms around me, and he began to sing 'The Good Ship Lollipop' in the most appalling voice I've ever heard. What a sight it must have been in that wild cabin on that doomed ship.

Where it might have led to I don't know, although I have some ideas, but whatever was intended to follow never did because suddenly there was a tremendous blow on the hull and a great square piece fell out of the side of the ship. The cabin woodwork splintered and a section of that dropped out also. The captain stopped singing and we both looked out of the shattered bulkhead into the night and the rolling ocean.

'I think I ought to be on the bridge,' said the captain, with what seemed to me to be something of an understatement. He got up from the stool, placed a peaked cap on his head and, in his boots and combinations, strode out to the storm.

By this time I was naturally frightened but I knew enough about ships to realize that there must be a life-jacket around somewhere. I found one that looked as though it had been a feast for mice and then discovered another in reasonable condition.

The revealing hole in the bulkhead was allowing large slops of sea into the cabin as the ship heeled to starboard. But it was not, at least, pouring through, although the place was awash around my ankles.

There was a wardrobe on one wall and I staggered to it and took out another pair of combinations and a short thick reefer jacket. I clambered into these garments and then pulled the life-jacket over me. All the time I kept telling myself to keep calm and think clearly. It was good advice.

I got outside the door and as I did so the *Charlie Harry II* gave the most pathetic dying groan and lurched to one side, never righting herself. I heard the sea roaring into the captain's cabin and it suddenly broke through the door behind me and rushed savagely around my legs. I cried out in horror and stumbled for the companionway.

It took all my strength to get to the open deck. Once there I saw instantly it was hopeless. Not only was the vessel sinking by the bow, but some incompetent sailor had triggered off a distress rocket which had shot straight through the bridge window and set the whole structure merrily on fire. We were both sinking and burning.

There was no sign of any of the crew, which even in my confused state I realized was only to be expected. They would logically have abandoned ship at the first opportunity, certainly before any order was given, always provided they could find a lifeboat or life-raft that had not rusted to its fittings.

Turning, I saw that the wheelhouse and the bridge were well ablaze and the sea was coming over the starboard side in great bites. I began to feel as alone as the boy on the burning deck. It must have been a violent pitch and shove that sent me into the sea, but suddenly there I was in the chilly water, hanging on to what at first seemed to be a large ornamental trunk. It had a convenient brass handle but, such were the distractions all around me, it was some time before I realized that my raft was a coffin. The ship was now several hundred yards away across the pitching waves, the fire and the water racing to devour her. All at once she gave up the struggle and let the ocean have her, descending with what seemed like an outrageous breaking of wind. The fire was gobbled by the sea, leaving only sudden blackness, and I was left floating with my life-saving coffin.

The sea was cold and dark all around me, but at least it was not as rough as I had imagined. Indeed, although the waves were large they seemed to roll in fairly orderly fashion and I floated well enough on them.

In the rolling and sliding of the sea I was tiring and the coat I had taken from the captain's cabin was weighing me down. I knew I would have to climb onto the coffin. I had gathered enough muscle to make an attempt to get onto the lid when a new advance of water conveniently lifted me and I made it first time. I doubt it there would have been a second chance. Now I wondered who might be inside.

Flat on the pine lid, in this outlandish situation, I hung onto the handles and, oddly, tried to read the inscription on the brass plate. My eyes had become used to the darkness and indeed I now realized that it was quite a bright night wide with stars and a trace of moon. Almost as soon as I had begun travelling in this odd way, I saw a light only a few waves away and shouted with all the power in my salty throat. No one appeared to hear me, at least they did not answer, but a couple of minutes later my coffin had drifted quite close to what I now saw was the ship's dinghy. It was the one they used for ferrying to and from the shore.

I paddled my coffin eagerly towards it and hung onto the stern. Exhausted now I heaved myself up and saw two prone figures in the bottom boards. One was Jock the mate, and the other the daft cabin boy. At first I thought they were dead, but true to form they were merely drunk.

It was no use expecting any help from them so I heaved myself over the stern, falling right on top of the cabin boy who only grunted. I even had the presence of mind to hitch the coffin onto the rope at the end of the dinghy so that we were towing it. Then, utterly spent, I crawled on my hands and knees and fell alongside the sprawled body of Jock.

He turned and nuzzled a whiskery, whisky-sodden face into mine. His eyes cracked into small crevices and he smiled dreamily.

'Och, 'tis ma bonnie lass, Jeanie McAllister,' he crooned. ''Tis fine to ha'ye with me, lass. Fine. Fine. Fine.'

We were only two hours in the small boat, which was just as well because, I learned later, within minutes of scrambling into the thing, Jock and the cabin boy had, typically, disposed of *all* the emergency rations and the bottle of medicinal brandy. They had opened the locker right away and tucked in as if it were a picnic, while the ship was burning and going down, while their shipmates were floating about in the sea and while I was travelling the waves on a coffin.

My uneasy feeling even in these dire circumstances, that I might be travelling with someone on the lower deck, as it were, was unfounded. It transpired that the coffin was kept on board for the personal use of the captain himself. His name was on the brass lid. He had a fear of dying at sea and he didn't like the thought of being tipped overboard sewn up in a canvas shroud with the ship's carpenter putting the final stitch through his nose in the traditional seafaring manner. He knew the incompetence of the carpenter.

It was a pity, in a way, that, having voyaged the coffin aboard the *Charlie Harry II* for ten years, he could not make use of it when the occasion arose. As it was, he apparently floated away in his combinations and was never seen again.

Of the rest of the crew, at the final count ashore, only the donkeyman was missing and he turned up in a bar in Bordeaux about a month later, sitting there waiting, he told the police, for his ship to come in.

Two hours after the *Charlie Harry II* sank, we were picked up by a French fishing boat and taken into a small port about a hundred miles up the coast from Bordeaux. The fishermen did not like the look of the coffin we were towing and cast it adrift with the dinghy. Perhaps it still sails the oceans of the earth, shunned by suspicious sailors, to become for ever one of the mysteries of the deep.

When they discovered that underneath the combinations and the life jacket I was wearing there was a female body, the French sailors became agitated and I thought at first they might think it unlucky to have a female on board, for some ships think it spells disaster – and judging by the experience of *Charlie Harry II* they might well be right. I was exhausted when they got me aboard and lay me first on the deck alongside Jock and the cabin boy, both of whom they were sure were dead. It was just dawn and they all gathered round to have a good luck at me. The French captain himself took off my life jacket and felt my heart. He was amazed and pleased with what he did feel under those soaked combinations and he carried me bodily down to his cabin for a reviving cognac. Fortunately he could see I was in no state for socializing and he gallantly allowed me to sleep alone in his bunk until we put into port in the morning.

We were taken to a small local hospital, where we found the rest of the crew, the donkeyman apart, sitting comfortably in bed smiling above their breakfasts. There were emotional reunions until I was taken away to a small private room where a nice worried young doctor examined me thoroughly and, for me, quite enjoyably in my drowsy state and pronounced that after a rest I would be fully recovered.

I must have slept for twenty-four hours and, awaking in a room full of calm sunshine, I luxuriated in unaccustomed comfort. I asked for a brush and did my hair and they gave me some coffee and a neat boiled egg. In the afternoon a representative from the British Consul in Bordeaux came to see me, a solemn and considerate man, who said he understood all my papers and belongings had gone down with the ship and he was sure I would want to contact someone at home to tell them I was safe. This caught me by surprise and at once saddened me. For a moment I realized there were few people indeed who would have missed me had I drowned that night. Not many tears would have been shed, even if anyone had realized I was aboard that ship. For all my gay and busy life, and the many men I had known, no one would have noticed I had gone. I did not have anyone. The last thing a whore can expect is to be remembered.

In the end I sent a telegram to Hal and Flossie who must have thought I had walked off for good. The representative from the Consul said that I came under the heading of 'Shipwrecked Mariners' and gave me what seemed like a large amount of French money before shaking my hand, smiling and leaving. It was the only time a man has ever left me in bed with money in my hand and never wanted anything in return.

Later that day I borrowed a robe and crept along the corridor of the small hospital to visit Jock and the rest of the crew. They were in a jovial mood, trying to make French nurses understand their quips and requirements, but as soon as he saw me Jock lapsed into melancholy.

'Ah, Nelly, dear,' he said guiltily. 'Since the crisis I've been thinking I should be telling you of Jeanie McAllister.'

'Not again,' I sighed. 'Soon you'll be able to tell *her*. As soon as you get home.'

'Na,' he mumbled. 'She doesna' exist, lassie. She's a mere figment of a poor man's distracted imagination.'

I was amazed. 'You mean all that moaning and groaning about Jeanie in the glen and the bagpipes, and all that stuff, was not true?'

'A figment,' he nodded. 'A sailor's got to have something, Nell. He needs to have something to remember, y'see, even if it's no' the truth.'

That was another thing I learned. A man would rather have anyone but a harlot. Even when he is in the arms of one.

That evening my life turned yet another of its famous odd corners and I moved into a time of luxury and strangeness which opened my surprisingly innocent eyes to many things.

I was in my room, now bored in my bed, when visitor was announced and in came one of the most beautiful women I have ever seen. She was tall and smiling, slender and with that grace of movement you either have throughout your life or you never have at all. She was about thirty-five, her clothes were of a style and quality beyond anything I had ever seen and there was about her an assurance, you might almost call it modest vanity, which I have since envied in some women and tried to copy myself. Indeed this lady, Madame Amantine Bougain, taught me all the manners and airs, the conversational tricks and charms, the very tactics of society that eventually enabled me to move and live among the most particular company, and have intercourse with many of its members. I had a lot to thank her for.

'I have read in the paper of your ordeal, you poor child,' she said after introducing herself. Her English was better than mine. There was just a flicker of an accent about it, but even that, I suspected, she could have eliminated if it had not been so effective and so charming.

'It is said that you clung to a coffin in the sea!' she exclaimed. 'Ooooh, that must have been so horrible for you!'

'It was empty,' I shrugged. 'There was nobody in it.'

She seemed delighted with the answer. 'Ah,' she smiled. 'You have a sense of humour also. And you are just as pretty as your picture in the newspaper shows.'

'My picture in the paper?' I asked, hardly able to believe that an unknown English girl, shanghaied by the randy crew of a doomed ship, and saved by a floating coffin, could have been of any value for a newspaper. From her bag she produced the cutting from the evening's paper. I must say I looked very grand, a heroine of the sea (which is what the paper called me), for the photograph had been taken just after we were landed from the French fishing boat.

Carefully I took the cutting from her. Her gentle perfume reached mw. Apart from Diana Seagram in London I had never met anyone like her before. Her hands were faultless, long fingers, the nails shaped and painted with minute care. She wore a glorious diamond ring and a wedding ring. I had a passing wonder what her husband might be like. Would he like me?

'Are you recovered?' she asked. I noticed that although her English was so good, she hesitated before each thing she said, as though making sure in her mind that it was correct. This was very charming too, of course, and when I knew her better I saw her using the trick to keep some dumbfounded man on tenterhooks while they conversed.

'I'm all right,' I said confidently. 'I could walk out of here now. But I don't know what they are going to do with us.'

'How did it happen that you, a young girl . . . How did you happen to be on that terrible ship?'

I must have blushed because she smiled to encourage me and in a moment my hesitation had vanished. 'I was kidnapped,' I confided. 'Well sort of. I'm afraid I had too much to drink and so did the crew and I ended up on their ship.'

Her eyes went wide. They were extraordinary; amber, like the eyes of a prize cat. Then she laughed, a fire-bubbling laugh that ran all over her body. 'Oooo-là-là!' she exclaimed. 'It is like a romance story!'

I laughed with her. 'Oh they were all right,' I said. 'The crew, when they realized what they had done, they were very kind and considerate. I had a cabin to myself and every attention.' I thought that was a truthful enough summary of what happened.

'In England,' she pursued. 'Your mama and papa know about this? They have been told of course?'

It seemed a good opportunity to tell her the story of my life, which I did, cutting out certain adventures and incidents, but giving a general summary of the things that had befallen me over the past few years. She listened, obviously fascinated, with tears when I told her about my mother and the bomb, and with laughter when I told her some of the other things. In the end she sat with her face hidden behind her fingers, looking at me through the little space between them. 'What a singular young lady you are, Nellee,' she said. 'Would you like to come and stay in my house? Until you are ready to go back to England?'

As she said it I could picture it, rising like a backcloth in a Christmas pantomime, the fairy castle, accompanied by fanfares and rainbows. It was not quite like that. For a start it was not a house but a very large apartment, but it had every touch of luxury and a great deal of excitement.

It was not difficult for her to arrange my discharge from the hospital the following day, since she appeared to have enormous influence in the area and a word from her was sufficient to make sure that everything was done with speed. At nine o'clock the next morning a complete new set of clothes arrived, all fitting to the inch, and an hour later a silent French motor car, with a silent chauffeur, arrived to take me from the hospital. I dashed in to say a quick farewell to the crew. Jock was heartbroken. 'I'd such plans for ye, lassie,' he moaned. 'Ye and me, roaming along the lochside in the dim of the day . . .'

'What about Jeanie McAllister?' I laughed and went out. I left quickly, hearing all the pleadings coming from the ward behind me. I ran down the corridor towards the glass doors that led to the new world, away from the hands and the fantasies of sailors, to where that marvellous motor car waited to take me to my new life. Madame Bougain had said it was for a few days, but I have always known, some instinct has never failed to tell me, when my life was about to become something different. And this was one of those moments.

CHAPTER TEN

Madame Amantine Bougain and her daughter Aurore lived in a white and wealthy apartment on a hillside that overlooked the tight streets of the town and the enormous sea that spread beyond. One room, very large, had french windows opening onto a roof garden and terrace, hung with bougainvillaea and other sweet flowers. The first morning I arrived we sat out there in the warm autumn air and talked and drank dry, colourless wine.

Aurore was as slender, as beautiful and as gentle in her manner as her mother. She had long hair and a fawn face and the same amber eyes. She was seventeen and still at school.

There was a Monsieur Bougain, but he was dismissed very quickly as 'living in Paris' and, apart from an early instance when we discussed his portrait, was hardly mentioned again during my stay, which in the end, all things considered, did not surprise me.

It might have been expected for me, a raw English country girl, even with my outgoing nature, to have felt clumsy and embarrassed in the company of these two fine French ladies. But they were so kind and so natural that not for a moment did they let me feel out of place. They admired my skin and my facial bones and even the texture of my hair, which was hardly looking in its glory after its submersion in the sea. We had lunch, served by a pretty maid on the terrace, and drank some more wine and Madame Bougain insisted that I repeat my life's adventures for the benefit of her young daughter. I can see them now, sitting with the casual sunshine on their elegant features, sighing contentedly and making small exclamations while I recounted the long story. At its conclusion they both sat there, as if waiting for some more, and when they realized I had come to the end, they both rose and kissed me, one on each cheek.

The next three days were like an expensive dream. I wandered about the beautiful apartment with its pictures and porcelain and stylish furniture, hardly daring to touch anything. I slept in a large downy bed with a latticed door onto a little balcony from which I could see the movements of the ships in the harbour. I waved sentimentally to them and their crews. Madame Bougain had insisted on taking me shopping several times and I was now attired like some princess in what seemed to me the most delicate of French fashions. I could hardly believe my good fortune. Then, standing on my balcony, looking out towards the port and remembering how all my life I had been *used*, I came to a conclusion that for all this there had to be a reason.

One strange thing about the apartment was the portrait of a florid and ugly man that dominated the entrance hall. If it is true that portrait painters always flatter their sitters then this man must have been a terrible sight in true life. On my third afternoon I was standing looking at it, the only unsightly thing in that tasteful place, when Amantine came, almost silently, to my elbow, and looking at the painting said: 'It is a rossignol. Our nightingale.'

'What does it mean?' I asked. 'Your nightingale.'

'It means something that is always with us, something that is hanging about and we cannot rid ourselves of it. Our rossignol is Monsieur Bougain.'

'He's very . . . impressive,' I said, not knowing what to say.

'His bank balance is but he is not,' she said. 'Will you come and listen to me play the harp?'

By this time nothing surprised me and I said that I would like to hear her play. She took me by the hand, as if I were a small girl, and led me to another room which had a piano and a large golden harp standing like some sort of footman near the sunlit window.

'Sit down, Nellee,' she said softly, 'and I will play.' She sat against the harp and touched it with real tenderness. 'This,' she said when she was ready, 'is Debussy.'

I would have known no difference, my experience of music being the lusty West Country songs we had to sing in school and the rowdy ballads with which the sailors at Weymouth accompanied their beer and spirits. But as she played, there came upon me a feeling like a dream: the room, the woman and the playing, each muted and fragile. It made me feel sweetly drowsy, as though we were in a garden, not a room.

'Did you enjoy that, Nellee?' she asked, rousing me from my trance. I saw that she was standing very close to where I was sitting. 'Embrace me, Nellee,' she asked. It was half an order. 'Put your arms about me.'

I put my arms about her waist, still sitting, and, my heart suddenly hurrying, looked up at her. The composed face was smiling down. Something unknown but compelling drew me up and I found myself in an embrace with her. Frantically I tried to organize my spinning mind. I tried to tell myself that this was just French friendship. Then she kissed me on the lips. I could feel her breasts against mine and her thighs flush against the front of my dress. The kiss and the feel of her went right through my body.

Nothing further happened. She was a very cool lady. She released me in a way that indicated that, after all, it was just a motherly kiss, and with a light laugh she took me by the hand and we went out onto the terrace where the pretty maid was laying out a fine tea service. I was still enthralled by what had taken place inside the music room. I could not believe it. If I had been held by some handsome prince I would not have been more pleased. After all the rough and terrible things I had known, to realize that someone so clean and so beautiful really *wanted* me was blissful. 'Oh Amantine,' I laughed as I went with her to the terrace and we came to the set table. 'I could just do with a nice cup of tea.'

In the mornings the light seemed to float in through the window. I would wake to find the sun golden all about the room and from the outside the softened sounds of the streets and the noises of the ships in the harbour and the outgoing sea.

For the first three mornings I lay in that soft and expensive bed, feeling my skin flush against the flimsy nightdress and wondering what amazing luck it was that had brought me into all this luxury. Rising from the bed on each of these days, I went to the window and then out onto the terrace, feeling so airy I swear I could have floated to the top edge of the hills above or to the town below. My shoulders felt the touch of the morning upon them and the bougainvillaea would crowd my head with its scent. The walls of the town appeared as a pale yellow, with the narrow streets sunk in shadow. Down the hill beyond a closed garden, with a wall low enough to see over the top, was the courtyard of a monastery of some kind, with a single silent bell and a few monks moving about like prisoners taking exercise. Standing high above it all on the balcony I felt truly rich and free, and I knew then that was how I would always want to be, and one day I would be in my own right.

On the fourth morning Aurore came through my door with the briefest knock while I was still drowsy in bed. The fresh light rippled all down her as she stood, paused inside the door. She was wearing a long pale garment that was gathered at the neck and prevented from opening by the inward slopes of her breasts. She had come in quickly, with no hesitation, but now she stood inside the door, her face fresh and composed, but not seeming to know what she wanted to do next.

'Aurore,' I said sleepily. 'Good morning.'

'Nellee,' she answered quietly and saying nothing more she walked across the space between the door and the bed. At the side of the bed there was another hesitation while I stared at her, my heart suddenly awake and banging like a bird at its bars.

At the edge of my bed she made another brief delay, but this was replaced by a small smile from her and an uncertain one from me. Did I understand what was about to happen? She carefully opened the side of the sheets and coverlet, and then leaned sideways and onto the bed so that the pale gown dropped open, still caught at the neck, like the entrance to a cool tent. Inside, in the shadows of the garment, I could see her body, the stomach curving inwards and then moulded into her thighs, warm and fawn, her legs bent beneath her bottom on the bed. The gown still sloped across the tops of her breasts but the under globes stood out, full and curved with no change in the colour of the skin. She leaned right across me, kissed me first on my doubting forehead and then, with a sudden consuming appetite, on the lips. I lay back gasping, my mouth agape. She was so wholesome and lovely. I could not help myself. It was as though my hands and arms had suddenly begun to float from the rest of my body. They went out to her slowly then, each hand almost leaping to the swollen skin of her bosom.

'You mustn't be late for school,' I said.

Her answer was to open the sheets wider and to climb right into the middle of the bed, her face intent on mine, searching it, mesmerizing me, her hands now delicately feeling my body. 'Mama sent me,' she said, as though that explained everything. Now her entire slender form merged into mine. She was much slimmer to hold than she was even to see, my one arm being plenty to encircle her waist and draw her closer to me. We kissed again, fully now, hanging on to it, a clean lovely kiss after all those rough, fish-and-drink soaked kisses I had known in the recent past. As she drew away she made to release the fastening at the throat of her gown, but I stopped her with my hand. Puzzled, then amused, she waited, but then seemed to realize how much I liked to see her in that sweet garment, flowing from her body like the wings of a butterfly.

We kissed again, our four breasts rubbing against each other like friendly cats. Mine were still within the bodice of my nightdress, although they were bursting to be released and caressed. Her cool hands went to them and, carefully, she brought them out from the silk like someone taking kittens from a basket. The sight and the feel of them excited her instantly and she pushed her head against them and ran her young tongue up their lobes and curled it around the nipples until I could feel my stomach boiling like a kettle. How long this went on I do not know. It seemed she would never tire of it and I lay back wallowing in the engulfing, loving feeling, something I had honestly never experienced before.

I could feel my whole body blushing, a warmth that spread from my knees to my ears, and my breasts swollen and almost bursting with the intense pleasantness. My hand fell to stroking her back and then her small buttocks, polishing them with the most gentle enjoyment for both of us. My fingers slid down between her damp legs and she lay back her head and groaned when I touched her. 'You like me a little, Nellee?' she inquired breathlessly, as if there might still be some doubt.

'I love you Aurore,' I choked. 'Honestly. More than anyone.'

Then to my astonishment, as though she had just remembered something urgent, she came from the trance into which she had so readily tumbled, and in a matter-of-fact voice, like someone recalling a lunch appointment, she said: 'We must go. Mama is expecting us.'

Without saying more, she slid like a python from the bed and came around to my side, taking my hand and leading me from the room. As I walked towards the door, entranced still, my nightdress finally dropped from me, as if it were exhausted, and lay around my feet on the floor.

'Leave it,' Aurore said, quietly but with authority. She looked at me closely, all up my body as if to make sure I was all there. Then she smiled that marvellously innocent smile again and whispered: 'Come. Mama waits for us.'

We went along the corridor like two children wandering around the house after rising too early from bed. I was naked and Aurore in her trailing gown. We held hands and walked without speaking along the padded corridor, with portraits of French poets staring down on us, lost for words. The pretty maid came up the stairs ahead and I gave a start but Aurore held more firmly to my fingers and the maid walked by without a second glance.

At the door to Amantine's bedroom Aurore knocked with great care, almost selecting the spot on the panel, and we heard her mother's musical voice call for us to enter. It was so strange. I felt as I had done before going to school. My heart began to echo within my chest again. Aurore opened the door.

Her mother, the stately Amantine, was lying like a queen in her huge bed, a fragile teacup in her hand, her hair and her face composed. I tried not to think of what might happen next.

'Mama,' said Aurore politely. 'I have brought Nellee.'

'Nellee,' she breathed happily from the bed and I felt the warmth run all through me, the lovely wonderful feeling of truly being wanted; welcome to someone so fine and extraordinary. I walked forward trembling but happy all over.

'Nellee darling,' Amantine said, her eyes soft but still fixing me. 'Please Nellee you will kneel by my bed.' It was an order.

'Kneel?' I asked, not in protest but surprise.

'As you do when you say your prayers,' she encouraged. 'By the bed.'

Dumbly I did as I was instructed. I slowed my movements as if I were performing a ritual, but within me my heart was racing. The sun was coming through the gauze curtain and I felt it run all over my back and my bottom as I dropped beside the bed. Aurore stood back and watched, her slender hands held before her like a choir girl, a sweet expression on her peaceful face.

As I knelt I let my head go forward to touch the bedcover and the body of Amantine. My hair had fallen wildly over my forehead and the bed. Nothing happened for what seemed a long time and then I felt her hand reach towards me and begin to stroke my hair and my neck. I had hardly cooled down from Aurore's caresses and now this firm willowy movement sent my blood quickening again. I reached up helplessly and groped for a touch of her, *any* touch. My fingers found her toes, as she swivelled so that she was sitting upright with her feet curled under her. I held onto her while she continued to stroke my hair and my neck, my ears and then my back.

'My dear Nellee,' she said firmly. 'Come to Amantine.'

She turned quickly on the bed now and her legs swung like a gymnast until she was sitting directly before my face, imprisoning my cheeks with her warm smooth thighs. I felt Aurore move behind me and then her hands holding my long hair. She gently brought my face up until I was looking into the eyes of Amantine sitting above me. Nell Luscombe's mistress.

Amantine's hands came down to my breasts, now staring up at her, still quick and full from the stroking of Aurore. Her fingers played as easily on my nipples as they had on that harp the previous day, until I was in such a state that, frankly, I would not have been surprised if my bosom had exploded with a loud bang. I was speechless and indeed what was there to say?

She moved forward a fraction on the bed so that her thighs and the deep, soft channel between her legs were open to me. She encouraged my head to it and, to my amazement, for I had never done anything like this before, I began to kiss it.

It was sweet and her body began to vibrate with the pleasure I gave. I was hardly conscious of Aurore moving in what seemed like the shadows behind, so enclosed was I in my lovely world, but I felt her flowing hair tickle my buttocks and the tops of my legs as I knelt against my mother. Instinctively I parted my legs to give her the passage she required and she lay against me and kissed me and lapped at me in the same way as I was doing to her mother.

It was unendurable. We wriggled, each just joined, the force of the pleasure running through us, one woman's body to another. I was experiencing both of them and if felt as though electricity was flying through my blood vessels. I began to shudder from my very foundations and I could not stop. I felt the same shaking going on in front of me and behind me and in a moment we were all clutching each other desperately as the travelling orgasm surged through us. It was the first time I had ever experienced a climax.

We tumbled then on to the floor, lying like beached fish, naked on the carpet, gasping, holding on to what ever parts of the others we could locate. The maid came in while we were like that, and after inquiring if Madame had finished with her tea tray, removed it from the side of Amantine's bed, stepping across our prostrate bodies to do so.

I loved it. I truly did. I might as well confess it. After all the crude times and the uncomfortable and stinking places, after all the foul advantages which had been taken of me, to find a loving and giving experience like this with two people so beautiful was something honestly wonderful.

Looking back on it now, and knowing what I now know, I still smile with pleasure. And to think I might have enjoyed it even more if I had been a lesbian. But you can't have everything.

Despite my busy sexual life among the fisherfolk of Weymouth and the adventures that had gone before it, I was still quite ignorant and innocent about many things. Homosexuality, for example, was something I had heard about, a subject of jokes and banter among the men I had come to know by the English Channel, but I had no idea of how people of the same sex made love, what methods were used to achieve their ends.

So, to me, my amazing experience with Amantine and Aurore was like falling into a rushing river and finding it full of warm and slow water. I knew nothing of their world and their enjoyable diversions until that time because in Dorset and Devon sex was simple. My loving with the beautiful mother and daughter was the most novel and luxurious thing that had happened in a life that was, admittedly, plain and often sordid. But for all my enjoyment of them and for all my enthusiasm for almost all the sexual things they did and taught me, and all the kindness and the cleanness that I appreciated so much, it was not possible for them to turn me into one of their sort. You are what you are, even as a professional sex-vendor, and nothing can change that. There have been times when the comfort and consideration of a female lover have been like a breath of gentle air after some of the depradations of the male sex, and I have welcomed them more than a few times. But although my body has been eased and sometimes entertained, my heart is not in it. It is always a mere diversion.

Amantine and Aurore, of course, sensed this very quickly with me and, for them, it was a matter of great regret, not only from their point of view but particularly for me. It was like going to a house of singers and having no real ear for a song. As Amantine put it: 'Men are all right in their place, but Nellee, there is nothing like the real thing.'

But we continued to be comfortable and gay in that exquisite home on the hill while the summer waned all around us, the sun a little more shy each day, the wind from the sea a trifle sharper. We lived a life of great leisure, and the days slipped easily and idly on. Aurore would go to school each morning in a plain grey dress with her hair tied tight behind her neck and come home each evening to tear off her garments and rush to embrace me on the terrace.

It must have seemed strange to outsiders that a girl so desirable should not give more than a dull glance to any man or boy. As she went to school each day, I would stand on the terrace with my morning glass of orange juice, and watch her walk down the steep hill into the town. Her carriage was that of a model, her sway timed to perfection, her head level and her arms and hands held delicately. There was undoubtedly a look of innocence on her face. Men and lads in houses, apartments, shops and gardens on her route used to hide in hedges, trees, on balconies and in windows just to glimpse her as she passed. I watched them clearly from the terrace, looking from above them. It was like seeing an army waiting in ambush, crouching, creeping, straining, just for a moment of her walk, and then to utter a wish or even a prayer of which she was the object. Once a middle-aged man, a fellow fat as a ball, actually fell out of the tree in his garden while he was hanging like a globular monkey in an effort to get just one more look at her backside as it undulated down the hill.

When I told Aurore of this casualty and of all the attention she received as she walked to school, she exploded with genuinely surprised laughter, loving to hear the details of the gauntlet she ran each day. She called Amantine to hear and we all rolled about with mirth at the poor stupidity of men. The following day Aurore, who had a lot of jokes in her, placed a pretty red garter above her right knee, just below the hem of her schooldress, so that it was exposed at every other step. My God, the effect that had! Amantine and I stood on the terrace and laughed until we cried at the antics of those poor, denied males.

When she had finally gone out of sight and beyond the view of those frustrated men and they had slunk back into their normal shadows, we sat down in the pale sunshine and Amantine, after thinking about it for a while, said very quietly. 'I must tell you, Nellee, that Aurore is not my true daughter.'

This surprised me considerably. I had thought how much alike they looked, but it was probably the young girl's style, her walk, her carriage, her clothes, her hair and the way she laughed and talked which made them seem related; things she had learned from Amantine.

'She came to me as you did, from nowhere,' she sighed. 'And as *you* will Nellee, one day she will leave and go back, or go to some other place. She was thirteen when I found her, her father had been killed in the war and her mother had vanished, as so many people did. She was living in a poor house in St Nazaire, with a devilish family. The husband was only waiting for her to grow for another year. He could hardly control his desires. Through some influence I have in that city I was able to bring her away to live here.'

'I could not help it. 'She learned everything from you?' I said. 'Everything?'

She did not seem offended, nor did she seem to consider than any offence was intended. 'She learned very well and easily,' Amantine smiled. 'But she was born with it. She is natural. Not like you Nellee, you will never be.'

'I know,' I said. I found myself saying it in a dull way, as if it were something in which I had failed. Something that gave me a sense of shame and regret. 'I can never be.'

'But,' she replied, half a sigh, half a laugh, 'it has been wonderful. You have enjoyed your stay here, Nellee?'

'Oh I have,' I said truthfully, 'I have so much, Amantine.' I was suddenly afraid that I had offended her after all and that I would be sent away. My fingers went out anxiously to touch her sunlit hands and she smiled her gratefulness.

'You have been beautiful to me,' she said. 'And also to Aurore.'

She laughed again and rose gracefully. 'Tomorrow,' she announced, 'there is to be a party. It is a house about thirty kilometres away, a most elegant house. There it is possible that you may meet a boy you would like. It will be a change for you.'

The house – I believe it was called Val de Plaisir or something like that, it was many years ago now – was more like a small château sited on one lump of a valley that was terraced with vines. We arrived in the late afternoon while there was still some sun lying in the floor of the valley and all along one side. As we approached between the slopes the house, which was on the sunny side, looked golden, as an apple does. It had some small turrets and a pennant was ruffling from the top of one of these, very bravely, giving it the look of a knight's fortress. I was thrilled to see it and so was Aurore who had never visited there before. She squeezed my hand as we sat in the back of the car, just girlish excitement, making some remark about how fairy-like the house looked in the sun. Amantine, who was in the front with the driver, turned to make some comment of her own, and her eyes went straight to our clasped hands. The look was so definite that both Aurore and I released fingers at once. It was over in a moment but in that instant I knew that we three would not be together for long. Where love is so is jealousy.

The owner of Val de Plaisir was a minor nobleman of some sort, as befits somebody with a small castle, and he greeted us as we left the car. He was florid and unappetizing, paying a lot of attention to us in turn, with many kisses and embraces. When he kissed me, a great slobbering smack full in the face, his hands went without hesitation to the underneath of my breasts as if he thought it necessary to hold him up. Had it been anywhere else I would have hit him (or charged him anyway), but here I could only blush. Blushing is something I could still, surprisingly, do. And I can now.

There were other cars, very expensive cars too, parked outside and there seemed to be relays of servants to fetch and carry our luggage into the house. Each of these servants. I noticed at once, whether male or female, was young and good looking. I began to wonder what the party was to be like.

'She is so beautiful,' the minor nobleman said for my benefit in English.

'Yes she is,' said Amantine. 'Very beautiful.'

Her voice troubled me. There was the jealousy again. I glanced at Aurore and saw that she had sensed it too. I felt a quick shot of sadness and a returning sense of my old loneliness. Before long, I thought, I will be going. It was to be sooner than I imagined.

Although small by comparison with some castles I have known, the house was hundreds of years old. I always have this strange idea that buildings grow with age as people do, or trees, and that something centuries old must naturally be spread everywhere. But it was very fine inside, with halls and paintings and a staircase down into the main room like the entrance of a stage.

A young manservant and a petite, pretty maid took me to my room although I only had one suitcase and a small valise. They fussed about with the curtains and the bed and the lights before finally leaving me and making exits each with a bow and a *wink*.

The room was airy and rich, and I was getting a taste for these things now. I undressed and, wrapped in my robe, lay on a large enveloping bed and considered the carved ceiling, imagining, not for the first time, that one day I would own something like this in England where I could be a lady and invite my friends. By then I would have some friends. Somewhere I would have to find some.

All at once I felt unsure and frightened. What was I going to do after this? After all this comfort and luxury, how would I again be able to face a tight bare room and grunting fishermen. I wanted to be rich and, as Flossie told Hal that night I had listened through the wall, I had only one talent, one advantage. There was only one thing for me. One way to travel – on my back. But for the future, I thought, I must rise in the world, learn more things, make new contacts and a new richer life; become a better class of whore. It was the only way I would get my castle and my friends.

Soon all this would end, all this fine fantasy, I felt sure of that. I could feel it approaching in the very looks that Amantine sent my way that day. Soon I would be on my own again. I had to know where I was going. Downstairs I heard a large clock chime. It was time to get ready. For what?

There are orgies and orgies and I have attended a few in my time, but never one quite like the affair that took place at Val de Plaisir that night. I have been present when such functions have developed into something not unlike a game of football, and others where people just sat around nibbling sedately at each other as if it were a Mothers' Union tea party. I have also been presiding ringmaster at an orgy for perverted elderly people, which was very worrying because the participants kept getting cramp and attacks of asthma and had to be banged on the backs. Once I also found myself in charge of a teenage orgy in Paris, where one boy cried bitterly because he was under the impression that he was going to play table tennis, and in London there was an orgy for shy people where the nearest they got to doing anything was shaking hands.

But at Val de Plaisir they were all apparently experienced orgiasts, myself apart at that early time in my career, and everyone knew what to expect and what was expected of them. It began with about forty people at dinner, a jolly but conventional affair, with the estate's output of claret being notably diminished, and then followed what seemed like a rowdy but decent party in the large room with the staircase, and here the dinner guests were joined by another group and, significantly, by all the men and maid servants of the house, the handsome young people I had noticed when we first arrived.

These youngsters seemed to be the organizers of the sexual activities, offering themselves, encouraging others to take off their clothes and stretch and roll on the many large cushions that were brought and rolled out and placed on the carpet for the purpose. The lights were dimmed and the whole affair was accompanied surrealistically by an elderly woman playing a mournful saxophone and a languid youth on the drums. They were the only people who remained clothed throughout the proceedings, even the police spies who were amongst us taking off their garments and taking part in the pursuit of both their work and sexual enjoyment.

It was very warm in the large room and the dimness of the light seemed to make it warmer. I sat on the fringe of the activity, not really knowing what to do, having no experience of this wide-spread form of sex, watching and wondering how I should take part. It was like being a child at school, hesitating on the edge of a playground game, wanting to join in but not sure how to go about it.

I had seen Amantine and Aurore only briefly since we had arrived at the small castle. Before dinner I had stood with them during cocktails. Not speaking French I feared that I would be adrift in the conversation without them. But at dinner they had been at distant places at the huge table and now I could not see them at all in the gloom. I began to suspect that before long I would not be wanted. Not by Amantine anyway.

Then Amantine herself appeared through the warm shadows. She was wearing a loose robe and I could see by the way it fell and the places where it touched her body as she walked that she was naked beneath it. She had with her a young girl, pretty but looking surly.

'This is Francie,' said Amantine. 'If you like her she is yours.'

She sounded like a cool, experienced saleswoman in a store. As though to add to the picture she tugged at a bow around the girl's neck and the long rose-pink garment Francie was wearing dropped swiftly away from her. I thought she shivered.

The girl was dark-skinned and slim with tight conical breasts like coat pegs in a Devon school. Her eyes dropped sulkily and she reached and pulled her hair cloak-like around her shoulders.

Amantine was regarding me, smiling to see if I approved. 'Nellee,' she said as though reminding me what was happening. 'Do you like her?' I felt uneasy. Stretching up towards her, I whispered close to her perfumed cheek: 'You said I might have a boy, for a change.'

Her smile then, I thought, was one of relief. Perhaps she was thinking Aurore was safe after all. 'Ah, you are right,' she nodded. 'I promised. Come, Francie.'

The girl let off a brief smile as if she too were relieved that nothing had come of our meeting, and took herself to some other place in the room more to her liking. I waited and in a few minutes Amantine came back accompanied by a white-skinned young man, his short, fair, curly hair looking like little flames in the beam of light above my head. He was wearing a short loin-cloth and an expression of happy insolence. He was not tall, but very broad across his chest and slim at the waist. His legs were thick and his skin like white paper. 'He'll do fine,' I said confidently to Amantine. 'He'll make a nice change.'

This young fellow's name was Etienne. That much he understood. I was Nellee and he was Etienne. After that word of mouth ceased. But he was a really unusual young fellow because he began to perform a series of acrobatics in front of me like a fairground tumbler in olden times. I sat there fascinated, but unable to make up my mind whether he was displaying himself peacock fashion or just limbering up for what was to follow.

No one, apart from me, took the slightest notice of these gymnastics, revealing though they were. He did a remarkable cartwheel and then stood on his head, stationary, like an upside-down statue. Since he wore nothing under his loin-cloth these antics resulted in a display of sexual attachment such as I had never seen.

As a fisherman's harlot, what with the confined spaces, the poor lighting, the pitching of the ship and the hurry, I never had much time for viewing. Now I sat astonished and admiring. He had a true sense of the theatre because he contrived to have the single lightbeam in that part of the room shine on the centre-piece of the exhibition in the most ingenious and alluring way.

It was a performance (although one he had certainly given on other occasions) just for me. The droning crone and the saxophone and the dim boy on the drums played on, long drawn-out, muted, tuneless, appropriate to the scene. All around were little heaps of people, playing slithering and sliding like one of those Dutch paintings were everyone plays in the snow. There was quite a lot of subdued beating going on, and biting, and a fair deal of tying with ropes and cords, not to mention one couple with a chain that could have pulled up a drawbridge. It was all a far cry from Hal's Café in Weymouth.

Etienne had now completed his circus performance and with a smug smile squatted in front of me and inserted his hands into the loose folds at the top of my gown. I made no move towards the boy because I felt, as a beginner, I ought to sit quietly and see what developed. What did develop was the sturdiest and palest jumbo I have ever seen. A true white elephant. (Years later I witnessed the feats of Swan-neck Swanson, the vile man of Cockfosters, who for sheer length could have left young Etienne standing.) Fascinated, I watched this pallid trunk creep beneath the hem of his loin-cloth as he fondled my breasts. An enjoyable bubble was growing inside me, like a pot coming to the boil. I realized that in the past I had been far too busy with sex to enjoy it. That required leisure.

My hands went out to this creeping creature which, amazingly, continued to wriggle away from its master. My horny sensation hardened in my stomach and for the first time in my life I was suddenly desperate. I made a move to throw myself back on the cushions but with a serious and experienced smile he restrained me. His fingers were magical, now stroking my hips and then cleaving into the pocket between my thighs. He moved his hands easily and delicately, like a bored man washing dishes, and through my half closed eyes I wondered how one so young could be so refined in this sort of activity.

His wrists pushed aside the last edge of my garments and I lay exposed to him. But, strangely, he seemed to get more enjoyment out of himself than out of me. It was as though *his* hands, not *my* breasts or what was between my legs, were the objects of his pleasure. By now I was in one hell of a state, sorely tempted to grab him and rape him. But there came an interruption, and it was obviously something they had all been awaiting, for there was a muted buzz of anticipation.

I found myself panting although I had not moved from the cushions. Etienne cooly eased himself up as if he had been engaged in a bit of carpentery, and watched with everyone else while Amantine, naked and very beautiful, walked with grace up to the landing of the central staircase. A gong sounded in the shadows. Breathing seemed to stop. All eyes were there. Two young men, wearing only coloured scarves around their throats, brought a harp onto the landing and a little stool with a satin cushion. On this Amantine placed her bare bottom and then leaned forward and took the harp between her legs like a tall golden lover. She began to play eerily, filling the place with the most overpowering sound. Everyone seemed to have forgotten what they had been doing previously and sat and watched and listened intently.

Then onto the stage, a collar and chain around her neck, her wrists secured, walked Marianne, the pretty maid from Amantine's apartment. She stepped straight and upright, her eyes closed. On the other end of the leather lead was a large, black-haired handsome woman. She carried a riding cane.

I felt my breast touched from one side and turning saw Aurore crouching like a naked hunter on one knee, looking at what was happening on the stairs. I responded to her touch, contacting her fingers in mine, although, truthfully, I felt a disappointment, a fear that she might have come to replace Etienne. But I need not have worried, in that place there was plenty for all.

The ritual on the landing, or the stage as it was, unfolded to gasps and sighs from the audience in the shadows, and to utter astonishment from me. Marianne was led to a stool, like a long piano stool, and bent across it by the big dark woman. This woman's expression was such that she might have been putting a cloth on a table. It was important to preserve the seriousness of the event, something I myself realized in later years when I was ringmaster at several orgies. Once a Conservative Member of Parliament was blackballed (in his case not an inappropriate term either) from the Westminster Strangeways Society because he could not stop laughing at moments like this. It spoils it for the others.

Poor Marianne, having been stretched across the stool, and with Amantine's fingers still brushing the harpstrings in the dimness behind, was tied by her wrists and legs to the stool. Her thighs were clamped by leather straps to the wooden legs, so she was bent over and could not move. Her hair trailed forward onto the ground before her. Her garment was opened behind.

'It will hurt,' I muttered to Aurore. 'It won't half.'

She smiled, still not taking her eyes from the stage. 'The girl likes it,' she said. 'Which in its way is a pity. Also she is well paid.'

At that moment the riding whip came down. People shrieked all over that room. I hid my eyes. Then I felt Etienne stir and put his white hands out to me, guiding me on to the cushions, still not taking his gaze from the stage. And Aurore, as casually as if she were joining in a dance, came to my side and began to caress my stomach while lifting her dilated eyes to see how the exhibition was progressing. As for Etienne – well he was enormous and energetic, that boy, moving like something driven by an engine.

I was now only aware of what we three were doing. My hands grasped part of him and part of her. I was aware of the harp music and the howls of Marianne the maid, but then everything happened in a dazzling instant. Etienne came, I came, and Aurore came, and an inspector of the French police arrived too.

He stood above us, while we lay gasping, and tapping us each politely on the shoulders, asked us to rise and provide him with names and addresses. All around similar policemen were making similar inquiries. It was a sad end to an unusual evening.

Never again was I to see Amantine and Aurore. After that moment of interruption in that exotic place they went from my life forever. When I was free and back in England again, I wrote to them, not wanting them to think I was ungrateful for their great friendship and kindness, but no reply came. Many years later, when I was able once more to visit that area of France, I went to the apartment and found that it was owned by a German diplomat who used it as a summer house. He was a wealthy, lonely man and he invited me in and walked around the rooms with me. The result was that I spent several days there in his company, a strange reliving of the past (although not quite!) but that is another story.

After the police raid on the Val de Plaisir (they had inserted spies into many of these orgies, drawing lots for who should be the lucky ones. In fact the raid was not made until every senior officer in the local division had claimed his turn as a spy), I was taken away by one police inspector, a mournful-looking man in uniform, one of those, I thought, given entrance to the castle by the spies inside. Presumably he was mournful because he missed the show. It was during the confusion within the orgy room that this officer approached me and, by a tap on the shoulder, motioned me to follow him. I had climbed back into my gown but was wearing nothing else, although compared to some around me I was decidedly overdressed. Policemen with smirks of enjoyment on their faces were taking off naked and semi-naked people to the vans parked outside. Three gendarmes were quarrelling over who should be permitted to release Marianne from her bondage across the piano stool. The big dark woman had struck an inspector with her riding crop and Amantine was gamely fighting them off from behind the strings of her harp. I saw Aurore in the distance passionately kissing a policewoman. She would always survive.

In all this confusion the morose inspector took me away, alone, and putting me into the back of a small Renault, he drove me silently away from the castle and towards Bordeaux.

I shivered with cold and worry in the back of the car. After a few miles I asked for a coat and, although he apparently spoke little or no English, my dumb-show of becoming frozen had its effect and he threw back a police greatcoat to me. It felt damp and musty, as though it had not been used for a long time, but after the first couple of minutes I was glad to have it around me. The seat of the car was made of some plastic material and kept sticking to the backs of my legs and my bare bottom. I felt very miserable.

After a drive of about half an hour we arrived at a dark building which contained one room and a small cell into which I was put. No other policeman appeared and I wondered why I had been singled out for this solitary confinement. It was warmer in there, but not much, and I crouched down on a bed in the corner of the cell throughout the whole night, feeling lost and cold.

At eight o'clock the following morning the inspector visited me and instructed me to stand up while he walked around me peering closely at my form. I had some bruises – made by Etienne or possibly Aurore – on my hip and he insisted that I lift the hem of my gown, so that he could study these minutely. Every now and then he would sanctimoniously write something in a black notebook.

I was given a breakfast of coffee and rolls and jam, served by a pop-eyed lad, who became so agitated by my presence that he slopped the coffee out of the jug all over my knee. He insisted, rather gallantly for one who looked incredibly stupid, in kneeling down and mopping it up with a handkerchief.

An hour later a stout, studious man with a gladstone bag entered the room and stood outside my cell eyeing me through the bars.

The inspector brought the keys and opened the door. 'Police doctor,' he informed me, pointing at the studious man. Then he left. The police doctor appeared very flustered, dropping things, and going red as a sunset in the face. Eventually he indicated that I should let my gown drop to the waist. With a shrug I let it fall. His eyes trembled. With shaking hand he produced a stethoscope and listened over almost every inch of my chest.

He asked to see my tongue and looked down at my throat, getting so close I thought I could have easily bitten off his head. Then he ran his fingers all over me, prodding and feeling me in places where no doctor had ever explored before. I sniffed: 'Doctor Livingstone, I presume,' but it was lost on him. He now had me standing with my gown around my ankles, shivering with chill and embarrassment. Then he stood in front of me and took one my breasts in each hand and weighed them, comparing one with the other like somebody judging turnips at a surburban garden show.

Only fear and uncertainty, reinforced by the appearance at regular intervals of the inspector's head around the door, prevented me from attacking the nasty little man. He grew in confidence as the examination went on and I continued to endure it, standing nude and flushed with shame. He even began to hum to himself, so happy was he in his work.

He eventually left with a polite, 'Good morning, mister,' which I thought in the circumstances was an error of some size. I sat on the cell stool and pulled my gown around me. I cried.

Later that day another police officer arrived with a tape measure and a notebook and proceeded to measure my body from every angle and every end. Once more it was insisted that I strip and stand for the examination while he ran the tape measure all over me, even noting the distance between the point of one breast and the other. He muttered 'Twenty-three centimetres' and wrote it down.

On the following day yet another police inspector arrived with a camera and a tripod which he proceeded to erect in the cell. This inspector then proceeded to photograph me, nude naturally, from every view and angle, taking hours, it seemed, to get the lighting the pose and the focus right.

Now by this time most people would have suspected something was amiss. But I was an ignorant country girl, suddenly thrown by a French policeman into a solitary cell. How was I to know what the procedures were? I had read about Devil's Island and about some of the terrible things that were done there.

It was while yet another inspector who was introduced as the police masseur was rolling up his sleeves that I realized that each of these men wore a uniform with a button missing from the right hand pocket. Each man was wearing *the same uniform*! They were changing into it before coming into my cell.

Suddenly I screamed and picking up the so-called masseur's bucket of mud I emptied it over his head. Then I laid into him with my stool, knocking him around the cell before finally he managed to crawl out of the barred door. He ran from the outer room cursing. He wanted his money back!

I was left alone for about an hour. Then the original inspector appeared and I told him what I thought about him and his perverted friends with every swear word I could summon. Without saying a word he manhandled poor me from the cell and hung me with shackles from the wall in the outer room. There I was suspended like some poor bastard from the middle ages, naked, and with the man in the uniform sitting drinking glass after glass of wine and gloating over me. Hanging there helpless in those cruel chains I shouted: 'I want to see the British Ambassador!'

The British Ambassador did not arrive, but the real police did. A few minutes later the outer door burst open and they burst in. They had a good time getting me down from the wall. They said my tormentor was a former policeman who had gone mad but was quite harmless. He had, however, been sane and crafty enough to insinuate himself into the police raid on the castle and, having got me in his private dungeon (under his house), he then hired out his uniform and my degradation to any of his friends who desired to practise their strange satisfactions on me.

In the police station they all rolled about laughing at the ingenuity of the bastard who had so debased me. I sat in the corner and cried and wished for the civilized fisherboys of Weymouth.

CHAPTER ELEVEN

My first marriage, to George Turnbull, champion of the two-foot paint roller, took place (solemnized, as they say) in the spring of my eighteenth year, 1951, in Dover.

Dover was the first place in England I reached when my adventure in the Bordeaux region of France was concluded. Glad as I was to see those cliffs protruding like large grinning teeth and to hear the English seagulls, I was again penniless. I left the ferry from France and walked into the town. It was the furthest I could afford to go and I was there for more than the next year and a half of my life.

People say that George Turnbull was as thick as paint itself, and paint, and the art of applying it to walls and other surfaces, was the great absorbing interest of his life. He was broad and young, with a kind, thoughtless face and an island of baldness in his thick hair where he obsessively scratched in a puzzled manner, because beyond his own glossy world he was a man of extreme indecision. Only when challenged by an unpaintable job or suspended in the sky with a giant roller and a bucket of white emulsion was he sure and in his element.

I arrived in Dover, feeling at once a stranger in my own country, in clothes and on a rail-boat ticket provided by the British Consul in Bordeaux from the store of such things he keeps for the stranded and destitute. The clothes would have looked better on Granny Lidstone of long ago, the ticket was third class (which meant hours across France on seats made of the hardest wood any bottom ever suffered) and they gave me only enough money judged to be sufficient for my needs until my first step on native soil.

Indeed as I stepped ashore from the ferry into the edgy autumn day I possessed only the garments I wore, plus my gown from the orgy at Val de Plaisir, and one brass token which I had somehow retained from the useless payments received aboard the doomed *Charlie Harry II*. Here was I, Nell Luscombe, once more starting life again.

I had spoken to hardly a soul on the long journey, although one or two Frenchmen on the train had looked at me with a prospective eye. But I was too tired in body and broken in spirit to respond. And so to Dover, in the blowy air, I was more solitary than I had every been since leaving my village in Devon. Instead of coming home, as I had dreamed, I was just like a stranger arriving in an unknown land. It was getting towards evening and the comfortable lights of the town seemed to mock me. There was a cold smeary rain in the air and the gulls were searching unnervingly in the dusk.

There seemed to be nothing I could do, nowhere I could go. Like some old lady, in my strange elderly clothes, I stood and began to cry. Looking back on that moment, I feel sure they were genuine tears but, with me, there was always a slightly theatrical touch about such emotion. I looked cagily through my wet fingers to see if I was arousing anyone's sympathy.

It was a policeman who came gallantly to my sobbing side. He decently put his cape around my shoulders and took me to the police canteen before accompanying me to the immigration authorities where I showed the temporary documents given to me by the Bordeaux Consul and told a little, but naturally only a little, of my story. There was a surge of rough British sympathy throughout the little warm office and a Salvation Army man and his wife were summoned from the town.

With the real kindness of their sort, they took me into their hostel in Dover and gave me a bed and some food. There was three other drifting girls in the room, two on their way out of the country and one not knowing where she was going next.

During the night the two outward-bound girls got up and went off to burgle a wine and spirits shop, which they had spied down the road.

They returned in an hour, scattering banknotes and with the Dover police two minutes behind them. They shot into the small dormitory and leapt into bed fully clothed, while the police banged on the hostel door downstairs. Peeping fearfully from over the edge of my bedclothes at all this, I looked down and saw three white five-pound notes lying on the moonlight on the floor. Like a lizard I slid from the sheets, collected them, rolled them up like a cigar and hid them where only the most personal of searches would have discovered them.

Then the police came with the poor, distressed Salvation Army lady. We had to get from our beds, two of us in our innocent nightdresses and the other two in incriminating trousers and sweaters. There was a dashing chase around the dormitory with the girls, the police in pursuit, going over the beds like some sort of steeplechase, and one-pound and five-pound notes flying all about, until eventually they were cornered and taken away. The hostel lady was weeping by this time and I went over the comfort her. I minced across to her, my legs hardly parting. I walked like a Japanese geisha girl, with the tiniest steps, but with a glad heart, for I knew that once more good providence had nudged my shoulder.

During my long wooden journey on the French trains, I had plenty of time to thing about what I should do when I reached England again. The number of people I knew as friends were accounted for on the fingers of one hand. There was Hal and Flossie in the café in Weymouth and the Commander and Diana Seagram in London. The only other person who would recognize me was my sister. I doubted whether my father would know me, or want to know now. It was not a very comforting list.

My sister and my father could be eliminated in the same brisk stroke. I was reluctant, too, to journey half-way across southern England merely to return to the scullery of Hal and Flossie, kind hearts though they had. In any case I had no wish to carry on business once more with the Weymouth fishing fleet. London beckoned temptingly, but I would not allow myself to contact Diana Seagram and certainly not the Commander in my destitute state.

I had it in mind to find my way to London – which with the lucky money that had floated my way I could now do – and to throw myself into the fortunes of that crowded and chancey city. I remembered the Italian who only wanted to whisper ruderies in my ear, and I thought there must be simpler ways of earning good living if they were only sought out. But, strangely perhaps, after all I had experienced, I was still nervous of the big town and more nervous of getting into a life of common vice, from which there might never be any escape. In my naïve way I had assured myself that all the amoral things I had done until then were merely temporary, a means to an end, and that once I had attained some stable form of living I would be able to cease and begin a normal life; sex would be a pastime, not a necessity.

For this reason I hesitated about going immediately to London. I also thought it prudent to wait for a few days because if I were seen boarding a train, questions might be asked as to how I came by the fare. When I went to the city I wanted to go firmly on my feet with no worries about making a living and finding a home. So I decided to stay, temporarily, right there in Dover, on the doorstep of England, until I had gathered enough substance to make a sure and steady change.

There was no thought in me, either, to open up business as a harlot in Dover, although the town being the busy port it is, I expect I would have prospered. Apart from the seafaring men (and I was sick of sailors anyway) there was, at that time, the first traffic of the great holiday activity to the Continent and back that came in later years. I could have in all probability set up a thriving business among travellers. I could have been the first and last whore in Britain.

That day I decided to remain in Dover I went out from the hostel, like the stout-hearted young girl nobody could deny I was, to find myself a job and a place where I could live. The job I found in a yellowing milk-bar in the town, working shifts, and I found a room above an undertaker's shop, spacious and warm and cheap since nobody else would take it because of what lay underneath. I had some uncertainty myself, but I decided it was a bargain and I took it. Walking down the street I saw coming towards me the other lost girl who had shared the dormitory at the hostel. She was glad to see me for she had no friends, and impulsively I asked her if she wanted to share a room. She embraced me in the street. Her name was Gwenny. She had walked from Wales. Round, talkative and irresponsible, she had lived half her life in fantasies, and she became my first real friend.

Suddenly I began to feel confident and assured again. It was very cosy there above the coffins with a view across the Channel, thrilling on screaming winter days and restful in the calm weather. We had a small gas cooker, a kettle and some pots and pans, two armchairs, a wardrobe and our beds. We used a bathroom down the corridor, which we shared with the business and which smelled of embalming fluid, and we had a key to let ourselves in through the shop when we came home late at night.

The first evening we moved in we bought a bottle of sweet, cheap sherry and drank to our health and our future. For the first time in my life I felt that I surely might have one. It was my home.

Gwenny, however, had a weakness. She was incapable of keeping a job for more than a week. Occasionally she had several posts in the same week, sometimes the employment only lasted a single day, and once she had two jobs in one day.

Born clumsy, she set fire to the Honeypot Tea Shop on her first afternoon, sending swarms of retired ladies tumbling into the street. She allowed a mass escape from the pet shop where they tolerated her for three days, permitting a monkey, a herd of white mice and three *tortoises* to run away.

Gwenny was then hired to push an elderly gentleman in his invalid chair and each afternoon she would trundle him along the seafront, dreaming her dreams, with the old fellow nodding off the sleep. One afternoon, Gwenny let go of the wheelchair to admire somebody's baby and the vehicle went bumping off by itself down the slipway and into the cold sea. The poor old man was up to his waist in waves when he woke up. Gwenny said she was sorry.

In these circumstances her money was uncertain and for much of the time we shared the room above the undertaker's it was my earnings from the milk bar which paid the rent and whatever food we could afford.

I was able to nibble at bits and pieces at the milk bar, although it was hardly filling or nourishing, and during Gwenny's brief career at the Home and Colonial we had plenty to eat every night because she always came home with half a dozen tins under her coat. They caught her after three days.

One of her real talents, however, was the ability to throw the most realistic epileptic fit I have ever seen. She did it one night in the room, scaring the wits from me, and we adapted this imitation to our needs by having her throw a fit in the grocery department of a store and while everyone's attention was diverted, I would put as much as I could into the shopping bag and make a run for it.

Two jolly humpers – young men who carried the loaded coffins for the undertakers – took us out to a public house sometimes or to the cinema. At funerals they would sit in the hearse with the coffin they had humped and would sing ribald songs under their breath while the procession made for the cemetery.

One night when we let ourselves into the shop below our room (something we now did as a matter of course, it seeming no different than, say, a sweet shop) I gave Gwenny a playful push. She was a solid round girl, and she stumbled back and collided with a coffin on its trestles, tipping it and depositing the body of a poor old dead man on to the floor.

We jumped about, horrified, squealing. There he was in his best suit, sprawled out on the floor as though he'd gone to sleep there.

'Oh God, Nelly, what are we going to do?' gasped Gwenny.

'Put him back,' I trembled. 'There's nothing else we can do. If they find him there they'll know it was us, and they'll throw us out.'

'I don't like it,' quivered Gwenny. 'Oh Nell, I don't at all.'

'Neither do I,' I admitted. 'But we got to do it. Come on, let's lift him back. Just pretend he's asleep. Kid ourselves.'

It was the most awful experience. In the light from the street coming in over the shop blinds, we crouched, one each end, and replaced the coffin and then bent to lift up the old dead man. God, we were petrified. We both trembled so much it was a wonder we did not shake the poor corpse to pieces. Then his false teeth fell out.

'Oh Christ, Nell!' Gwenny shrieked. 'His teeth. They've come out.'

They were sitting on the floor grinning invitingly at us like death itself. In some ghastly way they seemed worse than the actual corpse.

'Put him in,' I gasped. 'Get him back in the box.'

We lifted him up and dropped him into his coffin. The exit of his teeth had caused his mouth to relax into a gummy smile, as though he might be enjoying it. Once he was back we stood staring down at the teeth, luminous in the half-light.

'I can't,' whispered Gwenny. 'I can't pick them up Nell. Honest I can't.'

'Nor me,' I trembled. 'And we'd have to put them back in his mouth too.'

'Oh no!' she shuddered. 'Oh God, I couldn't. I just couldn't.'

'Let's throw them in the dustbin,' I suggested.

'No we can't,' she whispered superstitiously. 'It's tampering with the dead. And he'll need them. You know, weeping and gnashing of teeth and that, like they say in chapel.'

I had an idea. 'There's a coal scuttle in the back room,' I said. 'And there's a pair of fire tongs in it. Let's pick them up with them.'

She crept into the rear room and came back with the tongs. They were cumbersome for the job but between them we managed to pick up the teeth. Getting back into the mouth with them was a different matter. We kept dropping them on the corpse and in the coffin and having to fish them out again, until eventually, shaking every inch of the way, we manoeuvred them towards his gums and slotted them in. They did not go in straight and indeed they sat there grinning back at us in a most gruesome way. We could not stand it a minute longer. We shut the lid down and went upstairs. We spent the rest of the night clutching each other to fight off our nightmares.

Those months in Dover with Gwenny were, I suppose, now I come to think of it, the most sexually innocent of my adult life. I told her nothing of my immoral past, only describing the general things, and she was strangely incurious for a Welsh girl. She told me of her growing up in Wales and the things she had done since. But we exchanged little information about our private past. And in all the time we lived together, no man slept in our room. I was making up for the innocence and carefulness I had missed in earlier years. I was enjoying this life. I began to think that, after all, I might not be on a headlong course for an existence of casual sin. And it was while I was in this mood that I met George Turnbull and he asked me to marry him. He thought I was a virgin.

It was at a two shilling dance at a village hall a few miles outside Dover that we met. He was a big, dull man, his feet being especially large as I discovered during our first quickstep. He moved like a tractor, those enormous feet plonking down one after the other like caterpillar tracks; on his face there was ever an expression of good intention and earnestness. He was, I suppose, handsome in a stony sort of way but he was steady to the point of hardly appearing to move at all. The only time when George was seen to be truly alive was with the two-foot paint roller in his fists, and for that he was famous.

'I painted a ballroom last weekend,' he told me on that first night, after wrestling inwardly to find some form of conversation which might interest me. 'By myself.'

'By yourself?' I asked. 'A ballroom?'

'Three hundred feet long by seventy-five wide, by thirty high,' he quoted modestly, lowering his under-face into a pint beer mug. 'Wore out four rollers.' His decent frank eyes turned to me. 'If you want to come and see me working, I'm doing the front of the Red Lion next week,' he said. 'There'll be a lot of people watching.'

Walking through the town the following Wednesday, I saw a crowd filling one pavement and staring up at a building on the other side, their mouths open in the manner of upward gazing crowds. A policeman, presumably sent to disperse the obstruction, was fixed in the gutter also looking up as though some famous comet had appeared.

There was a ladder and at the top was the amazing George Turnbull, the Leonardo da Vinci of the Kent coast. He was performing at a tremendous rate, running his roller, as though it were part of him, over the flaky face of the Red Lion Hotel.

I felt a certain proprietorial pride as I watched him perform and saw how he continued to entrance the people, just like a tightrope man or acrobat, their heads moving hypnotically with the might strokes of his roller. Hurrying to the edge of the watchers, I waved and shouted and for a moment the famous man paused in his work, waving the roller in salute, an action which sent white paint sploshing over the crowd like seagull shit. 'Nell Luscombe!' he called down. 'Will you marry me?'

The watchers, all delighted, turned for my answers. There was nothing for it. 'Yes,' I shouted back. 'Yes I will.' People gazed at me with a sort of awe. I was to wed the great George Turnbull.

The only person who did not approve of the match was Gwenny, who knew she was incapable of leading a proper life alone, and I worried about her until, with unexpected fortune somebody she knew in Wales offered her a job as a tea girl.

'Where is it Gwenny?' I asked happily, but wondering if she would be able to cope.

She dropped her eyes because she knew that I was thinking of her clumsiness. 'In a steel smelting plant,' she mumbled.

But she was able to be my bridesmaid. It was something she later wrote, which gave her happy memories after her accident, while she was confined with eighteen steelworkers in the hospital at Ebbw Vale. That day she looked fascinating in the gown of turquoise through which she had, however, accidentally pushed her foot.

I was, naturally, in white. George Turnbull believed that he was taking an untouched maid to the altar, and who was I to spoil his day? In any event the previous years of my life were now fading behind me like a dream and here was I walking up the aisle as happy as any true and intact virgin.

During the service George seemed to be lost in a gaze that took in the entire east wall of the parish church, longing to measure it by rule of thumb and a squinting eye.

There was a lot of Kentish beer drunk at the reception, held in the same village hall where George and I had first danced. The groom, because of the paint that lodged in his throat, could roll away a dozen pints, one quickly on the heels of the pint before. The best man, a ruffian I can only now remember as Wild Mickey, was also an indiscriminate beer swigger and he and George, keeping pace with each other, fell to arguing drunkenly as to how long it would take to paint the interior of the hall where we were celebrating.

'Four days,' said Wild Mickey, pushing George on.

'Two days,' argued George, at once becoming belligerent. Nothing stirred him like paint. They drank more and the dispute became louder while I sat beside my new husband and tried to prevent an outburst of fists.

Eventually George, with a streak of beery gallantry, threw down a challenge. It was like some grand gentleman of the olden days. If he had not been standing there bulging out of his best blue suit, his neck hung over the edge of his collar, I would have imagined him in some silk ruffle with a sword ready in his hands. 'I'll paint this place I will,' he challenged. 'Before I takes my bride to bed tonight.'

There were howls and pleas all around, not the least from me, but there was nothing that could stop him then. Somebody was sent for his overalls and his rollers and paints and scaffold boards. While they were gone and I surrendered myself to gloom and Babycham, he drank another five pints of beer, took off his coat and strode up and down measuring the place out first with his giant feet and then with his thumb. Eventually when all his equipment had been brought by an obliging man with a milkcart, he clasped me to him and rubbed a rough kiss into my face. 'Wait for me Nell,' he breathed. 'Wait for me.'

Numb, dumb, I looked around the walls and the ceiling of the place. It had not seemed very big but now it seemed acres. I sat and began to cry, comforted by various women guests including Gwenny who had cut herself badly while opening a tin of peaches and had fresh blood all down the front of her dress, just above the hole in her skirt. All at once I felt I had to do something to stop him. Like a women trying to stop her man going to a pointless duel I howled: 'No! No! George Turnbull! Stop this madness now!'

Madness it may have been but it was too late. His overalls over his wedding suit, the confetti in his hair soon to be mingled with gobs of cream emulsion. George Turnbull set to, like an obsessed giant, to paint the walls. Everyone gasped at his speed and, sitting unattended at the table, I could not help but feel a certain pride as his roller covered the yards of wall so swiftly.

After four hours most of the guests had gone home and after another two I went also, leaving George solitary and still painting. Even Wild Mickey had gone. I walked alone (Gwenny became ill and had to be taken away) through the cold streets of Dover, a ghostly figure in a wedding dress, sobbing a little, but having a slight laugh between sobs.

We had booked a room for our honeymoon night at the same Red Lion Hotel from whose ramparts he had first proposed, and I wandered in, desolate, and went upstairs. The reception clerk instinctively realized what had happened. 'Gone off painting has he, Mrs Turnbull?' he said. The sound of my new name made the situation even more poignant. I nodded tearfully. 'There's nothing on earth is ever going to keep him from it,' he said solemnly. 'It's in his blood.'

I went to the room, bathed, put on my sad wedding nightdress and lay in bed waiting while the hours tolled by on the town clock. He came to bed an hour before dawn, stinking of topcoat and turpentine, but triumphant. He had done it! In two moments he was asleep. I smiled at his white face, so full of emulsion, and kissed his cheek. Poor fellow, I think now, he had few triumphs in his short life. I could hardly have denied him one on his wedding day.

He snored brilliantly all through what remained of that first night of our marriage. Perhaps it was overworked imagination but, lying there in the Dover dark, I convinced myself that a fine spray of paint was being fanned out with each snore. He lay on his back, his feet like tombstones. His large square rib cage would rise like a platform and then deflate, a pungent snore forcing into the room. It went on for hour upon hour. It was like lying with a machine. In the morning I would not have been surprised if he had done the ceiling in the night.

He had to go off to work in the morning, for he had left a coat of lime green drying somewhere and he could not leave it alone. Used as I was to all sorts of adversity and thoughtlessness on the part of men (why do they always call it 'mankind' I wonder?), I had a little, private cry, when he had gone, the whimper of a woman left for a wall.

I went around to see Gwenny who was under notice to leave the dry cleaning shop where she had been working since the beginning of that week. While I was there, sipping tea with her, a procession of customers came into the shop with wrong garments, burned clothes and one man bringing a pair of trousers with five creases in one leg. Gwenny dealt with them with the off-hand attitude of one who would be in another place at the end of the week. While we were there she chattily put a steam iron right through a shirt front. All sympathy for my problems, she comforted me with the thought that at least I had a husband who enjoyed his work. He could have painted all day long as far as I was concerned. It was the voluntary overtime he was so eager to work, what, in his trade, you might call extra-mural activity.

But on the evening of our first full day as wife and man he returned to the Red Lion Hotel (where they had given us a room for three nights, the cost to be set against future contract – a melancholy coincidence, as it happened), triumphant after yet another battle with paint and plasterwork. He spent the first hour of our evening describing every cornice, parapet and sash he had daubed that day and I realized then this would forever be the pattern of our lives together. Eventually, like an afterthought, he asked me how I had fared that day and I told him bluntly that I had been crying.

Genuinely astonished, he was further amazed to discover that I was not proud of the fact that he had painted the interior of a hall on our wedding night.

Sorry and concerned, he insisted that we went to our bed very early and I changed into my bridal nightdress feeling happier and softer. He modestly donned a pair of stiff pyjamas, apparently made from some sort of compressed wood shavings. I swear they creaked when he moved. Then, from under the bed he produced, with a kind of coy triumph, a parcel and an illustrated book on sex.

I sat in my bed, my beautiful unattended breasts lying half outside my nightdress, gazing in astonishment while this fucking novice opened the book at page one and began to read aloud. Worse was to follow, for the parcel contained the most horrifying collection of intercourse equipment I have ever seen. There were dozens of washable sheaths, jars of jelly and pots of French chalk (to dry out the sheaths after laundering them). There were pills and tablets enough to arouse a physical wreck. It was only a wonder that they had not included a puncture outfit. George smiled solidly as he looked up from the bundle.

'I didn't know rightly what to get, Nell,' he admitted. 'So I went and ordered the lot.'

It was one of the most humiliating nights I have ever spent with a man, not excluding my awful adventures aboard the *Charlie Harry II*. He even (Oh God, when I think of it!) produced a war surplus gas cape and spread it below my buttocks so that in the course of losing my virginity I would not damage the Red Lion sheets. When he had finally read the instructions (leaving the book open so he could refer to it) and had donned all his rubber, paste and jelly, and had taken two tablets (one meant for me) he hung poised above me. I couldn't help it. 'Why don't you give it a coat of paint as well, George?' I sighed.

The poor nincompoop eventually got himself pointed in the right direction and advanced on me like one of King Arthur's Knights, hanging with armour and with a blasted great lance sticking out in front.

What really worried him was that the instructions about what he kept calling 'piercing' could not be carried out. He kept pushing and probing with that look of intense puzzlement on his face, not understanding why he had not reached the expected resistance. Every now and then he would refer to the book and then have another poke. Eventually he lay against me panting and gave the matter thought. Then, tragedy smashed all over his face, he lifted himself up, and on his great elbows said: 'You *are* one Nell, ain't you?'

'One *what* George?' I asked, staring at the ceiling.

'One of them virgins?' he said. 'You ain't been with another man, have you?'

Still looking up I shook my head. 'I've never been with another man, George,' I recited.

'But something's supposed to happen,' he said miserably. 'Something's missing, Nell.'

The born dolt actually began looking around the bed for something that had vanished years before.

Fortunately he had another read and discovered that a girl could lose her physical virginity in a number of innocent ways, for example, on a horse or on a wall. Not knowing anything about horses I said it probably happened to me as a child and I spent hours astride our garden wall, sometimes hopping along it from end to end.

He buried his big, simple face in my breasts, which he seemed to have been saving for some emergency, and muttered: 'Damn that garden wall, Nelly. Damn it.'

'Oh dear,' I thought. 'Oh dear, Nelly Luscombe. What have you gone and done?'

But if George Turnbull as a lover left a girl breathless with boredom, he was a good and generous husband, giving me the settled silent life I had wanted after all the storms of my youth.

And he had a sense for the dramatic too, for he had prepared for me a great surprise – a little house of our own. Nothing had been said about where we were to live after our marriage and during our three days at the Red Lion, surprising as it seems now, I had not worried very much about it, believing that we would get some rooms in the town and make them our home. Perhaps I was secretly afraid of anything too permanent.

But on the third day we were wife and man, he arrived at the Red Lion in his rattling paint-splashed van and, smiling with stony mystery, he drove us from the town and inland to where a group of new houses sat on a hill like some sort of camp or fortress.

I thought that he was merely taking me to view some new professional triumph. We drew up in front of a small house shining like a painted box in the Dover sun. Still with that large fixed smile he led me to the door and with one of the few romantic gestures of his life he lifted me across the threshold. It was ours!

I am sure that I was never so overjoyed about anything, and even since then, even in my grand days to follow, never has that simple and sudden happiness been surpassed.

The realization that this was *my* house, my very own, took my breath away and I began to laugh crazily, jumping from his arms and running like a child from little room to little room, banging on the walls (recently painted of course) and trying to embrace the windows that looked out on sloping green fields, the roofs of Dover and the English Channel, grey in the distance like a broad street. He came and clumsily joined me at the window. I put my arms, my poor wandering homeless arms, about his hefty waist and we gazed out together.

'Look at the sea, Nell,' he said. 'It looks like it could do with a few undercoats and a nice gloss, don' it?'

It was difficult to answer that. I swear he would have liked to have given the rainbow a new top coat if the chance had been offered. And it was his work that had brought us our house. The builder was so keen to have George that he had given it to us rent free providing George would paint the houses all around him. He was to be allowed three days a week to do other work, so that he could earn the housekeeping, and the rest of the time paint the windows and doors of our neighbours. I realized I was married to a champion!

At first there were no neighbours. We were gladly marooned on that hill overlooking the sea, and I began to sense the happiness I had always felt might come if I could only find somewhere to settle, where every day would not bring a new trial or adventure. You could not be further from adventure than married to George Turnbull.

Three days a week his little van would trundle down the hill, all colours, like a large moving flower, and I would be left to the comfortable work of a young wife. Occasionally I would think of the hairy old days but, at that time, with no great longing. Then some people moved into the little estate and I was invited to coffee and tea and would stand gossiping on the muddy paths like any other woman. I began to dream about carpets and cocktail cabinets and perhaps even babies. Each day I lived in my house, doing the easy chores, while Frankie Lane and Johnny Ray sang to me from the radio.

George built a small shed in the garden where he kept his paints and where he spent much of his evening time pottering and making small things for the home. At one time I thought he was getting notions of parenthood himself because I went into his shed and saw that he was building something that looked very much like a cradle.

'What's that you're making in the shed George?' I asked him.

'Oh that,' he said. 'That's for the builder's yard. It's just a rat trap.'

Now of course, I realize that it was never in my nature to live that life, even if I had convinced myself that it was safe and happy. The change came with the seasons. Autumn was with us again and the wind blowing down the Channel made me lonely. In the town I met a man, Theo Baldwin, another painter, but a painter of canvases, not walls. He looked like that sort of painter ought to look, in his fifties, his hair long, grey-gold, his face lined with artistic worries. It was his voice that was so handsome.

'Mrs Turnbull,' he said on that day we first fell into conversation and introduced ourselves in the public bar of the Red Lion (so much of my life at that period was connected with that place). I was there waiting for George. We went out once a week to the films and I would meet him there. People in the cinema used to move away from us because of the smell of turps that hung about my husband, something to which I had now become accustomed. 'Mrs Turnbull,' said Theo Baldwin. 'You are a lady of great beauty you know. Would you permit me to paint you?'

Now I've seen enough films and suchlike about portrait painters to know that they want to have you pose in the nude and then, eventually, to persuade you to make love to them. Theo was not like that at all. He had me across the bed before he had ever touched a brush to the canvas.

I was shocked at myself more than at him. To think that I slipped into it so easily again after all my telling myself that I was cured and free of such things. But it happened as if it had all been arranged the moment I agreed to visit him at his studio in the town. And I went, eyes open, into it as if nothing had every happened to make me change my ways. Once a whore always a whore. Throughout the previous day I had felt guilty excitement simmering inside me. George rolled off in the morning with his brushes and rollers and his customary satisfied grin. I waited and made myself a cup of coffee. Then I sat on my plastic-topped stool in my fitted kitchen and tried to think clearly, to deliberately put this temptation behind me. It was as though I were praying. The radio played and the house felt safe like a cloak around my body. Was I to leave it and start a life of adventuring once more? Surely not. I was.

I left it until the last possible moment, in case something might happen, like George returning with lead-poisoning or a neighbour calling for a chat, which would play my hand for me and prevent me risking all this good, steady life I had managed to form. But at eleven o'clock no interruptions had occurred. It would not even rain to give me an excuse. Head bent, hellbent, I walked down the grassy slope of our hillside, with sea-wind in my face, feeling again the ghostly nudging presence of Nell Luscombe, travelling trollop from Weymouth. It's not surprising, I suppose, that I cannot, even now, visit a seaside place without hearing in its wind the whisper of a proposition.

Guiltily, I went into the town and, after walking along the main street, window-shopping, I snaked down a small alley where his home and studio lay. I trembled as I rang the bell and stood dumbly when he opened the door.

'Good girl, Nell,' he said like a secret agent meeting an accomplice. 'You got here.'

I walked into the gloomy house. There were paintings and canvases everywhere (he was not a particularly successful painter as far as actually selling his pictures was concerned) and I walked, still nervously, between them, trying to see what they portrayed.

'Come in here, my darling,' he said unhesitatingly. He was wearing a sort of loose smock with signs of the zodiac on it.

I felt out of practice and he took my uncertainty as some sort of innocence. I was loitering about and he was making circles around me like some artistic shark, putting out his hands and then withdrawing them without touching me.

'Proportions, proportions,' he muttered. It was like George measuring up a wall, with his thumb. Theo used his hands, holding them at angles like frames and advancing and backing away as if he were on elastic, until he came right in close and framed my right breast with his outspread fingers. 'Exquisite,' he murmured. 'Rotunda exquisite.'

'Thank you very much, Theo,' I said uncertainly. 'I can't stay long. I've got to go to Liptons.'

'Of course, of course,' he agreed. He was one of those people who keep saying things twice. 'Would you . . . would you just take your clothes off dear. At the top.'

I sighed. After all, I was there snared by my own irresistible attraction for grimy adventure so there was no point in being coy. I said nothing but began to undo the buttons on the front of my dress. Theo stepped back as if he expected an avalanche. I pulled the sleeves and shoulders of the dress down over my arms and let it hang there from the waist. I was wearing a slip and a bra. Theo started making more framing movements with his hands. 'Beautiful, beautiful,' he recited. 'Rotunda, rotunda.'

He kept up a commentary as I continued to strip. 'Skin, smooth, pink, curves, sublime, neck, sexually arousing, waist dainty, shoulders creamy, arms slender . . .' Then: 'Oh what a lovely pair of titties.' Flinging me back on the four poster spread behind me like a soft trap, he at once fastened on to my left nipple, as though making sure of a connection, so to speak, and then rolled passionately across to my other breast and hung on there. He went to and fro several times, spoiled for choice it seemed, in a long curve like a windscreen wiper.

'My darling, my darling,' he gabbled. 'My dear darling, my dear darling.'

His artistic beard was as stiff as one of George's abandoned paint brushes and he jabbed it all over my anatomy. He was wearing something or other under his zodiac robe and he tore this garment away and released a long thin appliance that sprang like a ship's bowsprit in a gale. He was taking a long time on his approach, so I wriggled out of the bottom half of my clothes and kicked them away down the bed. This gave him another excuse to explore and exclaim. He tracked over my lower landscape, nose down, beard tickling down between my legs, puffing, burrowing so deeply that I almost lost sight of his head altogether. He came out red-faced and breathless, like an inspector of drains, gave a pathetic moan and climbed close to me.

In a lifetime of beds and men I have known some strange performers, but Theo the artist was the most unusual I had met up to that time. He began using that long starved thing of his like a paintbrush, dipping it into my personal palette and painting my legs, my stomach and my bosom in the most odd fashion. I lay there, astonished, wondering where he would start work next. As he brushed me with his penis he muttered, eyes closed: 'Crimson . . . ochre . . . aquamarine . . . violet . . .' as if he were painting by numbers.

By the time he had finished this performance I was nicely on the boil, and ready for the real thing. Unfortunately what he had been about *was* the real thing as far as he was concerned and I left the studio puzzled and dissatisfied and clutching a small etching he had given me as a parting gift.

Several times more I visited Theo, each time emerging with a frown and a worthless drawing or painting which I dropped in somebody's dustbin. I would wait guiltily at home for my own painter, George, to return and satisfy me. But George was a man whose passions were less than occasional and after his tea he would go out to work in his little wooden shed, leaving me to wonder where I was going to dispose of my pent-up energy and love.

The answer was provided by Garth, a stringy young husband who lived three houses away. He had the haunted look of a man who hopes for and needs more than he gets. His wife was a jug-faced, fussy girl who went to evening classes for rug-making and it was during one of these absences and while George was working late over some expansive wall that Garth asked me if I would like to come into his house to see his cat's kittens. I would have had to have been as blind as a kitten not to see that he intended to show me more than that, because you can only take a certain amount of kittens and once you've seen one you've seen the litter; and anyway he had that dry, desperate look about him. When we had inspected the kittens, he asked me if I would like a drink and I could see his hand shaking as he poured it. He missed the glass with the first two lumps of ice.

'Nell,' he said through clenched teeth. 'The telephone's out there. Please, please ring nine-nine-nine for the police.'

'What's the emergency?' I said.

'There will be one shortly, Nell,' he muttered. 'I think I'm going to rape you.'

'Why tell the police?' I said. 'And what do you mean you *think*?' An explosion of amazed pleasure transformed his face.

'You mean . . . you mean . . . you'll let me?'

'Then it isn't rape,' I said. 'Not technically. If I let you.'

'Well call it what you like,' he gasped. 'We've got half a hour. Beryl will be knee deep in rug wool now.'

The use of his wife's name seemed to strengthen his resolve. He caught me by the wrists and kissed me agonizingly and we charged up the stairs. He had the curtains drawn and his trousers down in one swift sweep of his arm. I slipped out of my clothes while he stood transfixed on the far side of their bed which was covered by a hideous gold quilt.

'Oh God,' he whispered across the bed. 'I've watched you and watched you Nell, every day I've spied on you. I know every curve of your body by heart. It's been driving me mad and now you're here.'

'I'm here,' I smiled and nakedly leaned back across the quilt.

'Er . . . Nell . . . not that side . . . please. That's Beryl's side.' I sighed at his hypocrisy and moved over so I would not defile Beryl's bit of the bed. He was really hungry, poor soul, starved; holding me and caressing me with the enthusiasm of a man trying to rub away a stain.

We were both lying panting gratefully after it was over, when there came a ring on the front door chimes. Poor Garth went rigid with fear. His eyes seemed to revolve in his slim, pallid face.

'Lay low,' I whispered. 'They'll think there's nobody in.'

'But I'm *supposed* to be in,' he trembled. 'I'm baby-sitting. And it's bound to be someone from around here.'

'Better go down,' I said. 'Shall I stay.'

'No. Oh God, no.' He shook.

'I'll creep out the back door,' I decided for him. 'Trust to luck nobody sees me. Bye.'

He did not even answer, but tucked his tell-tale shirt into his trousers and stammered down the stairs. Long practice had made me able to dress quickly and I was only just behind him. I had intended to turn off and creep through the kitchen to the back door, but just as we reached the front door the letter box popped up and a pair of eyes pinned us.

'Open up Garth,' called the voice. 'I can see you, old boy. And that lovely Mrs Turnbull.'

The game was up before it was properly started. Garth shuddered forward and, ashen-faced (the back of his neck was ashen too), slowly opened the door. It was Bernard Winters, the motor car salesman who lived on the opposite side of the road. His face was all grinning triumph.

'Ho! Ho!' he exclaimed. 'Caught in the act, old boy. Nabbed you rotten.'

'Mrs Turnbull came in to see our kittens,' said Garth huffily. 'You're a bit much Bernard, a bit too much.'

Bernard laughed and patted us both on the shoulders and made man-of-the-world noises. He was a dark, handsome fellow, but a bit sure of himself.

Just how sure he was it did not take long to discover. I had hardly returned to my own sitting-room when our newly-installed telephone rang and it was Bernard. 'Nelly,' he said. '*I* think you're desirable too. Why don't you visit me sometime? Margaret goes to pottery on Thursdays.'

I paused. Then, right, I thought. This is the true crossroads. 'All right,' I answered calmly. 'It will cost you five pounds.'

'A fiver!' he exclaimed. 'Jesus, you're a girl, aren't you!'

'That's why I'm charging a fiver,' I said. I heard him guffaw over the line. 'I bet you didn't charge old Garth. He hasn't got a fiver to his name.'

'That's none of your business!' I said. 'It was a trial run. I was just seeing if I could still do it.'

'Christ you *are* something,' he said. 'All right, Nelly. On Thursday then, when Margaret's gone to pot.'

'Start saving your pennies,' I told him.

That's how it began. A one-girl vice ring in the middle of a little estate of boxy houses, stuck on a hilltop meadow in Kent. You don't have to explore far to find a market for flesh. I was passed from husband to husband like a secret game of rugby, gathering fivers as I went.

That first Thursday with Bernard Winters was worth a fiver of anybody's money, even mine. Here, at last, was an out-and-out bastard who enjoyed sex and especially illicit sex. He was genial, unhurried, unworried, getting me a couple of gins beforehand and a well-brewed cup of tea afterwards. Fortunately it was now the darkest side of winter so that moving about the district was not so difficult as it would have been on light evenings, although it occasionally meant climbing a garden fence or two. Bernard was not the type to merely pay up as a customer. It was his nature to get involved in business, and soon he was acting as my agent, with husbands all over the estate and even organized visits from Dover and the surrounding villages.

At first it was merely a quiet phone call from Bernard about Harry Venables, a draughtsman from the far end of the estate, whose wife was another Thursday potter. I paid Harry a half-hour visit and came away with my fiver. Then there was somebody else whose wife was doing French, flower arrangement and metal work for beginners. This man worked overtime on these evenings and then rushed home to spend his overtime on me. God only knows how it went on so long undetected.

The only real embarrassment was the money. I honestly did not know what to do with it. I thought of opening a bank account, but there was a risk of George discovering that. And it was not as though I could even go out and spend it. George would have soon noticed something new – although I would have dearly liked a refrigerator. Bernard offered to 'invest' my takings for me, but I prudently declined. What was I to do with this fortune that grew so readily as my contacts and customers increased?

Our house was so small and modern that there were no crannies or niches where such an amount in notes could be concealed. The garden was bare of possibilities – except for George's little hut down by the fence. One afternoon, when I was getting desperate with a hundred and fifty pounds in five and one pound notes under our mattress, I decided to look at the shed.

It was confined and crowded, full of tidy paint pots and brushes and his bench where he did his odd bits of carpentry and other work in the evenings. Suddenly I felt very sad for him and very guilty for what I was doing behind his back. Shamefully, I could imagine him in there at his lonely vice while I was sharing mine on some neighbouring bed.

Shame, however, would never find a hiding place for the money. I searched around with no success until, just as I was leaving and I was outside the workshed, I chanced to look down and I saw that the floor was raised from the ground a few inches leaving a hollow beneath. On his shelves were a line of jam-jars, some containing screws and nails and other oddments, but several standing empty. I took down one of the jars which had a screw-on lid and took it inside the house. My ill-gotten money curled in there very cosily and I returned to the garden and pushed it into the space under the floor. Within a few weeks it was joined by another, also full of notes. I had more than three hundred pounds.

The disgusting business was booming. I found myself morning, afternoons and often evenings making my way to some randy husband, with my bag containing one of the new electric vibrators which I had heard about and purchased as a professional aid.

There was a touch of pantomime about some of the visits I made. On one occasion the husband had been left to watch several simmering pans on the cooker. He explained smugly that his wife made her own jam and marmalade. Unfortunately he became engrossed during the next half hour and the forgotten pans flowed over and hung, black and burning, down the side of the cooker like lava from a volcano.

Another client had wailing two-year-old twins in his charge and we had to perform on the nursery bedroom carpet because they would not let daddy out of their sight until they were asleep. They were a couple of intensely ugly, chocolate-mouthed boys, and they stood at the side of their cot and leaned over and watched us on the floor, murmuring and muttering, like two yokels at a gate.

One man brought his father and we all three got into bed, me rolling log-like from one generation to the other. On another night I was the whore-in-residence at a blue-film performance attended by eight eager husbands.

Before long another jam-jar was stuffed with notes and I began to wonder where it would lead. George continued on his plodding life, apparently not noticing anything, not even my signs of fatigue. Then in the middle of one night, a terrible thing happened. I woke up and saw George standing against the window with a red glow reflected around the room.

'Nell,' he said ponderously, turning as he saw I was awake. 'My shed's on fire.'

With a screech much louder than justified the loss of a garden shed I rushed to the window beside him. It was burning furiously, just the bones of framework visible through the flames. His pots of paint were bursting like bombs. I almost choked just watching it. He went at his usual slow gait to telephone the fire brigade but by the time they arrived the little building was just hot ashes and the jam-jars had cracked and melted and my precious money had burned away. All that for nothing.

Two days later George Turnbull painted his last wall. It was at the side of the Red Lion, a blanked-out elevation with no windows or doors. He was painting it a jaunty blue and when I last saw him and waved to him he was on the top rung of the ladder using his two foot roller with his everyday cheerfulness and vigour.

I waved back and continued down the street to a grocery shop. While I was at the counter a commotion began outside and I saw people hurrying. Somehow I knew it was George. I put down my shopping basket and went to the door.

Down the street a crowd had gathered at the foot of the blank wall of the Red Lion. There was no doubt about it being my poor husband. From the new blue area at the top of the wall a great rounded streak of paint, a perfect quarter circle, curved down the wall like a layer of the rainbow. And at the foot of that rainbow there was not crock of gold but George Turnbull. He had reached too far, his ladder had toppled sideways, but faithful unto death, he had kept his roller against the surface all the way down, like a doomed aeroplane.

When I got to the crowd I could see it was terrible. To start with, dear, dying George was covered head to foot with blue paint. A policeman who had his head in his lap had it all over his trousers and tunic and it was rolling away, oddly like a bloodstain, from beneath the form of George. I took the blue head from the policeman and laid it properly on my lap. He died there a few minutes later, only opening his emulsion-covered mouth once and that was to say: 'I'm sorry Nell, but I always counted the jam-jars.'

The funeral was at the church where we had been married only a few months previously and all the neighbouring husbands came and stood around the grave but none of them would look up and look me in the eye. I went up the hill to our house, alone, adrift again, not knowing then whether the coroner's pronounced 'accidental death' was the truth and never to know.

That I had to be away from that place was obvious. I could not stay there now; there was no point. I packed the things I had and set off towards the town again, going somewhere I did not know. I sent a note to our best man, Wild Mickey, asking him to sell the contents of the house and always put fresh flowers on poor George's grave. I don't know whether he did.

Now was the time, I told myself, when at last I should go to London, where someone loose like me would be at home among my kind. But I still wavered, still afraid. I got on the London train but at Canterbury I got off again and wandered aimlessly down through the creaky old city until I saw the cheerful front of a fish and chip shop. I bought two shillings worth wrapped in paper and went into a small, cold park to eat them on a bench. I felt miserable and sorry for myself and sorry for poor dead George who had trusted me and asked for nothing, which was as much as he got.

The paper the fish and chips were wrapped in was *The Times* – Canterbury being the sort of town where fish and chips can be wrapped in *The Times*. I never read it in my life, except over Sir Waldo's shoulder, but sitting there in that wintry garden, with nowhere to turn my steps, I began to read the grease-smeared small advertisements on the front page. The third in the column I screwed up my eyes to read: 'Young nanny/companion required. Widower with three grown children. Resident France. Interviews London.'

There was a telephone number. I gaped at it and then slowly turned the newspaper up until I could see the date at the top of the page. It was only three days old. Almost mesmerized I got up from the bench and walked to the post office where I telephoned the number. Yes, I was experienced. Three years with Lord Sutton, two with the Duke of Dorset. References? Of course. Yes, I could be in London that evening. Seven o'clock. Thank you so much. Goodbye.

Still glazed I came out of the telephone box. Liar that I was I *knew* I was going to get the job. I was going to France once more. Nelly Luscombe had done it again.

CHAPTER TWELVE

Walking along the Promenade des Anglais, Nice, in the very spring of my life, the fine sun on the fine sea and France rising all around me, I could not help but think of the strange turns of fortune in my life and the chance that had brought me, a near penniless widow of Dover, to this rich and marvellous place.

There had been no trouble with Mr Sheridan who had advertised in *The Times*. I went to the house in Eaton Square and let my eyes shine. Poor Mr Sheridan's French wife had died a few months before (the poor lady had drowned in a revolving vat of flour while visiting a mill owned by her husband; a fate oddly similar to that suffered by my George). He had been interviewing a parade of starched women of the professional, housekeeper class and when I walked into his room you would have thought I was a summer's day. We discussed our twin tragedies and I dimmed my eyes accordingly and then he began telling me of his children, Sirie fifteen, Anton sixteen and Paul twenty-one, who was in military school in Paris. Slowly I turned up the lids of my country eyes and directed them on to his face. I could see he was not going to ask for references.

I was engaged immediately and I even received an advance of salary and was invited to make myself at home in that lovely house in Eaton Square. I was given a room overlooking the gardens and I stood in the window that very evening and watched the lights of London moving in the night. In three days I would be travelling to Nice, to a house, so he described, like a gem in the hills above the sea. A house called L'Horizon. I stood in the window and practised saying the name to myself. I felt rich and comfortable. Goodbye George Turnbull, goodbye Dover, I whispered.

I bought a new coat with some money given to me by a gentleman in Hyde Park, in payment for a ten minute trick in the back seat of his Rolls as the chaffeur cruised around the park. This was the first time I had performed in London and I was really pleased with it. For a start I had only been walking in the park – not even provocatively walking because I was not aware that Hyde Park was a place where this type of thing happened. It was a mild winter's day and I had found myself strolling by the water, looking at myself in the lake and giggling at the ducks, when the car drew up, silent as a ghost, and the driver startled me with a shout: 'Miss, are you working?'

It seemed a very curious question, but I answered honestly: 'Yes I am. I've just started.'

The next thing I knew was that I was in the back of the car with a lusty, lunchy sort of young businessman, ten pounds better off, and leaning back over the softest seats while he gave me the benefit of his better nature. It was really most luxurious, all the more so because it was so unexpected. He even had a nice little cocktail bar in the back of the car and he poured me a drink of champagne before depositing me within walking distance of Marble Arch. 'Goodbye, Nelly,' he called cheerfully, pulling up his trousers. 'And thank you so much.' A gentleman.

That afternoon I found Diana Seagram's house near Westminster and timidly rang the bell. She was, as always, the most kind lady and we sat and had tea while she gave me the news of the Commander and I told her at least some of my adventures. I wondered how she would have reacted if she knew that an hour before I had been rolling in a Rolls-Royce with someone from the City.

She told me that the Commander had gone to live in a house in Shropshire. She wanted to tell me something else, I could sense it, and eventually she decided she would.

'He has asked me to marry him,' she said quietly. She stared into her teacup as though she had just seen the answer there. A quick, unreasonable pang of jealousy touched me. 'What will you say?' I asked her. All at once we were not girl and woman but woman and woman. She looked up as though wanting help. It was the first time anyone like that had looked at me as though they needed advice.

'I truly don't know what to do, Nell,' she said shaking her head. 'We've known each other a long time. He and my husband were great friends, and now it seems almost like a merger of lost souls. He suffers a great deal, as you well know, but the worst thing is his frustration with his handicaps. He gets so violently angry with himself, you know.'

'I didn't know. I've never seen him angry.'

'No you wouldn't. He wouldn't let you see that. He wouldn't show you. But a man like that is bound to kick over at times. God, he can't walk, he just stumbles, and his voice sounds as if he's trying to speak through a tube. It hurts his pride.'

'Diana,' I said, feeling oddly wise. 'Do you love him?'

'No,' she said simply. 'No, Nell. Nor does he love me. As I said it would be a sort of merger of souls. But he needs me and I possibly need him, I don't know.'

We both knew that I could not tell her what to do. She had merely wanted to tell me the matter. We finished our tea in an aimless sort of way and I left her. We kissed each other at the doorstep and I felt the loneliness of her come through to me. How strange, I thought, that this woman with her poise and her house should really have nobody and here was I, now in fortune, going to a new life in a new rich place.

The day after I drove with Mr Sheridan in his large French car, retracing my journey to Dover which I had left in such despair shortly before. It seemed so odd going through those streets, seeing several people I knew, and going right by the wall of the Red Lion where George had died. Nothing had been done about continuing the painting of the big blank wall and looking out from my deep seat I saw again that terrible arc of blue that marked the crash dive of my late husband. The wall of death. His memorial.

Mr Sheridan had been silent most of the journey and now sat dozing beside me. I had only my thoughts. We returned to the ferry terminal from which I had emerged nearly two years before, without hope or money, after my adventures in France. Now I held out my passport with a certain smugness, a waif now a traveller.

We reached Paris by early evening and Mr Sheridan said he would have dinner in his room at the hotel, leaving me in the company of the chauffeur, a wooden-faced religious man called Perrington. He took me on a tour of all the dreadful and sinful places of that city, to show me, as he said, to what depths some poor creatures can fall. We went to a cabaret where a man with a dog-whip pretended to lay it across a naked girl who crawled across the stage.

'It makes me want to weep for her, Miss,' said Perrington, straining forward at every stroke. 'Imagine the degradation of that wretched young lady's soul.'

We remained dutifully for further equally disgraceful acts and then went along some streets, dozens of them, where the Paris prostitutes waited for customers, and Perrington again was almost in tears at their plight. He studied several very closely, even staring into their faces, as if he was wondering if it might be worth saving them. Apparently he had already made some attempt at this because several smiled as if they really knew him. After two hours of dragging around what seemed, even to me, to the the most sordid places, I was ready to return to the hotel. Mr Perrington, a bulky man who sweated, was almost breathless as we mounted some steps at Montmartre to visit a cabaret which he described as the most terrible in all of Paris.

He was a good judge. Even I sat there blinking at the depravity on the stage. My own sexual adventures, not excluding the exotic business near Bordeaux, were all light and purity compared with the performance displayed there that night. In any event, I do not approve of animals being involved in such matters, especially dumb sheep. As Mr Perrington became more annoyed so he seemed to swell with sweat. It oozed from every pore and he became more enraged as the acts went on. Then, not being able to stand it a moment longer, and despite my attempts to restrain him, he suddenly leapt to his feet and charged like a wet hippo down the aisle towards the stage shouting God's vengeance. He scattered the entire show, men, girls, sheep and everything else. One of the monkeys ran up the curtains. It was an amazing thing to see and I sat shaking but transfixed. Mr Perrington then flung himself on his knees and began to pray loudly for God's forgiveness for these people. The curious thing was that nobody did anything about him. Not immediately anyway. He was allowed to kneel there praying like fury, much to the obvious enjoyment of the cast of the orgy, who now stood back and watched (one naked girl cuddling the monkey and the other sitting astride the puzzled sheep) while the audience shouted and cat-called with huge gusto.

I stood up. 'Mr Perrington!' I called. Then, hardly knowing what to say, 'Mr Perrington. I think it's time we left!'

The people understood and there was tremendous applause from both the stage and the audience. I felt like Sarah Bernhardt. 'Mr Perrington,' I shouted again. 'Please.'

That was it. The whole show began a slow handclap and changed 'Mr Perrington . . . pleeeeese . . . Mr Perrington, pleeese.' I felt myself go scarlet in the dark. There was nothing for it. Shakily I stood and went, like some schoolteacher trying to instil discipline, down the aisle through the middle of the audience, jumped on to the stage and grasped hold of Mr Perrington who was still on his knees praying like fury. My appearance brought howls and wolf whistles from the people, mostly, but by no means all, men. The naked cast began to applaud and I looked about me embarrassed, but then began to feel rather thrilled by it all.

A beautiful bare black man came across the stage and put his arms around me, and a girl, the one with the sheep, came and kissed me on the cheek. The sheep put its nose up my skirt. Then there was a great hollow howl, Mr Perrington, who had seen the attention drift away from him, looked up with reddened eyes. The cast, after further embracing me, unceremoniously picked him up, took him to the side entrance and dumped him in the alley. When I hurried to him after several more naked hugs and kisses from the performers, he was sitting on the cobbles with his knee showing through a split in his trousers, very much like a large defeated boy. Without a word he got up and walked into the main street, where we took a taxi back to the hotel. All the way he was hushed, his eyes fixed straight ahead, but when we reached the hotel he took me by the elbow and said plaintively: 'I would be grateful, Miss, if no mention of this reached Mr Sheridan.' He paused and said secretly: 'I don't want word of my crusade to get around.'

The death of Mr Sheridan's young wife (his second) in the flour hopper (she had tumbled in and been whirled around and around in hundreds of tons of flour – she drowned in it before they could rescue her) had, it seemed, ruined the poor man's life. He sold the mill right away, retreated into his own thoughts, and would never again have any bread, biscuits, cakes or anything made with flour in his house.

He had apparently adored her. But she had been less popular with the other members of the household. Once at L'Horizon, in the kitchen, I asked Mr Perrington about the tragedy and he recounted it with smug enjoyment.

Fascinated I asked: 'How did she look when they got her out of the flour hopper?'

'White,' he replied with brief relish. 'Very white.'

The house was well named for it was set in the pines and hills above Nice, on the road to Grasse, looking over the random distant roofs of the city and on to the long blue sea. It had cool balconies and bougainvillaea lolling from the walls. It reminded me in that way of the terrace of Amantine and Aurore on the other coast of France. Mr Sheridan was, of course, very rich, and there were many beautiful things in the house. But he took little pleasure in any of them now that his wife was gone.

If I had thought at the outset that I had been engaged as a possible bed companion (and I *had* thought that) then I was in error. Never once did Mr Sheridan touch me or say anything untoward to me. He was kind but in an almost absent way. Sometimes however, I saw him glancing in my direction as if he felt guilty and, catching my eye one day when this happened, he looked quite crestfallen and felt he had to explain. 'When you move about the house, Nell, I sometimes catch a glimpse of my Giselle.' I felt very sorry for him.

But his children, the children of his first wife whom he had divorced, had apparently got over any effect of their stepmother's death. I thought perhaps she had been one of those people who can be intimately concerned with only one other person. For the children, once she had gone she had gone.

Sirie was slight and pretty in a wan way (strangely pale for a girl who lived much of her life within reach of the sun). Her black eyes never looked immediately to you, they wandered, almost floated upwards. They were full and lovely but they told you nothing. She was quiet, inward, given to reading filmstar magazines and listening idly to Chinese music. She was still at school and went silently every day dressed in a plain blue dress, driven by Perrington in the Citroen, her expression the same when she left in the morning as it was when she returned in the afternoon.

Anton, the younger son, was a year older and in many ways like his sister although he spent more time away from the house, driving a huge and dangerous motor cycle around the mountain roads. Before the death of his stepmother, his father had forbidden these journeys, but once she was dead he never bothered again.

My duties at L'Horizon could almost be defined as simply 'being there'. It appeared that I had been engaged not to perform tasks, or even take responsibilities, but simply to take the place left by the floury departure of Giselle. It was as if I were required to walk about, to occupy a chair, to complete the landscape of that house.

And yet I could have been in no way a replacement for the late Mrs Sheridan as far as her mourning husband was concerned. He made no demands on me except an occasional smile. I had seen pictures of Giselle and she had been an undoubtedly lovely woman, but with a sharp look in the very corners of the eyes, the sort of sharpness many French women have, as though they are keeping some clever secret. It was the look I had seen in the eyes of Amantine.

The children required me even less than their father. They were like a small secret society, spending much silent time in each other's company, sitting in the fine room or out under the trees on the sloping grass of the cool garden. Then, without a word, almost as if some signal had passed between them, they would rise and go their separate ways, she to her room to play her Chinese music and he to his great big red motor bike. When I saw them in the green garden, sometimes they reminded me of a pair of birds, like flamingoes.

I would do what I could around the house. There was a complete cast of servants and there was little left for me but to straighten a cushion or tend the potted plants on the terrace. After a few weeks in such a sunny, luxurious place I began to wonder what on earth I was doing there. I began to lounge about like the others, like some sun-tanned ghost, padding about the marble floors, cool and half-naked, while the silences of the place piled one on top of each other. I would sleep for an hour in the afternoon and then perhaps walk down to the town or the beach. I loved the shops, the Promenade des Anglais, the flowered squares and arcades of the town. The beach was always strewn with people like the dead after a battle. After a while, however, like the sea it became boring, eternally unaltered, lolling in the sun. It was a different kettle of fish to the cold but lively Channel I had always known. One night there was a storm that had been waiting in the mountains. It flew along the Riviera coast, flooding the streets and stirring up the sea. Early in the morning I ran down to see the waves banging on the shingle.

But the storm rode off and the coast was left as before, golden, hot and the same day after day. I sat in the shade of the terrace balcony, giant geraniums planted in pots on the verandah above, trailing down to give me shade. I drank a glass of dry, cold wine and wondered why I was so vacant and unhappy.

The gate of L'Horizon was at the foot of the garden with a long climbing drive right up to the house. It had two stone columns, flaking and covered with creeper, topped by a pair of ornamental pineapples. One morning, the sound of a show-off sports car came down the curling road from the hills, barking and breaking, and then it choked back as it ran along the road at the other side of the garden wall before swirling into the drive. It was a handsome green Alfa Romeo. It snorted and paused like a horse and then the driver turned it up the drive towards the house. I was sitting idly in the shadows, wearing a light wrap over my swimsuit.

I knew it was Paul, the elder son who was expected that day on leave from the Ecole Militaire in Paris. 'You will hear him making a lot of noise as he comes through the mountains,' Perrington forecast with a sniff. And so it proved.

From my idle shadows I carefully watched him bring the car more sedately up the drive. He was in uniform, round faced, leaning out like some pilot of the First World War taxi-ing his plane home after a dog fight. Paul was another romancer.

He was a pale, overfed young man – strange for a soldier – who walked about the house for the next few days in white slacks and a white shirt. He looked like a French cricketer. His attitude when he arrived was to be seen in his swagger but the lethargy of that house soon put its hand on him, as it did on everyone else, and he became bored and restless. Once or twice I could see him looking at me but he kept his distance until the third day when I was sunbathing beneath my window. Then, as though finally making up his mind, he walked beneath the trees and the trailers and sat in an attitude on a canvas chair next to me. His leg hung across the arm. He was in his whites and he remained immaculate and military in a stagey way. He would have jumped to attention at the least shout.

'Ennui,' he sighed. 'This house should have been named. Ennui. It's a place of boredom. Don't you feel bored?'

'Yes,' I said honestly. 'But I'm paid to be here.'

'I could go and sit in a café in the town,' he shrugged. 'I know many people there, you know, I am very popular.'

This raised my eyebrows, but I did not know whether it was boasting or the way he framed his English. 'Why not go and sit in the café then?' I suggested.

'I can't be troubled,' he sighed. 'It's hot and I feel just nothing. It's this house. I don't come here on leave, I die.' His forearms had become brown in the sun and so had his face. In the Military School he worked as an instructor in some kind of army office.

'What about Sirie and Anton?' I asked and this brought a thoughtful smile.

'Ah, the secret pair,' he said. 'They are just for themselves. I do not come into their thoughts very much as you can see. And as for my father, he is busy with his sorrows.'

'Yes, I know. It is very sad.'

'Yes. She was very white when they pulled her out you know. Giselle, I mean, from the vat.' He sniffed as though smelling the flour again.

'So I believe.'

'It was terrible. Like a dream. In fact I have a dream about her. There is a gigantic cake and Giselle is in the middle of it. It is not very nice.'

'No, it can't be.'

'Is there a chance that you might like to come to my room?' he said quite suddenly but without changing his tone. 'I could show you my birds.'

He did not have the nerve to look at me when he made this proposition but just stared ahead as though he had seen something fascinating at the far end of the lawns. But a small encampment of perspiration had gathered on his forehead, and his lips had become dry and hard.

'You have some birds?' I said. 'I did not know. No one mentioned them.'

'They wouldn't,' he shrugged. 'To my family they are a joke. Will you come and see?'

I could see it was taking every fibre of courage he had, which for a trainee officer was not a lot, to get me to that room. The plump Napoleon-like attitude he struck, where he would stare out like a field marshal over-seeing a battle, and his roaring sports car were both fronts for a shy and fearful youth.

'All right Paul,' I said, standing up and putting a beach wrap around my swimsuit. He stared at my bosom as I stood and his eyes went quickly down the length of my body to my thighs. He saw I had caught this and he blushed. 'The birds are very interesting,' he mumbled. 'My grandfather left them to me.'

I was pondering this while we walked into the house and the coolness fell over us. We walked without speaking up the stairs and along the top corridor to his room.

'Who feeds your birds?' I asked. 'When you are away? Nobody has mentioned them to me.'

He smiled strangely. 'There is no need,' he said. 'You will see.'

At that he opened his bedroom door and I stopped in astonishment. From the ceiling was suspended a full-sized stuffed swan, wings outstretched, beak fixed nastily ajar. And all around on shelves and stands were owls and gulls and various birds of prey. A stuffed pelican squatted beside the bed and there were two penguins on each side of the adjoining bathroom door.

'Christ!' I said.

'They used to frighten me,' he shrugged, closing the door behind us. 'But not now of course. When I was a little boy.'

'How amazing,' was all I could say.

'My grandfather,' he sighed. He sat on the bed right alongside the pelican. 'He collected them. He went mad.'

'I don't wonder,' I said staring around. The eyes looking through the feathers stared back from every corner.

Paul looked around morosely. 'He loved birds. He went all over the world to shoot them. But he was rich,' he added. 'Very rich, and when he died he made it a part of his will that I should have these creatures in my room. I was only five. He thought they might amuse me.'

I reached up and gave a touch at the swan's backside feathers. It rocked to and fro above the bed, its great neck casting a long shadow. 'Nice hobby for a lad,' I said.

'It was terrible,' he said, rolling his eyes at the eyes around the room. 'These monsters. I would lie, just a little boy, in my bed in terror unable to take my eyes away from these bastards. They flapped through all my nightmares and when I woke they were still there. Especially this fucker.' He jabbed his finger at the swan's undercarriage, but pulled it away again as if he were afraid to do it some hurt. He smiled wanly at me. 'Can you think what that was like? The fear. Every night?'

He looked at me hollowly, the grown youth once more a little boy surrounded by feathered fear. I felt a surge of pity for him, and my own needs, both sexual and maternal, began welling up within me. I began to unfasten the bra of my swimsuit.

His haunted stare became one of disbelief, his eyes wider than the owls'. His boyish mouth fell open and his hands began to make ineffectual movements towards me, away from me, and aimlessly in the air about him. I stood very still, by the bed, while he was rooted six feet away. I took the bra away slowly and smiled while I was doing it. My heavy breasts fell an inch when I took away the support. He was staring at my nipples and I knew they were returning the stare.

He made no movement at all now, but remained solidified, as if he were fearful that anything he did would shatter the moment. I wriggled out of the bottom half of the swimsuit and sat sedately on the bed. 'Come over here,' I invited. 'To me.'

He stumbled forward and fell on his knees in front of me, dropping his head into the cleft of my bosom and making a wet sort of moaning. I pushed him back firmly and unbuttoned his shirt. He scrambled out of the rest of his garments himself as if afraid I might vanish or change my mind. He had a body like a baby white elephant. He was pale and flabby but with an endearing innocence and eagerness. I lay back easily on the bed and invited him to me. He came clumsily to me and lay on top of me with the sigh of a boy who had reached the end of a long sorrowful journey.

I had to restrain him all the time we were making love. He would have run off like a stampede if I had not held him and coaxed him and whispered that everything was all right, that he had nothing to fear. Afterwards he lay against me weeping quietly.

'I thought that soldiers never cried,' I said tenderly. I was grateful to him too.

'Soldier,' he sniffed sarcastically. 'I'm no soldier. Just a fat clerk instructor in an army office. Until today I wondered if I was even a man. The only women I have known have not been for love. They have been the loose women of Paris. That sort, Nelly. Loose women.'

I was tempted to tell him that his luck had not changed. I patted him sympathetically. 'We cannot always choose our lovers, darling,' I said.

He lay completely still for some time. We cooled together. Then he did the most extraordinary thing. Slowly he levered himself away from me, a look of dawning wonder on his podgy face. When he was upright he threw his arms above him and emitted a whoop like a Red Indian.

Jumping from the bed he cried: 'I'm a man! I'm a real man!' and rushing about the room began throwing the owls everywhere.

I lay transfixed as he picked up the stupefied stuffed birds and hurled them across the room. They collided with walls and with each other, heads fell off, eyes rolled out, and there were feathers and frowsty stuffing flying all around.

'I'm free! I'm free!' he howled, capering about. 'Fucking oiseau!' He picked up the pelican from the beside and hurled it across the room, then he banged the pair of penguins together and threw them likewise. Then the swan. He loved that moment. His swinging arms sent the poor elongated thing see-sawing wildly above the bed. I lay there naked, backing away, hardly able to credit my eyes. The swan swung and then swung again. Then it began to break up like an aeroplane disintegrating in flight. I could almost imagine it squawk a final squawk.

Now the room was raining feathers and foul old stuffing. I removed a few bits of swan from my torso and, replacing my swimsuit, stood up and moved towards the door. Paul was standing, a nightmare figure, pale and naked in the middle of all this mayhem. He stopped and turned as I went. His light of triumph dimmed. Anxiety crammed his face. 'Nell,' he said. 'You leave – do you think I'm crazy?'

'No,' I replied. 'Just getting your own back. I'll go and get a dustpan and brush.'

In the evening, dinner being the only time when the entire family met together, Paul, a new smiling Paul, relaxed and assured, carried the conversation through what was generally an uncomfortable, quiet hour. The father was usually enclosed in his own thoughts and would only emerge to make an apologetic smile around the table and ask some slight question and then return to his own deep world. Sirie and Anton rarely spoke either, although it was never hostile, just enveloping. It seemed impossible for them to find a way out of the silence. We ate like monks.

Paul's transformation livened up the whole table. Everyone talked and smiled. Sirie and Anton exchanged glances and then smiled knowingly at each other, at their brother and at me. It was the best evening I had spent at the house and after a while I began to tell them something of my early life. As I told some of the things that had happened to me, a deep attention fell over the family. I only repeated the adventures that were repeatable but they kept their faces to me and even seemed to hold their breath as I told them about the village and my mother and the German bomb and all the things that followed, as though I was telling them of life in a country of which they had never heard.

No one laughed, even when I told them how we had ambushed Mr Fagence, the terrible man at the Bristol orphanage, before Davie and I ran away, or even when I described how the little boat had sunk below us in the river. I must have gone on with the story for a long time because the night wind began to come in through the french windows and stir about the room. Never before had I told the whole length of my adventure (when I described the shipwreck and the floating coffin, the girl's eyes widened like lamps in the dimming room) and I became very interested with it myself, as though seeing it from a distance for the first time.

When I had done, it had become dim in the room and both Sirie and Anton had tears running down their young cheeks. I began to feel quite pleased with myself.

When the evening was finished Mr Sheridan kissed me on the cheek and so did the two children (I think of them, or did then, as children because of their simplicity and sombreness). Paul and I sat in the subdued evening on the terrace and drank pastis, the drink from Marseilles. I had never tasted it before and even now I can sense vividly the peppermint feel of it and the taste of night air. Paul was attentive and hardly able to take his eyes from me. When we had finished our drinks we walked out to the front of the house to look over the dropping land to the brilliant lights of Nice and the glowing sea, to the moving headlights of the cars on the Corniche, and an aeroplane coming into land at the airport by the shore.

The romantic sights and sensations of the night were all around us, engulfing us and stretching far out to the horizon. We closed against each other and kissed with deep passion.

I took my arms from around him, rested my thick hair against his cheekbone, and reaching down undid his fly. It was a zip, only then coming into fashion, but so much easier than the fumbling buttons of old. They played havoc with a girl's fingernails. I felt his whole frame come to attention as I fumbled into the cave at the front of this trousers.

We went a few paces from the terrace, away from the diffuse lights of the house. The hard dry grass led in a slope down to an arbour where there was a large hammock, lying like a docked boat. We sat on that, romantically, like some couple from a chocolate box or birthday card. Then we eased ourselves back on the hammock and it creaked as if we had woken it up. It was amazing but within hours he had become a different man. He even looked different, firmer, stronger, the face more masculine, the eyes definite. He kissed me with passion and I returned the kiss. It was time for confessions.

'There is something I must tell you, Nell,' he said thoughtfully. 'It has been with me for what seems like a long time. I must tell someone of it. It is about Giselle.'

Giselle again. Self-raising from the flour. 'Yes, Paul,' I said. 'What about her?'

'She did not fall into the flour hopper. I pushed her.'

I must have become very good at surprises, having had a lot of practice, for I did not stiffen or make a sound. Instead I made myself relax even more against him. 'Did you hear me, Nelly? I pushed her.'

'That's what I thought you said,' I replied. 'Why did you do it?'

He held on to me. 'She was a monster,' he whispered. 'An evil spirit. She made us all cry in our different ways. The children hated her. My father she treated like an animal. And then she came to me one night, in the room with the birds, and she seduced me and tormented me, my own stepmother. Then she humiliated me so long and in so many evil ways that I could stand it no longer. We were all standing together looking at the mill and the flour swirled around and I gave her a little push. There was only a short rail and over she went. She was drowned in the flour. I am a murderer, Nelly.'

Thinking of it now I am astonished at my own calmness. My youth had taught me much. I turned his face to me. He was crying. I kissed the wet cheeks and then the mouth and felt for him below. 'It does not matter, Paul,' I murmured. 'I won't tell.'

CHAPTER THIRTEEN

When Paul had returned to Paris I was left with his guilty secret and my own loneliness. I did not love him but we had helped each other and I missed our hours together. Now around the house and in the town I felt as tight as a bomb. The weather became hotter, a haze shimmering through the mountains and the sun glaring along the coast. One afternoon, sitting in the shade of the garden, I saw Anton come in on his big, red motor cycle, and I began to study him carefully.

In all my life I had never set out to seduce any man or boy. It was always they that came towards me. Lying there with a lime juice in the shade of the hanging geraniums and the bougainvillaea, I thought about the possibilities of Anton, but curiously, at a loss as to how to go about it.

He walked up the lawn towards me, such a handsome boy, his red shirt open almost to the waist, his crash hat held below his arm like the helmet of a knight. He smiled from about fifteen yards away and said: 'Beautiful.' But I could not tell whether he meant me, Nell Luscombe, the day, the scenery or his roaring ride in the hills.

'I could hear you, Anton,' I smiled. 'I could hear you riding around the mountains.'

'From this place?' he seemed genuinely surprised and pleased. 'I was so far away for most of the time.'

'I know,' I nodded, sipping the lime. 'But the echoes came through the valleys and I could here the roaring from here. I knew it was you Anton. Nobody rides a motor cycle like you.'

It was a bit of bare-faced flattery to a mere boy, but he smiled as though wise enough to detect it. He walked the two or three paces left towards me, and said: 'You will be missing my brother Paul, Nellee.' Then he leaned forward, very calmly, and kissed me on the cheek. His lips were dry and young. I felt a shock of real delight go through me. But before I could look into his eyes he had straightened up and sauntered off towards the house. The sound of Chinese music was coming from Sirie's window.

Now, Nell Luscombe, I said to myself. You are a young woman, and a woman who has felt a good many beds on her bottom. Anton is sixteen and although he is a grown lad (and how beautifully grown!) it would be very wrong of you to take advantage of his youth and inexperience, even though the weather is so hot and you are so tight and horny, and the boy walks about so enticingly and sleeps his boy's sleep only yards from your door. There is no excuse. It is taking advantage of the young and it must be resisted. If at all possible.

I lay on my bed that night, the dark hours seeming even hotter than those of the day. I was naked with the crumpled top sheet drawn up between my legs. There were sounds coming from across the garden, creatures, and the midnight noises of Nice mumbling up to the open windows. My breasts were hard as marble and faintly luminous. From my pillow, I only had to squint down to see their outlines like the roof of some eastern temple with the nipples like oriental points. A bead of sweat wriggled down my stomach, my thighs and my private valley felt very heated and damp, my very skin seemed to throb. All I could think of was that boy lying, doubtless cool and sleeping, along the corridor. Restlessly I rose from the bed and went naked to the window. Why was I like this? Why could some women be born and live as wives or farm maids or office workers or assistants in a shop, like my own satisfied sister. Why could they go so calmly through their lives, unashamed, untormented, content? Why was it that I, a simple West Country girl should want so many desirable, undesirable things? I looked up at the stars that night, my stomach throbbing, my face damp, and wondered why God allowed such emotions. But the sky (or God if that is his face) just looked blankly back at me. It was no help. After calling on conscience, logic, religion, morality and all the others, I could only come to the conclusion that I was born randy.

Even the garden seemed ill-at-ease. I stepped onto the confined balcony outside my window and, as though I had trodden on a secret switch, a light came on and glowed behind the lace curtains of the window opposite, across the narrow paved courtyard. Anton's window.

I stiffened with excitement, standing naked as a statue but in the shadow. My blood began to rumble in my veins. There was a movement behind the curtains. I had my hands against the back of a small cane chair on the balcony and they felt wet. Dark air pressed against me.

Then, oh God I still thrill as I remember it now all these years later, the pale curtains of his room moved and Anton, naked as I was, stepped out onto the little balcony. Then the curtain moved again – and the lovely young Sirie, nude and slender, came out and stood beside him. What a moment! I remained and looked across at them and they looked at me. No words were said. I could have screamed. These things never happen in cold countries.

The two children, and it is impossible for me to think of them otherwise, stood like junior gods, slightly apart from each other. I could see the deep hair on his loins, and her little breasts like two dark eyes. Their hands moved across the space between them and joined. But neither their faces nor their bodies moved. The train of sweat trickled down my leg. 'Bit on the warm side tonight,' I called.

There was no reply (really I suppose it would be difficult to make one to an observation like that) and we continued to stand and gaze across at each other. A car went by beyond the garden wall on its way over the mountains. The top circle of its headlights curled over the wall. 'Please,' called Anton softly. 'You must visit us.'

'When?' I whispered nervously.

'This moment,' said Sirie. I thought I saw the shade of her smile.

'I will,' I said. 'I'll come now.'

I could hardly keep my fingers still as I pulled on my robe. I folded the silk around me, feeling it slide and roll against my skin. Quickly, and wondering why, I arranged my hair, opened the door and went like a ghost in a hurry along the shadows of the corridor. I tapped, merely touched Anton's door and pushed it open. All the doors in that house opened easily. I stepped in.

What can I say about the scene the met me when I entered the room? It was amazing, astounding me. It was dim and soundless, the only movement being the fidgeting of the lace curtain at the window. But at the far end, lit up like a religious scene, was a bed with an oval back and sitting up in that, meekly and beautifully, were the boy and girl, Sirie and Anton.

They were both unclothed to the waist, the sheet negligently lying over their thighs. The boy, manly and serious with a tuft of hair in the middle of his brown chest, his expression sober. The girl, slender as a deer, with the amber light lying sweetly over her slim torso and the dozy little breasts. She had that silent, puzzling smile as if she knew everything in the world but was not inclined to tell. Around each neck was a plain gold chain. They were side by side in bed, their shoulders touching. 'What an interesting bed,' I said throatily as I walked towards them.

They had been sleeping together since early childhood. When they were seven, they said, they were separated but on the first night Sirie got up from her bed and went immediately back to her brother. At ten they were told sternly that they must keep to their separate rooms, but they disobeyed and returned to the familiar reassurance of each other's bodies as soon as they could. When their father, who knew nothing of all this – or if he did he had taken no heed – married Giselle they had kept to their own rooms, but crept in to each other for an hour or two's company in the early hours. When she had died they had gone back to sleeping with each other again.

This was all explained in the most amusing and matter-of-fact way while I sat on their bed, like some aunt, and they sat upright projecting from the sheet, the damp light on their lovely bodies. My passion had, strangely, cooled, as if it were ashamed of its ambitions, and I was watching them and listening to them quite happily and with new and pleasant innocence.

'Nellee,' pleased Sirie. 'Tell us something more about your life's adventures.'

'Now?' I said.

'Ah, there is no better time. It is too hot to sleep,' said Sirie. 'And we love to hear people tell us stories, don't we Anton?'

'Yes we like that. You don't have to tell us the truth all the time. We do not mind if you make things from your imagination.'

'I'll tell you the truth,' I said. 'There is plenty of truth.'

Then, while those two naked beauties sat attentive as children, I told them of the days when I met the Commander and of the dirty lord who had put his hands up my dress when I was a servant at his breakfast table, and how I had taken revenge with the mousetrap. And the poor idiot son with his bean flicker.

At this they both broke into ripples of laughter and spontaneously leaned forward to kiss me. My hands went out to them and in leaning I touched his hard young chest and her small velvet breast.

When I had finished Anton said formally: 'We have something to tell you.'

'A secret,' confirmed Sirie.

'We have told no one but we must tell you,' he added. 'We have been waiting until Paul left us.' They glanced at each other as though uncertain who should speak. The girl nodded briefly at the boy and it was he who spoke.

'Nellee,' he said. 'You know that our stepmother Giselle is dead because she fell into the container of flour that goes round and around at the mill?'

I nodded dumbly. They knew about Paul then. 'She did not fall. She was pushed into the flour,' continued Anton.

'And *we* pushed her,' said Sirie smugly.

I felt my brain swim. 'You?' was all I could say. 'But Paul . . .'

'Hah! Paul told you it was him,' nodded Anton. 'I thought he would. It was not. He lies to protect us. We pushed her, Anton and Sirie.'

'But . . .'

'Because,' put in Sirie, 'she came into this, our room one night and came upon us like this together. She was very angry and said she would tell our father and we begged her not to. So she said she would punish us herself and she returned here the next night and used her golden hairbrush on our derrières, how do you say it?'

'Our arses,' put in Anton.

'Yes arses,' said Sirie.

Anton said: 'She made us ashamed and angry. And it hurt also. So the next day when we visited the mill we gave her a touch of our hands and, voilá! Into the flour she went.'

There was not a lot I could say. 'Of course I will not tell,' I promised. 'But Paul . . .'

'What he told you is not true,' said Anton firmly. 'He says it to make-believe he is romantic and tragic and, he believes, I suppose, to protect us. But we are safe. Nobody knows.'

Sirie smiled. 'When you have pushed your stepmother into a million kilos of flour,' she said logically, 'then it is something truly different is it not? It is no pleasure if you do not tell someone!'

They sat in bed, almost laughing at my expression. I was still sitting on the bed, and with that same spontaneous movement they so often showed, they turned back the sheet, moved a foot or so further apart and invited me into the middle.

It was all so logical, so amazingly innocent. I did not know how to respond. I glanced at each face and they were smiling confidently. So I climbed in, like a visiting cousin in a crowded house, and all three of us slid down naked beneath the sheet and slept.

It was still warm and dark when I felt the boy move against me. With an easy fish-like roll, he turned on me and with never a touch of exploration pushed his slim penis into me. The girl was snuggled into my other side, her breasts against my ribs, her mouth against my breast, and deeply asleep. Anton whispered as I woke and realized what he was about, 'Tomorrow I will take you on my motor cycle in the hills.'

Since my arrival at L'Horizon, Mr Sheridan had spent all those hours closed off in that room of his and I could not help but wonder during my listless days what he did or what he thought about in there. Then one morning he told me.

He was standing waiting, it seemed, in the corridor as I came in from the sun outside. 'It's you, Nell Luscombe,' he said, holding my hands.

'What is, Mr Sheridan?' I asked. He was staring at me, shaking his head, and coming into the gloom from the bright light I could not see him properly. 'It was you all the time.'

'Me, Mr Sheridan?' I continued. Had he found out about Sirie and Anton? Because of the light I was unsure whether it was a smile or a grimace coming towards me. It was a smile.

'Dante,' he said. 'Please call me Dante.'

'Yes of course, Dante.' That was encouraging anyway. 'What was me all the time, Dante?'

He took me by the arm and we walked into the cool house together. It seemed like a cave after the brassy sunshine outside. In the next few minutes he said more words to me than he had done in the whole time since our first interview in London. 'Come, Nell,' he smiled. 'I will show you my room.'

Another room! In this house there were always surprises in rooms. I walked with him, his hand still holding mine, wondering what I was to see this time. It turned out to be, for once, unremarkable. A solitary sort of room, a trifle stuffy, with a bedroom and bathroom adjoining it, with books and papers everywhere. The sort of room where a man spent a great deal of time alone.

The one remarkable piece of furniture was an enormous red velvet chair, high backed and wide-seated. 'That,' said Dante, seeing me looking at it, 'I call my thinking chair. I have been using it a great deal lately, Nell.'

He approached me familiarly, as though he had suddenly remembered why he had brought me to France in the first place. He was an attractive man, I suppose, with a good figure and the spreading of grey around the ears and temple which to so many young women brings unmentionable memories of their fathers. In my case, of course, it did not.

'For weeks, Nell,' he said, his hands on my elbows, 'I have been sitting here thinking of *someone*. Thinking, thinking. Making hopeless pictures of her. Never quite making them fit. I thought it was Giselle I was daydreaming about. I imagined her walking in English fields, along the beach in Rousillon, down a street in San Francisco. The backgrounds were all authentic. They fitted perfectly. But somehow the figure, the woman was wrong. And there was no face. I wondered where on earth the face had gone. Then, only last night I fitted another face to it. It was your face, Nell.'

I felt a flood of pity for him. Fitting faces to dreams here in this empty room. 'I'm glad you found me,' I said simply, as though I had been waiting for him all the time.

'May I kiss you?' he inquired seriously.

No one had ever asked me before. Quite often they expected a great deal more without asking. I was amazed and impressed at the politeness. 'Of course you can,' I laughed. 'I'm here.'

And he kissed me and as I returned that kiss, a whole nightmare began flashing in front of my imagination. I knew then the question he would ask. He would ask me to marry him. How could I marry a man when I had already been intimate with his sons? How?'

'Nell, let's sit in my chair,' he suggested. 'Will you?' I smiled and he sat in the huge red 'thinking chair', patted his knees and I sat on his lap. It felt enjoyable. Like a girl with a good father. 'You are a lovely young woman, Nell,' he said eventually. 'I am much older, but I have wealth and I can make you very comfortable and I would try to make you happy. If you will marry me?'

I put my fears aside quickly and decisively. 'Oh yes, Mr Sheridan . . . Dante,' I said. 'Please.'

You can hardly hesitate about an offer of that type, not when you've spent years as a sexual gypsy. Racing through my mind was the thought that somehow I would have to come to some arrangement with Sirie and Anton and, of course, Paul, but I felt sure they would understand. And there was the matter of Giselle and what I knew of her fate in the flour hopper.

He kissed me again, very lightly and decently, and we walked the length of the long, manly room to the bright window over the garden. Sirie was sitting in her usual ghostly way under the shade. She ruffled through the pages of a magazine but never paused to read anything or even look at a picture.

'Sirie is very bored, I'm afraid,' said Dante, putting his arm about my waist. Despite the weather he was wearing a jacket of some light, rough material and I liked the comforting touch of it around my bare midriff. 'They are strange children but I hope one day you will have something in common with them.'

'I'm sure I will,' I mumbled.

'I will not ask you to be mother to them,' he said. 'That is asking too much. And as for Paul . . .' He paused in a worried way as if he had suddenly thought about something concerning Paul. 'Well . . . he is not even younger than you,' he laughed quietly. 'He will not be able to call you "Mummy" will he!' I swallowed and joined the tail end of the laugh. Difficulties were already beginning to pile like hills on my horizon.

But immediately he reassured me. 'Sirie and Anton will be returning to Paris in a few weeks,' he said. 'I have arranged for them to start some new studies there. It is difficult to imagine what they will do for a living. Anton could be a motor bike mechanic I suppose, and Sirie would make a wonderful mistress for a rich man.' He made a noise of annoyance and I turned to see him blushing. 'What a thing for a father to say,' he tutted. 'What a thing.'

I was profoundly relieved to know that the two young people would not be in the house continuously. 'Dante,' I said. 'You are very sure aren't you? About marrying. It was *my* face you saw in your thoughts?'

He put his greying head against my cheek, very tiredly. 'It *was* you,' he said. 'You were very clear. And . . . Nell . . . I think there is something you should know about Giselle.'

'Oh now,' I thought. 'Not again.' I looked at him, trying to appear unknowing. 'What is that?' I asked.

'I pushed her into the hopper of flour at the mill,' he said simply. 'I loved her very much but she had hurt me so much that I took the opportunity to give her a nudge. The children were there, also Paul, but there were so many people on the gallery looking down that nobody saw me do it. She has been haunting me, of course, but I can conquer her. I feel it is something I have to tell you. You are marrying a man who has done his wife in.' I pulled back, but not forcefully, from his arm and regarded him with amazement.

'You killed Giselle?' I whispered. '*You* did it?'

'Yes. Does it worry you?'

By this time it was not so much worrying as intriguing. Why should they all want the credit for pushing her in the flour?

'I loved her overwhelmingly,' he said hopelessly. 'But she taunted me and tortured me, and the night before she even boasted that she had committed adultery with Paul, my own son. It was a lie, of course. A fabrication to injure me. I could not allow that sort of thing to be said. So

I gave her a jog. When they managed to get her out she looked very unpleasant. All white.'

'So I believe,' I answered stupidly, adding: 'Perrington told me.'

'Ah Perrington,' he nodded. 'Not always the silent chauffeur he appears to be.'

'Servants generally aren't,' I said, slipping very easily into the voice of the lady-of-the-house.

'A good chap,' he said, now apparently having completely disposed of his confession concerning Giselle. 'But sometimes strange. Do you know Nell, I discovered quite by chance that he goes on a sort of rampage in the dens of vice in Paris? He does it regularly, making out he's some kind of religious fanatic, trying to save everybody from sin.'

'No!' I managed to exclaim. 'Not our Perrington!'

'Our Perrington,' he said, accepting that I now owned Perrington too. 'It's apparently the way he gets his thrills. It's become so regular that half the erotic cabarets in Paris have come to know him, welcome him almost. People follow him from one cabaret to another, he is regarded as part of the entertainment.

I sighed. 'Well as long as he doesn't start that sort of thing in Nice.'

'Indeed, you're right, darling,' he agreed like a husband. 'He's a good chauffeur, and it's quite fun really, I suppose, to have a *tiny* bit of scandal in the house. It stops life becoming dull!'

It would be difficult to imagine two weddings further apart in style than my first and my second. Once more, of course, I married in white, but this time I knew the groom would not spend our first night painting the walls of the reception hall. In the event he spent it searching for the bride.

The ceremony at the large church of St Phillipe in Monte Carlo and the reception at the Hôtel de Paris were very costly, lavish and lovely, with hundreds of guests. For a family that kept so much to themselves, the Sheridans seemed to know an enormous number of people, who came in their cars and their finery.

In the church the atmosphere was thick and holy with incense clouding everywhere. Not wishing to be disqualified on a technicality, I had assured Dante that I was a Roman Catholic. The priest towered over us like some archangel. When the organ sounded and the choir sang it was so beautiful I would not have been surprised if my groom had started to rise to the ceiling.

And for this girl, who had been pulled by fishermen and wrecked by sailors, walking down the aisle, radiant in the reflections of the stained glass windows, through a large, rich, congregation, to the arm of my distinguished husband, it was a triumph.

My conversion to Roman Catholicism being so sudden it left some gaps in my knowledge as to what was going on in the church, but I joined in and chanted the tunes bravely with the rest, although the words I sang were 'Tom Pearce, Tom Pearce, lend me your grey mare.'

Incense drifted up my nose and the rosy light shone upon me. In the front pew, with all the family guests, sat the angelic pair, Sirie and Anton, and the upright and uniformed Paul, singing soberly and all three kissing me with perfect propriety after the ceremony.

There were three hundred guests at the reception, and sitting proudly next to Dante, my husband, a champagne glass hinged on my lip, and surveying the array of bobbing heads and the servants carving through the crowds, it came to me that the cost of this one extravagant day was probably more than the cost of my entire previous life put together.

But I was in no mood to think nostalgically of poorer days, although when a group of singers took the stage in front of the orchestra and sang French part-songs in harmony, my mind did return for a moment to that first wedding reception of mine, when Wild Mickey and some of poor George's painting pals sang 'Drink To Me Only'. It was a different world.

Then, as has been usual throughout this eventful existence of mine, something happened. Among the guests I had noticed, I could not help but notice, a funny little fellow with ill-fitting morning dress, moving in and out of the various tables. He looked like a street violinist, bald, small, saggy. Or a pickpocket, for he had a furtive way about him. I found my eye attracted towards him every time he appeared in view. He seemed to be alone, to know no one, but to be cruising around on some errand, a glass of champagne moving just in front of his nose. There was something ominously familiar about that stoop, about that walk.

Then, when the chanson group – two ladies in long white dresses and two men in brown tailed suits – were singing in fine French style, the little soiled man suddenly mounted the dais at their side. Then, relieved, I thought that he must be a musician or a vocalist perhaps, or a comedian. But the singers were at once upset by his presence, like a clutch of hens joined by a fox. They fidgeted and moved over, trying to keep their harmony and distance. Some guests began to snigger and then some to laugh outright and a cold, cold hand from years ago crept across my heart. The clown in the baggy trousers suddenly darted to the front of the singers, scattering them, and, throwing his arms wide, burst like a hideous off-key bird into: 'There's an old Mill by the Stream, Nellie Dean.'

'Oh God,' I thought. 'My fucking father!'

At the awful moment of realization, three bystanders approached and carried him still upright but bodily away from the dais and out of the room, his baggy legs running protestingly in mid-air as he went.

Over the heads of the amused people I could hear the cackling Devon voice shouting: 'She be *my* girl! My lovely daughter. Nell . . . ie!' I seemed to smell the cider reeking across the room, a memory that made me catch my breath, and for a strange moment saw my little home in Upcoombe and my childhood.

'Dante,' I whispered to my husband, 'I must just leave you for a moment dear. I'll be back very shortly.' He smiled his gentlemanly smile and I kissed his cheek. I got up for the moment, aware of my trembling, and the puzzled guests parted to let me through. I saw nothing but blurred faces. I ran the last three yards out of the door and saw my father still held by the three men who were discussing what to do with him.

Only one was needed to restrain him. The man had pinned him against the wall with one hand held on his chest, like a specimen moth. My father's face was yellow, his eyes bulged, his mouth dribbled.

'Please, please,' I asked, going towards them. 'Let him free. I . . . know him.' The man who held him let go obediently and my father dropped from the wall to the floor. His terrible iodine face turned to me and smiled, not with those jagged teeth of old but with a frightening set of new dentures that somehow seemed bigger than his mouth. 'Nelly my little maid,' he howled, staggering towards me.

For a moment I stood transfixed, helpless. Then (how could a daughter not?) I stumbled towards him and cried as I embraced his skeleton body.

'Oh Nelly,' he blubbered convincingly, 'I've been looking everywhere for you, my darling girl.'

'Dad,' I trembled. 'Dad . . .' I was crying now, wiping my eyes with the lace sleeve of my bridal dress. 'I've been and got married today.'

'I can bloody see that,' he said, immediately sour. 'And you didn't ask your old dad to give you away or even to come and have a drink with you.'

Something got caught in my throat and I felt my face redden. 'How could I?' I sobbed angrily. 'When you buggered off all those years ago? I haven't set eyes on you since!'

'Don't you shout at me my girl,' he snarled. 'You'm still my daughter!'

People began to look out of the main room and those passing in the foyer stopped to stare. The three men who had removed my father from the dais hovered around, obviously eager to remove him still further. Something had to be done, the bride at a society wedding could hardly be seen brawling with a derelict man.

My father, onto my indecision like a ferret, caught my hand: 'Come on outside a minute Nell. Then I'll go away. God's honour.'

Knowing him, I should have learned. But, just to save the embarrassment of that moment, and with only a quick guilty look about me, I followed him out of the door. Blood is thicker than champagne.

Innocent, bewildered, I followed him out to the steps of the hotel. 'I've got a car,' he said urgently, pulling me. 'Come on Nelly.'

A car! My senses were so fuddled I allowed myself to be dragged down the steps and a moment later the door of a big car at the kerb opened and I was flung into the back between two Negroes. My father, squeaking with triumph, jumped in beside the driver and we shot off at such a rate that I was thrown back between the black men. Stiff with terror, my white wedding dress up around my waist, I was fixed there, trying to scream but making no sound.

Eventually that stoatish face turned from the front seat and the layers of teeth smiled in the gloom. 'I read in the papers at home about you, Nell. "Society Wedding of Orphan Girl" it said. Read it with my own eyes. And bloody offended I was, as you can believe. After all you *do* have a father. So I decided to come here to see you on your happy day.'

'Where are we going?' I managed to demand. If the Negroes had not been holding hands across my front, I would have scratched his face. 'You'll be in prison for this! My husband . . .'

'Now stop it my girl,' he threatened. 'Just remember who it is you'm speaking to.' This piece of effrontery left me speechless. 'I came down here specially,' he said. 'Foreign parts. But I seem to have got into bad company, Nelly. I owe a lot of money for cards, and I told these gents that you'll be able to pay. You will won't you Nell? For your old dad?'

I don't suppose another woman in the entire world has ever spent another night like that. Not only was my distracted husband without me – and had the Riviera police and even the small Monte Carlo Army searching the towns and villages of the coast – but I danced on a table, clad only in my white bridal stockings and a suspender belt and I slept with a large hairy Corsican. Some women, I suppose, are simply born bad.

Certainly they had to give me some wild, doped, drink to make me do all the things I did, but I cannot help feeling that a *decent* woman would never have performed like that whatever she had been forced to take.

Inside some of us seems to be a casket of wickedness and it only needs to be unlocked for our lowest natures to take over. Looking back over the years of sin and regret I can only console myself with the thought that I am what I am. A trollop. My father and the other men took me to a sort of thieves' kitchen, a room behind a bar in the narrow streets of Nice. It was crowded with louts and whores and they were obviously waiting for me because I staggered through the door, encouraged by a sharp push from my father, and stood there in my wedding gown in the thick smoke, a huge approving roar went up from the bottle-crammed tables. What a sight I must have looked, crumpled white lace, and my flowered head-dress hung over my ear. I stood looking down on the riff-raff, furious but fearful. 'I'd like you to meet my friends,' my father said with his terrible smile.

What they gave me to drink I can only guess. At first I would not touch it, but a whole gang of them, not roughly, quite goodnaturedly in fact, poured some down my throat and it was easy for them after that.

I don't know how much the sneaky bastard had lost at cards (the suggestion that he should repay his debt with me had been made by him and planned after the people who ran this den had studied my picture in *Nice Matin*), but whatever it was I more than repaid the score that night.

There is not much of it I can remember, which is as well, but according to appreciative eye-witnesses, I was completely at home and entered into the spirit of the foul den and its low customers. The second and third drinks of whatever potion they were giving me did not seem so difficult to accept at the first and then I vaguely recall Spanish music twanging from somewhere and me mounting the large central table in my long lovely wedding dress. It was the most spectacular strip-tease ever seen in those parts, if only for the fact that everyone knew the costume was authentic. Off came my head flowers, off came the lace dress, off came the silk underclothes I had chosen so carefully for the delight of my husband, and eventually I danced brazenly in my satin shoes, my white wedding stockings and my suspender belt, and – God damn me – the veil I had worn so religiously in the church only hours before.

Like a nightmare I can still see the beaming criminal faces all about the edge of the table, the boards of the table itself, stretching out like a stage before me, the bouncing of my own bosom right under my nose, and I can still hear the rhythmic clapping, the randy shouts and my father's piping Devon voice over it all. 'That's my Nelly! You show them Nell! You show them!'

If I did nothing else I certainly *showed* them. To such an effect, apparently, that hot men were offering my father a fortune for the pleasure of the night with me. He was conducting this degrading auction while I was still banging the table with my heels (one of which I broke I recall, delicate shoes not being meant for Flamenco dancing). The owners of the place apparently moved in, however, and took the matter out of my father's hands and paid him a percentage from the highest bidder, the large and hairy Corsican. All this I heard next day from one of the whores who came by to see if I had survived – the Corsican apparently being a hard man to satisfy. She was weary but very pleased and said that my efforts had substantially increased her own earnings and those of her friends. My father, apparently, had gone off with his percentage, leaving his love for me and the promise that we would meet again someday. If he were in a condemned cell, I vowed to myself, then I would gladly go. Gladly.

I was in a cubicle bedroom. I had a vague memory that the Corsican had kept colliding with the confined walls. I sat on the edge of the bed, sore, sad, helpless, bedraggled, on what should have been the first wonderful morning of my life with Dante Sheridan, whom I had promised to cherish and love and be faithful to only the previous morning. I was naked. My poor stockings and the pretty belt were hanging over a light bracket just outside the door. I saw them as soon as I looked into the desolate room. Tables and chairs were thrown and scattered all over the place and an old woman was beginning to mop the floor. As I watched she picked up something from beneath a table, examined it disdainfully and threw it away. It landed on a pile of bottles in the corner. It was my expensive and beautiful wedding gown. There was a towel in my cubicle – it was the sort of place that short-time prostitutes use – and I wrapped it as best I could about my body, and, weeping now, I stumbled across the room to where she had thrown my dress. I picked it up. It had more holes in it than any lace dress ever had. It was splashed with wine and smeared with dirt. But it was all I had. With the mopping-up lady watching intently, I put it on, feeling the sad shame of what I had done, wishing my father dead and me dead also, but less painfully.

Head down, I walked out of that wretched place, not knowing where I was going. I could never go back to L'Horizon now, I would not let Dante suffer for what I was like. For what my family was like. I would have to go out again on my poor travels. I could never go home.

As it happened I did not have to travel far. I walked through the blank, sunless alleys, until I reached a small square. There was a café and I sat, huddled at a table, my dress hanging down like a soiled rag. The waiter arrived and with that blankness cultivated by all waiters in that part of the world, he took my order for coffee without a lift of the eyebrow at my wretched condition. I had no money. But it did not matter. Just as I was about to drink it I felt a hand on my shoulder and an English voice said: 'Make it another coffee, will you?'

Slowly I looked up and there, smooth and suave and handsome in the Riviera morning sun, was my Davie. My Davie from long, long ago.

CHAPTER FOURTEEN

Davie had lived in Marseilles and at other places along the coast while he pursued his career of burglar, bank robber and general thief. Those years before, when we were on our childish journey through the West Country after running from the institution at Bristol, I had often watched him and thought to myself that he was bound to be an exceptional person when he grew up. I remember, on those nights when we were little fugitives, when we were resting in some place, how I would ask him what he wanted to be when he was a man and he would sit and seriously consider it with his confident attitude, giving the impression that he would be offered all the most wonderful positions in the world and would merely have to thumb through them and take his pick.

'Nell,' he used to say then, ''tis a difficult thing to make up my mind. I reckon all the places in the world have been discovered now so I don't see any use in me being a navigator. There's acting I suppose, on the films. Or I could be a famous sportsman.'

'I didn't know you could play sport, Davie,' I had said.

'Oh I could learn,' he replied. 'Any sport.'

'Or I could be a boss,' he went on. 'Like of factories, and have cars and cigars. I'd be a doctor, one of those surgeons with the masks on, but I can't abide blood, Nell. Can't abide it.'

As it turned out he did wear a mask to his work, even if it were in a bank rather than in the operating theatre. He had made his first bank raid before I met him again in Monte Carlo. It was in Antibes, and according to his own account had been executed with great audacity and cleverness, but with no luck. The haul only amounted to about two hundred francs, due to some incompetence by the cashier who handed it across. But as an artistic operation, he said, it was perfection.

'I realized Nell,' he said gravely when we were driving high above the sea on that first day we met again, 'it came to me like a flash from heaven, that there's no room for people like me in the world, the ordinary, legal world. It's all fixed against you. It doesn't matter how clever you are, there's your place – down there at the bottom – and that's where you have to be, so that's it. So I reckoned I would put my talent where they would make the most for me.'

I nodded. The breakneck rocky road soared above the patterns of the sea and rose up towards the silk blue sky. I was still in my torn and defaced wedding dress, but now the sun warmed me. I wondered how my husband Dante was getting on without me. I felt sad for him, but I looked at the grown-up profile of Davie, my childhood hero, sitting beside me and squeezed his arm because I knew that it was him I had loved all these years. Even though I had almost forgotten him.

'I think you're right, Davie,' I agreed. 'You could have done anything, you could.'

'Anything,' he agreed grimly. 'Anything.'

His voice now was a strange muddle of Devon, London and Marseilles French. He had been on the Mediterranean for two years, working for various small gangs to gain experience, he said, before branching out on his own. He told me he had been very successful and had stolen a lot of money, art treasures and other good things.

'Somebody in my position can't trust *anybody*, Nell,' he said, making the car screech. It was a rugged Renault, not very new but chosen for it's anonymity, he explained. 'When I've got to know you better again, then I'll tell you some of my secrets.'

His apartment just off the port quarter in Marseilles was suitably impressive, good light rooms and a view over the docked shipping and the quays, but far enough away not to have the hot, dusty noises that blew from there every day of the summer. The only thing amiss with it was that it seemed a shade feminine, the décor and the oddments and especially the main bedroom which had lace and chintz and smelled of perfume. In one closet I found a whole rack full of women's clothes.

'Well,' explained Davie carefully. 'I don't really *own* it, see, I'm renting it from a lady.'

'But she's left all her clothes and things,' I laughed uncertainly.

'Yes, well, as a matter of fact, she's away where she doesn't need all these things at the moment and she asked me if I'd mind keeping them.'

I went to the wardrobe and ran my fingers along the materials. They slid over my fingertips like water ripples. 'These are very nice,' I said. 'Very expensive. She must be rich.'

'Yes,' he nodded. 'Very rich.'

'Listen Davie,' I laughed. 'Don't be embarrassed, darling. I haven't seen you for years, why feel embarrassed about living with a woman here? I could hardly expect you to wait for me. I didn't wait for you. My God, I got married only yesterday.' Then I added anxiously, 'Perhaps you shouldn't have brought me here. Will she be back soon?'

'Not for five years,' he said, sitting on the bed and doggedly lighting a cigarette. 'She's in prison.'

'Oh dear, what happened?'

'She got herself caught,' he answered.

'Oh. So she let you have the flat while she's in there.'

I could see the old, small slice of shiftiness in his face. It was amazing to recognize it again after all these years.

'Well, if you really want to know, Nell,' he said. 'She doesn't actually *know* I'm living here. I just sort of moved in when she got put away. I had a key. But I reckoned she owed me a few favours. I mean, I set her up in the area. She had to clear out of Paris. So I'm keeping the place aired now, see?'

I could not help but laugh at him. Here was the half-apologetic half-defiant Davie I had just glimpsed in childhood. I moved towards him because he looked so juvenile in his sulk and touched him intimately for the first time in years. We had kissed outside the café where he had found me, but apart from my hand resting on his knee during the drive, there had been no contact between us.

'Are you alone now, Davie?' I asked slightly mocking. 'Don't nobody want you?'

For a moment I was afraid he was going to reincarnate one of his sudden childish outbursts of temper. It was still there, rotten within him. But he stemmed it and smiled cagily. 'I'm never alone Nell,' he said. 'Never. I've got thousands who know me down here, contacts, friends. That's how I knew where to find you. Eyes and ears everywhere. It's in the newspapers you know.' He sounded a trifle jealous then. 'Pictures, everything. Beautiful bride abducted and all that stuff. A photo of your husband crying into his hands. Very sad and touching I must say. He's got a lot of money hasn't he?'

'He's a good, nice man,' I said, looking straight at him.

'Why are you here then?' he asked craftily.

'Because I'm not sure I'm a good nice woman,' I replied still stiffly. 'I can't go back now. I don't belong with him.'

'And you think you belong with me?'

'I might. I started off with you. Where's the newspapers with my picture?'

'There's none here,' he said. 'You can see some later.' Then after a wait: 'Do you want to do it again?' In a way I thought it was more like an inquiry.

'Again?' I laughed. 'Remember the last time Davie? Us two? In that warehouse, the night the war was over.'

'Oh . . . Oh yes, I remember,' he said as if he had only just been able to. 'Only kids we were then.'

'Oh Davie.' I was smiling when I moved towards him but by the time I had reached his chest with my cheek I felt desolate.

I thought it was strange but he seemed uncertain, almost as if he were out of practice, or shy. I opened his shirt for him and rubbed his chest. He seemed a little surprised that I should know what to do.

I undid his trousers but he got out of the rest of his clothes himself, in the way of a small boy who does not like his mother to help him when he imagines he can manage alone. He grinned a little embarrassed at me. I could see he was not excited. 'Why don't you have a bath then, Nelly,' he said surprisingly, 'and get that old wedding dress off.'

I was naturally surprised at his fastidiousness. He had come a long way from the warehouse in Plymouth. 'Yes,' I said. 'I suppose I'd better, I feel scruffy.'

'It's there,' he said, pointing at the bathroom. 'While you're in there, I'll do my press-ups.'

Now I was blinking at every sentence. 'Press-ups,' I said wanly. He nodded encouragement, so I said: 'Yes, you'd better, Davie.' I went into the bathroom, full of perfumes and talc and enormous sponges, with a replica of the little boy statue from Brussels who provided the bathwater by peeing at an enormous rate and volume into the bath. I regarded myself in the full-length mirror. I looked like some Spanish countess ravaged by bandits. My face was grubby, my hair screwed into knots and bundles, and that poor, lovely white dress like some crumpled tablecloth in a teashop.

But when I had taken the gown away from my body and I was naked, I stood reassured before the glass. My legs curved and slender, my waist tight, my breasts full and ripe and my arms slim and fawn from the sun. I had grown well since I last saw Davie.

The bath was swirling with warm green-blue water, embroidered with bubbles. I turned off the manikin and stood in the drifting steam. I could hear Davie grunting in the other room. Although I had hardly put my foot into the comfortable water, I paused, then got out again and pushed the door. He was really doing his exercises, not press-ups, but standing on his head, nude, legs straight as flagpoles in the air, as slender as mine, his penis hanging long and limp over, pointing at his chin like a small pistol.

I applauded jokingly through the crack of the door. Then I called: 'Come in and wash my back, Davie.'

Moving towards the bath I stepped in and at the same time heard him drop his feet back to the ground. He padded towards the door and, quaintly, knocked.

'Come in,' I called from the suds. 'I'm only bare.'

He opened the door and, pausing, took in the sight of me in the luxurious bath. I was sitting up, the upper mounds of my bosom floating on the water line, skin slippery and shining. I could see he was staring, as though amazed that one person could have grown so much. I grinned at his expression and eased myself back into the water, so that my bosom became fully in sight, two hulls, keel up. The water ran in tides over the flats of my belly and gurgled down the gully between my legs as I eased myself further so that he could see more.

'How old are you, Nell?' he asked to my amusement.

'Four months older than you, remember,' I replied.

'You're a beautiful big girl,' he said inadequately. A sudden dream, a trance had come upon him as if he could not bring himself to make any action. He seemed to be searching for another compliment. 'You got lovely hair,' he said eventually. 'Masses of it.'

He stepped forward then in the steam, his member remaining limp, and rubbed his fingers against my stomach. He kneeled at the side of the bath and reached for the scented soap. I handed it to him, and thoughtfully added one of the sponges. I watched him intently but he did not look deeply or even directly into my eyes. He moved like a monk doing a religious chore, slowly and with only a kind of languid interest.

His face was still Davie, narrow and indifferent, but an anxiety pinned across it. He looked intent and worried. I eased myself on my elbows from the soft suds. Like a mildly romantic laundryman he slowly soaped and washed me, and to my further amazement began to whistle in a tuneless languid way. He seemed to spend hours on my stomach and breasts driving me crazy with his rubbing, then he mentioned that he would like me to kneel, motioning me over with his hands. I did so. He slowly lathered the tops of my legs and then went through between them, first with the soap, then the sponge, then his fingers, absent mindedly, lazily. I was aching more than I would have thought possible by then. My eyes were down to slits. I felt as though my own breath were stifling me and any words I tried to say became moans before they came from my lips. God I felt so soapy, so randy.

'Nell, turn,' he muttered dismally, and I swirled slowly around until my back was towards him, He paid as much attention to my shoulder blades as he had to the front of my body, his one hand around to the front and holding my bursting bosom, just as if he were keeping me steady, while he soaped and sponged my back. Then he began to tamper around with my bottom. He slowed, and went slower and slower. Once I thought he must have dropped off to sleep because he stopped whistling and even moving for several moments, leaving me so tight I wanted to screech. But then he was back again, his fingers and that sponge reaching, touching every inch. Never can I recall feeling so clean and so dirty at the same moment. This boundless torment went on for half an hour or more. I kept seeing him, behind my closed eyes, as a lad, sitting opposite me in the bath that first night in Bristol. The night when he had shyly asked me if he could touch my breast and I had let him.

'If Mr Fagence could only see us now,' I managed to say.

He replied in his astonishingly matter-of-fact voice. 'No chance of that. He died four years ago. I went to his funeral.'

I could not handle all this at the same time so I said nothing. Davie took my hand and led me from the bath. He gave me some towels and a nod as if to indicate it was time I did something to myself. But he was soon back with a phial of oil which he proceeded to massage into my skin. I stood naked, helpless, hands hung by my side, blushing with desire. He used it on the palms of his hands around my legs and buttocks and his fingers in every place, drawing little haloes of oil around my nipples. For some reason I remembered from childhood the man who had swollen and swollen and finally blown up in the coffin in the front room. I felt sure I would be sharing a similar violent fate. Then to my relief Davie led me back to the bedroom. I went carefully.

He gave me a feathery push back on to the bed and I tumbled there in luxury and anticipation, while he climbed towards me, still, astonishingly, with that lazy jumbo of his long and limp. It seemed to be the last thing he worried about. He hung above me and then with a tired sigh, relaxed and fell on to my body. We rolled together, locked, and made love, but without great passion. More an end than a means. It seemed it had all gone before and this was merely the way of releasing the enclosed tensions. It was brief and almost formal. Then we lay uneasily together in the silent hot afternoon room with the sounds snorting up from the streets of Marseilles and a ship somewhere grunting in the sun. The aroma of the bath and the oils hung around us like a cloud on a mountain. We lay flesh to flesh. I thought he was dozing.

'Davie?' I whispered, never being one to let well alone.

'What you want, Nell?'

'I thought you were asleep.'

'No, I'm thinking, Nell.'

'What about?'

'I was thinking it was a nice change to have a woman again – after all this time.'

That left me wide awake and staring at the ceiling for a long time. Davie had a boyfriend, a Catalan queen called René, sometimes known as the Perpignan Pompadour. I should have known all those years before, I suppose, when he walked through Devon wearing girl's clothes so casually, although he undoubtedly did not know himself. Now it was a matter for a shrug. I decided immediately that I did not love him although I still felt responsible to him and for him in an odd way. To me he remained the lost boy despite all the change and the bravado. I could still see him hanging out of the window, while Mr Fagence swung him by the wrists.

'How did you mean you went to Mr Fagence's funeral?' I asked him.

The sly grin settled on his face. We were sitting on the small balcony with the smell of the streets rising to us.

'Wouldn't you have done?' he said. 'I got my own back on that bastard. I went to work in Bristol after I left school, in a lousy blacksmiths – although I learned a few things *there* I can tell you. Anyway one day I saw in the paper that old Fagence had kicked off, so I went to the funeral, keeping quiet and well to the back. She was there, Mrs Fagence of course, all bowed and black, the old cow. Glad to see the back of him, I suppose. I just kept out of the way until the cemetery. The family were all around the grave as they lowered him in all sniffing and sobbing and the like. I sort of pushed my way in a bit between them and I started to giggle.'

'Giggle? God what happened?' I stared at him knowing he was quite capable of doing it.

'Nothing for a bit. The vicar bloke kept on muttering the prayers and everybody started sneaking glances around and I just giggled a bit more and more until I was laughing out loud. Then I turned away and went laughing and skipping down the graveyard path. I got my own back in the end, didn't I Nell?'

To tell the truth I was shocked. 'But it was a funeral, Davie. He couldn't hear you.'

'I just wish he could,' said Davie, not realizing I was reproving him. 'That would have been even better.'

That was the first afternoon of our reunion. René the Perpignan Pompadour turned up about four, lisping for a drink and prancing about the place in a yellow sharkskin suit. He was swarthy and mean-looking, which made his piping voice and mannerisms all the more strange. He was one of a group, a gang would be an exaggeration, of associates of Davie that had gathered about him both as friends and occasional partners.

They were the biggest collection of quaints and misfits I have ever seen. They drifted in and out of the apartment, had a look (mostly disapproving) at me, and drifted out again. Their lives consisted of moving up and down the Côte d'Azur living on their wits and fingers.

There was Lennie, the Lizard of the Lounge, who hung about hotels poncing and trying to see what he could pick up both human and material. An hour after he first saw me he told me that he loved me eternally. He was not bad looking but with a fatal furtiveness about him. One night when I was drunk at a party I let him roam all over me and eventually, mostly because I was too far gone to move, I permitted him to achieve what he proclaimed as the ambition of his life. It was so unimpressive (most of his endearments seemed to be directed at himself, which is no way to make friends with a lover) that I could have easily missed it altogether. When he asked again I said I did not have a spare minute and he went through my life from that moment with a perpetual sulk. He was, however, quite talented as far as drawing off wealth from old ladies staying in rich hotels along the coast, and in compromising careless men with photographs taken of them interlocked with girls that he had obtained. He was not, in general, an attractive person.

There was Sir Robart McAndrew, a flushed and flabby man who claimed to be a noble Scotsman and wore a dirty and disreputable kilt, the sporran as bare as a pig's ear. He relied on the kilt as an object of curiosity to make the acquaintance of the people he later cheated or robbed. He and his ways were exposed by a genuine Scots nobleman who perceived that Sir Robart's kilt was assembled from three different tartans (clans who had been enemies for centuries) and chased him along the beach at St Raphael with the knife he wore in his sock held for the kill. Sir Robart only escaped by running into the sea and swimming ponderously to a rock, from which he had to be rescued late at night, when the real Scotsman had gone grumbling back to his hotel.

Then there was Antibes Annie, a sloven who was a good safecracker. She had fingers like screwdrivers. She had opened one or two difficult boxes at various places along the Riviera over the years but what she did with the proceeds was a mystery. She certainly never spent them on herself. It was rumoured that she had a kept man who was a police department official and this may have been true because her information was excellent. She drank blackcurrant juice which had given her a permanently purple tongue.

These people were not settled members of Davie's gang, which was just as well since they would not all be in Marseilles prison instead of only going there in relays. He frequently worked by himself, or so he said, and when he needed help he brought in contact men from the organization in Marseilles. He said they were impressed with his cool attitude. They must also have been impressed with his lies, and not aware of the feet of clay I could now see so obviously in those pigskin shoes.

When this collection of disreputables met, slouched in smoke and making nasty noises in their throats, the bottle on the stained table replaced every few minutes, I would sit in the background and wonder how Davie had come to gain (although this is hardly the word) such friends and confidants.

When they were not slurring or slurping, when one of them wasn't folded face down on the table racked by a fit of coughing, they would plan all sorts of improbable raids and crimes. If boasts had been deeds they would have cleared every casino between Bains du Boulon and San Remo. But only rarely was anything decided and when they did work together they usually bungled it to such an extent that the police were at the scene of the crime almost before they were.

Antibes Annie went to gaol and so did Lennie the Lizard. He wept in the court and begged for mercy, while Annie, to her credit, filed her iron hard fingernails, setting the teeth of everyone on edge. The judge gave her two years.

'I think they're a joke,' I said to Davie. 'All of them. All your so-called criminal friends. Weak-kneed, incompetent riff-raff.'

He tried to put on his deep look, as though there were machinations I could never hope to understand. We had little sex after the first time, just the occasional flurry after a bath, because the Perpignan Pompadour kept turning up to take him out somewhere. I did not mind. I had a roof over my head. My only worry was when I had to sit and wait for the gang to return after one of their occasional sorties, biting my nails and wondering who would get back and how close the police were on their tails. I had written to Dante, a letter full of the true shame I felt at leaving him on our wedding day, not telling him the details, not mentioning my father, but merely saying that suddenly I had fallen among low people, which was saying the same thing.

'I'm better when I work by myself,' muttered Davie, still full of himself. 'Then I only have to trust myself, but sometimes I need the others.'

I sniffed. 'You don't need *them*,' I said. 'Not that clutch of nincompoops. And even when you work by yourself it's not exactly spectacular, not from what I've seen.' Predictably he rose to that.

'What do you mean by that?' he demanded, the Devon coming through in his tone. 'What do you mean by that, Nell Luscombe?'

I looked loftily. 'Well when like last week you come in with a diamond bracelet worth millions, so you said, and they're selling them in St

Tropez for ten francs a throw, I think you're working on the wrong lines.'

The sulk puffed on his face. 'Anyone can make a mistake,' he said. 'That woman usually wears good stuff.'

'Davie, hardly *anything* works. Twice you've tried that trick of robbing a bank by pretending you're going to make a deposit there – and twice you've run out with less than you took in. That's not crime, it's not even good business sense.'

His sulk rolled down to his throat. His sullen eyes turned up to me. 'It's just that I'm having a terrible run of luck, that's all. God, there's so much loot around here, hotels, apartments, yachts.'

The fact was, for all his bravado, he had neither the luck nor the technique that brings its own luck. The weak side of his character displayed itself in his work.

'Hotels, apartments and yachts,' I repeated remorselessly. 'You were caught red-handed in that flat at Bandol and the old sod who caught you made you go to bed with him.'

He shrugged. 'It was better than the police,' he said. Then, remembering: 'Not much better, but better.'

I sat him down patiently. We were moving about the apartment like two mooching cats. 'Listen,' I said. 'Either quit this place or do something else for a living. You'll end up inside a cell, and French prisons are like French restaurants, you're there for a long time.'

Davie looked hopeless. 'What can I do, Nell? I've not been trained have I? I can only do whatever comes along.' He walked to the window and looked over the sweaty port. 'And I'm not slaving away doing work like those stupid bastards down there.'

'In that case,' I said quietly, and because I had thought it all out, '*I'll* be your partner.'

He turned from the window in astonishment. 'You, Nell? You come in with me?'

'It would be better company that you've been keeping lately,' I said.

He walked back across the room. 'It might work,' he nodded. 'It just might. I could teach you everything.'

'Don't bother,' I smiled. 'We want to be successful, don't we?'

I thought he was going to make some retaliation but instead he dumped himself in a chair, the thought still imprinted on his face. 'It's not a bad idea,' he agreed. 'We split. Sixty-forty. No seventy-thirty.'

I poured two glasses of wine. 'Right,' I said. 'We're partners in crime. As long as you're happy with thirty per cent.'

Our first bank raid in partnership on the Juan les Pins branch of the Banque des Alpes Maritimes. It was perfectly positioned for my plan, its rear door opening on to a close street, and a short covered alley leading from that street and on to the seafront and the fashionable beach. The beach was important.

I believed I had a real aptitude for this sort of crime. It would be short, sharp, simple, but with a spice of ingenuity. As I explained it Davie's wry face rearranged itself into a smile. 'I reckon it might easily work, Nell,' he nodded. 'You got a lot of cunning.'

The plan was that we should go to the beach at Juan les Pins, hire one of the beach cabins and sunbathe for an hour. Then Davie would return to the cabin and dress, leaving me lying alongside his empty deckchair. In the cabin he would take our coloured beach bag, one of the duffle-bag variety with a draw string, and turn it inside out. The inside I would line with black material and there would be two eye holes cut out. There was another, larger beach bag for the money we would steal and this was also reversed so it had a black exterior.

At eleven in the morning, Davie would walk into the bank through the rear entrance after coming from the beach. We arranged for a little crooked man from Marseilles to block the front entrance by capsizing a handcart loaded with apples right in the doorway. Davie, now wearing the beach bag hood, would produce a gun and get the money put in the second bag and leave by the back door. Taking of his mask he would reverse it so that it became a beach bag again. Then he would walk through the alley and on to the beach, go into the cabin and strip down to his swim-trunks. He would take the cash from the second bag, reverse it, replace the cash, and then walk back to his place on the beach beside me. We would lie there like any other couple taking in the sun, our coloured beach bags by our side, one loaded with loot, and wait until the excitement had died down.

Whatever his weaknesses in other directions, Davie, given the guidance, was cool and daring enough to carry such a scheme through with ease. Was he lucky enough?

After an hour on the beach, during which time we had ensured that we had a conversation with the beach attendant, so that he would remember that we were on his stretch of territory, I touched Davie's wrist and he winked, rose quietly and went back to the changing cabin with the two beach bags, the duffle bag inside the larger one. Three minutes later he walked out in shirt, slacks and sandals, carrying the large bag, and slipped into the alley without fuss.

I lay back with my eyes closed. It hardly seemed fair to pray for the success of such a venture but I did anyway, hoping God might be in a liberal frame of mind. After two minutes I heard the commotion in the street as the apple cart was tipped on schedule. Nothing more happened and I remained unmoving until, four minutes later, Davie came quietly down the sand again in his trunks and sat down casually beside me. He winked. It was done. I felt so elated. I grinned up at the sun.

After a further three minutes there came the expected uproar from the street behind us. The police sirens and the noise of excitement. With the other people on the beach we turned idly as though we too were mildly wondering what had happened. The loot was sitting right between us, and our crooked little friend from Marseilles, who had slipped off immediately he had upset the apples, would be heading home by now.

We remained on the beach until the sun began to run down towards the rim of the sea and then casually packed our belongings and went hand in hand from the place, wishing the attendant 'Bon soir' as we went.

By that time Juan was peaceful with indolent men playing boule under the pines and the dreamy late-afternoon feeling and light over everything. Outside the bank a policeman was standing guard on that quaint way the police have of guarding something once the deed is already done. We wished him a pleasant evening as we strolled by.

As a precaution against being stopped by any road blocks the police might put up, we had delayed until the roads along the coast were crowded with early evening cars. They would not hold up the entire Côte d'Azur at that time of day. As we drove towards Marseilles we saw police cars and motor cyclists by the rocky edges of the road scanning traffic, but we sailed by them with identical smiles.

It was not until we reached the apartment that we dared to open the bag to see how much the escapade had netted. We ran laughing up the stairs, like mischievous children, and locked ourselves in before opening the bag.

It was like opening a large Christmas present. The money was all in beautiful thousand franc notes. I peeled one from the top and ran it luxuriously through my fingers. In the bag there were francs to the value of £10,000. We sat and gazed at each other in awe at what we had done.

'Davie,' I whispered. 'What are we going to do with it all?'

The answer came within five minutes, for six of the most sinister men I have ever had the displeasure of seeing on a doorstep came into the apartment and asked politely for a joining subscription to the Brotherhood of Marseilles. The crooked little fellow who had spilled the apples for us had then spilled the beans about us. He was with them. Everthing was done without violence. We were allowed to keep a thousand pounds each for our trouble.

After that, however, we were permitted to practise but not in a spectacular way. The Brotherhood made clear to us that if we intended to work along the coast of the Côte d'Azur we had first to serve our apprenticeship as petty thieves. The big brothers looked after the major crimes.

There was no alternative but to work on a less ambitious plane until we were ready to perform one final major coup – after which we would escape to some other part of the world where the Brotherhood could not levy their dues.

We cleared a suite at the Hôtel Victor Hugo in Menton of jewellery including a pearl necklace so heavy that it felt like a horse collar to me. Unfortunately this particular piece was so well known and had been photographed so many times that we could not find a fence who would touch it. Eventually we got rid of it to a shaky man at Lyon who paid us half and promised half but who disappeared the next day leaving us with a loss on the operation.

There was better fortune at St Raphael, however, where Davie purloined a fine yacht owned by a French industrialist who had gone ashore with his guests for dinner. He watched the two crew members left behind creep ashore for an unofficial drink and then started her up and took her miles out to sea. I met him out there in a small motor boat borrowed from a jetty up the coast. We loaded everything of value on board, including a projector and a whole collection of wicked films, money, jewellery, champagne and three cases of Scotch, into the motor boat and cruised away with it.

What we had gained so far meant that our living had become more comfortable. I took driving lessons and bought myself a red Alfa Romeo, which I drove like the richest girl in the world on the roads of the Azure coast. I took myself a lover, a comparatively honest and handsome Frenchman who owned a restaurant in the fashionable part of Marseilles, one of the most charming men between sheets that I can remember. He always kissed my hand before and after the event. Davie was pleased because it meant that he no longer had to provide for my needs and he himself had moved up sexually and socially. He became, as he described it, unofficially engaged to a bronzed but homely Niçois boxing champion. Davie spent hours at the gym and they sparred around happily together, both southpaws.

The summer was drifting with each day now and the coast became subdued and thoughtful. I was thinking too; wondering where we should make our big take. We discussed various plans and possibilities and then, one warm day in October, we were sitting, Davie and I, at a pavement café near the apartment when the alarm bell of a small branch bank on the opposite side of the avenue began ringing. It stopped after a few minutes and then began again and eventually a police car arrived and we watched a bank official explaining something to the officers. I touched Davie's hand and nodded that we should stroll that way. Several people had stopped and were watching the conversation between the man from the bank, now joined by two others and the police. We stood with them, a couple of idlers, moved only by curiosity.

The bank officials were gesticulating, explaining profusely that the bell had a fault and the police were complaining at being brought out on a false alarm and repeating that it was not the first time it had happened. People living in that district had been woken in the middle of the night. There was a lot of French puffing of cheeks and spreading of hands, and the officials promised that they would again have the bell checked and corrected. The police went sourly away and the small crowd dispersed. We went back to the apartment and stood out on the balcony studying the exterior of the bank building through a pair of binoculars we had purloined from the yacht we stole.

'What's the idea then, Nell?' asked Davie. 'How d'you think we're going to get in?'

I sat down and had a drink and thought about it. It did not take me long. I had a natural aptitude for the business.

The evening we carried out the raid we had dinner in a small fish restaurant directly opposite the bank. It was warm for the time of year and it was not uncomfortable to eat outside so we sat at one of the pavement tables and watched the bank. Its all-night lights showed drowsily over the tops of the windows and the glass panel at the top of the door. A cat sat on the doorstep for and hour and washed itself eight times. Eventually it strolled on its way and so did the people in the street. We stood up, paid our bill and walked back to the apartment.

Davie had been out a few afternoons previously and returned with a pocket radio transmitter which, he promised, was guaranteed to activate any burglar alarm. We now took this and walked, like any midnight strollers, back along the avenue. In the shadows of the bank we concealed ourselves and Davie directed the radio waves towards the top of a barred window and fraction higher than our heads. In ten seconds the alarm began obediently ringing. My heart leapt like a rabbit but Davie calmed me and we walked from the shadows and went across the avenue to a small park, open to the street and popular with late lovers. There we sat on a bench. Davie's familiar arm around me. I smiled at him and he at me. We watched.

The alarm continued shrilling along the street and squares of irate light began appearing in the darkened upper stories of the apartments and buildings. Someone complained from his window: 'Stop that machine! Where's the police?' Other people responded from across the street. Nobody gave a thought that it might be a genuine alarm, it had rung wolf too many times. 'That thing had been going mad for weeks,' shouted someone else.

The bored night police arrived without haste. They also had been called to too many false alarms. A few minutes later a Renault drove up with the flustered cashier who had the keys. Davie touched me lightly on the arm in the shadows of the park. 'Our man,' he whispered.

As soon as the door was opened the alarm was switched off and the neighbours in the avenue noisily pulled down their windows and the lights went off. A couple remained hanging out of the window to shout insults at the bank official and he, being in just as ruffled a mood as they, bawled insults back up the street. He went into the bank with the police, and finding nothing amiss returned to the pavement. The door was locked again and the men wished each other a sullen 'Bon nuit'. Whereupon a man from a window shouted: 'Bon nuit! Merde! Bon matin!' The bank man blew the Marseilles equivalent of a raspberry and everyone went home. After ten minutes Davie and I rose from the bench and, while I kept watch, he returned to the dark side of the bank where he once more activated the alarm. He came grinning back to the dim overhung park.

Up went the windows, on went the lights. People began shouting to each other all up and down the street. It was as though some famous victory had been announced in the middle of the night. This time the police did not even bother to appear. After three minutes (he could have barely had time to get back into his bed) the bank man appeared in his Renault, and waving his pale fist at all the fists protruding from the surrounding windows, he unlocked the bank and went in. The alarm bell stopped. The windows banged, lights went off. Davie, pulling a nylon stocking over his face, walked across to the bank, strolled in the door, and put a gun in the bank man's ribs.

Pulling my stocking mask over my nose and chin I walked casually from the park and into the bank. I closed the door easily behind me. Davie was taking the official's keys from his stiff fingers. The man's face looked as if it had suddenly been frozen. His eyes protruded and his mouth was fixed in a small amazed circle.

Everything until then had gone beautifully to our schedule. I could feel myself flushed with the thrill of it. Davie's eyes were like bright points, shining through the mesh of the mask. Then things began to go wrong. The bank man had a heart attack.

He simply toppled down to our feet and lay there turning blue. Davie and I looked at each other with horror. There was no doubt it was genuine, no one could put on an act like that. 'Davie,' I said, aghast. 'We'll have to call an ambulance.'

We tried no further crimes for a month, so demoralized were we with our latest thwarted attempt. It was not so much incompetence as fate.

The Côte d'Azur newspapers were full of the story of the 'Chevalier' bank thieves who had saved the cashier's life by calling for help and losing the loot. We were glad to hear he had not expired, but pictures of him sitting smirking like a hero in the hospital were not much compensation for us for all that risk and no reward.

Silence fell over us and some of Davie's former associates, the pink, puffing Sir Robart and the Perpignan pouf, came around to drink and gloat. This made me angry and Davie more sullen, but from his sullenness came the idea for our last and most fearful operation. He had been brewing it all day and half the night. At three in the morning he rose from the bed and went out onto the balcony to smoke. Seeing the red dot out there and knowing he had been restless, I got up myself and went out to him. We were a good distance above the street. I stood by him and we looked out to the weary, early-morning lights of the ships in port. The avenue below had a yellow silence. Not even a cat or dog walked there.

'What have you thought of?' I asked him. It felt very good standing together like this. It was a shame we could not have been lovers, that he had changed.

'I have a plan,' he nodded. 'A good plan.'

'Not a bank again. I don't think I could stand another bank.'

He shook his head seriously. 'Not a bank, Nell. A *house*, a *rich* house.'

'But they all have burglar alarms and dogs and suchlike,' I said. 'How many house gangs have been put out of business down here? Dozens. There's always hidden safes, and getting rid of the stuff afterwards, and having somebody to . . .'

I stopped because he had broken into a sardonic smile and it was still on me. Then I realized what he meant. 'No . . .' I said. 'No Davie. We can't . . . I couldn't do it.'

'L'Horizon,' he said. 'The perfect place. You know every inch of it. You know what's there. And if we get caught, you could always say you'd come back for something you'd forgotten.'

I shook my head, still hardly able to believe what he was suggesting.

'No,' I said. 'Not poor Dante. Not L'Horizon.'

I stood beneath the trees in the garden, watching the light in Dante's bedroom, brimming with a mixture of guilt and nostalgia. The perfume of the late Riviera flowers that climbed the walls to the balcony of my bedroom came to touch me like a soft hand. It had been six months to the day since our wedding. I wondered how my husband was.

Davie came like a wraith through the shrubbery and studied the house as if he were an expert viewing a painting. He knew now where everything was, each room and what it contained, or, at least, what it had contained when I was last there.

There were no dogs, for Dante did not care for animals around the place. There was an elaborate burglar system, but I knew that one cellar half-window was not wired or at least had not been wired when I had been at the house.

Davie nodded to me with his head and we eased our way through the shrubbery and a curtain of elephant grass at one flank of the lawn. Davie seemed to know the way better than I did. He was soon at the cellar window, a half circle set close to the ground and sunk deeply into the stonework. There were weeds and cobwebs there and a dust as solid as cement in the crack. This window had never been intended to be opened so there were no hinges or locks to bother us. But it was set into the wall just as formidably as one of the actual stones.

But glass is always removable and, lying out on his stomach, Davie worked with a diamond cutter until he had carefully removed all three panes of glass from the low window. Then, with a pocket hacksaw, he went easily through the uprights. We could get in.

At least Davie could. He was still as thin as a ballet dancer and with no bottom or other projecting parts to bar his progress his slide into the house was simple. My legs and hips and waist were inserted without difficulty into the cellar, but the ledge of my bosom became jammed against the ledge of the window and there were anxious minutes of tugging and levering before I was able to drop down breathlessly beside Davie in the dark underground room.

There had never been a key to the cellar, and it opened dustily but without fuss and we crept upstairs into the house. How strange it was, going through those shadows again. Everything as far as I could see was as before, the air of warm boredom, the silence, the patterns of pallid light through the windows. I paused at the bottom of the main staircase and listened up the well of the stairs. Was Dante, I wondered, with a woman in his room? I doubted it. The light was on and it showed in tight strips around his door. He must have been in there as he ever was, reading or brooding. Poor Dante.

At that moment his door swung open soundlessly. I thought my heart had crashed from my body. I stood stiff against the wall, while my husband stood on the landing above me. I could see his legs. Davie moved like a snake, backing lithely away down the passage in the direction from which we had come. I could not follow for Dante would see me. I thought he might call or go to the telephone for the police, or at least rouse the servants. But he was quite casual. He began to step down the stairs. Sinking back into a recess I watched as he came down the stairs and walked right by me. He was wearing a robe over his pyjamas, and his hair was like dull silver in the dim light. He paced steadily through the gloom. He stopped and I guessed he was at the light switch. He touched it and the whole passage was lit. Then he walked on and I heard him go around the corner to the front hall of the house. I might have reached a window or another door then, but I did the strangest thing in my life. I ran up the stairs and into his bedroom. It took me twenty seconds to strip myself and get naked into the large soft bed. I pulled my sheet down so that it only just touched the underside of my breasts. Then I waited.

His footsteps returned along the corridor, the light went out down there and he climbed the stairs. He was at the same pace.

As soon as he walked into the room he saw me, his lost wife, lying beautifully in more ways than one. Astonishment jumped into his eyes. He made a half step forward, then stopped. 'Nell,' he said. 'Nell.'

From the bed, the light lying on me. I smiled at him.

'Hello Dante,' I whispered. 'I've come back.'

CHAPTER FIFTEEN

For the next ten years I was Mrs Dante Sheridan, a pleasant and affluent experience at first, but one which soured when suspicion and nostalgia, a potent and nasty mixture, entered into our life. My husband became at first casual, then distant and eventually hostile. For my part I was good to him while he was good to me but after that I betrayed him. In addition he became almost mad with the renewed haunting of Giselle, eventually it became oppressive to live with him. Frankly I was not all that sorry when he hanged himself from the cedar tree in our garden in England.

We had moved to England very soon after my returning to him that difficult night at L'Horizon when Davie and I broke into the house. Dante, who although quiet was far from stupid, realized what I was about but forgave me for it in bed and questioned me no more about it. I told him nearly all the truth about my disappearance from our wedding feast and he generously forgave me that too. In fact I awoke on that morning, after my prodigal's return, with the sun of a new life once more shining in my eyes. I was determined that never again would I be dissuaded from this good and exceedingly comfortable life as the wife of a rich and attentive man.

Davie was caught by the Riviera police a week or so later when bungling a burglary at St Raphael. He was sent for five years to the prison at, appropriately, Nancy, where he apparently had quite a comfortable and privileged time, because after his release he set up house with one of the warders.

Our house in England was called Banham Court, comfortable Queen Anne, set among the trees, streams and purple moorland of southern Hampshire. Here I learned to ride, to be a firm member of the Conservative Party, to entertain a household of guests at the weekend.

At first I was novel enough for Dante to banish the self-raising ghosts of the floury Giselle and the frowns fell away from my husband as I entered into the rural English life at his side. He seemed to fit so much more easily into the damper English society and his solitude of the hot summer in France was all forgotten. I bought a lovely mare called Charlotte Brontë and we would sometimes ride across the blowy open country as far as Winchester, ten miles away, and back in a morning, racing the clouds all the way.

But Dante always remained thoughtful and a trifle slow in company and there were cocksure young men in the country who gave me looks across dinner tables and rooms that were both puzzled by my faithfulness and full of invitations to end it. It gave me a strange delight to joke with them, encourage them and dance with them, but always to leave them at the end unasked. Dante observed me at these games and would nod an approving smile across the room in my direction. He even began to wink.

I thought perhaps we were both cured; he of his trying memories and me of my natural-born shamelessness, and so we might have been, but for his gradual lapse into quietness with the occasional bursts of downright ill-temper. This I later discovered (when it was too late, of course) was brought about by his financial difficulties in his many business interests and not because of anything I had done.

It was in this period of my life, with leisure and money but with little work for me to do, that I began to read. Until that time I had hardly ever picked up more than a magazine, but, with the enthusiasm of a discoverer, I now began to read from the library at Banham Court and also to buy books as they were published and reviewed. Being of my disposition of course, and ever ambitious, I even began to write adventures, both real from my life and imaginary, although I never showed these to anyone but kept them locked in a bureau in my dressing room. At this time, too, I began to take elocution lessons, secretly again, for I wanted to surprise Dante. Each time we had a dinner party or other company I would insert some of my new sounds, getting away from my old anonymous voice (a voice which had, over the years, lost even the individuality of its West Country roots). But nobody ever noticed, not even Dante.

Dante used to hunt twice a week in the season but I did not enjoy this and after two or three attempts to keep up with horses and the conversation, both before and after the kill, I excused myself. Instead I took Brontë on silent and solitary rides through the forest and the open Hampshire land.

It was on these lonely expeditions that I began to meet, by chance at first, but later with too much regularity for it to be an accident, a young man called John Thornbury who lived in a village ten miles away, towards Winchester, and who, like me, chose to ride away from the crowd. His wife was a compulsive invalid and he was always alone.

I suppose it was almost inevitable that he should be my first lover since my return to Dante at L'Horizon. For six years I had kept my pact and been faithful to my husband, but now was coming the time when he began to drift away from me and I from him. Instinctively I knew that before long I would have to find another man, a temporary man, and by the same sense I knew that it would be John Thornbury.

He was a handsome and quiet man and our first meetings were shy and indecisive, our rides taking us across open country, slowly at first and then breaking into a good gallop as soon as we could see the sun reflecting on the stones of Winchester Cathedral. We asked little of each other then, only an occasional word, and company.

Then, when I decided quite abruptly one day that the time had come to take him as a lover, I found that he had been waiting for just as long. It was May, with the first real warmth in the season's sun. We had ridden across the open moorland of the New Forest and found ourselves in one of the glades that has remained secret and hidden from most people since the place was a hunting ground of kings. There were thick trees in that part and they hung low, while the new ferns reached high from the banks and knolls making a roof of green tracery above us. There, in the very nub of that green wood, was a small clear stream and we stopped to let the horses drink.

'When I was a little girl,' I said, 'there was a stream like this right behind the little house where I lived.'

'Where was that, Nell?' he said. We had dismounted and were standing as close as we had ever stood with that sudden knowing feeling locking us together.

'In Devonshire,' I said. I knew I had to be the first one to do anything so I turned against him and put my arms about him, lifting my face and kissing him on his face. He responded at once, enfolding me and kissing me in return.

'What part of Devon?' he asked as our faces parted. 'I know it quite well down there.'

'Upcoombe, in the south.'

His mouth was against my neck and his hands went to feel and clutch my breasts. My blood began to warm for the first time in a year. 'The South Hams,' he said reflectively.

'That's right.' My voice was getting very tight, so was my chest.

'I was reading about it the other evening,' he said unbuttoning my shirt. 'A man called John Lelland, in the seventeenth century, wrote a book about Devon.'

'Did he?' I had the swelling of his member against me now. I pressed my hands around it. 'A book?'

'Yes. He called it the fruitfullest part of all Devon.'

'The South Hams?'

'Yes. Down there. Can you get your jodhpurs off, Nell?'

'They're one hell of a job, John,' I said breathlessly. 'They're not meant for making love. Have you got a knife of something we could split the seams with?'

'No knife. Got a corkscrew, though, in my jacket here. Want to try it?'

'Christ yes, I'm so hungry for you. Let's lie down over there, beneath that hawthorn, it looks lovely with the bloom on it, doesn't it.'

'Yes beautiful,' he replied. 'It's really summer now. I'm very hungry for you too, Nelly. Here's the corkscrew.'

I took it from him and while we both lay back and giggled foolishly I used the point of it to unpick the seam of his breeches between legs. 'I'll be careful,' I promised. 'For both our sakes.'

Like many things that look difficult, it worked with surprising ease. The thread pulled away and he was open at the front and underneath. I was tempted to put my hands in and bring it out to my mouth at once, but he firmly held me and took the corkscrew from me and in the same painstaking way unpicked the seams of my jodhpurs. God only knows what any forest wonderer would have thought if he had come across the scene, a man using a corkscrew between a lady's legs. Now I did feel for him and brought his dear, imprisoned thing out into the sunshine. I kissed it right away and he undid my shirt completely and began to suck hungrily at my breasts. Soon we were joined in a frenzied outdoor game. The horses dozed and the birds sang and we were relieved and our spirits happy again.

We rode back circumspectly until we reached the place where we went our separate ways. We did not kiss but merely let our hands touch.

Several times we made love in the forest after that, although it never became a habit. Somehow we both seemed to sense when it would be, for I would wear my jodhpurs parted at the middle seam – a pair which I normally kept well hidden – and so would he. We never needed a corkscrew again.

Dante had many business interests, although they never again included anything to do with milling flour, and he travelled to many parts of the world in pursuit of them, sometimes taking me with him. He would not, as he put it, let me tax my brain with these matters and he rarely discussed them, although at times I overheard things upon which, had he any confidence in my judgement, I might have had some worthwhile thoughts. But he never considered me like that. I was just a face and a body who was at his side. It was a pity. I felt wasted.

During the middle part of our marriage, at the time when we began to drift, we made one long journey over several months throughout American and Canada. Dante was delivering a series of lectures on business techniques. He had become quite renowned for this particular subject and throngs of businessmen would pack the halls wherever we went. Sometimes I would go to the convention centres or the huge rooms in ornate hotels to see him deliver his conclusions on commercial methods and I was astonished how popular he was. They would applaud tremendously and shake his hand and slap him on the back (although he discouraged this in his studied English way by saying to the enthusiasts 'no slapping on the back please, it hurts'). It was as if he had won an election or something. He would come down from the platform, a small but assured smile on his jaw, give me a quick nod and hold out his hand for me to join him. American women were always gushing around him, making noises like blowholes and telling me how lucky I was to be married to such a remarkable brain.

There were receptions and dinners and I had some beautiful clothes and jewellery and received many complimentary looks from the businessmen. But they were always good-mannered, contained and courtly, no matter what they were thinking inside. With them business, the making of money, always came first.

But when the day was over and we were being driven back to our hotel suite, a weary quiet would drop like a curtain between us; not a comfortable quiet of two people content in each other's company, but the sharp quiet of a husband and wife who have nothing to say. I knew he was thinking of another woman, and worse than that, she could never be attained, she could never disillusion him, so that he could have her and then return to me, his wife. Because she was dead.

Towards the end of that long and increasingly dispiriting journey, we arrived at Miami Beach where he was to take part in a convention.

I was not looking forward to it. It was May and the weather was hot and humid. But there was a novelty.

'Nell,' Dante said in that manner of his which suggested that he had forgotten to tell you something long before. 'We're having a boat here in Miami. It's a luxury thing of course, all mod cons. You'll be able to sunbathe. You won't want to be at the convention centre, will you?'

It was not a question. The boat sounded attractive, but I knew it would be lonely. It was on the inter-coastal waterway which runs up the Florida shore, only a few hundred yards inland from the ocean and the beaches, moored in an inlet, a large, beautiful, white, boring boat. By the end of the day I had counted thirty-two pelicans creaking overhead, sunbathed for as long as I dared, had a secret swim in the canal, and drunk half a bottle of gin.

Dante returned about eight and we went to a restaurant only a few hundred yards away on the beach. One of his business associates met us there and throughout the meal they talked about their eternal methods and techniques, while I felt myself almost crying with unhappiness. God, how I wished his marriage methods had been more successful. We returned to the boat and he worked on his papers until the cool empty hours. I could hear him breathing in the main saloon of the boat. On impulse, I rose from the bed and walked to him in my nightdress, hoping that the sight of me might remind him that I was his wife. He looked up from his papers, blinking, puzzled, as if he did not know me.

'Nell,' he said awkwardly. 'I thought you were sleeping.'

I moved two paces closer to him, entering the circle of his lamplight, near enough for him to touch me if he needed or wanted to. He did not move. A look of desolation passed across his face.

'Why don't you come to bed with me?' I said quietly.

'I know. I know,' he muttered. 'I've been busy, you know Nelly. Conventions.'

'Are you ever going to spend some time with me again Dante? What about *our* conventions?'

'Of course. Don't be silly. It's just now.' His arm moved across the spread papers. 'You can see how it is.'

'Yes,' I admitted, dullness filling me like chilly grey water. 'Yes, I can see how it is.'

In the morning he went off early to his convention. I lay in the sleeping cabin staring at the bulkhead of the boat. During the night the off-hand slapping of water against the hull had made me dream that I was a girl in Weymouth again, out with the rude fisherboys. That was a long journey back.

I showered and put on a swimsuit and robe, then took a cup of coffee to the area at the stern of the boat where there were some canvas chairs and a table. There was another vessel, a large opulent-looking craft, moored stern to ours and almost as soon as I sat down a brown and grey man appeared, sat at the table opposite and began drinking whisky.

'Morning,' he began right away, lifting an old peaked cap. 'Real nice day. Hardly a spit of wind.' He gobbed heavily over the side and watched as it plopped straight into the water.

He had that Spencer Tracy sort of face, sunned and knotted, with splendid eyes and chopped grey hair. His arms, protruding from the short sleeves of a shirt faded to the point of being colourless, were like pieces of wood and his knees and legs were the same where they emerged from his canvas shorts.

'It's certainly fine,' I replied. It was oddly like talking to a neighbour over a garden wall. 'Is that your boat?'

'Ain't she pretty,' he replied, without answering. He swirled the bourbon around his glass and swallowed it like medicine. He made a face then poured another. 'Worth over a million dollars,' he said. He was not boasting.

'Are you by yourself on board?'

'Sure. I got a couple of Cubans who crew for me. But they wanted to go and see their mommy, so I let them. They used to make men down in Cuba. Want to go fishing?'

It was one of those times. I knew it. The coffee cup was half way to my lip and I let it stay there. 'I'd love it,' I said. 'But won't we need more help?'

'Ever been on a boat fishing?' he sniffed, regarding me critically across a few feet that separated the sterns. He seemed to be wondering if my arms would be strong enough. 'Out at sea, I mean. Out there in the ocean.'

I nodded honestly. 'A long time ago,' I said. 'But I did. I went fishing in the English seas.'

'Guess you'll fish anywhere then. Come aboard then, lady, let's get her cast off.'

Feeling as though I was playing some well-rehearsed part, I got up as I was and taking nothing from the boat I clambered across the rails and stood beside him. He shook hands formally.

'Ben Castairs,' he said. 'Pleased to meet you, lady.'

'Nell Sheridan,' I said, then added. 'Er . . . Mrs Nell Sheridan.'

His face gave a kind of humph at this. '*Mrs* Nell Sheridan is it?' he remarked. 'Well. I'm *Mister* Ben Castairs, but it ain't going to make any difference . . . Not to us fishing. Have a slug of bourbon before we cast off.'

The spirit burned my throat and brought tears to my eyes. He went forward and fired the engine. For the first time in months I knew that I was going to be happy that day. Just to show I knew what I was about, I cast off fore and aft and the lovely big vessel, like a swan, turned in her own length and eased herself through the waterway, her nose bowing eagerly as if she smelled the sea.

Sunshine flew along the deck, green palm trees waved over the limp water, gulls and pelicans lay flat against the perfect sky. I went to the wheelhouse with him and stood by his side, just as I had stood by the boy Rainbow's side all those spent years ago. God, Dante would be gabbling from the platform by now. If only he could see me!

'Any good with a cooking stove, woman?' asked Ben. I could see the spreading sea at the mouth of the waterway.

'Want something?' I asked, quickly adopting his short speech.

''Course I want something. Otherwise I wouldn'a asked. Git down and see what you can git in a pan.'

I went below. There was a saloon, expensively furnished and with a rank of books along a shelf. As I went by I leaned towards them and raised my forehead. Sex manuals, every one. How to do it, why you do it, why you can't do it, why you shouldn't do it, all the American best sellers on a topic of unfailing fascination. I grinned and cast a glance back to where his thick bare legs were just visible astride the wheelhouse.

'Are these yours?' I shouted up to him. 'All these sex books?'

'They're the wife's,' he replied at once. 'She likes to read about that stuff. And I'm glad, because while she's busy reading about it she don't come looking to me. Right?'

'Right,' I laughed back in the American way. I went to the galley. Everything was easy, an age away from the old spitting, spilling stoves of the Weymouth boats. I made breakfast of bacon and eggs, toast and coffee and we ate together on the wheelhouse as the shining ocean grew wider and wider about us.

'You must be very wealthy,' I said, my mouth full. 'With this boat.'

'Millionaire.' He waved his toast in his matter-of-fact bragging. 'Got so much I don't know what to do with it all. Next season maybe I'll get a new boat or a new wife. Maybe both. A bigger boat and a smaller wife.' He laughed uproariously at his joke and the bow bucked as though it heard the joke too.

He wiped the egg off the corners of his mouth with the last piece of toast, then tucked that away into his mouth too. He had fine flat teeth and his eyes were pale like the sea. 'Can you take her?' he said. 'I'll get the tackle set up.'

With more show of confidence that I was feeling I stood and took the wheel. I could feel her moving, trying to get her own way like a strong horse. Firmly I brought her back on course.

'That-a-girl!' he said. 'Keep her head right.'

'Okay Popeye!' I shouted. I do not know why I called him that; it simply came out. I heard him laugh hugely as he went to walk towards the tackle. Then he turned and gave me a smack with his hand across my backside, before going off towards the stern.

I stood against the wheel, a sensation of warmth and expectation all over me. I had never made love to an older man than my husband, who was then fifty-eight. That, I had a feeling, was something which would be changed before the sun set that night on the far edge of Florida.

What a fisherman he was. He had the most beautiful back I had ever seen on any man, the muscles built tightly in ridges and yet full of ease and suppleness. In three hours we caught half a dozen marlin, some yellow tails and a small grinning shark. I could hear myself laughing with triumph, holding on to him, helping to draw them in.

Then I went to the galley and got together everything for a salad and I opened a bottle of cold white wine. We put the sea anchor down while we sat in the stern and ate and drank. It appeared that we were alone on the long ocean, the sun and the birds for company, the land low on the rim of the water. It began to feel like one of the best days of my life.

When we had finished we lolled there, lulled by the sea. I looked at his strong brown face with its close crop of grey hair thrusting out from under his cap. 'Popeye,' I said quietly.

'Yep,' he said just as calmly.

'I was wondering if you would like to make some love.'

'Strange thing, Nell,' he replied, still without changing his tone. 'I was just wonderin' that myself.'

We spent the next half an hour on the open deck, the sun burning first one back, then the other. He was the strongest and most energetic lover I had ever experienced and we savoured every rolling moment. When we eventually lay back he caressed my nipples with his hard hands and said thoughtfully: 'Shit, but you're a fine healthy girl. I ain't seen quality like this, not in years.'

He had made me satisfied too, taken all the tension from me, filled me and quietened my appetite. I would have liked to stay with him forever.

But the sun was trailing and I knew that, by the nature of things, I would have to return to my husband, to entertain yet another clutch of dollar-grubbing men with labels on their lapels (as if they were likely to get lost), eyeing me only from the greatest of distances, the respect of business.

Popeye sensed my reduced mood. 'Guess we'd better turn this tub around,' he said squinting towards the sun and the horizon. 'Ain't going to be able to stay out here for the rest of our lives, Nell.'

I put my naked arms to his hard chest and pulled my breasts to his stomach again. It was as firm as a board. 'Once more Popeye,' I whispered. 'Once more before I have to go back to him.'

He smiled gently, a surprising smile from one so hardened, and moved against me gain. He had a beautiful penis, so smooth it might have been carved. Not a knot-hole or a bump anywhere. He pressed it softly into me and we joined without a murmur. My cheek close to that hard scrubby hair by his ear, I groaned with the rough pleasure of him. His lips, firm and dry, went against my neck.

'God,' I breathed when we had finished. 'What could you have been like when you were twenty?'

'Shy,' he answered flatly. 'Very shy.' We dropped over the side and swam naked against the vessel. Then we climbed aboard again and he went forward, sadly, I like to feel for I was sad too that our day was nearly complete, to the wheelhouse, pulling his old shorts up around his backside. I did not put my clothes on immediately but went up there with him, naked, and stood alongside him. I felt that we had been familiars all our lives.

'I gotta tell you something, Nell,' he said after being quiet for some time.

'Don't tell me you can't marry me,' I laughed. 'They all say that.'

'Nope it ain't that. It's the matter of this boat. I don't own her. In fact I never been aboard her till last night.'

I was genuinely astonished.

'I ain't kidding,' he shrugged. 'I was in a bar and this guy gave me the keys and told me to go and help myself. I was drunk and he was drunk, so I don't rightly know who he was. But it was real nice of him.'

I put my naked arms around him. 'She's been yours today, anyway,' I said. 'Ours.'

'Sure has,' he nodded. 'But I ain't no millionaire, neither. I been bumming up and down the Eastern seaboard for years. From Maine to Cape Hateras, the Carolinas, Savannah too. That's a goddam place, Savannah. Building boats, sailing them, all that sort of stuff. But I never did make enough money to be a millionaire.'

'I know millionaires who would give a lot to have what you've got,' I said truthfully, holding him against me.

He ruminated and turned the wheel carefully. 'Sure, sure,' he replied eventually. 'All I got is my health and strength.'

That evening when the plastic men with their plastic name tags and their plastic talk were crowding the saloon of our boat and I was in my evening gown and Popeye was alone on the boat on the next berth, I heard a car draw up and voices and footsteps. I went to the stern and saw some policemen taking Popeye ashore. My heart went cold. I called to him and he turned. I looked around, no one had followed me to the deck.

'That guy who gave me the keys to the boat – he didn't own it neither!' he called jovially. 'Goodbye Nell.'

'Goodbye Popeye,' I echoed sadly. I waved as they drove him away and I turned and went back to my rich famous husband and his nasal friends. The very best things in life sometimes come unexpectedly and then only for a little while.

Once Dante fell into his unhappy valley he never again returned to the contented ways he had managed briefly to achieve with me. At about three o'clock one April morning I woke and found he had gone from the room. I sensed that he had been absent for a long time, and feeling inside his bed I found it cold. Uneasily I got up and went to the mullioned window which overlooked the stepped lawns of the house. The cedar tree spread its enormous branches like fingers trying to hold the night. A weary moon was yawning on the skyline. Looking down I saw what at first I thought must be a ghost.

It stalked, white along the shadows and into the long streaks of low moonlight, a thoughtful, sorry sort of ghost. I realized it could only be Dante once more communing with his dead, but never gone, Giselle.

Secretly I eased the window open and peered out. He muttered as he wandered and our household cat sat on the sundial at the centre of the lawn and watched with astonishment. Well it might too, for Dante was clad in a long silk dress, elegant and white, if a little old-fashioned by then. Giselle's.

Somehow I was not really shocked. I had always known that it was still lying with him. I had hoped that it would dry and disappear with time. I retreated to my bed feeling solitary again; all the things I had gained, wealth, experience, even (so I thought and hoped) love, all ashes. Nelly Luscombe was once more on her own.

I sat up in bed cursing quietly to myself. Should I now, once more get up and go, take to the road and see what new life it would lead me. The thought did not attract me. In the old days I had fled from nothing, only expecting to find nothing at the end of the journey. Anything better was a bonus. But here I had a life, a staff, a house, money and recognition. Could I balance them against married unhappiness and live with it? The thought came to me. It said that I could no longer run away. I was too old.

In fact I was now thirty. I rolled in the bed to see if I still felt luxurious. I thought I did. I had taken to wearing calico nightdresses – some of them eighty years old that I had brought from an antique shop in Winchester. The smooth ordinariness of the old cloth against my skin that night, now I was on my own again, made me remember the solitary nights in similar nightdresses all those years ago in childhood. Slowly, as if the bed were the sea, I eased myself lower and lower into its deepness and safety and waited for Dante to return from his haunting.

He padded guiltily into the room, now in his pyjamas, and pausing, whispered 'Nelly . . . Nelly.' I knew he did not want me for anything, even less for comfort, but was only testing to see if I had woken. I let out a dreamy snore from beneath the sheets and I heard him grunt and climb back into his bed, to join his own dreams.

We had spent the previous evening at Sir Bernard Buffling's house in the Vale of Pewsey and, although Dante had been his usual and quietly withdrawn self, I noticed that several times he had looked intensely at one of Buffling's nieces, a pale, fair, empty girl in her twenties. And it was this, I later realized, which had provoked his transvestite walk.

There were no more nocturnal walkings for some time after, but towards the end of the month we went to a grim Conservative Gala Ball and once again, as I was dancing, I saw Dante standing alone at the side of the floor and staring blatantly at a similar type of blonde girl. That night he again sidled from the bed and this time I followed.

It was a big secret sort of house, riddled with corridors and tunnels and rooms folded away and easily overlooked. I trailed him to the north wing and, crouched and sad, watched him unlock a cupboard within a cupboard and produce not one but a whole section of his dead wife's dresses. It was amazing. He held them against him, comparing one with another, eventually selecting a pale blue number with thin shoulder straps and a mouldy looking corsage. He took his pyjamas off and wriggled into the dress, making little whining noises to himself. Then he went wandering.

I waited until he was muttering and pacing the lawn beneath the spreading hands of the cedar tree and then, creeping back, I opened the first cupboard and found the second, with the key left in the lock. I turned it and pulled the door. Inside was Giselle's complete wardrobe, dresses, coats, shoes, and lots of expensive underwear. I felt my lip curl in disgust. I ran my hands through it, feeling that old unwanted, unneeded sensation seeping through my veins like creeping damp. 'Fuck you,' I whispered to the clothes.

Three days later, on an afternoon of dizzy, springtime sunshine, with the county rivers shining and the Hampshire birds full of song, I returned from my forest ride to see him (at a distance of a mile too, which was most disconcerting) dangling by the neck from the lowest and largest branch of the cedar tree.

He swung gently in time with the April breeze, the long pale nightdress almost touching the ground beneath his useless feet. I rode carefully up the hill, not hurrying for I knew I was too late and there was no need for hurrying. Indeed it had been too late for two years. I took the mare to the stable block and called Jarman, the groom. He came from the tack-room, a spidery man, his face crammed with lines and creases. 'Jarman,' I said. 'Please come and help me with the master.'

A lifetime of dealing with the foibles and dramas of horses had, I suppose, toughened him for the minor turns of human histrionics and he turned the corner with me to come upon the dangling Dante with only the merest flicker shading his expression, only half a step of hesitation in his walk. 'I'll get a ladder, Madam,' he said politely. 'People in that way are very difficult to get without a ladder.'

He ambled away calmly and returned with the ladder. Between us we managed to get the wobbly body of Dante down from its gibbet and on to the lawn. As we stretched him out there, the springtime sun streaking teasingly across his dulled face, Jarman sniffed and said: 'I ain't never seen the master wearing that nightdress before.'

Looking down at the deeply dead Dante, a small swelling of pity rose within me. 'Do you think we could make it look like natural causes?' I said hopefully to Jarman.'It looks very bad like this.'

'I doubt it Madam,' he said sizing up the corpse. 'It would take some believing that would.'

'Well at least let's get that ridiculous nightdress of him and put him to bed,' I said. 'It's all so undignified like this.'

'You're right Madam,' he agreed. 'People will probably talk.' He gave the alternatives some thought, walking in a small horseman's circle around the body. The two housemaids and the cook were off duty at that time of the afternoon or the whole thing would have become too complicated. 'Maybe,' muttered Jarman, 'we could put him across the back of old Nightmare and send him off on a gallop across country. We could make out the master fell off and broke his neck. Or we could drop him in the river and say he drowned.'

The vision of the three of us riding across country with Dante held upright between Jarman and me, had its touch of romance, but I doubted if we could carry it off. And Dante floating down the river would look just as suicidal as ever.

'I think the best thing we can do is put his pyjamas on and get him into bed,' I said. 'Maybe we'll get away with pretending it's a coronary. We'll get Doctor Finneston. He's bound to be drunk.'

It was difficult not to admire his aplomb. 'Come on Mr Dante, Sir,' he said, just as if he were helping him on to his horse. 'Up we come.' He attempted to carry the corpse by himself but he was a very short man and poor Dante kept slipping over the back and trailing his dead head close to the ground. So I took my husband's feet and Jarman took the shoulders and we carried him into the house and into the bedroom.

The worse part was getting the hideous nightdress from him. She had fearful taste that Giselle, whatever her other qualities, and it did not suit Dante any better. He had however caught part of the material in his hand, probably the last movement of his life, and we tried to prise his fingers free of the silk. They would not let go. In death he was still difficult. But we managed to pull the silk through until he was free. After that, Jarman, touching his groom's forelock tactfully, left the room and I was alone with Dante.

Seeing him stretched out there, the first time I had seen him naked for about a year, it occurred to me that my husband had been a strong figure of a man and I felt a proper pang of regret that things had not been different between us. But it was too late even for regret. It was no use standing and admiring him. I took his pyjamas from their drawer, a conservative striped design, and with much pulling and tugging eventually got him dressed in them. Then I put his hand on his chest in the manner of one who might have suffered a sudden pain from his heart. The rope had made a nasty mark around his neck but I optimistically turned up the collar of his jacket in the hope this might hide some of the evidence. Then, when all was set, I called Dr Finneston, an Irish bottleman who could always be relied upon to give a false diagnosis, certainly in life.

Dr Finneston was in an early afternoon stupor but agreed to come at once, although, as he put it, death is never that urgent. He came into the room, brought up by the marvellous Jarman, as expressionless as a sleeping donkey, the doctor breathing a fiery cloud of whisky before him. He gave Dante the most cursory of examinations, before nodding carefully and saying: 'This man is dead.'

'Was it a heart attack?' I prompted, managing to squeeze a tear out of my eye. 'A coronary?'

'Aye, I'd say that's what it was by the look of him. A very sad day for you both, I've no doubt.' He stumbled towards the window, seemingly suddenly conscious of the alcohol he exploded with every breath, and stood blowing the fumes out into the garden.

'There's a very strange piece of rope hanging from the cedar tree down there,' he observed. 'Chopped off. As if man might have hanged himself from it. It matches, I've no doubt, the nasty contusion around Mr Sheridan's neck. It looks like he might have hanged himself and then come up here to his bedroom to die quietly.'

At the inquest evidence was given that Dante's financial affairs were in a stormy state, something of which I was quite unaware. It made me feel a little better, however, knowing his death was not only prompted by his longings for Giselle.

Everyone for miles around was there, of course, in the coroner's court, cramming every seat and bench and lined up six deep against the terrible treacle-coloured tiles at the back. Jarman assured me that it was a mark of respect for my late husband to have so many people at the inquest.

I was summoned to the witness box by an usher calling my name like an echo without a voice. All around us they rustled with anticipation and I stepped forward, slowly, with dignity, feeling within me the guilty thrill of the tragic actress. Pace by pace I went towards the witness stand, recited clearly the binding oath, and then waited for the questions that I knew must come my way.

The coroner had a face like a fat parrot. He leaned over to get a better look at me in my fine black clothes. 'Mrs Sheridan,' he moaned. 'Tell us, in your own words, the events of this most sad afternoon.'

My voice retreated into my bosom and I described how I had found Dante swinging from the tree, but omitting the details of the nightdress which had remained a secret known only to myself and Jarman.

'Why, Mrs Sheridan,' said the coroner, 'did you take your husband to the bedroom and dress him in his pyjamas?'

My chin went down to my chest again. 'I was trying to keep him warm,' I whispered. 'I was trying to get him into bed. I thought warmth might . . .'

'Bring about a recovery,' he finished for me. 'Well I've heard stranger things in this court, I must say. But not many.'

They brought in a verdict of suicide while the balance of the mind was disturbed and then everyone emptied out into the young spring sun of the street. Several people came to me and patted my arm and made sympathetic noises, but I noticed how a great many women, most of whom I knew by name, backed away from me. In that stratum of life it was not permitted to let one's husband get away with much, particularly suicide.

Everyone seemed to drift away across the streets, into the pubs for the discussion of the case, into cars and on buses, leaving me oddly alone on the pavement. The house servants, those of whom had been permitted to attend, and of course Jarman, remained with me, but a pace behind. He said we were waiting for the car. The coroner and the clerk came out and both raised their hats. The coroner wished me a pleasant remainder of the day. I was wondering about the remainder of my life. I turned around and the handful of staff who had come with me were staring at the back of my neck.

Everyone else had gone. The striped sunshine of the street was undisturbed now. It was a small street and there was no traffic. It was not until then that I realized that everyone was blaming me for what had happened, because he had hanged himself. I suppose I, the wife was the natural one to blame. The thought struck me with such force – and my basic innocence was such that it had never occurred to me before. I have frequently been wicked but never intentionally cruel. Cruelty is the pastime of respectable people.

'I think we had better go home,' I said to Jarman. Surely *he* did not think it was my fault. His expression, as normal, said nothing. 'Home,' I repeated. 'Everbody else seems to have gone.'

As though he had been awaiting some movement, Perrington the chaffeur eased my car around the corner. It was strange how we had been just left there like that, on the pavement. Even as the car drew up I wanted to begin running. Just to get away from it. I would have to wait for Dante's burial. Then I would go again. On my own.

One of the most difficult things in the world, I suppose, is to throw a successful funeral. The basic circumstances are set against it, of course, and yet people expect it to be handled properly like any other social occasion and if it does not go right they grumble just as they would about a mismanaged wedding.

Fortunately the arrangements were taken care of by Dante's London solicitor, Maurice Benning, a long, careful and considerate man who knew more about Dante's life and dealings than anyone. All I had to do was to supervise the catering arrangements and look mournful at the graveside. This, as it turned out, was quite difficult, since it was decided that Dante's hunter, Roulette, should be part of the funeral procession, trotting saddled but riderless through the streets, with Jarman, face composed with horsey sorry, at the halter. Roulette enjoyed the affair tremendously, pawing and neighing and finally enlivening everything by letting go the most colourful and noisy fart as the last rites were recited.

It rattled magnificently in the churchyard air and stopped the clergyman in the middle of his ashes and dust. I felt myself begin to laugh inside and had to concentrate heavily on the lid of the coffin so as not to allow the laugh to burst out.

Dante's children, Paul, Anton and Sirie, came from France for the funeral, of course, although in the years since our marriage they had hardly seen their father at all. He had pulled away from them and they from him, and considering our intimacies in the early days at L'Horizon, they treated me with remarkable resentment and disdain. They had accepted me as an employee of their father's, as a confidant and a companion, even, briefly, as a lover. But never as a step-mother. Now they acted out the day of the funeral with sullen faces as if they felt not so much bereaved as cheated.

Sirie and Anton, who, predictably, had grown into two of the most strikingly beautiful people, still lived together in Paris. Her habitual paleness suited the funeral perfectly, her black lace mantilla edging that sulky face and those downcast eyes. She looked more disgusted than sorrowing. He looked remarkably handsome in black and white, his fair hair just stirring in the graveyard breeze. They stood sides touching, aloof, perfect, and yet somehow amazingly rotten. Their polite mutterings of comfort to me were only just off the edge of insults. But I smiled to let them know I understood.

Paul, on the other hand, was more obvious. His languid fat had scarcely been held in check through the years during which he had clawed his way to the rank of full Lieutenant in the kitchen corps of the French army. His sulks were less subtle than those of his brother and sister.

'There is *nothing*,' he said, bending close over my glass of sherry at the reception in the house following the burial. 'Nothing at all. You know that?'

'Nothing what?' I asked genuinely. People everywhere thought only of what wealth or what lack of wealth a dead man left behind. No one has loved money more than I, but it has always been my own, earned by me, not acquired, not borrowed, not inherited. I always thought of Dante's wealth as his. And the same went for his debts.

'There is *no* money!' rasped Paul through his fluffy pink lips. 'He was broke, bankrupt, penniless. The lawyer will tell you.'

I shrugged. 'What did you expect?' I asked.

He pouted, the way I remember him pouting in his room that day, a boy's sulk, unsure, unmanly, standing there among his stuffed birds.

'I thought he was rich,' he said blatantly. 'But I find *this* – only debts, mortgages, stupid investments. Not even this house is left.'

'You've still got your owls, haven't you, Paul?' I said. 'Or have you punched them all to pieces now?'

He glared at me. 'Another thing I want to tell you, Mrs Sheridan,' he said bitterly. '*Nobody* killed Giselle. She jumped into the flour herself. Everybody lied, thinking they were covering for my father.'

'Well I'm glad that's cleared up,' I sighed. 'I was waiting to hear that the butler did it.' I turned from him, determined now to make sure it was the last word with him. 'Goodbye Paul,' I said. 'Give my love to the owls.'

Every sentence Mr Benning spoke was delivered with great deliberation as though he examined each word for libel before he uttered it. He had about him, however, a stuffy legal kindness and when he approached me after we had put Dante away he touched my arm and spoke softly.

'I'm afraid, Mrs Sheridan,' he intoned, 'that you will be able to touch nothing. Not the house or anything else. Dante was in a difficult situation. Deep trouble I'm afraid.'

'Not as deep as he's in now,' I suggested quietly. I thought the corner of a grin took root on the extreme side of his mouth but it thought the better of it.

'Is there anything here that you could call your own?' he went on. 'Separate from anything which Dante provided?'

'There's my soul,' I said. 'Can I keep that?'

'No one can take that from you but God,' he said. 'And he would need a writ and a good reason. Anything else? Your clothes, of course, no one could argue about those.'

I thought about it. Once again I realized that I had nothing. Then I said: 'My horse. I paid for that myself, so it must be mine, mustn't it?'

'Your horse,' he ruminated. 'Well, I'd say it was borderline. What would you intend to do with it?'

'I may have to eat it if all you say is true, Mr Benning,' I smiled. 'But my thought at the moment is that I may just mount it and ride away from this arseholing place.'

Not a wrinkle disturbed his expression. I suppose you hear everything as a lawyer. 'That,' he smiled quietly after some thought, 'might be a very good idea. I am giving you this advice very unofficially, you understand, but if I were you I'd ride like fury. Get right away from this . . . arseholing place, as you put it.'

It was sound judgement. Everybody went, my stepchildren with their hateful bird-like pecks on each of my cheeks (I have never seen them since), everybody else full of sherry, chablis, pâté and assorted cold meats. They went off over the lawns towards their motor cars, gossiping among themselves, never once caring to look back to see me standing at the window alone, watching them. If I found it difficult to cry for Dante, I suppose, I might have had some reasonable excuse to cry for myself. Through the house I walked and wandered, not feeling any great love or gratefulness to it, but simply wondering what my next roof would be. Left in the world with nothing but a horse.

It became dark mercifully early, rain clouds coming low and swiftly across the land and the trees. I sat in the drawing room by the unlit fire, gradually drinking my way through a bottle of champagne. The creditors would never get that. At nine o'clock, only waiting for the chimes to fade, I stood up and walked through the darkening corridors. I had sent all the servants packing as soon as the funeral fun had finished, only Jarman remaining in his cottage next to the stables. Walking through the house I stamped my feet heavily, defiantly at each step, until I arrived at Dante's secret cupboard. I opened the outer door and then the one within that. 'Come out, Giselle dear,' I called. It would not have surprised me to find that somehow her collection of clothes had been spirited away, but they were still there in their smug rows. One by one at first, and then by the armful, I took out her fine tat, my eyes now filling with jealous tears. How could any man marry someone and keep this sort of thing hidden away?

I opened a window in the upper corridor and tossed out the stuff by the armful. It floated down through the darkness to the lawn like a flight of dumbstruck angels. Then another load, then another, dresses, night-clothes, underclothes and shoes. I threw them all, in a controlled rage, my face wet, my lips trembling with her name. When I had finished and the cupboard was bare, I stood panting at the window and saw it all scattered on the lawns. Two dresses were hung on the tree where Dante himself had dangled.

Calmed at last I walked carefully down to the casement door below and went into the night. Oppressive clouds hung almost to the ground. A nightbird screamed far away and I could hear the horses were uneasy. First I gathered all the garments I had thrown and made them into a pile on the grass, just below Dante's gibbet branch. I walked over to the garage where there was always a spare can of petrol and took this back and emptied it over Giselle's clothes.

I did not light the pyre immediately. I went inside, changed my clothes, and took my handbag, then I walked to the stables and quietly saddled Brontë, who seemed glad to see me. I led her out on to the drive and she stood and watched me go to the pile of soaked clothes and throw a final match to them. They flared spitefully at once and Brontë gave a concerned snort. But I went quickly to her, pulled myself on to her back, and turned her away. I rode briskly away from the house, across the open country, along the ridge of little hills and down to the shingle road. On the brow of the last small hill I allowed myself to turn and look back at the flames rolling up from the darkness in front of the house. I could see some of the windows throwing back the reflections of the fire. I let out what began as a laugh but emerged as a sob, and then wheeling the horse I set out to ride through the darkness of the English night. Once more I was on the road.

John Thornbury's house was about a mile short of the town in the bottom of a wooded hollow so deep that the house seemed to be crouching, the top windows looking nervously over the upper ground from under their roofs. At that hour of the night the wood had, it seemed, closed in even tighter. Brontë eyed it unhappily but I encouraged her through it and we came to the yard beneath the back windows of the house. There was a light showing in the panes below the eaves. I hoped his wife had taken her sleeping pills.

I sat on my horse and gave the hoot of an owl, so realistically that a real owl fell out of the eaves just above my head and flapped furiously away. The light grew stronger at the window and I saw it was John. Indistinct as it was I thought I saw him smile. He opened the window. 'A midnight rider,' he called down softly. 'What news?'

'No news,' I called back. 'Only I buried my husband today.'

'I know. I was there. One of the thousands. I heard his horse fart at the graveside.'

'It did too. Listen. I have to sell Brontë'

'Come in,' he whispered. 'All the doors are bolted. Can you climb up here, Nell?'

'She's asleep?'

'Whistling through her teeth. Can you climb?'

It was no trouble, and it had a touch of romance which we both enjoyed much better than him simply coming down to open the door. There was a window sill and an easy haul to the flat roof over the door. Then another few steps along a ledge and finally to his window. He hauled me in.

'Beautiful,' he said holding me.

'It was easy. This house is built for burglars.'

He put his long rough arms around me, letting his hands rest comfortingly against my backside. 'How are you Nell?' he said genuinely.

'Unwanted, cast out. Running like a fugitive – again,' I said. 'That's why I want to sell Brontë. I'm going to London and I need some cash. I can't touch anyting in the house. Dante owed millions.'

'So I hear.' He kissed me now, the friendly kiss of a man I had known I could trust. He paused, then said: 'It's funny, I was feeling alone too. I was wondering only an hour ago how you were.'

'Is Cecily no better?'

'Not one bit. I'm trapped with her. That's the worst type of loneliness. At least you're free. She's going really bonkers, I think. She came in screaming last night, said there was a grey ghost in riding boots in the yard . . . You really want to sell Brontë do you?'

'I have to. I have to start a life.'

'Would you take five hundred?'

'That's very fair.'

'Splendid. She's a lovely animal. I'll give you half cash, half cheque. Is that all right?'

I nodded. He squeezed my hands and then went away from the room. He came back with an envelope and handed it to me.

'Do you want a receipt?'

'No. We're friends.'

'She's down in the yard. I shall miss her. She's very kind and dependable.'

'Not many people are like that.'

'No. Thank you John.'

I kissed him for thanks.

'Will you stay for a while?' he asked.

'No. There's a train at midnight. I want to get on it.'

'I'm sorry. I'll just have to remember the last time.'

'I will too.' We both laughed softly as friends do. He knew I was going and took me again towards the window. Brontë was staring up, waiting for me to emerge. I felt very sad about her. She knew me very well. I kissed John again and put my foot over the window sill.

'What will you do in London, Nell?' he asked finally.

'What I should have done years ago, dear,' I replied. 'I'm going to be a high-class harlot.'

CHAPTER SIXTEEN

Even after all these years I had no real idea how to go about it. By now the ladies who had patrolled Curzon Street and Shepherd Market in the days of my youth and wonder were no more. Their descendants had been banned from the pavements on threat of prison, and they now plied their trade in the confines of rooms and drinking clubs, with no fresh air and no walking; not nearly such a healthy life.

The train arrived in London in the steamy early hours and it was obvious that it was no time to begin a new career. On the other hand it was important, I realized, to start as soon as I could, otherwise my capital would be eroded.

When Dante and I had stayed in London on occasional visits we had always taken a suite at Burridges in Mayfair and now, at the early solitary hour, I turned naturally towards the luxurious homeliness of that famous hotel. A suite, I reasoned, I could not afford, but a room was not beyond me. Burridges, with its chandeliers, its traditions, its fine courtesy and its almost family relationship with its special rich and regular customers. The thought suddenly caught me. What better place to set up a small whoring business!

The notion entranced me. All the way through the blank streets in the taxi it occupied my mind. When I arrived at those famous portals, the late, pale lamps shining through the panes and curtains, I could almost envisage a modest red light shining there too.

I was a guest who was known to them well, and they even turned some poor young under-manager out from whatever cubby-hole he was occupying to greet me. This familiarity could only be of help. Who would suspect Mrs Dante Sheridan of operating an illicit room on one of the finest hotels in the world?'

The under-manager, once he had rubbed the sleep from his eyes and straightened his tails, accompanied me to my room and I must have mystified him not only by my lack of luggage (explained by my complaints of misfortune and mix-up) but my obvious and detailed examination of the bed and bathroom facilities.

'Splendid,' I said enthusiastically bouncing on the bed. 'It will do just fine.'

The young man stood red-faced while the porter who had carried the key observed me with astonishment. 'Er . . . I hope you have a pleasant stay, Mrs Sheridan,' said the young man. They backed towards the door, still looking at me strangely. Before they went the under-manager said gravely: 'We were, of course, madam, terribly sorry to hear about Mr Dante. Please accept our deepest sympathies.'

I accepted it sadly and graciously and they went out, looking puzzled. Then I stripped naked and lay back on the large bed. I felt weary but free. Now, at last, I was back. Once more I could lead the life that came so naturally to me. The life to which I belonged.

The morning, naturally, brought a great many second thoughts, not concerned, needless to say, with the morality or properness of the plan but merely the mechanics. How to collect customers?

In a place like Burridges, it was obviously not the done thing to solicit in the foyer, standing provocatively swinging a door key. They would hardly have allowed that even from a guest of my standing. I could advertise discreetly, I thought, but it would not take long for that to be exposed. What I really needed was an agent. Someone to quietly point clients in my direction. Someone I could trust.

As a beginning I questioned the waiters who brought my breakfast trolley about the status of the guests at present staying at the hotel. There were the usual small princes, a maharajah and two or three sheikhs, but this was before sheikhs were fashionable. There were the usual English society names, some of whom I knew and I would need to avoid, and a lot of Americans. It was obviously a situation for a reconnaissance.

After breakfast I navigated the lounges and the foyer, attempting to look interesting but chaste. I sat elegantly in one room and then in another. Then I circled the entrance hall, made a foray up and down the street, and then returned to the foyer. The hall porter and some of the staff began to notice. Did madam require assistance?

I thanked them and declined with grace, backing towards the lift. As the doors closed I heard the porter say to the doorman 'Racked with grief, I've no doubt. Racked with it.'

I occupied the remainder of the morning trying to think how to begin my business. At lunchtime the answer was dropped neatly but quietly into my lap in that efficient way fate often had with those who need her.

My solitary lunch was taken in the grillroom and I found myself placed at the next table to a large and apparent lonely young man, plump-faced, who devastated his food with rural relish. We fell into conversation in a way which, I supposed, would have scandalized the older Burridges customers. He was a Yorkshire landowner in London to conclude a deal for beef. That much I understood. But he was one of those people who believe that everyone knows as much about, and is equally interested in, their business as well as they themselves. We were soon in a world of poundage and pedigree agricultural shows and artificial insemination. Somehow it seemed quite easy that we continued the conversation from the grillroom and up the stairs until we found ourselves, in the most natural way, outside my room. I then began a protracted point about horses and during the course of this I led him easily into the room.

Only inside the door did he react to the situtation. He may have been from the country but he was no bumpkin. 'By Christ, there's a nice bed!' he exclaimed. 'By God, you know I *do* fancy a lie down!'

'It's twenty pounds,' I said to him before I thought the better of it. Then not wanting to lose him. 'Fifteen in the afternoons.'

'Oh, right,' he nodded solemnly. 'You've got a little shagging business going 'ave you lass? I wondered what you were about chatting me up like that.' He sniffed like I suppose he sniffed when bidding at a cattle auction. 'Well,' he said, looking at the hefty watch around his huge, red-haired wrist. 'A've got an appointment at four, matter of some heifers, but it's only 'alf past two. Yes, why not, lass? Let's have one.'

It seemed like magic. I took his money and had my clothes off and was prostrate on the bed in only a moment. He gazed at me with slow appreciation. 'By Jesus, you've got some form on you,' he said. 'Beautiful. Aye, right gradely. Here I come.'

He was a grand looking chap himself, though a bit carpeted in rough hair, not unlike that on some cattle. He climbed athletically above me, briefly kissed each of my nipples in the manner of an uncle greeting two nieces, and then unerringly entered me.

He was not one to make a meal of it and within five minutes we were lying together, him smoking a large cigar, deep in post-coital conversation.

''Ow long have you been about this game then?' he inquired. 'In this hotel, I mean. It's not generally known for its shagging, you know. More for its roast beef.'

I had to tell him. 'You're the first one,' I confessed. 'But I want to set up a regular business if I can. There trouble is you can't be too obvious here. The staff watch everyone like vultures anyway. I've got to find a way of building up a clientele.'

'Well,' he said ponderously thinking. 'Ah know one or two who'd be only too pleased to come along and give you a fuck. And I know some cricketers too. The season starts at the end of the month. It's no bother to me, I like to see a lass trying to get on by her own efforts. There's too many sit at home. There'll be the word going round, don't worry, but discreet, like.'

I was so pleased, I offered him a refund of half the fee, but he waved it aside with the cigar. 'No lass,' he said kindly. 'It were not half a fuck, so I don't want half the money back. You keep it. Good luck to you.'

Two hours was all I had to wait for my next customer. He was in a hurry, banging urgently on the door and almost falling into the room when I opened it. He was a middle-aged man in a city grey suit, bowler and umbrella, red in the face from running, completely out of breath. Worried by the state of him I helped him to a chair, opened his winged collar and got him a glass of water. After a while he smiled through his sweat: 'Got in here in time, anyway. I . . . I wasn't sure what time you closed.'

The young Yorkshireman had sent him with a warm recommendation. 'We've been doing some business,' he explained when his lungs were working normally again. 'I'm a solicitor.' He laughed throatily. 'We're both in the same line, in fact. Anyway I hear it's fifteen pounds, is that right?'

'Twenty after six o'clock,' I replied, thinking I ought to get these matters in order right from the beginning. We both looked at our watches. 'Is it time of arrival, or the time intercourse actually takes place?' he inquired, his solicitor's mind taking over. 'If it's the first then I got here with three minutes to spare, if it's the second then we're going to have to move terribly quickly.'

I had to laugh. 'We'll make it time of arrival', I said.

'Oh good,' he replied. 'You have a sort of sliding scale, do you? I must say I think it's a grand idea doing it here at Burridges. Such comfort, such elegance, good beds. But don't they notice the customers coming up to you?'

'You're only the second,' I admitted. 'I only started today. I expect they will notice in time.'

'Only the second! Then my Yorkshire friend was the first! How marvellous.' He began to undress enthusiastically. There are some men who want to undress you (always the same types who cannot undo a button or a hook and eye) and others who want you to undress them, just like their mothers did, and a third sort who don't want the preliminaries. This man had his clothes off like somebody in a comic obstacle race. 'You ought to try the fire escape, you know,' he said thoughtfully. He sat down quietly, naked in the chair while I undressed, feeling a trifle disconcerted at his concern with the technicalities.

My breasts came from their covering, round and ripe. 'I worked on the fire regulations for this hotel,' he said, not seeming to notice. 'If I remember, there's a fire escape just along this corridor. You ought to bring your clients up that way, certainly after dark. Let's see, you get to it by going along East Audley Street and turning right into a little alley. Yes, that's it. Remember the situation well.'

Patiently I sat down. We faced each other, both professionals, both clients. 'Even if they caught you at it,' he mused, 'I wonder which section of the act they could use. You're not keeping a disorderly house. You're not soliciting. Hmm, interesting. Listen if they *do* nab you, here's my card. Give me a call.' Automatically he reached for where his waistcoat pocket would normally be. His fingers touching his bare chest woke him up to the situation. 'Oh dear, sorry,' he smiled thinly. 'I do chatter on, don't I?'

'I was beginning to wonder who was consulting who about what,' I said.

'Yes, quite. Well I came here about *my* problems, not yours. Can we start right away? A few minutes with you will give me the fortitude to face my wife for another evening. Here's the money. Fifteen pounds, we said. Could you give me a receipt?'

'A receipt!'

'Er . . . yes . . . sorry. Unusual, I know, but I have to cover myself. Here, I've got some blank paper if I can find my briefcase, just jot down something like "Inquiries *re* fire escapes. Mayfair." That'll do. Scribble a signature underneath. They don't check very thoroughly. Good, thank you very much.'

I finished signing. I sat back and looked at him oddly. We had been naked for several minutes and nobody had laid a finger on anybody up to that time. 'Sorry,' he waffled. 'Taking up your precious time. Well, I'm pretty well ready now.' He tried putting the receipt into a pocket in his bare chest, blushed with embarrassment again, and filed it in his briefcase. 'London,' he muttered. 'All rush. All bustle. No time to breathe.'

He fussed around for several more minutes, folding his trousers in their creases and arranging his stiff collar tidily on the dressing table. I waited, my patience diminishing. 'Is there anything else before we start? I asked sarcastically. 'You wouldn't like some tea by any chance?'

'No time, no time,' he fluttered. Then he realized. 'Oh you're pulling my leg. Pull the other one.'

I reached out and pulled the middle one. I almost tugged him towards me, pushed him back on the bed and mounted him from above. He liked that. 'Ah yes, the dominance syndrome,' he murmured. 'Yes very unusual. Tried to get the wife to do this, but the silly bitch keeps falling off. Yes. Splendid. Most acceptable.'

He did not stop all the way through. In contrast to his fussing beforehand, he climaxed very quickly and efficiently, glancing at his watch immediately afterwards and noting: 'One minute forty-three seconds.'

After that I had to lie back and watch him. In a vivid series of jerks and jumps he got himself washed, dressed, collar fixed, bowler on, umbrella over arm, and then pointed like some greyhound towards the door, he again consulted his watch and said: 'Ten minutes to get the six-fifty. Cheery-bye.' And out he flew.

After that first day my business grew with gratifying speed. At all hours of the day and into the night gentlemen might have been observed – but fortunately were not – creeping up the fire escape of Burridges or coming in with casual boldness through the main foyer and up to the third floor by the lift. The cocktail bar and even the grillroom took on the form of a waiting room, with clients drinking or sometimes having a meal, while they waited for an appointment. They came from a variety of sources, my fame, or infamy if you like, and my telephone extension being passed around quickly by word of mouth. Lunchtime became particularly busy with pin-striped men rushing across the city by taxi for a ten minute session before returning renewed to their bulls and their bears. One man regularly brought his sandwiches and a bottle of good wine which we always shared, the only disadvantage being that he invariably left crumbs in the sheets.

Late afternoon would bring the going-home brigade, coming in one after the other from their offices, their eyes on their watches and muttering about British Rail and London Transport. I became quite and expert on surburban timetables and certainly, with some of my regular clients, I knew to the very stroke when they would have to be finished and on their way to their homeward train. By heart I began to know the frequency of services to Tunbridge Wells, Horsham, Basingstoke and, appropriately, Effingham Junction.

Early evening would bring gentlmen in evening dress. One left the notes of a speech he was going to make at the Dorchester under my pillow and, very agitated, had to rush back for them at the last minute. Then midnight would bring the inevitable sequence of well-dined chaps, who had to be cautioned about making a noise in the corridors or on the fire escape, and there was an occasional early hours emergency call from some fellow who had missed his last train or had his car stolen or was in some way stranded.

Even the cricketers promised by my very first customer began to materialize as May grew longer. I was told that my activities had a profound effect on that year's matches, and one team had a brilliant, and as far as I was concerned profitable, arrangement whereby they sent to my room a particularly clever batsman or bowler who was due to play against them the following day. I undertook to make sure that his performance – on the field that is – was below expectations.

Naturally I found I was making money hand over fist (although that is hardly anatomically accurate), and my account at my Park Lane bank was healthier by the day. Unfortunately many men were not satisfied with what nature intended and requests for diversions were soon being made. I had to lay in a stock of costumes, ironmongery and implements of chastisement that faintly disgusted me. Indeed it was this aspect of the business that finally revealed me for what I was, and sent the general manager of Burridges to begin a new career as the publican of The Hanging Grapes on the Great West Road.

Three of my regular irregulars, as it were, the punishment addicts, always arrived together and underwent their session at the same time, never speaking a word nor even apparently recognizing each other even though they were all Members of Parliament (from different parties). This half hour was probably the most sexless of the week, for it involved me doing nothing more than putting one in the pillory, which I had arranged to have smuggled into the hotel in kit form and which could be erected in a few minutes in the middle of the floor. He would take off his clothes and hang there, head and arms imprisoned like some pathetic pick-pocket from the Middle Ages. One of his companions demanded to be stood naked in a corner wearing a dunce's cap and boringly recited his multiplication tables, while the third required to be beaten with a stick of fresh, wet celery.

It was when this strange tri-partite activity was taking place, with me wearing my school matron's costume, that the management of Burridges decided to raid my room. Without even the courtesy of a knock on the door the general manager, the house detective and half a dozen staff who came out of curiosity flung themselves into the room. I was just raising the celery to deliver the first of the half dozen blows that the client required across his bent, bare bottom.

'Mrs Sheridan!' howled the manager. 'What in God's name is happening here?'

I remained cool. 'Let me see,' I ruminated. 'That man in the corner is a dunce saying his tables, this chap is a naughty boy in the pillory and I'm just about to give this one a crack with a stick of fresh, wet celery. That's all.'

The three clients all began to howl like children because they thought they would be recognized and I insisted that the management troops withdraw while the gentlemen regained their everyday clothes, attitudes and reputations and were allowed to leave, unobserved, by the fire escape. I guessed rightly that Burridges wanted to make as little fuss as possible. A scandal like this must not be allowed to come to the ears of the newspapers.

For the same reason they waived my bill for the week and hurried me off the premises. They were shuddering around my room getting my luggage and props shifted when a man appeared through the window of the fire escape, a tall, sallow man with grinning eyes and small moustache. I attempted to wave him away, but he was not in the least put out by the obvious dismantling of my business. In front of the general manager, the manager and those who were fussing around, he bowed and said: Mrs Sheridan, I am delighted to meet you. This is my card. I hope I can be of some service to you in the near future.' Then he replaced his bowler hat, bowed and made his exit the same way as he had arrived – through the fire escape window. Entranced by the performance I looked at the card before the aghast faces of the hotel men. It said 'Pierre Arthur Bickerstaff', and beneath that modestly: 'First Rate Businessman.'

CHAPTER SEVENTEEN

Pierre Arthur Bickerstaff had attained the difficult distinction of being a rogue and a fraud without being a hypocrite. In my past and many dealings wih dishonest persons, particularly in my Riviera days with Davie, they had, almost without exception, made excuses of ill-fortune and the cruelty of the world as the reasons for their thievery and worse.

They were snivellers, moaners, cowerers, belly-ache bandits. Pierre Arthur Bickerstaff was a bastard without alibis.

I went to see him, in one of his offices in a financial house of the City of London, about a week after he had presented his card with such style in such strange circumstances. I had money and the ambition to make more. But I needed guidance.

He sat behind a desk only marginally less elegant and polished than he was, around him sombre panelled walls, decorated with paintings and photographs of shipwrecks, which was something of a hobby as well as a business interest with him. I sat opposite, set his card upon the desk, and said bluntly: 'Well, what do you do?'

His response was unforgettable. He leaned back in his black upholstered chair, put his thumbs in the armholes of his striped waistcoat (he also wore what he always described as his 'near-Old Etonian' tie) and recited, without appearing to pause for breath.

'Pierre Arthur Bickerstaff,' he intoned, 'was born, circa 1928 or thereabouts, at Buxton, the lovely Derbyshire spa, of a French mother, Madam Lisette Reynaud, of Alsace, and an English father, Arthur Bickerstaff, a roving dealer, sometime of Dingle in the city of Liverpool. His schooling was of a desultory nature but through endeavour, cleverness and some artistic cheating, he rose quickly but steadily through the strata of business life, arriving in the City of London at the early age of eighteen. He was called to the army but served only three days before being honourably discharged with a pension, whereupon he returned to a relieved City to begin what has certainly been one of the most remarkable careers of this business century.

'Mrs Sheridan, you are now looking at that same Pierre Arthur Bickerstaff. You ask what do I do? The answer is everything, but only a little of each. I am, you might say, a wheeler and a dealer who has been known to double-wheel and double-deal. I have been very rich and very poor, unkempt and kempt, but always with prospects ahead. I have dealt with shipbuilding and shipwrecking, the insurance aspects that is, I have moved in every sort of commodity in the share market and once I was almost admitted, through error I must confess, as a member of the Stock Exchange and of Lloyds. Since that disappointment I have preferred to play the part of an *éminence grise*, a pimpernel, a flitting ghost of the financial alleys. Everyone thinks they know me, few actually do. But my touch is everywhere, Mrs Sheridan, I am the least well-known person in London and the best least-known man.' He smiled conclusively. 'In fact nobody knows how famous I am.'

He then told me he could get me cheap groceries, petrol, collections of Green Shield Stamps or interests in Bolivian tin mines. He also had a friend who ran children's parties and owned his own cowboy suit.

I sat fascinated and amazed. 'None of that interests me,' I said, however. He remained blithe. 'I did not think it would,' he said. 'But it's entertaining isn't it? It's merely a patter I have learned by heart and I like to use on the occasional person.'

I applauded gently. 'Very nice too,' I said. 'Very entertaining. Now, what did you want with me?'

'Well, frankly Nell, that particular afternoon when I appeared through the fire escape window, I had come for a fuck, but I quickly ascertained that your game was up and Burridges were hurrying you away. There was nothing in the gossip columns was there?'

'They were scared stiff of publicity,' I pointed out.

'Of course. You should have blackmailed them. That must have been worth a couple of thousand at least.'

'I didn't think of it.'

'*Exactement.* That's why you need Pierre Arthur Bickerstaff,' he said. He rose from the desk. He was very tall and slim, the pinstripes seeming to go on for miles, like railway tracks. 'Let's have a drink,' he suggested. 'I have just taken a rare consignment of Moroccan champagne, so much less fussy than the French variety I always think. Will you have a glass?'

I said I would and watched him lope around the room like a giraffe until he opened a concealed wall cupboard and produced his Moroccan champagne. As he progressed, the photographs of the shipwrecks passed behind him like a cinematograph. 'Tragedies of the sea,' he said, sensing my look, pointing the long finger as he went by. 'Each one a ring on the Lutine Bell and a wringing of a hundred hearts. You were in a shipwreck once, I understand, Nelly.'

His knowledge shocked me. I was very impressed. 'How in the world did you now that?' I asked.

'Ah, newspaper cuttings, records, I have them all available. When I became interested in you I had a little research done and among the social chit-chat of the past few years, all worthless, appeared a photograph of you as a young lady being helped ashore in France after a vessel had foundered. You were but very young at the time, I think.'

Dumbfounded I reached out and took the champagne from him. 'You certainly seem to know your business,' I said. 'But I'd still like to know . . .'

'Your good health, Nelly,' he said, raising his glass. 'I have a notion that this might be a propitious day for both of us.'

I raised my glass but said nothing. I couldn't take my eyes from him. Every movement was long and accomplished, every word, every expression an entertainment. 'Moroccan champagne,' he beamed over his glass. 'Not bad for a poor lad from Derbyshire, eh?'

Like a snake he suddenly curled and slid around the desk. Once more he was in his businesslike position, thumbs tucked into the waistcoat, confidence in every slim line of his face. His moustache twitched enticingly. 'I have two propositions to make,' he said eventually. 'I hope that you will find them both of interest. Firstly may I say that your setting up business in Burridges Hotel had a touch of genius about it, and being of that nature myself, I was quick to acknowledge it. Unfortunately that sort of traffic was bound to be discovered eventually. Did you know that the takings in the little bar downstairs were up thirty per cent? That was your customers waiting until you were free. Yes, a marvellous stroke, but one that could not be sustained.

'My suggestion is based on the fact that a great proportion of your fortunate clients came from the City of London. Indeed I first heard your name and game whispered in a tavern in Leadenhall Street. If you now merely rented yourself the conventional flat in the Curzon Street area you would only be duplicating a service which is already overloaded. Your attraction was not only your undoubted beauty but the uniqueness of your bedroom.

'What I would now like to put forward is that you should transfer your business to the City of London itself, away from the traditional haunts of illicit pleasure. No one, as far as I am aware, has ever set up a knocking shop within the City. And yet it is crying out for it. There's money there, God knows, great pressures and the need to relax and unfold, and always the odd couple of hours in the day when the market gets a bit dull. The City has everything, banks, finance houses, legal institutions, even Fleet Street for God's sake, and they're randy enough down there, insurance bustle and business. Every business in fact but yours.'

I sat feeling my mouth drop lower as he continued. He smiled at my fascination. 'Not bad, eh?' he said. 'And it could all be daytime business. By seven o'clock, apart from the odd dinner or reunion, the place is as dead as a fish's eye. Your evenings would be your own.'

'It's . . . it's never been done before?' I said.

'Not as far as I know. For diversions of that sort the frustrated financier and the steaming stockbroker either have to travel east to the lower confines of Aldgate Pump and thereabouts, which is not of great quality or salubriousness, or get in a taxi and make their way to the opposite side of London to the more usual places, as before mentioned. We must set you up in luxury, an apartment or a penthouse worthy of your beauty and desirability. It would not even be illegal, for a cat house only becomes a cat house in the eyes of the law when there is more than one cat using it. Neither would you need to solicit business. I will be your agent and send the right people your way. For this service I will charge a set fifteen per cent. All expenses to come from income.'

He smiled dazzlingly. His teeth were carnivorous. 'I think it sounds interesting,' I said at last.

'Good, good. Well done Nelly,' he enthused. 'Think – you could be the *Young* Lady of Threadneedle Street!'

'What was the other thing you mentioned? The other proposal?' I asked cautiously.

'Ah yes, that *other* proposal,' he mused. He looked down at the desk and then directly at me again. 'Well, it's simply this. The whole scheme would be a lot easier to handle if you married me.'

We were married a month later, very secretly, in the registrar's office at Bognor Regis, a very secret place, and we spent our honeymoon through a series of thunderstorms in the Commercial and Regent Hotel in that town. I was still supposedly in mourning for Dante Sheridan but Pierre's need for secrecy was even greater (for very good business reasons he did not want our union to be known), thus our resort to Bognor.

I wore white, as has been the custom at my weddings, but this time reduced it to a linen costume and a small white hat. Pierre wore his pinstripes – I can never remember seeing him in anything else – he even wore pinstriped pyjamas – and the only other people in attendance were the registrar and a council workman we invited in off the street to act as a witness, for a small fee.

If the wedding was unpretentious, the honeymoon was the most enjoyable I had ever had, which I suppose was not difficult. Pierre was a breezy companion, always talking or reciting or singing, which he did rather well in an old-fashioned Victorian manner. Our sexual union, which we saved for the wedding night, another old-fashioned touch, was easily and happily achieved since we had nothing to hope or fear from each other. During our three days in the Commercial and Regent Hotel he bought the hotel and resold it at a modest profit without ever using any money of his own. In many ways he was someone you could admire.

In between thunderstorms we would go out to get something to eat or to breathe some strong sea air and he would walk beside me telling a continuous stream of jokes. Most of them were very funny. But it was the way we staggered along, holding hands, in the gusty wind or began running when it started to rain again, all the time keeping up a breathless commentary of funny stories. That was what was so enjoyable. In a strange way he began to make me feel young again. One afternoon we went to a tea-dance in a hall along the front and I found myself waltzing and tangoing with this lean, elegant and surprising husband, while powdery ladies and furtive men shared pots of tea and crumpets and the band played wheezily.

Before leaving London he had set about obtaining an apartment for me within the business bounds of the City and when we returned, by chauffeur-driven Bentley, it was ready to be visited. Pierre had been living in St John's Wood and we kept that house as our home. The other would be a workplace.

It was a sumptuous workplace, five rooms spread across the top floor of an office building, and soon carpeted and furnished with every need, including a circular bed with an oyster shell canopy. The City men, he said, were partial to a little fantasy.

We stood at the living-room window looking down at the scurrying heads of London. 'See them beetling about down there,' he said, not sarcastically but with a certain fondness. 'Rush from the brokers to the Stock Exchange, from the banks to the insurance houses, from the shipping offices to the financiers. Busy, busy, busy. But each must pause at some time and each must have thoughts away from this turmoil of money. And you, Nelly, will provide the satisfactions they seek. Down there are your lovers.'

He discovered somewhere an old Japanese proverb which said: 'In the hustle and bustle of the market place there is much money to be made. But under the Cherry Tree there is rest.'

He had this printed on small but distinguished looking cards with merely a telephone number below. These were distributed to discreet customers; our apartment immediately became known as the Cherry Tree, and Nelly Luscombe was in its foliage.

On the first day of opening Pierre sent me a magnificent bunch of red roses. We had installed a tongue-tied Turkish housemaid who stood poised to answer the door while I lay at the centre of the oyster shell on my round bed, looking very fine in a pink nightgown. It took only half an hour for the first phone call, but the customer, when he arrived, was something of a surprise.

It was a heatwave in the street and he arrived, wet with perspiration, handing the astonished maid his briefcase and his jacket with one thrust as he came through the front door. He advanced on me in his shirt and braces, a large, excited man.

'It's going up!' he said. 'Up and up.'

'The Bank Rate?' I asked.

'No, the bloody temperature dear. God, it's like Panama down there. Be glad to get my togs off. How much is it?'

I must confess I felt a bit hurt by his attitude. After all my careful and romantic arranging of myself on the bed I had expected at least a compliment on how I looked. He dropped his trousers without ceremony. 'At least they're out at last,' he went on. 'The bloody Aussies. Bastards they are. England fielded well for once. Got their fingers out.'

All I could do was nod at this stream of uninteresting information. But I learned in time that the City Englishman would rather talk about anything other than what he was doing or about to do with me.

'Shallots!' one cried as he climbed across my bed. 'Can't grow shallots in my garden. Try as I may.' Others would tell me about their wives, usually their shortcomings, or the girls at the office who wore their skirts too high, or their golf swing had gone to pieces (this, quite often, with a demonstration, standing there naked, erect and swishing an imaginary golf club).

Every whore gets used to it. She must be an actress and an athlete, a lover and a mother, a listener and occasionally an adviser. She is put-upon almost as frequently as she is laid-upon. She must never, except in the most outrageous circumstances, lose her temper. She must be able to turn on love as though it were a tap, but she must expect nothing in return except money. A woman who gives herself to love must never expect to receive it. One moment she is the object of every desire, high and frequently low, an oasis, a resting place, a comforter, and the next she is abandoned for the demands of the five-thirty to Sevenoaks. Two things she must have, understanding and a strong back.

The Cherry Tree was a great success from the first day. I remember Pierre calling me in the early evening. 'How much did we take?' he asked.

'Eighty-seven pounds,' I said.

'I'll come and pick you up,' he whispered fondly. 'Tonight we will go somewhere special for dinner.'

Our life together was surprisingly simple. At weekends we would go out from St John's Wood to Richmond and take a boat down the river and have tea in some place with a garden and trees crowding the water.

Or we would go down the park on a Sunday and sit in the chairs and listen to the band in the bandstand. Pierre would wear his white shirt open at the collar at weekends and he would lean back in his pinstriped suit and warble away to himself and to me while the band trumped out some overture or some music hall melody. It used to give me such pleasure just to see him enjoying himself. We would leave the music-makers and walk across the park to the public house where we would sit holding hands and drinking lemonade shandies and after that we would walk home to our house. With this unlikely man I was beginning to find peace.

We were never anything less than comfortable and occupied in each other's company. He always told me jokes, thousands of them, and I enjoyed his antics while he told them. On impulse, to amuse me, he would take a parked bicycle and ride it down the street, or he would take off his shoes and socks and paddle in a roadside puddle like a boy. We made love only on Sunday nights because he did not want to tire me for business commitments.

The week at Cherry Tree would start quietly, but about midday those who had been running the matter over in their minds at the weekend would begin to telephone and sidle in. Monday afternoon was frequently the busiest few hours of the week and I would be quite glad when seven o'clock arrived and they all went home to their wives and the streets of the City were deserted and hushed. Usually I would walk to the taxi rank among the cats and town dogs sniffing around, with janitors going for their evening pint and charladies waiting for their buses home. It was so empty then it was like being in Devon again.

There were, of course, times when my customers were kind enough to give me information about financial matters that were to my considerable advantage. I remember, one stockbroker who, riding me like a national hunt jockey, gasped between jumps 'Tanlings, buy Tanlings, Nelly. There's a takeover bid.'

This was followed by other genuine information and I got myself a stockbroker and phoned him between assignations, frequently making ten times as much from the phone call as I had done from the performance which led to the whisper.

Some Members of Parliament who had been my customers at Burridges and who had dealings in the City continued as clients, but at the Cherry Tree I discontinued the satisfactions which required so much equipment and embarrassment. I simply could not get used to the idea that those who governed us should want to be governed themselves in such curious and elementary ways. The City customers, because they were for the most part fairly quickly in and out (sometimes in the space of a coffee break), had no time at all for shackles and such-like and I was glad to exclude it.

From my activities in the City I began to get invitations to travel with various gentlemen. At first I refused on the grounds that I, of all people, could not leave the business. Then fees of such enticement, plus the attraction of a visit to Paris, Zurich, Toronto, or New York, were offered and I asked Pierre Arthur what I ought to do. To my amazement he was touchingly shocked at the very idea.

'Nelly, I am *not* permitting my wife to travel abroad with another man,' he announced with the logic that was his alone. 'It's quite scandalous.'

However when the amounts on offer began to look like three hundred pounds he regarded it more charitably and said it might be good for me. The change would broaden my outlook and there would be some social life for me to enjoy. Yes, I could go. But I had to be home by the weekend. We were going to Kew Gardens. The daffodils were out.

My role on these visits varied with the circumstances of my host or employer. Sometimes it would be a businessman who could openly enjoy having me with him at social functions and for dinner. Or perhaps it would be some hole-in-the-corner man who tucked me away in a room and then would sneak in when he could with an elaborate system of knocking on the door. One of these furtive fornicators did not pay me one visit throughout our trip to Washington and I discovered later that his wife had followed him unexpectedly and he had had to pay attention to her requirements. I spent the entire four days watching television and eating chocolates. Naturally he still had to pay.

Sir Courtney Bellow took me with him several times, a charming old fellow with a white moustache like a pair of horns. He was so busy and so absent-minded that he often forgot about me altogether and would return exhausted to the hotel after some trying session with the International Monetary Fund, and be amazed and delighted to find me waiting in bed.

'Good God, Nelly! Damned forgot you were here, dear. Had a nice day? Hope so. Absolute fucker myself. Be with you in a moment.' He would pour himself a gigantic scotch and take it into the bathroom with him. After some twenty minutes I would go in and find him fast asleep in the bath, pushing furrows across the water like some benevolent snoring walrus. I would have to get him out, dry him, dress him in his flowered pyjamas and roll him into bed. He was a lovely old fellow.

There was a treasury official, a young ambitious man, determined to get his money's worth, who would tear back to the hotel to screw me between sessions of whatever conference he was attending. He would come in like a middle distance runner, taking his clothes off as he came through the door, slam himself on top of me, have it, then dash for the debating table again. By the end of the day it cannot have been much fun for the delegate sitting next to him.

After every foreign assignment, no matter where, I returned alone and Pierre would be at the airport to meet me with a slim but glad smile, a bunch of flowers and the latest limerick or joke. He would collect the money from me (half paid on leaving, half on return) and whisk us home to St John's Wood where I would rest before going out to the pub or the park on my husband's arm. It was becoming a fine life.

It was not always possible for me to take every phone call that came for an appointment at the Cherry Tree, and the Turkish maid, who gradually became less tongue-tied, sometimes made these appointments for me.

It was as a result of one of her arrangements that one afternoon a diminutive telegram boy, bicycle clips, peaked cap and a deadly squint behind rimless spectacles arrived at the door. He was shown in and I swayed out in a long blue silk negligée, expecting a client, to be confronted by those small wild eyes and hanging mouth.

'Oh,' I said, half covering up my front. 'Just leave it then.'

'Just leave wot?' he asked, his eyes even further askance.

'The telegram,' I said. 'You're a telegram boy aren't you?'

'This ain't the uniform of the Coldstream Guards, lady,' he sniffed. 'But there ain't no telegram. I came for the other.'

'The *other*?' I was sincerely shocked.

'Yeah, you know, the *other*, what you can get in 'ere. Is it you?'

I felt giddy.'What? Who . . . who sent you?'

He sniffed. 'I got sent. Let's leave it like that. Listen . . . missus, I know this is where it is.'

I had sat down. Now I got up sternly. 'I think you'd better clear off, young man,' I ordered. 'Come on. Hop it.'

He looked so crushed I took my hand from his arm. 'Aw, hang about,' he said. 'I got the money. I was looking forward to it.'

I sat down heavily. The maid, who was hovering about like a thrush on a window sill, went to open the door, but I waved her away. I reached out and brought the boss-eyed boy closer. 'I really think you ought to go son,' I said. 'It's not right.'

'I got the money,' he said again. 'Look.' From his pocket he took four five pound notes. 'I won the office sweep, see. For the most goals in the month. I can spend it on anything I want. And . . . I want . . . you know . . . Don't kick me out, missus. It took all the guts I got to come 'ere in the first place.'

There was nothing I could say. I sat there and studied him. His face was bright with eagerness. 'I'm not sure it's not illegal,' I said half to myself. 'At your age.'

'Sixteen in March, I was. So it's all right. I found out for you. In fact lady, there ain't such thing as under age for boys with women, only girls with dirty old men. I know a bloke in a solicitor's and he told me. It's true. But I want to undress myself.'

'Oh Christ,' I said.

'Here's the money,' he said, holding out two of the five pounds notes. 'Ten quid. Or do I get half price?'

'I don't think you get anything,' I decided firmly. 'Come on. Off you go. Home to your mum.'

He looked stunned. 'No,' he whispered. 'Don't send me away. I'm old enough. And I won't tell anybody. Straight.'

To my own surprise I began to wonder whether he ought to keep his glasses on or take them off, whether that reckless squint would be too much to look at when it was roaming free. He smiled in a juvenile way. 'If I don't get it now I don't reckon I ever will,' he said, playing the card carefully. 'Girls don't like me because I'm so bleeding ugly.'

My heart and my hand went out to him simultaneously. He grinned because he knew he had won. 'I'll get my fings off,' he said. 'Don't look.'

I went almost entranced to the bed. I lay back against the oyster shell and waited for him to appear. In less than a minute he had scampered around the bathroom door without his glasses and came laughing towards me. He stopped when he saw the bed. 'Blimey, that's somefink, that bed, innit?' he said. 'Like them fings wot you get jellied eels in dahn the Mile End Road.'

He was white and skinny as a stick. But he had plenty of confidence now. He climbed exuberantly on to the bed and pushed his small skinny head straight into my bosom. 'I like them,' he sighed, 'ever so.'

He knew where everything else was too, despite taking off his spectacles. I still could hardly believe this was happening and I almost leapt from the bed when he lifted my hem and made straight for me with his junior jumbo.

'My name's Fred,' he said before making another movement. His manner suggested he thought we ought to be introduced.

'I'm Nelly,' I said dazedly. 'Pleased to meet you.'

He was the sweetest lad ever, I swear. No expert lover could have been more kind, more gentle or enjoyable. Every now and then he lifted those madly crossed eyes and smiled. 'Are you all right down there?'

'I thought you'd never done this before,' I found myself whispering. I had never felt so flattered in my life. 'That's what you said.'

'Not to a *lady*,' he said, pausing to pass on the information. 'I've done it with a couple of girls in our alley. One was my sister. She's cross-eyed as well.' He sighed and went into my woman's warmth again. 'This is the first time I've done it without taking the bleeding skin off my knees.'

Needless, perhaps, to say, at the conclusion when he was once more uniformed and ready to go on his messenger's way, I offered to toss him double or quits for the ten pounds. We did. He won.

The Cherry Tree blossomed, as you might say, for almost two years. It became a comfortable, unexciting existence, weekends in the park in summer or at the Science Museum or Madam Tussaud's waxworks in the winter, and weekdays on the round bed. We, and I include Pierre Arthur because he handled all the contacts, built up a clientele that would have graced *Who's Who, The Directory of Directors, Debrett* and *Crockford's Clerical Directory*. I had regular assignations with a sly but jolly rural dean from Somerset who was most energetic between the sheets and who then talked to me of the error of my life for a hour afterwards. He had the full rounded voice of the West Country man and he reminded me of my long lost home.

One morning the same nostalgia, although more sudden and poignant, touched me when I received a letter with the postmark 'Upcoombe, Devon.' The handwriting was round and honest. It could only be from my sister Mary.

She wrote:

Dear Nell,

I am sending this to the last address I knew you were at, although we read in the papers that your poor husband had hung himself. We also saw that he had lost all his money which was very bad luck. This time I am writing to tell you that our Dad is dead too. He fell down in the street in Plymouth (drunk as usual) and was run over by a taxi. He never changed. Just before he died there on the road he got enough strength to punch the taxi driver in the face. The police said there was more blood from the taxi driver than there was from our poor Dad. They took him to hospital in the same ambulance as Dad, but Dad was dead by then. Anyhow he's dead for sure. He had two thousand pounds in the bank and the solicitor says that it's a thousand for each of us, though I don't expect you'll need yours. Dad was buried here, right alongside our Mum's grave (if you can remember where that is). They are back together anyway but Fred my husband says there's no cider where he is so he can't get drunk anymore. Fred's really witty sometimes.

I still work at the bakery and Fred is a pigman at Upcoombe and we have five children, four boys and a girl who looks just like you did then.

I hope one day you will come in for a cup of tea and see your sister again.

> Your sister,
> *Mary.*

God knows why but I sat on the bed and had a little cry for my father. Then I pictured the little old bastard lying in the Plymouth street and punching the taxi driver in the face before dying. It made me laugh and then remember all the terrible things he had always done, the bomb he made from his army mess tins, the marching behind our mum's coffin with that shotgun and firing it across her grave, the terrible thing he did when he abducted me from my own wedding in France and sold me to pay his gambling debts. I wondered how he would fare on Judgement Day. He would probably get off with a caution.

Two months later I received a cheque from a solicitor in Plymouth for a thousand pounds. I sent the money to the person in charge of the old folks' home in the town to provide cider every day for the people there. I said it was from the Luscombe Cider Memorial Fund.

Towards the end of our second year of marriage and business I began to notice a marked decline in my number of daily appointments. At first they dropped to half a dozen and then to four, then two and after than I was glad to hear the doorbell ring as I sat disgruntled and watched afternoon television. I mentioned this to Pierre Arthur but he was quite airy and unworried about it. 'There's not the cash about, dear,' he said. 'Uncertainty in the City and suchlike. We are a country on the downward path.'

He seemed to take the matter so calmly that I began to be concerned.

Takings had dropped by seventy per cent and I was finding it difficult to fill my time. I even considered taking a part-time position somewhere else.

One afternoon a nice, gentlemanly fellow, a solicitor from Lincoln's Inn, was sharing my round bed and I mentioned this slump to him. 'Yes, yes, Nell,' he replied. 'It's a great pity. You have always given such satisfaction, such good measure. I'm sure the new girl can't match you for that.'

I lay back against the oyster shell, feeling myself go pale all down my naked body. 'The new girl?' I muttered. 'There's a new girl?'

He looked professionally aghast at having given away a secret. 'Oh dear, Nell,' he said. 'You didn't know. Oh dear, oh dear.'

Even then I concluded, naturally, that this was some rival organization set up to take away the business. 'Just wait,' I muttered. 'Just wait until Pierre Arthur knows about this.'

'I think, my dear,' said the solicitor, 'I think you'll find he knows already.'

There was a fairground that weekend on Hampstead Heath and I knew that Pierre Arthur would want to go there. I said nothing to him about my discovery until, on the Saturday evening, we were sitting high above London at the top of the big wheel. It paused at the top and we could see the widespread lights of the city below and feel the thrill of being suspended in the air.

Pierre Arthur had been acting the card that evening, as he so often did, making quick jokes, singing a ditty about coming to the fair, and holding my hand. Within me my heart was like a piece of stone for, with that instinct formed by long experience, I knew that something was going to finish us that night. It would be our last few hours in each other's company. So I laughed with him for a final time. We rode on the dodgem cars and roundabouts, him like some eccentric teenager making zooming noises over the handlebars of a tin motorbike. I sat on a funny ostrich and watched him with tears just behind my eyes.

We fired at moving targets and bit into clouds of candyfloss. He seemed to be no different from the way he always was, the eternal boyish businessman. Then we took our ride on the wheel.

When we were stopped at the height of the great wheel with the fairground music gurgling up to us from the revolving lights below and then darkness stretching away across the open heath to the limpid lights of London, I pressed his hand and said in the most ordinary voice I could make: 'Pierre Arthur, who is the new girl you have working for you?'

For the only time since our first meeting I saw him shaken out of his composure. He climbed back quickly but the look had been there, rushing to his face.

'Girl? New girl?'

'You've opened a new apartment,' I said steadily, still holding his slim hand. 'All the customers have been going there.'

'Not all,' he protested. 'Only some, Nelly.'

'Who *is* she?' His admission, although I had been awaiting it, was crushing.

He let out a manic laugh which shrieked across the fairground night and even made people in the din below look up towards us. I could see their faces like coins. 'Well . . . she's just a girl, Nell. An apprentice. I thought I'd try her out to take some work off your shoulders . . . if that's the right thing to say.'

He tried to laugh again but he could see I was not joining in. The man controlling the big wheel began to let it down gently. 'Who is she?' I repeated. 'Come on.'

Just a girl called Connie,' he said, almost blurting it out. 'Just a kid. A beginner.'

'How old?'

'Oh, I don't know . . . twenty-one, twenty-two, something like that.'

Just the mention of the age entered me like a chill. I was now in my thirties. The big wheel reached the bottom and Pierre Arthur helped me out, making an automatic joke to the attendant. I had released his hand now and we began to walk in the same direction but separately. In the two years we had known each other we had never once quarrelled.

'Look Nell,' he said pleadingly. 'It's time you gave it a rest. For your own sake. Let somebody else do it.'

'You didn't tell me,' I said quietly. 'You kept it from me.'

'I would have. Of course I would have. It was going to be a surprise.'

'It was a surprise. A nasty one.'

'Don't you think it's a good idea? Logically now? Honestly? When you're successful you open a branch office. This is all it is. Hah! That's a good one! A branch of the Cherry Tree! What about that Nell?'

'Bugger off,' I said briefly. 'Go away from me.'

He looked around to the front of my face. He could see I was angry and crying. 'I suppose you had to . . . to try her out first,' I snivelled.

Well, what's in that, it was just a . . .'

I didn't give him time to finish. 'Adulterer!' I bellowed. 'Dirty adulterer.'

People turned everywhere. Some smirked, some looked shocked and accusing. Pierre Arthur went red in the lights.

What about you?' he blurted back at me. 'Ten times a day.'

Exclamations went up all around. People began to gather for a close look. 'That's business,' I howled. '*Your* bloody business.'

'It's *all* business!' he shouted back, not caring now. 'All of it. She's just business. And so are *you!*'

It stunned me that he said it. But all at once I saw that it was true. He did not love me. And *now* I had found out after coming to care for him so much.

'Oh,' I bawled. 'Oh, now you've said it Pierre Arthur Bickerstaff!' I picked a coconut from a box standing by a stall and heaved it savagely at him. It actually bounced off his head and went on to shatter what was alleged to be a cut-glass flower vase on the shelf of prizes. Pierre Arthur fell down in the Hampstead mud and the two showmen, one short of a coconut and the other of a glass vase, started shouting. People gathered around my husband as if he were some sideshow himself. I ran away from the fairground lights and over the black heath, sobbing, running, running. Running again.

CHAPTER EIGHTEEN

That same night I went back to Weymouth. I did not know why; perhaps with some idea of escaping to youth, if not to innocence. After running down the slope of Hampstead Heath I reached a main road and from there took a taxi to Waterloo Station. At that moment I was running anywhere. Had my passport been in my handbag I would have gone to London Airport.

There was a melancholy lateness about Waterloo, the station concourse blowing with stray paper, most of the platform gates pulled and the damp night air lying over everything. There were some tramps huddled on the wooden seats bent almost double in sleep. I stood, isolated, looking at the indicator board. I would have gone to any place. Then I saw that a quarter to two in the morning there was a train to Weymouth. I decided to return.

The tramps sat like a scruffy oasis in the station desert. There was nothing for me to do but sit in the waiting room or pace the concourse, and somehow I gravitated towards the tramps. There was a space on one of the benches and I sat there, pulling my coat around my neck.

The bundle of rags to my left stirred and a cracked woman's voice came from it. She was speaking from the middle of the bundle and she did not look up.

'You on the road?' she asked.

'Yes,' I answered. 'I suppose I am.'

''Ow long you been on the road?'

'All my life.'

'It gets cold don't it?'

'Yes, it's cold.'

'And those church bleeders ain't come round with the soup tonight, neither. Can't trust nobody.'

'No,' I said with feeling. 'You can't trust nobody.'

'You going to Wimbledon this year, Eustace?' one of the other tramps suddenly inquired of the pile of rags at the far end of the benches.

'Course,' replied the rags. 'Never miss Wimbledon do I?'

'Same as me with Ascot and 'enley Regatta,' the first tramp called across. 'Never miss.'

'It gets cold on the road,' said the lady tramp next to me. 'Those church bleeders.'

I thought I ought to get them something to eat. Murmuring 'Excuse me,' I rose carefully from the bench and went through the station archway to where I could see a wan light in the café across the street. It was an Italian restaurant and they had just closed. There was a man wearily sweeping up but he opened the door when I banged on the glass. From him I purchased a large saucepan full of spaghetti which we reheated on the stove. I poured in all the Bolognaise sauce he had left, paid him and carried the saucepan back to the station benches.

The tramps, to my relief, all had their own spoons and forks and they crouched around the saucepan delving into the hot spaghetti and the thick sauce. The dark station air was warmed by the aroma. Then the lady tramp, my neighbour on the bench, paused and looked up, her spoon half way to her ragged mouth. 'Mind you,' she said. 'For myself I like it with a sprinkling of Parmesan cheese, and a nice glass of good red wine.'

It was strange to be in Weymouth again. We change but some things never do. It could have been the same breath of wind, the same day of sunshine, the same clouds and the self-same sea that rolled and grumbled forever to the beach.

I went to the Eden Roc Hotel, a rich place, unheard of in my days in the town, and in the morning stood in the bowl of the bay window of my room to look out across the fine grey patterns of the Channel on that cloudy day. There were ships hugging the horizon and I saw a small fishing boat working off-shore. Perhaps young Rainbow was still hauling out there in the sightless sea.

I did not hurry. I had risen late after the cold, stopping journey in the train carrying myself and the newspapers from London, and I had a quiet lunch in the almost vacant hotel dining room, and then walked down to the harbour. I felt like a ghost. The town that came to meet me was familiar enough, the buildings along the front, the clock and the flowers, for many things change less than we would have them change in our imagination.

But when I got to the quay and the place where Hal's Café ('always something hot') had been in those early days of my adventures, it had vanished and in its place was a tarty little coffee bar where three indolent teenagers lolled at a table and listened to music banging from a juke box. No one had ever heard of any people called Hal and Flossie. They had gone.

The wind pushed the clouds from the sky in the late afternoon and freed the sun. It splashed along the beach and the mounds of the waves and I remembered how many times I had walked that same sand in the icy winter of my girlhood there. There were some early visitors on the beach, making the most of the discomfiting wind, playing with children, lying with their faces to the sun. I walked among them, still in the clothes

I had worn at the Hampstead fairground the previous night that now seemed very long ago.

This place of my past set me thinking that I must take stock and plan for my future. My tears for Pierre Arthur Bickerstaff were dry and almost forgotten, for I do not grieve for long; if nothing else, I am resilient. I felt a residue of anger towards him for his amateur (as distinct from my professional) infidelity and with this I firmly closed the door on him and the period we had known.

For once, though, I was not changing lives penniless. Thanks both to my efforts beneath the oyster shell canopy and the investments I had made from advice offered in that same situation I had £32,850 in my bank account. I was free and rich. I also felt a certain oldness.

Back in the hotel I lay down for an hour and thought of what future I might have. I had many acquaintances, but hardly a friend, an occupied past but an uncertain future. I took my clothes off to bathe and stood before the mirror, remembering, for some reason, how I had done so long ago in girlhood, in front of the cottage looking-glass when Davie and I were in our runaway days. Considering the use to which it had been put, the body of Nelly Luscombe had survived well. The curves were fuller, but still symmetrical, the skin touched with small pockets and wrinkles but I had looked after it; it remained creamy. It was the eyes and the mouth and the breasts where the tiredness showed. I sat on the bed and crossed my legs. My thighs bulged. In a few years I would be forty. It was time I did something else for a living.

In the night I dreamed there was a storm with tiny ships trembling in great seas. I was on the bridge of a trawler with the Commander and, in the logic of dreams, we were playing housey-housey while the tempest spilled around us.

'House!' he was calling in that hurt, croaky voice. 'House Nelly! House!'

The dream so stirred me that I almost fell out of bed in the waves and awoke on my knees in an attitude of prayer. I rose and stumbled to the window. It was the loveliest calm night, moon travelling high, the sea silver, the land smooth. I sat by the window for a while, watching it and following the lights of a few fishing boats a mile or two out. I wondered if some fruity, willing Weymouth girl was out there with the lusty crews. Perhaps not these nights.

Because the dream was still with me and it had disturbed me so much I was reluctant to return to bed. For a while I missed the attentive Pierre Arthur, but I thought that at that moment his attentions were most probably on his new apprentice lover and I dismissed his face from my mind. But the nameless restlessness provoked by the sea perhaps, once familiar, now a new sensation again, would not go. I began to dress.

Outside among the silver and the shadows it was chilly and I tugged my coat against my body. The dozing hall porter had presumably seen odder things in his life and he had merely wished me a pleasant walk as he turned the large key in the door. I walked immediately towards the shoreline.

Every step, even across the grass, seemed to sound in the standing night. The air pressed cold against my eyes, the heaving of the Channel became more distinct. Then, almost at the beach, I saw the surprising sight of a Rolls-Royce parked on the grass with its headlights dipped. Walking towards it I saw that the door was open and there was a man sitting on the step looking down towards the beach. And on the beach, clear in the moon, was a young boy dancing to the sound of the sea. I looked towards the man, and he towards me, and we saw that we knew each other.

He was Derek Blane, a prominent Member of Parliament, who had been a business acquaintance of Dante. He had visited us and I had met him again, after Dante's death, at Zurich during one of my professional visits as the guest of a British delegate to a conference there.

We exchanged greetings as naturally as if it were the middle of the day not the night, and at his invitation I sat beside him on the doorstep of the Rolls. He was a dark, slender, sharp-faced man, then a good deal more good-humoured than he looked. I remembered thinking that about him before. The laugh would suddenly break from the serious and lined face, so quickly and easily that it came as a surprise.

'That's my son, Simon,' he said, nodding at the lad making ballet movements on the beach. 'He wants to be a dancer.'

'He certainly seems to have the dedication,' I said, hardly knowing how to reply. 'Practising in the middle of the night.'

Derek sighed. 'I'm told that he is really very good,' he said. 'He is now ten and they say he could become an exceptional dancer. And he loves it. He has been going down to the beach in the day and dancing in the firm sand. People have been gathering around to laugh at him but he's taken no notice at all. His eyes just glaze over when he is dancing and he doesn't see anybody.'

'People are like that,' I agreed. 'It's ignorance.'

'But,' he added, 'suddenly even they become quiet and they watch him and they realize what he is doing and just how talented he is. And at the end they stand and applaud. Some people come back every day. It's very funny, actually, because when they clap it sort of wakes him up. He blinks at them as though he has just come out of a trance.'

I watched the shadowy boy on the beach. His movements were like a graceful ghost or perhaps a sprite. The moon lay over the white sea, caught his shadow and threw it across the sand.

'He doesn't even need music, does he?' I said quietly.

'Not al all. In fact he comes down here at this time of night because it is so silent and the waves and sometimes the wind makes the noises he wants. The strange thing is, Nell, he is such a masculine kid. He's the best footballer I've seen in years at his age.'

'If he moves like that it's not surprising,' I said. I waited, then added: 'Where's his mother, Derek?'

He looked directly ahead and said: 'At this moment I would think that she is in bed with one of my political opponents. That's what hurts. If it were one of our side than it would not seem as if you were defeated in every direction.'

'Oh dear,' I said inadequately.

'And you, Nell?'

I thought it was improbable that he would know about the Cherry Tree and my occupation there for, although Members of Parliament were among the regular climbers of those City stairs, the secret was only spread very carefully. He was not, I thought, the sort of man who might have heard it.

'I married again after Dante's death,' I said simply. 'But it seems as if that's finished now, too. Only just. That's why I came down to Weymouth. I spent some time here when I was a girl.'

'That's why I find you wandering abroad by moonlight then,' he nodded. 'Trying to think things out?'

'No,' I said certainly. 'I've done all that. All the thinking out. It's done, finished. But it happened rather suddenly and it's left me in space. At the moment I really have nothing to do in my life, nothing at all.'

'I imagine you'll soon repair the situation,' he smiled. 'I seem to remember thinking that, even as a wife of Dante, you had a good deal more potential than anyone gave you credit for.'

I smiled too. 'I was holding myself in,' I shrugged. 'Dante was not the sort of husband to let me *do* anything.'

The boy had completed his dance. He concluded with a marvellous bow to the moon and the sea. I began to applaud and his father, after a quick glance sideways at me, joined in. It was as though he had never thought of it before. The boy jogged up from the beach. He was wearing a track suit and he looked like an athlete. He had his father's serious dark expression. He looked up at us from the rising shingle, surprised at the clapping and at my appearance there, but then grinned and came forward to be introduced.

'We will be leaving in a few hours, Nell,' said Derek. 'Are you staying down here in Weymouth for a while?'

'I expect so,' I said. 'I want to look up some old friends. You never know, I might even find myself.'

They got into the car. 'Goodbye,' he said shyly. 'Would you mind if I telephoned you at your hotel this evening?'

'Please do,' I said. 'I'd like that. It's the Eden Roc.'

He regarded me steadily for a moment and I returned the same look. Then he smiled and we all shook hands. He drove the large, silent car towards the moonlight, and I turned and walked up the slope away from the sea. I could hear it muttering knowingly behind my back.

That unusual, casual meeting was yet another hinge to my life, another entrance to another place. Derek Blane was exceptionally intelligent and stable for a Member of Parliament and despite his betraying wife and his own sharp good looks and his manner he had none of the reputation for womanizing that many of the less appealing men in the House had achieved. I think that our affair was his first for many years.

He had, however, heavy political ambitions and when we met he was on the verge of a seat in the Cabinet. We had to be secret. Discretion being the better part of my life, this was no trouble for me and his normally solemn face was as good a shield against prayers as I have known.

Royal Ascot week arrived within ten days of our meeting and we set out in our hats and finery for the course, but each day made a circuit before we arrived and went to a small, beautiful hotel, where we made love all the afternoon. The first time I playfully kept my picture hat on my head while the rest of me was naked and he sat in the bed entranced, while I paraded as the Ascot ladies do (and were doing at the moment on our bedroom television set). 'And here is the Honourable Lady Nelly Luscombe,' he intoned from the sheet. 'A delightful hat of turquoise feathers, a fine shade for an exquisite face, skin like porcelain, the finest pair of breasts in all the land, shapely waist, an intriguing little posy at the meeting of the legs . . . and . . . God knows what else.'

I went to him on the bed and, still arrayed in my wide hat, I lay above him and stroked his fine skin, letting him ease himself into me. He was a composed but deeply passionate lover and I found it difficult to keep my hat on my head.

We drank champagne and ate from a Fortnum's picnic basket. That morning I had gone to the bank and checked the sum of £32,850 in my account. Apart from the fun of a pound on the Grand National or the Derby, stretched perhaps to ten pounds on the rare occasions I had been taken to a race meeting, I had no experience of betting. I told Derek nothing of it but I had gambled away a thousand pounds on that first afternoon while we were making love. As we embraced in that warm hotel room, the horses carrying my faith were being beaten by varying distances on the course three miles away.

On the second day of Ascot we again dressed in our finery and with our champagne and pâté enjoyed the afternoon in naked privacy at the hotel. We made love between and during the races and talked and learned to like each other and enjoyed the novelty of our situation. 'What are you doing Henley Regatta week?' I asked him breathlessly as we lay panting against each other after a torrid period that lasted through the running of the Ascot Gold Cup. 'Those rowing races last a lot longer,' I pointed out.

'There's the Lord's Test Match too,' he grinned from beside me. 'Five days of it.'

It was intriguing matching our actions to the voice of the commentator ('And here's the favourite. He's coming again.') and we enjoyed the pantomime almost as much as the lovemaking. On that afternoon I lost another thousand pounds to the bookmakers.

Had Derek known of what the horses who laboured on the screen behind my back were costing me, I could not have given him any logic for my sudden plunge into such uncontrolled betting. It was partly, I suppose, that £30,000 seemed a rounder figure than £32,850. It seemed a flatter base from which I could restart my life.

On the third day of Ascot I put the remaining £850 on a treble wager, three horses called Devon Fields, Bedfellow and Future Uncertain, all of which had to win their races. I still said nothing to Derek Blane and we smiled at our private joke as we met once more, he in topper and tails and me in an orange hat decorated with small ducks' eggs.

At the hotel they hardly gave us a glance. It was one of those London fringe hotels, a pretty, lawned place on the Thames where couples go not only to have sex but to be romantic as well. The staff was probably used to unusual situations.

Devon Fields won at four to one and I mentally rang up £3,400 while Derek was kissing my neck and I was stroking his loins (a whore achieves this facility of cashing-up while touching-up through long practice). I said nothing about the win or the wager, however, but when Bedfellow loped past the post two lengths ahead of the next horse, and at three to one, I began to take some heed of what was going on at the racecourse.

'What's the matter, Nelly?' asked Derek from the bed, seeing my attention wandering. 'What's upset you?'

I still didn't let him know. I kissed him and laughed and tried to keep my excitement still. Future Uncertain was running in the four-thirty and the hour between Bedfellow's win and then was the longest of my life. My lover could not understand what was worrying me.

At the start of the race we were sprawled across the bed and he was wanting me again (he was very healthy for an MP), his hands were rolling against my breasts and his tongue was pressed into my navel. But he could see that my heart was not in it. My eyes were wandering around at the twenty-two inch screen.

'Ah,' he said knowingly. 'It's that that's annoying you. Right, let's turn it off.'

I raced him to the knob. 'No. No. It's not that darling! Truly. Leave it on please.'

'Then what is it?' he pleaded. 'You've suddenly changed.'

'Very shortly I'll tell you,' I said trembling.

'It's not me is it? You're not tired of me?'

I reached out for him, anything to take my mind off that bloody race, and turned him onto the bed. I heard the commentator shout 'They're off!' as we embraced. In all my life I've never had a few minutes like that. We were doing it and I kept hearing 'and third . . . Future Uncertain . . . and he's moving up . . . he's in second place . . . four furlongs to go.'

It was more than I could stand. Like a wrestler I rolled over front down on the bed, motioning that my surprised and interrupted lover should mount me from the rear. I had to watch that screen.

'God help me Nell!' he cried. 'What the hell's going on?'

'Derek,' I moaned. 'Oh Derek, darling.' I half turned my head backwards towards him riding my rear like a jockey himself. 'That horse – Future Uncertain. I've got a fortune on it!'

There never was a *coitus interruptus* like that. He rolled and slid from my back and we lay clutching each other while Future Uncertain fought it out, ear by ear, with the favourite. 'How much?' he kept jabbering in my ear. 'For God's sake, how much?'

'Thousands,' I jabbered back. 'Ten thousand. 'Oh Christ, I can't look! I can't!'

Future Uncertain won it by a sneeze. We lay like two dead people on the bed. 'Nelly,' he croaked. 'You've won a fortune. What . . . what . . . odds?'

'Something like four to one,' I said. My face was soaking with sweat and tears. We waited, prostrated. Then they announced it, Future Uncertain, as six to one. I moaned and lay close to him. 'There was ten thousand two hundred pounds riding on him,' I whispered. 'I had a treble. They all won. Oh darling . . . sixty-one thousand two hundred pounds!'

The following week, on impulse, I went to Diana Seagram's house in Westminster and, after waiting for a moment to give myself the opportunity to change my mind, I walked to the door and rang the bell.

I arrived at the hour she was about to leave forever. I found her sitng sorrily among trunks and packing cases and she was delighted to see me. It was odd to visit her again after the interval of years, lines traced on the beautiful skin, the eyes tired but her figure still slim, her voice always soft. The voice can always stay beautiful.

'You find me at a melancholy moment, Nelly,' she said after we had embraced. 'After all these years I have decided to give up this house. I am retiring to Sevenoaks to join the senior citizens, the legion of the damned.'

'You're hardly ready for that,' I said. 'You look just the same.'

'And you have become a woman of the world,' she smiled. 'Just as we always knew you would.'

'How is he?' I asked tentatively. 'The Commander.'

'Oh just the same.' She laughed, I thought a shade guiltily. 'A trifle short on patience and temper.'

Her eyes came up slowly to me now for she knew what my next question would be. 'You . . . you didn't get married then?'

Diana shrugged. 'No. I decided against it. A merger is a big thing, bigger than marriage in its way. As I told you at the time, that's all he proposed – well, *we* proposed really – a merger of souls. In the end we . . . we didn't do it. He is still stumping about up in Shropshire and I am here. At the moment.'

We sat down. She on a tin trunk, me on a chair. The years seemed to have reversed us. 'We have read something about your life, Nelly,' she said cautiously. 'It has not all been happy has it? We discussed whether one or the other of us should write to you but we decided against it. Sometimes one can fare better without sympathy.'

'Dante,' I sighed. 'My husband. Yes, it was very unpleasant. There have been other things, a lot, good and bad. Mine's just been one of those lives. All I can say is it hasn't been dull.'

I looked up at her as though expecting her to guess what I had done with those years, but if she did, she did not show it. 'You've escaped that dullness anyway,' she said. 'I've had more than enough, I think, chiefly brought upon my own head. Sometimes it does not pay to lead a life that's too comfortable, emotionally comfortable I mean,' she smiled wryly. 'I'm quite looking forward to playing fast and loose in Sevenoaks.'

As she spoke I was still looking around the room, remembering it from that first sun-filled day when I had walked into it, a rosy apprentice lover from the breezy seaside. Now she was leaving and I was looking for somewhere to live. 'Diana,' I said carefully, 'this house. What will it cost?'

'Nelly!' she almost cried out. 'Nelly . . . you think *you* might . . .?'

I found myself blushing as though even the thought should have been beyond me. 'Yes,' I nodded. 'I *did* think. Would it be . . .'

'Possible? Well of course, Nelly. How marvellous. There is only a short lease left, about five years, so if you would be willing to take it on for that period the landlord could hardly ask a fortune. It would be wonderful wouldn't it? A sort of passing on to a new generation of friends.'

My hands went involuntarily out to her and hers to mine. We were, as ever, comfortable with each other, like sisters. We both burst into laughter. She rose from the trunk. 'Do you remember it?' she said excitedly. 'All the rooms? Come on, let me remind you'

She held out her hand like a girl and I gave her mine and we went through the house, as voluble as exploring children. It was a tall, slim house, elegant as a tall man may be elegant, with more rising rooms and corridors than I ever remembered. It was almost devoid of furniture now and our steps echoed as we went from one door to another. The bedrooms were large with the sun splashing through the vacant windows. And one of those windows, I saw, was filled with a vista of pointing towers and turrets and the great grey clock of the Houses of Parliament.

The house that became known, and indeed notorious, as Strangeways never had a name, only a number, 184, Westminster Terrace Gardens. The Members of Parliament who frequented it over the next few years became, unofficially, The Strangeways Society. At the famous court case, of course, this was alleged, by my defence, to be a collection of MPs dedicated to prison reform.

None of this had been my intention when I took over the lease from Diana Seagram. I only thought of it as an indulgence. The grand London home of Nelly Luscombe from Devon, the completion of a neat circle begun many years before, and probably the place to entertain the occasional rich lover: perhaps, some time, another husband.

Poor Pierre Arthur had sent me telegrams and tea-roses, had phoned and pleaded and, once I moved in, walked up and down outside the house for so many days that it was rumoured among the neighbours that he was a special detective guarding an important new resident. But I was never good at retying knots and now I decided quite calmly and sharply that his part of my life was used up, finished. In one of his many tearstained letters to me (held, I suspected, for a few moments below a slow-dripping tap) he promised that he would disband the Cherry Tree and its branch and that we would regain our happy life in the parks and showgrounds and museums of London with me no longer required to work at all. But this I refused, my door to his life being firmly closed, and, eventually, as I guessed he would, he made the best of it and recruited another, younger lady to lie on the round bed framed by the oyster shell. Gradually he backed away and bowed out of my life and I was not to see him again until that New Year's Eve utterly ruined by his untimely death.

My affair with Derek Blane developed easily and steadily and when I moved into Strangeways he would frequently visit me when the House of Commons was sitting. Before long his friends came too, their lady friends and occasionally even their wives. There were dinner parties when wives and lady friends (the wives at least unknowing) sat at the same table. Derek was acknowledged as host on many of these occasions. His wife had asked for a divorce and it was generally and, by me, comfortably accepted that when this was over and my divorce from Pierre Arthur was complete, that – with my recent past miraculously hidden – we could marry. I had become a famous hostess, due to marry a man who might one day become Prime Minister.

One of the several troubles with Members of Parliament, of course, is that they talk, and they drink as well. They also fancy themselves with women. I was careful, naturally, to exclude from Strangeways any of the half dozen or so who had engaged in dealings with me at the Cherry Tree or at Burridges, but I realized now that I must have been in a fool's dream to think that this would remain untold for long.

At the dinner table one evening I found my knee being fumbled below the cloth by a port-faced old bastard who had been fancied for high office years before, but had missed by a whisker and had taken his revenge on both the country and the party ever since. I made a joke of the incident at first, althouth the finger crawling like a fat caterpillar up my thigh filled me with distaste. It is different when you are pawed for money. Eventually, when he ignored my whispered warnings, I stuck a fork firmly into his hand. He let out a boozy cry and pulled his hand away. It was late, a lot had been drunk around the table and few people noticed it. We confronted each other. His eyes became dull and nasty and he said: 'Come on Nelly Luscombe. You didn't mind when you had that little love spot in the City, did you? Nor at Burridges. I've heard all about that, Nelly. The goings on.'

He froze into hurt silence then and soon left, but I knew it would not be long before the shadows of my past came creeping along like an unwelcome evening to shroud me once more.

It took two weeks. The morning newspapers had said that Derek was to be invited into the Cabinet in a government reshuffle and at four in the afternoon he arrived himself. Standing at the window I watched him jump from a taxi and come hurrying up the steps. His face was like a hatchet.

I tried. 'Didn't they ask you to be Foreign Secretary after all?' I said when he came into the drawing-room. 'You look so fierce, Derek.'

He stood immobilized at the door. The terrible thing was I knew that he loved me. He faltered, then walked forward and embraced me with genuine love for the final time. We kissed and he turned and went to the window, staring out towards Westminster and his future.

'Nelly, God, Nelly, I've got to ask you about something,' he said. 'I've got to ask you if something is true or not.'

'I promise – I cannot tell a lie,' I said, trying to ease it. 'Like George Washington.'

He turned to me and jumped at the phrase. 'Is that a saying from the Cherry Tree?' he asked bitterly. 'You remember the Cherry Tree, don't you.'

Within me I shivered. But I controlled my answer. 'I'm unlikely to forget it,' I said defiantly. 'But it's all over now.'

He seemed shattered by the answer even though he must have expected it. 'Christ,' he stumbled. 'How *could* you?'

That made me angry. 'How could I *what*? To make a sodding living, that's how Derek. How was I to know I was going to meet a better class of person?'

He backed away from the sarcasm. 'I could hardly believe it,' he whispered. 'You – doing that.'

'I've done it for you,' I pointed out. 'Many times.'

'There's a difference!' he shouted now. 'For God's sake, Nelly!'

'Because I got paid? I'll say there was. It kept me fed and clothed for a start.'

'Don't tell me that. That's rubbish. You . . . you of all people Nell Luscombe. You need never have done it for money. Never!' He bawled the word at me. He was in a scarcely controlled frenzy. I backed into the room and stood behind a chair. In that moment, however, I knew he was speaking the truth. I need never have done it. It was always easy. It was the most convenient of all professions.

'Well Derek I did.' I felt that I was going to cry. 'But . . . that's finished. It's all past.'

'If you think that you must be simple,' he retorted.

'I am.'

'For God's sake how can you imagine that something of that kind could be hidden? It's a bloody miracle that it didn't come out before.'

'Who told you?' I said conversationally. It was too late to save anything.

He looked up. His face was like a sheet. 'The Prime Minister,' he muttered. 'Who else?'

'I never screwed the Prime Minister,' I said callously.

'Nelly, don't make a joke of it. Don't you see. Everybody knew but me, it seems. Somebody put the poison in for me. If the news of this Cabinet job had not already been leaked to the press, I doubt if I'd have got it. Anyway, he's told me to . . .'

'Get rid of me,' I suggested.

'Not in those words, but that's what he meant. Can't you see . . .?'

'Very well indeed,' I said. 'But don't worry. You don't have to get rid of me Derek, because I'm getting rid of *you*. Go out of that door and point yourself towards Downing Street and keep going, boy. Don't look back or you won't be a pillar of the society – you'll be a pillar of fucking salt!'

I left him standing ashen in the room. I went unhurriedly up the stairs and closed my bedroom door. He had some political books and files in there. I took them to the window and dropped them on his head as he left the house. He turned and shook his fist at me as he scrabbled around trying to pick them up. I laughed at him and turned away from the casement.

That time I cried a bit longer than usual. Not just for him, not many of my tears are for men, but for myself again. The moment I went out in that fishing boat with Rainbow, all those years before, I had set the pattern of my life. There was no cure for it. But I was running out of places to go.

It was six months later that I made the decision to turn my elegant house in Westminster Terrace Gardens into a luxury salon for Members of Parliament and others in need. The idea had been lingering ever since the disgraceful walkout of Derek Blane, bartering love for office, and had been willingly promoted by several of his fellow Members who had neither his scruples nor his hopes of glory.

The firm and final suggestion, in fact, came from one of Derek Blane's Cabinet colleagues, an older man, surer, and one who would never have put power before pleasure. His name was Sir Berthold Wick and even in his sixties he could live up to his singular boast of an erection tall enough to match a pile of thirty-three two-shilling pieces topped by an old fashioned threepenny bit. Towards the end of this time (he died in the bath tub while taking a dip with his wife's maid and his own faithful bull terrier), he found to his chagrin that he could not manage the threepenny bit.

He was a large, gentle, grey man, and once I had returned (so easily I'm afraid) to my old ways, we spent many a convivial hour together in my bed. Indeed he half seriously suggested, after cutting his return to the Commons rather finely on an important vote, that a division bell should be installed in my house. But he was without cant and even his necessary political hypocrisy was performed tongue-in-cheek. One day, speaking of a fellow minister, he sighed: 'That man my dear, would stay at a hotel, leave without paying the bill *and* steal the Gideon Bible.'

'You know Nelly dear,' he murmured one afternoon while we were drinking gin in the drawing room. 'You're not using this fine house to the best of its capacity. You have all these rooms, why not turn it into a nice little brothel. Get some decent honest tarts in. The boys at the House would love it.'

He took no heed of my half-hearted protestations, merely hooding his rheumy eyes and continuing speaking as so often he did when rudely interrupted in the Commons: 'You could have a room for this and a room for that. You know what varying degrees of interest Members have. You'd make a fortune, me dear.'

I went to Monte Carlo for a month and thought about it. It was running the risk of the law, for I had never managed other whores before, always working alone. But being on the Riviera again, thinking about past years, L'Horizon, the distant Dante, the hopeless Davie, and standing outside the Hôtel de Paris from whence I was kidnapped in my wedding gown by my own father, I came to the conclusion that my life was never meant to run placidly.

Returning, fortuitously, on the day Her Majesty opened Parliament in the autumn, I decided, watching the ranked, blanked faces of the politicians assembled in the House to hear the Speech, that I should have a grand opening of Strangeways, as it became known, just before the Christmas Recess.

It began in a luxurious but conventional way, with carefully invited guests being entertained to cocktails by four engaging and easy-going girls who had been selected with equal care. Evening gowns with wide views, special grooming, cheerfulness, understanding, intelligence and physical fitness were required. Each evening a piano played.

There were five dim bedrooms on the first floor and two more above. In the basement was a dancing room with a mirrored floor and there were two other rooms below ground where some of the more exotic diversions were permitted and which, perhaps needless to say, proved in time to be the most popular in the house.

Amateur dramatics night was invariably crowded (during one Commons debate on the Future of the Isle of Wight Watercress Industry it was said that there were more Members to be seen at Strangeways than in the House itself). On these theatrical nights we arranged to put on various charades which excited individuals and groups in the most spectacular way and for this we had to keep a wardrobe of costumes including such bizarre items as Red Riding Hood's cloak, a Florence Nightingale outfit, two Rasputin costumes, various Roman and Greek robes and togas, some whips and nastier looking implements of punishment, chains, shackles, and other ironmongery, slave disguises, guardsman's uniforms and a small stuffed mule.

More girls were recruited and I was able to manage my establishment from a velvet chair in the main salon, spending my evenings drinking, eating and conversing with some of the country's most respected and responsible figures. Our champagne consumption became legendary. It was not necessary for me to take part in any of the sexual activities if I did not choose, although I quite liked to play the part of the Bleeding Nun of Lindenburg, in an occasional melodrama we produced. I could choose my bed partners as I wished and charge them twice as much as girls half my age.

Our door was knocked many times. Others came to hear of Strangeways and actors, actresses and that sort would join in by special invitation. It was amazing how after a night of devoted debauchery everyone emptied into the morning streets and became again the idols of society they were popularly seen to be.

Our operations continued for four years – spanning two Governments and many changes of fortune in individual power – and Strangeways

became an established place of entertainment for officials and participants in Commonwealth Prime Ministers' Conferences, the casts of
Broadway shows playing in London's West End, Church Conventions,
reunions of senior officers and occasional groups from overseas, Japanese
and Germans in particular. We also held a complimentary Police Night
once every few months.

My young ladies were acknowledged as being the most attractive and
kindest in London and the guests appreciated this. There was Molly
Burtenshaw, a red-haired Yorkshire girl, who never sent an unsmiling
man from her room. Members of Parliament would stalk into Strangeways, their teeth clenched after frustrating debates and political
skullduggery, and Molly would be summoned to be considerate to them.
They would return to the rough-edged world calmed, satisfied,
Mollified.

There was Angelica Brownjohn, who sang sweet ballads at the piano
and the same songs, in lower, softer key, into her client's ear while he
enjoyed her embrace. She wore leopardskin tights and had raven hair.
Her parents in Wiltshire knew nothing about her activities and imagined
that she was unemployed. When she visited them they would give her
groceries and second-hand garments to take back to London, believing
she was in need. Once she returned aghast from a weekend at home with
a consignment of headless plastic gnomes, obtained for her by her father.
The heads, provided in a separate box, had to be screwed on the bodies,
and the manufacturers paid a pound for every five hundred of these
completed monstrosities. She had to make some sort of show to please her
father and she completed almost a thousand gnomes and earned nearly
two pounds before becoming exhausted. Encouraged by her industry he
then provided a further cargo and she brought these despairingly to
Strangeways where the upshot was the extraordinary spectacle of harlots
and visiting Members of Parliament busily fixing plastic heads on to
plastic gnomes. After this questions were asked in the House about the
low rates paid to outworkers by exploiting manufacturers.

Cynthie Broad, one of our original hostesses, lived in a suburban house
with her sister, who was a secretary and imagined Cynthie went off each
night to work as a waitress in a nightclub. Eventually she discovered
what her sister did and was dreadfully shocked until she discovered how
much her sister earned and for what effort. A week later she was on the
staff as well.

They were all marvellous girls. We had a West Indian hostess, Teresa
Longmate, who had great influence on some of the immigration debates
in the Commons, Lucy Wing, a Chinese girl whose oriental anatomy was
a constant source of conjecture and interest. She did a marvellous act
sliding naked down the banister of the main staircase. There were two
French ladies of noble families who had been sent to London as *au pair*
girls to learn how to make a coal fire and placate screaming children and
scheming husbands.

It was, in its manner, rather like a luxurious harem, a comfortable,
warm, secret place, where, at a price, even the most difficult ego, the most

tormented soul could be provided for and even the most outrageous appetite, the most pathetic need, could be satisfied and the recipient sent out into the world cleansed and sane, lighter in spirit and, of course, in pocket.

It was eleven thirty on New Year's Eve and the festivities at Strangeways were developing towards an almost inevitable orgy which traditionally took place while Big Ben struck the year almost outside the window. There were a good many stranded foreigners with us that night and a good gathering of people from Mayfair and the West End, but rather less Members of Parliament, due to their being reluctantly exiled to their constituencies for the Christmas Recess.

My comfortable duties over the past year and more had resulted in my putting on some nicely rounded poundage and I was astride the thick and happy legs of some Teutonic industrialist who liked larger sizes. We were singing traditional German songs such as 'We March Against England' when the telephone rang almost at my elbow and from it came the terrible and lonely voice of Pierre Arthur Bickerstaff. He said he was dying.

I left the New Year to my guests and hurried out into the damp night. People were shouting good drunken wishes in the streets and there were party lights in many windows. A timely taxi came by and I took it and was in St John's Wood in fifteen minutes.

Oh God, what a night that was! It was bad enough going back to the house, our old familiar place, our dwelling shared in the days when we went to the park and the river. Nostalgia swamped me like nausea, a silent wave of it all the more poignant because the noises of celebration had now drifted away and the path and the trees were wet and dark and from the house came a solitary uncomfortable light. Trembling I walked to the front door. It was standing six inches open. I touched it and walked in.

He had been living there with some idiot girl chemist and the place stank of ether and ammonia and the other smelly pieces of her trade. As soon as I went through the door I could hear him coughing in the kitchen. The solitary light was in there. Shaking I walked in.

He was sitting on the floor, his back propped against a kitchen cupboard. His face was set in an awful mask. But even then he tried to smile when he saw me, the most terrible sight.

'Pierre Arthur,' I whispered, crouching down by him and taking his freezing hand. 'What have you done?'

'I'll tell you what he's done.' She came out of the other room, out of the shadows. It was his girl, a yawning creature scratching her own back. 'He mistook something very nasty for custard powder. He had a lot to drink and he tasted it. He likes custard you know.'

'Don't tell me, I'm his wife,' I snapped. 'I know he likes custard. Is the doctor coming?'

'I've just managed to reach him,' she said. 'He was out celebrating. There's nothing we can do anyway. I've given him an emetic, but it's too late. That stuff would go through steel.'

And with that, all delivered in tones of utmost boredom, she pulled a scraggy blanket around her shoulders and walked out of the front door. I bent over poor Pierre Arthur and pulled him to my bosom. His hand still felt the same there, except it was rather more limp. Outside I heard the doctor's car pull up on the gravel and the man came in full of bonhomie and scotch, with a paper hat stuffed in his dinner jacket pocket.

He bent over and briefly examined Pierre Arthur. He glanced at me and saw I was convivially dressed also and that I had my coat. 'You know him well?' he inquired.

'He's my husband,' I replied throatily.

'He's not now dear. I'm afraid he's dead.' He took out a pocket watch. 'Bang on midnight too. Fascinating. It's a toss-up which year he died in.'

CHAPTER NINETEEN

For the next two years Strangeways entertained and prospered in Westminster. Some of the more healthy denizens of the House of Lords took to coming there and, since they always had to have things different from the members of the Commons, to them the house became known as Kinky Court.

It became necessary to take on other girls, and they were, of course, always of marked beauty, charm and great stamina. One, who acquired the name of Dirty Dierdre, was a sweet redhead, the daughter of an earl, and she proved a great favourite with certain left-wing MPs who, I was gratified to see, had the same weaknesses and appetites as the most conservative Tory. She entertained regularly a notorious neo-communist who, astride this aristocratic beauty, would leap about with revolutionary fervour and cry: 'Forward the Oppressed!'

Who the spoilsport was I never did discover. It may have been one of the Socialists, riven by conscience, it may have been a sneaky Tory, aspiring to office, or it may have been a peer admonished for some outrageous perversion which endangered the well-being of the girl involved. Their Lordships, in fact, were far more difficult to accommodate than their colleagues in the Lower House whose demands were normally more humble. Whether it was the rot of the aristocracy, the long shadow of the public schools, or some other flaw, I cannot tell, but I soon grew to know what the expression 'a belted earl' really meant. During those long, dozing sessions in the House, filled with lunch and wine, they dreamed unruly dreams that woke them grunting and brought them shuffling to my door in the hope and expectation of the dreams being gratified. Some of their abnormalities could be accommodated but others were so outrageous that I would not allow my girls to take part. I once found a terrified young lady, legs apart, stretched out on a bed with a titled man, old enough to be her grandfather, *and* in full ermine and red robes and coronet, ceremonially running an ornate sword between her thighs. He argued that it was not sharp. Other activites emanating from that regal place included the use of chocolate spread, lemon curd, fire irons, dog collars, recordings of Melba, false moustaches (for the girl) and other oddities. A fee of one hundred and fifty pounds was offered by a Scots peer who wanted to ride a district nurse's bicycle over a tethered whore. This was never taken up.

My own sexual life had now reverted to an amateur basis. I no longer had to live by bed alone. Life was prosperous. In the Portobello Road antique market one Saturday I met a young man who sold bogus watches with a smile and he charmingly asked me to go and have a pint with him. His name was Albert Farthing, he was a Hackney Cockney, and his lovemaking was fierce and uncomplicated.

'Look at that, Nell,' he would say, stretched full on my bed, admiring what God had blessed him with. 'Ever seen the like of that? Like a lucky dog's bone, ain't it?'

When I first undressed for him and lay indolently, my breasts lolling, so that he could see me, he crouched at the foot of the bed like a lean alley cat, eyeing me along all my landscape. 'I reckon the look of you, Nell,' he said genuinely. 'I like a body what's been lived in.'

He was amazed, then scornful, of the idiosyncracies of those who were paying clients of the house. 'Disgusting,' he grunted when he realized some of the things that went on. 'This sort of thing gives fucking a bad name.' And he was particularly outraged when, one evening, I showed him the mirrored dance floor. A slow waltz was playing and four customers were dancing with my girls.

'They 'unchbacks or something?' asked Albert, nodding at the slowly revolving men, each with his head bent forward.

'No,' I smiled and whispered. 'They're looking down into the mirror.'

'What they doing that for?' he asked innocently.

'Because the girls don't wear anything under their dresses.'

Even in the dim lights I could see the shock encompass Albert's face. 'Oh the dirty sods,' he breathed. 'The rotten dirty little sods. And these are the buggers who keep putting up the income tax.'

However simple his outlook, Albert was an enduring lover and I enjoyed his energy, his hard, Cockney body and his homespun filth. He loved to tell jokes and we would spend an hour or more, cooling off on the bed after making love, while he regaled me with the newest foul anecdotes, riddles and rhymes.

The raid by the police on Strangeways came, appropriately, on St Valentine's Night. We had organized a grand fancy dress orgy (strictly invitation only) and this was in progress when Albert rushed through the back door. 'Nelly!' he shouted across the room. 'The Law's everywhere!'

I turned angrily at first, for shouting was not allowed at Strangeways, but immediately I realized what he meant I sounded a pre-arranged alarm signal – three blasts on a coastguard's whistle. We had practised this drill reguarly but had never needed to use it.

We always enjoyed good relations with individual police officers from Scotland Yard and the London police stations. We never paid protection money to anyone, but policemen were always welcome and were permitted trade discounts, as indeed were editors and other journalists. I never thought they would turn and bite the hand that caressed them. But they do and they did.

Fortunately the front and back doors were kept locked and when the demanding banging began we were able to delay them for a few precious minutes, while the bolts were clumsily drawn, and rearrange the salon.

When the police were finally admitted, two dozen customers, half of them Members of Parliament, and a dozen of my girls were sitting primly watching Albert Farthing dropping into a spiritualist's trance. The lights were dim, the drinks hidden, the dress of everyone decently adjusted.

'What's going on here?' demanded the first police inspector through the door. 'What's this you're up to?'

Albert was superb. As the lights went up he went into an uncontrollable fit of shouting, rolling and raving, and had to be calmed and restrained before anything else could be done.

'Now you've done it,' I threatened the inspector. 'Now you've done it. Don't you know it can be fatal to disturb a medium in a trance.'

'Trance my arse,' he said rudely. 'We know what's going on here.'

'We were just trying to contact the other side,' I told him acidly. 'Now you've ruined it. We were just getting through, too.'

They were everywhere by now, of course, running through the building like spiders, every boudoir, every bathroom, every cupboard (except one which they somehow missed) and every chest. I always contended they found nothing incriminating (there is no law against having silk sheets on all the beds, mirrors on the ceilings – not to mention one on the floor – and a full scale model of a slave galley in the conservatory) but they were satisfied enough for their purposes. They took everybody's name, although those of the Members of Parliament somehow floated out of the police car window on the way back from the raid, and I was arrested and taken to their police station.

They kept me all night in their cheerless charge room, with questions and answers and cups of limp tea. My solicitor came down at four o'clock in the morning and told me I was in serious trouble. For that sort of advice I had to pay him.

I was released on bail of £5,000 after appearing in the magistrate's court the following morning, tired and drained and charged with keeping a brothel, living on the earnings of prostitution, and procuring for an immoral purpose.

In tatters I went out into the street and took a taxi back to my house. There were photographers and police everywhere. The police had been through everything, even lifting the paper from the walls, presumably to see if it contained filthy drawings and writings. I got them out as soon as I could without going altogether mad and sat amongst the debris of my life, drinking gin, alone again. Then, from far away it seemed, I heard a echoing banging.

'Christ! Lord Corwellian!' I almost shouted to myself.

I ran from the room and down to the basement to open a concealed cupboard which the police, for all their efforts, had failed to find. Inside, hanging by his hands, wearing only a surgical support, was the Ninth Earl of Corwellian, an elderly man who derived his sensual enjoyment by being suspended thus in this secret cupboard. Hurriedly I cut him down. He collapsed in a thin naked heap on the floor.

'Oh Nelly,' he sighed. 'I thought you'd forgotten me hanging up here. I was kicking the door with my heels.' He looked up, poor old ravaged bugger, and smiled. 'But I've had a lovely time,' he sighed. 'It was a truly wonderful night.'

I dressed him and led him to the door where he waved happily and went hobbling off in the direction of the House of Lords. As I was about to close the door I saw a face looking at me from the gate. It was Diana Seagram. She was pale and uncomfortable but she appeared to know nothing of the events at her former house, although the newspapers with the episode were already on the streets, nor did she make any comment on the condition in which the house had been left by the police. Probably she knew everything but said nothing.

Instead she said: 'I have just had news that . . .' she hesitated '. . . that the Commander is very ill. They say he's dying.'

My face went cold. We regarded each other strangely, like rivals.

'He wants to see you,' she said. 'Will you go?'

'Oh of course. You are coming too?'

'No,' she shrugged with what was the first trace of bitterness I had ever seen in her. 'It's you he wants, Nell.'

It was very strange going to see him again. I went north at once that afternoon, weary though I was after my night with the police and their questions. Most of the way I dozed in the soft, deep back seat of the chauffeured car while rain melted against the windows and the February day darkened early.

Years had gone since I had last seen him. It was difficult to recall how many. The thought that I was only going to him again at what were the last few days of his life filled me with regret. I wondered why, in fact, I *had* kept away from him. Perhaps it was because I thought he might see how I had used my life, and I would want to hide that from him.

It was difficult to know what to expect. When the driver found the house, ten miles from Shrewsbury, it turned out that night to be an uncomfortable, grey Victorian place, in a few acres of anonymous parkland. Misgivings crowded in on me as we drove along the trees of the drive. Who would be there? His family? What would they think of me, a trollop arriving out of the night?

The door was opened by a lead-faced woman with already pursed lips.

She knew who I was and indicated that this excluded the need for all but the minimum of conversation. She led me through the uncared-for house to a large cold bedroom and said she would tell the Commander I had arrived. I would have liked a drink or a cup of tea but I was afraid to ask. I looked about the walls and then out into the dreary landing. God, if I'd been with him all these years he would not have had to die in a dismal place like this.

The ashen-faced woman returned and surprisingly jerked her thumb towards the outside corridor. 'He says he wants to see you now,' she muttered. 'He don't think he's going to last the night. For once in his life I reckon he's right.'

With this depressing forecast delivered, she turned and I nervously followed her down the passage. She paused at a large carved door and banged on it with her fist. A roar came from within. 'Come in! Come in, Nell.'

The wonderful thing about him was how his very presence, frail though it was now, lifted my spirits and my heart. There he was sitting quite jauntily in bed, his face like driftwood, but with a wonderful grin of greeting for me. 'Push off, Martha,' he amiable ordered the doleful woman. 'Let's have some smiles around here.' He opened his pyjama arms to me and I hurried forward, my heart glad, just as it had been when I had greeted him as a girl. We hugged each other, me falling on my knees by the bedside and burying my tearful face in his hard cheek and he patting and comforting me in the way he had always done. Dear God, what had I done with all those years?

He eased me away from the bedside. 'Let's have a look at you, Nell,' he grinned. 'God, but you look fine. The beautiful little girl become the beautiful woman.'

I was attempting to calm myself. 'And you?' I eventually said. 'How do you feel?'

'Well they say I've had it,' he said in a matter-of-fact voice. 'But it's not the first occasion. I've had a good many death beds in my time, Nell.' His eyes, steady blue amongst the creases in his face, were alive. 'See over there, in the cabinet. There's a bottle of champagne on ice. They tried to stop me getting it. But I fooled them. I even hobbled down to purloin the ice when nobody was looking.'

I went to the cabinet and took the cold bucket and its bottle back to the bed. 'I think we deserve a drink,' he said strongly. His voice was less of a croak than it had been in the old days. 'Open it up, Nell. Let's have a toast.'

There were some glasses in the cabinet also and I returned with these. Despite his brave words he had no strength to open the bottle so I did. 'Performed like an expert,' he observed from his sheets. 'You've had a lot of champagne have you, Nell?'

'Some of it less than vintage,' I smiled.

'I've followed your fortunes occasionally in the newspapers and the gossip magazines,' he said seriously. 'You've used your time, had a full life.'

'Misfortunes too,' I pointed out. I had the cork free now and as the white tongue of the stuff came over the lip I poured it into our glasses. We lifted them together. 'To you Nell,' he said.

'And I drink to you,' I said, almost choking with the feeling of the moment.

When we had drunk I pulled a chair to the bedside and sat holding his firm but faded hand. 'The first time we met I was stuck in bed,' he remembered. 'And here I am again.'

'It suits you,' I smiled. 'Do you remember when we went on the Serpentine and I rowed you around in the boat? And the time when you came to the Manor when I was a kitchen maid, and the day you met me at Waterloo when I first came to London from Weymouth?'

I could not help it. I hung forward and buried my face and my thick hair in his neck and his cheek, against his old wounds. He put his hand tenderly around my hair and stroked it. 'It's not too difficult, is it,' he said. 'Remembering our joint past. There has not been a great deal of it.'

'I'm so sorry,' I sniffed. 'I should have come to see you before. It's just that . . .' Whatever the excuse or confession I was about to make was interrupted by a fist hammering on the door.

'It's old cheery,' said the Commander. 'Come in Mrs Modley.'

The glum woman entered bowed over a trolley on which, I was glad to see, was set a meal for two. She managed to demonstrate her overwhelming disapproval of me by ignoring my polite appreciation and only speaking to him. 'I thought we might have dinner together,' he said when she had shuffled out. 'She's a miserable old boot isn't she? Been here years. Asked me the other day what I expected her to do when I've gone to glory. She'll be out of a job she said. She blames me for everything. Even for dying. But she's been here about a million years. Poor old thing.'

'Who else is in the house?' I asked, arranging the cutlery and the plates for us. We had another glass of champagne and there was a bottle of burgundy on the cloth, already opened. The meal was a beef casserole which was excellent. I was very hungry.

'I've got various relatives flitting in and out just to see if I'm still one of the living,' he joked. 'I wouldn't bore you with them Nell. It's bad enough having to bore myself with them. Dying's difficult enough without the crew all around. They all hope to get a million quid.'

'Who actually *says* you're dying?' I inquired. 'I mean, have you got any proof?'

'Good girl,' he laughed. 'That's my Nell. Well only what the damned doctor says and he's in his dotage. Probably beat me to it yet. Ha! Be quite funny to go downstairs and announce that the doctor had passed away wouldn't it! God, I'd enjoy that.'

'So really it's just a rumour,' I said. The food and the wine were warming us. I was glad this was how it had turned out. 'A wild rumour.'

'Not according to those that are supposed to know,' he replied. 'According to these alleged specialists, all these bits of string and lumps of metal that have been holding this poor bloody frame together since the war are in a terrible state and I'm liable to disintegrate more than actually die. I mean, I'll end up a pile of random bits, all fallen apart. They'll be able to bury me in a brown paper parcel.'

It started from that point. I began to fill in the years, telling him about the days and adventures of my life, those of which I was actually ashamed. I did not tell him I had been arrested and charged that previous night. He sat listening, his grin growing and receding on his handsome face, his eyes full of interest. Occasionally he would explode with laughter and I would laugh too while I went over some story again. It was while we were amused like this that Mrs Modley returned for the trolley and wheeled it out like a hearse, asking at the door, 'Is there anything else, sir?' There was not. And there would never be again.

We had finished the champagne and the wine. I had eaten most of the food. He found that too difficult. The rain brushed across the large ugly windows and the time grew late. He seemed smaller, exhausted. I arranged his pillows for him. He thought I was going. 'Can you stay a little longer, Nell?' he said.

'Much longer,' I said. I rose. 'I'll be back in a few minutes. Don't go away.'

'I won't,' he promised, now very subdued. He watched me go to the door as though fearful that I was going to leave and not tell him. 'I'll be five minutes,' I promised again. 'I'll be back, then we can talk all night.'

'Good girl, Nell,' he said from the bed. He looked small and isolated there. I returned and kissed him firmly on the cheek and then left the room.

Going to my own room I undressed and put on my nightdress and my robe. Then I went back along the corridor and quietly opened his door. He was still propped up, waiting anxiously. When he saw me a strange smile cracked his lips. 'And not before time, either,' he said throatily.

I climbed into the bed beside him and after a while put out the light. I was conscious how vibrant, how alive my body was against his frailness. Lying against him softly. I put my warm arms about him and cradled his head into the fullness of my breasts. My heart was so crowded I could hardly trust myself to speak and we only said a few words before we closed our eyes. I was overcome with the tiredness of my long night and long day and the emotion of these last hours.

Several times I awoke in the night and he was breathing peacefully, his hand against my thigh, his face still resting on my breast. Before I slept I wondered what might have been if our lives had been joined all those years before. The way I felt that night I was full of sorrow for those wasted years.

At four o'clock I thought I heard him snore but when I awoke in early daylight he was dead, still lying close to me. At least we had spent one night together.

My trial took place at the Central Criminal Court three months later, before Mr Justice Bonner. The very name of the place chilled me. Central Criminal Court meant Crippen, Christie and murderers of that type. I preferred to call it the Old Bailey which seemed less sordid and, indeed, had a touch of the theatrical about it.

It was, as all trials are, an entertainment for everyone but the accused in the dock. The public seats were filled as soon as the doors opened and there were crowds left outside to view me as I went in. On the first morning, not realizing the immensity of the attraction of such an occasion, I arrived at the court by taxi and fully believed that the moving throng held back by the police in front of the building must have been there to catch a glimpse of someone else. For a moment I thought perhaps even the Queen was making a visit to the court.

But the instant my head appeared from the taxi there was a rumble from them, as if a motor had been started, and they began to press against the policemen's arms. I looked out, still misunderstanding, and then, as I stepped to the pavement, I realized with a perverse thrill that they had come to see *me*. Nelly Luscombe was infamous.

As I stepped, as steadily as I could, to the door of the court, where my counsel, James Threadgold, waited in his robes and a little bib, the excitement gathered like a small wind blowing through the streets. There was a growing buzz, the sucking in and blowing out of breath, the clucking of disapproving tongues, the little squeaks as lips were pursed, and over all that the comments.

I was wearing an olive velvet suit, a cream blouse and a curling hat. I felt smart. From behind the shopping baskets and the briefcases came the voices like darts.

'Don't look like a prossie, do she?'

'Brazen bitch.'

'Taking men from their wives and children.'

'Go back to your knocking shop!'

The choice British hypocrisy was counterbalanced by a call from some scaffolding clinging to a building across the road. From there a workman shouted through an improvised loudhailer: 'Give the judge one, Nelly. He'll let you off with a caution!'

James Threadgold put his experienced arm on my shaking shoulder and led me into the merciful shadows of the court. I was shaking, a pint of tears ready to run. 'Those people,' I managed to say. 'God, talk about going to the guillotine. Do I have to come in that way every day?'

I felt him smile. 'Nell,' he said, 'by the end of the week they'll be cheering you.'

'I hope the jury isn't like that,' I said, walking with him.

'Oh God, so do I,' he said fervently.

'What could I get?' I had never asked him before and I was too frightened to make other inquiries.

'Five years,' he said stonily.

'Five. Oh God.'

'Keep calm, Nelly,' he said quietly. 'Especially in the witness box. I'll keep calm too. Let the others do the shouting. You never know, we might just win.'

There are few things, of course, that the public and the newspapers savour more than the brutal baring of people's morals. Alongside a sexual trial the most gross of murders becomes commonplace. There is a preference for beds even over blood.

Standing in the dock, my fingers resting on the ledge where many notorious hands had touched before, I felt as lonely as I had never done in a life that has had its share of loneliness. The court reminded me of some form of animal auction room, with the shoulders and the faces of the bidders projecting from booths all around. It was an especially warm day for early summer and the sun hung through the windows like a series of banners. Five years. The two words revolved inside my head. Five years in a prison where you could not even feel it rain.

James Threadgold sat reassuringly just in front of my place in the dock. His assistant, a young fellow called Morton, was hopelessly in love with me. During the weeks before the trial, after the hearings at the magistsrate's court, he had been overcome with what can only be described as a sickness for me although he had never uttered a word of it. I would catch him gazing at my full bosom and he would go scarlet and begin to stutter. 'Nelly,' he said dolefully that morning, before the opening of the trial. 'If they put you away, I will never rest until you are free once more.'

'Nor me,' I smiled at him.

The counsel for the Crown was Peter Crowburn QC, a hard and handsome man, tanned from April ski-ing in Europe, the edges of his gown in symmetrical lines, the papers in his hands used theatrically, his eyes full of menace for me, his voice clipping away like the clipping of scissors. On that first morning he sat below me and to my left, unmoving as wood, staring directly ahead, waiting for the judge. His papers were piled with tidy confidence before him, he did not whisper to his junior. He gave the appearance that the matter was cut and dried and I would soon be on my way to prison. Looking at him later from the witness box, I could not help but think that he would have made a fine lover.

There were so many reporters behind the press enclosure that it looked like an overcrowded lifeboat. They jostled and whispered snarls to each other as they tired to make their notes. The jury sat timidly in their pen. Everyone waited.

The chimes of the City outside the window marked ten thirty and as though he had been awaiting the cue Mr Justice Bonner materialized through a door which suddenly opened in the panelling behind his raised position. He looked sad but kind, weighed down by his robes and responsibilities. Everyone stood, counsel bowed, the judge bowed, I did a clumsy curtsy. The most important day in the full life of Nelly Luscombe was about to commence.

The Queen versus Nell Luscombe began with a voice. I still remember it better than almost any other thing in my life. It was very like someone calling through a hollow tube and it reached every rafter and every ear of that courtroom where I stood accused.

'Nell Luscombe, you are accused that on the fourteenth day of February this year and on divers other days you, being the householder of 184, Westminster Terrace Gardens, London, SW1, did cause those premises to be used for the purpose of prostitution. How do you plead? Guilty or not guilty?'

'Not guilty, sir.'

'Further, that on the fourteenth day of February this year and on diverse other days you were a prostitute using these premises for the purposes of prostitution. How do you plead? Guilty or not guilty?'

'Not guilty, sir.'

'Further that on the fourteenth of February this year and on divers other days as 184, Westminster Terrace Gardens, SW1, you did procure Lady Diedre Mountjoy, Molly Burtenshaw, Angelican Brownjohn, Cynthia Broad, Teresa Longmate, Lucy Wing and others to be prostitutes. How do you plead? Guilty or not guilty?'

'Not guilty.'

'Further, that on the fourteenth day of February this year and on divers other days at 184, Westminster Terrace Gardens, SW1, you did live on the earnings of prostitution. How do you plead? Guilty or not guilty?'

'Not guilty.'

I did not like to lie in that bold way but I could not let myself go to prison for five years.

For two days the healthy and handsome Mr Crowburn outlined the case for the prosecution and called his witnesses. The police had been watching the house for weeks and produced time-tables of the comings and goings of many men. I had wondered why the gang repairing the gas-main across the street had been so long about it and had worked such unsocial hours into the night.

Some of the unusual finds at Strangeways, including an oar from the model slave galley, ropes, whips, canes, rubber things and a variety of beautifully photographed pornography, were trotted out in the solemn courtroom like an inventory of some ancient uncovered Egyptian tomb. Small museum-like men went into the witness box and read out the scientific analysis of stains found on beds and cushions. Watching them I wondered if they ever, beneath those frozen faces, secretly gloated over their finds; I wondered how their lovemaking was with their wives.

'A great deal of money was found at this house and you may think Miss Luscombe shows every sign of being a wealthy woman,' said the elegant counsel in his elegant tones. 'I will eventually put it to you, members of the jury, that here was a veritable harem, a place of available sin, a house of disgust and disgrace, in short a brothel, a bordello in the very heart of Westminster. And to keep a brothel is against the laws of England. It is a serious offence and I ask you to believe that Miss Luscombe is guilty of that offence. The observations of the police officers, the exotic and devilish implements of sexual depravity, the testimony of witnesses show that the very nature of this establishment is in no doubt.'

It sounded very damning to me. The timid eyes of the jury – with their fat, respectable foreman – turned one by one to me. I returned them a tired smile. They looked away.

Strange as it seems, and I did not realize it then, it was a trial I could never lose. Too many famous names were involved. The prosecution were hampered from the start and as the proceedings went on I began to sense the frustration of Peter Crowburn as he sought to condemn me on diminishing evidence.

Then, in the middle of the following night, itchy-eyed and sleepless, alone in my bed, I had a telephone call. It was my erstwhile lover, Derek Blane.

'Nell, I am speaking from New Zealand,' he whispered.

'Why are you whispering then?' I said dryly. 'Nobody will hear you from there.'

'Don't fool about Nelly,' he said. 'It's this damned trial. It's going to put a lot of people in jeopardy you realize.'

'I'm one of them,' I answered.

'God, they must have been fools to prosecute. I've been abroad for three months. I'd no idea . . .'

'It could topple the Government,' I said. I sat up on the pillow with sudden hope. 'Names might be named.'

'That sounds like blackmail.'

'It's you who is telephoning me,' I pointed out.

'We both need help,' he rasped.

God, I thought, how different from those afternoons at Ascot.

'Listen Nell,' he went on, 'whatever you do – no names. I am going to take whatever action I can from here. Understand? It may be too late but I'll try. It's such a bloody mess.'

'It looks like that to me too,' I said.

'No names, then. I'll try and do something.'

I heard him slam down the phone all those miles away.

'Nelly,' said James Threadgold at the end of the second day and the prosecution case. 'They have not produced one witness – thank God MPs don't tell tales – nor one decent bit of evidence, which says that you took *money* from the people who visited your house. That is the one matter they must prove. I think if our case is tidy, and I will endeavour to make it so, and if our witnesses keep their heads under cross-examination, then we must have a chance. Above all it depends on you, Nelly. How you perform in the witness box. Your fate is truly in your own hands, dear girl.'

My cross-examination began on the morning of the fourth day. Outside the court the spectators were just as numerous but, as James Threadgold had foretold, they had warmed to me as each day's proceedings were reported in the newspapers. Now, although there were still the individual insulters, others shouted encouragement and there was even a modest burst of applause – the sort you might hear at a village cricket match – as I left the taxi and made for the door of the court.

Within the courtroom there was now a familiarity also. It was like becoming accustomed to a fresh place of work. Ushers and policemen nodded to me and the jury seemed more at ease in their box. Peter Crowburn even smiled minutely at me from his robes. But I thought that it was his ploy. It was the tiger's smile.

Mr Justice Bonner made his entry to the City chimes. His robes seemed to get heavier for him each day and he smiled a trifle wearily as he sat down, his wig hanging like the ears of some doleful and unusual dog.

I went to the witness box immediately. I had stood there the previous afternoon while my counsel questioned me gently on my life and the events which had brought me to the court. That was an easy journey. Now came the moment for which the Old Bailey audience had been waiting. A woman who for days had been knitting in the public gallery stilled her needles to pay attention. Noses were blown. I stood in my wooden pen, calm at the top but feeling my knees were like wool. Counsel for the prosecution showed no sign of the difficulties and frustrations which, behind the scenes, were piling upon him. He took his time. He shuffled with his papers, sniffed, looked around, dropped his pen, and showed no general hurry to rise. Everyone watched him. The air of suspense thickened. I knew he had begun to play his weakened hand.

Then the judge, with the smallest lean forward, said: 'Mr Crowburn, are you intending to keep a lady waiting?' The words warmed me.

'I am sorry, my Lord,' Peter Crowburn said, hurrying to his feet. There was a small flush around the dark hair curling about his ears.

'Don't apologize to me,' murmured the judge.

'I do apologize, ma'am,' said the lawyer more grandly than was necessary. He bowed towards me, boxed in with the Bible and my fears.

'Your apology is accepted,' I returned quietly. My stomach was beginning to move. I must be calm, I must think every step. Five years under one roof would be a long time.

'Your true name is Mrs Nell Bickerstaff,' he began carefully. 'You are a widow.'

'That is correct,' I said. 'But I prefer to be called by my maiden name of Luscombe.'

'You are known by that name – Nell Luscombe,' he murmured. 'So be it. And you reside at 184, Westminster Terrace Gardens, London, SW1, the premises which are in fact the core of this case.'

'I do.'

'Would you like to tell us your age, Miss Luscombe?'

'No. Of course if the court thinks it is necessary, I will. But otherwise I would prefer not.'

'The court may well think it is necessary, indeed to have a definite bearing on one aspect of this matter,' he replied smugly. 'But, if you prefer so, I will not press you at this time. You prefer to be called Miss Luscombe, although it is a fact, is it not, that you have been married a number of times?'

'Three times,' I answered. 'And three times widowed.'

A little sigh, like the smallest of breezes, came from the gallery. The judge glanced up disapprovingly.

'Could you tell us a little about your husbands. Their names for example.'

I saw an expression of alarm take root on my counsel's face. But James remained seated and waiting. He had his fists clenched white on the table before him.

'I have been Mrs Turnbull, Mrs Sheridan and Mrs Bickerstaff.'

'And Mr Turnbull, Mr Sheridan and Mr Bickerstaff are no longer with us? Would it be true to say that each of these gentlemen died in somewhat unusual circumstances, in a violent manner, and . . .'

James was on his feet now. His face scarlet with anger. 'My Lord,' he said. 'I object most strongly to this manner of questioning the defendant. What difference does it make to these charges if Miss Luscombe had a dozen husbands and they all came to the most extraordinary ends? It matters nothing whatsoever.'

'I believe it does,' muttered Peter Crowburn as he sat down.

'Mr Crowburn,' observed the judge equably. 'That may be so, but I think at the moment all we really require to know is that Miss Luscombe has been married and widowed three times.'

The QC began a scowl but thought better of it, bowed his acknowledgement and then turned to me. 'So be it,' he said. 'Let us then go to matters which I hope may be deemed to have more validity in the case. Miss Luscombe, would you say that you are, and have been, an exceptionally sensual woman, or even a little stronger, a *sexual* woman.'

'Yes, I have had quite a lot to do with it.'

'Good. Yes. You have had not only husbands but many lovers also.'

'A great variety,' I answered.

'Variety also. Yes. Would you go perhaps further? Miss Luscombe, are you, have you ever been, a prostitute?'

'I have been. I am not now.'

'But you have been a prostitute?'

'I liked to think of myself a courtesan. I don't like the word prostitute.'

He arched his excessive eyebrows. 'You don't? Well I think it is a word acceptable in this court. We all know what it means. We are talking about a woman who sells, or hires anyway, her body for sexual purposes.'

'It sounds much better when you put it like that,' I said tartly.

'Well that is the way I intended to put it. A prostitute. Now, could you tell the jury when this mode of life, this prostitution began. Can you remember that Miss Luscombe?'

'Very well. When I was about sixteen. I was without parents or home or friends. I was working in a café in Weymouth and I went out with a young fisherman in a boat. I had intercourse with him and his father gave me half-a-crown.'

'His father? Half-a-crown?'

'It seemed a lot then. The father had given me to his son as a sort of birthday present. His name was Rainbow. He had lovely dark hair, like yours Mr Crowburn.'

He went dull red. There was a small rumble in the court and I thought I saw a small twitch at the edge of the mouth of Mr Justice Bonner.

'Thank you,' sniffed the QC. 'That's very flattering, I'm sure. What happened after that?'

'I used to oblige the fishermen. I made a few pounds.'

'And you've continued making more than a few pounds ever since?'

'Not at all. After that I went to France and on my return to England I met my first husband and we married. A good many years went by before I found the need to do it again.'

'The *need*?' He seized on the word. Although I did not realize it fully, I sensed there was something wrong, something desperate about him. The telephone voice of Derek Blane came to my mind: 'I'll try and do something.' In fact he had done something; people had to be protected. But Peter Crowburn's own integrity would not let him give up. His case against me became a personal one.

'What *need* is that, Miss Luscombe? A financial need, or was it an emotional need, a need to have intercourse with as many men as possible, and to take money for that intercourse? In other words, the need of a *compulsive prostitute*, a person who becomes a harlot for other motives than just money. A woman who cannot resist the calling.'

God, I thought, he had put his finger on it right away. There it was. What I knew I had always been, a compulsive harlot.

He knew it too. He stood cooling. His experience would not allow him to leap yet. It was too early.

'With the court's permission,' he said. 'I will read the synonyms for prostitute as listed in Roget's *Thesaurus*. They are as follows: Prostitute, adultress, advoutress, courtesan, strumpet, tart, hustler, chippy, broad, harlot, whore, punk, fille de joie, woman of the street, street-walker, cyprian, miss, piece, frail sister, fallen woman, demirep, wench, trollop, trull, baggage, hussy, drab, bitch, jade, skit, wanton, fornicatress, Jezabel, Messalina, Delilah, Thais, Phryne, Aspasia, Lais, lorette, coquette, petite dame, grisette, demi-mondaine, white slave, doxy fancy woman, kept woman, chère amie, bona roba, mistress, pandar, bawd, mackerel, wittol.'

He paused and drew a stage breath.

'Hooker,' I pointed out quietly. 'You missed out hooker.'

'All right. Hooker too. Can you see yourself under those headings, Miss Luscombe?'

'Some of them,' I agreed. 'I don't like the sound of being a mackerel or a wittol.'

'Would you agree that you are a woman of ill-repute?'

'I am a woman of excellent repute, sir.'

'Perhaps you might like to tell us how you think a prostitute could be described. Since you are in the business.'

'Since I *was* in the business,' I corrected. I had no difficulty in framing the words. I had lain many a night hour running them through my mind. 'A prostitute,' I said patiently. 'Well she must be something of an actress and an athlete. She must be a mother, a daughter, a mistress. She must be able to switch on love and switch it off again. She must realize that she is a man's heart's desire at one moment and a cast-off the next. She must learn the art of loneliness and there is one thing she can never expect. She can never expect love.'

That staggered him. It staggered the court. I could see their new amazement all around me. 'Oh,' said Peter Crowburn hollowly. 'You sound as if you learned that off by heart.'

'I have, sir,' I said. 'I've had a long time to learn it.'

It must have taken two or three minutes for the atmosphere to clear. James Threadgold was staring at me in pleased disbelief, Morton was sitting as a crouch, his mouth agape. Mr Justice Bonner asked if I would like a glass of water. I accepted it and a blushing usher brought it on a neat tray. He came forward with it as if he were offering his heart.

Counsel for the prosecution would not allow the skirmish to become a battle. He skirted around like a prowling tiger for several minutes asking routine and innocuous questions about my purchase of the lease of 184, Westminster Terrace Gardens. Then he began steadily to move into the attack again.

'Surely,' he said. 'A house in that position, in that part of London, must have cost a great deal. Also it was furnished in great style. You must be a wealthy woman, Miss Luscombe.'

'I have money,' I said.

'How did you come by that money?'

'My own work,' I said. 'I saved. I had some good investments, In my profession not all the whispers were of passion. Some were tips for the Stock Exchange.'

'You must have had excellent information. The market had not been at its brightest. To have earned the sort of money you have would have kept yourself very busy. Are you sure it did not come from the sexual efforts of others? The young ladies who disported themselves in your house, for example?'

'The bulk of the money for the house and furnishings came from one afternoon's racing at Ascot,' I told him simply, as though it was the most logical of matters. 'I won in excess of £60,000. On three horses.'

There was a sound like escaping gas around the courtroom. This time Mr Justice Bonner appeared to join in.

'You won £60,000 at Ascot?' queried Peter Crowburn. 'Sixty thousand?'

'I was not actually there, at Ascot. I was three miles from the course. In bed.'

'You can, I assume, prove this amazing piece of fortune?'

'The gentleman whose company I was keeping could corroborate my story,' I said. I laughed quietly inside as I pictured Derek Blane reading that in the newspaper. 'But I would not embarrass him by calling him as proof. The bookmakers would confirm it. They remember it very well.'

He sniffed optimistically as if he expected no one to believe me. 'And with this pile of winnings and your fortunate investments, you purchased the house at Westminster Terrace Gardens?'

'I did. The lease, that is.'

'What, madam, was your object in taking that house?' He emphasized the 'madam'.

'For years it had been the home of a friend,' I told him. 'She was leaving it and I was looking for somewhere to live. It was one of those happy coincidences.'

'It was also a coincidence, was it not, that this house was so conveniently placed to the Houses of Parliament.'

'Yes, I have a great many friends in both Houses of Parliament and I enjoyed being a hostess to them. So many of the poor creatures are far from home, you know Mr Crowburn, and they have absolutely nowhere to go.'

'Oh, Miss Luscombe you will have me in tears,' he said sarcastically.

'It's very sad,' I replied. 'They are like lost souls.'

He said, abruptly blunt: 'I would like to put it to you that Members of Parliament and others visited your house for sexual activity with the prostitutes you housed there. *And for those services they paid in cash!*'

'That is not true,' I lied. 'They came there as friends.'

'Why then, tell me, was your house known as Strangeways? It was, was it not? Strangeways.'

'That was just a joke. Some Members interested in prison reform came there and they pulled my leg about the place being like a gaol. They said it was like Strangeways Prison, that's how it started.'

'The truth is, is it not,' his voice was much harder now, as if it had broken through a crust. 'The truth is that the joke referred to the sexual perversions that could be enjoyed, *at a price*, under *your* roof. Sexual services provided by *you*, Nell Luscombe.' Suddenly he shouted and frightened me. '*That is the truth, is it not?*'

'No it is *not*,' I cried back. Suddenly he had me trembling. I caught James Threadgold's worried eye. 'That's not true!'

'All the police observations, all the evidence of the sexual equipment found in that house, then, is wrong. How do you explain the whips then? Go on, Miss Luscombe, explain that.'

'I like to be whipped!' I howled. It was not true of course. The tears were coursing down my face. 'I like those things. So do others. Or perhaps *you* cannot understand that.'

'Indeed I cannot,' he observed with personal menace. 'What I do seem to understand though is that these activities did take place and that you enticed and procured the younger girls to perform these perversions and to receive payment for what we might call their pains. You, madam, say you had no need of the money. That may be true, but now we are back – are we not, madam – at the point where I suggested that you are a prostitute by compulsion, not by necessity.' His face had grown darker as if a bruise were coming out. He hurled the words at me. I could not stop trembling and crying. There was no respite, no breathing space, no mercy. Peter Crowburn, harried as he was from high places, was not going to stop now. He would pursue me if no one else would. I faced him. Now it was him and me. He came at me like a tiger.

'I put it to you and to the jury that you encouraged this *filth*, this *infamy*, for your own personal sexual satisfaction. Now madam, here we come to your age again – I said it was pertinent. I apologize for this impoliteness, but would you agree that getting beyond the bloom of youth, now you are feeling and knowing your age, even if you don't care to divulge it. Now you can get *others* to work for you to give *you* satisfaction. So you can watch, observe and enjoy the sensations. So you can use the facilities offered by your ill-famed house. So that you, Nell Luscombe, a lifelong sexual addict, can squeeze the last ounce of pleasure out of the sexual life you know is slipping away. So you debauch young girls, make them perform these acts with men, and get *your* kicks, *kicks* madam I said, in that way. Is that not true? I put it to you plainly. You are a prostitute by proxy. Now – because it is *too late* for you, madam. Too late!' He shouted the final words at me.

Now I was on my emotional knees. Tears were splattering my cheeks and my chin, my whole being vibrated with a great, sorry, outrageous rage. I could feel my very bones trembling. All I remember is looking at him and seeing him in that very same state, furious, shaking, shouting. It was astonishing. We confronted each other like a pair of warring, wounded sealions. Then my own fury rose and engulfed me.

I do not remember clearly the next minute. I can still hear myself shouting 'Too late for me? Too late is it?' And then I was tearing at the buttons on the front of my blouse, pulling it open and with one movement breaking the clasps between the cups of my brassière. My proud and beautiful breasts tumbled out, large, creamy, superbly nippled, free! 'There!' I bawled at him. 'Now tell me it's too late!'

For seconds that seemed like years there was a stillness. The whole courtroom was petrified. I remember the expression on Peter Crowburn's face and the sagging mouth of James Threadgold and young Morton. Then uproar. Ushers, policemen, converged on my exposed person. I felt the room turning, quite slowly, around me and I fell in a faint in the bottom of the witness box.

In the circumstances it was the best thing I could have done.

'Nell,' said James Threadgold, squeezing my arm, 'something has happened. They've chucked it. I damn well know they've chucked it. Something has gone on somewhere. They're going to back down.'

I smiled confidently at him but he did not understand what I knew. He was still cautious however and he wanted to make sure.

'Nell,' he said coyly, 'as soon as the judge begins his summing up to the jury, stand on the left-hand side of the dock. See, where the beam of sunshine is. Stand in that sunbeam, Nell. Try to look like Joan of Arc.'

It was the last day of my trial. Nobody who had been present throughout would ever be quite the same again. I now faced not only the original accusations but a singular charge of Contempt of Court.

I walked two paces sideways – the dock being large enough to accommodate several prisoners at the same time – and stood where the streak of sunshine struck as it came through the clouds and the windows. It had faded temporarily and I stood, listening to the somnolent words of the judge as he directed the jury, like a father trying to give understanding to children. They were to forget everything that had taken place in that court, he said, apart from the facts that had been presented to them. That would have required a miracle.

'*You* and only you must decide whether this extraordinary lady operated her house as a place of ill-repute, for gain, for *money*, and whether she made herself available there, for *money* and procured others to do likewise. But I emphasize that you must be satisfied that the prosecution have shown beyond doubt that whatever took place at Miss Luscombe's house was for money, for her financial gain.'

He turned towards me at this point and their twelve pairs of eyes followed him and, God bless me, at that moment the sun came out and streamed down through the big windows upon me. I could feel it lightening my hair. I tilted my chin. Like Joan of Arc.

They retired to think about their verdict. James sat quietly by me. I was still drained by it all. I felt at that moment that I would have welcomed a quiet five years in prison. Eventually I whispered, 'What do you think, James?'

'I think we'll get an acquittal,' he said calmly. 'Poor Crowburn. Something shot his case from under him. They have not produced one little turd of evidence to show that any money changed hands. It is fortunate too that the gentlemen who were present in the house were all properly attired and, in any event, since they're what they are, politicians, were always highly unlikely to be caught as witnesses.'

He put the tips of his fingers together in his mouth as though considering a prayer, but thought again about it. 'I have never seen Peter Crowburn get into such a mess as that,' he said, a note of sympathy in his voice. 'I understand his wife left him last week. That may have been behind his outburst. Even Queen's Counsel are not immune from inner conflict. Also they gave him a shitty case to handle. I think he's been betrayed. I think we will win, Nell.'

I felt very grateful to him and touched his hand. He smiled seriously. 'On the other hand, for your truly stupendous Contempt of Court, you could go to prison for six months,' he said. 'You can bare you heart, your soul or your conscience in the Old Bailey, but not your bosom.'

I stood facing them, judge and jury, my stomach shaking within me, my face burning, my hands wet. The four charges were read again and each time the judge leaned towards the jury and asked: 'Do you find the accused guilty or not guilty as charged?'

And four times the voice from the big-bellied foreman sounded surprisingly small. But how sweet.

'Not guilty,' he said.

I felt relief engulf me. My legs wobbled, my view became fuzzy with tears. All around me the sound from the people came like the starting of a dynamo.

'Nell Luscombe, you have been found not guilty by this court of the four charges brought against you.' The judge's words came to me as though they were being sung by a baritone angel. His dogged face seemed many miles away up there at the end of the court. 'On those counts you will, therefore, be discharged.'

He wrinkled his expression. His wig wobbled. 'Miss Luscombe, do you think that you could stand out of that fortuitous sunbeam? Yes, thank you. That is much less dramatic.'

I stood in the cool now, the rays gone from my hair. 'There is now the matter,' he said, 'of the very serious Contempt of Court. I have taken into account the extreme stress you found yourself under and also that there was no mean measure of provocation on the part of the counsel for the prosecution.'

Peter Crowburn stared ahead, not a finger moving. He had a fine strong back. I wondered why his wife had gone. 'On the other hand,' continued Mr Justice Bonner, 'it constitutes one of the gravest contempts I have ever witnessed in a court of law. I was very tempted to send you to gaol without any option. However I decided, in view of the other verdicts, that I shall impose upon you a fine of two thousand pounds with the added punishment of three months in prison . . .' There seemed a year until the next words. '. . . This to be in the form of a suspended sentence.' He leaned towards me in the distance. 'Miss Luscombe . . . you must *never, ever* do that sort of thing in the Central Criminal Court again.'

'No sir,' I whispered. 'I won't. I'm sorry.'

With James Threadgold and the adoring Morton I went out into the free London sunlight, my heart welling with emotion. Outside were my lovely girls, Dirty Diedre, Angelica, Suzy and the others, to surround me and kiss me for the photographers. They would be famous forever.

A furtive man appeared at my elbow. 'Miss Luscombe,' he said. 'I am Detective Sergeant Parry. I congratulate you on the verdict.'

'Thank you,' I said surprised.

'I wondered if at some time I could have a few words with you about the late Mr Pierre Arthur Bickerstaff? Just routine, you understand?

'You don't *think* . . .'

'We never *think* anything Miss Luscombe. Just routine, nothing to fret about.'

I stood amazed. Then I laughed. I had just been proved innocent of a crime of which I was guilty. I was not afraid of their questions about poor Pierre Arthur although to this day they have pursued me.

'Any time,' I said lightly.

'Thank you Miss Luscombe,' he said, touching his pork pie hat. He sidled away.

There was an enormous turncoat crowd, cheering and happy now that I Nelly Luscombe had won the day – and with what sensations. Something made me turn and in the shadows of the door to the court I could see the solitary Peter Crowburn. I could not help it. I turned back, away from everyone, re-entered that now un-frightening place and confronted him. His face, and certainly his heart, were loaded.

'I suppose it's easy for me now,' I said to him. 'But I wanted to say I am sorry for that demonstration in the witness box.'

He smiled wanly and we shook hands. 'Don't apologize,' he said. I got what I deserved. You are a very beautiful woman, Nelly.' We smiled together and I wondered if we had planted a seed. He grinned boyishly.

'And the sunbeam trick was brilliant. I must remember it. Goodbye Nelly.'

'Goodbye Peter,' I did not return to the crowded front of the court, but went through its landings and corridors, guided by a pleased usher to a small back door. As we passed by the inner doors of each courtroom I knew that in every one justice was being done, or not, as the case was.

Outside again I was in a brief shadowed street. A taxi was idling at the kerb as if it had waiting for me for days. I got in and sat, suddenly deflated and sad, on the long seat.

'Where to madam,' the driver asked. His 'madam' was different.

'Take me home please,' I said wearily.

'Where's home?' he asked.

'Devon,' I said on impulse. 'Take me to Devon.'

It was an evening returned from childhood. May, with warm Devon air and an airy lightness, the day drifting only reluctantly towards the sea. The hamlet seemed empty of people, only voices calling from houses, gardens with flowers crammed behind their stone walls, birds in trees and cats on walls.

I had walked the mile from Hopewell, over the unchanging hill, drinking from a bottle of gin as I went. Tomorrow, I promised, I would go and see my sister Mary, her good husband, and her children, all the things she had gained. But now, empty once more, without substance, I needed to see if the ghosts of long ago were still lingering.

At the top of the hill, and how small it seemed now, as though it had shrivelled with its ageing. I looked down and saw my stream below still moving through green banks. Where our homely terrace had been was now a smart run of mews-like houses with bogus Georgian windows and coach lamps at the doors. I did not look at them. They had taken the old place away, foundations, earth, heart and all.

The gin was making me drunk and I had not eaten since breakfast that day. The taxi driver had declined to drive me to Devon but taken me to Paddington in time for the train. I was still in my Old Bailey clothes, my hat awry, my shoes biting my feet. With another swig from the gin bottle I made the last few yards to the bank of the brook.

Miraculously it was just as it had always been. Just as solitary too. Midges, the descendants of those who whirled there long before, were dancing over the darkening water. The day had finally decided to go. Crying, inebriated, I sat on the damp bank and watched the water. I let my shoes and my stockings dangle down into it. I was alone there as I had so often been. The cold water embalmed my feet. I had to do it. Taking a large swig from the gin bottle I laid it on the bank and then undressed. I put all my clothes in a pile on the grass and, naked, stumbled drunkenly down into the clear, cold, shallow current.

Then I sat down and let the water run about my middle-aged thighs. A sort of mad melancholy held me. I reached for the bottle, had another mouthful, and began to sing a little Devon song.

Bare Nell Luscombe was back.

That Old Gang of Mine

'Please don't rob me. I'm just a little old lady.

'So am I,' said the voice behind the mask.

At four-thirty on the afternoon of 27 January, this year, a bus returning to Miami and Fort Lauderdale with tourists who had been visiting a Seminole Indian Reservation was held up at gun-point, twenty-eight miles west of Andytown on the Florida Everglades Parkway.

The ambush took place on a dirt road two miles from the main highway. The tourist guide was held hostage and the passengers robbed of everything of value.

Three hooded gangsters carried out the robbery. Two women accomplices were also involved. The ages of the five robbers totalled 320 years – an average of 64 years per gun.

CHAPTER ONE

'*This is Station WAIA, Miami, a bee ... utiful morning, people. We expect a high of seventy-eight degrees today, a low of sixty-two tonight, with a twenty per cent chance of rain. It's real good to be alive ... Station WAIA, your music way, serving the Golden Coast from the Palm Beaches to Key West.*'

The pelican cruising down from Palm Beach, Florida, towards the islands of the Keys that January day had fine flying weather. A gentle wind sniffed from the south-west but there were few clouds and the long golden arm of Miami Beach was in good shape. A remote storm in the night had disturbed the sea and there were surfers at Pompano; at Fort Lauderdale basking ranks of vacationing college students, boys and girls, blew bubble gum. Rich old widows in bikinis and pastel pink knee boots, which hid their varicose veins, sunbathed at the Fontainbleu Hotel and many blocks down, along Ocean Drive, South Miami, two thousand elderly folk sat on small chairs beneath the sea-grape trees.

The Golden Coast to which radio station WAIA, Miami, refers in its call sign stretches for two hundred miles from Palm Beach on the Atlantic seaboard of Florida, through Boca Raton, Pompano, Fort Lauderdale, Hollywood, and a dozen other seaside conurbations, through Miami Beach, separated from Miami proper by fine lakes and lagoons, and then south to the curving small islands of the Florida Keys which terminate in the city of Key West, the most southerly in the United States.

South Miami Beach lies roughly halfway down the distance, an area gradually diminishing to squalor, in contrast to the expensive real estate only a couple of miles to the north. Once it was *the* Miami Beach, but now it slips a little with each season. It has become a museum of art deco buildings of the nineteen-twenties, inhabited by a tribe of old people, ninety per cent of them Jewish, many impoverished. They have colonized it with that special talent they have for colonizing; it has kosher shops and kosher hotels, synagogues, talking places like salt beef bars and selected shady trees and Jewish social centres. The accents and dialogue of twenty old countries can be heard on Washington Avenue or Ocean Drive. For these are the people who once arrived in America for a new life. Now they have almost had that life and they sit in their collapsible canvas chairs and watch the sail boats and the automobiles of the new generations.

There is not much money about, the people do not live or eat extravagantly, but they stick together beneath the Florida sun. They believe that it lengthens their days, days spent in inactivity or in pseudo-pastimes. The people are no longer useful. Frequently they have been sent to South Miami Beach by families who have ceased to have time or space for them. A cynic has called the place God's Waiting Room.

As the ungainly pelican creaked on his journey that morning he might have spotted on the South Beach a solitary figure in red vest and shorts, running steadily with the shore line, a man known as Ari the Greek, sixty years of age. Although at that moment he was unaware of it, he was about to become involved in one of the most bizarre series of crimes in the history of the state of Florida.

He ran every day on the beach. Most of his fellow pensioners sat where the grass was clean and cool beneath the sea-grape trees, but there were a few who were on the sand and they exchanged waves and words as he jogged by.

'Hiya Ari! Still running?'

'If I'm running I'm living!' the Greek called back, hardly panting. He had a strong Mediterranean face although he had lived in Jackonsville, Florida most of his life. In Prohibition days he had been a bootlegger, then he had operated a pancake house and later branched out into hotdogs. His hair was just a memory and his large nose seemed to have features all its own, like a second face. He drew abreast of a barefoot woman in a red dress, plump as a strawberry. They called her Molly Mandy and she was searching for treasure with a metal detector. She saw Ari call to her but she did not hear because of the dishes clamped over her ears. She obligingly pulled one of the dishes away and extended the exposed ear towards Ari.

'What d'yer say, Ari?'

'I said have you found something? Like treasure?'

'Jeez, I swear this machine makes you deaf.' She switched off the detector. 'Now what d'yer say?'

Ari jogged on the spot as though fearful of letting his momentum run down. A dollop of sweat careered down his nose and hit the sand at his feet making a hole like a bullet. 'Molly, I said have you found anything?' he repeated patiently. 'Like treasure?'

'Sure, sure,' Molly nodded. She had serene Jewish features, deep, dark eyes, broad forehead, hair grey but neat. She should have been sitting in the comfortable house of her elder son in White Plains, New York, where he was important with the telephone company, but his wife did not like her being around there. They had told her she would like it better down on Miami Beach in the sun. She had innocently believed them. 'Yesterday I found gold like Fort Knox never had, Ari,' she joked. 'Ten million dollars in gold! How about that! But I figured I just couldn't give up looking. Like it's a hobby.'

'I know just how you feel.' nodded Ari understandingly. 'Like I'm in the American Olympics team. It provides something to do.'

He slipped into gear and started off again. ''Bye now, take care,' Molly called automatically after him. She clamped the dogs around her ears and returned to searching the empty sand. Half an hour later she found a nickle and a dime.

Ari habitually terminated the beach section of his run by the comfort station coyly labelled 'Boys' and 'Girls', near the place where the City of Miami, with a stroke of tactless genius, had erected a large concrete calendar recording the time, date, day and year. If there was anything the many people in that region did not need it was a calendar. Had they been more militant they might have blown it up. As it was Ari projected a spirited raspberry at the object's timeful face which brought a wry laugh from some old men playing dominoes in the shade. Ari did that every day. It was not much of a defiance, but it was something.

The Greek crossed Ocean Drive, the street running parallel with the sea, but divided from the beach by the grass and the sea-grape trees. He went up Eighth Street onto Washington Avenue. It was hot now and his padding feet made prints in the sidewalk dust. There was a kosher shop advertising guaranteed clean water at twenty-five cents a jug, bring your own jug. He curled his lip because he did not go along with all these Jewish precautions, but it made him feel thirsty and he began to look forward to the lime juice he always drank after his exercise.

There was a small funeral on Washington. They never had big funerals in those parts because, in general, people did not enjoy attending them. This was just two cars, one with the coffin and the other with a clutch of bland and blank mourners. The cortège had halted at the traffic signals and the driver leaned out and mopped his brow with an appropriately black handkerchief. Ari, as if he were a motor vehicle, pulled up and ticked over also, his old but muscled legs slowing carefully like pistons. He knew the hearse driver, a violently cheerful young man who also drove a truck for an anti-bug, delousing company doing business with the small hotels. They often joked about the young man scatching a living.

'Who's travelling?' asked Ari, watching the traffic lights. He nodded casually back towards the coffin.

'Guy called Sylvester, I think,' replied the driver. 'Resident at the Beau Park.'

'Don't remember him,' shrugged Ari.

'Not many do,' said Herbie casually. 'There was no interest. He left ten dollars each to pay for some mourners.'

'If it's gonna be like that I ain't going.' Ari snorted like a horse through his nose.

'Maybe you'll be next, Ari.' warned Herbie cheerfully. 'All that running could kill you, man.'

'If I'm running I'm living,' recited the dogged Greek. The lights changed and he went into gear and got away ahead of the funeral. 'Goddamn you,' he said over his shoulder.

The conversation had worried him, so he went to the Kress Bargain Store and paid the man a dollar to test his blood pressure. The man sat all day at a small table at the entrance and tested many people's blood pressures. Some came back every day, some twice a day. A doctor would have charged ten dollars. At a dollar a pressure, it was a give-away.

The man who wore a proper white coat, wound the tourniquet around

Ari's arm, pumped on a rubber globe, while Ari watched both his arm and the registering arrow anxiously.

'It's okay, Ari,' said the pressureman. 'Same as before. You ain't going nowhere yet.'

'I get these headaches . . .' Ari began hopefully.

The man pointed sternly to the notice which said: 'Please do not ask for medical advice.' He said: 'If I knew about headaches, Ari, I'd be a doctor now, wouldn't I? Not a gas pump attendant for humans. That'll be a dollar.'

Loose Bruce got off the Greyhound bus at the depot just across the street from the Shelbourne Hotel where beauty queens used to imprint their feet in wet concrete on the forecourt. He was twenty-five years old, tall, stringy, with a casual face and a sloppy way of walking. He had been a car washer and a waiter in various parts of New York State and then had taken a job as an usher in a pornographic movie theatre off Times Square, but had been fired after being found asleep during working hours. He had taken the bus to Miami Beach because it was January in New York and he understood they had a different January in Florida. As he sloped from the bus depot with his canvas bag and his scarred jeans he was grateful to feel the sun on his face.

Walking across the street he stood on the sidewalk examining the feet of Miss Americas and Miss Universes, immortalized in concrete. Ari the Greek, who was passing by at the end of his run, loitered too. The footprints had stopped when the district began to fade, when they started to build Miami again, forty blocks north.

'Sure had big feet some of them beauties,' observed Ari. Loose Bruce nodded. The inhabitants of the district made a habit of talking to young people whenever they were available. They believed it kept them in touch.

'Not many girls around here now, huh?' said Bruce, looking at the big toe of Barbara Ann Morley, of Gary, Indiana. A family of busy blank ants had gathered in its depression.

'You have to look real hard,' admitted Ari. 'But we got some real nice *old* ladies. The young girls, they're all up at Fort Lauderdale and so's the young fellas.'

'So I'm too far south,' nodded Loose Bruce. 'That figures. Know anywhere I can stay?'

The Greek squinted at him with amazement. 'You want to *stay*?' he said. 'A young guy like you and you want to stay? Here?'

Bruce chewed on imaginary gum. 'Don't they allow anybody under eighty?' he asked.

'Eighty? Jeez. How old d'you think I am? Come on, take a guess.' Ari did a little trot on the spot and showed his teeth.

'Oh, man I don't know. I really couldn't tell at all,' replied Bruce cautiously. 'I guess about seventy.'

Fury gathered like a cloud around Ari's great nose. 'Seventy! Goddamn you, you're ten years out! Ten whole years!'

Bruce looked at him again. 'Mister,' he said admiringly, 'you sure look great for eighty.'

'I'm *sixty*! You blind young bastard!' retorted Ari. 'Get a load of those legs, son.' He displayed the gnarled calves hanging from his running shorts. 'Take a look. They ain't no old man's legs.'

'Sorry,' said Bruce genuinely. 'I mean I can never tell the ages of older folks – or babies either. I guess you look fine for sixty. I hope I look like you when I'm sixty. I hope I can still run.'

'If I'm running I'm living,' recited Ari a little mollified. He seemed to be measuring Bruce. 'You could try where I live,' he said. 'I reckon they'll have a bed to fit you. Sunny Gables Hotel, on the ocean. It's real nice. They have a guy come and plays the banjo in the evening.'

'Sounds the place I could be looking for,' said Bruce doubtfully. 'What's the rate?'

'Forty-five dollars a week, but maybe if the boss-woman likes you she'll give you a reduction. There's a vacancy right now because a guy fell out of bed last week and they took him to the hospital. I don't figure he'll be back.'

They began to walk towards the beach, Loose Bruce tall, with his bag on his shoulder like a sailor, Ari, almost a foot shorter, loping at his side, pausing every twenty yards for a spasm of frenzied running on the spot.

'They got a burlesque up the street,' he said informatively. 'I took a look at it on my birthday. Jesus, the girls sure have got boobs these days. I figure it's the good food, the nutrition, that does that. In my day the young girls didn't get that sort of eating. Some of the older women around here ain't too bad. In fact some of them's real comfortable. But the routine takes so long you kinda lose interest. Your mind wanders. Know what I mean? And if you do anything to them – any little thing – it's a bet they start crying and thinking about their husbands, who are dead years ago. In the main it's no good. Not for women.'

Bruce took the information in. 'Well,' he said, 'that don't worry me. I'm not planning too much in that way right now. I just feel I'll stick around and get the feel of the place. Forty dollars you calculate?'

'Maybe less. Mrs Nissenbaum maybe would like a young face about the joint. And she's a widow too. South Miami Beach is kinda hung with widows.'

'That's just the room, forty dollars,' said Bruce thoughtfully. He only had seventy in the world. 'For a week.'

'It ain't for a year,' said Ari. 'That's for your room. Right. I got an efficiency, that's a room with a cooking pot. There's a stove to put it on, but mine don't work. The pot leaks anyway. It's a non-efficient efficiency, you could say. So I got it reduced. Maybe you could get a job.'

'I'll sure need one,' admitted Bruce.

'Mortician, that's a good deal around these parts,' said Ari sombrely. 'Busy, busy. Never out of work.'

'Black never suited me,' said Bruce, shaking his head. 'Maybe I could be a swimming instructor.'

'You a good swimmer then?'

'No, I can't swim. But maybe around here they wouldn't notice.'
'They wouldn't,' agreed Ari.

As though coming as a comment on their words they walked out onto
Ocean Drive and Bruce saw what it was like. The beach and the sea were
empty, just touching each other as if for company. But on the grass
between the sand and the street there were hundreds and hundreds of old
folk.

They massed like many-coloured penguins along a lonely shore,
moving, still, chattering, silent, all bunched together beneath the fanned
branches of the trees. Jazzy shirts and pants, bright hats above
sunburned faces, extravagant robes and dresses. Bruce stopped in
astonishment. They were around tables playing chess and cards and
dominoes; they sang and danced in groups to the accompaniment of
ancient violins and desperately blown trumpets; they wrote letters to
remote loved ones who only occasionally replied, and read out extracts to
their uninterested neighbours. They sat singly, a transistor radio
clamped to the ear, they fed the seabirds and the sparrows, or they
merely sat dozing or awake and staring at the enormous shining sea as if
wondering what the hell it was.

'Jesus Christ,' breathed Bruce.

'Not too loud. He may arrive,' mentioned Ari. 'You get the feeling
down here that he's kinda loitering. Eighty-five per cent of the people
here are Jewish and they worry in case they did the wrong thing by Jesus,
if you get me. When you get older you get things like that on your mind.
I'm Greek Orthodox so He don't bother me.'

'I just never saw so many old folks,' said Bruce.

'They clear them out of the rest of the country,' said Ari. 'They get
swept down here, like a corner. God's Waiting Room they call this place.'

They walked south on Ocean Drive. A frail couple went in the
opposite direction between them wheeling a supermarket basket trolley.
It contained their suitcases and other worldly belongings.

'Moving,' said Ari, giving a brief nod towards the pair.

'Very moving,' agreed Bruce. 'Real sad. Have they had to quit where
they lived?'

'That's what I said, didn't I? They're *moving*. I don't know where.
Maybe they're going to the penthouse at the Fontainbleu.' The
commonplace sight had evoked no sympathy in him. He stopped on the
sidewalk. 'Listen, kid,' he said. 'Let me go ahead and do some
negotiating for you. Mrs Nissenbaum, she respects me because I'm not
Jewish, see? Maybe I can get you a good deal for your room. Okay?'

'Okay,' said Bruce. 'That sure is nice of you.'

'To the Greek, kindness is only second to avarice,' said Ari baring his
teeth. 'Stick around. Go and see the ocean, it's real neat. I'll be back.'

He loped away, still pausing every so often to perform his strange
running-on-the-spot routine. He threw out a few ghostly punches too
before continuing on his way to the Sunny Gables Hotel. Loose Bruce
watched him go, shrugged and grinned and, throwing his bag over his
shoulder again, walked through the people and the sea-grape trees

towards the beach.

In contrast to the market-place atmosphere of the Ocean Drive lawns, the beach was almost deserted. The sea was clear, long indolent waves curling towards Florida, still echoing the storm of the night before. There was a lookout watch tower with a man gazing out over the empty waves to sky where the pelicans and the seagulls flew. Bruce sat idly on a low wall and watched the lookout. He could only see half his head, chopped grey hair under a ragged, dirty white tugboat cap.

The half a head nodded rhythmically as though the man was talking or singing to himself. Bruce wondered what was the age limit for lifeguards. Not that there seemed to be any risk of ever having to make a rescue. The ocean at South Beach was empty.

At that moment a fat woman in a rainbow bathing suit waddled onto the beach near where Bruce was standing and proceeded towards the shoreline. The lifeguard seemed to have been waiting for her.

'Mrs Blum,' he called in a friendly way through his loud-hailer. The voice was firm, not old. '*Not* today, Mrs Blum, you promised.'

The rainbow woman half turned and waved a dismissive hand towards him. She shouted something that Bruce did not catch.

'Mrs Blum, come on back right now. *Please, Mrs Blum!*' called the guard.

Bruce turned and saw the numerous old folk now gathering by the parapet of the wall behind him, watching the developing scene with keen interest. 'This time she'll do it,' forecast a tiny bald man. 'You just see. This time she'll do it.'

'Mrs BLUM!' echoed the despairing shout from the lookout tower. 'YOU COME BACK HERE THIS MINUTE! MRS BLUM . . .!'

She had now reached the fringe of the ocean and, after pausing, then stepping with fat daintiness over the first waves, she strode boldly into the rollers advancing on her. Bruce heard the lifeguard mutter, 'Shit, Mrs Blum,' as he slid down the ladder. Below the prematurely grey hair the rest of him was about thirty-five years of age. He was wearing a sun-faded track suit and he ran across the sand in athletic fashion. Bruce had slowly risen to his feet and now began to saunter, then run, after him. Mrs Blum had become like a multi-coloured playball in the great green sea.

The lifeguard plunged into the waves. A mutter of surprised approval came from the spectators on the parapet. 'There, Thelma, I told you he could swim. He wasn't kidding,' said the tiny man with the bald head.

'The water ain't very deep there,' answered Thelma in a flat tone, pleasurably anticipating tragedy. 'You wait till that guy has to get into *deep* water. Or wait till there's a killer shark. He won't go, no sir, he won't go.'

The bald man had a lifetime's experience of not arguing with Thelma beyond a sentence or so. They watched the lifeguard wrestling with slippery Mrs Blum. Her ringed colours spun in the waves. Twice she knocked the man backwards with powerful dorsal sweeps of her fat forearm. Bravely he struggled from the water and tried to get his arms fixed about her. He could not get a hold. He had salt in his eyes and brine in his throat. He was not, he repeated to himself, a very good lifeguard. He had a nasty vision of Mrs Blum eventually rescuing him. 'Please, Mrs Blum, cooperate,' he pleaded. Then Loose Bruce arrived and the lifeguard saw him gratefully.

The two men closed on her, but Mrs Blum was not finished. She began to howl the name of her late husband whom, she bellowed defiantly, she intended to join. 'Arnie!' she cried above the rollers. 'Arnie, come and get me Arnie!'

She turned and brilliantly knocked Bruce backwards into the waves. The lifeguard had to help him to his feet, letting go of Mrs Blum who made a final suicide bid, lying face down in the water, her multi-coloured backside rolling like some Walt Disney whale in the swell. This time the two men managed to turn her over and tow her towards the beach. The final effort had exhausted the old lady and now she was a dead weight in their arms as they struggled for the sand. Her eyes were closed and her mouth hung open like a large cave. But she was breathing.

'I ain't doing no resuscitation,' said Bruce as he looked down at the mouth. 'It ain't my responsibility.'

'Don't put ideas into Mrs Blum's head,' whispered the lifeguard urgently. He looked down at the large coloured expanse. 'Resuscitation could take six months.'

Mrs Blum unhinged one eyelid to get a look at Bruce and closed it quickly again.

'She does this often?' said Bruce.

'Twice a week. At least twice,' nodded the lifeguard. 'It's her only contact with a man.' He looked expectantly up the beach and waved. Two men with a stretcher were coming towards them but with no urgency. They had obviously seen it all before. They even paused while one of them bent to pick up an unusual shell from the sand. 'That's the first time she's got that far out,' continued the lifeguard. 'Maybe she's been practising. One day I'm going to wake up on this sand with her blowing into *my* mouth.' He closed his eyes and shuddered briefly. Then he leaned gratefully across the coloured satin mountain that was Mrs Blum. 'My name's Oswald,' he said. 'I like to be called Ossie.'

'I don't blame you,' said Bruce reaching across. 'I'm Bruce. I just got here.'

'Glad you arrived in time,' said Ossie. The two shook hands across the meridian of Mrs Blum. It was the beginning of a partnership.

'What I gotta tell you,' said Ari the Greek loping along beside the wet Bruce, 'is that there's two hotels. The Sunny Gables and the Waving Palms, one right next to the other, if you get me. There's Mrs Nissenbaum, she runs Sunny Gables, and Miss Nissenbaum runs the Waving Palms. Like they're sisters-in-law. One is uglier than the other, but I don't know which.'

'She don't have to be Miss America,' shrugged Bruce. 'Just so I can get a room and get dry. Life-saving is very wet.'

'It's no problem, not as I see it,' Ari assured him seriously. They had walked three blocks along Ocean Drive. Some people looked at Bruce with curiosity but not many. They were mostly elderly and they walked with their own enclosing thoughts, not taking much notice of anything else. Eventually the two men stopped short of a tired building that managed to reach eight floors. It looked as though it had hunched shoulders in the way of a tall, old man. Across the front were letters tipped at various angles with the words Sunny Gables Hotel and beneath that the inducement: 'Come Swing With Us'.

Three old ladies nodded approvingly at Bruce from their seats on the narrow porch. They could have been operated by clockwork. Bruce nodded back and nervously tried to wipe some of the wet from his shirt.

Immediately next door was a similarly weary building. One letter of its name had vanished so that it announced itself as Waving –alms Hotel. It boasted 'We Swing More', apparently as a taunt to the hotel next door, and added 'Pullmanettes' and 'Condos'.

'Who are they?' asked Bruce.

'You sleep in a pullmanette and you sleep in a condo, which is a condominium,' said Ari. 'There ain't a lot of room. It's good practice for when you're dead and in your grave.'

Bruce saw the Greek's expression alter. He followed his eyes and saw an almost fearsome woman arrive on the top step of the Sunny Gables Hotel. Another lady of comparable aspect came out onto the porch of the adjoining hotel.

'Mrs Nissenbaum of the Sunny Gables and Miss Nissenbaum of the Waving Palms,' whispered Ari. 'Get what I mean?'

Bruce could. Dark, ugly and truculent, they stood on their separate doorsteps. The Sunny Gables Nissenbaum was the shorter of the two, so there was less of her to be ugly. But it was the only thing in her favour. He looked up like some boy slave put forward for auction.

'Too late, Sadie, he's coming in here,' said the Sunny Gables Nissenbaum nastily to her sister-in-law. She pointed an enormous finger towards Bruce.

'And plenty you'll charge him,' said the Waving Palms Nissenbaum. 'And goddam little he'll get for it.'

Bruce stared up one to the other. Two grey men came out into the porch of the Waving Palms and nodded in support of their landlady. The three women on the front of Sunny Gables had never stopped nodding.

'You'll be happy here,' Sunny Gables Nissenbaum promised, waving Bruce towards the steps. 'We could do with a young face.'

'You sure could,' said her sister-in-law coarsely. She put in a rival bid. 'Here, my boy, you pay two dollars less than you pay there. How much she charges, we charge two dollars less. You got a deal.'

Bewildered, Bruce looked at Ari. The indecision brought Mrs Nissenbaum heavily down the steps of Sunny Gables and she caught him by the wet arm and hurried him into the house. 'He'll be sorry,' shouted the Waving Palms Nissenbaum after them.

'That woman,' sneered her sister-in-law once they were in the small lobby. 'Haggling. She's so Jewish.' She noticed Bruce's state apparently for the first time. 'Why is he all wet?' She looked at Bruce but asked the question of Ari, as if the responsibility must be his.

'Since arriving in this area,' said Ari patiently, 'this boy has rescued a woman from the sea. Am I speaking the truth, son?'

Bruce nodded modestly but Mrs Nissenbaum remained unimpressed. 'There's too many women here,' she said. 'Better to leave her. Conserve the men, okay. Let the ocean have the women, I say.' There was a brief pause, then she said. 'Thirty dollars a week for the room.'

Bruce glanced gratefully at Ari who winked in return. 'That's very nice of you,' he said to Mrs Nissenbaum. He had time to study her now. She was a wooden woman with jowls and heavily reddened lips. Her hair was accidentally tinted several colours and her eyelashes laden with mascara. Detachable lashes projected like teeth.

'Maybe if you feel at home I could give you a better deal still,' she said brazenly. She cocked her eye and the right eyelash broke partially free and curled upwards giving her the fierce questioning aspect of a war god in a Chinese opera. Bruce involuntarily shivered. 'I think thirty dollars is real generous, Mrs Nissenbaum,' he said.

She knew the eyelash was adrift but it did not worry her. She reached up and pulled it back into position on her lid. 'In advance,' she said firmly, holding out her hand. 'I got to take a week in advance.'

'Sure,' said Bruce, reaching for his pocket. His seventy dollars came out like a wet wedge of tobacco. He looked at it doubtfully. 'I guess it neeeds drying out,' he suggested.

'That'll teach you to run after women, even them that's drowning,' sniffled Mrs Nissenbaum. 'Okay, I'll take the thirty when it's aired. Ari will show you the room. No members of the opposite sex, that means women, allowed in the room after nine o'clock, no dogs and cats, no parties, noise, drunkenness or drugs. What I says, that goes. Okay?'

'Okay,' nodded Bruce. 'I don't figure on getting a dog or a cat anyway.'

'And there ain't no women around after nine o'clock anyway,' added Ari.

Mrs Nissenbaum loosed off an enormous smile that completely wrecked her face. Her false teeth appeared to be floating in the cavern of her mouth. 'Welcome to Sunny Gables then,' she said. A hand like a spade came out and folded over his. Bruce winced. 'I'm sure we'll be friends,' she continued. 'This is a great little place to live. You just swing with us. Ari will tell you, won't you Ari?'

Ari's nose bowed meekly. 'A great little place, Mrs Nissenbaum,' he agreed. 'Just a great place.'

'Some of the beds are new,' she continued. 'And the water's clean. And in the evening we have a guy comes and plays the banjo.'

In the early evening, as promised, the man who played the banjo arrived at Sunny Gables and set up a little dais upon which he sat to play to the guests. Loose Bruce walked into the lobby after the performance had begun and stood at the rear behind the rows of chairs, looking over the heads of the old folk as if they were children.

The banjoist was dressed, for some reason, in a kind of old-fashioned military uniform with which went a sombrero. Bruce wondered if he might have been in the Mexican army at some time. His voice, however, was mid-American. Once, long before, he had been able to sing as well as play the banjo, but although he tried gallantly now, the higher notes took off into silence with only a smile in the eyes and a moving of the mouth to show that they were being attempted. When he had real trouble with a few notes, or he slipped up on remembering the words, which he also did at times, the audience sportingly joined in to push him up the hill. With some it seemed that their voices were the strongest part of their bodies and they entered the spirit with almost raucous abandon.

A great favourite seemed to be *They Tried To Tell Us We're Too Young* – 'as sung by my own personal friend, the late, great, Nat King Cole.' Everybody joined in and Bruce stood awkwardly outside the company, too embarrassed to join it. He knew the words, however, and after being pushed and prodded by several eager old people in the back row of the seats, he began to mouth them silently. When the song had finished a long delicate hand reached up and took his, encouraging him to take a chair. He sat down awkwardly.

'I'm K-K-K-Katy,' said a beautiful, grey-haired lady. 'I'm not trying to st-st-steal you, young man. I already have somebody who loves me.'

'That's nice,' was all Bruce could think of under the circumstances. 'That's very nice indeed.'

'He is an ex-theatrical st-strong man,' she recited, keeping her voice well modulated, below the sound of the banjo man's tune. 'He was known as Lou the Barbender. He's J-J-Jewish, you know.'

Bruce had never met anyone like this before. 'Jewish?' he echoed, as though she had said he was Gibraltese. 'That's very interesting.'

Katy bent closer. She had a fine perfume about her hair. He wondered why girls did not smell like that now. 'He lives next door,' she whispered, 'In the other Niss-Niss-Nissenbaum place. Enemy territory. We have to meet in secret.'

That for the moment seemed to exhaust the information she was inclined to give about herself and her lover. The banjoist, with a unique blend of the slang of three generations, exclaimed: 'Bounce me, brother, we're going back to rock, because this is where it all is!'

An appreciative snort came from the audience and they began to sway about while he lurched himself into some barely recognizable tunes of the fifties. A lady came round with a tray of drinks and, impecunious though he was, Bruce felt like he ought to ask if Katy would like one. She seemed overwhelmed with pleasure.

'Th-th-that's real kind of you, young fellow,' she told him. 'I'd like a Kosher Cola.'

Bruce trying to look as if he bought Kosher Colas every day, took the drink and paid his thirty cents. A pale, slim man in a faded but still shapely suit came in, his hair carefully combed, a boot-lace tie at his neck and a pair of fawn spats topping his polished black boots. He sat down with the casualness of a dude and turned on the television that stood in the corner. He took no notice of the banjo-player but turned the volume of the cowboy series he had selected until it was to his satisfaction. Then he sat back easily to watch.

'That's Joe D-Danziger. They call him Sidewalk Joe,' whispered Katy seeing Bruce watching the man. 'He used to be a g-g-gangster, you know. In New York. Nobody crosses him.'

'He looks dangerous,' agreed Bruce, looking at the man's frail hands against his cheek.

'I don't really think he is,' confided Katy. 'I guess he re-retired from that life a long time ago.' She looked around. 'Like all of us.'

Bruce looked towards the other side of the room. 'Who's that?' he nodded. 'The lady tearing the pages out of the book?'

'That's Molly Manders. Everybody calls her Molly Mandy. She looks for treasure on the South Beach. Her granddaughter's got a motor cycle. I've seen it.'

Bruce was becoming accustomed to the inconsequential sentences. 'Why would she be doing that? Tearing pages from her book?' he inquired.

'Once she's read a page she r-r-rips it out,' shrugged Katy as if it were perfectly natural. 'No point in c-c-carrying around pages you've read, now is there? When you get older you learn to conserve your energy.'

With a sudden rattle of his banjo, the player indicated that his evening's performance was almost through. Immediately everyone got to their feet and attempted to stand stiffly. Bruce was the last one up. 'It's the National Anthem of our country,' said Katy as if he had recently arrived from Mars. Do you know it?'

'Yes . . . sure,' mumbled Bruce. He tried to remember how long ago he had last sung the words.

'It's a lovely song,' said Katy, skipping a couple of bars. 'We ought to be real pleased and proud to be Americans.'

CHAPTER TWO

Mornings begin early on South Miami Beach. As the first sun pushes through the streets, so the people emerge from the shabby little hotels and hurry along Washington Avenue to the fruit and bread shops. At the fruit store they know there will be bruised and damaged produce being sold at half price and at the bakery the same bargains in day-old bread and cakes.

Ari the Greek scorned such scavenging, as he called it. 'I got my pride still,' he said to Loose Bruce as they trotted along the beach in the warming morning. 'Sure I pick up my social security with the rest of the people, but me, I spend it in style. I buy *fresh* fruit and *new* goddam bread. Maybe I gave the apples a little push so they fall on the floor and then I get a discount on account of them being damaged, but that ain't the same as lining up at dawn for the left-overs. There's no style in that, son. No style.'

Bruce found himself puffing a little as they trotted the long beach. The early waves fell nonchalantly on the sand almost at their feet.

In the distance behind them the cruise liners from the Caribbean were lined along the quays in the port, ahead the tall buildings of contemporary Miami Beach stood like topless palms along the shore. At that distance the sand diminished into early mist. Pelicans flew creak to creak and the municipal trash cart bearing its label 'Rubbish Gobbler' cruised Ocean Drive. There were a lot of cats and dogs mooching the streets and along the shore, because the old people liked pets. Mostly they were not allowed to keep animals in their rooms, but they adopted strays and fed them regularly in appointed places with scraps saved from their own tables.

'See that,' said Ari pointing to four people feeding dogs and cats in a yard between two blocks. 'It don't matter what happens to humans as long as the animals get fed.'

'Seems to me,' puffed Bruce, 'that all these people about here need *something* to *do*.'

'Sure, sure,' agreed Ari. Bruce watched his clockwork legs with admiration. There was brown perspiration like rusty water on his face and his large nose wobbled as he ran, as though it were on a hinge, but he spoke without panting. 'They *got* things to do,' he added, nodding his nose towards a man sitting facing but not seeing the ocean, a transistor radio clamped to his ear. In the other ear was a deaf aid. 'But they ain't the *right* things. Feeding the birds and the cats, dancing, playing cards and dominoes, arguing, all that sort of stuff. But it ain't real, son. There ain't no ambition around these parts.'

They came within shouting distance of the lifeguard's watchtower. Bruce had done enough running. 'Ari,' he said, 'I guess I'll have a word with my buddy up there.'

'You're bushed,' grinned Ari. 'You ain't used to it.'

'No, I'm in good shape. Just thought I'd see him. Keep running.'

'While I'm running I'm living.' Ari's slogan floated back over the sand as he trotted on. The sun eased itself higher. The ocean was unoccupied except for a cargo ship moving indolently towards Port Everglades. Bruce climbed the ladder to the lifeguard platform.

'Busy?' he asked.

'Nope. But you never know in these parts,' drawled Ossie. His matted grey hair hung over his brown forehead. There was a hole in his antique hat. 'Could be an out-of-season hurricane. Could be an invasion from Cuba. Or Mrs Blum could make another run for eternity. You just never can tell, man.'

They stood on the platform and turned from the shore to the grass and the sea-grape trees. The multi-coloured costumes of the old folk of South Miami Beach were coming from many directions, from the lateral streets and the steps of the cramped hotels, many of them carrying flimsy fold-up chairs. Groups were already forming on the grass. Greetings were called, newly arrived letters were waved ('I got word from my son, the sailor.'), musical instruments were tuned, cards were shuffled. On the small enclosed terraces and balconies of the hotels others sat looking wistfully at the activity on the ocean front. They did not move very much. They just sat and watched and if anyone could think of something to say they said it and the others were grateful. A discussion of whether a walk was possible that day might occupy half an hour.

'Something new every day,' shrugged Ossie, looking out over the people. 'Non-stop excitement, man. Ever seen anything like this?'

'Not till now,' admitted Bruce shaking his head. 'What the hell are *you* doing here, anyway?'

'Now that's what I was going to ask you,' said Ossie.

'I heard the sun was out down here,' replied Bruce. 'I just didn't realize what it was shining on. Is there anybody under sixty for miles?'

'Pompano, Fort Lauderdale,' said Ossie nodding his head along the shore towards the vague, warm distance. 'Daytona Beach, that's the place. Plenty of chicks up there, so I hear. The kids drive around in cars on the beach. Or Key West.' He revolved and nodded in the other direction towards the unseen Florida islands. 'They got all the hippy people down there. That's where all the flowers have gone. You can smell the grass burning.'

'Maybe I'll head that way. Down the Keys.'

'It's nice, so they say. A guy told me there's a lot of hot, wild screwing goes on and people have iguanas and frogs as pets. And they all sit on the quay and watch the sun set, and they clap when it goes down. It's different, I guess.'

'What the hell *are* you doing here?' repeated Bruce.

'Well, it's kinda peaceful. The other thing that old folks are – they're kinda peaceful.'

'Mrs Blum didn't seem so peaceful. I still got the bruises.'

'Right. But she's the exception. The rest keep good and quiet. I was in Vietnam and when I got back I didn't enjoy getting the blame for it, you know? Sometimes I got blamed for losing and sometimes I got blamed for not losing sooner, and sometimes I got blamed for not losing, and sometimes I got blamed for being there at all. Christ, I didn't know what the hell it was all about. I just went and I came back and every bastard's throwing shit at me. So I figured that down here it would be peaceful and it sure is.'

'Sure. But there don't seem a lot of future to me. Where d'you live?'

'I got an apartment. It's okay. I was sharing with a girl from Omaha who kinda wandered in this direction, just like you. But she's gone. She went off with one of the old guys. One with a lot of dough. I guess she saw more future in that.'

'So what d'you do?'

'I just sit here and then I go home. There's a diner next to the place I live so I eat there. I get drunk pretty regular and last week I went to the burlesque. They got big boobs those chicks there.'

'It's the food, the nourishment,' said Bruce knowingly.

'Could be. There's a broad does things with a snake. It's real neat. But it ain't like doing the genuine thing. Going there, I mean. There's no future in that either.'

'How old are you?' said Bruce.

'Just about thirty-five,' said Ossie.

'You look older, pal. It's this place growing on you.'

They stood looking out over the grass. The people now numbered more than a thousand. 'We ought to think of something they could do,' decided Bruce. 'Maybe organize a revolution.'

'Right,' nodded Ossie. 'Lead them on Washington. All the old biddies and the old guys, burning and raping and pillaging on the way.'

'There ought to be something,' said Bruce thoughtfully.

As they watched, a heavy red motor cycle eased down as it cruised throatily into Ocean Drive. It came to a stop outside Sunny Gables and Bruce and Ossie stopped speaking and stood on the watchtower admiring its bright powerful form. 'Gee, it's not too often you see a sight like that down these parts,' said Ossie. 'Beautiful.'

The rider, slight in black jacket and jeans, pulled away a vivid orange helmet and visor. At a shake of the head a sunlit cascade of fair hair rolled down. Bruce grabbed Ossie's binoculars. 'A Yamaha Mama,' he breathed as he looked. 'And beautiful, so beautiful.'

Ossie forced the return of the glasses and turned them on the girl. He felt the breeze of Bruce going past him. 'I'll tell you what she's like later,' the younger man called as he stumbled hurriedly down the ladder. Ossie was quickly after him, sliding expertly on the wooden rail. They landed in a heap on the sand and then ran towards the street, dodging through the assemblies of old people, and braking a few yards short of the girl who was looking towards the entrance to Sunny Gables. She heard their breathing and turned and saw them.

'Nice little runabout you got there,' said Bruce, looking patronizingly at the broad red back and silver shoulders of the machine. It glistened like a sweating horse in the sunshine.

'It gets me from A to B,' she answered evenly. 'And I take my grandma on it. I'm waiting for her now.'

'Molly,' said Bruce, pleased he had remembered. 'Molly Mandy.'

'Mrs Manders, that's right,' said the girl. 'You know her?'

'Well, in a way. We're fellow guests.' He nodded at Nissenbaum's hotel.

'There? You?'

'I like old folks.' He smiled winningly at her. 'And younger folks. I just have no firm preferences. Look at my friend here. He's old.'

'I'm Ossie,' said Ossie stepping forward modestly. 'Old Ossie.'

'And me, I'm young Bruce. Loose Bruce they call me,' Bruce grinned with boyish assurance.

'You should get somebody to tighten you up with a wrench,' said the girl.

'I'd sure like to ride that bike,' said Bruce easily.

Surprisingly she nodded. 'Okay. Get on the back. I'll drive.'

Bruce's eyebrows went up with pleasure. 'You wait and keep grandma glad,' he said to Ossie. 'We'll be back next week.'

'Five minutes,' forecast the girl. She eased her tight backside across the saddle and Bruce climbed on behind. He rubbed his hands with brief chivalry on his jeans and placed them with careful enjoyment around her waist. 'Not too tight, Loose Bruce,' she called over her shoulder. 'I'm not going to leave you, sonny.'

She kicked the started and the motor cycle growled like an animal. It strained to be off and she did not contain the urge for long. They roared south on Ocean Drive and were gone in a moment into the Miami dust. Ossie sat down on the grass and waited.

Molly Mandy appeared on the steps of Sunny Gables wearing a purple motor cycle outfit and a green crash helmet. Ossie introduced himself and told her what had happened.

'And this younger guy's gone off with Gabby, has he?' she said, looking concerned. 'Poor fellow.'

She and Ossie exchanged comments on the heat of the Florida day. Although they had never met before he had seen her with her metal detector on the beach and she had seen him sitting above in his watchtower and they had exchanged waves. 'Glad you came down to earth,' she said with a smile. 'You looked like some kind of angel sitting up there.'

Within five minutes Gabby was back, curving in dust along Eighth Street and guiding the thick wheels along the sidewalk. Loose Bruce, pale down to his shoulders, dismounted unsteadily. The girl pushed back her visor, kissed her grandmother, and glanced back at her passenger.

'I guess you really enjoyed that, didn't you, Bruce?' she inquired. 'I certainly did.'

'Yes,' muttered Bruce uneasily. 'Very different. I'm glad we missed the ocean liner on the quay. I don't go for collisions with ocean liners.'

Gabby smiled fully at Ossie. 'Maybe you'd like a little ride someday?' she suggested.

'Thanks,' replied Ossie with great care. 'When I dice, I like to dice with dice.'

'Okay,' she said easily. 'Get aboard grandma.'

Molly laughed with delight and got into her helmet. The old lady clutched the young waist and the machine eased forward picking up speed as it drove once more south of Ocean Drive.

'Some experience, I guess?' suggested Ossie.

'Great,' breathed Bruce. 'Just getting your legs around something as special as that is just great.'

Ossie shrugged. 'You didn't seem to appreciate it too much.'

'I wasn't talking about the motor bike,' said Bruce.

K-K-K-Katy was preparing to go to the weekly twenty-five cent dance at the South Miami Beach Community Centre. It was always an event to which she looked forward and she sang short snatches of old stage songs, the words adorned by her attractive speech impediment. On occasions, years ago, she had used it to devastating effect. Allied to a baby face and flawless blue eyes, the stutter had made men tremble.

She had been a chorus girl in the wanton days of the thirties in Buffalo, and she still had the long legs and the urchin grin. She was proud of both and decided gratefully that they were now with her for good. All the charms you were going to lose, she calculated, you lost by the time you were sixty and she had just seen that birthday off.

The weekly dances had recently taken on a new significance for now she was escorted by her one-time strong man, Lou the Barbender. He had toured every state and had even astonished the populace in Cuba and Mexico. Their paths, they decided, must have touched at times in their respective heydays because they remembered many of the same names. They had fallen into conversation one morning beneath the sea-grape trees and now they were in love. It was strange, K-K-K-Katy reflected, how love reverted in these late days to the childish extremes of holding hands and stealing kisses. Lou still had immensely strong hands, and he could still bend thin iron bars and tear two thirds of a telephone directory down the middle, and she still had the lips that had been desired by so many in the past years. Occasionally she wondered where all those suitors had gone.

The room was small and overburdened with Katy's wordly goods. There were trunks and suitcases, hundreds of smiling dead photographs, faded paper flowers, press cuttings, knick-knacks she had accumulated over the years and two dozen dresses hanging from the picture rail around the walls. These included the wedding dress that she had never worn. She had been ready and eager to marry a nice Jewish financier in Chicago in 1941 when he was called, not to the war which had opened only a week before, but to gaol for frauds that kept him there for the next twenty years. When he came out he said he had thought about it and changed his mind about marriage and so the dress remained unused. She wondered if, perhaps, after all, it was not too late for the dress. Lou would look remarkably fine in a tail coat (she knew he had one because he had mentioned he had kept such a garment from the days of his act). And she knew for sure that the dress would still fit her because every year, on her birthday, she tried it on.

She had bathed in the one bathroom on that floor of the Sunny Gables Hotel where she had lived for the past five years, and had been delayed because, as occasionally happened, one of the other guests, a fat man, had become wedged in the narrow bathtub and needed to be levered out by some of the stronger male residents.

Now she selected a fine lavender dress that swept down her long legs and put a saucy flower in her ear. She could still do a shoulder high kick and she performed several of these, standing facing down the narrow room with the window wide open in case of miscalculations. She sang a few bars of a song, worked up a movement, and then flung the leg spectacularly towards the ceiling one, two, three times. She smiled with satisfaction and then waited for the banging downstairs. It came on schedule, one, two, three, four ill-tempered thumps on their ceiling with a rubber-ended walking stick. They always did that when she kicked. In her youth, when she could really kick high, people used to complain from the room above.

Cheerfully she went downstairs and onto the confined balcony in front of the hotel. Several of the inmates were sitting out there staring in the direction of the setting sun as though wondering why and where it was going. She said a bright word to them and two nodded kindly but the others did not take much notice. She was still considered a flapper.

She timed her exit excellently, for as she went out with the paling daylight, Lou the Barbender, uncomfortably resplendent in his tailed suit, appeared on the porch of the Waving Palms Hotel only a few feet away. She smiled and he grinned shyly but they did not speak, and would not do so until they were two blocks away. The rival Nissenbaums appeared a minute later, both having suspicions of the alliance, and confronted each other truculently over the wooden fence that divided their dominions.

'Fraud,' said the Sunny Gables Nissenbaum.

'Skinflint,' replied her sister-in-law.

That was all. They sniffed the South Beach air and, their salvos fired, turned and retreated into their doors. They did it every evening.

Two safe blocks away, Katy held on to Lou's great hand. She sniffed at the warm evening, smiled at the calm palms, and felt that there were possibilities abounding. She allowed her dancing shoes to sound loudly on the sidewalk and did a short, complicated triple step between some ornamental trees. Lou smiled his admiration. She felt very good; like a young girl going to a college ball. She had a strong intuition that something was going to happen to her soon. She could not have realized just how much.

Loose Bruce had wanted to go to the burlesque show, but Ossie had dissuaded him, saying that at the weekly dance in the Community Centre there was always complimentary food and plenty of it and some of the old guys carried whisky flasks in their pockets.

They lined up at the door without attracting a great amount of interest. Old folk have generally seen everything and one more surprise is not surprising. Bruce towered over the line for the pay booth and Ossie was only just shorter. Behind them among the elderly chatter they heard the girl's voice talking to her grandmother. They turned simultaneously, their heads almost colliding as they twisted inwards. She looked up and regarded the two hopefuls faces coolly.

'Wow,' the girl said to the old lady. 'Old folks get younger all the time.'

'Never did see *two* of them fellows here before,' said the grandmother.

'Maybe they're a cabaret act,' the girl whispered loudly. 'They look kinda strange, like that.'

Bruce and Ossie paid their twenty-five cents each and hung about inside the door.

'Why don't you go to the washroom?' suggested Bruce watching for the girl to enter.

'I never do,' replied Ossie coolly. 'The old guys ask you to zip them up.'

They loitered beside a dusty indoor palm until the girl and the old lady came in.

'Hi,' said Bruce with what he believed was a long smile.

'Hi,' said Ossie touching his forehead with what he imagined was a sign of good manners.

'Good evening,' said the girl soberly. She looked superb in a cool blue dress. Her face was lovely but her eyes without encouragement. 'Come on grandma, let's find you a chair,' she said briskly.

Bruce and Ossie followed behind as they walked. They watched the graceful loop of the girl's backside alongside the little plodding bumps of the old lady. 'Man,' said Bruce thoughtfully, 'I sure don't care for your date.'

'How much does that job of yours pay?' asked Bruce. 'Being a beach guard?'

Ossie picked his teeth carefully. 'About enough,' he drawled. 'And expenses.'

'Expenses! Jesus, how can you get expenses? You can't *spend* anything. You just sit there on your ass all day looking at the goddam ocean. Christ, you don't move unless Mrs Blum makes a run for it.'

'And bonuses,' continued Ossie. They were sitting on the Community Centre chairs watching the old folk dancing in a large revolving oval, moving as if they were some substance in a slow mixer.

'Now I've heard it all! What kind of bonuses?'

'Ten dollars for a rescue. That's the rate.'

'Ten bucks. Did Mrs Blum rate ten bucks?'

'Sure.'

'Well, what about my fifty per cent? I rescued half of Mrs Blum. The heavy half.'

'Twenty per cent,' offered Ossie easily. 'It's my pitch remember. When I get paid, you get paid. Okay? Two bucks.'

'Cheapskate,' said Loose Bruce. But his face brightened. 'Say, you're real slow man. Why not get a few of the old women to make like they're drowning. *Give* them a dollar a time. You'd be *nine bucks* in profit every time! Ten rescues a day would be worth it. Ninety bucks, seven days a week, that makes . . .'

'They get suspicious,' Ossie pointed out solemnly. 'The authorities. The guy I took the job from tried that. Got his own folks to be like they were drowning. Come to remember it, his ma really *did* drown. While he was pulling out his sister, his ma drowned. So it don't work.'

'You've got a negative outlook,' complained Bruce. 'According to you *nothing* works. Something's got to.'

He looked about him. Again it came to him that he was in an unreal world. The old folks performing their polkas and other odd ancient dances as if some time machine had projected him to a past age. Ossie, who had seen it before, sat munching free sandwiches and drinking sarsparilla, his grey head nodding to the music as if he at least partly understood it. The women heavily outnumbered the men and many ladies danced together, some clutched to each other as if they were in danger of sinking. At that time of life, however, they had abandoned any feminine shyness and soon two plump and beaming sisters advanced upon Bruce and Ossie and demanded that they get to their feet and dance.

Neither knew what foot went first but excuses were loudly elbowed aside and they found themselves in the revolving crowd bouncing up and down and in and out to some Slovak dance from years back.

They saw that the girl was dancing, however, and the jig conveniently gave way to another, a progressive dance where the people stood in lines, stayed with a partner for a few steps and turns and then moved on to someone else. Bruce adeptly inserted himself three places from the girl and soon they came face to face. They clapped hands together as the dance required.

'This is beautiful,' said Bruce. 'Gee, I love this dance. What's your name?'

She sighed. 'Okay. My name's Gwendolina but everyone calls me Gabby.'

'I don't wonder,' said Bruce.

She grimaced, then laughed. 'I'm from St Pete's, Florida, and the lady you are about to hold in your arms is my grandmother. You'll like her. Goodbye.'

Bruce found himself pushed along the line by the eager Ossie, who grinned happily at the girl he now turned in his hold. 'I'm in steady employment,' he said, 'and my name's Ossie. I'm a lifesaver.'

'I'm not drowning,' she said, disentangling his arms. 'Yet.'

Bruce quickly broke out of sequence and slipped into the line again on the left side of Ossie, so that when the dancers moved up again he was facing the girl. 'It's me again,' he smiled winningly. 'I'm Bruce.'

'I'm Bruce, fly me,' said the girl wryly.

'Loose Bruce,' called Ossie sideways down the danceline. 'Ask him why he's called Loose Bruce. Go on, ask him.'

'I'm six feet almost one inch, fair hair, brown eyes, friendly nature and alone.'

'Alone? I wonder why that could be?' said Gabby.

'You're spoiling the dance,' he said sharply to Ossie.

'Sorry. I'm not sure how to do this one. I'm just all confused,' said Ossie moving in on Gabby. He smiled his mature smile at her. 'I save people from the ocean,' he said. 'All day.'

'He gets ten dollars a time,' Bruce called up the line. 'He wants you to put your grandmother in the sea and he'll split it with you. He's all heart.'

The dance stopped and everyone clapped, Bruce and Ossie louder than anyone. 'They spoiled it,' said the five foot man who had been looking forward to dancing with Gabby. 'They shouldn't be allowed in here.'

Ossie smiled overwhelmingly at him and then at the puffy lady at his side. She blushed pink and, nagging, pulled the small man away. Gabby and her grandmother sat down and Ossie and Bruce sat on either side of them, Ossie triumphantly next to the girl. 'Why don't you join us,' suggested Gabby caustically.

'Gabby,' said the old lady. 'Are these two trying to pick us up?'

'I'm afraid so, grandma.'

'Well I don't want to be picked up. I'm fancy free. My heart's my own.'

A man with red bursting cheeks pranced to the centre of the floor and threw his arms wide. 'Ladies and gentlemen, nice people,' he beamed. 'Now we come to the time of the cabaret. You all like the cabaret, don't you?' There was a chorus of approval. 'Yes of course. Well tonight we have your old favourite, Lou the Barbender, the strongest man on Miami Beach. Also a lady who's just come down from Pittsburgh who can sing, and a gentleman who's real hot playing the zither.'

The two young men watched almost mesmerized as a big woman in a blood-red dress rushed immediately onto stage, pushed the compère violently to one side and flung herself into a hideous song with enormous and tuneless gusto. All around the people groaned and buried their heads in their elderly hands; some shouted rudely at her to quit. But she appeared not to hear, went right through three verses and the terrible chorus, eyes closed, mouth wide, not caring for anyone or anything. She left the stage to a fusillade of catcalls and boos. The compère returned shakily. 'Thanks people, I just knew you would enjoy that,' he smiled.

'Mother Courage,' said Ossie. 'That's who she is. Mother Courage.'

'They've all got guts,' put in Gabby turning to him. 'You need guts to survive down here.'

'I figure they ought to *do* something,' said Bruce, anxious to talk with her. 'Not dancing or singing. Not *made up* things. Get me? Something they'd be a hundred per cent occupied with. You know?'

'I don't know. But I see what you mean,' she said. 'Like building a dam or riding pony express.'

'Something like that,' agreed Ossie.

'My grandma searches for treasure with a metal detector,' said Gabby quite proudly.

'I've seen her,' said Ossie. 'When she finds it I'm going to help her carry it home.'

Lou the Barbender had now taken the centre of the floor. He lifted a ten pound weight with his little finger, a feat which brought excited gasps from the encircling ladies. He was red-faced in his tailed suit and every one of his shirt buttons had burst, but he looked formidable in an old-fashioned way.

Bruce looked beyond the strong man to where the man they called Sidewalk Joe, the old New York gangster, sat like a well preserved dandy at the edge of the floor. Bruce turned and caught Ossie's eye. He briefly jerked his head sideways and the two young men stood up carefully and, with an excusing nod to Gabby and her grandmother, sidled their way through the audience to the deserted sandwich table. They both picked up leftover segments of bread and put them in their mouths.

'I've got it, said Bruce. 'It's beautiful.'

'Okay,' said Ossie sceptically. 'What is it?'

'Crime,' said Bruce seriously, biting into the rye bread. 'Organized crime.'

CHAPTER THREE

Captain of Detectives Albert Salvatore drove over the Julia Tuttle Causeway from Miami Beach towards the City of Miami at eight o'clock on a shining Florida morning. His head told him that his police college reunion he had attended the previous night at a hotel on the beach had been a raucous experience. He had been obliged to telephone his wife Betty at midnight to report that he was in no condition to negotiate his passage home and had slept on an uncomfortable floor in a room in the hotel.

The splendid but everyday crystal air and water of the region was all about him, with sail boats and power boats on the lagoons and the habitual Goodyear silver blimp in the sky. And had he been a reflective sort of man, which he was not, he might have given thought to Julia Tuttle after whom the concrete causeway on which he drove was named. Mrs Tuttle, an adventurous widow, had literally discovered Miami less than a century before when it was swamp and jungle and inhabited only by Seminoles. She had sailed down the Miami River with her family, a piano and a pair of Jersey cows and found herself in a region of such warm lushness that she sent a sprig of orange blossom to Henry Flagler the railroad builder in New York. By this he could see, on that cold January day in 1895, that Miami was without frost. So he built a railroad to the south and opened up the great vacation city.

From the Julia Tuttle Causeway, Salvatore could look over silvery lagoons to both north and south, joining the long peninsular of Miami Beach and the island of Key Biscayne to the city of Miami. Further north the lagoons thinned to become the amazing and little know Intra-Coastal Waterway, a canal running almost the whole length of the eastern seaboard of the United States. In winter, using lakes and rivers and the canal itself, small boats from as far north as Canada could voyage to Florida and into the Caribbean without once having to risk the open sea. From the point where the wide lagoons bottlenecked into the slim canal the banks were joined by a series of cantilever bridges, opening at their centre to allow the passage of larger craft. There were ten of those mechanical bridges between Hollywood Beach at the northern extreme of Miami Beach proper to West Palm Beach several miles further up the coast. They crossed the Intra-Coastal Waterway at Hollywood, where there were two bridges, Fort Lauderdale, Pompano Beach, Boca Raton, Delray Beach, Lake Worth, Palm Beach and West Palm Beach. Each bridge carried above it a highway connecting Route A95 and the Florida Turnpike with the beach resorts. That morning Captain Albert Salvatore had, perhaps fortunately, no inkling of the drama and frustration these cantilever bridges were to cause him in his pursuit of the most unusual gang of criminals Florida, probably even the entire United States, had ever known.

He was not, and this he admitted even to himself, the most spectacular of police officers, nor did he look it. He was slighty undersized, but slim enough, with a worried face that continued its habitual frown right up to the summit of his head via a channel naked of hair. He found this embarrassing and his wife Betty blamed it on his scratching his head when puzzled or frustrated, which was frequently. On special occasions he tried to conceal this channel by combing the hair from its sides over the exposed skin. His children had been heard to refer to him as 'Old River Head' and this had frightened and annoyed him. He was running out of people whom he could love and who loved him in return.

Crime in greater Miami contained a high element of misdemeanours which the police officially referred to as 'self-adjusting'. This included various feuds within the Miami branch of the Mafia or between the Mafia and other organizations whose members appeared in the area on spring vacations as regularly as the big league baseball teams who came there to tune up for the new season. These crimes, while they had to be investigated, could generally be relied upon to look after themselves, vengeance and sometimes even justice being delivered within the framework of the secret society itself. The same went for political crimes, a bomb explosion or a shooting, among the many Cubans who had settled in Florida following the coming to power of Fidel Castro in Havana. The various factions within the tempestuous Cuban community occasionally took primitive revenge on each other. But the Cuban eye for the Cuban eye was the same as the Mafia tooth for the Mafia tooth. All that remained for the police to do was to take photographs and police notes.

There was a third area of self-righting crime, the hot-weather misdemeanour of passion, usually domestic, which required no great effort either to solve or to bring to justice. These three types of activity took up a fair part of Salvatore's professional life and he could handle them. Handle them with such ease, in fact, that the recent intrusion of a man called George Zaharran, a retired policeman, into his working hours, a minor thing in itself, had become a major intrusion and irritant.

He guessed that Zaharran would turn up somewhere that morning because it was Monday and he had become a habit on Monday. Salvatore owed him professional favours from the distant past but he found it difficult to find the opportunity, or the inclination, to repay them now. Zaharran was elderly, fat and almost immovable. He had set himself up as a private investigator, or a criminalistic inquirer and investigator, as he preferred to be known, had, over two or three years, achieved a series of almost spectacular failures and was now begging for work.

Zaharran, in fact, did not appear until after eleven that morning – thus lulling Salvatore into false complacency – and then it was in the coffee shop where the police detective went for a twenty minute break from his office.

It was all but impossible for Zaharran to conceal himself anywhere, this added to an enormous slowness of movement being one of his prime failure factors, and even though he contrived to sit shadowed by a large and dusty indoor plant in the coffee shop, Salvatore immediately spotted him. But it was too late to escape. Zaharran emerged.

He was like a brown elephant, wearing fawn shirt and trousers, lumbering forward, small-eyed, large-limbed, fat-bodied, with a look of pleasured astonishment on his worn face. 'But Captain Salvatore . . . what a break . . . I just didn't know you numbered among the clientele of this place! May I buy you a cup of coffee?'

Salvatore sighed. 'Jesus Harry Christ,' he said. 'You *know* I come in here, Zaharran. Every goddam day I come in here. And now you're in here also. You bother me at my office and you bother me now when I'm taking a private cup of coffee. Why not come to my home maybe?'

'My cover's blown,' sighed Zaharran sitting heavily on the stool next to the policeman.

'Like it always was,' returned Salvatore unkindly.

'In the early days I was good,' said Zaharran, more in reminiscence that protest. 'You got to give me that. I helped you a lot then. Remember the case at Key Biscayne – the big house robbery? And the kidnapped kid at Pompano . . .?'

'Okay, okay. But that's gone. You're retired, Zaharran. Why don't you be like other retired guys and retire?'

'If I gave up the work of detection I would just go to pieces,' said Zaharran illogically. Salvatore stared at the human wreck beside him. He melted sufficiently to order a second cup of coffee which he passed to Zaharran.

'Coffee,' beamed Zaharran, his face a movement of creases. 'Now you buy me coffee. You're seeing things my way.'

'I don't,' said Salvatore bluntly. 'You're retired and that's retired. If you want to go on investigating then get your own cases.' He tried logic. 'Listen, we got trained cops, plenty of trained cops. How can I pass on even a crumb to you? How can I? How can I justify the cost?'

Zaharran felt about his fawn pockets and produced a bent business card. It said 'George Zaharran, Criminalistic Inquirer and Investigator. Formerly of the Police.' 'Here,' he said as if making a donation. 'Take this with you, captain.'

'Jesus Lionel Christ,' sighed Salvatore. 'I have plenty of these already. I got a whole drawer full of them.' He held the battered card between two fingers. 'And they don't get any cleaner either. I guess the Sanitation Department might have a case against you Zaharran, handing out dirty cards like this.'

'Let them try,' shrugged Zaharran. 'I'd sue them for violation of civil rights. Violation of the rights of the elderly, the poor and the needy.' He looked thoughtful. 'Maybe I could sue you for that, Salvatore, or the police department. Violation of the rights of the elderly, the poor and the needy.'

'We do it all the time,' said Salvatore unimpressed. 'It's no good violating the rights of the big people is it? You can't win.'

He finished his coffee and rose. 'Got to go,' he said. 'Lots to be done.'

'Wish I could help,' said Zaharran sadly. 'I miss it like hell, you know. Maybe some small routine cases. Missing children, stray dogs . . .'

'We have all the personnel we need. You should concentrate on divorce, Zaharran, like most private investigators do. That pays.'

Zaharran made a worse face than he had. 'No dice,' he said. 'I always fall out of trees and I'm too big to get under a bed. I know, I've tried.' He leaned forward with last minute urgency and fumbled again in his gaping pocket. He produced a small sheaf of business cards encircled with an elastic band. He separated them hurriedly and handed them one by one to the reluctant Salvatore.

'Zaharran Real Estate' said the first card. 'Zaharran Paper Novelties' said another. 'Zaharran Mailed Astrology' said a third. And as an additional reminder, 'George Zaharran, Criminalistic Inquirer and Investigator. Formerly of the Police' said the fourth.

Salvatore sighed and took the cards. 'If you should ever feel yourself in requirement of any of those services,' prompted Zaharran, 'do not hesitate to call me. I can recommend the mailed astrology personally.'

Nothing was going to stop Salvatore leaving now. He reached the sunshine of the door. Zaharran called after him: 'The businesses are for sale too . . . Five thousand . . . a thousand dollars the lot . . .'

But the policeman had gone. Zaharran gathered himself together, asked the man behind the counter if he wanted any paper novelties. He did not. So Zaharran himself lumbered out into the sad eternal sunshine.

The potent aroma of lokshen pudding hung over South Miami Beach. It drifted from the kitchens of the compressed hotels and out onto the dry sidewalks of Ocean Drive, Washington Avenue and the short streets between them. In Flamingo Park it loitered about the trees in the late sunshine, it wafted to the windows of The Four Seasons Nursing Home, it triumphed even in competition with the Latin smells that issued from the Cuban eating places. It was a balm and a reassurance to the thousands of Jewish people in the twilight streets. While there was lokshen pudding there was hope.

'Jeez, that Jerusalem smell gets everywhere,' protested Ari the Greek sitting under the Tree of Knowledge in Flamingo Park. He did not know why it was called the Tree of Knowledge, it was just that it had a notice to that effect and Ari, in general, believed what notices said. Also, it seemed appropriate to him that an outnumbered Greek should sit beneath its boughs.

'It's bad enough being a fit kinda guy down here,' he confided to Bruce who sat one side of him. Ossie sat on the other considering him quizzically. 'I mean the ladies, they outnumber the guys by plenty to one. So they bother you. "Can I do anything for you Ari?" "Gee Ari, you sure look young and healthy." "Don't you get lonely Ari?" The shit that's circulated in these parts, you would not believe. When a guy's on his feet and breathing down here, he's in trouble, just believe Ari. And get the smell of that pudding.'

'We thought up an idea,' said Bruce getting in while Ari took a breath.

'Yeah, an idea for business,' said Ossie. Ossie had been fired that day as a beach guard. They said he wasn't working hard enough. There were not enough rescues on the books. He had an idea they were looking for an excuse to get rid of him.

'Business!' exclaimed Ari. 'Business! Listen kid, let me tell *you* about business. Don't tell me. And especially business in these parts and this locality.'

'We had an idea . . .' restarted Bruce hopefully.

'Teeth,' said Ari with conviction. 'Now teeth are good business. Have you just seen the teeth they sell around here? Jeez, but an alligator couldn't accommodate some of the teeth they sell in these parts. Just you see how many folks are about South Miami with their faces all screwed up. That's the teeth they've got. Get good teeth and you've got good business. And taking blood pressure. Now *there's* a good business. You don't need no stock, no capital. All you have is a Band Aid and a pump and you charge a buck a time to tell people they're still alive. A buck to find you're still alive! And walking sticks! Now there's another racket. What you got to pay for a walking stick is robbery . . .'

'Robbery,' put in Bruce quickly but quietly. 'That's what we had in mind. Robbery.'

Ari's nose was trembling all over his face. 'And just to get a pair of reading glasses! So you can see the bad news in the newspaper. They charge you . . .' He braked. 'What did you mention, son? Robbery, you said?'

'Sure, robbery, that's what I said,' nodded Bruce. 'I said robbery.'

'Robbery,' confirmed Ossie from the other side.

'And kidnapping.'

'Hold-ups.'

'Burglaries.'

'Frauds.'

'Extortion.'

For once Ari was silent. His mouth opened and shut a few times.

'Ari,' said Bruce patiently. 'We're thinking of forming a select group of the people around here.'

'Like a gang?' nodded Ari with unusual accuracy.

'Okay, a gang. There'll be Ossie and me and maybe half a dozen of your generation. Four guys and two old ladies, or three and three. We'll work on the details. We use hoods and gloves. We pick off selected targets in the South Florida region. A break-in here, a hold-up there. You know the sort of things.'

'But no violence. We'll avoid violence.'

'Yeah, you need to avoid violence if you figure on getting your gang from these parts,' said Ari practically. 'Half the poor bastards can't stand up.'

'We've got to pick carefully,' put in Bruce. 'Hand selected. They've got to be fit.' He waited, then added pointedly, 'Like you, Ari.'

The nose turned towards him like the bow of a ship turning to port. The Mediterranean eyes were sharp. 'You want me, *me*, to get myself mixed up in this?' he said accusingly. 'Me? Say I got caught and put in prison. I can't afford that kind of time, son. Jeez, even probation would be a life sentence to somebody my age.'

'There's money in crime,' encouraged Ossie.

'There is,' agreed Ari. 'I'm going in for blackmail. Twenty bucks or I tell the cops.'

'And it gives you something to *do*,' emphasized Ossie. 'You can't just go on running all your life.'

'But I just run on the beach and down the street,' Ari pointed out innocently. 'I ain't got no highway patrol up my ass. Mine's legal running.' He glared at them, but with a touch of uncertainty. 'The whole thing's crazy,' he muttered.

'Listen Ari,' said Ossie. 'You're a guy of *action*. You can *do* things. You may be sixty but you can *do* things. But what do you *do*? Tell me that, what do you *do* down here on South Miami Beach?'

'I run,' said Ari predictably. 'And son, while I'm running I'm living.'

'Sure. But you ain't running nowhere. And you ain't living nohow. Don't you feel like a little excitement now and then? Don't you kinda feel that you'd like to *use* yourself . . .?'

'Sure, sure,' agreed Ari gently. 'But there's business and there's business. Why don't you give the teeth a whirl. There's not many folks satisfied with their teeth. There's real good money in . . .'

'Robbery,' said Bruce again. 'Nothing violent or unpleasant. Just now and then a neat little robbery and get out quick, back here to Ocean Drive. And that's the beauty of it. The cops will never guess that the operators come from down here. Like you say, most of the people have trouble standing up. It's a perfect cover.'

'And what will you guys do? Wait for the old folks at home?'

'Aw, Ari, would we?' Ossie was pained. 'We'll be right there with you. We'll plan it all and we'll be there. You've got people down here with plenty of cool, and they're fit even if they're old, and they've got experience in a million things.'

'Not many in robbing,' pointed out Ari. 'Anyway, what experience do you guys have? What crime experience?'

The young men looked shamefaced. Neither replied for a moment, then Loose Bruce looked up and said: 'Not much. We'll come clean about that. Not a big deal.'

'I once slugged a guy straight through a bar window,' admitted Ossie.

'And I used to steal my mother's clothes and sell them,' muttered Bruce.

'For Chrissake,' said Ari in mock admiration. 'That's sure powerful stuff.'

'What about you?' asked Bruce shrewdly.

Ari looked reminiscent. 'Well I naturally ain't told anybody about it, but I used to steal horseshoes in Chicago. When I was a boy. Steal them and sell them.'

'Not exactly Dillinger's scene,' said Bruce.

'You asked me what I'd done. And a little bootlegging down here in these parts in the Prohibition days.' He smiled fondly at the memory. 'They was good times. I made some dough too. Everybody knew Ari the Greek then.'

'If you could have some more good times,' suggested Ossie, 'you could be Ari the Greek again.'

Ari's wide mouth spread in a grin beneath the parapet of his nose. 'Well, I guess it might be interesting. And I ain't busy just now. And if they catch me and give me twenty years. I'll cheat by dying. Okay, you got a deal.'

Delighted, Bruce and Ossie shook the old Greek's hand. 'Right,' whispered Bruce. 'Now we need you to recruit the others. You know the fittest and the people who might be interested around these parts. Just draw up a list and we'll take a look at each one, then you can move in. Then when we've got the gang we've got to get the guns.'

Ari's face contracted against his nose. 'Guns? You said no violence.'

'Okay. Right, no violence. But you got to have guns, Ari. You got to be fierce, otherwise there's no point. Who ever heard of a gang without guns?'

Sidewalk Joe was sitting in his usual place in the shade of the giant calendar. He was dealing the cards but like the other old men around the table he could not resist a sidelong glance at the concrete reminder that while he played poker his days were numbered. The big square said it was 17 January, the time was 10.46 am and the temperature was seventy-six and climbing. It was going to be the usual day on South Miami Beach.

'Morry,' said Joe, looking at a piece of paper at his elbow. 'As of this moment you owe eighty-six.' He was wearing his light brown suit, a homburg and spats over his black boots.

Morry nodded agreement over his cards. Joe ran a strong finger down the paper. 'And Charlie. You're down seventy-one. Benny you owe just thirty.' He added the totals carefully with some satisfaction. 'That's one hundred and eighty-seven cents altogether, which according to my calculations is one dollar, eighty-seven cents.'

'This game could hit the roof,' muttered Benny. 'All that dough.' He whistled softly and shook his head.

Joe said: 'Okay, let's play.'

The sun travelled across the populated lawns, snaking between the sea-grape trees. Someone began to pluck on a Jew's harp. He played it well and some of the old people smiled in memory and rocked their heads gently to the faraway tune. The grass area was filling up as the folks converged on it from the hotels, all carrying their square canvas chairs. Some pigeons and a clutch of seagulls waited patiently in two groups for well-wishers who they knew would soon come to feed them on scraps rescued from early morning trash cans. A family of Florida sparrows sat separately but also expectantly. Lonely people often befriended birds.

Mrs Blum, ready to make her first suicide bid of the week, was sharply disappointed to see that the familiar grey-haired and handsome young beachguard had been replaced in the watchtower by a large plain woman. She vowed to complain to the authorities. It would be no fun being rescued anymore.

Ari the Greek sat carefully in the shade watching Sidewalk Joe and the others crouched over their poker game. Mrs Blum plodded by him bulging from her many coloured swimsuit and muttering disconsolately. On the beach he could see the solitary searcher Molly Mandy stepping slowly, her metal detector held out before her oddly like a reverse dog on a lead.

They had made out a list, Harry, Bruce and Ossie, a dozen names of which they had eliminated seven for various reasons such as arthritis, bad eyesight and liability to panic under fire. The names remaining were Ari himself, Sidewalk Joe, Lou the Barbender, K-K-K-Katy and Molly Mandy.

Ari knew better than to break up Sidewalk Joe's poker school, as he sat peacefully in his raft of shade while it changed course with the sun's journey through the bright sky. After an hour Joe rose from his collapsible chair and carrying it with him (everybody carried their small chair when they moved even if it were only a few yards) he approached Ari. As he had been sitting with his back to Ari this impressed the Greek a good deal.

'How d'yer know I was looking for you, Joe?' asked Ari moving up to make a piece of shade available.

Joe opened his little chair and occupied the shade. 'I got the scent of you, Ari,' said Joe. 'I just felt like you was in this area.'

They sat, like the two elderly men they were, looking out at the people and the ocean. Joe nodded towards the seabirds sitting watching the people, taking turns to curve off for a noisy white flight in the blue. 'Baygulls,' said Joe. 'Jewish seagulls.'

'So I hear,' replied Ari amiably.

'I hear things too,' said Joe. 'I heard things and I see things.'

Ari looked at him with a mixture of alarm and admiration. 'You do,

Joe? That's smart. Very smart. And what about do you do this seeing and hearing?'

'Who's the two young guys?' asked Joe. 'Like I see them at the dance. Like I see them in earnest session with you in Flamingo Park. Like they look like guys do when they're working something out, when they're looking for action. I seen it all before. What they planning? Robbing the Social Security? I don't mind. The Social Security been robbing me for years.'

Ari nodded admiringly. 'I knew you couldn't lose the nose.'

Joe glanced at him. 'You couldn't lose your nose either Ari. Christ, that's some nose you got.'

'From a Jew that's a compliment,' nodded Ari. 'But I was not speaking of the physical organ of the nose. I was talking about the way you smell things out. Like situations.'

'What's the deal? I was getting bored playing poker for pennies.'

'I figured that. We wondered if you'd be interested in joining a little business hustle. Just a quiet heist or two. No violence.'

'These two guys. They want somebody to do their dirty work,' guessed Joe. 'Innocent old men.'

'They'll be right there,' promised Ari. 'And it's splits. Not the Federal Bank. Just pee-wee league stuff. It'll be great, Joe. Just like the old days for you.'

'In New York City,' murmured Joe, his bright eyes clouding sentimentally. 'They was good times, Ari. Forty years ago now. Good times. I worked with three gangs who got wiped out, all except me. Real good times.' He returned to the present. 'But not now, old friend. I couldn't do that now. I ain't stole nothing in years. Only the usual things, fruit, bread and that sort of material.'

Ari moved closer in the shade. The gulls were disturbed by a dog and whirled around the heads of the people, screaming abuse. Before Ari could speak Joe became engrossed with the birds. 'Barbecued gull,' he said. 'Now that could be a great idea. Catch 'em and cook 'em.'

'Oily,' said Ari. 'Kosher maybe, but oily.'

'I was just dreaming,' said Joe. 'So you want me to join the operation? Who else is on the payroll?'

'I got to keep that a secret until the gang is all got together. You understand that now, don't you? I have a feeling you're interested, Joe.'

'Sure I'm interested. I get weary taking cents off these millionaires. But I don't want to shoot anybody. Got that. I'm too old to kill people. That's for the birds.'

'No shooting,' said Ari sincerely. 'That's already in the rules and regulations. But we got to have guns because it won't look like we mean business without guns. You can't hold-up a mail truck with a wooden leg can you?'

'Right. No. That figures. Okay, I'm in.' He stood and folded his chair. Ari shook Joe's hand warmly. Joe looked around cautiously. 'Take it easy, Greek,' he said. 'Cut out the warm friendship stuff. When people see a Jew and a Greek shaking hands they know something suspicious is likely.'

Ari swallowed and then grinned and said loudly, 'Thank you, thank you sir, for your generous contribution to the Orthodox Church.'

'Great,' muttered Joe sourly. 'I can see I'm going to enjoy working with you.' Joe returned to the poker school and Ari walked through the people towards the ocean, deep green and blue embroidered with a double cuff of surf. An old compatriot tried to waylay him to tell of his boyhood in the Peloponnese, but Ari had heard it eight times already and had excused himself, leaving the old man looking thoughtfully around for someone else to tell.

Down on the sand, a patient figure in the sun, Molly Mandy dowsed for treasure. The metal detector swung easily, regularly, in front of her, her ears enveloped and engrossed in the earphones. Ari eased himself over the parapet wall and walked towards her. She did not detect him until he was a few yards away. Then she heard the metal lace-holes of his shoes. 'You ain't running, Ari,' she said surprised. 'You tired of living?'

'Today I made it early, real early,' said Ari. 'Because I got business.'

She took the earphones away from her head and handed them generously to him. 'Just listen in to that,' she invited. 'I guess you can fit your ears in. It's a good thing you don't listen through that nose.'

Good-humouredly Ari acknowledged the remark and put the earphones to his head. Molly Mandy moved the detector to and fro on the beach. Ari launched a slow, big smile. 'I like it,' he said. 'It's beautiful. Just beautiful.'

'Like the music of the stars,' she said sweetly. 'And folks ask me what pleasure I get from this? Sure I find things – but also it makes lovely music.'

Ari returned the earphones to her. He hesitated, dug his toes in the sand and said: 'Molly, I got something to ask you. A couple of years ago, I hear, you found some guns buried down here on the beach.'

'Right,' she replied readily. 'Lots of guns. I still have them in my room. Would you like to see them?'

'I would, Molly,' said Ari gratefully. 'I sure would.'

CHAPTER FOUR

Lou the Barbender was worried. He walked, bowed, along Washington Avenue, a large man among the smaller old folk on the sidewalk. He wondered whether he ought to spend a dollar on a blood pressure check but he dismissed the notion. He liked to be lifting a weight or bending some iron at the time they took the pressure but that always drew a crowd and today he did not feel like a crowd.

Some days he met K-K-K-Katy in a steamy coffee shop along the avenue, a favourite with many of the South Miami folk because although the air conditioning was not efficient, it had daily bargains in food. He was heading that way now. He wondered how Katy would take to the idea of becoming a criminal so late in life.

The bargain of the day was unexciting. The owner had painted across the window 'SPAVLOV'S DO IT AGAIN! Today's great Special: Rice, Noodles and Chicken. NOW WITH FREE BREAD!'

Katy had ordered the special. The waiter came back with the plate and recited. 'Rice, Noodles and Chicken. Now with free bread.' He put the plates down.

'I know, I know,' sighed Lou. 'Spavlov's have done it again. Free bread for God's sake. What d'you want? That my eyes should sparkle?'

'S-S-Something's happened,' said Katy when the man had grumbled at people who bit the hand that fed them and gone off. 'I can tell, Lou, b-baby. What's gone on? Maybe a bar you couldn't bend?'

'It's serious,' Lou told her. 'Very and most serious. I have to put a straight proposition to you, Katy.'

'T-T-This is i-i-it,' said Katy to herself. Curiously she often stuttered when talking to herself. 'M-m-marriage.'

'What could that b-b-b-be, honey?' she inquired, leaning over her rice. The free bread fell from the plate but she deftly caught it before it hit the floor.

'It could change your life, and mine,' said Lou. His face was large with emotion. 'For ever and ever.'

'It often does,' she said girlishly. 'But we won't mind.' She wondered if she ought to do a few high kicks. She felt like it. Old people are just young people with nothing to lose. They often feel free to be eccentric. Katy got up and did three high kicks in the coffee shop. Lou and most of the other customers watched her passively then, when she had sat down again, he leaned towards her.

'Can I interest you in joining a gang?' he said bluntly.

'A g-g-g-gang?' She was as astounded as she was disappointed. 'I thought you were asking me to marry you, Lou.'

'I will, I will,' he said as if the matter had been settled long before. 'But this is a different question. We've been invited to join a gang. You and me.'

'A gang?' she almost shouted and he put a heavy hand on her mouth. Her eyes revolved and he released her.

'Like Al Capone. That kind. But older folks.'

'And what's it for?' she whispered.

'What gangs are for. Robbing, kidnapping and such activities.'

'Gee, it sounds exciting. But who asked? Somebody crazy? I don't want to join if the man is crazy.'

'Ari,' said Lou. 'You know him, the Greek. The guy who runs in those little pants.'

'He's got a gang? He don't look like he's got a gang.'

'He's collecting one. Well, he's the front man see. There's two young guys behind it. They figure it will give some of the more active people around here something to do.'

'It sure sounds nice,' said Katy seriously. 'But I wouldn't like to break the law.'

'Gangs *have* to break the law,' said Lou patiently. 'That's why they're gangs.'

'I see. Yes, that's logical I guess. But I don't enjoy the sight of blood. If it was a different colour it wouldn't be so bad. Like pale blue. So I couldn't guarantee to shoot anybody, Lou. I just couldn't see myself doing it. Not unless I really didn't sympathize with them.'

'There's no violence planned,' said Lou. 'None *planned*, I said. But in the gang business it could develop. It just could. That's why they asked me. I'm strong.'

'But why me? I'm just a little old lady.'

'You're a girl,' he said suddenly softly. Their eyes met and she blushed and laid her shapely hand on his.

'So we get married as well, do we? she whispered. 'I mean you did mention it in passing just now.'

'Yes, sure, sure. But we'd better not have any kids, Katy. The gang business being risky.'

Her eyes shone happily towards him. 'It was sure a funny proposal,' she said. 'But I accept. I've loved you ever since I saw you bite through that pack of cards.'

'There was no aces and no kings,' he said modestly. 'But it was my own teeth. So we join the gang then?'

'Oh sure, it sounds fine. But . . . but what do they calculate to steal? I mean things are guarded. You couldn't even walk out of here with a piece of their free bread without the alarm going off.'

Lou nodded his heavy head. 'Okay, okay. You're right Katy. But it's going to be all scheduled see. Every detail. And these guys figure that nobody is going to suspect a gang of old folks to be operating the crimes. You get it?'

'What if the cops get us?' said Katy. 'They'll put me in a women's prison and you in a men's prison. It's no use being married if we're in different prisons, now is it? What's the sense of that?'

'We *don't* get caught, that's all,' said Lou decisively. 'If we do we say we thought it was for charity.' Thought lay thickly on his brow. 'For myself, Katy, I'd like to do it. I been missing the excitement these past few years. After what I've done. You know I've been in the theatres in every state and in Mexico and Cuba. I was the strong man of Havana before Fidel Castro had any chance of growing a beard. I guess I'd like to take a final fling.'

She laid her hand on his again and looked at him intensely. 'Right, let's do it. Let's join,' she said. 'Who knows, maybe we can steal a few things for our new home.'

'Guns,' said Molly as she led Ari up the winding stairs of Sunny Gables Hotel. 'Sure I got guns. When I dug them up on the beach I thought maybe I ought to tell the police, but then I thought, maybe not. I figured they might come in useful someday, like if Fidel Castro invaded the United States. So I stored them.'

She opened the door of her room and felt a small blush in the gloom of the passage. 'No man has ever been in this room, Ari. Not since Melford died.'

'I'll respect that, Molly,' said the Greek. 'I only want to view the guns.'

'So you shall.' She worked the lock with some difficulty and then let the door creak open. Ari looked in. Right opposite on a sideboard against the wall was a Russian one-man rocket firer.

Dumbstruck, Ari stepped cautiously in the room. 'I keep that one there for decoration,' said Molly blithely. 'I think it's just cute. The others are in the bathroom.'

Modestly she led Ari through the tight living room, pausing to indicate a dim photograph. 'That was Melford with the Elks,' she whispered. 'There, that's him, smiling. He was a great Elk, Melford, and he enjoyed smiling. But even Elks die.'

'It's a common happening,' agreed Ari. 'Myself I try to avoid the matter. I think maybe I'll get overlooked and I'll be around for ever. But I guess that won't happen.'

'You don't get luck like that,' agreed Molly seriously. 'Not on South Miami Beach. Somebody goes every day. Here's the guns.'

She opened the bathroom door and Ari's eyes bulged. Ranged around the walls was a complete armoury, pistols, short rifles, grenades, sub-machine guns and a flame thrower displayed over the toilet cistern. 'Jeez,' muttered Ari. 'Jeez.'

'Melford mounted them. Before he died of course. He was with me when I found them buried on the South Beach. Melford thought they must be something to do with all the Cubans we have down here. They're into guns, the Cubans you know, I found them with my detector. Gee, it was like the Fifth Symphony when I got this lot on the earphones. They were only just under the sand in a kind of box. Melford said it had Soviet writing on the side.'

'And you . . . you and Melford,' said Ari still staring, 'just dug them up and brought them here?'

'Just like that,' she said proudly. 'We had a car then and we loaded them in and unloaded after dark.'

Ari gingerly touched the butt of one of the pistols. 'Ammunition,' he muttered. 'How about ammunition?'

'There's no ammunition,' she shrugged. 'We didn't find any. Except one little itsy-bitsy bullet and that's right over here. Above the washbasin. I hide it among my lipsticks. Don't you think that's clever, Ari?'

'A stroke of genius,' nodded Ari, still looking disbelievingly at all the guns, 'hiding the bullet. But no ammunition?'

'Well we figured, Melford and me, that if there was ever any complications concerning our guns we could always say there was no ammunition so there was no danger, was there?'

'They're Russian guns, and Russian ammunition is hard to come by,' admitted Ari. 'You don't see a lot of it around.' He reached up and brought down the pistol he had touched. It felt ugly in his hand, heavy and menacing. 'Not a pretty baby,' he said. 'But just what we need.'

'Who's we?' inquired Molly without suspicion. She was another who could not easily be surprised. 'Why do you want the guns, Ari?'

Ari knew he might as well tell her. He had thought of making some excuse about a hunting trip but since there was no ammunition he could hardly expect Molly to believe that. 'We've got a gang,' he said looking straight at her.

'Gee, how nice!' she said warmly, her hands clasping. 'Are you going to rob people?'

'That's the general idea,' he nodded. 'But we don't want nobody getting hurt, and especially the members of the gang. It's just a kind of hobby. Something to amuse a few folks around here.'

'Well,' she said decisively, 'if you have *my* guns, *I* want to be a member of the gang. I'm getting bored with treasure hunting anyway.' She put out her hand and took the pistol from him. Suddenly she whirled on him, thrust her legs apart and, crouching, jabbed the muzzle at him. 'Okay buster,' she said, trying for a harsh deep voice. 'Hand over the goodies.'

Ari swallowed uneasily. The aperture of the weapon was pointing at his nose. 'Not the nose please, Molly,' he said, 'that's an easy target.' Cautiously he took the gun from her. 'I mean, you're sure it's not loaded?'

'No, sir,' she assured him. 'My Melford checked every single one. But he said the grenades work okay. You just have to pull the pin out. See, like . . .'

Ari just beat her to the pin. 'No, leave it where it is, Molly. You should just *not* do anything like that.'

Prudently he led the old lady from the bathroom. He still had the gun. He sat down, staring at it thoughtfully. 'And you want to join?' he asked, his old eyes rising.

'I've *got* to join,' she said triumphantly. 'I insist. No Molly, no hardware.'

'I need to make a call,' said Ari. 'You don't have a phone, do you?'

To his surprise she did, housed beneath a knitted tea cosy on the sideboard. He pushed the Russian rocket firer gently away and dialled the number. 'Boss,' he said, when Loose Bruce had answered, 'she's got the guns. Enough for an army. All clean. Yes, just great ain't it. There's two other items of news. The first is she wants to join. If she don't we don't get the munitions. Sure . . . sure . . . she's fit. She walks miles on the beach every day and she's watched *Kojak* because she does the cop's crouch with a pistol. So I guess she'll be fine.

'Sure . . . sure. Okay, I'll tell her. What's that? Oh yeah, the other item of news. We've got everything here, everything but a ballistic missile, it seems to me. But there's a difficulty. It's all Ruskie stuff meant for Castro. It was buried in the beach somehow. Everything. But the only ammo is *one* bullet. Yeah, that's right. You got it. One. I guess we'll have to conserve our ammunition.'

Loose Bruce looked carefully along the row of lined, expectant faces. They sat on the chairs and on the bed in Ari's room at Sunny Gables Hotel, Ari himself squatting on his light canvas chair. Ossie arranged himself awkwardly on the table behind Bruce. Because he had no job and little cash Ossie had now moved into a small room at the hotel, he and Bruce having shone twin smiles at Mrs Nissenbaum who melted and agreed to take the rent at the end of the month.

Outside it was a sullen day. Clouds lay heavily on the sea and the air was warm as soup. The ancient air conditioning box fitted to Ari's window heaved and grunted as if it were containing some captive animal.

Bruce looked along the eager faces. Ossie's eyes followed his track. What they saw was not encouraging and yet, ironically, just what they wanted. This collection of has-beens with their bright eyes and old limbs looked like anything but a gang intent on criminal pursuits.

Ari the Greek sat on his beach chair trying to look strong, his prow of a nose pushed out, his eyes steady, his muscles below his sweatshirt flexed, ready for action. Next to him sat Molly Mandy who, for effect, had brought with her the detector with which she scoured the beach. She held the upright lightly with one hand, like a soldier leaning on a rifle. Sidewalk Joe fingered his bootlace tie and narrowed his New York eyes.

Lou the Barbender was next, the large face spread like a map, intent on every word which had been said. He kept inserting short encouraging remarks into the discussion. 'My strength is still my own.' 'I can break in anywhere.' 'I can handle three cops at once.'

Next to him, her delicate hand in his heavy paw, sat K-K-K-Katy, her fine legs crossed, so excellent that both Bruce and Ossie found their eyes continually drawn that way. If ever I get to go dating a sixty-year-old woman, Bruce thought, that's the one I'm going to date.

'It's important,' Bruce heard himself saying, 'that everyone here realizes what all this is about. We don't want any backers-out later who'll say they didn't get the idea straight. The group will carry out criminal activities. Is that clear? Robbery, hold-up, kidnapping. Criminal activities. Okay?'

All the heads nodded. Only Ari spoke his agreement.

'This could put us all behind bars. Is that understood?' said Bruce. Again the heads nodded. Ari's this time as well.

'And, although we will avoid it if we can, there could be some violence.'

'There could be some violence,' repeated Molly Mandy as if she were looking forward to it. The rest nodded.

'Now, this is the last call. Anybody want to quit? I'm asking you to speak up now.'

Nobody wanted to quit. Their heads shook all along the line.

'Okay, that's settled. Now I'm going to hand you over to Ossie, who's the tactical guy. He was in Vietnam. He's going to tell you what to do next.'

'What about the profits?' asked Sidewalk Joe. 'How about the split?'

Bruce said: 'Equal shares, after the deduction of expenses.'

Sidewalk looked back steadily, then nodded. Nobody else said anything. Bruce felt uneasy. 'Right,' he swallowed. 'Now Ossie is going to go over our plans. Questions and suggestions afterwards. We're going to run this gang on democratic lines.'

'You can't,' interrupted Joe again. 'You can't run a gang like that, son. I know. There's got to be a big guy, the boss, and there's got to be a not-so-big guy and he's the second boss.'

Ossie looked at him. 'Bruce and me thought we kinda fitted those roles,' he said. 'If that's okay with you, Sidewalk?'

'Sure it's okay. It's just important to know, that's all. The bosses always get the longest stretch in the penitentiary. We got to know who they are.'

'Okay, we'll take that responsibility,' swallowed Bruce. 'Now, can we get down to business? Okay Ossie, let them hear it.'

Ossie leaned forward but doubt was still touching his face as he looked at them. 'We have a plan,' he said 'For the first assignment. We've gotten a real nice lot of Russian guns, mostly pistols, but I might as well tell you the bad news now. There's only one bullet.'

He heard Sidewalk Joe say 'Christ', but he went on talking. 'Maybe this is not such a bad thing. If there's no ammunition, nobody here is going to the penitentiary for murder.'

'It's not the penitentiary I'm worried about,' said Katy thoughtfully. 'It's going up to God with a murder on my conscience. Now that I wouldn't care for.'

'Right,' agreed Ossie. 'So if there's no bullets nobody gets hurt.'

'What do we have to do, yell "bang"?' asked Sidewalk.

Ossie sighed. 'We use the guns as threats.'

'And what if we find we got guns against us?' said Sidewalk. 'Like fuzz guns.'

'We run,' shrugged Ossie. 'Or we surrender.'

'Good thinking,' said Sidewalk.

'Got any better ideas? The way we figure it we ain't going to have call to use any guns anyway. They're just kinda props. It's just for effect, Mr Sidewalk.'

'Which guy has the bullet?' asked Lou.

'Me,' put in Bruce decisively. 'I may have to blow my brains out.'

'Right,' Ossie began again. 'Any more questions about the guns?'

'Excuse me,' said Katy shyly. 'But I can't use a gun. Up to now I've never had a reason.'

'That's okay, Katy,' said Ossie. 'Tomorrow, if we can fix transportation, we are going on a little trip.'

'Goody,' he heard Molly Mandy whisper. 'Oh, goody.' He shuddered.

'I know a place,' he went on, 'that's pretty quiet. It's off one of the Everglades tracks and we can take a couple of hours for instruction without anyone seeing us.'

'There's alligators in the Everglades,' pointed out Molly nervously. 'I don't care for alligators.'

'And snakes,' added Katy. 'Fl-fl-flying snakes.'

Ossie sighed. 'I'm afraid, ladies,' he said, 'that we have to take some risks. The whole operation is a risk. Now there's still time to back out. Anyone want to back out?'

Nobody did. Katy lowered her eyes. Ossie went on. 'We're going to have some weapons training. I'll handle that with maybe some assistance from Sidewalk, okay?'

'Maybe we ought to take some water pistols and bows and arrows,' suggested Sidewalk sourly.

'I can shoot a bow and arrow,' said Mandy.

'For Chrissakes,' put in Bruce angrily. 'Can we just get this matter straight without making a musical out of it? Okay. We go to the Everglades tomorrow. And I want you to keep your eyes open in that vicinity because that's where we're planning to run our first hold-up.'

'Are we going to rob the Seminoles?' said Lou blinking ponderously. 'Ain't no good robbing the Seminoles. They're poor Indians. They ain't got a bean.'

Ossie sighed. 'No, it's not that. But we think we have an idea how to make some good pickings in that area. First, we got to get this training done. We got to look right. We got to *scare* people. Okay?'

'Okay,' they all agreed.

'Right. We meet here at ten tomorrow morning. Got that? Ten. Anyone you know can fix transportation?'

'I know a guy with a little bus,' said Sidewalk unexpectedly. 'I can get that.'

'Great. What about the dough?'

'Nothing,' said Sidewalk. 'I just have to lean on him a little.'

'That's the sort of talk I want to hear,' put in Bruce encouragingly. 'Let's be like that. Let's lean on people.'

They went out singly, at intervals of two minutes, in case of observation. Molly Mandy was the last to go. She turned at the door and said to Bruce and Ossie, 'Well, off I go to practise looking *fierce*.' She ground her teeth as she went out.

Bruce and Ossie sat down and looked at each other disconsolately. 'Jesus,' said Bruce. 'What are we going to do with this goddam bunch? I ask you?'

'Make them into a gang,' replied Ossie. 'You wait. It'll work.'

'I've got a name for them,' said Bruce sombrely. 'The Ocean Drive Delinquent Society – the ODDS.'

'It sure fits,' nodded Ossie.

CHAPTER FIVE

South Florida's Everglades Parkway, otherwise known and marked on maps as Alligator Alley, cuts directly, east to west, across the foot of the state from Naples on the Gulf of Mexico to Miami on the Atlantic, a distance of about a hundred miles. After Naples there are no settlements of any size, apart from Seminole Indian Reservations, until Andytown is reached just short of Miami–Fort Lauderdale.

The Seminoles, once the proud water-Indians of the region, are now reduced to an area of rough country to the north of the highway, with one large compound to the south. The rest of the area is swamp, saw-grass and entwined trees, the home of the alligator, snake, swimming bear, panther, bald eagle and flamingo. It is accessible only by air-boat, a light craft powered by a large fan on its stern, and tenuous man-made walkways linking occasional firm islands in the four hundred square miles of watery jungle.

There are, in addition, a few dirt roads turning off the main highway and pushing for a mile or so into the Everglades, generally to places of interest to tourists.

At one of these attractions, a bogus Seminole encampment, a bus-load of tourists from the Miami–Fort Lauderdale area were watching an Indian wrestle with an alligator. The air was humid and there was no great enthusiasm from the audience, their guide from Smileytime Tours, the Seminole called Blue Squirrel, or the alligator itself, now lying somnolently on its back. Molly Mandy watched with only half-attention, her mind on other things. The tourist guide was a red-cheeked young man with a croaky voice. 'Now folks,' he called. 'Just watch that critter's tail when Blue Squirrel turns him on his front again. He don't like what's been going on and Blue Squirrel sure needs to watch that sneaky tail.'

Blue Squirrel reached carefully and turned the five foot alligator onto its feet again. Its tail struck at him spitefully and he jumped. A minor buzz of interest came from the tourists.

The Smileytime guide called out: 'And that ladies and gentlemen is the end of the performance today. I guess you want to show your appreciation to Blue Squirrel in the usual way.'

The people applauded and Molly Mandy in a brightly flowered straw hat slipped away towards a wigwam which bore the sign 'Telephone'. The audience drifted, leaving the Indian looking annoyed. 'Mean bastards,' he said to the alligator. 'Every time that guy says "show your appreciation", they think it's enough to *clap*. Never a goddam dime.' The alligator opened its jaws as if laughing at the joke. Blue Squirrel closed them again with a firm push of his foot.

Molly Mandy was in the wigwam. 'Everglades one,' she whispered into the phone. 'Everglades one calling Everglades two.'

'E-E-Everglades two,' said the excited K-K-K-Katy in a call box three miles away on the highway.

'We're just leaving. Okay?'

'Okay. We're ready. G-G-Good luck, M-Molly.'

Molly left the wigwam. The rest of the party was already aboard the bus. The stripe-shirted guide, sweat running down his chin, was stretched on his toes counting his charges.

'Wait for me!' shouted Molly running towards them holding her pretty flowered hat in place.

'Ah!' exclaimed the guide, 'I thought maybe the Seminoles had got you.'

'Wish they would,' said Molly brightly as she boarded the bus. 'We women don't have fun like that these days.'

Some of the passengers laughed but she got a few frowns and turned-away faces as she went down the aisle. She reached her place next to a stiff-looking woman who had said she was from Boston. Molly settled herself. 'You *know* what the Indians do to white women,' she mentioned mischievously. The Boston lady shuddered.

It had been very hot and the majority of the tourists were from Canada and the Northern United States. The doors closed and the bus started along the track towards the main highway. The people sat gratefully in the air conditioning and discussed the afternoon's diversions.

'I got to tell you, Marge, to me that alligator looked just like it was made of rubber.'

'Doped,' said Marge decisively. 'Doped snout to tail. That Indian didn't have a scratch or a mark on him. Doped.'

The driver sighed idly into the mirror. Every day he heard the same comments, the same complaints. They did not believe those parrots at the Parrot Jungle really rode bicycles and roller skates. It was all a trick, rubber parrots worked by electricity, wasn't this sun hot, and the whole of Florida was below water level and one good tidal wave would drown the whole state, and the hotel charged too much for drinks, and, gee, wasn't it hot, those guys had to be cruel to make those dolphins do those tricks, anyway they were rubber dolphins, worked by electricity, same as the alligators and the parrots. Never mind, they just had two feet of snow in New York State. God, this dirt road is sure bumpy. The Mafia ran everything in Miami, even a dum-dum knew that. The horse racing and the Jai-alai games and the dog tracks. You couldn't win anywhere. Florida was out to rob you. Gee this road. And what's that, Al, some guy off his motor cycle? Lying in the dirt road . . .

Katy felt very hot and uncomfortable in the motor cycle gear, and the crash helmet hung like a ton on her head. She lay face down in the red dust, a centipede walking determinedly towards her left eye. She watched it nervously. To her relief it did a smart left turn when it realized that her eyelash was not another centipede. It marched past her view like a platoon of soldiers.

The motor cycle was spreadeagled in the dirt a dozen yards away, a long convincing scar cut into the track by its handlebars. She had offered to attempt to ride the machine, but Ossie had said it would be just as realistic if it were a set-up. He rode the bike along the track to make the tyre impressions and skidded it at the decided point.

She heard the bus come around the bend and hoped that the driver wasn't too tired or preoccupied to see her. It would be a shame to miss the very first operation. She smiled at the dust under her nose as she heard the engine check and then come to a halt.

In the sawgrass a few yards from the bus Ari and Lou crouched, the useless Russian pistols in their hands. On the other side of the track Sidewalk Joe waited, similarly mis-armed. Bruce and Ossie watched through binoculars two hundred yards up the track. All wore hoods which reached to their waists.

'Right,' whispered Bruce. 'It's stopped. Any second now.'

The door of the bus slid open and the guide and the driver appeared on the step. At the windows the faces of the tourists pressed to get a better view. From the undergrowth on either side the three masked figures stepped out simultaneously. Everybody in the bus screamed.

'Okay,' said Sidewalk Joe, moving in first, according to plan. 'This is what they used to call a stick-up.' He pushed the large Russian gun into the tourist guide's projecting middle. 'What's your name, son?'

The young man, his face crimson with alarm, swallowed. It seemed like he would never make it. 'Larry,' he said painfully. 'Larry K. Burlestone.'

'Right,' said Sidewalk Joe beneath his mask. 'Larry K. Burlestone. You're going to be the late Larry K. Burlestone if these people don't contribute to my benevolent fund.' He shouted the words up the bus. The passengers were sitting stiff with apprehension. 'Okay, my buddies will be coming along the bus for contributions. We'll accept anything and everything. Any trouble and lovely Larry here will be ready for the mortician. And the same goes for anybody else who tries to pull anything.'

Lou and Ari moved into the bus. Each had a canvas bag for the loot. Molly watched them as they advanced. She clutched her purse realistically.

'Rape! Rape!' cried a plump woman, half way along the centre aisle.

'We don't do requests, lady,' muttered Ari standing along the centre aisle. He leaned forward and took off her necklace, opened her pocketbook and helped himself to a billfold. All around the other passengers were surrendering their valuables, some fearfully, some sullenly, some with brave curses. Lou took Molly's handbag.

'I've counted it,' warned Molly from the edge of her mouth. 'Every last cent.'

Lou was quietly collecting the belongings of three New England gentlemen. They handed them over haughtily. Lou smiled below his hood. 'This is where you say "you'll never get away with this",' he reminded them. None of them spoke.

Ari opened the wallet of a large scornful-looking man and was confronted by the man's photograph and an FBI identification card. Ari's breath stopped for a moment. He handed the wallet back. 'Nice to have you aboard, sir,' he said from beneath the hood.

Lou was patiently making his way along his section of the bus. 'Contributions please,' he recited. 'All gratefully received.'

A quarrelsome woman refused to be parted from a diamond and emerald ring. 'Never,' she said bluntly to Ari. 'Just for a start, mister, it won't come off that finger. It never has come off.'

'Gee, I'm sorry,' said Ari. He called towards the front of the bus. 'Charley, get a hacksaw.'

'It came off! exclaimed the woman at once. 'That's the first time it's come off in twenty years!'

Ari examined it. 'Nice stuff, lady,' he said. 'You should look after rocks like this. Hope it's insured.' He dropped it into his bag. He looked around. The others were finished and making their way towards the door at the front.

'Ladies and gentlemen, on behalf of the poor of South Florida, we would like to thank you for your response to our appeal,' said Sidewalk Joe. 'You been real generous. We've got to be on our way, but we will always remember you and we hope you will remember us. We are going to take your guide Larry K. along with us for a while. That's just to make sure you stay good and quiet. If you all stay in your seats and button up for ten minutes you'll find that Larry will come back to you – all his pieces joined onto his other pieces. If you don't, then we may have to separate him.' A shudder, beginning with Larry himself, echoed down the bus.

'I'd like to say something,' said Larry bravely. 'Is that possible, sir?'

'Just don't shout "Help",' replied Sidewalk. 'Okay, go ahead.'

'Ladies and gentlemen,' said Larry turning his sweat-soaked face to his customers. 'Smileytime Tours apologize for this interruption. We hope that you will still remember us next time you are planning a tour in Florida.' His smile was yellow. 'Smileytime, anytime – that's our slogan.'

There was a predictably mixed chorus of cheers and groans and outright boos from the robbed passengers. Lawsuits were already being planned. Larry was taken from the bus by the gang. The driver was warned once again not to move a yard. The gang and their hostage stepped out into the heavy sun. Katy had gone off on a prearranged route, leaving the motor cycle, which they had stolen, lying in the dust in the path of the bus.

From their concealment two hundred yards away Bruce and Ossie watched. 'They're on their way,' said Bruce. 'All to plan. Let's blow.'

They climbed through the undergrowth and pushed their way to a clearing in the swamp. A Volkswagen mini-bus was parked there. Ossie climbed into the driving seat and started the engine. Bruce opened the rear doors. A moment later the three hooded members of the gang and the prisoner came through the sawgrass. Larry K. was hoisted into the back of the Volkswagen and the others sat around him, still in their hoods.

'This will ruin Smileytime Tours,' said Larry loyally.

'Shit,' said Sidewalk Joe. 'Great publicity, all the newspapers, TV, radio. Everybody will want to tour with Smileytime.'

Larry brightened. 'You sure?' he asked. 'You really think that could happen?'

'Sure,' put Ari. 'You'll get more loot from this than we did. Just wait and see.'

After five minutes they dropped Larry K. by the side of the dirt road at a place where he had a long walk to a phone and a longer walk to the Everglades Parkway. He sat down resignedly at the side of the swamp waiting for his bus to pick him up.

The gang were joined by Katy, who appeared from the vegetation, and they set off for the main highway in soaring spirits.

They took their hoods away, each one revealing a sweating face smirking with triumph. 'Great! It was great!' hooted Ari. 'It worked! We did it!'

Lou embraced him so heavily he winced and Sidewalk grinned his New York grin. Katy giggled and Bruce and Ossie shouted their relief.

'We got some nice trinkets,' said Ari looking down into his canvas bag. 'Some real pretty things.'

'Put it away,' said Sidewalk sharply. 'Jeez! Never look at the takings until the door is locked.'

Ari looked up shamefacedly but the warning was timely because now they had reached the Everglades Parkway and Ossie had turned the vehicle east towards Andytown. Occasional cars passed in either direction and a worried silence fell on them. Then at the traffic lights at the termination of the parkway a highway patrol car drew easily alongside.

'Sing,' hissed Bruce. 'Everybody sing.'

It was Katy who began. In her old piping voice she opened up. She sang '*That old gang who sang heart-of-my-heart,*' and the others joined in robustly.

The highway patrol men grinned and one leaned from the car and called to Ossie: 'All had a good day?'

'Oh a great day, thank you officer,' he grinned back. 'Everybody.'

The policeman waved cheerfully as the lights changed. 'One thing I like to see,' he said to his driver, 'is old folks having a good time.'

The headquarters of Dade County Police is on Biscayne Boulevard, Miami. It was here that the victims of the Everglades bus hold-up were taken. Three hours had elapsed since the robbery, the Florida sun had sunk without a trace, and the tourists were becoming irritated and hungry. They sat on benches around the large, untidy but boring room waiting their turn to step to one of the tables where the policemen sat and wrote laborious lists of valuables stolen by the gang.

Molly Mandy was conscious of a small blush of apprehension as she was beckoned forward to one of the tables. But the officer who was listing took it as natural nervousness of the police – a sound deduction – and he smiled professionally at her as he nodded towards the seat on the other side of the table.

'Now, ma'am, this won't take too long. First your name and address.'

'Molly Belle Mandifield,' she lied primly, touching her gentle finger-tips together. 'I'm not going to tell you my age, I'll tell you where I live. I live at 1017, Pine Street, Longville, South Carolina.' That was a lie also, but she had wisely decided to keep the law away from South Miami Beach.

'And you're on vacation in Florida?'

'Yes. And I've had a real good time, till now.'

'Local address?'

She decided to bluff it out. 'Sunshine Apartments, Pompano Beach,' she said, naming a hotel where she had once spent three days on her first arrival in South Florida. She had doubts about the untruth. 'But I'm leaving tomorrow,' she added firmly. 'Going home. And I'm glad, just take it from me, I'm glad.'

'Okay, I see. Well, we'll get in touch if we find out who did this to you.'

'What do you mean "if"?' she inquired, leaning forward as though she were the interrogator. 'Is there any *doubt* that you're going to catch them? I hope not.'

The policeman looked pained as if he were personally disappointed in her. 'We hope not too, lady, but we got a few million people in this corner of the US and maybe they could hide. We've not heard of this gang before. This is the first time they've tried anything.'

'I hope you're watching the ports and airports and the state boundaries,' sniffed Molly. 'I hope you remember that.'

'Night and day,' sighed the policeman. 'We've got them trapped in sixty thousand square miles. Now can we get down the list of your missing property?'

'Okay,' she replied sweetly. 'Eight dollars, thirty-five cents, my ruby ring and good luck travel charm.'

'Like a medallion on a chain?'

'Right,' affirmed Molly. 'It's supposed to take care of me when I travel.'

'It quit on the job. Anything else?'

'No.' Molly dabbed at her eyes. 'I'm just a poor robbed woman.'

The policeman looked up with a suspicion of sympathy. 'Sure, sure,' he muttered. 'I'm sorry lady. We'll get them, don't worry.'

'I'll pray for you,' said Molly turning away. As she did so she raised her eyes towards the ceiling.

Captain Salvatore sat disconsolately on the edge of his desk in the police station office. He was thinking, his sparsely covered head bent, his eyes dull, his top lip hanging over the bottom.

He spread a sheaf of statements in his hairy hand like an ape playing cards. 'Hooded hoods!' he snorted. 'Guns, scared old ladies. For Chrissake, what is this, I ask you?'

Detective Stewart, a blinking young man, shrugged: 'It's armed robbery, chief,'

Salvatore regarded him painfully and then revolved thoughtfully to the other policeman in the room, Detective Cook.

'I'll tell you something, Cookie,' he said, nodding towards Stewart. 'Our boy here has sure improved since he went on his refresher course at police school. It's armed robbery, he says. Jesus Harold Christ! I *know* it's armed robbery. I already made that deduction, Stewart. What I meant was, for Godsake, this is Florida! Sunshine, citrus, palm trees, safe swimming in the ocean. Nice people getting a suntan. It ain't Harlem.' Salvatore sighed, the effort shaking his frame. 'Tourists, the state's most valuable commodity. Robbed, in broad daylight. In Florida sunshine!' He seemed to take it as a personal hurt. His unkempt face sagged.

'We don't know any gang in this state who operates like that,' ventured Cook. 'Hooded, guns . . .'

Stewart tried. 'Maybe it's the Purvisco Mob,' he said. 'Down for a vacation.'

Salvatore stared at him desperately. 'The Purvisco Mob? You get more beautiful by the hour, Stewart. The last operation the Purvisco gang pushed got them a million bucks from the State Deposit Bank in Chicago.' Dull-eyed he looked down at the list in his hand. 'Two pearl earrings, imitation,' he read. 'A pair of sunglasses, eight dollars, a diamond ring, a ruby ring, imitation. Three candy bars, genuine.' He paused and looked up sourly at Stewart. 'Does that sound like the Purvisco Mob?'

Stewart looked aggrieved. 'It was only an idea,' he said.

'And a lousy one,' said Salvatore. 'I can't see me telling it to the chief. Who was the FBI man on the bus?'

'Guy called Brown, I expect that's an alias,' shrugged Stewart. 'Nobody in the FBI is called Brown.'

His captain's odd eyebrows went up in the direction of Cook. 'What was he doing?' repeated Salvatore. 'Have we checked him?'

'He was on vacation,' said Cook. 'He likes seeing Indians fight alligators. He's okay. I've checked him. And his name's Brown.'

The Ocean Drive Delinquent Society returned quickly to South Miami Beach, scattered with hardly a flutter and merged with the hundreds of inhabitants of God's Waiting Room. In turn they deposited the bags of loot taken from the bus in the bathroom of Molly's narrow apartment, among the armoury of Russian weapons.

At nine that evening they rendezvoused in the apartment, K-K-K-Katy bringing with her a bottle of genuine New York French Champagne. 'I was saving it for something to celebrate,' she said before looking in Lou the Barbender's direction and pouring a measure in each glass held by the gang. 'But maybe we've got something.'

'Beautiful,' murmured Loose Bruce, sipping at his glass. 'Just beautiful.'

'It sure seemed like it,' said Ossie cautiously. 'But ladies and gentlemen, we're waiting for Molly to get back. She's been held up with the police for quite a time.'

'I l-l-l-liked it,' said Katy decisively. 'Gee, it was so exciting! And that gun felt so comforting.'

'Like old times,' nodded Sidewalk Joe contentedly. 'Took me right back to the thirties. Maybe it wanted a little more drama, like there was no shooting, no ketchup, and nobody turned stool pigeon or double crossed, but it was close enough.'

Ari said: 'Jeez, did you see those folks' faces? People sure don't like being robbed.'

'How much did we get? That's what I want to know,' said Sidewalk quietly. 'I just know it ain't much.'

'Right,' said Ossie. 'You're right. But it was the first pitch. That's what matters. We did it.'

'Maybe we should have waited until some millionaires went to see the Indian wrestle the alligator,' suggested Lou solidly. 'Maybe it would have been big time then.'

'And maybe not,' put in Katy. 'All the m-m-millionaires I've ever known never had a cent on them. It's all in banks and safe deposits and stock. They don't go around loaded.'

There came three soft knocks on the door, followed by two others. 'Molly,' said Bruce. He rose from the table and opened it. Molly slid in like a spy.

'Was it okay?' said Bruce right away.

'Oh, just wonderful,' she smiled. 'There's a poor cop called Captain Salvatore going bananas at police headquarters. They just got no idea. No idea. Gee, is that champagne? Oh, you kept some. That's real sweet. I like the bubbles in my eyes.'

'What happened then?' asked Ossie when she had taken a long drink from the glass. 'Did you get through with the questioning okay? You handled it?'

'Easy,' she said blandly. 'Like falling in love. Gave them a list of what was stolen from me. By the way, can I have my pocket book back?' She looked accusingly at the Greek. 'It was you, Ari, I could tell even with the hood. The way you keep doing that cute little run. It must be a nervous twitch, Ari. You did it in the bus.'

'Watch that, Ari,' warned Bruce. 'It's a clue. We don't want to hand out no clues. No jogging when we're robbing.'

'We're going to do some more soon are we? Say we are,' said Molly. 'I want to be under a hood next time.'

Ossie studied the line of waiting, anticipatory faces. 'It's something we've got to discuss,' he said. 'First, I guess we all want to see what we made on the operation.' He reached for the first canvas bag and carefully slid the contents onto the table. It made a pile of wallets, jewellery, cigarette cases, lighters and cash. The robbers leaned over. Ossie began to sort it, pushing the money to one side. Bruce began to count that. Katy put a jeweller's eyeglass to her eye and examined the trinkets critically. Every bag was emptied, each set of contents sorted and counted. Eventually Ossie turned to them.

'Four hundred and ninety-three dollars, thirty-seven cents,' he said. 'Assorted jewellery, such as you can see. It's not dynamite. There's a couple of nice cigarette cases, but they've got initials on them and those would have to be removed before we sell them.'

A small pout of unhappiness blew from Molly's face. 'Sell them?' she repeated. 'Sell them? Somehow that seems so dishonest.'

The heads of the gang turned to her in slow astonishment. Bruce and Ossie matched eyebrows. Ossie said gently, 'So is armed robbery dishonest, Molly. In fact it would be pretty well impossible to run a gang like this without some element of dishonesty.'

'I know, I know,' sighed Molly. 'You think I'm crazy. It's just that doing the robbery's exciting and there's a risk. But, well, how can I explain it? Selling the stuff seems . . . well . . . mean.'

'I know a fence,' said Sidewalk practically. 'He'll take everything, but his rate ain't so good.'

'Maybe we would show a better profit by each taking a few things to the pawnbrokers and secondhand shops,' said Katy. 'A little at a time.'

'We need a fence,' said Ossie decisively. 'I vote we give Sidewalk the assignment of getting this arranged.'

'You're supposed to fix a fence before you do the job, son,' warned Sidewalk. 'That's why you don't have the stuff hanging around where people can smell it out.'

'I know, I know,' sighed Ossie. 'But we're beginners, remember. Next time we'll have things arranged a little more on the line. And that's another thing. Next time. Now do we vote that we're going on to do something else? Now we know we can handle a crime are we going to try and improve on it, or does anyone want to quit now?'

Nobody wanted to quit, although Molly insisted quietly: 'I'd be a whole heap happier if we didn't have to *sell* it.' No one took any notice of her.

Katy got up and putting the loot in two of the bags she carried it up to the bathroom. The money she left on the table and Bruce divided it up equally between them. He put the bills in his pocket. 'Now at least I can eat,' he said.

From below them came the sound of somebody playing an evening piano. They played sadly and badly and the fractured notes floated like memories.

'You'll be hearing soon,' said Bruce as one by one they sidled out into the warm corridor. 'Just be ready.'

He and Ossie went out of the elderly hotel and walked along Ocean Drive and across Washington Avenue. They went to a bar next to the burlesque show. It was half-dark in there, a blue rinse light coming from the television set hoisted up near the ceiling at the far end. Three or four male customers gazed up as if the machine was bringing them some celestial message. Ossie and Bruce went to the far end of the counter and turned their backs on the screen.

'So what do you think?' said Bruce.

'Well it worked. I mean it *worked*, didn't it? These old guys seem to slide right into it. And apart from Molly not wanting to sell the stuff, the old ladies seem right there, with it.'

'Less than five hundred bucks in cash, phoney rings and some dented cigarette cases ain't exactly the great train robbery,' pointed out Bruce. 'We might as well get jobs.'

'Right, okay. I agree,' said Ossie. 'But now we know they can do it. Next time we'll strike something rich.'

'Like what's rich?' said Bruce. 'You got any ideas?'

'A house,' said Ossie quietly. 'Jesus, this area's full of loaded houses.'

'A burglary,' said Bruce.

'You're quick, real quick. What I think we should do is to smell around for a while. Keep our eyes on the newspapers maybe. Then when we come up with something considerable, go to work on it.'

'It'll be quieter than a stick-up,' agreed Bruce finishing his beer. They went out and got some hot pastrami sandwiches from a take-away, and cans of beer from a package store. Ocean Drive was quiet except for the insistent pushing sound of the waves.

'My dad always thought I'd make a good preacher,' said Ossie biting into the sandwich as he walked along.

'Shows how wrong fathers can be,' mumbled Bruce with his mouth full.

'Maybe I'll still be, one day,' said Ossie. 'I got a feeling for it. I just see all these old folk sitting along here in the day and, man, you know, I just feel like getting up there on a box or something and giving them the Jesus call.'

'They're Jewish,' Bruce pointed out through the bread. 'Ninety per cent Jewish. They'd say "Jesus, who needs it?"'

'So it would be hard. I don't give a shit. I tell you sometimes up there on the beach tower I've been tempted, you know seriously tempted, to start throwing my arms about and start shouting things.'

'You want to be loved,' Bruce told him.

'I guess that's it.'

They reached the Sunny Gables Hotel, looking sick in the orange floodlight which was thrown across its front. 'Maybe if we make a few more bucks,' said Bruce, 'I'll get me a better room. That one I got is so small I can turn the air conditioning on just by breaking wind.'

'You don't say.'

'Sure. It's enough to work the thermostat. Just breaking wind.'

'You got some nice habits,' said Ossie.

They walked into the front of the hotel. Gabby was standing in the shadows. They saw she was pointing a gun at them. They stopped and regarded her with alarm.

'Okay, you two,' she said quietly. 'I want to know what you're doing with my grandma.'

She looked very businesslike behind the small hole of the gun. She jabbed it towards them and ushered them towards the stairs.

'Put your hands over your heads,' she said firmly. 'And don't put them down.'

'You're enjoying this,' murmured Bruce. 'Domination over men.' He caught Ossie's grinning eye. They both raised their hands and allowed themselves to be prodded up the stairs. Gabby was three stairs behind them.

'Don't try to pull anything,' she warned sombrely. 'I promise I'll shoot.'

'We ain't pulled anything in weeks,' answered Bruce easily. He could tell by the back of Ossie's neck that he was smiling. Ossie's got the bullet, he thought. The stairs were narrow and turning and they could hear hesitant footsteps scraping down. They were on the first landing and the elevator clanked open almost at Ossie's elbow.

'In there,' said Gabby. 'Go on. Get in.' She pushed the snout of the gun into Bruce's middle. 'You get it if anybody tries anything.' Obediently they got into the elevator. It was old and trembling. Most of the residents of Sunny Gables were afraid to use it, the elderly having a profound distrust of the elderly.

'Which floor is your room?' she said to Bruce. 'I want to go there. Right now.'

'Gee, I thought you'd never ask,' he answered. He pressed the button for the eighth floor which was the top. The jerk caught the girl off balance and they both hurriedly caught her and steadied her. She regarded them with deep dislike.

'I want to know what you guys have been doing,' she muttered. She rattled the gun in Bruce's ribs.

At the next floor a thin, weak-eyed man was waiting and he stepped into the cage, somehow blindly inserting himself between Gabby and Bruce. Gabby found herself with the gun pointing at the old man. She manoeuvered it behind his thin back until it was covering Bruce again. He grinned sympathetically. The thin old man focussed his eyes carefully on the elevator door and when it stopped at the next floor staggered out with tiny steps. He had not spoken to them.

'That guy,' said Ossie conversationally to Bruce. 'Have you noticed? All day he goes up and down in the elevator. Every time I get in this elevator he's either aboard or he gets aboard.'

'I noticed,' said Bruce. 'Maybe he doesn't know where he lives.'

'Maybe he lives in ths elevator,' said Ossie. 'Right here.'

They were completely ignoring Gabby. Her expression hardened. 'You two think you know all the answers don't you? Oh yes, you're real smarties. I might have known you were up to something. Using an old lady's guns. Jesus, how low can some people get?'

They had reached the eighth. Bruce and Ossie with exaggerated politeness stood back to allow Gabby to exit, but she pushed them both out with a nudge of the gun. 'Okay, where?' she said.

'Right here,' said Bruce reaching the door. 'I hope it's not too untidy, lady.'

'There may be blood on the floor before to long,' she replied. She was keeping up the hardness, but they knew she was unsure because of their lack of concern at the gun. They walked into the room. Bruce quietly let off wind and the air conditioning obligingly whirred. Ossie nodded at the feat. 'I'm impressed,' he said.

'What's it all about?' insisted Gabby at once.

'Grandma didn't tell you?'

'She wouldn't say.'

'Great. Good for Molly.'

The familiarity of the name immediately angered the girl. 'Jesus, you are such shit!' she burst out. 'She's seventy. Come on you bastards, what was it all for?'

'For armed robbery,' shrugged Bruce. Ossie nodded. 'You *need* a gun for armed robbery,' he added solicitously.

Gabby's large eyes opened larger. The muzzle of the revolver dropped and so did her attractive mouth. Loose Bruce and Ossie grinned together. 'Robbery . . .?' she said at last. 'Robbery? My grandma . . .?'

Bruce said: 'Well on this raid she didn't have the gun because she was the plant, you get me? We need somebody among the er . . . victims . . . and that was Molly. She had a good time, believe me.'

'I ought to shoot you, both of you,' she muttered.

'It ain't no good,' said Bruce easily. 'That weapon ain't loaded. We got the guns but there's only one bullet. And he's got that.' He nodded backwards at Ossie. Ossie looked puzzled. 'No man, you've got it,' he said.

Bruce went serious and pale. 'But you . . .'

'You had it,' said Ossie quietly.

'I've got it,' said the girl firmly. 'It's in the gun.'

They whitened together. 'Jesus, Gabby, baby, watch what you're doing!' pleaded Bruce. 'Point it at *him*.'

'I was brought up with guns,' said Gabby. 'My old man was a game ranger. What's in this could go right through both of you. And maybe it will.'

'Look,' said Ossie hurriedly. 'Let's have a little sense in this. We wouldn't have let your grandma have a loaded gun.'

'No,' said Bruce fervently. 'Not for anything, Gabby. We thought there was only one bullet and we thought one of *us* had it.'

'One of you may yet get it,' she said. 'My grandma stole it from you. Great gang leaders you are. Letting a little old lady steal your ammunition.' She was very sure of herself now.

Expertly she flicked open the chamber of the gun as if to make sure the bullet had not got out. Both men jumped on her in the instant. Bruce caught the gun and Ossie caught the girl. She could fight and the room was narrow. Ossie fell over Bruce and Bruce got Ossie's boot in the chest. The girl rolled beneath them. The table fell over and one of its legs collapsed. Bruce managed to sit astride her. Ossie pushed him aside and muttered, 'I'll hold her, I'm stronger.'

'It's rape now, is it?' spat Gabby. 'You horny bastards.'

'Nobody's getting raped unless it's me,' Ossie assured her. 'We just wanted the gun and the bullet on our side. Now are you going to be a good girl?'

She nodded sullenly. Gently he got from above her. Her lovely breasts heaved under her sweater. The man and the girl regarded each other. Bruce, seeing the expressions, moved in quickly and helped her into the chair again. All three sat down panting. Bruce had the gun. Ossie took it from him and dropped the bullet from the chamber. 'Next time,' he said to Bruce, 'I'll make you sign for it.'

One hour and fifteen cans of beer later they thought they had convinced her. She kept pace, argument by argument, and can by can, with them, but in the end she shrugged. 'Okay,' she said. 'I'll go and talk to her again. I want to make quite sure she knows what she's doing.'

'Like I say, it's only occupational therapy,' said Ossie persuasively. His strong eyes regarded her seriously and she had to look away after holding onto the gaze for a moment. 'These old people down here,' he went on, 'just need something . . . a little excitement. We aim to provide it.'

Gabby hung her head thoughtfully. 'I want to go and talk to her again,' she repeated. 'I want to hear it from her. Okay?'

Bruce looked doubtful. But Ossie said: 'Okay. But don't try anything, sweetheart.'

'I know,' she said. 'She's in it too. I won't tell any tales. Don't worry your junior heads.'

She went out. Bruce and Ossie drank another can of beer each silently. Then Bruce said: 'You're too old, man. She's my generation.'

'That's right,' agreed Ossie. 'That's why I've got a lap start. Just see, sonny, she'll come to daddy.'

'Listen, we *can't*,' said Bruce. 'We could screw up everything if we both start making pitches for her.'

'Maybe she'll have a say,' pointed out Ossie logically. 'Women have a curious idea they can make up their own minds. Anyway, don't let it bug you – or me. And have a little sympathy, man. Jesus, you're so young you'll have them by the hundred before you're too old and tired. Me, I'm nearly through, it could be my last chance.'

'You poor old bastard,' commented Bruce looking at the cheerful brown face and the chopped grey hair. 'My heart bleeds. It bleeds.'

They had another two cans of beer before the girl came back. She came quietly into the room. Bruce farted silently and set the air conditioning going. 'At least the air conditioning works in here,' she said. 'My grandma's only goes when it thinks it will.'

'Maybe I'll fix it for her,' offered Bruce.

Ossie smiled. 'What did she say, the old lady?' he asked.

Gabby sat, surrendered, on the chair. 'I've got to tell you that grandma told me she loved every minute,' she sighed. 'She's not crazy about spending the loot, but she liked doing the job. I've never seen her so frisky. To tell you the truth I only came back from St Petersburg because

I was worried so much about her. She used to be such fun, like a young girl, but this place, this graveyard, is getting to her. And when I get back today she's hopping about like a buck rabbit.'

'Maybe she'll make enough to get away from South Miami Beach altogether,' said Ossie cagily. 'Go some place where she can be old and content and not have to live in a crummy hotel like this. What do *you* do for her, anyway?'

It was a shrewd inquiry. She hesitated. 'Not enough,' she admitted. 'But I worry. That's why I came back. Just now I'm not in a very strong situation myself. I had some trouble. I got mixed up with a guy who has a wife and it hit the fan just a few weeks ago. And he's got a vice-presidency and kids. I don't have a job or even a proper home of my own right now. God, I just had to sell my motor cycle, and that was hard, really hard.'

Bruce did not like the way the conversation seemed to have been carried on without him, almost as if nobody expected he was mature enough to understand. 'She got any other family, your grandma?' he said solidly. 'Don't anybody else take an interest?'

Gabby looked carefully towards him. Ossie smiled to himself. 'Well, no, not really,' said Gabby. 'They don't give a damn. They sent her off down here before I was old enough to stop them. Go and have a good time on Miami Beach, they said. The sun always shines down there. Jesus, the sun! What the hell's the sun? If somebody cut their throat down here they'd put them out in the sun to get better.'

'Right,' said Bruce gravely. 'That's absolutely one hundred per cent right.'

'What are you going to do next?' inquired Gabby expectantly.

'The gang?' said Ossie. 'Oh well, we were just getting around to thinking about that. It's still in the planning sequence you understand.'

'We can't reveal anything at this stage,' said Bruce importantly.

'Are you interested?' said Ossie, more to the point. He leaned towards her. Bruce looked annoyed that he had not said it. Gabby's face came up to meet Ossie's and nodded. She shrugged. 'I'm right out on a limb myself. People keep throwing dirt at me anyway. Maybe I could deserve some of it. Sure, why not?'

The young man and the older man regarded her passively, their beer cans held negligently. She appeared to have forgotten them, to have gone down into some cellar of her own. Her brown neck was arched forward and her beautiful profile became thoughtful, the lids and lashes dropped low over the large eyes. The air conditioning stopped and Bruce, silently lifting his leg, started it again. The girl said, 'That's the neatest way I ever saw of starting it.' It was an aside. Bruce looked shocked and ashamed. Ossie nodded approvingly towards Gabby.

'Okay, what did the stick-up make?' she asked eventually.

Bruce and Ossie turned to each other, their separate embarrassments meeting halfway. 'Well,' Ossie hesitated, 'it didn't show much of a profit. Not that much.'

'It was a kind of try-out,' aplogized Bruce. 'Just to see if it could be done.'

'How much?' she insisted.

'Oh, roughly about five hundred dollars,' said Ossie.

'Approximately that,' confirmed Bruce as though trying to share the blame.

'Big time eh? You could have sold the guns for more than that.'

'Right. Okay. But we'll need the guns again. And next time we'll be after bigger fry,' said Ossie.

'What's it to be next time? Busting into a juke box?'

'Listen,' said Ossie leaning forward and touching her arm with his can of beer, 'you just joined.'

'Sure, he's right,' said Bruce. 'We were only waiting for *you* before going into the big-time.'

'Just as well I got here,' she said, ignoring the sarcasm. 'Seems like it wasn't a minute too soon.'

Ossie looked at her squarely with such concentration that she had to lift her head and return the look. 'One thing, baby,' he said slowly. 'One thing you're not going to do and that's take over.'

She converted her calm stare into a shrugging laugh. 'Okay. Okay,' she agreed. 'I'm not going to spoil your party. You Tarzan, me Jane.'

'What about me?' said Bruce.

'There's only Boy left,' said Gabby.

Gabby and Ossie both laughed at Bruce's lost face. Ossie tapped him on the head with his beer can. 'Don't take it too hard, son. It's *our* gang. She's just been coopted.'

'*Our Gang* is right,' commented Gabby. Before they could reply she had lapsed into her thoughts again.

Bruce opened three more beers. The last three. 'What are we supposed to be thinking about?' he asked the other two.

'The next target,' said Ossie patiently. 'Where the ODDS strike next.'

'What's the ODDS?' asked Gabby almost absently. 'What's it stand for?'

'Ocean Drive Delinquent Society,' replied Bruce smugly. 'Don't you think that's a smart name?'

'It is, it is,' agreed Gabby, forestalling any further argument. 'The Lostra Nostra.'

Ossie opened his mouth but she got there first again. 'There's a three million dollar house at Palm Beach,' she said thoughtfully. 'It's called something Spanish, Casa Velentia, that kind of place. I saw it in the Miami newspaper. They're having some sort of gala night there for charity. Why don't we just look into the possibilities. If we can get in during the extravaganza . . .'

'What's an extravaganza?' asked Bruce.

'The night,' Ossie said. 'It means the charity night, see?'

'Why didn't she just say?' sulked Bruce.

'If we get in,' she went on, ignoring the exchange, 'while all the guests are there, we might find there's some pickings. Maybe from the people themselves – they're bound to be loaded at that sort of party. Or maybe we can hook onto a few treasures from the house itself. It will be a matter of finding out what the possibilities are.'

'Casing the joint,' said Bruce smugly. 'Reconnoitring.'

'Just so,' agreed Gabby easily.

'When's the charity night?' asked Ossie grinning at them. 'How long do we have for planning?'

'In a couple of weeks, I seem to remember,' said Gabby. 'I'll check with the newspaper. How does it sound?'

'Sounds okay,' said Bruce like a military tactician. 'Worth taking a look I'd say.'

'What's the charity?' asked Ossie. He leaned back for some more beer but realized it had all gone. 'How many beers have you drunk?' he asked Gabby.

'Jesus, I don't know,' she said. 'You hand me them, I drink them. The charity is the Senior Citizens' Goodwill Fund.'

'What better?' said Ossie. 'We qualify right away.'

CHAPTER SIX

The members of the Ocean Drive Delinquent Society gathered in Molly Mandy's room. It was their third meeting that week, and they arrived, their excitement and expectancy scarely contained in their expressions. Carefully they moved the Russian flame thrower from the sideboard and all stood around while Ossie opened a drawn plan. Gabby and Bruce stood slightly behind him.

'It would seem, ladies and gentlemen, that if we're lucky, this operation at Palm Beach is tailor-made for us.' He looked around like the chairman at a board meeting. 'We have given you time to familiarize yourselves with the surroundings of the house, Casa Velentia, and here we have an architect's drawing of the place, which Katy managed to extract from the municipality at Palm Beach without the municipality being aware of it. Good work Katy.'

Katy blushed and, half standing, gave a little old-fashioned bow. 'Th-Th-Thank you,' she said. 'I just went in there and said I was an interior designer and I needed the plan, and they gave it to me. They were real nice.'

Ossie and Bruce both smiled fondly at her, causing her blush to surface again. 'In this operation – which Gabby will explain in detail in a moment – we need three inside helpers and the rest will have their own responsibilities in carrying out the raid.'

Molly Mandy shyly raised her hand. 'Ossie,' she said quietly. 'Could I please be one of the ones who wears a hood this time?'

'Everybody will get a chance to wear a hood in time,' said Ossie. He paused, circled the faces. Molly smiled her motherly smile, Sidewalk adusted the bright buckle on his spats, Katy crossed her legs, Ari's eyes looked a long way behind his nose and Lou worked the strength of one set of fingers against the others, bending them one way and another, like a man wrestling with himself. Katy glanced at his hands affectionately before going back to the strategy unfolded on the plan.

'We've discussed this matter in great detail,' said Ossie. 'We want it to go right and we want to make sure we come out with a profit. So if you'd give your attention to Gabby, she will run through the plan for the operation.'

Gabby stepped forward and there was an endearing little round of applause for her, originating from her grandmother but being taken up generously all around. 'The girl's got brains,' confided Molly Mandy in a loud whisper to Sidewalk Joe. 'That's what this outfit needs – brains.' Bruce and Ossie looked at each other and winced.

Gabby performed a short bow. Ossie observed her closely. So did Bruce. The tight shirt over the excellent breasts, the brown arms and brown arched neck, the face beautiful and sure.

'Ladies and gentlemen,' she said, 'I want to tell you the general outline for our plan for the robbery of Casa Velentia . . .'

'Can I wear the hood this time?' put in her grandmother at once. 'Please?'

'You just have *got* to wait, grandma,' said Gabby. 'Everybody will have an important part to play.'

'I'd still like to wear the hood,' muttered Molly. 'After all, I made them.'

'I made the gloves,' nodded Katy. 'Crochetwork – it's a lost art.'

Gabby sighed and ignored them. 'There's going to be a lot of good things going for us in this operation,' she said. 'A lot. For a start, the charity gala is in aid of the Senior Citizens' Goodwill Fund of Palm Beach. The house belongs to Mr and Mrs Peter Van der Vatt and they plan to have a few tame old folks present to give it some atmosphere. Like exhibits. We have arranged that two of our members will be among the tame old folk. That will be pretty useful when it comes to creating a diversion.' She looked along the faces, each watching her pointedly. 'We'll require two people with strong acting ability for that part,' she said.

'I was an actress, you know,' put in Katy with modest enthusiasm. She glanced around. 'Well, a chorus girl anyway.'

'I still want to wear the hood,' muttered Molly doggedly.

'Grandma,' threatened Gabby 'button up or I'll put the hood on now.'

Molly looked chastened and fixed her upper lip deliberately across the lower as though charging it with the responsibility of silence. Her eyes remained firmly and fondly upon Gabby.

Gabby continued. 'We've carried out a little research on Casa

Velentia,' she said. She picked up the architect's plan. 'It's a real nice place. The main reception will be in the salon which opens out onto the garden, the swimming pool and the beach. The room we are most interested in is the room directly above this salon.' She brushed a slim fawn finger like a feather across the map. Bruce and Ossie watched the beautiful finger intently. Gabby glanced up, saw their expressions and pursed her lips as if cautioning them to pay attention to the map.

'In the room above the salon,' she said, returning to the drawing, 'there is a safe. There are a lot of goodies in the house itself but the real sweet things are in that safe.'

'What kind of safe?' asked Sidewalk Joe. 'There's all kinds.'

'Yeah, what kind? How strong?' confirmed Lou professionally.

'That's where we've stalled,' admitted Gabby. 'We don't know as yet. All we *do* know is it's concealed. It's in the wall or maybe the floor.'

'It's a long time since I busted a safe,' said Sidewalk. 'Safes have changed.'

'On the other hand,' said Gabby, 'our information is that no new safe has been fitted in the house for at least fifteen years.'

'If it needs strength, I've got strength,' said Lou. He looked at his fingers as though counting them. Kate glanced at him and then at his powerful hands with soft admiration. Lou caught her eye and blushed through his elderly tan. 'Sure I have,' he repeated.

'Concealed safes,' said Sidewalk, 'are pretty much the same. They ain't got enough room to be too fancy. If we can't open it by hand we can always blow it open.'

'That will be very noisy,' said Molly thoughtfully, 'blowing it open.'

Sidewalk nodded patiently. 'It will be,' he conceded. 'Real noisy.'

Bruce looked across at him. 'You can get some explosive?' he said.

'I guess so,' nodded Sidewalk. 'Me, I can always get explosive.'

Ari the Greek looked at him with long-standing admiration. 'He always could get things,' he said half to himself. 'Sidewalk Joe. Always could.'

'We'll fill in more details before Wednesday,' nodded Gabby. 'Just now I think maybe we ought to fix who is going to do what.'

The gang leaned forward in anticipation. 'Katy and Ari ought to be our plants,' said Gabby decisively. 'We thought this out and – in the event of us needing a diversion – one of them has got to throw a good, realistic heart attack. Okay?'

'That's Katy,' said Ari firmly. 'I don't like pretending those things. Not heart attacks. Like it's tempting Providence.'

'Sure,' agreed Katy. 'I'd like to do that. Can't say I ever had much scope for tragedy. Not as a chorus girl.'

'You don't,' agreed Lou sagely. 'Not in the chorus. Not as a general rule.'

They waited for him to finish. He looked around, embarrassed, muttered, 'Well you don't,' and shut his mouth firmly.

'Okay, that's agreed,' said Gabby. 'And we need a waiter. I have a thought for a waiter – Bruce.'

'Me?' exclaimed Bruce, backing away. 'A waiter? But I drop things.'

'Sure,' said Gabby sarcastically. 'That's going to be a great help. But we need you, Bruce, to keep things coordinated on the lower floor, in the salon and to help Katy and Ari get clear if we blow the job. It won't be difficult to get you in there as a waiter. Just try not to start dropping trays until it's time, that's all.'

Bruce nodded. 'I'll practise,' he promised.

'We need a look-out,' continued Gabby. 'Someone to keep watch for trouble outside, while we're working in the house. That will be you, grandma.'

'But my hood. What about my hood?' insisted Molly plaintively. 'You promised.'

'We need you as a look-out,' said Gabby firmly. 'Because you can *whistle* real loud. And we need a look-out who can whistle if there's trouble coming.'

Molly smiled. 'Sure can,' she said. She put her fingers into her mouth and let go an ear-wrenching whistle.

They all fell away from her, consternation on their faces. 'Sounds like some crazy bird,' said Sidewalk staring at her.

'I can whistle too,' put in K-K-Katy quietly. She put her fingers to her lips and after a hesitation not unlike her habitual stutter let go an even louder shriek. It was like Molly's, only longer. The gang held back, amazement, admiration and protest on their faces. Katy smiled sweetly. 'At one time,' she said confidingly to Gabby, 'all American girls could whistle.'

'It's a lost art,' agreed Molly.

'Let's not search for it,' suggested Gabby. 'Okay. Check. We've got the look-outs and we've got the plants, we've got the waiter. The others – there's Lou, Sidewalk, Ossie and me – we'll do the job on the safe.'

'Maybe I could ask a question,' said Ari.

'Sure, questions are welcome.'

'Why do we have to rob the safe with so many people in the house? Maybe it would be easier just to get in there when there was only the family at home.'

Sidewalk Joe looked at him impatiently. 'All the best house robberies used to be done when the place was full of folks,' he said. 'Nobody notices a few more faces around and a little noise nobody notices. And a lot of folks is like a smokescreen when it comes to getting away too. Get it?'

Ari looked abashed and said: 'Yes, I see, Sidewalk. I was only a no-good bootlegger. I was never in the big time. But I see the point. Believe me, I see the point.'

'Anything else?' put in Ossie.

Bruce said: 'One thing we ought to get right is the raid party. The guys who are going to get into the upstairs room will be dressed like they're going to the gala.'

'In fact they *will* be going to the gala,' added Gabby. 'Tuxedos, everything. We'll have some tickets specially stolen. They won't know. It's going to be easier getting into that room from inside than out. But we'll need to get away through the window, so somebody will have to be outside with a rope ladder to throw it to the window. That should be the look-out.' She regarded her grandmother doubtfully. 'Could you throw a rope up to the window, grandma?'

Molly looked scornful. 'Sure I can. I can throw a rope like I can whistle.' They backed away quickly in case she whistled again but she did not. She just smiled and said. 'I'll throw the rope.'

Gabby nodded. Lou said: 'I got my own tuxedo. It's smart, real smart. I'd like to wear that.'

'Right, that's okay,' agreed Bruce. 'There's nothing like a well dressed gang. But everybody, the waiter, that's me, the tame old folks, Katy and Ari, the look-out and the safe gang will all have their hoods with them, okay? If it all hits the fan and you can get your hood on, then get it on smart. Then run like hell.'

Charity begins in everybody's home in Palm Beach, Florida. There are few weeks in the season when there are no benefits or galas in aid of some worthy cause. These are invariably well patronized and always by the same people. Some are not especially generous in either heart or pocket, but it is socially required to attend such functions, to note who is missing and who is present, how much they give, and then to host a richer and more ostentatious charity ball or benefit at a later time.

Mr and Mrs Peter Van der Vatt, an elegant, wealthy couple in their thirties, had planned for half a year, organizing the details of their gala night for the Senior Citizens' Goodwill Fund. Casa Velentia, their expensive and expansive home, was ideal for such an event. Its neo-colonial arches and verandas looked out serenely over inch-clipped lawns to a swimming pool like a bevelled turquoise and then down the gentle slope to the ocean, a limb of it captured in a stone boat dock where their several boats were tethered. At night amber lights and lanterns oozed from the house, there were diffuse illuminations among the flowered shrubs and burning brands along the ocean shore. All around the elegant Florida palms bowed in the night breeze as though approving every touch and detail.

Two hundred guest were expected, at a hundred dollars a plate, and as they strolled about the grounds an hour before the scheduled start of the event, watching the musicians setting up their music, checking that the chefs were abreast of time, and that the barbecue was glowing, that the glasses were shining, the Van der Vatts experienced only one regret. It was a pity, they agreed, that their own household servants were insufficient to fulfil the needs of so many guests.

It had been necessary to import outside help and some of the temporary staff looked anything but the correct thing in such surroundings. There was, Mrs Van der Vatt noted particularly, one young, tall, fair man – obviously uncomfortable in his waiter's suit, who had already knocked a salver of glassware sideways and now, even as they walked from their measured lawns towards the wide terrace doors of the house, was scraping a trembling pile of vanilla ice cream from the seat of a chair.

He looked up as they approached and had the grace to blush.

'It kinda slipped,' he said apologetically. 'Ice cream does.'

Mrs Van der Vatt winced as he picked up a great gob in his hand and dropped it back into the dish. She rolled her eyes at her distinguished husband but said nothing. Taking his sympathetic arm she went with him into the house.

The sight of the main room reassured them. It was a salon with fine proportions, copied from one of the most famous colonial houses in Virginia, dominated by an exquisite chandelier especially made for the Van der Vatts by Claudio Picci in Florence. Below this, sitting like a stalagmite under a stalactite, was an ornate cake of great girth. It was iced and curled and embossed. At its summit were two miniature old people, the man in a frock coat, the lady in an old-fashioned dress, each supported by a walking stick, the other hands coyly touching. Around the third layer of the cake was inscribed 'Palm Beach Senior Citizens' Goodwill Fund'. It was an impressive work of charity. It was intended to be.

There were some tasteful paintings rivetted to the walls and some good drawings tucked away into modest niches. A portrait of Mr Van der Vatt's father (for it was he, Cornelius Van der Vatt, who had bought Casa Velentia for them as a wedding present ten years before) sat regally above the carved fireplace.

It was in this room, penned in a small minstrels' gallery, that the musicians would play, with an additional Cuban guitarist strumming down by the shore for the enrichment of any romantic moments that the guests might enjoy there. He was also keeping an eye on the boats. At the last party some high spirits had taken one of the more sumptuous craft and rammed the dock wall with it, causing it to sink immediately. The Van der Vatts did not want that sort of expensive unpleasantness again.

'Honey,' said Peter Van der Vatt, 'I want to tell you, I think it's just perfect. I don't see how it could be improved.'

'I think so too,' she said with elegant modesty. Then her voice changed. 'Even so, we're bound to get some bitchy remarks from some people, the Costellos for sure. Have you ever seen a woman take a bite out of anything – but anything – making the face she makes? You'd think the whole goddam world was out to poison her. That look of suspicion.'

'Maybe the world is,' he sniffed. He looked around thoughtfully. 'Baby,' he said, 'these old folks we've invited. They're going to be okay are they? I mean . . . okay?'

'Sure, sure,' she said, understanding at once what he meant. 'I told the welfare authorities that we wanted them clean and civilized – and quiet. We don't want them making a fuss or drinking too much. But at the same time it's no good having them too well turned out. They've got to have just a suspicion of poverty, darling, otherwise, you know what people are, they'll just wonder why they're giving money to people who are okay anyway.'

'And that's no way to get the biggest subscription for any charity in Palm Beach,' he smiled fondly. 'No way at all.'

'It's fixed,' she said confidentially. 'I told them to send half a dozen senior citizens who look a bit sad and just a little threadbare. They know what I mean.'

'Right,' he nodded. 'It's no good having the merchandise looking better than the people who are paying for it.'

They did not consider there was any lack of charity in their observations. To them they were practical, basic economics, the sort of considered thinking that had made both families rich and powerful and the givers of the best benefits in South Florida. Charity was proverbially cold. It was no good being sentimental about it.

When the tame old folks arrived an hour later Teresa Van der Vatt had planned it so that there would be a sufficient number of guests present to give them heartfelt applause as they trooped through the house and onto the lawns, but not so many that the demonstration would put a brake on the more pleasurable events of the evening.

The six dowdy old people had been carefully selected by the welfare office, who were particularly pleased with the pair who had come forward (not many old folks wanted to volunteer) and who seemed to have all the steadfast humility that was required by the occasion. This pair had also been recommended by that nice young lady from St Petersburg who spent so much time helping the elderly of South Miami Beach pass the time of day.

Ari the Greek and K-K-K-Katy were almost bursting with the excitement of their mission. As they walked with the other selected tame old people, two men and two modest women, through the ranks of the guests at Casa Velentia, Katy performed a short stagey shuffle, which brought a patronizing burst of extra applause from the watchers.

'Now wasn't that just cute, Wilbur? Did you see? She did a dear little dance.'

Ari, not to be left out, suddenly broke into his running-and-sparring routine which delighted the audience further. 'Wow, that old guy's fitter than me, Audrey. Just look how he moves. What a mover. Real great!'

A group of the guests waylaid Katy and asked her name, squeals of delight coming from them as she told them what it was with an embroidered version of her celebrated stutter. 'They d-d-didn't call me after the song,' she added to their enchantment. 'They c-c-c-called the song K-K-K-Katy after *me*. I'm that a-a-ancient!'

Just then Ari caught the eye of Loose Bruce the bogus waiter, balancing a difficult tray and trying to send out warning signals about becoming too conspicuous by their antics. Ari got the message and moved closer to Katy. 'Cool it Katy,' he whispered. 'We don't want to get too much attention. We don't want them to remember us after tonight. Not to remember us too well.'

Katy simmered down and walked more sedately. Ari was about to begin shadow boxing again, something he did without thinking, when Bruce's gaze found him once more across the heads of the guests and he dropped his fists and slowed his feet.

A worrying photographer and a bleak lady journalist materialized through the crowd, and the tame old people were halted while photographs were taken of Mr and Mrs Van der Vatt posing smiling with their guests and then with the old people themselves. The columnist agitated her pencil, whirling it around like an épée, jabbing at each of the elderly folk in turn to demand their names.

Then the short procession corralled into the house for photographs with the giant iced cake surmounted by the two miniature figures. There was no doubt about it that this was the centrepiece of Mrs Van der Vatt's dreams of making her evening as spectacular as possible. It was a cake like a castle, four tiers, carved, embossed, finished with great art. It was so tall that its summit was only two feet below the centre crystal of the fine and famous chandelier.

The musicians in their pen began playing their spidery waltz and down by the shore the Cuban guitarist sang calypsos from the West Indies, where he had never been. The lights eased through the flowers and trees, the palms slyly nudged each other: the sound of conversation, polite laughter, touching greetings and touching glasses mingled with the insinuating music. The night was airy and warm. There was a strong possibility of a moon.

Loose Bruce looked at his watch as he attempted to serve drinks without drenching everyone. The movement of turning his wrist emptied a glass of champagne wastefully onto the ground and he grinned with wry embarrassment at the astonished lady who was holding out her hand in readiness to receive it.

Ari and Katy were holding court by the swimming pool. Ari, who told a good tale when given the opportunity, had the men gravefaced and the women reaching for their handkerchiefs as he related some touching but completely fictitious episode of his younger life. Katy, her face suitably subdued, listened too and realistically reached out and held his gnarled hand. The society ladies blinked, the men swallowed visibly.

Three hundred yards away, in a concealed grove, the other members of the Ocean Drive Delinquent Society quietly left two cars. Everyone knew where to go and what to do when they got there. Ossie, Lou the Barbender and Sidewalk wore tuxedos and smiles. Gabby was in a long and rippling evening dress below which she wore a set of overalls. Molly appeared modest and becoming in her gown. Her hood was in her handbag.

Molly, with Sidewalk as her escort, went first, strolling surely through the front gates of Casa Velentia, producing stolen tickets for the perusal of the security guard. 'Gee, honey,' Molly said loudly, unable to resist embroidering the occasion, 'I feel like tonight we're doing something in a real good cause.'

'For folks not as fortunate as ourselves,' echoed Sidewalk. It was a far cry from the old New York hoodlum days.

Gabby, on Ossie's arm, followed two minutes later. Lou strolled alongside them like a large keeper. They produced the tickets and Gabby smiled brilliantly at the gateman. He blushed under his lamps and smiled back. 'It looks like Mrs Van der Vatt's done it again,' mentioned

Gabby to Ossie, squeezing his arm.

'There's nobody throws a benefit like the Van der Vatts,' agreed Ossie.

Gabby turned to Lou. 'Come on Daddy, we're going to miss all the fun.'

Lou's face became crammed with surprise because he was not the most facile of men. Then he grinned and said: 'Okay, daughter, I don't want to miss it neither.' The gateman's pleased smile took in all of them and he waved them on.

Loose Bruce saw them right away. He turned his face to where Ari and Katy were holding court and latched onto Ari's eye. They both nodded.

Gabby eased herself through the crowd. Inside the house there were people sitting on the fine staircase and others moving up and down betwen them. Gabby saw the grand iced cake with its symbolic figures and winced. Ossie took a glass from the tray offered by Bruce. He handed it to Gabby who looked coolly around before sipping it. 'The rooms upstairs are all open,' said Bruce quietly. 'Room "A" as we had it on the plan is the place to change. It has a door directly into room "B" and the door is unlocked, but I still don't know where the safe is.'

It's in room "B". We'll have to find it,' said Ossie quietly over the rim of his champagne. His voice made furrows on the surface.

'Okay Gabby, let's move.'

Lou took a glass from Bruce's tray and emptied it quickly. He caught the younger man's warning look, took another and lifted it more sedately to his large lips. 'Room "A",' muttered Bruce. 'Pass it on to Sidewalk.'

'I got it,' said Lou with more confidence than either he or Bruce felt. 'Everything's going to be fine.' He moved away, to where Sidewalk, his back to the room, was admiring an obtuse drawing. 'Room "A",' he said from the corner of his mouth, standing behind the old New Yorker and looking in the other direction. 'The door's open. In one minute.'

'Okay pal,' said Sidewalk. He was apparently absorbed in the picture. Within himself he felt the warmth of danger, the twist of excitement in his gut that he had been missing all these years. This was true therapy; better than poker any day.

At the side of the grounds Molly stationed herself among the guests, patrolling a path that gave her a view of both the front and rear entrance of Casa Velentia.

She was observing the gate near the beach, ostensibly standing and admiring the profile of the Cuban guitarist against the creamy sky. His proverbial song floated through the trees. She smiled, suddenly pleased to realize the words.

'*Some folks buy and some folks pay.*
Some folks come and steal it away.
Whatever you got, you won't have long.
This is the story of this song.'

She put her hand in her handbag and felt the hood and the shape of the pistol.

It was ten o'clock. The Van der Vatts' exquisite Boule wall clock chimed its exquisite chimes, attracting as many glances as if it had produced a cuckoo. For the members of the Ocean Drive Delinquent Society it was Zero Hour.

Gabby slipped into the small ante-chamber they had designated room 'A' in their plans. There was a cool excitement about her, a sensation trapped burning in her stomach and showing nowhere in her outward calm. At least she too was *doing* something. The room was furnished as a dressing room with two subdued lights and an illuminated mirror. She undid her long dress, forcing herself not to hurry, and folded it carefully before putting it into a plastic bag. She was not going to leave that behind. Now she was wearing the dark overalls that her clever grandmother had made. She turned to the mirror, approved of the fit around her bottom and tidied her hair. The door opened carefully behind her and Ossie came in. He grinned when he saw her at the mirror. Lou and Sidewalk Joe were just behind him. Sidewalk locked the door.

'Nice party,' said Ossie finishing a glass of champagne. He put it unhurriedly on the dressing table. There was no need of conversation. Each took out his hood and put it on. Lou found himself sweating and made two attempts before he could locate his head. Sidewalk took a piece of gum from his mouth and casually parked it on the side of the dressing table before easing on his hood. It is difficult to chew gum under a hood.

Each had a gun. Gabby had the one with the bullet. She had insisted on that and they had not argued. The girl glanced around her through the eye-holes of her hood. Her large eyes filled the spaces. She nodded at Ossie. He had a strange feeling that she had taken command.

Bruce had said the communicating door was open. Now, the others watching, Ossie turned the handle anxiously. It opened soundlessly and they crept like thieves into the gloom of a generous library. Sidewalk and Ossie had the torches. Lou checked the window. Below in the shrubbery he could see the upturned face of Molly. He waved without hurry as though he were on the street. Molly acknowledged the signal then swung the lightly weighted rope and threw it like a sailor. Lou grabbed for it wildly. He was a strong man but with no finesse. He caught it awkwardly and pulled it in, hand over hand. The other end was attached to a nylon handle. Lou secured it clumsily but safely to the pipe of an air conditioning duct. He waved confirmation to Molly who sank into the shrubbery like a lady sinking into a lake. Then Lou turned into the room. They were searching for the safe. Gabby looked towards him and he patted the knot that held the ladder. She lifted her hand in acknowledgement and waved him to help find the safe. It was Lou who saw the bump in the floor below the table.

'I got it I think,' he said close to Ossie's ear. He pointed. Below the table there was a smooth, regular bump under the carpet.

Ossie crouched and went below the table. Sidewalk dropped down too. He ran his hand over the carpet like a man stroking a cat. 'Could be,' he nodded at Ossie.

Lou lifted the heavy table by himself and placed it gently aside. Ossie knelt close to the carpet and felt the swelling again. He glanced sideways and Sidewalk wordlessly handed him a knife. He pushed it into the carpet and made a slit. The gleam of brass came through as he eased the carpet aside. 'Looks like it is,' he whispered tensely, running the knife crossways. He pulled the segmented carpet clear. Beneath it, now revealed, was a round brass plate like a small hill. He glanced up at Lou. The strong man bent and felt the plate. He nodded. Ossie looked towards Sidewalk. He nodded too.

The mound was about the size of a large dinner plate but Lou's outsize hands spanned it without difficulty. He placed his powerful fingers against the metal and pressed before turning the pressure to the right. Nothing happened. He turned the force left and then right again. The plate moved.

The others eased back to give him room. Beneath the hoods they were all set-faced and sweating. Gabby glanced towards the door. The sounds of the party drifted through to them. She looked back at Lou.

The Jewish Barbender was carefully turning the plate and it was obediently rising from its setting. 'It's just the cover,' muttered Sidewalk. 'The safe's underneath. Watch it ain't wired, buddy.'

Lou nodded. He reached up and took Gabby's slim hand. She knelt beside him. He took her fingers and guided them towards the edge of the plate, now raised a quarter of an inch from its fitting. Gabby glanced at him. 'Wires,' he whispered. 'Feel for wires.'

She fingered carefully around the edge of the brass and eventually had made the full circle. 'Nothing,' she said. 'Can't feel any wires.'

Lou nodded and went back to his task. Then someone tried the door and they stiffened as the handle turned and turned again. Gabby unhurriedly drew her gun. The others saw her and stared through the eye holes of their hoods. Ossie's eyes met hers. She lowered the weapon. Someone laughed outside the door and then went away.

They breathed and crouched again. It was very tight and hot under the hoods. Lou lifted his off his face. He was layered with sweat. His big hands went back to the plate. He turned again. Easier now. He turned it twice and felt it disengage from its thread. With extreme caution, like a man de-fusing a mine, he laid the brass disc aside. Beneath it was another brass plate, concave with a large nut of the same metal hugging a bolt. Lou looked quizzically at Sidewalk. Sidewalk scratched his chin through his hood. 'It's another goddam cover,' he said quietly. 'Try it.'

Lou began turning the nut, about the size of a coffee cup. The brass slid beautifully around on its thread. Gabby had a passing thought that it was an elegant safe, if inconvenient. The nut came away easily. Lou had it in his hand.

At that instant they knew they had done something wrong. There was an eerie creaking below them and the floor trembled as if in an earthquake. Alarm jumped to the faces below the masks.

Then, suddenly, convulsively, the projecting bolt from which the nut had been taken shuddered and disappeared before their eyes. There was a terrible crash below and many cries.

In the room beneath them, the great chandelier, made specially by

Claudio Picci in Florence, descended from the ceiling and crashed through the giant ice cake with the little elderly figures on its summit. The miniature candy man shot from the top like a high diver. The thousand crystals and their curved ironwork decimated the cake and thundered into a cascade across the table, scattering delicacies and drinks over every edge.

The people all around reeled back in horror, the men shouting and cursing, the women howling hysterically. Peter Van der Vatt and his wife stood immobilized. K-K-K-Katy, remembering her instruction to have a heart attack at the first sign of any emergency, threw herself backwards with an awe-inspiring cry. Ari caught her and shouted for assistance. Nobody answered.

'That ceiling's coming down next!' shouted the society columnist, filling her pad gleefully. 'Everybody scram!'

There followed a disgracefully mad scramble towards the safety of the open air. Several heavy men actuallly stood on poor prostrate Katy, pushing Ari aside in his efforts to protect her.

Ari got her to her feet. 'B-B-Bastards!' she cried. 'Kick an old lady when she's down!'

'I don't think the heart attack routine is going to work,' suggested Ari in a whisper. 'They've screwed it. We'd better get going.'

Above them the would-be-robbers looked down through the massive hole in the floor like people peering down a well. 'Jesus,' breathed Ossie. 'We've fucked it up. Let's blow.' They blew.

At both gates there was a rush of people to get away from Casa Velentia. Many believed the whole house would explode any second. Others in disorder cried: 'Terrorists! Cuban terrorists!'

At her watching post Molly Mandy witnessed the panic. She knew what had happened. 'They blew it,' muttered Molly to herself. She joined the running crowd.

In five minutes the house and grounds were almost deserted. The police and fire brigade arrived to find Mr and Mrs Van der Vatt standing amid the wreckage of their extravagant cake and their expensive chandelier. Down by the ocean the Cuban calypso singer, who had witnessed much in his life and remained unimpressed, and anyway was paid by the hour, leaned back against an equally imperturbable palm tree and sang:

> *'People they come, people they pay.*
> *There come a big bang – people go away.'*

It seemed to Detective Salvatore that the chief looked like God in a bad mood. Hubert Morriston sat, heavy and hunched, behind the extensive desk at Miami Police Headquarters, his eyebrows brooding, his mouth a tight line, his chin a deep police blue. From hand to knuckled hand he tossed a viciously-honed dagger which had once been an exhibit in one of Florida's most carnal crimes and which he now used as a paper knife.

'I knocked,' apologized Salvatore as he went tentatively into the office. 'I just didn't hear whether you called me in, chief.'

'I heard you, Salvatore,' grunted Morriston. 'I heard you fine. I was just trying to make up my mind whether I wanted to see you this morning or whether maybe I could put off the evil day.'

'I'm sorry, chief, but I don't *plan* the crime in this district, I just try and find who's committed it.'

For a moment the detective thought that his superior was about to throw the knife in an attempt to part his already sparse hair. But the chief grasped it instead, tightly with both hands as if forcing himself not to give in to the temptation. 'I *know* what you do, Albert,' he said with exaggerated patience. 'At least I know what you're *supposed* to do. But for Chrissake, there's crime and there's crime. Okay, a few dead Cubans after a shoot-out is one thing, but this terrible business at the lovely home of Mr and Mrs Peter Van der Vatt is something else, and something else I don't like.'

'Can I sit down, chief?' asked Salvatore. 'I don't feel so good today.'

The chief looked as though he might refuse the request, instead he grunted. 'Take a seat but don't get too comfortable because this is not a comfortable situation. Hooded mobsters in one of the fanciest homes in Florida. And in the middle of a goddam benefit.'

'Chief,' said Salvatore painfully, 'please remember, they didn't get away with anything. Not a dime. There was no larceny.'

Morriston stared at him, an elongated stare, like a shaft, as if he could not believe what he was hearing. 'Detective Salvatore,' he said eventually, 'they brought the whole fucking ceiling down. A chandelier worth fifty thousand dollars and a cake of great sentimental value.' Salvatore thought his chief was going to begin an explosion of shouting and he minutely edged his chair away, but Morriston seemed to find at the very moment of ignition a small reserve of unsuspected inner calm.

'You and me, Salvatore, we're just men. Everyday Joes. We got nice houses and nice kids and nice wives. Okay?'

'I got a nice house,' agreed Salvatore. 'I ain't so keen on the wife and kids.'

'Okay, okay. But what I'm trying to put to you is that we don't have no chandeliers worth fifty thousand dollars and made by some brilliant bastard in Italy. We don't have that kind of ornament in our homes, now do we?'

Salvatore, reassured by the new quiet in his chief, nodded. 'Maybe we we could help to fix it. To piece it together,' he joked. 'It sure seems a lot of dough for a light fitting.'

'Light fitting!' Morriston had used up the inner calm. His face blew up before Salvatore's eyes. 'Light fucking fitting! Jesus Christ, Salvatore, how did you ever get to be a cop? This is fifty thousand bucks worth of broken, beautiful glass. And guess what, Salvatore – the insurers don't want to pay up because it was in the course of a robbery. The Van der Vatts are insured for damage and they're insured for robbery . . .'

'But they're not insured for damage during a robbery,' sighed Salvatore knowingly. 'Which means?'

'Which means we're in big shit. Lots of it.' Morriston quietened as though the realization that they were in it together turned down his anger. 'What do we have to go on? Anything? Anything at all? Speak to me, Salvatore.'

Salvatore backed down from repeating the obvious. He grappled for words.

'Speak to me, Salvatore,' repeated Morriston. It was a mutter, half a threat, half a plea. 'Just tell me *something* I can tell the commissioner because Mr and Mrs Van der Vatt have already told the commissioner what they think and I got to tell him something different. Anything different.'

'Hooded gang,' shrugged Salvatore. 'Same as the bus robbery. Fingerprints on a champagne glass and a wad of parked gum in the room next to the library. We're having them checked but it takes time, chief. And the FBI go fishing on Thursday. You try calling them.'

'How did the guy *get* a glass of champagne?' asked Morriston quickly. 'I mean did he go down to the party in his hood and take a glass of champagne and walk about drinking it like the goddam invisible man?'

Salvatore frowned. 'No, chief. I guess he must have been one of the guests. On the other hand, there's no proof that the glass was anything to do with the robbery. Maybe the gang didn't ever go in that room. Maybe somebody else put it down there while he was having a quick screw. We just don't know.'

'People,' sighed Morriston, 'don't have quick screws at Mrs Van der Vatt's parties. Or even slow screws. They're not that kind of party. Maybe we ought to make a list of things we don't know. There's so many I keep forgetting.'

'We could pull some suspects in,' said Salvatore hopefully. 'You know, the same guys we always pull in. At least it gives you something to tell the commissioner.' He looked at Morriston carefully, then said decisively: 'I'll get them pulled in.'

Morriston began staring again. Salvatore did not enjoy it when he stared. 'Why don't we call Rent-a-Suspect?' Morriston said. 'Ten custom-made suspicious characters at a hundred bucks a time. You ought to consider that, Salvatore. Seriously consider it. You won't solve any crimes, but at least you'll *look* like you're busy.'

'What else can I do, chief? I've got five men on the case. What else?'

'Get your ass off that chair and walk around in circles in your office until you've thought of something! That's what! I'll tell the commissioner to tell the Van der Vatts that you're seriously considering the matter. Boy, that'll satisfy them! They'll go home smiling all over their million dollar faces.'

Salvatore rose, shrugging as he did so. 'I'll try,' he said. 'I'll really try, chief.' He made for the door. 'This job is okay when you've just got the Mafia and the Cubans to deal with. At least with them you know where to look.'

'I think maybe you ought to apply to join the Mafia, Salvatore,' said Morriston. 'You'll be safer there. I'll get you an application form.'

Salvatore habitually opened one eye and then the other as though he expected each day to attack him as soon as he awoke. This day was Sunday, he told himself as soon as he had examined the horizon revealed by the first eye. That was good because he was, unless the circumstances were exceptional, relieved of the hassle of the office. But it was also bad because it meant he could anticipate the hassle from his family. Sometimes it was easier to handle the office hassle because, at least up to a certain level, there he was boss. At home he was the last of a long line.

His normally morose spirits took a dive to an even lower level when he remembered that all the neighbours he did not like were coming to his house for a lunchtime barbecue. He hated the people and he hated barbecues because he was the one who had to do the cooking and the dry fumes of the charcoal always got into his head. His only consolation was in imagining that the grilling meat he turned on the spits was the bodies of those guests who surrounded him with their hideous Sunday neighbourliness.

'Albert!' Betty's voice came wearily up the stairs to him. He pretended to be still asleep. If he did that she sometimes went away. This time she didn't.

'Albert!' she called again flatly. 'The children say there's a dead man on the lawn.'

'Tell him to go away,' Salvatore called back. She must know their children were congenital liars.

'He's dead, I tell you. How can I tell him to go away if he's dead?'

'Problems, problems,' grumbled Salvatore. 'Why can't anybody solve their problems without consulting me.'

'You're supposed to be a cop,' she shouted back.

'It's Sunday, for God's sake,' he said. He rolled reluctantly from the bed. He did not believe there was a dead man on his lawn, so he took a cautious look at himself in the mirror.

He never looked any better. Even he had to admit that. His hair was fleeing altogether, his eyes were holding up sullen bags. Daringly he poked out his tongue. 'Oh God,' he said. 'A dead man.'

To see the lawn it was necessary to go into the next room. He did not hurry. He put on his robe and stretched his arms before grumblingly going out into the passage and into the room of his son. He looked from the window and saw them standing almost religiously around the stretched out body of a large, living, fat man.

'Zaharran!' he bellowed angrily. 'Get off my lawn! Get out of here you bum!'

'He's dead,' called the eldest son, Franco. 'How can he answer?'

'He's not dead,' Salvatore howled back. 'You quarter-wit!'

Betty called up the stairs. 'Albert, go and see. We've got people coming, remember. If there's a body on the lawn, get rid of it. Somebody's done it to get revenge on you, I expect.'

Dispiritedly he went to the head of the stairs. 'People get revenge on me all the time,' he pointed out loudly. 'Revenge is all I get from people. But that man ain't dead, Betty. That man ain't capable of doing a decent living thing like dying. He has come here to bother me, to attract attention to himself.'

'To get revenge?' she suggested from the bottom of the stairs.

'Revenge. Sure revenge. That's what he wants also. Everybody wants it.'

'Well go and see what it's all about,' she sighed. 'It's too much for me all this. If he is dead then get him moved. Then get the barbecue going. You can find out who killed him tomorrow.'

'Okay, okay, okay,' he recited the words as he descended the stairs. He wrapped the robe tighter around him, although the morning was growing hot. His scowl increased as he strode down the lawn.

His four children for once acknowledged his superior presence and backed away. Zaharran was lying like a dumped pile of sand. His battered face was as composed as it would ever be, his hands were clasped religiously across his great stomach.

'He's dead as dead,' said Francesca, the youngest girl. 'I'm going to get him some flowers.'

'He's not dead!' The children jumped as their father shouted.

Betty was leaning out of the kitchen window. 'Is he dead?' she called in the same voice she used to ask if the Sunday newspapers had arrived. 'Or isn't he?'

'He's not dead!' cried Salvatore again, turning round and directing the verdict to her. He pushed his slippered foot forward and touched Zaharran. 'In the first place,' he said in his detective's voice, 'note how the hands are clasped across his gut.'

'That's how dead people are,' said Clara, the second daughter. 'I've seen it in hospital films on TV.'

'Idiot,' Salvatore told her. She poked out her tongue at him. 'They put the hands across the body *after* death. Nobody *dies* in that position.'

The children, who hated disappointments, wanted the man to be dead. Franco said: 'Maybe somebody killed him and then put his hands across there, like as a mark of respect.'

'How do you kill somebody then respect them?' asked Salvatore. He was now enjoying his superiority. 'Idiot. Anyway, you may like to notice that the dead body is breathing. See, it's rising up and down. That's called breathing.'

'Death convulsions,' said Clara. 'There's things called death convulsions. I know. It's on TV.'

'Zaharran,' said Salvatore to the body. 'Get up. You're frightening the children.'

'No he's not,' protested little Francesca. 'Can we bury him? I want to bury him.'

'Zaharran,' repeated Salvatore, 'get up or I get the garden hose on you.'

The heavily folded eyes reluctantly opened like those of a tortoise. The children gasped and backed away before coming forward again to view the miracle. A fissure appeared in the prostrate man's face. It was his smile. 'Captain Salvatore?' he breathed. 'What . . . what am I doing here?'

'Playing dead,' answered Salvatore. 'And if you don't beat it, and quick, you won't just be *playing* dead.'

'But I collapsed,' pleaded Zaharran, his eyes widening with what he faintly hoped might look like innocence. 'Collapsed, blacked out. And I wake up right here in your yard. What a coincidence.'

'It's my *lawn*,' Salvatore pointed out. 'These houses don't have yards, they have lawns. The grass you are bruising with your body, Zaharran, is my lawn.'

'Could . . . could I ask for a drink?' inquired the big man pitifully.

'I'll get you one,' said Clara eagerly. She moved towards the house.

'Water,' her father called after her. 'Just water.'

'With maybe a little Scotch,' Zaharran called too.

'I will. I will,' the girl called back.

Salvatore continued to glower down at the human hulk. 'We got people coming for a barbecue,' he said. 'We're going to be using the lawn.'

'Okay, okay,' acknowledged Zaharran. He put up a hand as big as a sail. The children stared at it. 'I maybe wondered if you needed a few leads on the masked gang, that's all.'

'Zaharran . . . George,' said Salvatore moving urgently forward. His children stared at the change in his attitude. Their father knelt by the prostrate man and helped him into a sitting position. 'Scotch!' he bellowed over his shoulder. 'Plenty of Scotch. Not too much water.'

He almost fell on his knees beside Zaharran. 'You've got something?' he pressed. 'You know something? I don't have to warn you about withholding evidence, do I? George? What have you found out?'

'Nothing,' said Zaharran simply. 'Not a thing.'

'Jesus Harry Christ!' bawled Salvatore. 'What's all this about then?'

'I got some ideas, that's all.'

'Ideas? Is that all?'

'That's what I said. Ideas. But they're good ideas. I just want to know if you'll retain me on the case. So I can follow them up.'

Clara appeared with the Scotch and water. 'Take that Scotch back,' shouted her father. 'Get back with it.'

'But you . . . but you . . .' pleaded the girl.

'I don't care. Take it back.' He leaned threateningly over Zaharran. 'Don't bother me any more, Zaharran,' he said. 'Or I have you arrested. Vagrancy. I could get you for vagrancy. I know I could.'

Zaharran considered it, then shook his bison head. 'No way,' he said. 'I have a home.'

'Wandering abroad then. Or trespass. Yes, I could get you for trespass.' He glared at the big man. 'Anyway, why am I discussing this with you? Get your ass off my grass and beat it.'

Zaharran rose slowly. The children backed away and looked at him respectfully, something they had never afforded their father. The older man began to shuffle towards the gate. 'There's a reward?' he said.

'Reward? For God's sake, you know there's a reward. You read the newspapers.'

'I'll work for that,' said Zaharran as if making the decision right there. 'I'll operate on my own.'

'Do that,' growled Salvatore. 'But keep out of my hair.'

Zaharran stared at the policeman's famished hair but said nothing. He lounged towards the gate. Francesca hurried forward and opened it for him. He raised his unkempt hat. She smiled. 'I sure wish you were my daddy,' she said.

The members of the Ocean Drive Delinquent Society, hung with gloom and disappointment, sat beneath the Tree of Knowledge in Flamingo Park, South Miami Beach. It was a day of fresh wind which seemed to spring on impulse from the ocean, thrilling the gulls and cormorants and the planing pelicans, but keeping most of the human denizens of the district away from the shore. The old gang with Ossie and Bruce sat in the way of a class receiving instruction, with Gabby facing them. Indeed there were often to be seen small groups like this sitting in small semi-moons along the lawns of Ocean Drive, studying Hebrew history and destiny, Mexican embroidery, book binding, philately, the art of the jazz drummer and such subjects, so the meeting beneath the tree attracted little attention.

'Anybody can make a mistake,' pleaded Lou the Barbender, the shame of the crashing chandelier still pressing his strong shoulders. 'I didn't know it wasn't a safe. I'm just strong, not brainy.'

Gabby shrugged. 'There's no blame. It was a joint responsibility,' she said. 'If anything, the fault lies with the leadership. We just made a mess of it.'

'The chandelier made a mess of the cake,' reminisced Ari. 'I saw it. It's a sight you don't generally see, a chandelier go crash through a cake. Not something you can experience every day. Very rare . . .'

They were not inclined to let him finish. 'Okay, okay,' said Ossie firmly. 'The post mortem's over. We screwed it up.'

'More like unscrewed it,' said Bruce making a turning motion with his hand. Nobody even smiled. He shrugged and returned to disappointed silence.

'Now we come to the crunch question,' continued Ossie as though no one had spoken. 'Do we quit or do we have another try? On the law of averages we've just got to get something right soon. On the other hand we've taken a lot of risks for not much return. I think we need a vote on it.' As he put the proposition to them a cop left a police car along Ocean Drive and walked idly to take a look at the rough seascape. He was screened from the group by the foliage of the Tree of Knowledge and nobody saw him until a moment after Ossie had put the question. 'Do we try another crime or do we declare this society closed?'

'Try another crime,' they all answered loudly, not one of them feeling that it was sufficient merely to raise a hand. Elderly persons, like children, like to assert themselves vocally. The words 'Try another crime' came out strongly just as the strolling policeman rounded the tree. He could hardly have failed to have heard it. Gabby paled as she looked across the heads of the gang and saw the blue uniform appear. Ossie was swift.

'Okay,' he said with extra loudness. 'We'll try another time.'

The cop smiled a fatherly smile when he saw the small class. He was a well-nourished policeman, amiable and ambling, with a smile dropping easily into well-used creases on his warm face. 'What's the lesson today, teacher?' he said to Gabby, approving in his look that one so young was aiding the old.

'Aspects of presidential responsibility,' Gabby replied at once. 'The class are trying to learn some of the Articles of the Constitution.'

'That's interesting,' said the cop, expanding his face into an even bigger smile. 'What they going to do with it when they know?' He did not wait or require an answer. 'Maybe,' he suggested, 'I could come by with my buddy one day and give you a lecture on police work. I been a cop twenty years. Seen things you'd never believe.'

'Oh, we'd like that, wouldn't we now class?' enthused Gabby.

'Oh sure, great.' 'Yes please, sir.' 'Oh boy, I can't wait,' echoed the gang, all nodding and returning the policeman's smile. 'Can we see how your gun works?' asked Molly, always the one to ask the additional question. 'I'd like to see that.'

'I promise,' said the decent cop. 'I won't promise to shoot anybody but I promise to show you. Maybe next week. I'm on this patrol next week as well.'

'Tuesday,' said Ossie decisively. He wanted to get rid of the man.

'Right, Tuesday then,' beamed the officer. 'Same time, same place. Gee, I'll enjoy that too. Look after yourselves.'

He waved and sauntered on towards the crashing green ocean. The gang remained silent, watching him go. He suddenly turned and saw their expressions. 'Just carry on,' he called back. 'Don't let me disturb the lesson. I'm just a cop.'

'Everybody wave,' ordered Ossie quietly. The gang all waved towards the friendly cop and he waved back before continuing his walk to the beach.

CHAPTER SEVEN

Gabbie and Ossie were walking by the sea at night. The wind and the day had gone, drifting in close company across the flat land towards the Gulf of Mexico, leaving the Miami night in its customary condition, warm and blue, with the firm promise of a later moon.

The girl and the man walked a yard apart over the sand. Neither was wearing shoes. They had hardly spoken for five minutes. They progressed thoughtfully as if each were alone.

'Listen,' he said eventually but without looking towards her. 'If you want to quit and go back to St Pete's I'm certain everyone will understand. I would.'

'You trying to ditch me?' She stared down as if she had lost something in the shingle.

'No, not at all, Gabby. It's just been such a bomb.'

'We'll think of something. Next time it will work. I know it.'

He glanced at her and the beginnings of a grin touched his face. She continued walking, ploughing her feet into the sand, her face and her breasts pushed forward like an intrepid explorer in an unknown place. She did not return his look. They were walking towards an horizon of waiting stars. Across the sky, among the stars, a plane moved like a small spark.

'Do you think I'm beautiful?' Gabby suddenly asked. She still did not look at him and they continued their walking.

'Yes,' he said simply. 'Excessively.'

'I think you're beautiful too,' she said. 'I go for men with untidy grey hair.'

'Maybe when we do a successful robbery I'll get it cut,' he said.

They returned to their silent journey. For several minutes neither acknowledged that the other was even there. It was Gabby who spoke again. 'Where are we headed?' she asked, looking behind her and suddenly realizing how far they had travelled along the beach. The sand faded far behind them and the white stripes of the sea showed clearly for a great distance.

'Don't ask me,' he said. 'We just started walking.'

They stopped, Ossie turning back and looking into the distance. The lights of Miami Beach were heavily along the shore. She extended her hand to him. He had been waiting for it. Their faces turned and their eyes met frankly for the first time.

'The boy's not going to like this,' said Ossie. 'Bruce is crazy about you.'

'I was never very enthusiastic about youth,' Gabby replied. 'Not even my own. I can't wait to be thirty. But maybe we won't tell him. Okay?'

'Okay,' he agreed. 'We won't tell.' For a moment neither seemed to know what was expected of them next. There was no awkwardness about it; they simply stood there, facing each other, a gap still between his rough blue shirt and her breasts, their hands still held. He grinned. 'What happens now?' he said.

'You're not so old you can't remember,' she said. 'How old are you anyway?'

'Going on,' he said. 'Beyond that I'm not prepared to comment.'

'You're beautiful,' she repeated softly. 'I don't know why I didn't see it before.'

'You've been too busy being a gang leader,' he smiled. He had been a tired man for a long time. Suddenly he felt a freshness come from her and pass into him.

She said: 'I love your tired face. I love the weary blue eyes and the lines on your forehead and the . . .'

'Maybe I can get a word in,' he said. 'You are the most stunning girl in

America, well in Florida . . . okay, let's settle for Ocean Drive.'

'Thanks. Do you feel like kissing me?'

'I'd forgotten,' he said. 'I thought that was old fashioned.'

They leaned towards each other curiously, like experimenting children, and they kissed without fuss. Then he moved a pace across the sand and put his hard arms quietly about her waist and eased her body to him. The breasts pushed softly against his shirt, as though begging attention. Gabby's arms travelled up around his dark neck and she pressed her face to his. He felt himself stir in his gut and his groin. It had been a long time.

'You look older than you are,' she whispered against the rough sides of his hair.

'I got old suddenly,' he said. 'Overnight.'

'When you were a soldier?'

'Yes. That makes you old.'

'Are you going to kiss me properly.'

'I was going to but we got talking.'

'Do it now.'

'Sure, I'll try and remember how it goes.'

He kissed her fully as she had asked. She began tugging at him, pulling him to the sand. He eased her down gently. Where they lay there was the bole of a felled palm tree. She was exploring his face, touching her fingers over its contours. 'I love your skin,' she said.

'Try not to poke my eye out,' he said gently. They were almost lying against the trunk of the fallen palm. 'This could be a giant's leg,' he suggested, touching it with his arm. 'He's been washed up from the ocean and he's stretched out here but nobody notices him because he's too big.'

'Like Gulliver,' she said. 'Do you like telling stories?'

'Well it's been a secret ambition of mine, you know, a story-teller. I'd be great in one of those Eastern market places. But up to now I haven't had much scope. You've got to have someone to tell the stories *to*. It's no good telling yourself because you've always heard the goddam things.'

Gabby stretched herself along his whole body. His shirt was only fastened with one button. It came away as she tried to undo it. 'The shirt's going rotten,' he said. 'It's the air down here.'

'I'll buy a new one,' she promised. 'A button I mean.'

She lay her young cheek against his rough chest and he felt her plentiful hair cascading around his neck and across his shoulder. 'Once upon a time,' he began, 'there was a giant who carelessly lost a leg on Miami Beach. And along came two people and found that leg . . .'

Gabby began to ease his trousers from his hips.

'What's this, they thought when they saw the leg.' His voice was controlled with difficulty because she was rubbing his stomach with her fingers and then she began to slide them down. They felt slim and luxurious on the enclosed parts of his body, but he continued with his story, closing his eyes. 'When they realized it was a giant's leg, they right away set out to find a giant with only one leg, left leg . . . leg left . . .'

Now she had stripped him. He could feel the sand against his back and his buttocks. He still remained with his eyes closed. He could feel her taking off her clothes. She kneeled up, away from him, but now sitting astride his loins. His hands searched and went at once to her naked breasts. The touch went like a shock through him. The first finger and thumb of each hand carefully squeezed the nipples. He opened his eyes and saw what she was like. 'Jesus Christ,' he breathed. 'What a beautiful sight.'

His hands stroked her shoulders, went below her armpits and ran down her hip bones. They made a hollow on each side and he rested his hands there. 'What happened next?' she asked. 'In the story?'

'Sorry, I got distracted,' he said. His eyes were held on hers now. Her hands were laid flat against his chest. 'You're sitting on my penis,' he mentioned.

'I wondered what it was,' she said throatily. She slowly descended across his body and lay on top of him, their toes meeting, their knees side by side, their thighs against each other. She put her hand down to him and brought him into her. In no time the tiredness had gone from his face. He was smiling and so was she. They lay together for some minutes, the sea and the traffic on Ocean Drive sounded.

'I ran away from St Pete's because of an older guy,' she said thoughtfully.

'You said,' he said. 'You mentioned it.'

'Sure. He was married and a big executive and that stuff. He still says he's quitting everything and coming down here to get me. He sends me letters.'

'That's thoughtful. If he gets down here will you go?'

'I don't know,' she shrugged. 'I guess I will.'

'Oh. We're keeping this from Bruce, okay?'

'Yes, we'll keep it a secret. It's more fun like that.'

They fell more silent than the immediate night. Then he said, 'What are we going to do with the old folks – the gang?'

She smiled in the dimness. 'Kidnapping,' she said slowly. 'I've a feeling maybe we should try kidnapping.'

Miami Beach's Hotel De Luxe Mon Desir sits with ponderous magnificence on a narrow neck of sand and land between the ocean and the narrow waters of the Intra-Coastal Waterway. From its fine and enormous main swimming pool a jetty runs over the sun-deck and extends for a hundred feet into the sunny Atlantic.

At ten o'clock in the morning Gabby with Ossie and Bruce on either flank lounged on sun-beds beside the pool, along with a scattering of other early sunbathers, and casually watched the double glass doors issuing from the hotel. At five minutes past ten they opened and through them came an elderly man in a wheeled chair but wearing a bathing costume. He was propelled by a tall, claylike figure in the uniform of a chauffeur. The pair were Mr Cyril M. Hoffner, a millionaire from the Mid-West, and Landers his personal servant and bodyguard.

The trio watched carefully as Landers pushed his employer towards the sun-deck and then ran the wheeled carriage up a wooden ramp and onto the jetty. At a strong but measured stride the servant pushed the old man towards the open ocean. Bruce raised himself on his elbow. The others eased themselves up so they could see also.

At the end of the jetty Landers halted and then, after the briefest pause, he tightened his grasp on the vehicle, lifted, and emptied the old man into the sea.

Gabby, Bruce and Ossie observed this with amazement. A woman reeking of coconut oil sun lotion, who had watched the same performance, saw their consternation and laughed. 'He does that every day,' she said. 'I thought he was trying to drown the old guy too. But he's just going for his swim. He's some character.'

'Certainly seems to be,' acknowledged Gabby. The woman leaned back on her sun-bed and began to anoint herself with a further libation of oil. She pulled her large sunglasses over her face. The trio watched the ocean and saw Cyril M. Hoffner swimming through the easy waves to a point on the sun-deck where Landers had taken the chair. The big servant knelt and eased the old man from the water with no trouble. He wrapped him in a bath robe and sedately turned and wheeled him back towards the hotel.

The Sweetheart Bar in the Hotel De Luxe Mon Desir is casually lit, the bartenders are discreet and watchful; it is a place of illicit couplings of various sorts and where they mix a famous Vodka Collins. The bar is in the shape of a heart.

The Hotel De Luxe Mon Desir itself is one of the largest and most ornate on Miami Beach with fifteen hundred bedrooms, shops, hair and beauty salons, three swimming pools, a life-saver, a golf professional, a gourmet restaurant, and a dwindling clientele. It was built in the late nineteen forties when Miami suddenly burgeoned after the war. It sought to remain obtrusively select by refusing to display its name.

It was the vacation haunt of the very wealthy who felt at home among its golden chandeliers, heavily draped curtains and pseudo-Louis furniture. Many came down from the wintry north in their private cruisers, voyaging from New York City, or even further north, in ease along the Intra-Coastal Waterway, travelling into the gradual sunshine, waiting politely for the many cantilever bridges to be opened to allow them to pass, and eventually tying up only a hundred yards from the main door of the Hotel De Luxe Mon Desir. For many of the visitors the most hazardous and uncomfortable part of the entire journey was traversing the six lanes of the highway that divides the hotel from the waterway. Special staff were on duty to escort the elderly or the nervous to the door of the hotel.

Cyril M. Hoffner was an annual migratory visitor. He was the man whose youthful brainchild had been the Hoffner Widespread Manure Distributor, a device which had given many of America's farmers cause for gratitude and had, of course, made Mr Hoffner one of the richest men in the Mid-West. Every year he would travel in January to New York to visit his sixth wife and then board his fine cruiser *Marilyn Monroe VII* (Mr Hoffner tended to get through a lot of cruisers and lots of wives) for his pilgrimage to Miami Beach and the De Luxe Mon Desir. Although Mr Hoffner had taken to travelling about in a wheeled chair, there was nothing crippling him, but he was seventy-three and had become obsessively lazy.

Ossie, Gabby and Bruce stood at the Sweetheart Bar and observed Mr Cyril M. Hoffner as Landers propelled him across the great ornate lobby of the hotel in the early evening. He was on his way for his daily perusal of the Dow Jones tape. It had not given him cause for anxiety for years but he liked to think he was still in contact with the market. He was a man of sullen temper on occasion, although in his off-guard moments he had been heard to sing to himself snatches of traditional western songs. His words to the propelling Landers usually came singly. 'Forward.' 'Stop.' 'Back,' as if the servant was a human gear box, and Landers never spoke at all unless it could not be avoided. Bruce observed the massive, brooding man, six foot three from his boots to his scowl, with shoulders spread wide like the wings of a Boeing.

'Who's going to look after the ape?' asked Bruce quietly as they sat at the Sweetheart Bar.

'I thought maybe you could handle him,' smiled Ossie. 'Tough kid like you.'

'I never went to war,' said Bruce. 'You did.'

'He'll be easier to handle than a war,' replied Ossie.

'It'll be over quicker too,' said Gabby enigmatically.

Hoffner and Landers had gone from their view into the Dow Jones corner. They knew he would be back in less than two minutes. On cue the invalid chair with the great pushing servant reappeared around one of the hotel's famous bogus classical columns.

'Shit,' muttered Loose Bruce hiding behind his glass. 'That guy gets bigger with every step. Maybe Ari the Greek can handle him. At least Ari can run.'

'Once we've got the boss, the rest will be no trouble,' said Gabby quietly. The two bartenders were down at the pointed end of the bar, out of hearing. 'We just need the hostage,' she continued. 'That's what hi-jacking is all about. Power through persuasion.'

'There's three crew on the boat,' said Ossie. 'Brothers.'

'It gets better,' grumbled Bruce. 'All the time it gets better.' Gabby and Ossie continued drinking and watching Mr Hoffner being trundled across the lobby.

'The beauty of it is,' whispered Gabby, 'we won't need to hustle him or carry him to his boat. We can just wheel him there.'

'It will need to be about this time of the evening,' said Ossie looking at his watch. 'Seven. When he's going to look at the stock market report. We can count on him doing that. And there'll be just enough daylight to get the boat away from the dock, down the waterway and out into the sea before it's dark.'

Bruce looked apprehensive. 'Can you handle a boat like that, Ossie?'

he asked. 'I couldn't. Anyway I get to feeling sick.'

'I thought you might,' mentioned Gabby.

'The crew will handle the boat,' said Ossie. 'We just press them.'

The map showed the eastern tail of the Florida coastline, curling down from Boca Raton to Palm Beach and finally into the long dotted tail of islands terminating at the humid old city of Key West. Ossie was taking the briefing. The members of the Ocean Drive Delinquent Society sat attentively. Molly Mandy leaned forward and pointed to Boca Raton. 'My sister-in-law lives at Boca,' she announced, smiling around as if it were an attainment.

'And it's real nice there at Boca,' said Katy. 'M-M-My cousin gets there every season.'

'No,' put in Ossie firmly. 'No, ladies, Molly's sister-in-law has *not* met Katy's cousin. Can we take that as understood? Please ladies, we're trying to plan a hi-jacking, not play happy families.'

'Sorry,' muttered Katy. 'We just like a little social chit-chat.'

'Where would we be without it?' agreed Molly.

'Later, later,' said Ossie.

'Yes, please ladies, cut it out,' said Gabby.

'You didn't know your great aunt at Boca,' said Molly, determined to get the final throw.

'No, okay. You must tell me some other year, grandma. Right. Ossie, get back to it before they start again.'

'On Wednesday, 16 February, at 7.05 pm we will abduct Mr Cyril M. Hoffner, one of America's wealthiest men, from the lobby of the Hotel De Luxe Mon Desir, Miami Beach. Mr Hoffner spends most of his time in a wheeled chair pushed by a man called Landers who looks as though he might be a buddy of Tarzan. However, we will eliminate Mr Landers. I'll give you details later. Mr Hoffner will be persuaded at gunpoint to keep quiet until he is taken across the street, still in the wheeled chair of course, to his cruiser, *Marilyn Monroe VII*, which is moored directly across from the hotel. Right?'

'Right,' they all echoed. Their faces were beginning to shine.

'Steps will have been taken to make sure the boat is ready for sea as soon as we get the old guy aboard. We will get away as soon as possible, within two or three minutes. Landers, incidentally, will be taking the trip with us, so there's no reason for anybody at the De Luxe Mon Desir to suspect anything's wrong.'

'How does the old guy travel?' asked Sidewalk. He drew on a thin cheroot. 'Does he stay in his chair?'

'Good question,' nodded Ossie. 'He has a special ramp so the carriage can be wheeled onto the deck of the boat, and the saloon and his cabin have been designed so that he can run the chair right through. There is also a special kind of rack on the deck and another on the roof of the cabin. The wheels of the carriage can be locked into either of these so that on a fine day he can sit out in the sun.'

'Why is the p-p-poor man in this chair?' asked Katy, her habitual kindness surfacing. 'We won't do him any harm, will we? Carrying him off like this?'

'Our imformation,' put in Gabby, 'is that there's nothing at all wrong with him. He's elderly but he's strong.'

'He's just a lazy old bum,' put in Bruce. The others looked sharply at him and he bit his lip. 'I mean . . . devil,' he said. The elderly folk nodded, acknowledging the apology, and returned their attention to Ossie and the map.

'Look,' he said. 'We'll take any further questions later. Just now I want to go on to what happens once we get the cruiser to sea. Using Mr Cyril Mr Hoffner as our hostage we will see to it that the crew head south, then south-west, down along the Florida Keys to this point here.' He indicated an inlet on the map. 'That's Dove Key, a small island at present unoccupied, although there are a couple of vacation houses on it. It has a good dock, and we can get the boat in there easily. It should be safe there for maybe twenty-four hours before the coastguard or anyone else takes an interest. By that time we – and Mr Hoffner – will be safely back in South Miami Beach.'

'Back here?' asked Ari speaking for them all. 'Jeez, what's the use of sailing all the way down *there*, just to come back *here*?'

'Exactly, that's the idea, Ari. Katy and Lou will take two cars down to the Keys and they will wait for us on the Intra-Ocean Highway at Marathon, just along the coast here from Dove Key. Marathon is one of the few places along the coast where it is possible to hide an automobile. The rest of the highway is too narrow – just a road going from island to island with no turnings. But Marathon is a fatter kind of place. We can have the cars waiting there without making people suspicious. The road itself passes directly through Dove Key so that won't be any problem. We get Cyril M. from the cruiser, immobilize the crew and our pal Landers, then we drive back to Miami. When the coastguard, or whoever it is, finds the boat it will be concluded that we've gone somewhere further down the Keys, probably to Key West, and that that's where we've got him hidden away. But we will be right back here where we started, with Mr Hoffner a guest right in this hotel.'

'He's not coming in my room,' said Molly Mandy immediately and firmly. 'There's no man spending the night in my room. My late Melford wouldn't like that at all.' She paused. 'No man of seventy-three anyway.'

'He's going to stay in Bruce's room,' smiled Ossie. He watched Bruce's eyebrows shooting up.

'Shit and corruption, why me?' protested the young man. 'There's no goddam room in there as it is! God, I have to go outside to scratch.' He looked pleadingly at Ossie and Gabby. 'There's just no room for a wheeled chair,' he mumbled. 'Honest.'

'Okay, we'll take a rain check on that,' agreed Ossie. 'Maybe he could go in the bathroom at Katy's.' He smiled at Katy.

'I would do my best,' said the old chorus girl. 'I s-s-surely would. But it w-w-would be pretty difficult when I wanted to use the bathroom.'

'I don't agree with it,' said Lou solidly. He glowered at Ossie and flexed his fingers.

Gabby said firmly: 'Here we are, right on schedule again. Getting nowhere. For the present never mind where we'll keep him. Let's plan how we're going to *get* him.'

Her grandmother raised a frail, compelling hand. 'I would like to ask one, little-bitty question, dear,' she said gently. 'How much are we going to ask for him, this rich Mr Cyril Mr Hoffner? I don't think we ought to be too greedy.'

'A million dollars,' said Ossie as convincingly as he could.

'But we'll settle for a hundred bucks and trading stamps,' grumbled Sidewalk. 'If things go like they always do.'

'Okay, okay,' conceded Gabby. 'So it hasn't worked out so far. But this time it will. I just know it.' She paused and regarded them carefully. 'We want a million dollars,' she said.

At seven in the evening it was what they called the Happy Hour in the Sweetheart Bar. A bulging black man loomed over the piano, producing some mellifluous sounds both from the keyboard and from his throat, the latter an amazingly high pitch coming from such a deep source.

The place was redolent with widows. They sat around, in their vivid, unsuitable gowns; pastel predators, their hair and faces of many hues, eyeing each other and any male who entered the bar whether escorting a lady or not. Bruce had been sitting for half an hour alone, observing the movements around in the hotel, and had already been on the end of many widow's winks, knowing nudges, and the blunt offer of a free vacation in Honolulu if he cared to take it in the company of a lady with ice blue hair, several years older than his mother.

Gabby and Ossie appeared immediately on seven. 'We've secured the boat,' said Ossie quietly to Bruce. 'It'll be ready to sail in ten minutes from now.'

'Now we've got to get the man,' said Bruce. 'The quicker the better. These old women are monsters, man.'

At seven-five precisely Cyril M. Hoffner, wheeled by the mountainous Landers, appeared on the main concourse of the De Luxe Mon Desir's lobby. The hoary millionaire wore his customary sour expression, enhanced by the extreme lighting of the surroundings. He looked grey and belligerent as the blunt-faced servant pushed him towards the Dow Jones Averages.

Bruce left the bar with a tentative farewell wave to the clutch of widows. 'A whole *month* in Honolulu!' the one who had made the promise called shamelessly after him. 'All for free.' He shuddered when he thought of the cost. He began to walk towards the door. The pale-blue haired lady lapsed into a sulk and barked at the barman for another rye and dry.

Bruce's eyes followed the slow progress of Mr Hoffner over the large concourse of the lobby. The place was placid, the clerks at their reception desk around the corner, the shops now closed, the guests changing for dinner. Bruce saw Ossie and Gabby leave their bar stools and stroll towards the corner where the tape machine clacked out its fortunes. He eyed the small side door to the garden. He moved closer behind Landers.

Gabby made her move then. She approached seductively and confronted Cyril M. Hoffner with a smile and a gun.

'Please Mr Hoffner,' she said, 'make no sound. I don't want to have to use this.'

To her consternation an enormous grin slashed across his face. 'God, oh God,' he breathed delightedly. 'Don't tell me I'm being hi-jacked.'

'You are,' said Ossie from behind, his Russian pistol pushed into the massive ribs of Landers. The expression on the great face scarcely changed. 'Please don't cause any trouble.'

'Goddam it,' said Mr Hoffner, enormously pleased, 'I don't fucking well intend to. It's not every day a guy gets hi-jacked in his wheeled chair. Shit almighty – I'll be all over the papers.'

Bruce on the other side of Landers felt a chill sensation enter his stomach. Why didn't things ever work out right?

The crew of the *Marilyn Monroe VII* consisted of three brothers known to their friends as Ding, Dong, and Belle. When their employer was wheeled onto the deck via the special ramp, they were lined up against the wall of the saloon, rigid with enjoyable horror, covered by guns held in the hands of hooded figures.

'We resisted, Mr Hoffner, we *resisted*,' Ding called out as Ossie manoeuvered the old man's chair aboard. They had crossed the six lane highway without trouble, two younger people kindly pushing an old invalid across the road, with Landers like an out-size doctor in attendance. There had been no difficulty, in fact Cyril M. Hoffner had chortled enthusiastically all the way from the hotel. Ossie was glad when they reached the deck.

'Resisted?' echoed Mr Hoffner glaring at Ding. 'If you did, son, it's the first goddam time ever.'

Dong, who was the tallest and darkest of the three brothers, eyed Ossie speculatively. 'I ought to warn you that this is piracy,' he whispered primly. 'For this you can be put in irons.'

'Gee, can you?' said his brother Belle, his eyes shining. 'Gee, you don't say.'

'Is this vessel ready for sea?' asked Gabby glancing at the hooded figures of Sidewalk, Ari the Greek and Molly.

'We've wound the clockwork up,' volunteered Ding. 'Why have these guys got masks on and you don't?'

'They're real ugly,' said Ossie. 'We thought they might scare you. Now let's get this show on the road. Start the engine. Come on, get going.'

'Sure, get going,' said Mr Hoffner enthusiastically. 'Otherwise we'll be caught.'

Bruce took the chair and propelled it deeper into the saloon, the wheels running between the special guide rails. He bent and pushed over two steel clips which held the rims and kept the chair stable. 'What are you going to do with me?' inquired the hostage with beaming interest. 'Throw me to the sharks?'

'It depends,' said Bruce ominously. Mr Hoffner grinned.

The engine of the boat growled and then roared like a dog disturbed in the night. They all felt the vessel vibrate. 'We're asking a million bucks for you,' said Bruce, he hoped coolly. He went to the cabin hatch and stood watching the traffic curling along Collins Avenue.

The vessel eased from the mooring, Ding calling playfully: 'Cast off for'ard,' and 'Cast off behind.'

Cyril M. Hoffner laughed at Bruce until he coughed. 'Jesus Christ,' he said. 'A million! Who are you going to get to pay that kind of dough?'

'Your family,' said Bruce, trying to sound confident. 'Your business associates.'

'Boy, have you got it wrong,' gurgled the old man. 'My family! Christ, they'd *give* a million bucks to see me rubbed out.' He laughed outright. 'And my business associates, *they'd* pay two million!' He looked around them. 'I guess you just got yourself a liability,' he said. 'A real lulu.'

'We'll see,' put in Gabby with more sureness that she felt. 'I think you'll be worth something to somebody.'

'My momma liked me, but she ain't in a position to pay because she's dead,' reflected the old man. 'There may be a few others who want to keep me alive for reasons of their own.' He shook his head. 'But a million bucks. No way. Maybe five hundred, stretching to a thousand, but not a million.'

Gabby eyed Ossie and they went out onto the deck together. It was cool on the waterway with the cruiser going easily between the high buildings and streaming highway on one side and the low-slung houses of the more expensive people of Miami Beach on the other.

'Is he kidding?' asked Gabby.

'He's kidding,' said Ossie, attempting to sound convincing. 'He's just a wily old bastard who works out a situation like lightning. That's how he became who he is. No, he's worth ransom money. Maybe not a million. But money.'

The daylight was running away from Miami Beach now, going quickly from the shore and over the block buildings of the main city across the lagoons. Lights mixed with stars and the sea was glowing with its own peculiar iridescence. Later there would be a moon.

The *Marilyn Monroe VII* grunted eagerly towards the passage to the ocean as though enjoying her role in the adventure. Ossie felt Gabby's shoulder but after touching his hand in return she whispered. 'Cut it out, we're working.'

Belle was at the wheel with the hooded Sidewalk alongside him.

'Which way, Mystery Man?' asked Belle lightly.

'Out through the ocean channel,' answered Sidewalk pointing to the water junction ahead. Belle rang to ease the vessel's speed.

'Never been kidnapped before,' said Belle conversationally. 'When it happened I'd always kinda hoped it would be an Arab.'

'We used to rub out guys like you in the old days in New York,' muttered Sidewalk, finding it difficult to cope with the situation. 'Beat 'em up and rub 'em out.'

'Why ever did they stop?' sighed Belle. 'Must be heaven. Incidentally, I love your spats.'

'Shut your mouth and drive the boat,' returned Sidewalk. He could already feel the large easing of the open sea. He felt his stomach give a warning lurch.

Belle felt the first wave too. 'Beautiful,' he said. 'Just beautiful. Sure looks like we're heading for a fun sea tonight.'

Below in the saloon Cyril M. Hoffner felt the hunting movement of the boat also. He grinned with anticipation. Molly Mandy and Ari were sitting one each side of him. Even through their hoods he could see their consternation. 'Going to blow a little, I guess,' he said easily. 'Maybe even more than a little.'

Ossie climbed back into the saloon. 'Where are we heading, son?' inquired Mr Hoffner. His mood appeared to become more buoyant with each rise of the bow.

'Towards the Keys,' said Ossie. There was no harm in telling him now.

'Ah, then we'll really be in for some excitement,' confirmed the captive with patent relish. 'When the wind's coming up from Dry Tortugas it whoops around them Keys. And I can feel it coming up. We'll be rattling like a trashcan soon.'

'The boat is safe I suppose?' The inquiry came from beneath the hood of Molly Mandy.

The hostage blinked in surprise. He bent forward and intently examined Molly through her eye-holes. 'Jeez, a woman,' he breathed. He leaned closer so that his eyeball was almost on hers. 'I'm right, I know I'm right. It's an old gal. This gets better and better.'

'Mr Hoffner,' said Gabby coming from the hatch. 'Please sit still. And button up.'

'Don't get excited with me, young lady,' the captive replied affably enough. 'You're going to need me before the night is out.'

Ossie saw that Gabby already had spray on her face. She wiped it away. He could feel an unpleasant sheen of sweat on his forehead. The cabin was moving irregularly in the growling sea.

'If it gets real exciting will you let me go to the top?' requested Mr Hoffner like a boy. Ossie and Gabby stared back at him.

'The top?' said Ossie. 'You mean on deck?'

'No. On top of the cabin. On the roof. I always go to the roof if it blows,' he said eagerly. 'The crew think I'm crazy, but boy I love it. It's been the most exciting thing I've ever known. Until now anyway.'

'Maybe, maybe,' answered Ossie vaguely. He too felt the situation was taking on the only too familiar feel of failure. By now the victim should have been cowed and writing begging letters to his relatives. Instead Mr Hoffner was the only happy man in the cabin. The *Marilyn Monroe VII* rolled and added a lurch. Ossie moved prudently towards the door.

'Aw, come on son,' pleaded the captive. 'Just get me out onto the cabin roof now. Before it gets too bad for you to stand. I tell you what, I'll write a good ransom note for you then, I promise. To my nephew in Philadelphia – the one that likes me, I think. Is that a deal?'

Ossie looked at the old man strangely. Then he glanced sideways at Gabby. 'I'm going to take a look at the sea,' he said. 'There's no way we're going to put you out there and see you washed overboard. We need you, Mr Hoffner. We need you.'

'Like hell you need me,' the old man grinned. The contortion sat strangely on his face as if it were unaccustomed to being there. 'Sure son,' he ruminated. 'I'm the most important person on this vessel. Don't think I don't *know* that. You guys are going to look goddam stupid without your hostage.'

Gabby and Ossie nodded together. 'We could have used somebody smart like you on our side,' acknowledged Gabby. 'Okay, we'll get you on the deck if we can.'

Mr Hoffner pushed his grin even further. 'You've got to humour me,' he said with relish. 'Just keep on with the humouring.'

Gabby and Ossie went carefully out onto the deck. The moon had now cleared the horizon and was peering down at the sea as though searching for something it had lost. A sailor would have categorized the conditions as fair, with medium swell. The *Marilyn Monroe VII* was running up one side of the liquid hills and down the other, the bright moon lighting the oily flanks, the waves and the refined whiteness of the vessel's decks. Gabby held Ossie's arm, too tightly for it to be a mere romantic touch. 'Jesus,' she breathed. 'How far have we got to go like this?'

'Seventy miles,' he answered. 'Maybe it will calm soon. I don't care for it either.'

'Bruce is all yellow down there,' said Gabby nodding at the cabin. 'I can't tell with the others because of the hoods. But I bet they don't look any better without them. What are we going to do, Ossie?'

'Get me to the deck!' The voice, like an answer, came from the saloon. They looked back to see the extended neck of Mr Hoffner jutting out like that of a strangely wheeled tortoise. 'I want to be up top!' he shouted. 'I want to rule the sea!'

'Okay, okay, Mr Hoffner,' Ossie replied. His stomach seemed to be rising to his neck. 'You win.'

'I already know that!' the hostage called back triumphantly. 'Now do as I say or I won't be a good victim.' They heard him laugh wildly at his joke. 'The crew know how to put me up there.'

He put his fingers into the sides of his mouth and blew a shrieking whistle. Ding and Dong appeared obediently. 'Mr Hoffner wants to go up top,' said Ding flashing his eyelashes at Ossie. 'Is that all right, sailor?'

'Get him up,' growled Ossie.

With accustomed ease they manoeuvered the wheeled chair onto the deck, deftly fixed it to a lift platform and while Gabby and Ossie watched, astonished, raised it to the level of the cabin roof. It was all done as if the ship were becalmed. Ossie watched with reluctant admiration while they slotted the wheeled chair into the retaining fitting on the cabin roof. Ding hurried below and reappeared with a reefer jacket which he proceeded to put on his employer. Then Dong, as though taking part in some well rehearsed ritual, leapt lightly from the roof, using a vertical stanchion to swing himself round and down, and brought up from the cabin an unopened bottle of Scotch whisky. He and his brother strapped Mr Hoffner firmly into his invalid chair, placed the bottle of Scotch in his hands and, smartly saluting, jumped down to the deck again.

There was one further touch, one further embellishement to the extraordinary scene to bemuse Ossie and Gabby. The old man was now perched high and astride his boat like some ancient fighting king mounted upon a huge and armoured warhorse. The vessel plunged and heaved over the long regular waves and the hostage shouted with the sheer abandoned enjoyment of it. There was little wind now and in front of him, in any case, there was a protective glass shield. Mr Hoffner snorted with freedom and gladness. Then came the final touch. He reached and turned first one switch and then another. The first illuminated the entire vessel, lighting it like a flashing ghost as it charged across the empty sea of silver and purple. Then, at the second switch, there burst out a brilliantly amplified recording of *The Ride of the Valkyries* played by the Berlin Philharmonic Orchestra under Bruno Walter.

What a sight it was! Any wandering fishing boat that night would have seen the dipping, rising cruiser, vividly lit, with an old man strapped in a wheeled chair in its cabin roof, and that old man frantically conducting the flying music of Wagner as it issued over the heavy sea.

From the cabin, the sickly kidnappers, Bruce, Molly and Sidewalk, the latter pair now having abandoned their masks, looked out hollow eyed, upwards to the amazing sight on the roof. Bruce closed his lids with despair and *mal der mer*. The others, yellow-gilled, stared and let their mouths drop into gapes.

'I think we've got a lulu here,' sighed Gabby.

At three in the morning the *Marilyn Monroe VII* struck a coral reef half a mile off-shore at Key Largo. By this time the kidnappers had all been rendered helpless by the passion of the sea. Mr Hoffner had shortly before been returned to the cabin and was sleeping soundly in his chair with the bottle of Scotch almost drained but held conqueringly in his fist. Ding and Dong were playing Monopoly for cents and Belle, brimming with bourbon, was at the wheel. Ossie, holding onto the wheelhouse just prior to the collision, could not bear to take one more look at the dipping and rising moon. He knew they had failed again.

'Get this thing inshore,' he muttered to Belle. 'This is where we quit. Where the hell are we anyway?'

Belle, breathing Jack Daniels everywhere, consulted the chart. 'Just there, baby,' he smiled angelically. 'I guess.'

'What d'you mean, you guess? Don't you know?'

Belle looked amiably, quizzically, at the chart. 'I really don't know this coast,' he said. 'But if we're on course that *could* be Key Largo.' He wiped the chart exaggeratedly with his hand. 'If it's a dead mosquito,' he said benignly, 'we're lost.'

'Stop screwing about and get us in,' said Ossie. 'Just get us to the land.'

Belle bent at the knees and took another swig at the bourbon bottle. 'Key Largo here we come,' he said, happily turning the wheel. 'And real fast. Real fast.' He put the engine into full ahead and with power to match her elegance the boat curved shorewards towards the single string of lights showing where the road strung itself across the islands of the Florida Keys.

'Steady, boy, steady,' said Belle as if the vessel were racing ahead of her own accord.

Ossie looked doubtfully at him. 'What about rocks and things?' he said.

'We haven't got an inshore chart for here,' beamed Belle, a camp smile. 'So I guess the quicker we get there the better. I don't think there's too much danger.'

At that moment *Marilyn Monroe VII* scuttled across the reef less than a fathom down and took a large slice out of her bottom boards. Everyone was thrown to the deck by the force. But the gallant vessel, like a horse jumping an injurious barrier, went on with its own force and skidded through a lagoon before hitting shallow sand a mile off-shore.

'Abandon the goddam ship!' bellowed the voice of Cyril M. Hoffner from the cabin. The *Marilyn Monroe VII* halted spectacularly as if baulking at a fence. Everyone aboard was thrown forwards, threshing about on the deck or the floor of the saloon. The steering wheel came off its mounting and Belle was left bemusedly holding it in his hands.

Ossie got to his feet and gained the rail. Then the nose of the vessel was dipping as though it had smelled something on the sea-bed. He judged the distance to the shore by the lights. Gabby staggered alongside him. 'Anything wrong?' she inquired laconically.

'Let's get the old man into a boat or we'll have a murder rap on our hands,' muttered Ossie. He need not have worried. The faithful Landers now appeared on the deck carrying Cyril M. Hoffner like a child. Ding, Dong and Belle followed in orderly and serene fashion, Ding and Dong carrying the wheeled chair between them, Belle with a fresh bottle of Scotch and a case containing the ship's papers.

Mr Hoffner was laughing uproariously as the waves bit into his luxury cruiser. 'Goodbye Marilyn Monroe the seventh!' he shouted. 'Hello Marilyn Monroe the eighth!' This struck him as an enormous joke because he broke up into further laughter, hooting like a funny baby in the enormous hands of Landers.

The crew did not bother to launch the small lifeboat. Instead, one after the other in an apparently well-timed and rehearsed act, they dropped into the sea, which, Ossie was relieved to observe, came only up to their armpits. They held the wheeled chair above their heads like African tribesmen carrying a chieftain's seat. And, like a chieftain, Cyril M. Hoffner was placed in the chair and borne in some majesty towards the shore.

'Let's get going,' said Gabby to Ossie. 'This hulk's going to turn over before too long.'

Ossie sighed. 'Could be that's the best thing that could happen to us.' He turned and saw his woebegone gang assembled on the deck, sick-faced every one, eyeing each other and eyeing the dark washing sea. 'Okay, abandon ship,' he grunted.

'They'll have the cops waiting on shore,' put in Bruce dolefully.

'Let's get there first then,' said Ossie.

He put Molly Mandy onto his shoulders and climbed into the ocean. The others followed one at a time. They went into the water up to their necks, and began a sad, liquid tramp towards the island.

There was no chance of getting to the shore first. When eventually Ossie helped Molly Mandy up the gradual sand from the dim sea, Cyril M. Hoffner and his odd henchmen were arranged on the darkened and deserted beach in almost regal formation, the chair like a throne in the centre of the four attendants. The Ocean Drive Delinquent Society looked a sorry clique, its old members bent almost double on the beach, water running from their garments while Bruce, Ossie and Gabby stood despairingly like some hapless native subjects standing to ask a favour of a local potentate.

'Jesus,' said Cyril M. Hoffner after surveying them. 'You guys are the greatest collection of bums I've ever seen. Hi-jack! You couldn't low-jack.' He stared at Ossie as though demanding an answer.

'Things go wrong,' shrugged Ossie.

'All the time,' put in Bruce.

Mr Hoffner began to laugh. Polite grins appeared on the set faces of Ding, Dong and Belle, although Landers, even more menacing when wet, remained wooden-featured, the awful eyes glaring from beneath soaked and dripping eyebrows. Not a soul had come to the beach from Key Largo. Occasional cars drifted along the inter-island highway, their lights carving the darkness, but from the settlement came only muted sounds, the easy wind in the wires of docked boats, a dog calling, dimmed voices.

The strange inquisition on the beach continued. 'What were you bums hoping to get anyway?' asked Mr Hoffner, managing to still his laughter.

'Experience,' replied Gabby at once. 'We're hoping to gain experience, Mr Hoffner.'

'And boy, oh boy, do you sure need it,' the old man agreed. He glanced along the set piece again. It was like a scene in a classic tragedy. Molly had sunk to her knees on the shingle by the waterline. Ari was solicitously hovering over her but she sent him away saying she was fine. 'I just felt like praying,' she grunted.

Cyril M. Hoffner, victim turned victor, now paused as though considering judgement. 'Okay, okay,' he said at length. 'You gave me the greatest belly-laugh I've had in years. I've never seen such goddam incompetence. It's made me feel years younger just to know that you kids can screw things up too. You ought to get the old folks to put you straight. Anyway, I guess I owe you that.'

He paused, the faces all on him. He was a natural winner. 'I was going 'to get a new boat anyway,' he said eventually. 'And she was insured. And nobody here is going to mention it wasn't an accident.' He looked at his henchman with a confident scowl. Then he looked back at the gang. 'So beat it,' he said.

'Beat it?' said Ossie. 'You mean go?'

'I mean go,' said Mr Hoffner. 'Just go.'

They went. The younger members of the gang helped their elders, and they staggered up the beach towards the sparse lights of Key Large. From far behind they heard a shout of triumphant mirth.

CHAPTER EIGHT

Loose Bruce was moodily drinking a blackcurrant juice in the Ragtime Coffee Shop on Collins Avenue, when in the mirror behind the counter he saw Gabby come through the street door. He concluded that Ari the Greek must have told her he was there because she made directly for him and climbed on the next stool.

'Hi,' he said quietly. 'Want a blackcurrant juice?'

'Back to high school,' she said. Then she shrugged. 'Sure, why not. Maybe I could go back to school too.'

He asked the waitress for the same again and she brought the drinks in plastic containers. 'We all ought to go back to school,' said Bruce a little bitterly. 'The way we performed on our big hi-jacking. We've got a lot to learn, I guess.'

She touched his shoulder sympathetically and at once he felt it was more than just a touch. He glanced at her. She was smiling refectively. 'Well at least we gave Cyril M. Hoffner a new lease of life,' she said. 'That should keep him laughing until the old bastard's a hundred years old.'

'I guess it's demoralized everybody,' said Bruce, drinking the dark liquid through his straw. 'If we decided to quit the entire business right now – as of this moment – then I can't see anybody arguing. It was just so *embarrassing*. There's no way you can run a criminal organization like that, Gabby.'

The girl touched his arm again, this time to warn him to keep his voice down, but Bruce was acutely conscious of the contact. 'Ossie gone off on his fishing?' he said.

'An hour ago,' she confirmed. 'He needs to be alone, he says. Just him and the sea and the stars. He's been really grouchy since the Hoffner thing.'

'But night fishing,' shrugged Bruce. 'I just don't understand any guy going out there to sea, on all that liquid, from choice. Shit, it was bad enough on that cruiser, but sitting in a row-boat all night. Man, that's not for me.'

'He enjoys his quiet times,' said Gabby. 'He's quite a contemplative guy really. I suppose he's older and he's seen a lot more than we have and when you get older you get more thoughtful.'

Bruce felt himself stir. For the first time since he rode with her on the motorcycle she had grouped herself with him. She had said 'we'. 'He sure has,' he nodded at her in the mirror. Her face looked very soft and relaxed in the lights of the coffee shop. He could see her eyes were looking at him in the glass. 'But if I wanted to be alone, and I don't,' he continued, 'I'd go off and sit in Flamingo Park or just go to my room.'

'Do you still work the air conditioning with your ass?' she laughed.

'Sure I do. It's not too difficult when you practise.' He waited. 'You like older guys, don't you, Gabby? I mean the sort . . . well, okay, Ossie for example. You like the way they have things worked out, nice and wise and calm. You like the grey hair around the edges, don't you?'

She laughed again, quietly. 'That's me Bruce. I was crazy about my dad. But he preferred my mom, which I guess is the way it has to be.'

'Was the guy in St Petersburg, the one who motivated you to come away, was he older? Like Ossie?'

'About the same age,' she agreed.

'Touch of grey hair?'

She nodded sadly now. 'Grey hair. The wholesome girl's daddy fantasy. You know, the knowing eyes, and the sure grin, and on his very *last* open sports car – and the big job and the wife and the kids. In other words – disaster.'

'You really felt strong for him, huh?'

She sighed. 'I don't know. I never know how strong you're supposed to feel about anybody. I've never worked out the measurements. All I know is the last time I saw rainbows was when I was eleven. I look for them now and listen hard for chimes but I don't see or hear anything. This guy was okay, I suppose. I felt for him and I was hurt, very deep too, when he threw me out. But I didn't cry the day after. Now he writes me to say that – guess what? – it was me after all he wanted and threatening to come down and take me back.'

Bruce's eyebrows ascended a little. 'You don't say? And what if he arrives?'

She shook her head. 'I'd tell him to go screw himself. At least I *think* I'd tell him to go and screw himself. When it came to it I expect I'd swallow my pride and just get into the car and go.'

'I really wish I could help,' said Bruce looking directly at her in the glass. 'I'd honestly like to help you, Gabby.'

'Maybe we could help each other,' she said with a frank laugh. 'I feel like I need someone just now.'

'Right now?' he said, still not looking away from their reflections. 'Like right now, when you've finished that blackcurrant juice?'

'Pretty much right now,' she replied.

Bruce turned to her and grinned. 'Maybe I could get a hair colour spray and put a few patches of grey in this,' He ran his hand through his untidy fair hair.

Now they were facing each other on the stools. She put her fingers up to touch his face and smiled teasingly. 'The grey hair needs to be other places as well,' she said slyly. 'That's how it really turns me on.'

'Oh,' he nodded. 'I see. Well, I have to be a little careful spraying things in that region. I once sprayed on what I thought was deodorant and it turned out to be hair lacquer. That was a terrible experience, believe me.'

She laughed outright and they bent forward and kissed. 'You mustn't tell Ossie,' she said. 'Promise. I just wouldn't like him to know.'

'He won't,' said Bruce eagerly. He paused. 'Are you saying what I think you're saying?' he asked.

'You're slow for a young guy,' she smiled. 'Maybe that's a good thing. Sure, that's what I'm saying. I'm depressed and I'm hungry and I don't mean for a pizza either. Maybe you could show me how to work the air conditioning in your room.'

Bruce dropped the money on the floor as he was hurrying to pay the check. Gabby knelt to help him pick it up. 'Hurry Bruce,' she whispered in his ear. 'I may die of night starvation.'

'I'm hurrying,' he whispered back. 'My hands are just shaking, that's all.' He handed her the money. 'Here, you give it over the counter. I may drop it again. I can't believe this is happening.'

She paid and they went out onto the street. 'Let's run,' he said eagerly.

He took her hand and they began to run along the street. She laughed at the childishness of it.

'We won't go to my room,' he panted. 'The bed creaks and everybody hears it. I just have to scratch my ass and they all start banging on the walls.'

'We can't go to my place,' puffed Gabby, keeping pace with him 'Grandma's at home.'

'Ossie's' he said, out of breath. 'He'll be out all night, fishing, and his bed can't creak as bad as mine. Okay?'

'Okay. Ossie's,' she said.

They dropped to a prudent walk as they reached the block where the Sunny Gables was located. 'Go ahead,' said Bruce. 'I'll count to a hundred and follow you. It won't look so suspicious.'

'Right, I'll do that,' said Gabby, out of breath. 'You just take a rest. I don't want you to be exhausted before we make it.'

'I'll breathe oxygen,' he promised. 'I'll be right there with you, don't worry.'

She kissed him lightly and walked down the sidewalk. He watched her go under the evening lights and almost hugged himself with anticipation as her backside swayed sweetly. There was a brass plate on the railings by which he had halted. He looked at his reflection in it and showed his teeth. 'Lonely no more, man,' he muttered. He counted to seventy, which was as long as his patience would allow, and then walked after Gabby.

Miss Nissenbaum and Mrs Nissenbaum were having their evening confrontation on their respective front porches. 'I'm cutting my rates next week,' said the Sunny Gables Nissenbaum.

'So you cut the food last week,' rasped her sister-in-law.

'Evening ladies,' said Bruce breezily as he went eagerly up the steps. His Nissenbaum smiled and the other scowled. 'I bet he don't pay any rent,' she alleged. 'Or not much.'

'He pays,' Mrs Nissembaum lied boastfully. 'Just beautifully.'

She turned grandly with the remark and left her rival standing outside. 'Punk,' snarled the sister-in-law. 'Punk.'

All the rooms at the Sunny Gables had keys but few of the locks worked. Mrs Nissenbaum said it was a good thing in its way because with so many elderly residents there might be emergencies. Even the bathroom was unlockable, the users being advised to sing. Ossie's room was easily entered and Bruce walked in and right into the naked arms of Gabby.

He stared at her disbelievingly in the gloom. 'I considered there was no point in wasting time,' she said, smiling uncertainly at his expression.

'No point at all,' he whispered breathlessly. He was naked with her in ten seconds. As they went back onto the bed it emitted the most terrible iron creak that either had ever heard. They froze with apprehension, then Bruce said: 'The hell, who cares,' and they returned to their embrace.

Throughout the next ten minutes the old man in the room on the other side of the wall was bent almost double with his ear pressed to a drinking glass which in turn was pressed to the thin wall like a listening trumpet. The creaking and twanging of the springs were within a few inches of him, just the other side of the flimsy screen of wood and plaster. He leaned closer eagerly. His wife called him from the bed at the other end of their small room. She was in bed knitting a pair of socks.

'Hal, what are you doing listening against the wall?' she asked. 'What is going on in there?'

'The Flip Wilson show,' he lied brilliantly. 'They have the television right next to here. I can hear every word. It's real good, Annie, real good.'

The Miami office of Smileytime Tours was decorated with murals of large, good-time grins. Overpowering open lips and happy teeth looked down from the walls of the lobby as Zaharran waited. He selected each monstrous painting in turn and returned the grin with a grimace.

'Mr Burlestone, our tour director, will see you now, Mr Zaharran.' The voice interrupted a particularly rude face he was projecting towards the back of the lobby. The expression was still nailed to his face when he turned at the girl's voice. He removed it hurriedly.

'Oh, sure, good,' he said. The girl was sharp in a peppermint uniform, green and white stripes curved over her curves. Zaharran sighed inwardly and tried to pat his hair flat. She turned her provocative backside on him and swayed off ahead of his haunted eyes.

'So he's tour director now, your Mr Burlestone?' he called after the girl. His shambling amble had already left him yards behind her incisive steps. Her legs were opening and closing like scissors.

'Sure he is,' she sang over her shoulder with the briefest turn of her head. 'Best one we ever had.'

Zaharran's luxuriant but ragged eyebrows often reacted to the strange ways of the world. They did so now, rising ponderously like twin hedgehogs at the thought of Larry K. Burlestone, the beleaguered guide on the Everglades bus first robbed by the masked gang, now being an executive of Smileytime Tours. The peppermint girl stopped almost reverently outside the panelled door marked with Mr Burlestone's name. Zaharran thought her fingers actually touched, caressed the gold lettering before closing into the delicate fist that knocked upon the panel.

'Larry K. Burlestone says come in,' came a jovial shout from within.

'What a guy,' breathed the girl.

'Sure, what a guy,' agreed Zaharran in a puzzled tone.

They went in. The girl's face sweetened into a beatific smile as she saw the fat young man behind the desk. It was a big desk; to Zaharran it looked as if he were driving it. He was wearing a shirt of the same design and material as her dress except that the stripes were crimson. He rolled his young, well-fed eyes at her and Zaharran, three feet away, felt her quiver. 'Mr Burlestone,' said the girl. 'This' – she abruptly shut off her smile and looked at Zaharran as she might have looked at a mangy camel – 'this is Mr Zaharran.'

'Thank you, thank you, Selina,' said Mr Burlestone, rising heavily from the desk. It was like a striped sun coming up. The girl made a little bob with her bottom and, after another disparaging look at Zaharran, left the room.

'Are there any tours I can go on with her?' asked Zaharran. 'Like on a bicycle?'

'Ha!' The laugh was sweaty. So was the hand that shook Zaharran's. 'We aim to please at Smileytime.' Burlestone looked at the card which the visitor had sent ahead. 'And what service can we do for George Zaharran, Criminalistic Inquirer and Investigator?' he read. 'I guess it's about the bus hold-up, is it?'

'Sure,' nodded Zaharran. 'Unless there's some different crime you'd like to talk about. Something maybe I could solve for you. Something simple?'

Mr Burlestone indicated first one chair, then checking Zaharran's bulk, went through a half circle and offered another more suited to the load it would have to bear. Zaharran sat down gratefully. His back was beginning to ache. He had suffered with his back lately. Maybe he would have to lie down before too long. There was a pause, but Mr Burlestone was not going to speak first.

'I expected you to be in the basement, servicing the oil in the buses,' began Zaharran. 'Or showing the tourists how to walk through a snake pit. But instead you're Larry K. Burlestone, tour director no less. How come, Larry?'

'Just great business,' beamed Larry Burlestone with jovial frankness. 'Just great. Have to turn folks away all the time. Since the hold-up just everybody in the United States wants to travel on the same bus on the same route. They're just *dying* to be robbed, Mr Zaharran. That's how folks are.'

'I can understand that,' nodded Zaharran heavily.

'My God, I thought I'd be right out on my ass when the robbery happened. Goodbye Smileytime Tours. So did the bosses, including the bum who was sitting behind this desk. But when the news got around and the business rolled up, it just hit them that we'd struck gold. Extra buses, extra novelties. We call it the Hold-Up Trail now and we even have a staged robbery take place in the exact spot where the real crime was committed. We have the masked gang and the guns and every goddam thing. Folks love it. It's put the fucking Indian and his weary fucking alligator right out of business, I can tell you. Who the hell wants to see a guy fighting an old 'gator when there's a fun robbery?'

The old, heavy detective shook his head solemnly. 'Maybe you could co-ordinate the Indian and the alligator in the robbery,' he suggested. 'Have him take it onto the bus and threaten to bite anybody who didn't hand over the loot.'

For a moment a spark lit Larry's face. Then it died. 'Shit no,' he said. 'Every goddam fag in the Protection of Wildlife and the Preservation of the American Indian would go crazy. It's too much trouble. I guess we do pretty well right now. How are the police getting along with the investigation? Not too good, I guess or you wouldn't be here.'

'Not good at all,' Zaharran agreed. 'The same gang tried a burglary at a big house in Palm Beach, you probably read. They screwed that up too, but they sure caused a disturbance.'

'Right,' agreed Larry, looking suddenly sad. 'We tried to arrange with the people there, Van der Vatt or some fucking name, to have a Smilytime Tour around the damaged house. But they were pretty shitty about the idea. It was a pity.'

'They would be,' agreed Zaharran sagely. 'The Van der Vatts ain't bus tour sort of folk.'

Larry looked down at the card again. 'So the police have brought in outside help,' he said. 'George Zaharran, Criminalistic Inquirer and Investigator.' Zaharran did not disillusion him. Instead he handed him his other business cards.

'I also do mail order astrology, real estate and novelties,' mentioned Zaharran. 'Maybe we could do business some time. For example I could provide you with five thousand inch-high plastic dolls, each one dressed like a robber, you know, little masks, everything. You could give them to the customers as a kind of souvenir.'

'I like that,' said Larry seriously. 'You know, I really *like* that. Let me think about it. You cost it out. Give me some figures, huh?'

'Okay. But right now I'm a criminalistic investigator and inquirer right? What I came for was to get you to go over the things that took place on that day, the day of the robbery.'

'Christ, I've been over it so many times I dream it,' protested Larry. 'What else can I tell you?'

'You ain't told *me* nothing,' pointed out Zaharran. 'Others, yes. But me, no. Maybe I find something different. Working with mailed astrology and novelties, not to mention real estate, sure keeps you fresh for criminalistic work if you understand me. Just go through it again for George Zaharran, will you?'

Larry Burlestone sighed but made no more protests. He leaned back heavily in the important chair, put his large hands across his young outsized stomach and closed his eyes as if he were about to tell a bedside story to himself.

Zaharran himself closed his eyes and the two large men sat like some dozing mystics exchanging the secrets of centuries. Burlestone described the events of the previous 27 January in a supressed tourist guide voice, whilst the detective listened, only moving to manoeuvre his back into a less painful position.

Eventually Larry came to the end of his story and his trance and wiped his brow with a peppermint-striped handkerchief. 'And that, Mr Zaharran, was all there was to it. Like I said, it seemed like disaster at the time.'

Zaharran searched for something to wipe his brow. He did not have a handkerchief. Larry Burlestone saw his problem and obligingly handed his over. The detective gratefully accepted the gesture, wiping his face and his neck and then pocketing the handkerchief.

'It gets steamy in here,' agreed Larry. 'It's because the air conditioning's not functioning too well. We sacked the guy who looks after it and it looks like he took a few parts of the machinery as well. You can't trust any bastard, can you?'

'It's getting more difficult,' agreed Zaharran. 'Now I would be grateful if you could just think if anything else happened that day. Anything unusual at all. Apart from the stick-up.'

Larry thought. 'Nothing. It was just another boring Everglades tour.'

'Just go through what you remember, Larry. When you were at the Indian wrestling with the alligator. Anything different there?'

'Nothing. I'm sure of that. It all went to schedule. Those things are so in the groove, with the same dumb people, and the same dumb questions – you know: "Is it a rubber alligator?" and crap like that – that I'd have noticed if anything different had gone on. No, nothing.'

'I take it the bus was on time.'

'All but a couple of minutes. We were minimally late leaving the reservation because some old lady was in the wigwam.'

'What's the wigwam? The john?'

'Yes. There's a comfort station shaped like a wigwam. We have to remember to call it a wigwam not a teepee! But there's another wigwam that has the public telephone. She was making a call and we had to keep the bus waiting for her.'

Zaharran sat up quickly but heavily. 'Making a call? Why would you want to make a call from the Everglades for Godsake?'

Larry shrugged. 'I don't know. But people do. That's why the phone is there. Maybe she was calling the ASPCA about the Indian being lousy to the alligator. People do you know, regularly.'

'Or she might just have been giving the starting signal to the gang,' said Zaharran.

'Oh come on, Zaharran,' said Burlestone with a look of boyish petulance. 'She was just a little old lady. I can see her now runnung for the bus. She looked like she could drop dead before she got there.'

'You don't remember her name by any chance?'

'Well no, but I could think of it. There's a group photograph of all the people on that tour, taken at the Monkey Jungle on the outgoing trip. I could pick her out on that. The police should have her address and other details. But Zaharran, you're not starting on the right foot. Believe me, brother.'

Zaharran shrugged with emphasized heaviness. 'There ain't any other foot I can start on,' he said. 'They used up all the feet. Anything else?'

He could see immediately there was. He always knew by instinct. 'What else?' he repeated. He leaned forward and felt his back stab him. 'What else have you got Larry? Not anything you've been hiding is there? Come on, tell Uncle Zaharran – or I'll get you for withholding evidence.'

'Well,' hesitated Burlestone quietly. 'There *was* something and it's kinda been on my conscience, but nobody had any proof that it was anything to do with the armed robbery. But anyway, maybe I ought to show you and get the record straight.'

'Sure, maybe you'd better.'

His big doleful eyes watched carefully as the fat young man went to a cupboard in the corner of the office. He returned with a white woollen glove and handed it to Zaharran. 'A glove,' he said as if Zaharran would not know what it was. 'It's just a glove.'

'Where did you get it?'

'It was found on the bus after the hold-up. It may have been one of the customers dropped it, but it's certainly unusual for people to wear woollen gloves in Florida.'

'You ought to have been a cop,' sniffed Zaharran. 'But apart from being a glove, Burlestone, it's withheld evidence.'

The young man glanced up, quick apprehension in his tubby eyes. 'Yes, sure, but we didn't know. I mean *I* didn't. It was just there. It could have been anything.'

'The gang were wearing gloves,' remembered Zaharran. 'And it wasn't to keep them warm either.'

'Fingerprints?' suggested Burlestone, hurrying to get on the right side again. 'They didn't want to leave fingerprints, huh?'

'You get cuter. Maybe also to hide their hands?'

'Why would they want to do that? Hide their hands?'

Zaharran did not answer. 'Withheld evidence,' he intoned, holding up the glove. 'Why did you keep it?' He could see he had scared Larry K.

Burlestone. The young man ran his finger over his lips.

'It didn't come to light right away after the robbery,' he pleaded. 'One of our couriers found it when he went out to the bus and he put it in his pocket thinking it belonged to one of the passengers. He's a blockhead.'

'But then you thought you'd keep it. Show it to the tourists. "This, ladies and gentlemen, is a real glove worn by one of the robbers." That kind of thing. Good business.'

Burlestone shrugged. 'We haven't done it yet. But we were thinking along those lines.' He looked miserably at the glove. 'I guess we should have turned it in to the police,' he mumbled.

But Zaharran seemed to have lost interest in his guilt. He held the white glove delicately between a large dirty finger and a bulging thumb. 'That's a real neat glove,' he said, seemingly to himself. 'Real neat. This is not just machine-knitting or crap like that, you know. This is expert work. This is what they call crochet work. It's difficult to learn, you understand. And there's not too many people can do that sort of work today. There's no patience around, you know Burlestone, no interest in finer things.'

Burlestone was puzzled. 'Yes indeed,' he agreed doubtfully. 'I'm always saying that to myself. I tell the people around here all the time.'

'This is the sort of glove that a little old lady could make, but not too many other people. The lady who made the call from the wigwam. Now could it have belonged to her?'

Burlestone tried to show his eagerness to help. He was still worried about withholding evidence. 'I don't think so, Mr Zaharran. I mean I can't be exactly sure, but I don't think she was wearing gloves. I helped her onto the bus when we were leaving the Indian and alligator show and I'm sure I would have remembered if she'd had gloves. They're quite rare in these parts as I said before. People don't wear them.'

Zaharran sniffed. 'Yeah, sure,' he mumbled, 'I remember you saying that.'

Burlestone looked pleased he had remembered. He looked even more pleased when Zaharran rose painfully to leave. 'There won't be any trouble will there?' he asked. 'About the glove? I mean I did show it to you voluntarily. I could have held it back. All I want to do is help.'

'I'll tell lies for you,' promised Zaharran without enthusiasm. 'There's nothing else, is there? Not one thing? Nothing more you can suddenly remember, like one of the gang was your uncle?'

The fat face blanched and trembled before an uncertain smile secured it. 'Oh, you're funny too,' gushed Burlestone. 'Yes sir, you're funny.' His face dropped to seriousness. 'No, there's nothing else. On my honour.'

'I believe you,' said Zaharran flatly. 'Now I'll need to see the group photograph you mentioned and maybe you could pick out the old lady who used the wigwam.'

Burlestone pressed a button on his desk. 'That's easy,' he said, obviously relieved that something was. 'We can do that right now.' They waited after he had called for the photograph, then feeling he ought to say something, Burlestone said with his professional smile almost restored: 'If you'd ever like to take one of our tours, please tell me, Mr Zaharran. It will be with our compliments. Maybe you'd like to take a trip through the Everglades.'

Zaharran smiled his ghastly, creased smile. 'No thanks, son,' he said. 'I spend my life in the jungle.'

Detective Salvatore saw Zaharran stumble out of a bus on Biscayne Boulevard and make towards the main door of police headquarters. He howled to himself and hurried from his office to waylay him before he reached the elevator. In that building the elevators took their time and Salvatore was sure he could stop Zaharran before he entered the doors. However, when he reached the ground floor Zaharran was not waiting there. Salvatore ran up the stairs and arrived out of breath in his office to find the criminalistic inquirer and investigator sitting like a large untidy mole behind his desk.

'For Chrissake,' puffed Salvatore, 'get out from there! Beat it! Jesus Charles Christ, I don't want anybody to see you in this office. I want you away from here. Now get going.' He made to pull at the big man's arm.

Zaharran yawned and ponderously removed himself from the chair, coughed, and complained about his aching back. 'I just can't hide. There's no way I can hide in a whole city, let alone in a crummy office like this. You want me to get under the desk?'

'Get out,' said Salvatore uncompromisingly.

'I've got something,' said Zaharran rolling up his bushy eyebrows. 'A lead. Evidence.'

Salvatore stalled. 'No, I don't believe you,' he said.

Zaharran grinned. Salvatore said: 'Okay, let's get some coffee.'

The detective knew the policeman would not throw him out now. 'This gets too much,' he said, pleased. 'Can I have some French fries as well? I didn't get any breakfast.'

'You'd better not be fooling,' said Salvatore. 'Come on before the whole goddam police department knows you're here.' He tugged at the large man's arm. It was like a mouse trying to pull a boulder. But Zaharran turned his large frame to the door and ambled toward it under his own motivation. Salvatore followed him agitatingly, giving him tentative pushes towards the landing and the elevator.

They went to a coffee shop three blocks away, which Salvatore hoped was far enough for him not to be observed. Zaharran was sweating when they reached there but he still said he wanted French fries. Salvatore sighed and ordered them with coffee. 'Okay, what have you got?' he demanded, as if the food and drink had to be repaid with information or at least reassurance.

'I've got a glove,' said Zaharran quietly. From a baggy pocket he produced the crochet-worked glove and dangled it like a ghostly hand before Salvatore. The policeman reached out to touch it but Zaharran eased it away. 'My evidence,' he pointed out. 'You forget, buddy, that if I don't crack this case, I don't get paid. Once I'm on a retainer, I'll start sharing the goodies.'

Salvatore looked flustered. He stared at the glove. 'Sure George,' he said. 'I'm real sorry. I'm going to try and fix something for you. I'll have to get it under the heading of expenses or maybe I can get something out of the welfare fund. After all, you are an ex-cop.'

'Thanks,' answered Zaharran heavily. The portion of French fries appeared in front of him and, cheered by their appearance, he handed the glove without further argument to Salvatore. The policeman examined it. 'Full of holes,' he said. 'Whoever made this thing kept dropping stitches.'

'It's meant to be like that,' sighed Zaharran through the French fries. 'It's goddam crochet work. It's special work. It's like cheese. When it's full of holes it's special see? It's the same thing. That was made by an old lady. They don't make them like that anymore. It was found at the scene of one of your robberies.'

'You don't *know* that it belonged to one of the gang, though?'

'They wore gloves. Not many people wear gloves in Florida.'

'Fingerprints,' shrugged Salvatore. 'They didn't want to leave fingerprints.'

'Okay, detective. But that's a fancy glove for all that. Maybe they wore gloves to hide something else. Like they wore masks to hide their mugs.'

'Their hands? But why should they want to hide their hands?'

Zaharran poured coffee on top of the French fries in his mouth. 'Because they got veins and callouses and they're thin. Things like that maybe. Because they're *old* hands.'

'Old hands?' Salvatore's coffee cup was hinged to his lip.

'Right. And in more ways than one, Salvatore. My guess is that this is someone who has come out of retirement.'

'A dame too?' said Salvatore. He allowed the cup to tip over his lip. He wiped the coffee away from his chin and his hand. 'An old dame?'

'Guys and dolls,' said Zaharran. 'All over again. Remember the raid on the Van der Vatts' place during the benefit for old folks? And they had old folks there, right? Sort of demonstrating them. Showing people what old folks looked like and where their benefit money was going. And at the bus hold-up there was an old lady who had to make a phone call just before the bus left. My guess is she was tipping off the rest of the gang in ambush.'

'I'll get you expenses,' promised Salvatore eagerly, his eyes brighter than they had been for weeks. 'I'll also get a grant from the welfare fund.'

'Can I have some more French fries?' asked Zaharran.

'Sure, sure. And some more coffee?' said Salvatore eagerly. 'Waiter, more coffee and another portion of French fries for my friend.'

The waiter moved smoothly up the counter as if he were on wheels running along a rail. 'In general,' he said, 'we don't serve French fries on their own. They got to be with something. Like hamburger, hot dog, frankfurter. But not generally by themselves, you understand.'

'Frank, George?' asked Salvatore.

'Frank, Albert,' acknowledged Zaharran.

'Frank, Charlie,' said Salvatore to the waiter. 'And French fries.'

'Frank, Carlo,' called the waiter to the man who was doing the frying.

Zaharran said: 'Will you get somebody to check out the details that old lady gave when she came into headquarters from the robbery. Her name and address and everything. I've seen her in the group photograph. I take it they were photographed in the office too?'

'Sure they were,' said Salvatore. 'We had each one photographed while they were making their statements of complaint. I'll get them to you so you can pick her out. Then we'll make a check. Anything else?'

The waiter glided towards them with the coffee and frank and fries. Zaharran took a bite from the frank. 'This is living,' he said.

'Grants from welfare are limited,' said Salvatore, almost to himself. 'But I can get expenses for you, George. Jesus William Christ, we got men charging expenses for just breathing. I knew you would come up with something.'

Zaharran said heavily. 'I'd also like to take a look at the photographs taken at the benefit at Palm Beach. Not just the police photos, but all those taken by the society column craphounds. Can you fix that?'

'We've got the file in the office,' said Salvatore. His expression fell. 'But I think I'd better bring it around to your place. Having you around headquarters is not good for me. Nobody talks like a cop to a cop, you know that. They tell tales like old ladies.'

'I know, I know,' mumbled Zaharran. 'Just get the file. Bring it over to me on Washington. The place is difficult to find. But you'll find it. You're a detective.'

Salvatore went at his customary worried slouch along Washington Avenue sidewalk, dodging slowly in and out of the crowded life of that section of South Miami Beach. He had left his car three blocks away and now he was sorry. All over the pavement people were talking. Hot smells and voices came from the cooking shops along the route and there was a line fifteen yards long at a diner that sold half-price lunches after three-thirty. They also served early dinners before five-thirty. The two hours were the busiest of their day. Some people stayed and ate both meals. The afternoon sun was cutting directly down the avenue. Ladies blinked under antiquated straw bonnets, to which many had added a flower or two, and men sweated as they carried bags of groceries. Salvatore, carrying a folio under his arm, searched the shop fronts for the name of George Zaharran.

'Hi, honey,' called a fat lady with big lips from a bench in front of one of the peeling hotels. 'Want to swing?'

He stared at her, scarcely crediting what he thought he had heard. 'I'm looking for George Zaharran,' he said. 'He's above a salt beef bar. Know him?'

'No, baby,' she replied as if she had learned the lines especially for the moment. 'But if you find him, bring him too. I got a nice friend.'

He smiled, still uncertain that he had got the right sense of it, and continued his passage. Some Cubans were discussing the world in a corner. There were a few coloured people in the street. But the faces all about him were the faces of retired white Americans. Some of them had dogs, and one man, much admired, had a parrot in a cage. A group of elderly folk were bent close to the bars because the man had mentioned that the parrot could sing. Salvatore paused in interest, because he liked parrots and sometimes went alone to the Parrot Jungle where they rode bicycles and roller skates. The man said he would only tell the parrot to sing if everyone donated a quarter to its upkeep. Within ten seconds he was alone in the street.

Eventually Salvatore saw the sign in the window of the salt beef bar, a cardboard square with the announcement: 'George Zaharran. Criminalistic Inquirer and Investigator. Formerly of the Police.'

At the door of the salt beef bar he was confronted with a steaming mass of customers besieging the counter for end-of-the range bargain sandwiches; those who had obtained their bargains were eating them violently and talking at the same time. It seemed to Salvatore that there had just been some emergency. But he was wrong. It was just the normal daily conversation in the establishment.

He elbowed his way through the crowd to a small steamy door at the extreme end. On this the title 'George Zaharran. Criminalistic Inquirer and Investigator,' also appeared. It had been defaced in various ways by the customers of the salt beef bar, one of whom had written the unkind words 'He don't know nothing' under the name. At the deepest end of the place it seemed the customers were even thicker on the ground and even more vociferous. It was like forcing his way through a creek of Jewish crocodiles; all around him were gnashing jaws and feverish arguments. He had to diswedge several voluble men from behind the door before he could open it towards him and see that he had to climb a flight of hidden wooden stairs to the office of the old policeman.

At the top of the stairs was another door on which appeared several name plates. 'Zaharran Mailed Astrology,' and 'Zaharran Real Estate.' 'Zaharran Paper Novelties,' said another. 'George Zaharran, Criminalistic Inquirer and Investigator' was a more sober plate half way down the door. Salvatore knocked.

'Come on in for Chrissake,' croaked Zaharran's voice.

Salvatore pushed the door. It opened to reveal the enormous man lying flat on his back on a short length of carpet placed in front of a similarly large and untidy desk. He was aiming a pistol at the ceiling. As Salvatore entered he fired a sucker-dart against the plaster. 'Got him,' he grunted with satisfaction.

'Who was it, Batman?' asked Salvatore without humour.

'A fly,' Zaharran told him. 'Flies make great target practice. They're real difficult to hit. You should get your boys trying it.'

'I can see the commissioner walking in on a dozen cops firing sucker-darts at the headquarters ceiling,' said Salvatore sourly. 'I can just see it.'

'Cheaper than range practice,' said Zaharran, still making no attempt to get up from the floor. 'Save the taxpayer's money on bullets.'

'And then you have to spend the taxpayer's money on ceiling repairs,' argued Salvatore, who could always find a reason. 'Forget it. If we need any flies killed we'll call you. I've got those pictures you wanted to see. I had to smuggle them out.'

'Great. Did you check on the old lady's address? Mrs Molly Manders, remember?'

'I've got somebody checking it out,' said Salvatore sitting down. He stared at Zaharran bleakly. 'It's real difficult discussing things with you like this, George,' he complained. 'In that position, I mean. Can't you get up and sit behind the desk or somewhere.'

'Not even somewhere, pal. It's my back. It keeps going. It just goes. The only way I can get it into shape again is to lie on the floor like this. For an hour. And I've only been down here' – he looked at his watch – 'twenty-one minutes. If you want a normal discussion you'll have to wait or come back another time. I'm sorry, but that's the way the pisspot spills.'

Salvatore grimaced and argued no further. 'I'll call the bureau,' he said, reaching for the phone. 'Maybe they've got the information on the old lady by now.' He put the receiver to his long narrow ear, and began to dial. A look of querulous puzzlement took over his face. He shook the instrument. 'What's wrong with this thing?' he said.

'It ain't connected,' admitted Zaharran from the floor. 'I didn't pay. Things have been bad, captain, I told you that. It's just there as an ornament, a decoration, in case I get somebody come to call. It looks better if a private eye has got a phone.'

'You've got it right there,' sighed Salvatore. He put down the receiver. 'Okay, where do I phone?'

'Downstairs. If you can get through that rabble down there, you'll find a phone on the hook on the back wall. Next to the Jewish Racing Calendar.'

'Shit,' said Salvatore, with studied impatience. He looked down at the spreadeagled body and the prostrate face. 'If you crack this case and get the reward will you pay the bill and get the phone reconnected? You will won't you?'

'I promise,' nodded Zaharran eagerly. 'Right after I get the electricity and the water put back. Just now I have to read by candlelight after seven o'clock and I have to walk two blocks and cross the street to wash my hands. It's no pleasure for me, I can tell you, no pleasure at all. Maybe if I get the reward I'll be able to afford all sorts of goodies, like underwear and hot drinks.'

Salvatore was at the door. He went ill-temperedly down the uncovered wooden stairs into the crowd of the salt beef bar. As soon as he had gone Zaharran eased his body up as if it were on a strong hinge and reached for Salvatore's folio. He slipped the photographs out of the cover and quickly, his large thumbs and fingers moving like a shuttle, he went through them.

They were the photographs taken by the society photographer at Mrs Van de Vatt's party. There were duplicate prints of each. Swiftly his veined eyes went across the faces. He stopped suddenly and brought one photograph close up to his eye. His ragged smile appeared. He slid the photograph clear of the others and pushed it under the piece of carpet upon which he was sitting. Then he replaced the folio and lay tiredly back on the floor again.

Eventually Salvatore's stamping steps could be heard. He came in looking as though he had been brawling. 'That's my idea of Hebrew Hell,' he said nodding back fiercely down the stairs. 'I'm glad I ain't going where that lot are going. Jesus Jacob Christ, I didn't think you could get so many people into one lousy room. And they're all pushing and shoving and talking at the same time. Some bastard had his beard in my face the whole time I was on the phone.' He sat down and looked steadily at Zaharran. 'Okay,' he said. 'You were right. They've checked the address Molly Manders gave. It don't exist. There's no such street. I guess we should have checked them all out before, but it would have been a long job and there just didn't seem any need.'

'Fine, fine,' Zaharran nodded at him. 'That's not bad to go on. Now, how about these pictures?'

Salvatore took the folio and took out the prints. He handed the whole batch to Zaharran who examined each one with the nape of his neck flat on the floor and the photographs held, each one at a time, over his head like a canopy.

'Swell occasion,' said Zaharran, staring up as if the picture was miles above him. 'Just look at all the rich ladies and gentlemen. They're the sort that get robbed. Just look at all of them. Ain't no good robbing poor people. And that's Mrs Van der Vatt, I recognize her. I always read the society columns when I pick up an old newspaper in the park. Ah, and these are the old folks they led around the ring by the noses, eh?'

'It was *for* them,' said Salvatore defensively. 'For old people's charity.'

'We need it,' agreed Zaharran. 'Gee, I wish I could have been there. Maybe there's a kind of list for these functions. Maybe there's some place where you can put your name down. Like a bureau. I should get down there and tell them I'm available.'

Salvatore looked uncomfortable. 'I'm sure to get you expenses,' he said doubtfully. 'If I have to go without myself I'll get something. Okay? Now do you see anything in the photographs.'

'Nothing,' lied Zaharran, 'except a lot of people having a good time.' He passed them up to Salvatore. 'I guess you'd better just leave me to get on with it, captain,' he said. 'Don't pull your detectives off the case or anything, I may fail.'

'There's no way I'm going to do that, so don't worry,' said Salvatore getting up from the chair. 'Not that they've turned up anything so far. If you get something big or even not-so-big, you'll put us on to it I guess.'

'Oh sure. Then you can have the reward for the police Christmas party,' said Zaharran.

'Okay, okay. But don't double-cross me, just don't double-cross me. I'll get a description circulated of this Molly Manders woman.'

Zaharran eased himself up on his hinge. An anxiety had taken over his vast face. He grinned pleadingly towards Salvatore, his teeth like the broken railings of a park. 'No, please captain, give me a break too. Let it lie will you for a few days? Well, a couple of weeks. I need to work without a lot of hassle going on. I think I can find her.'

Salvatore stared at him. 'You mean that?'

'Right now I mean it,' Zaharran assured him. 'As true as I'm sitting on this floor.'

Salvatore looked doubtful. 'Okay. You turned her up. You can keep her. Just temporarily. But if there's any more raids or anything, I'm putting a warrant out for her. Got that?'

'Got that,' agreed Zaharran. 'And I also got a backache.'

Salvatore got to the door and with a silent nod went out.

Zaharran eased himself to the horizontal and waited until the footfalls had gone down the stairs. He heard the hubbub as the lower door opened. Nobody could come back up those stairs without his hearing. He rolled over like a walrus onto his side and withdrew the photograph he had taken from beneath the carpet. He held it above his eyes and grinned. 'Ari the Greek,' he muttered to himself. 'All these years and he's still got that same goddam nose.'

Zaharran took a disintegrating suitcase with him and wandered with studied aimlessness along Ocean Drive going south. It was mid-afternoon and the sun filled the air with heat. Even the grass seemed to sag and the sea-grape trees hung their heads. The ocean was banded blue and green and frilled white. It was almost unattended, vacant as the sky. Three thousand old folks congregated on the humid grass bordering the beach for their unending convention. It never became too hot. The sun gave life and life was worth having.

The ex-policeman's normal appearance was such as to merge almost faultlessly with the background. He was wearing a large pair of multi-creased azure trousers and a Honolulu shirt he acquired long before Hawaii became the forty-ninth state. He sported a pair of moderately clean white shoes although his socks were of differing colours. His other clothes bulged like blisters from his split suitcase. Only one item had he added to his normal appearance. He now wore a dun-coloured wig, not as a disguise since even the most disinterested, distant and distorted eye could have immediately seen it for what it was, but because he had been given it by a dying well-wisher and until now had not had the opportunity to display it. The wig was not a particularly good fit and the perspiration on his head caused it to slip forward like a pancake on his forehead, but a mere faulty adornment like that was unlikely to cause comment in that region. Many people had wigs that did not fit.

Zaharran was looking for Ari the Greek. The Prohibition days when he had known him were now far distant, and the detective hoped that Ari's memory was not so active as his own. However, even with the beacon of his unique nose, Ari was no easy quarry amid the elderly thousands along Ocean Drive. Zaharran walked the length of the lawns and gardens first, keeping to the sidewalk, apparently meandering aimlessly, his suitcase banging from a pendulous arm which it seemed to stretch to twice the length of the other one. But from beneath the fringe of the slipping wig he watched as carefully as an Indian in the grass. The insistent heat of the Florida day began to broil him and he had to squat on a bench for a while. On the grass before him was a man playing a sorrowful cello while another attempted harmony on the musical spoons. It was a difficult combination but they had managed over months of experiment and rehearsal, so Zaharran imagined, to make a melody and form a descant and they applied themselves to this with deep concern. Outsized seagulls stood on the grass listening, heads cocked, and being soulful creatures, finding the rhythm to their liking.

Zaharran found it soothing too and his big shaggy head soon began to nod. A pleasant haze enveloped him and an infant snore wriggled from his lips. The sound of the snore was enough to bring him awake and he sat up with a start and looked about him quietly, as if ashamed at sleeping on duty. As he did so a squat figure in red vest and running shorts trotted towards him, spinning at apparently inspired intervals to perform a spasm of shadow boxing. Zaharran's hooded eyes shone quietly. He had found Ari the Greek.

The nose was unmistakable, bobbing away in front of its owner as though loosely hinged to his face. Zaharran three-quarters closed his eyes and hunched down as if in untroubled sleep. He felt the wig slide forward but this time he was grateful for its added concealment. From the crevices of his eyes and from beneath the thatch of the wig he observed Ari the Greek carefully.

Ari, he decided, looked good. There was no doubt about that. He had to be in his sixties now, thought Zaharran, but he seemed as active and as lithe as ever. The ex-policeman, who had once been boxing champion of his state force, felt a touch of envy to which his back added a twinge of pain.

Ari the Greek sparred by him, revolving on a complicated pattern of footwork in front of the men playing the cello and spoons. His feet obligingly danced to the time of their music for a moment but he did not look at them nor they at him. It was the same with the chess players and the Slavonic dancers along the same path. On South Miami Beach everyone did what the new generation liked to call 'their own thing' without interference from others. Among the old folks it was called courtesy.

Zaharran permitted his eyelids to lift a degree more to follow Ari's progress. He could not hope to follow him on foot, especially with the burden of the suitcase, and he was grateful as well as interested when he saw the Greek begin jogging on the spot while he conversed with two young men in denims who appeared through the screen of old people. Zaharran settled back and observed. It was quite rare to see young folks in this part, especially young folks who talked intently to old folk. He gave a little start when a striking girl in jeans and a white shirt with military chevrons just above her brown arm walked from the opposite direction and joined them.

He wished that the cello and spoons would quit for a while, so he might catch a fragment of what they were saying. It was a serious matter, he could see, for none was smiling. The girl kept pushing her glance around furtively as if keeping watch. The rendezvous lasted only a couple of minutes before the party split in three, Ari continuing on his jogging run towards the ocean, the girl and the older of the two men walking towards Ocean Drive and the youngest man sitting on the grass and gazing at the diminishing figures of the other two. His expression was moody. Zaharran could sense the old detective magic working. He had almost forgotten the feeling. Today was the day he was getting the breaks.

Loose Bruce sat for a while on the grass wondering if Ossie would notice if he took Gabby to Daytona Beach when they made some money out of a robbery. The sun seemed to concentrate on him and he succumbed to its drowsing touch. Zaharran was pleased to see him lie back on the tough grass and close his eyes. The young man was not prostrate for long. He sat up, blinked, and then removed his cowboy boots and socks. He set them on the grass beside him, wriggled his toes and then the rest of his feet in the sunshine and with a sigh settled back again to doze.

Zaharran could tell when a man was really sleeping and when he was only napping. He had been inside too many prisons and watched too many prisoners not to know. The deep breathing told you nothing, only the small movements of the eyelashes giving away whether a man is in sleep or only feigning or napping. Eventually Bruce's eyes began the tiny butterfly movement that told the detective that he would not be easily disturbed.

The cello man and the spoons player were having a sudden but acute dispute about some aspect of their duet. It became acrimonious. The spoons man raised his spoons threateningly and the cello man raised his cello, projecting the pointed end towards his fellow player. He looked like an aged knight with a fat lance. They paused two paces apart and then burst into mutual friendly laughter and shook hands. They settled down to play again and, as if he had been waiting for the cover of the music, Zaharran got up and moved largely but easily along the path towards the sleeping Bruce.

Although there were dozens of people all around, they were so occupied with their various activities, whether it was bridge, reading, talking, dancing or listening to a transistor radio held against the ear, that no one noticed him. He approached Bruce and almost without pausing in his walk and by means of the merest stoop he bent and stole the young man's boots.

Loose Bruce wandered footloose, barefoot, disconsolate along the grass of Ocean Drive. His eyes searched ahead among the hundreds of sitters beneath the sun. His astonishment at finding, on walking from his grassy sleep, that his cowboy boots had vanished was only matched by his puzzlement that anyone in that old-fashioned region should even have considered the outrage.

Zaharran circled him patiently, like a threadbare shark, his shabby suitcase in one hand and the purloined boots in the other. He waited on his moment and then, smooth and casual, approached Bruce from behind. 'Hey there, son,' he said with gruff cheerfulness. 'You wouldn't be looking for these now, would you?' Bruce turned quickly and beamed as he saw Zaharran holding out the boots.

'Gee, yes, thanks,' said Bruce, the words tumbling out gratefully. 'Where did you find them?'

'Right down by the ocean,' lied Zaharran blithely. 'Standing there on the shore, their toes pointing to sea, just like they was thinking of walking in after whoever it was that usually has their feet in them. I figured the guy had gone for good. I made the sign of the cross, picked them up and brought them here. Then I saw you walking around like some barefoot boy. Here, take them.'

He handed Bruce the boots and watched paternally while the young man sat down and eased them on his feet. 'No socks with them?' inquired Bruce. 'The socks went too.'

'Not a sock,' confirmed Zaharran. 'Guess you'll have to say goodbye to the socks. They're probably floating to Cuba.'

'Thank God I got the boots,' said Bruce. 'I ain't got any others.' He stood up on the grass and looked down fondly at the boots as one would look at twins recently lost and found. Then he glanced at Zaharran and held out his hand. 'My name's Bruce,' he said. 'I'm sure grateful mister.'

'George,' said Zaharran. 'I'm George.'

'That's neat and easy,' returned Bruce. He glanced at the suitcase. 'What are you doing in these parts?'

'Travelling,' shrugged Zaharran. 'Just going south. But I guess there's not much more south left. Only the ocean.' He glanced around. 'I guess this is where I'm going, right here.' The people were leaving the grass now because the afternoon was advanced, the sun slinking over the western buildings of Miami and the diners were offering their cut-rate meals to early eaters. They left the grass and the sea-grape trees in their droves, most of them carrying the little light chairs that were their badge of office and their physical and moral support.

'Got anywhere to stay?' asked Bruce. He sat on the bench and began to polish his boots fiercely with a piece of newspaper as though comforting them on their return. Zaharran smiled inwardly, grateful for the young man's making things easy for him.

'Not a single place,' he said. 'I was just considering that maybe I ought to start looking. It's just that I don't have much money. So I got to be careful. Can't stay at the Fontainbleu.'

'Nor me,' agreed Bruce. 'I stay right over there. See, under the trees.' He pointed under and up. 'See, Sunny Gables Hotel. It's okay. And the lady don't charge overmuch. You just have to smile at her.'

'A good Christian action,' suggested Zaharran.

'In her case no. Her name's Mrs Nissenbaum. You'll have to get your religions straightened out if you're considering moving in there.'

Zaharran tried to look as if the idea had never occurred to him. 'You think there might be a room?' he asked, thrusting forward eagerly. 'And the rent not too high?'

'Come along with me,' Bruce offered cheerfully. 'I can fix it for you, George.'

They shook hands solemnly and Bruce picked up the older man's suitcase and turned towards Sunny Gables. The wig slipped spectacularly over Zaharran's forehead and he pushed it back impatiently. It stuck out of centre. He did not care. He was always grateful if someone did his work for him. He stepped out heavily alongside Bruce.

'Where you from?' asked the young man. 'Where did you come from to go south?'

'Savannah,' replied Zaharran who had once been to Savannah. 'I been there for a couple of years. That's north from here, you know.'

'Sure,' nodded Bruce, thinking there was nothing strange in the remark. 'Generally speaking if you're heading south it's the north you come from. That's nearly always the case.'

The logic caused Zaharran's wig to slide again as he raised his bearish eyebrows. He moved it carefully this time to a safer location on his head and looked speculatively ahead as they crossed Ocean Drive. On the outside terrace of Sunny Gables sat a line of old folk, looking at the world like a jury, set eyes, set faces, apart from small movements of the jaw. There was not much movement or conversation, although one lady did rise to brush a fly from a potted plant. She knocked at it seven or eight times with a battered magazine as though it were a locust. The insect escaped but the plant was destroyed by the onslaught. She stared at it in dismay and tried to prop up the broken stems and leaves only to see them flop hopelessly again. She shrugged and manoeuvred the plant pot behind some others.

The faces in the chairs viewed Bruce's approach with a suitcase and a prospective guest with mixed reactions. 'No room,' croaked one man glaring at the following Zaharran like one bull seal objecting to the approach of another to his harem. 'All sold out. Full up.'

'There's room,' argued a lady next to him, smiling beguilingly at Zaharran.

'Yes, there's room,' echoed two others. 'Plenty of room.' They were visibly cheered by the advent of a new male.

Bruce paused at the top of the short flight of steps which led to the hotel. 'Ladies and gentlemen,' he said, setting the suitcase down on the stone. It had only just lasted the journey. 'This is George, from Savannah. He was heading south.'

'Then why don't he keep going?' asked the disgruntled man. 'There's no room. Just keep moving.'

'There's room,' snarled the grey lady at his elbow. 'You know darn well there's room. You're just jealous because he's ten years younger than you.'

'Hah!' snorted the man. 'His wig's ten years older. Hah!'

Bruce jerked his head towards the door and Zaharran walked after him towards the hotel lobby, raising his wig carefully as he departed from the terrace, an action which brought hoots of appreciation from the old ladies and further grumbles from the man. 'In the old days, I'd have beaten that guy to a pulp,' the man said, his trembling hands clutching his walking stick. But the fury passed quickly. He sat back and the dying sun touched his face and soon he was drifting into the sleep which occupied so much of his days and nights.

Lou Yen Lew's is a noted Kosher Chinese Restaurant on Washington Avenue, South Miami Beach. It is an ornate place, like a prayer house with cooking smells, with pictures of the Great Wall, Shanghai Harbour and former President Nixon on the walls, and ventilated by great sweeping old ceiling fans.

Some of the more well-off old people eat there and others make it a place for commemorations and celebrations. One Jewish widow went there every year for ten years to mark the anniversary of her husband's death and every time wept copiously into her Kosher wun tun soup. The staff, from Cochin China, grew to know the date and placed a pile of clean napkins on the table, a kindly gesture typical of the Chinese Jew. In the eleventh year the widow did not arrive and they knew that she had gone to join her husband and would cry no more. It was just one of the small dramas that are to be found every day on South Miami Beach.

Sidewalk Joe and some of his acquaintances used to visit Lou Yen Lew's every Monday night for other reasons.

There would be eight or ten participants around the table. They would eat first, simply, cheaply and late, and then, when the other customers had gone from the restaurant and a look-out had been placed on the door, they would get down to the true business of the evening.

Each table was equipped with a turntable upon which were placed the various Chinese dishes. It was revolved by hand during the meal. But once the eating was finished this circulating top became the sort of gambling machine frowned on by the Miami authorities.

A simple arrow – usually a six inch nail – was placed on the table with the pointed end touching the rim. Bets were placed at the centre and the wheel was then spun.

Around the table the gamblers watched its whirl and the winner, who found the nail pointing at his chest at the end of the spin, would collect sometimes as much as ten dollars.

The sessions, like all gaming sequences, were performed with a seriousness bordering on the grim. The lights in the restaurant were diminished and the spinning wheel illuminated by a single beam which made the six inch nail shine like the blade of a silver sword. The faces all around the circle were set, the shadows trapped in the creases of the skin, and even the winner, by some unwritten but acknowledged rule, was only permitted to smile seriously.

On the day after the arrival at South Miami Beach of George Zaharran, Loose Bruce had sought out Sidewalk Joe in his daytime pitch by Ocean Drive where he played in the aged men's poker school and asked his permission to take his new friend to the secret wheel of fortune at Lou Yen Lew's. Zaharran hovered like a large shadow beneath a sea-grape tree some distance away and he nodded a grim greeting when he saw Sidewalk Joe turn his head towards him.

'Has the guy got any real dough?' asked Sidewalk, turning back to Bruce. 'I don't care to play for pennies.' He looked down at the paltry stakes of his poker school. 'I have to, but I don't care for it.'

'He's got a few bucks,' Bruce assured him. 'He's played at games in Savannah.'

'He ain't going to sing about it?' asked Joe doubtfully. He took another glance at the big, waiting figure beneath the branches. 'It's something we don't want any songs about.'

'Sure, I understand that,' said Bruce. 'He's to be trusted, Joe, I know he is. He's moved into the Sunny Gables. He's looking for some action at the table.' He leaned closer to Joe's old jagged ear. 'Ossie thinks maybe he could be some help with our other operation.'

Joe looked at him sharply. Throughout the conversation he had been dealing the cards with expert off-hand swiftness. His eyes reverted to the table. Bruce bent nearer and reassured him. 'Nobody's told him. Jesus, do you think we'd tell *anybody*? It's just that he might be useful. He's that sort of guy.'

'Bring him,' said Sidewalk out of the corner of his mouth, in the traditional gangster manner. 'Tonight. Mind he don't forget his dough. Or his tongue. Okay?'

'Okay, Sidewalk. Thanks.'

Joe was already pushing up the bets a quarter a time. Bruce saw that he had two kings, a queen and two aces and he'd only picked up one card. He went back to George, nodding the affirmative as he went. Zaharran smiled.

That night in Lou Yen Lew's the table was spinning. It was not the smooth revolution of the genuine gaming wheel, for there were little undulations and slower and faster places on the circular jogging journey of the Chinese roundabout and thus there were seats at the edge of the board which were more popular than others because of the increased odds in the pointing nail stopping there. So lots were drawn for the places at the table and it was a rule when, very rarely, a trusted newcomer was introduced, that he had to sit at the chair where the wheel was known to travel by with the most speed. That seat was left for Zaharran.

Loose Bruce introduced George around the table. Sidewalk, in grey waistcoated suit and mended shirt, inquired, during the interval in the game: 'And do you have another name to go with George, mister?'

'Seltzer,' replied Zaharran blandly. 'Like Alka Seltzer. That fizzy stuff.'

Nobody said anything. The wheel had begun to spin. Given a firm push the wheel would travel around for a minute or so before coming to its hesitant stop. The house was a big one for that school, a dollar a bet. The Chinese waiters, drawn by their inborn fascination for gambling, crowded at the back of the chairs. Often they split a fifty-fifty bet with the player sitting nearest to them.

Zaharran's head could descend into his body on occasions, in the manner of a ponderous, half-withdrawn turtle. It was almost as if its weight was too much for the neck, which contracted in coils to accommodate it.

Now from its low position it moved infinitesimally from side to side, the eyes following the pointing curved journey of the nail but at the same time taking in the fixed faces around the rim of the table. Sitting immediately opposite was Ari the Greek, his nose making little pushing movements to urge the wheel. It was a nose like an extra hand. Gabby was to Ari's left. Zaharran noted her animated beauty appreciatively. Ossie was next to Gabby, his strong face watching the spin intently, his tough grey hair scattered untidily across his forehead. Bruce sat next to him, the sunburned expression full of naïve hope and the eyes innocently expectant. Zaharran took in Ossie and Bruce. Considered them carefully. He wondered which one slept with the girl.

There were other players but, unless Zaharran's policeman's instinct was awry, they were not the people he sought. They were old men with gnarled hands and dulled eyes. But at the far side, in the best seat, suspiciously watching even the Miami fly that alighted for a brief ride on the table, was Sidewalk. Zaharran knew a genuine, old New York gangster when he saw one.

The table slowed as though it had become weary performing for them. Zaharran saw the eyes of Sidewalk and Ari rise to him even before it had commenced its final three circuits, soon to be joined by the eyes of the other players as it slowed obediently and the nail came to rest pointing directly at Zaharran's breastbone. He reached out without hurry and took the money.

'This is a good game,' he smiled at Sidewalk.

'Beginner's luck,' said Bruce nervously. He looked tentatively at Sidewalk and then at Zaharran.

Gabby said: 'Grab it while you can.'

'Sure is beginner's luck,' nodded Zaharran, taking care not to look up from the money he had accumulated. He stuffed it into the pocket of the voluminous trousers and threw the final dollar into the centre of the wheel as his wager for the next game. 'Anybody want to change seats?' he inquired, looking about him with fat innocence. Nobody did.

Sidewalk fluttered his dollar into the centre and the others followed suit. Sidewalk spun the wheel as he always did.

Zaharran glanced at the embarrassed Bruce and smiled diffidently at Gabby. 'I wonder can I do it again?' he said ingenuously. 'I just wonder?'

Twice more during the course of the evening he won and at the conclusion of the session he was thirty dollars richer. Sidewalk was last from the table. 'George,' he said, getting up elegantly. His shoes caught the light. 'We got another game we play. Like to take a chance?'

Ossie moved close to Sidewalk. 'Watch it, man,' he whispered. 'Don't make any trouble. Trouble makes trouble. Understand?'

'Sure,' said Sidewalk amiably. 'I don't have any trouble in mind.' He walked towards Zaharran and put his hand on the fat arm. There was no reaction but a guarded smile. 'It's a great game,' he said. 'And quick. We take the cards and we throw them up at the fan there.'

Zaharran looked up to where the huge old-fashioned fan cleft the air above their heads. 'And when they come down?' he asked.

'When they come down every guy catches a card while it's still flying, see? Whoever gets the highest card wins the loot. Okay?'

'I've got a better idea,' said Zaharran.

'I thought you could have,' said Sidewalk. 'What is it, friend?'

'Just you and me, Mr Sidewalk. We'll play the game. Twenty-five bucks we put down. Then we throw the cards into the fan.'

'Twenty-five bucks?' Everyone looked anxiously at Sidewalk. That was a lot of money on South Miami Beach. A grin broke unexpectedly on his face although it disappeared again quickly, as if it had no right to be there. 'Okay, you got a bet. What's twenty-five bucks anyway?'

The old men all looked at each other and shrugs were exchanged. 'What's twenty-five bucks, anyway?' they echoed to each other. 'What's twenty-five bucks?'

They gathered around the rivals. The Chinese waiters stood in one clutch as if ready collectively to defend themselves in trouble. Ossie and Bruce, sensing the tension, glanced unsurely at each other. Gabby wondered how much twenty-five dollars meant to Sidewalk. All of twenty-five dollars she guessed. Sidewalk pushed the pack of cards towards her. 'Okay,' he said. 'You throw, lady.'

'You sure you want to go through with this?' said Gabby. She hesitated. 'For twenty-five dollars?' She looked at Zaharran and then hard at Sidewalk. Sidewalk nodded and Zaharran said: 'Throw them, little lady.'

Gabby did. She shuffled and tidied the pack. Ari the Greek said: 'No need to shuffle them, Gabby. The fan shuffles 'em.' Then she threw them into the revolving blades of the fan.

The cards seemed to hang in the close air for a moment and then the four blades caught them and flung them to all corners of the room. As they floated down Sidewalk grabbed a card in mid-air and so did Zaharran. Sidewalk immediately slapped his down on the table. 'Queen,' he said quietly. 'Of Spades.'

'Eight of Hearts,' sighed Zaharran, throwing his on the floor. He reached into his deep trousers and counted out twenty-five dollars for Sidewalk. Sidewalk laughed and so did everyone, including the relieved waiters. 'I'll buy you a beer, mister,' said Sidewalk shaking Zaharran by the hand.

'Thanks, I need one,' said Zaharran. He did too. It was not every day that he threw away a winning card, a King of Diamonds. If Salvatore ever paid his expenses he would make sure the twenty-five dollars was included.

Gabby lay naked in Ossie's arms in the beach tower which had for so long been the scene of his employment. She stirred uneasily and he looked questioningly at her in the diffuse moonlight.

'Something wrong?' he said. 'You don't seem too happy, Gabby.'

'Me? No, I'm okay, Ossie. I guess you can't expect to be as kookie as I am and be calm and happy all the time. It's a tough combination.'

'I *know*,' he guessed. 'You got another letter from Prince Charming in St Pete's. He's coming for you on his white horse with his shining lance in his hand.'

'Stop it,' she half-laughed. As she said it a droopy-faced pelican dropped dozily onto the rail of the watch tower and sat there ridiculously, observing them with hooded eyes.

'Oh God,' said Gabby. 'Now we have an audience.'

'Beat it,' said Ossie to the pelican. The bird obeyed but was back within two minutes with two colleagues. They sat, their huge beaks hanging like pockets, each watching the naked humans with unembarrassed interest. Ossie clapped his hands at them but they only flew a few yards before returning.

Gabby laughed. 'Maybe they think we're a couple of big fish. Maybe they haven't seen naked people laying flat before. Maybe we'd better split.'

'Let's split,' agreed Ossie. 'We'll go to my room. If that's all right with you.'

Gabby only hesitated momentarily. They had never been together in his room. She had only been there with Loose Bruce. 'Okay,' she said. 'As long as you don't have a creaky bed.'

'It creaks,' he told her. 'But I've never seen a pelican in there. Let's go.'

He stood up and put his pants and shirt on. She put a brief dress around her body and pulled her panties up beneath it. 'Okay?' she said addressing the pelicans. 'The show's over. Hope you had a good time.'

As the humans went down the steps of the watch tower the birds croaked a little and flew away as if disappointed. Ossie took Gabby's hand and she felt his assurance flowing into her. They walked along the beach and then up over the lawns to Ocean Drive and separately into the Sunny Gables Hotel. It was late. The banjo player had gone, Mrs Nissenbaum was eating her supper, and the old man who cleaned up the place in return for his room was dusting the leaves of the rubber plant. He hardly noticed the two people. He was very intent on the leaves and he wiped each leaf carefully. Mrs Nissenbaum liked clean leaves.

They went swiftly to his room and stood together in the gloom. He undid the buttons of the dress and she pulled her panties to her knees with her hand and then the rest of the way with one foot. She took his shirt away and he let his pants fall to his ankles.

They were instinctive lovers and once they looked at each other in the dimness of the room they closed together with no further words, their bodies touching firmly and enjoyably all the way down. He moved his hands up her thighs to her hip bones and then to her small stomach and below.

Ossie smiled at her in the wan light and she returned the smile and put her lips to his hard chest. They shuffled one pace to the bed and he eased her onto it. There came a loud twang of old bed springs. They clutched each other, transfixed with it.

In the next room the old husband opened his eyes at the noise. He glanced quickly at his old wife. She snored softly. He left the bed and crept to his voyeur's position by the wall. All day he had been secretly at work with a chisel and had made a peep-hole through the plaster. Eagerly his eye went to it. He could see the dim figures on the bed a few feet away. He heard Gabby whisper: 'Take it easy now, darling, this bed's like a bell.'

They moved again and the twang resounded through the room. He looked at her anxiously in the dark. 'Maybe nobody will hear,' he whispered. 'Maybe they're all asleep.'

'They'll hear,' she forecast grimly. 'When it does that I feel like the Hunchback of Notre Dame.'

Holding each other's ribs they attempted a tentative roll across the mattress. There came some muted creaks and groans from the bed beneath their bodies but nothing major. Ossie smiled down at her in the half light. Gabby smiled back. Then, like some booby trap being sprung, the most resonant twang that ever issued from a bedspring vibrated through the room. They lay stiff, waiting.

There came a furious banging from beneath the floor as if someone were buried alive down there. Muffled shouts issued up. Ossie swore fluently.

'To hell with it,' he said to the girl. 'I pay for this room. At least, I'm going to pay for it when I get enough dough. And while I rent it, I do what I like in it.'

'Not if Mrs Nissenbaum finds out,' pointed out Gabby. Her body was hot and her eyes sleepy. 'Come on Ossie,' she said urgently, 'let's give it another pitch.'

'They're only jealous,' he whispered. Carefully he manoeuvered himself to her, feeling her soft flesh on his, thigh mounting thigh. The bed remained quiet but they were not fooled by it. It was merely waiting in ambush.

Ossie and Gabby moved into each other, easily and softly as familiars do. They knew each other now, every hill and culvert of the lover's body. He kissed her face and she returned the kiss from beneath him. It was very hot in the room. Ossie felt full. He moved harder into her. Twang!

The bed emitted the loudest noise to date. It was as if one spring had been jammed below another and had been released by some movement of their lovemaking. Twang. It sounded again. That did it. From every side, it seemed, from above and particularly below, the elderly inhabitants of Sunny Gables Hotel set up a fusillade of protest. Banging, kicking, shouting. Except the room to the left, where the old man sat and waited and watched. He was not complaining.

'You bastards are spoiling the late, late show!' howled a denizen to the right.

'So what?' bellowed Ossie back. 'You're spoiling *my* late, late show. Fuck off the lot of you! You old bums!'

Gabby was somewhere below him howling with laughter. He put his hand gently over her mouth. 'I think we're going to have to finish this some other time, baby,' he said. 'Mrs Nissembaum will be on her way up soon.'

Gabby nodded mirthful agreement. She rolled from the bed looking like a wet fish. She put her meagre clothes on and kissing him briefly went out of the door and down the stairs, just as the old folks were coming out of their doors all around. In their nightdresses, nightcaps and ancient pyjamas they converged on Ossie's door and there they were grouped, hammering with their bony fists, when Mrs Nissembaum thumped her way up the stairs and made her way through them like a riot cop pushing aside a mob.

'That's guy's disturbing us!' one man said, prodding Mrs Nissenbaum with a stick.

'He ruined the late, late show.'

'He does things in bed.'

'Disgraceful at this time of night.'

'Are you in there!' shouted Mrs Nissenbaum, rapping her knuckles on the door. 'Come on, young man, are you in there!' Her eyelash had fallen across her eye like a seal. She pushed it back into place. 'Answer me, mister!'

Ossie let out a huge echoing yawn. The bedspring harped again as he eased himself from the horizontal position. 'What's the racket?' he called towards the door. 'Who's making all the noise?'

'Open this door, please,' ordered Mrs Nissenbaum grimly. 'It's Mrs Nissenbaum. Come on, young man, open up.'

The door opened and Ossie appeared there, yawning, eyes blinking, naked with a long manilla envelope held in front of his private parts. 'Mrs Nissenbaum,' he inquired amid the gasps of the old ladies, 'why are you making all this noise.'

In the next room, the old husband left the hole in the wall and retreated to his bed and his old, snoring wife.

Sidewalk Joe said: 'Listen, just listen to me. We either got to get something going soon. Like quick. Or we'd just better forget the whole goddam thing.'

Ossie nodded. 'You mean the confidence will disappear.'

'Jesus,' said Gabby. 'Since when did we have any confidence?'

'I've got a suggestion,' said Bruce. They were sitting in Flamingo Park under the Tree of Knowledge. It was a fine Florida day with no clouds, no wind and no waves. The sun had the sky to itself.

Bruce looked around, surprised that he was being given unusual hearing room. There were only four of them under the tree, for it was the morning most people went to collect their social security and there were always long lines at the office on Collins Avenue. Sidewalk, who retained some of his old privileges as a gang boss, had an arrangement whereby he could dispatch an emissary to collect his. He now smoked a cigar and looked with the others at Bruce, but with no great hope.

'What I want to say, to suggest, anyway, is that we bring in another guy. That guy George.'

A groan passed from one to another. 'We need another hand in this outfit like we need fleas,' said Gabby. 'Jesus, we don't make enough dough to go round as it is.'

'One thing we've never had,' pursued Bruce, 'that's luck. Not once have we had a lucky break. It's always gone the other way. Now George, now there's a lucky man.'

'If we want a mascot why don't we get a black cat or something?' asked Ossie sourly. 'Or a tattoo on our ass?'

'Just a minute. Give me a break,' insisted Bruce. 'I know that guy. I've talked to him a lot since he came here. He *makes* his luck. He's not just hoping it will come along. The things that guy's done! New York, Philly, Savannah, all over. He's told me. He could be the one to turn it for us.' He paused and looked around at their doubting faces. 'And we sure need somebody.'

Zaharran made a massive sight sprawled on his narrow bed in the Sunny Gables Hotel. He was stripped to the waist, his chest hairy and his stomach enormous. He was smoking a dubious cigar and the smoke hung around him like rainclouds around a mountain. His instinct told him that he might be getting a caller and it was right. After he had been prone there for an hour, had rested his nagging back and smoked three evil cigars, there came a knock and Loose Bruce and Ossie walked in at his call.

'Hi,' he said, his huge head revolving towards them as if moved by a slow mechanism. 'What's this, a raid?'

'Kind of,' smiled Ossie. He was still not feeling sure about George.

'We just wanted to talk to you,' said Bruce, who was sure, but was worried that the others had already made him responsible for the results of the new man's recruitment to the gang. 'We got a proposition to make. If you're interested.'

'Oh God,' groaned Zaharran. He rolled his eyes. 'It's not work is it? I ain't fit to work, that's for sure, son. I ain't hardly fit enough to lie here. It's my back. I got agony all the way down from my neck to my ass.'

'No, no, it's not work, not exactly,' Ossie assured him. He looked around the close room. There was the customary small armchair and a stool. He pulled the armchair forward for the full three feet it would travel without colliding with anything and made to sit on it.

'The left hand leg at the front,' warned Zaharran, without moving. 'It's come off. You have to keep your weight towards the back. What do you guys want anyway?'

Bruce sat on the stool and pulled it nearer to the bed like a doctor with a patient. Ossie manoeuvered his backside into the armchair and eased his weight away from the left front corner. The chair wobbled but he managed a balance.

'It's like this,' Bruce began. He paused with uncertainty.

'Like what?' asked Zaharran. His retired policeman's heart was beating hopefully. He even glanced down in case its palpitations might be visible through the hair on his chest.

'Well, George, you seem like a guy who's got all his nuts and bolts. You've been around. New York, Savannah and places. And you've *done* things. Am I right?'

Zaharran turned his expression half an inch towards the young man.

'Sure,' he said. 'I've *done* things. Yesterday, for instance, I had a crap. What kind of things?'

'Crime,' Ossie put it bluntly. Bruce looked at him half grateful, half annoyed.

'Yes, like crime,' said Bruce. 'Remember, you told me, George.'

'Oh that,' smiled George. The smile wandered down his face like a trickle of water. 'Crime. Well, sure, I've tried my hand at everything including crime. But I did two years in South Carolina State Prison and that kinda cured me. It's quite a cure, believe me.'

'That was for the thing you did in Savannah,' prompted Bruce. 'You told me, remember?'

Zaharran dismissed the thought with a wave of the decomposed cigar. It curved through the air like a burning aeroplane. Its odour had reached both the younger men and they wiped their eyes. 'That's all gone and past,' said Zaharran. 'I didn't mean to bore you with those things, son. I was just passing the time of day. We seem to have plenty of that to pass down here.'

'That's just it,' said Ossie on cue. 'Some of the people down here have found they don't care just to hang about until they're dead. So they *do* something. They take *action*, George.'

Zaharran ordered his heart to stop banging. He eased himself up on his thick, pale elbows. His great sweaty face revolved from one to the other as if it were on oiled castors. 'What?' he asked. 'What do they do?'

Bruce glanced at Ossie. It was the signal for him to continue. 'So far, not much,' he said carefully. 'But we have a group of people down here who like to take part in a little excitement. A little robbery and that sort of thing.'

Zaharran erupted into outsized, convincing laughter. 'Ho! Oh, Jesus Christ!' He roared. 'That's the best yet! Robbery! The poor old bastards from around here?'

'Right,' said Ossie quietly.

'Right,' repeated Bruce more sharply. They felt hurt at his mirth. Zaharran looked at their serious faces and burst into a further peal. Bruce produced his Russian pistol and stuck it into his fleshy belly. Zaharran stopped laughing.

'No bullet would ever penetrate that, sonny,' he said seriously. 'Move it up to the ribs. Give it a fair chance.'

For some reason Bruce took the advice. He moved the gun up to the ribs. 'This is a Russian gun,' he said. 'A Muscof 43. It could make a hole in you as big as a plate.'

'That's if it was loaded,' sighed Zaharran. He pushed the muzzle of the gun away. 'Okay, so you're serious. I guessed you guys didn't just go around doing good works down here. And the chick also. So what's the plot, the scene like you say today. Yeah, what the hell's the scene?'

Bruce put the gun into his shirt. He was glad he had not misjudged the older man's nerve. 'We've got some associates,' he said carefully. 'Just a few. Already we've tried out some things and they worked, well almost. They would have worked even better if we'd had someone with experience and *luck*. We figure you could be that someone. The pickings are good George, real good.'

'I didn't like it in South Carolina State,' said George, shaking his large head. 'In fact, I really disliked it a great deal. I don't reckon Florida State Penitentiary's any goddam better. It's worse from what I understand.'

Ossie leaned forward and tipped over the chair. He ended on his knees by the bed. 'You don't have to pray,' observed Zaharran. 'Those measures are unnecessary.'

Embarrassed, Ossie got up and balanced himself on the chair again. 'If we get caught you could just say you're of unsound mind, you're mad. At your age it sounds plausible.'

The eyebrows, thick as twin moustaches, went up. 'Thanks a million,' Zaharran said. 'So I end up in the state asylum. That's a great consolation.' He paused, then thought he had gone far enough. 'Okay,' he said. 'What's in it?'

Boyish joy lit Bruce's face. He leaned forward eagerly. 'You mean you'll consider it? Oh, that's terrific.'

Zaharran sighed. 'Well, to tell you guys the truth, I was lying here, like when you knocked on the door of this salon, wondering what to do with the rest of my life. Maybe, I thought, I could go pearl-diving, or get out to Africa and catch lions and tigers and crap like that, or walk the tightrope in a circus. The possibilities were just endless. On the other hand, I thought there was quite a good chance I might just lie here and rot. And then they'd take me out and stuff me into a hole in the unholy ground and that would be that for good old George. So what you have proposed seems reasonable enough to me.'

'Great,' put in Ossie. 'Just great.' The chair overturned and he tumbled forward as he held out his hand. 'Everything will be great from now on, I know it will,' he said.

'Why from now on?' said Zaharran sagely. 'So far not so good?'

'Not so good,' Ossie admitted for Bruce. 'We've done three operations to date and we're showing a loss.'

'Oh, that *ain't* good,' agreed Zaharran. 'That ain't good at all. If there's anything that should pay, it's crime. What's the next thing you got in mind? Can you tell me?'

'Sure, but later,' said Ossie. 'We'd like the others to be there.'

'They're good,' Bruce assured him. 'They've had lousy luck, but believe me they're real good.'

'They sure sound like it,' said Zaharran scratching his belly.

Zaharran's fist, the size of a plucked chicken, indicated the plan pinned on Molly's wall right next to her photograph of her Melford and the Elks. 'The US National Trust Bank,' he said in his heavy voice, 'is located on Broward, right here on this corner of the block. At the rear of the bank is a narrow street and pretty much opposite the rear door of the bank is another door that gives into Meggison's Funeral Parlour.'

'That's where I'm going,' nodded Molly conversationally at Katy.

'Soon, if you don't button up,' said Ossie, but so nobody heard.

'Meggison's you'll know because it has a kinda slogan over the back door giving the name and the words: "Trust Us With Your Loved Ones".'

'That's why I'm going,' whispered Molly to Katy. 'I think that's so nice, don't you?'

Ossie kept his teeth firmly together and Gabby looked at him as though she hated him before cautioning her grandmother to be quiet. Molly pouted a little, but dropped obediently into silence.

Zaharran continued. 'Now I know, and I'm not telling anybody *how* I know, that every Tuesday morning at nine o'clock there's a consignment of cash, all used notes, that comes in from small banks in the country areas. Our aim is to ... er, obtain ... yes, obtain this money and transport it out of the area by means of one of Meggison's funeral hearses. We figure a slow but safe getaway.'

He watched the faces suddenly brightening around him. He was like a new general propounding strategy to a previously defeated and deflated army. Ari the Greek and Lou the Barbender looked at him with dawning admiration, Sidewalk Joe creased his eyes and nodded affirmatively over his thin cigar. Katy touched Molly's arm and whispered: 'You'll get to ride with Meggison's sooner than you thought.' Molly smiled appreciatively. Gabby and Ossie watched the reactions and Bruce grinned all around with proprietorial smugness.

'Our colleague Ari the Greek, although I could not at the time enlighten him as to why, has contacted his young friend who is a hearse driver for Meggison's and has learned that next Tuesday morning a loaded hearse, if you'll pardon the expression, will be waiting in the Meggison garage to take a deceased body to the cemetery. That funeral is timed for eleven o'clock. We have to make sure we drive it out of there in plenty of time. There won't be anybody at Meggison's except a clerk who arrives about eight-thirty – and, of course, the deceased in the coffin which will be already loaded into the hearse. It will be necessary to make sure the clerk is immobilized, of course, so that we have time to get away with the funeral. But nothing violent. We only want one body.

'Our entry into the bank will be as follows . . .'

On Monday evening Molly Mandy, suitably attired in faded coveralls and mop cap, arrived at the side of the bank just behind the group of half-a-dozen cleaning women who regularly entered the bank at that time. 'Nearly late,' she confided to the security guard who let her in without a murmur. She went briskly to the third floor of the building and locked herself in an executive bathroom. She was equipped with sandwiches and a flask of coffee and she slept fitfully on the carpet. No one disturbed her and at seven o'clock the next morning she went casually down the stairs and put a gun in the back of the security guard on duty at the back of the building. At her suggestion he opened a rear door and into the bank came Bruce, Ossie, Gabby, Sidewalk and George. Katy with her resounding whistle was placed at a strategic point on the block as a lookout. Ari the Greek and Lou the Barbender, wearing boiler suits and carrying window-cleaners' buckets, were entering Meggison's funeral parlour.

They found the hearse as expected, standing ready to leave, with the coffin already aboard. A second funeral car stood behind it. A man came towards them from an office in the corner of the garage and Ari produced his Russian pistol. The employee gaped. 'The bank's across the street,' he said hurriedly. 'You guys have got the wrong block.' They tied and gagged him neatly and put him back in his office. Then they took off their boiler suits and brushed down the decent black mourning clothes they wore underneath.

Bruce and Ossie entered the bank carrying the components of the Russian rocket launcher which had for so long been an adornment of Molly's sideboard. Wearing their hoods they went swiftly but quietly to the panelled office of the manager, Mr Walter J. Smithly, where they set up the weapon on the desk, its unpleasant mouth facing the door.

When the staff of the bank arrived at eight-thirty each one was admitted by the security guard and then accompanied to the safe-deposit room by the masked Gabby and Sidewalk, each holding a gun. Nobody argued.

At eight forty-five Mr Smithly himself arrived for the day's business and, upon entering his office, found himself confronted by a Soviet Dov Anti-Personnel Missile Launcher Mark III.

The weapon was intended to look much more threatening than a mere hand gun and it had the desired effect on Mr Smithly who was only a year from retirement. 'I have to tell you that if you do not obey our orders, this weapon can take your head off,' said Ossie quietly from below the mask. 'You understand that?'

'I really don't want that to happen,' Mr Smithly told them mildly. 'I'm playing golf this afternoon.'

Zaharran blinked in admiration below the mask. He wondered if they made bank managers like this anymore. Ossie motioned the man to sit down in a corner chair and Bruce turned the rocket firer a fraction to cover him. 'That's been outmoded these five years,' said the bank manager, nodding with interest at the weapon. 'It's amazing how this old hardware gets around.'

'It still shoots,' said Ossie briefly.

'Right. I bet it does. Be quite difficult to patch a guy up after a hit with one of those,' agreed Mr Smithly. He was a tanned, fit-looking man and he had not gone pale. He began to practise short-pitch golf shots in the chair, closing his knees together and making economical sweeping movements with his hands.

'I guess it's the ten o'clock Wells Fargo you're after,' he said. 'Sometimes they're late. They stop for coffee at the second bank. But they shouldn't be too long.'

Ossie said: 'You're pretty cool about this, mister.'

'Oh, I am,' said Mr Smithly. 'And why not? There's no way I'm going to have my head taken off by that thing. I'm due to retire to Boca Raton next year. I'm looking forward to uninterrupted golf. There's some real nice golf at Boca.'

'You don't say?'

'I do. And in any case, I'll certainly get some glory from this. It's not every bank manager gets robbed at the end of a rocket launcher. Pictures in the newspapers. My grandchildren will be tickled pink. And to think I thought this was going to be just another day at the bank.'

Mr Smithly chatted on amiably while they waited. He even produced some photographs of his grandchildren, which the masked Molly moved forward to view until Sidewalk ushered her back. He told them there was a coffee machine outside and gave Gabby a handful of quarters for the coffee. 'That's a nice hand for a bank robber,' he observed as she took the coins. Ossie bit his lip between his teeth beneath his hood.

But then, for once, things began to go right. The security van turned up promptly at ten and the cases of used bank notes were brought in through the side entrance. Gabby went to the safe deposit room and returned with Mr Smithly's bespectacled secretary. She sat staring into the bad end of the rocket launcher while her boss went into the outer office and calmly signed for the consignment of notes. One hundred thousand dollars.

'Looks like a real nice day, Mr Smithly,' said one of the visiting guards as the cases were checked.

'It usually is in these parts,' replied Mr Smithly easily. 'It seems you can't get used to Miami after Cleveland, John.'

'You're right, sir,' said John jovially. 'I wake every day expecting it to be snowing. But it never is.' He took the papers. 'Thanks Mr Smithly,' he said blithely. Smithly had written: 'We are being held at rocket point by robbers,' on the consignment sheet but the breezy John didn't notice. He put the papers in his pocket and went out into the shining street.

'Have a nice day,' he called over his shoulder.

Ossie looked down at the assembled boxes of money. His heart was rising. 'Mr Smithly,' he said, keeping his voice as level as the bank manager's had been, 'I want to tell you it's been a great pleasure. You're a nice man, and brave too. If I ever need some financial advice I'll come to you.'

'The US National Trust Bank is here to serve,' recited Mr Smithly with the trace of a smile. 'I'd like to shoot the lot of you, but since it's you who has the hardware there's no way I can do that. And I'm not risking any lives in this bank for the sake of a few thousand dollars. There's plenty of dollars around.'

'Very sound, very sensible,' put in Bruce.

'We are going, taking the money with us of course,' continued Ossie. 'Everybody is to remain in the safe deposit room downstairs for ten minutes. You are to stay here. I'm afraid we're going to have to take your secretary along with us to make sure this is done.'

The girl gave a frightened start and for the first time Mr Smithly reacted. 'What about me?' he said. 'Take me. I'm just as good a hostage.'

'No, we'll take her. But don't worry. She's not going to be hurt. Not if everything's kept quiet. We want ten minutes start, that's all, Mr Smithly. If nobody bugs us she'll be dropped on the Tuttle Causeway. You can have her picked up from there. If they do bug us you can pick her up from the harbour. Okay, let's go.'

The last words were directed at the gang. They moved swiftly, picking up the boxes and carrying them towards the rear door. Bruce stayed crouched behind the rocket launcher. Gabby took hold of the secretary's arm and silently led her towards the door of the office. When she reached it the secretary suddenly turned back and kissed Mr Smithly full on the mouth. He reacted with an amazement he had not shown throughout the entire drama. He looked at the masked Zaharran and raised his eyebrows with a touch of pleasurable anticipation.

'Goodbye Mr Smithly, darling,' said the girl when Gabby got her to the door again. 'I will always remember you.'

'Don't worry, Freda,' he said, wiping his mouth. 'You'll be back in no time. We won't call the police until we know you're safe. I'm sure these gentlemen will keep their word.'

Gabby took the girl out of the office, the gun a foot away from her girdle. When they were almost at the rear door and out of Mr Smithly's view, she abruptly turned her and made her go downstairs to where the rest of the staff were in the safe deposit room. Gabby opened the door and nudged her in with the rest.

Ossie nodded at Molly. She went out and into the street. Katy was on the other sidewalk. Molly waved and the wave was answered. The two old ladies went towards the rear door of Meggison's.

Ari the Greek and Lou the Barbender were standing in their funeral clothes beside the hearse and the second car in Meggison's Funeral Parlour when Molly and then Katy came carefully in through the side door.

'Gee, you look neat,' said Molly to the men. 'Real sad.'

Katy kissed Lou earnestly. 'You look like you're dressed for a wedding,' she whispered.

Lou blushed. 'One day, sweetheart,' he answered throatily.

The two ladies looked into the hearse at the bright coffin. 'Who is it?' whispered Katy. 'Anybody we know?'

'No names,' said Ari, shaking his nose. 'We don't want no sentiment entering into this. You'd better get a move on, girls.'

The feathery pair hurried away to a small ante-room and there, surrounded by vases of flowers and wreaths, they reversed their street clothes, the bright Miami colours turned to reveal black linings which became their mourning dresses. In two minutes they were sitting sedately and sombrely beside Ari and Lou in the rear seats of the car to follow the hearse. They waited expectantly. On time the side street door opened and Gabby, Ossie and Bruce came in, followed quickly by Sidewalk Joe and the lumbering Zaharran. Ossie and Bruce dismantled the missile projector and, casually lifting the coffin lid, placed it carefully alongside the body of the late citizen lying there. Ossie wondered if some archaeologist of the distant future might conjure some intriguing theories of how an old man came to be buried with such a lethal weapon beside him.

The money was in three canvas bags and these were put into the second funeral car, under the feet of the mourners. The gang were all now rid of their masks and they changed their clothes standing alongside the hearse, reversing anything and everything so that in a few minutes they were all rigid in burial black. They made the change smoothly and without hurry.

Bruce sat at the wheel of the hearse and, glancing at his watch, nodded. Sidewalk drove the second car. George operated the street door of the garage, got into the second car and the two vehicles slid reverently out into the Florida day.

They drove at a dead march pace, ten miles an hour, around a one-way street and past the front of the bank. With great caution nine pairs of eyes swivelled to take in the scene. The bank was silent. Nobody had moved to give the alarm.

The funeral sailed serenely by, hardly noticed by anyone on the sidewalk. Bruce steadied his hand on the wheel. He leaned over to Ossie.

'Listen pal, where are we heading? Is this a Jewish funeral or some other kind?'

'Jesus,' said Ossie. 'I forgot to ask.'

'Great,' mutterd Gabby. 'Now what do we do?'

'Go to the Jewish cemetery,' said Lou almost below his breath. 'And if they don't expect us there, go to the other goddam place.'

'I vote we leave this wagon train by the side of the road and beat it,' said Bruce. 'It ain't going to make any difference to the guy in the box.'

'We can't,' protested Katy. 'Not just leave the poor man.' But it was unconvincing. She added: 'Maybe we can . . . but . . . somewhere . . . nice.'

They pulled to a stop in the car park of Miami's Hialeah Race Course. At that time of day the vast area was deserted. 'I promised we'd take them back,' said Ari. 'I told the guy. I said he could have them back in time for the funeral.'

'We'll pass him another hundred dollars,' said Ossie. 'The quicker we get clear the better. Okay?'

They left the hearse and its coffin parked decently and getting into the second funeral car they drove away. It was a big race afternoon at Hialeah and the coffin remained there until nightfall, the centre of interest and speculation for thousands.

'One hundred thousand bucks,' breathed Ossie. 'At last we got it right!'

The loot was piled on the table in Molly's room, like a haphazard wall, the notes in wrinkled bundles of a hundred. All around the members of the Ocean Drive Delinquent Society sat as if attending at some shrine.

'And it's all real,' said Bruce, easing forward to touch the notes. 'Every goddam buck. And all ours.'

'More than ten thousand each,' breathed Katy. 'A girl could get married on that.' She rolled her eyes at Lou. He coughed and grinned sheepishly.

Gabby said: 'I suggest we deduct ten thousand dollars for expenses. For this and for future operations. Anyone object?'

No one did. 'Well, I guess we'd better start giving out the Christmas presents,' said Gabby. 'Ain't no good just looking at the stuff.' She broke a section from the wall of the notes and counted it into each lap, starting with Katy and ending with George. Only Molly seemed unsure. 'I still think it seems just a little dishonest,' she whispered to her granddaughter.

'Okay,' Gabby said decisively, 'we'll take yours and share it around evenly. Is that what you want, grandma?'

Molly closed her mouth and closed her hands about her ten thousand.

'Just one thing,' Ossie said, looking around warningly. 'Don't everybody go out splashing this stuff around. Sit on it for a while. Nobody buys a car or a mink. Okay? Just let the situation cool. If we don't, somebody's going to get wise. I vote we split up now. Just disperse quietly and say nothing. We'll have another operation for you before long.'

Zaharran remained after the others. He sat there, a large hunched figure, his ten thousand dollars in his lap. 'Well, George,' breathed Bruce gratefully, 'we're sure glad you joined. You brought us some know-how and some luck. I hope you feel the same about it.'

'Sure, sure,' answered Zaharran. His wig slipped forward as he nodded and, since his hands were full of money, he indicated to the young man that he would be glad of some assistance in putting the hairpiece back in place. Bruce obliged. 'I never had so much dough,' said the older man. 'And it was all so easy.'

He rose and went to his small suitcase which he had left in the room. He opened it and stowed the money carefully. Then, like some unkempt roadside salesman, he went out into the close, star-lit night. His mind was travelling like a roundabout. Then he patted his little case reassuringly and laughed to himself all the way down Ocean Drive.

CHAPTER NINE

Zaharran was asleep on the floor of his little office when Salvatore came in after knocking once. The knock was insufficient to wake the big man and the policeman stood looking down at him as God might look down from heaven upon an extinct volcano. The visitor however was not, at the best of times, given to poetic reflection and especially not today. He nudged Zaharran with first one foot and then the other.

One eye opened down there. 'I ain't no football,' said Zaharran. 'I don't like folks kicking me.' With heavy difficulty he levered himself up onto his elbows and worked his face about to try and settle it into its daytime creases. 'You're living dangerously, Salvatore,' he continued as he tried to get up from the floor. The policeman got his arm and helped him with a heave. 'Have a care with the back,' warned Zaharran. He did a cumbersome swivel movement and his backside closed with the chair. He sat down and looked at Salvatore. 'Living dangerously,' he repeated. 'You should know better than to creep up on a guy in my line of work when he's sleeping. I might have knocked you over with my forty-five.'

'With your snore, maybe,' sighed Salvatore. 'You heard the news? They did it again, the bastards. They robbed a bank this time.'

'Sure, I heard the radio before I went to sleep,' nodded Zaharran. 'They seem like they're getting better.'

'Jesus Alvin Christ,' said Salvatore. 'Is that the best you got for me? *They're getting better!* Do I need a detective to tell me they're getting better?'

'An elementary deduction,' admitted Zaharran sagely. 'While I ain't retained on a financial basis, what do you expect? So what gives?'

'They took a girl, a secretary from the bank, to cover themselves. They said they would leave her on the Tuttle Causeway, but instead they just pushed her into the strongroom with all the rest of the staff.' Salvatore sighed deeply. 'And get this,' he said. 'They stole a funeral!' Zaharran's eyebrows ascended and he whistled. 'Yeah they hi-jacked a funeral,' said Salvatore. 'There's a funeral parlour right across the street from the bank and they got away in a hearse. They took it – with the guy in the coffin – to Hialeah.' He put his head in his hands. 'I need help, Zaharran. I was hoping you might have come up with something.'

'Not much,' lied Zaharran. This was it, he thought. From now on the die was cast. He'd never had ten thousand dollars in cash before. 'I've been circulating down on Ocean Drive. It's real nice down there on the beach. The ocean's kinda of lazy and they have some funny pelicans and lots of . . .'

'Stop!' howled Salvatore. 'I don't want a guided tour around the district! Fuck the pelicans!'

'That's an indictable offence, I shouldn't wonder,' said Zaharran. He leaned forward. 'Okay, listen Salvatore. It's no consolation to you, I know. But I'm watching. That's all I can tell you. I'm watching.'

'Great,' sighed Salvatore. 'I get a grant for you – a hundred and fifty dollars no less – from the pension fund and all you can tell me is you're watching. That's big dough for watching, Zaharran.'

'Did you bring the money with you?' asked Zaharran practically. 'I mean now?'

'No,' Salvatore snapped. 'It has to go through channels. You know that. Maybe it will get through by the end of the month.'

Zaharran sighed. 'By which time I am lying down there on the floor and when you come in and kick me, I don't move. And why don't I move? Because I'm lying dead, that's why.'

'I'm going,' said Salvatore. 'I really am. I come out of that crazy goddam office, with everybody yelling on my head, and come here hoping to get some good news, or maybe even a little sympathy, and all you can tell me is that I might find you lying dead. A great big deal that would be. What sort of sympathy have you got? What sort, I ask you?'

Zaharran regarded him with a face crammed with sorrow. 'I'll tell you what I'll do, Salvatore,' he said. 'I'll sell my novelty business to you. And the astrology by mail, cheap. That could be a winner. All it needs is a little foresight. You could quit the force and put all your efforts into it.'

Salvatore regarded him balefully. 'I'm going home,' he said. 'I'm going home to my wife and family. They don't love me either, but I got a roof and a door there. I'm protected.'

'Listen, pal,' said Zaharran. He was genuinely sorry for Salvatore, but he kept thinking that he had never seen ten thousand dollars before. 'Listen, I'm working on it, Okay? That's the best news I've got for you.'

Loose Bruce and Gabby were sail-surfing off Key Biscayne, balanced with young grace on the fibreglass hulls while the fresh wind pushed into the vividly striped sails. They were half a mile out and the sea was vacant. Neither wore any clothes, his shorts and her bikini were tied each to the single masts of their craft. The wind and the sun whirled about them. Their browned bodies bent easily as they manoeuvred the sail-boats. They laughed with exhilaration.

'I'd like to get to know you better, lady,' called Bruce as he curled his craft closer to hers. He bent it away again before she had time to answer.

'Never better than you do,' she called after him. She watched him dip into the side of an ambitious wave and brace himself as the sail-board met the challenge and rose triumphantly.

'You're crazy,' she yelled happily. 'Mad!'

A long wild sand spit ventured out into the sea from Key Biscayne with a group of palms standing on it like marooned folk waiting for rescue. The white houses and other buildings on Key Biscayne, beyond the spit, were just visible among the greenery as they moved towards it and cars moved busily across the causeway and along the ocean front.

They both knew where they were heading. They shifted their weight and coaxed the single sails of their novel craft with the wind. Now with its strength right behind them they headed at speed for the beach. They both began to shout, feeling the naked exhilaration. Gabby's blue and white striped sail stretched taut beside her and over her head and Bruces's red diamond on a white sheet was in the full swell of the sea wind. They rode over the waves like two horsemen bearing banners.

The sail boards sliced fast over the last remaining water and the pair turned them expertly at the optimum moment, so that they slid beautifully onto the low shelf of beach. They kept the momentum and tumbled ashore, rolling delightedly onto the easy white sand. Bruce turned and caught the girl in his brown arms and they rolled across the beach. They lay laughing at the end of it, covered with spray and with sand adhering to the spray. They kissed and parted laughing because their lips were sandy. Bruce rose and took the girl's hand. They went back to the fringe of the water and caught the sail-boards which were fidgeting in the low water, trying to free themselves from the beach. They pulled them clear, then bent and rolled into the sea again to wash away the sand.

They stood up in the shallow water and admired each other's nakedness. Her hand went out and caught hold of him. His head dropped forward when she touched him and he pushed his fair rough hair into the smooth vale between her large breasts. His hands went to their flanks and he pressed them to his cheeks. They looked up at each other and grinned now, the time for laughter having gone. 'I've been getting hungry for you, Gabby,' he said seriously.

He picked her up and put her across his hard shoulder, smacking her buttocks playfully as he did so. She giggled and returned the smack, hanging down his back like a large shining fish. 'No fighting,' he warned. 'If there's any fighting, I do it. Okay?'

'Okay,' she said. 'I'll go along with that.'

Bruce unloaded her none too gently on the sand. 'I've got sand all stuck to me again,' she whispered as he knelt over her.

'We're stuck with it,' he said. He kissed her on the face and then on the lips. 'Want to come on top?' he inquired.

'Sure. Today I want to be boss lady.'

'Right, start climbing,' said Bruce. He lay back into the warmth of the beach, feeling it across his shoulder blades and his backside and the backs of his legs. She climbed on him, an immediate dreaminess overcoming her so that her movements were at once slowed, her face taking on an uncertain smile as if she did not know what was to occur next, her eyes half closed. Bruce grinned with anticipation, his hands went about the deep indentations on her waist and he eased her into position. Her face broke into a series of small spasms as she settled on him. Then, when they were together, she fell carefully forward and rested her breasts against his tight chest and her thick hair against his face.

They lay on the beach and the sun lay on them. The considerate frond of a palm tree occasionally stretched itself in the breeze to give them some momentary shade. Its shadow fanned across their forms as they moved slowly. It was no time for passion. It was too hot. They took it easily and quietly like young people do who feel there might be many more times ahead. Gabby groaned as she rode him at a little canter. He lay easing himself up to her and down into the sand again in compliment to her movements. The whole time they did not alter their pace, not even hurrying, as so many do, towards the end. They came as they went, almost idly.

Afterwards they lay for several minutes, dopey against each other, a few small movements coming from her in a lazy effort to gain another sensation. Their bodies were sweating, glistening like lizards. Their eyes remained closed, their skin relaxed.

It was while they were in this semi-embrace that they were spotted by a large Florida crab, staggering like an afternoon drunk along the usually deserted shoreline. He had little experience of humans and their habits, even less their sexual fashions, and the entangled limbs and adjacent trunks lying so quietly on the sand took his curiosity.

He advanced without fear or caution and upon reaching the side of the girl's thigh took a deep crablike breath and began to climb. Gabby, believing the touches came from Bruce's fingers, remained placid and it was only when the crab mounted the back of her thigh and was there resting that she demurred. 'Baby,' she whispered. 'You've just got to cut those fingernails.'

Bruce who had one hand on her naked backside and the other trailing idly in the sand moved both hands to her waist and half opened his eyes. 'Is that two hands you've got around my middle?' asked the girl half rising and waking rapidly. 'Two?'

'Two,' he confirmed, puzzled but unworried. 'Sorry about the fingernails.'

'Bruce, there's something on my leg,' she muttered. Her eyes widened and she looked backwards over her shoulder to see the crab's bright black eyes regarding her with the insolence of the conqueror. For a second she was immobilized, then she flung herself sideways from Bruce with a cry that set the gulls and pelicans wheeling in worried circles in the sky.

The crab, self-preservation rating higher even than curiosity in its priorities, slid from her leg like a sailor abandoning a ship. It scampered away to the familiarity of the sea. Gabby screamed again and Bruce, after sitting up in alarm, began hooting with laughter as the hind quarters of the crab scuttled away across the sand.

'This is station WAIA, Miami, serving the golden coast from the Palm Beaches to the Florida Keys. Here is the weather for twenty-four hours to six pm tomorrow. It's getting hotter folks. Tonight there will be clear skies and a high of seventy-five degrees, a low of sixty-two, and a ten per cent chance of rain. Tomorrow a high of eighty-five and clear skies, little breeze and a calm sea. Today is April fourteenth and this is WAIA your music way . . .'

After Easter, in those latitudes, the sun gets hotter along the southern ocean coast, the humidity thickens and the wintering people go away. During the torrid summer the Florida beaches are left to the everyday inhabitants and those who cannot afford to move.

Along Ocean Drive in that month, competition among the retired people for a place in the shade of the sea-grape trees increased and there were occasional arguments and disputes in the vivid dialects that so many of the denizens could summon, sometimes even involving the use of fists and what force could be fired in the elderly breast. It was not easy to keep a temper in that off-season heat.

Ari the Greek got up very early on those days for his run. The sun was just swelling from below the Atlantic when he trotted from the front porch of the Sunny Gables Hotel and went on his jogging journey along the amber beach and eventually along Ocean Drive and the streets back to the hotel. He was so early these mornings that the Washington Avenue store was not open when he passed it so he could not go in for a blood pressure test. He needed to make a special journey late in the day.

His blood pressure was all right but Ari's conscience was bothering him. He had not spent a cent of the illicit money that had come his way. It remained in a box hidden at the back of the cupboard in his room. It seemed to call in an increasing nagging voice, calling out that he had, at his age, committed a major felony. Bootlegging was different and it was so long ago.

He even confided these misgivings to Molly, who at that season took her metal detector to the beach as early as Ari went on his run. 'Maybe I'm old fashioned or crazy,' he sighed, 'but I get all that loot out and I say to myself, "Ari," I say, "who needs it!".'

Molly nodded, for she understood him well. Without looking up but continuing to weave her curved patterns with her metal detector, even obliging Ari to move his sneaker-clad feet out of the way, she said: 'It didn't seem so bad when we were losing, if you get what I mean, Ari. When we made a hash of the jobs it seemed to be okay. Kinda square and fair. But I got to tell you I've been worried too. It ain't the thought of getting caught. I keep wondering if that poor guy at the bank got into trouble. The manager, I mean. He seemed such a nice man, just like my Melford, I thought, and he was just about due to retire.'

'Nearly one of us,' said Ari sadly.

'Not the sort at all we should have threatened with that rocket firer,' she continued pensively.

The machine she was using gave a whirr in her ears. Ari heard it and his face sharpened with interest. 'What is it, Molly?' he asked. 'Something big?'

'A quarter at the most,' she shrugged. 'Probably a dime. I can tell by the tone.' She produced a small garden fork and proceeded to prod and scrape the sand. Ari watched with interest. Eventually the now rising sun touched off a glint of silver and Molly bent and recovered a coin, a dime, from the sand.

'It ain't much,' she said, looking fondly, 'but at least it's lost – not stolen.'

Ari's face clouded and she looked up and saw he was troubled. 'I'd better be on my way,' he said. 'Once the sun gets up this running ain't so funny. 'Bye, Molly.'

''Bye, Ari. Have a nice day.' She smiled her motherly smile and Ari, after glancing at the sun as if it were particularly pursuing him, jogged away.

'Keep running,' she called, beginning to sweep the sand with the detector again. 'Just keep running, Ari.'

'Sure,' he called back over his shoulder. 'While I'm running I'm living.' He did a quick spasm of shadow boxing. 'It won't make me rich, but I'm living,' he said to himself. He wondered, once again, what the hell he was supposed to do with ten thousand dollars.

Lou the Barbender and K-K-K-Katy sat holding hands at the Parrot Jungle watching a bright cockatoo pedal a tiny cycle along a tightrope. 'That's so cute,' sighed K-K-K-Katy. 'Makes you feel you want children of your own.'

'I hope they don't look like parrots,' put in Lou gently. 'I'm allergic to feathers.'

She laughed her silvery girl's laugh and nudged him. 'I mean seeing all the children enjoying this,' she said. 'I didn't mean they would *be* like the parrots.'

'I liked the little one on the roller skates best,' said Lou. 'The parrot. That's real neat.'

They watched the remainder of the novel performance and then went unhurriedly from the amphitheatre to walk around the tropical gardens alive with shouting birds. Lou bought two ice creams and they sat admiring a row of exquisitely-hued cockatoos, large as chickens, who perched and posed for round-eyed photographs and cackled: 'Watch the birdie.'

'I know we won't have children,' said Katy, patting his hand and speaking carefully. 'We're just a little too late. But if we did I wouldn't want them to know their parents robbed a bank.'

She was looking at his big cheek, his strong nose and his suntanned forehead. His eyes remained forward, staring as if he was trying to identify one cockatoo especially. 'Nor me, honey,' he said gruffly. 'I'd like them to tell the other kids that their daddy was the strongest man in America and their mommy had the prettiest legs. But not that we robbed a bank. No, I don't go for that.'

'It don't seem right getting married on stolen money either, Lou,' she whispered. Now she wanted to get it all off her conscience. 'It won't help us to be happy. We'll always have to live with it.'

He nodded ponderously, still considering the coloured birds. 'Maybe God will strike me dead on our wedding night,' he forecast gloomily. 'Dead like stone – and then you'll have my share to worry about as well. Twenty thousand bucks on your conscience, Katy. I couldn't leave you with that sort of legacy.'

'I wouldn't want it,' she sighed. 'Gee, I want to get married, Lou. More than anybody knows. But it's not the way to finance it. I want us to save up what we get legally. We could save enough in a year. We don't need much.'

Lou shrugged in agreement. 'A year now ain't going to make any difference, honey,' he said, apparently addressing a huge turquoise and yellow bird which was leaning forward, intent on every word. 'We're not going to get any older in a year.'

'That's right!' exclaimed the bird. 'That's right! That's right, buddy! That's right!' He rocked to and fro with the excitement of what he had said and let loose a huge screech to emphasize the point. Katy laughed and Lou nodded his head in slow wisdom.

'He seems to agree,' said Katy, squeezing Lou's arm. They had finished the ice cream and now they went, her delicate hand in his big paw, towards the exit to the park where their excursion bus was waiting. Other people were going the same way. Katy bent her head against Lou's shoulder. 'It's not that I don't enjoy doing it, baby,' she said. A young couple walking the same way and two feet from them both turned and registered surprise. 'I love every second of it,' continued Katy, oblivious of the attention she was getting. 'It's the most exciting thing ever. But it's the consequences. When I open the box and see all those little faces looking at me . . . so accusingly.'

The young couple swallowed jointly and hurried ahead. 'Jesus, what d'you know,' breathed the boy. 'And *we're* supposed to be the kookie generation.'

Molly Mandy, her best hat on her head and determination in her elderly heart, left the front door of the Sunny Gables Hotel and headed for the post office on Washington Avenue. She was carrying a supermarket shopping bag and in the bag, parcelled with the utmost care, was a package containing ten thousand dollars. It was addressed to the manager of the United States National Trust Bank on Broward Boulevard, Miami, and contained a note which said:

Dear Manager,
I am sending this money back to you because I can't sleep for it. It's more than I have ever seen in my life before but I was brought up not to steal, even from those who have plenty, and so I am sending it back to you with my compliments. This is only my share of the money taken from your bank in the raid but I am sure you will be glad to see it back safely.

> Yours faithfully,
> *A Robber*

Her heart banged like a gong all the way along Washington Avenue. She was sure she would meet some other member of the Ocean Drive Delinquent Society and her guilt would show. But the street was much as it always was, hot on one side, shaded on the other. The hot side was very hot, for it was afternoon and the sun was striking along its whole length, but she braved the discomfort in the exchange for fewer people. She reached the post office and went in gratefully. The clerk took the parcel and weighed it. His eyebrows went up. 'That packet is going to cost a packet, lady,' he said.

'It's worth it, mister,' she said mysteriously. 'Every cent.'

Five minutes later she came out of the building feeling years younger and pounds lighter. She chose the shaded side of the street and walked like a girl in springtime, swinging her hips, a smile gracing her face and her hat at a jaunty angle. She said 'Hi!' and 'Good afternoon,' and 'Great to see you,' to people she did not even know.

One person she did not see had watched her walk to the post office and had followed in her wake, had sat on a seat opposite while she deposited the parcel, and had observed her lighthearted exit from the building and her sunny progress down the street once more.

It was Zaharran. He was smiling a knowing smile.

The riverboat *Florida King* left Fort Lauderdale every afternoon at two for a cruise along the green-banked miles of the inland waterways. It was built like the Mississippi paddle steamers of older days, with many decks, brightly painted bows and superstructure. It carried three hundred passengers seated on rows along the decks one above the other. As it made its two hour voyage it looked, from the banks, like a giant sandwich, with the tourists as the filling.

It was a popular excursion because what the area lacked in geographical variety and history it made up for in opulence. Immediately the steamer left Fort Lauderdale pier and headed for the creeks and canals it voyaged on tranquil green water cushioned by the lawns and trees and glaring white houses of the very rich indeed.

The tourists, fortunate enough to be able to visit this last leg of the United States when it was winter elsewhere in the land, gazed with a mixture of interest and envy as the homes of the wealthy slid by. Sometimes a person was to be seen in a deck chair on a lawn, the ship's guide would announce his or her household name over the loud-speaker and the entire three hundred trippers would wave and call.

Sometimes the household name would wave wearily back and the tourists could then go home to Wisconsin and Ohio and say they had exchanged greetings with a multi-millionaire.

Overhanging the water were willows and palms, hibiscus and brilliant tulip trees, giving it a hybrid aspect, part temperate, part tropical. Each pure white house had a landing stage or a boat dock and the slender and luxurious craft, tethered like pets, moved, idle and rich, in the wash of the large riverboat.

'On your left, folks – look left, not right, sir – just below that big, beautiful tree, the one that touches the water, is the lovely home of George C. Peckin, President of the United Whisky Importers and a dozen other corporations. That house – believe it or not – is called Scotch Corner.' The guide had recited it a hundred times over the microphone but he tried to sound lively.

An appreciative titter drifted over the packed rows on the paddle-steamer, but too many were staring at the shaded luxury being indicated to appreciate the joke. Ossie, Gabby, Bruce and Sidewalk sat on one row. K-K-K-Katy, Lou the Barbender, Ari and Molly, and Zaharran sat in the row behind. Their heads, like the rest of the two hundred and ninety heads on the vessel, moved obediently from one side of the waterway to the other, as if following some slow and travelling tennis game.

'These wonderful homes have been built by famous industrialists and politicians and some by film stars. Not *all* the stars are in California, folks. The house coming up on the left is the home of Miss Tottie di Milo . . . that house just on the strip of land projecting into the waterway, with the luxury cabin cruiser moored there. I wonder who can be visiting today . . .?'

The mansion was still a hundred yards ahead but many of the eager sightseers could not wait so they stood and leaned this way and that trying to get a view around the screening trees and perhaps catch a glimpse of the famous movie star and her visitors.

'You remember the movie *Where the Boys Are*, folks?' A chorus of vague assent came from the sandwiched decks. 'Well that was one movie made right here in Fort Lauderdale. And the boys are still here, and the girls I'm glad to say . . .'

The ponderous showboat had now drawn abreast of the house of Tottie di Milo. As it eased along the waterway, it cleared the trees and the dazzling white home unrolled before the thrilled eyes of the tourists. 'Wow, what a shack, ladies and gentlemen,' enthused the guide who said it twice a day. 'A lovely home. Miss Tottie is resting after making a movie. And when you're a big girl like Tottie di Milo you sure need your rest!'

The tourists sniggered dutifully. The guide continued to shout. 'Next week she is throwing a great big bonanza party for all the society people and the show people who happen to be in Florida right now. I sure would like to get a pass to that, wouldn't you? What a bullfight that is going to be!'

An envious buzz of assent rose from the decks. 'One thing that's truly unique about the house,' went on the man indestructibly. 'It has a river – yes, people, you heard right, a real, wet river – running right through the salon. It empties into the waterway just by the boat dock. There's not too many houses, even in wonderful Florida, that have a genuine one hundred per cent river going through them.'

The chorus of amazement at the news was overcome by an even louder emission as the people spotted a bikini-clad figure issuing from the widespread reflecting doors of the house. The glass flashed in the sunlight as she came out. Right on cue. 'And my goodness, are we in luck!' the commentator gabbled. 'Wow! It's Miss Tottie di Milo herself!'

There was such a rush to the left hand side of the ship it seemed to wallow and list that way. 'Steady, steady,' came the warning. 'Don't capsize the boat. It's all we have.'

'I'll capsize it if that broad rescues me,' said Ari the Greek ruminatively. Zaharran sniffed heavily and moved to the other side of the boat as if hoping that his weight would counterbalance the list.

'Miss Tottie has come out to say hello,' announced the commentator excitedly. 'Give her a wave, folks. Show her we love her!'

There was multiple waving and the riverboat lurched sluggishly. The goddess, posed and poised on the bank, waved a bandanna and flashed her famous teeth in the sun. She was joined by two obediently playful dogs and then by a long, loping figure in shorts wearing a hawser of gold chain around his neck.

'Gee and look who's here!' bellowed the commentator. 'None other than Herb Specter, folks. I guess you've all seen the movie *Skin and Skin*. Mr Specter was the star of that movie.'

Excitement aboard the *Florida King* was reaching the proportions of a mutiny. Molly and K-K-K-Katy urgently joined the mass hoping to see Herb Specter, Molly standing unceremoniously on Ossie's lap to do so. He struggled painfully but patiently.

'Only this morning, folks, I read that Herb had left his wife back in Hollywood, California, and was entering a new romance. Well now we know who it is don't we? We have it exclusive!'

A huge chorus of satisfaction and acclaim rose from the crammed tourists. They waved with renewed fury and Tottie and Herb waved back with dignified movements, like royalty, from the lawns that sloped to the water. Eventually the boat eased itself further away and reluctantly and raggedly the people sat down. The hull righted itself.

'Could you ask the captain if we could get real close on the way back?' a lady called to the guide. 'I'd sure like to take a picture.'

The commentator smiled grimly. He said below his breath, 'We'll beach the fucking ship and you can get an autograph.' He waved to her, indicating that they would do their best.

Molly sat down again, perspiring with the efforts she had made to gain a vantage point. 'It's just great to see the greats, isn't it just?' she said to her granddaughter. Gabby rolled her eyes and patted her grandmother's hand.

Zaharran, still on the far side of the deck, was confronted by a big, flowered lady who demanded the restoration of her seat. 'I was just keeping the boat upright,' he grunted and lumbered back to the opposite rail. He looked down at Ossie and Ossie saw an expression in his bulbous eye. The big man leaned over the rail and consulted the water as if he were sounding the fathoms. Ossie got up and stood beside him.

'You found what we came for? asked Ossie quietly.

'Ah,' said Zaharran lazily. 'I was just thinking what a great coincidence it is that the lady over there . . . in the house . . . with the boobs and the ape . . .'

'Tottie di Milo,' said Ossie. 'What were the thoughts?'

'Yeah, that's her. What a coincidence that she should be having a big, big party next week, with all the society and all the stars and suchlike, and there's us looking for another operation.'

'How do we get in?' asked Ossie quietly. 'The place is bound to have security all around it. She's that sort of star.'

'Well, she's got a living river running through the place,' sniffed Zaharran. He smiled through the sniff. 'That ain't too bad for a start.'

CHAPTER TEN

They sat in a silent, shadowy circle in Molly Mandy's room, the central light falling on the plan that Ossie had spread over the table. Already there was a suppressed excitement about them, the faces inching forward, alive with anticipation and interest. For the Ocean Drive Delinquent Society there was no source of adrenalin like the plotting of another raid.

'Obviously the river that goes through the salon of Old Creek House is not much more than a stream,' said Ossie pointing to the appropriate part of the plan. 'It is no Mississippi.'

An elderly audible smile came from those around. K-K-K-Katy reached and found Lou's hand, Ari exchanged some sort of left-hand jabs with an invisible opponent, Zaharran sat like a pile of wet cement, small ripples of movement going over his large body, but his eyes steady and intent. Gabby looked at the composed Ossie and then at the youthful Bruce, his brown face like copper in the subdued light. Inwardly she shrugged.

'The river,' Ossie went on, 'is in fact ten feet wide and four deep. But that's a constant depth. It's got a square concrete base even if it's been planted with various reeds and stuff like that. It runs almost down the centre of the main room and out through an arched tunnel into the waterway. That's the way we are going in.'

He drew a small circle on the map with his fingers. 'Just here, almost at the back of the room, where the faucet feeds the water into the river there is a kind of round ornamental pool with fish and this is kept separate from the river itself by a removable metal grille. That grill we will use as a mooring for the boat. Okay?'

Doubtfully Ossie looked around the circle. 'I take it you've all at least seen pictures of an Everglades fan-boat. Maybe you've seen a real one, or on television. It's a flat-bottomed skiff, designed for use in the swamps where there's no great depth of water and where there's a lot of weed and other crud that would catch in the propellers of any other type of craft. It can be used in as little as five inches of water, so we should have depth to spare. It's propelled by a fan mounted on the stern, an outsized version of one of the desk fans you see in people's offices or homes.

'We've had a long talk about this, Gabby and Bruce and myself, and we think that this fan-boat is just about right for our requirements. It's narrow enough to get through the tunnel from the river to the house and it has no draught to speak of so we'll have plenty of water below the hull. There's one disadvantage. At the most it will carry six people.' He glanced at the large Zaharran. 'Five if we take George,' he said. He smiled apologetically but Zaharran merely nodded acknowledgement. 'We also need a look-out,' went on Ossie. 'And two people to have the getaway cars ready – in the right place at the right time.'

He paused and then said. 'Personally I'm sorry about this because it's George's brainchild, but if he wouldn't mind . . .'

'Don't worry about me, son,' said Zaharran shaking his head in slow motion. 'I'll fix the cars. I'll be there when you get ashore.'

'Great. Thanks. We need six for the operation, I think. Would Katy mind being the look-out? She's really good at that.'

'I don't mind, dear,' said Katy. 'I can wh-wh-whistle.'

Molly clasped her hands in front of her face with excitement. 'Oh good, goody, good,' she said. Then her face clouded. 'I made a mess of my mask,' she confessed. 'I was trying to drink coffee when I was wearing it. Just kinda practising, you understand. And you can't drink it like that. I'll have to send it to the valet service.'

Gabby, among others, closed her eyes. 'I wouldn't do that, grandma,' she advised. 'They may get a little suspicious having a mask and a hood in at the valet service.'

'You're darn right,' said Molly emphatically. 'I'm sure glad you mentioned it, dear. Okay, I'll get the coffee out myself.' She looked up benignly oblivious of the defeated looks she was getting. 'What's next?' she asked brightly.

Ossie coughed. He said slowly: 'Yes, well, next . . . You really won't take the mask to the valet service, will you, Molly . . .? No, good. Just try and remember. It might be like taking the guns to the pawn shop, if you understand what I mean.'

'Sure I see,' nodded Molly blandly. 'I'm not completely crazy.'

'Good, good,' said Ossie. 'That's very reassuring. Now, there's the small matter of obtaining the fan-boat. Our good friend and colleague Sidewalk here knows where they keep the fan-boats at night and he and Ari are going to borrow one for a while.'

'It's a yard where they renovate them,' said Sidewalk Joe. 'It ain't too difficult. And it ain't that far away either, so that will make it easier. I've always wanted to drive one of them things.'

Ossie nodded at him. 'Fine. Now the details will be worked out between Gabby, Bruce and myself, as usual. Maybe George wouldn't mind remaining behind as well. His know-how was pretty useful last time.' George's head nodded. 'I guess that's all, ladies and gentlemen,' said Ossie. 'Don't talk about it, even among yourselves. You never know who's got ears that may be functioning even in South Miami.' He smiled at the joke, but they didn't smile back.

Molly leaned over to Ari and said: 'What did he say?'

'I don't know,' said Ari. 'I didn't hear.'

'Wednesday,' said Ossie a little more loudly. 'Assemble here at nine. We plan to enter the house at ten-thirty and be out with the profits by ten-forty. Any further questions?'

There were none. The old gang went out singly to their small rooms. Gabby, Ossie and Bruce said goodnight to each one. Zaharran moved towards the table. He was going to be in charge of the getaway cars. The perfect trap. Now he had them. If he wanted them.

Tottie di Milo had experienced some little difficulty in getting together enough fun people for her party, because Fort Lauderdale at that time of the year was not the place where the fun people gathered. She was saved, however, by the surprising advent of Frankie Moon, the popular singer, who had come down from New York to give an in-person concert in Miami. He had with him various members of his travelling world, his dumb wife, his two dumb mistresses and his children by various alliances and marriages. His musicians were the famous Billy Bolon group and they had their various affiliates, and there were some supporting singers and a progressive comedian. She asked them all to her party and they all accepted, there not being a great deal of excitement in Miami out of season.

She also invited neighbours of Old Creek House who happened to be in residence, including George C. Peckin, the president of United Whisky Importers, who had a group of business associates and their wives as his guests at his waterway home.

Miss di Milo was busy completing her late guest list a few days before the party when there was a telephone call from the Miami Police Department.

'I've done nothing,' she said immediately in her famous film voice. At any time of the day or evening, even if she had been awake for hours, it was the voice of a voluptuous woman just roused from sleep. The voice of a long-haired lovely, speaking with her eyes closed.

'Oh,' she sighed. 'You're *not* going to arrest me? Oh I'm so glad, captain, so glad.'

Captain Salvatore on the receiving end of this honey permitted himself to enjoy the sensation. Betty, his wife, had just nagged him for ten minutes on that same phone. 'No, Miss di Milo,' he breathed. 'We're not arresting you, much as we would appreciate your company. The area of this bureau could do with a little glamour.'

'You're just *so* kind,' she breathed. 'I'm afraid I don't look very glamorous just now. I'm just in an old pink silk robe. Nothing else at all. Not one little thing.'

Salvatore bit his lip fiercely at the thought. He returned to business. 'Miss di Milo, you're having a society party, so I understand, in a few days.'

'News travels,' she whispered. 'Just a hundred little people. All close friends.'

'Sure, sure. I bet you've got more than that too. It's just that I'd appreciate it if I could come over and take up some of your time discussing your security arrangements.'

'Security?' She seemed to wake up at the word. 'Why? What's wrong with my security, captain? I have a little guard at the gate all the time.'

'I know, Miss di Milo, I know. But you may know from the newspapers that we've had a gang operating in the Miami area over the past few weeks. They already made one raid on a party at a home in Palm Beach. So we're just keeping a surveillance on social events like the one you're proposing to have on Wednesday. And especially social gatherings that are mentioned in the newspapers. There was an item in the *Miami News* about your party last night.'

'A gang?' she resumed her wondrous, embedded voice. 'A gang of robbers?'

'Masked robbers,' confirmed Salvatore.

'Masked? But, oh, that's terrifying. I'm shaking all over, captain. Somehow I've just got to calm down.'

Salvatore blinked at the phone he was holding. 'It's just a precaution, Mis di Milo. Don't let it bother you. All we want to do is have the house watched. A patrol car or maybe two on the streets leading to the property. Perhaps I could just call and familiarize you with the plans.'

'Any time,' she breathed. 'I'd just love to be familiarized.'

Salvatore put the phone down and, standing up quickly as if hoping to catch his reflection by surprise, looked in the mirror on the wall. Without much hope he tried to arrange his sparse hair so that it covered more of his scalp. He smiled courageously and brushed his teeth with his finger. Then he picked up the intercom phone. 'Detective Cook,' he said. 'Are you solving big crimes?'

'No, captain. I'm looking in the newspaper to see what's on TV tonight.'

'Well get off your ass, Cookie. We're going to see a lovely lady. Well I am. You can sit in the car.'

Tottie di Milo wondered what she should do while she waited for the policeman. She had bathed luxuriously and attended to the ritual of her make-up. She thought perhaps she ought to put some clothes on and this she did, although she often felt better without. But when she had dressed the detective had still not arrived. Habitually she found it difficult to fill in vacuous moments and she sat down and stood up again several times in front of a full length mirror, each time adopting a different pose, trying urgently to decide which did the most for her.

Then she brightened because she had an idea and generally they came slowly. She went down to the main salon of her beautiful house, to where the living river flowed through the floor. At the ornamental pool at the top end of the huge semi-circular room she took a bowl of freshly cut meat and began to feed the new acquisitions that would, she was sure, be the sensation of the party. Two Everglades alligators.

The gang left the two cars on a short jetty near Fort Lauderdale Bridge, one of the series of cantilever bridges which opened to allow large vessels to progress along the Intra-Coastal Waterway, the operation being worked by a man in a small wheelhouse on the beach side.

Zaharran and Lou the Barbender stayed with the cars. K-K-K-Katy had already taken up her look-out post in a telephone booth in the street leading to Tottie di Milo's house. Around the corner out of Katy's view, and Katy out of their's, Detective Cook and two policemen sat in a car beneath some trees. Another patrol car was two hundred yards away.

The remaining members of the Ocean Drive Delinquent Society embarked on the fan-boat which Ari and Sidewalk had casually stolen and brought to the jetty. It was ten o'clock on a thundery night and the waterway was shaded although the lights of the district shone all around and the bridge was busy with cars. The robbers arranged themselves carefully, three on each side of the slight craft. Ossie and Bruce in the bow, Gabby and Molly next to Sidewalk and Ari behind them. Nobody was hooded yet. Molly held her hood like a present to be opened at Christmas. Her lively eyes were brimming with excitement and apprehension, and they widened even further when a touch from Sidewalk on the starter of the boat sent the fan whirring softly and the boat moving through the dark, silky water.

Sidewalk kept as close as was prudent to the right-hand bank, easing the odd vessel along with all the quiet he could manage. A few disturbed waterbirds croaked as they passed but there were no other alarms. Like commandos the gang crouched on the slight deck. They were approaching the neck of the waterway where the lights of Old Creek House could be seen filtering through the trees. Music, which travels well across water, floated to them. Bruce turned and gave a shadow of a nod to the others. Unhurriedly they began to put on their hoods. Bruce and Ossie mounted a useless Russian mortar in the bow of the boat. They eased its barrel down to the horizontal because it looked more menacing like that. Then Molly Mandy, in the excitement of putting on her hood, fumbled and dropped it into the water.

'Oh dear,' she whispered. 'Mine's gone over the side.'

Ossie turned around with Bruce. Both immediately turned to the front again and uttered swearwords. Gabby looked helpless. 'We've got to get it,' she said. 'She'll be recognized if we don't.'

'And I *do* want to wear it,' pleaded Molly. 'I *do* so.'

Tight-faced, Sidewalk turned the shallow boat around in as brief a circle as he could. They found the missing hood floating towards them but it had gone by before anyone could grab it, so they had to circle again and chase it up the river. Eventually Ari fished it from the waterway and handed it silently to Molly. 'I'll wring it out,' she said brightly.

'I'll wring her out if she does it again,' said Ossie to Bruce under his breath.

Gabby leaned forward in whispered anger. 'Drop dead,' she muttered. 'If you take old people on a goddam picnic you expect jam to be spilt.'

'Okay, okay,' sighed Ossie. 'Do what you can. We're behind the schedule.'

'You always were,' said Gabby rudely. She helped her grandmother to twist the water from the hood. They were now moving slowly towards the lawns of the house. The music issued more firmly through the trees. They could recognize the tune. Ossie leaned back and handed a hood to Molly. 'Better wear this,' he said without looking at her. 'Otherwise you'll get pneumonia.'

'That's mine,' protested Bruce.

'You're young,' said Ossie. 'You wear the wet hood.'

'I'll get neuralgia,' complained Bruce. 'Or toothache. I suffer hell from toothache.'

He took the wet hood from Molly nevertheless and pulled it over his head. Ossie looked around. He could see they were as ready as they would ever be.

'Okay?' he whispered.

The hooded heads nodded.

'Right,' he said. 'Get ready. We're going in.'

It was beginning to look like a good party. Tottie di Milo in her most angelic gown held the hand of her new lover, Herb Specter, and beamed around at all her guests as if she knew and loved them all.

The wide semi-circle of the salon made an excellent place for such a function, particularly on a night, such as this, of gathering off-season thunder. People did not enjoy being out of doors on lawns and patios in threatening weather and the living river flowing through the huge room lent it an added and welcome coolness.

Tottie's new alligators had naturally been a great attraction, with the guests gathering around the pool at the headwaters of the river, so to speak, laughing at them and cajoling them from the safety of the low barrier rail. The alligators, for their parts, bared their teeth hungrily, never having seen so many people at one time.

'It must be like looking at the greatest feast you ever saw – and not being able to touch a morsel,' philosophized Captain Salvatore. He spoke to himself, and possibly the alligators, for Miss di Milo apart, he had never met anyone in the room before and nobody had bothered to introduce him. When she had invited him as her guest he was flattered and delighted. But now he wondered whether he should have been there. It did not feel comfortable. He also realized that his gun was making a bulge in the coat of his best suit.

Hidden music eased its way through the room, glasses and laughter sounded. The singer Frankie Moon with his dumb wife, his dumb mistresses, his tribe of musicians, dancers, whoo-whoo singers, agents, managers and paid admirers, arrived late, to plan. They were in their normal extravagant mood and infused the party with a lot of noise. Frankie Moon himself got a lot of laughs by pouring a glass of bourbon down the yawning throat of one of the Everglades alligators as it came up and glared from the pool.

'Gee,' shouted Mr George C. Peckin of United Whisky, 'I'm real glad that was only bourbon, Mr Moon. If it had been our imported Scotch that 'gator would have been out of that darned pool looking for more!'

It got a laugh as such inanities get laughs at parties. Salvatore abruptly found himself in conversation with Tottie and trying desperately not to look down the front of her dress. Its angelic folds fell away unangelically from the shoulders revealing the twin hills of which Miss de Milo was so proud and which had gone a considerable way to making her famous.

'I feel really safe with you around, Captain Salvatore,' she said with a sigh that expanded her bosom even more spectacularly and had Salvatore's eyes desperately swinging for somewhere else to look. Her skin was like coffee cream, swollen and sweet with the material of the dress only just making an horizon below which, he knew, oh he knew, hid the loveliest pink buds in the world. God, he would have given half his pension, *fuck it, all his pension*, just to see them and perhaps touch them and a few other things for a couple of hours. After that he could die, he wouldn't care. Her suntan went zooming right down her cleavage. Jesus Bernard Christ, she must sunbathe in the skin. God, if only he could get a view of them.

'It's certainly kind of you to invite me,' he managed to say through all his imaginings. 'I don't think we need worry too much about any interruptions. But just in case, I have two patrol cars on surveillance, one at each end of the street. Everyone who comes in and out is checked.'

'Is there something wrong with your arm, Captain Salvatore?' she suddenly inquired solicitously. 'Why does it stand away from your body like that? Is it a wound of some sort?'

Salvatore blushed. 'It's my gun,' he explained. 'It don't really fit this suit.'

'Your gun?' she said in a thrilled voice. 'You have your *gun* with you?' She descended to a conspiratorial whisper. 'Guns turn me on so.'

Salvatore smiled like he hoped a television cop would smile. 'Always have this baby with me, Miss di Milo.' He patted the weapon and grimaced as it dug uncomfortably into his chest.

'Tottie,' she invited. He felt sure she let her dress slip forward. 'Please call me Tottie, Captain.'

Salvatore felt a warmth coming up like steam from his boots. Jesus Henry Christ, maybe this sort of woman liked beleaguered police officers with sparse hair and ill-fitting suits. 'Albert,' he whispered.

He looked around. Herb Specter, a big bastard there was no doubt, was sprawled on a couch with one of Frankie Moon's dumb mistresses. Maybe it was one of those parties he had heard about. He felt the gun moving with his deepening breaths and the strong beat of his heart.

'I'm calling you Captain,' she smiled. 'It sounds so much braver. And I want to try on your little gun.'

'My gun?' Salvatore stared at her bosom. 'But it's in a shoulder holster Miss di . . . I mean Tottie. Here, I'll show you.' With theatrical secrecy he quickly opened his coat and revealed the gun in its holster. He could feel his own eyes shining and a warmth rushing through his veins. All at once his head seemed thick with hair.

'Gee, that's neat,' she said. 'Come on, Captain, let me try it. Please – just once.' Unbelievably she pulled away the front of her dress at one side revealing a whole flank of exquisite bosom. 'There's room down there,' she said plaintively. 'Plenty of room for a little gun like that. Let me get you another drink.'

She poured a huge glass of champagne. 'It's difficult,' he said with difficulty. 'Difficult to get the holster off . . . and on. Maybe you'd just like to see the gun.'

Inwardly he cursed himself for being a timid fool but he quickly retrieved the situation. The champagne had given him daring. 'Oh no, maybe you could just get the holster to fit,' he said. 'But I don't want to take it off here. It's too public – and against police regulations, truly.'

'If there's a room where I could take my harness off,' he suggested, his confidence growing wild, 'then you could go to your room and try it. It might be difficult to get it on without er . . . some . . . adjustments . . .'

She winked at him hugely. 'We'll both go,' she decided to his explosive delight. 'We're both in this together.' She glanced quickly at Herb Specter who had now sunk deeper into the couch and almost deeper into the red-haired dumb mistress. 'Herb's having one of his celibate nights,' she said. 'He won't object. Come on, Honey Captain.'

Honey Captain blushed all down his chest. He knew it wasn't happening but, God almighty, she was holding his hand. He thought he needed another drink to keep the vision steady but she was insistent. 'I have some champagne in my room,' she said. 'We can drink while we're adjusting.'

Tottie flitted slightly ahead of him towards one of the distant doors around the circular wall. He glanced quickly around and went at a policeman's creep after her. Nobody seemed to notice. Salvatore thought his heart was going to spoil everything by leaping like an idiot clean out of his chest. He had a fleeting 'if the boys could see me now' thought, went through the door as if he were raiding a cat-house, and followed her though a series of snaking passages until they were at a door which opened at the touch of her fingers.

Salvatore had never seen a beautiful film star's bedroom before. She stood there on the thick carpet, her luxury body suddenly enfolded by the voluptuousness of the room. Salvatore felt so full he wanted to cry.

'Honey Captain,' she said in a voice no weightier than a sigh. The bedroom seemed to have an effect on her also. She suddenly became dreamy, wafty, and she moved over the carpet, her feet below her gown hardly seemed to brush the floor. Nor did Salvatore's.

'Honey Captain,' she repeated, 'you must sit on my bed.'

'Bed?' he answered hollowly. '*Your* bed?'

'Yes,' she said firmly, pointing to the high altar of the room. Pink, heart-shaped, with silks and frills and pillows like ice cream. Salvatore stared at it as if it were the electric chair at Sing Sing and he had been invited to sit in it.

'But *your* bed?' he said hoarsely. 'Are you certain?'

'Sure – I only let people I really love get onto my little bed – even just to sit on it,' she said with sudden coyness. Salvatore knew he was going to wake up in one of his own cells on a charge of drunken fantasy, if there were such a charge. Jesus Bill Christ, she was pouring them more champagne. This was easy, easier than screwing his Betty in the back of his car all those years ago. Betty had kicked like hell. This vision was pouring champagne. She floated towards him, a glass in each hand; the glasses floated before her. He took one, hardly able to stand the devastation of her eyes. He almost missed his mouth when he tried to drink. With a playful push she sat him on the bed. He saw his own knees lock together like a virgin's and he pulled them forcibly apart. 'Now about this little gun,' she said, moving so close her perfume and her warmth added to his giddiness.

'The gun, yes, surely, the gun,' he gabbled, blowing little bubbles of champagne from the top of the glass. 'You wanted to see . . . to fit my gun.'

'That's why we came, didn't we?' she smiled overwhelmingly. 'I only invite gentlemen in here for very special reasons.'

Salvatore thought if there was any more of this he would end up a jabbering lunatic. He tried to reach for the gun with the same hand as held the champagne glass. She laughed like a little bell. 'Crazy man,' she said, taking the glass from him. 'You can't reach it like that. You're getting a little confused . . .' She leaned towards him and blatantly kissed him on the brow. 'I can't think why you're getting confused.'

'I'll have . . . have to take my coat off,' drooled Salvatore. 'If that's all right with you . . . in here.'

'There's no better place,' she whispered. 'Just wait a moment, don't go away.'

For a terrible moment he thought she was leaving because she got up and went towards the door. But, to his suffocating delight, it was only to turn the key. She turned across the room and smiled that internationally famous smile. Her bosom seemed halfway to him. 'There,' she said. 'Now you can take your coat off, Honey Captain.'

He struggled out of the stiff best suit coat and sat there in his trousers, his white shirt and gun. 'Oh, it's too beautiful,' she sighed hurrying to him. 'It's real neat, the way it cuddles into your shoulder. Oh, I'd really like to wear that, please. It would turn me right on.'

His fingers rushed to the buckle and, fumble though he did, he got the harness from around his body in quick time. He took hold of the gun in the holster and handed it to her like a knight surrendering his sword to a noble lady. 'Is it loaded?' she asked.

'Yes . . . no. I can't remember,' he confessed. 'All that seems so long ago Miss di Milo . . . Tottie. I guess it's not. Yes, I remember it clearly – it is. So please be careful.'

'It's you who's loaded,' she joked, silkily kissing him again, this time on the cheek and then on the edge of the mouth which he moved swiftly sideways to catch the kiss. Her full breast lolled across his shoulder. If he died later that night he would not have given a damn.

With a long, delighted, deepening smile she held the harness like the coils of a delicate dead snake. He watched her fine cream fingers run along its length and imagined them doing the same along his backbone. Then she got to the holster, bulging and polished. She removed the gun and set it aside with careful casualness. Then she began to massage the holster with her pink nails, running them over the worn, soft leather, and then, turning the palm sensually, revolving over the leather bulge at the end. Salvatore watched every movement of her fingers as though they were caressing his skin. His eyes grew wider and wider until they hurt.

'Beautiful,' she said throbbingly, still fondling the holster. 'So sexy, Honey Captain.' His eyes came up like slowly moving moons and glowed at him. He could actually feel them on the skin of his face. He gulped at the champagne as a man in a desert might gulp at saving water. There was nothing left in the glass but he was unable to notice.

'You want another drink?' she said, noticing. His hand went to her urgently. 'No, no thanks, Tottie. Just don't move. Don't go away. You may never come back . . .'

She laughed in a whisper. 'The little thing you put the gun into really sways me, darling,' she said. 'It turns me on just like nothing's ever going to be able to turn me off again.'

'Would you . . . would you care to . . . er, try it on?' he inquired like a lingerie salesman with a speech impediment. 'I'll help – it's kinda difficult.'

'Sure, please,' answered Tottie. There were some noises coming from the party but they were two corridors and many ages away as far as Salvatore was concerned. He would have shot anyone who had come into the room just now and would have stood a fair chance with a plea of self defence. She eased her lovely body and picked up the gun. 'And this,' she breathed, 'is beautiful, really beautiful. It double turns me on. Yes . . . double.'

She held the police revolver in both hands, abandoning the holster and the harness like used toys. She rubbed it in her hands and closed her eyes with the feel of it. Salvatore with exquisite alarm saw her breasts heaving more quickly than ever. Jesus Cyril Christ, it was all going to happen; he *knew* it was going to happen. Why couldn't the boys from the precinct see him now? He'd show them! He'd show Betty! He'd show her! By God, he would.

'It fits,' she murmured, her eyes half hinging towards him. She had picked up the harness from the bed again and had slipped the gun into the holster. 'So snug,' she said. She began to move it with blatant sensuousness in and out, in and out, up and down, up and down.

This was more than a police captain of twenty year's involuntary blamelessness could stand. Salvatore's hands, trembling on the ends of his shaking arms, went out to touch her. They homed onto the right, blatant breast. He hovered like a man seeking a landing place in a planet and then sumptuously closing onto the flesh and holding onto it, soft and warm and vibrant. Tottie did not seem to notice. Men frequently had their hands on her bosom. 'I want to put the gun on,' she said in her normal voice. 'Will you help, darling?'

Salvatore was beyond words. He withdrew his hands with enormous difficulty, as if they were metal on a magnet, but was immediately rewarded because she bent and kissed his thumbs, left then right, as they were reluctantly moving back towards him. Then, with the merest easing of those laden eyes towards him, she slipped out of the top of the dress and pushed away the encumbrance of the lace bra. There she was, beautifully spread out and displayed, yards of bulging cream skin, it seemed, and large rosy nipples. 'Okay God, you can come and get me now,' challenged Salvatore.

'God's seen them already,' she said a little primly. 'Do you like them, Captain Honey?'

It was the most fatuous question Salvatore had ever heard. 'Big,' he managed to mutter. 'Big and . . . big.'

'Thirty-nine inches at the last count,' she said, smiling fondly down at them. Like a careful housewife she brused an imaginary piece of dust from the surface. Salvatore reached out and obligingly did the same. She continued to smile.

'Just tidying up,' he explained lamely. Then he reached out again and deliberately pressed one nipple and then the other with his bell-ringing finger. That was it. With a sob he abruptly collapsed forward onto all the magnificence and buried his face and even his ears deeply into it.

'Poor Captain,' said Tottie, stroking the sparse tundra hair at the back of his neck. 'Poor, poor Captain.'

Salvatore emerged, because he urgently needed to breathe. She leaned forward and kissed his wet face. 'It was real nice in there Tottie,' he shuddered. 'Real cosy. Like . . . like . . . home.'

'Did you find what you were looking for?' she inquired with a familiar laugh. She abruptly moved a yard further away from him. 'Now I want to get this gun belt thing on. You help, Honey Captain.'

He did not care a damn what he did now. Haplessly he lifted the gun from the holster and put it on the silken bed. Her fingers went to it and caressed it fondly. He took the harness and, never for a moment able to take his tormented eyes from her bosom, he fumbled with buckles and straps and eventually got the contraption undone. 'Excuse me, Tottie,' he said, leaning towards her. 'This has to go round your . . . er, top.'

'Put it round then, baby,' she droned. 'Just hang it on me.'

From the eerie distant past he could hear the voice of his instructor at the police academy calling out the instructions necessary for the fixing of a shoulder holster. The voice echoed from the days when he was a clean-faced kid, all eager to serve the people and the law of the country. How things had changed. Jesus Willard Christ.

'I'll need to get very close to get this on you, Tottie,' he mentioned nervously. 'Very, very close, indeed.'

'Be my guest,' she said, moving forward the yard she had previously retreated. 'Honey Captain.'

He passed the main strap around her back, leaning against those lovely human pillows as he did so. Then came the strap around the front.

He failed twice. 'I'll have to kinda . . . hold these two still,' he said and put his hand firmly below her right breast before she had time to do it herself. He got the strap below that and then held the left breast still while he did the same that side. It was like holding a pound of warm jelly. Clumsily he buckled the straps and then fitted the revolver holster below the armpit so the side wall of the splendid gland decorating that side was lying snugly against it.

'That seems to be safe,' he said, professionally patting the holster into place and then arranging the breast more comforatbly. 'I don't think that will move.'

'Now . . . put the gun in, please,' she requested. Her voice was a husky drone. Her opaque eyes were on the holster. Trembling he picked up the gun. He checked the safety catch. 'We don't want any accidents now do we, please?' he murmured. 'Not in that locality.'

He slotted the weapon into the leather container. Her eyes closed. 'That's dreamy,' she whispered. 'Oh God, that's dreamy.' She began to rub her hands over the gun, the holster and the harness and then massage her nipples with her palms. 'I really like it, Captain,' she said as though she had forgotten him but then suddenly remembered he was there. 'I honestly do. It's so good. So very good.'

It's time, thought Salvatore. Now go and get it, you jerk. He made himself move forward, but she slid from beneath him with an unhurried agility born of extended practice. Suddenly the wonderful body was heading towards the door. Salvatore sat shipwrecked on the bed, his arms going beseechingly towards her as she went. At the handle she called back. 'I must show this to Herb, darling. It'll really turn him on too.'

She unlocked the door and was gone into the corridor and towards the crowded party in the salon. Salvatore sobbed with frustration. He rose hopelessly from the bed and sadly ran his hand down the luxurious quilt. Then he hitched himself together and went, a figure of disappointment and despondency, towards the door. He could hear the sounds of excitement coming from the main room. What an entrance she must have made.

Salvatore followed. He got to the main room just as Tottie di Milo was displaying the gun, and much more besides, to a group of entranced guests at one side of the room. Her lover Herb's eyes were wide with anticipation. Other guests were moving over to see what there was to see. Male shouts and exclamations of appreciation, like those from a football crowd, and some startled envious cries from the ladies filled the room.

Then there came a new diversion. Through the tunnel leading from the waterway came a humming that abruptly filled both the tunnel and the room. It was as though a creature from another world had made its arrival. All the people turned. Even the vision of Tottie di Milo was unable to hold them. Through the tunnel and into the living river of that extraordinary room roared the sharp little fan-boat and aboard it, armed and amazing, were the hooded members of the Ocean Drive Delinquent Society.

Salvatore, eyes unbelieving, mouth like granite, reached for the gun he didn't have.

Naturally at first the guests thought it was all part of the entertainment, especially when Tottie herself suddenly opened wild fire with the police revolver she had been so lovingly displaying. Certain that the bullets were blanks, everyone laughed when she began shooting, but the laughter curdled when one of the wild shots brought a large oriental vase in fragments to the floor. Herb managed to stand up from beneath the nerve-wracked wreckage of Frankie Moon's dumb mistress and attempted to take the gun from the trembling Tottie. She refused to be parted from it.

The hooded Gabby, stepping ashore from the fan-boat, pushed her Russian pistol into Tottie's slim waist to make the point. Tottie dropped the gun. Gabby checked it, saw it was empty, and kicked it aside.

'Okay, everybody, just listen,' ordered Ossie loudly. 'If nobody fools about anymore we can get this over with nice and quick and you can get on with the party.'

The gang were deployed three one side of the artificial living river and two the other. Bruce remained aboard the fan-boat, the propeller now idling to a standstill. He lay behind the fierce horizontal barrel of the unloaded Soviet mortar. The guests, collectively shaking, had backed towards the semi-circular walls of the room, which was where they were wanted. Around the walls they formed a nervous half-moon.

'Please take it from me, folks,' continued Ossie, waving his pistol like a rich man waves a cigar, 'we've come on business. Anybody who tries to stop us doing business will have only seconds to regret it. Okay?'

Gabby shouted. 'Let's hear you!'

'Okay.' 'Yes.' Surely.' The words tumbled from the crowd to be followed by stares and mumbles towards Gabby, now that they realized it was a woman below the mask.

Gabby nodded towards Ossie. 'Right,' he ordered. 'This is how we play the game.' He was enjoying himself. It was going right. 'Everybody empties their wallets, their pocket-books, purses, pockets, right onto the floor in front of them. All the way along there, see. Then everybody takes off watches, jewellery and anything else of value and places it – get me – *places* it, so it stays undamaged, in the same spot. Our collectors will be circulating.'

Salvatore felt he had to do something. 'And if we don't?' he said bravely, Tottie standing just in the corner of his eye.

It was Gabby who answered. She took a step towards him and nodded backwards at Bruce behind the menacing mortar. 'If you don't we blast everybody,' she said quietly.

'Ball brain!' Tottie called at Salvatore. He bit his lip with hurt.

'Okay,' he mumbled, stepping back. 'I only asked.'

'No more questions,' said Ossie. 'It's not a debate. Right, empty the goodies. Come on – move.'

Bruce in the bow swung the mortar first to one side and then the other.

Its grim barrel and wide mouth made it a serious sight. Sidewalk, Ari and Molly began to prod the captives on their side of the river and Ossie and Gabby encouraged them on the other. The people reached for their movable wealth from pockets and wrists and fingers. They placed the valuables on the floor until on each side of the room there was a high-tide mark of glittering trinkets, cash, and leather wallets and pocketbooks. On her bank of the river Molly took a canvas bag and began to scoop the loot into it. Gabby did likewise on her side. A sniffling woman complained to Molly: 'Please don't rob me. I'm just a little old lady.'

'So am I,' said the voice behind the mask.

It was all accomplished speedily. 'Now,' called Ossie. 'Has anybody forgotten anything? I bet there *is* somebody.' He leaned forward and took a fat wallet from the coat of a stiff-faced man. 'Personal things,' said the man. 'Private things.'

'Stand over there,' ordered Ossie, looking fiercely into the man's eyes. 'We're going to shoot you.'

The words brought a fresh avalanche of wallets and other valuables piling on the floor. From both sides of the room they appeared. Salvatore's police badge was with them. Ossie picked it up and felt himself go pale inside. He felt for the policeman's gun. 'It's not there,' said Salvatore resignedly. 'The broad had it, remember. The broad who called me a ball brain.'

A cop in the house spurred Ossie to get it over with now. He gave a low whistle and the members of the gang backed towards the captive river and their slim craft. 'Sidewalk,' whispered Ossie.

'Okay, I'm going,' came the return whisper. Sidewalk Joe climbed aboard and started the fan. It whirred softly and the boat fidgeted. They knew they would have to reverse through the tunnel. That would be the tricky part of the operation.

'We're going out ass-first,' Ossie called to the white-faced crowd on either side of the room. He pointed to the mortar. 'But just take it from me folks, that weapon will be pointing straight back into this room. If we hear a pin drop before we're clear we'll fire it. If the ladies present don't know what a piece of hardware like that does, maybe their husbands would just whisper it to them.'

He was about to signal the other members of the gang to step carefully aboard the fan-boat when he heard Sidewalk's soft curses. He half looked round. 'The reverse ain't working,' muttered Sidewalk. 'It can't make it.' Ossie swore but still calmly. 'It was in the repair yard,' Sidewalk reminded him.

'Never mind why,' snapped Ossie. He looked up. The semi-circular crowd could see there was something wrong. 'Stand still!' he bawled. He waved his pistol and Bruce swung the mortar from side to side. The guests stood still.

Gabby leaned to Sidewalk. 'Turn the boat in the pond,' she said, nodding at the circular oriental pool. 'You can get it around in there.'

'Good girl,' said Ossie. He whispered to Sidewalk who nodded. Gabby edged towards the metal grille gate that separated the pond from the river. It had a removable bolt. She took it out and with Ari holding the other side of the grille eased it up and out of its housing.

'Watch the alligators,' laughed Tottie di Milo suddenly. 'They haven't been fed.'

'Button up,' barked Gabby. 'Or I'll shoot you where you're biggest.' She was feeling the strain.

'Tell the alligators to button up,' giggled Tottie.

They did not believe her. The 'gators were lying at the bottom of the pool away from the lights and it was only when Sidewalk and Bruce, temporarily forsaking the mortar, began to push the fan-boat around the pond, just big enough for the manoeuvre, that the truth surfaced. The wooden mouth of a large, hungry Everglades alligator suddenly appeared at the low edge of the boat within inches of Bruce's hand. Then another long, ragged jaw surfaced alongside the first.

The creatures were jostling each other to get to the most obtainable man they had seen for some time.

'Oh Christ!' exclaimed Bruce. 'She's right!'

Sidewalk stepped ashore smartly. Bruce was quickly after him. Ossie was staring at the vertical jaws. But Gabby was still aware. 'Turn it round,' she said sharply. 'Get it out of there.'

Gingerly the young man and the old gangster returned to the deck and eased the craft around full circle. The alligators had a snap or two at the smooth hull but could get a hold of nothing. Then the bow was pointing the right way again, out towards the waterway. 'Get the gate back,' said Ossie to Ari and Gabby. 'We don't want those bastards following us.' The pair slotted the gate into its housing. Sidewalk pressed the starter button and the fan whirred. With relief and with their loot the gang boarded the small craft. The robbed guests were standing against the walls. Then at the moment Ossie was about to say: 'Let's go,' Tottie broke drunkenly away from the protective arms of Herb and recklessly running forward plunged up to her lovely armpits in the river, blocking the river and their exit. 'Nobody ain't going from here,' she howled extravagantly. 'You bastards!'

The gang stared horrified. Salvatore, Herb and some of the more gallant were about to advance to her. Gabby turned her gun and shouted at them to get back.

The boozy Tottie was a different problem. She floated magnificently on the river, her great breasts like life preservers, bobbing on the water. 'Nobody leaves,' she shouted. 'It's over my dead body.'

'Okay,' shouted Gabby decisively. 'Let the 'gators out.'

Everybody's eyebrows, inside and outside of masks, shot up. But the girl was serious. 'Let them loose!' she called again. Ari, his nose pale and trembling beneath the hood, climbed from the boat to the shore. He pulled the pin from the grating and lifted the grille. The alligators, now awake and aware, made a move for the open river. Herb and Salvatore made a dash towards the floating Tottie again, but Tottie was no fool. With a wet howl she got herself from the living river and staggered into the embracing arms of her guests and admirers.

'Give it the lot,' said Ossie to Sidewalk. He did. The fan screamed and the small narrow boat shot forward and into the tunnel almost leaving its crew behind. They hung on by inches. Through the tunnel they roared and out into the concealing dark of the Intra-Coastal Waterway. The alligators, hardly able to believe their luck, slid out after them.

Screams and cries filled the house behind them. Women fainted on both banks of the artificial river. Salvatore made a run for the telephone.

CHAPTER ELEVEN

'Yes, for Chrissake!' shouted Salvatore into the phone. 'A fan-boat. That's what I said. I know, I saw them. Listen they can only go two ways, up the waterway or down the waterway . . . Oh, okay, okay, or across the waterway . . . We got two cars right here. Get Cook to pick me up and send Stewart south along US One. We'll go north. Right, let's move . . .'

He made for the door and then returned to get his gun and the holster from Tottie who was letting off small screams in a corner surrounded by numerous well-wishers and spectators. (It was not often you could see a famous actress virtually nude to the waist apart from a gun-belt, letting off small screams.)

'I just need to have my gun, honey,' said Salvatore briskly. He somehow felt better now. More assured. He was not a great policeman but he was a better policeman than a lover. At least he understood the basics. 'My gun please, Miss di Milo,' he repeated. 'I need to have my gun.'

'Take your fucking gun,' said the lady ungraciously. 'Causing all this trouble.'

He was tempted to argue the point but he knew there was no time. He took the gun and was pushed out of the way by the sanctimoniously concerned Herb who retrieved the belt from Tottie's bosom region and handed it scornfully to him. Salvatore strapped it on right away, enjoying the brief quasi-heroic moment, before turning for the door. The bell outside was chiming urgently. That would be Cook.

'Goodbye,' he called gallantly like a knight errant leaving on a mission.

'Fuck off,' Tottie called after him. 'I'll sue you, you bastard. You've lost my alligators.' This last thought, which had apparently just occurred to her, prompted a new spasm of longer wails and hysterical half-sentences. Salvatore went.

Cook was waiting outside. 'Why no all-cars call?' he asked desperately as they hurried towards the patrol car. 'We could have picked them up by now.'

'This is personal,' muttered Salvatore getting into the front seat. The two bemused patrolmen sat in the back. 'I want to get those bastards myself.' Cook started to move towards the gates. 'Go north on US One,' ordered Salvatore. 'Follow the waterway. If they're going north we should be able to hear that fan a mile away. Never mind the siren.'

The look-out, Katy, watched the patrol car pull away and put her hand to her mouth. It was too late to whistle now. But she tried it. She put her fingers to her mouth and let forth a tremendous hoot. Then – according to orders – she walked swiftly from the scene and got a bus back to South Miami Beach.

Cook rushed the car along the streets parallel with the waterway, every now and then pulling up by some private jetty or landing stage so that Salvatore could run eagerly to the edge and listen into the night. At the third pause he heard them. The unique whirr of the fan-boat's propeller. Exultantly he jumped back into the patrol car. 'We got them!' he shouted. 'Half-a-mile up-river. Come on Cookie, for Chrissake!'

Zaharran and Lou the Barbender were waiting with the cars at the planned place between Fort Lauderdale and Pompano Beach. It was an anxious time and Zaharran was grateful that Lou was inclined to fill in the elongated minutes by telling him some of the astonishing feats of strength he had performed in his prime years.

Eventually the droning of Lou's narrative was overtaken by another drone. Zaharran, whose ears were in better shape than almost any other part of his ill-used body, sat up and quietened the strong man. 'They're coming,' he whispered. 'They're on their way.' He looked at his enormous watch around his enormous wrist. 'They're late.'

The two large men jumped with identical awkwardness from the car and Lou went to the wheel of the second vehicle parked twenty yards away. They watched the dark, limp canal intensely. Then like a moth in the gloom they saw the fan-boat approaching. They started the engines of the cars, then went back to the wooden landing stage to help their fellow conspirators ashore.

The fan-boat edged nearer. Even from the shore Zaharran and Lou could see the dim approaching smiles. 'You made it,' whispered Zaharran.

'Sure,' answered Ossie. 'We made it. But we've got to move quick now.'

The loot bags were carefully handed ashore. The fan had been stilled by Sidewalk and the frail boat fidgeted alongside the jetty. They put the bags into the front car and then helped everybody ashore.

'Let's beat it,' said Gabby. 'They're feeling sore back there. And there was that cop. He'll know what to do.'

'There was a cop?' asked Zaharran.

'Sure, he was at the party.'

Zaharran whistled.

Ossie, Bruce and Gabby jumped in the first car with Zaharran at the wheel. Sidewalk, Ari and Molly were in the second with Lou driving.

'I sure hope Katy's clear,' said Lou.

'She'll have taken off quick, don't worry,' said Ari. 'She'll be back at Sunny Gables by now.'

They started off quickly through the quiet street. Another ten seconds and they would have been clear and into the main road traffic of US One, indistinguishable from any other car, but while they were still running along the waterside street, Salvatore's police car turned from a side junction. Each knew who the other was.

'Cops,' breathed Ossie. 'Go like shit.' Zaharran put his foot down. He heard the car behind begin to rush after them.

'It's them!' Salvatore shouted triumphantly to Cook, so loudly that Cook winced and pulled his ear away. 'Go for them, Cookie, let's get the bastards.'

Cook had to perform a difficult manoeuvre at the junction to get the police car pointing the right way. He tried going onto the sidewalk, but misjudged the distance and had to back down again to avoid hitting a street lamp. Salvatore cursed him vividly.

But they knew what the cars looked like now. 'Why not call all cars?' pleaded Cook, ramming the car's nose along the street. 'We got them, boss. We can sew them up.'

'Shut your ass,' said Salvatore rudely. 'I'm getting these babies by myself. I know what I'm doing, Cookie boy, you just drive and fast. I'll show that Betty.'

They were half a mile behind, siren now going, when Zaharran turned onto the highway leading to the cantilever bridge at Pompano Beach. Lou's car was a yard behind them. Zaharran swerved out so he could see the police in his driving mirror. His driving skill caused Ossie and Bruce to glance at each other. He flashed his brake lights and Lou swerved inside and came level. 'Beat it over the bridge,' Zaharran shouted to Lou. He was giving the orders. 'Wait the other side.'

Now everyone was staring at the fat man. He grunted. 'I know what I'm doing.' Again Ossie's eybrows went up. Gabby stared at Ossie then at Bruce. Zaharran turned. 'I know,' he repeated. 'Gabby – get over there to the bridge house. Stick a gun in the guy's ribs and get the bridge up. Do it!'

She reacted quickly to his tone. She jumped from the car. 'Then take off,' said Zaharran. 'Anywhere.'

The girl ran through the traffic to the far side of the highway. Zaharran started the car over the bridge. The police siren was getting nearer through the traffic at the back. 'Who are you anyway?' said Ossie.

'A friend,' Zaharran answered coolly. 'A friend who maybe will get you out of this situation. The cops will have an "all cars" alert out now, so hold tight.' He drove the car over the bump of the cantilever. Behind them they could hear the drawbridge warning clanging.

Gabby, her hood down, her Russian automatic in the back of the trembling operator, watched the cantilever arms of the bridge rising like a man making a slow surrender. The bell was sounding and the barrier was down, the red lights flashing. The traffic stopped. Above the bell she could hear the nearing irritable sound of the police siren. She judged it as well as she could. 'Now buddy,' she said, 'just keep that bridge up there for as long as you can. Okay?'

'Okay, young lady,' said the bridge operator. 'I don't want to die. It's my birthday.'

'Happy birthday,' said Gabby. The bridge was almost up now, its fingers seeming to point to something in the sky. She heard the police car stop. She backed out, put the gun away and ran easily down a narrow street into the anonymous darkness. As she went she began wondering about Zaharran.

Salvatore was spitting with rage. 'That fucking bridge!' he kept shouting. 'That goddam fucking bridge!' He sent one of the patrolmen running to the bridge house. He glared at Cook as if it were his fault.

'All cars?' suggested Cook blandly. 'Want to make the call?'

'No! I'll give the orders!' Salvatore howled. Oh God, he couldn't lose them now. What lousy goddam luck. 'Get Stewart,' he grunted. 'And quick.'

Cook got the other patrol car on the radio. Salvatore grabbed the instrument. 'Where are you?' demanded Salvatore.

'Going south on US One,' he said. 'We're at Hollywood Beach.'

'Okay, turn around. Go across the bridge at Lauderdale. Suspects now on ocean side US A-One-A heading north or south. I don't know. They've fucked us at Pompano Bridge. Okay?'

'Okay, we're going,' answered Stewart. 'Why not make it all cars, chief?'

'Do what I say!' howled Salvatore. 'I'm doing this!'

The Pompano Bridge before them was now descending, the patrolman having persuaded the frightened bridge keeper that it was the right thing to do, and that he was personally safe. The policeman ran as he saw the patrol car moving around the waiting traffic and jumped into the rear just as it was accelerating towards the falling arm of the bridge. 'A woman,' he said breathlessly closing the door. 'She stuck a gun into the guy and told him to put the bridge up.'

Salvatore cursed. Even as he did so Stewart, to the south, was crossing the Fort Lauderdale drawbridge towards the ocean. As he did so the policeman beside him called a warning and along the opposite lane, going in the other direction, roared the two fugitive cars. As Stewart braked and reached the summit of the bridge, it began to yawn open, horrifying the police crew. The car went nose-first down an ever-steepening hill. Bruce, a gun in the ribs of the bridge keeper, watched it coolly, then stepped back and ran into the shadows. Stewart's car came down the incline and slewed around in the road. Then Salvatore's car arrived. Now both cars were on the same side of the bridge.

Salvatore stared unbelievingly at the other police car. 'It's the Keystone fucking cops!' he bawled. He began to use his radio, swore again, and leaned out of the window. 'Stewart, you jerk. Where are they?'

'On the other side of the bridge,' answered Stewart. 'Shall I call all cars?'

Salvatore blasphemed again. Jesus Malcolm Christ, why couldn't they get anything right? 'Stay there,' he shouted. 'Wait till the goddam bridge is down then get over it. Go north on US One, okay?'

He guessed right for once. He shouted at Cook loud enough to frighten that officer and Cook turned their own car north along Collins and towards the bridge at Boca Raton. They reached the bridge and mounting the middle reservation, skimmed by the traffic. Like Stewart on the previous drawbridge they had just reached the summit when the road began to lift under their wheels. Salvatore went crazy. He knew what was going to happen and it did. The fugitive cars came in the opposite direction and the police car, passing them, had no alternative but to run down the ever increasing angle of the slope onto the wrong bank of the waterway. As they arrived on the other side so Stewart's car turned the corner at the end of the street. Stewart saw what had happened and grinned with mean satisfaction.

'Serve the bastard right,' he said to himself.

Salvatore ran to the bridge house himself. The Boca Raton bridge operator was ashen-faced, leaning on his little desk. He saw the policeman with enormous relief. 'A guy with a mask . . . and a gun,' he mumbled. 'He had a *real* gun.' It was too late to look into the shadows now. Salvatore decided on one last throw. He ordered both cars south down the ocean side of the waterway. He sent Stewart over Pompano Bridge and his own car ran onto the cantilever at Fort Lauderdale. To his astonishment parked casually by the side of the bridge house was one of the runaway cars.

Salvatore ran over, his still unloaded gun waving, and followed by his panting policemen. Sitting in the driving seat, reading the *Miami News*, was Zaharran. He turned and gave Salvatore a huge creased smile.

Salvatore felt sick. 'Oh God,' he said, almost like a prayer. 'What the fuck is this guy doing here?'

'This guy,' said Zaharran slowly, 'is reading the sports page of the paper, because this guy just might as well occupy himself doing that because this guy just had a month's work screwed up by some cops.'

Leaning wearily against the hull of the car Salvatore said: 'You had them? You got them?'

'Sure I had them,' said Zaharran just as wearily. 'Right here. I was among them. I was right in there. I was ready to spring the trap. I even had the loot, Salvatore, right here in this automobile. But suddenly we get ambushed by the cops and suddenly I try to stall the car and suddenly they think maybe I'm working for the cops and suddenly they put a big Russian gun in my ear. I'm lucky to be siting here with my entire head.'

'Okay, okay,' said Salvatore more eagerly. 'But you got them. You got descriptions?'

'Sure. Every face was the same. Covered with a hood with two eye slits. That any good to you? I never saw them without masks. After tonight I would have been all right with them. They would have trusted me. But you blew it, Captain Salvatore, you blew it.'

'How the fuck could we know?' demanded Salvatore angrily. 'You didn't tell us nothing.'

'Okay, you didn't blow it. It just got blown.' He folded the newspaper deliberately. 'There's a chance I might get the loot back,' he suggested. Salvatore's face brightened. 'And most of the dough from the bank,' added Zaharran.

'You can? You can do that?' Stewart's car arrived on their side of the bridge but Salvatore waved him away impatiently.

'Maybe, but I have to be left alone. Already I got some of the cash sent back to the bank. Ten thousand bucks in a package by post. Right?'

'Right,' said Salvatore. 'That was you then?'

'Who else? Santa Claus? But don't bug me. I got to do it my way. And only *I* know about my way.' He turned a slow old eye to Salvatore. 'For the reward.'

'For the entire bank haul there's ten thousand bucks,' said Salvatore. 'You know that.'

'What about tonight's? Will there be something for receiving that?'

'Well not yet. Jesus Harold Christ, it only just happened an hour ago. But I guess there will be. I guess that can be arranged. You can really get that stuff back?'

'I think so. But on my *own*. Okay Salvatore?'

'Okay, if that's what you want.'

'That's just what I want,' said Zaharran. 'I don't want any official screwing up of this. Maybe you'll let me know tomorrow about the reward for tonight's stuff. I'm already running at a deficit on this case.'

Salvatore nodded. 'Maybe next time we'll get the bastards,' he said. 'I got a feeling we will. Where did they come from Zaharran.'

'Philadelphia,' lied Zaharran easily. 'They came down from Philly.'

'I might have guessed,' said Salvatore seriously.

'And they won't be operating in the Miami area again,' continued Zaharran. 'They're splitting.'

'That's the best news so far. Where are they splitting to? Back to Philly?'

'Alaska,' sniffed Zaharran. 'Alaska, I heard.'

'Wouldn't you just know,' said Salvatore.

'Okay Mr Zaharran,' said Gabby. 'So you came to find us. Why didn't you find us?'

Zaharran sat in Bruce's room facing the three young ones. Bruce farted and restarted the air conditioning which had been faltering. Zaharran looked at him appreciatively. 'A short-term discomfort for long-term benefits,' he said quizzically. He looked around at them. 'I don't know,' he said, going back to the question. 'I came to find you, but somehow I didn't. I guess I got fond of the older folks. I'm an old folk myself, see. I sympathize because I have the same problems. I get lonely and bored and frustrated like hell. I guess you could say I'm an old folk first and a retired cop second. And I never did have ten thousand bucks in cash before. That was too much of a temptation for a poor man.'

'You've sent that back too?' said Bruce.

'Sure. I didn't get a choice. Not after I'd collected all the rest from you. The bank got its cash back. It's a real nice deal for them. And Miss Tottie di Milo's friends got all their trinkets back and a story to tell their friends. And nobody is going to be any the wiser about you. As far as the cops are concerned you've taken off. For Alaska. So I guess everybody's more or less happy.'

'What about you?' asked Ossie. 'You pick up the rewards?'

'Sure I do. I've been working, remember. This is my profession. I have to live don't I?' They agreed that he had to live. 'You'll be moving out I guess,' he said, eyeing them suggestively. 'Somewhere not too near. Like China.'

'That direction,' nodded Ossie. 'We're just going, right now. We came to say goodbye.'

Solemnly Zaharran shook hands with each of them and they went out leaving him sitting in the room. He released wind to try and start the air conditioning. It didn't work. He was getting old.

Ossie, Bruce and Gabby walked down the stairs with their respective meagre belongings. Suddenly they felt a yawning awkwardness between them. Nobody spoke. They went outside the Sunny Gables Hotel and stood on the uncomfortably hot sidewalk. Nobody seemed to want to make the first move. Then a new model Cadillac cruised along Ocean Drive and stopped right there by them. A bronzed, middle-aged man was at the wheel. Bruce and Ossie realized, with sinking hearts, who he was. He smiled handsomely and opened the door. Gabby quickly kissed Bruce and then Ossie and while they stood speechless stepped into the car and embraced the man. Then she leaned out of the automobile and dropped something into Ossie's hand. He looked down at it. 'It's the bullet we never used,' said Gabby. 'Maybe it was as well. It's a dud.' The car eased itself along the street and turned a corner towards Washington Avenue.

'Jesus help me,' said Bruce at last. 'And I thought she was crazy about me.'

'And me,' shrugged Ossie.

If the pelican cruising along from the Keys towards Fort Lauderdale that May day had cared to note – and pelicans, being forever lost in thought, are not, as a general rule, observant birds – it would have seen small changes along South Miami Beach. There were fewer people sitting under the sea-grape trees along Ocean Drive, the terraces of the larger hotels, a few blocks to the north, were less populated and those that sat were off-season people. The waves were too dull for the surfers and the day too hot to encourage the rich widows to display themselves in their bikinis and pink boots. No students blew bubble gum at Hallendale. The voice of Station WAIA was hung with weariness.

'What can I say folks you don't already know. South Florida is having the hottest

day of the year so far. Phew! At noon the pointer got to ninety-eight degrees and the
humidity is way, way up. Roll on November we say, don't you? WAIA your music
way, serving the golden coast from the Palm Beaches to Key West . . .'

Lou the Barbender and K-K-Katy were practising for their wedding, sitting in her humid, gown-hung room, he perspiring in his tailed coat and stiff collar, she wearing her unused wedding dress. On the following day they were to be married. Sidewalk Joe, playing poker now beneath the sea-grape trees, was to be their special guest.

Ari the Greek waited until evening before he took his run. As he left Sunny Gables Hotel, which would be his home forever, the rival Nissenbaums came out, arms folded, for their evening confrontation. The sun had dipped dramatically, gorged and red, grinning after a day's demonstration of its prowess. A small, apologetic breeze arrived late from the Atlantic and fussed around like an inadequate rescue team trying to alleviate a large disaster. Ocean Drive was still warm under foot but once he had crossed the street towards the ocean Ari felt the little touch of the zephyr on his great nose and was grateful. He made a brief shadow-boxing turn and then began to jog towards the beach. He went very easily, at not much more than walking pace, but before he had cleared the sea-grape trees there was a sheen of sweat across his old brow. The concrete calendar on Ocean Drive showed it was 17 July, eight-fifteen pm and still seventy-four degrees. Ari poked his tongue out at it as he passed.

He was not surprised to see Molly Mandy on the beach, her metal detector performing its habitual concentric circles.

He approached from behind and noted how, in the reduced light, the big earphones clamped to her small head gave her the silhouette of Minnie Mouse. He smiled at the image.

Thoughtfully he made a detour, still jogging, so that he did not startle her. He was a dozen yards to her right when she saw him from the corner of her intent eyes.

'Hi, Ari,' she called.

'Hi there, Molly, hot day.'

'Sure was. You still running?'

'Still running,' he confirmed, increasing the pace of his jogging on the spot just to demonstrate the point. 'While I'm running I'm living.'

She nodded, acknowledging the philosophy. 'And I'm still looking,' she said, staring at the darkening sand at her feet. 'Bye, Ari.'

'Bye, Molly,' he answered. He slipped into gear and jogged away from her. She looked up from her search and watched him go. On impulse she called after him. 'Ari – you and me ought to go into business sometime.'

He slowed and jogged on the spot, half turned and then continued. 'Teeth,' he shouted back. 'Now there's a real *good* business. Teeth.'